Complete Stories of Henry James

HENRY JAMES

Henry James

COMPLETE STORIES
1864–1874

THE LIBRARY OF AMERICA

The paper used in this publication meets the
minimum requirements of the American National Standard for
Information Sciences—Permanence of Paper for Printed
Library Materials, ANSI Z39.48—1984.

Distributed to the trade in the United States
by Penguin Putnam Inc.
and in Canada by Penguin Books Canada Ltd.

Library of Congress Catalog Number: 98–53919
For cataloging information, see end of Notes.
ISBN 1–883011–70–1

First Printing
The Library of America—111

Manufactured in the United States of America

JEAN STROUSE
WROTE THE NOTES FOR THIS VOLUME

Contents

A Tragedy of Error

A LOW English phaeton was drawn up before the door of the post office of a French seaport town. In it was seated a lady, with her veil down and her parasol held closely over her face. My story begins with a gentleman coming out of the office and handing her a letter.

He stood beside the carriage a moment before getting in. She gave him her parasol to hold, and then lifted her veil, showing a very pretty face. This couple seemed to be full of interest for the passers by, most of whom stared hard and exchanged significant glances. Such persons as were looking on at the moment saw the lady turn very pale as her eyes fell on the direction of the letter. Her companion saw it too, and instantly stepping into the place beside her, took up the reins, and drove rapidly along the main street of the town, past the harbor, to an open road skirting the sea. Here he slackened pace. The lady was leaning back, with her veil down again, and the letter lying open in her lap. Her attitude was almost that of unconsciousness, and he could see that her eyes were closed. Having satisfied himself of this, he hastily possessed himself of the letter, and read as follows:

SOUTHAMPTON, *July 16th, 18–*

MY DEAR HORTENSE: You will see by my postmark that I am a thousand leagues nearer home than when I last wrote, but I have hardly time to explain the change. M. P—— has given me a most unlooked-for *congé.* After so many months of separation, we shall be able to spend a few weeks together. God be praised! We got in here from New York this morning, and I have had the good luck to find a vessel, the *Armorique,* which sails straight for H——. The mail leaves directly, but we shall probably be detained a few hours by the tide; so this will reach you a day before I arrive: the master calculates we shall get in early Thursday morning. Ah, Hortense! how the time drags! Three whole days. If I did not write from New York, it is because I was unwilling to torment you with an expectancy which, as it is, I venture to hope, you will find long enough. Farewell. To a warmer greeting!

Your devoted

C. B.

I

When the gentleman replaced the paper on his companion's lap, his face was almost as pale as hers. For a moment he gazed fixedly and vacantly before him, and a half-suppressed curse escaped his lips. Then his eyes reverted to his neighbor. After some hesitation, during which he allowed the reins to hang so loose that the horse lapsed into a walk, he touched her gently on the shoulder.

'Well, Hortense,' said he, in a very pleasant tone, 'what's the matter; have you fallen asleep?'

Hortense slowly opened her eyes, and, seeing that they had left the town behind them, raised her veil. Her features were stiffened with horror.

'Read that,' said she, holding out the open letter.

The gentleman took it, and pretended to read it again.

'Ah! M. Bernier returns. Delightful!' he exclaimed.

'How, delightful?' asked Hortense; 'we mustn't jest at so serious a crisis, my friend.'

'True,' said the other, 'it will be a solemn meeting. Two years of absence is a great deal.'

'O Heaven! I shall never dare to face him,' cried Hortense, bursting into tears.

Covering her face with one hand, she put out the other toward that of her friend. But he was plunged in so deep a reverie, that he did not perceive the movement. Suddenly he came to, aroused by her sobs.

'Come, come,' said he, in the tone of one who wishes to coax another into mistrust of a danger before which he does not himself feel so secure but that the sight of a companion's indifference will give him relief. 'What if he does come? He need learn nothing. He will stay but a short time, and sail away again as unsuspecting as he came.'

'Learn nothing! You surprise me. Every tongue that greets him, if only to say *bon jour*, will wag to the tune of a certain person's misconduct.'

'Bah! People don't think about us quite as much as you fancy. You and I, *n'est-ce-pas?* we have little time to concern ourselves about our neighbors' failings. Very well, other people are in the same box, better or worse. When a ship goes to pieces on those rocks out at sea, the poor devils who are pushing their way to land on a floating spar, don't bestow many glances on those who are battling with the waves beside them. Their eyes are fastened to the shore, and all their care is for their own safety. In life we are all afloat on a tumultuous sea; we are all struggling toward some *terra firma* of wealth or love or leisure. The roaring of the waves we kick up about us and the spray we dash into our eyes deafen and blind us to the sayings and doings of our fellows. Provided we climb high and dry, what do we care for them?'

'Ay, but if we don't? When we've lost hope ourselves, we want to make others sink. We hang weights about their necks, and dive down into the dirtiest pools for stones to cast at them. My friend, you don't feel the shots which are not aimed at you. It isn't of you the town talks, but of me: a poor woman throws herself off the pier yonder, and drowns before a kind hand has time to restrain her, and her corpse floats over the water for all the world to look at. When her husband comes up to see what the crowd means, is there any lack of kind friends to give him the good news of his wife's death?'

'As long as a woman is light enough to float, Hortense, she is not counted drowned. It's only when she sinks out of sight that they give her up.'

Hortense was silent a moment, looking at the sea with swollen eyes.

'Louis,' she said at last, 'we were speaking metaphorically: I have half a mind to drown myself literally.'

'Nonsense!' replied Louis; 'an accused pleads "not guilty," and hangs himself in prison. What do the papers say? People talk, do they? Can't you talk as well as they? A woman is in the wrong from the moment she holds her tongue and refuses battle. And that you do too often. That pocket handkerchief is always more or less of a flag of truce.

'I'm sure I don't know,' said Hortense indifferently; 'perhaps it is.'

There are moments of grief in which certain aspects of the subject of our distress seems as irrelevant as matters entirely foreign to it. Her eyes were still fastened on the sea. There was another silence. 'O my poor Charles!' she murmured, at length, 'to what a hearth do you return!'

'Hortense,' said the gentleman, as if he had not heard her, although, to a third person, it would have appeared that it was because he had done so that he spoke: 'I do not need to tell you that it will never happen to me to betray our secret. But I will answer for it that so long as M. Bernier is at home no mortal shall breathe a syllable of it.'

'What of that?' sighed Hortense. 'He will not be with me ten minutes without guessing it.'

'Oh, as for that,' said her companion, dryly, 'that's your own affair.'

'Monsieur de Meyrau!' cried the lady.

'It seems to me,' continued the other, 'that in making such a guarantee, I have done my part of the business.'

'Your part of the business!' sobbed Hortense.

M. de Meyrau made no reply, but with a great cut of the whip sent the horse bounding along the road. Nothing more was said. Hortense lay back in the carriage with her face buried in her handkerchief, moaning. Her companion sat upright, with contracted brows and firmly set teeth, looking straight before him, and by an occasional heavy lash keeping the horse at a furious pace. A wayfarer might have taken him for a ravisher escaping with a victim worn out with resistance. Travellers to whom they were known would perhaps have seen a deep meaning in this accidental analogy. So, by a *détour*, they returned to the town.

When Hortense reached home, she went straight up to a little boudoir on the second floor, and shut herself in. This room was at the back of the house, and her maid, who was at that moment walking in the long garden which stretched down to the water, where there was a landing place for small boats, saw her draw in the window blind and darken the room, still in her bonnet and cloak. She remained alone for a couple of hours. At five o'clock, some time after the hour at which she was usually summoned to dress her mistress for the evening, the maid knocked at Hortense's door, and offered her services. Madame called out, from within, that she had a *migraine*, and would not be dressed.

'Can I get anything for madame?' asked Josephine; 'a *tisane*, a warm drink, something?'

'Nothing, nothing.'

'Will madame dine?'

'No.'

'Madame had better not go wholly without eating.'

'Bring me a bottle of wine—of brandy.'

Josephine obeyed. When she returned, Hortense was standing in the doorway, and as one of the shutters had meanwhile been thrown open, the woman could see that, although her mistress's hat had been tossed upon the sofa, her cloak had not been removed, and that her face was very pale. Josephine felt that she might not offer sympathy nor ask questions.

'Will madame have nothing more?' she ventured to say, as she handed her the tray.

Madame shook her head, and closed and locked the door.

Josephine stood a moment vexed, irresolute, listening. She heard no sound. At last she deliberately stooped down and applied her eye to the keyhole.

This is what she saw:

Her mistress had gone to the open window, and stood with her back to the door, looking out at the sea. She held the bottle by the neck in one hand, which hung listlessly by her side; the other was resting on a glass half filled with water, standing, together with an open letter, on a table beside her. She kept this position until Josephine began to grow tired of waiting. But just as she was about to arise in despair of gratifying her curiosity, madame raised the bottle and glass, and filled the latter full. Josephine looked more eagerly. Hortense held it a moment against the light, and then drained it down.

Josephine could not restrain an involuntary whistle. But her surprise became amazement when she saw her mistress prepare to take a second glass. Hortense put it down, however, before its contents were half gone, as if struck by a sudden thought, and hurried across the room. She stooped down before a cabinet, and took out a small opera glass. With this she returned to the window, put it to her eyes, and again spent some moments in looking seaward. The purpose of this proceeding Josephine could not make out. The only result visible to her was that her mistress suddenly dropped the lorgnette on the table, and sank down on an armchair, covering her face with her hands.

Josephine could contain her wonderment no longer. She hurried down to the kitchen.

'Valentine,' said she to the cook, 'what on earth can be the matter with Madame? She will have no dinner, she is drinking brandy by the glassful, a moment ago she was looking out to sea with a lorgnette, and now she is crying dreadfully with an open letter in her lap.'

The cook looked up from her potato-peeling with a significant wink.

'What can it be,' said she, 'but that monsieur returns?'

II.

At six o'clock, Josephine and Valentine were still sitting together, discussing the probable causes and consequences of the event hinted at by the latter. Suddenly Madame Bernier's bell rang. Josephine was only too glad to answer it. She met her mistress descending the stairs, combed, cloaked, and veiled, with no traces of agitation, but a very pale face.

'I am going out,' said Madame Bernier; 'if M. le Vicomte comes, tell him I am at my mother-in-law's, and wish him to wait till I return.'

Josephine opened the door, and let her mistress pass; then stood watching her as she crossed the court.

'Her mother-in-law's,' muttered the maid; 'she has the face!'

When Hortense reached the street, she took her way, not through the town, to the ancient quarter where that ancient lady, her husband's mother, lived, but in a very different direction. She followed the course of the quay, beside the harbor, till she entered a crowded region, chiefly the residence of fishermen and boatmen. Here she raised her veil. Dusk was beginning to fall. She walked as if desirous to attract as little observation as possible, and yet to examine narrowly the population in the midst of which she found herself. Her dress was so plain that there was nothing in her appearance to solicit attention; yet, if for any reason a passer by had happened to notice her, he could not have helped being struck by the contained intensity with which she scrutinized every figure she met. Her manner was that of a person seeking to recognize a long-lost friend, or perhaps, rather, a long-lost enemy, in a crowd. At last she stopped before a flight of steps, at the foot of which was a landing place for half a dozen little boats, employed to carry passengers between the two sides of the port, at times when the drawbridge above was closed for the passage of vessels. While she stood she was witness of the following scene:

A man, in a red woollen fisherman's cap, was sitting on the top of the steps, smoking the short stump of a pipe, with his face to the water. Happening to turn about, his eye fell on a little child, hurrying along the quay toward a dingy tenement close at hand, with a jug in its arms.

'Hullo, youngster!' cried the man; 'what have you got there? Come here.'

The little child looked back, but, instead of obeying, only quickened its walk.

'The devil take you, come here!' repeated the man, angrily, 'or I'll wring your beggarly neck. You won't obey your own uncle, eh?'

The child stopped, and ruefully made its way to its relative, looking around several times toward the house, as if to appeal to some counter authority.

'Come, make haste!' pursued the man, 'or I shall go and fetch you. Move!'

The child advanced to within half a dozen paces of the steps, and then stood still, eyeing the man cautiously, and hugging the jug tight.

'Come on, you little beggar, come up close.'

The youngster kept a stolid silence, however, and did not budge. Suddenly its self-styled uncle leaned forward, swept out his arm, clutched hold of its little sunburnt wrist, and dragged it toward him.

'Why didn't you come when you were called?' he asked, running his disengaged hand into the infant's frowsy mop of hair, and shaking its head until it staggered. 'Why didn't you come, you unmannerly little brute, eh?—eh?—eh?' accompanying every interrogation with a renewed shake.

The child made no answer. It simply and vainly endeavored to twist its neck around under the man's gripe, and transmit some call for succor to the house.

'Come, keep your head straight. Look at me, and answer me. What's in that jug? Don't lie.'

'Milk.'

'Who for?'

'Granny.'

'Granny be hanged.'

The man disengaged his hands, lifted the jug from the child's feeble grasp, tilted it toward the light, surveyed its contents, put it to his lips, and exhausted them. The child, although liberated, did not retreat. It stood watching its uncle drink until he lowered the jug. Then, as he met its eyes, it said:

'It was for the baby.'

For a moment the man was irresolute. But the child seemed to have a foresight of the parental resentment, for it had hardly spoken when it darted backward and scampered off, just in time to elude a blow from the jug, which the man sent clattering at its heels. When it was out of sight, he faced about to the water again, and replaced the pipe between his teeth with a heavy scowl and a murmur that sounded to Madame Bernier very like—'I wish the baby'd choke.'

'Hortense was a mute spectator of this little drama. When it was over, she turned around, and retraced her steps twenty yards with her hand to her head. Then she walked straight back, and addressed the man.

'My good man,' she said, in a very pleasant voice, 'are you the master of one of these boats?'

He looked up at her. In a moment the pipe was out of his mouth, and a broad grin in its place. He rose, with his hand to his cap.

'I am, madame, at your service.'

'Will you take me to the other side?'

'You don't need a boat; the bridge is closed,' said one of his comrades at the foot of the steps, looking that way.

'I know it,' said Madame Bernier; 'but I wish to go to the cemetery, and a boat will save me half a mile walking.'

'The cemetery is shut at this hour.'

'*Allons*, leave madame alone,' said the man first spoken to. 'This way, my lady.'

Hortense seated herself in the stern of the boat. The man took the sculls.

'Straight across?' he asked.

Hortense looked around her. 'It's a fine evening,' said she; 'suppose you row me out to the lighthouse, and leave me at the point nearest the cemetery on our way back.'

'Very well,' rejoined the boatman; 'fifteen sous,' and began to pull lustily.

'*Allez*, I'll pay you well,' said Madame.

'Fifteen sous is the fare,' insisted the man.

'Give me a pleasant row, and I'll give you a hundred,' said Hortense.

Her companion said nothing. He evidently wished to appear not to have heard her remark. Silence was probably the most dignified manner of receiving a promise too munificent to be anything but a jest.

For some time this silence was maintained, broken only by the trickling of the oars and the sounds from the neighboring shores and vessels. Madame Bernier was plunged in a sidelong scrutiny of her ferryman's countenance. He was a man of about thirty-five. His face was dogged, brutal, and sullen. These indications were perhaps exaggerated by the dull monotony of his exercise. The eyes lacked a certain rascally gleam which had appeared in them when he was so *empressé* with the offer of his services. The face was better then—that is, if vice is better than ignorance. We say a countenance is 'lit up' by a smile; and indeed that momentary flicker does the office of a candle in a dark room. It sheds a ray upon the dim upholstery of our souls. The visages of poor men, generally, know few alternations. There is a large class of human beings whom fortune restricts to a single change of expression, or, perhaps, rather to a single expression. Ah me! the faces which wear either nakedness or rags; whose repose is stagnation, whose activity vice; ignorant at their worst, infamous at their best!

'Don't pull too hard,' said Hortense at last. 'Hadn't you better take breath a moment?'

'Madame is very good,' said the man, leaning upon his oars. 'But if you had taken me by the hour,' he added, with a return of the vicious grin, 'you wouldn't catch me loitering.'

'I suppose you work very hard,' said Madame Bernier.

The man gave a little toss of his head, as if to intimate the inadequacy of any supposition to grasp the extent of his labors.

'I've been up since four o'clock this morning, wheeling bales and boxes on the quay, and plying my little boat. Sweating without five minutes' intermission. *C'est comme ça.* Sometimes I tell my mate I think I'll take a plunge in the basin to dry myself. Ha! ha! ha!'

'And of course you gain little,' said Madame Bernier.

'Worse than nothing. Just what will keep me fat enough for starvation to feed on.'

'How? you go without your necessary food?'

'Necessary is a very elastic word, madame. You can narrow it down, so that in the degree above nothing it means luxury. My necessary food is sometimes thin air. If I don't deprive myself of that, it's because I can't.'

'Is it possible to be so unfortunate?'

'Shall I tell you what I have eaten to-day?'

'Do,' said Madame Bernier.

'A piece of black bread and a salt herring are all that have passed my lips for twelve hours.'

'Why don't you get some better work?'

'If I should die to-night,' pursued the boatman, heedless of the question, in the manner of a man whose impetus on the track of self-pity drives him past the signal flags of relief, 'what would there be left to bury me? These clothes I have on might buy me a long box. For the cost of this shabby old suit, that hasn't lasted me a twelvemonth, I could get one that I wouldn't wear out in a thousand years. *La bonne idée!*'

'Why don't you get some work that pays better?' repeated Hortense.

The man dipped his oars again.

'Work that pays better? I must work for work. I must earn that too. Work is wages. I count the promise of the next week's employment the best part of my Saturday night's pocketings. Fifty casks rolled from the ship to the storehouse mean two things: thirty sous and fifty more to roll the next day. Just so a crushed hand, or a dislocated shoulder, mean twenty francs to the apothecary and *bon jour* to my business.

'Are you married?' asked Hortense.

'No, I thank you. I'm not cursed with that blessing. But I've an old mother, a sister, and three nephews, who look to me for support. The old woman's too old to work; the lass is too lazy, and the little ones are too young. But they're none of them too old or young to be hungry, *allez*. I'll be hanged if I'm not a father to them all.'

There was a pause. The man had resumed rowing. Madame Bernier sat motionless, still examining her neighbor's physiognomy. The sinking sun, striking full upon his face, covered it with an almost lurid glare. Her own features being darkened against the western sky, the direction of them was quite indistinguishable to her companion.

'Why don't you leave the place?' she said at last.

'Leave it! how?' he replied, looking up with the rough avidity with which people of his class receive proposals touching their interests, extending to the most philanthropic suggestions that mistrustful eagerness with which experience has taught them to defend their own side of a bargain—the only form of proposal that she has made them acquainted with.

'Go somewhere else,' said Hortense.

'Where, for instance!'

'To some new country—America.'

The man burst into a loud laugh. Madame Bernier's face bore more evidence of interest in the play of his features than of that discomfiture which generally accompanies the consciousness of ridicule.

'There's a lady's scheme for you! If you'll write for furnished apartments, *là-bas*, I don't desire anything better. But no leaps in the dark for me. America and Algeria are very fine words to cram into an empty stomach when you're lounging in the sun, out of work, just as you stuff tobacco into your pipe and let the smoke curl around your head. But they fade away before a cutlet and a bottle of wine. When the earth grows so smooth and the air so pure that you can see the American coast from the pier yonder, then I'll make up my bundle. Not before.'

'You're afraid, then, to risk anything?'

'I'm afraid of nothing, *moi*. But I am not a fool either. I don't want to kick away my *sabots* till I am certain of a pair of shoes. I can go barefoot here. I don't want to find water where I counted on land. As for America, I've been there already.'

'Ah! you've been there?'

'I've been to Brazil and Mexico and California and the West Indies.'

'Ah!'

'I've been to Asia, too.'

'Ah!'

'*Pardio*, to China and India. Oh, I've seen the world! I've been three times around the Cape.'

'You've been a seaman then?'

'Yes, ma'am; fourteen years.'

'On what ship?'

'Bless your heart, on fifty ships.'

'French?'

'French and English and Spanish; mostly Spanish.'

'Ah?'

'Yes, and the more fool I was.'

'How so?'

'Oh, it was a dog's life. I'd drown any dog that would play half the mean tricks I used to see.'

'And you never had a hand in any yourself?'

'*Pardon*, I gave what I got. I was as good a Spaniard and as great a devil as any. I carried my knife with the best of them, and drew it as quickly, and plunged it as deep. I've got scars, if you weren't a lady. But I'd warrant to find you their mates on a dozen Spanish hides!'

He seemed to pull with renewed vigor at the recollection. There was a short silence.

'Do you suppose,' said Madame Bernier, in a few moments—'do you remember—that is, can you form any idea whether you ever killed a man?'

There was a momentary slackening of the boatman's oars. He gave a sharp glance at his passenger's countenance, which was still so shaded by her position, however, as to be indistinguishable. The tone of her interrogation had betrayed a simple, idle curiosity. He hesitated a moment, and then gave one of those conscious, cautious, dubious smiles, which may cover either a criminal assumption of more than the truth or a guilty repudiation of it.

'*Mon Dieu!*' said he, with a great shrug, 'there's a question! . . . . . I never killed one without a reason.'

'Of course not,' said Hortense.

'Though a reason in South America, *ma foi!*' added the boatman, 'wouldn't be a reason here.'

'I suppose not. What would be a reason there?'

'Well, if I killed a man in Valparaiso—I don't say I did, mind—it's because my knife went in farther than I intended.'

'But why did you use it at all?'

'I didn't. If I had, it would have been because he drew his against me.'

'And why should he have done so?'

'*Ventrebleu!* for as many reasons as there are craft in the harbor.'

'For example?'

'Well, that I should have got a place in a ship's company that he was trying for.'

'Such things as that? is it possible?'

'Oh, for smaller things. That a lass should have given me a dozen oranges she had promised him.'

'How odd!' said Madame Bernier, with a shrill kind of laugh. 'A man who owed you a grudge of this kind would just come up and stab you, I suppose, and think nothing of it?'

'Precisely. Drive a knife up to the hilt into your back, with an oath, and slice open a melon with it, with a song, five minutes afterward.'

'And when a person is afraid, or ashamed, or in some way unable to take revenge himself, does he—or it may be a woman—does she, get some one else to do it for her?'

'*Parbleu!* Poor devils on the look-out for such work are as plentiful all along the South American coast as *commission-aires* on the street corners here.' The ferryman was evidently surprised at the fascination possessed by this infamous topic for so lady-like a person; but having, as you see, a very ready tongue, it is probable that his delight in being able to give her information and hear himself talk were still greater. 'And then down there,' he went on, 'they never forget a grudge. If a fellow doesn't serve you one day, he'll do it another. A Spaniard's hatred is like lost sleep—you can put it off for a time, but it will gripe you in the end. The rascals always keep their promises to themselves. . . . . An enemy on shipboard is jolly fun. It's like bulls tethered in the same field. You can't stand still half a minute except against a wall. Even when he makes friends with you, his favors never taste right. Messing with him is like drinking out of a pewter mug. And so it is everywhere. Let your shadow once flit across a Spaniard's path, and he'll always see it there. If you've never lived in any but these damned clockworky European towns, you can't imagine the state of things in a South American seaport—one half the population waiting round the corner for the other half. But I don't see that it's so much better here, where every man's a spy on every other. There you meet an assassin at every turn, here a *sergent de ville*. . . . . At all events, the life *là bas* used to remind me, more than anything else, of sailing in a shallow channel, where you don't know what infernal rock you may ground on. Every man has a standing account with his neighbor, just as madame has at her *fournisseur's*; and, *ma foi*, those are the only accounts they settle. The master of the *Santiago* may pay me one of these days for the pretty names I heaved after him when we parted company, but he'll never pay me my wages.'

A short pause followed this exposition of the virtues of the Spaniard.

'You yourself never put a man out of the world, then?' resumed Hortense.

'Oh, *que si!* . . . . Are you horrified?'

'Not at all. I know that the thing is often justifiable.'

The man was silent a moment, perhaps with surprise, for the next thing he said was:

'Madame is Spanish?'

'In that, perhaps, I am,' replied Hortense.

Again her companion was silent. The pause was prolonged. Madame Bernier broke it by a question which showed that she had been following the same train of thought.

'What is sufficient ground in this country for killing a man?'

The boatman sent a loud laugh over the water. Hortense drew her cloak closer about her.

'I'm afraid there is none.'

'Isn't there a right of self-defence?'

'To be sure there is—it's one I ought to know something about. But it's one that *ces messieurs* at the Palais make short work with.'

'In South America and those countries, when a man makes life insupportable to you, what do you do?'

'*Mon Dieu!* I suppose you kill him.'

'And in France?'

'I suppose you kill yourself. Ha! ha! ha!'

By this time they had reached the end of the great breakwater, terminating in a lighthouse, the limit, on one side, of the inner harbor. The sun had set.

'Here we are at the lighthouse,' said the man; 'it's growing dark. Shall we turn?'

Hortense rose in her place a few moments, and stood looking out to sea. 'Yes,' she said at last, 'you may go back—slowly.' When the boat had headed round she resumed her old position, and put one of her hands over the side, drawing it through the water as they moved, and gazing into the long ripples.

At last she looked up at her companion. Now that her face caught some of the lingering light of the west, he could see that it was deathly pale.

'You find it hard to get along in the world,' said she: 'I shall be very glad to help you.'

The man started, and stared a moment. Was it because this remark jarred upon the expression which he was able faintly to discern in her eyes? The next, he put his hand to his cap.

'Madame is very kind. What will you do?'

Madame Bernier returned his gaze.

'I will trust you.'

'Ah!'

'And reward you.'

'Ah? Madame has a piece of work for me?'

'A piece of work,' Hortense nodded.

The man said nothing, waiting apparently for an explanation. His face wore the look of lowering irritation which low natures feel at being puzzled.

'Are you a bold man?'

Light seemed to come in this question. The quick expansion of his features answered it. You cannot touch upon certain subjects with an inferior but by the sacrifice of the barrier which separates you from him. There are thoughts and feelings and glimpses and foreshadowings of thoughts which level all inequalities of station.

'I'm bold enough,' said the boatman, 'for anything *you* want me to do.'

'Are you bold enough to commit a crime?'

'Not for nothing.'

'If I ask you to endanger your peace of mind, to risk your personal safety for me, it is certainly not as a favor. I will give you ten times the weight in gold of every grain by which your conscience grows heavier in my service.'

The man gave her a long, hard look through the dim light.

'I know what you want me to do,' he said at last.

'Very well,' said Hortense; 'will you do it?'

He continued to gaze. She met his eyes like a woman who has nothing more to conceal.

'State your case.'

'Do you know a vessel named the *Armorique*, a steamer?'

'Yes; it runs from Southampton.'

'It will arrive to-morrow morning early. Will it be able to cross the bar?'

'No; not till noon.'

'I thought so. I expect a person by it—a man.'

Madame Bernier appeared unable to continue, as if her voice had given way.

'Well, well?' said her companion.

'He's the person'—she stopped again.

'The person who—?'

'The person whom I wish to get rid of.'

For some moments nothing was said. The boatman was the first to speak again.

'Have you formed a plan?'

Hortense nodded.

'Let's hear it.'

'The person in question,' said Madame Bernier, 'will be impatient to land before noon. The house to which he returns will be in view of the vessel if, as you say, she lies at anchor. If he can get a boat, he will be sure to come ashore. *Eh bien!*— but you understand me.'

'Aha! you mean my boat—*this* boat?'

'O God!'

Madame Bernier sprang up in her seat, threw out her arms, and sank down again, burying her face in her knees. Her companion hastily shipped his oars, and laid his hands on her shoulders.

'*Allons donc*, in the devil's name, don't break down,' said he; 'we'll come to an understanding.'

Kneeling in the bottom of the boat, and supporting her by his grasp, he succeeded in making her raise herself, though her head still drooped.

'You want me to finish him in the boat?'

No answer.

'Is he an old man?'

Hortense shook her head faintly.

'My age?'

She nodded.

'*Sapristi!* it isn't so easy.'

'He can't swim,' said Hortense, without looking up; 'he— he is lame.'

'*Nom de Dieu!*' The boatman dropped his hands. Hortense looked up quickly. Do you read the pantomime?

'Never mind,' added the man at last, 'it will serve as a sign.'

'*Mais oui*. And besides that, he will ask to be taken to the Maison Bernier, the house with its back to the water, on the extension of the great quay. *Tenez*, you can almost see it from here.'

'I know the place,' said the boatman, and was silent, as if asking and answering himself a question.

Hortense was about to interrupt the train of thought which she apprehended he was following, when he forestalled her.

'How am I to be sure of my affair?' asked he.

'Of your reward? I've thought of that. This watch is a pledge of what I shall be able and glad to give you afterward. There are two thousand francs' worth of pearls in the case.'

'*Il faut fixer la somme,*' said the man, leaving the watch untouched.

'That lies with you.'

'Good. You know that I have the right to ask a high price.'

'Certainly. Name it.'

'It's only on the supposition of a large sum that I will so

much as consider your proposal. *Songez donc*, that it's a MURDER you ask of me.'

'The price—the price?'

'Tenez,' continued the man, 'poached game is always high. The pearls in that watch are costly because it's worth a man's life to get at them. You want me to be your pearl diver. Be it so. You must guarantee me a safe descent,—it's a descent, you know—ha!—you must furnish me the armor of safety; a little gap to breathe through while I'm at my work—the thought of a capful of Napoleons!'

'My good man, I don't wish to talk to you or to listen to your sallies. I wish simply to know your price. I'm not bargaining for a pair of chickens. Propose a sum.'

The boatman had by this time resumed his seat and his oars. He stretched out for a long, slow pull, which brought him closely face to face with his temptress. This position, his body bent forward, his eyes fixed on Madame Bernier's face, he kept for some seconds. It was perhaps fortunate for Hortense's purpose at that moment—it had often aided her purposes before—that she was a pretty woman.* A plain face might have emphasized the utterly repulsive nature of the negotiation. Suddenly, with a quick, convulsive movement, the man completed the stroke.

'Pas si bête! propose one yourself.'

'Very well,' said Hortense, 'if you wish it. *Voyons:* I'll give you what I can. I have fifteen thousand francs' worth of jewels. I'll give you them, or, if they will get you into trouble, their value. At home, in a box I have a thousand francs in gold. You shall have those. I'll pay your passage and outfit to America. I have friends in New York. I'll write to them to get you work.'

'And you'll give your washing to my mother and sister, *hein?* Ha! ha! Jewels, fifteen thousand francs; one thousand more makes sixteen; passage to America—first class—five hundred francs; outfit—what does Madame understand by that?'

---

*I am told that there was no resisting her smile; and that she had at her command, in moments of grief, a certain look of despair which filled even the roughest hearts with sympathy, and won over the kindest to the cruel cause.

'Everything needful for your success *là-bas*.'

'A written denial that I am an assassin? *Ma foi*, it were better not to remove the impression. It's served me a good turn, on this side of the water at least. Call it twenty-five thousand francs.'

'Very well; but not a sous more.'

'Shall I trust you?'

'Am I not trusting you? It is well for you that I do not allow myself to think of the venture I am making.'

'Perhaps we're even there. We neither of us can afford to make account of certain possibilities. Still, I'll trust you, too. . . . . *Tiens!*' added the boatman, 'here we are near the quay.' Then with a mock-solemn touch of his cap, 'Will Madame still visit the cemetery?'

'Come, quick, let me land,' said Madame Bernier, impatiently.

'We *have* been among the dead, after a fashion,' persisted the boatman, as he gave her his hand.

III.

It was more than eight o'clock when Madame Bernier reached her own house.

'Has M. de Meyrau been here?' she asked of Josephine.

'Yes, ma'am; and on learning that Madame was out, he left a note, *chez monsieur*.'

Hortense found a sealed letter on the table in her husband's old study. It ran as follows:

'I was desolated at finding you out. I had a word to tell you. I have accepted an invitation to sup and pass the night at C——, thinking it would look well. For the same reason I have resolved to take the bull by the horns, and go aboard the steamer on my return, to welcome M. Bernier home—the privilege of an old friend. I am told the *Armorique* will anchor off the bar by daybreak. What do you think? But it's too late to let me know. Applaud my *savoir faire*—you will, at all events, in the end. You will see how it will smoothe matters.'

'Baffled! baffled!' hissed Madame, when she had read the note; 'God deliver me from my friends!' She paced up and down the room several times, and at last began to mutter to herself, as people often do in moments of strong emotion: 'Bah! but he'll never get up by daybreak. He'll oversleep himself, especially after to-night's supper. The other will be before him. . . . . Oh, my poor head, you've suffered too much to fail in the end!'

Josephine reappeared to offer to remove her mistress's things. The latter, in her desire to reassure herself, asked the first question that occurred to her.

'Was M. le Vicomte alone?'

'No, madame; another gentleman was with him—M. de Saulges, I think. They came in a hack, with two portmanteaus.'

Though I have judged best, hitherto, often from an exaggerated fear of trenching on the ground of fiction, to tell you what this poor lady did and said, rather than what she thought. I may disclose what passed in her mind now:

'Is he a coward? is he going to leave me? or is he simply going to pass these last hours in play and drink? He might have stayed with me. Ah! my friend, you do little for me, who do so much for you; who commit murder, and—Heaven help me!—suicide for you! . . . . But I suppose he knows best. At all events, he will make a night of it.'

When the cook came in late that evening, Josephine, who had sat up for her, said:

'You've no idea how Madame is looking. She's ten years older since this morning. Holy mother! what a day this has been for her!'

'Wait till to-morrow,' said the oracular Valentine.

Later, when the women went up to bed in the attic, they saw a light under Hortense's door, and during the night Josephine, whose chamber was above Madame's, and who couldn't sleep (for sympathy, let us say), heard movements beneath her, which told that her mistress was even more wakeful than she.

IV.

There was considerable bustle around the *Armorique* as she anchored outside the harbor of H——, in the early dawn of the following day. A gentleman, with an overcoat, walking stick, and small valise, came alongside in a little fishing boat, and got leave to go aboard.

'Is M. Bernier here?' he asked of one of the officers, the first man he met.

'I fancy he's gone ashore, sir. There was a boatman inquiring for him a few minutes ago, and I think he carried him off.

M. de Meyrau reflected a moment. Then he crossed over to the other side of the vessel, looking landward. Leaning over the bulwarks he saw an empty boat moored to the ladder which ran up the vessel's side.

'That's a town boat, isn't it?' he said to one of the hands standing by.

'Yes, sir.'

'Where's the master?'

'I suppose he'll be here in a moment. I saw him speaking to one of the officers just now.'

De Meyrau descended the ladder, and seated himself at the stern of the boat. As the sailor he had just addressed was handing down his bag, a face with a red cap looked over the bulwarks.

'Hullo, my man!' cried De Meyrau, 'is this your boat?'

'Yes, sir, at your service,' answered the red cap, coming to the top of the ladder, and looking hard at the gentleman's stick and portmanteau.

'Can you take me to town, to Madame Bernier's, at the end of the new quay?'

'Certainly, sir,' said the boatman, scuttling down the ladder, 'you're just the gentleman I want.'

An hour later Hortense Bernier came out of the house, and began to walk slowly through the garden toward the terrace which overlooked the water. The servants, when they came down at an early hour, had found her up and dressed, or rather, apparently, not undressed, for she wore the same clothes as the evening before.

'Tiens!' exclaimed Josephine, after seeing her, 'Madame gained ten years yesterday; she has gained ten more during the night.'

When Madame Bernier reached the middle of the garden

she halted, and stood for a moment motionless, listening. The next, she uttered a great cry. For she saw a figure emerge from below the terrace, and come limping toward her with outstretched arms.

The Story of a Year

MY STORY begins as a great many stories have begun
within the last three years, and indeed as a great many
have ended; for, when the hero is despatched, does not the
romance come to a stop?

In early May, two years ago, a young couple I wot of
strolled homeward from an evening walk, a long ramble
among the peaceful hills which inclosed their rustic home.
Into these peaceful hills the young man had brought, not the
rumor, (which was an old inhabitant,) but some of the reality
of war,—a little whiff of gunpowder, the clanking of a sword;
for, although Mr. John Ford had his campaign still before
him, he wore a certain comely air of camp-life which stamped
him a very Hector to the steady-going villagers, and a very
pretty fellow to Miss Elizabeth Crowe, his companion in this
sentimental stroll. And was he not attired in the great brightness of blue and gold which befits a freshly made lieutenant?
This was a strange sight for these happy Northern glades; for,
although the first Revolution had boomed awhile in their
midst, the honest yeomen who defended them were clad in
sober homespun, and it is well known that His Majesty's
troops wore red.

These young people, I say, had been roaming. It was plain
that they had wandered into spots where the brambles were
thick and the dews heavy,—nay, into swamps and puddles
where the April rains were still undried. Ford's boots and
trousers had imbibed a deep foretaste of the Virginia mud; his
companion's skirts were fearfully bedraggled. What great enthusiasm had made our friends so unmindful of their steps?
What blinding ardor had kindled these strange phenomena: a
young lieutenant scornful of his first uniform, a well-bred
young lady reckless of her stockings?

Good reader, this narrative is averse to retrospect.

Elizabeth (as I shall not scruple to call her outright) was
leaning upon her companion's arm, half moving in concert
with him, and half allowing herself to be led, with that in-

stinctive acknowledgment of dependence natural to a young
girl who has just received the assurance of lifelong protection.
Ford was lounging along with that calm, swinging stride
which often bespeaks, when you can read it aright, the answering consciousness of a sudden rush of manhood. A spectator might have thought him at this moment profoundly
conceited. The young girl's blue veil was dangling from his
pocket; he had shouldered her sun-umbrella after the fashion
of a musket on a march: he might carry these trifles. Was
there not a vague longing expressed in the strong expansion
of his stalwart shoulders, in the fond accommodation of his
pace to hers,—her pace so submissive and slow, that, when he
tried to match it, they almost came to a delightful standstill,—a silent desire for the whole fair burden?

They made their way up a long swelling mound, whose top
commanded the sunset. The dim landscape which had been
brightening all day to the green of spring was now darkening
to the gray of evening. The lesser hills, the farms, the brooks,
the fields, orchards, and woods, made a dusky gulf before the
great splendor of the west. As Ford looked at the clouds, it
seemed to him that their imagery was all of war, their great
uneven masses were marshalled into the semblance of a battle.
There were columns charging and columns flying and standards floating,—tatters of the reflected purple; and great
captains on colossal horses, and a rolling canopy of cannon-
smoke and fire and blood. The background of the clouds, indeed, was like a land on fire, or a battle-ground illumined by
another sunset, a country of blackened villages and crimsoned
pastures. The tumult of the clouds increased; it was hard to
believe them inanimate. You might have fancied them an
army of gigantic souls playing at football with the sun. They
seemed to sway in confused splendor; the opposing squadrons
bore each other down; and then suddenly they scattered,
bowling with equal velocity towards north and south, and
gradually fading into the pale evening sky. The purple pen-
nons sailed away and sank out of sight, caught, doubtless,
upon the brambles of the intervening plain. Day contracted
itself into a fiery ball and vanished.

Ford and Elizabeth had quietly watched this great mystery
of the heavens.

"That is an allegory," said the young man, as the sun went under, looking into his companion's face, where a pink flush seemed still to linger: "it means the end of the war. The forces on both sides are withdrawn. The blood that has been shed gathers itself into a vast globule and drops into the ocean."

"I'm afraid it means a shabby compromise," said Elizabeth. "Light disappears, too, and the land is in darkness."

"Only for a season," answered the other. "We mourn our dead. Then light comes again, stronger and brighter than ever. Perhaps you'll be crying for me, Lizzie, at that distant day."

"Oh, Jack, didn't you promise not to talk about that?" says Lizzie, threatening to anticipate the performance in question.

Jack took this rebuke in silence, gazing soberly at the empty sky. Soon the young girl's eyes stole up to his face. If he had been looking at anything in particular, I think she would have followed the direction of his glance; but as it seemed to be a very vacant one, she let her eyes rest.

"Jack," said she, after a pause, "I wonder how you'll look when you get back."

Ford's soberness gave way to a laugh.

"Uglier than ever. I shall be all incrusted with mud and gore. And then I shall be magnificently sun-burnt, and I shall have a beard."

"Oh, you dreadful!" and Lizzie gave a little shout. "Really, Jack, if you have a beard, you'll not look like a gentleman."

"Shall I look like a lady, pray?" says Jack.

"Are you serious?" asked Lizzie.

"To be sure. I mean to alter my face as you do your misfitting garments,—take in on one side and let out on the other. Isn't that the process? I shall crop my head and cultivate my chin."

"You've a very nice chin, my dear, and I think it's a shame to hide it."

"Yes, I know my chin's handsome; but wait till you see my beard."

"Oh, the vanity!" cried Lizzie, "the vanity of men in their faces! Talk of women!" and the silly creature looked up at her lover with most inconsistent satisfaction.

"Oh, the pride of women in their husbands!" said Jack, who of course knew what she was about.

"You're not my husband, Sir. There's many a slip"—— But the young girl stopped short.

" 'Twixt the cup and the lip," said Jack. "Go on. I can match your proverb with another. 'There's many a true word,' and so forth. No, my darling: I'm not your husband. Perhaps I never shall be. But if anything happens to me, you'll take comfort, won't you?"

"Never!" said Lizzie, tremulously.

"Oh, but you must; otherwise, Lizzie, I should think our engagement inexcusable. Stuff! who am I that you should cry for me?"

"You are the best and wisest of men. I don't care; you *are*."

"Thank you for your great love, my dear. That's a delightful illusion. But I hope Time will kill it, in his own good way, before it hurts any one. I know so many men who are worth infinitely more than I—men wise, generous, and brave—that I shall not feel as if I were leaving you in an empty world."

"Oh, my dear friend!" said Lizzie, after a pause, "I wish you could advise me all my life."

"Take care, take care," laughed Jack; "you don't know what you are bargaining for. But will you let me say a word now? If by chance I'm taken out of the world, I want you to beware of that tawdry sentiment which enjoins you to be 'constant to my memory.' My memory be hanged! Remember me at my best,—that is, fullest of the desire of humility. Don't inflict me on people. There are some widows and bereaved sweethearts who remind me of the peddler in that horrible murder-story, who carried a corpse in his pack. Really, it's their stock in trade. The only justification of a man's personality is his rights. What rights has a dead man?—Let's go down."

They turned southward and went jolting down the hill.

"Do you mind this talk, Lizzie?" asked Ford.

"No," said Lizzie, swallowing a sob, unnoticed by her companion in the sublime egotism of protection; "I like it."

"Very well," said the young man, "I want my memory to help you. When I am down in Virginia, I expect to get a vast deal of good from thinking of you,—to do my work better, and to keep straighter altogether. Like all lovers, I'm horribly selfish. I expect to see a vast deal of shabbiness and baseness and turmoil, and in the midst of it all I'm sure the inspiration of patriotism will sometimes fail. Then I'll think of you. I love you a thousand times better than my country, Liz.—Wicked? So much the worse. It's the truth. But if I find your memory makes a milksop of me, I shall thrust you out of the way, without ceremony,—I shall clap you into my box or between the leaves of my Bible, and only look at you on Sunday."

"I shall be very glad, Sir, if that makes you open your Bible frequently," says Elizabeth, rather demurely.

"I shall put one of your photographs against every page," cried Ford; "and then I think I shall not lack a text for my meditations. Don't you know how Catholics keep little pictures of their adored Lady in their prayer-books?"

"Yes, indeed," said Lizzie; "I should think it would be a very soul-stirring picture, when you are marching to the front, the night before a battle,—a poor, stupid girl, knitting stupid socks, in a stupid Yankee village."

Oh, the craft of artless tongues! Jack strode along in silence a few moments, splashing straight through a puddle; then, ere he was quite clear of it, he stretched out his arm and gave his companion a long embrace.

"And pray what am I to do," resumed Lizzie, wondering, rather proudly perhaps, at Jack's averted face, "while you are marching and countermarching in Virginia?"

"Your duty, of course," said Jack, in a steady voice, which belied a certain little conjecture of Lizzie's. "I think you will find the sun will rise in the east, my dear, just as it did before you were engaged."

"I'm sure I didn't suppose it wouldn't," says Lizzie.

"By duty I don't mean anything disagreeable, Liz," pursued the young man. "I hope you'll take your pleasure, too. I wish you might go to Boston, or even to Leatherborough, for a month or two."

"What for, pray?"

"What for? Why, for the fun of it: to 'go out,' as they say."

"Jack, do you think me capable of going to parties while you are in danger?"

"Why not? Why should I have all the fun?"

"Fun? I'm sure you're welcome to it all. As for me, I mean to make a new beginning."

"Of what?"

"Oh, of everything. In the first place, I shall begin to improve my mind. But don't you think it's horrid for women to be reasonable?"

"Hard, say you?"

"Horrid,—yes, and hard too. But I mean to become so. Oh, girls are such fools, Jack! I mean to learn to like boiled mutton and history and plain sewing, and all that. Yet, when a girl's engaged, she's not expected to do anything in particular."

Jack laughed, and said nothing; and Lizzie went on.

"I wonder what your mother will say to the news. I think I know."

"What?"

"She'll say you've been very unwise. No, she won't: she never speaks so to you. She'll say I've been very dishonest or indelicate, or something of that kind. No, she won't either: she doesn't say such things, though I'm sure she thinks them. I don't know what she'll say."

"No, I think not, Lizzie, if you indulge in such conjectures. My mother never speaks without thinking. Let us hope that she may think favorably of our plan. Even if she doesn't"——

Jack did not finish his sentence, nor did Lizzie urge him. She had a great respect for his hesitations. But in a moment he began again.

"I was going to say this, Lizzie: I think for the present our engagement had better be kept quiet."

Lizzie's heart sank with a sudden disappointment. Imagine the feelings of the damsel in the fairy-tale, whom the disguised enchantress had just empowered to utter diamonds and pearls, should the old beldame have straightway added that for the present mademoiselle had better hold her tongue. Yet the disappointment was brief. I think this enviable young lady would have tripped home talking very hard to herself, and have been not ill pleased to find her little mouth turning into a tightly clasped jewel-casket. Nay, would she not on this occasion have been thankful for a large mouth,—a mouth huge and unnatural,—stretching from ear to ear? Who wish to cast their pearls before swine? The young lady of the pearls was, after all, but a barnyard miss. Lizzie was too proud of

Jack to be vain. It's well enough to wear our own hearts upon our sleeves; but for those of others, when intrusted to our keeping, I think we had better find a more secluded lodging.

"You see, I think secrecy would leave us much freer," said Jack,—"leave *you* much freer."

"Oh, Jack, how can you?" cried Lizzie. "Yes, of course; I shall be falling in love with some one else. Freer! Thank you, Sir!"

"Nay, Lizzie, what I'm saying is really kinder than it sounds. Perhaps you *will* thank me one of these days."

"Doubtless! I've already taken a great fancy to George Mackenzie."

"Will you let me enlarge on my suggestion?"

"Oh, certainly! You seem to have your mind quite made up."

"I confess I like to take account of possibilities. Don't you know mathematics are my hobby? Did you ever study algebra? I always have an eye on the unknown quantity."

"No, I never studied algebra. I agree with you, that we had better not speak of our engagement."

"That's right, my dear. You're always right. But mind, I don't want to bind you to secrecy. Hang it, do as you please! Do what comes easiest to you, and you'll do the best thing. What made me speak is my dread of the horrible publicity which clings to all this business. Nowadays, when a girl's engaged, it's no longer, 'Ask mamma,' simply; but, 'Ask Mrs. Brown, and Mrs. Jones, and my large circle of acquaintance,—Mrs. Grundy, in short.' I say nowadays, but I suppose it's always been so."

"Very well, we'll keep it all nice and quiet," said Lizzie, who would have been ready to celebrate her nuptials according to the rites of the Esquimaux, had Jack seen fit to suggest it.

"I know it doesn't look well for a lover to be so cautious," pursued Jack; "but you understand me, Lizzie, don't you?"

"I don't entirely understand you, but I quite trust you."

"God bless you! My prudence, you see, is my best strength. Now, if ever, I need my strength. When a man's a-wooing, Lizzie, he is all feeling, or he ought to be; when he's accepted, then he begins to think."

"And to repent, I suppose you mean."

"Nay, to devise means to keep his sweetheart from repenting. Let me be frank. Is it the greatest fools only that are the best lovers? There's no telling what may happen, Lizzie. I want you to marry me with your eyes open. I don't want you to feel tied down or taken in. You're very young, you know. You're responsible to yourself of a year hence. You're at an age when no girl can count safely from year's end to year's end."

"And you, Sir!" cries Lizzie; "one would think you were a grandfather."

"Well, I'm on the way to it. I'm a pretty old boy. I mean what I say. I may not be entirely frank, but I think I'm sincere. It seems to me as if I'd been fibbing all my life before I told you that your affection was necessary to my happiness. I mean it out and out. I never loved any one before, and I never will again. If you had refused me half an hour ago, I should have died a bachelor. I have no fear for myself. But I have for you. You said a few minutes ago that you wanted me to be your adviser. Now you know the function of an adviser is to perfect his victim in the art of walking with his eyes shut. I sha'n't be so cruel."

Lizzie saw fit to view these remarks in a humorous light. "How disinterested!" quoth she: "how very self-sacrificing! Bachelor indeed! For my part, I think I shall become a Mormon!"—I verily believe the poor misinformed creature fancied that in Utah it is the ladies who are guilty of polygamy.

Before many minutes they drew near home. There stood Mrs. Ford at the garden-gate, looking up and down the road, with a letter in her hand.

"Something for you, John," said his mother, as they approached. "It looks as if it came from camp.—Why, Elizabeth, look at your skirts!"

"I know it," says Lizzie, giving the articles in question a shake. "What is it, Jack?"

"Marching orders!" cried the young man. "The regiment leaves day after to-morrow. I must leave by the early train in the morning. Hurray!" And he diverted a sudden gleeful kiss into a filial salute.

They went in. The two women were silent, after the manner of women who suffer. But Jack did little else than laugh and talk and circumnavigate the parlor, sitting first here and then there,—close beside Lizzie and on the opposite side of the room. After a while Miss Crowe joined in his laughter, but I think her mirth might have been resolved into articulate heart-beats. After tea she went to bed, to give Jack opportunity for his last filial *épanchements*. How generous a man's intervention makes women! But Lizzie promised to see her lover off in the morning.

"Nonsense!" said Mrs. Ford. "You'll not be up. John will want to breakfast quietly."

"I shall see you off, Jack," repeated the young lady, from the threshold.

Elizabeth went up stairs buoyant with her young love. It had dawned upon her like a new life,—a life positively worth the living. Hereby she would subsist and cost nobody anything. In it she was boundlessly rich. She would make it the hidden spring of a hundred praiseworthy deeds. She would begin the career of duty: she would enjoy boundless equanimity: she would raise her whole being to the level of her sublime passion. She would practise charity, humility, piety;—in fine, all the virtues: together with certain *morceaux* of Beethoven and Chopin. She would walk the earth like one glorified. She would do homage to the best of men by inviolate secrecy. Here, by I know not what gentle transition, as she lay in the quiet darkness, Elizabeth covered her pillow with a flood of tears.

Meanwhile Ford, down-stairs, began in this fashion. He was lounging at his manly length on the sofa, in his slippers.

"May I light a pipe, mother?"

"Yes, my love. But please be careful of your ashes. There's a newspaper."

"Pipes don't make ashes.—Mother, what do you think?" he continued, between the puffs of his smoking; "I've got a piece of news."

"Ah?" said Mrs. Ford, fumbling for her scissors; "I hope it's good news."

"I hope you'll think it so. I've been engaging myself"—puff,—puff—"to Lizzie Crowe." A cloud of puffs between his mother's face and his own. When they cleared away, Jack felt his mother's eyes. Her work was in her lap. "To be married, you know," he added.

In Mrs. Ford's view, like the king in that of the British Constitution, her only son could do no wrong. Prejudice is a stout bulwark against surprise. Moreover, Mrs. Ford's motherly instinct had not been entirely at fault. Still, it had by no means kept pace with fact. She had been silent, partly from doubt, partly out of respect for her son. As long as John did not doubt of himself, he was right. Should he come to do so, she was sure he would speak. And now, when he told her the matter was settled, she persuaded herself that he was asking her advice.

"I've been expecting it," she said, at last.

"You have? why didn't you speak?"

"Well, John, I can't say I've been hoping it."

"Why not?"

"I am not sure of Lizzie's heart," said Mrs. Ford, who, it may be well to add, was very sure of her own.

Jack began to laugh. "What's the matter with her heart?"

"I think Lizzie's shallow," said Mrs. Ford; and there was that in her tone which betokened some satisfaction with this adjective.

"Hang it! she is shallow," said Jack. "But when a thing's shallow, you can see to the bottom. Lizzie doesn't pretend to be deep. I want a wife, mother, that I can understand. That's the only wife I can love. Lizzie's the only girl I ever understood, and the first I ever loved. I love her very much,—more than I can explain to you."

"Yes, I confess it's inexplicable. It seems to me," she added, with a bad smile, "like infatuation."

Jack did not like the smile; he liked it even less than the remark. He smoked steadily for a few moments, and then he said,—

"Well, mother, love is notoriously obstinate, you know. We shall not be able to take the same view of this subject: suppose we drop it."

"Remember that this is your last evening at home, my son," said Mrs. Ford.

"I do remember. Therefore I wish to avoid disagreement."

There was a pause. The young man smoked, and his mother sewed, in silence.

"I think my position, as Lizzie's guardian," resumed Mrs. Ford, "entitles me to an interest in the matter."

"Certainly, I acknowledged your interest by telling you of our engagement."

Further pause.

"Will you allow me to say," said Mrs. Ford, after a while, "that I think this a little selfish?"

"Allow you? Certainly, if you particularly desire it. Though I confess it isn't very pleasant for a man to sit and hear his future wife pitched into,—by his own mother, too."

"John, I am surprised at your language."

"I beg your pardon," and John spoke more gently. "You mustn't be surprised at anything from an accepted lover.— I'm sure you misconceive her. In fact, mother, I don't believe you know her."

Mrs. Ford nodded, with an infinite depth of meaning; and from the grimness with which she bit off the end of her thread it might have seemed that she fancied herself to be executing a human vengeance.

"Ah, I know her only too well!"

"And you don't like her?"

Mrs. Ford performed another decapitation of her thread.

"Well, I'm glad Lizzie has one friend in the world," said Jack.

"Her best friend," said Mrs. Ford, "is the one who flatters her least. I see it all, John. Her pretty face has done the business."

The young man flushed impatiently.

"Mother," said he, "you are very much mistaken. I'm not a boy nor a fool. You trust me in a great many things; why not trust me in this?"

"My dear son, you are throwing yourself away. You deserve for your companion in life a higher character than that girl."

I think Mrs. Ford, who had been an excellent mother, would have liked to give her son a wife fashioned on her own model.

"Oh, come, mother," said he, "that's twaddle. I should be thankful, if I were half as good as Lizzie."

"It's the truth, John, and your conduct—not only the step you've taken, but your talk about it—is a great disappointment to me. If I have cherished any wish of late, it is that my darling boy should get a wife worthy of him. The household governed by Elizabeth Crowe is not the home I should desire for any one I love."

"It's one to which you should always be welcome, Ma'am," said Jack.

"It's not a place I should feel at home in," replied his mother.

"I'm sorry," said Jack. And he got up and began to walk about the room. "Well, well, mother," he said at last, stopping in front of Mrs. Ford, "we don't understand each other. One of these days we shall. For the present let us have done with discussion. I'm half sorry I told you."

"I'm glad of such a proof of your confidence. But if you hadn't, of course Elizabeth would have done so."

"No, Ma'am, I think not."

"Then she is even more reckless of her obligations than I thought her."

"I advised her to say nothing about it."

Mrs. Ford made no answer. She began slowly to fold up her work.

"I think we had better let the matter stand," continued her son. "I'm not afraid of time. But I wish to make a request of you: you won't mention this conversation to Lizzie, will you? nor allow her to suppose that you know of our engagement? I have a particular reason."

Mrs. Ford went on smoothing out her work. Then she suddenly looked up.

"No, my dear, I'll keep your secret. Give me a kiss."

II.

I have no intention of following Lieutenant Ford to the seat of war. The exploits of his campaign are recorded in the public journals of the day, where the curious may still peruse them. My own taste has always been for unwritten history, and my present business is with the reverse of the picture.

After Jack went off, the two ladies resumed their old homely life. But the homeliest life had now ceased to be repulsive to Elizabeth. Her common duties were no longer wearisome: for the first time, she experienced the delicious companionship of thought. Her chief task was still to sit by the window knitting soldiers' socks; but even Mrs. Ford could not help owning that she worked with a much greater diligence, yawned, rubbed her eyes, gazed up and down the road less, and indeed produced a much more comely article. Ah, me! if half the lovesome fancies that flitted through Lizzie's spirit in those busy hours could have found their way into the texture of the dingy yarn, as it was slowly wrought into shape, the eventual wearer of the socks would have been as light-footed as Mercury. I am afraid I should make the reader sneer, were I to rehearse some of this little fool's diversions. She passed several hours daily in Jack's old chamber: it was in this sanctuary, indeed, at the sunny south window, overlooking the long road, the wood-crowned heights, the gleaming river, that she worked with most pleasure and profit. Here she was removed from the untiring glance of the elder lady, from her jarring questions and commonplaces; here she was alone with her love,—that greatest commonplace in life. Lizzie felt in Jack's room a certain impress of his personality. The idle fancies of her mood were bodied forth in a dozen sacred relics. Some of these articles Elizabeth carefully cherished. It was rather late in the day for her to assert a literary taste,—her reading having begun and ended (naturally enough) with the ancient fiction of the "Scottish Chiefs." So she could hardly help smiling, herself, sometimes, at her interest in Jack's old college tomes. She carried several of them to her own apartment, and placed them at the foot of her little bed, on a book-shelf adorned, besides, with a pot of spring violets, a portrait of General McClellan, and a likeness of Lieutenant Ford. She had a vague belief that a loving study of their well-thumbed verses would remedy, in some degree, her sad intellectual deficiencies. She was sorry she knew so little: as sorry, that is, as she might be, for we know that she was shallow. Jack's omniscience was one of his most awful attributes. And yet she comforted herself with the thought, that, as he had forgiven her ignorance, she herself might surely forget it.

Happy Lizzie, I envy you this easy path to knowledge! The
volume she most frequently consulted was an old German
"Faust," over which she used to fumble with a battered lexi-
con. The secret of this preference was in certain marginal
notes in pencil, signed "J." I hope they were really of Jack's
making.

Lizzie was always a small walker. Until she knew Jack, this
had been quite an unsuspected pleasure. She was afraid, too,
of the cows, geese, and sheep,—all the agricultural *spectra* of
the feminine imagination. But now her terrors were over.
Might she not play the soldier, too, in her own humble way?
Often with a beating heart, I fear, but still with resolute, elastic steps, she revisited Jack's old haunts; she tried to love
Nature as he had seemed to love it; she gazed at his old sunsets; she fathomed his old pools with bright plummet glances,
as if seeking some lingering trace of his features in their
brown depths, stamped there as on a fond human heart; she
sought out his dear name, scratched on the rocks and trees,—
and when night came on, she studied, in her simple way, the
great starlit canopy, under which, perhaps, her warrior lay
sleeping; she wandered through the green glades, singing
snatches of his old ballads in a clear voice, made tuneful with
love,—and as she sang, there mingled with the everlasting
murmur of the trees the faint sound of a muffled bass, borne
upon the south wind like a distant drum-beat, responsive to a
bugle. So she led for some months a very pleasant idyllic life,
face to face with a strong, vivid memory, which gave everything and asked nothing. These were doubtless to be (and she
half knew it) the happiest days of her life. Has life any bliss so
great as this pensive ecstasy? To know that the golden sands
are dropping one by one makes servitude freedom, and
poverty riches.

In spite of a certain sense of loss, Lizzie passed a very blissful summer. She enjoyed the deep repose which, it is to be
hoped, sanctifies all honest betrothals. Possible calamity
weighed lightly upon her. We know that when the columns of
battle-smoke leave the field, they journey through the heavy
air to a thousand quiet homes, and play about the crackling
blaze of as many firesides. But Lizzie's vision was never
clouded. Mrs. Ford might gaze into the thickening summer

dusk and wipe her spectacles; but her companion hummed her old ballad-ends with an unbroken voice. She no more ceased to smile under evil tidings than the brooklet ceases to ripple beneath the projected shadow of the roadside willow. The self-given promises of that tearful night of parting were forgotten. Vigilance had no place in Lizzie's scheme of heavenly idleness. The idea of moralizing in Elysium!

It must not be supposed that Mrs. Ford was indifferent to Lizzie's mood. She studied it watchfully, and kept note of all its variations. And among the things she learned was, that her companion knew of her scrutiny, and was, on the whole, indifferent to it. Of the full extent of Mrs. Ford's observation, however, I think Lizzie was hardly aware. She was like a reveller in a brilliantly lighted room, with a curtainless window, conscious, and yet heedless, of passers-by. And Mrs. Ford may not inaptly be compared to the chilly spectator on the dark side of the pane. Very few words passed on the topic of their common thoughts. From the first, as we have seen, Lizzie guessed at her guardian's probable view of her engagement: an abasement incurred by John. Lizzie lacked what is called a sense of duty; and, unlike the majority of such temperaments, which contrive to be buoyant on the glistening bubble of Dignity, she had likewise a modest estimate of her dues. Alack, my poor heroine had no pride! Mrs. Ford's silent censure awakened no resentment. It sounded in her ears like a dull, soporific hum. Lizzie was deeply enamored of what a French book terms her *aises intellectuelles.* Her mental comfort lay in the ignoring of problems. She possessed a certain native insight which revealed many of the horrent inequalities of her pathway; but she found it so cruel and disenchanting a faculty, that blindness was infinitely preferable. She preferred repose to order, and mercy to justice. She was speculative, without being critical. She was continually wondering, but she never inquired. This world was the riddle; the next alone would be the answer.

So she never felt any desire to have an "understanding" with Mrs. Ford. Did the old lady misconceive her? it was her own business. Mrs. Ford apparently felt no desire to set herself right. You see, Lizzie was ignorant of her friend's promise. There were moments when Mrs. Ford's tongue itched to speak. There were others, it is true, when she dreaded any explanation which would compel her to forfeit her displeasure. Lizzie's happy self-sufficiency was most irritating. She grudged the young girl the dignity of her secret; her own actual knowledge of it rather increased her jealousy, by showing her the importance of the scheme from which she was excluded. Lizzie, being in perfect good-humor with the world and with herself, abated no jot of her personal deference to Mrs. Ford. Of Jack, as a good friend and her guardian's son, she spoke very freely. But Mrs. Ford was mistrustful of this semi-confidence. She would not, she often said to herself, be wheedled against her principles. Her principles! Oh for some shining blade of purpose to hew down such stubborn stakes! Lizzie had no thought of flattering her companion. She never deceived any one but herself. She could not bring herself to value Mrs. Ford's good-will. She knew that Jack often suffered from his mother's obstinacy. So her unbroken humility shielded no unavowed purpose. She was patient and kindly from nature, from habit. Yet I think, that, if Mrs. Ford could have measured her benignity, she would have preferred, on the whole, the most open defiance. "Of all things," she would sometimes mutter, "to be patronized by that little piece!" It was very disagreeable, for instance, to have to listen to *portions* of her own son's letters.

These letters came week by week, flying out of the South like white-winged carrier-doves. Many and many a time, for very pride, Lizzie would have liked a larger audience. Portions of them certainly deserved publicity. They were far too good for her. Were they not better than that stupid war-correspondence in the "Times," which she so often tried in vain to read? They contained long details of movements, plans of campaigns, military opinions and conjectures, expressed with the emphasis habitual to young sub-lieutenants. I doubt whether General Halleck's despatches laid down the law more absolutely than Lieutenant Ford's. Lizzie answered in her own fashion. It must be owned that hers was a dull pen. She told her dearest, dearest Jack how much she loved and honored him, and how much she missed him, and how delightful his last letter was, (with those beautifully drawn diagrams,) and the village gossip, and how stout and strong his mother continued to be,—and again, how she loved, etc., etc., and that she remained his loving L. Jack read these effusions as became one so beloved. I should not wonder if he thought them very brilliant.

The summer waned to its close, and through myriad silent stages began to darken into autumn. Who can tell the story of those red months? I have to chronicle another silent transition. But as I can find no words delicate and fine enough to describe the multifold changes of Nature, so, too, I must be content to give you the spiritual facts in gross.

John Ford became a veteran down by the Potomac. And, to tell the truth, Lizzie became a veteran at home. That is, her love and hope grew to be an old story. She gave way, as the strongest must, as the wisest will, to time. The passion which, in her simple, shallow way, she had confided to the woods and waters reflected their outward variations; she thought of her lover less, and with less positive pleasure. The golden sands had run out. Perfect rest was over. Mrs. Ford's tacit protest began to be annoying. In a rather resentful spirit, Lizzie forbore to read any more letters aloud. These were as regular as ever. One of them contained a rough camp-photograph of Jack's newly bearded visage. Lizzie declared it was "too ugly for anything," and thrust it out of sight. She found herself skipping his military dissertations, which were still as long and written in as handsome a hand as ever. The "too good," which used to be uttered rather proudly, was now rather a wearisome truth. When Lizzie in certain critical moods tried to qualify Jack's temperament, she said to herself that he was too literal. Once he gave her a little scolding for not writing oftener. "Jack can make no allowances," murmured Lizzie. "He can understand no feelings but his own. I remember he used to say that moods were diseases. His mind is too healthy for such things; his heart is too stout for ache or pain. The night before he went off he told me that Reason, as he calls it, was the rule of life. I suppose he thinks it the rule of love, too. But his heart is younger than mine,—younger and better. He has lived through awful scenes of danger and bloodshed and cruelty, yet his heart is purer." Lizzie had a horrible feeling of being *blasée* of this one affection. "Oh, God bless him!" she cried. She

felt much better for the tears in which this soliloquy ended.
I fear she had begun to doubt her ability to cry about Jack.

III.

Christmas came. The Army of the Potomac had stacked its
muskets and gone into winter-quarters. Miss Crowe received
an invitation to pass the second fortnight in February at
the great manufacturing town of Leatherborough. Leatherborough is on the railroad, two hours south of Glenham, at
the mouth of the great river Tan, where this noble stream ex-
pands into its broadest smile, or gapes in too huge a fashion
to be disguised by a bridge.

"Mrs. Littlefield kindly invites you for the last of the
month," said Mrs. Ford, reading a letter behind the tea-urn.

It suited Mrs. Ford's purpose—a purpose which I have not
space to elaborate—that her young charge should now go
forth into society and pick up acquaintances.

Two sparks of pleasure gleamed in Elizabeth's eyes. But, as
she had taught herself to do of late with her protectress, she
mused before answering.

"It is my desire that you should go," said Mrs. Ford, taking silence for dissent.

The sparks went out.

"I intend to go," said Lizzie, rather grimly. "I am much
obliged to Mrs. Littlefield."

Her companion looked up.

"I intend you shall. You will please to write this morning."

For the rest of the week the two stitched together over
muslins and silks, and were very good friends. Lizzie could
scarcely help wondering at Mrs. Ford's zeal on her behalf.
Might she not have referred it to her guardian's principles?
Her wardrobe, hitherto fashioned on the Glenham notion of
elegance, was gradually raised to the Leatherborough standard of fitness. As she took up her bedroom candle the night
before she left home, she said,—

"I thank you very much, Mrs. Ford, for having worked so
hard for me,—for having taken so much interest in my outfit.
If they ask me at Leatherborough who made my things, I
shall certainly say it was you."

Mrs. Littlefield treated her young friend with great kindness. She was a good-natured, childless matron. She found Lizzie very ignorant and very pretty. She was glad to have so great a beauty and so many lions to show.

One evening Lizzie went to her room with one of the maids, carrying half a dozen candles between them. Heaven forbid that I should cross that virgin threshold—for the present! But we will wait. We will allow them two hours. At the end of that time, having gently knocked, we will enter the sanctuary. Glory of glories! The faithful attendant has done her work. Our lady is robed, crowned, ready for worshippers.

I trust I shall not be held to a minute description of our dear Lizzie's person and costume. Who is so great a recluse as never to have beheld young ladyhood in full dress? Many of us have sisters and daughters. Not a few of us, I hope, have female connections of another degree, yet no less dear. Others have looking-glasses. I give you my word for it that Elizabeth made as pretty a show as it is possible to see. She was of course well-dressed. Her skirt was of voluminous white, puffed and trimmed in wondrous sort. Her hair was profusely ornamented with curls and braids of its own rich substance. From her waist depended a ribbon, broad and blue. White with coral ornaments, as she wrote to Jack in the course of the week. Coral ornaments, forsooth! And pray, Miss, what of the other jewels with which your person was decorated,—the rubies, pearls, and sapphires? One by one Lizzie assumes her modest gimcracks: her bracelet, her gloves, her handkerchief, her fan, and then—her smile. Ah, that strange crowning smile!

An hour later, in Mrs. Littlefield's pretty drawing-room, amid music, lights, and talk, Miss Crowe was sweeping a grand curtsy before a tall, sallow man, whose name she caught from her hostess's redundant murmur as Bruce. Five minutes later, when the honest matron gave a glance at her newly started enterprise from the other side of the room, she said to herself that really, for a plain country-girl, Miss Crowe did this kind of thing very well. Her next glimpse of the couple showed them whirling round the room to the crashing thrum of the piano. At eleven o'clock she beheld them linked by their finger-tips in the dazzling mazes of the reel. At half-past eleven she discerned them charging shoulder to shoulder in the serried columns of the Lancers. At midnight she tapped her young friend gently with her fan.

"Your sash is unpinned, my dear.—I think you have danced often enough with Mr. Bruce. If he asks you again, you had better refuse. It's not quite the thing.—Yes, my dear, I know. —Mr. Simpson, will you be so good as to take Miss Crowe down to supper?"

I'm afraid young Simpson had rather a snappish partner.

After the proper interval, Mr. Bruce called to pay his respects to Mrs. Littlefield. He found Miss Crowe also in the drawing-room. Lizzie and he met like old friends. Mrs. Littlefield was a willing listener; but it seemed to her that she had come in at the second act of the play. Bruce went off with Miss Crowe's promise to drive with him in the afternoon. In the afternoon he swept up to the door in a prancing, tinkling sleigh. After some minutes of hoarse jesting and silvery laughter in the keen wintry air, he swept away again with Lizzie curled up in the buffalo-robe beside him, like a kitten in a rug. It was dark when they returned. When Lizzie came in to the sitting-room fire, she was congratulated by her hostess upon having made a "conquest."

"I think he's a most gentlemanly man," says Lizzie.

"So he is, my dear," said Mrs. Littlefield; "Mr. Bruce is a perfect gentleman. He's one of the finest young men I know. He's not so young either. He's a little too yellow for my taste; but he's beautifully educated. I wish you could hear his French accent. He has been abroad I don't know how many years. The firm of Bruce and Robertson does an immense business."

"And I'm so glad," cries Lizzie, "he's coming to Glenham in March! He's going to take his sister to the water-cure."

"Really?—poor thing! She has very good manners."

"What do you think of his looks?" asked Lizzie, smoothing her feather.

"I was speaking of Jane Bruce. I think Mr. Bruce has fine eyes."

"I must say I like tall men," says Miss Crowe.

"Then Robert Bruce is your man," laughs Mr. Littlefield. "He's as tall as a bell-tower. And he's got a bell-clapper in his head, too."

"I believe I will go and take off my things," remarks Miss Crowe, flinging up her curls.

Of course it behooved Mr. Bruce to call the next day and see how Miss Crowe had stood her drive. He set a veto upon her intended departure, and presented an invitation from his sister for the following week. At Mrs. Littlefield's instance, Lizzie accepted the invitation, despatched a laconic note to Mrs. Ford, and stayed over for Miss Bruce's party. It was a grand affair. Miss Bruce was a very great lady: she treated Miss Crowe with every attention. Lizzie was thought by some persons to look prettier than ever. The vaporous gauze, the sunny hair, the coral, the sapphires, the smile, were displayed with renewed success. The master of the house was unable to dance; he was summoned to sterner duties. Nor could Miss Crowe be induced to perform, having hurt her foot on the ice. This was of course a disappointment; let us hope that her entertainers made it up to her.

On the second day after the party, Lizzie returned to Glenham. Good Mr. Littlefield took her to the station, stealing a moment from his precious business-hours.

"There are your checks," said he; "be sure you don't lose them. Put them in your glove."

Lizzie gave a little scream of merriment.

"Mr. Littlefield, how can you? I've a reticule, Sir. But I really don't want you to stay."

"Well, I confess," said her companion.—"Hullo! there's your Scottish chief! I'll get him to stay with you till the train leaves. He may be going. Bruce!"

"Oh, Mr. Littlefield, don't!" cries Lizzie. "Perhaps Mr. Bruce is engaged."

Bruce's tall figure came striding towards them. He was astounded to find that Miss Crowe was going by this train. Delightful! He had come to meet a friend who had not arrived.

"Littlefield," said he, "you can't be spared from your business. I will see Miss Crowe off."

When the elder gentleman had departed, Mr. Bruce conducted his companion into the car, and found her a comfortable seat, equidistant from the torrid stove and the frigid door. Then he stowed away her shawls, umbrella, and reticule. She would keep her muff? She did well. What a pretty fur!

"It's just like your collar," said Lizzie. "I wish I had a muff for my feet," she pursued, tapping on the floor.

"Why not use some of those shawls?" said Bruce; "let's see what we can make of them."

And he stooped down and arranged them as a rug, very neatly and kindly. And then he called himself a fool for not having used the next seat, which was empty; and the wrapping was done over again.

"I'm so afraid you'll be carried off!" said Lizzie. "What would you do?"

"I think I should make the best of it. And you?"

"I would tell you to sit down *there*"; and she indicated the seat facing her. He took it. "Now you'll be sure to," said Elizabeth.

"I'm afraid I shall, unless I put the newspaper between us." And he took it out of his pocket. "Have you seen the news?"

"No," says Lizzie, elongating her bonnet-ribbons. "What is it? Just look at that party."

"There's not much news. There's been a scrimmage on the Rappahannock. Two of our regiments engaged,—the Fifteenth and the Twenty-Eighth. Didn't you tell me you had a cousin or something in the Fifteenth?"

"Not a cousin, no relation, but an intimate friend,—my guardian's son. What does the paper say, please?" inquires Lizzie, very pale.

Bruce cast his eye over the report. "It doesn't seem to have amounted to much; we drove back the enemy, and recrossed the river at our ease. Our loss only fifty. There are no names," he added, catching a glimpse of Lizzie's pallor,—"none in this paper at least."

In a few moments appeared a newsboy crying the New York journals.

"Do you think the New York papers would have any names?" asked Lizzie.

"We can try," said Bruce. And he bought a "Herald," and unfolded it. "Yes, there *is* a list," he continued, some time after he had opened out the sheet. "What's your friend's name?" he asked, from behind the paper.

"Ford,—John Ford, second lieutenant," said Lizzie.

There was a long pause.

At last Bruce lowered the sheet, and showed a face in which Lizzie's pallor seemed faintly reflected.

"There *is* such a name among the wounded," he said; and, folding the paper down, he held it out, and gently crossed to the seat beside her.

Lizzie took the paper, and held it close to her eyes. But Bruce could not help seeing that her temples had turned from white to crimson.

"Do you see it?" he asked; "I sincerely hope it's nothing very bad."

"*Severely,*" whispered Lizzie.

"Yes, but that proves nothing. Those things are most unreliable. *Do* hope for the best."

Lizzie made no answer. Meanwhile passengers had been brushing in, and the car was full. The engine began to puff, and the conductor to shout. The train gave a jog.

"You'd better go, Sir, or you'll be carried off," said Lizzie, holding out her hand, with her face still hidden.

"May I go on to the next station with you?" said Bruce.

Lizzie gave him a rapid look, with a deepened flush. He had fancied that she was shedding tears. But those eyes were dry; they held fire rather than water.

"No, no, Sir; you must not. I insist. Good bye."

Bruce's offer had cost him a blush, too. He had been prepared to back it with the assurance that he had business ahead, and, indeed, to make a little business in order to satisfy his conscience. But Lizzie's answer was final.

"Very well," said he, "*good* bye. You have my real sympathy, Miss Crowe. Don't despair. We shall meet again."

The train rattled away. Lizzie caught a glimpse of a tall figure with lifted hat on the platform. But she sat motionless, with her head against the window-frame, her veil down, and her hands idle.

She had enough to do to think, or rather to feel. It is fortunate that the utmost shock of evil tidings often comes first. After that everything is for the better. Jack's name stood printed in that fatal column like a stern signal for despair. Lizzie felt conscious of a crisis which almost arrested her

breath. Night had fallen at midday: what was the hour? A
tragedy had stepped into her life: was she spectator or actor?
She found herself face to face with death: was it not her own
soul masquerading in a shroud? She sat in a half-stupor. She
had been aroused from a dream into a waking nightmare. It
was like hearing a murder-shriek while you turn the page of
your novel. But I cannot describe these things. In time the
crushing sense of calamity loosened its grasp. Feeling lashed
her pinions. Thought struggled to rise. Passion was still,
stunned, floored. She had recoiled like a receding wave for a
stronger onset. A hundred ghastly fears and fancies strutted a
moment, pecking at the young girl's naked heart, like sand-
pipers on the weltering beach. Then, as with a great mur-
murous rush, came the meaning of her grief. The flood-gates
of emotion were opened.

At last passion exhausted itself, and Lizzie thought. Bruce's
parting words rang in her ears. She did her best to hope. She
reflected that wounds, even severe wounds, did not necessarily mean death. Death might easily be warded off. She would
go to Jack; she would nurse him; she would watch by him;
she would cure him. Even if Death had already beckoned, she
would strike down his hand: if Life had already obeyed, she
would issue the stronger mandate of Love. She would stanch
his wounds; she would unseal his eyes with her kisses; she
would call till he answered her.

Lizzie reached home and walked up the garden path. Mrs.
Ford stood in the parlor as she entered, upright, pale, and
rigid. Each read the other's countenance. Lizzie went towards
her slowly and giddily. She must of course kiss her patroness.
She took her listless hand and bent towards her stern lips.
Habitually Mrs. Ford was the most undemonstrative of
women. But as Lizzie looked closer into her face, she read the
signs of a grief infinitely more potent than her own. The formal kiss gave way: the young girl leaned her head on the old
woman's shoulder and burst into sobs. Mrs. Ford acknowledged those tears with a slow inclination of the head, full of a
certain grim pathos: she put out her arms and pressed them
closer to her heart.

At last Lizzie disengaged herself and sat down.

"I am going to him," said Mrs. Ford.

Lizzie's dizziness returned. Mrs. Ford was going,—and she, she?

"I am going to nurse him, and with God's help to save him."

"How did you hear?"

"I have a telegram from the surgeon of the regiment"; and Mrs. Ford held out a paper.

Lizzie took it and read: "Lieutenant Ford dangerously wounded in the action of yesterday. You had better come on."

"I should like to go myself," said Lizzie: "I think Jack would like to have me."

"Nonsense! A pretty place for a young girl! I am not going for sentiment; I am going for use."

Lizzie leaned her head back in her chair, and closed her eyes. From the moment they had fallen upon Mrs. Ford, she had felt a certain quiescence. And now it was a relief to have responsibility denied her. Like most weak persons, she was glad to step out of the current of life, now that it had begun to quicken into action. In emergencies, such persons are tacitly counted out; and they as tacitly consent to the arrangement. Even to the sensitive spirit there is a certain meditative rapture in standing on the quiet shore, (beside the ruminating cattle,) and watching the hurrying, eddying flood, which makes up for the loss of dignity. Lizzie's heart resumed its peaceful throbs. She sat, almost dreamily, with her eyes shut.

"I leave in an hour," said Mrs. Ford. "I am going to get ready.—Do you hear?"

The young girl's silence was a deeper consent than her companion supposed.

IV.

It was a week before Lizzie heard from Mrs. Ford. The letter, when it came, was very brief. Jack still lived. The wounds were three in number, and very serious; he was unconscious; he had not recognized her; but still the chances either way were thought equal. They would be much greater for his recovery nearer home; but it was impossible to move him. "I write from the midst of horrible scenes," said the poor lady.

Subjoined was a list of necessary medicines, comforts, and delicacies, to be boxed up and sent.

For a while Lizzie found occupation in writing a letter to Jack, to be read in his first lucid moment, as she told Mrs. Ford. This lady's man-of-business came up from the village to superintend the packing of the boxes. Her directions were strictly followed; and in no point were they found wanting. Mr. Mackenzie bespoke Lizzie's admiration for their friend's wonderful clearness of memory and judgment. "I wish we had that woman at the head of affairs," said he. " 'Gad, I'd apply for a Brigadier-Generalship."—"I'd apply to be sent South," thought Lizzie. When the boxes and letter were despatched, she sat down to await more news. Sat down, say I? Sat down, and rose, and wondered, and sat down again. These were lonely, weary days. Very different are the idleness of love and the idleness of grief. Very different is it to be alone with your hope and alone with your despair. Lizzie failed to rally her musings. I do not mean to say that her sorrow was very poignant, although she fancied it was. Habit was a great force in her simple nature; and her chief trouble now was that habit refused to work. Lizzie had to grapple with the stern tribulation of a decision to make, a problem to solve. She felt that there was some spiritual barrier between herself and repose. So she began in her usual fashion to build up a false repose on the hither side of belief. She might as well have tried to float on the Dead Sea. Peace eluding her, she tried to resign herself to tumult. She drank deep at the well of self-pity, but found its waters brackish. People are apt to think that they may temper the penalties of misconduct by self-commiseration, just as they season the long after-taste of beneficence by a little spice of self-applause. But the Power of Good is a more grateful master than the Devil. What bliss to gaze into the smooth gurgling wake of a good deed, while the comely bark sails on with floating pennon! What horror to look into the muddy sediment which floats round the piratic keel! Go, sinner, and dissolve it with your tears! And you, scoffing friend, there is the way out! Or would you prefer the window? I'm an honest man forevermore.

One night Lizzie had a dream,—a rather disagreeable one, —which haunted her during many waking hours. It seemed to her that she was walking in a lonely place, with a tall, dark-eyed man who called her wife. Suddenly, in the shadow of a tree, they came upon an unburied corpse. Lizzie proposed to dig him a grave. They dug a great hole and took hold of the corpse to lift him in; when suddenly he opened his eyes. Then they saw that he was covered with wounds. He looked at them intently for some time, turning his eyes from one to the other. At last he solemnly said, "Amen!" and closed his eyes. Then she and her companion placed him in the grave, and shovelled the earth over him, and stamped it down with their feet.

He of the dark eyes and he of the wounds were the two constantly recurring figures of Lizzie's reveries. She could never think of John without thinking of the courteous Leatherborough gentleman, too. These were the *data* of her problem. These two figures stood like opposing knights, (the black and the white,) foremost on the great chess-board of fate. Lizzie was the wearied, puzzled player. She would idly finger the other pieces, and shift them carelessly hither and thither; but it was of no avail: the game lay between the two knights. She would shut her eyes and long for some kind hand to come and tamper with the board; she would open them and see the two knights standing immovable, face to face. It was nothing new. A fancy had come in and offered defiance to a fact; they must fight it out. Lizzie generously inclined to the fancy, the unknown champion, with a reputation to make. Call her *blasée*, if you like, this little girl, whose record told of a couple of dances and a single lover, heartless, old before her time. Perhaps she deserves your scorn. I confess she thought herself ill-used. By whom? by what? wherein? These were questions Miss Crowe was not prepared to answer. Her intellect was unequal to the stern logic of human events. She expected two and two to make five: as why should they not for the nonce? She was like an actor who finds himself on the stage with a half-learned part and without sufficient wit to extemporize. Pray, where is the prompter? Alas, Elizabeth, that you had no mother! Young girls are prone to fancy that when once they have a lover, they have everything they need: a conclusion inconsistent with the belief entertained by many persons, that life begins with love. Lizzie's fortunes became old stories to her before she had half read them through. Jack's wounds and danger were an old story. Do not suppose that she had exhausted the lessons, the suggestions of these awful events, their inspirations, exhortations, —that she had wept as became the horror of the tragedy. No: the curtain had not yet fallen, yet our young lady had begun to yawn. To yawn? Ay, and to long for the afterpiece. Since the tragedy dragged, might she not divert herself with that well-bred man beside her?

Elizabeth was far from owning to herself that she had fallen away from her love. For my own part, I need no better proof of the fact than the dull persistency with which she denied it. What accusing voice broke out of the stillness? Jack's nobleness and magnanimity were the hourly theme of her clogged fancy. Again and again she declared to herself that she was unworthy of them, but that, if he would only recover and come home, she would be his eternal bond-slave. So she passed a very miserable month. Let us hope that her childish spirit was being tempered to some useful purpose. Let us hope so.

She roamed about the empty house with her footsteps tracked by an unlaid ghost. She cried aloud and said that she was very unhappy; she groaned and called herself wicked. Then, sometimes, appalled at her moral perplexities, she declared that she was neither wicked nor unhappy; she was contented, patient, and wise. Other girls had lost their lovers: it was the present way of life. Was she weaker than most women? Nay, but Jack was the best of men. If he would only come back directly, without delay, as he was, senseless, dying even, that she might look at him, touch him, speak to him! Then she would say that she could no longer answer for herself, and wonder (or pretend to wonder) whether she were not going mad. Suppose Mrs. Ford should come back and find her in an unswept room, pallid and insane? or suppose she should die of her troubles? What if she should kill herself?—dismiss the servants, and close the house, and lock herself up with a knife? Then she would cut her arm to escape from dismay at what she had already done; and then her courage would ebb away with her blood, and, having so far pledged herself to despair, her life would ebb away with her courage; and then, alone, in darkness, with none to help her, she would vainly scream, and thrust the knife into her temple, and swoon to death. And Jack would come back, and burst into the house, and wander through the empty rooms, calling her name, and for all answer get a death-scent! These imaginings were the more creditable or discreditable to Lizzie, that she had never read "Romeo and Juliet." At any rate, they served to dissipate time,—heavy, weary time,—the more heavy and weary as it bore dark foreshadowings of some momentous event. If that event would only come, whatever it was, and sever this Gordian knot of doubt!

The days passed slowly: the leaden sands dropped one by one. The roads were too bad for walking; so Lizzie was obliged to confine her restlessness to the narrow bounds of the empty house, or to an occasional journey to the village, where people sickened her by their dull indifference to her spiritual agony. Still they could not fail to remark how poorly Miss Crowe was looking. This was true, and Lizzie knew it. I think she even took a certain comfort in her pallor and in her failing interest in her dress. There was some satisfaction in displaying her white roses amid the apple-cheeked prosperity of Main Street. At last Miss Cooper, the Doctor's sister, spoke to her:—

"How is it, Elizabeth, you look so pale, and thin, and worn out? What you been doing with yourself? Falling in love, eh? It isn't right to be so much alone. Come down and stay with us awhile,—till Mrs. Ford and John come back," added Miss Cooper, who wished to put a cheerful face on the matter.

For Miss Cooper, indeed, any other face would have been difficult. Lizzie agreed to come. Her hostess was a busy, unbeautiful old maid, sister and housekeeper of the village physician. Her occupation here below was to perform the forgotten tasks of her fellow-men,—to pick up their dropped stitches, as she herself declared. She was never idle, for her general cleverness was commensurate with mortal needs. Her own story was, that she kept moving, so that folks couldn't see how ugly she was. And, in fact, her existence was manifest through her long train of good deeds,—just as the presence of a comet is shown by its tail. It was doubtless on the above principle that her visage was agitated by a perpetual laugh.

Meanwhile more news had been coming from Virginia.

"What an absurdly long letter you sent John," wrote Mrs. Ford, in acknowledging the receipt of the boxes. "His first lucid moment would be very short, if he were to take upon himself to read your effusions. Pray keep your long stories till he gets well." For a fortnight the young soldier remained the same,—feverish, conscious only at intervals. Then came a change for the worse, which, for many weary days; however, resulted in nothing decisive. "If he could only be moved to Glenham, home, and old sights," said his mother, "I should have hope. But think of the journey!" By this time Lizzie had stayed out ten days of her visit.

One day Miss Cooper came in from a walk, radiant with tidings. Her face, as I have observed, wore a continual smile, being dimpled and punctured all over with merriment,—so that, when an unusual cheerfulness was super-diffused, it re-sembled a tempestuous little pool into which a great stone has been cast.

"Guess who's come," said she, going up to the piano, which Lizzie was carelessly fingering, and putting her hands on the young girl's shoulders. "Just guess!"

Lizzie looked up.

"Jack," she half gasped.

"Oh, dear, no, not that! How stupid of me! I mean Mr. Bruce, your Leatherborough admirer."

"Mr. Bruce! Mr. Bruce!" said Lizzie. "Really?"

"True as I live. He's come to bring his sister to the Water-Cure. I met them at the post-office."

Lizzie felt a strange sensation of good news. Her finger-tips were on fire. She was deaf to her companion's rattling chron-icle. She broke into the midst of it with a fragment of some triumphant, jubilant melody. The keys rang beneath her flash-ing hands. And then she suddenly stopped, and Miss Cooper, who was taking off her bonnet at the mirror, saw that her face was covered with a burning flush.

That evening, Mr. Bruce presented himself at Doctor Cooper's, with whom he had a slight acquaintance. To Lizzie he was infinitely courteous and tender. He assured her, in very pretty terms, of his profound sympathy with her in her cousin's danger,—her cousin he still called him,—and it seemed to Lizzie that until that moment no one had begun to be kind. And then he began to rebuke her, playfully and in excellent taste, for her pale cheeks.

"Isn't it dreadful?" said Miss Cooper. "She looks like a ghost. I guess she's in love."

"He must be a good-for-nothing lover to make his mistress look so sad. If I were you, I'd give him up, Miss Crowe."

"I didn't know I looked sad," said Lizzie.

"You don't now," said Miss Cooper. "You're smiling and blushing. A'n't she blushing, Mr. Bruce?"

"I think Miss Crowe has no more than her natural color," said Bruce, dropping his eye-glass. "What have you been doing all this while since we parted?"

"All this while? it's only six weeks. I don't know. Nothing. What have you?"

"I've been doing nothing, too. It's hard work."

"Have you been to any more parties?"

"Not one."

"Any more sleigh-rides?"

"Yes. I took one more dreary drive all alone,—over that same road, you know. And I stopped at the farm-house again, and saw the old woman we had the talk with. She remembered us, and asked me what had become of the young lady who was with me before. I told her you were gone home, but that I hoped soon to go and see you. So she sent you her love"——

"Oh, how nice!" exclaimed Lizzie.

"Wasn't it? And then she made a certain little speech; I won't repeat it, or we shall have Miss Cooper talking about your blushes again."

"I know," cried the lady in question: "she said she was very"——

"Very what?" said Lizzie.

"Very h-a-n-d—— what every one says."

"Very handy?" asked Lizzie. "I'm sure no one ever said that."

"Of course," said Bruce; "and I answered what every one answers."

"Have you seen Mrs. Littlefield lately?"

"Several times. I called on her the day before I left town, to see if she had any messages for you."

"Oh, thank you! I hope she's well."

"Oh, she's as jolly as ever. She sent you her love, and hoped you would come back to Leatherborough very soon again. I told her, that, however it might be with the first message, the second should be a joint one from both of us."

"You're very kind. I should like very much to go again.—Do you like Mrs. Littlefield?"

"Like her? Yes. Don't you? She's thought a very pleasing woman."

"Oh, she's very nice.—I don't think she has much conversation."

"Ah, I'm afraid you mean she doesn't backbite. We've always found plenty to talk about."

"That's a very significant tone. What, for instance?"

"Well, we *have* talked about Miss Crowe."

"Oh, you have? Do you call that having plenty to talk about?"

"We *have* talked about Mr. Bruce,—haven't we, Elizabeth?" said Miss Cooper, who had her own notion of being agreeable.

It was not an altogether bad notion, perhaps; but Bruce found her interruptions rather annoying, and insensibly allowed them to shorten his visit. Yet, as it was, he sat till eleven o'clock—a stay quite unprecedented at Glenham.

When he left the house, he went splashing down the road with a very elastic tread, springing over the starlit puddles, and trolling out some sentimental ditty. He reached the inn, and went up to his sister's sitting-room.

"Why, Robert, where have you been all this while?" said Miss Bruce.

"At Dr. Cooper's."

"Dr. Cooper's? I should think you had! Who's Dr. Cooper?"

"Where Miss Crowe's staying."

"Miss Crowe? Ah, Mrs. Littlefield's friend! Is she as pretty as ever?"

"Prettier,—prettier,—prettier. *Tara-ta! tara-ta!*"

"Oh, Robert, do stop that singing! You'll rouse the whole house."

V.

Late one afternoon, at dusk, about three weeks after Mr. Bruce's arrival, Lizzie was sitting alone by the fire, in Miss Cooper's parlor, musing, as became the place and hour. The Doctor and his sister came in, dressed for a lecture.

"I'm sorry you won't go, my dear," said Miss Cooper. "It's a most interesting subject: 'A Year of the War.' All the battles and things described, you know."

"I'm tired of war," said Lizzie.

"Well, well, if you're tired of the war, we'll leave you in peace. Kiss me good-bye. What's the matter? You look sick. You are homesick, a'n't you?"

"No, no,—I'm very well."

"Would you like me to stay at home with you?"

"Oh, no! pray, don't!"

"Well, we'll tell you all about it. Will they have programmes, James? I'll bring her a programme.—But you really feel as if you were going to be ill. Feel of her skin, James."

"No, you needn't, Sir," said Lizzie. "How queer of you, Miss Cooper! I'm perfectly well."

And at last her friends departed. Before long the servant came with the lamp, ushering Mr. Mackenzie.

"Good evening, Miss," said he. "Bad news from Mrs. Ford."

"Bad news?"

"Yes, Miss. I've just got a letter stating that Mr. John is growing worse and worse, and that they look for his death from hour to hour.—It's very sad," he added, as Elizabeth was silent.

"Yes, it's very sad," said Lizzie.

"I thought you'd like to hear it."

"Thank you."

"He was a very noble young fellow," pursued Mr. Mackenzie.

Lizzie made no response.

"There's the letter," said Mr. Mackenzie, handing it over to her.

Lizzie opened it.

"How long she is reading it!" thought her visitor. "You can't see so far from the light, can you, Miss?"

"Yes," said Lizzie.—"His poor mother! Poor woman!"

"Ay, indeed, Miss,—she's the one to be pitied."

"Yes, she's the one to be pitied," said Lizzie. "Well!" and she gave him back the letter.

"I thought you'd like to see it," said Mackenzie, drawing on his gloves; and then, after a pause,—"I'll call again, Miss, if I hear anything more. Good night!"

Lizzie got up and lowered the light, and then went back to her sofa by the fire.

Half an hour passed; it went slowly; but it passed. Still lying there in the dark room on the sofa, Lizzie heard a ring at the door-bell, a man's voice and a man's tread in the hall. She rose and went to the lamp. As she turned it up, the parlor-door opened. Bruce came in.

"I was sitting in the dark," said Lizzie; "but when I heard you coming, I raised the light."

"Are you afraid of me?" said Bruce.

"Oh, no! I'll put it down again. Sit down."

"I saw your friends going out," pursued Bruce; "so I knew I should find you alone.—What are you doing here in the dark?"

"I've just received very bad news from Mrs. Ford about her son. He's much worse, and will probably not live."

"Is it possible?"

"I was thinking about that."

"Dear me! Well that's a sad subject. I'm told he was a very fine young man."

"He was,—very," said Lizzie.

Bruce was silent awhile. He was a stranger to the young officer, and felt that he had nothing to offer beyond the commonplace expressions of sympathy and surprise. Nor had he exactly the measure of his companion's interest in him.

"If he dies," said Lizzie, "it will be under great injustice."

"Ah! what do you mean?"

"There wasn't a braver man in the army."

"I suppose not."

"And, oh, Mr. Bruce," continued Lizzie, "he was so clever and good and generous! I wish you had known him."

"I wish I had. But what do you mean by injustice? Were these qualities denied him?"

"No indeed! Every one that looked at him could see that he was perfect."

"Where's the injustice, then? It ought to be enough for him that you should think so highly of him."

"Oh, he knew that," said Lizzie.

Bruce was a little puzzled by his companion's manner. He watched her, as she sat with her cheek on her hand, looking at the fire. There was a long pause. Either they were too friendly or too thoughtful for the silence to be embarrassing. Bruce broke it at last.

"Miss Crowe," said he, "on a certain occasion, some time ago, when you first heard of Mr. Ford's wounds, I offered you my company, with the wish to console you as far as I might for what seemed a considerable shock. It was, perhaps, a bold offer for so new a friend; but, nevertheless, in it even then my heart spoke. You turned me off. Will you let me repeat it? Now, with a better right, will you let me speak out all my heart?"

Lizzie heard this speech, which was delivered in a slow and hesitating tone, without looking up or moving her head, except, perhaps, at the words "turned me off." After Bruce had ceased, she still kept her position.

"You'll not turn me off now?" added her companion.

She dropped her hand, raised her head, and looked at him a moment: he thought he saw the glow of tears in her eyes. Then she sank back upon the sofa with her face in the shadow of the mantel-piece.

"I don't understand you, Mr. Bruce," said she.

"Ah, Elizabeth! am I such a poor speaker. How shall I make it plain? When I saw your friends leave home half an hour ago, and reflected that you would probably be alone, I determined to go right in and have a talk with you that I've long been wanting to have. But first I walked half a mile up the road, thinking hard,—thinking how I should say what I had to say. I made up my mind to nothing, but that somehow or other I should say it. I would trust,—I *do* trust to your frankness, kindness, and sympathy, to a feeling corresponding to my own. Do you understand that feeling? Do you know

that I love you? I do, I do, I do! You *must* know it. If you
don't, I solemnly swear it. I solemnly ask you, Elizabeth, to
take me for your husband."

While Bruce said these words, he rose, with their rising
passion, and came and stood before Lizzie. Again she was
motionless.

"Does it take you so long to think?" said he, trying to read
her indistinct features; and he sat down on the sofa beside her
and took her hand.

At last Lizzie spoke.

"Are you sure," said she, "that you love me?"

"As sure as that I breathe. Now, Elizabeth, make me as sure
that I am loved in return."

"It seems very strange, Mr. Bruce," said Lizzie.

"What seems strange? Why should it? For a month I've
been trying, in a hundred dumb ways, to make it plain; and
now, when I swear it, it only seems strange!"

"What do you love me for?"

"For? For yourself, Elizabeth."

"Myself? I am nothing."

"I love you for what you are,—for your deep, kind heart,
—for being so perfectly a woman."

Lizzie drew away her hand, and her lover rose and stood
before her again. But now she looked up into his face, questioning when she should have answered, drinking strength
from his entreaties for her replies. There he stood before her,
in the glow of the firelight, in all his gentlemanhood, for her
to accept or reject. She slowly rose and gave him the hand she
had withdrawn.

"Mr. Bruce, I shall be very proud to love you," she said.

And then, as if this effort was beyond her strength, she half
staggered back to the sofa again. And still holding her hand,
he sat down beside her. And there they were still sitting when
they heard the Doctor and his sister come in.

For three days Elizabeth saw nothing of Mr. Mackenzie. At
last, on the fourth day, passing his office in the village, she
went in and asked for him. He came out of his little back parlor with his mouth full and a beaming face.

"Good-day, Miss Crowe, and good news!"

"*Good* news?" cried Lizzie.

"Capital!" said he, looking hard at her, while he put on his spectacles. "She writes that Mr. John—won't you take a seat?—has taken a sudden and unexpected turn for the better. Now's the moment to save him; it's an equal risk. They were to start for the North the second day after date. The surgeon comes with them. So they'll be home—of course they'll travel slowly—in four or five days. Yes, Miss, it's a remarkable Providence. And that noble young man will be spared to the country, and to those who love him, as I do."

"I had better go back to the house and have it got ready," said Lizzie, for an answer.

"Yes, Miss, I think you had. In fact, Mrs. Ford made that request."

The request was obeyed. That same day Lizzie went home. For two days she found it her interest to overlook, assiduously, a general sweeping, scrubbing, and provisioning. She allowed herself no idle moment until bed-time. Then—— But I would rather not be the chamberlain of her agony. It was the easier to work, as Mr. Bruce had gone to Leatherborough on business.

On the fourth evening, at twilight, John Ford was borne up to the door on his stretcher, with his mother stalking beside him in rigid grief, and kind, silent friends pressing about with helping hands.

> "Home they brought her warrior dead,
>   She nor swooned nor uttered cry."

It was, indeed, almost a question, whether Jack was not dead. Death is not thinner, paler, stiller. Lizzie moved about like one in a dream. Of course, when there are so many sympathetic friends, a man's family has nothing to do,—except exercise a little self-control. The women huddled Mrs. Ford to bed; rest was imperative; she was killing herself. And it was significant of her weakness that she did not resent this advice. In greeting her, Lizzie felt as if she were embracing the stone image on the top of a sepulchre. She, too, had her cares anticipated. Good Doctor Cooper and his sister stationed themselves at the young man's couch.

The Doctor prophesied wondrous things of the change of climate; he was certain of a recovery. Lizzie found herself very shortly dealt with as an obstacle to this consummation. Access to John was prohibited. "Perfect stillness, you know, my dear," whispered Miss Cooper, opening his chamber-door on a crack, in a pair of very creaking shoes. So for the first evening that her old friend was at home Lizzie caught but a glimpse of his pale, senseless face, as she hovered outside the long train of his attendants. If we may suppose any of these kind people to have had eyes for aught but the sufferer, we may be sure that they saw another visage equally sad and white. The sufferer? It was hardly Jack, after all.

When Lizzie was turned from Jack's door, she took a covering from a heap of draperies that had been hurriedly tossed down in the hall: it was an old army-blanket. She wrapped it round her, and went out on the verandah. It was nine o'clock; but the darkness was filled with light. A great wanton wind— the ghost of the raw blast which travels by day—had arisen, bearing long, soft gusts of inland spring. Scattered clouds were hurrying across the white sky. The bright moon, careering in their midst, seemed to have wandered forth in frantic quest of the hidden stars.

Lizzie nestled her head in the blanket, and sat down on the steps. A strange earthy smell lingered in that faded old rug, and with it a faint perfume of tobacco. Instantly the young girl's senses were transported as they had never been before to those far-off Southern battle-fields. She saw men lying in swamps, puffing their kindly pipes, drawing their blankets closer, canopied with the same luminous dusk that shone down upon her comfortable weakness. Her mind wandered amid these scenes till recalled to the present by the swinging of the garden-gate. She heard a firm, well-known tread crunching the gravel. Mr. Bruce came up the path. As he drew near the steps, Lizzie arose. The blanket fell back from her head, and Bruce started at recognizing her.

"Hullo! You, Elizabeth? What's the matter?"

Lizzie made no answer.

"Are you one of Mr. Ford's watchers?" he continued, coming up the steps; "how is he?"

Still she was silent. Bruce put out his hands to take hers, and bent forward as if to kiss her. She half shook him off, and retreated toward the door.

"Good heavens!" cried Bruce; "what's the matter? Are you moon-struck? Can't you speak?"

"No,—no,—not to-night," said Lizzie, in a choking voice. "Go away,—go away!"

She stood holding the door-handle, and motioning him off. He hesitated a moment, and then advanced. She opened the door rapidly, and went in. He heard her lock it. He stood looking at it stupidly for some time, and then slowly turned round and walked down the steps.

The next morning Lizzie arose with the early dawn, and came down stairs. She went into the room where Jack lay, and gently opened the door. Miss Cooper was dozing in her chair. Lizzie crossed the threshold, and stole up to the bed. Poor Ford lay peacefully sleeping. There was his old face, after all,—his strong, honest features refined, but not weakened, by pain. Lizzie softly drew up a low chair, and sat down beside him. She gazed into his face,—the dear and honored face into which she had so often gazed in health. It was strangely handsomer: body stood for less. It seemed to Lizzie, that, as the fabric of her lover's soul was more clearly revealed,—the veil of the temple rent wellnigh in twain,—she could read the justification of all her old worship. One of Jack's hands lay outside the sheets,—those strong, supple fingers, once so cunning in workmanship, so frank in friendship, now thinner and whiter than her own. After looking at it for some time, Lizzie gently grasped it. Jack slowly opened his eyes. Lizzie's heart began to throb; it was as if the stillness of the sanctuary had given a sign. At first there was no recognition in the young man's gaze. Then the dull pupils began visibly to brighten. There came to his lips the commencement of that strange moribund smile which seems so ineffably satirical of the things of this world. O imposing spectacle of death! O blessed soul, marked for promotion! What earthly favor is like thine? Lizzie sank down on her knees, and, still clasping John's hand, bent closer over him.

"Jack,—dear, dear Jack," she whispered, "do you know me?"

The smile grew more intense. The poor fellow drew out his other hand, and slowly, feebly placed it on Lizzie's head, stroking down her hair with his fingers.

"Yes, yes," she murmured; "you know me, don't you? I am Lizzie, Jack. Don't you remember Lizzie?"

Ford moved his lips inaudibly, and went on patting her head.

"This is home, you know," said Lizzie; "this is Glenham. You haven't forgotten Glenham? You are with your mother and me and your friends. Dear, darling Jack!"

Still he went on, stroking her head; and his feeble lips tried to emit some sound. Lizzie laid her head down on the pillow beside his own, and still his hand lingered caressingly on her hair.

"Yes, you know me," she pursued; "you are with your friends now forever,—with those who will love and take care of you, oh, forever!"

"I'm very badly wounded," murmured Jack, close to her ear.

"Yes, yes, my dear boy, but your wounds are healing. I will love you and nurse you forever."

"Yes, Lizzie, our old promise," said Jack: and his hand fell upon her neck, and with its feeble pressure he drew her closer, and she wet his face with her tears.

Then Miss Cooper, awakening, rose and drew Lizzie away.

"I am sure you excite him, my dear. It is best he should have none of his family near him,—persons with whom he has associations, you know."

Here the Doctor was heard gently tapping on the window, and Lizzie went round to the door to admit him.

She did not see Jack again all day. Two or three times she ventured into the room, but she was banished by a frown, or a finger raised to the lips. She waylaid the Doctor frequently. He was blithe and cheerful, certain of Jack's recovery. This good man used to exhibit as much moral elation at the prospect of a cure as an orthodox believer at that of a new convert: it was one more body gained from the Devil. He assured Lizzie that the change of scene and climate had already begun to tell: the fever was lessening, the worst symptoms disappearing. He answered Lizzie's reiterated desire to do something by directions to keep the house quiet and the sick-room empty.

Soon after breakfast, Miss Dawes, a neighbor, came in to

relieve Miss Cooper, and this indefatigable lady transferred her attention to Mrs. Ford. Action was forbidden her. Miss Cooper was delighted for once to be able to lay down the law to her vigorous neighbor, of whose fine judgment she had always stood in awe. Having bullied Mrs. Ford into taking her breakfast in the little sitting-room, she closed the doors, and prepared for "a good long talk." Lizzie was careful not to break in upon this interview. She had bidden her patroness good morning, asked after her health, and received one of her temperate osculations. As she passed the invalid's door, Doctor Cooper came out and asked her to go and look for a certain roll of bandages, in Mr. John's trunk, which had been carried into another room. Lizzie hastened to perform this task. In fumbling through the contents of the trunk, she came across a packet of letters in a well-known feminine handwriting. She pocketed it, and, after disposing of the bandages, went to her own room, locked the door, and sat down to examine the letters. Between reading and thinking and sighing and (in spite of herself) smiling, this process took the whole morning. As she came down to dinner, she encountered Mrs. Ford and Miss Cooper, emerging from the sitting-room, the good long talk being only just concluded.

"How do you feel, Ma'am?" she asked of the elder lady, —"rested?"

For all answer Mrs. Ford gave a look—I had almost said a scowl—so hard, so cold, so reproachful, that Lizzie was transfixed. But suddenly its sickening meaning was revealed to her. She turned to Miss Cooper, who stood pale and fluttering beside the mistress, her everlasting smile glazed over with a piteous, deprecating glance; and I fear her eyes flashed out the same message of angry scorn they had just received. These telegraphic operations are very rapid. The ladies hardly halted: the next moment found them seated at the dinner-table with Miss Cooper scrutinizing her napkin-mark and Mrs. Ford saying grace.

Dinner was eaten in silence. When it was over, Lizzie returned to her own room. Miss Cooper went home, and Mrs. Ford went to her son. Lizzie heard the firm low click of the lock as she closed the door. Why did she lock it? There was something fatal in the silence that followed. The plot of her little tragedy thickened. Be it so: she would act her part with the rest. For the second time in her experience, her mind was lightened by the intervention of Mrs. Ford. Before the scorn of her own conscience, (which never came,) before Jack's deepest reproach, she was ready to bow down,—but not before that long-faced Nemesis in black silk. The leaven of resentment began to work. She leaned back in her chair, and folded her arms, brave to await results. But before long she fell asleep. She was aroused by a knock at her chamber-door. The afternoon was far gone. Miss Dawes stood without.

"Elizabeth, Mr. John wants very much to see you, with his love. Come down very gently: his mother is lying down. Will you sit with him while I take my dinner?—Better? Yes, ever so much."

Lizzie betook herself with trembling haste to Jack's bedside.

He was propped up with pillows. His pale cheeks were slightly flushed. His eyes were bright. He raised himself, and, for such feeble arms, gave Lizzie a long, strong embrace.

"I've not seen you all day, Lizzie," said he. "Where have you been?"

"Dear Jack, they wouldn't let me come near you. I begged and prayed. And I wanted so to go to you in the army; but I couldn't. I wish, I wish I had!"

"You wouldn't have liked it, Lizzie. I'm glad you didn't. It's a bad, bad place."

He lay quietly, holding her hands and gazing at her.

"Can I do anything for you, dear?" asked the young girl. "I would work my life out. I'm so glad you're better!"

It was some time before Jack answered,—

"Lizzie," said he, at last, "I sent for you to look at you.— You are more wondrously beautiful than ever. Your hair is brown,—like—like nothing; your eyes are blue; your neck is white. Well, well!"

He lay perfectly motionless, but for his eyes. They wandered over her with a kind of peaceful glee, like sunbeams playing on a statue. Poor Ford lay, indeed, not unlike an old wounded Greek, who at falling dusk has crawled into a temple to die, steeping the last dull interval in idle admiration of sculptured Artemis.

"Ah, Lizzie, this is already heaven!" he murmured.

"It will be heaven when you get well," whispered Lizzie.

He smiled into her eyes:—

"You say more than you mean. There should be perfect truth between us. Dear Lizzie, I am not going to get well. They are all very much mistaken. I am going to die. I've done my work. Death makes up for everything. My great pain is in leaving you. But you, too, will die one of these days; remember that. In all pain and sorrow, remember that."

Lizzie was able to reply only by the tightening grasp of her hands.

"But there is something more," pursued Jack. "Life *is* as good as death. Your heart has found its true keeper; so we shall all three be happy. Tell him I bless him and honor him. Tell him God, too, blesses him. Shake hands with him for me," said Jack, feebly moving his pale fingers. "My mother," he went on,—"be very kind to her. She will have great grief, but she will not die of it. She'll live to great age. Now, Lizzie, I can't talk any more; I wanted to say farewell. You'll keep me farewell,—you'll stay with me awhile,—won't you? I'll look at you till the last. For a little while you'll be mine, holding my hands—so—until death parts us."

Jack kept his promise. His eyes were fixed in a firm gaze long after the sense had left them.

In the early dawn of the next day, Elizabeth left her sleepless bed, opened the window, and looked out on the wide prospect, still cool and dim with departing night. It offered freshness and peace to her hot head and restless heart. She dressed herself hastily, crept down stairs, passed the death-chamber, and stole out of the quiet house. She turned away from the still sleeping village and walked towards the open country. She went a long way without knowing it. The sun had risen high when she bethought herself to turn. As she came back along the brightening highway, and drew near home, she saw a tall figure standing beneath the budding trees of the garden, hesitating, apparently, whether to open the gate. Lizzie came upon him almost before he had seen her. Bruce's first movement was to put out his hands, as any lover might; but as Lizzie raised her veil, he dropped them.

"Yes, Mr. Bruce," said Lizzie, "I'll give you my hand once more,—in farewell."

"Elizabeth!" cried Bruce, half stupefied, "in God's name, what do you mean by these crazy speeches?"

"I mean well. I mean kindly and humanely to you. And I mean justice to my old—old love."

She went to him, took his listless hand, without looking into his wild, smitten face, shook it passionately, and then, wrenching her own from his grasp, opened the gate and let it swing behind her.

"No! no! no!" she almost shrieked, turning about in the path. "I forbid you to follow me!"

But for all that, he went in.

A Landscape Painter

D O YOU remember how, a dozen years ago, a number of our friends were startled by the report of the rupture of young Locksley's engagement with Miss Leary? This event made some noise in its day. Both parties possessed certain claims to distinction: Locksley in his wealth, which was believed to be enormous, and the young lady in her beauty, which was in truth very great. I used to hear that her lover was fond of comparing her to the Venus of Milo; and, indeed, if you can imagine the mutilated goddess with her full complement of limbs, dressed out by Madame de Crinoline, and engaged in small talk beneath the drawing-room chandelier, you may obtain a vague notion of Miss Josephine Leary. Locksley, you remember, was rather a short man, dark, and not particularly good-looking; and when he walked about with his betrothed, it was half a matter of surprise that he should have ventured to propose to a young lady of such heroic proportions. Miss Leary had the gray eyes and auburn hair which I have always assigned to the famous statue. The one defect in her face, in spite of an expression of great candor and sweetness, was a certain lack of animation. What it was besides her beauty that attracted Locksley I never discovered: perhaps, since his attachment was so short-lived, it was her beauty alone. I say that his attachment was of brief duration, because the rupture was understood to have come from him. Both he and Miss Leary very wisely held their tongues on the matter; but among their friends and enemies it of course received a hundred explanations. That most popular with Locksley's well-wishers was, that he had backed out (these events are discussed, you know, in fashionable circles very much as an expected prize-fight which has miscarried is canvassed in reunions of another kind) only on flagrant evidence of the lady's—what, faithlessness?—on overwhelming proof of the most *mercenary* spirit on the part of Miss Leary. You see, our friend was held capable of doing battle for an "idea." It must be owned that this was a novel charge; but, for myself, having long known Mrs. Leary, the mother, who was a widow with four daughters, to be an inveterate old screw, I took the liberty of accrediting the existence of a similar propensity in her eldest born. I suppose that the young lady's family had, on their own side, a very plausible version of their disappointment. It was, however, soon made up to them by Josephine's marriage with a gentleman of expectations very nearly as brilliant as those of her old suitor. And what was *his* compensation? That is precisely my story.

Locksley disappeared, as you will remember, from public view. The events above alluded to happened in March. On calling at his lodgings in April, I was told he had gone to the "country." But towards the last of May I met him. He told me that he was on the look-out for a quiet, unfrequented place on the sea-shore, where he might rusticate and sketch. He was looking very poorly. I suggested Newport, and I remember he hardly had the energy to smile at the simple joke. We parted without my having been able to satisfy him, and for a very long time I quite lost sight of him. He died seven years ago, at the age of thirty-five. For five years, accordingly, he managed to shield his life from the eyes of men. Through circumstances which I need not detail, a large portion of his personal property has come into my hands. You will remember that he was a man of what are called elegant tastes: that is, he was seriously interested in arts and letters. He wrote some very bad poetry, but he produced a number of remarkable paintings. He left a mass of papers on all subjects, few of which are adapted to be generally interesting. A portion of them, however, I highly prize,—that which constitutes his private diary. It extends from his twenty-fifth to his thirtieth year, at which period it breaks off suddenly. If you will come to my house, I will show you such of his pictures and sketches as I possess, and, I trust, convert you to my opinion that he had in him the stuff of a great painter. Meanwhile I will place before you the last hundred pages of his diary, as an answer to your inquiry regarding the ultimate view taken by the great Nemesis of his treatment of Miss Leary,—his scorn of the magnificent Venus Victrix. The recent decease of the one person who had a voice paramount to mine in the disposal of Locksley's effects enables me to act without reserve.

Cragthorpe, June 9th.—I have been sitting some minutes, pen in hand, pondering whether on this new earth, beneath this new sky, I had better resume these occasional records of my idleness. I think I will at all events make the experiment. If we fail, as Lady Macbeth remarks, we fail. I find my entries have been longest when my life has been dullest. I doubt not, therefore, that, once launched into the monotony of village life, I shall sit scribbling from morning till night. If nothing happens—— But my prophetic soul tells me that something *will* happen. I am determined that something shall,—if it be nothing else than that I paint a picture.

When I came up to bed half an hour ago, I was deadly sleepy. Now, after looking out of the window a little while, my brain is strong and clear, and I feel as if I could write till morning. But, unfortunately, I have nothing to write about. And then, if I expect to rise early, I must turn in betimes. The whole village is asleep, godless metropolitan that I am! The lamps on the square without flicker in the wind; there is nothing abroad but the blue darkness and the smell of the rising tide. I have spent the whole day on my legs, trudging from one side of the peninsula to the other. What a trump is old Mrs. M——, to have thought of this place! I must write her a letter of passionate thanks. Never before, it seems to me, have I known pure coast-scenery. Never before have I relished the beauties of wave, rock, and cloud. I am filled with a sensuous ecstasy at the unparalleled life, light, and transparency of the air. I am stricken mute with reverent admiration at the stupendous resources possessed by the ocean in the way of color and sound; and as yet, I suppose, I have not seen half of them. I came in to supper hungry, weary, footsore, sunburnt, dirty,—happier, in short, than I have been for a twelvemonth. And now for the victories of the brush!

June 11th.—Another day afoot and also afloat. I resolved this morning to leave this abominable little tavern. I can't stand my feather-bed another night. I determined to find some other prospect than the town-pump and the "drug-store." I questioned my host, after breakfast, as to the possibility of getting lodgings in any of the outlying farms and cottages. But my host either did not or would not know anything about the matter. So I resolved to wander forth and seek my fortune,—to roam inquisitive through the neighborhood, and appeal to the indigenous sentiment of hospitality. But never did I see a folk so devoid of this amiable quality. By dinner-time I had given up in despair. After dinner I strolled down to the harbor, which is close at hand. The brightness and breeziness of the water tempted me to hire a boat and resume my explorations. I procured an old tub, with a short stump of a mast, which, being planted quite in the centre, gave the craft much the appearance of an inverted mushroom. I made for what I took to be, and what is, an island, lying long and low, some three or four miles, over against the town. I sailed for half an hour directly before the wind, and at last found myself aground on the shelving beach of a quiet little cove. *Such* a little cove! So bright, so still, so warm, so remote from the town, which lay off in the distance, white and semi-circular! I leaped ashore, and dropped my anchor. Before me rose a steep cliff, crowned with an old ruined fort or tower. I made my way up, and about to the landward entrance. The fort is a hollow old shell. Looking upward from the beach, you see the harmless blue sky through the gaping loopholes. Its interior is choked with rocks and brambles, and masses of fallen masonry. I scrambled up to the parapet, and obtained a noble sea-view. Beyond the broad bay I saw miniature town and country mapped out before me; and on the other hand, I saw the infinite Atlantic,—over which, by the by, all the pretty things are brought from Paris. I spent the whole afternoon in wandering hither and thither over the hills that encircle the little cove in which I had landed, heedless of the minutes and my steps, watching the sailing clouds and the cloudy sails on the horizon, listening to the musical attrition of the tidal pebbles, killing innocuous suckers. The only particular sensation I remember was that of being ten years old again, together with a general impression of Saturday afternoon, of the liberty to go in wading or even swimming, and of the prospect of limping home in the dusk with a wondrous story of having *almost* caught a turtle. When I returned, I found—but I know very well what I found, and I need hardly repeat it here for my mortification. Heaven knows I never was a practical character. What thought I about the tide? There lay the old tub, high and dry, with the rusty anchor protruding from the flat green stones and the shallow puddles left by the receding wave. Moving the boat an inch, much more a dozen yards, was quite beyond my strength. I slowly reascended the cliff, to see if from its summit any help was discernible. None was within sight; and I was about to go down again in profound dejection, when I saw a trim little sail-boat shoot out from behind a neighboring bluff, and advance along the shore. I quickened pace. On reaching the beach, I found the new-comer standing out about a hundred yards. The man at the helm appeared to regard me with some interest. With a mute prayer that his feeling might be akin to compassion, I invited him by voice and gesture to make for a little point of rocks a short distance above us, where I proceeded to join him. I told him my story, and he readily took me aboard. He was a civil old gentleman, of the seafaring sort, who appeared to be cruising about in the evening breeze for his pleasure. On landing, I visited the proprietor of my old tub, related my misadventure, and offered to pay damages, if the boat shall turn out in the morning to have sustained any. Meanwhile, I suppose, it is held secure against the next tidal revolution, however insidious.—But for my old gentleman. I have decidedly picked up an acquaintance, if not made a friend. I gave him a very good cigar; and before we reached home, we had become thoroughly intimate. In exchange for my cigar, he gave me his name; and there was that in his tone which seemed to imply that I had by no means the worst of the bargain. His name is Richard Blunt, "though most people," he added, "call me Captain, for short." He then proceeded to inquire my own titles and pretensions. I told him no lies, but I told him only half the truth; and if he chooses to indulge mentally in any romantic understatements, why, he is welcome, and bless his simple heart! The fact is, that I have broken with the past. I have decided, coolly and calmly, as I believe, that it is necessary to my success, or, at any rate, to my happiness, to abjure for a while my conventional self, and to assume a simple, natural character. How can a man be simple and natural who is known to have a hundred thousand a year? That is the supreme curse. It's bad enough to have it: to be known to have it, to be known only because you have it, is most damnable. I suppose I am too proud to be successfully rich. Let me see how poverty will serve my turn. I have taken a fresh start. I have determined to stand upon my own merits. If they fail me, I shall fall back upon my millions; but with God's help I will test them, and see what kind of stuff I am made of. To be young, to be strong, to be poor,—such, in this blessed nineteenth century, is the great basis of solid success. I have resolved to take at least one brief draught from the pure founts of inspiration of my time. I replied to the Captain with such reservations as a brief survey of these principles dictated. What a luxury to pass in a poor man's mind for his brother! I begin to respect myself. Thus much the Captain knows: that I am an educated man, with a taste for painting; that I have come hither for the purpose of cultivating this taste by the study of coast scenery, and for my health. I have reason to believe, moreover, that he suspects me of limited means and of being a good deal of an economist. Amen! *Vogue la galère!* But the point of my story is in his very hospitable offer of lodgings. I had been telling him of my ill success of the morning in the pursuit of the same. He is an odd union of the gentleman of the old school and the old-fashioned, hot-headed merchant-captain. I suppose that certain traits in these characters are readily convertible.

"Young man," said he, after taking several meditative puffs of his cigar, "I don't see the point of your living in a tavern, when there are folks about you with more house-room than they know what to do with. A tavern is only half a house, just as one of these new-fashioned screw-propellers is only half a ship. Suppose you walk round and take a look at my place. I own quite a respectable house over yonder to the left of the town. Do you see that old wharf with the tumble-down warehouses, and the long row of elms behind it? I live right in the midst of the elms. We have the dearest little garden in the world, stretching down to the water's edge. It's all as quiet as anything can be, short of a graveyard. The back windows, you know, overlook the harbor; and you can see twenty miles up the bay, and fifty miles out to sea. You can paint to yourself there the livelong day, with no more fear of intrusion than if you were out yonder at the light-ship. There's no one but myself and my daughter, who's a perfect lady, Sir. She teaches music in a young ladies' school. You see, money's an object, as they say. We have never taken boarders yet, because none ever came in our track; but I guess we can learn the ways. I suppose you've boarded before; you can put us up to a thing or two."

There was something so kindly. and honest in the old man's weather-beaten face, something so friendly in his address, that I forthwith struck a bargain with him, subject to his daughter's approval. I am to have her answer tomorrow. This same daughter strikes me as rather a dark spot in the picture. Teacher in a young ladies' school,—probably the establishment of which Mrs. M—— spoke to me. I suppose she's over thirty. I think I know the species.

June 12th, A. M.—I have really nothing to do but to scribble. "Barkis is willing." Captain Blunt brought me word this morning that his daughter smiles propitious. I am to report this evening; but I shall send my slender baggage in an hour or two.

P. M.—Here I am, housed. The house is less than a mile from the inn, and reached by a very pleasant road, skirting the harbor. At about six o'clock I presented myself. Captain Blunt had described the place. A very civil old negress admitted me, and ushered me into the garden, where I found my friends watering their flowers. The old man was in his house-coat and slippers. He gave me a cordial welcome. There is something delightfully easy in his manners,—and in Miss Blunt's, too, for that matter. She received me very nicely. The late Mrs. Blunt was probably a well-bred woman. As for Miss Blunt's being thirty, she is about twenty-four. She wore a fresh white dress, with a violet ribbon at her neck, and a rose-bud in her button-hole,—or whatever corresponds thereto on the feminine bosom. I thought I discerned in this costume a vague intention of courtesy, of deference, of celebrating my arrival. I don't believe Miss Blunt wears white muslin every day. She shook hands with me, and made me a very frank little speech about her hospitality. "We have never had any inmates before," said she; "and we are consequently new to the business. I don't know what you expect. I hope you don't expect a great deal. You must ask for anything you want. If we can give it, we shall be very glad to do so; if we can't, I give you warning that we shall refuse outright." Bravo, Miss Blunt! The best of it is, that she is decidedly beautiful,—and in the grand manner: tall, and rather plump. What is the orthodox description of a pretty girl?—white and red? Miss Blunt is not a pretty girl, she is a handsome woman. She leaves an impression of black and red; that is, she is a florid brunette. She has a great deal of wavy black hair, which encircles her head like a dusky glory, a smoky halo. Her eyebrows, too, are black, but her eyes themselves are of a rich blue gray, the color of those slate-cliffs which I saw yesterday, weltering under the tide. Her mouth, however, is her strong point. It is very large, and contains the finest row of teeth in all this weary world. Her smile is eminently intelligent. Her chin is full, and somewhat heavy. All this is a tolerable catalogue, but no picture. I have been tormenting my brain to discover whether it was her coloring or her form that impressed me most. Fruitless speculation! Seriously, I think it was neither; it was her movement. She walks a queen. It was the conscious poise of her head, the unconscious "hang" of her arms, the careless grace and dignity with which she lingered along the garden-path, smelling a red red rose! She has very little to say, apparently; but when she speaks, it is to the point, and if the point suggests it, with a very sweet smile. Indeed, if she is not talkative, it is not from timidity. Is it from indifference? Time will elucidate this, as well as other matters. I cling to the hypothesis that she is amiable. She is, moreover, intelligent; she is probably quite reserved; and she is possibly very proud. She is, in short, a woman of character. There you are, Miss Blunt, at full length,—emphatically the portrait of a lady. After tea, she gave us some music in the parlor. I confess that I was more taken with the picture of the dusky little room, lighted by the single candle on the piano, and by the *effect* of Miss Blunt's performance, than with its meaning. She appears to possess a very brilliant touch.

June 18th.—I have now been here almost a week. I occupy two very pleasant rooms. My painting-room is a vast and rather bare apartment, with a very good southern light. I have decked it out with a few old prints and sketches, and have already grown very fond of it. When I had disposed my artistic odds and ends in as picturesque a fashion as possible, I called in my hosts. The Captain looked about silently for some moments, and then inquired hopefully if I had ever tried my hand at a ship. On learning that I had not yet got to ships, he relapsed into a deferential silence. His daughter smiled and questioned very graciously, and called everything beautiful and delightful; which rather disappointed me, as I had taken her to be a woman of some originality. She is rather a puzzle;—or is she, indeed, a very commonplace person, and the fault in me, who am forever taking women to mean a great deal more than their Maker intended? Regarding Miss Blunt I have collected a few facts. She is not twenty-four, but twenty-seven years old. She has taught music ever since she was twenty, in a large boarding-school just out of the town, where she originally got her education. Her salary in this establishment, which is, I believe, a tolerably flourishing one, and the proceeds of a few additional lessons, constitute the chief revenues of the household. But Blunt fortunately owns his house, and his needs and habits are of the simplest kind. What does he or his daughter know of the great worldly theory of necessities, the great worldly scale of pleasures? Miss Blunt's only luxuries are a subscription to the circulating library, and an occasional walk on the beach, which, like one of Miss Brontë's heroines, she paces in company with an old Newfoundland dog. I am afraid she is sadly ignorant. She reads nothing but novels. I am bound to believe, however, that she has derived from the perusal of these works a certain practical science of her own. "I read all the novels I can get," she said yesterday; "but I only like the good ones. I do so like Zanoni, which I have just finished." I must set her to work at some of the masters. I should like some of those fretful New-York heiresses to see how this woman lives. I wish, too, that half a dozen of *ces messieurs* of the clubs might take a peep at the present way of life of their humble servant. We breakfast at eight o'clock. Immediately afterwards, Miss Blunt, in a shabby old bonnet and shawl, starts off to school. If the weather is fine, the Captain goes out a-fishing, and I am left to my own devices. Twice I have accompanied the old man.

The second time I was lucky enough to catch a big bluefish, which we had for dinner. The Captain is an excellent specimen of the sturdy navigator, with his loose blue clothes, his ultra-divergent legs, his crisp white hair, and his jolly thick-skinned visage. He comes of a seafaring English race. There is more or less of the ship's cabin in the general aspect of this antiquated house. I have heard the winds whistle about its walls, on two or three occasions, in true mid-ocean style. And then the illusion is heightened, somehow or other, by the extraordinary intensity of the light. My painting-room is a grand observatory of the clouds. I sit by the half-hour, watching them sail past my high, uncurtained windows. At the back part of the room, something tells you that they belong to an ocean sky; and there, in truth, as you draw nearer, you behold the vast, gray complement of sea. This quarter of the town is perfectly quiet. Human activity seems to have passed over it, never again to return, and to have left a kind of deposit of melancholy resignation. The streets are clean, bright, and airy; but this fact seems only to add to the intense sobriety. It implies that the unobstructed heavens are in the secret of their decline. There is something ghostly in the perpetual stillness. We frequently hear the rattling of the yards and the issuing of orders on the barks and schooners anchored out in the harbor.

June 28th.—My experiment works far better than I had hoped. I am thoroughly at my ease; my peace of mind quite passeth understanding. I work diligently; I have none but pleasant thoughts. The past has almost lost its terrors. For a week now I have been out sketching daily. The Captain carries me to a certain point on the shore of the harbor, I disembark and strike across the fields to a spot where I have established a kind of *rendezvous* with a particular effect of rock and shadow, which has been tolerably faithful to its appointment. Here I set up my easel, and paint till sunset. Then I retrace my steps and meet the boat. I am in every way much encouraged. The horizon of my work grows perceptibly wider. And then I am inexpressibly happy in the conviction that I am not wholly unfit for a life of (moderate) labor and (comparative) privation. I am quite in love with my poverty, if I may call it so. As why should I not? At this rate I don't spend eight hundred a year.

July 12th.—We have been having a week of bad weather: constant rain, night and day. This is certainly at once the brightest and the blackest spot in New England. The skies can smile, assuredly; but how they can frown! I have been painting rather languidly, and at a great disadvantage, at my window. . . . . Through all this pouring and pattering, Miss Blunt sallies forth to her pupils. She envelopes her beautiful head in a great woollen hood, her beautiful figure in a kind of feminine Mackintosh; her feet she puts into heavy clogs, and over the whole she balances a cotton umbrella. When she comes home, with the rain-drops glistening on her red cheeks and her dark lashes, her cloak bespattered with mud, and her hands red with the cool damp, she is a profoundly wholesome spectacle. I never fail to make her a very low bow, for which she repays me with an extraordinary smile. This working-day side of her character is what especially pleases me in Miss Blunt. This holy working-dress of loveliness and dignity sits upon her with the simplicity of an antique drapery. Little use has she for whalebones and furbelows. What a poetry there is, after all, in red hands! I kiss yours, Mademoiselle. I do so because you are self-helpful; because you earn your living; because you are honest, simple, and ignorant (for a sensible woman, that is); because you speak and act to the point; because, in short, you are so unlike—certain of your sisters.

July 16th.—On Monday it cleared up generously. When I went to my window, on rising, I found sky and sea looking, for their brightness and freshness, like a clever English water-color. The ocean is of a deep purple blue; above it, the pure, bright sky looks pale, though it bends with an infinite depth over the inland horizon. Here and there on the dark breezy water gleams the white cap of a wave, or flaps the white cloak of a fishing-boat. I have been sketching sedulously; I have discovered, within a couple of miles' walk, a large, lonely pond, set in quite a grand landscape of barren rocks and grassy slopes. At one extremity is a broad outlook on the open sea; at the other, deep buried in the foliage of an apple-orchard,

stands an old haunted-looking farm-house. To the west of the
pond is a wide expanse of rock and grass, of beach and marsh.
The sheep browse over it as upon a Highland moor. Except a
few stunted firs and cedars, there is not a tree in sight. When
I want shade, I seek it in the shelter of one of the great mossy
boulders which upheave their scintillating shoulders to the
sun, or of the long shallow dells where a tangle of blackberry-
bushes hedges about a sky-reflecting pool. I have encamped
over against a plain, brown hillside, which, with laborious patience, I am transferring to canvas; and as we have now had
the same clear sky for several days, I have almost finished
quite a satisfactory little study. I go forth immediately after
breakfast. Miss Blunt furnishes me with a napkin full of bread
and cold meat, which at the noonday hours, in my sunny solitude, within sight of the slumbering ocean, I voraciously convey to my lips with my discolored fingers. At seven o'clock I
return to tea, at which repast we each tell the story of our
day's work. For poor Miss Blunt, it is day after day the same
story: a wearisome round of visits to the school, and to the
houses of the mayor, the parson, the butcher, the baker,
whose young ladies, of course, all receive instruction on the
piano. But she doesn't complain, nor, indeed, does she look
very weary. When she has put on a fresh calico dress for tea,
and arranged her hair anew, and with these improvements flits
about with that quiet hither and thither of her gentle footsteps, preparing our evening meal, peeping into the teapot,
cutting the solid loaf,—or when, sitting down on the low
door-step, she reads out select scraps from the evening paper,—or else, when, tea being over, she folds her arms, (an attitude which becomes her mightily,) and, still sitting on the
door-step, gossips away the evening in comfortable idleness,
while her father and I indulge in the fragrant pipe, and watch
the lights shining out, one by one, in different quarters of the
darkling bay: at these moments she is as pretty, as cheerful, as
careless as it becomes a sensible woman to be. What a pride
the Captain takes in his daughter! And she, in return, how
perfect is her devotion to the old man! He is proud of her
grace, of her tact, of her good sense, of her wit, such as it is.
He thinks her to be the most accomplished of women. He
waits upon her as if, instead of his old familiar Esther, she

were a newly inducted daughter-in-law. And indeed, if I were
his own son, he could not be kinder to me. They are certainly—nay, why should I not say it?—*we* are certainly a very
happy little household. Will it last forever? I say *we*, because
both father and daughter have given me a hundred assurances—he direct, and she, if I don't flatter myself, after the
manner of her sex, indirect—that I am already a valued friend.
It is natural enough that I should have gained their good-will.
They have received at my hands inveterate courtesy. The way
to the old man's heart is through a studied consideration of
his daughter. He knows, I imagine, that I admire Miss Blunt.
But if I should at any time fall below the mark of ceremony,
I should have an account to settle with him. All this is as it
should be. When people have to economize with the dollars
and cents, they have a right to be splendid in their feelings. I
have prided myself not a little on my good manners towards
my hostess. That my bearing has been without reproach is,
however, a fact which I do not, in any degree, set down here
to my credit; for I would defy the most impertinent of men
(whoever he is) to forget himself with this young lady, without leave unmistakably given. Those deep, dark eyes have a
strong prohibitory force. I record the circumstance simply because in future years, when my charming friend shall have become a distant shadow, it will be pleasant, in turning over
these pages, to find written testimony to a number of points
which I shall be apt to charge solely upon my imagination. I
wonder whether Miss Blunt, in days to come, referring to the
tables of her memory for some trivial matter-of-fact, some
prosaic date or half-buried landmark, will also encounter this
little secret of ours, as I may call it,—will decipher an old faint
note to this effect, overlaid with the memoranda of intervening years. Of course she will. Sentiment aside, she is a woman
of an excellent memory. Whether she forgives or not I know
not; but she certainly doesn't forget. Doubtless, virtue is its
own reward; but there is a double satisfaction in being polite
to a person on whom it *tells*. Another reason for my pleasant
relations with the Captain is, that I afford him a chance to
rub up his rusty old cosmopolitanism, and trot out his little
scraps of old-fashioned reading, some of which are very
curious. It is a great treat for him to spin his threadbare

yarns over again to a sympathetic listener. These warm July evenings, in the sweet-smelling garden, are just the proper setting for his amiable garrulities. An odd enough relation subsists between us on this point. Like many gentlemen of his calling, the Captain is harassed by an irresistible desire to romance, even on the least promising themes; and it is vastly amusing to observe how he will auscultate, as it were, his auditor's inmost mood, to ascertain whether it is prepared for the absorption of his insidious fibs. Sometimes they perish utterly in the transition: they are very pretty, I conceive, in the deep and briny well of the Captain's fancy; but they won't bear being transplanted into the shallow inland lakes of my land-bred apprehension. At other times, the auditor being in a dreamy, sentimental, and altogether unprincipled mood, he will drink the old man's salt-water by the bucketful and feel none the worse for it. Which is the worse, wilfully to tell, or wilfully to believe, a pretty little falsehood which will not hurt any one? I suppose you can't believe wilfully; you only pretend to believe. My part of the game, therefore, is certainly as bad as the Captain's. Perhaps I take kindly to his beautiful perversions of fact, because I am myself engaged in one, because I am sailing under false colors of the deepest dye. I wonder whether my friends have any suspicion of the real state of the case. How should they? I fancy, that, on the whole, I play my part pretty well. I am delighted to find it come so easy. I do not mean that I experience little difficulty in foregoing my hundred petty elegancies and luxuries,—for to these, thank Heaven, I was not so indissolubly wedded that one wholesome shock could not loosen my bonds,—but that I manage more cleverly than I expected to stifle those innumerable tacit allusions which might serve effectually to belie my character.

Sunday, July 20th.—This has been a very pleasant day for me; although in it, of course, I have done no manner of work. I had this morning a delightful *tête-à-tête* with my hostess. She had sprained her ankle, coming down stairs; and so, instead of going forth to Sunday school and to meeting, she was obliged to remain at home on the sofa. The Captain, who is of a very punctilious piety, went off alone. When I came into the parlor, as the church-bells were ringing, Miss Blunt asked me if I never went to meeting.

"Never when there is anything better to do at home," said I.

"What is better than going to church?" she asked, with charming simplicity.

She was reclining on the sofa, with her foot on a pillow, and her Bible in her lap. She looked by no means afflicted at having to be absent from divine service; and, instead of answering her question, I took the liberty of telling her so.

"I *am* sorry to be absent," said she. "You know it's my only festival in the week."

"So you look upon it as a festival," said I.

"Isn't it a pleasure to meet one's acquaintance? I confess I am never deeply interested in the sermon, and I very much dislike teaching the children; but I like wearing my best bonnet, and singing in the choir, and walking part of the way home with"——

"With whom?"

"With any one who offers to walk with me."

"With Mr. Johnson, for instance," said I.

Mr. Johnson is a young lawyer in the village, who calls here once a week, and whose attentions to Miss Blunt have been remarked.

"Yes," she answered, "Mr. Johnson will do as an instance."

"How he will miss you!"

"I suppose he will. We sing off the same book. What are you laughing at? He kindly permits me to hold the book, while he stands with his hands in his pockets. Last Sunday I quite lost patience. 'Mr. Johnson,' said I, 'do hold the book! Where are your manners?' He burst out laughing in the midst of the reading. He will certainly have to hold the book to-day."

"What a 'masterful soul' he is! I suppose he will call after meeting."

"Perhaps he will. I hope so."

"I hope he won't," said I, roundly. "I am going to sit down here and talk to you, and I wish our *tête-à-tête* not to be interrupted."

"Have you anything particular to say?"

"Nothing so particular as Mr. Johnson, perhaps."

Miss Blunt has a very pretty affectation of being more matter-of-fact than she really is.

"His rights, then," said she, "are paramount to yours."

"Ah, you admit that he has rights?"

"Not at all. I simply assert that you have none."

"I beg your pardon. I have claims which I mean to enforce. I have a claim upon your undivided attention, when I pay you a morning call."

"Your claim is certainly answered. Have I been uncivil, pray?"

"Not uncivil, perhaps, but inconsiderate. You have been sighing for the company of a third person, which you can't expect me to relish."

"Why not, pray? If I, a lady, can put up with Mr. Johnson's society, why shouldn't you, one of his own sex?"

"Because he is so outrageously conceited. You, as a lady, or at any rate as a woman, like conceited men."

"Ah, yes; I have no doubt that I, as a woman, have all kinds of improper tastes. That's an old story."

"Admit, at any rate, that our friend is conceited."

"Admit it? Why, I have said so a hundred times. I have told him so."

"Indeed! It has come to that, then?"

"To what, pray?"

"To that critical point in the friendship of a lady and gentleman, when they bring against each other all kinds of delightful charges of moral obliquity. Take care, Miss Blunt! A couple of intelligent New-Englanders, of opposite sex, young, unmarried, are pretty far gone, when they begin morally to reprobate each other. So you told Mr. Johnson that he is conceited? And I suppose you added, that he was also dreadfully satirical and skeptical? What was his rejoinder? Let me see. Did he ever tell you that you were a little bit affected?"

"No: he left that for you to say, in this very ingenious manner. Thank you, Sir."

"He left it for me to deny, which is a great deal prettier. Do you think the manner ingenious?"

"I think the matter, considering the day and hour, very

profane, Mr. Locksley. Suppose you go away and let me read my Bible."

"Meanwhile," I asked, "what shall I do?"

"Go and read yours, if you have one."

"I haven't."

I was nevertheless compelled to retire, with the promise of a second audience in half an hour. Poor Miss Blunt owes it to her conscience to read a certain number of chapters. What a pure and upright soul she is! And what an edifying spectacle is much of our feminine piety! Women find a place for everything in their commodious little minds, just as they do in their wonderfully subdivided trunks, when they go on a journey. I have no doubt that this young lady stows away her religion in a corner, just as she does her Sunday bonnet,—and, when the proper moment comes, draws it forth, and reflects while she assumes it before the glass, and blows away the strictly imaginary dust: for what worldly impurity can penetrate through half a dozen layers of cambric and tissue-paper? Dear me, what a comfort it is to have a nice, fresh, holiday faith!—When I returned to the parlor, Miss Blunt was still sitting with her Bible in her lap. Somehow or other, I no longer felt in the mood for jesting. So I asked her soberly what she had been reading. Soberly she answered me. She inquired how I had spent my half-hour.

"In thinking good Sabbath thoughts," I said. "I have been walking in the garden." And then I spoke my mind. "I have been thanking Heaven that it has led me, a poor, friendless wanderer, into so peaceful an anchorage."

"Are you, then, so poor and friendless?" asked Miss Blunt, quite abruptly.

"Did you ever hear of an art-student under thirty who wasn't poor?" I answered. "Upon my word, I have yet to sell my first picture. Then, as for being friendless, there are not five people in the world who really care for me."

"*Really* care? I am afraid you look too close. And then I think five good friends is a very large number. I think myself very well off with a couple. But if you are friendless, it's probably your own fault."

"Perhaps it is," said I, sitting down in the rocking-chair; "and yet, perhaps, it isn't. Have you found me so very

repulsive? Haven't you, on the contrary, found me rather sociable?"

She folded her arms, and quietly looked at me for a moment, before answering. I shouldn't wonder if I blushed a
little.

"You want a compliment, Mr. Locksley; that's the long and
short of it. I have not paid you a compliment since you have
been here. How you must have suffered! But it's a pity you
couldn't have waited awhile longer, instead of beginning to
angle with that very clumsy bait. For an artist, you are very
inartistic. Men never know how to wait. 'Have I found you
repulsive? haven't I found you sociable?' Perhaps, after all,
considering what I have in my mind, it is as well that you
asked for your compliment. I have found you charming. I say
it freely; and yet I say, with equal sincerity, that I fancy very
few others would find you so. I can say decidedly that you are
not sociable. You are entirely too particular. You are considerate of me, because you know that I know that you are so.
There's the rub, you see: I know that you know that I know
it. Don't interrupt me; I am going to be eloquent. I want you
to understand why I don't consider you sociable. You call Mr.
Johnson conceited; but, really, I don't believe he's nearly as
conceited as yourself. You are too conceited to be sociable;
he is not. I am an obscure, weak-minded woman,—weak-
minded, you know, compared with men. I can be patronized,—yes, that's the word. Would you be equally amiable
with a person as strong, as clear-sighted as yourself, with a
person equally averse with yourself to being under an obligation? I think not. Of course it's delightful to charm people.
Who wouldn't? There is no harm in it, as long as the charmer
does not sit up for a public benefactor. If I were a man, a
clever man like yourself, who had seen the world, who was
not to be charmed and encouraged, but to be convinced and
refuted, would you be equally amiable? It will perhaps seem
absurd to you, and it will certainly seem egotistical, but I consider myself sociable, for all that I have only a couple of
friends,—my father and the principal of the school. That is, I
mingle with women without any second thought. Not that I
wish you to do so: on the contrary, if the contrary is natural
to you. But I don't believe you mingle in the same way with

men. You may ask me what I know about it. Of course I know nothing: I simply guess. When I have done, indeed, I mean to beg your pardon for all I have said; but until then, give me a chance. You are incapable of listening deferentially to stupid, bigoted persons. I am not. I do it every day. Ah, you have no idea of what nice manners I have in the exercise of my profession! Every day I have occasion to pocket my pride and to stifle my precious sense of the ridiculous,—of which, of course, you think I haven't a bit. It is, for instance, a constant vexation to me to be poor. It makes me frequently hate rich women; it makes me despise poor ones. I don't know whether you suffer acutely from the narrowness of your own means; but if you do, I dare say you shun rich men. I don't. I like to go into rich people's houses, and to be very polite to the ladies of the house, especially if they are very well-dressed and ignorant and vulgar. All women are like me in this respect; and all men more or less like you. That is, after all, the text of my sermon. Compared with us, it has always seemed to me that you are arrant cowards,—that we alone are brave. To be sociable, you must have a great deal of pluck. You are too fine a gentleman. Go and teach school, or open a corner grocery, or sit in a law-office all day, waiting for clients: *then* you will be sociable. As yet, you are only agreeable. It *is* your own fault, if people don't care for you. You don't care for them. That you should be indifferent to their applause is all very well; but you don't care for their indifference. You are amiable, you are very kind, and you are also very lazy. You consider that you are working now, don't you? Many persons would not call it work."

It was now certainly my turn to fold my arms.

"And now," added my companion, as I did so, "I beg your pardon."

"This was certainly worth waiting for," said I. "I don't know what answer to make. My head swims. I don't know whether you have been attacking me or praising me. So you advise me to open a corner grocery, do you?"

"I advise you to do something that will make you a little less satirical. You had better marry, for instance."

"*Je ne demande pas mieux.* Will you have me? I can't afford it."

"Marry a rich woman."

I shook my head.

"Why not?" asked Miss Blunt. "Because people would accuse you of being mercenary? What of that? I mean to marry the first rich man who offers. Do you know that I am tired of living alone in this weary old way, teaching little girls their gamut, and turning and patching my dresses? I mean to marry the first man who offers."

"Even if he is poor?"

"Even if he is poor, ugly, and stupid."

"I am your man, then. Would you take me, if I were to offer?"

"Try and see."

"Must I get upon my knees?"

"No, you need not even do that. Am I not on mine? It would be too fine an irony. Remain as you are, lounging back in your chair, with your thumbs in your waistcoat."

If I were writing a romance now, instead of transcribing facts, I would say that I knew not what might have happened at this juncture, had not the door opened and admitted the Captain and Mr. Johnson. The latter was in the highest spirits.

"How are you, Miss Esther? So you have been breaking your leg, eh? How are you, Mr. Locksley? I wish I were a doctor now. Which is it, right or left?"

In this simple fashion he made himself agreeable to Miss Blunt. He stopped to dinner and talked without ceasing. Whether our hostess had talked herself out in her very animated address to myself an hour before, or whether she preferred to oppose no obstacle to Mr. Johnson's fluency, or whether she was indifferent to him, I know not; but she held her tongue with that easy grace, that charming tacit intimation of "We could, an we would," of which she is so perfect a mistress. This very interesting woman has a number of pretty traits in common with her town-bred sisters; only, whereas in these they are laboriously acquired, in her they are severely natural. I am sure, that, if I were to plant her in Madison Square to-morrow, she would, after one quick, all-compassing glance, assume the *nil admirari* in a manner to drive the greatest lady of them all to despair. Johnson is a man of excellent intentions, but no taste. Two or three times I looked at Miss Blunt to see what impression his sallies were making upon her. They seemed to produce none whatever. But I know better, *moi*. Not one of them escaped her. But I suppose she said to herself that her impressions on this point were no business of mine. Perhaps she was right. It is a disagreeable word to use of a woman you admire; but I can't help fancying that she has been a little *soured*. By what? Who shall say? By some old love affair, perhaps.

July 24th.—This evening the Captain and I took a half-hour's turn about the harbor. I asked him frankly, as a friend, whether Johnson wants to marry his daughter.

"I guess he does," said the old man; "and yet I hope he don't. You know what he is: he's smart, promising, and already sufficiently well off. But somehow he isn't for a man what my Esther is for a woman."

"That he isn't!" said I; "and honestly, Captain Blunt, I don't know who is"——

"Unless it's yourself," said the Captain.

"Thank you. I know a great many ways in which Mr. Johnson is more worthy of her than I."

"And I know one in which you are more worthy of her than he,—that is, in being what we used to call a gentleman."

"Miss Esther made him sufficiently welcome in her quiet way, on Sunday," I rejoined.

"Oh, she respects him," said Blunt. "As she's situated, she might marry him on that. You see, she's weary of hearing little girls drum on the piano. With her ear for music," added the Captain, "I wonder she has borne it so long."

"She is certainly meant for better things," said I.

"Well," answered the Captain, who has an honest habit of deprecating your agreement, when it occurs to him that he has obtained it for sentiments which fall somewhat short of the stoical,—"well," said he, with a very dry expression of mouth, "she's born to do her duty. We are all of us born for that."

"Sometimes our duty is rather dreary," said I.

"So it be; but what's the help for it? I don't want to die without seeing my daughter provided for. What she makes by teaching is a pretty slim subsistence. There was a time when I thought she was going to be fixed for life, but it all blew over. There was a young fellow here from down Boston way, who came about as near to it as you can come, when you actually don't. He and Esther were excellent friends. One day Esther came up to me, and looked me in the face, and told me she was engaged.

" 'Who to?' says I, though of course I knew, and Esther told me as much. 'When do you expect to marry?' I asked.

" 'When John grows rich enough,' says she.

" 'When will that be?'

" 'It may not be for years,' said poor Esther.

"A whole year passed, and, as far as I could see, the young man came no nearer to his fortune. He was forever running to and fro between this place and Boston. I asked no questions, because I knew that my poor girl wished it so. But at last, one day, I began to think it was time to take an observation, and see whereabouts we stood.

" 'Has John made his fortune yet?' I asked.

" 'I don't know, father,' said Esther.

" 'When are you to be married?'

" 'Never!' said my poor little girl, and burst into tears. 'Please ask me no questions,' said she. 'Our engagement is over. Ask me no questions.'

" 'Tell me one thing,' said I: 'where is that d—d scoundrel who has broken my daughter's heart?'

"You should have seen the look she gave me.

" 'Broken my heart, Sir? You are very much mistaken. I don't know who you mean.'

" 'I mean John Banister,' said I. That was his name.

" 'I believe Mr. Banister is in China,' says Esther, as grand as the Queen of Sheba. And there was an end of it. I never learnt the ins and outs of it. I have been told that Banister is accumulating money very fast in the China trade."

August 7th.—I have made no entry for more than a fortnight. They tell me I have been very ill; and I find no difficulty in believing them. I suppose I took cold, sitting out so late, sketching. At all events, I have had a mild intermittent fever. I have slept so much, however, that the time has seemed rather short. I have been tenderly nursed by this kind old gentleman, his daughter, and his maid-servant. God bless them, one and all! I say his daughter, because old Dorothy informs me that for half an hour one morning, at dawn, after a night during which I had been very feeble, Miss Blunt relieved guard at my bedside, while I lay wrapt in brutal slumber. It is very jolly to see sky and ocean once again. I have got myself into my easy-chair by the open window, with my shutters closed and the lattice open; and here I sit with my book on my knee, scratching away feebly enough. Now and then I peep from my cool, dark sick-chamber out into the world of light. High noon at midsummer! What a spectacle! There are no clouds in the sky, no waves on the ocean. The sun has it all to himself. To look long at the garden makes the eyes water. And we—"Hobbs, Nobbs, Stokes, and Nokes"—propose to paint that kingdom of light. *Allons, donc!*

The loveliest of women has just tapped, and come in with a plate of early peaches. The peaches are of a gorgeous color and plumpness; but Miss Blunt looks pale and thin. The hot weather doesn't agree with her. She is overworked. Confound it! Of course I thanked her warmly for her attentions during my illness. She disclaims all gratitude, and refers me to her father and Mrs. Dorothy.

"I allude more especially," said I, "to that little hour at the end of a weary night, when you stole in like a kind of moral Aurora, and drove away the shadows from my brain. That morning, you know, I began to get better."

"It was indeed a very little hour," said Miss Blunt. "It was about ten minutes." And then she began to scold me for presuming to touch a pen during my convalescence. She laughs at me, indeed, for keeping a diary at all. "Of all things," cried she, "a sentimental man is the most despicable."

I confess I was somewhat nettled. The thrust seemed gratuitous.

"Of all things," I answered, "a woman without sentiment is the most unlovely."

"Sentiment and loveliness are all very well, when you have time for them," said Miss Blunt. "I haven't. I'm not rich enough. Good morning."

Speaking of another woman, I would say that she flounced

out of the room. But such was the gait of Juno, when she moved stiffly over the grass from where Paris stood with Venus holding the apple, gathering up her divine vestment, and leaving the others to guess at her face——

Juno has just come back to say that she forgot what she came for half an hour ago. What will I be pleased to like for dinner?

"I have just been writing in my diary that you flounced out of the room," said I.

"Have you, indeed? Now you can write that I have bounced in. There's a nice cold chicken down-stairs," etc., etc.

August 14th.—This afternoon I sent for a light wagon, and treated Miss Blunt to a drive. We went successively over the three beaches. What a time we had, coming home! I shall never forget that hard trot over Weston's Beach. The tide was very low; and we had the whole glittering, weltering strand to ourselves. There was a heavy blow yesterday, which had not yet subsided; and the waves had been lashed into a magnificent fury. Trot, trot, trot, trot, we trundled over the hard sand. The sound of the horse's hoofs rang out sharp against the monotone of the thunderous surf, as we drew nearer and nearer to the long line of the cliffs. At our left, almost from the lofty zenith of the pale evening sky to the high western horizon of the tumultuous dark-green sea, was suspended, so to speak, one of those gorgeous vertical sunsets that Turner loved so well. It was a splendid confusion of purple and green and gold,—the clouds flying and flowing in the wind like the folds of a mighty banner borne by some triumphal fleet whose prows were not visible above the long chain of mountainous waves. As we reached the point where the cliffs plunge down upon the beach, I pulled up, and we remained for some moments looking out along the low, brown, obstinate barrier at whose feet the impetuous waters were rolling themselves into powder.

August 17th.—This evening, as I lighted my bedroom candle, I saw that the Captain had something to say to me. So I waited below until the old man and his daughter had performed their usual picturesque embrace, and the latter had given me that hand-shake and that smile which I never failed to exact.

"Johnson has got his discharge," said the old man, when he had heard his daughter's door close up-stairs.

"What do you mean?"

He pointed with his thumb to the room above, where we heard, through the thin partition, the movement of Miss Blunt's light step.

"You mean that he has proposed to Miss Esther?"

The Captain nodded.

"And has been refused?"

"Flat."

"Poor fellow!" said I, very honestly. "Did he tell you himself?"

"Yes, with tears in his eyes. He wanted me to speak for him. I told him it was no use. Then he began to say hard things of my poor girl."

"What kind of things?"

"A pack of falsehoods. He says she has no heart. She has promised always to regard him as a friend: it's more than I will, hang him!"

"Poor fellow!" said I; and now, as I write, I can only repeat, considering what a hope was here broken, Poor fellow!

August 23d.—I have been lounging about all day, thinking of it, dreaming of it, spooning over it, as they say. This is a decided waste of time. I think, accordingly, the best thing for me to do is, to sit down and lay the ghost by writing out my story.

On Thursday evening Miss Blunt happened to intimate that she had a holiday on the morrow, it being the birthday of the lady in whose establishment she teaches.

"There is to be a tea-party at four o'clock in the afternoon for the resident pupils and teachers," said Miss Esther. "Tea at four! what do you think of that? And then there is to be a speech-making by the smartest young lady. As my services are not required, I propose to be absent. Suppose, father, you take us out in your boat. Will you come, Mr. Locksley? We shall have a nice little picnic. Let us go over to old Fort Pudding, across the bay. We will take our dinner with us, and send Dorothy to spend the day with her sister, and put the house-key in our pocket, and not come home till we please."

I warmly espoused the project, and it was accordingly carried into execution the next morning, when, at about ten o'clock, we pushed off from our little wharf at the garden-foot. It was a perfect summer's day: I can say no more for it. We made a quiet run over to the point of our destination. I shall never forget the wondrous stillness which brooded over earth and water, as we weighed anchor in the lee of my old friend,—or old enemy,—the ruined fort. The deep, translucent water reposed at the base of the warm sunlit cliff like a great basin of glass, which I half expected to hear shiver and crack as our keel ploughed through it. And how color and sound stood out in the transparent air! How audibly the little ripples on the beach whispered to the open sky! How our irreverent voices seemed to jar upon the privacy of the little cove! The mossy rocks doubled themselves without a flaw in the clear, dark water. The gleaming white beach lay fringed with its deep deposits of odorous sea-weed, gleaming black. The steep, straggling sides of the cliffs raised aloft their rugged angles against the burning blue of the sky. I remember, when Miss Blunt stepped ashore and stood upon the beach, relieved against the heavy shadow of a recess in the cliff, while her father and I busied ourselves with gathering up our baskets and fastening the anchor—I remember, I say, what a figure she made. There is a certain purity in this Cragthorpe air which I have never seen approached,—a lightness, a brilliancy, a *crudity*, which allows perfect liberty of self-assertion to each individual object in the landscape. The prospect is ever more or less like a picture which lacks its final process, its reduction to unity. Miss Blunt's figure, as she stood there on the beach, was almost *criarde*; but how lovely it was! Her light muslin dress, gathered up over her short white skirt, her little black mantilla, the blue veil which she had knotted about her neck, the crimson shawl which she had thrown over her arm, the little silken dome which she poised over her head in one gloved hand, while the other retained her crisp draperies, and which cast down upon her face a sharp circle of shade, out of which her cheerful eyes shone darkly and her happy mouth smiled whitely,—these are some of the hastily noted points of the picture.

"Young woman," I cried out, over the water, "I do wish you might know how pretty you look!"

"How do you know I don't?" she answered. "I should think I might. You don't look so badly, yourself. But it's not I; it's the accessories."

"Hang it! I am going to become profane," I called out again.

"Swear ahead," said the Captain.

"I am going to say you are devilish pretty."

"Dear me! is that all?" cried Miss Blunt, with a little light laugh, which must have made the tutelar sirens of the cove ready to die with jealousy down in their submarine bowers.

By the time the Captain and I had landed our effects, our companion had tripped lightly up the forehead of the cliff—in one place it is very retreating—and disappeared over its crown. She soon reappeared with an intensely white hand-kerchief added to her other provocations, which she waved to us, as we trudged upward, carrying our baskets. When we stopped to take breath on the summit, and wipe our fore-heads, we of course rebuked her who was roaming about idly with her parasol and gloves.

"Do you think I am going to take any trouble or do any work?" cried Miss Esther, in the greatest good-humor. "Is not this my holiday? I am not going to raise a finger, nor soil these beautiful gloves, for which I paid a dollar at Mr. Daw-son's in Cragthorpe. After you have found a shady place for your provisions, I would like you to look for a spring. I am very thirsty."

"Find the spring yourself, Miss," said her father. "Mr. Locksley and I have a spring in this basket. Take a pull, Sir."

And the Captain drew forth a stout black bottle.

"Give me a cup, and I will look for some water," said Miss Blunt. "Only I'm so afraid of the snakes! If you hear a scream, you may know it's a snake."

"Screaming snakes!" said I; "that's a new species."

What nonsense it all sounds like now! As we looked about us, shade seemed scarce, as it generally is, in this region. But Miss Blunt, like the very adroit and practical young person she is, for all that she would have me believe the contrary, soon discovered a capital cool spring in the shelter of a pleasant little dell, beneath a clump of firs. Hither, as one of the young gentlemen who imitate Tennyson would say, we brought our basket, Blunt and I; while Esther dipped the cup, and held it dripping to our thirsty lips, and laid the cloth, and on the grass disposed the platters round. I should have to be a poet, indeed, to describe half the happiness and the silly poetry and purity and beauty of this bright long summer's day. We ate, drank, and talked; we ate occasionally with our fingers, we drank out of the necks of our bottles, and we talked with our mouths full, as befits (and excuses) those who talk wild nonsense. We told stories without the least point. Blunt and I made atrocious puns. I believe, indeed, that Miss Blunt herself made one little punkin, as I called it. If there had been any superfluous representative of humanity present, to register the fact, I should say that we made fools of ourselves. But as there was no fool on hand, I need say nothing about it. I am conscious myself of having said several witty things, which Miss Blunt understood: *in vino veritas.* The dear old Captain twanged the long bow indefatigably. The bright high sun lingered above us the livelong day, and drowned the prospect with light and warmth. One of these days I mean to paint a picture which in future ages, when my dear native land shall boast a national school of art, will hang in the *Salon Carré* of the great central museum, (located, let us say, in Chicago,) and remind folks—or rather make them forget—Giorgione, Bordone, and Veronese: A Rural Festival; three persons feasting under some trees; scene, nowhere in particular; time and hour, problematical. Female figure, a big *brune;* young man reclining on his elbow; old man drinking. An empty sky, with no end of expression. The whole stupendous in color, drawing, feeling. Artist uncertain; supposed to be Robinson, 1900. That's about the programme.

After dinner the Captain began to look out across the bay, and, noticing the uprising of a little breeze, expressed a wish to cruise about for an hour or two. He proposed to us to walk along the shore to a point a couple of miles northward, and there meet the boat. His daughter having agreed to this proposition, he set off with the lightened pannier, and in less than half an hour we saw him standing out from shore. Miss Blunt and I did not begin our walk for a long, long time. We sat and talked beneath the trees. At our feet, a wide cleft in the hills—almost a glen—stretched down to the silent beach. Beyond lay the familiar ocean-line. But, as many philosophers have observed, there is an end to all things. At last we got up. Miss Blunt said, that, as the air was freshening, she believed she would put on her shawl. I helped her to fold it into the proper shape, and then I placed it on her shoulders, her crimson shawl over her black silk sack. And then she tied her veil once more about her neck, and gave me her hat to hold, while she effected a partial redistribution of her hair-pins. By way of being humorous, I placed her hat on my own head; at which she was kind enough to smile, as with downcast face and uplifted elbows she fumbled among her braids. And then she shook out the creases of her dress, and drew on her gloves; and finally she said, "Well!"—that inevitable tribute to time and morality which follows upon even the mildest forms of dissipation. Very slowly it was that we wandered down the little glen. Slowly, too, we followed the course of the narrow and sinuous beach, as it keeps to the foot of the low cliffs. We encountered no sign of human life. Our conversation I need hardly repeat. I think I may trust it to the keeping of my memory: I think I shall be likely to remember it. It was all very sober and sensible,—such talk as it is both easy and pleasant to remember; it was even prosaic,—or, at least, if there was a vein of poetry in it, I should have defied a listener to put his finger on it. There was no exaltation of feeling or utterance on either side; on one side, indeed, there was very little utterance. Am I wrong in conjecturing, however, that there was considerable feeling of a certain quiet kind? Miss Blunt maintained a rich, golden silence. I, on the other hand, was very voluble. What a sweet, womanly listener she is!

September 1st.—I have been working steadily for a week. This is the first day of autumn. Read aloud to Miss Blunt a little Wordsworth.

September 10th. Midnight.—Worked without interruption, —until yesterday, inclusive, that is. But with the day now closing—or opening—begins a new era. My poor vapid old diary, at last you shall hold a *fact*.

For three days past we have been having damp, chilly weather. Dusk has fallen early. This evening, after tea, the Captain went into town,—on business, as he said: I believe, to attend some Poorhouse or Hospital Board. Esther and I went into the parlor. The room seemed cold. She brought in the lamp from the dining-room, and proposed we should have a little fire. I went into the kitchen, procured an armful of wood, and while she drew the curtains and wheeled up the table, I kindled a lively, crackling blaze. A fortnight ago she would not have allowed me to do this without a protest. She would not have offered to do it herself,—not she!— but she would have said that I was not here to serve, but to be served, and would have pretended to call Dorothy. Of course I should have had my own way. But we have changed all that. Esther went to her piano, and I sat down to a book. I read not a word. I sat looking at my mistress, and thinking with a very uneasy heart. For the first time in our friendship, she had put on a dark, warm dress: I think it was of the material called alpaca. The first time I saw her she wore a white dress with a purple neck-ribbon; now she wore a black dress with the same ribbon. That is, I remember wondering, as I sat there eying her, whether it *was* the same ribbon, or merely another like it. My heart was in my throat; and yet I thought of a number of trivialities of the same kind. At last I spoke.

"Miss Blunt," I said, "do you remember the first evening I passed beneath your roof, last June?"

"Perfectly," she replied, without stopping.

"You played this same piece."

"Yes; I played it very badly, too. I only half knew it. But it is a showy piece, and I wished to produce an effect. I didn't know then how indifferent you are to music."

"I paid no particular attention to the piece. I was intent upon the performer."

"So the performer supposed."

"What reason had you to suppose so?"

"I'm sure I don't know. Did you ever know a woman to be able to give a reason, when she has guessed aright?"

"I think they generally contrive to make up a reason, afterwards. Come, what was yours?"

"Well, you *stared* so hard."

"Fie! I don't believe it. That's unkind."

"You said you wished me to invent a reason. If I really had one, I don't remember it."

"You told me you remembered the occasion in question perfectly."

"I meant the circumstances. I remember what we had for tea; I remember what dress I wore. But I don't remember my feelings. They were naturally not very memorable."

"What did you say, when your father proposed my coming?"

"I asked how much you would be willing to pay?"

"And then?"

"And then, if you looked 'respectable'."

"And then?"

"That was all. I told father to do as he pleased."

She continued to play. Leaning back in my chair, I continued to look at her. There was a considerable pause.

"Miss Esther," said I, at last.

"Yes."

"Excuse me for interrupting you so often. But,"—and I got up and went to the piano,—"but I thank Heaven that it has brought you and me together."

She looked up at me and bowed her head with a little smile, as her hands still wandered over the keys.

"Heaven has certainly been very good to us," said she.

"How much longer are you going to play?" I asked.

"I'm sure I don't know. As long as you like."

"If you want to do as I like, you will stop immediately."

She let her hands rest on the keys a moment, and gave me a rapid, questioning look. Whether she found a sufficient answer in my face I know not; but she slowly rose, and, with a very pretty affectation of obedience, began to close the instrument. I helped her to do so.

"Perhaps you would like to be quite alone," she said. "I suppose your own room is too cold."

"Yes," I answered, "you've hit it exactly. I wish to be alone. I wish to monopolize this cheerful blaze. Hadn't you better go into the kitchen and sit with the cook? It takes you women to make such cruel speeches."

"When we women are cruel, Mr. Locksley, it is without knowing it. We are not wilfully so. When we learn that we have been unkind, we very humbly ask pardon, without even knowing what our crime has been." And she made me a very low curtsy.

"I will tell you what your crime has been," said I. "Come and sit by the fire. It's rather a long story."

"A long story? Then let me get my work."

"Confound your work! Excuse me, but I mean it. I want you to listen to me. Believe me, you will need all your thoughts."

She looked at me steadily a moment, and I returned her glance. During that moment I was reflecting whether I might silently emphasize my request by laying a lover's hand upon her shoulder. I decided that I might not. She walked over and quietly seated herself in a low chair by the fire. Here she patiently folded her arms. I sat down before her.

"With you, Miss Blunt," said I, "one must be very explicit. You are not in the habit of taking things for granted. You have a great deal of imagination, but you rarely exercise it on the behalf of other people." I stopped a moment.

"Is that my crime?" asked my companion.

"It's not so much a crime as a vice," said I; "and perhaps not so much a vice as a virtue. Your crime is, that you are so stone-cold to a poor devil who loves you."

She burst into a rather shrill laugh. I wonder whether she thought I meant Johnson.

"Who are you speaking for, Mr. Locksley?" she asked.

"Are there so many? For myself."

"Honestly?"

"Honestly doesn't begin to express it."

"What is that French phrase that you are forever using? I think I may say, '*Allons, donc!*'"

"Let us speak plain English, Miss Blunt."

" 'Stone-cold' is certainly very plain English. I don't see the relative importance of the two branches of your proposition. Which is the principal, and which the subordinate clause,

—that I am stone-cold, as you call it, or that you love me, as you call it?"

"As I call it? What would you have me call it? For God's sake, Miss Blunt, be serious, or I shall call it something else. Yes, I love you. Don't you believe it?"

"I am open to conviction."

"Thank God!" said I.

And I attempted to take her hand.

"No, no, Mr. Locksley," said she,—"not just yet, if you please."

"Action speaks louder than words," said I.

"There is no need of speaking loud. I hear you perfectly."

"I certainly sha'n't whisper," said I; "although it is the custom, I believe, for lovers to do so. Will you be my wife?"

"I sha'n't whisper, either, Mr. Locksley. Yes, I will."

And now she put out her hand.—That's my fact.

September 12th.—We are to be married within three weeks.

September 19th.—I have been in New York a week, transacting business. I got back yesterday. I find every one here talking about our engagement. Esther tells me that it was talked about a month ago, and that there is a very general feeling of disappointment that I am not rich.

"Really, if you don't mind it," said I, "I don't see why others should."

"I don't know whether you are rich or not," says Esther; "but I know that I am."

"Indeed! I was not aware that you had a private fortune," etc., etc.

This little farce is repeated in some shape every day. I am very idle. I smoke a great deal, and lounge about all day, with my hands in my pockets. I am free from that ineffable weariness of ceaseless *giving* which I experienced six months ago. I was shorn of my hereditary trinkets at that period; and I have resolved that *this* engagement, at all events, shall have no connection with the shops. I was balked of my poetry once; I sha'n't be a second time. I don't think there is much danger of this. Esther deals it out with full hands. She takes a

very pretty interest in her simple outfit,—showing me tri-
umphantly certain of her purchases, and making a great
mystery about others, which she is pleased to denominate
table-cloths and napkins. Last evening I found her sewing
buttons on a table-cloth. I had heard a great deal of a certain
gray silk dress; and this morning, accordingly, she marched
up to me, arrayed in this garment. It is trimmed with velvet,
and hath flounces, a train, and all the modern improvements
generally.

"There is only one objection to it," said Esther, parading
before the glass in my painting-room: "I am afraid it is above
our station."

"By Jove! I'll paint your portrait in it," said I, "and make
our fortune. All the other men who have handsome wives will
bring them to be painted."

"You mean all the women who have handsome dresses,"
said Esther, with great humility.

Our wedding is fixed for next Thursday. I tell Esther that it
will be as little of a wedding, and as much of a marriage, as
possible. Her father and her good friend the schoolmistress
alone are to be present.—My secret oppresses me considerably; but I have resolved to keep it for the honeymoon, when
it may take care of itself. I am harassed with a dismal apprehension, that, if Esther were to discover it now, the whole
thing would be à refaire. I have taken rooms at a romantic little watering-place called Clifton, ten miles off. The hotel is already quite free of city-people, and we shall be almost alone.

September 28th.—We have been here two days. The little
transaction in the church went off smoothly. I am truly sorry
for the Captain. We drove directly over here, and reached the
place at dusk. It was a raw, black day. We have a couple of
good rooms, close to the savage sea. I am nevertheless afraid
I have made a mistake. It would perhaps have been wiser to
go inland. These things are not immaterial: we make our own
heaven, but we scarcely make our own earth. I am writing at
a little table by the window, looking out on the rocks, the
gathering dusk, and the rising fog. My wife has wandered
down to the rocky platform in front of the house. I can see
her from here, bareheaded, in that old crimson shawl, talking

to one of the landlord's little boys. She has just given the little fellow a kiss, bless her heart! I remember her telling me once that she was very fond of little boys; and, indeed, I have noticed that they are seldom too dirty for her to take on her knee. I have been reading over these pages for the first time in—I don't know when. They are filled with *her*,—even more in thought than in word. I believe I will show them to her, when she comes in. I will give her the book to read, and sit by her, watching her face,—watching the great secret dawn upon her.

Later.—Somehow or other, I can write this quietly enough; but I hardly think I shall ever write any more. When Esther came in, I handed her this book.

"I want you to read it," said I.

She turned very pale, and laid it on the table, shaking her head.

"I know it," she said.

"What do you know?"

"That you have a hundred thousand a year. But believe me, Mr. Locksley, I am none the worse for the knowledge. You intimated in one place in your book that I am born for wealth and splendor. I believe I am. You pretend to hate your money; but you would not have had me without it. If you really love me,—and I think you do,—you will not let this make any difference. I am not such a fool as to attempt to talk here about my sensations. But I remember what I said."

"What do you expect me to do?" I asked. "Shall I call you some horrible name and cast you off?"

"I expect you to show the same courage that I am showing. I never said I loved you. I never deceived you in that. I said I would be your wife. So I will, faithfully. I haven't so much heart as you think; and yet, too, I have a great deal more. I am incapable of more than one deception.—Mercy! didn't you see it? didn't you know it? see that I saw it? know that I knew it? It was diamond cut diamond. You deceived me; I deceived you. Now that your deception ceases, mine ceases. *Now* we are free, with our hundred thousand a year! Excuse me, but it sometimes comes across me! *Now* we can be good and honest and true. It was all a make-believe virtue before."

"So you read that thing?" I asked: actually—strange as it may seem—for something to say.

"Yes, while you were ill. It was lying with your pen in it, on the table. I read it because I suspected. Otherwise I shouldn't have done so."

"It was the act of a false woman," said I.

"A false woman? No,—simply of a woman. I am a woman, Sir." And she began to smile. "Come, *you* be a man!"

A Day of Days

M R. HERBERT MOORE, a gentleman of some note in the scientific world, and a childless widower, finding himself at last unable to reconcile his sedentary habits with the management of a household, had invited his only sister to come and superintend his domestic affairs. Miss Adela Moore had assented the more willingly to his proposal, as by her mother's death she had recently been left without a formal protector. She was twenty-five years of age, and was a very active member of what she and her friends called society. She was almost equally at home in the very best company of three great cities, and she had encountered most of the adventures which await a young girl on the threshold of life. She had become rather hastily and imprudently engaged, but she had eventually succeeded in disengaging herself. She had spent a Summer in Europe, and she had made a voyage to Cuba with a dear friend in the last stage of consumption, who had died at the hotel in Havana. Although by no means beautiful in person she was yet thoroughly pleasing, rejoicing in what young ladies are fond of calling an *air*. That is, she was tall and slender, with a long neck, a low forehead and a handsome nose. Even after six years of "society," too, she still had excellent manners. She was, moreover, mistress of a very pretty little fortune, and was accounted clever without detriment to her amiability, and amiable without detriment to her wit. These facts, as the reader will allow, might have ensured her the very best prospects; but he has seen that she had found herself willing to forfeit her prospects and bury herself in the country. It seemed to her that she had seen enough of the world and of human nature, and that a couple of years of seclusion might not be unprofitable. She had begun to suspect that for a girl of her age she was unduly old and wise— and, what is more, to suspect that others suspected as much. A great observer of life and manners, so far as her opportunities went, she conceived that it behooved her to organize the results of her observation into principles of conduct and of belief. She was becoming—so she argued—too impersonal, too critical, too intelligent, too contemplative, too just. A woman had no business to be so just. The society of nature, of the great expansive skies and the primeval woods, would prove severely unpropitious to her excessive intellectual growth. She would spend her time in the fields and live in her feelings, her simple sense, and the perusal of profitable books from Herbert's library.

She found her brother very prettily housed at about a mile's distance from the nearest town, and at about six miles' distance from another town, the seat of a small college, before which he delivered a weekly lecture. She had seen so little of him of late years that his acquaintance was almost to make; but it was very soon made. Herbert Moore was one of the simplest and least aggressive of men, and one of the most patient and delicate of students. He had a vague notion that Adela was a young woman of extravagant pleasures, and that, somehow, on her arrival, his house would be overrun with the train of her attendant revellers. It was not until after they had been six months together that he discovered that his sister was a model of diligence and temperance. By the time six months more had passed, Adela had bought back a delightful sense of youth and *naïveté*. She learned, under her brother's tuition, to walk—nay, to climb, for there were great hills in the neighborhood—to ride and to botanize. At the end of a year, in the month of August, she received a visit from an old friend, a girl of her own age, who had been spending July at a watering-place, and who was about to be married. Adela had begun to fear that she had lapsed into an almost irreclaimable rusticity, and had suffered a permanent diminution of the social facility for which she had formerly been distinguished; but a week spent in *tête-à-tête* with her friend convinced her not only that she had not forgotten much that she had feared, but also that she had not forgotten much that she had hoped. For this, and other reasons, her friend's departure left her slightly depressed. She felt lonely and even a little elderly. She had lost another illusion. Laura B., for whom a year ago she had entertained a serious regard, now impressed her as a very flimsy little person, who talked about her lover with almost indecent flippancy.

Meanwhile, September was slowly running its course. One

morning Mr. Moore took a hasty breakfast and started to catch the train for S., whither a scientific conference called him, which might, he said, release him that afternoon in time for dinner at home, and might on the other hand detain him until the evening. It was almost the first time during Adela's rustication that she had been left alone for several hours. Her brother's quiet presence was inappreciable enough; yet now that he was at a distance she nevertheless felt a singular sense of freedom; a sort of return of those days of early childhood, when, through some domestic catastrophe, she had for an infinite morning been left to her own devices. What should she do? she asked herself, half laughing. It was a fair day for work: but it was a still better one for play. Should she drive into town and pay a long-standing debt of morning calls? Should she go into the kitchen and try her hand at a pudding for dinner? She felt a delicious longing to do something illicit, to play with fire, to discover some Bluebeard's closet. But poor Herbert was no Bluebeard. If she were to burn down his house he would exact no amends. Adela went out to the veranda, and, sitting down on the steps, gazed across the country. It was apparently the last day of Summer. The sky was faintly blue; the woody hills were putting on the morbid colors of Autumn; the great pine grove behind the house seemed to have caught and imprisoned the protesting breezes. Looking down the road toward the village, it occurred to Adela that she might have a visit, and so kindly was her mood that she felt herself competent to a chat with one of her rustic neighbors. As the sun rose higher, she went in and established herself with a piece of embroidery in a deep, bow window in the second story, which, betwixt its muslin curtains and its external frame-work of vines, commanded most insidiously the principal approach to the house. While she drew her threads, she surveyed the road with a deepening conviction that she was destined to have a caller. The air was warm, yet not hot; the dust had been laid during the night by a gentle rain. It had been from the first a source of complaint among Adela's new friends that her courtesies were so thoroughly indiscriminating. Not only had she lent herself to no friendships, but she had committed herself to no preferences. Nevertheless, it was with a by no means impartial fancy that

she sat thus expectant at her casement. She had very soon
made up her mind that, to answer the exactions of the hour,
her visitor should perforce be of the other sex, and as, thanks
to the somewhat uncompromising indifference which, during
her residence, she had exhibited to the *jeunesse dorée* of the
county, her roll-call, in this her hour of need, was limited to a
single name, so her thoughts were now centered upon the
bearer of that name, Mr. Madison Perkins, the Unitarian minister. If, instead of being Miss Moore's story, this were Mr.
Perkins's, it might easily be condensed into the one pregnant
fact that he was very far gone in love for our heroine.
Although of a different faith from his, she had been so well
pleased with one of his sermons, to which she had allowed
herself to lend a tolerant ear, that, meeting him some time afterward, she had received him with what she considered a
rather knotty doctrinal question; whereupon, gracefully waiving the question, he had asked permission to call upon her
and talk over her "difficulties." This short interview had enshrined her in the young minister's heart; and the half-dozen
occasions on which he had subsequently contrived to see her
had each contributed an additional taper to her shrine. It is
but fair to add, however, that, although a captive, Mr. Perkins
was as yet no captor. He was simply an honorable young man,
who happened at this moment to be the most sympathetic
companion within reach. Adela, at twenty-five years of age,
had both a past and a future. Mr. Perkins reëchoed the one,
and foreshadowed the other.

So, at last, when, as the morning waned toward noon,
Adela descried in the distance a man's figure treading the
grassy margin of the road, and swinging his stick as he came,
she smiled to herself with some complacency. But even while
she smiled she became conscious of a most foolish acceleration of the process of her heart. She rose, and resenting her
gratuitous emotion, stood for a moment half resolved to have
herself denied. As she did so, she glanced along the road
again. Her friend had drawn nearer, and, as the distance less-
ened, lo! it seemed to her that he was not her friend. Before
many moments her doubts were removed. The gentleman
was a stranger. In front of the house three roads diverged
from a great spreading elm. The stranger came along the

opposite side of the highway, and when he reached the elm stopped and looked about him as if to verify a direction. Then he deliberately crossed over. Adela had time to see, unseen, that he was a shapely young man, with a bearded chin and a straw hat. After the due interval, Becky, the maid, came up with a card somewhat rudely superscribed in pencil:

THOMAS LUDLOW,
New York.

Turning it over in her fingers, Adela saw that the reverse of a card had been used, abstracted from the basket on her own drawing-room table. The printed name on the other side was dashed out; it ran: *Mr. Madison Perkins.*

"He asked me to give you this, ma'am," said Becky. "He helped himself to it out of the tray."

"Did he ask for me by name?"

"No, ma'am, he asked for Mr. Moore. When I told him Mr. Moore was away, he asked for some of the family. I told him you were all the family, ma'am."

"Very well," said Adela, "I will go down." But, begging her pardon, we will precede her by a few steps.

Tom Ludlow, as his friends called him, was a young man of twenty-eight, concerning whom you might have heard the most various opinions; for as far as he was known (which, indeed, was not very far), he was at once one of the best liked and one of the best hated of men. Born in one of the lower *strata* of New York society, he was still slightly incrusted, if we may so express it, with his native soil. A certain crudity of manners and of aspect proved him to be one of the great majority of the ungloved. On this basis, however, he was a sufficiently good-looking fellow: a middle-sized, agile figure; a head so well shaped as to be handsome; a pair of inquisitive, responsive eyes, and a large, manly mouth, constituting his heritage of beauty. Turned upon the world at an early age, he had, in the pursuit of a subsistence, tried his head at everything in succession, and had generally found it to be quite as hard as the opposing substance; and his figure may have been thought to reflect this sweet assurance in a look of somewhat aggressive satisfaction with things in general, himself included. He was a man of strong faculties and a strong will, but it is doubtful whether his feelings were stronger than he. He was liked for his directness, his good humor, his general soundness and serviceableness; he was disliked for the same qualities under different names; that is, for his impudence, his offensive optimisms, and his inhuman avidity for facts. When his friends insisted upon his noble disinterestedness, his enemies were wont to reply it was all very well to ignore, to nullify oneself in the pursuit of science, but that to suppress the rest of mankind coincidentally betrayed an excess of zeal. Fortunately for Ludlow, on the whole, he was no great listener; and even if he had been, a certain plebeian thick-skinnedness would have been the guaranty of his equanimity; although it must be added that, if, like a genuine democrat, he was very insensitive, like a genuine democrat, too, he was amazingly proud. His tastes, which had always been for the natural sciences, had recently led him to paleontology, that branch of them cultivated by Herbert Moore; and it was upon business connected with this pursuit that, after a short correspondence, he had now come to see him.

As Adela went in to him, he came out with a bow from the window, whence he had been contemplating the lawn. She acknowledged his greeting.

"Miss Moore, I believe," said Ludlow.

"Miss Moore," said Adela.

"I beg your pardon for this intrusion, but as I had come from a distance to see Mr. Moore on business, I thought I might venture either to ask at headquarters how he may most easily be reached, or even to charge you with a message." These words were accompanied with a smile before which it was Adela's destiny to succumb—if this is not too forcible a term for the movement of feeling with which she answered them.

"Pray make no apologies," she said. "We hardly recognize such a thing as intrusion in the country. Won't you sit down? My brother went away only this morning, and I expect him back this afternoon."

"This afternoon? indeed. In that case I believe I'll wait. It was very stupid of me not to have dropped a word beforehand. But I have been in the city all Summer long, and I shall not be sorry to screw a little vacation out of this business. I'm prodigiously fond of the country, and I very seldom get a glimpse of it."

"It's possible," said Adela, "that my brother may not come home until the evening. He was uncertain. You might go to him at S."

Ludlow reflected a moment, with his eyes on his hostess. "If he does return in the afternoon, at what hour will he arrive?"

"At three."

"And my own train leaves at four. Allow him a quarter of an hour to come from town and myself a quarter of an hour to get there (if he would give me his vehicle, back), I should have half an hour to see him. We couldn't do much talk, but I could ask him the essential questions. I wish chiefly to ask him for some letters. It seems a pity to take two superfluous— that is, possibly superfluous—railway journeys of an hour apiece, for I should probably come back with him. Don't you think so?" he asked, very frankly.

"You know best," said Adela. "I'm not particularly fond of the journey to S., even when it's absolutely necessary."

"Yes; and then this is such a lovely day for a good long ramble in the fields. That's a thing I haven't done since I don't know when. I'll stay." And he placed his hat on the floor beside him.

"I'm afraid, now that I think of it," said Adela, "that there is no train until so late an hour that you would have very little time left on your arrival to talk with my brother before the hour at which he himself might have determined to start for home. It's true that you might induce him to remain till the evening."

"Dear me! I shouldn't like to do that. It might be very inconvenient for him. Besides I shouldn't have time. And then I always like to see a man in his own home—or in my own home; a man, that is, whom I have any regard for—and I have a very great regard for your brother, Miss Moore. When men meet at a half-way house, neither feels at his ease. And then this is such an uncommonly pretty place of yours," pursued Ludlow, looking about him.

"Yes, it's a very pretty place," said Adela.

Ludlow got up and walked to the window. "I want to look

at your view," said he. "A lovely view it is. You're a happy woman, Miss Moore, to live before such a prospect."

"Yes, if pretty scenery can make one happy, I ought to be happy." And Adela was glad to regain her feet and stand on the other side of the table, before the window.

"Don't you think it can?" asked Ludlow, turning around. "I don't know, though, perhaps it can't. Ugly sights can't make you unhappy, necessarily. I've been working for a year in one of the narrowest, darkest, dirtiest, and busiest streets in New York, with rusty bricks and muddy gutters for scenery. But I think I can hardly set up to be miserable. I wish I could. It might be a claim on your favor." As he said these words, he stood leaning against the window-shutter, without the curtain, with folded arms. The morning light covered his face, and, mingled with that of his broad laugh, showed Adela that it was a very pleasant face.

"Whatever else he may be," she said to herself as she stood within the shade of the other curtain, playing with the paper-knife which she had plucked from the table. "I think he is honest. I am afraid he isn't a gentleman—but he is not a simpleton." She met his eye frankly for a moment. "What do you want of my favor?" she asked, with an abruptness of which she was acutely conscious. "Does he wish to make friends," she pursued, "or does he merely wish to pay me a vulgar compliment? There is bad taste, perhaps, in either case, but especially in the latter." Meanwhile her visitor had already answered her.

"What do I want of your favor? Why, I want to make the most of it." And Ludlow blushed at his own audacity.

Adela, however, kept her color. "I'm afraid it will need all your pulling and stretching," she said, with a little laugh.

"All right. I'm great at pulling and stretching," said Ludlow, with a deepening of his great masculine blush, and a broad laugh to match it.

Adela glanced toward the clock on the mantle. She was curious to measure the duration of her acquaintance with this breezy invader of her privacy, with whom she so suddenly found herself bandying florid personalities. She had known him some eight minutes.

Ludlow observed her movement. "I'm interrupting you and detaining you from your own affairs," he said; and he moved toward his hat. "I suppose I must bid you good morning." And he picked it up.

Adela stood at the table and watched him cross the room. To express a very delicate feeling in terms comparatively broad, she was loth to have him go. She divined, too, that he was loth to go. The knowledge of this feeling on his part, however, affected her composure but slightly. The truth is—we say it with all respect—Adela was an old hand. She was modest, honest and wise; but, as we have said, she had a past—a past of which importunate swains in the guise of morning-callers had been no inconsiderable part; and a great dexterity in what may be called outflanking these gentlemen, was one of her registered accomplishments. Her liveliest emotion at present, therefore, was less one of annoyance at her companion than of surprise at her own gracious impulses, which were yet undeniable. "Am I dreaming?" she asked herself. She looked out of the window, and then back at Ludlow, who stood grasping his hat and stick, contemplating her face. Should she bid him remain? "He is honest," she repeated; "why should not I be honest for once?" "I'm sorry you are in a hurry," she said aloud.

"I am in no hurry," he answered.

Adela turned her face to the window again, and toward the opposite hills. There was a moment's pause.

"I thought *you* were in a hurry," said Ludlow.

Adela gave him her eyes. "My brother would be very glad to have you remain as long as you like. He would expect me to offer you what little hospitality is in my power."

"Pray, offer it then."

"That's easily done. This is the parlor, and there, beyond the hall, is my brother's study. Perhaps you would like to look at his books and his collections. I know nothing about them, and I should be a very poor guide. But you are welcome to go in and use your discretion in examining what may interest you."

"This, I take it, would be but another way of bidding you good-morning."

"For the present, yes."

"But I hesitate to take such liberties with your brother's treasures as you prescribe."

"Prescribe, sir? I prescribe nothing."

"But if I decline to penetrate into Mr. Moore's *sanctum,* what alternative remains?"

"Really—you must make your own alternative."

"I think you mentioned the parlor. Suppose I choose that."

"Just as you please. Here are some books, and, if you like, I will bring you some magazines. Can I serve you in any other way? Are you tired by your walk? Would you like a glass of wine?"

"Tired by my walk?—not exactly. You are very kind, but I feel no immediate desire for a glass of wine. I think you needn't trouble yourself about the magazines, either. I am not exactly in the mood to read." And Ludlow pulled out his watch and compared it with the clock. "I'm afraid your clock is fast."

"Yes;" said Adela, "very likely."

"Some ten minutes. Well, I suppose I had better be walking;" and, coming toward Adela, he extended his hand.

She gave him hers. "It's a day of days for a long, slow ramble," she said.

Ludlow's only rejoinder was his hand-shake. He moved slowly toward the door, half accompanied by Adela. "Poor fellow!" she said to herself. The lattice summer-door admitted into the entry a cool, dusky light, in which Adela looked pale. Ludlow divided its wings with his stick, and disclosed a landscape, long, deep and bright, framed by the pillars of the veranda. He stopped on the threshold, swinging his stick. "I hope I shan't lose my way," he said.

"I hope not. My brother will not forgive me if you do."

Ludlow's brows were slightly contracted by a frown, but he contrived to smile with his lips. "When shall I come back?" he asked abruptly.

Adela found but a low tone—almost a whisper—at her command, to answer. "Whenever you please," she said.

The young man turned about, with his back to the bright doorway, and looked into Adela's face, which was now covered with light. "Miss Moore," said he, "it's very much against my will that I leave you at all."

Adela stood debating within herself. What if her companion should stay? It would, under the circumstances, be an adventure; but was an adventure necessarily unadvisable? It lay wholly with herself to decide. She was her own mistress, and she had hitherto been a just mistress. Might she not for once be a generous one? The reader will observe in Adela's meditation the recurrence of this saving clause "for once." It rests upon the simple fact that she had begun the day in a romantic mood. She was prepared to be interested; and now that an interesting phenomenon had presented itself, that it stood before her in vivid human—nay, manly—shape, instinct with reciprocity, was she to close her hand to the liberality of fate? To do so would be to court mischance; for it would involve, moreover, a petty insult to human nature. Was not the man before her fairly redolent of honesty, and was that not enough? He was not what Adela had been used to call a gentleman. To this conviction she had made a swallow's flight; but from this assurance she would start. "I have seen" (she thus concluded) "all the gentlemen can show me; let us try something new."

"I see no reason why you should run away so fast, Mr. Ludlow," she said, aloud.

"I think," cried Ludlow, "it would be the greatest piece of folly I ever committed."

"I think it would be a pity," said Adela, with a smile.

"And you invite me into your parlor again? I come as your visitor, you know. I was your brother's before. It's a simple enough matter. We are old friends. We have a broad, common ground in your brother. Isn't that about it?"

"You may adopt whatever theory you please. To my mind, it is, indeed, a very simple matter."

"Oh, but I wouldn't have it too simple," said Ludlow, with a mighty smile.

"Have it as you please."

Ludlow leaned back against the doorway. "Your kindness is too much for me, Miss Moore," said he. "I am passive; I am in your hands; do with me what you please. I can't help contrasting my fate with what it might have been but for you. A quarter of an hour ago I was ignorant of your existence; you weren't in my programme. I had no idea your brother had a sister. When your servant spoke of 'Miss Moore,' upon my word I expected something rather elderly—something venerable—some rigid old lady, who would say, 'exactly,' and 'very well, sir,' and leave me to spend the rest of the morning tilting back in a chair on the hotel piazza. It shows what fools we are to attempt to forecast the future."

"We must not let our imagination run away with us in any direction," said Adela.

"Imagination? I don't believe I have any. No, madam," and Ludlow straightened himself up, "I live in the present. I write my programme from hour to hour—or, at any rate, I will in the future."

"I think you are very wise," said Adela. "Suppose you write a programme for the present hour. What shall we do? It seems to me a pity to spend so lovely a morning in-doors. I fancy this is the last day of Summer. We ought to celebrate it. How would you like a walk?" Adela had decided that, to reconcile her favors with the proper maintenance of her dignity, her only course was to play the perfect hostess. This decision made, very naturally and gracefully she played her part. It was the one possible part. And yet it did not preclude those delicate sensations with which her novel episode seemed charged: it simply legitimated them. A romantic adventure on so classical a basis would assuredly hurt no one.

"I should like a walk very much," said Ludlow; "a walk with a halt at the end of it."

"Well, if you will consent to a short halt at the beginning of it," said Adela, "I will be with you in a very few minutes." When she returned, in her little hat and shawl, she found her friend seated on the veranda steps. He arose and gave her a card.

"I have been requested, in your absence, to hand you this," he said.

Adela read with some compunction the name of Mr. Madison Perkins.

"Has he been here?" she asked. "Why didn't he come in?"

"I told him you were not at home. If it wasn't true then, it was going to be true so soon that the interval was hardly worth taking account of. He addressed himself to me, as I seemed from my position to be quite at home here; but I confess he looked at me as if he doubted my word. He hesitated as to whether he should confide his name to me, or whether he should confide it in that shape to the entry table. I think he wished to show me that he suspected my veracity, for he was making rather grimly for the table when I, fearing that once inside the house he might encounter the living truth, informed him in the most good-humored tone possible that I would take charge of his little tribute."

"I think, Mr. Ludlow, that you are a strangely unscrupulous man. How did you know that Mr. Perkins's business was not urgent?"

"I didn't know it. But I knew it could be no more urgent than mine. Depend upon it, Miss Moore, you have no case against me. I only pretend to be a man; to have admitted that charming young gentleman would have been heroic."

Adela was familiar with a sequestered spot, in the very heart of the fields, as it seemed to her, to which she now proposed to conduct her friend. The point was to select a goal neither too distant nor too near, and to adopt a pace neither too rapid nor too slow. But, although Adela's happy valley was a good two miles away, and they had measured the interval with the very *minimum* of speed, yet most sudden seemed their arrival at the stile over which Adela was used to strike into the meadows. Once on the road, she felt a precipitate conviction that there could be no evil in an adventure so essentially wholesome as that to which she had lent herself, and that there could be no guile in a spirit so deeply sensitive to the sacred influences of Nature, and to the melancholy aspect of incipient Autumn as that of her companion. A man with an unaffected relish for small children is a man to inspire young women with a generous confidence; and so, in a lesser degree, a man with a genuine feeling for the simple beauties of a common New England landscape may not unreasonably be accepted by the daughters of the scene as a person worthy of their esteem. Adela was a great observer of the clouds, the trees and the streams, the sounds and colors, the echoes and reflections native to her adopted home; and she experienced an honest joy at the sight of Ludlow's keen appreciation of these modest facts. His enjoyment of them, deep as it was, however, had to struggle against that sensuous depression natural to a man who has spent the Summer in a close and fetid laboratory in the heart of a great city, and against a sensation of a less material order—the feeling that Adela was a delightful girl. Still, naturally a great talker, he celebrated his impressions in a generous flow of good-humored eloquence. Adela resolved within herself that he was decidedly a companion for the open air. He was a man to make use, even to abuse, of the wide horizon and the high ceiling of Nature. The freedom of his gestures, the sonority of his voice, the keenness of his vision, the general vivacity of his manners, seemed to necessitate and to justify a universal absence of barriers. They crossed the stile, and waded through the long grass of several successive meadows, until the ground began to rise, and stony surfaces to crop through the turf, when, after a short ascent, they reached a broad plateau, covered with boulders and shrubs, which lost itself on one side in a short, steep cliff, whence fields and marshes stretched down to the opposite river; and on the other, in scattered clumps of pine and maple, which gradually thickened and multiplied, until the horizon in that quarter was blue with a long line of woods. Here was both sun and shade—the unobstructed sky, or the whispering dome of a circle of pines. Adela led the way to a sunny seat among the rocks, which commanded the course of the river, and where a cluster of trees would lend an admonitory undertone to their conversation.

Before long, however, its muffled eloquence became rather importunate, and Adela remarked upon the essential melancholy of the phenomenon.

"It has always seemed to me," rejoined Ludlow, "that the wind in the pines expresses tolerably well man's sense of a coming change, simply *as* a change."

"Perhaps it does," said Adela. "The pines are forever rustling, and men are forever changing."

"Yes, but they can only be said to express it when there is some one there to hear them; and more especially some one in whose life a change is, to his own knowledge, going to take place. Then they are quite prophetic. Don't you know Longfellow says so?"

"Yes, I know Longfellow says so. But you seem to speak from your own feeling."

"I do."

"Is there a change pending in your life?"

"Yes, rather an important one."

"I believe that's what men say when they are going to be married," said Adela.

"I'm going to be divorced, rather. I'm going to Europe."

"Indeed! soon?"

"To-morrow," said Ludlow, after an instant's pause.

"Oh!" said Adela. "How I envy you!"

Ludlow, who sat looking over the cliff and tossing stones down into the plain, observed a certain inequality in the tone of his companion's two exclamations. The first was nature, the second art. He turned his eyes upon her, but she had turned hers away upon the distance. Then, for a moment, he retreated within himself and thought. He rapidly surveyed his position. Here was he, Tom Ludlow, a hard-headed son of toil, without fortune, without credit, without antecedents, whose lot was cast exclusively with vulgar males, and who had never had a mother, a sister nor a well-bred sweetheart to pitch his voice for the feminine tympanum; who had seldom come nearer an indubitable young lady than, in a favoring crowd, to receive a mechanical "thank you" (as if he were a policeman), for some ingeniously provoked service; here he found himself up to his neck in a sudden pastoral with the most ladyish young woman in the land. That it was in him to enjoy the society of such a woman (provided, of course, she were not a fool), he very well knew; but he had not yet suspected that it was possible for him (in the midst of more serious cares) to obtain it. Was he now to infer that this final gift was his—the gift of pleasing women who were worth the pleasing? The inference was at least logical. He had made a good impression. Why else should a modest and discerning girl have so speedily granted him her favor? It was with a little thrill of satisfaction that Ludlow reflected upon the directness of his course. "It all comes back," he said to himself, "to my old theory, that a process can't be too simple. I used no arts. In such an enterprise I shouldn't have known where to begin. It was my ignorance of the regulation method that served me. Women like a gentleman, of course; but they like a man better." It was the little touch of nature he had discerned in Adela's tone that had set him thinking; but as compared with the frankness of his own attitude it betrayed after all no undue emotion. Ludlow had accepted the fact of his adaptability to the idle mood of a cultivated woman in a thoroughly rational spirit, and he was not now tempted to exaggerate its bearings. He was not the man to be intoxicated by success—this or any other. "If Miss Moore," he pursued, "is so wise—or so foolish—as to like me half an hour for what I am, she is welcome. Assuredly," he added, as he gazed at her intelligent profile, "she will not like me for what I am not." It needs a woman, however, far more intelligent than (thank heaven!) most women are—more intelligent, certainly, than Adela was—to guard her happiness against a strong man's consistent assumption of her intelligence; and doubtless it was from a sense of this general truth, as Ludlow still gazed, he felt an emotion of manly tenderness. "I wouldn't offend her for the world," he thought. Just then, Adela, conscious of his gaze, looked about; and before he knew it, Ludlow had repeated aloud, "Miss Moore, I wouldn't offend you for the world."

Adela glanced at him for a moment with a little flush that subsided into a smile. "To what dreadful injury is that the prelude?" she asked.

"It's the prelude to nothing. It refers to the past—to any possible displeasure I may have caused you."

"Your scruples are unnecessary, Mr. Ludlow. If you had given me offence, I should not have left you to apologize for it. I should not have left the matter to occur to you as you sat dreaming charitably in the sun."

"What would you have done?"

"Done? nothing. You don't imagine I would have rebuked you—or snubbed you—or answered you back, I take it. I would have left undone—what, I can't tell you. Ask yourself what I have done. I'm sure I hardly know myself," said Adela, with some intensity. "At all events, here I am sitting with you in the fields, as if you were a friend of years. Why do you speak of offence?" And Adela (an uncommon accident with her) lost command of her voice, which trembled ever so slightly. "What an odd thought! why should you offend me? Do I invite it?" Her color had deepened again, and her eyes had brightened. She had forgotten herself, and before speaking had not, as was her wont, sought counsel of that staunch conservative, her taste. She had spoken from a full heart—a heart which had been filling rapidly since the outset of their walk with a feeling almost passionate in its quality, and which that little blast of prose which had brought her Ludlow's announcement of his departure, had caused to overflow. The reader may give this feeling such a name as he pleases. We will content ourselves with saying that Adela had played with fire so effectually that she had been scorched. The slight vehemence of the speech just quoted had covered her sensation of pain.

"You pull one up rather short, Miss Moore," said Ludlow. "A man says the best he can."

Adela made no reply. For a moment she hung her head. Was she to cry out because she was hurt? Was she to introduce her injured soul as an impertinent third into the company? No! here our reserved and contemplative heroine is herself again. Her part was still to be the perfect young lady. For our own part, we can imagine no figure more bewitching than that of the perfect young lady under these circumstances; and if Adela had been the most accomplished coquette in the world she could not have assumed a more becoming expression than the air of languid equanimity which now covered her features. But having paid this generous homage to propriety, she felt free to suffer. Raising her eyes from the ground, she abruptly addressed her companion with this injunction:

"Mr. Ludlow," said she, "tell me something about yourself."

Ludlow burst into a laugh. "What shall I tell you?"

"Everything."

"Everything? Excuse me, I'm not such a fool. But do you know that's a delicious request you make? I suppose I ought to blush and hesitate; but I never yet blushed or hesitated in the right place."

"Very good. There is one fact. Continue. Begin at the beginning."

"Well, let me see. My name you know. I'm twenty-eight years old."

"That's the end," said Adela.

"But you don't want the history of my babyhood, I take it. I imagine that I was a very big, noisy and ugly baby: what's called a 'splendid infant.' My parents were poor, and, of course, honest. They belonged to a very different set—or 'sphere,' I suppose you call it—from any you probably know. They were working people. My father was a chemist in a small way, and I fancy my mother was not above using her hands to turn a penny. But although I don't remember her, I am sure she was a good, sound woman; I feel her occasionally in my own sinews. I myself have been at work all my life, and a very good worker I am, let me tell you. I'm not patient, as I imagine your brother to be—although I have more patience than you might suppose—but I'm plucky. If you think I'm over-egotistical, remember 'twas you began it. I don't know whether I'm clever, and I don't much care; that word is used only by unpractical people. But I'm clear-headed, and inquisitive, and enthusiastic. That's as far as I can describe myself. I don't know anything about my character. I simply suspect I'm a pretty good fellow. I don't know whether I'm grave or gay, lively or severe. I don't know whether I'm high-tempered or low-tempered. I don't believe I'm 'high-toned.' I fancy I'm good-natured enough, inasmuch as I'm not nervous. I should not be at all surprised to discover I was prodigiously conceited; but I'm afraid the discovery wouldn't cut me down, much. I'm desperately hard to snub, I know. Oh, you would think me a great brute if you knew me. I should hesitate to say whether I am of a loving turn. I know I'm desperately tired of a number of persons who are very fond of me; I'm afraid I'm ungrateful. Of course as a man speaking to a woman, there's nothing for it but to say I'm selfish; but I hate to talk about such windy abstractions. In the way of positive facts: I'm not educated. I know no Greek and very little Latin. But I can honestly say that first and last I have read a great many books—and, thank God, I have a memory! And I have some tastes, too. I'm very fond of music. I have a good old voice of my own: *that* I can't help knowing; and I'm not one to be bullied about pictures. Is that enough? I'm conscious of an utter inability to say anything to the point. To put myself in a nutshell, I suppose I'm simply a working man; I have his virtues and I have his defects. I'm a very common fellow."

"Do you call yourself a very common fellow because you really believe yourself to be one, or because you are weakly tempted to disfigure your rather flattering catalogue with a great final blot?"

"I'm sure I don't know. You show more subtlety in that one question than I have shown in my whole string of affirmations. You women are strong on asking witty questions. Seriously, I believe I *am* a common fellow. I wouldn't make the admission to every one though. But to you, Miss Moore, who sit there under your parasol as impartial as the Muse of History, to you I own the truth. I'm no man of genius. There is something I miss; some final distinction I lack; you may call it what you please. Perhaps it's humility. Perhaps you can find it in Ruskin, somewhere. Perhaps it's patience—perhaps it's imagination. I'm vulgar, Miss Moore. I'm the vulgar son of vulgar people. I use the word, of course, in it's strictest sense. So much I grant you at the outset, and then I walk ahead."

"Have you any sisters?"

"Not a sister; and no brothers, nor cousins, nor uncles, nor aunts."

"And you sail for Europe to-morrow?"

"To-morrow, at ten o'clock."

"To be away how long?"

"As long as I possibly can. Five years if possible."

"What do you expect to do in those five years?"

"Study."

"Nothing but study?"

"It will all come back to that, I fancy. I hope to enjoy myself reasonably, and to look at the world as I go. But I must not waste time; I'm growing old."

"Where are you going?"

"To Berlin. I wanted to get letters from your brother."

"Have you money? Are you well off?"

"Well off? Not I, no. I'm poor. I travel on a little money that has just come to me from an unexpected quarter: an old debt owing my father. It will take me to Germany and keep me for six months. After that I shall work my way."

"Are you happy? Are you contented?"

"Just now I'm pretty comfortable, thank you."

"But will you be so when you get to Berlin?"

"I don't promise to be contented; but I'm pretty sure to be happy."

"Well!" said Adela, "I sincerely hope you may be."

"Amen!" said Ludlow.

Of what more was said at this moment, no record may be given. The reader has been put into possession of the key of our friends' conversation; it is only needful to say that substantially upon this key, it was prolonged for half an hour more. As the minutes elapsed, Adela found herself drifting further and further away from her anchorage. When at last she compelled herself to consult her watch, and remind her companion that there remained but just time enough for them to reach home, in anticipation of her brother's arrival, she knew that she was rapidly floating seaward. As she descended the hill at her companion's side, she felt herself suddenly thrilled by an acute temptation. Her first instinct was to close her eyes upon it, in the trust that when she opened them again it would have vanished; but she found that it was not to be so uncompromisingly dismissed. It importuned her so effectually, that before she had walked a mile homeward, she had succumbed to it, or had at least given it the pledge of that quickening of the heart which accompanies a bold resolution. This little sacrifice allowed her no breath for idle words, and she accordingly advanced with a bent and listening head. Ludlow marched along, with no apparent diminution of his habitual buoyancy of mien, talking as fast and as loud as at the outset. He adventured a prophecy that Mr. Moore would not have returned, and charged Adela with a humorous message of regrets. Adela had begun by wondering whether the approach of their separation had wrought within him any sentimental depression at all commensurate with her own, with that which sealed her lips and weighed upon her heart; and now she was debating as to whether his express declaration that he felt "awfully blue" ought necessarily to remove her doubts. Ludlow followed up this declaration with a very pretty review of the morning, and a sober valedictory which, whether intensely felt or not, struck Adela as at least nobly bare of flimsy compliments. He might be a common fellow—but he was certainly a very uncommon one. When they reached the garden gate, it was with a fluttering heart that Adela scanned the premises for some accidental sign of her brother's presence. She felt that there would be an especial fitness in his not having returned. She led the way in. The hall table was bare of his hat and overcoat. The only object it displayed was Mr. Perkins's card, which Adela had deposited there on her exit. All that was represented by that little white ticket seemed a thousand miles away. Finally, Mr. Moore's absence from his study was conclusive against his return.

As Adela went back thence into the drawing-room, she simply shook her head at Ludlow, who was standing before the fire-place; and as she did so, she caught her reflection in the mantel-glass. "Verily," she said to herself, "I have travelled far." She had pretty well unlearned the repose of the Veres of Vere. But she was to break with it still more completely. It was with a singular hardihood that she prepared to redeem the little pledge which had been extorted from her on her way home. She felt that there was no trial to which her generosity might now be called which she would not hail with enthusiasm. Unfortunately, her generosity was not likely to be challenged; although she nevertheless had the satisfaction of assuring herself at this moment that, like the mercy of the Lord, it was infinite. Should she satisfy herself of her friend's? or should she leave it delightfully uncertain? These had been the terms of what has been called her temptation, at the foot of the hill. But inasmuch as Adela was by no means strictly engaged in the pursuit of pleasure, and as the notion of a grain of suffering was by no means repugnant to her, she had resolved to obtain possession of the one essential fact of her case, even though she should be at heavy costs to maintain it.

"Well, I have very little time," said Ludlow; "I must get my dinner and pay my bill and drive to the train." And he put out his hand.

Adela gave him her own, and looked him full in the eyes. "You are in a great hurry," said she.

"It's not I who am in a hurry. It's my confounded destiny. It's the train and the steamer."

"If you really wished to stay you wouldn't be bullied by the train and the steamer."

"Very true—very true. But *do* I really wish to stay?"

"That's the question. That's what I want to know."

"You ask difficult questions, Miss Moore."

"I mean they shall be difficult."

"Then, of course, you are prepared to answer difficult ones."

"I don't know that that's of course, but I am."

"Well, then, do you wish me to stay? All I have to do is to throw down my hat, sit down and fold my arms for twenty minutes. I lose my train and my ship. I stay in America, instead of going to Europe."

"I have thought of all that."

"I don't mean to say it's a great deal. There are pleasures and pleasures."

"Yes, and especially the former. It is a great deal."

"And you invite me to accept it?"

"No; I ought not to say that. What I ask of you is whether, if I should so invite you, you would say 'yes.' "

"That makes the matter very easy for you, Miss Moore. What attractions do you hold out?"

"I hold out nothing whatever, sir."

"I suppose that means a great deal."

"It means what it seems to mean."

"Well, you are certainly a most interesting woman, Miss Moore—a charming woman."

"Why don't you call me 'fascinating' at once, and bid me good morning?"

"I don't know but that I shall have to come to that. But I will give you no answer that leaves you at an advantage. Ask me to stay—command me to stay, if that suits you better— and I will see how it sounds. Come, you must not trifle with a man." He still held Adela's hand, and they had been looking frankly into each other's eyes. He paused, waiting for an answer.

"Good-by, Mr. Ludlow," said Adela. "God bless you!" And she was about to withdraw her hand; but he held it.

"Are we friends?" said he.

Adela gave a little shrug of her shoulders. "Friends of three hours."

Ludlow looked at her with some sternness. "Our parting could at best hardly have been sweet," said he; "but why should you make it bitter, Miss Moore?"

"If it's bitter, why should you try to change it?"

"Because I don't like bitter things."

Ludlow had caught a glimpse of the truth—that truth of which the reader has had a glimpse—and he stood there at once thrilled and annoyed. He had both a heart and a conscience. "It's not my fault," he cried to the latter; but he was unable to add, in all consistency, that it was his misfortune. It would be very heroic, very poetic, very chivalric, to lose his steamer, and he felt that he could do so for sufficient cause— at the suggestion of a fact. But the motive here was less than a fact—an idea; less than an idea—a fancy. "It's a very pretty little romance as it is," he said to himself. "Why spoil it? She is an admirable girl: to have learned that is enough for me." He raised her hand to his lips, pressed them to it, dropped it, reached the door and bounded out of the garden gate.

The day was ended.

My Friend Bingham

CONSCIOUS as I am of a deep aversion to stories of a painful nature, I have often asked myself whether, in the events here set forth, the element of pain is stronger than that of joy. An affirmative answer to this question would have stood as a veto upon the publication of my story, for it is my opinion that the literature of horrors needs no extension. Such an answer, however, I am unwilling to pronounce; while, on the other hand, I hesitate to assume the responsibility of a decided negative. I have therefore determined to leave the solution to the reader. I may add, that I am very sensible of the superficial manner in which I have handled my facts. I bore no other part in the accomplishment of these facts than that of a cordial observer; and it was impossible that, even with the best will in the world, I should fathom the emotions of the actors. Yet, as the very faintest reflection of human passions, under the pressure of fate, possesses an immortal interest, I am content to appeal to the reader's sympathy, and to assure him of my own fidelity.

Towards the close of summer, in my twenty-eighth year, I went down to the seaside to rest from a long term of work, and to enjoy, after several years of separation, a *tête-à-tête* with an intimate friend. My friend had just arrived from Europe, and we had agreed to spend my vacation together by the side of the sounding sea, and within easy reach of the city. On taking possession of our lodgings, we found that we should have no fellow-idlers, and we hailed joyously the prospect of the great marine solitudes which each of us declared that he found so abundantly peopled by the other. I hasten to impart to the reader the following facts in regard to the man whom I found so good a companion.

George Bingham had been born and bred among people for whom, as he grew to manhood, he learned to entertain a most generous contempt,—people in whom the hereditary possession of a large property—for he assured me that the facts stood in the relation of cause and effect—had extinguished all intelligent purpose and principle. I trust that I do not speak rhetorically when I describe in these terms the combined ignorance and vanity of my friend's progenitors. It was their fortune to make a splendid figure while they lived, and I feel little compunction in hinting at their poverty in certain human essentials. Bingham was no declaimer, and indeed no great talker; and it was only now and then, in an allusion to the past as the field of a wasted youth, that he expressed his profound resentment. I read this for the most part in the severe humility with which he regarded the future, and under cover of which he seemed to salute it as void at least (whatever other ills it might contain) of those domestic embarrassments which had been the bane of his first manhood. I have no doubt that much may be said, within limits, for the graces of that society against which my friend embodied so violent a reaction, and especially for its good-humor,—that home-keeping benevolence which accompanies a sense of material repletion. It is equally probable that to persons of a simple constitution these graces may wear a look of delightful and enduring mystery; but poor Bingham was no simpleton. He was a man of opinions numerous, delicate, and profound. When, with the lapse of his youth, he awoke to a presentiment of these opinions, and cast his first interrogative glance upon the world, he found that in his own little section of it he and his opinions were a piece of melancholy impertinence. Left, at twenty-three years of age, by his father's death, in possession of a handsome property, and absolute master of his actions, he had thrown himself blindly into the world. But, as he afterwards assured me, so superficial was his knowledge of the real world,—the world of labor and inquiry,—that he had found himself quite incapable of intelligent action. In this manner he had wasted a great deal of time. He had travelled much, however; and, being a keen observer of men and women, he had acquired a certain practical knowledge of human nature. Nevertheless, it was not till he was nearly thirty years old that he had begun to live for himself. "By myself," he explained, "I mean something else than this monstrous hereditary faculty for doing nothing and thinking of nothing." And he led me to believe, or I should rather say he allowed me to believe, that at this moment he had made a serious attempt to study. But upon this point he was not very

explicit; for if he blushed equally for the manner in which he
had slighted his opportunities, he blushed equally for the
manner in which he had used them. It is my belief that he had
but a limited capacity for study, and I am certain that to the
end of his days there subsisted in his mind a very friendly relation between fancies and facts.

Bingham was *par excellence* a moralist, a man of sentiment.
I know—he knew himself—that, in this busy Western world,
this character represents no recognized avocation; but in the
absence of such avocation, its exercise was nevertheless very
dear to him. I protest that it was very dear to me, and that,
at the end of a long morning devoted to my office-desk, I
have often felt as if I had contributed less to the common
cause than I have felt after moralizing—or, if you please, sentimentalizing—half an hour with my friend. He was an idler,
assuredly; but his candor, his sagacity, his good taste, and,
above all, a certain diffident enthusiasm which followed its
objects with the exquisite trepidation of an unconfessed and
despairing lover,—these things, and a hundred more, redeemed him from vulgarity. For three years before we came
together, as I have intimated, my impressions of my friend
had rested on his letters; and yet, from the first hour which
we spent together, I felt that they had done him no wrong.
We were genuine friends. I don't know that I can offer better proof of this than by saying that, as our old personal relations resumed their force, and the time-shrunken outlines of
character filled themselves out, I greeted the reappearance of
each familiar foible on Bingham's part quite as warmly as I
did that of the less punctual virtue. Compared, indeed, with
the comrade of earlier years, my actual companion was a well-
seasoned man of the world; but with all his acquired humility and his disciplined *bonhomie*, he had failed to divest
himself of a certain fastidiousness of mind, a certain formalism of manner, which are the token and the prerogative
of one who has not been obliged to address himself to practical questions. The charm bestowed by these facts upon
Bingham's conversation—a charm often vainly invoked in
their absence—is explained by his honest indifference to their
action, and his indisposition to turn them to account in the
interest of the picturesque,—an advantage but too easy of

conquest for a young man, rich, accomplished, and endowed with good looks and a good name. I may say, perhaps, that to a critical mind my friend's prime distinction would have been his very positive refusal to drape himself, after the current taste, with those brilliant stuffs which fortune had strewn at his feet.

Of course, a great deal of our talk bore upon Bingham's recent travels, adventures, and sensations. One of these last he handled very frankly, and treated me to a bit of genuine romance. He had been in love, and had been cruelly jilted, but had now grown able to view the matter with much of the impartial spirit of those French critics whose works were his favorite reading. His account of the young lady's character and motives would indeed have done credit to many a clever *feuilleton*. I was the less surprised, however, at his severely dispassionate tone, when, in retracing the process of his opinions, I discerned the traces—the ravages, I may almost say—of a solemn act of renunciation. Bingham had forsworn marriage. I made haste to assure him that I considered him quite too young for so austere a resolve.

"I can't help it," said he; "I feel a foreboding that I shall live and die alone."

"A foreboding?" said I. "What's a foreboding worth?"

"Well, then, rationally considered, my marriage is improbable."

"But it's not to be rationally considered," I objected. "It belongs to the province of sentiment."

"But you deny me sentiment. I fall back upon my foreboding."

"That's not sentiment,—it's superstition," I answered. "Your marrying will depend upon your falling in love; and your falling in love will certainly not depend upon yourself."

"Upon whom, then?"

"Upon some unknown fair one,—Miss A, B, or C."

"Well," said Bingham, submissively, "I wish she would make haste and reveal herself."

These remarks had been exchanged in the hollow of a cliff which sloped seaward, and where we had lazily stretched ourselves at length on the grass. The grass had grown very long and brown; and as we lay with our heads quite on a level with it, the view of the immediate beach and the gentle breakers was so completely obstructed by the rank, coarse herbage, that our prospect was reduced to a long, narrow band of deep blue ocean traversing its black fibres, and to the great vault of the sky. We had strolled out a couple of hours before, bearing each a borrowed shot-gun and accompanied by a friendly water-dog, somewhat languidly disposed towards the slaughter of wild ducks. We were neither of us genuine sportsmen, and it is certain that, on the whole, we meant very kindly to the ducks. It was at all events fated that on that day they should suffer but lightly at our hands. For the half-hour previous to the exchange of the remarks just cited, we had quite forgotten our real business; and, with our pieces lost in the grass beside us, and our dog, weary of inaction, wandering far beyond call, we looked like any straw-picking truants. At last Bingham rose to his feet, with the asseveration that it would never do for us to return empty-handed. "But, behold," he exclaimed, as he looked down across the breadth of the beach, "there is our friend of the cottage, with the sick little boy."

I brought myself into a sitting posture, and glanced over the cliff. Down near the edge of the water sat a young woman, tossing stones into it for the amusement of a child, who stood lustily crowing and clapping his hands. Her title to be called our friend lay in the fact, that on our way to the beach we had observed her issuing from a cottage hard by the hotel, leading by the hand a pale-faced little boy, muffled like an invalid. The hotel, as I have said, was all but deserted, and this young woman had been the first person to engage our idle observation. We had seen that, although plainly dressed, she was young, pretty, and modest; and, in the absence of heavier cares, these facts had sufficed to make her interesting. The question had arisen between us, whether she was a native of the shore, or a visitor like ourselves. Bingham inclined to the former view of the case, and I to the latter. There was, indeed, a certain lowliness in her aspect; but I had contended that it was by no means a rustic lowliness. Her dress was simple, but it was well made and well worn; and I noticed that, as she strolled along, leading her little boy, she cast upon sky and sea the lingering glance of one to whom, in their integrity, these were unfamiliar objects. She was the wife of some small tradesman, I argued, who had brought her child to the seaside by the physician's decree. But Bingham declared that it was utterly illogical to suppose her to be a mother of five years' motherhood; and that, for his part, he saw nothing in her appearance inconsistent with rural influences. The child was her nephew, the son of a married sister, and she a sentimental maiden aunt. Obviously the volume she had in her hand was Tennyson. In the absence on both sides of authentic data, of course the debate was not prolonged; and the subject of it had passed from our memories some time before we again met her on the beach. She soon became aware of our presence, however; and, with a natural sense of intrusion, we immediately resumed our walk. The last that I saw of her, as we rounded a turn in the cliff which concealed the backward prospect, was a sudden grasp of the child's arm, as if to withdraw him from the reach of a hastily advancing wave.

Half an hour's further walk led us to a point which we were not tempted to exceed. We shot between us some half a dozen birds; but as our dog, whose talents had been sadly misrepresented, proved very shy of the deep water, and succeeded in bringing no more than a couple of our victims to shore, we resolved to abstain from further destruction, and to return home quietly along the beach, upon which we had now descended.

"If we meet our young lady," said Bingham, "we can gallantly offer her our booty."

Some five minutes after he had uttered these words, a couple of great sea-gulls came flying landward over our heads, and, after a long gyration in mid-air, boldly settled themselves on the slope of the cliff at some three hundred yards in front of us, a point at which it projected almost into the waves. After a momentary halt, one of them rose again on his long pinions and soared away seaward; the other remained. He sat perched on a jutting boulder some fifteen feet high, sunning his fishy breast.

"I wonder if I could put a shot into him," said Bingham.

"Try," I answered; and, as he rapidly charged and levelled his piece, I remember idly repeating, while I looked at the great bird,

> "God save thee, ancient mariner,
>   From the fiends that plague thee thus!
>   Why look'st thou so? 'With my cross-bow
>   I shot the albatross.'"

"He's going to rise," I added.

But Bingham had fired. The creature rose, indeed, half sluggishly, and yet with too hideous celerity. His movement drew from us a cry which was almost simultaneous with the report of Bingham's gun. I cannot express our relation to what followed it better than by saying that it exposed to our sight, beyond the space suddenly left vacant, the happy figure of the child from whom we had parted but an hour before. He stood with his little hands extended, and his face raised toward the retreating bird. Of the sickening sensation which assailed our common vision as we saw him throw back his hands to his head, and reel downwards out of sight, I can give no verbal account, nor of the rapidity with which we crossed the smooth interval of sand, and rounded the bluff.

The child's companion had scrambled up the rocky bank towards the low ledge from which he had fallen, and to which access was of course all too easy. She had sunk down upon the stones, and was wildly clasping the boy's body. I turned from this spectacle to my friend, as to an image of equal woe. Bingham, pale as death, bounded over the stones, and fell on his knees. The woman let him take the child out of her arms, and bent over, with her forehead on a rock, moaning. I have never seen helplessness so vividly embodied as in this momentary group.

"Did it strike his head?" cried Bingham. "What the devil was he doing up there?"

"I told him he'd get hurt," said the young woman, with harrowing simplicity. "To shoot straight at him!—He's killed!"

"Great heavens! Do you mean to say that I saw him?" roared Bingham. "How did I know he was there? Did you see us?"

The young woman shook her head. "Of course I didn't see you. I saw you with your guns before. Oh, he's killed!"

"He's not killed. It was mere duck shot. Don't talk such

stuff.—My own poor little man!" cried George. "Charles, where *were* our eyes?"

"He wanted to catch the bird," moaned our companion. "Baby, my boy! open your eyes. Speak to your mother. For God's sake, get some help!"

She had put out her hands to take the child from Bingham, who had half angrily lifted him out of her reach. The senseless movement with which, as she disengaged him from Bingham's grasp, he sank into her arms, was clearly the senselessness of death. She burst into sobs. I went and examined the child.

"He *may* not be killed," I said, turning to Bingham; "keep your senses. It's not your fault. We *couldn't* see each other."

Bingham rose stupidly to his feet.

"She must be got home," I said.

"We must get a carriage. Will you go or stay?"

I saw that he had seen the truth. He looked about him with an expression of miserable impotence. "Poor little devil!" he said, hoarsely.

"Will you go for a carriage?" I repeated, taking his hand, "or will you stay?"

Our companion's sobs redoubled their violence.

"I'll stay," said he. "Bring some woman."

I started at a hard run. I left the beach behind me, passed the white cottage at whose garden gate two women were gossiping, and reached the hotel stable, where I had the good fortune to find a vehicle at my disposal. I drove straight back to the white cottage. One of the women had disappeared, and the other was lingering among her flowers,—a middle-aged, keen-eyed person. As I descended and hastily addressed her, I read in her rapid glance an anticipation of evil tidings.

"The young woman who stays with you—" I began.

"Yes," she said, "my second-cousin. Well?"

"She's in trouble. She wants you to come to her. Her little boy has hurt himself." I had time to see that I need fear no hysterics.

"Where did you leave her?" asked my companion.

"On the beach."

"What's the matter with the child?"

"He fell from a rock. There's no time to be lost." There

was a certain antique rigidity about the woman which was at once irritating and reassuring. I was impelled both to quicken her apprehensions and to confide in her self-control. "For all I know, ma'am," said I, "the child is killed."

She gave me an angry stare. "For all you know!" she exclaimed. "Where were your wits? Were you afraid to look at him?"

"Yes, half afraid."

She glanced over the paling at my vehicle. "Am I to get into that?" she asked.

"If you will be so good."

She turned short about, and re-entered the house, where, as I stood out among the dahlias and the pinks, I heard a rapid opening and shutting of drawers. She shortly reappeared, equipped for driving; and, having locked the house door, and pocketed the key, came and faced me, where I stood ready to help her into the wagon.

"We'll stop for the doctor," she began.

"The doctor," said I, "is of no use."

A few moments of hard driving brought us to my starting-point. The tide had fallen perceptibly in my absence; and I remember receiving a strange impression of the irretrievable nature of the recent event from the sight of poor Bingham, standing down at the low-water-mark, and looking sea-ward with his hands in his pockets. The mother of his little victim still sat on the heap of stones where she had fallen, pressing her child to her breast. I helped my companion to descend, which she did with great deliberation. It is my belief that, as we drove along the beach, she derived from the expression of Bingham's figure, and from the patient aversion of his face, a suspicion of his relation to the opposite group. It was not till the elder woman had come within a few steps of her, that the younger became aware of her approach. I merely had time to catch the agonized appeal of her upward glance, and the broad compassion of the other's stooping movement, before I turned my back upon their encounter, and walked down towards my friend. The monotonous murmur of the waves had covered the sound of our wagon-wheels, and Bingham stood all unconscious of the coming of relief,—distilling I know not what divine relief from the simple beauty of sea and sky. I had laid my hand on his shoulder before he turned about. He looked towards the base of the cliff. I knew that a great effusion of feeling would occur in its natural order; but how should I help him across the interval?

"That's her cousin," I said at random. "She seems a very capable woman."

"The child is quite dead," said Bingham, for all answer. I was struck by the plainness of his statement. In the comparative freedom of my own thoughts I had failed to make allowance for the embarrassed movement of my friend's. It was not, therefore, until afterwards that I acknowledged he had thought to better purpose than I; inasmuch as the very simplicity of his tone implied a positive acceptance (for the moment) of the dreadful fact which he uttered.

"The sooner they get home, the better," I said. It was evident that the elder of our companions had already embraced this conviction. She had lifted the child and placed him in the carriage, and she was now turning towards his mother and inviting her to ascend. Even at the distance at which I stood, the mingled firmness and tenderness of her gestures were clearly apparent. They seemed, moreover, to express a certain indifference to our movements, an independence of our further interference, which—fanciful as the assertion may look—was not untinged with irony. It was plain that, by whatever rapid process she had obtained it, she was already in possession of our story. "Thank God for strong-minded women!" I exclaimed;—and yet I could not repress a feeling that it behooved me, on behalf of my friend, to treat as an equal with the vulgar movement of antipathy which he was destined to encounter, and of which, in the irresistible sequence of events, the attitude of this good woman was an index.

We walked towards the carriage together. "I shall not come home directly," said Bingham; "but don't be alarmed about me."

I looked at my watch. "I give you two hours," I said, with all the authority of my affection.

The new-comer had placed herself on the back seat of the vehicle beside the sufferer, who on entering had again possessed herself of her child. As I went about to mount in front, Bingham came and stood by the wheel. I read his purpose in his face,—the desire to obtain from the woman he had wronged some recognition of his *human* character, some confession that she dimly distinguished him from a wild beast or a thunderbolt. One of her hands lay exposed, pressing together on her knee the lifeless little hands of her boy. Bingham removed his hat, and placed his right hand on that of the young woman. I saw that she started at his touch, and that he vehemently tightened his grasp.

"It's too soon to talk of forgiveness," said he, "for it's too soon for me to think intelligently of the wrong I have done you. God has brought us together in a very strange fashion."

The young woman raised her bowed head, and gave my friend, if not just the look he coveted, at least the most liberal glance at her command,—a look which, I fancy, helped him to face the immediate future. But these are matters too delicate to be put into words.

I spent the hours that elapsed before Bingham's return to the inn in gathering information about the occupants of the cottage. Impelled by that lively intuition of calamity which is natural to women, the housekeeper of the hotel, a person of evident kindliness and discretion, lost no time in winning my confidence. I was not unwilling that the tragic incident which had thus arrested our idleness should derive its earliest publicity from my own lips; and I was forcibly struck with the exquisite impartiality with which this homely creature bestowed her pity. Miss Horner, I learned, the mistress of the cottage, was the last representative of a most respectable family, native to the neighboring town. It had been for some years her practice to let lodgings during the summer. At the close of the present season she had invited her kinswoman, Mrs. Hicks, to spend the autumn with her. That this lady was the widow of a Baptist minister; that her husband had died some three years before; that she was very poor; that her child had been sickly, and that the care of his health had so impeded her exertions for a livelihood, that she had been intending to leave him with Miss Horner for the winter, and obtain a "situation" in town;—these facts were the salient points of the housekeeper's somewhat prolix recital.

The early autumn dusk had fallen when Bingham returned. He looked very tired. He had been walking for several hours, and, as I fancied, had grown in some degree familiar with his new responsibilities. He was very hungry, and made a vigorous attack upon his supper. I had been indisposed to eat, but the sight of his healthy appetite restored my own. I had grown weary of my thoughts, and I found something salutary in the apparent simplicity and rectitude of Bingham's state of mind.

"I find myself taking it very quietly," he said, in the course of his repast. "There is something so absolute in the nature of the calamity, that one is compelled to accept it. I don't see how I could endure to have mutilated the poor little mortal. To kill a human being is, after all, the least injury you can do him." He spoke these words deliberately, with his eyes on mine, and with an expression of perfect candor. But as he paused, and in spite of my perfect assent to their meaning, I could not help mentally reverting to the really tragic phase of the affair; and I suppose my features revealed to Bingham's scrutiny the process of my thoughts. His pale face flushed a burning crimson, his lips trembled. "Yes, my boy!" he cried; "that's where it's damnable." He buried his head in his hands, and burst into tears.

We had a long talk. At the end of it, we lit our cigars, and came out upon the deserted piazza. There was a lovely starlight, and, after a few turns in silence, Bingham left my side and strolled off towards a bend in the road, in the direction of the sea. I saw him stand motionless for a long time, and then I heard him call me. When I reached his side, I saw that he had been watching a light in the window of the white cottage. We heard the village bell in the distance striking nine.

"Charles," said Bingham, "suppose you go down there and make some offer of your services. God knows whom the poor creatures have to look to. She has had a couple of men thrust into her life. She must take the good with the bad."

I lingered a moment. "It's a difficult task," I said. "What shall I say?"

Bingham silently puffed his cigar. He stood with his arms folded, and his head thrown back, slowly measuring the starry sky. "I wish she could come out here and look at that sky," he said at last. "It's a sight for bereaved mothers. Somehow, my dear boy," he pursued, "I never felt less depressed in my life. It's none of my doing."

"It would hardly do for me to tell her that," said I.

"I don't know," said Bingham. "This isn't an occasion for the exchange of compliments. I'll tell you what you may tell her. I suppose they will have some funeral services within a day or two. Tell her that I should like very much to be present."

I set off for the cottage. Its mistress in person introduced me into the little parlor.

"Well, sir?" she said, in hard, dry accents.

"I've come," I answered, "to ask whether I can be of any assistance to Mrs. Hicks."

Miss Horner shook her head in a manner which deprived her negation of half its dignity. "What assistance is possible?" she asked.

"A man," said I, "may relieve a woman of certain cares—"

"O, men are a blessed set! You had better leave Mrs. Hicks to me."

"But will you at least tell me how she is,—if she has in any degree recovered herself?"

At this moment the door of the adjoining room was opened, and Mrs. Hicks stood on the threshold, bearing a lamp,—a graceful and pathetic figure. I now had occasion to observe that she was a woman of decided beauty. Her fair hair was drawn back into a single knot behind her head, and the lamplight deepened the pallor of her face and the darkness of her eyes. She wore a calico dressing-gown and a shawl.

"What do you wish?" she asked, in a voice clarified, if I may so express it, by long weeping.

"He wants to know whether he can be of any assistance," said the elder lady.

Mrs. Hicks glanced over her shoulder into the room she had left. "Would you like to look at the child?" she asked, in a whisper.

"Lucy!" cried Miss Horner.

I walked straight over to Mrs. Hicks, who turned and led the way to a little bed. My conductress raised her lamp aloft, and let the light fall gently on the little white-draped figure. Even the bandage about the child's head had not dispelled his short-lived prettiness. Heaven knows that to remain silent was easy enough; but Heaven knows, too, that to break the silence—and to break it as I broke it—was equally easy. "He must have been a very pretty child," I said.

"Yes, he was very pretty. He had black eyes. I don't know whether you noticed."

"No, I didn't notice," said I. "When is he to be buried?"

"The day after to-morrow. I am told that I shall be able to avoid an inquest."

"Mr. Bingham has attended to that," I said. And then I paused, revolving his petition.

But Mrs. Hicks anticipated it. "If you would like to be present at the funeral," she said, "you are welcome to come. —And so is your friend."

"Mr. Bingham bade me ask leave. There is a great deal that I should like to say to you for him," I added, "but I won't spoil it by trying. It's his own business."

The young woman looked at me with her deep, dark eyes. "I pity him from my heart," she said, pressing her hands to her breast. "I had rather have my sorrow than his."

"They are pretty much one sorrow," I answered. "I don't see that you can divide it. You are two to bear it. Bingham is a wise, good fellow," I went on. "I have shared a great many joys with him. In Heaven's name," I cried, "don't bear hard on him!"

"How can I bear hard?" she asked, opening her arms and letting them drop. The movement was so deeply expressive of weakness and loneliness, that, feeling all power to reply stifled in a rush of compassion, I silently made my exit.

On the following day, Bingham and I went up to town, and on the third day returned in time for the funeral. Besides the two ladies, there was no one present but ourselves and the village minister, who of course spoke as briefly as decency allowed. He had accompanied the ladies in a carriage to the graveyard, while Bingham and I had come on foot. As we turned away from the grave, I saw my friend approach Mrs. Hicks. They stood talking beside the freshly-turned earth, while the minister and I attended Miss Horner to the carriage. After she had seated herself, I lingered at the door, exchanging sober commonplaces with the reverend gentleman. At last Mrs. Hicks followed us, leaning on Bingham's arm.

"Margaret," she said, "Mr. Bingham and I are going to stay

here awhile. Mr. Bingham will walk home with me. I'm *very* much obliged to you, Mr. Bland," she added, turning to the minister and extending her hand.

I bestowed upon my friend a glance which I felt to be half interrogative and half sympathetic. He gave me his hand, and answered the benediction by its pressure, while he answered the inquiry by his words. "If you are still disposed to go back to town this afternoon," he said, "you had better not wait for me. I may not have time to catch the boat."

I of course made no scruple of returning immediately to the city. Some ten days elapsed before I again saw Bingham; but I found my attention so deeply engrossed with work, that I scarcely measured the interval. At last, one morning, he came into my office.

"I take for granted," I said, "that you have not been all this time at B——."

"No; I've been on my travels. I came to town the day after you came. I found at my rooms a letter from a lawyer in Baltimore, proposing the sale of some of my property there, and I seized upon it as an excuse for making a journey to that city. I felt the need of movement, of action of some kind. But when I reached Baltimore, I didn't even go to see my correspondent. I pushed on to Washington, walked about for thirty-six hours, and came home."

He had placed his arm on my desk, and stood supporting his head on his hand, with a look of great physical exhaustion.

"You look very tired," said I.

"I haven't slept," said he. "I had such a talk with that woman!"

"I'm sorry that you should have felt the worse for it."

"I feel both the worse and the better. She talked about the child."

"It's well for her," said I, "that she was able to do it."

"She wasn't able, strictly speaking. She began calmly enough, but she very soon broke down."

"Did you see her again?"

"I called upon her the next day, to tell her that I was going to town, and to ask if I could be useful to her. But she seems to stand in perfect isolation. She assured me that she was in want of nothing."

"What sort of a woman does she seem to be, taking her in herself?"

"Bless your soul! I can't take her in herself!" cried Bingham, with some vehemence. "And yet, stay," he added; "she's a very pleasing woman."

"She's very pretty."

"Yes; she's very pretty. In years, she's little more than a young girl. In her ideas, she's one of 'the people.' "

"It seems to me," said I, "that the frankness of her conduct toward you is very much to her credit.

"It doesn't offend you, then?"

"Offend me? It gratifies me beyond measure."

"I think that, if you had seen her as I have seen her, it would interest you deeply. I'm at a loss to determine whether it's the result of great simplicity or great sagacity. Of course, it's absurd to suppose that, ten days ago, it could have been the result of anything but a beautiful impulse. I think that to-morrow I shall again go down to B——."

I allowed Bingham time to have made his visit and to have brought me an account of his further impressions; but as three days went by without his re-appearance, I called at his lodgings. He was still out of town. The fifth day, however, brought him again to my office.

"I've been at B—— constantly," he said, "and I've had several interviews with our friend."

"Well; how fares it?"

"It fares well. I'm forcibly struck with her good sense. In matters of mind—in matters of soul, I may say—she has the touch of an angel, or rather the touch of a woman. That's quite sufficient."

"Does she keep her composure?"

"Perfectly. You can imagine nothing simpler and less sentimental than her manner. She makes me forget myself most divinely. The child's death colors our talk; but it doesn't confine or obstruct it. You see she has her religion: she can afford to be natural."

Weary as my friend looked, and shaken by his sudden subjection to care, it yet seemed to me, as he pronounced these words, that his eye had borrowed a purer light and his voice a fresher tone. In short, where I discerned it, how I detected it, I know not; but I felt that he carried a secret. He sat poking with his walking-stick at a nail in the carpet, with his eyes dropped. I saw about his mouth the faint promise of a distant smile,—a smile which six months would bring to maturity.

"George," said I, "I have a fancy."

He looked up. "What is it?"

"You've lost your heart."

He stared a moment, with a sudden frown. "To whom?" he asked.

"To Mrs. Hicks."

With a frown, I say, but a frown that was as a smile to the effect of my rejoinder. He rose to his feet; all his color deserted his face and rushed to his eyes.

"I beg your pardon if I'm wrong," I said.

Bingham had turned again from pale to crimson. "Don't beg *my* pardon," he cried. "You may say what you please. Beg *hers!*" he added, bitterly.

I resented the charge of injustice. "I've done *her* no wrong!" I answered. "I haven't said," I went on with a certain gleeful sense that I was dealing with massive truths,—"I haven't said that she had lost her heart to you!"

"Good God, Charles!" cried Bingham, "what a horrid imagination you have!"

"I am not responsible for my imagination."

"Upon my soul, I hope *I'm* not!" cried Bingham, passionately. "I have enough without that."

"George," I said, after a moment's reflection, "if I thought I had insulted you, I would make amends. But I have said nothing to be ashamed of. I believe that I have hit the truth. Your emotion proves it. I spoke hastily; but you must admit that, having caught a glimpse of the truth, I couldn't stand indifferent to it."

"The truth! the truth! What truth?"

"Aren't you in love with Mrs. Hicks? Admit it like a man."

"Like a man! Like a brute. Haven't I done the woman wrong enough?"

"Quite enough, I hope."

"Haven't I turned her simple joys to bitterness?"

"I grant it."

"And now you want me to insult her by telling her that I love her?"

"I want you to tell her nothing. What you tell her is your own affair. Remember that, George. It's as little mine as it is the rest of the world's."

Bingham stood listening, with a contracted brow and his hand grasping his stick. He walked to the dusty office-window and halted a moment, watching the great human throng in the street. Then he turned and came towards me. Suddenly he stopped short. "God forgive me!" he cried; "I believe I do love her."

The fountains of my soul were stirred. "Combining my own hasty impressions of Mrs. Hicks with yours, George," I said, "the consummation seems to me exquisitely natural."

It was in these simple words that we celebrated the sacred fact. It seemed as if, by tacit agreement, the evolution of this fact was result enough for a single interview.

A few days after this interview, in the evening, I called at Bingham's lodgings. His servant informed me that my friend was out of town, although he was unable to indicate his whereabouts. But as I turned away from the door a hack drew up, and the object of my quest descended, equipped with a travelling-bag. I went down and greeted him under the gas-lamp.

"Shall I go in with you?" I asked; "or shall I go my way?"

"You had better come in," said Bingham. "I have some-thing to say.—I have been down to B——," he resumed, when the servant had left us alone in his sitting-room. His tone bore the least possible tinge of a confession; but of course it was not as a confessor that I listened.

"Well," said I, "how is our friend?"

"Our friend—" answered Bingham. "Will you have a cigar?"

"No, I thank you."

"Our friend— Ah, Charles, it's a long story."

"I sha'n't mind that, if it's an interesting one."

"To a certain extent it's a painful one. It's painful to come into collision with incurable vulgarity of feeling."

I was puzzled. "Has that been your fortune?" I asked.

"It has been my fortune to bring Mrs. Hicks into a great

deal of trouble. The case, in three words, is this. Miss Horner has seen fit to resent, in no moderate terms, what she calls the 'extraordinary intimacy' existing between Mrs. Hicks and myself. Mrs. Hicks, as was perfectly natural, has resented her cousin's pretension to regulate her conduct. Her expression of this feeling has led to her expulsion from Miss Horner's house."

"Has she any other friend to turn to?"

"No one, except some relatives of her husband, who are very poor people, and of whom she wishes to ask no favors."

"Where has she placed herself?"

"She is in town. We came up together this afternoon. I went with her to some lodgings which she had formerly occupied, and which were fortunately vacant."

"I suppose it's not to be regretted that she has left B——. She breaks with sad associations."

"Yes; but she renews them too, on coming to town."

"How so?"

"Why, damn it," said Bingham, with a tremor in his voice, "the woman is utterly poor."

"Has she no resources whatever?"

"A hundred dollars a year, I believe,—worse than nothing."

"Has she any marketable talents or accomplishments?"

"I believe she is up to some pitiful needle-work or other. Such a woman! O horrible world!"

"Does *she* say so?" I asked.

"She? No indeed. She thinks it's all for the best. I suppose it is. But it seems but a bad best."

"I wonder," said I, after a pause, "whether I might see Mrs. Hicks. Do you think she would receive me?"

Bingham looked at me an instant keenly. "I suppose so," said he. "You can try."

"I shall go, not out of curiosity," I resumed, "but out of—"

"Out of what?"

"Well, in fine, I should like to see her again."

Bingham gave me Mrs. Hicks's address, and in the course of a few evenings I called upon her. I had abstained from bestowing a fine name upon the impulse which dictated this act; but I am nevertheless free to declare that kindliness and courtesy had a large part in it. Mrs. Hicks had taken up her residence in a plain, small house, in a decent by-street, where, upon presenting myself, I was ushered into a homely sitting-room (apparently her own), and left to await her coming. Her greeting was simple and cordial, and not untinged with a certain implication of gratitude. She had taken for granted, on my part, all possible sympathy and good-will; but as she had regarded me besides as a man of many cares, she had thought it improbable that we should meet again. It was no long time before I became conscious of that generous charm which Bingham had rigorously denominated her good-sense. Good-sense assuredly was there, but good-sense mated and prolific. Never had I seen, it seemed to me, as the moments elapsed, so exquisitely modest a use of such charming faculties,—an intelligence so sensible of its obligations and so indifferent to its privileges. It was obvious that she had been a woman of plain associations: her allusions were to homely facts, and her manner direct and unstudied; and yet, in spite of these limitations, it was equally obvious that she was a person to be neither patronized, dazzled, nor deluded. O the satisfaction which, in the course of that quiet dialogue, I took in this sweet infallibility! How it effaced her loneliness and poverty, and added dignity to her youth and beauty! It made her, potentially at least, a woman of the world. It was an anticipation of the self-possession, the wisdom, and perhaps even in some degree of the wit, which comes through the experience of society,—the result, on Mrs. Hicks's part, of I know not what hours of suffering, despondency, and self-dependence. With whatever intentions, therefore, I might have come before her, I should have found it impossible to address her as any other than an equal, and to regard her affliction as anything less than an absolute mystery. In fact, we hardly touched upon it; and it was only covertly that we alluded to Bingham's melancholy position. I will not deny that in a certain sense I regretted Mrs. Hicks's reserve. It is true that I had a very informal claim upon her confidence; but I had gone to her with a half-defined hope that this claim would be liberally interpreted. It was not even recognized; my vague intentions of counsel and assistance had lain undivined; and I departed with the impression that my social horizon had been considerably enlarged, but that my charity had by no means secured a pensioner.

Mrs. Hicks had given me permission to repeat my visit, and after the lapse of a fortnight I determined to do so. I had seen Bingham several times in the interval. He was of course much interested in my impressions of our friend; and I fancied that my admiration gave him even more pleasure than he allowed himself to express. On entering Mrs. Hicks's parlor a second time, I found him in person standing before the fireplace, and talking apparently with some vehemence to Mrs. Hicks, who sat listening on the sofa. Bingham turned impatiently to the door as I crossed the threshold, and Mrs. Hicks rose to welcome me with all due composure. I was nevertheless sensible that my entrance was ill-timed; yet a retreat was impossible. Bingham kept his place on the hearth-rug, and mechanically gave me his hand,—standing irresolute, as I thought, between annoyance and elation. The fact that I had interrupted a somewhat passionate interview was somehow so obvious, that, at the prompting of a very delicate feeling, Mrs. Hicks hastened to anticipate my apologies.

"Mr. Bingham was giving me a lecture," she said; and there was perhaps in her accent a faint suspicion of bitterness. "He will doubtless be glad of another auditor."

"No," said Bingham, "Charles is a better talker than listener. You shall have two lectures instead of one." He uttered this sally without even an attempt to smile.

"What is your subject?" said I. "Until I know that, I shall promise neither to talk nor to listen."

Bingham laid his hand on my arm. "He represents the world," he said, addressing our hostess. "You're afraid of the world. There, make your appeal."

Mrs. Hicks stood silent a moment, with a contracted brow and a look of pain on her face. Then she turned to me with a half-smile. "I don't believe you represent the world," she said; "you are too good."

"She flatters you," said Bingham. "You wish to corrupt him, Mrs. Hicks."

Mrs. Hicks glanced for an instant from my friend to myself. There burned in her eyes a far-searching light, which consecrated the faint irony of the smile which played about her

lips. "O you men!" she said,—"you are so wise, so deep!"
It was on Bingham that her eyes rested last; but after a
pause, extending her hand, she transferred them to me. "Mr.
Bingham," she pursued, "seems to wish you to be admitted
to our counsels. There is every reason why his friends should
be my friends. You will be interested to know that he has
asked me to be his wife."

"Have you given him an answer?" I asked.

"He was pressing me for an answer when you came in. He
conceives me to have a great fear of the judgments of men,
and he was saying very hard things about them. But they have
very little, after all, to do with the matter. The world may
heed it, that Mr. Bingham should marry Mrs. Hicks, but it
will care very little whether or no Mrs. Hicks marries Mr.
Bingham. You are the world, for me," she cried with beautiful inconsequence, turning to her suitor; "I know no other."
She put out her hands, and he took them.

I am at a loss to express the condensed force of these rapid
words,—the amount of passion, of reflection, of experience,
which they seemed to embody. They were the simple utterance of a solemn and intelligent choice; and, as such, the
whole phalanx of the Best Society assembled in judgment
could not have done less than salute them. What honest
George Bingham said, what I said, is of little account. The
proper conclusion of my story lies in the highly dramatic fact
that out of the depths of her bereavement—out of her loneliness and her pity—this richly gifted woman had emerged, responsive to the passion of him who had wronged her all but
as deeply as he loved her. The reader will decide, I think, that
this catastrophe offers as little occasion for smiles as for tears.
My narrative is a piece of genuine prose.

It was not until six months had elapsed that Bingham's
marriage took place. It has been a truly happy one. Mrs.
Bingham is now, in the fulness of her bloom, with a single exception, the most charming woman I know. I have often assured her—once too often, possibly—that, thanks to that
invaluable good-sense of hers, she is also the happiest. She has
made a devoted wife; but—and in occasional moments of
insight it has seemed to me that this portion of her fate is a
delicate tribute to a fantastic principle of equity—she has never

again become a mother. In saying that she has made a devoted wife, it may seem that I have written Bingham's own
later history. Yet as the friend of his younger days, the comrade of his *belle jeunesse*, the partaker of his dreams, I would
fain give him a sentence apart. What shall it be? He is a truly
incorruptible soul; he is a confirmed philosopher; he has
grown quite stout.

Poor Richard

MISS WHITTAKER'S garden covered a couple of acres, behind and beside her house, and at its farther extremity
was bounded by a narrow meadow, which in turn was bor-
dered by the old disused towing-path beside the river, at this
point a slow and shallow stream. Its low flat banks were unadorned with rocks or trees, and a towing-path is not in itself
a romantic promenade. Nevertheless, here sauntered bareheaded, on a certain spring evening, the mistress of the acres
just mentioned and many more beside, in sentimental converse with an impassioned and beautiful youth.

She herself had been positively plain, but for the frequent
recurrence of a magnificent broad smile,—which imparted
loveliness to her somewhat plebeian features,—and (in another degree) for the elegance of her dress, which expressed
one of the later stages of mourning, and was of that voluminous abundance proper to women who are massive in person,
and rich besides. Her companion's good looks, for very good
they were, in spite of several defects, were set off by a shabby
suit, as carelessly worn as it was inartistically cut. His manner,
as he walked and talked, was that of a nervous, passionate
man, wrought almost to desperation; while her own was that
of a person self-composed to generous attention. A brief silence, however, had at last fallen upon them. Miss Whittaker
strolled along quietly, looking at the slow-mounting moon,
and the young man gazed on the ground, swinging his stick.
Finally, with a heavy blow, he brought it to earth.

"O Gertrude!" he cried, "I despise myself."

"That's very foolish," said Gertrude.

"And, Gertrude, I adore you."

"That's more foolish still," said Gertrude, with her eyes
still on the moon. And then, suddenly and somewhat impatiently transferring them to her companion's face, "Richard,"
she asked, "what do you mean when you say you adore
me?"

"Mean? I mean that I love you."

"Then, why don't you say what you mean?"

The young man looked at her a moment. "Will you give me leave," he asked, "to say *all* that I mean?"

"Of course." Then, as he remained silent, "I listen," added Gertrude.

Yet he still said nothing, but went striking vehemently at the weeds by the water's edge, like one who may easily burst into tears of rage.

"Gertrude!" he suddenly exclaimed, "what more do you want than the assurance that I love you!"

"I want nothing more. That assurance is by itself delightful enough. You yourself seemed to wish to add something more."

"Either you won't understand me," cried Richard, "or"—flagrantly vicious for twenty seconds—"you can't!"

Miss Whittaker stopped and looked thoughtfully into his face. "In our position," she said, "if it becomes you to sacrifice reflection to feeling, it becomes me to do the reverse. Listen to me, Richard. I *do* understand you, and better, I fancy, than you understand yourself."

"O, of course!"

But she continued, heedless of his interruption. "I thought that, by leaving you to yourself awhile, your feelings might become clearer to you. But they seem to be growing only more confused. I have been so fortunate, or so unfortunate, I hardly know which,"—and she smiled faintly,—"as to please you. That's all very well, but you must not make too much of it. Nothing can make me happier than to please you, or to please any one. But here it must stop with you, as it stops with others."

"It does not stop here with others."

"I beg your pardon. You have no right to say that. It is partly out of justice to others that I speak to you as I am doing. I shall always be one of your best friends, but I shall never be more. It is best I should tell you this at once. I might trifle with you awhile and make you happy (since upon such a thing you are tempted to set your happiness) by allowing you to suppose that I had given you my heart; but the end would soon come, and then where should we be? You may in your disappointment call me heartless now,—I freely give you leave to call me anything that may ease your mind,—

but what would you call me then? Friendship, Richard, is a
heavenly cure for love. Here is mine," and she held out her
hand.

"No, I thank you," said Richard, gloomily folding his arms.
"I know my own feelings," and he raised his voice. "Haven't
I lived with them night and day for weeks and weeks? Great
Heaven, Gertrude, this is no fancy. I'm not of that sort. My
whole life has gone into my love. God has let me idle it away
hitherto, only that I might begin it with you. Dear Gertrude,
hear me. I have the heart of a man. I know I'm not respectable, but I devoutly believe I'm lovable. It's true that
I've neither worked, nor thought, nor studied, nor turned a
penny. But, on the other hand, I've never cared for a woman
before. I've waited for you. And now—now, after all, I'm to
sit down and be *pleased!* The Devil! Please other men,
madam! Me you delight, you intoxicate."

An honest flush rose to Gertrude's cheek. "So much the
worse for you!" she cried with a bitter laugh. "So much the
worse for both of us! But what is your point? Do you wish to
marry me?"

Richard flinched a moment under this tacit proposition
suddenly grown vocal; but not from want of heart. "Of
course I do," he said.

"Well, then, I only pity you the more for your consistency.
I can only entreat you again to rest contented with my friendship. It's not such a bad substitute, Richard, as I understand
it. What my love might be I don't know,—I couldn't answer
for that; but of my friendship I'm sure. We both have our duties in this matter, and I have resolved to take a liberal view of
mine. I might lose patience with you, you know, and dismiss
you,—leave you alone with your dreams, and let you break
your heart. But it's rather by seeing more of me than by seeing less, that your feelings will change."

"Indeed! And yours?"

"I have no doubt they will change, too; not in kind, but in
degree. The better I know you, I am sure, the better I shall
like you. The better too you will like me. Don't turn your
back upon me. I speak the truth. You will get to entertain a
serious opinion of me,—which I'm sure you haven't now, or
you wouldn't talk of my intoxicating you. But you must be

patient. It's a singular fact that it takes longer to like a woman than to love her. A sense of intoxication is a very poor feeling to marry upon. You wish, of course, to break with your idleness, and your bad habits,—you see I am so thoroughly your friend that I'm not afraid of touching upon disagreeable facts, as I should be if I were your mistress. But you are so indolent, so irresolute, so undisciplined, so uneducated,"— Gertrude spoke deliberately, and watched the effect of her words,— "that you find a change of life very difficult. I propose, with your consent, to appoint myself your counsellor. Henceforth my house will be open to you as to my dearest friend. Come as often and stay as long as you please. Not in a few weeks, perhaps, nor even in a few months, but in God's good time, you will be a noble young man in working order,—which I don't consider you now, and which I know you don't consider yourself. But I have a great opinion of your talents," (this was very shrewd of Gertrude,) "and of your heart. If I turn out to have done you a service, you'll not want to marry me then."

Richard had silently listened, with a deepening frown. "That's all very pretty," he said; "but"—and the reader will see that, in his earnestness, he was inclined to dispense with courtesy—"it's rotten,—rotten from beginning to end. What's the meaning of all that rigmarole about the inconsistency of friendship and love? Such talk is enough to drive one mad. Refuse me outright, and send me to the Devil, if you must; but don't bemuddle your own brains at the same time. But one little word knocks it all to pieces: I want you for my wife. You make an awful mistake in treating me as a boy,—an awful mistake. I *am* in working order. I have begun life in loving you. I have broken with drinking as effectually as if I hadn't touched a drop of liquor for twenty years. I hate it, I loathe it. I've drunk my last. No, Gertrude, I'm no longer a boy,—you've cured me of that. Hang it, that's why I love you! Don't you see? Ah, Gertrude!"—and his voice fell, — "you're a great enchantress! You have no arts, you have no beauty even, (can't a lover deal with facts now?) but you are an enchantress without them. It's your nature. You are so divinely, damnably honest! That excellent speech just now was meant to smother my passion; but it has only inflamed it. You

will say it was nothing but common sense. Very likely; but
that is the very point. Your common sense captivates me. It's
for that that I love you."

He spoke with so relentless a calmness that Gertrude was
sickened. Here she found herself weaker than he, while the
happiness of both of them demanded that she should be
stronger.

"Richard Clare," she said, "you are unkind!" There was a
tremor in her voice as she spoke; and as she ceased speaking,
she burst into tears. A selfish sense of victory invaded the
young man's breast. He threw his arm about her; but she
shook it off. "You are a coward, sir!" she cried.

"Oho!" said Richard, flushing angrily.

"You go too far; you persist beyond decency."

"You hate me now, I suppose," said Richard, brutally, like
one at bay.

Gertrude brushed away her tears. "No indeed," she answered, sending him a dry, clear glance. "To hate you, I
should have to have loved you. I pity you still."

Richard looked at her a moment. "I don't feel tempted to
return the feeling, Gertrude," said he. "A woman with so
much head as you needs no pity."

"I have not head enough to read your sarcasm, sir; but I
have heart enough to excuse it, and I mean to keep a good
heart to the end. I mean to keep my temper, I mean to be
just, I mean to be conclusive, and not to have to return to
this matter. It's not for my pleasure, I would have you know,
that I am so explicit. I have nerves as well as you. Listen,
then. If I don't love you, Richard, in your way, I don't; and
if I can't, I can't. We can't love by will. But with friendship,
when it is once established, I believe the will and the reason
may have a great deal to do. I will, therefore, put the whole
of my mind into my friendship for you, and in that way we
shall perhaps be even. Such a feeling—as I shall naturally
show it—will, after all, not be very different from that other
feeling you ask—as I should naturally show it. Bravely to reconcile himself to such difference as there is, is no more than
a man of honor ought to do. Do you understand me?"

"You have an admirable way of putting things. 'After
all,' and 'such difference as there is'! The difference is the

difference of marriage and no-marriage. I suppose you don't mean that you are willing to live with me without that ceremony?"

"You suppose correctly."

"Then why do you falsify matters? A woman is either a man's wife, or she isn't."

"Yes; and a woman is either a man's friend, or she isn't."

"And you are mine, and I'm an ungrateful brute not to rest satisfied! That's what you mean. Heaven knows you're right," —and he paused a moment, with his eyes on the ground. "Don't despise me, Gertrude," he resumed. "I'm not so ungrateful as I seem. I'm very much obliged to you for the pains you have taken. Of course I understand your not loving me. You'd be a grand fool if you did; and you're no fool, Gertrude."

"No, I'm no fool, Richard. It's a great responsibility,—it's dreadfully vulgar; but, on the whole, I'm rather glad."

"So am I. I could hate you for it; but there is no doubt it's why I love you. If you were a fool, you might love me; but I shouldn't love you, and if I must choose, I prefer that."

"Heaven has chosen for us. Ah, Richard," pursued Gertrude, with admirable simplicity, "let us be good and obey Heaven, and we shall be sure to be happy,"—and she held out her hand once more.

Richard took it and raised it to his lips. She felt their pressure and withdrew it.

"Now you must leave me," she said. "Did you ride?"

"My horse is at the village."

"You can go by the river, then. Good night."

"Good night."

The young man moved away in the gathering dusk, and Miss Whittaker stood for a moment looking after him.

To appreciate the importance of this conversation, the reader must know that Miss Gertrude Whittaker was a young woman of four-and-twenty, whose father, recently deceased, had left her alone in the world, with a great fortune, accumulated by various enterprises in that part of the State. He had appointed a distant and elderly kinswoman, by name Miss Pendexter, as his daughter's household companion; and an old friend of his own, known to combine shrewdness with integrity, as her financial adviser. Motherless, country-bred, and homely-featured, Gertrude on arriving at maturity had neither the tastes nor the manners of a fine lady. Of a robust and active make, with a warm heart, a cool head, and a very pretty talent for affairs, she was, in virtue both of her wealth and of her tact, one of the chief figures of the neighborhood. These facts had forced her into a prominence which she made no attempt to elude, and in which she now felt thoroughly at home. She knew herself to be a power in the land; she knew that, present and absent, she was continually talked about as the rich Miss Whittaker; and although as modest as a woman need be, she was neither so timid nor so nervous as to wish to compromise with her inevitable distinctions. Her feelings were indeed, throughout, strong, rather than delicate; and yet there was in her whole nature, as the world had learned to look at it, a moderation, a temperance, a benevolence, an orderly freedom, which bespoke universal respect. She was impulsive, and yet discreet; economical, and yet generous; humorous, and yet serious; keenly discerning of human distinctions, and yet almost indiscriminately hospitable; with a prodigious fund of common sense beneath all; and yet beyond this,—like the priest behind the king,—and despite her broadly prosaic, and as it were secular tone, a certain latent suggestion of heroic possibilities, which he who had once become insensible of it (supposing him to be young and enthusiastic) would linger about her hoping to detect, as you might stand watchful of a florid and vigorous dahlia, which for an instant, in your passage, should have proved deliciously fragrant. It is upon the actual existence, in more minds than one, of a mystifying sense of this sweet and remote perfume, that our story is based.

Richard Clare and Miss Whittaker were old friends. They had in the first place gone democratically to the town school together as children; and then their divergent growth, as boy and girl, had acknowledged an elastic bond in a continued intimacy between Gertrude and Fanny Clare, Richard's sister, who, however, in the fulness of time had married, and had followed her husband to California. With her departure the old relations of habit between her brother and her friend had slackened, and gradually ceased. Richard had grown up a rebellious and troublesome boy, with a disposition combining stolid apathy and hot-headed impatience in equal proportions. Losing both of his parents before he was well out of his boyhood, he had found himself at the age of sixteen in possession actual, and as he supposed uncontested, of the paternal farm. It was not long, however, before those turned up who were disposed to question his immediate ability to manage it; the result of which was, that the farm was leased for five years, and that Richard was almost forcibly abducted by a maternal uncle, living on a farm of his own some three hundred miles away. Here our young man spent the remainder of his minority, ostensibly learning agriculture with his cousins, but actually learning nothing. He had very soon established, and had subsequently enjoyed without a day's interval, the reputation of an ill-natured fool. He was dull, disobliging, brooding, lowering. Reading and shooting he liked a little, because they were solitary pastimes; but to common duties and pleasures he proved himself as incompetent as he was averse. It was possible to live with him only because he was at once too selfish and too simple for mischief. As soon as he came of age he resumed possession of the acres on which his boyhood had been passed, and toward which he gravitated under an instinct of mere local affection, rather than from any intelligent purpose. He avoided his neighbors, his father's former associates; he rejected, nay, he violated, their counsel; he informed them that he wanted no help but what he paid for, and that he expected to work his farm for himself and by himself. In short, he proved himself to their satisfaction egregiously ungrateful, conceited, and arrogant. They were not slow to discover that his incapacity was as great as his conceit. In two years he had more than undone the work of the late lessee, which had been an improvement on that of the original owner. In the third year, it seemed to those who observed him that there was something so wanton in his errors as almost to impugn his sanity. He appeared to have accepted them himself, and to have given up all pretence of work. He went about silent and sullen, like a man who feels that he has a quarrel with fate. About this time it became generally known that he was often the worse for liquor; and he hereupon acquired the deplorable reputation of a man worse than

unsociable,—a man who drinks alone,—although it was still
doubtful whether this practice was the cause or the effect of
his poor crops. About this time, too, he resumed acquaintance with Gertrude Whittaker. For many months after his return he had been held at his distance, together with most of
his rural compeers, by the knowledge of her father's bitter
hostility to all possible suitors and fortune-hunters; and then,
subsequently, by the illness preceding the old man's death;
but when at last, on the expiration of her term of mourning,
Miss Whittaker had opened to society her long blockaded
ports, Richard had, to all the world's amazement, been
among the first to profit by this extension of the general privilege, and to cast anchor in the wide and peaceful waters of
her friendship. He found himself at this moment, considerably to his surprise, in his twenty-fourth year, that is, a few
months Gertrude's junior.

It was impossible that she should not have gathered from
mere juxtaposition a vague impression of his evil repute and
of his peculiar relation to his neighbors, and to his own affairs. Thanks to this impression, Richard found a very warm
welcome,—the welcome of compassion. Gertrude gave him a
heavy arrear of news from his sister Fanny, with whom he had
dropped correspondence, and, impelled by Fanny's complaints of his long silence, ventured upon a friendly admonition that he should go straight home and write a letter to
California. Richard sat before her, gazing at her out of his
dark eyes and not only attempting no defence of his conduct,
but rejoicing dumbly in the utter absence of any possible defence, as of an interruption to his companion's virtue. He
wished that he might incontinently lay bare all his shortcomings to her delicious reproof. He carried away an extraordinary sense of general alleviation; and forthwith began a series
of visits, which in the space of some ten weeks culminated in
the interview with which our narrative opens. Painfully diffident in the company of most women, Richard had not from
the first known what it was to be shy with Gertrude. As a man
of the world finds it useful to refresh his social energies by an
occasional *tête-à-tête* of an hour with himself, so Richard, with
whom solitude was the rule, derived a certain austere satisfaction from an hour's contact with Miss Whittaker's consoling

good sense, her abundance, her decent duties and comforts. Gradually, however, from a salutary process, this became almost an æsthetic one. It was now pleasant to go to Gertrude, because he enjoyed the contagion of her own repose,—because he witnessed her happiness without a sensation of envy, —because he forgot his own entanglements and errors,— because finally, his soul slept away its troubles beneath her varying glance, very much as his body had often slept away its weariness in the shade of a changing willow. But the soul, like the body, will not sleep long without dreaming; and it will not dream often without wishing at last to tell its dreams. Richard had one day ventured to impart his visions to Gertrude, and the revelation had apparently given her serious pain. The fact that Richard Clare (of all men in the world!) had somehow worked himself into an intimacy with Miss Whittaker very soon became public property among their neighbors; and in the hands of these good people, naturally enough, received an important addition in the inference that he was going to marry her. He was, of course, esteemed a very lucky fellow, and the prevalence of this impression was doubtless not without its effect on the forbearance of certain long-suffering creditors. And even if she was not to marry him, it was further argued, she yet might lend him money; for it was assumed without question that the necessity of raising money was the mainspring of Richard's suit. It is needless to inform the reader that this assumption was—to use a homely metaphor—without a leg to stand upon. Our hero had faults enough, but to be mercenary was not one of them; nor was an excessive concern on the subject of his debts one of his virtues. As for Gertrude, wherever else her perception of her friend's feelings may have been at fault, it was not at fault on this point. That he loved her as desperately as he declared, she indeed doubted; but it never occurred to her to question the purity of his affection. And so, on the other hand, it was strictly out of her heart's indifference that she rejected him, and not for the disparity of their fortunes. In accepting his very simple and natural overtures to friendship, in calling him "Richard" in remembrance of old days, and in submitting generally to the terms of their old relations, she had foreseen no sentimental catastrophe. She had viewed her friend from

the first as an object of lively material concern. She had espoused his interests (like all good women, Gertrude was ever
more or less of a partisan) because she loved his sister, and because she pitied himself. She would stand to him *in loco
sororis*. The reader has seen that she had given herself a long
day's work.

It is not to be supposed that Richard's sober retreat at the
close of the walk by the river implied any instinct of resignation to the prospects which Gertrude had opened to him. It
is explained rather by an intensity of purpose so deep as to
fancy that it can dispense with bravado. This was not the end
of his suit, but the beginning. He would not give in until he
was positively beaten. It was all very well, he reflected, that
Gertrude should reject him. Such a woman as she ought
properly to be striven for, and there was something ridiculous
in the idea that she should be easily won, whether by himself
or by another. Richard was a slow thinker, but he thought
more wisely than he talked; and he now took back all his angry boasts of accomplished self-mastery, and humbly surveyed
the facts of the case. He was on the way to recovery, but he
was by no means cured, and yet his very humility assured him
that he was curable. He was no hero, but he was better than
his life; he was no scholar, but in his own view at least he was
no fool. He was good enough to be better; he was good
enough not to sit by the hour soaking his slender brains in
whiskey. And at the very least, if he was not worthy to possess
Gertrude, he was yet worthy to strive to obtain her, and to
live forevermore upon the glory of having been formally refused by the great Miss Whittaker. He would raise himself
then to that level from which he could address her as an
equal, from which he could borrow that authority of which
he was now so shamefully bare. How he would do this, he
was at a loss to determine. He was conscious of an immense
fund of brute volition, but he cursed his barbarous ignorance,
as he searched in vain for those high opposing forces the defeat of which might lend dignity to his struggle. He longed
vaguely for some continuous muscular effort, at the end of
which he should find himself face to face with his mistress.
But as, instead of being a Pagan hero, with an enticing task-
list of impossibilities, he was a plain New England farmer,

with a bad conscience, and nature with him and not against him,—as, after slaying his dragon, after breaking with liquor, his work was a simple operation in common sense,—in view of these facts he found but little inspiration in his prospect. Nevertheless he fronted it bravely. He was not to obtain Gertrude by making a fortune, but by making himself a man, by learning to think. But as to learn to think is to learn to work, he would find some use for his muscle. He would keep sober and clear-headed; he would retrieve his land and pay his debts. Then let her refuse him if she could,—or if she dared, he was wont occasionally to add.

Meanwhile Gertrude on her side sat quietly at home, revolving in her own fashion a dozen ideal schemes for her friend's redemption and for the diversion of his enthusiasm. Not but that she meant rigorously to fulfil her part of the engagement to which she had invited him in that painful scene by the river. Yet whatever of that firmness, patience, and courtesy of which she possessed so large a stock she might still oppose to his importunities, she could not feel secure against repeated intrusion (for it was by this term that she was disposed to qualify all unsanctioned transgression of those final and immovable limits which she had set to her immense hospitality) without the knowledge of a partial change at least in Richard's own attitude. Such a change could only be effected through some preparatory change in his life; and a change in his life could be brought about only by the introduction of some new influence. This influence, however, was very hard to find. However positively Gertrude had dwelt upon the practical virtue of her own friendship, she was now on further reflection led sadly to distrust the exclusive use of this instrument. He was welcome enough to that, but he needed something more. It suddenly occurred to her, one morning after Richard's image had been crossing and recrossing her mental vision for a couple of hours with wearisome pertinacity, that a world of good might accrue to him through the friendship of a person so unexceptionable as Captain Severn. There was no one, she declared within herself, who would not be better for knowing such a man. She would recommend Richard to his kindness, and him she would recommend to Richard's— what? Here was the rub! Where was there common ground between Richard and such a one as he? To request him to like Richard was easy; to ask Richard to like him was ridiculous. If Richard could only know him, the work were done; he couldn't choose but love him as a brother. But to bespeak Richard's respect for an object was to fill him straightway with aversion for it. Her young friend was so pitiable a creature himself, that it had never occurred to her to appeal to his sentiments of compassion. All the world seemed above him, and he was consequently at odds with all the world. If some worthy being could be found, even less favored of nature and of fortune than himself, to such a one he might become attached by a useful sympathy. There was indeed nothing particularly enviable in Captain Severn's lot, and herein Richard might properly experience a fellow-feeling for him; but nevertheless he was apparently quite contented with it, and thus he was raised several degrees above Richard, who would be certain to find something aggressive in his equanimity. Still, for all this, Gertrude would bring them together. She had a high estimate of the Captain's generosity, and if Richard should wantonly fail to conform to the situation, the loss would be his own. It may be thought that in this enterprise Captain Severn was somewhat inconsiderately handled. But a generous woman will freely make a missionary of the man she loves. These words suggest the propriety of a short description of the person to whom they refer.

Edmund Severn was a man of eight-and-twenty, who, having for some time combated fortune and his own inclinations as a mathematical tutor in a second-rate country college, had, on the opening of the war, transferred his valor to a more heroic field. His regiment of volunteers, now at work before Richmond, had been raised in Miss Whittaker's district, and beneath her substantial encouragement. His soldiership, like his scholarship, was solid rather than brilliant. He was not destined to be heard of at home, nor to leave his regiment; but on many an important occasion in Virginia he had proved himself in a modest way an excellently useful man. Coming up early in the war with a severe wound, to be nursed by a married sister domiciled in Gertrude's neighborhood, he was, like all his fellow-sufferers within a wide circuit, very soon honored with a visit of anxious inquiry from Miss Whittaker, who was as yet known to him only by report, and who transmitted to him the warmest assurances of sympathy and interest, together with the liveliest offers of assistance; and, incidentally as it were to these, a copious selection from the products of her hot-house and store-room. Severn had taken the air for the first time in Gertrude's own great cushioned barouche, which she had sent to his door at an early stage of his convalescence, and which of course he had immediately made use of to pay his respects to his benefactress. He was confounded by the real humility with which, on this occasion, betwixt smiles and tears, she assured him that to be of service to such as him was for her a sacred privilege. Never, thought the Captain as he drove away, had he seen so much rustic breadth combined with so much womanly grace. Half a dozen visits during the ensuing month more than sufficed to convert him into what is called an admirer; but, as the weeks passed by, he felt that there were great obstacles to his ever ripening into a lover. Captain Severn was a serious man; he was conscientious, discreet, deliberate, unused to act without a definite purpose. Whatever might be the intermediate steps, it was necessary that the goal of an enterprise should have become an old story to him before he took the first steps. And, moreover, if the goal seemed a profitable or an honorable station, he was proof against the perils or the discomforts of the journey; while if, on the other hand, it offered no permanent repose, he generally found but little difficulty in resisting the incidental allurements. In pursuance of this habit, or rather in obedience to this principle, of carefully fixing his programme, he had asked himself whether he was prepared to face the logical results of a series of personal attentions to our heroine. Since he had determined a twelvemonth before not to marry until, by some means or another, he should have evoked a sufficient income, no great change had taken place in his fortunes. He was still a poor man and an unsettled one; he was still awaiting his real vocation. Moreover, while subject to the chances of war, he doubted his right to engage a woman's affections: he shrank in horror from the thought of making a widow. Miss Whittaker was one in five thousand. Before the luminous fact of her existence, his dim ideal of the desirable wife had faded into vapor. But should he allow this fact to in-

validate all the stern precepts of his reason? He could no more
afford to marry a rich woman than a poor one. When he
should have earned a subsistence for two, then he would be
free to marry whomsoever he might fancy,—a beggar or an
heiress. The truth is, that the Captain was a great deal too
proud. It was his fault that he could not bring himself to forget the difference between his poverty and Gertrude's wealth.
He would of course have resented the insinuation that the superior fortune of the woman he loved should really have force
to prevent him from declaring his love; but there is no doubt
that in the case before us this fact arrested his passion in its
origin. Severn had a most stoical aversion to being in debt. It
is certain that, after all, he would have made a very graceful
debtor to his mistress or his wife; but while a woman was as
yet neither his mistress nor his wife, the idea of being be-
holden to her was essentially distasteful to him. It would have
been a question with one who knew him, whether at this
juncture this frigid instinct was destined to resist the warmth
of Gertrude's charms, or whether it was destined gradually to
melt away. There would have been no question, however, but
that it could maintain itself only at the cost of great suffering
to its possessor. At this moment, then, Severn had made up
his mind that Gertrude was not for him, and that it behooved
him to be sternly vigilant both of his impulses and his impressions. That Miss Whittaker, with a hundred rational cares,
was anything less than supremely oblivious of him, individually, it never occurred to him to suspect. The truth is, that
Gertrude's private and personal emotions were entertained in
a chamber of her heart so remote from the portals of speech
that no sound of their revelry found its way into the world.
She constantly thought of her modest, soldierly, scholarly
friend as of one whom a wise woman might find it very
natural to love. But what was she to him? A local roadside
figure,—at the very most a sort of millionnaire Maud
Muller,—with whom it was pleasant for a lonely wayfarer to
exchange a friendly "good-morning." Her duty was to fold
her arms resignedly, to sit quietly on the sofa, and watch a
great happiness sink below the horizon. With this impression
on Gertrude's part it is not surprising that Severn was not
wrenched out of himself. The prodigy was apparently to be

wrought—if wrought at all—by her common, unbought sweetness. It is true that this was of a potency sufficient almost to work prodigies; but as yet its effect upon Severn had been none other than its effect upon all the world. It kept him in his kindliest humor. It kept him even in the humor of talking sentiment; but although, in the broad sunshine of her listening, his talk bloomed thick with field-flowers, he never invited her to pluck the least little daisy. It was with perfect honesty, therefore, that she had rebutted Richard's insinuation that the Captain enjoyed any especial favor. He was as yet but another of the pensioners of her good-nature.

The result of Gertrude's meditations was, that she despatched a note to each of her two friends, requesting them to take tea with her on the following day. A couple of hours before tea-time she received a visit from one Major Luttrel, who was recruiting for a United States regiment at a large town, some ten miles away, and who had ridden over in the afternoon, in accordance with a general invitation conveyed to him through an old lady who had bespoken Miss Whittaker's courtesy for him as a man of delightful manners and wonderful talents. Gertrude, on her venerable friend's representations, had replied, with her wonted alacrity, that she would be very glad to see Major Luttrel, should he ever come that way, and then had thought no more about him until his card was brought to her as she was dressing for the evening. He found so much to say to her, that the interval passed very rapidly for both of them before the simultaneous entrance of Miss Pendexter and of Gertrude's guests. The two officers were already slightly known to each other, and Richard was accordingly presented to each of them. They eyed the distracted-looking young farmer with some curiosity. Richard's was at all times a figure to attract attention; but now he was almost picturesque (so Severn thought at least) with his careless garments, his pale face, his dark mistrustful eyes, and his nervous movements. Major Luttrel, who struck Gertrude as at once very agreeable and the least bit in the world disagreeable, was, of course, invited to remain,—which he straightway consented to do; and it soon became evident to Miss Whittaker that her little scheme was destined to miscarry. Richard practised a certain defiant silence, which, as she feared, gave him eventually a decidedly ridiculous air. His companions displayed toward their hostess that half-avowed effort to shine and to outshine natural to clever men who find themselves concurring to the entertainment of a young and agreeable woman. Richard sat by, wondering, in splenetic amazement, whether he was an ignorant boor, or whether they were only a brace of inflated snobs. He decided, correctly enough, in substance, for the former hypothesis. For it seemed to him that Gertrude's consummate accommodation (for as such he viewed it) of her tone and her manner to theirs added prodigiously (so his lover's instinct taught him) to her loveliness and dignity. How magnanimous an impulse on Richard's part was this submission for his sweetheart's sake to a fact damning to his own vanity, could have been determined only by one who knew the proportions of that vanity. He writhed and chafed under the polish of tone and the variety of allusion by which the two officers consigned him to insignificance; but he was soon lost in wonder at the mettlesome grace and vivacity with which Gertrude sustained her share of the conversation. For a moment it seemed to him that her tenderness for his equanimity (for should she not know his mind,—she who had made it?) might reasonably have caused her to forego such an exhibition of her social accomplishments as would but remind him afresh of his own deficiencies; but the next moment he asked himself, with a great revulsion of feeling, whether he, a conscious suitor, should fear to know his mistress in her integrity. As he gulped down the sickening fact of his comparative, nay, his absolute ignorance of the great world represented by his rivals, he felt like anticipating its consequences by a desperate sally into the very field of their conversation. To some such movement Gertrude was continually inviting him by her glances, her smiles, her questions, and her appealing silence. But poor Richard knew that, if he should attempt to talk, he would choke; and this assurance he imparted to his friend in a look piteously eloquent. He was conscious of a sensation of rage under which his heart was fast turning into a fiery furnace, destined to consume all his good resolutions. He could not answer for the future now. Suddenly, as tea was drawing to a close, he became aware that Captain Severn had lapsed into a silence very nearly as profound as his own, and that he was covertly watching the progress of a lively dialogue between Miss Whittaker and Major Luttrel. He had the singular experience of seeing his own feelings reflected in the Captain's face; that is, he discerned there an incipient jealousy. Severn too was in love!

On rising from table, Gertrude proposed an adjournment to the garden, where she was very fond of entertaining her friends at this hour. The sun had sunk behind a long line of hills, far beyond the opposite bank of the river, a portion of which was discernible through a gap in the intervening wood. The high-piled roof and chimney-stacks, the picturesquely crowded surface, of the old patched and renovated farm-house which served Gertrude as a villa, were ruddy with the declining rays. Our friends' long shadows were thrown over the short grass, Gertrude, having graciously anticipated the gentlemen's longing for their cigars, suggested a stroll toward the river. Before she knew it, she had accepted Major Luttrel's arm; and as Miss Pendexter preferred remaining at home, Severn and Richard found themselves lounging side by side at a short distance behind their hostess. Gertrude, who had marked the reserve which had suddenly fallen upon Captain Severn, and in her simplicity had referred it to some unwitting failure of attention on her own part, had hoped to repair her neglect by having him at her own side. She was in some degree consoled, however, by the sight of his happy juxtaposition with Richard. As for Richard, now that he was on his feet and in the open air, he found it easier to speak.

"Who is that man?" he asked, nodding toward the Major.

"Major Luttrel, of the —th Artillery."

"I don't like his face much," said Richard.

"Don't you?" rejoined Severn, amused at his companion's bluntness. "He's not handsome, but he looks like a soldier."

"He looks like a rascal, I think," said Richard.

Severn laughed outright, so that Gertrude glanced back at him. "Dear me! I think you put it rather strongly. I should call it a very intelligent face."

Richard was sorely perplexed. He had expected to find acceptance for his bitterest animadversions, and lo! here was the Captain fighting for his enemy. Such a man as that was no rival. So poor a hater could be but a poor lover. Nevertheless, a certain new-born mistrust of his old fashion of measuring human motives prevented him from adopting this conclusion as final. He would try another question.

"Do you know Miss Whittaker well?" he asked.

"Tolerably well. She was very kind to me when I was ill. Since then I've seen her some dozen times."

"That's a way she has, being kind," said Richard, with what he deemed considerable shrewdness. But as the Captain merely puffed his cigar responsively, he pursued, "What do you think of her face?"

"I like it very much," said the Captain.

"She isn't beautiful," said Richard, cunningly.

Severn was silent a moment, and then, just as Richard was about to dismiss him from his thoughts, as neither formidable nor satisfactory, he replied, with some emphasis, "You mean she isn't pretty. She *is* beautiful, I think, in spite of the irregularity of her face. It's a face not to be forgotten. She has no features, no color, no lilies nor roses, no attitudes; but she has *looks*, expressions. Her face has *character*; and so has her figure. It has no 'style,' as they call it; but that only belongs properly to a work of art, which Miss Whittaker's figure isn't, thank Heaven! She's as unconscious of it as Nature herself."

Severn spoke Richard's mind as well as his own. That "She isn't beautiful" had been an extempore version of the young man's most sacred dogma, namely, She is beautiful. The reader will remember that he had so translated it on a former occasion. Now, all that he felt was a sense of gratitude to the Captain for having put it so much more finely than he, the above being his choicest public expression of it. But the Captain's eyes, somewhat brightened by his short but fervid speech, were following Gertrude's slow steps. Richard saw that he could learn more from them than from any further oral declaration; for something in the mouth beneath them seemed to indicate that it had judged itself to have said enough, and it was obviously not the mouth of a simpleton. As he thus deferred with an unwonted courtesy to the Captain's silence, and transferred his gaze sympathetically to Gertrude's shapely shoulders and to her listening ear, he gave utterance to a tell-tale sigh,—a sigh which there was no mistaking. Severn looked about; it was now his turn to scrutinize.

"Good Heavens!" he exclaimed, "that boy is in love with her!"

After the first shock of surprise, he accepted this fact with rational calmness. Why shouldn't he be in love with her? *"Je le suis bien,"* said the Captain; "or, rather, I'm not." Could it be, Severn pursued, that he was a favorite? He was a mannerless young farmer; but it was plain that he had a soul of his own. He almost wished, indeed, that Richard might prove to be in Gertrude's good graces. "But if he is," he reflected, "why should he sigh? It is true that there is no arguing for lovers. I, who am out in the cold, take my comfort in whistling most impertinently. It may be that my friend here groans for very bliss. I confess, however, that he scarcely looks like a favored swain."

And forthwith this faint-hearted gentleman felt a twinge of pity for Richard's obvious infelicity; and as he compared it with the elaborately defensive condition of his own affections, he felt a further pang of self-contempt. But it was easier to restore the equilibrium of his self-respect by an immediate cession of the field, than by contesting it against this wofully wounded knight. "Whether he wins her or not, he'll fight for her," the Captain declared; and as he glanced at Major Luttrel, he felt that this was a sweet assurance. He had conceived a singular distrust of the Major.

They had now reached the water's edge, where Gertrude, having arrested her companion, had turned about, expectant of her other guests. As they came up, Severn saw, or thought that he saw (which is a very different thing), that her first look was at Richard. The "admirer" in his breast rose fratricidal for a moment against the quiet observer; but the next, it was pinioned again. "Amen," said the Captain; "it's none of my business."

At this moment, Richard was soaring most heroically. The end of his anguish had been a sudden intoxication. He surveyed the scene before him with a kindling fancy. Why should he stand tongue-tied in sullen mistrust of fortune, when all nature beckoned him into the field? There was the river-path where, a fortnight before, he had found an eloquence attested by Gertrude's tears. There was sweet Gertrude herself, whose hand he had kissed and whose waist he had clasped. Surely, he

was master here! Before he knew it, he had begun to talk,—
rapidly, nervously, and almost defiantly. Major Luttrel having
made an observation about the prettiness of the river, Richard
entered upon a description of its general course and its superior beauty upon his own place, together with an enumeration
of the fish which were to be found in it, and a story about a
great overflow ten years before. He spoke in fair, coherent
terms, but with singular intensity and vehemence, and with
his head thrown back and his eyes on the opposite bank. At
last he stopped, feeling that he had given proof of his manhood, and looked towards Gertrude, whose eyes he had been
afraid to meet until he had seen his adventure to a close. But
she was looking at Captain Severn, under the impression that
Richard had secured his auditor. Severn was looking at
Luttrel, and Luttrel at Miss Whittaker; and all were apparently
so deep in observation that they had marked neither his
speech nor his silence. "Truly," thought the young man, "I'm
well out of the circle!" But he was resolved to be patient still,
which was assuredly, all things considered, a very brave resolve. Yet there was always something spasmodic and unnatural in Richard's magnanimity. A touch in the wrong place
would cause it to collapse. It was Gertrude's evil fortune to
administer this touch at present. As the party turned about
toward the house, Richard stepped to her side and offered her
his arm, hoping in his heart—so implicitly did he count upon
her sympathy, so almost boyishly, finally, did he depend upon
it—for some covert token that his heroism, such as it was, had
not been lost upon her.

But Gertrude, intensely preoccupied by the desire to repair
her fancied injustice to the Captain, shook her head at him
without even meeting his eye. "Thank you," she said; "I want
Captain Severn," who forthwith approached.

Poor Richard felt his feet touch the ground again. He felt
that he could have flung the Captain into the stream. Major
Luttrel placed himself at Gertrude's other elbow, and Richard
stood behind them, almost livid with spite, and half resolved
to turn upon his heel and make his way home by the river.
But it occurred to him that a more elaborate vengeance
would be to follow the trio before him back to the lawn, and
there make it a silent and scathing bow. Accordingly, when

they reached the house, he stood aloof and bade Gertrude a grim good-night. He trembled with eagerness to see whether she would make an attempt to detain him. But Miss Whittaker, reading in his voice—it had grown too dark to see his face at the distance at which he stood—the story of some fancied affront, and unconsciously contrasting it, perhaps, with Severn's clear and unwarped accents, obeyed what she deemed a prompting of self-respect, and gave him, without her hand, a farewell as cold as his own. It is but fair to add, that, a couple of hours later, as she reviewed the incidents of the evening, she repented most generously of this little act of justice.

PART II.

Richard got through the following week he hardly knew how. He found occupation, to a much greater extent than he was actually aware of, in a sordid and yet heroic struggle with himself. For several months now, he had been leading, under Gertrude's inspiration, a strictly decent and sober life. So long as he was at comparative peace with Gertrude and with himself, such a life was more than easy; it was delightful. It produced a moral buoyancy infinitely more delicate and more constant than the gross exhilaration of his old habits. There was a kind of fascination in adding hour to hour, and day to day, in this record of his new-born austerity. Having abjured excesses, he practised temperance after the fashion of a novice: he raised it (or reduced it) to abstinence. He was like an unclean man who, having washed himself clean, remains in the water for the love of it. He wished to be religiously, superstitiously pure. This was easy, as we have said, so long as his goddess smiled, even though it were as a goddess indeed,—as a creature unattainable. But when she frowned, and the heavens grew dark, Richard's sole dependence was in his own will,—as flimsy a trust for an upward scramble, one would have premised, as a tuft of grass on the face of a perpendicular cliff. Flimsy as it looked, however, it served him. It started and crumbled; but it held, if only by a single fibre. When Richard had cantered fifty yards away from Gertrude's gate in a fit of stupid rage, he suddenly pulled up his horse

and gulped down his passion, and swore an oath, that, suffer
what torments of feeling he might, he would not at least
break the continuity of his gross physical soberness. It was
enough to be drunk in mind; he would not be drunk in
body. A singular, almost ridiculous feeling of antagonism to
Gertrude lent force to this resolution. "No, madam," he cried
within himself, "I shall *not* fall back. Do your best! I shall
keep straight." We often outweather great offences and afflic-
tions through a certain healthy instinct of egotism. Richard
went to bed that night as grim and sober as a Trappist monk;
and his foremost impulse the next day was to plunge headlong into some physical labor which should not allow him a
moment's interval of idleness. He found no labor to his taste;
but he spent the day so actively, in the mechanical annihila-
tion of the successive hours, that Gertrude's image found no
chance squarely to face him. He was engaged in the work of
self-preservation,—the most serious and absorbing work possible to man. Compared to the results here at stake, his passion for Gertrude seemed but a fiction. It is perhaps difficult
to give a more lively impression of the vigor of this passion,
of its maturity and its strength, than by simply stating that it
discreetly held itself in abeyance until Richard had set at rest
his doubts of that which lies nearer than all else to the heart
of man,—his doubts of the strength of his will. He answered
these doubts by subjecting his resolution to a course of such
cruel temptations as were likely either to shiver it to a myriad
of pieces, or to season it perfectly to all the possible requirements of life. He took long rides over the country, passing
within a stone's throw of as many of the scattered wayside
taverns as could be combined in a single circuit. As he drew
near them he sometimes slackened his pace, as if he were
about to dismount, pulled up his horse, gazed a moment,
then, thrusting in his spurs, galloped away again like one pursued. At other times, in the late evening, when the window-
panes were aglow with the ruddy light within, he would walk
slowly by, looking at the stars, and, after maintaining this
stoical pace for a couple of miles, would hurry home to his
own lonely and black-windowed dwelling. Having successfully
performed this feat a certain number of times, he found
his love coming back to him, bereft in the interval of its

attendant jealousy. In obedience to it, he one morning leaped upon his horse and repaired to Gertrude's abode, with no definite notion of the terms in which he should introduce himself.

He had made himself comparatively sure of his will; but he was yet to acquire the mastery of his impulses. As he gave up his horse, according to his wont, to one of the men at the stable, he saw another steed stalled there which he recognized as Captain Severn's. "Steady, my boy," he murmured to himself, as he would have done to a frightened horse. On his way across the broad court-yard toward the house, he encountered the Captain, who had just taken his leave. Richard gave him a generous salute (he could not trust himself to more), and Severn answered with what was at least a strictly just one. Richard observed, however, that he was very pale, and that he was pulling a rosebud to pieces as he walked; whereupon our young man quickened his step. Finding the parlor empty, he instinctively crossed over to a small room adjoining it, which Gertrude had converted into a modest conservatory; and as he did so, hardly knowing it, he lightened his heavy-shod tread. The glass door was open and Richard looked in. There stood Gertrude with her back to him, bending apart with her hands a couple of tall flowering plants, and looking through the glazed partition behind them. Advancing a step, and glancing over the young girl's shoulder, Richard had just time to see Severn mounting his horse at the stable door, before Gertrude, startled by his approach, turned hastily round. Her face was flushed hot, and her eyes brimming with tears.

"You!" she exclaimed, sharply.

Richard's head swam. That single word was so charged with cordial impatience that it seemed the death-knell of his hope. He stepped inside the room and closed the door, keeping his hand on the knob.

"Gertrude," he said, "you love that man!"

"Well, sir?"

"Do you confess it?" cried Richard.

"Confess it? Richard Clare, how dare you use such language? I'm in no humor for a scene. Let me pass."

Gertrude was angry; but as for Richard, it may almost be said that he was mad. "One scene a day is enough, I suppose," he cried. "What are these tears about? Wouldn't he have you? Did he refuse you, as you refused me? Poor Gertrude!"

Gertrude looked at him a moment with concentrated scorn. "You fool!" she said, for all answer. She pushed his hand from the latch, flung open the door, and moved rapidly away.

Left alone, Richard sank down on a sofa and covered his face with his hands. It burned them, but he sat motionless, repeating to himself, mechanically, as if to avert thought, "You fool! you fool!" At last he got up and made his way out.

It seemed to Gertrude, for several hours after this scene, that she had at this juncture a strong case against Fortune. It is not our purpose to repeat the words which she had exchanged with Captain Severn. They had come within a single step of an *éclaircissement*, and when but another movement would have flooded their souls with light, some malignant influence had seized them by the throats. Had they too much pride?—too little imagination? We must content ourselves with this hypothesis. Severn, then, had walked mechanically across the yard, saying to himself, "She belongs to another"; and adding, as he saw Richard, "and such another!" Gertrude had stood at her window, repeating, under her breath, "He belongs to himself, himself alone." And as if this was not enough, when misconceived, slighted, wounded, she had faced about to her old, passionless, dutiful past, there on the path of retreat to this asylum Richard Clare had arisen to forewarn her that she should find no peace even at home. There was something in the violent impertinence of his appearance at this moment which gave her a dreadful feeling that fate was against her. More than this. There entered into her emotions a certain minute particle of awe of the man whose passion was so uncompromising. She felt that it was out of place any longer to pity him. He was the slave of his passion; but his passion was strong. In her reaction against the splendid civility of Severn's silence, (the real antithesis of which would have been simply the perfect courtesy of explicit devotion,) she found herself touching with pleasure on the fact of Richard's brutality. He at least had ventured to insult her. He had loved her enough to forget himself. He had dared to make himself odious in her eyes, because he had cast away his sanity. What cared he for the impression he made? He cared only for the impression he received. The violence of this reaction, however, was the measure of its duration. It was impossible that she should walk backward so fast without stumbling. Brought to her senses by this accident, she became aware that her judgment was missing. She smiled to herself as she reflected that it had been taking holiday for a whole afternoon. "Richard was right," she said to herself. "I am no fool. I can't be a fool if I try. I'm too thoroughly my father's daughter for that. I love that man, but I love myself better. Of course, then, I don't deserve to have him. If I loved him in a way to merit his love, I would sit down this moment and write him a note telling him that if he does not come back to me, I shall die. But I shall neither write the note nor die. I shall live and grow stout, and look after my chickens and my flowers and my colts, and thank the Lord in my old age that I have never done anything unwomanly. Well! I'm as He made me. Whether I can deceive others, I know not; but I certainly can't deceive myself. I'm quite as sharp as Gertrude Whittaker; and this it is that has kept me from making a fool of myself and writing to poor Richard the note that I wouldn't write to Captain Severn. I needed to fancy myself wronged. I suffer so little! I needed a sensation! So, shrewd Yankee that I am, I thought I would get one cheaply by taking up that unhappy boy! Heaven preserve me from the heroics, especially the economical heroics! The one heroic course possible, I decline. What, then, have I to complain of? Must I tear my hair because a man of taste has resisted my unspeakable charms? To be charming, you must be charmed yourself, or at least you must be able to be charmed; and that apparently I'm not. I didn't love him, or he would have known it. Love gets love, and no-love gets none."

But at this point of her meditations Gertrude almost broke down. She felt that she was assigning herself but a dreary future. Never to be loved but by such a one as Richard Clare was a cheerless prospect; for it was identical with an eternal spinsterhood. "Am I, then," she exclaimed, quite as passionately as a woman need do,—"am I, then, cut off from a woman's dearest joys? What blasphemous nonsense! One thing is plain: I am made to be a mother; the wife may take

care of herself. I am made to be a wife; the mistress may take
care of *her*self. I am in the Lord's hands," added the poor girl,
who, whether or no she could forget herself in an earthly
love, had at all events this mark of a spontaneous nature, that
she could forget herself in a heavenly one. But in the midst of
her pious emotion, she was unable to subdue her conscience.
It smote her heavily for her meditated falsity to Richard, for
her miserable readiness to succumb to the strong temptation
to seek a momentary resting-place in his gaping heart. She recoiled from this thought as from an act cruel and immoral.
Was Richard's heart the place for her now, any more than it
had been a month before? Was she to apply for comfort
where she would not apply for counsel? Was she to drown her
decent sorrows and regrets in a base, a dishonest, an extemporized passion? Having done the young man so bitter a
wrong in intention, nothing would appease her magnanimous
remorse (as time went on) but to repair it in fact. She went so
far as keenly to regret the harsh words she had cast upon him
in the conservatory. He had been insolent and unmannerly;
but he had an excuse. Much should be forgiven him, for he
loved much. Even now that Gertrude had imposed upon her
feelings a sterner regimen than ever, she could not defend
herself from a sweet and sentimental thrill—a thrill in which,
as we have intimated, there was something of a tremor—at
the recollection of his strident accents and his angry eyes. It
was yet far from her heart to desire a renewal, however brief,
of this exhibition. She wished simply to efface from the young
man's morbid soul the impression of a real contempt; for she
knew—or she thought that she knew—that against such an
impression he was capable of taking the most fatal and inconsiderate comfort.

Before many mornings had passed, accordingly, she had a
horse saddled, and, dispensing with attendance, she rode
rapidly over to his farm. The house door and half the windows stood open; but no answer came to her repeated summons. She made her way to the rear of the house, to the
barn-yard, thinly tenanted by a few common fowl, and across
the yard to a road which skirted its lower extremity and was
accessible by an open gate. No human figure was in sight;
nothing was visible in the hot stillness but the scattered and

ripening crops, over which, in spite of her nervous solicitude, Miss Whittaker cast the glance of a connoisseur. A great uneasiness filled her mind as she measured the rich domain apparently deserted of its young master, and reflected that she perhaps was the cause of its abandonment. Ah, where was Richard? As she looked and listened in vain, her heart rose to her throat, and she felt herself on the point of calling all too wistfully upon his name. But her voice was stayed by the sound of a heavy rumble, as of cart-wheels, beyond a turn in the road. She touched up her horse and cantered along until she reached the turn. A great four-wheeled cart, laden with masses of newly broken stone, and drawn by four oxen, was slowly advancing towards her. Beside it, patiently cracking his whip and shouting monotonously, walked a young man in a slouched hat and a red shirt, with his trousers thrust into his dusty boots. It was Richard. As he saw Gertrude, he halted a moment, amazed, and then advanced, flicking the air with his whip. Gertrude's heart went out towards him in a silent Thank God! Her next reflection was that he had never looked so well. The truth is, that, in this rough adjustment, the native barbarian was duly represented. His face and neck were browned by a week in the fields, his eye was clear, his step seemed to have learned a certain manly dignity from its attendance on the heavy bestial tramp. Gertrude, as he reached her side, pulled up her horse and held out her gloved fingers to his brown dusty hand. He took them, looked for a moment into her face, and for the second time raised them to his lips.

"Excuse my glove," she said, with a little smile.

"Excuse mine," he answered, exhibiting his sunburnt, work-stained hand.

"Richard," said Gertrude, "you never had less need of excuse in your life. You never looked half so well."

He fixed his eyes upon her a moment. "Why, you have forgiven me!" he exclaimed.

"Yes," said Gertrude, "I have forgiven you,—both you and myself. We both of us behaved very absurdly, but we both of us had reason. I wish you had come back."

Richard looked about him, apparently at loss for a rejoinder. "I have been very busy," he said, at last, with a simplicity of tone slightly studied. An odd sense of dramatic effect prompted him to say neither more nor less.

An equally delicate instinct forbade Gertrude to express all the joy which this assurance gave her. Excessive joy would have implied undue surprise; and it was a part of her plan frankly to expect the best things of her companion. "If you have been busy," she said, "I congratulate you. What have you been doing?"

"O, a hundred things. I have been quarrying, and draining, and clearing, and I don't know what all. I thought the best thing was just to put my own hands to it. I am going to make a stone fence along the great lot on the hill there. Wallace is forever grumbling about his boundaries. I'll fix them once for all. What are you laughing at?"

"I am laughing at certain foolish apprehensions that I have been indulging for a week past. You're wiser than I, Richard. I have no imagination."

"Do you mean that *I* have? I haven't enough to guess what you *do* mean."

"Why, do you suppose, have I come over this morning?"

"Because you thought I was sulking on account of your having called me a fool."

"Sulking, or worse. What do I deserve for the wrong I have done you?"

"You have done me no wrong. You reasoned fairly enough. You are not obliged to know me better than I know myself. It's just like you to be ready to take back that bad word, and try to make yourself believe that it was unjust. But it was perfectly just, and therefore I have managed to bear it. I *was* a fool at that moment,—a stupid, impudent fool. I don't know whether that man had been making love to you or not. But you had, I think, been feeling love for him,—you looked it; I should have been less than a man, I should be unworthy of your—your affection, if I had failed to see it. I did see it,—I saw it as clearly as I see those oxen now; and yet I bounced in with my own ill-timed claims. To do so was to be a fool. To have been other than a fool would have been to have waited, to have backed out, to have bitten my tongue off before I spoke, to have done anything but what I did. I have no right to claim you, Gertrude, until I can woo you better than that.

It was the most fortunate thing in the world that you spoke as you did: it was even kind. It saved me all the misery of groping about for a starting-point. Not to have spoken as you did would have been to fail of justice; and then, probably, I should have sulked, or, as you very considerately say, done worse. I had made a false move in the game, and the only thing to do was to repair it. But you were not obliged to know that I would so readily admit my move to have been false. Whenever I have made a fool of myself before, I have been for sticking it out, and trying to turn all mankind—that is, *you* —into a a fool too, so that I shouldn't be an exception. But this time, I think, I had a kind of inspiration. I felt that my case was desperate. I felt that if I adopted my folly now I adopted it forever. The other day I met a man who had just come home from Europe, and who spent last summer in Switzerland. He was telling me about the mountain-climbing over there,—how they get over the glaciers, and all that. He said that you sometimes came upon great slippery, steep, snow-covered slopes that end short off in a precipice, and that if you stumble or lose your footing as you cross them hori-zontally, why you go shooting down, and you're gone; that is, but for one little dodge. You have a long walking-pole with a sharp end, you know, and as you feel yourself sliding,—it's as likely as not to be in a sitting posture,—you just take this and ram it into the snow before you, and there you are, stopped. The thing is, of course, to drive it in far enough, so that it won't yield or break; and in any case it hurts infernally to come whizzing down upon this upright pole. But the inter-ruption gives you time to pick yourself up. Well, so it was with me the other day. I stumbled and fell; I slipped, and was whizzing downward; but I just drove in my pole and pulled up short. It nearly tore me in two; but it saved my life."
Richard made this speech with one hand leaning on the neck of Gertrude's horse, and the other on his own side, and with his head slightly thrown back and his eyes on hers. She had sat quietly in her saddle, returning his gaze. He had spoken slowly and deliberately; but without hesitation and without heat. "This is not romance," thought Gertrude, "it's reality." And this feeling it was that dictated her reply, divesting it of romance so effectually as almost to make it sound trivial.

"It was fortunate you had a walking-pole," she said.

"I shall never travel without one again."

"Never, at least," smiled Gertrude, "with a companion who has the bad habit of pushing you off the path."

"O, you may push all you like," said Richard. "I give you leave. But isn't this enough about myself?"

"That's as you think."

"Well, it's all I have to say for the present, except that I am prodigiously glad to see you, and that of course you will stay awhile."

"But you have your work to do."

"Dear me, never you mind my work. I've earned my dinner this morning, if you have no objection; and I propose to share it with you. So we will go back to the house." He turned her horse's head about, started up his oxen with his voice, and walked along beside her on the grassy roadside, with one hand in the horse's mane, and the other swinging his whip.

Before they reached the yard-gate, Gertrude had revolved his speech. "Enough about himself," she said, silently echoing his words. "Yes, Heaven be praised, it *is* about himself. I am but a means in this matter,—he himself, his own character, his own happiness, is the end." Under this conviction it seemed to her that her part was appreciably simplified. Richard was learning wisdom and self-control, and to exercise his reason. Such was the suit that he was destined to gain. Her duty was as far as possible to remain passive, and not to interfere with the working of the gods who had selected her as the instrument of their prodigy. As they reached the gate, Richard made a trumpet of his hands, and sent a ringing summons into the fields; whereupon a farm-boy approached, and, with an undisguised stare of amazement at Gertrude, took charge of his master's team. Gertrude rode up to the door-step, where her host assisted her to dismount, and bade her go in and make herself at home, while he busied himself with the bestowal of her horse. She found that, in her absence, the old woman who administered her friend's household had re-appeared, and had laid out the preparations for his mid-day meal. By the time he returned, with his face and head shining from a fresh ablution, and his shirt-sleeves decently concealed by a coat, Gertrude had apparently won the complete confidence of the good wife.

Gertrude doffed her hat, and tucked up her riding-skirt, and sat down to a *tête-à-tête* over Richard's crumpled table-cloth. The young man played the host very soberly and naturally; and Gertrude hardly knew whether to augur from his perfect self-possession that her star was already on the wane, or that it had waxed into a steadfast and eternal sun. The solution of her doubts was not far to seek; Richard was absolutely at his ease in her presence. He had told her indeed that she intoxicated him; and truly, in those moments when she was compelled to oppose her dewy eloquence to his fervid importunities, her whole presence seemed to him to exhale a singularly potent sweetness. He had told her that she was an enchantress, and this assertion, too, had its measure of truth. But her spell was a steady one; it sprang not from her beauty, her wit, her figure,—it sprang from her character. When she found herself aroused to appeal or to resistance, Richard's pulses were quickened to what he had called intoxication, not by her smiles, her gestures, her glances, or any accession of that material beauty which she did not possess, but by a generous sense of her virtues in action. In other words, Gertrude exercised the magnificent power of making her lover forget her face. Agreeably to this fact, his habitual feeling in her presence was one of deep repose,—a sensation not unlike that which in the early afternoon, as he lounged in his orchard with a pipe, he derived from the sight of the hot and vaporous hills. He was innocent, then, of that delicious trouble which Gertrude's thoughts had touched upon as a not unnatural result of her visit, and which another woman's fancy would perhaps have dwelt upon as an indispensable proof of its success. "Porphyro grew faint," the poet assures us, as he stood in Madeline's chamber on Saint Agnes' eve. But Richard did not in the least grow faint now that his mistress was actually filling his musty old room with her voice, her touch, her looks; that she was sitting in his unfrequented chairs, trailing her skirt over his faded carpet, casting her perverted image upon his mirror, and breaking his daily bread. He was not fluttered when he sat at her well-served table, and trod her muffled floors. Why, then, should he be fluttered now? Gertrude was herself in all places, and (once granted that she was at peace) to be at her side was to drink peace as fully in one place as in another.

Richard accordingly ate a great working-day dinner in Gertrude's despite, and she ate a small one for his sake. She asked questions moreover, and offered counsel with most sisterly freedom. She deplored the rents in his table-cloth, and the dismemberments of his furniture; and although by no means absurdly fastidious in the matter of household elegance, she could not but think that Richard would be a happier and a better man if he were a little more comfortable. She forbore, however, to criticise the poverty of his *entourage*, for she felt that the obvious answer was, that such a state of things was the penalty of his living alone; and it was desirable, under the circumstances, that this idea should remain implied.

When at last Gertrude began to bethink herself of going, Richard broke a long silence by the following question: "Gertrude, *do* you love that man?"

"Richard," she answered, "I refused to tell you before, because you asked the question as a right. Of course you do so no longer. No. I do not love him. I have been near it,—but I have missed it. And now good by."

For a week after her visit, Richard worked as bravely and steadily as he had done before it. But one morning he woke up lifeless, morally speaking. His strength had suddenly left him. He had been straining his faith in himself to a prodigious tension, and the chord had suddenly snapped. In the hope that Gertrude's tender fingers might repair it, he rode over to her towards evening. On his way through the village, he found people gathered in knots, reading fresh copies of the Boston newspapers over each other's shoulders, and learned that tidings had just come of a great battle in Virginia, which was also a great defeat. He procured a copy of the paper from a man who had read it out, and made haste to Gertrude's dwelling.

Gertrude received his story with those passionate imprecations and regrets which were then in fashion. Before long, Major Luttrel presented himself, and for half an hour there was no talk but about the battle. The talk, however, was chiefly between Gertrude and the Major, who found considerable ground for difference, she being a great radical and he a decided conservative. Richard sat by, listening apparently, but with the appearance of one to whom the matter of the discourse was of much less interest than the manner of those engaged in it. At last, when tea was announced, Gertrude told her friends, very frankly, that she would not invite them to remain,—that her heart was too heavy with her country's woes, and with the thought of so great a butchery, to allow her to play the hostess,—and that, in short, she was in the humor to be alone. Of course there was nothing for the gentlemen but to obey; but Richard went out cursing the law, under which, in the hour of his mistress's sorrow, his company was a burden and not a relief. He watched in vain, as he bade her farewell, for some little sign that she would fain have him stay, but that as she wished to get rid of his companion civility demanded that she should dismiss them both. No such sign was forthcoming, for the simple reason that Gertrude was sensible of no conflict between her desires. The men mounted their horses in silence, and rode slowly along the lane which led from Miss Whittaker's stables to the high-road. As they approached the top of the lane, they perceived in the twilight a mounted figure coming towards them. Richard's heart began to beat with an angry foreboding, which was confirmed as the rider drew near and disclosed Captain Severn's features. Major Luttrel and he, being bound in courtesy to a brief greeting, pulled up their horses; and as an attempt to pass them in narrow quarters would have been a greater incivility than even Richard was prepared to commit, he likewise halted.

"This is ugly news, isn't it?" said Severn. "It has determined me to go back to-morrow."

"Go back where?" asked Richard.

"To my regiment."

"Are you well enough?" asked Major Luttrel. "How is that wound?"

"It's so much better that I believe it can finish getting well down there as easily as here. Good by, Major. I hope we shall meet again." And he shook hands with Major Luttrel. "Good by, Mr. Clare." And, somewhat to Richard's surprise, he stretched over and held out his hand to him.

Richard felt that it was tremulous, and, looking hard into

his face, he thought it wore a certain unwonted look of excitement. And then his fancy coursed back to Gertrude, sitting where he had left her, in the sentimental twilight, alone with her heavy heart. With a word, he reflected, a single little word, a look, a motion, this happy man whose hand I hold can heal her sorrows. "Oh!" cried Richard, "that by this hand I might hold him fast forever!"

It seemed to the Captain that Richard's grasp was needlessly protracted and severe. "What a grip the poor fellow has!" he thought. "Good by," he repeated aloud, disengaging himself.

"Good by," said Richard. And then he added, he hardly knew why, "Are you going to bid good by to Miss Whittaker?"

"Yes. Isn't she at home?"

Whether Richard really paused or not before he answered, he never knew. There suddenly arose such a tumult in his bosom that it seemed to him several moments before he became conscious of his reply. But it is probable that to Severn it came only too soon.

"No," said Richard; "she's not at home. We have just been calling." As he spoke, he shot a glance at his companion, armed with defiance of his impending denial. But the Major just met his glance and then dropped his eyes. This slight motion was a horrible revelation. He had served the Major too.

"Ah? I'm sorry," said Severn, slacking his rein,—"I'm sorry." And from his saddle he looked down toward the house more longingly and regretfully than he knew.

Richard felt himself turning from pale to consuming crimson. There was a simple sincerity in Severn's words which was almost irresistible. For a moment he felt like shouting out a loud denial of his falsehood: "She is there! she's alone and in tears, awaiting you. Go to her—and be damned!" But before he could gather his words into his throat, they were arrested by Major Luttrel's cool, clear voice, which in its calmness seemed to cast scorn upon his weakness.

"Captain," said the Major, "I shall be very happy to take charge of your farewell."

"Thank you, Major. Pray do. Say how extremely sorry I was. Good by again." And Captain Severn hastily turned his horse about, gave him his spurs, and galloped away, leaving his friends standing alone in the middle of the road. As the sound of his retreat expired, Richard, in spite of himself, drew a long breath. He sat motionless in the saddle, hanging his head.

"Mr. Clare," said the Major, at last, "that was very cleverly done."

Richard looked up. "I never told a lie before," said he.

"Upon my soul, then, you did it uncommonly well. You did it so well I almost believed you. No wonder that Severn did."

Richard was silent. Then suddenly he broke out, "In God's name, sir, why don't you call me a blackguard? I've done a beastly act!"

"O, come," said the Major, "you needn't mind that, with me. We'll consider that said. I feel bound to let you know that I'm very, very much obliged to you. If you hadn't spoken, how do you know but that I might?"

"If you had, I would have given you the lie, square in your teeth."

"Would you, indeed? It's very fortunate, then, I held my tongue. If you will have it so, I won't deny that your little improvisation sounded very ugly. I'm devilish glad I didn't make it, if you come to that."

Richard felt his wit sharpened by a most unholy scorn,—a scorn far greater for his companion than for himself. "I am glad to hear that it did sound ugly," he said. "To me, it seemed beautiful, holy, and just. For the space of a moment, it seemed absolutely right that I should say what I did. But you saw the lie in its horrid nakedness, and yet you let it pass. You have no excuse."

"I beg your pardon. You are immensely ingenious, but you are immensely wrong. Are you going to make out that I am the guilty party? Upon my word, you're a cool hand. I *have* an excuse. I have the excuse of being interested in Miss Whittaker's remaining unengaged."

"So I suppose. But you don't love her. Otherwise—"

Major Luttrel laid his hand on Richard's bridle. "Mr. Clare," said he, "I have no wish to talk metaphysics over this

matter. You had better say no more. I know that your feelings
are not of an enviable kind, and I am therefore prepared to be
good-natured with you. But you must be civil yourself. You
have done a shabby deed; you are ashamed of it, and you wish
to shift the responsibility upon me, which is more shabby still.
My advice is, that you behave like a man of spirit, and swallow your apprehensions. I trust that you are not going to
make a fool of yourself by any apology or retraction in any
quarter. As for its having seemed holy and just to do what you
did, that is mere bosh. A lie is a lie, and as such is often excusable. As anything else,—as a thing beautiful, holy, or
just,—it's quite inexcusable. Yours was a lie to you, and a lie
to me. It serves me, and I accept it. I suppose you understand
me. I adopt it. You don't suppose it was because I was frightened by those big black eyes of yours that I held my tongue.
As for my loving or not loving Miss Whittaker, I have no report to make to you about it. I will simply say that I intend,
if possible, to marry her."

"She'll not have you. She'll never marry a cold-blooded
rascal."

"I think she'll prefer him to a hot-blooded one. Do you
want to pick a quarrel with me? Do you want to make me lose
my temper? I shall refuse you that satisfaction. You have been
a coward, and you want to frighten some one before you go
to bed to make up for it. Strike me, and I'll strike you in self-
defence, but I'm not going to mind your talk. Have you anything to say? No? Well, then, good evening." And Major
Luttrel started away.

It was with rage that Richard was dumb. Had he been but
a cat's-paw after all? Heaven forbid! He sat irresolute for an
instant, and then turned suddenly and cantered back to
Gertrude's gate. Here he stopped again; but after a short
pause he went in over the gravel with a fast-beating heart. O,
if Luttrel were but there to see him! For a moment he fancied
he heard the sound of the Major's returning steps. If he
would only come and find him at confession! It would be so
easy to confess before him! He went along beside the house
to the front, and stopped beneath the open drawing-room
window.

"Gertrude!" he cried softly, from his saddle.

Gertrude immediately appeared. "You, Richard!" she exclaimed.

Her voice was neither harsh nor sweet; but her words and her intonation recalled vividly to Richard's mind the scene in the conservatory. He fancied them keenly expressive of disappointment. He was invaded by a mischievous conviction that she had been expecting Captain Severn, or that at the least she had mistaken his voice for the Captain's. The truth is that she had half fancied it might be,—Richard's call having been little more than a loud whisper. The young man sat looking up at her, silent.

"What do you want?" she asked. "Can I do anything for you?"

Richard was not destined to do his duty that evening. A certain infinitesimal dryness of tone on Gertrude's part was the inevitable result of her finding that that whispered summons came only from Richard. She was preoccupied. Captain Severn had told her a fortnight before, that, in case of news of a defeat, he should not await the expiration of his leave of absence to return. Such news had now come, and her inference was that her friend would immediately take his departure. She could not but suppose that he would come and bid her farewell, and what might not be the incidents, the results, of such a visit? To tell the whole truth, it was under the pressure of these reflections that, twenty minutes before, Gertrude had dismissed our two gentlemen. That this long story should be told in the dozen words with which she greeted Richard, will seem unnatural to the disinterested reader. But in those words, poor Richard, with a lover's clairvoyance, read it at a single glance. The same resentful impulse, the same sickening of the heart, that he had felt in the conservatory, took possession of him once more. To be witness of Severn's passion for Gertrude,—that he could endure. To be witness of Gertrude's passion for Severn,—against that obligation his reason rebelled.

"What is it you wish, Richard?" Gertrude repeated. "Have you forgotten anything?"

"Nothing! nothing!" cried the young man. "It's no matter!"

He gave a great pull at his bridle, and almost brought his horse back on his haunches, and then, wheeling him about on himself, he thrust in his spurs and galloped out of the gate.

On the highway he came upon Major Luttrel, who stood looking down the lane.

"I'm going to the Devil, sir!" cried Richard. "Give me your hand on it."

Luttrel held out his hand. "My poor young man," said he, "you're out of your head. I'm sorry for you. You haven't been making a fool of yourself?"

"Yes, a damnable fool of myself!"

Luttrel breathed freely. "You'd better go home and go to bed," he said. "You'll make yourself ill by going on at this rate."

"I—I'm afraid to go home," said Richard, in a broken voice. "For God's sake, come with me!"—and the wretched fellow burst into tears. "I'm too bad for any company but yours," he cried, in his sobs.

The Major winced, but he took pity. "Come, come," said he, "we'll pull through. I'll go home with you."

They rode off together. That night Richard went to bed miserably drunk; although Major Luttrel had left him at ten o'clock, adjuring him to drink no more. He awoke the next morning in a violent fever; and before evening the doctor, whom one of his hired men had brought to his bedside, had come and looked grave and pronounced him very ill.

PART III.

In country districts, where life is quiet, incidents do duty as events; and accordingly Captain Severn's sudden departure for his regiment became very rapidly known among Gertrude's neighbors. She herself heard it from her coachman, who had heard it in the village, where the Captain had been seen to take the early train. She received the news calmly enough to outward appearance, but a great tumult rose and died in her breast. He had gone without a word of farewell! Perhaps he had not had time to call upon her. But bare civility would have dictated his dropping her a line of writing,— he who must have read in her eyes the feeling which her lips

refused to utter, and who had been the object of her tender-
est courtesy. It was not often that Gertrude threw back into
her friends' teeth their acceptance of the hospitality which it
had been placed in her power to offer them; but if she now
mutely reproached Captain Severn with ingratitude, it was because he had done more than slight her material gifts: he had
slighted that constant moral force with which these gifts were
accompanied, and of which they were but the rude and vulgar token. It is but natural to expect that our dearest friends
will accredit us with our deepest feelings; and Gertrude had
constituted Edmund Severn her dearest friend. She had not,
indeed, asked his assent to this arrangement, but she had
borne it out by a subtile devotion which she felt that she had
a right to exact of him that he should repay,—repay by letting
her know that, whether it was lost on his heart or not, it was
at least not lost to his senses,—that, if he could not return it,
he could at least remember it. She had given him the flower
of her womanly tenderness, and, when his moment came, he
had turned from her without a look. Gertrude shed no tears.
It seemed to her that she had given her friend tears enough,
and that to expend her soul in weeping would be to wrong
herself. She would think no more of Edmund Severn. He
should be as little to her for the future as she was to him.

It was very easy to make this resolution: to keep it,
Gertrude found another matter. She could not think of the
war, she could not talk with her neighbors of current events,
she could not take up a newspaper, without reverting to her
absent friend. She found herself constantly harassed with the
apprehension that he had not allowed himself time really to
recover, and that a fortnight's exposure would send him back
to the hospital. At last it occurred to her that civility required
that she should make a call upon Mrs. Martin, the Captain's
sister; and a vague impression that this lady might be the de-
pository of some farewell message—perhaps of a letter—
which she was awaiting her convenience to present, led her at
once to undertake this social duty. The carriage which had
been ordered for her projected visit was at the door, when,
within a week after Severn's departure, Major Luttrel was announced. Gertrude received him in her bonnet. His first care
was to present Captain Severn's adieus, together with his re-

grets that he had not had time to discharge them in person.
As Luttrel made his speech, he watched his companion narrowly, and was considerably reassured by the unflinching
composure with which she listened to it. The turn he had
given to Severn's message had been the fruit of much mischievous cogitation. It had seemed to him that, for his purposes, the assumption of a hasty, and as it were mechanical,
allusion to Miss Whittaker, was more serviceable than the assumption of no allusion at all, which would have left a boundless void for the exercise of Gertrude's fancy. And he had
reasoned well; for although he was tempted to infer from her
calmness that his shot had fallen short of the mark, yet, in
spite of her silent and almost smiling assent to his words, it
had made but one bound to her heart. Before many minutes,
she felt that those words had done her a world of good. "He
had not had time!" Indeed, as she took to herself their full expression of perfect indifference, she felt that her hard, forced
smile was broadening into the sign of a lively gratitude to the
Major.

Major Luttrel had still another task to perform. He had
spent half an hour on the preceding day at Richard's bedside,
having ridden over to the farm, in ignorance of his illness, to
see how matters stood with him. The reader will already have
surmised that the Major was not pre-eminently a man of conscience: he will, therefore, be the less surprised and shocked
to hear that the sight of the poor young man, prostrate,
fevered, and delirious, and to all appearance rapidly growing
worse, filled him with an emotion the reverse of creditable. In
plain terms, he was very glad to find Richard a prisoner in
bed. He had been racking his brains for a scheme to keep his
young friend out of the way, and now, to his exceeding satisfaction, Nature had relieved him of this troublesome care. If
Richard was condemned to typhoid fever, which his symptoms seemed to indicate, he would not, granting his recovery,
be able to leave his room within a month. In a month, much
might be done; nay, with energy, all might be done. The
reader has been all but directly informed that the Major's
present purpose was to secure Miss Whittaker's hand. He was
poor, and he was ambitious, and he was, moreover, so well
advanced in life—being thirty-six years of age—that he had

no heart to think of building up his fortune by slow degrees. A man of good breeding, too, he had become sensible, as he approached middle age, of the many advantages of a luxurious home. He had accordingly decided that a wealthy marriage would most easily unlock the gate to prosperity. A girl of a somewhat lighter calibre than Gertrude would have been the woman—we cannot say of his heart; but, as he very generously argued, beggars can't be choosers. Gertrude was a woman with a mind of her own; but, on the whole, he was not afraid of her. He was abundantly prepared to do his duty. He had, of course, as became a man of sense, duly weighed his obstacles against his advantages; but an impartial scrutiny had found the latter heavier in the balance. The only serious difficulty in his path was the possibility that, on hearing of Richard's illness, Gertrude, with her confounded benevolence, would take a fancy to nurse him in person, and that, in the course of her ministrations, his delirious ramblings would force upon her mind the damning story of the deception practised upon Captain Severn. There was nothing for it but bravely to face this risk. As for that other fact, which many men of a feebler spirit would have deemed an invincible obstacle, Luttrel's masterly understanding had immediately converted it into the prime agent of success,—the fact, namely, that Gertrude's heart was preoccupied. Such knowledge as he possessed of the relations between Miss Whittaker and his brother officer he had gained by his unaided observations and his silent deductions. These had been logical; for, on the whole, his knowledge was accurate. It was at least what he might have termed a good working knowledge. He had calculated on a passionate reactionary impulse on Gertrude's part, consequent on Severn's simulated offence. He knew that, in a generous woman, such an impulse, if left to itself, would not go very far. But on this point it was that his policy bore. He would not leave it to itself: he would take it gently into his hands, attenuate it, prolong it, economize it, and mould it into the clew to his own good-fortune. He thus counted much upon his skill and his tact; but he likewise placed a becoming degree of reliance upon his solid personal qualities,—qualities too sober and too solid, perhaps, to be called *charms*, but thoroughly adapted to inspire confidence.

The Major was not handsome in feature; he left that to younger men and to lighter women; but his ugliness was of a masculine, aristocratic, intelligent stamp. His figure, moreover, was good enough to compensate for the absence of a straight nose and a fine mouth; and his general bearing offered a most pleasing combination of the gravity of the man of affairs and the versatility of the man of society.

In her sudden anxiety on Richard's behalf, Gertrude soon forgot her own immaterial woes. The carriage which was to have conveyed her to Mrs. Martin's was used for a more disinterested purpose. The Major, prompted by a strong faith in the salutary force of his own presence, having obtained her permission to accompany her, they set out for the farm, and soon found themselves in Richard's chamber. The young man was wrapped in a heavy sleep, from which it was judged imprudent to arouse him. Gertrude, sighing as she compared his thinly furnished room with her own elaborate apartments, drew up a mental list of essential luxuries which she would immediately send him. Not but that he had received, however, a sufficiency of homely care. The doctor was assiduous, and the old woman who nursed him was full of rough good-sense.

"He asks very often after you, Miss," she said, addressing Gertrude, but with a sly glance at the Major. "But I think you'd better not come too often. I'm afraid you'd excite him more than you'd quiet him."

"I'm afraid you would, Miss Whittaker," said the Major, who could have hugged the goodwife.

"Why should I excite him?" asked Gertrude. "I'm used to sick-rooms. I nursed my father for a year and a half."

"O, it's very well for an old woman like me, but it's no place for a fine young lady like you," said the nurse, looking at Gertrude's muslins and laces.

"I'm not so fine as to desert a friend in distress," said Gertrude. "I shall come again, and if it makes the poor fellow worse to see me, I shall stay away. I am ready to do anything that will help him to get well."

It had already occurred to her that, in his unnatural state, Richard might find her presence a source of irritation, and she was prepared to remain in the background. As she returned to her carriage, she caught herself reflecting with so much pleasure upon Major Luttrel's kindness in expending a couple of hours of his valuable time on so unprofitable an object as poor Richard, that, by way of intimating her satisfaction, she invited him to come home and dine with her.

After a short interval she paid Richard a second visit, in company with Miss Pendexter. He was a great deal worse; he lay emaciated, exhausted, and stupid. The issue was doubtful. Gertrude immediately pushed forward to M——, a larger town than her own, sought out a professional nurse, and arranged with him to relieve the old woman from the farm, who was worn out with her vigilance. For a fortnight, moreover, she received constant tidings from the young man's physician. During this fortnight, Major Luttrel was assiduous, and proportionately successful.

It may be said, to his credit, that he had by no means conducted his suit upon that narrow programme which he had drawn up at the outset. He very soon discovered that Gertrude's resentment—if resentment there was—was a substance utterly impalpable even to his most delicate tact, and he had accordingly set to work to woo her like an honest man, from day to day, from hour to hour, trusting so devoutly for success to momentary inspiration, that he felt his suit dignified by a certain flattering *faux air* of genuine passion. He occasionally reminded himself, however, that he might really be owing more to the subtle force of accidental contrast than Gertrude's life-long reserve—for it was certain she would not depart from it—would ever allow him to measure.

It was as an honest man, then, a man of impulse and of action, that Gertrude had begun to like him. She was not slow to perceive whither his operations tended; and she was almost tempted at times to tell him frankly that she would spare him the intermediate steps, and meet him at the goal without further delay. It was not that she was prepared to love him, but she would make him an obedient wife. An immense weariness had somehow come upon her, and a sudden sense of loneliness. A vague suspicion that her money had done her an incurable wrong inspired her with a profound distaste for the care of it. She felt cruelly hedged out from human sympathy by her bristling possessions. "If I had had five hundred dollars a year," she said in a frequent parenthesis, "I might have pleased him." Hating her wealth, accordingly, and chilled by her isolation, the temptation was strong upon her to give herself up to that wise, brave gentleman who seemed to have adopted such a happy medium betwixt loving her for her money and fearing her for it. Would she not always stand between men who would represent the two extremes? She would anticipate security by an alliance with Major Luttrel.

One evening, on presenting himself, Luttrel read these thoughts so clearly in her eyes, that he made up his mind to speak. But his mind was burdened with a couple of facts, of which it was necessary that he should discharge it before it could enjoy the freedom of action which the occasion required. In the first place, then, he had been to see Richard Clare, and had found him suddenly and decidedly better. It was unbecoming, however,—it was impossible,—that he should allow Gertrude to linger over this pleasant announcement.

"I tell the good news first," he said, gravely. "I have some very bad news, too, Miss Whittaker."

Gertrude sent him a rapid glance. "Some one has been killed," she said.

"Captain Severn has been shot," said the Major,—"shot by a guerilla."

Gertrude was silent. No answer seemed possible to that uncompromising fact. She sat with her head on her hand, and her elbow on the table beside her, looking at the figures on the carpet. She uttered no words of commonplace regret; but she felt as little like giving way to serious grief. She had lost nothing, and, to the best of her knowledge, *he* had lost nothing. She had an old loss to mourn,—a loss a month old, which she had mourned as she might. To give way to passion would have been but to impugn the solemnity of her past regrets. When she looked up at her companion, she was pale, but she was calm, yet with a calmness upon which a single glance of her eye directed him not inconsiderately to presume. She was aware that this glance betrayed her secret; but in view both of Severn's death and of the Major's attitude, such betrayal mattered less. Luttrel had prepared to act upon her hint, and to avert himself gently from the topic, when

Gertrude, who had dropped her eyes again, raised them with a slight shudder. "I'm cold," she said. "Will you shut that window beside you, Major? Or stay, suppose you give me my shawl from the sofa."

Luttrel brought the shawl, placed it on her shoulders, and sat down beside her. "These are cruel times," he said, with studied simplicity. "I'm sure I hardly know what's to come of it all."

"Yes, they are cruel times," said Gertrude. "They make one feel cruel. They make one doubt of all he has learnt from his pastors and masters."

"Yes, but they teach us something new also."

"I'm sure I don't know," said Gertrude, whose heart was so full of bitterness that she felt almost malignant. "They teach us how mean we are. War is an infamy, Major, though it *is* your trade. It's very well for you, who look at it professionally, and for those who go and fight; but it's a miserable business for those who stay at home, and do the thinking and the sentimentalizing. It's a miserable business for women; it makes us more spiteful than ever."

"Well, a little spite isn't a bad thing, in practice," said the Major. "War is certainly an abomination, both at home and in the field. But as wars go, Miss Whittaker, our own is a very satisfactory one. It involves something. It won't leave us as it found us. We're in the midst of a revolution, and what's a revolution but a turning upside down? It makes sad work with our habits and theories and our traditions and convictions. But, on the other hand," Luttrel pursued, warming to his task, "it leaves something untouched, which is better than these,—I mean our feelings, Miss Whittaker." And the Major paused until he had caught Gertrude's eyes, when, having engaged them with his own, he proceeded. "I think they are the stronger for the downfall of so much else, and, upon my soul, I think it's in them we ought to take refuge. Don't you think so?"

"Yes, if I understand you."

"I mean our serious feelings, you know,—not our tastes nor our passions. I don't advocate fiddling while Rome is burning. In fact it's only poor, unsatisfied devils that are tempted to fiddle. There is one feeling which is respectable and hon-

orable, and even sacred, at all times and in all places, whatever
they may be. It doesn't depend upon circumstances, but they
upon it; and with its help, I think, we are a match for any circumstances. I don't mean religion, Miss Whittaker," added
the Major, with a sober smile.

"If you don't mean religion," said Gertrude, "I suppose
you mean love. That's a very different thing."

"Yes, a very different thing; so I've always thought, and so
I'm glad to hear you say. Some people, you know, mix them
up in the most extraordinary fashion. I don't fancy myself an
especially religious man; in fact, I believe I'm rather otherwise. It's my nature. Half mankind are born so, or I suppose
the affairs of this world wouldn't move. But I believe I'm a
good lover, Miss Whittaker."

"I hope for your own sake you are, Major Luttrel."

"Thank you. Do you think now you could entertain the
idea for the sake of any one else?"

Gertrude neither dropped her eyes, nor shrugged her
shoulders, nor blushed. If anything, indeed, she turned somewhat paler than before, as she sustained her companion's
gaze, and prepared to answer him as directly as she might.

"If I loved you, Major Luttrel," she said, "I should value
the idea for my own sake."

The Major, too, blanched a little. "I put my question con-
ditionally," he answered, "and I have got, as I deserved, a conditional reply. I will speak plainly, then, Miss Whittaker. *Do*
you value the fact for your own sake? It would be plainer still
to say, Do you love me? but I confess I'm not brave enough
for that. I will say, Can you? or I will even content myself with
putting it in the conditional again, and asking you if you
could; although, after all, I hardly know what the *if* understood can reasonably refer to. I'm not such a fool as to ask of
any woman—least of all of you—to love me contingently. You
can only answer for the present, and say yes or no. I shouldn't
trouble you to say either, if I didn't conceive that I had given
you time to make up your mind. It doesn't take forever to
know James Luttrel. I'm not one of the great unfathomable
ones. We've seen each other more or less intimately for a good
many weeks; and as I'm conscious, Miss Whittaker, of having
shown you my best, I take for granted that if you don't fancy

me now, you won't a month hence, when you shall have seen my faults. Yes, Miss Whittaker, I can solemnly say," continued the Major, with genuine feeling, "I have shown you my best, as every man is in honor bound to do who approaches a woman with those predispositions with which I have approached you. I have striven hard to please you,"—and he paused. "I can only say, I hope I have succeeded."

"I should be very insensible," said Gertrude, "if all your kindness and your courtesy had been lost upon me."

"In Heaven's name, don't talk about courtesy," cried the Major.

"I am deeply conscious of your devotion, and I am very much obliged to you for urging your claims so respectfully and considerately. I speak seriously, Major Luttrel," pursued Gertrude. "There is a happy medium of expression, and you have taken it. Now it seems to me that there is a happy medium of affection, with which you might be content. Strictly, I don't love you. I question my heart, and it gives me that answer. The feeling that I have is not a feeling to work prodigies."

"May it at least work the prodigy of allowing you to be my wife?"

"I don't think I shall over-estimate its strength, if I say that it may. If you can respect a woman who gives you her hand in cold blood, you are welcome to mine."

Luttrel moved his chair and took her hand. "Beggars can't be choosers," said he, raising it to his mustache.

"O Major Luttrel, don't say that," she answered. "I give you a great deal; but I keep a little,—a little," said Gertrude, hesitating, "which I suppose I shall give to God."

"Well, I shall not be jealous," said Luttrel.

"The rest I give to you, and in return I ask a great deal."

"I shall give you all. You know I told you I'm not religious."

"No, I don't want more than I give," said Gertrude.

"But, pray," asked Luttrel, with a delicate smile, "what am I to do with the difference?"

"You had better keep it for yourself. What I want is your protection, sir, and your advice, and your care. I want you to take me away from this place, even if you have to take me down to the army. I want to see the world under the shelter of your name. I shall give you a great deal of trouble. I'm a mere mass of possessions: what I am, is nothing to what I have. But ever since I began to grow up, what I am has been the slave of what I have. I am weary of my chains, and you must help me to carry them,"—and Gertrude rose to her feet as if to inform the Major that his audience was at an end.

He still held her right hand; she gave him the other. He stood looking down at her, an image of manly humility, while from his silent breast went out a brief thanksgiving to favoring fortune.

At the pressure of his hands, Gertrude felt her bosom heave. She burst into tears. "O, you must be very kind to me!" she cried, as he put his arm about her, and she dropped her head upon his shoulder.

When once Richard's health had taken a turn for the better, it began very rapidly to improve. "Until he is quite well," Gertrude said, one day, to her accepted suitor, "I had rather he heard nothing of our engagement. He was once in love with me himself," she added, very frankly. "Did you ever suspect it? But I hope he will have got better of that sad malady, too. Nevertheless, I shall expect nothing of his good judgment until he is quite strong; and as he may hear of my new intentions from other people, I propose that, for the present, we confide them to no one."

"But if he asks me point-blank," said the Major, "what shall I answer?"

"It's not likely he'll ask you. How should he suspect anything?"

"O," said Luttrel, "Clare is one that suspects everything."

"Tell him we're not engaged, then. A woman in my position may say what she pleases."

It was agreed, however, that certain preparations for the marriage should meanwhile go forward in secret; and that the marriage itself should take place in August, as Luttrel expected to be ordered back into service in the autumn. At about this moment Gertrude was surprised to receive a short note from Richard, so feebly scrawled in pencil as to be barely legible. "Dear Gertrude," it ran, "don't come to see me just

yet. I'm not fit. You would hurt me, and *vice versa*. God bless
you! R. CLARE." Miss Whittaker explained his request, by the
supposition that a report had come to him of Major Luttrel's
late assiduities (which it was impossible should go unobserved); that, leaping at the worst, he had taken her engagement for granted; and that, under this impression, he could
not trust himself to see her. She despatched him an answer,
telling him that she would await his pleasure, and that, if
the doctor would consent to his having letters, she would
meanwhile occasionally write to him. "She will give me good
advice," thought Richard impatiently; and on this point,
accordingly, she received no account of his wishes. Expecting
to leave her house and close it on her marriage, she spent
many hours in wandering sadly over the meadow-paths and
through the woodlands which she had known from her childhood. She had thrown aside the last ensigns of filial regret,
and now walked sad and splendid in the uncompromising colors of an affianced bride. It would have seemed to a stranger
that, for a woman who had freely chosen a companion for life,
she was amazingly spiritless and sombre. As she looked at her
pale cheeks and heavy eyes in the mirror, she felt ashamed
that she had no fairer countenance to offer to her destined
lord. She had lost her single beauty, her smile; and she would
make but a ghastly figure at the altar. "I ought to wear a
calico dress and an apron," she said to herself, "and not this
glaring finery." But she continued to wear her finery, and to
lay out her money, and to perform all her old duties to the
letter. After the lapse of what she deemed a sufficient interval,
she went to see Mrs. Martin, and to listen dumbly to her nar-
ration of her brother's death, and to her simple eulogies.

Major Luttrel performed his part quite as bravely, and
much more successfully. He observed neither too many things
nor too few; he neither presumed upon his success, nor mis-
trusted it. Having on his side received no prohibition from
Richard, he resumed his visits at the farm, trusting that, with
the return of reason, his young friend might feel disposed to
renew that anomalous alliance in which, on the hapless
evening of Captain Severn's farewell, he had taken refuge
against his despair. In the long, languid hours of his early convalescence, Richard had found time to survey his position, to

summon back piece by piece the immediate past, and to frame a general scheme for the future. But more vividly than anything else, there had finally disengaged itself from his meditations a profound aversion to James Luttrel.

It was in this humor that the Major found him; and as he looked at the young man's gaunt shoulders, supported by pillows, at his face, so livid and aquiline, at his great dark eyes, luminous with triumphant life, it seemed to him that an invincible spirit had been sent from a better world to breathe confusion upon his hopes. If Richard hated the Major, the reader may guess whether the Major loved Richard. Luttrel was amazed at his first remark.

"I suppose you're engaged by this time," Richard said, calmly enough.

"Not quite," answered the Major. "There's a chance for you yet."

To this Richard made no rejoinder. Then, suddenly, "Have you had any news of Captain Severn?" he asked.

For a moment the Major was perplexed at his question. He had assumed that the news of Severn's death had come to Richard's ears, and he had been half curious, half apprehensive as to its effect. But an instant's reflection now assured him that the young man's estrangement from his neighbors had kept him hitherto and might still keep him in ignorance of the truth. Hastily, therefore, and inconsiderately, the Major determined to confirm this ignorance. "No," said he; "I've had no news. Severn and I are not on such terms as to correspond."

The next time Luttrel came to the farm, he found the master sitting up in a great, cushioned, chintz-covered armchair which Gertrude had sent him the day before out of her own dressing-room.

"Are you engaged yet?" asked Richard.

There was a strain as if of defiance in his tone. The Major was irritated. "Yes," said he, "we *are* engaged now."

The young man's face betrayed no emotion.

"Are you reconciled to it?" asked Luttrel.

"Yes, practically I am."

"What do you mean by practically? Explain yourself."

"A man in my state can't explain himself. I mean that, however I feel about it, I shall accept Gertrude's marriage."

"You're a wise man, my boy," said the Major, kindly.

"I'm growing wise. I feel like Solomon on his throne in this chair. But I confess, sir, I don't see how she could have you."

"Well, there's no accounting for tastes," said the Major, good-humoredly.

"Ah, if it's been a matter of taste with her," said Richard, "I have nothing to say."

They came to no more express understanding than this with regard to the future. Richard continued to grow stronger daily, and to defer the renewal of his intercourse with Gertrude. A month before, he would have resented as a bitter insult the intimation that he would ever be so resigned to lose her as he now found himself. He would not see her for two reasons: first, because he felt that it would be—or that at least in reason it ought to be—a painful experience to look upon his old mistress with a coldly critical eye; and secondly, because, justify to himself as he would his new-born indifference, he could not entirely cast away the suspicion that it was a last remnant of disease, and that, when he stood on his legs again in the presence of those exuberant landscapes with which he had long since established a sort of sensuous communion, he would feel, as with a great tumultuous rush, the return of his impetuous manhood and of his old capacity. When he had smoked a pipe in the outer sunshine, when he had settled himself once more to the long elastic bound of his mare, then he would see Gertrude. The reason of the change which had come upon him was that she had disappointed him,—she whose magnanimity it had once seemed that his fancy was impotent to measure. She had accepted Major Luttrel, a man whom he despised; she had so mutilated her magnificent heart as to match it with his. The validity of his dislike to the Major, Richard did not trouble himself to examine. He accepted it as an unerring instinct; and, indeed, he might have asked himself, had he not sufficient proof? Moreover he labored under the sense of a gratuitous wrong. He had suffered an immense torment of remorse to drive him into brutishness, and thence to the very gate of death, for an offence which he had deemed mortal, and which was after all but a phantasm of his impassioned conscience. What a fool he had been! a fool for his nervous fears, and a fool for his penitence. Marriage with Major Luttrel,—such was the end of Gertrude's fancied anguish. Such, too, we hardly need add, was the end of that idea of reparation which had been so formidable to Luttrel. Richard had been generous; he would now be just.

Far from impeding his recovery, these reflections hastened it. One morning in the beginning of August, Gertrude received notice of Richard's presence. It was a still, sultry day, and Miss Whittaker, her habitual pallor deepened by the oppressive heat, was sitting alone in a white morning-dress, languidly fanning aside at once the droning flies and her equally importunate thoughts. She found Richard standing in the middle of the drawing-room, booted and spurred.

"Well, Richard," she exclaimed, with some feeling, "you're at last willing to see me!"

As his eyes fell upon her, he started and stood almost paralyzed, heeding neither her words nor her extended hand. It was not Gertrude he saw, but her ghost.

"In Heaven's name what has happened to you?" he cried. "Have *you* been ill?"

Gertrude tried to smile in feigned surprise at his surprise; but her muscles relaxed. Richard's words and looks reflected more vividly than any mirror the dejection of her person; and this, the misery of her soul. She felt herself growing faint. She staggered back to a sofa and sank down.

Then Richard felt as if the room were revolving about him, and as if his throat were choked with imprecations,—as if his old erratic passion had again taken possession of him, like a mingled legion of devils and angels. It was through pity that his love returned. He went forward and dropped on his knees at Gertrude's feet. "Speak to me!" he cried, seizing her hands. "Are you unhappy? Is your heart broken? O Gertrude! what have you come to?"

Gertrude drew her hands from his grasp and rose to her feet. "Get up, Richard," she said. "Don't talk so wildly. I'm not well. I'm very glad to see you. *You* look well."

"I've got my strength again,—and meanwhile you've been failing. You're unhappy, you're wretched! Don't say you're not, Gertrude: it's as plain as day. You're breaking your heart."

"The same old Richard!" said Gertrude, trying to smile again.

"Would that you were the same old Gertrude! Don't try to smile; you can't!"

"I *shall*!" said Gertrude, desperately. "I'm going to be married, you know."

"Yes, I know. I don't congratulate you."

"I have not counted upon that honor, Richard. I shall have to do without it."

"You'll have to do without a great many things!" cried Richard, horrified by what seemed to him her blind self-immolation.

"I have all I ask," said Gertrude.

"You haven't all *I* ask then! You haven't all your friends ask."

"My friends are very kind, but I marry to suit myself."

"You've not suited yourself!" retorted the young man. "You've suited—God knows what!—your pride, your despair, your resentment." As he looked at her, the secret history of her weakness seemed to become plain to him, and he felt a mighty rage against the man who had taken a base advantage of it. "Gertrude!" he cried, "I entreat you to go back. It's not for my sake,—I'll give you up,—I'll go a thousand miles away, and never look at you again. It's for your own. In the name of your happiness, break with that man! Don't fling yourself away. Buy him off, if you consider yourself bound. Give him your money. That's all he wants."

As Gertrude listened, the blood came back to her face, and two flames into her eyes. She looked at Richard from head to foot. "You are not weak," she said, "you are in your senses, you are well and strong; you shall tell me what you mean. You insult the best friend I have. Explain yourself! you insinuate foul things,—speak them out!" Her eyes glanced toward the door, and Richard's followed them. Major Luttrel stood on the threshold.

"Come in, sir!" cried Richard. "Gertrude swears she'll believe no harm of you. Come and tell her that she's wrong! How can you keep on harassing a woman whom you've brought to this state? Think of what she was three months ago, and look at her now!"

Luttrel received this broadside without flinching. He had overheard Richard's voice from the entry, and he had steeled his heart for the encounter. He assumed the air of having been so amazed by the young man's first words as only to have heard his last; and he glanced at Gertrude mechanically as if to comply with them. "What's the matter?" he asked, going over to her, and taking her hand; "are you ill?" Gertrude let him have her hand, but she forbore to meet his eyes.

"Ill! of course she's ill!" cried Richard, passionately. "She's dying,—she's consuming herself! I know I seem to be playing an odious part here, Gertrude, but, upon my soul, I can't help it. I look like a betrayer, an informer, a sneak, but I don't feel like one! Still, I'll leave you, if you say so."

"Shall he go, Gertrude?" asked Luttrel, without looking at Richard.

"No. Let him stay and explain himself. He has accused you,—let him prove his case."

"I know what he is going to say," said Luttrel. "It will place me in a bad light. Do you still wish to hear it?"

Gertrude drew her hand hastily out of Luttrel's. "Speak, Richard!" she cried, with a passionate gesture.

"I will speak," said Richard. "I've done you a dreadful wrong, Gertrude. How great a wrong, I never knew until I saw you to-day so miserably altered. When I heard that you were to be married, I fancied that it was no wrong, and that my remorse had been wasted. But I understand it now; and *he* understands it, too. You once told me that you had ceased to love Captain Severn. It wasn't true. You never ceased to love him. You love him at this moment. If he were to get another wound in the next battle, how would you feel? How would you bear it?" And Richard paused for an instant with the force of his interrogation.

"For God's sake," cried Gertrude, "respect the dead!"

"The dead! Is he dead?"

Gertrude covered her face with her hands.

"You beast!" cried Luttrel.

Richard turned upon him savagely. "Shut your infernal mouth!" he roared. "You told me he was alive and well!"

Gertrude made a movement of speechless distress.

"You would have it, my dear," said Luttrel, with a little bow.

Richard had turned pale, and began to tremble. "Excuse me, Gertrude," he said, hoarsely, "I've been deceived. Poor, unhappy woman! Gertrude," he continued, going nearer to her, and speaking in a whisper, "*I* killed him."

Gertrude fell back from him, as he approached her, with a look of unutterable horror. "I and *he*," said Richard, pointing at Luttrel.

Gertrude's eyes followed the direction of his gesture, and transferred their scorching disgust to her suitor. This was too much for Luttrel's courage. "You idiot!" she shouted at Richard, "speak out!"

"He loved you, though you believed he didn't," said Richard. "I saw it the first time I looked at him. To every one but you it was as plain as day. Luttrel saw it too. But he was too modest, and he never fancied you cared for him. The night before he went back to the army, he came to bid you good by. If he had seen you, it would have been better for every one. You remember that evening, of course. We met him, Luttrel and I. He was all on fire,—he meant to speak. I knew it, you knew it, Luttrel: it was in his fingers' ends. I intercepted him. I turned him off,—I lied to him and told him you were away. I was a coward, and I did neither more nor less than that. I knew you were waiting for him. It was stronger than my will,—I believe I should do it again. Fate was against him, and he went off. I came back to tell you, but my damnable jealousy strangled me. I went home and drank myself into a fever. I've done you a wrong that I can never repair. I'd go hang myself if I thought it would help you." Richard spoke slowly, softly, and explicitly, as if irresistible Justice in person had her hand upon his neck, and were forcing him down upon his knees. In the presence of Gertrude's dismay nothing seemed possible but perfect self-conviction. In Luttrel's attitude, as he stood with his head erect, his arms folded, and his cold gray eye fixed upon the distance, it struck him that there was something atrociously insolent; not insolent to him,—for that he cared little enough,—but insolent to Gertrude and to the dreadful solemnity of the hour. Richard

sent the Major a look of the most aggressive contempt. "As
for Major Luttrel," he said, "*he* was but a passive spectator.
No, Gertrude, by Heaven!" he burst out; "he was worse than
I! I loved you, and he didn't!"

"Our friend is correct in his facts, Gertrude," said Luttrel,
quietly. "He is incorrect in his opinions. I *was* a passive spectator of his deception. He appeared to enjoy a certain authority with regard to your wishes,—the source of which I
respected both of you sufficiently never to question,—and I
accepted the act which he has described as an exercise of it.
You will remember that you had sent us away on the ground
that you were in no humor for company. To deny you, therefore, to another visitor, seemed to me rather officious, but
still pardonable. You will consider that I was wholly ignorant
of your relations to that visitor; that whatever you may have
done for others, Gertrude, to me you never vouchsafed a
word of information on the subject, and that Mr. Clare's
words are a revelation to me. But I am bound to believe
nothing that he says. I am bound to believe that I have injured you only when I hear it from your own lips."

Richard made a movement as if to break out upon the
Major; but Gertrude, who had been standing motionless with
her eyes upon the ground, quickly raised them, and gave him
a look of imperious prohibition. She had listened, and she had
chosen. She turned to Luttrel. "Major Luttrel," she said,
"you *have* been an accessory in what has been for me a serious grief. It is my duty to tell you so. I mean, of course, a
profoundly unwilling accessory. I pity you more than I can tell
you. I think your position more pitiable than mine. It is true
that I never made a confidant of you. I never made one of
Richard. I had a secret, and he surprised it. You were less fortunate." It might have seemed to a thoroughly dispassionate
observer that in these last four words there was an infinitesimal touch of tragic irony. Gertrude paused a moment while
Luttrel eyed her intently, and Richard, from a somewhat tardy
instinct of delicacy, walked over to the bow-window. "This is
the most painful moment of my life," she resumed. "I hardly
know where my duty lies. The only thing that is plain to me
is, that I must ask you to release me from my engagement. I
ask it most humbly, Major Luttrel," Gertrude continued, with

warmth in her words, and a chilling coldness in her voice,—a coldness which it sickened her to feel there, but which she was unable to dispel. "I can't expect that you should give me up easily; I know that it's a great deal to ask, and"—she forced the chosen words out of her mouth—"I should thank you more than I can say if you would put some condition upon my release. You have done honorably by me, and I repay you with ingratitude. But I can't marry you." Her voice began to melt. "I have been false from the beginning. I have no heart to give you. I should make you a despicable wife."

The Major, too, had listened and chosen, and in this trying conjuncture he set the seal to his character as an accomplished man. He saw that Gertrude's movement was final, and he determined to respect the inscrutable mystery of her heart. He read in the glance of her eye and the tone of her voice that the perfect dignity had fallen from his character,—that his integrity had lost its bloom; but he also read her firm resolve never to admit this fact to her own mind, nor to declare it to the world, and he honored her forbearance. His hopes, his ambitions, his visions, lay before him like a colossal heap of broken glass; but he would be as graceful as she was. She had divined him; but she had spared him. The Major was inspired.

"You have at least spoken to the point," he said. "You leave no room for doubt or for hope. With the little light I have, I can't say I understand your feelings, but I yield to them religiously. I believe so thoroughly that you suffer from the thought of what you ask of me, that I will not increase your suffering by assuring you of my own. I care for nothing but your happiness. You have lost it, and I give you mine to replace it. And although it's a simple thing to say," he added, "I must say simply that I thank you for your implicit faith in my integrity,"—and he held out his hand. As she gave him hers, Gertrude felt utterly in the wrong; and she looked into his eyes with an expression so humble, so appealing, so grateful, that, after all, his exit may be called triumphant.

When he had gone, Richard turned from the window with an enormous sense of relief. He had heard Gertrude's speech, and he knew that perfect justice had not been done; but still there was enough to be thankful for. Yet now that his duty was accomplished, he was conscious of a sudden lassitude.

Mechanically he looked at Gertrude, and almost mechanically he came towards her. She, on her side, looking at him as he walked slowly down the long room, his face indistinct against the deadened light of the white-draped windows behind him, marked the expression of his figure with another pang. "He has rescued me," she said to herself; "but his passion has perished in the tumult. Richard," she said aloud, uttering the first words of vague kindness that came into her mind, "I forgive you."

Richard stopped. The idea had lost its charm. "You're very kind," he said, wearily. "You're far too kind. How do you know you forgive me? Wait and see."

Gertrude looked at him as she had never looked before; but he saw nothing of it. He saw a sad, plain girl in a white dress, nervously handling her fan. He was thinking of himself. If he had been thinking of her, he would have read in her lingering, upward gaze, that he had won her; and if, so reading, he had opened his arms, Gertrude would have come to them. We trust the reader is not shocked. She neither hated him nor despised him, as she ought doubtless in consistency to have done. She felt that he was abundantly a man, and she loved him. Richard on his side felt humbly the same truth, and he began to respect himself. The past had closed abruptly behind him, and tardy Gertrude had been shut in. The future was dimly shaping itself without her image. So he did not open his arms.

"Good by," he said, holding out his hand. "I may not see you again for a long time."

Gertrude felt as if the world were deserting her. "Are you going away?" she asked, tremulously.

"I mean to sell out and pay my debts, and go to the war."

She gave him her hand, and he silently shook it. There was no contending with the war, and she gave him up.

With their separation our story properly ends, and to say more would be to begin a new story. It is perhaps our duty, however, expressly to add, that Major Luttrel, in obedience to a logic of his own, abstained from revenge; and that, if time has not avenged him, it has at least rewarded him. General Luttrel, who lost an arm before the war was over, recently married Miss Van Winkel of Philadelphia, and seventy

thousand a year. Richard engaged in the defence of his country, on a captain's commission, obtained with some difficulty.
He saw a great deal of fighting, but he has no scars to show.
The return of peace found him in his native place, without a
home, and without resources. One of his first acts was to call
dutifully and respectfully upon Miss Whittaker, whose circle
of acquaintance had apparently become very much enlarged,
and now included a vast number of gentlemen. Gertrude's
manner was kindness itself, but a more studied kindness than
before. She had lost much of her youth and her simplicity.
Richard wondered whether she had pledged herself to spinsterhood, but of course he didn't ask her. She inquired very
particularly into his material prospects and intentions, and offered most urgently to lend him money, which he declined to
borrow. When he left her, he took a long walk through her
place and beside the river, and, wandering back to the days
when he had yearned for her love, assured himself that no
woman would ever again be to him what she had been.
During his stay in this neighborhood he found himself impelled to a species of submission to one of the old agricultural
magnates whom he had insulted in his unregenerate days, and
through whom he was glad to obtain some momentary employment. But his present position is very distasteful to him,
and he is eager to try his fortunes in the West. As yet, however, he has lacked even the means to get as far as St. Louis.
He drinks no more than is good for him. To speak of
Gertrude's impressions of Richard would lead us quite too
far. Shortly after his return, she broke up her household, and
came to the bold resolution (bold, that is, for a woman
young, unmarried, and ignorant of manners in her own country) to spend some time in Europe. At our last accounts she
was living in the ancient city of Florence. Her great wealth, of
which she was wont to complain that it excluded her from
human sympathy, now affords her a most efficient protection.
She passes among her fellow-countrymen abroad for a very
independent, but a very happy woman; although, as she is by
this time twenty-seven years of age, a little romance is occasionally invoked to account for her continued celibacy.

The Story of a Masterpiece

N<small>O LONGER AGO</small> than last Summer, during a six weeks' stay at Newport, John Lennox became engaged to Miss Marian Everett of New York. Mr. Lennox was a widower, of large estate, and without children. He was thirty-five years old, of a sufficiently distinguished appearance, of excellent manners, of an unusual share of sound information, of irreproachable habits and of a temper which was understood to have suffered a trying and salutary probation during the short term of his wedded life. Miss Everett was, therefore, all things considered, believed to be making a very good match and to be having by no means the worst of the bargain.

And yet Miss Everett, too, was a very marriageable young lady—the pretty Miss Everett, as she was called, to distinguish her from certain plain cousins, with whom, owing to her having no mother and no sisters, she was constrained, for decency's sake, to spend a great deal of her time—rather to her own satisfaction, it may be conjectured, than to that of these excellent young women.

Marian Everett was penniless, indeed; but she was richly endowed with all the gifts which make a woman charming. She was, without dispute, the most charming girl in the circle in which she lived and moved. Even certain of her elders, women of a larger experience, of a heavier calibre, as it were, and, thanks to their being married ladies, of greater freedom of action, were practically not so charming as she. And yet, in her emulation of the social graces of these, her more fully licensed sisters, Miss Everett was quite guiltless of any aberration from the strict line of maidenly dignity. She professed an almost religious devotion to good taste, and she looked with horror upon the boisterous graces of many of her companions. Beside being the most entertaining girl in New York, she was, therefore, also the most irreproachable. Her beauty was, perhaps, contestable, but it was certainly uncontested. She was the least bit below the middle height, and her person was marked by a great fulness and roundness of outline; and yet, in spite of this comely ponderosity, her movements were perfectly light and elastic. In complexion, she was a genuine blonde—a warm blond; with a midsummer bloom upon her cheek, and the light of a midsummer sun wrought into her auburn hair. Her features were not cast upon a classical model, but their expression was in the highest degree pleasing. Her forehead was low and broad, her nose small, and her mouth—well, by the envious her mouth was called *enormous*. It is certain that it had an immense capacity for smiles, and that when she opened it to sing (which she did with infinite sweetness) it emitted a copious flood of sound. Her face was, perhaps, a trifle too circular, and her shoulders a trifle too high; but, as I say, the general effect left nothing to be desired. I might point out a dozen discords in the character of her face and figure, and yet utterly fail to invalidate the impression they produced. There is something essentially uncivil, and, indeed, unphilosophical, in the attempt to verify or to disprove a woman's beauty in detail, and a man gets no more than he deserves when he finds that, in strictness, the aggregation of the different features fails to make up the total. Stand off, gentlemen, and let *her* make the addition. Beside her beauty, Miss Everett shone by her good nature and her lively perceptions. She neither made harsh speeches nor resented them; and, on the other hand, she keenly enjoyed intellectual cleverness, and even cultivated it. Her great merit was that she made no claims or pretensions. Just as there was nothing artificial in her beauty, so there was nothing pedantic in her acuteness and nothing sentimental in her amiability. The one was all freshness and the others all *bonhommie*.

John Lennox saw her, then loved her and offered her his hand. In accepting it Miss Everett acquired, in the world's eye, the one advantage which she lacked—a complete stability and regularity of position. Her friends took no small satisfaction in contrasting her brilliant and comfortable future with her somewhat precarious past. Lennox, nevertheless, was congratulated on the right hand and on the left; but none too often for his faith. That of Miss Everett was not put to so severe a test, although she was frequently reminded by acquaintances of a moralizing turn that she had reason to be very thankful for Mr. Lennox's choice. To these assurances Marian listened with a look of patient humility, which was extremely becoming. It was as if for *his* sake she could consent even to be bored.

Within a fortnight after their engagement had been made known, both parties returned to New York. Lennox lived in a house of his own, which he now busied himself with repairing and refurnishing; for the wedding had been fixed for the end of October. Miss Everett lived in lodgings with her father, a decayed old gentleman, who rubbed his idle hands from morning till night over the prospect of his daughter's marriage.

John Lennox, habitually a man of numerous resources, fond of reading, fond of music, fond of society and not averse to politics, passed the first weeks of the Autumn in a restless, fidgetty manner. When a man approaches middle age he finds it difficult to wear gracefully the distinction of being engaged. He finds it difficult to discharge with becoming alacrity the various *petits soins* incidental to the position. There was a certain pathetic gravity, to those who knew him well, in Lennox's attentions. One-third of his time he spent in foraging in Broadway, whence he returned half-a-dozen times a week, laden with trinkets and gimcracks, which he always finished by thinking it puerile and brutal to offer his mistress. Another third he passed in Mr. Everett's drawing-room, during which period Marian was denied to visitors. The rest of the time he spent, as he told a friend, God knows how. This was stronger language than his friend expected to hear, for Lennox was neither a man of precipitate utterance, nor, in his friend's belief, of a strongly passionate nature. But it was evident that he was very much in love; or at least very much off his balance.

"When I'm with her it's all very well," he pursued, "but when I'm away from her I feel as if I were thrust out of the ranks of the living."

"Well, you must be patient," said his friend; "you're destined to live hard, yet."

Lennox was silent, and his face remained rather more sombre than the other liked to see it.

"I hope there's no particular difficulty," the latter resumed; hoping to induce him to relieve himself of whatever weighed upon his consciousness.

"I'm afraid sometimes I—afraid sometimes she doesn't really love me."

"Well, a little doubt does no harm. It's better than to be too sure of it, and to sink into fatuity. Only be sure you love her."

"Yes," said Lennox, solemnly, "that's the great point."

One morning, unable to fix his attention on books and papers, he bethought himself of an expedient for passing an hour.

He had made, at Newport, the acquaintance of a young artist named Gilbert, for whose talent and conversation he had conceived a strong relish. The painter, on leaving Newport, was to go to the Adirondacks, and to be back in New York on the first of October, after which time he begged his friend to come and see him.

It occurred to Lennox on the morning I speak of that Gilbert must already have returned to town, and would be looking for his visit. So he forthwith repaired to his studio.

Gilbert's card was on the door, but, on entering the room, Lennox found it occupied by a stranger—a young man in painter's garb, at work before a large panel. He learned from this gentleman that he was a temporary sharer of Mr. Gilbert's studio, and that the latter had stepped out for a few moments. Lennox accordingly prepared to await his return. He entered into conversation with the young man, and, finding him very intelligent, as well as, apparently, a great friend of Gilbert, he looked at him with some interest. He was of something less than thirty, tall and robust, with a strong, joyous, sensitive face, and a thick auburn beard. Lennox was struck with his face, which seemed both to express a great deal of human sagacity and to indicate the essential temperament of a painter.

"A man with that face," he said to himself, "does work at least worth looking at."

He accordingly asked his companion if he might come and look at his picture. The latter readily assented, and Lennox placed himself before the canvas.

It bore a representation of a half-length female figure, in a costume and with an expression so ambiguous that Lennox remained uncertain whether it was a portrait or a work of fancy: a fair-haired young woman, clad in a rich mediæval dress, and looking like a countess of the Renaissance. Her figure was relieved against a sombre tapestry, her arms loosely folded, her head erect and her eyes on the spectator, toward whom she seemed to move—*"Dans un flôt de velours traînant ses petits pieds."*

As Lennox inspected her face it seemed to reveal a hidden likeness to a face he well knew—the face of Marian Everett. He was of course anxious to know whether the likeness was accidental or designed.

"I take this to be a portrait," he said to the artist, "a portrait 'in character.' "

"No," said the latter, "it's a mere composition: a little from here and a little from there. The picture has been hanging about me for the last two or three years, as a sort of receptacle of waste ideas. It has been the victim of innumerable theories and experiments. But it seems to have survived them all. I suppose it possesses a certain amount of vitality."

"Do you call it anything?"

"I called it originally after something I'd read—Browning's poem, 'My Last Duchess.' Do you know it?"

"Perfectly."

"I am ignorant of whether it's an attempt to embody the poet's impression of a portrait actually existing. But why should I care? This is simply an attempt to embody my own private impression of the poem, which has always had a strong hold on my fancy. I don't know whether it agrees with your own impression and that of most readers. But I don't insist upon the name. The possessor of the picture is free to baptize it afresh."

The longer Lennox looked at the picture the more he liked it, and the deeper seemed to be the correspondence between the lady's expression and that with which he had invested the heroine of Browning's lines. The less accidental, too, seemed that element which Marian's face and the face on the canvas possessed in common. He thought of the great poet's noble lyric and of its exquisite significance, and of the physiognomy of the woman he loved having been chosen as the fittest exponent of that significance.

He turned away his head; his eyes filled with tears. "If I

were possessor of the picture," he said, finally, answering the artist's last words, "I should feel tempted to call it by the name of a person of whom it very much reminds me."

"Ah?" said Baxter; and then, after a pause—"a person in New York?"

It had happened, a week before, that, at her lover's request, Miss Everett had gone in his company to a photographer's and had been photographed in a dozen different attitudes. The proofs of these photographs had been sent home for Marian to choose from. She had made a choice of half a dozen—or rather Lennox had made it—and the latter had put them in his pocket, with the intention of stopping at the establishment and giving his orders. He now took out his pocket-book and showed the painter one of the cards.

"I find a great resemblance," said he, "between your Duchess and that young lady."

The artist looked at the photograph. "If I am not mistaken," he said, after a pause, "the young lady is Miss Everett."

Lennox nodded assent.

His companion remained silent a few moments, examining the photograph with considerable interest; but, as Lennox observed, without comparing it with his picture.

"My Duchess very probably bears a certain resemblance to Miss Everett, but a not exactly intentional one," he said, at last. "The picture was begun before I ever saw Miss Everett. Miss Everett, as you see—or as you know—has a very charming face, and, during the few weeks in which I saw her, I continued to work upon it. You know how a painter works—how artists of all kinds work: they claim their property wherever they find it. What I found to my purpose in Miss Everett's appearance I didn't hesitate to adopt; especially as I had been feeling about in the dark for a type of countenance which her face effectually realized. The Duchess was an Italian, I take it; and I had made up my mind that she was to be a blonde. Now, there is a decidedly southern depth and warmth of tone in Miss Everett's complexion, as well as that breadth and thickness of feature which is common in Italian women. You see the resemblance is much more a matter of type than of expression. Nevertheless, I'm sorry if the copy betrays the original."

"I doubt," said Lennox, "whether it would betray it to any other perception than mine. I have the honor," he added, after a pause, "to be engaged to Miss Everett. You will, therefore, excuse me if I ask whether you mean to sell your picture?"

"It's already sold—to a lady," rejoined the artist, with a smile; "a maiden lady, who is a great admirer of Browning."

At this moment Gilbert returned. The two friends exchanged greetings, and their companion withdrew to a neighboring studio. After they had talked a while of what had happened to each since they parted, Lennox spoke of the painter of the Duchess and of his remarkable talent, expressing surprise that he shouldn't have heard of him before, and that Gilbert should never have spoken of him.

"His name is Baxter—Stephen Baxter," said Gilbert, "and until his return from Europe, a fortnight ago, I knew little more about him than you. He's a case of improvement. I met him in Paris in '62; at that time he was doing absolutely nothing. He has learned what you see in the interval. On arriving in New York he found it impossible to get a studio big enough to hold him. As, with my little sketches, I need only occupy one corner of mine, I offered him the use of the other three, until he should be able to bestow himself to his satisfaction. When he began to unpack his canvases I found I had been entertaining an angel unawares."

Gilbert then proceeded to uncover, for Lennox's inspection, several of Baxter's portraits, both of men and women. Each of these works confirmed Lennox's impression of the painter's power. He returned to the picture on the easel. Marian Everett reappeared at his silent call, and looked out of the eyes with a most penetrating tenderness and melancholy.

"He may say what he pleases," thought Lennox, "the resemblance *is*, in some degree, also a matter of expression. Gilbert," he added, wishing to measure the force of the likeness, "whom does it remind you of?"

"I know," said Gilbert, "of whom it reminds *you*."

"And do you see it yourself?"

"They are both handsome, and both have auburn hair. That's all I can see."

Lennox was somewhat relieved. It was not without a

feeling of discomfort—a feeling by no means inconsistent with his first moment of pride and satisfaction—that he thought of Marian's peculiar and individual charms having been subjected to the keen appreciation of another than himself. He was glad to be able to conclude that the painter had merely been struck with what was most superficial in her appearance, and that his own imagination supplied the rest. It occurred to him, as he walked home, that it would be a not unbecoming tribute to the young girl's loveliness on his own part, to cause her portrait to be painted by this clever young man. Their engagement had as yet been an affair of pure sentiment, and he had taken an almost fastidious care not to give himself the vulgar appearance of a mere purveyor of luxuries and pleasures. Practically, he had been as yet for his future wife a poor man—or rather a man, pure and simple, and not a millionaire. He had ridden with her, he had sent her flowers, and he had gone with her to the opera. But he had neither sent her sugar-plums, nor made bets with her, nor made her presents of jewelry. Miss Everett's female friends had remarked that he hadn't as yet given her the least little betrothal ring, either of pearls or of diamonds. Marian, however, was quite content. She was, by nature, a great artist in the *mise en scène* of emotions, and she felt instinctively that this classical moderation was but the converse presentment of an immense matrimonial abundance. In his attempt to make it impossible that his relations with Miss Everett should be tinged in any degree with the accidental condition of the fortunes of either party, Lennox had thoroughly understood his own instinct. He knew that he should some day feel a strong and irresistible impulse to offer his mistress some visible and artistic token of his affection, and that his gift would convey a greater satisfaction from being sole of its kind. It seemed to him now that his chance had come. What gift could be more delicate than the gift of an opportunity to contribute by her patience and good-will to her husband's possession of a perfect likeness of her face?

On that same evening Lennox dined with his future father-in-law, as it was his habit to do once a week.

"Marian," he said, in the course of the dinner, "I saw, this morning, an old friend of yours."

"Ah," said Marian, "who was that?"

"Mr. Baxter, the painter."

Marian changed color—ever so little; no more, indeed, than was natural to an honest surprise.

Her surprise, however, could not have been great, inasmuch as she now said that she had seen his return to America mentioned in a newspaper, and as she knew that Lennox frequented the society of artists. "He was well, I hope," she added, "and prosperous."

"Where did you know this gentleman, my dear?" asked Mr. Everett.

"I knew him in Europe two years ago—first in the Summer in Switzerland, and afterward in Paris. He is a sort of cousin of Mrs. Denbigh." Mrs. Denbigh was a lady in whose company Marian had recently spent a year in Europe—a widow, rich, childless, an invalid, and an old friend of her mother. "Is he always painting?"

"Apparently, and extremely well. He has two or three as good portraits there as one may reasonably expect to see. And he has, moreover, a certain picture which reminded me of you."

"His 'Last Duchess'?" asked Marian, with some curiosity. "I should like to see it. If you think it's like me, John, you ought to buy it up."

"I wanted to buy it, but it's sold. You know it then?"

"Yes, through Mr. Baxter himself. I saw it in its rudimentary state, when it looked like nothing that I should care to look like. I shocked Mrs. Denbigh very much by telling him I was glad it was his 'last.' The picture, indeed, led to our acquaintance."

"And not *vice versa*," said Mr. Everett, facetiously.

"How *vice versa*?" asked Marian, innocently. "I met Mr. Baxter for the first time at a party in Rome."

"I thought you said you met him in Switzerland," said Lennox.

"No, in Rome. It was only two days before we left. He was introduced to me without knowing I was with Mrs. Denbigh, and indeed without knowing that she had been in the city. He was very shy of Americans. The first thing he said to me was that I looked very much like a picture he had been painting."

"That you realized his ideal, etc."

"Exactly, but not at all in that sentimental tone. I took him to Mrs. Denbigh; they found they were sixth cousins by marriage; he came to see us the next day, and insisted upon our going to his studio. It was a miserable place. I believe he was very poor. At least Mrs. Denbigh offered him some money, and he frankly accepted it. She attempted to spare his sensibilities by telling him that, if he liked, he could paint her a picture in return. He said he would if he had time. Later, he came up into Switzerland, and the following Winter we met him in Paris."

If Lennox had had any mistrust of Miss Everett's relations with the painter, the manner in which she told her little story would have effectually blighted it. He forthwith proposed that, in consideration not only of the young man's great talent, but of his actual knowledge of her face, he should be invited to paint her portrait.

Marian assented without reluctance and without alacrity, and Lennox laid his proposition before the artist. The latter requested a day or two to consider, and then replied (by note) that he would be happy to undertake the task.

Miss Everett expected that, in view of the projected renewal of their old acquaintance, Stephen Baxter would call upon her, under the auspices of her lover. He called in effect, alone, but Marian was not at home, and he failed to repeat the visit. The day for the first sitting was therefore appointed through Lennox. The artist had not as yet obtained a studio of his own, and the latter cordially offered him the momentary use of a spacious and well-lighted apartment in his house, which had been intended as a billiard room, but was not yet fitted up. Lennox expressed no wishes with regard to the portrait, being content to leave the choice of position and costume to the parties immediately interested. He found the painter perfectly well acquainted with Marian's "points," and he had an implicit confidence in her own good taste.

Miss Everett arrived on the morning appointed, under her father's escort, Mr. Everett, who prided himself largely upon doing things in proper form, having caused himself to be introduced beforehand to the painter. Between the latter and Marian there was a brief exchange of civilities, after which they addressed themselves to business. Miss Everett professed the most cheerful deference to Baxter's wishes and fancies, at the same time that she made no secret of possessing a number of strong convictions as to what should be attempted and what should be avoided.

It was no surprise to the young man to find her convictions sound and her wishes thoroughly sympathetic. He found himself called upon to make no compromise with stubborn and unnatural prejudices, nor to sacrifice his best intentions to a short-sighted vanity.

Whether Miss Everett was vain or not need not here be declared. She had at least the wit to perceive that the interests of an enlightened sagacity would best be served by a painting which should be good from the painter's point of view, inasmuch as these are the painting's chief end. I may add, moreover, to her very great credit, that she thoroughly understood how great an artistic merit should properly attach to a picture executed at the behest of a passion, in order that it should be anything more than a mockery—a parody—of the duration of that passion; and that she knew instinctively that there is nothing so chilling to an artist's heat as the interference of illogical self-interest, either on his own behalf or that of another.

Baxter worked firmly and rapidly, and at the end of a couple of hours he felt that he had begun his picture. Mr. Everett, as he sat by, threatened to be a bore; laboring apparently under the impression that it was his duty to beguile the session with cheap aesthetic small talk. But Marian good-humoredly took the painter's share of the dialogue, and he was not diverted from his work.

The next sitting was fixed for the morrow. Marian wore the dress which she had agreed upon with the painter, and in which, as in her position, the "picturesque" element had been religiously suppressed. She read in Baxter's eyes that she looked supremely beautiful, and she saw that his fingers tingled to attack his subject. But she caused Lennox to be sent for, under the pretense of obtaining his adhesion to her dress. It was black, and he might object to black. He came, and she read in his kindly eyes an augmented edition of the assurance conveyed in Baxter's. He was enthusiastic for the black dress, which, in truth, seemed only to confirm and enrich, like a grave maternal protest, the young girl's look of undiminished youth.

"I expect you," he said to Baxter, "to make a masterpiece."

"Never fear," said the painter, tapping his forehead. "It's made."

On this second occasion, Mr. Everett, exhausted by the intellectual strain of the preceding day, and encouraged by his luxurious chair, sank into a tranquil sleep. His companions remained for some time, listening to his regular breathing; Marian with her eyes patiently fixed on the opposite wall, and the young man with his glance mechanically travelling between his figure and the canvas. At last he fell back several paces to survey his work. Marian moved her eyes, and they met his own.

"Well, Miss Everett," said the painter, in accents which might have been tremulous if he had not exerted a strong effort to make them firm.

"Well, Mr. Baxter," said the young girl.

And the two exchanged a long, firm glance, which at last ended in a smile—a smile which belonged decidedly to the family of the famous laugh of the two angels behind the altar in the temple.

"Well, Miss Everett," said Baxter, going back to his work; "such is life!"

"So it appears," rejoined Marian. And then, after a pause of some moments: "Why didn't you come and see me?" she added.

"I came and you weren't at home."

"Why didn't you come again?"

"What was the use, Miss Everett?"

"It would simply have been more decent. We might have become reconciled."

"We seem to have done that as it is."

"I mean 'in form.'"

"That would have been absurd. Don't you see how true an instinct I had? What could have been easier than our meeting? I assure you that I should have found any talk about the past, and mutual assurances or apologies extremely disagreeable."

Miss Everett raised her eyes from the floor and fixed them

on her companion with a deep, half-reproachful glance, "Is the past, then," she asked, "so utterly disagreeable?"

Baxter stared, half amazed. "Good heavens!" he cried, "of course it is."

Miss Everett dropped her eyes and remained silent.

I may as well take advantage of the moment, rapidly to make plain to the reader the events to which the above conversation refers.

Miss Everett had found it expedient, all things considered, not to tell her intended husband the whole story of her acquaintance with Stephen Baxter; and when I have repaired her omissions, the reader will probably justify her discretion.

She had, as she said, met this young man for the first time at Rome, and there in the course of two interviews had made a deep impression upon his heart. He had felt that he would give a great deal to meet Miss Everett again. Their reunion in Switzerland was therefore not entirely fortuitous; and it had been the more easy for Baxter to make it possible, for the reason that he was able to claim a kind of roundabout relationship with Mrs. Denbigh, Marian's companion. With this lady's permission he had attached himself to their party. He had made their route of travel his own, he had stopped when they stopped and been prodigal of attentions and civilities. Before a week was over, Mrs. Denbigh, who was the soul of confiding good nature, exulted in the discovery of an invaluable kinsman. Thanks not only to her naturally unexacting disposition, but to the apathetic and inactive habits induced by constant physical suffering, she proved a very insignificant third in her companions' spending of the hours. How delightfully these hours were spent, it requires no great effort to imagine. A suit conducted in the midst of the most romantic scenery in Europe is already half won. Marian's social graces were largely enhanced by the satisfaction which her innate intelligence of natural beauty enabled her to take in the magnificent scenery of the Alps. She had never appeared to such advantage; she had never known such perfect freedom and frankness and gayety. For the first time in her life she had made a captive without suspecting it. She had surrendered her heart to the mountains and the lakes, the eternal snows and the pastoral valleys, and Baxter, standing by, had intercepted it. He felt his long-projected Swiss tour vastly magnified and beautified by Miss Everett's part in it—by the constant feminine sympathy which gushed within earshot, with the coolness and clearness of a mountain spring. Oh! if only it too had not been fed by the eternal snows! And then her beauty—her indefatigable beauty—was a continual enchantment. Miss Everett looked so thoroughly in her place in a drawing-room that it was almost logical to suppose that she looked well nowhere else. But in fact, as Baxter learned, she looked quite well enough in the character of what ladies call a "fright"— that is, sunburnt, travel-stained, over-heated, exhilarated and hungry—to elude all invidious comparisons.

At the end of three weeks, one morning as they stood together on the edge of a falling torrent, high above the green concavities of the hills, Baxter felt himself irresistibly urged to make a declaration. The thunderous noise of the cataract covered all vocal utterance; so, taking out his sketch-book, he wrote three short words on a blank leaf. He handed her the book. She read his message with a beautiful change of color and a single rapid glance at his face. She then tore out the leaf.

"Don't tear it up!" cried the young man.

She understood him by the movement of his lips and shook her head with a smile. But she stooped, picked up a little stone, and wrapping it in the bit of paper, prepared to toss it into the torrent.

Baxter, uncertain, put out his hand to take it from her. She passed it into the other hand and gave him the one he had attempted to take.

She threw away the paper, but she let him keep her hand.

Baxter had still a week at his disposal, and Marian made it a very happy one. Mrs. Denbigh was tired; they had come to a halt, and there was no interruption to their being together. They talked a great deal of the long future, which, on getting beyond the sound of the cataract, they had expeditiously agreed to pursue in common.

It was their misfortune both to be poor. They determined, in view of this circumstance, to say nothing of their engagement until Baxter, by dint of hard work, should have at least quadrupled his income. This was cruel, but it was imperative, and Marian made no complaint. Her residence in Europe had enlarged her conception of the material needs of a pretty woman, and it was quite natural that she should not, close upon the heels of this experience, desire to rush into marriage with a poor artist. At the end of some days Baxter started for Germany and Holland, portions of which he wished to visit for purposes of study. Mrs. Denbigh and her young friend repaired to Paris for the Winter. Here, in the middle of February, they were rejoined by Baxter, who had achieved his German tour. He had received, while absent, five little letters from Marian, full of affection. The number was small, but the young man detected in the very temperance of his mistress a certain delicious flavor of implicit constancy. She received him with all the frankness and sweetness that he had a right to expect, and listened with great interest to his account of the improvement in his prospects. He had sold three of his Italian pictures and had made an invaluable collection of sketches. He was on the high road to wealth and fame, and there was no reason their engagement should not be announced. But to this latter proposition Marian demurred—demurred so strongly, and yet on grounds so arbitrary, that a somewhat painful scene ensued. Stephen left her, irritated and perplexed. The next day, when he called, she was unwell and unable to see him; and the next—and the next. On the evening of the day that he had made his third fruitless call at Mrs. Denbigh's, he overheard Marian's name mentioned at a large party. The interlocutors were two elderly women. On giving his attention to their talk, which they were taking no pains to keep private, he found that his mistress was under accusal of having trifled with the affections of an unhappy young man, the only son of one of the ladies. There was apparently no lack of evidence or of facts which might be construed as evidence. Baxter went home, *la mort dans l'áme*, and on the following day called again on Mrs. Denbigh. Marian was still in her room, but the former lady received him. Stephen was in great trouble, but his mind was lucid, and he addressed himself to the task of interrogating his hostess. Mrs. Denbigh, with her habitual indolence, had remained unsuspicious of the terms on which the young people stood.

"I'm sorry to say," Baxter began, "that I heard Miss Everett accused last evening of very sad conduct."

"Ah, for heaven's sake, Stephen," returned his kinswoman, "don't go back to that. I've done nothing all Winter but defend and palliate her conduct. It's hard work. Don't make me do it for you. You know her as well as I do. She was indiscreet, but I know she is penitent, and for that matter she's well out of it. He was by no means a desirable young man."

"The lady whom I heard talking about the matter," said Stephen, "spoke of him in the highest terms. To be sure, as it turned out, she was his mother."

"His mother? You're mistaken. His mother died ten years ago."

Baxter folded his arms with a feeling that he needed to sit firm. "*Allons*," said he, "of whom do you speak?"

"Of young Mr. King."

"Good heavens," cried Stephen. "So there are two of them?"

"Pray, of whom do *you* speak?"

"Of a certain Mr. Young. The mother is a handsome old woman with white curls."

"You don't mean to say there has been anything between Marian and Frederic Young?"

"*Voilà!* I only repeat what I hear. It seems to me, my dear Mrs. Denbigh, that you ought to know."

Mrs. Denbigh shook her head with a melancholy movement. "I'm sure I don't," she said. "I give it up. I don't pretend to judge. The manners of young people to each other are very different from what they were in my day. One doesn't know whether they mean nothing or everything."

"You know, at least, whether Mr. Young has been in your drawing-room?"

"Oh, yes, frequently. I'm very sorry that Marian is talked about. It's very unpleasant for me. But what can a sick woman do?"

"Well," said Stephen, "so much for Mr. Young. And now for Mr. King."

"Mr. King is gone home. It's a pity he ever came away."

"In what sense?"

"Oh, he's a silly fellow. He doesn't understand young girls."

"Upon my word," said Stephen, "with expression," as the music sheets say, "he might be very wise and not do that."

"Not but that Marian was injudicious. She meant only to be amiable, but she went too far. She became adorable. The first thing she knew he was holding her to an account."

"Is he good-looking?"

"Well enough."

"And rich?"

"Very rich, I believe."

"And the other?"

"What other—Marian?"

"No, no; your friend Young."

"Yes, he's quite handsome."

"And rich, too?"

"Yes, I believe he's also rich."

Baxter was silent a moment. "And there's no doubt," he resumed, "that they were both far gone?"

"I can only answer for Mr. King."

"Well, I'll answer for Mr. Young. His mother wouldn't have talked as she did unless she'd seen her son suffer. After all, then, it's perhaps not so much to Marian's discredit. Here are two handsome young millionaires, madly smitten. She refuses them both. She doesn't care for good looks and money."

"I don't say that," said Mrs. Denbigh, sagaciously. "She doesn't care for those things alone. She wants talent, and all the rest of it. Now, if you were only rich, Stephen—" added the good lady, innocently.

Baxter took up his hat. "When you wish to marry Miss Everett," he said, "you must take good care not to say too much about Mr. King and Mr. Young."

Two days after this interview, he had a conversation with the young girl in person. The reader may like him the less for his easily-shaken confidence, but it is a fact that he had been unable to make light of these lightly-made revelations. For him his love had been a passion; for *her*, he was compelled to believe, it had been a vulgar pastime. He was a man of a violent temper; he went straight to the point.

"Marian," he said, "you've been deceiving me."

Marian knew very well what he meant; she knew very well that she had grown weary of her engagement and that, however little of a fault her conduct had been to Messrs. Young and King, it had been an act of grave disloyalty to Baxter. She felt that the blow was struck and that their engagement was clean broken. She knew that Stephen would be satisfied with no half-excuses or half-denials; and she had none others to give. A hundred such would not make a perfect confession. Making no attempt, therefore, to save her "prospects," for which she had ceased to care, she merely attempted to save her dignity. Her dignity for the moment was well enough secured by her natural half-cynical coolness of temper. But this same vulgar placidity left in Stephen's memory an impression of heartlessness and shallowness, which in that particular quarter, at least, was destined to be forever fatal to her claims to real weight and worth. She denied the young man's right to call her to account and to interfere with her conduct; and she almost anticipated his proposal that they should consider their engagement at an end. She even declined the use of the simple logic of tears. Under these circumstances, of course, the interview was not of long duration.

"I regard you," said Baxter, as he stood on the threshold, "as the most superficial, most heartless of women."

He immediately left Paris and went down into Spain, where he remained till the opening of the Summer. In the month of May Mrs. Denbigh and her *protégé* went to England, where the former, through her husband, possessed a number of connections, and where Marian's thoroughly un-English beauty was vastly admired. In September they sailed for America. About a year and a half, therefore, had elapsed between Baxter's separation from Miss Everett and their meeting in New York.

During this interval the young man's wounds had had time to heal. His sorrow, although violent, had been short-lived, and when he finally recovered his habitual equanimity, he was very glad to have purchased exemption at the price of a simple heart-ache. Reviewing his impressions of Miss Everett in a calmer mood, he made up his mind that she was very far from being the woman of his desire, and that she had not really been the woman of his choice. "Thank God," he said to himself, "it's over. She's irreclaimably light. She's hollow, trivial, vulgar." There had been in his addresses something hasty and feverish, something factitious and unreal in his fancied passion. Half of it had been the work of the scenery, of the weather, of mere juxtaposition, and, above all, of the young girl's picturesque beauty; to say nothing of the almost suggestive tolerance and indolence of poor Mrs. Denbigh. And finding himself very much interested in Velasquez, at Madrid, he dismissed Miss Everett from his thoughts. I do not mean to offer his judgment of Miss Everett as final; but it was at least conscientious. The ample justice, moreover, which, under the illusion of sentiment, he had rendered to her charms and graces, gave him a right, when free from that illusion, to register his estimate of the arid spaces of her nature. Miss Everett might easily have accused him of injustice and brutality; but this fact would still stand to plead in his favor, that he cared with all his strength for truth. Marian, on the contrary, was quite indifferent to it. Stephen's angry sentence on her conduct had awakened no echo in her contracted soul.

The reader has now an adequate conception of the feelings with which these two old friends found themselves face to face. It is needful to add, however, that the lapse of time had very much diminished the force of those feelings. A woman, it seems to me, ought to desire no easier company, none less embarrassed or embarrassing, than a disenchanted lover; premising, of course, that the process of disenchantment is thoroughly complete, and that some time has elapsed since its completion.

Marian herself was perfectly at her ease. She had not retained her equanimity—her philosophy, one might almost call it—during that painful last interview, to go and lose it now. She had no ill feeling toward her old lover. His last words had been—like all words in Marian's estimation—a mere *façon de parler*. Miss Everett was in so perfect a good humor during these last days of her maidenhood that there was nothing in the past that she could not have forgiven.

She blushed a little at the emphasis of her companion's remark; but she was not discountenanced. She summoned up her good humor. "The truth is, Mr. Baxter," she said, "I feel at the present moment on perfect good terms with the world; I see everything *en rose*; the past as well as the future."

"I, too, am on very good terms with the world," said Baxter, "and my heart is quite reconciled to what you call the past. But, nevertheless, it's very disagreeable to me to think about it."

"Ah then," said Miss Everett, with great sweetness, "I'm afraid you're not reconciled."

Baxter laughed—so loud that Miss Everett looked about at her father. But Mr. Everett still slept the sleep of gentility. "I've no doubt," said the painter, "that I'm far from being so good a Christian as you. But I assure you I'm very glad to see you again."

"You've but to say the word and we're friends," said Marian.

"We were very foolish to have attempted to be anything else."

" 'Foolish,' yes. But it was a pretty folly."

"Ah no, Miss Everett. I'm an artist, and I claim a right of property in the word 'pretty.' You mustn't stick it in there. Nothing could be pretty which had such an ugly termination. It was all false."

"Well—as you will. What have you been doing since we parted?"

"Travelling and working. I've made great progress in my trade. Shortly before I came home I became engaged."

"Engaged?—*à la bonne heure*. Is she good?—is she pretty?"

"She's not nearly so pretty as you."

"In other words, she's infinitely more good. I'm sure I hope she is. But why did you leave her behind you?"

"She's with a sister, a sad invalid, who is drinking mineral waters on the Rhine. They wished to remain there to the cold weather. They're to be home in a couple of weeks, and we are straightway to be married."

"I congratulate you, with all my heart," said Marian.

"Allow me to do as much, sir," said Mr. Everett, waking up; which he did by instinct whenever the conversation took a ceremonious turn.

Miss Everett gave her companion but three more sittings, a large part of his work being executed with the assistance of

photographs. At these interviews also, Mr. Everett was present, and still delicately sensitive to the soporific influences of
his position. But both parties had the good taste to abstain
from further reference to their old relations, and to confine
their talk to less personal themes.

PART II.

One afternoon, when the picture was nearly finished, John
Lennox went into the empty painting-room to ascertain the
degree of its progress. Both Baxter and Marian had expressed
a wish that he should not see it in its early stages, and this, accordingly, was his first view. Half an hour after he had entered
the room, Baxter came in, unannounced, and found him sitting before the canvas, deep in thought. Baxter had been furnished with a house-key, so that he might have immediate and
easy access to his work whenever the humor came upon him.

"I was passing," he said, "and I couldn't resist the impulse
to come in and correct an error which I made this morning,
now that a sense of its enormity is fresh in my mind." He sat
down to work, and the other stood watching him.

"Well," said the painter, finally, "how does it satisfy you?"

"Not altogether."

"Pray develop your objections. It's in your power materially
to assist me."

"I hardly know how to formulate my objections. Let me, at
all events, in the first place, say that I admire your work immensely. I'm sure it's the best picture you've painted."

"I honestly believe it is. Some parts of it," said Baxter,
frankly, "are excellent."

"It's obvious. But either those very parts or others are singularly disagreeable. That word isn't criticism, I know; but I
pay you for the right to be arbitrary. They are too hard, too
strong, of too frank a reality. In a word, your picture fright-
ens me, and if I were Marian I should feel as if you'd done me
a certain violence."

"I'm sorry for what's disagreeable; but I meant it all to be
real. I go in for reality; you must have seen that."

"I approve you; I can't too much admire the broad and
firm methods you've taken for reaching this same reality. But

you can be real without being brutal—without attempting, as one may say, to be *actual*."

"I deny that I'm brutal. I'm afraid Mr. Lennox, I haven't taken quite the right road to please you. I've taken the picture too much *au sérieux*. I've striven too much for completeness. But if it doesn't please you it will please others."

"I've no doubt of it. But that isn't the question. The picture is good enough to be a thousand times better."

"That the picture leaves room for infinite improvement, I, of course, don't deny; and, in several particulars, I see my way to make it better. But, substantially, the portrait is there. I'll tell you what you miss. My work isn't 'classical;' in fine, I'm not a man of genius."

"No; I rather suspect you are. But, as you say, your work isn't classical. I adhere to my term *brutal*. Shall I tell you? It's too much of a study. You've given poor Miss Everett the look of a professional model."

"If that's the case I've done very wrong. There never was an easier, a less conscious sitter. It's delightful to look at her."

"Confound it, you've given all her ease, too. Well, I don't know what's the matter. I give up."

"I think," said Baxter, "you had better hold your verdict in abeyance until the picture is finished. The classical element is there, I'm sure; but I've not brought it out. Wait a few days, and it will rise to the surface."

Lennox left the artist alone; and the latter took up his brushes and painted hard till nightfall. He laid them down only when it was too dark to see. As he was going out, Lennox met him in the hall.

"*Exegi monumentum*," said Baxter; "it's finished. Go and look at your ease. I'll come to-morrow and hear your impressions."

The master of the house, when the other had gone, lit half a dozen lights and returned to the study of the picture. It had grown prodigiously under the painter's recent handling, and whether it was that, as Baxter had said, the classical element had disengaged itself, or that Lennox was in a more sympathetic mood, it now impressed him as an original and powerful work, a genuine portrait, the deliberate image of a human face and figure. It was Marian, in very truth, and Marian most patiently measured and observed. Her beauty was there, her sweetness, and her young loveliness and her aerial grace, imprisoned forever, made inviolable and perpetual. Nothing could be more simple than the conception and composition of the picture. The figure sat peacefully, looking slightly to the right, with the head erect and the hands—the virginal hands, without rings or bracelets—lying idle on its knees. The blonde hair was gathered into a little knot of braids on the top of the head (in the fashion of the moment), and left free the almost childish contour of the ears and cheeks. The eyes were full of color, contentment and light; the lips were faintly parted. Of color in the picture, there was, in strictness, very little; but the dark draperies told of reflected sunshine, and the flesh-spaces of human blushes and pallors, of throbbing life and health. The work was strong and simple, the figure was thoroughly void of affectation and stiffness, and yet supremely elegant.

"That's what it is to be an artist," thought Lennox. "All this has been done in the past two hours."

It was his Marian, assuredly, with all that had charmed him—with all that still charmed him when he saw her: her appealing confidence, her exquisite lightness, her feminine enchantments. And yet, as he looked, an expression of pain came into his eyes, and lingered there, and grew into a mortal heaviness.

Lennox had been as truly a lover as a man may be; but he loved with the discretion of fifteen years' experience of human affairs. He had a penetrating glance, and he liked to use it. Many a time when Marian, with eloquent lips and eyes, had poured out the treasures of her nature into his bosom, and he had taken them in his hands and covered them with kisses and passionate vows; he had dropped them all with a sudden shudder and cried out in silence, "But ah! where is the heart?" One day he had said to her (irrelevantly enough, doubtless), "Marian, where *is* your heart?"

"*Where*—what do you mean?" Miss Everett had said.

"I think of you from morning till night. I put you together and take you apart, as people do in that game where they make words out of a parcel of given letters. But there's always one letter wanting. I can't put my hand on your heart."

"My heart, John," said Marian, ingeniously, "is the whole word. My heart's everywhere."

This may have been true enough. Miss Everett had distributed her heart impartially throughout her whole organism, so that, as a natural consequence, its native seat was somewhat scantily occupied. As Lennox sat and looked at Baxter's consummate handiwork, the same question rose again to his lips; and if Marian's portrait suggested it, Marian's portrait failed to answer it. It took Marian to do that. It seemed to Lennox that some strangely potent agency had won from his mistress the confession of her inmost soul, and had written it there upon the canvas in firm yet passionate lines. Marian's person was lightness—her charm was lightness; could it be that her soul was levity too? Was she a creature without faith and without conscience? What else was the meaning of that horrible blankness and deadness that quenched the light in her eyes and stole away the smile from her lips? These things were the less to be eluded because in so many respects the painter had been profoundly just. He had been as loyal and sympathetic as he had been intelligent. Not a point in the young girl's appearance had been slighted; not a feature but had been forcibly and delicately rendered. Had Baxter been a man of marvellous insight—an unparalleled observer; or had he been a mere patient and unflinching painter, building infinitely better than he knew? Would not a mere painter have been content to paint Miss Everett in the strong, rich, objective manner of which the work was so good an example, and to do nothing more? For it was evident that Baxter had done more. He had painted with something more than knowledge—with imagination, with feeling. He had almost *composed*; and his composition had embraced the truth. Lennox was unable to satisfy his doubts. He would have been glad to believe that there was no imagination in the picture but what his own mind supplied; and that the unsubstantial sweetness on the eyes and lips of the image was but the smile of youth and innocence. He was in a muddle—he was absurdly suspicious and capricious; he put out the lights and left the portrait in kindly darkness. Then, half as a reparation to his mistress, and half as a satisfaction to himself, he went up to spend an hour with Marian. She, at least, as he found, had no scruples.

She thought the portrait altogether a success, and she was very willing to be handed down in that form to posterity. Nevertheless, when Lennox came in, he went back into the painting-room to take another glance. This time he lit but a single light. Faugh! it was worse than with a dozen. He hastily turned out the gas.

Baxter came the next day, as he had promised. Meanwhile poor Lennox had had twelve hours of uninterrupted reflection, and the expression of distress in his eyes had acquired an intensity which, the painter saw, proved it to be of far other import than a mere tribute to his power.

"Can the man be jealous?" thought Baxter. Stephen had been so innocent of any other design than that of painting a good portrait, that his conscience failed to reveal to him the source of his companion's trouble. Nevertheless he began to pity him. He had felt tempted, indeed, to pity him from the first. He had liked him and esteemed him; he had taken him for a man of sense and of feeling, and he had thought it a matter of regret that such a man—a creature of strong spiritual needs—should link his destiny with that of Marian Everett. But he had very soon made up his mind that Lennox knew very well what he was about, and that he needed no enlightenment. He was marrying with his eyes open, and had weighed the risks against the profits. Every one had his particular taste, and at thirty-five years of age John Lennox had no need to be told that Miss Everett was not quite all that she might be. Baxter had thus taken for granted that his friend had designedly selected as his second wife a mere pretty woman—a woman with a genius for receiving company, and who would make a picturesque use of his money. He knew nothing of the serious character of the poor man's passion, nor of the extent to which his happiness was bound up in what the painter would have called his delusion. His only concern had been to do his work well; and he had done it the better because of his old interest in Marian's bewitching face. It is very certain that he had actually infused into his picture that force of characterization and that depth of reality which had arrested his friend's attention; but he had done so wholly without effort and without malice. The artistic half of Baxter's nature exerted a lusty dominion over the human half—fed upon its disappointments and grew fat upon its joys and tribulations. This, indeed, is simply saying that the young man was a true artist. Deep, then, in the unfathomed recesses of his strong and sensitive nature, his genius had held communion with his heart and had transferred to canvas the burden of its disenchantment and its resignation. Since his little affair with Marian, Baxter had made the acquaintance of a young girl whom he felt that he could love and trust forever; and, sobered and strengthened by this new emotion, he had been able to resume with more distinctness the shortcomings of his earlier love. He had, therefore, painted with feeling. Miss Everett could not have expected him to do otherwise. He had done his honest best, and conviction had come in unbidden and made it better.

Lennox had begun to feel very curious about the history of his companion's acquaintance with his destined bride; but he was far from feeling jealous. Somehow he felt that he could never again be jealous. But in ascertaining the terms of their former intercourse, it was of importance that he should not allow the young man to suspect that he discovered in the portrait any radical defect.

"Your old acquaintance with Miss Everett," he said, frankly, "has evidently been of great use to you."

"I suppose it has," said Baxter. "Indeed, as soon as I began to paint, I found her face coming back to me like a half-remembered tune. She was wonderfully pretty at that time."

"She was two years younger."

"Yes, and I was two years younger. Decidedly, you are right. I *have* made use of my old impressions."

Baxter was willing to confess to so much; but he was resolved not to betray anything that Marian had herself kept secret. He was not surprised that she had not told her lover of her former engagement; he expected as much. But he would have held it inexcusable to attempt to repair her omission.

Lennox's faculties were acutely sharpened by pain and suspicion, and he could not help detecting in his companion's eyes an intention of reticence. He resolved to baffle it.

"I am curious to know," he said, "whether you were ever in love with Miss Everett?"

"I have no hesitation in saying Yes," rejoined Baxter;

fancying that a general confession would help him more than a particular denial. "I'm one of a thousand, I fancy. Or one, perhaps, of only a hundred. For you see I've got over it. I'm engaged to be married."

Lennox's countenance brightened. "That's it," said he. "Now I know what I didn't like in your picture—the point of view. I'm not jealous," he added. "I should like the picture better if I were. You evidently care nothing for the poor girl. You have got over your love rather too well. You loved her, she was indifferent to you, and now you take your revenge." Distracted with grief, Lennox was taking refuge in irrational anger.

Baxter was puzzled. "You'll admit," said he, with a smile, "that it's a very handsome revenge." And all his professional self-esteem rose to his assistance. "I've painted for Miss Everett the best portrait that has yet been painted in America. She herself is quite satisfied."

"Ah!" said Lennox, with magnificent dissimulation; "Marian is generous."

"Come, then," said Baxter; "what do you complain of? You accuse me of scandalous conduct, and I'm bound to hold you to an account." Baxter's own temper was rising, and with it his sense of his picture's merits. "How have I perverted Miss Everett's expression? How have I misrepresented her? What does the portrait lack? Is it ill-drawn? Is it vulgar? Is it ambiguous? Is it immodest?" Baxter's patience gave out as he recited these various charges. "Fiddlesticks!" he cried; "you know as well as I do that the picture is excellent."

"I don't pretend to deny it. Only I wonder that Marian was willing to come to you."

It is very much to Baxter's credit that he still adhered to his resolution not to betray the young girl, and that rather than do so he was willing to let Lennox suppose that he had been a rejected adorer.

"Ah, as you say," he exclaimed, "Miss Everett is so generous!"

Lennox was foolish enough to take this as an admission. "When I say, Mr. Baxter," he said, "that you have taken your revenge, I don't mean that you've done so wantonly or consciously. My dear fellow, how could you help it? The disappointment was proportionate to the loss and the reaction to the disappointment."

"Yes, that's all very well; but, meanwhile, I wait in vain to learn wherein I've done wrong."

Lennox looked from Baxter to the picture, and from the picture back to Baxter.

"I defy you to tell me," said Baxter. "I've simply kept Miss Everett as charming as she is in life."

"Oh, damn her charms!" cried Lennox.

"If you were not the gentleman, Mr. Lennox," continued the young man, "which, in spite of your high temper, I believe you to be, I should believe you—"

"Well, you should believe me?"

"I should believe you simply bent on cheapening the portrait."

Lennox made a gesture of vehement impatience. The other burst out laughing and the discussion closed. Baxter instinctively took up his brushes and approached his canvas with a vague desire to detect latent errors, while Lennox prepared to take his departure.

"Stay!" said the painter, as he was leaving the room; "if the picture really offends you, I'll rub it out. Say the word," and he took up a heavy brush, covered with black paint.

But Lennox shook his head with decision and went out. The next moment, however, he reappeared. "You *may* rub it out," he said. "The picture is, of course, already mine."

But now Baxter shook his head. "Ah! now it's too late," he answered. "Your chance is gone."

Lennox repaired directly to Mr. Everett's apartments. Marian was in the drawing-room with some morning callers, and her lover sat by until she had got rid of them. When they were alone together, Marian began to laugh at her visitors and to parody certain of their affectations, which she did with infinite grace and spirit. But Lennox cut her short and returned to the portrait. He had thought better of his objections of the preceding evening; he liked it.

"But I wonder, Marian," he said, "that you were willing to go to Mr. Baxter."

"Why so?" asked Marian, on her guard. She saw that her

lover knew something, and she intended not to commit herself until she knew how much he knew.

"An old lover is always dangerous."

"An old lover?" and Marian blushed a good honest blush.
But she rapidly recovered herself. "Pray where did you get
that charming news?"

"Oh, it slipped out," said Lennox.

Marian hesitated a moment. Then with a smile: "Well, I
was brave," she said. "I went."

"How came it," pursued Lennox, "that you didn't tell
me?"

"Tell you what, my dear John?"

"Why, about Baxter's little passion. Come, don't be
modest."

Modest! Marian breathed freely. "What do you mean, my
dear, by telling your wife not to be modest? Pray don't ask me
about Mr. Baxter's passions. What do I know about them?"

"Did you know nothing of this one?"

"Ah, my dear, I know a great deal too much for my comfort. But he's got bravely over it. He's engaged."

"Engaged, but not quite disengaged. He's an honest fellow, but he remembers his *penchant*. It was as much as he
could do to keep his picture from turning to the sentimental.
He saw you as he fancied you—as he wished you; and he has
given you a little look of what he imagines moral loveliness,
which comes within an ace of spoiling the picture. Baxter's
imagination isn't very strong, and this same look expresses, in
point of fact, nothing but insanity. Fortunately he's a man of
extraordinary talent, and a real painter, and he has made a
good portrait in spite of himself."

To such arguments as these was John Lennox reduced, to
stifle the evidence of his senses. But when once a lover begins
to doubt, he cannot cease at will. In spite of his earnest efforts
to believe in Marian as before, to accept her without scruple
and without second thought, he was quite unable to repress
an impulse of constant mistrust and aversion. The charm was
broken, and there is no mending a charm. Lennox stood half-
aloof, watching the poor girl's countenance, weighing her
words, analyzing her thoughts, guessing at her motives.

Marian's conduct under this trying ordeal was truly heroic. She felt that some subtle change had taken place in her future husband's feelings, a change which, although she was power-less to discover its cause, yet obviously imperilled her prospects. Something had snapped between them; she had lost half of her power. She was horribly distressed, and the more so because that superior depth of character which she had all along gladly conceded to Lennox, might now, as she conjectured, cover some bold and portentous design. Could he meditate a direct rupture? Could it be his intention to dash from her lips the sweet, the spiced and odorous cup of being the wife of a good-natured millionaire? Marian turned a tremulous glance upon her past, and wondered if he had dis-covered any dark spot. Indeed, for that matter, might she not defy him to do so? She had done nothing really amiss. There was no visible blot in her history. It was faintly discolored, in-deed, by a certain vague moral dinginess; but it compared well enough with that of other girls. She had cared for noth-ing but pleasure; but to what else were girls brought up? On the whole, might she not feel at ease? She assured herself that she might; but she nevertheless felt that if John wished to break off his engagement, he would do it on high abstract grounds, and not because she had committed a naughtiness the more or the less. It would be simply because he had ceased to love her. It would avail her but little to assure him that she would kindly overlook this circumstance and remit the obligations of the heart. But, in spite of her hideous ap-prehensions, she continued to smile and smile.

The days passed by, and John consented to be still engaged. Their marriage was only a week off—six days, five days, four. Miss Everett's smile became less mechanical. John had appar-ently been passing through a crisis—a moral and intellectual crisis, inevitable in a man of his constitution, and with which she had nothing to do. On the eve of marriage he had ques-tioned his heart; he had found that it was no longer young and capable of the vagaries of passion, and he had made up his mind to call things by their proper names, and to admit to himself that he was marrying not for love, but for friendship, and a little, perhaps, for prudence. It was only out of regard for what he supposed Marian's own more exalted theory of the matter, that he abstained from revealing to her this common-sense view of it. Such was Marian's hypothesis.

Lennox had fixed his wedding-day for the last Thursday in October. On the preceding Friday, as he was passing up Broadway, he stopped at Goupil's to see if his order for the framing of the portrait had been fulfilled. The picture had been transferred to the shop, and, when duly framed, had been, at Baxter's request and with Lennox's consent, placed for a few days in the exhibition room. Lennox went up to look at it.

The portrait stood on an easel at the end of the hall, with three spectators before it—a gentleman and two ladies. The room was otherwise empty. As Lennox went toward the picture, the gentleman turned out to be Baxter. He proceeded to introduce his friend to his two companions, the younger of whom Lennox recognized as the artist's betrothed. The other, her sister, was a plain, pale woman, with the look of ill health, who had been provided with a seat and made no attempt to talk. Baxter explained that these ladies had arrived from Europe but the day before, and that his first care had been to show them his masterpiece.

"Sarah," said he, "has been praising the model very much to the prejudice of the copy."

Sarah was a tall, black-haired girl of twenty, with irregular features, a pair of luminous dark eyes, and a smile radiant of white teeth—evidently an excellent person. She turned to Lennox with a look of frank sympathy, and said in a deep, rich voice:

"She must be very beautiful."

"Yes, she's very beautiful," said Lennox, with his eyes lingering on her own pleasant face. "You must know her—she must know you."

"I'm sure I should like very much to see her," said Sarah.

"This is very nearly as good," said Lennox. "Mr. Baxter is a great genius."

"I know Mr. Baxter is a genius. But what is a picture, at the best? I've seen nothing but pictures for the last two years, and I haven't seen a single pretty girl."

The young girl stood looking at the portrait in very evident admiration, and, while Baxter talked to the elder lady, Lennox bestowed a long, covert glance upon his *fiancée*. She had brought her head into almost immediate juxtaposition with that of Marian's image, and, for a moment, the freshness and the strong animation which bloomed upon her features seemed to obliterate the lines and colors on the canvas. But the next moment, as Lennox looked, the roseate circle of Marian's face blazed into remorseless distinctness, and her careless blue eyes looked with cynical familiarity into his own.

He bade an abrupt good morning to his companions, and went toward the door. But beside it he stopped. Suspended on the wall was Baxter's picture, *My Last Duchess*. He stood amazed. Was *this* the face and figure that, a month ago, had reminded him of his mistress? Where was the likeness now? It was as utterly absent as if it had never existed. The picture, moreover, was a very inferior work to the new portrait. He looked back at Baxter, half tempted to demand an explanation, or at least to express his perplexity. But Baxter and his sweetheart had stooped down to examine a minute sketch near the floor, with their heads in delicious contiguity.

How the week elapsed, it were hard to say. There were moments when Lennox felt as if death were preferable to the heartless union which now stared him in the face, and as if the only possible course was to transfer his property to Marian and to put an end to his existence. There were others, again, when he was fairly reconciled to his fate. He had but to gather his old dreams and fancies into a faggot and break them across his knee, and the thing were done. Could he not collect in their stead a comely cluster of moderate and rational expectations, and bind them about with a wedding favor? His love was dead, his youth was dead; that was all. There was no need of making a tragedy of it. His love's vitality had been but small, and since it was to be short-lived it was better that it should expire before marriage than after. As for marriage, that should stand, for that was not of necessity a matter of love. He lacked the brutal consistency necessary for taking away Marian's future. If he had mistaken her and overrated her, the fault was his own, and it was a hard thing that she should pay the penalty. Whatever were her failings, they were profoundly involuntary, and it was plain that with regard to himself her intentions were good. She would be no companion, but she would be at least a faithful wife.

With the help of this grim logic, Lennox reached the eve of his wedding day. His manner toward Miss Everett during the preceding week had been inveterately tender and kind. He felt that in losing his love she had lost a heavy treasure, and he offered her instead the most unfailing devotion. Marian had questioned him about his lassitude and his preoccupied air, and he had replied that he was not very well. On the Wednesday afternoon, he mounted his horse and took a long ride. He came home toward sunset, and was met in the hall by his old housekeeper.

"Miss Everett's portrait, sir," she said, "has just been sent home, in the most beautiful frame. You gave no directions, and I took the liberty of having it carried into the library. I thought," and the old woman smiled deferentially, "you'd like best to have it in your own room."

Lennox went into the library. The picture was standing on the floor, back to back with a high arm-chair, and catching, through the window, the last horizontal rays of the sun. He stood before it a moment, gazing at it with a haggard face.

"Come!" said he, at last, "Marian may be what God has made her; but *this* detestable creature I can neither love nor respect!"

He looked about him with an angry despair, and his eye fell on a long, keen poinard, given him by a friend who had bought it in the East, and which lay as an ornament on his mantel-shelf. He seized it and thrust it, with barbarous glee, straight into the lovely face of the image. He dragged it downward, and made a long fissure in the living canvas. Then, with half a dozen strokes, he wantonly hacked it across. The act afforded him an immense relief.

I need hardly add that on the following day Lennox was married. He had locked the library door on coming out the evening before, and he had the key in his waistcoat pocket as he stood at the altar. As he left town, therefore, immediately after the ceremony, it was not until his return, a fortnight later, that the fate of the picture became known. It is not necessary to relate how he explained his exploit to Marian and how he disclosed it to Baxter. He at least put on a brave face. There is a rumor current of his having paid the painter an enormous sum of money. The amount is probably exaggerated, but there can be no doubt that the sum was very large. How he has fared—how he is destined to fare—in matrimony, it is rather too early to determine. He has been married scarcely three months.

The Romance of Certain Old Clothes

TOWARD the middle of the eighteenth century there lived in the Province of Massachusetts a widowed gentlewoman, the mother of three children. Her name is of little account: I shall take the liberty of calling her Mrs. Willoughby, —a name, like her own, of a highly respectable sound. She had been left a widow after some six years of marriage, and had devoted herself to the care of her children. These latter grew up in a manner to reward her tender care and to gratify her fondest hopes. The first-born was a son, whom she had called Bernard, after his father. The others were daughters,— born at an interval of three years apart. Good looks were traditional in the family, and these young persons were not likely to allow the tradition to perish. The boy was of that fair and ruddy complexion and of that athletic mould which in those days (as in these) were the sign of genuine English blood,—a frank, affectionate young fellow, a capital son and brother, and a steadfast friend. Clever, however, he was not; the wit of the family had been apportioned chiefly to his sisters. Mr. Willoughby had been a great reader of Shakespeare, at a time when this pursuit implied more penetration of mind than at the present day, and in a community where it required much courage to patronize the drama even in the closet; and he had wished to record his admiration of the great poet by calling his daughters out of his favorite plays. Upon the elder he had bestowed the charming name of Viola; and upon the younger, the more serious one of Perdita, in memory of a little girl born between them, who had lived but a few weeks.

When Bernard Willoughby came to his sixteenth year, his mother put a brave face upon it, and prepared to execute her husband's last request. This had been an earnest entreaty that, at the proper age, his son should be sent out to England, there to complete his education at the University of Oxford, which had been the seat of his own studies. Mrs. Willoughby valued her son three times as much as she did her two daughters together; but she valued her husband's wishes more. So she swallowed her sobs, and made up her boy's trunk and his simple provincial outfit, and sent him on his way across the seas. Bernard was entered at his father's college, and spent five years in England, without great honor, indeed, but with a vast deal of pleasure and no discredit. On leaving the University he made the journey to France. In his twenty-third year he took ship for home, prepared to find poor little New England (New England was very small in those days) an utterly intolerable place of abode. But there had been changes at home, as well as in Mr. Bernard's opinions. He found his mother's house quite habitable, and his sisters grown into two very charming young ladies, with all the accomplishments and graces of the young women of Britain, and a certain native-grown gentle *brusquerie* and wildness, which, if it was not an accomplishment, was certainly a grace the more. Bernard privately assured his mother that his sisters were fully a match for the most genteel young women in England; whereupon poor Mrs. Willoughby quite came into conceit of her daughters. Such was Bernard's opinion, and such, in a tenfold higher degree, was the opinion of Mr. Arthur Lloyd. This gentleman, I hasten to add, was a college-mate of Mr. Bernard, a young man of reputable family, of a good person and a handsome inheritance; which latter appurtenance he prepared to invest in trade in this country. He and Bernard were warm friends; they had crossed the ocean together, and the young American had lost no time in presenting him at his mother's house, where he had made quite as good an impression as that which he had received, and of which I have just given a hint.

The two sisters were at this time in all the freshness of their youthful bloom; each wearing, of course, this natural brilliancy in the manner that became her best. They were equally dissimilar in appearance and character. Viola, the elder,—now in her twenty-second year,—was tall and fair, with calm gray eyes and auburn tresses; a very faint likeness to the Viola of Shakespeare's comedy, whom I imagine as a brunette (if you will), but a slender, airy creature, full of the softest and finest emotions. Miss Willoughby, with her rich, fair skin, her fine arms, her majestic height, and her slow utterance, was not cut out for adventures. She would never have put on a man's jacket and hose; and, indeed, being a very plump beauty, it is perhaps as well that she wouldn't. Perdita, too, might very well have exchanged the sweet melancholy of her name against something more in consonance with her aspect and disposition. She was a positive brunette, short of stature, light of foot, with dark brown eyes full of fire and animation. She had been from her childhood a creature of smiles and gayety; and so far from making you wait for an answer to your speech, as her handsome sister was wont to do (while she gazed at you with her somewhat cold gray eyes), she had given you the choice of half a dozen, suggested by the successive clauses of your proposition, before you had got to the end of it.

The young girls were very glad to see their brother once more; but they found themselves quite able to maintain a reserve of good-will for their brother's friend. Among the young men their friends and neighbors, the *belle jeunesse* of the Colony, there were many excellent fellows, several devoted swains, and some two or three who enjoyed the reputation of universal charmers and conquerors. But the home-bred arts and the somewhat boisterous gallantry of these honest young colonists were completely eclipsed by the good looks, the fine clothes, the respectful *empressement*, the perfect elegance, the immense information, of Mr. Arthur Lloyd. He was in reality no paragon; he was an honest, resolute, intelligent young man, rich in pounds sterling, in his health and comfortable hopes, and his little capital of uninvested affections. But he was a gentleman; he had a handsome face; he had studied and travelled; he spoke French, he played on the flute, and he read verses aloud with very great taste. There were a dozen reasons why Miss Willoughby and her sister should forthwith have been rendered fastidious in the choice of their male acquaintance. The imagination of women is especially adapted to the various little conventions and mysteries of polite society. Mr. Lloyd's talk told our little New England maidens a vast deal more of the ways and means of people of fashion in European capitals than he had any idea of doing. It was delightful to sit by and hear him and Bernard discourse upon the fine people and fine things they had seen. They would all gather round the fire after tea, in the little wainscoted parlor,—quite innocent then of any intention of being picturesque or of being anything else, indeed, than economical, and saving the expense of stamped papers and tapestries,—and the two young men would remind each other, across the rug, of this, that, and the other adventure. Viola and Perdita would often have given their ears to know exactly what adventure it was, and where it happened, and who was there, and what the ladies had on; but in those days a well-bred young woman was not expected to break into the conversation of her own movement or to ask too many questions; and the poor girls used therefore to sit fluttering behind the more languid—or more discreet—curiosity of their mother.

That they were both very nice girls Arthur Lloyd was not slow to discover; but it took him some time to satisfy himself as to the balance of their charms. He had a strong presentiment—an emotion of a nature entirely too cheerful to be called a foreboding—that he was destined to marry one of them; yet he was unable to arrive at a preference, and for such a consummation a preference was certainly indispensable, inasmuch as Lloyd was quite too much of a young man to reconcile himself to the idea of making a choice by lot and being cheated of the heavenly delight of falling in love. He resolved to take things easily, and to let his heart speak. Meanwhile, he was on a very pleasant footing. Mrs. Willoughby showed a dignified indifference to his "intentions," equally remote from a carelessness of her daughters' honor and from that hideous alacrity to make him commit himself, which, in his quality of a young man of property, he had but too often encountered in the venerable dames of his native islands. As for Bernard, all that he asked was that his friend should take his sisters as his own; and as for the fair creatures themselves, however each may have secretly longed for the monopoly of Mr. Lloyd's attentions, they observed a very decent and modest and contented demeanor.

Towards each other, however, they were somewhat more on the offensive. They were good sisterly friends, betwixt whom it would take more than a day for the seeds of jealousy to sprout and bear fruit; but the young girls felt that the seeds had been sown on the day that Mr. Lloyd came into the house. Each made up her mind that, if she should be slighted, she would bear her grief in silence, and that no one should be any the wiser; for if they had a great deal of love, they had also a great deal of pride. But each prayed in secret, nevertheless, that upon *her* the glory might fall. They had need of a vast deal of patience, of self-control, and of dissimulation. In those days a young girl of decent breeding could make no advances whatever, and barely respond, indeed, to those that were made. She was expected to sit still in her chair with her eyes on the carpet, watching the spot where the mystic handkerchief should fall. Poor Arthur Lloyd was obliged to undertake his wooing in the little wainscoted parlor, before the eyes of Mrs. Willoughby, her son, and his prospective sister-in-law. But youth and love are so cunning that a hundred little signs and tokens might travel to and fro, and not one of these three pair of eyes detect them in their passage. The young girls had but one chamber and one bed between them, and for long hours together they were under each other's direct inspection. That each knew that she was being watched, however, made not a grain of difference in those little offices which they mutually rendered, or in the various household tasks which they performed in common. Neither flinched nor fluttered beneath the silent batteries of her sister's eyes. The only apparent change in their habits was that they had less to say to each other. It was impossible to talk about Mr. Lloyd, and it was ridiculous to talk about anything else. By tacit agreement they began to wear all their choice finery, and to devise such little implements of coquetry, in the way of ribbons and top-knots and furbelows as were sanctioned by indubitable modesty. They executed in the same inarticulate fashion a little agreement of sincerity on these delicate matters. "Is it better so?" Viola would ask, tying a bunch of ribbons on her bosom, and turning about from her glass to her sister. Perdita would look up gravely from her work, and examine the decoration. "I think you had better give it another loop," she would say, with great solemnity, looking hard at her sister with eyes that added, "upon my honor." So they were forever stitching and trimming their petticoats, and pressing out their muslins, and contriving washes and ointments and cosmetics, like the ladies in the household of the Vicar of Wakefield. Some three or four months went by; it grew to be midwinter, and as yet Viola knew that if Perdita had nothing more to boast of than she, there was not much to be feared from her rivalry. But Perdita by this time, the charming Perdita, felt that her secret had grown to be tenfold more precious than her sister's.

One afternoon Miss Willoughby sat alone before her toilet-glass, combing out her long hair. It was getting too dark to see; she lit the two candles in their sockets on the frame of her mirror, and then went to the window to draw her curtains. It was a gray December evening; the landscape was bare and bleak, and the sky heavy with snow-clouds. At the end of the long garden into which her window looked was a wall with a little postern door, opening into a lane. The door stood ajar, as she could vaguely see in the gathering darkness, and moved slowly to and fro, as if some one were swaying it from the lane without. It was doubtless a servant-maid. But as she was about to drop her curtain, Viola saw her sister step within the garden, and hurry along the path toward the house. She dropped the curtain, all save a little crevice for her eyes. As Perdita came up the path, she seemed to be examining something in her hand, holding it close to her eyes. When she reached the house she stopped a moment, looked intently at the object, and pressed it to her lips.

Poor Viola slowly came back to her chair, and sat down before her glass, where, if she had looked at it less abstractedly, she would have seen her handsome features sadly disfigured by jealousy. A moment afterwards, the door opened behind her, and her sister came into the room, out of breath, and her cheeks aglow with the chilly air.

Perdita started. "Ah," said she, "I thought you were with mamma." The ladies were to go to a tea-party, and on such occasions it was the habit of one of the young girls to help their mother to dress. Instead of coming in, Perdita lingered at the door.

"Come in, come in," said Viola. "We've more than an hour yet. I should like you very much to give a few strokes to my hair." She knew that her sister wished to retreat, and that she could see in the glass all her movements in the room. "Nay, just help me with my hair," she said, "and I'll go to mamma."

Perdita came reluctantly, and took the brush. She saw her sister's eyes, in the glass, fastened hard upon her hands. She had not made three passes, when Viola clapped her own right hand upon her sister's left, and started out of her chair. "Whose ring is that?" she cried, passionately, drawing her towards the light.

On the young girl's third finger glistened a little gold ring, adorned with a couple of small rubies. Perdita felt that she need no longer keep her secret, yet that she must put a bold face on her avowal. "It's mine," she said proudly.

"Who gave it to you?" cried the other.

Perdita hesitated a moment. "Mr. Lloyd."

"Mr. Lloyd is generous, all of a sudden."

"Ah no," cried Perdita, with spirit, "not all of a sudden. He offered it to me a month ago."

"And you needed a month's begging to take it?" said Viola, looking at the little trinket; which indeed was not especially elegant, although it was the best that the jeweller of the Province could furnish. "I shouldn't have taken it in less than two."

"It isn't the ring," said Perdita, "it's what it means!"

"It means that you're not a modest girl," cried Viola. "Pray does mamma know of your conduct? does Bernard?"

"Mamma has approved my 'conduct,' as you call it. Mr. Lloyd has asked my hand, and mamma has given it. Would you have had him apply to you, sister?"

Viola gave her sister a long look, full of passionate envy and sorrow. Then she dropped her lashes on her pale cheeks, and turned away. Perdita felt that it had not been a pretty scene; but it was her sister's fault. But the elder girl rapidly called back her pride, and turned herself about again. "You have my very best wishes," she said with a low courtesy. "I wish you every happiness, and a very long life."

Perdita gave a bitter laugh. "Don't speak in that tone," she cried. "I'd rather you cursed me outright. Come sister," she added, "he couldn't marry both of us."

"I wish you very great joy," Viola repeated mechanically, sitting down to her glass again, "and a very long life, and plenty of children."

There was something in the sound of these words not at all to Perdita's taste. "Will you give me a year, at least?" she said. "In a year I can have one little boy,—or one little girl at least. If you'll give me your brush again, I'll do your hair."

"Thank you," said Viola. "You had better go to mamma. It isn't proper that a young lady with a promised husband should wait on a girl with none."

"Nay," said Perdita, good-humoredly, "I have Arthur to wait upon me. You need my service more than I need yours."

But her sister motioned her away, and she left the room. When she had gone, poor Viola fell on her knees before her dressing-table, buried her head in her arms, and poured out a flood of tears and sobs. She felt very much the better for this effusion of sorrow. When her sister came back, she insisted upon helping her to dress, and upon her wearing her prettiest things. She forced upon her acceptance a bit of lace of her own, and declared that now that she was to be married she should do her best to appear worthy of her lover's choice. She discharged these offices in stern silence; but, such as they were, they had to do duty as an apology and an atonement; she never made any other.

Now that Lloyd was received by the family as an accepted suitor, nothing remained but to fix the wedding-day. It was appointed for the following April, and in the interval preparations were diligently made for the marriage. Lloyd, on his side, was busy with his commercial arrangements, and with establishing a correspondence with the great mercantile house to which he had attached himself in England. He was therefore not so frequent a visitor at Mrs. Willoughby's as during the months of his diffidence and irresolution, and poor Viola had less to suffer than she had feared from the sight of the mutual endearments of the young lovers. Touching his future sister-in-law Lloyd had a perfectly clear conscience. There had not been a particle of sentiment uttered between them, and he had not the slightest suspicion that she coveted anything more than his fraternal regard. He was quite at his ease; life promised so well, both domestically and financially. The lurid clouds of revolution were as yet twenty years beneath the horizon, and that his connubial felicity should take a tragic turn it was absurd, it was blasphemous, to apprehend. Meanwhile at Mrs. Willoughby's there was a greater rustling of silks, a more rapid clicking of scissors, and flying of needles than ever. Mrs. Willoughby had determined that her daughter should carry from home the most elegant outfit that her money could buy, or that the country could furnish. All the sage women in the county were convened, and their united taste was brought to bear on Perdita's wardrobe. Viola's situation, at this moment, was assuredly not to be envied. The poor girl had an inordinate love of dress, and the very best taste in the world, as her sister perfectly well knew. Viola was tall, she was full and stately, she was made to carry stiff brocade and masses of heavy lace, such as belong to the toilet of a rich man's wife. But Viola sat aloof, with her beautiful arms folded and her head averted, while her mother and sister and the venerable women aforesaid worried and wondered over their materials, oppressed by the multitude of their resources. One day there came in a beautiful piece of white silk, brocaded with heavenly blue and silver, sent by the bridegroom himself,—it not being thought amiss in those days that the husband elect should contribute to the bride's *trousseau*. Perdita was quite at loss to imagine a pattern and trimmings which should do sufficient honor to the splendor of the material.

"Blue's your color, sister, more than mine," she said with appealing eyes. "It's a pity it's not for you. You'd know what to do with it."

Viola got up from her place, and looked at the great shining fabric as it lay spread over the back of a chair. Then she took it up in her hands and felt it,—lovingly, as Perdita could see,—and turned about toward the mirror with it. She let it roll down to her feet, and flung the other end over her shoulder, gathering it in about her waist with her white arm bare to the elbow. She threw back her head, and looked at her image, and a hanging tress of her auburn hair fell upon the gorgeous surface of the silk. It made a dazzling picture. The women standing about uttered a little "Ah!" of admiration. "Yes, indeed," said Viola, quietly, "blue is my color." But Perdita could see that her fancy had been stirred, and that she would now fall to work and solve all their silken riddles. And indeed she behaved very well, as Perdita, knowing her insatiable love of millinery, was quite ready to declare. Yards and yards of lovely silks and satins, of muslins, velvets, and laces, passed through her cunning hands, without a word of envy coming from her lips. Thanks to her efforts, when the wedding-day came Perdita was prepared to espouse more of the vanities of life than any fluttering young bride who had yet challenged the sacramental blessing of a New England divine.

It had been arranged that the young couple should go out and spend the first days of their wedded life at the country house of an English gentleman,—a man of rank, and a very kind friend to Lloyd. He was an unmarried man; he professed himself delighted to withdraw and leave them for a week to their billing and cooing. After the ceremony at church,—it had been performed by an English priest,—young Mrs. Lloyd hastened back to her mother's house to change her wedding gear for a riding-dress. Viola helped her to effect the change, in the little old room in which they had been fond sisters together. Perdita then hurried off to bid farewell to her mother, leaving Viola to follow. The parting was short; the horses were at the door, and Arthur impatient to start. But Viola had not followed, and Perdita hastened back to her room, opening the door abruptly. Viola, as usual, was before the glass, but in a position which caused the other to stand still, amazed. She had dressed herself in Perdita's cast-off wedding veil and wreath, and on her neck she had hung the heavy string of pearls which the young girl had received from her husband as a wedding-gift. These things had been hastily laid aside, to await their possessor's disposal on her return from the country. Bedizened in this unnatural garb, Viola stood at the mirror, plunging a long look into its depths, and reading Heaven knows what audacious visions. Perdita was shocked and pained. It was a hideous image of their old rivalry come to life again. She made a step toward her sister, as if to pull off the veil and the flowers. But catching her eyes in the glass, she stopped.

"Farewell, Viola," she said. "You might at least have waited till I had got out of the house." And she hurried away from the room.

Mr. Lloyd had purchased in Boston a house which, in the taste of those days, was considered a marvel of elegance and comfort; and here he very soon established himself with his young wife. He was thus separated by a distance of twenty miles from the residence of his mother-in-law. Twenty miles in that primitive era of roads and conveyances were as good as a hundred at the present day, and Mrs. Willoughby saw but little of her daughter during the first twelvemonth of her marriage. She suffered in no small degree from her absence; and her affliction was not diminished by the fact that Viola had fallen into a spiritless and languid state, which made change of scene and of air essential to her restoration. The real cause of the young girl's dejection the reader will not be slow to suspect. Mrs. Willoughby and her gossips, however, deemed her complaint a purely physical one, and doubted not that she would obtain relief from the remedy just mentioned. Her mother accordingly proposed on her behalf a visit to certain relatives on the paternal side, established in New York, who had long complained that they were able to see so little of their New England cousins. Viola was despatched to these good people, under a suitable escort, and remained with them for several months. In the interval her brother Bernard, who had begun the practice of the law, made up his mind to take a wife. Viola came home to the wedding, apparently cured of her heartache, with honest roses and lilies in her face, and a proud smile on her lips. Arthur Lloyd came over from Boston to see his brother-in-law married, but without his wife, who was expecting shortly to be confined. It was nearly a year since Viola had seen him. She was glad—she hardly knew why—that Perdita had stayed at home. Arthur looked happy, but he was more grave and solemn than before his marriage. She thought he looked "interesting,"—for although the word in its modern sense was not then invented, we may be sure that the idea was. The truth is, he was simply preoccupied with his wife's condition. Nevertheless he by no means failed to observe Viola's beauty and splendor, and how she quite effaced the poor little bride. The allowance that Perdita had enjoyed for her dress had now been transferred to her sister, who certainly made the most of it. On the morning after the wedding, he had a lady's saddle put on the horse of the servant who had come with him from town, and went out with the young girl for a ride. It was a keen, clear morning in January; the ground was bare and hard, and the horses in good condition,—to say nothing of Viola, who was charming in her hat and plume, and her dark blue riding-coat, trimmed with fur. They rode all the morning, they lost their way, and were obliged to stop for dinner at a farm-house. The early winter dusk had fallen when they got home. Mrs. Willoughby met them with a long face. A messenger had arrived at noon from Mrs. Lloyd; she was beginning to be ill, and desired her husband's immediate return. The young man swore at the thought that he had lost several hours, and that by hard rid-ing he might already have been with his wife. He barely con-sented to stop for a mouthful of supper, but mounted the messenger's horse and started off at a gallop.

He reached home at midnight. His wife had been delivered of a little girl. "Ah, why weren't you with me?" she said, as he came to her bedside.

"I was out of the house when the man came. I was with Viola," said Lloyd, innocently.

Mrs. Lloyd made a little moan, and turned about. But she continued to do very well, and for a week her improvement was uninterrupted. Finally, however, through some excess of diet or of exposure, it was checked, and the poor lady grew rapidly worse. Lloyd was in despair. It very soon became evi-dent that the relapse was fatal. Mrs. Lloyd came to a sense of her approaching end, and declared that she was reconciled with death. On the third evening after the change took place she told her husband that she felt she would not outlast the night. She dismissed her servants, and also requested her mother to withdraw,—Mrs. Willoughby having arrived on the preceding day. She had had her infant placed on the bed be-side her, and she lay on her side, with the child against her breast, holding her husband's hands. The night-lamp was hid-den behind the heavy curtains of the bed, but the room was illumined with a red glow from the immense fire of logs on the hearth.

"It seems strange to die by such a fire as that," the young woman said, feebly trying to smile. "If I had but a little of such fire in my veins! But I've given it all to this little spark of mortality." And she dropped her eyes on her child. Then rais-ing them she looked at her husband with a long penetrating gaze. The last feeling which lingered in her heart was one of mistrust. She had not recovered from the shock which Arthur had given her by telling her that in the hour of her agony he had been with Viola. She trusted her husband very nearly as well as she loved him; but now that she was called away forever, she felt a cold horror of her sister. She felt in her soul that Viola had never ceased to envy her good fortune; and a year of happy security had not effaced the young girl's image, dressed in her wedding garments, and smiling with fancied triumph. Now that Arthur was to be alone, what might not Viola do? She was beautiful, she was engaging; what arts might she not use, what impression might she not make upon the young man's melancholy heart? Mrs. Lloyd looked at her husband in silence. It seemed hard, after all, to doubt of his constancy. His fine eyes were filled with tears; his face was convulsed with weeping; the clasp of his hands was warm and passionate. How noble he looked, how tender, how faithful and devoted! "Nay," thought Perdita, "he's not for such as Viola. He'll never forget me. Nor does Viola truly care for him; she cares only for vanities and finery and jewels." And she dropped her eyes on her white hands, which her husband's liberality had covered with rings, and on the lace ruffles which trimmed the edge of her night-dress. "She covets my rings and my laces more than she covets my husband."

At this moment the thought of her sister's rapacity seemed to cast a dark shadow between her and the helpless figure of her little girl. "Arthur," she said, "you must take off my rings. I shall not be buried in them. One of these days my daughter shall wear them,—my rings and my laces and silks. I had them all brought out and shown me to-day. It's a great wardrobe, —there's not such another in the Province; I can say it without vanity now that I've done with it. It will be a great inheritance for my daughter, when she grows into a young woman. There are things there that a man never buys twice, and if they're lost you'll never again see the like. So you'll watch them well. Some dozen things I've left to Viola; I've named them to my mother. I've given her that blue and silver; it was meant for her; I wore it only once, I looked ill in it. But the rest are to be sacredly kept for this little innocent. It's such a providence that she should be my color; she can wear my gowns; she has her mother's eyes. You know the same fashions come back every twenty years. She can wear my gowns as they are. They'll lie there quietly waiting till she grows into them,—wrapped in camphor and rose-leaves, and keeping their colors in the sweet-scented darkness. She shall have black hair, she shall wear my carnation satin. Do you promise me, Arthur?"

"Promise you what, dearest?"

"Promise me to keep your poor little wife's old gowns."

"Are you afraid I'll sell them?"

"No, but that they may get scattered. My mother will have them properly wrapped up, and you shall lay them away under a double-lock. Do you know the great chest in the attic, with the iron bands? There's no end to what it will hold. You can lay them all there. My mother and the housekeeper will do it, and give you the key. And you'll keep the key in your secretary, and never give it to any one but your child. Do you promise me?"

"Ah, yes, I promise you," said Lloyd, puzzled at the intensity with which his wife appeared to cling to this idea.

"Will you swear?" repeated Perdita.

"Yes, I swear."

"Well—I trust you—I trust you," said the poor lady, looking into his eyes with eyes in which, if he had suspected her vague apprehensions, he might have read an appeal quite as much as an assurance.

Lloyd bore his bereavement soberly and manfully. A month after his wife's death, in the course of commerce, circumstances arose which offered him an opportunity of going to England. He embraced it as an alleviation to his sadness. He was absent nearly a year, during which his little girl was tenderly nursed and cherished by her grandmother. On his return he had his house again thrown open, and announced his intention of keeping the same state as during his wife's lifetime. It very soon came to be predicted that he would marry again, and there were at least a dozen young women of whom one may say that it was by no fault of theirs that, for six months after his return, the prediction did not come true. During this interval he still left his little daughter in Mrs. Willoughby's hands, the latter assuring him that a change of residence at so tender an age was perilous to her health. Finally, however, he declared that his heart longed for the little creature's presence, and that she must be brought up to town. He sent his coach and his housekeeper to fetch her home. Mrs. Willoughby was in terror lest something should befall her on the road; and, in accordance with this feeling, Viola offered to ride along with her. She could return the next day. So she went up to town with her little niece, and Mr. Lloyd met her on the threshold of his house, overcome with her kindness and with gratitude. Instead of returning the next day, Viola stayed out the week; and when at last she reappeared, she had only come for her clothes. Arthur would not hear of her coming home, nor would the baby. She cried and moaned if Viola left her; and at the sight of her grief Arthur lost his wits, and swore that she was going to die. In fine, nothing would suit them but that Viola should remain until the little thing had grown used to strange faces.

It took two months for this consummation to be brought about; for it was not until this period had elapsed that Viola took leave of her brother-in-law. Mrs. Willoughby had fretted and fumed over her daughter's absence; she had declared that it was not becoming, and that it was the talk of the town. She had reconciled herself to it only because, during the young girl's visit, the household enjoyed an unwonted term of peace. Bernard Willoughby had brought his wife home to live, between whom and her sister-in-law there existed a bitter hostility. Viola was perhaps no angel; but in the daily practice of life she was a sufficiently good-natured girl, and if she quarrelled with Mrs. Bernard it was not without provocation. Quarrel, however, she did, to the great annoyance not only of her antagonist, but the two spectators of these constant altercations. Her stay in the household of her brother-in-law, therefore, would have been delightful, if only because it removed her from contact with the object of her antipathy at home. It was doubly—it was ten times—delightful, inasmuch as it kept her near the object of her old passion. Mrs. Lloyd's conjectures had fallen very far short of the truth touching Viola's feeling for her husband. It had been a passion at first and a passion it remained,—a passion of whose radiant heat, tempered to the delicate state of his feelings, Mr. Lloyd very soon felt the influence. Lloyd, as I have said, was no paragon; it was not in his nature to practise an ideal constancy. He had not been many days in the house with his sister-in-law before he began to assure himself that she was, in the language of that day, a devilish fine woman. Whether Viola really practised those insidious arts that her sister had been tempted to impute to her it is needless to inquire. It is enough to say that she found means to appear to the very best advantage. She used to seat herself every morning before the great fireplace in the dining-room, at work upon a piece of tapestry, with her little niece disporting herself on the carpet at her feet, or on the train of her dress, and playing with her woollen balls. Lloyd would have been a very stupid fellow if he had remained insensible to the rich suggestions of this charming picture. He was prodigiously fond of his little girl, and was never weary of taking her in his arms and tossing her up and down, and making her crow with delight. Very often, however, he would venture upon greater liberties than the little creature was yet prepared to allow, and she would suddenly vociferate her displeasure. Viola would then drop her tapestry, and put out her handsome hands with the serious smile of the young girl whose virgin fancy has revealed to her all a mother's healing arts. Lloyd would give up the child, their eyes would meet, their hands would touch, and Viola would extinguish the little girl's sobs upon the snowy folds of the kerchief that crossed her bosom. Her dignity was perfect, and nothing could be less obtrusive than the manner in which she accepted her brother-in-law's hospitality. It may be almost said, perhaps, that there was something harsh in her reserve. Lloyd had a provoking feeling that she was in the house, and yet that she was unapproachable. Half an hour after supper, at the very outset of the long winter evenings, she would light her candle, and make the young man a most respectful courtesy, and march off to bed. If these were arts, Viola was a great artist. But their effect was so gentle, so gradual, they were calculated to work upon the young widower's fancy with such a finely shaded *crescendo*, that, as the reader has seen, several weeks elapsed before Viola began to feel sure that her return would cover her outlay. When this became morally certain, she packed up her trunk, and returned to her mother's house. For three days she waited; on the fourth Mr. Lloyd made his appearance, a respectful but ardent suitor. Viola

heard him out with great humility, and accepted him with infinite modesty. It is hard to imagine that Mrs. Lloyd should
have forgiven her husband; but if anything might have disarmed her resentment, it would have been the ceremonious
continence of this interview. Viola imposed upon her lover
but a short probation. They were married, as was becoming,
with great privacy,—almost with secrecy,—in the hope, perhaps, as was waggishly remarked at the time, that the late
Mrs. Lloyd wouldn't hear of it.

The marriage was to all appearance a happy one, and each
party obtained what each had desired,—Lloyd "a devilish fine
woman," and Viola—but Viola's desires, as the reader will
have observed, have remained a good deal of a mystery. There
were, indeed, two blots upon their felicity; but time would,
perhaps, efface them. During the three first years of her marriage Mrs. Lloyd failed to become a mother, and her husband
on his side suffered heavy losses of money. This latter circumstance compelled a material retrenchment in his expenditure,
and Viola was perforce less of a great lady than her sister had
been. She contrived, however, to sustain with unbroken consistency the part of an elegant woman, although it must be
confessed that it required the exercise of more ingenuity than
belongs to your real aristocratic repose. She had long since ascertained that her sister's immense wardrobe had been se-
questrated for the benefit of her daughter, and that it lay
languishing in thankless gloom in the dusty attic. It was a revolting thought that these glorious fabrics should wait on the
bidding of a little girl who sat in a high chair, and ate bread-
and-milk with a wooden spoon. Viola had the good taste,
however, to say nothing about the matter until several
months had expired. Then, at last, she timidly broached it to
her husband. Was it not a pity that so much finery should be
lost?—for lost it would be, what with colors fading, and
moths eating it up, and the change of fashions. But Lloyd
gave so abrupt and peremptory a negative to her inquiry, that
she saw that for the present her attempt was vain. Six months
went by, however, and brought with them new needs and
new fancies. Viola's thoughts hovered lovingly about her sister's relics. She went up and looked at the chest in which they
lay imprisoned. There was a sullen defiance in its three great

padlocks and its iron bands, which only quickened her desires. There was something exasperating in its incorruptible immobility. It was like a grim and grizzled old household servant, who locks his jaws over a family secret. And then there was a look of capacity in its vast extent, and a sound as of dense fulness, when Viola knocked its side with the toe of her little slipper, which caused her to flush with baffled longing. "It's absurd," she cried; "it's improper, it's wicked," and she forthwith resolved upon another attack upon her husband. On the following day, after dinner, when he had had his wine, she bravely began it. But he cut her short with great sternness.

"Once for all, Viola," said he, "it's out of the question. I shall be gravely displeased if you return to the matter."

"Very good," said Viola. "I'm glad to learn the value at which I'm held. Great Heaven!" she cried, "I'm a happy woman. It's a delightful thing to feel one's self sacrificed to a caprice!" And her eyes filled with tears of anger and disappointment.

Lloyd had a good-natured man's horror of a woman's sobs, and he attempted—I may say he condescended—to explain. "It's not a caprice, dear, it's a promise," he said,—"an oath."

"An oath? It's a pretty matter for oaths! and to whom, pray?"

"To Perdita," said the young man, raising his eyes for an instant, but immediately dropping them.

"Perdita,—ah, Perdita!" And Viola's tears broke forth. Her bosom heaved with stormy sobs,—sobs which were the long-deferred counterpart of the violent fit of weeping in which she had indulged herself on the night when she discovered her sister's betrothal. She had hoped, in her better moments, that she had done with her jealousy; but here it raged again as fierce as ever. "And pray what right," she cried, "had Perdita to dispose of my future? What right had she to bind you to meanness and cruelty? Ah, I occupy a dignified place, and I make a very fine figure! I'm welcome to what Perdita has left! And what has she left? I never knew till now how little! Nothing, nothing, nothing!"

This was very poor logic, but it was very good passion. Lloyd put his arm around his wife's waist and tried to kiss her, but she shook him off with magnificent scorn. Poor fellow! he had coveted a "devilish fine woman," and he had got one. Her scorn was intolerable. He walked away with his ears tingling,—irresolute, distracted. Before him was his secretary, and in it the sacred key which with his own hand he had turned in the triple lock. He marched up and opened it, and took the key from a secret drawer, wrapped in a little packet which he had sealed with his own honest bit of blazonry. *Teneo*, said the motto,—"I hold." But he was ashamed to put it back. He flung it upon the table beside his wife.

"Keep it!" she cried. "I want it not. I hate it!"

"I wash my hands of it," cried her husband. "God forgive me!"

Mrs. Lloyd gave an indignant shrug of her shoulders, and swept out of the room, while the young man retreated by another door. Ten minutes later Mrs. Lloyd returned, and found the room occupied by her little step-daughter and the nursery-maid. The key was not on the table. She glanced at the child. The child was perched on a chair with the packet in her hands. She had broken the seal with her own little fingers. Mrs. Lloyd hastily took possession of the key.

At the habitual supper-hour Arthur Lloyd came back from his counting-room. It was the month of June, and supper was served by daylight. The meal was placed on the table, but Mrs. Lloyd failed to make her appearance. The servant whom his master sent to call her came back with the assurance that her room was empty, and that the women informed him that she had not been seen since dinner. They had in truth observed her to have been in tears, and, supposing her to be shut up in her chamber, had not disturbed her. Her husband called her name in various parts of the house, but without response. At last it occurred to him that he might find her by taking the way to the attic. The thought gave him a strange feeling of discomfort, and he bade his servants remain behind, wishing no witness in his quest. He reached the foot of the staircase leading to the topmost flat, and stood with his hand on the banisters, pronouncing his wife's name. His voice trembled. He called again, louder and more firmly. The only sound which disturbed the absolute silence was a faint echo of his own voice, repeating his question under the great eaves. He nevertheless felt irresistibly moved to ascend the staircase.

It opened upon a wide hall, lined with wooden closets, and terminating in a window which looked westward, and admitted the last rays of the sun. Before the window stood the great chest. Before the chest, on her knees, the young man saw with amazement and horror the figure of his wife. In an instant he crossed the interval between them, bereft of utterance. The lid of the chest stood open, exposing, amid their perfumed napkins, its treasure of stuffs and jewels. Viola had fallen backward from a kneeling posture, with one hand supporting her on the floor and the other pressed to her heart. On her limbs was the stiffness of death, and on her face, in the fading light of the sun, the terror of something more than death. Her lips were parted in entreaty, in dismay, in agony; and on her bloodless brow and cheeks there glowed the marks of ten hideous wounds from two vengeful ghostly hands.

A Most Extraordinary Case

L ATE in the spring of the year 1865, just as the war had come to a close, a young invalid officer lay in bed in one of the uppermost chambers of one of the great New York hotels. His meditations were interrupted by the entrance of a waiter, who handed him a card superscribed *Mrs. Samuel Mason*, and bearing on its reverse the following words in pencil: "Dear Colonel Mason, I have only just heard of your being here, ill and alone. It's too dreadful. Do you remember me? Will you see me? If you do, I think you *will* remember me. I insist on coming up. M. M."

Mason was undressed, unshaven, weak, and feverish. His ugly little hotel chamber was in a state of confusion which had not even the merit of being picturesque. Mrs. Mason's card was at once a puzzle and a heavenly intimation of comfort. But all that it represented was so dim to the young man's enfeebled perception that it took him some moments to collect his thoughts.

"It's a lady, sir," said the waiter, by way of assisting him.

"Is she young or old?" asked Mason.

"Well, sir, she's a little of both."

"I can't ask a lady to come up here," groaned the invalid.

"Upon my word, sir, you look beautiful," said the waiter. "They like a sick man. And I see she's of your own name," continued Michael, in whom constant service had bred great frankness of speech; "the more shame to her for not coming before."

Colonel Mason concluded that, as the visit had been of Mrs. Mason's own seeking, he would receive her without more ado. "If she doesn't mind it, I'm sure I needn't," said the poor fellow, who hadn't the strength to be over-punctilious. So in a very few moments his visitor was ushered up to his bedside. He saw before him a handsome, middle-aged blond woman, stout of figure, and dressed in the height of the fashion, who displayed no other embarrassment than such as was easily explained by the loss of breath consequent on the ascent of six flights of stairs.

"Do you remember me?" she asked, taking the young man's hand.

He lay back on his pillow, and looked at her. "You used to be my aunt,—my aunt Maria," he said.

"I'm your aunt Maria, still," she answered. "It's very good of you not to have forgotten me."

"It's very good of you not to have forgotten *me*," said Mason, in a tone which betrayed a deeper feeling than the wish to return a civil speech.

"Dear me, you've had the war and a hundred dreadful things. I've been living in Europe, you know. Since my return I've been living in the country, in your uncle's old house on the river, of which the lease had just expired when I came home. I came to town yesterday on business, and accidentally heard of your condition and your whereabouts. I knew you'd gone into the army, and I had been wondering a dozen times what had become of you, and whether you wouldn't turn up now that the war's at last over. Of course I didn't lose a moment in coming to you. I'm *so* sorry for you." Mrs. Mason looked about her for a seat. The chairs were encumbered with odds and ends belonging to her nephew's wardrobe and to his equipment, and with the remnants of his last repast. The good lady surveyed the scene with the beautiful mute irony of compassion.

The young man lay watching her comely face in delicious submission to whatever form of utterance this feeling might take. "You're the first woman—to call a woman—I've seen in I don't know how many months," he said, contrasting her appearance with that of his room, and reading her thoughts.

"I should suppose so. I mean to be as good as a dozen." She disembarrassed one of the chairs, and brought it to the bed. Then, seating herself, she ungloved one of her hands, and laid it softly on the young man's wrist. "What a great full-grown young fellow you've become!" she pursued. "Now, tell me, are you very ill?"

"You must ask the doctor," said Mason. "I actually don't know. I'm extremely uncomfortable, but I suppose it's partly my circumstances."

"I've no doubt it's more than half your circumstances. I've seen the doctor. Mrs. Van Zandt is an old friend of mine; and when I come to town, I always go to see her. It was from her I learned this morning that you were here in this state. We had begun by rejoicing over the new prospects of peace; and from that, of course, we had got to lamenting the numbers of young men who are to enter upon it with lost limbs and shattered health. It happened that Mrs. Van Zandt mentioned several of her husband's patients as examples, and yourself among the number. You were an excellent young man, miserably sick, without family or friends, and with no asylum but a suffocating little closet in a noisy hotel. You may imagine that I pricked up my ears, and asked your baptismal name. Dr. Van Zandt came in, and told me. Your name is luckily an uncommon one: it's absurd to suppose that there could be two Ferdinand Masons. In short, I felt that you were my husband's brother's child, and that at last I too might have my little turn at hero-nursing. The little that the Doctor knew of your history agreed with the little that I knew, though I confess I was sorry to hear that you had never spoken of our relationship. But why should you? At all events you've got to acknowledge it now. I regret your not having said something about it before, only because the Doctor might have brought us together a month ago, and you would now have been well."

"It will take me more than a month to get well," said Mason, feeling that, if Mrs. Mason was meaning to exert herself on his behalf, she should know the real state of the case. "I never spoke of you, because I had quite lost sight of you. I fancied you were still in Europe; and indeed," he added, after a moment's hesitation, "I heard that you had married again."

"Of course you did," said Mrs. Mason, placidly. "I used to hear it once a month myself. But I had a much better right to fancy you married. Thank Heaven, however, there's nothing of that sort between us. We can each do as we please. I promise to cure you in a month, in spite of yourself."

"What's your remedy?" asked the young man, with a smile very courteous, considering how sceptical it was.

"My first remedy is to take you out of this horrible hole. I talked it all over with Dr. Van Zandt. He says you must get into the country. Why, my dear boy, this is enough to kill you outright,—one Broadway outside of your window and another outside of your door! Listen to me. My house is directly on the river, and only two hours' journey by rail. You know I've no children. My only companion is my niece, Caroline Hofmann. You shall come and stay with us until you are as strong as you need be,—if it takes a dozen years. You shall have sweet, cool air, and proper food, and decent attendance, and the devotion of a sensible woman. I shall not listen to a word of objection. You shall do as you please, get up when you please, dine when you please, go to bed when you please, and say what you please. I shall ask nothing of you but to let yourself be very dearly cared for. Do you remember how, when you were a boy at school, after your father's death, you were taken with measles, and your uncle had you brought to our own house? I helped to nurse you myself, and I remember what nice manners you had in the very midst of your measles. Your uncle was very fond of you; and if he had had any considerable property of his own, I know he would have remembered you in his will. But of course he couldn't leave away his wife's money. What I wish to do for you is a very small part of what he would have done, if he had only lived, and heard of your gallantry and your sufferings. So it's settled. I shall go home this afternoon. To-morrow morning I shall despatch my man-servant to you with instructions. He's an Englishman. He thoroughly knows his business, and he will put up your things, and save you every particle of trouble. You've only to let yourself be dressed, and driven to the train. I shall, of course, meet you at your journey's end. Now don't tell me you're not strong enough."

"I feel stronger at this moment than I've felt in a dozen weeks," said Mason. "It's useless for me to attempt to thank you."

"Quite useless. I shouldn't listen to you. And I suppose," added Mrs. Mason, looking over the bare walls and scanty furniture of the room, "you pay a fabulous price for this bower of bliss. Do you need money?"

The young man shook his head.

"Very well then," resumed Mrs. Mason, conclusively, "from this moment you're in my hands."

The young man lay speechless from the very fulness of his

heart; but he strove by the pressure of his fingers to give her some assurance of his gratitude. His companion rose, and lingered beside him, drawing on her glove, and smiling quietly with the look of a long-baffled philanthropist who has at last discovered a subject of infinite capacity. Poor Ferdinand's weary visage reflected her smile. Finally, after the lapse of years, he too was being cared for. He let his head sink into the pillow, and silently inhaled the perfume of her sober elegance and her cordial good-nature. He felt like taking her dress in his hand, and asking her not to leave him,—now that solitude would be bitter. His eyes, I suppose, betrayed this touching apprehension,—doubly touching in a war-wasted young officer. As she prepared to bid him farewell, Mrs. Mason stooped, and kissed his forehead. He listened to the rustle of her dress across the carpet, to the gentle closing of the door, and to her retreating footsteps. And then, giving way to his weakness, he put his hands to his face, and cried like a homesick school-boy. He had been reminded of the exquisite side of life.

Matters went forward as Mrs. Mason had arranged them. At six o'clock on the following evening Ferdinand found himself deposited at one of the way stations of the Hudson River Railroad, exhausted by his journey, and yet excited at the prospect of its drawing to a close. Mrs. Mason was in waiting in a low basket-phaeton, with a magazine of cushions and wrappings. Ferdinand transferred himself to her side, and they drove rapidly homeward. Mrs. Mason's house was a cottage of liberal make, with a circular lawn, a sinuous avenue, and a well-grown plantation of shrubbery. As the phaeton drew up before the porch, a young lady appeared in the doorway. Mason will be forgiven if he considered himself presented *ex officio*, as I may say, to this young lady. Before he really knew it, and in the absence of the servant, who, under Mrs. Mason's directions, was busy in the background with his trunk, he had availed himself of her proffered arm, and had allowed her to assist him through the porch, across the hall, and into the parlor, where she graciously consigned him to a sofa which, for his especial use, she had caused to be wheeled up before a fire kindled for his especial comfort. He was unable, however, to take advantage of her good offices.

Prudence dictated that without further delay he should betake himself to his room.

On the morning after his arrival he got up early, and made an attempt to be present at breakfast; but his strength failed him, and he was obliged to dress at his leisure, and content himself with a simple transition from his bed to his arm-chair. The chamber assigned him was designedly on the ground-floor, so that he was spared the trouble of measuring his strength with the staircase,—a charming room, brightly carpeted and upholstered, and marked by a certain fastidious freshness which betrayed the uncontested dominion of women. It had a broad high window, draped in chintz and crisp muslin and opening upon the greensward of the lawn. At this window, wrapped in his dressing-gown, and lost in the embrace of the most unresisting of arm-chairs, he slowly discussed his simple repast. Before long his hostess made her appearance on the lawn outside the window. As this quarter of the house was covered with warm sunshine, Mason ventured to open the window and talk to her, while she stood out on the grass beneath her parasol.

"It's time to think of your physician," she said. "You shall choose for yourself. The great physician here is Dr. Gregory, a gentleman of the old school. We have had him but once, for my niece and I have the health of a couple of dairy-maids. On that one occasion he—well, he made a fool of himself. His practice is among the 'old families,' and he only knows how to treat certain old-fashioned, obsolete complaints. Anything brought about by the war would be quite out of his range. And then he vacillates, and talks about his own maladies *à lui*. And, to tell the truth, we had a little repartee which makes our relations somewhat ambiguous."

"I see he would never do," said Mason, laughing. "But he's not your only physician?"

"No: there is a young man, a newcomer, a Dr. Knight, whom I don't know, but of whom I've heard very good things. I confess that I have a prejudice in favor of the young men. Dr. Knight has a position to establish, and I suppose he's likely to be especially attentive and careful. I believe, moreover, that he's been an army surgeon."

"I knew a man of his name," said Mason. "I wonder if this

is he. His name was Horace Knight,—a light-haired, near-sighted man."

"I don't know," said Mrs. Mason; "perhaps Caroline knows." She retreated a few steps, and called to an upper window: "Caroline, what's Dr. Knight's first name?"

Mason listened to Miss Hofmann's answer,—"I haven't the least idea."

"Is it Horace?"

"I don't know."

"Is he light or dark?"

"I've never seen him."

"Is he near-sighted?"

"How in the world should I know?"

"I fancy he's as good as any one," said Ferdinand. "With you, my dear aunt, what does the doctor matter?"

Mrs. Mason accordingly sent for Dr. Knight, who, on arrival, turned out to be her nephew's old acquaintance. Although the young men had been united by no greater intimacy than the superficial comradeship resulting from a winter in neighboring quarters, they were very well pleased to come together again. Horace Knight was a young man of good birth, good looks, good faculties, and good intentions, who, after a three years' practice of surgery in the army, had undertaken to push his fortune in Mrs. Mason's neighborhood. His mother, a widow with a small income, had recently removed to the country for economy, and her son had been unwilling to leave her to live alone. The adjacent country, moreover, offered a promising field for a man of energy,—a field well stocked with large families of easy income and of those conservative habits which lead people to make much of the cares of a physician. The local practitioner had survived the glory of his prime, and was not, perhaps, entirely guiltless of Mrs. Mason's charge, that he had not kept up with the progress of the "new diseases." The world, in fact, was getting too new for him, as well as for his old patients. He had had money invested in the South,—precious sources of revenue, which the war had swallowed up at a gulp; he had grown frightened and nervous and querulous; he had lost his presence of mind and his spectacles in several important conjunctures; he had been repeatedly and distinctly fallible; a vague dissatisfaction pervaded the breasts of his patrons; he was without competitors: in short, fortune was propitious to Dr. Knight. Mason remembered the young physician only as a good-humored, intelligent companion; but he soon had reason to believe that his medical skill would leave nothing to be desired. He arrived rapidly at a clear understanding of Ferdinand's case; he asked intelligent questions, and gave simple and definite instructions. The disorder was deeply seated and virulent, but there was no apparent reason why unflinching care and prudence should not subdue it.

"Your strength is very much reduced," he said, as he took his hat and gloves to go; "but I should say you had an excellent constitution. It seems to me, however,—if you will pardon me for saying so,—to be partly your own fault that you have fallen so low. You have opposed no resistance; you haven't cared to get well."

"I confess that I haven't,—particularly. But I don't see how you should know it."

"Why, it's obvious."

"Well, it was natural enough. Until Mrs. Mason discovered me, I hadn't a friend in the world. I had become demoralized by solitude. I had almost forgotten the difference between sickness and health. I had nothing before my eyes to remind me in tangible form of that great mass of common human interests for the sake of which—under whatever name he may disguise the impulse—a man continues in health and recovers from disease. I had forgotten that I ever cared for books or ideas, or anything but the preservation of my miserable carcass. My carcass had become quite too miserable to be an object worth living for. I was losing time and money at an appalling rate; I was getting worse rather than better; and I therefore gave up resistance. It seemed better to die easy than to die hard. I put it all in the past tense, because within these three days I've become quite another man."

"I wish to Heaven I could have heard of you," said Knight. "I would have made you come home with me, if I could have done nothing else. It was certainly not a rose-colored prospect; but what do you say now?" he continued, looking around the room. "I should say that at the present moment rose-color was the prevailing hue."

Mason assented with an eloquent smile.

"I congratulate you from my heart. Mrs. Mason—if you don't mind my speaking for her—is so thoroughly (and, I should suppose, incorrigibly) good-natured, that it's quite a surprise to find her extremely sensible."

"Yes; and so resolute and sensible in her better moments," said Ferdinand, "that it's quite a surprise to find her good-natured. She's a fine woman."

"But I should say that your especial blessing was your servant. He looks as if he had come out of an English novel."

"My especial blessing! You haven't seen Miss Hofmann, then?"

"Yes: I met her in the hall. She looks as if she had come out of an American novel. I don't know that that's great praise; but, at all events, I make her come out of it."

"You're bound in honor, then," said Mason, laughing, "to put her into another."

Mason's conviction of his newly made happiness needed no enforcement at the Doctor's hands. He felt that it would be his own fault if these were not among the most delightful days of his life. He resolved to give himself up without stint to his impressions,—utterly to vegetate. His illness alone would have been a sufficient excuse for a long term of intellectual laxity; but Mason had other good reasons besides. For the past three years he had been stretched without intermission on the rack of duty. Although constantly exposed to hard service, it had been his fortune never to receive a serious wound; and, until his health broke down, he had taken fewer holidays than any officer I ever heard of. With an abundance of a certain kind of equanimity and self-control,—a faculty of ready self-adaptation to the accomplished fact, in any direction,—he was yet in his innermost soul a singularly nervous, over-scrupulous person. On the few occasions when he had been absent from the scene of his military duties, although duly authorized and warranted in the act, he had suffered so acutely from the apprehension that something was happening, or was about to happen, which not to have witnessed or to have had a hand in would be matter of eternal mortification, that he can be barely said to have enjoyed his recreation. The sense of lost time was, moreover, his perpetual bugbear,—the feeling that precious hours were now fleeting uncounted, which in more congenial labors would suffice almost for the building of a monument more lasting than brass. This feeling he strove to propitiate as much as possible by assiduous reading and study in the intervals of his actual occupations. I cite the fact merely as an evidence of the uninterrupted austerity of his life for a long time before he fell sick. I might triple this period, indeed, by a glance at his college years, and at certain busy months which intervened between this close of his youth and the opening of the war. Mason had always worked. He was fond of work to begin with; and, in addition, the complete absence of family ties had allowed him to follow his tastes without obstruction or diversion. This circumstance had been at once a great gain to him and a serious loss. He reached his twenty-seventh year a very accomplished scholar, as scholars go, but a great dunce in certain social matters. He was quite ignorant of all those lighter and more evanescent forms of conviviality attached to being somebody's son, brother, or cousin. At last, however, as he reminded himself, he was to discover what it was to be the nephew of somebody's husband. Mrs. Mason was to teach him the meaning of the adjective *domestic*. It would have been hard to learn it in a pleasanter way. Mason felt that he was to learn something from his very idleness, and that he would leave the house a wiser as well as a better man. It became probable, thanks to that quickening of the faculties which accompanies the dawning of a sincere and rational attachment, that in this last respect he would not be disappointed. Very few days sufficed to reveal to him the many excellent qualities of his hostess,—her warm capacious heart, her fairness of mind, her good temper, her good taste, her vast fund of experience and of reminiscence, and, indeed, more than all, a certain passionate devotedness, to which fortune, in leaving her a childless widow, had done but scant justice. The two accordingly established a friendship,—a friendship that promised as well for the happiness of each as any that ever undertook to meddle with happiness. If I were telling my story from Mrs. Mason's point of view, I take it that I might make a very good thing of the statement that this lady had deliberately and solemnly conferred her affection upon my hero; but I am compelled to let it stand in this simple shape. Excellent, charming person that she was, she had every right to the rich satisfaction which belonged to a liberal—yet not too liberal—estimate of her guest. She had divined him,—so much the better for her. That it was very much the better for him is obviously one of the elementary facts of my narrative; a fact of which Mason became so rapidly and profoundly sensible, that he was soon able to dismiss it from his thoughts to his life,—its proper sphere.

In the space of ten days, then, most of the nebulous impressions evoked by change of scene had gathered into substantial form. Others, however, were still in the nebulous state,—diffusing a gentle light upon Ferdinand's path. Chief among these was the mild radiance of which Miss Hofmann was the centre. For three days after his arrival Mason had been confined to his room by the aggravation of his condition consequent upon his journey. It was not till the fourth day, therefore, that he was able to renew the acquaintance so auspiciously commenced. When at last, at dinner-time, he reappeared in the drawing-room, Miss Hofmann greeted him almost as an old friend. Mason had already discovered that she was young and gracious; he now rapidly advanced to the conclusion that she was uncommonly pretty. Before dinner was over, he had made up his mind that she was neither more nor less than beautiful. Mrs. Mason had found time to give him a full account of her life. She had lost her mother in infancy, and had been adopted by her aunt in the early years of this lady's widowhood. Her father was a man of evil habits,—a drunkard, a gambler, and a rake, outlawed from decent society. His only dealings with his daughter were to write her every month or two a begging letter, she being in possession of her mother's property. Mrs. Mason had taken her niece to Europe, and given her every advantage. She had had an expensive education; she had travelled; she had gone into the world; she had been presented, like a good republican, to no less than three European sovereigns; she had been admired; she had had half a dozen offers of marriage to her aunt's knowledge, and others, perhaps, of which she was ignorant, and had refused them all. She was now twenty-six years of age, beautiful, accomplished, and *au mieux* with her bankers.

She was an excellent girl, with a will of her own. "I'm very fond of her," Mrs. Mason declared, with her habitual frankness; "and I suppose she's equally fond of me; but we long ago gave up all idea of playing at mother and daughter. We have never had a disagreement since she was fifteen years old; but we have never had an agreement either. Caroline is no sentimentalist. She's honest, good-tempered, and perfectly discerning. She foresaw that we were still to spend a number of years together, and she wisely declined at the outset to affect a range of feelings that wouldn't stand the wear and tear of time. She knew that she would make a poor daughter, and she contented herself with being a good niece. A capital niece she is. In fact we're almost sisters. There are moments when I feel as if she were ten years older than I, and as if it were absurd in me to attempt to interfere with her life. I never do. She has it quite in her own hands. My attitude is little more than a state of affectionate curiosity as to what she will do with it. Of course she'll marry, sooner or later; but I'm curious to see the man of her choice. In Europe, you know, girls have no acquaintances but such as they share with their parents and guardians; and in that way I know most of the gentlemen who have tried to make themselves acceptable to my niece. There were some excellent young men in the number; but there was not one—or, rather, there was but one—for whom Caroline cared a straw. That one she loved, I believe; but they had a quarrel, and she lost him. She's very discreet and conciliating. I'm sure no girl ever before got rid of half a dozen suitors with so little offence. Ah, she's a dear, good girl!" Mrs. Mason pursued. "She's saved me a world of trouble in my day. And when I think what she might have been, with her beauty, and what not! She has kept all her suitors as friends. There are two of them who write to her still. She doesn't answer their letters; but once in a while she meets them, and thanks them for writing, and that contents them. The others are married, and Caroline remains single. I take for granted it won't last forever. Still, although she's *not* a sentimentalist, she'll not marry a man she doesn't care for, merely because she's growing old. Indeed, it's only the sentimental girls, to my belief, that do that. They covet a man for his money or his looks, and then give the feeling some fine name. But there's one thing, Mr. Ferdinand," added Mrs. Mason, at the close of these remarks, "you will be so good as not to fall in love with my niece. I can assure you that she'll not fall in love with you, and a hopeless passion will not hasten your recovery. Caroline is a charming girl. You can live with her very well without that. She's good for common daylight, and you'll have no need of wax-candles and ecstasies."

"Be reassured," said Ferdinand, laughing. "I'm quite too attentive to myself at present to think of any one else. Miss Hofmann might be dying for a glance of my eye, and I shouldn't hesitate to sacrifice her. It takes more than half a man to fall in love."

At the end of ten days summer had fairly set in; and Mason found it possible, and indeed profitable, to spend a large portion of his time in the open air. He was unable either to ride or to walk; and the only form of exercise which he found practicable was an occasional drive in Mrs. Mason's phaeton. On these occasions Mrs. Mason was his habitual companion. The neighborhood offered an interminable succession of beautiful drives; and poor Ferdinand took a truly exquisite pleasure in reclining idly upon a pile of cushions, warmly clad, empty-handed, silent, with only his eyes in motion, and rolling rapidly between fragrant hedges and springing crops, and beside the outskirts of woods, and along the heights which overlooked the river. Detested war was over, and all nature had ratified the peace. Mason used to gaze up into the cloudless sky until his eyes began to water, and you would have actually supposed he was shedding sentimental tears. Besides these comfortable drives with his hostess, Mason had adopted another method of inhaling the sunshine. He used frequently to spend several hours at a time on a veranda beside the house, sheltered from the observation of visitors. Here, with an arm-chair and a footstool, a cigar and half a dozen volumes of novels, to say nothing of the society of either of the ladies, and sometimes of both, he suffered the mornings to pass unmeasured and uncounted. The chief incident of these mornings was the Doctor's visit, in which, of course, there was a strong element of prose,—and very good prose, as I may add, for the Doctor was turning out an excellent fellow. But, for the rest, time unrolled itself like a gentle strain of music. Mason knew so little, from direct observation, of the *vie intime* of elegant, intelligent women, that their habits, their manners, their household motions, their principles, possessed in his view all the charm of a spectacle,—a spectacle which he contemplated with the indolence of an invalid, the sympathy of a man of taste, and a little of the awkwardness which women gladly allow, and indeed provoke, in a soldier, for the pleasure of forgiving it. It was a very simple matter to Miss Hofmann that she should be dressed in fresh crisp muslin, that her hands should be white and her attitudes felicitous; she had long since made her peace with these things. But to Mason, who was familiar only with books and men, they were objects of constant, half-dreamy contemplation. He would sit for half an hour at once, with a book on his knees and the pages unturned, scrutinizing with ingenious indirectness the simple mass of colors and contours which made up the physical personality of Miss Hofmann. There was no question as to her beauty, or as to its being a warm, sympathetic beauty, and not the cold perfection of poetry. She was the least bit taller than most women, and neither stout nor the reverse. Her hair was of a dark and lustrous brown, turning almost to black, and lending itself readily to those multitudinous ringlets which were then in fashion. Her forehead was broad, open, and serene; and her eyes of that deep and clear sea-green that you may observe of a summer's afternoon, when the declining sun shines through the rising of a wave. Her complexion was the color of perfect health. These, with her full, mild lips, her generous and flexible figure, her magnificent hands, were charms enough to occupy Mason's attention, and it was but seldom that he allowed it to be diverted. Mrs. Mason was frequently called away by her household cares, but Miss Hofmann's time was apparently quite her own. Nevertheless, it came into Ferdinand's head one day, that she gave him her company only from a sense of duty, and when, according to his wont, he had allowed this impression to ripen in his mind, he ventured to assure her that, much as he valued her society, he should be sorry to believe that her gracious bestowal of it interfered with more profitable occupations. "I'm no companion," he said. "I don't pretend to be one. I sit here deaf and dumb, and blind and halt, patiently waiting to be healed,—waiting till this vagabond Nature of ours strolls my way, and brushes me with the hem of her garment."

"I find you very good company," Miss Hofmann replied on this occasion. "What do you take me for? The hero of a hundred fights, a young man who has been reduced to a shadow in the service of his country,—I should be very fastidious if I asked for anything better."

"O, if it's on theory!" said Mason. And, in spite of Miss Hofmann's protest, he continued to assume that it *was* on theory that he was not intolerable. But she remained true to her post, and with a sort of placid inveteracy which seemed to the young man to betray either a great deal of indifference or a great deal of self-command. "She thinks I'm stupid," he said to himself. "Of course she thinks I'm stupid. How should she think otherwise? She and her aunt have talked me over. Mrs. Mason has enumerated my virtues, and Miss Hofmann has added them up: total, a well-meaning bore. She has armed herself with patience. I must say it becomes her very well." Nothing was more natural, however, than that Mason should exaggerate the effect of his social incapacity. His remarks were desultory, but not infrequent; often trivial, but always good-humored and informal. The intervals of silence, indeed, which enlivened his conversation with Miss Hofmann, might easily have been taken for the confident pauses in the talk of old friends.

Once in a while Miss Hofmann would sit down at the piano and play to him. The veranda communicated with the little sitting-room by means of a long window, one side of which stood open. Mason would move his chair to this aperture, so that he might see the music as well as hear it. Seated at the instrument, at the farther end of the half-darkened room, with her figure in half-profile, and her features, her movements, the color of her dress, but half defined in the cool obscurity, Miss Hofmann would discourse infinite melody. Mason's eyes rested awhile on the vague white folds of her dress, on the heavy convolutions of her hair, and the gentle movement of her head in sympathy with the music. Then a single glance in the other direction revealed another picture,—the dazzling midday sky, the close-cropped lawn, lying almost black in its light, and the patient, round-backed gardener, in white shirtsleeves, clipping the hedge or rolling the gravel. One morning, what with the music, the light, the heat, and the fragrance of the flowers,—from the perfect equilibrium of his senses, as it were,—Mason manfully went to sleep. On waking he found that he had slept an hour, and that the sun had invaded the veranda. The music had ceased; but on looking into the parlor he saw Miss Hofmann still at the piano. A gentleman was leaning on the instrument with his back toward the window, intercepting her face. Mason sat for some moments, hardly sensible, at first, of his transition to consciousness, languidly guessing at her companion's identity. In a short time his observation was quickened by the fact that the picture before him was animated by no sound of voices. The silence was unnatural, or, at the least, disagreeable. Mason moved his chair, and the gentleman looked round. The gentleman was Horace Knight. The Doctor called out, "Good morning!" from his place, and finished his conversation with Miss Hofmann before coming out to his patient. When he moved away from the piano, Mason saw the reason of his friends' silence. Miss Hofmann had been trying to decipher a difficult piece of music, the Doctor had been trying to assist her, and they had both been brought to a stop.

"What a clever fellow he is!" thought Mason. "There he stands, rattling off musical terms as if he had never thought of anything else. And yet, when he talks medicine, it's impossible to talk more to the point." Mason continued to be very well satisfied with Knight's intelligence of his case, and with his treatment of it. He had been in the country now for three weeks, and he would hesitate indeed to affirm that he felt materially better; but he felt more comfortable. There were moments when he feared to push the inquiry as to his real improvement, because he had a sickening apprehension that he would discover that in one or two important particulars he was worse. In the course of time he imparted these fears to his physician. "But I may be mistaken," he added, "and for this reason. During the last fortnight I have become much more sensible of my condition than while I was in town. I then accepted each additional symptom as a matter of course. The more the better, I thought. But now I expect them to give an account of themselves. Now I have a positive wish to recover."

Dr. Knight looked at his patient for a moment curiously. "You are right," he said; "a little impatience is a very good thing."

"O, I'm not impatient. I'm patient to a most ridiculous extent. I allow myself a good six months, at the very least."

"That is certainly not unreasonable," said Knight. "And will you allow me a question? Do you intend to spend those six months in this place?"

"I'm unable to answer you. I suppose I shall finish the summer here, unless the summer finishes me. Mrs. Mason will hear of nothing else. In September I hope to be well enough to go back to town, even if I'm not well enough to think of work. What do you advise?"

"I advise you to put away all thoughts of work. That is imperative. Haven't you been at work all your life long? Can't you spare a pitiful little twelvemonth to health and idleness and pleasure?"

"Ah, pleasure, pleasure!" said Mason, ironically.

"Yes, pleasure," said the Doctor. "What has she done to you that you should speak of her in that manner?"

"O, she bothers me," said Mason.

"You are very fastidious. It's better to be bothered by pleasure than by pain."

"I don't deny it. But there is a way of being indifferent to pain. I don't mean to say that I have found it out, but in the course of my illness I have caught a glimpse of it. But it's beyond my strength to be indifferent to pleasure. In two words, I'm afraid of dying of kindness."

"O, nonsense!"

"Yes, it's nonsense; and yet it's not. There would be nothing miraculous in my not getting well."

"It will be your fault if you don't. It will prove that you're fonder of sickness than health, and that you're not fit company for sensible mortals. Shall I tell you?" continued the Doctor, after a moment's hesitation. "When I knew you in the army, I always found you a step beyond my comprehension. You took things too hard. You had scruples and doubts about everything. And on top of it all you were devoured with the mania of appearing to take things easily and to be perfectly indifferent. You played your part very well, but you must do me the justice to confess that it *was* a part."

"I hardly know whether that's a compliment or an impertinence. I hope, at least, that you don't mean to accuse me of playing a part at the present moment."

"On the contrary. I'm your physician; you're frank."

"It's not because you're my physician that I'm frank," said Mason. "I shouldn't think of burdening you in that capacity with my miserable caprices and fancies"; and Ferdinand paused a moment. "You're a man!" he pursued, laying his hand on his companion's arm. "There's nothing here but women, Heaven reward them! I'm saturated with whispers and perfumes and smiles, and the rustling of dresses. It takes a man to understand a man."

"It takes more than a man to understand you, my dear Mason," said Knight, with a kindly smile. "But I listen."

Mason remained silent, leaning back in his chair, with his eyes wandering slowly over the wide patch of sky disclosed by the window, and his hands languidly folded on his knees. The Doctor examined him with a look half amused, half perplexed. But at last his face grew quite sober, and he contracted his brow. He placed his hand on Mason's arm and shook it gently, while Ferdinand met his gaze. The Doctor frowned, and, as he did so, his companion's mouth expanded into a placid smile. "If you don't get well," said Knight,—"if you don't get well—" and he paused.

"What will be the consequences?" asked Ferdinand, still smiling.

"I shall hate you," said Knight, half smiling too.

Mason broke into a laugh. "What shall I care for that?"

"I shall tell people that you were a poor, spiritless fellow,— that you are no loss."

"I give you leave," said Ferdinand.

The Doctor got up. "I don't like obstinate patients," he said.

Ferdinand burst into a long loud laugh, which ended in a fit of coughing.

"I'm getting too amusing," said Knight; "I must go."

"Nay, laugh and grow fat," cried Ferdinand. "I promise to

get well." But that evening, at least, he was no better, as it turned out, for his momentary exhilaration. Before turning in for the night, he went into the drawing-room to spend half an hour with the ladies. The room was empty, but the lamp was lighted, and he sat down by the table and read a chapter in a novel. He felt excited, light-headed, light-hearted, half-intoxicated, as if he had been drinking strong coffee. He put down his book, and went over to the mantelpiece, above which hung a mirror, and looked at the reflection of his face. For almost the first time in his life he examined his features, and wondered if he were good-looking. He was able to conclude only that he looked very thin and pale, and utterly unfit for the business of life. At last he heard an opening of doors overhead, and a rustling of voluminous skirts on the stairs. Mrs. Mason came in, fresh from the hands of her maid, and dressed for a party.

"And is Miss Hofmann going?" asked Mason. He felt that his heart was beating, and that he hoped Mrs. Mason would say no. His momentary sense of strength, the mellow lamplight, the open piano, and the absence, of the excellent woman before him, struck him as so many reasons for her remaining at home. But the sound of the young lady's descent upon the stairs was an affirmative to his question. She forthwith appeared upon the threshold, dressed in crape of a kind of violent blue, with desultory clusters of white roses. For some ten minutes Mason had the pleasure of being witness of that series of pretty movements and preparations with which women in full dress beguile the interval before their carriage is announced; their glances at the mirror, their slow assumption of their gloves, their mutual revisions and felicitations.

"Isn't she lovely?" said Miss Hofmann to the young man, nodding at her aunt, who looked every inch the handsome woman that she was.

"Lovely, lovely, lovely!" said Ferdinand, so emphatically, that Miss Hofmann transferred her glance to him; while Mrs. Mason good-humoredly turned her back, and Caroline saw that Mason was engaged in a survey of her own person.

Miss Hofmann smiled discreetly. "I wish very much you might come," she said.

"I shall go to bed," answered Ferdinand, simply.

"Well, that's much better. We shall go to bed at two o'clock. Meanwhile I shall caper about the rooms to the sound of a piano and fiddle, and Aunt Maria will sit against the wall with her toes tucked under a chair. Such is life!"

"You'll dance then," said Mason.

"I shall dance. Dr. Knight has invited me."

"Does he dance well, Caroline?" asked Mrs. Mason.

"That remains to be seen. I have a strong impression that he does not."

"Why?" asked Ferdinand.

"He does so many other things well."

"That's no reason," said Mrs. Mason. "Do you dance, Ferdinand?"

Ferdinand shook his head.

"I like a man to dance," said Caroline, "and yet I like him not to dance."

"That's a very womanish speech, my dear," said Mrs. Mason.

"I suppose it is. It's inspired by my white gloves and my low dress, and my roses. When once a woman gets on such things, Colonel Mason, expect nothing but nonsense.—Aunt Maria," the young lady continued, "will you button my glove?"

"Let me do it," said Ferdinand. "Your aunt has her gloves on."

"Thank you." And Miss Hofmann extended a long white arm, and drew back with her other hand the bracelet from her wrist. Her glove had three buttons, and Mason performed the operation with great deliberation and neatness.

"And now," said he, gravely, "I hear the carriage. You want me to put on your shawl."

"If you please,"—Miss Hofmann passed her full white drapery into his hands, and then turned about her fair shoulders. Mason solemnly covered them, while the waiting-maid, who had come in, performed the same service for the elder lady.

"Good by," said the latter, giving him her hand. "You're not to come out into the air." And Mrs. Mason, attended by her maid, transferred herself to the carriage. Miss Hofmann gathered up her loveliness, and prepared to follow. Ferdinand stood leaning against the parlor door, watching her; and as she rustled past him she nodded farewell with a silent smile. A characteristic smile, Mason thought it,—a smile in which there was no expectation of triumph and no affectation of reluctance, but just the faintest suggestion of perfectly good-humored resignation. Mason went to the window and saw the carriage roll away with its lighted lamps, and then stood looking out into the darkness. The sky was cloudy. As he turned away the maidservant came in, and took from the table a pair of rejected gloves. "I hope you're feeling better, sir," she said, politely.

"Thank you, I think I am."

"It's a pity you couldn't have gone with the ladies."

"I'm not well enough yet to think of such things," said Mason, trying to smile. But as he walked across the floor he felt himself attacked by a sudden sensation, which cannot be better described than as a general collapse. He felt dizzy, faint, and sick. His head swam and his knees trembled. "I'm ill," he said, sitting down on the sofa; "you must call William."

William speedily arrived, and conducted the young man to his room. "What on earth had you been doing, sir?" asked this most irreproachable of serving-men, as he helped him to undress.

Ferdinand was silent a moment. "I had been putting on Miss Hofmann's shawl," he said.

"Is that all, sir?"

"And I had been buttoning her glove."

"Well, sir, you must be very prudent."

"So it appears," said Ferdinand.

He slept soundly, however, and the next morning was the better for it. "I'm certainly better," he said to himself, as he slowly proceeded to his toilet. "A month ago such an attack as that of last evening would have effectually banished sleep. Courage, then. The Devil isn't dead, but he's dying."

In the afternoon he received a visit from Horace Knight. "So you danced last evening at Mrs. Bradshaw's," he said to his friend.

"Yes, I danced. It's a great piece of frivolity for a man in my position; but I thought there would be no harm in doing it just once, to show them I know how. My abstinence in future will tell the better. Your ladies were there. I danced with Miss Hofmann. She was dressed in blue, and she was the most beautiful woman in the room. Every one was talking about it."

"I saw her," said Mason, "before she went off."

"You should have seen her there," said Knight. "The music, the excitement, the spectators, and all that, bring out a woman's beauty."

"So I suppose," said Ferdinand.

"What strikes me," pursued the Doctor, "is her—what shall I call it?—her vitality, her quiet buoyancy. Of course, you didn't see her when she came home? If you had, you would have noticed, unless I'm very much mistaken, that she was as fresh and elastic at two o'clock as she had been at ten. While all the other women looked tired and jaded and used up, she alone showed no signs of exhaustion. She was neither pale nor flushed, but still light-footed, rosy, and erect. She's solid. You see I can't help looking at such things as a physician. She has a magnificent organization. Among all those other poor girls she seemed to have something of the inviolable strength of a goddess"; and Knight smiled frankly as he entered the region of eloquence. "She wears her artificial roses and dew-drops as if she had gathered them on the mountain-tops, instead of buying them in Broadway. She moves with long steps, her dress rustles, and to a man of fancy it's the sound of Diana on the forest-leaves."

Ferdinand nodded assent. "So you're a man of fancy," he said.

"Of course I am," said the Doctor.

Ferdinand was not inclined to question his friend's estimate of Miss Hofmann, nor to weigh his words. They only served to confirm an impression which was already strong in his own mind. Day by day he had felt the growth of this impression. "He must be a strong man who would approach her," he said to himself. "He must be as vigorous and elastic as she herself, or in the progress of courtship she will leave him far behind. He must be able to forget his lungs and his liver and his digestion. To have broken down in his country's defence, even, will avail him nothing. What is that to her? She needs a man who has defended his country without breaking down,—a being complete, intact, well seasoned, invulnerable. Then,—then," thought Ferdinand, "perhaps she will consider him. Perhaps it will be to refuse him. Perhaps, like Diana, to whom Knight compares her, she is meant to live alone. It's certain, at least, that she is able to wait. She will be young at forty-five. Women who are young at forty-five are perhaps not the most interesting women. They are likely to have felt for nobody and for nothing. But it's often less their own fault than that of the men and women about them. This one at least *can* feel; the thing is to move her. Her soul is an instrument of a hundred strings, only it takes a strong hand to draw sound. Once really touched, they will reverberate for ever and ever."

In fine, Mason was in love. It will be seen that his passion was not arrogant nor uncompromising; but, on the contrary, patient, discreet, and modest,—almost timid. For ten long days, the most memorable days of his life,—days which, if he had kept a journal, would have been left blank,—he held his tongue. He would have suffered anything rather than reveal his emotions, or allow them to come accidentally to Miss Hofmann's knowledge. He would cherish them in silence until he should feel in all his sinews that he was himself again, and then he would open his heart. Meanwhile he would be patient; he would be the most irreproachable, the most austere, the most insignificant of convalescents. He was as yet unfit to touch her, to look at her, to speak to her. A man was not to go a wooing in his dressing-gown and slippers.

There came a day, however, when, in spite of his high resolves, Ferdinand came near losing his balance. Mrs. Mason had arranged with him to drive in the phaeton after dinner. But it befell that, an hour before the appointed time, she was sent for by a neighbor who had been taken ill.

"But it's out of the question that you should lose your drive," said Miss Hofmann, who brought him her aunt's apologies. "If you are still disposed to go, I shall be happy to take the reins. I shall not be as good company as Aunt Maria, but perhaps I shall be as good company as Thomas." It was settled, accordingly, that Miss Hofmann should act as her aunt's substitute, and at five o'clock the phaeton left the door. The first half of their drive was passed in silence; and almost the first words they exchanged were as they finally drew near to a space of enclosed ground, beyond which, through the trees at its farther extremity, they caught a glimpse of a turn in the river. Miss Hofmann involuntarily pulled up. The sun had sunk low, and the cloudless western sky glowed with rosy yellow. The trees which concealed the view flung over the grass a great screen of shadow, which reached out into the road. Between their scattered stems gleamed the broad white current of the Hudson. Our friends both knew the spot. Mason had seen it from a boat, when one morning a gentleman in the neighborhood, thinking to do him a kindness, had invited him to take a short sail; and with Miss Hofmann it had long been a frequent resort.

"How beautiful!" she said, as the phaeton stopped.

"Yes, if it wasn't for those trees," said Ferdinand. "They conceal the best part of the view."

"I should rather say they indicate it," answered his companion. "From here they conceal it; but they suggest to you to make your way in, and lose yourself behind them, and enjoy the prospect in privacy."

"But you can't take a vehicle in."

"No: there is only a footpath, although I have ridden in. One of these days, when you're stronger, you must drive to this point, and get out, and walk over to the bank."

Mason was silent a moment,—a moment during which he felt in his limbs the tremor of a bold resolution. "I noticed the place the day I went out on the water with Mr. McCarthy. I immediately marked it as my own. The bank is quite high, and the trees make a little amphitheatre on its summit. I think there's a bench."

"Yes, there are two benches," said Caroline.

"Suppose, then, we try it now," said Mason, with an effort.

"But you can never walk over that meadow. You see it's broken ground. And, at all events, I can't consent to your going alone."

"That, madam," said Ferdinand, rising to his feet in the phaeton, "is a piece of folly I should never think of proposing. Yonder is a house, and in it there are people. Can't we drive thither, and place the horse in their custody?"

"Nothing is more easy, if you insist upon it. The house is occupied by a German family with a couple of children, who are old friends of mine. When I come here on horseback they always clamor for 'coppers.' From their little garden the walk is shorter."

So Miss Hofmann turned the horse toward the cottage, which stood at the head of a lane, a few yards from the road. A little boy and girl, with bare heads and bare feet,—the former members very white and the latter very black,—came out to meet her. Caroline greeted them good-humoredly in German. The girl, who was the elder, consented to watch the horse, while the boy volunteered to show the visitors the shortest way to the river. Mason reached the point in question without great fatigue, and found a prospect which would have repaid even greater trouble. To the right and to the left, a hundred feet below them, stretched the broad channel of the seaward-shifting waters. In the distance rose the gentle masses of the Catskills with all the intervening region vague and neutral in the gathering twilight. A faint odor of coolness came up to their faces from the stream below.

"You can sit down," said the little boy, doing the honors.

"Yes, Colonel, sit down," said Caroline. "You've already been on your feet too much."

Ferdinand obediently seated himself, unable to deny that he was glad to do so. Miss Hofmann released from her grasp the skirts which she had gathered up in her passage from the phaeton, and strolled to the edge of the cliff, where she stood for some moments talking with her little guide. Mason could only hear that she was speaking German. After the lapse of a few moments Miss Hofmann turned back, still talking—or rather listening—to the child.

"He's very pretty," she said in French, as she stopped before Ferdinand.

Mason broke into a laugh. "To think," said he, "that that little youngster should forbid us the use of two languages! Do you speak French, my child?"

"No," said the boy, sturdily, "I speak German."

"Ah, there I can't follow you!"

The child stared a moment, and then replied, with pardonable irrelevancy, "I'll show you the way down to the water."

"There I can't follow you either. I hope *you*'ll not go, Miss

Hofmann," added the young man, observing a movement on Caroline's part.

"Is it hard?" she asked of the child.

"No, it's easy."

"Will I tear my dress?"

The child shook his head; and Caroline descended the bank under his guidance.

As some moments elapsed before she reappeared, Ferdinand ventured to the edge of the cliff, and looked down. She was sitting on a rock on the narrow margin of sand, with her hat in her lap, twisting the feather in her fingers. In a few moments it seemed to Ferdinand that he caught the tones of her voice, wafted upward as if she were gently singing. He listened intently, and at last succeeded in distinguishing several words; they were German. "Confound her German!" thought the young man. Suddenly Miss Hofmann rose from her seat, and, after a short interval, reappeared on the platform. "What did you find down there?" asked Ferdinand, almost savagely.

"Nothing,—a little strip of a beach and a pile of stones."

"You *have* torn your dress," said Mason.

Miss Hofmann surveyed her drapery. "Where, if you please?"

"There, in front." And Mason extended his walking-stick, and inserted it into the injured fold of muslin. There was a certain graceless *brusquerie* in the movement which attracted Miss Hofmann's attention. She looked at her companion, and, seeing that his face was discomposed, fancied that he was annoyed at having been compelled to wait.

"Thank you," she said; "it's easily mended. And now suppose we go back."

"No, not yet," said Ferdinand. "We have plenty of time."

"Plenty of time to catch cold," said Miss Hofmann, kindly.

Mason had planted his stick where he had let it fall on withdrawing it from contact with his companion's skirts, and stood leaning against it, with his eyes on the young girl's face. "What if I do catch cold?" he asked abruptly.

"Come, don't talk nonsense," said Miss Hofmann.

"I never was more serious in my life." And, pausing a moment, he drew a couple of steps nearer. She had gathered her shawl closely about her, and stood with her arms lost in it, holding her elbows. "I don't mean that quite literally," Mason continued. "I wish to get well, on the whole. But there are moments when this perpetual self-coddling seems beneath the dignity of man, and I'm tempted to purchase one short hour of enjoyment, of happiness, at the cost—well, at the cost of my life if necessary!"

This was a franker speech than Ferdinand had yet made; the reader may estimate his habitual reserve. Miss Hofmann must have been somewhat surprised, and even slightly puzzled. But it was plain that he expected a rejoinder.

"I don't know what temptation you may have had," she answered, smiling; "but I confess that I can think of none in your present circumstances likely to involve the great sacrifice you speak of. What you say, Colonel Mason, is half—"

"Half what?"

"Half ungrateful. Aunt Maria flatters herself that she has made existence as easy and as peaceful for you—as stupid, if you like—as it can possibly be for a—a clever man. And now, after all, to accuse her of introducing temptations."

"Your aunt Maria is the best of women, Miss Hofmann," said Mason. "But I'm not a clever man. I'm deplorably weak-minded. Very little things excite me. Very small pleasures are gigantic temptations. I would give a great deal, for instance, to stay here with you for half an hour."

It is a delicate question whether Miss Hofmann now ceased to be perplexed; whether she discerned in the young man's accents—it was his tone, his attitude, his eyes that were fully significant, rather than his words—an intimation of that sublime and simple truth in the presence of which a wise woman puts off coquetry and prudery, and stands invested with perfect charity. But charity is nothing if not discreet; and Miss Hofmann may very well have effected the little transaction I speak of, and yet have remained, as she did remain, gracefully wrapped in her shawl, with the same serious smile on her face. Ferdinand's heart was thumping under his waistcoat; the words in which he might tell her that he loved her were fluttering there like frightened birds in a storm-shaken cage. Whether his lips would form them or not depended on the next words she uttered. On the faintest sign of defiance or of impatience he would really give her something to coquet withal. I repeat that I do not undertake to follow Miss Hofmann's feelings; I only know that her words were those of a woman of great instincts. "My dear Colonel Mason," she said, "I wish we might remain here the whole evening. The moments are quite too pleasant to be wantonly sacrificed. I simply put you on your conscience. If you believe that you can safely do so,—that you'll not have some dreadful chill in consequence,—let us by all means stay awhile. If you do not so believe, let us go back to the carriage. There is no good reason, that I see, for our behaving like children."

If Miss Hofmann apprehended a scene,—I do not assert that she did,—she was saved. Mason extracted from her words a delicate assurance that he could afford to wait. "You're an angel, Miss Hofmann," he said, as a sign that this kindly assurance had been taken. "I think we had better go back."

Miss Hofmann accordingly led the way along the path, and Ferdinand slowly followed. A man who has submitted to a woman's wisdom generally feels bound to persuade himself that he has surrendered at discretion. I suppose it was in this spirit that Mason said to himself as he walked along, "Well, I got what I wanted."

The next morning he was again an invalid. He woke up with symptoms which as yet he had scarcely felt at all; and he was obliged to acknowledge the bitter truth that, small as it was, his adventure had exceeded his strength. The walk, the evening air, the dampness of the spot, had combined to produce a violent attack of fever. As soon as it became plain that, in vulgar terms, he was "in for it," he took his heart in his hands and succumbed. As his condition grew worse, he was fortunately relieved from the custody of this valuable organ, with all it contained of hopes delayed and broken projects, by several intervals of prolonged unconsciousness.

For three weeks he was a very sick man. For a couple of days his recovery was doubted of. Mrs. Mason attended him with inexhaustible patience and with the solicitude of real affection. She was resolved that greedy Death should not possess himself, through any fault of hers, of a career so full of bright possibilities and of that active gratitude which a good-natured elderly woman would relish, as she felt that of her *protégé* to be. Her vigils were finally rewarded. One fine morning poor long-silent Ferdinand found words to tell her that he was better. His recovery was very slow, however, and it ceased several degrees below the level from which he had originally fallen. He was thus twice a convalescent,—a sufficiently miserable fellow. He professed to be very much surprised to find himself still among the living. He remained silent and grave, with a newly contracted fold in his forehead, like a man honestly perplexed at the vagaries of destiny. "It must be," he said to Mrs. Mason,—"it must be that I am reserved for great things."

In order to insure absolute quiet in the house, Ferdinand learned Miss Hofmann had removed herself to the house of a friend, at a distance of some five miles. On the first day that the young man was well enough to sit in his arm-chair Mrs. Mason spoke of her niece's return, which was fixed for the morrow. "She will want very much to see you," she said. "When she comes, may I bring her into your room?"

"Good heavens, no!" said Ferdinand, to whom the idea was very disagreeable. He met her accordingly at dinner, three days later. He left his room at the dinner hour, in company with Dr. Knight, who was taking his departure. In the hall they encountered Mrs. Mason, who invited the Doctor to remain, in honor of his patient's reappearance in society. The Doctor hesitated a moment, and, as he did so, Ferdinand heard Miss Hofmann's step descending the stair. He turned towards her just in time to catch on her face the vanishing of a glance of intelligence. As Mrs. Mason's back was against the staircase, her glance was evidently meant for Knight. He excused himself on the plea of an engagement, to Mason's regret, while the latter greeted the younger lady. Mrs. Mason proposed another day,—the following Sunday; the Doctor assented, and it was not till some time later that Ferdinand found himself wondering why Miss Hofmann should have forbidden him to remain. He rapidly perceived that during the period of their separation this young lady had lost none of her charms; on the contrary, they were more irresistible than ever. It seemed to Mason, moreover, that they were bound together by a certain pensive gentleness, a tender, submissive look, which he had hitherto failed to observe. Mrs. Mason's own remarks assured him that he was not the victim of an illusion.

"I wonder what is the matter with Caroline," she said. "If it were not that she tells me that she never was better, I should believe she is feeling unwell. I've never seen her so simple and gentle. She looks like a person who has a great fright,—a fright not altogether unpleasant."

"She has been staying in a house full of people," said Mason. "She has been excited, and amused, and preoccupied; she returns to you and me (excuse the juxtaposition,—it exists)—a kind of reaction asserts itself." Ferdinand's explanation was ingenious rather than plausible.

Mrs. Mason had a better one. "I have an impression," she said, "George Stapleton, the second of the sons, is an old admirer of Caroline's. It's hard to believe that he could have been in the house with her for a fortnight without renewing his suit, in some form or other."

Ferdinand was not made uneasy, for he had seen and talked with Mr. George Stapleton,—a young man very good-looking, very good-natured, very clever, very rich, and very unworthy, as he conceived, of Miss Hofmann. "You don't mean to say that your niece has listened to him," he answered, calmly enough.

"Listened, yes. He has made himself agreeable, and he has succeeded in making an impression,—a temporary impression," added Mrs. Mason with a business-like air.

"I can't believe it," said Ferdinand.

"Why not? He's a very nice fellow."

"Yes,—yes," said Mason, "very nice indeed. He's very rich too." And here the talk was interrupted by Caroline's entrance.

On Sunday the two ladies went to church. It was not till after they had gone that Ferdinand left his room. He came into the little parlor, took up a book, and felt something of the stir of his old intellectual life. Would he ever again know what it was to work? In the course of an hour the ladies came in, radiant with devotional millinery. Mrs. Mason soon went out again, leaving the others together. Miss Hofmann asked Ferdinand what he had been reading; and he was thus led to declare that he really believed he should, after all, get the use of his head again. She listened with all the respect which an intelligent woman who leads an idle life necessarily feels for a clever man when he consents to make her in some degree the confidant of his intellectual purposes. Quickened by her delicious sympathy, her grave attention, and her intelligent questions, he was led to unbosom himself of several of his dearest convictions and projects. It was easy that from this point the conversation should advance to matters of belief and hope in general. Before he knew it, it had done so; and he had thus the great satisfaction of discussing with the woman on whom of all others his selfish and personal happiness was most dependent those great themes in whose expansive magnitude persons and pleasures and passions are absorbed and extinguished, and in whose austere effulgence the brightest divinities of earth remit their shining. Serious passions are a good preparation for the highest kinds of speculation. Although Ferdinand was urging no suit whatever upon his companion, and consciously, at least, making use in no degree of the emotion which accompanied her presence, it is certain that, as they formed themselves, his conceptions were the clearer for being the conceptions of a man in love. And, as for Miss Hofmann, her attention could not, to all appearances, have been more lively, nor her perception more delicate, if the atmosphere of her own intellect had been purified by the sacred fires of a responsive passion.

Knight duly made his appearance at dinner, and proved himself once more the entertaining gentleman whom our friends had long since learned to appreciate. But Mason, fresh from his contest with morals and metaphysics, was forcibly struck with the fact that he was one of those men from whom these sturdy beggars receive more kicks than halfpence. He was nevertheless obliged to admit, that, if he was not a man of principles, he was thoroughly a man of honor. After dinner the company adjourned to the piazza, where, in the course of half an hour, the Doctor proposed to Miss Hofmann to take a turn in the grounds. All around the lawn there wound a narrow footpath, concealed from view in spots by clusters of shubbery. Ferdinand and his hostess sat watching their retreating figures as they slowly measured the sinuous strip of gravel; Miss Hofmann's light dress and the Doctor's white waistcoat gleaming at intervals through the dark verdure. At the end of twenty minutes they returned to the house. The Doctor came back only to make his bow and to take his departure; and, when he had gone, Miss Hofmann retired to her own room. The next morning she mounted her horse, and rode over to see the friend with whom she had stayed during Mason's fever. Ferdinand saw her pass his window, erect in the saddle, with her horse scattering the gravel with his nervous steps. Shortly afterwards Mrs. Mason came into the room, sat down by the young man, made her habitual inquiries as to his condition, and then paused in such a way as that he instantly felt that she had something to tell him. "You've something to tell me," he said; "what is it?"

Mrs. Mason blushed a little, and laughed. "I was first made to promise to keep it a secret," she said. "If I'm so transparent now that I have leave to tell it, what should I be if I hadn't? Guess."

Ferdinand shook his head peremptorily. "I give it up."

"Caroline is engaged."

"To whom?"

"Not to Mr. Stapleton,—to Dr. Knight."

Ferdinand was silent a moment; but he neither changed color nor dropped his eyes. Then, at last, "Did she wish you not to tell me?" he asked.

"She wished me to tell no one. But I prevailed upon her to let me tell *you*."

"Thank you," said Ferdinand with a little bow—and an immense irony.

"It's a great surprise," continued Mrs. Mason. "I never suspected it. And there I was talking about Mr. Stapleton! I don't see how they have managed it. Well, I suppose it's for the best. But it seems odd that Caroline should have refused so many superior offers, to put up at last with Dr. Knight."

Ferdinand had felt for an instant as if the power of speech was deserting him; but volition nailed it down with a great muffled hammer-blow.

"She might do worse," he said mechanically.

Mrs. Mason glanced at him as if struck by the sound of his voice. "You're not surprised, then?"

"I hardly know. I never fancied there was anything between

them, and yet, now that I look back, there has been nothing against it. They have talked of each other neither too much nor too little. Upon my soul, they're an accomplished couple!" Glancing back at his friend's constant reserve and self-possession, Ferdinand—strange as it may seem—could not repress a certain impulse of sympathetic admiration. He had had no vulgar rival. "Yes," he repeated gravely, "she might do worse."

"I suppose she might. He's poor, but he's clever; and I'm sure I hope to Heaven he loves her!"

Ferdinand said nothing.

"May I ask," he resumed at length, "whether they became engaged yesterday, on that walk around the lawn?"

"No; it would be fine if they had, under our very noses! It was all done while Caroline was at the Stapletons'. It was agreed between them yesterday that she should tell me at once."

"And when are they to be married?"

"In September, if possible. Caroline told me to tell you that she counts upon your staying for the wedding."

"Staying where?" asked Mason, with a little nervous laugh.

"Staying here, of course,—in the house."

Ferdinand looked his hostess full in the eyes, taking her hand as he did so. " 'The funeral baked meats did coldly furnish forth the marriage tables.' "

"Ah, hold your tongue!" cried Mrs. Mason, pressing his hand. "How can you be so horrible? When Caroline leaves me, Ferdinand, I shall be quite alone. The tie which binds us together will be very much slackened by her marriage. I can't help thinking that it was never very close, when I consider that I've had no part in the most important step of her life. I don't complain. I suppose it's natural enough. Perhaps it's the fashion,—come in with striped petticoats and pea-jackets. Only it makes me feel like an old woman. It removes me twenty years at a bound from my own engagement, and the day I burst out crying on my mother's neck because your uncle had told a young girl I knew, that he thought I had beautiful eyes. Now-a-days I suppose they tell the young ladies themselves, and have them cry on their own necks. It's a great saving of time. But I shall miss Caroline all the same; and then, Ferdinand, I shall make a great deal of you."

"The more the better," said Ferdinand, with the same laugh; and at this moment Mrs. Mason was called away.

Ferdinand had not been a soldier for nothing. He had received a heavy blow, and he resolved to bear it like a man. He refused to allow himself a single moment of self-compassion. On the contrary, he spared himself none of the hard names offered by his passionate vocabulary. For not guessing Caroline's secret, he was perhaps excusable. Women were all inscrutable, and this one especially so. But Knight was a man like himself,—a man whom he esteemed, but whom he was loath to credit with a deeper and more noiseless current of feeling than his own, for his own was no babbling brook, betraying its course through green leaves. Knight had loved modestly and decently, but frankly and heartily, like a man who was not ashamed of what he was doing, and if he had not found it out it was his own fault. What else had he to do? He had been a besotted day-dreamer, while his friend had simply been a genuine lover. He deserved his injury, and he would bear it in silence. He had been unable to get well on an illusion; he would now try getting well on a truth. This was stern treatment, the reader will admit, likely to kill if it didn't cure.

Miss Hofmann was absent for several hours. At dinner-time she had not returned, and Mrs. Mason and the young man accordingly sat down without her. After dinner Ferdinand went into the little parlor, quite indifferent as to how soon he met her. Seeing or not seeing her, time hung equally heavy. Shortly after her companions had risen from table, she rode up to the door, dismounted, tired and hungry, passed directly into the dining-room, and sat down to eat in her habit. In half an hour she came out, and, crossing the hall on her way up stairs, saw Mason in the parlor. She turned round, and, gathering up her long skirts with one hand, while she held a little sweet-cake to her lips with the other, stopped at the door to bid him good day. He left his chair, and went towards her. Her face wore a somewhat weary smile.

"So you're going to be married," he began abruptly.

Miss Hofmann assented with a slight movement of her head.

"I congratulate you. Excuse me if I don't do it with the last grace. I feel all I dare to feel."

"Don't be afraid," said Caroline, smiling, and taking a bite from her cake.

"I'm not sure that it's not more unexpected than even such things have a right to be. There's no doubt about it?"

"None whatever."

"Well, Knight's a very good fellow. I haven't seen him yet," he pursued, as Caroline was silent. "I don't know that I'm in any hurry to see him. But I mean to talk to him. I mean to tell him that if he doesn't do his duty by you, I shall—"

"Well?"

"I shall remind him of it."

"O, I shall do that," said Miss Hofmann.

Ferdinand looked at her gravely. "By Heaven! you know," he cried with intensity, "it must be either one thing or the other."

"I don't understand you."

"O, I understand myself. You're not a woman to be thrown away, Miss Hofmann."

Caroline made a gesture of impatience. "I don't understand you," she repeated. "You must excuse me. I'm very tired." And she went rapidly up stairs.

On the following day Ferdinand had an opportunity to make his compliments to the Doctor. "I don't congratulate you on doing it," he said, "so much as on the way you've done it."

"What do you know about the way?" asked Knight.

"Nothing whatever. That's just it. You took good care of that. And you're to be married in the autumn?"

"I hope so. Very quietly, I suppose. The parson to do it, and Mrs. Mason and my mother and you to see it's done properly." And the Doctor put his hand on Ferdinand's shoulder.

"O, I'm the last person to choose," said Mason. "If he were to omit anything, I should take good care not to cry out." It is often said, that, next to great joy, no state of mind

is so frolicsome as great distress. It was in virtue of this truth,
I suppose, that Ferdinand was able to be facetious. He kept
his spirits. He talked and smiled and lounged about with the
same deferential languor as before. During the interval before
the time appointed for the wedding it was agreed between the
parties interested that Miss Hofmann should go over and
spend a few days with her future mother-in-law, where she
might partake more freely and privately than at home of the
pleasure of her lover's company. She was absent a week; a
week during which Ferdinand was thrown entirely upon his
hostess for entertainment and diversion,—things he had a
very keen sense of needing. There were moments when it
seemed to him that he was living by mere force of will, and
that, if he loosened the screws for a single instant, he would
sink back upon his bed again, and never leave it. He had forbidden himself to think of Caroline, and had prescribed a
course of meditation upon that other mistress, his first love,
with whom he had long since exchanged pledges,—she of a
hundred names,—work, letters, philosophy, fame. But, after
Caroline had gone, it was supremely difficult not to think of
her. Even in absence she was supremely conspicuous. The
most that Ferdinand could do was to take refuge in books,—
an immense number of which he now read, fiercely, passionately, voraciously,—in conversation with Mrs. Mason, and in
such society as he found in his path. Mrs. Mason was a great
gossip,—a gossip on a scale so magnificent as to transform the
foible into a virtue. A gossip, moreover, of imagination, dealing with the future as well as the present and the past,—with
a host of delightful half-possibilities, as well as with stale
hyper-verities. With her, then, Ferdinand talked of his own
future, into which she entered with the most outspoken
and intelligent sympathy. "A man," he declared, "couldn't
do better; and a man certainly would do worse." Mrs. Mason
arranged a European tour and residence for her nephew, in
the manner of one who knew her ground. Caroline once married, she herself would go abroad, and fix herself in one of the
several capitals in which an American widow with an easy income may contrive to support existence. She would make her
dwelling a base of supplies—a *pied à terre*—for Ferdinand,
who should take his time to it, and visit every accessible spot

in Europe and the East. She would leave him free to go and
come as he pleased, and to live as he listed; and I may say
that, thanks to Mrs. Mason's observation of Continental
manners, this broad allowance covered in her view quite as
much as it did in poor Ferdinand's, who had never been out
of his own country. All that she would ask of him would be
to show himself say twice a year in her drawing-room, and to
tell her stories of what he had seen; that drawing-room which
she already saw in her mind's eye,—a compact little *entresol*
with tapestry hangings in the doorways and a coach-house in
the court attached. Mrs. Mason was not a severe moralist; but
she was quite too sensible a woman to wish to demoralize her
nephew, and to persuade him to trifle with his future,—that
future of which the war had already made light, in its own
grim fashion. Nay, she loved him; she thought him the cleverest, the most promising, of young men. She looked to the day
when his name would be on men's lips, and it would be a
great piece of good fortune to have very innocently married
his uncle. Herself a great observer of men and manners, she
wished to give him advantages which had been sterile in her
own case.

In the way of society, Ferdinand made calls with his hostess, went out twice to dine, and caused Mrs. Mason herself to
entertain company at dinner. He presided on these occasions
with distinguished good grace. It happened, moreover, that
invitations had been out some days for a party at the
Stapletons',—Miss Hofmann's friends,—and that, as there
was to be no dancing, Ferdinand boldly announced his intention of going thither. "Who knows?" he said; "it may do me
more good than harm. We can go late, and come away early."
Mrs. Mason doubted of the wisdom of the act; but she finally
assented, and prepared herself. It was late when they left
home, and when they arrived the rooms—rooms of exceptional vastness—were at their fullest. Mason received on this
his first appearance in society a most flattering welcome, and
in a very few moments found himself in exclusive possession
of Miss Edith Stapleton, Caroline's particular friend. This
young lady has had no part in our story, because our story is
perforce short, and condemned to pick and choose its constituent elements. With the least bit wider compass we might

long since have whispered to the reader, that Miss Stapleton
—who was a charming girl—had conceived a decided preference for our Ferdinand over all other men whomsoever. That
Ferdinand was utterly ignorant of the circumstance is our excuse for passing it by; and we linger upon it, therefore, only
long enough to suggest that the young girl must have been
very happy at this particular moment.

"Is Miss Hofmann here?" Mason asked as he accompanied
her into an adjoining room.

"Do you call that being here?" said Miss Stapleton, looking
across the apartment. Mason, too, looked across.

There he beheld Miss Hofmann, full-robed in white, standing fronted by a semicircle of no less than five gentlemen,—
all good-looking and splendid. Her head and shoulders rose
serene from the *bouillonnement* of her beautiful dress, and she
looked and listened with that half-abstracted air which is pardonable in a woman beset by half a dozen admirers. When
Caroline's eyes fell upon her friend, she stared a moment, surprised, and then made him the most gracious bow in the
world,—a bow so gracious that her little circle half divided itself to let it pass, and looked around to see where the deuce
it was going. Taking advantage of this circumstance, Miss
Hofmann advanced several steps. Ferdinand went towards
her, and there, in sight of a hundred men and as many
women, she gave him her hand, and smiled upon him with
extraordinary sweetness. They went back together to Miss
Stapleton, and Caroline made him sit down, she and her
friend placing themselves on either side. For half an hour
Ferdinand had the honor of engrossing the attention of the
two most charming girls present,—and, thanks to this distinction, indeed the attention of the whole company. After which
the two young ladies had him introduced successively to every
maiden and matron in the assembly in the least remarkable for
loveliness or wit. Ferdinand rose to the level of the occasion,
and conducted himself with unprecedented gallantry. Upon
others he made, of course, the best impression, but to himself
he was an object almost of awe. I am compelled to add, however, that he was obliged to fortify himself with repeated
draughts of wine; and that even with the aid of this artificial
stimulant he was unable to conceal from Mrs. Mason and his

physician that he was looking far too much like an invalid to be properly where he was.

"Was there ever anything like the avidity of these dreadful girls?" said Mrs. Mason to the Doctor. "They'll let a man swoon at their feet sooner than abridge a *tête-à-tête* that amuses them. Then they'll have up another. Look at little Miss McCarthy, yonder, with Ferdinand and George Stapleton before her. She's got them contradicting each other, and she looks like a Roman fast lady at the circus. What does she care so long as she makes her evening? They like a man to look as if he were going to die,—it's interesting."

Knight went over to his friend, and told him sternly that it was high time he should be at home and in bed. "You're looking horribly," he added shrewdly, as Ferdinand resisted.

"You're *not* looking horribly, Colonel Mason," said Miss McCarthy, a very audacious little person, overhearing this speech.

"It isn't a matter of taste, madam," said the Doctor, angrily; "it's a fact." And he led away his patient.

Ferdinand insisted that he had not hurt himself, that, on the contrary, he was feeling uncommonly well; but his face contradicted him. He continued for two or three days more to play at "feeling well," with a courage worthy of a better cause. Then at last he let disease have its way. He settled himself on his pillows, and fingered his watch, and began to wonder how many revolutions he would still witness of those exquisite little needles. The Doctor came, and gave him a sound rating for what he called his imprudence. Ferdinand heard him out patiently; and then assured him that prudence or imprudence had nothing to do with it; that death had taken fast hold of him, and that now his only concern was to make easy terms with his captor. In the course of the same day he sent for a lawyer and altered his will. He had no known relatives, and his modest patrimony stood bequeathed to a gentleman of his acquaintance who had no real need of it. He now divided it into two unequal portions, the smaller of which he devised to William Bowles, Mrs. Mason's man-servant and his personal attendant; and the larger— which represented a considerable sum—to Horace Knight.

He informed Mrs. Mason of these arrangements, and was pleased to have her approval.

From this moment his strength began rapidly to ebb, and the shattered fragments of his long-resisting will floated down its shallow current into dissolution. It was useless to attempt to talk, to beguile the interval, to watch the signs, or to count the hours. A constant attendant was established at his side, and Mrs. Mason appeared only at infrequent moments. The poor woman felt that her heart was broken, and spent a great deal of time in weeping. Miss Hofmann remained, naturally, at Mrs. Knight's. "As far as I can judge," Horace had said, "it will be a matter of a week. But it's the most extraordinary case I ever heard of. The man was steadily getting well." On the fifth day he had driven Miss Hofmann home, at her suggestion that it was no more than decent that she should give the young man some little sign of sympathy. Horace went up to Ferdinand's bedside, and found the poor fellow in the languid middle condition between sleeping and waking in which he had passed the last forty-eight hours. "Colonel," he asked gently, "do you think you could see Caroline?"

For all answer, Ferdinand opened his eyes. Horace went out, and led his companion back into the darkened room. She came softly up to the bedside, stood looking down for a moment at the sick man, and then stooped over him.

"I thought I'd come and make you a little visit," she said. "Does it disturb you?"

"Not in the least," said Mason, looking her steadily in the eyes. "Not half as much as it would have done a week ago. Sit down."

"Thank you. Horace won't let me. I'll come again."

"You'll not have another chance," said Ferdinand. "I'm not good for more than two days yet. Tell them to go out. I wish to see you alone. I wouldn't have sent for you, but, now that you're here, I might as well take advantage of it."

"Have you anything particular to say?" asked Knight, kindly.

"O, come," said Mason, with a smile which he meant to be good-natured, but which was only ghastly; "you're not going to be jealous of me at this time of day."

Knight looked at Miss Hofmann for permission, and then

left the room with the nurse. But a minute had hardly elapsed before Miss Hofmann hurried into the adjoining apartment, with her face pale and discomposed.

"Go to him!" she exclaimed. "He's dying!"

When they reached him he was dead.

In the course of a few days his will was opened, and Knight came to the knowledge of his legacy. "He was a good, generous fellow," he said to Mrs. Mason and Miss Hofmann, "and I shall never be satisfied that he mightn't have recovered. It was a most extraordinary case." He was considerate enough of his audience to abstain from adding that he would give a great deal to have been able to make an autopsy. Miss Hofmann's wedding was, of course, not deferred. She was married in September, "very quietly." It seemed to her lover, in the interval, that she was very silent and thoughtful. But this was certainly natural under the circumstances.

A Problem

SEPTEMBER was drawing to an end, and with it the honeymoon of two young persons in whom I shall be glad to interest the reader. They had stretched it out in sovereign contempt of the balance of the calendar. That September hath thirty days is a truth known to the simplest child; but our young lovers had given it at least forty. Nevertheless, they were on the whole not sorry to have the overture play itself out, and to see the curtain rise on the drama in which they had undertaken the leading parts. Emma thought very often of the charming little house which was awaiting her in town, and of the servants whom her dear mother had promised to engage; and, indeed, for that matter, the young wife let her imagination hover about the choice groceries with which she expected to find her cupboards stocked through the same kind agency. Moreover, she had left her wedding-gown at home—thinking it silly to carry her finery into the country—and she felt a great longing to refresh her memory as to the particular shade of a certain lavender silk, and the exact length of a certain train. The reader will see that Emma was a simple, unsophisticated person, and that her married life was likely to be made up of small joys and vexations. She was simple and gentle and pretty and young; she adored her husband. He, too, had begun to feel that it was time they were married in earnest. His thoughts wandered back to his counting-room and his vacant desk, and to the possible contents of the letters which he had requested his fellow-clerk to open in his absence. For David, too, was a simple, natural fellow, and although he thought his wife the sweetest of human creatures —or, indeed, for that very reason—he was unable to forget that life is full of bitter inhuman necessities and perils which muster in force about you when you stand idle. He was happy, in short, and he felt it unfair that he should any longer have his happiness for nothing.

The two, therefore, had made up their trunks again, and ordered the vehicle in time for the morrow's train. Twilight had come on, and Emma sat at the window empty-handed, taking a silent farewell of the landscape, which she felt that they had let into the secret of their young love. They had sat in the shade of every tree, and watched the sunset from the top of every rock.

David had gone to settle his account with the landlord, and to bid good-by to the doctor, who had been of such service when Emma had caught cold by sitting for three hours on the grass after a day's rain.

Sitting alone was dull work. Emma crossed the threshold of the long window, and went to the garden gate to look for her husband. The doctor's house was a mile away, close to the village. Seeing nothing of David, she strolled along the road, bareheaded, in her shawl. It was a lovely evening. As there was no one to say so to, Emma said so, with some fervor, to herself; and to this she added a dozen more remarks, equally original and eloquent—and equally sincere. That David was, ah! so good, and that she ought to be so happy. That she would have a great many cares, but that she would be orderly, and saving, and vigilant, and that her house should be a sanctuary of modest elegance and good taste; and, then, that she might be a mother.

When Emma reached this point, she ceased to meditate and to whisper virtuous nothings to her conscience. She rejoiced; she walked more slowly, and looked about at the dark hills, rising in soft undulations against the luminous west, and listened to the long pulsations of sound mounting from woods and hedges and the margins of pools. Her ears rang, and her eyes filled with tears.

Meanwhile she had walked a half-mile, and as yet David was not in sight. Her attention, however, was at this moment diverted from her quest. To her right, on a level with the road, stretched a broad, circular space, half meadow, half common, enclosed in the rear by a wood. At some distance, close to the wood, stood a couple of tents, such as are used by the vagrant Indians who sell baskets and articles of bark. In front, close to the road, on a fallen log, sat a young Indian woman, weaving a basket, with two children beside her. Emma looked at her curiously as she drew near.

"Good evening," said the woman, returning her glance with hard, bright black eyes. "Don't you want to buy something?"

"What have you got to sell?" asked Emma, stopping.

"All sorts of things. Baskets, and pincushions, and fans."

"I should like a basket well enough—a little one—if they're pretty."

"Oh, yes, they're pretty, you'll see." And she said something to one of the children, in her own dialect. He went off, in compliance, to the tents.

While he was gone, Emma looked at the other child, and pronounced it very handsome; but without touching it, for the little savage was in the last degree unclean. The woman doggedly continued her work, examining Emma's person from head to foot, and staring at her dress, her hands, and her rings.

In a few moments the child came back with a number of baskets strung together, followed by an old woman, apparently the mother of the first. Emma looked over the baskets, selected a pretty one, and took out her purse to pay for it. The price was a dollar, but Emma had nothing smaller than a two-dollar note, and the woman professed herself unable to give change.

"Give her the money," said the old woman, "and, for the difference, I'll tell your fortune."

Emma looked at her, hesitating. She was a repulsive old squaw, with sullen, black eyes, and her swarthy face hatched across with a myriad wrinkles.

The younger woman saw that Emma looked a little frightened, and said something in her barbarous native gutturals to her companion. The latter retorted, and the other burst out into a laugh.

"Give me your hand," said the old woman, "and I'll tell your fortune." And, before Emma found time to resist, she came and took hold of her left hand. She held it awhile, with the back upwards, looking at its fair surface, and at the diamonds on her third finger. Then, turning up the palm, she began to mutter and grumble. Just as she was about to speak, Emma saw her look half-defiantly at some one apparently behind her. Turning about, she saw that her husband had come up unperceived. She felt relieved. The woman had a horribly vicious look, and she exhaled, moreover, a strong odor of whiskey. Of this David immediately became sensible.

"What is she doing?" he asked of his wife.

"Don't you see? She's telling my fortune."

"What has she told you?"

"Nothing yet. She seems to be waiting for it to come to her."

The squaw looked at David cunningly, and David returned her gaze with ill-concealed disgust. "She'll have to wait a long time," he said to his wife. "She has been drinking."

He had lowered his voice, but the woman heard him. The other began to laugh, and said something in her own tongue to her mother. The latter still kept Emma's hand and remained silent.

"This your husband?" she said, at last, nodding at David.

Emma nodded assent. The woman again examined her hand. "Within the year," she said, "you'll be a mother."

"That's wonderful news," said David. "Is it to be a boy or a girl?"

The woman looked hard at David. "A girl," she said. And then she transferred her eyes to Emma's palm.

"Well, is that all?" said Emma.

"She'll be sick."

"Very likely," said David. "And we'll send for the doctor."

"The doctor'll do no good."

"Then we shall send for another," said Emma, laughing—but not without an effort.

"He'll do no good. She'll die."

The young squaw began to laugh again. Emma drew her hand away, and looked at her husband. He was a little pale, and Emma put her hand into his arm.

"We're very much obliged to you for the information," said David. "At what age is our little girl to die?"

"Oh, very young."

"How young?"

"Oh, very young." The old woman seemed indisposed to commit herself further, and David led his wife away.

"Well," said Emma, "she gave us a good dollar's worth."

"I think," said David, "she had been giving herself a good dollar's worth. She was full of liquor."

From this assurance Emma drew for twenty-four hours to come a good deal of comfort. As for David, in the course of an hour he had quite forgotten the prophecy.

The next day they went back to town. Emma found her house all that she had desired, and her lavender silk not a shade too pale, nor her train an inch too short. The winter came and went, and she was still a very happy woman. The spring arrived, the summer drew near, and her happiness increased. She became the mother of a little girl.

For some time after the child was born Emma was confined to her room. She used to sit with the infant on her lap, nursing her, counting her breathings, wondering whether she would be pretty. David was at his place of business, with his head full of figures. A dozen times Emma recurred to the old woman's prophecy, sometimes with a tremor, sometimes with indifference, sometimes almost with defiance. Then, she declared that it was silly to remember it. A tipsy old squaw—a likely providence for her precious child. She was, perhaps, dead herself by this time. Nevertheless, her prophecy was odd; she seemed so positive. And the other woman laughed so disagreeably. Emma had not forgotten that laugh. She might well laugh, with her own lusty little savages beside her.

The first day that Emma left her room, one evening, at dinner, she couldn't help asking her husband whether he remembered the Indian woman's prediction. David was taking a glass of wine. He nodded.

"You see it's half come true," said Emma. "A little girl."

"My dear," said David, "one would think you believed it."

"Of course she'll be sick," said Emma. "We must expect that."

"Do you think, my dear," pursued David, "that it's a little girl because that venerable person said so?"

"Why no, of course not. It's only a coincidence."

"Well, then, if it's merely a coincidence, we may let it rest. If the old woman's *dictum* was a real prediction, we may also let it rest. That it has half come true lessens the chances for the other half."

The reader may detect a flaw in David's logic; but it was quite good enough for Emma. She lived upon it for a year, at the end of which it was in a manner put to the test.

It were certainly incorrect to say that Emma guarded and cherished her little girl any the more carefully by reason of the old woman's assurance; her natural affection was by itself a guaranty of perfect vigilance. But perfect vigilance is not infallible. When the child was a twelvemonth old it fell grievously sick, and for a week its little life hung by a thread. During this time I am inclined to think that Emma quite forgot the sad prediction suspended over the infant's head; it is certain, at least, that she never spoke of it to her husband, and that he made no attempt to remind her of it. Finally, after a hard struggle, the little girl came out of the cruel embrace of disease, panting and exhausted, but uninjured. Emma felt as if her child was immortal, and as if, henceforth, life would have no trials for her. It was not till then that she thought once more of the prophecy of the swarthy sybil.

She was sitting on the sofa in her chamber, with the child lying asleep in her lap, watching the faint glow of returning life in its poor little wasted cheeks. David came in from his day's labor and sat down beside her.

"I wonder," said Emma, "what our friend Magawisca—or whatever her name is—would say to that."

"She would feel desperately snubbed," said David. "Wouldn't she, little transcendent convalescent?" And he gently tickled the tip of his little girl's nose with the end of his moustache. The baby softly opened her eyes, and, vaguely conscious of her father, lifted her hand and languidly clutched his nose. "Upon my soul," said David, "she's positively boisterous. There's life in the old dog yet."

"Oh, David, how can you?" said Emma. But she sat watching her husband and child with a placid, gleeful smile. Gradually, her smile grew the least bit serious, and then vanished, though she still looked like the happy woman that she was. The nurse came up from supper, and took possession of the baby. Emma let it go, and remained sitting on the sofa. When the nurse had gone into the adjoining room, she laid her hand in one of her husband's.

"David," she said, "I have a little secret."

"I've no doubt," said David, "that you have a dozen. You're the most secretive, clandestine, shady sort of woman I ever came across."

It is needless to say that this was merely David's exuberant humor; for Emma was the most communicative, sympathetic soul in the world. She practised, in a quiet way, a passionate devotion to her husband, and it was a part of her religion to make him her confidant. She had, of course, in strictness, very little to confide to him. But she confided to him her little, in the hope that he would one day confide to her what she was pleased to believe his abundance.

"It's not exactly a secret," Emma pursued; "only I've kept it so long that it almost seems like one. You'll think me very silly, David. I couldn't bear to mention it so long as there was any chance of truth in the talk of that horrible old squaw. But now, that it's disproved, it seems absurd to keep it on my mind; not that I really ever felt it there, but if I said nothing about it, it was for your sake. I'm sure you'll not mind it; and if you don't, David, I'm sure I needn't."

"My dear girl, what on earth is coming?" said David. " 'If you don't, I'm sure I needn't!'—you make a man's flesh crawl."

"Why, it's another prophecy," said Emma.

"Another prophecy? Let's have it, then, by all means."

"But you don't mean, David, that you're going to believe it?"

"That depends. If it's to my advantage, of course I shall."

"To your advantage! Oh, David!"

"My dear Emma, prophecies are not to be sneered at. Look at this one about the baby."

"Look at the baby, I should say."

"Exactly. Isn't she a girl? hasn't she been at death's door?"

"Yes; but the old woman made her go through."

"Nay; you've no imagination. Of course, they pull off short of the catastrophe; but they give you a good deal, by the way."

"Well, my dear, since you're so determined to believe in them, I should be sorry to prevent you. I make you a present of this one."

"Was it a squaw, this time?"

"No, it was an old Italian—a woman who used to come on Saturday mornings at school and sell us sugar-plums and trinkets. You see it was ten years ago. Our teachers used to dislike her; but we let her into the garden by a back-gate. She used to carry a little tray, like a pedler. She had candy and cakes, and kid-gloves. One day, she offered to tell our fortunes with cards. She spread out her cards on the top of her tray, and half a dozen of us went through the ceremony. The rest were afraid. I believe I was second. She told me a long rigmarole that I have forgotten, but said nothing about lovers or husbands. That, of course, was all we wanted to hear; and, though I was disappointed, I was ashamed to ask any questions. To the girls who came after me, she promised successively the most splendid marriages. I wondered whether I was to be an old maid. The thought was horrible, and I determined to try and conjure such a fate. 'But I?' I said, as she was going to put up her cards; 'am I never to be married?' She looked at me, and then looked over her cards again. I suppose she wished to make up for her neglect. 'Ah, you, Miss,' she said—you are better off than any of them. You are to marry twice!' Now, my dear," Emma added, "make the most of that." And she leaned her head on her husband's shoulder and looked in his face, smiling.

But David smiled not at all. On the contrary, he looked grave. Hereupon, Emma put by her smile, and looked grave, too. In fact, she looked pained. She thought it positively unkind of David to take her little story in such stiff fashion.

"It's very strange," said David.

"It's very silly," said Emma. "I'm sorry I told you, David."

"I'm very glad. It's extremely curious. Listen, and you'll see—I, too, have a secret, Emma."

"Nay, I don't want to hear it," said Emma.

"You shall hear it," said the young man. "I never mentioned it before, simply because I had forgotten it—utterly forgotten it. But your story calls it back to my memory. I, too, once had my fortune told. It was neither a squaw nor a gypsy. It was a young lady, in company. I forget her name. I was less than twenty. It was at a party, and she was telling people's fortunes. She had cards; she pretended to have a gift. I don't know what I had been saying. I suppose that, as boys of that age are fond of doing, I had been showing off my wit at the expense of married life. I remember a young lady introducing me to this person, and saying that here was a young man who declared he never would marry. Was it true? She looked at her cards, and said that it was completely false, and that I should marry twice. The company began to laugh. I was mortified. 'Why don't you say three times?' I said. 'Because,' answered the young lady, 'my cards say only twice.' " David had got up from the sofa, and stood before his wife. "Don't you think it's curious?" he said.

"Curious enough. One would say you thought it something more."

"You know," continued David, "we can't both marry twice."

"You know," cried Emma. "Bravo, my dear. 'You know' is delightful. Perhaps you would like me to withdraw and give you a chance."

David looked at his wife, half surprised at the bitterness of her words. He was apparently on the point of making some conciliatory speech; but he seemed forcibly struck, afresh, with the singular agreement of the two predictions. "Upon my soul!" he said, "it's preternaturally odd!" He burst into a fit of laughter.

Emma put her hands to her face and sat silent. Then, after a few moments: "For my part," she said, "I think it's extremely disagreeable!" Overcome by the effort to speak, she burst into tears.

Her husband again placed himself at her side. He still took the humorous view of the case—on the whole, perhaps, indiscreetly. "Come, Emma," he said, "dry your tears, and consult your memory. Are you sure you've never been married before?"

Emma shook off his caresses and got up. Then, suddenly turning around, she said, with vehemence, "And you, sir?"

For an answer David laughed afresh; and then, looking at his wife a moment, he rose and followed her. *"Où diable la jalousie va-t-elle se nicher?"* he cried. He put his arm about her, she yielded, and he kissed her. At this moment a little wail went up from the baby in the neighboring room. Emma hastened away.

Where, indeed, as David had asked, will jealousy stow herself away? In what odd, unlikely corners will she turn up? She made herself a nest in poor Emma's innocent heart, and, at her leisure, she lined and feathered it. The little scene I have just described left neither party, indeed, as it found them. David had kissed his wife and shown the folly of her tears, but he had not taken back his story. For ten years he hadn't thought of it; but, now that he had been reminded of it, he was quite unable to dismiss it from his thoughts. It besieged him, and harassed and distracted him; it thrust itself into his mind at the most inopportune moments; it buzzed in his ears and danced among the columns of figures in his great folio account books. Sometimes the young lady's prediction conjoined itself with a prodigious array of numerals, and roamed away from its modest place among the units into the hundreds of thousands. David read himself a million times a husband. But, after all, as he reflected, the oddity was not in his having been predestined, according to the young lady, to marry twice; but in poor Emma having drawn exactly the same lot. It was a conflict of oracles. It would be an interesting inquiry, although now, of course, quite impracticable, to ascertain which of the two was more to be trusted. For how under the sun could both have revealed the truth? The utmost ingenuity was powerless to reconcile their mutual incompatibility. Could either of the soothsayers have made her statement in a figurative sense? It seemed to David that this was to fancy them a grain too wise. The simplest solution— except not to think of the matter at all, which he couldn't bring himself to accomplish—was to fancy that each of the prophecies nullified the other, and that when he became Emma's husband, their counterfeit destinies had been put to confusion.

Emma found it quite impossible to take the matter so easily. She pondered it night and day for a month. She admitted that the prospect of a second marriage was, of necessity, unreal for one of them; but her heart ached to discover for which of them it was real. She had laughed at the folly of the Indian's threat; but she found it impossible to laugh at the extraordinary coincidence of David's promised fate with her own. That it was absurd and illogical made it only the more painful. It filled her life with a horrible uncertainty. It seemed to indicate that whether or no the silly gossip of a couple of jugglers was, on either side, strictly fulfilled; yet there was some dark cloud hanging over their marriage. Why should an honest young couple have such strange things said of them? Why should they be called upon to read such an illegible

riddle? Emma repented bitterly of having told her secret. And
yet, too, she rejoiced; for it was a dreadful thought that
David, unprompted to reveal his own adventure should have
kept such a dreadful occurrence locked up in his breast, shedding, Heaven knows what baleful influence, on her life and
fortunes. Now she could live it down; she could combat it,
laugh at it. And David, too, could do as much for the mysterious prognostic of his own extinction. Never had Emma's
fancy been so active. She placed the two faces of her destiny
in every conceivable light. At one moment, she imagined that
David might succumb to the pressure of his fancied destiny,
and leave her a widow, free to marry again; and at another
that he would grow enamored of the thought of obeying his
own oracle, and crush her to death by the masculine vigor of
his will. Then, again, she felt as if her own will were strong,
and as if she bore on her head the protecting hand of fate.
Love was much, assuredly, but fate was more. And here, indeed, what was fate but love? As she had loved David, so she
would love another. She racked her poor little brain to conjure up this future master of her life. But, to do her justice, it
was quite in vain. She could not forget David. Nevertheless,
she felt guilty. And then she thought of David, and wondered
whether he was guilty, too—whether he was dreaming of another woman.

In this way it was that Emma became jealous. That she was
a very silly girl I don't pretend to deny. I have expressly said
that she was a person of a very simple make; and in proportion to the force of her old straightforward confidence in her
husband, was that of her present suspicion and vagaries.

From the moment that Emma became jealous, the household angel of peace shook its stainless wings and took a
melancholy flight. Emma immediately betrayed herself. She
accused her husband of indifference, and of preferring the society of other women. Once she told him that he might, if he
pleased. It was à *propos* of an evening party, to which they had
both been asked. During the afternoon, while David was still
at his business, the baby had been taken sick, and Emma had
written a note to say that they should not be able to come.
When David returned, she told him of her note, and he
laughed and said that he wondered whether their intended

hostess would fancy that it was his practice to hold the baby. For his part, he declared that he meant to go; and at nine o'clock he appeared, dressed. Emma looked at him, pale and indignant.

"After all," she said, "you're right. Make the most of your time."

These were horrible words, and, as was natural, they made a vast breach between the husband and wife.

Once in awhile Emma felt an impulse to take her revenge, and look for happiness in society, and in the sympathy and attention of agreeable men. But she never went very far. Such happiness seemed but a troubled repose, and the world at large had no reason to suspect that she was not on the best of terms with her husband.

David, on his side, went much further. He was gradually transformed from a quiet, home-keeping, affectionate fellow, into a nervous, restless, querulous man of pleasure, a diner-out and a haunter of clubs and theatres. From the moment that he detected their influence on his life, he had been unable to make light of the two prophecies. Then one, now the other, dominated his imagination, and, in either event, it was impossible to live as he would have lived in ignorance. Sometimes, at the thought of an early death, he was seized with a passionate attachment to the world, and an irresistible desire to plunge into worldly joys. At other moments, thinking of his wife's possible death, and of her place being taken by another woman, he felt a fierce and unnatural impatience of all further delay in the evolution of events. He wished to annihilate the present. To live in expectation so acute and so feverish was not to live. Poor David was occasionally tempted by desperate expedients to kill time. Gradually the perpetual oscillation from one phase of his destiny to the other, and the constant change from passionate exaltation to equally morbid depression, induced a state of chronic excitement, not far removed from insanity.

At about this moment he made the acquaintance of a young unmarried woman whom I may call Julia—a very charming, superior person, of a character to exert a healing, soothing influence upon his troubled spirit. In the course of time, he told her the story of his domestic revolution. At first, she was very much amused; she laughed at him, and called him superstitious, fantastic, and puerile. But he took her levity so ill, that she changed her tactics, and humored his delusion.

It seemed to her, however, that his case was serious, and that, if some attempt were not made to arrest his growing alienation from his wife, the happiness of both parties might depart forever. She believed that the flimsy ghost of their mysterious future could be effectually laid only by means of a reconciliation. She doubted that their love was dead and gone. It was only dormant. If she might once awaken it, she would retire with a light heart, and leave it lord of the house.

So, without informing David of her intention, Julia ventured to call upon Emma, with whom she had no personal acquaintance. She hardly knew what she should say; she would trust to the inspiration of the moment; she merely wished to kindle a ray of light in the young wife's darkened household. Emma, she fancied, was a simple, sensitive person, she would be quickly moved by proffered kindness.

But, although she was unacquainted with Emma, the young wife had considerable knowledge of Julia. She had had her pointed out to her in public. Julia was handsome. Emma hated her. She thought of her as her husband's temptress and evil genius. She assured herself that they were longing for her death, so that they might marry. Perhaps he was already her lover. Doubtless they would be glad to kill her. In this way it was that, instead of finding a gentle, saddened, sensitive person, Julia found a bitter, scornful woman, infuriated by a sense of insult and injury. Julia's visit seemed to Emma the climax of insolence. She refused to listen to her. Her courtesy, her gentleness, her attempt at conciliation, struck her as a mockery and a snare. Finally, losing all self-control, she called her a very hard name.

Then Julia, who had a high temper of her own, plucked up a spirit, and struck a blow for her dignity—a blow, however, which unfortunately rebounded on David. "I had steadily refused, Madam," she said, "to believe that you are a fool. But you quite persuade me."

With these words she withdrew. But it mattered little to Emma whether she remained or departed. She was conscious only of one thing, that David had called her a fool to another woman. "A fool?" she cried. "Truly I have been. But I shall be no longer."

She immediately made her preparations for leaving her husband's house, and when David came home he found her with her child and a servant on the point of departure. She told him in a few words that she was going to her mother's, that in his absence he had employed persons to insult her in her own house, it was necessary that she should seek protection in her family. David offered no resistance. He made no attempt to resent her accusation. He was prepared for anything. It was fate.

Emma accordingly went to her mother's. She was supported in this extraordinary step, and in the long months of seclusion which followed it, by an exalted sense of her own comparative integrity and virtue. She, at least, had been a faithful wife. She had endured, she had been patient. Whatever her destiny might be, she had made no indecent attempt to anticipate it. More than ever she devoted herself to her little girl. The comparative repose and freedom of her life gave her almost a feeling of happiness. She felt that deep satisfaction which comes upon the spirit when it has purchased contentment at the expense of reputation. There was now, at least, no falsehood in her life. She neither valued her marriage nor pretended to value it.

As for David, he saw little of any one but Julia. Julia, I have said, was a woman of great merit and of perfect generosity. She very soon ceased to resent the check she had received from Emma, and not despairing, still, of seeing peace once more established in the young man's household, she made it a matter of conscience to keep David by her influence in as sane and unperverted a state of mind as circumstances would allow. "She may hate me," thought Julia, "but I'll keep him for her." Julia's, you see, in all this business was the only wise head.

David took his own view of their relations. "I shall certainly see you as often as I wish," he declared. "I shall take consolation where I find it. She has her child—her mother. Does she begrudge me a friend? She may thank her stars I don't take to drink or to play."

For six months David saw nothing of his wife. Finally, one evening, when he was at Julia's house, he received this note:

"Your daughter died this morning, after several hours' suffering. She will be buried to-morrow morning.   E."

David handed the note to Julia. "After all," he said, "she was right."

"Who was right, my poor friend?" asked Julia.

"The old squaw. We cried out too soon."

The next morning he went to the house of his mother-in-law. The servant, recognizing him, ushered him into the room in which the remains of his poor little girl lay, ready for burial. Near the darkened window stood his mother-in-law, in conversation with a gentleman—a certain Mr. Clark—whom David recognized as a favorite clergyman of his wife, and whom he had never liked. The lady, on his entrance, made him a very grand curtsy—if, indeed, that curtsy may be said to come within the regulations which govern salutations of this sort, in which the head is tossed up in proportion as the body is depressed—and swept out of the room. David bowed to the clergyman, and went and looked at the little remnant of mortality which had once been his daughter. After a decent interval, Mr. Clark ventured to approach him.

"You have met with a great trial, sir," said the clergyman.

David assented in silence.

"I suppose," continued Mr. Clark, "it is sent, like all trials, to remind us of our feeble and dependent condition—to purge us of pride and stubbornness—to make us search our hearts and see whether we have not by chance allowed the noisome weeds of folly to overwhelm and suffocate the modest flower of wisdom."

That Mr. Clark had deliberately prepared this speech, with a view to the occasion, I should hesitate to affirm. Gentlemen of his profession have these little parcels of sentiment ready to their hands. But he was, of course, acquainted with Emma's estrangement from her husband (although not with its original motives), and, like a man of genuine feeling, he imagined that under the softening action of a common sorrow, their two hardened hearts might be made to melt and again to flow into one. "The more we lose, my friend," he pursued, "the more we should cherish and value what is left."

"You speak to very good purpose, sir," said David; "but I, unfortunately, have nothing left."

At this moment the door opened, and Emma came in—pale, and clad in black. She stopped, apparently unprepared to see her husband. But, on David's turning toward her, she came forward.

David felt as if Heaven had sent an angel to give the lie to his last words. His face flushed—first with shame, and then with joy. He put out his arms. Emma halted an instant, struggling with her pride, and looked at the clergyman. He raised his hand, with a pious sacramental gesture, and she fell on her husband's neck.

The clergyman took hold of David's hand and pressed it; and, although, as I have said, the young man had never been particularly fond of Mr. Clark, he devoutly returned the pressure.

"Well," said Julia, a fortnight later—for in the interval Emma had been brought to consent to her husband's maintaining his acquaintance with this lady, and even herself to think her a very good sort of person—"well, I don't see but that the terrible problem is at last solved, and that you have each been married twice."

De Grey: A Romance

I T WAS the year 1820, and Mrs. De Grey, by the same token,
as they say in Ireland (and, for that matter, out of it), had
reached her sixty-seventh spring. She was, nevertheless, still a
handsome woman, and, what is better yet, still an amiable
woman. The untroubled, unruffled course of her life had left
as few wrinkles on her temper as on her face. She was tall and
full of person, with dark eyes and abundant white hair, which
she rolled back from her forehead over a cushion, or some
such artifice. The freshness of youth and health had by no
means faded out of her cheeks, nor had the smile of her imperturbable courtesy expired on her lips. She dressed, as became a woman of her age and a widow, in black garments, but
relieved with a great deal of white, with a number of handsome rings on her fair hands. Frequently, in the spring, she
wore a little flower or a sprig of green leaves in the bosom of
her gown. She had been accused of receiving these little floral
ornaments from the hands of Mr. Herbert (of whom I shall
have more to say); but the charge is unfounded, inasmuch as
they were very carefully selected from a handful cut in the
garden by her maid.

That Mrs. De Grey should have been just the placid and
elegant old lady that she was, remained, in the eyes of the
world at large, in spite of an abundance of a certain sort of evidence in favor of such a result, more or less of a puzzle and
a problem. It is true, that every one who knew anything
about her knew that she had enjoyed great material prosperity, and had suffered no misfortunes. She was mistress in her
own right of a handsome property and a handsome house;
she had lost her husband, indeed, within a year after marriage;
but, as the late George De Grey had been of a sullen and
brooding humor,—to that degree, indeed, as to incur the suspicion of insanity,—her loss, leaving her well provided for,
might in strictness have been accounted a gain. Her son,
moreover, had never given her a moment's trouble; he had
grown up a charming young man, handsome, witty, and wise;
he was a model of filial devotion. The lady's health was good;

she had half a dozen perfect servants; she had the perpetual company of the incomparable Mr. Herbert; she was as fine a figure of an elderly woman as any in town; she might, therefore, very well have been happy and have looked so. On the other hand, a dozen sensible women had been known to declare with emphasis, that not for all her treasures and her felicity would they have consented to be Mrs. De Grey. These ladies were, of course, unable to give a logical reason for so strong an aversion. But it is certain that there hung over Mrs. De Grey's history and circumstances a film, as it were, a shadow of mystery, which struck a chill upon imaginations which might easily have been kindled into envy of her good fortune. "She lives in the dark," some one had said of her. Close observers did her the honor to believe that there was a secret in her life, but of a wholly undefined character. Was she the victim of some lurking sorrow, or the mistress of some clandestine joy? These imputations, we may easily believe, are partially explained by the circumstance that she was a Catholic, and kept a priest in her house. The unexplained portion might very well, moreover, have been discredited by Mrs. De Grey's perfectly candid and complacent demeanor. It was certainly hard to conceive, in talking with her, to what part of her person one might pin a mystery,—whether on her clear, round eyes or her handsome, benevolent lips. Let us say, then, in defiance of the voice of society, that she was no tragedy queen. She was a fine woman, a dull woman, a perfect gentlewoman. She had taken life, as she liked a cup of tea,—weak, with an exquisite aroma and plenty of cream and sugar. She had never lost her temper, for the excellent reason that she had none to lose. She was troubled with no fears, no doubts, no scruples, and blessed with no sacred certainties. She was fond of her son, of the church, of her garden, and of her toilet. She had the very best taste; but, morally, one may say that she had had no history.

Mrs. De Grey had always lived in seclusion; for a couple of years previous to the time of which I speak she had lived in solitude. Her son, on reaching his twenty-third year, had gone to Europe for a long visit, in pursuance of a plan discussed at intervals between his mother and Mr. Herbert during the whole course of his boyhood. They had made no

attempt to forecast his future career, or to prepare him for a
profession. Strictly, indeed, he was at liberty, like his late father, to dispense with a profession. Not that it was to be
wished that he should take his father's life as an example. It
was understood by the world at large, and, of course, by Mrs.
De Grey and her companion in particular, that this gentleman's existence had been blighted, at an early period, by an
unhappy love-affair; and it was notorious that, in consequence, he had spent the few years of his maturity in gloomy
idleness and dissipation. Mrs. De Grey, whose own father was
an Englishman, reduced to poverty, but with claims to high
gentility, professed herself unable to understand why Paul
should not live decently on his means. Mr. Herbert declared
that in America, in any walk of life, idleness was indecent; and
that he hoped the young man would—nominally at least—select a career. It was agreed on both sides, however, that there
was no need for haste; and that it was proper, in the first
place, he should see the world. The world, to Mrs. De Grey,
was little more than a name; but to Mr. Herbert, priest as he
was, it was a vivid reality. Yet he felt that the generous and intelligent youth upon whose education he had lavished all the
treasures of his tenderness and sagacity, was not unfitted,
either by nature or culture, to measure his sinews against its
trials and temptations; and that he should love him the better
for coming home at twenty-five an accomplished gentleman
and a good Catholic, sobered and seasoned by experience,
sceptical in small matters, confident in great, and richly replete with good stories. When he came of age, Paul received
his walking-ticket, as they say, in the shape of a letter of credit
for a handsome sum on certain London bankers. But the
young man pocketed the letter, and remained at home, poring over books, lounging in the garden, and scribbling heroic
verses. At the end of a year, he plucked up a little ambition,
and took a turn through the country, travelling much of the
way on horseback. He came back an ardent American, and
felt that he might go abroad without danger. During his absence in Europe he had written home innumerable long letters,—compositions so elaborate (in the taste of that day,
recent as it is) and so delightful, that, between their pride in
his epistolary talent, and their longing to see his face, his

mother and his ex-tutor would have been at a loss to determine whether he gave them more satisfaction at home or abroad.

With his departure the household was plunged in unbroken repose. Mrs. De Grey neither went out nor entertained company. An occasional morning call was the only claim made upon her hospitality. Mr. Herbert, who was a great scholar, spent all his hours in study; and his patroness sat for the most part alone, arrayed with a perfection of neatness which there was no one to admire (unless it be her waiting-maid, to whom it remained a constant matter of awe), reading a pious book or knitting under-garments for the orthodox needy. At times, indeed, she wrote long letters to her son,—the contents of which Mr. Herbert found it hard to divine. This was accounted a dull life forty years ago; now, doubtless, it would be considered no life at all. It is no matter of wonder, therefore, that finally, one April morning, in her sixty-seventh year, as I have said, Mrs. De Grey suddenly began to suspect that she was lonely. Another long year, at least, was to come and go before Paul's return. After meditating for a while in silence, Mrs. De Grey resolved to take counsel with Father Herbert.

This gentleman, an Englishman by birth, had been an intimate friend of George De Grey, who had made his acquaintance during a visit to Europe, before his marriage. Mr. Herbert was a younger son of an excellent Catholic family, and was at that time beginning, on small resources, the practice of the law. De Grey met him in London, and the two conceived a strong mutual sympathy. Herbert had neither taste for his profession nor apparent ambition of any sort. He was, moreover, in weak health; and his friend found no difficulty in persuading him to accept the place of travelling companion through France and Italy. De Grey carried a very long purse, and was a most liberal friend and patron; and the two young men accomplished their progress as far as Venice in the best spirits and on the best terms. But in Venice, for reasons best known to themselves, they bitterly and irretrievably quarrelled. Some persons said it was over a card-table, and some said it was about a woman. At all events, in consequence, De Grey returned to America, and Herbert repaired to Rome.

He obtained admission into a monastery, studied theology, and finally was invested with priestly orders. In America, in his thirty-third year, De Grey married the lady whom I have described. A few weeks after his marriage he wrote to Herbert, expressing a vehement desire to be reconciled. Herbert felt that the letter was that of a most unhappy man; he had already forgiven him; he pitied him, and after a short delay succeeded in obtaining an ecclesiastical mission to the United States. He reached New York and presented himself at his friend's house, which from this moment became his home. Mrs. De Grey had recently given birth to a son; her husband was confined to his room by illness, reduced to a shadow of his former self by repeated sensual excesses. He survived Herbert's arrival but a couple of months; and after his death the rumor went abroad that he had by his last will settled a handsome income upon the priest, on condition that he would continue to reside with his widow, and take the entire charge of his boy's education.

This rumor was confirmed by the event. For twenty-five years, at the time of which I write, Herbert had lived under Mrs. De Grey's roof as her friend and companion and counsellor, and as her son's tutor. Once reconciled to his friend, he had gradually dropped his priestly character. He was of an essentially devout temperament, but he craved neither parish nor pulpit. On the other hand, he had become an indefatigable student. His late friend had bequeathed to him a valuable library, which he gradually enlarged. His passion for study, however, appeared singularly disinterested, inasmuch as, for many years, his little friend Paul was the sole witness and receptacle of his learning. It is true that he composed a large portion of a History of the Catholic Church in America, which, although the manuscript exists, has never seen, and, I suppose, is never destined to see, the light. It is in the very best keeping, for it contains an immense array of facts. The work is written, not from a sympathetic, but from a strictly respectful point of view; but it has a fatal defect,—it lacks unction.

The same complaint might have been made of Father Herbert's personal character. He was the soul of politeness, but it was a cold and formal courtesy. When he smiled, it was, as the French say, with the end of his lips, and when he took your hand, with the end of his fingers. He had had a charming face in his younger days, and, when gentlemen dressed their hair with powder, his fine black eyes must have produced the very best effect. But he had lost his hair, and he wore on his naked crown a little black silk cap. Round his neck he had a black cravat of many folds, without any collar. He was short and slight, with a stoop in his shoulders, and a handsome pair of hands.

"If it were not for a sad sign to the contrary," said Mrs. De Grey, in pursuance of her resolve to take counsel of her friend, "I should believe I am growing younger."

"What is the sign to the contrary?" asked Herbert.

"I'm losing my eyes. I can't see to read. Suppose I should become blind."

"And what makes you suspect that you are growing young again?"

"I feel lonely. I lack company. I miss Paul."

"You will have Paul back in a year."

"Yes; but in the mean while I shall be miserable. I wish I knew some nice person whom I might ask to stay with me."

"Why don't you take a companion,—some poor gentlewoman in search of a home? She would read to you, and talk to you."

"No; that would be dreadful. She would be sure to be old and ugly. I should like some one to take Paul's place,—some one young and fresh like him. We're all so terribly old, in the house. You're at least seventy; I'm sixty-five" (Mrs. De Grey was pleased to say); "Deborah is sixty, the cook and coachman are fifty-five apiece."

"You want a young girl then?"

"Yes, some nice, fresh young girl, who would laugh once in a while, and make a little music,—a little sound in the house."

"Well," said Herbert, after reflecting a moment, "you had better suit yourself before Paul comes home. You have only a year."

"Dear me," said Mrs. De Grey; "I shouldn't feel myself obliged to turn her out on Paul's account."

Father Herbert looked at his companion with a penetrating

glance. "Nevertheless, my dear lady," he said, "you know what I mean."

"O yes, I know what you mean,—and you, Father Herbert, know what I think."

"Yes, madam, and, allow me to add, that I don't greatly care. Why should I? I hope with all my heart that you'll never find yourself compelled to think otherwise."

"It is certain," said Mrs. De Grey, "that Paul has had time to play out his little tragedy a dozen times over."

"His father," rejoined Herbert, gravely, "was twenty-six years old."

At these words Mrs. De Grey looked at the priest with a slight frown and a flushed cheek. But he took no pains to meet her eyes, and in a few moments she had recovered, in silence, her habitual calmness.

Within a week after this conversation Mrs. De Grey observed at church two persons who appeared to be strangers in the congregation: an elderly woman, meanly clad, and evidently in ill health, but with a great refinement of person and manner; and a young girl whom Mrs. De Grey took for her daughter. On the following Sunday she again found them at their devotions, and was forcibly struck by a look of sadness and trouble in their faces and attitude. On the third Sunday they were absent; but it happened that during the walk, going to confession, she met the young girl, pale, alone, and dressed in mourning, apparently just leaving the confessional. Something in her gait and aspect assured Mrs. De Grey that she was alone in the world, friendless and helpless; and the good lady, who at times was acutely sensible of her own isolation in society, felt a strong and sympathetic prompting to speak to the stranger, and ask the secret of her sorrow. She stopped her before she left the church, and, addressing her with the utmost kindness, succeeded so speedily in winning her confidence that in half an hour she was in possession of the young girl's entire history. She had just lost her mother, and she found herself in the great city penniless, and all but houseless. They were from the South; her father had been an officer in the navy, and had perished at sea, two years before. Her mother's health had failed, and they had come to New York, ill-advisedly enough, to consult an eminent physician.

He had been very kind, he had taken no fees, but his skill had been applied in vain. Their money had melted away in other directions,—for food and lodging and clothing. There had been enough left to give the poor lady a decent burial; but no means of support save her own exertions remained for the young girl. She had no relatives to look to, but she professed herself abundantly willing to work. "I look weak," she said, "and pale, but I'm really strong. It's only that I'm tired,—and sad. I'm ready to do anything. But I don't know where to look." She had lost her color and the roundness and elasticity of youth; she was thin and ill-dressed; but Mrs. De Grey saw that at her best she must be properly a very pretty creature, and that she was evidently, by rights, a charming girl. She looked at the elder lady with lustrous, appealing blue eyes from under the hideous black bonnet in which her masses of soft light hair were tucked away. She assured her that she had received a very good education, and that she played on the piano-forte. Mrs. De Grey fancied her divested of her rusty weeds, and dressed in a white frock and a blue ribbon, reading aloud at an open window, or touching the keys of her old not unmelodious spinnet; for if she took her (as she mentally phrased it) Mrs. De Grey was resolved that she would not be harassed with the sight of her black garments. It was plain that, frightened and faint and nervous as she was, the poor child would take any service unconditionally. She kissed her then tenderly within the sacred precinct, and led her away to her carriage, quite forgetting her business with her confessor. On the following day Margaret Aldis (such was the young girl's name) was transferred in the same vehicle to Mrs. De Grey's own residence.

This edifice was demolished some years ago, and the place where it stood forms at the present moment the very centre of a turbulent thoroughfare. But at the period of which I speak it stood on the outskirts of the town, with as vast a prospect of open country in one direction as in the other of close-built streets. It was an excellent old mansion, moreover, in the best taste of the time, with large square rooms and broad halls and deep windows, and, above all, a delightful great garden, hedged off from the road by walls of dense verdure. Here, steeped in repose and physical comfort, rescued

from the turbid stream of common life, and placed apart in
the glow of tempered sunshine, valued, esteemed, caressed,
and yet feeling that she was not a mere passive object of charity, but that she was doing her simple utmost to requite her
protectress, poor Miss Aldis bloomed and flowered afresh.
With rest and luxury and leisure, her natural gayety and
beauty came back to her. Her beauty was not dazzling, indeed, nor her gayety obtrusive; but, united, they were the
flower of girlish grace. She still retained a certain tenuity and
fragility of aspect, a lightness of tread, a softness of voice, a
faintness of coloring, which suggested an intimate acquaintance with suffering. But there seemed to burn, nevertheless,
in her deep blue eyes the light of an almost passionate vitality;
and there sat on her firm, pale lips the utterance of a determined, devoted will. It seemed at times as if she gave herself
up with a sensuous, reckless, half-thankless freedom to the
mere consciousness of security. It was evident that she had an
innate love of luxury. She would sometimes sit, motionless,
for hours, with her head thrown back, and her eyes slowly
wandering, in a silent ecstasy of content. At these times
Father Herbert, who had observed her attentively from the
moment of her arrival (for, scholar and recluse as he was, he
had not lost the faculty of appreciating feminine grace),—at
these times the old priest would watch her covertly and marvel at the fantastic, soulless creature whom Mrs. De Grey had
taken to her side. One evening, after a prolonged stupor of
this sort, in which the young girl had neither moved nor spoken, sitting like one whose soul had detached itself and was
wandering through space, she rose, on Mrs. De Grey's at last
giving her an order, and moved forward as if in compliance;
and then, suddenly rushing toward the old woman, she fell
on her knees, and buried her head in her lap and burst into a
paroxysm of sobs. Herbert, who had been standing by, went
and laid one hand on her head, and with the other made over
it the sign of the cross, in the manner of a benediction,—
a consecration of the passionate gratitude which had finally
broken out into utterance. From this moment he loved her.

Margaret read aloud to Mrs. De Grey, and on Sunday
evenings sang in a clear, sweet voice the chants of their
Church, and occupied herself constantly with fine needle-

work, in which she possessed great skill. They spent the long summer mornings together, in reading and work and talk. Margaret told her companion the simple, sad details of the history of which she had already given her the outline; and Mrs. De Grey, who found it natural to look upon them as a kind of practical romance organized for her entertainment, made her repeat them over a dozen times. Mrs. De Grey, too, honored the young girl with a recital of her own biography, which, in its vast vacuity, produced upon Margaret's mind a vague impression of grandeur. The vacuity, indeed, was relieved by the figure of Paul, whom Mrs. De Grey never grew weary of describing, and of whom, finally, Margaret grew very fond of thinking. She listened most attentively to Mrs. De Grey's eulogies of her son, and thought it a great pity he was not at home. And then she began to long for his return, and then, suddenly, she began to fear it. Perhaps he would dislike her being in the house, and turn her out of doors. It was evident that his mother was not prepared to contradict him. Perhaps—worse still—he would marry some foreign woman, and bring her home, and she would turn wickedly jealous of Margaret (in the manner of foreign women). De Grey, roaming through Europe, took for granted, piously enough, that he was never absent from his good mother's thoughts; but he remained superbly unconscious of the dignity which he had usurped in the meditations of her humble companion. Truly, we know where our lives begin, but who shall say where they end? Here was a careless young gentleman whose existence enjoyed a perpetual echo in the soul of a poor girl utterly unknown to him. Mrs. De Grey had two portraits of her son, which, of course, she lost no time in exhibiting to Margaret, —one taken in his boyhood, with brilliant red hair and cheeks, the lad's body encased in a bright blue jacket, and his neck encircled in a frill, open very low; the other, executed just before his departure, a handsome young man in a buff waistcoat, clean shaven, with an animated countenance, dark, close-curling auburn hair, and very fine eyes. The former of these designs Margaret thought a very pretty child; but to the other the poor girl straightway lost her heart,—the more easily that Mrs. De Grey assured her, that, although the picture was handsome enough, it conveyed but the faintest idea of her boy's adorable flesh and blood. In a couple of months arrived a long-expected letter from Paul, and with it another portrait,—a miniature, painted in Paris by a famous artist. Here Paul appeared a far more elegant figure than in the work of the American painter. In what the change consisted it was hard to tell; but his mother declared that it was easy to see that he had spent two years in the best company in Europe.

"O, the best company!" said Father Herbert, who knew the force of this term. And, smiling a moment with inoffensive scorn, he relapsed into his wonted gravity.

"I think he looks very sad," said Margaret, timidly.

"Fiddlesticks!" cried Herbert, impatiently. "He looks like a coxcomb. Of course, it's the Frenchman's fault," he added, more gently. "Why on earth does he send us his picture at all? It's a great piece of impertinence. Does he think we've forgotten him? When I want to remember my boy, I have something better to look to than that flaunting bit of ivory."

At these words the two ladies went off, carrying the portrait with them, to read Paul's letter in private. It was in eight pages, and Margaret read it aloud. Then, when she had finished, she read it again; and in the evening she read it once more. The next day, Mrs. De Grey, taking the young girl quite into her confidence, brought out a large packet containing his earlier letters, and Margaret spent the whole morning in reading them over aloud. That evening she took a stroll in the garden alone,—the garden in which *he* had played as a boy, and lounged and dreamed as a young man. She found his name—his beautiful name—rudely cut on a wooden bench. Introduced, as it seemed to her that she had been by his letters, into the precincts of his personality, the mystery of his being, the magic circle of his feelings and opinions and fancies; wandering by his side, unseen, over Europe, and treading, unheard, the sounding pavements of famous churches and palaces, she felt that she tasted for the first time of the substance and sweetness of life. Margaret walked about for an hour in the starlight, among the dusky, perfumed alleys. Mrs. De Grey, feeling unwell, had gone to her room. The young girl heard the far-off hum of the city slowly decrease and expire, and then, when the stillness of the night was unbroken, she came back into the parlor across the long window, and lit one of the great silver candlesticks that decorated the ends of the mantel. She carried it to the wall where Mrs. De Grey had suspended her son's miniature, having first inserted it in an immense gold frame, from which she had expelled a less valued picture. Margaret felt that she must see the portrait before she went to bed. There was a certain charm and ravishment in beholding it privately by candlelight. The wind had risen,—a warm west wind,—and the long white curtains of the open windows swayed and bulged in the gloom in a spectral fashion. Margaret guarded the flame of the candle with her hand, and gazed at the polished surface of the portrait, warm in the light, beneath its glittering plate of glass. What an immensity of life and passion was concentrated into those few square inches of artificial color! The young man's eyes seemed to gaze at her with a look of profound recognition. They held her fascinated; she lingered on the spot, unable to move. Suddenly the clock on the chimney-piece rang out a single clear stroke. Margaret started and turned about, at the thought that it was already half past ten. She raised her candle aloft to look at the dial-plate; and perceived three things: that it was one o'clock in the morning, that her candle was half burnt out, and that some one was watching her from the other side of the room. Setting down her light, she recognized Father Herbert.

"Well, Miss Aldis," he said, coming into the light, "what do you think of it?"

Margaret was startled and confused, but not abashed. "How long have I been here?" she asked, simply.

"I have no idea. I myself have been here half an hour."

"It was very kind of you not to disturb me," said Margaret, less simply.

"It was a very pretty picture," said Herbert.

"O, it's beautiful!" cried the young girl, casting another glance at the portrait over her shoulder.

The old man smiled sadly, and turned away, and then, coming back, "How do you like our young man, Miss Aldis?" he asked, apparently with a painful effort.

"I think he's very handsome," said Margaret, frankly.

"He's not so handsome as that," said Herbert.

"His mother says he's handsomer."

"A mother's testimony in such cases is worth very little. Paul is well enough, but he's no miracle."

"I think he looks sad," said Margaret. "His mother says he's very gay."

"He may have changed vastly within two years. Do you think," the old man added, after a pause, "that he looks like a man in love?"

"I don't know," said Margaret, in a low voice. "I never saw one."

"Never?" said the priest, with an earnestness which surprised the young girl.

She blushed a little. "Never, Father Herbert."

The priest's dark eyes were fixed on her with a strange intensity of expression. "I hope, my child, you never may," he said, solemnly.

The tone of his voice was not unkind, but it seemed to Margaret as if there were something cruel and chilling in the wish. "Why not I as well as another?" she asked.

The old man shrugged his shoulders. "O, it's a long story," he said.

The summer passed away and flushed into autumn, and the autumn slowly faded, and finally expired in the cold embrace of December. Mrs. De Grey had written to her son of her having taken Margaret into her service. At this time came a letter in which the young man was pleased to express his satisfaction at this measure. "Present my compliments to Miss Aldis," he wrote, "and assure her of my gratitude for the comfort she has given my dear mother,—of which, indeed, I hope before very long to inform her in person." In writing these good-natured words Paul De Grey little suspected the infinite reverberation they were to have in poor Margaret's heart. A month later arrived a letter, which was handed to Mrs. De Grey at breakfast. "You will have received my letter of December 3d," it began (a letter which had miscarried and failed to arrive), "and will have formed your respective opinions of its contents." As Mrs. De Grey read these words, Father Herbert looked at Margaret; she had turned pale. "Favorable or not," the letter continued, "I am sorry to be obliged to bid you undo them again. But my engagement to Miss L. is broken off. It had become impossible. As I made no attempt to give you a history of it, or to set forth my motives, so I shall not now attempt to go into the logic of the rupture. But it's broken clean off, I assure you. Amen." And the letter passed to other matters, leaving our friends sadly perplexed. They awaited the arrival of the missing letter; but all in vain; it never came. Mrs. De Grey immediately wrote to her son, urgently requesting an explanation of the events to which he had referred. His next letter, however, contained none of the desired information. Mrs. De Grey repeated her request. Whereupon Paul wrote that he would tell her the story when he had reached home. He hated to talk about it. "Don't be uneasy, dear mother," he added; "Heaven has insured me against a relapse. Miss L. died three weeks ago at Naples." As Mrs. De Grey read these words, she laid down the letter and looked at Father Herbert, who had been called to hear it. His pale face turned ghastly white, and he returned the old woman's gaze with compressed lips and a stony immobility in his eyes. Then, suddenly, a fierce, inarticulate cry broke from his throat, and, doubling up his fist, he brought it down with a terrible blow on the table. Margaret sat watching him, amazed. He rose to his feet, seized her in his arms, and pressed her on his neck.

"My child! my child!" he cried, in a broken voice, "I have always loved you! I have been harsh and cold and crabbed. I was fearful. The thunder has fallen! Forgive me, child. I'm myself again." Margaret, frightened, disengaged herself, but he kept her hand. "Poor boy!" he cried, with a tremulous sigh.

Mrs. De Grey sat smelling her vinaigrette, but not visibly discomposed. "Poor boy!" she repeated, but without a sigh, —which gave the words an ironical sound.—"He had ceased to care for her," she said.

"Ah, madam!" cried the priest, "don't blaspheme. Go down on your knees, and thank God that *we* have been spared that hideous sight!"

Mystified and horrified, Margaret drew her hand from his grasp, and looked with wondering eyes at Mrs. De Grey. She smiled faintly, touched her forefinger to her forehead, tapped it, raised her eyebrows, and shook her head.

From counting the months that were to elapse before

Paul's return, our friends came to counting the weeks, and then the days. The month of May arrived; Paul had sailed from England. At this time Mrs. De Grey opened her son's room, and caused it to be prepared for occupation. The contents were just as he had left them; she bade Margaret come in and see it. Margaret looked at her face in his mirror, and sat down a moment on his sofa, and examined the books on his shelves. They seemed a prodigious array; they were in several languages, and gave a deep impression of their owner's attainments. Over the chimney hung a small sketch in pencil, which Margaret made haste to inspect,—a likeness of a young girl, skilfully enough drawn. The original had apparently been very handsome, in the dark style; and in the corner of the sketch was written the artist's name,—*De Grey.* Margaret looked at the portrait in silence, with quickened heart-beats.

"Is this Mr. Paul's?" she asked at last of her companion.

"It belongs to Paul," said Mrs. De Grey. "He used to be very fond of it, and insisted upon hanging it there. His father sketched it before our marriage."

Margaret drew a breath of relief. "And who is the lady?" she asked.

"I hardly know. Some foreign person, I think, that Mr. De Grey had been struck with. There's something about her in the other corner."

In effect, Margaret detected on the opposite side of the sketch, written in minute characters, the word "*obiit,* 1786."

"You don't know Latin, I take it, my dear," said Mrs. De Grey, as Margaret read the inscription. "It means that she died thirty-four good years ago."

"Poor girl!" said Margaret, softly. As they were leaving the room, she lingered on the threshold and looked about her, wishing that she might leave some little memento of her visit. "If we knew just when he would arrive," she said, "I would put some flowers on his table. But they might fade."

As Mrs. De Grey assured her that the moment of his arrival was quite uncertain, she left her fancied nosegay uncut, and spent the rest of the day in a delightful tremor of anticipation, ready to see the dazzling figure of a young man, equipped with strange foreign splendor, start up before her and look at her in cold surprise, and hurry past her in search of his mother. At every sound of footsteps or of an opening door she laid down her work, and listened curiously. In the evening, as if by a common instinct of expectancy, Father Herbert met Mrs. De Grey in the front drawing-room,—an apartment devoted exclusively to those festivities which never occurred in the annals of this tranquil household.

"A year ago to-day, madam," said Margaret, as they all sat silent among the gathering shadows, "I came into your house. To-day ends a very happy year."

"Let us hope," said Father Herbert, sententiously, "that to-morrow will begin another."

"Ah, my dear lady!" cried Margaret, with emotion; "my good father,—my only friends,—what harm can come to me with you? It was you who rescued me from harm." Her heart was swollen with gratitude, and her eyes with rising tears. She gave a long shudder at the thought of the life that might have been her fate. But, feeling a natural indisposition to obtrude her peculiar sensations upon the attention of persons so devoutly absorbed in the thought of a coming joy, she left her place, and wandered away into the garden. Before many minutes, a little gate opened in the paling, not six yards from where she stood. A man came in, whom, in the dim light, she knew to be Paul De Grey. Approaching her rapidly, he made a movement as if to greet her, but stopped suddenly, and removed his hat.

"Ah, you're Miss—the young lady," he said.

He had forgotten her name. This was something other, something less felicitous, than the cold surprise of the figure in Margaret's vision. Nevertheless, she answered him, audibly enough: "They are in the drawing-room; they expect you."

He bounded along the path, and entered the house. She followed him slowly to the window, and stood without, listening. The silence of the young man's welcome told of its warmth.

Paul De Grey had made good use of his sojourn in Europe; he had lost none of his old merits, and had gained a number of new ones. He was by nature and culture an intelligent, amiable, accomplished fellow. It was his fortune to possess a peculiar, indefinable charm of person and manner. He was tall and slight of structure, but compact, firm, and active, with a clear, fair complexion, an open, prominent brow, crisp auburn hair, and eyes—a glance, a smile—radiant with youth and intellect. His address was frank, manly, and direct; and yet it seemed to Margaret that his bearing was marked by a certain dignity and elegance—at times even verging upon formalism—which distinguished it from that of other men. It was not, however, that she detected in his character any signs of that strange principle of melancholy which had exerted so powerful an action upon the other members of the household (and, from what she was able to gather, on his father). She fancied, on the contrary, that she had never known less levity associated with a more exquisite mirth. If Margaret had been of a more analytical turn of mind, she would have told herself that Paul De Grey's nature was eminently aristocratic. But the young girl contented herself with understanding it less, and secretly loving it more; and when she was in want of an epithet, she chose a simpler term. Paul was like a ray of splendid sunshine in the dull, colorless lives of the two women; he filled the house with light and heat and joy. He moved, to Margaret's fancy, in a circle of almost supernatural glory. His words, as they fell from his lips, seemed diamonds and pearls; and, in truth, his conversation, for a month after his return, was in the last degree delightful. Mrs. De Grey's house was *par excellence* the abode of leisure,—a castle of indolence; and Paul in talking, and his companions in listening, were conscious of no jealous stress of sordid duties. The summer days were long, and Paul's daily fund of loquacity was inexhaustible. A week after his arrival, after breakfast, Father Herbert contracted the habit of carrying him off to his study; and Margaret, passing the half-open door, would hear the changeful music of his voice. She begrudged the old man, at these times, the exclusive enjoyment of so much eloquence. She felt that with his tutor, Paul's talk was far wiser and richer than it was possible it should be with two simple-minded women; and the young girl had a pious longing to hear him, to see him, at his best. A brilliant best it was to Father Herbert's mind; for Paul had surpassed his fondest hopes. He had amassed such a store of knowledge; he had learned all the good that the old man had enjoined upon him; and, although he had not wholly ignored the evil against which the priest had warned him, he judged it so wisely and wittily! Women and priests, as a general thing, like a man none the less for not being utterly innocent. Father Herbert took an unutterable satisfaction in the happy development of Paul's character. He was more than the son of his loins: he was the child of his intellect, his patience, and devotion.

The afternoons and evenings Paul was free to devote to his mother, who, out of her own room, never dispensed for an hour with Margaret's attendance. This, thanks to the young girl's delicate tact and sympathy, had now become an absolute necessity. Margaret sat by with her work, while Paul talked, and marvelled at his inexhaustible stock of gossip and anecdote and forcible, vivid description. He made cities and churches and galleries and playhouses swarm and shine before her enchanted senses, and reproduced the people he had met and the scenery through which he had travelled, until the young girl's head turned at the rapid succession of images and pictures. And then, at times, he would seem to grow weary, and would sink into silence; and Margaret, looking up askance from her work, would see his eyes absently fixed, and a faint smile on his face, or else a cold gravity, and she would wonder what far-off memory had called back his thoughts to that unknown European world. Sometimes, less frequently, when she raised her eyes, she found him watching her own figure, her bent head, and the busy movement of her hands. But (as yet, at least) he never turned away his glance in confusion; he let his eyes rest, and justified his scrutiny by some simple and natural remark.

But as the weeks passed by, and the summer grew to its fulness, Mrs. De Grey contracted the habit of going after dinner to her own room, where, we may respectfully conjecture, she passed the afternoon in dishabille and slumber. But De Grey and Miss Aldis tacitly agreed together that, in the prime and springtime of life, it was stupid folly to waste in any such fashion the longest and brightest hours of the year; and so they, on their side, contracted the habit of sitting in the darkened drawing-room, and gossiping away the time until within an hour of tea. Sometimes, for a change, they went across the garden into a sort of summer-house, which occupied a central point in the enclosure, and stood with its face averted from

the mansion, and looking to the north, and with its sides covered with dense, clustering vines. Within, against the wall, was
a deep garden bench, and in the middle a table, upon which
Margaret placed her work-basket, and the young man the
book, which, under the pretence of meaning to read, he usually carried in his hand. Within was coolness and deep shade
and silence, and without the broad glare of the immense summer sky. When I say there was silence, I mean that there was
nothing to interrupt the conversation of these happy idlers.
Their talk speedily assumed that desultory, volatile character,
which is the sign of great intimacy. Margaret found occasion
to ask Paul a great many questions which she had not felt at
liberty to ask in the presence of his mother, and to demand
additional light upon a variety of little points which Mrs. De
Grey had been content to leave in obscurity. Paul was perfectly communicative. If Miss Aldis cared to hear, he was
assuredly glad to talk. But suddenly it struck him that her attitude of mind was a singular provocation to egotism, and
that for six weeks, in fact, he had done nothing but talk about
himself,—his own adventures, sensations, and opinions.

"I declare, Miss Aldis," he cried, "you're making me a
monstrous egotist. That's all you women are good for. I shall
not say another word about Mr. Paul De Grey. Now it's your
turn."

"To talk about Mr. Paul De Grey?" asked Margaret, with a
smile.

"No, about Miss Margaret Aldis,—which, by the way, is a
very pretty name."

"By the way, indeed!" said Margaret. "By the way for you,
perhaps. But for me, my pretty name is all I have."

"If you mean, Miss Aldis," cried Paul, "that your beauty is
all in your name—"

"I'm sadly mistaken. Well, then, I don't. The rest is in my
imagination."

"Very likely. It's certainly not in mine."

Margaret was, in fact, at this time, extremely pretty; a little
pale with the heat, but rounded and developed by rest and
prosperity, and animated—half inspired, I may call it—with
tender gratitude. Looking at her as he said these words, De
Grey was forcibly struck with the interesting character of her

face. Yes, most assuredly, her beauty was a potent reality. The charm of her face was forever refreshed and quickened by the deep loveliness of her soul.

"I mean literally, Miss Aldis," said the young man, "that I wish you to talk about yourself. I want to hear *your* adventures. I demand it,—I need it."

"My adventures?" said Margaret. "I have never had any."

"Good!" cried Paul; "that in itself is an adventure."

In this way it was that Margaret came to relate to her companion the short story of her young life. The story was not all told, however, short as it was, in a single afternoon; that is, a whole week after she began, the young girl found herself setting Paul right with regard to a matter of which he had received a false impression.

"Nay, he is married," said Margaret; "I told you so."

"O, he is married?" said Paul.

"Yes; his wife's an immense fat woman."

"O, his wife's an immense fat woman?"

"Yes; and he thinks all the world of her."

"O, he thinks all the world of her!"

It was natural that, in this manner, with a running commentary supplied by Paul, the narrative should proceed slowly. But, in addition to the observations here quoted, the young man maintained another commentary, less audible and more profound. As he listened to this frank and fair-haired maiden, and reflected that in the wide world she might turn in confidence and sympathy to other minds than his,—as he found her resting her candid thoughts and memories on his judgment, as she might lay her white hand on his arm,—it seemed to him that the pure intentions with which she believed his soul to be peopled took in her glance a graver and higher cast. All the gorgeous color faded out of his recent European reminiscences and regrets, and he was sensible only of Margaret's presence, and of the tender rosy radiance in which she sat and moved, as in a sort of earthly halo. Could it be, he asked himself, that while he was roaming about Europe, in a vague, restless search for his future, his end, his aim, these things were quietly awaiting him at his own deserted hearth-stone, gathered together in the immaculate person of the sweetest and fairest of women? Finally, one day, this view of the case struck him so forcibly, that he cried out in an ecstasy of belief and joy.

"Margaret," he said, "my mother found you in church, and there, before the altar, she kissed you and took you into her arms. I have often thought of that scene. It makes it no common adoption."

"I'm sure I have often thought of it," said Margaret.

"It makes it sacred and everlasting," said Paul. "On that blessed day you came to us for ever and ever."

Margaret looked at him with a face tremulous between smiles and tears. "For as long as you will keep me," she said. "Ah, Paul!" For in an instant the young man had expressed all his longing and his passion.

With the greatest affection and esteem for his mother, Paul had always found it natural to give precedence to Father Herbert in matters of appeal and confidence. The old man possessed a delicacy of intellectual tact which made his sympathy and his counsel alike delightful. Some days after the conversation upon a few of the salient points of which I have lightly touched, Paul and Margaret renewed their mutual vows in the summer-house. They now possessed that deep faith in the sincerity of their own feelings, and that undoubting delight in each other's reiterated protests, which left them nothing to do but to take their elders into their confidence. They came through the garden together, and on reaching the threshold Margaret found that she had left her scissors in the garden hut; whereupon Paul went back in search of them. The young girl came into the house, reached the foot of the staircase, and waited for her lover. At this moment Father Herbert appeared in the open doorway of his study, and looked at Margaret with a melancholy smile. He stood, passing one hand slowly over another, and gazing at her with kindly, darksome looks.

"It seems to me, Mistress Margaret," he said, "that you keep all this a marvellous secret from your poor old Doctor Herbert."

In the presence of this gentle and venerable scholar, Margaret felt that she had no need of vulgar blushing and simpering and negation. "Dear Father Herbert," she said, with heavenly simpleness, "I have just been begging Paul to tell you."

"Ah, my daughter,"—and the old man but half stifled a sigh,—"it's all a strange and terrible mystery."

Paul came in and crossed the hall with the light step of a lover.

"Paul," said Margaret, "Father Herbert knows."

"Father Herbert knows!" repeated the priest,—"Father Herbert knows everything. You're very innocent for lovers."

"You're very wise, sir, for a priest," said Paul, blushing.

"I knew it a week ago," said the old man, gravely.

"Well, sir," said Paul, "we love you none the less for loving each other so much more. I hope you'll not love us the less."

"Father Herbert thinks it's 'terrible,' " said Margaret, smiling.

"O Lord!" cried Herbert, raising his hand to his head as if in pain. He turned about, and went into his room.

Paul drew Margaret's hand through his arm and followed the priest. "You suffer, sir," he said, "at the thought of losing us,—of our leaving you. That certainly needn't trouble you. Where should we go? As long as you live, as long as my mother lives, we shall all make but a single household."

The old man appeared to have recovered his composure. "Ah!" he said; "be happy, no matter where, and I shall be happy. You're very young."

"Not so young," said Paul, laughing, but with a natural disinclination to be placed in too boyish a light. "I'm six-and-twenty. *J'ai vécu,*—I've lived."

"He's been through everything," said Margaret, leaning on his arm.

"Not quite everything." And Paul, bending his eyes, with a sober smile, met her upward glance.

"O, he's modest," murmured Father Herbert.

"Paul's been all but married already," said Margaret.

The young man made a gesture of impatience. Herbert stood with his eyes fixed on his face.

"Why do you speak of that poor girl?" said Paul. Whatever satisfaction he may have given Margaret on the subject of his projected marriage in Europe, he had since his return

declined, on the plea that it was extremely painful, to discuss
the matter either with his mother or with his old tutor.

"Miss Aldis is perhaps jealous," said Herbert, cunningly.

"O Father Herbert!" cried Margaret.

"There is little enough to be jealous of," said Paul.

"There's a fine young man!" cried Herbert. "One would
think he had never cared for her."

"It's perfectly true."

"Oh!" said Herbert, in a tone of deep reproach, laying his
hand on the young man's arm. "Don't say that."

"Nay, sir, I shall say it. I never said anything less to her. She
enchanted me, she entangled me, but, before Heaven, I never
loved her!"

"O, God help you!" cried the priest. He sat down, and
buried his face in his hands.

Margaret turned deadly pale, and recalled the scene which
had occurred on the receipt of Paul's letter, announcing the
rupture of his engagement. "Father Herbert," she cried,
"what horrible, hideous mystery do you keep locked up in
your bosom? If it concerns me,—if it concerns Paul,—I demand of you to tell us."

Moved apparently by the young girl's tone of agony to a
sense of the needfulness of self-control, Herbert uncovered
his face, and directed to Margaret a rapid glance of entreaty.
She perceived that it meant that, at any cost, she should be
silent. Then, with a sublime attempt at dissimulation, he put
out his hands, and laid one on each of his companions' shoulders. "Excuse me, Paul," he said, "I'm a foolish old man. Old
scholars are a sentimental, a superstitious race. We believe still
that all women are angels, and that all men—"

"That all men are fools," said Paul, smiling.

"Exactly. Whereas, you see," whispered Father Herbert,
"there are no fools but ourselves."

Margaret listened to this fantastic bit of dialogue with a
beating heart, fully determined not to content herself with
any such flimsy explanation of the old man's tragical allusions.
Meanwhile, Herbert urgently besought Paul to defer for a few
days making known his engagement to his mother.

The next day but one was Sunday, the last in August. The
heat for a week had been oppressive, and the air was now

sullen and brooding, as if with an approaching storm. As she left the breakfast-table, Margaret felt her arm touched by Father Herbert.

"Don't go to church," he said, in a low voice. "Make a pretext, and stay at home."

"A pretext?—"

"Say you've letters to write."

"Letters?" and Margaret smiled half bitterly. "To whom should I write letters?"

"Dear me, then say you're ill. I give you absolution. When they're gone, come to me."

At church-time, accordingly, Margaret feigned a slight indisposition; and Mrs. De Grey, taking her son's arm, mounted into her ancient deep-seated coach, and rolled away from the door. Margaret immediately betook herself to Father Herbert's apartment. She saw in the old man's face the portent of some dreadful avowal. His whole figure betrayed the weight of an inexorable necessity.

"My daughter," said the priest, "you are a brave, pious girl—"

"Ah!" cried Margaret, "it's something horrible, or you wouldn't say that. Tell me at once!"

"You need all your courage."

"Doesn't he love me?—Ah, in Heaven's name, speak!"

"If he didn't love you with a damning passion, I should have nothing to say."

"O, then, say what you please!" said Margaret.

"Well then,—you must leave this house."

"Why?—when?—where must I go?"

"This moment, if possible. You must go anywhere,—the further the better,—the further from *him*. Listen, my child," said the old man, his bosom wrung by the stunned, bewildered look of Margaret's face; "it's useless to protest, to weep, to resist. It's the voice of fate!"

"And pray, sir," said Margaret, "of what do you accuse me?"

"I accuse no one. I don't even accuse Heaven."

"But there's a reason,—there's a motive—"

Herbert laid his hand on his lips, pointed to a seat, and, turning to an ancient chest on the table, unlocked it, and drew from it a small volume, bound in vellum, apparently an old illuminated missal. "There's nothing for it," he said, "but to tell you the whole story."

He sat down before the young girl, who held herself rigid and expectant. The room grew dark with the gathering storm-clouds, and the distant thunder muttered.

"Let me read you ten words," said the priest, opening at a fly-leaf of the volume, on which a memorandum or register had been inscribed in a great variety of hands, all minute and some barely legible. "God be with you!" and the old man crossed himself. Involuntarily, Margaret did the same. " 'George De Grey,' " he read, " 'met and loved, September, 1786, Antonietta Gambini, of Milan. She died October 9th, same year. John De Grey married, April 4th, 1749, Henrietta Spencer. She died May 7th. George De Grey engaged himself October, 1710, to Mary Fortescue. She died October 31st. Paul De Grey, aged nineteen, betrothed June, 1672, at Bristol, England, to Lucretia Lefevre, aged thirty-one, of that place. She died July 27th. John De Grey, affianced January 10th, 1649, to Blanche Ferrars, of Castle Ferrars, Cumberland. She died, by her lover's hand, January 12th. Stephen De Grey offered his hand to Isabel Stirling, October, 1619. She died within the month. Paul De Grey exchanged pledges with Magdalen Scrope, August, 1586. She died in childbirth, September, 1587.' " Father Herbert paused. "Is it enough?" he asked, looking up with glowing eyes. "There are two pages more. The De Greys are an ancient line; they keep their records."

Margaret had listened with a look of deepening, fierce, passionate horror,—a look more of anger and of wounded pride than of terror. She sprang towards the priest with the lightness of a young cat, and dashed the hideous record from his hand.

"What abominable nonsense is this!" she cried. "What does it mean? I barely heard it; I despise it; I laugh at it!"

The old man seized her arm with a firm grasp. "Paul De Grey," he said, in an awful voice, "exchanged pledges with Margaret Aldis, August, 1821. She died—with the falling leaves."

Poor Margaret looked about her for help, inspiration, comfort of some kind. The room contained nothing but serried lines of old parchment-covered books, each seeming a grim repetition of the volume at her feet. A vast peal of thunder resounded through the noonday stillness. Suddenly her strength deserted her; she felt her weakness and loneliness, the grasp of the hand of fate. Father Herbert put out his arms, she flung herself on his neck, and burst into tears.

"Do you still refuse to leave him?" asked the priest. "If you leave him, you're saved."

"Saved?" cried Margaret, raising her head; "and Paul?"

"Ah, there it is.—He'll forget you."

The young girl pondered a moment. "To have him do that," she said, "I should apparently have to die." Then wringing her hands with a fresh burst of grief, "Is it certain," she cried, "that there are no exceptions?"

"None, my child"; and he picked up the volume. "You see it's the first love, the first passion. After that, they're innocent. Look at Mrs. De Grey. The race is accursed. It's an awful, inscrutable mystery. I fancied that you were safe, my daughter, and that that poor Miss L. had borne the brunt. But Paul was at pains to undeceive me. I've searched his life, I've probed his conscience: it's a virgin heart. Ah, my child, I dreaded it from the first. I trembled when you came into the house. I wanted Mrs. De Grey to turn you off. But she laughs at it,—she calls it an old-wife's tale. *She* was safe enough; her husband didn't care two straws for her. But there's a little dark-eyed maiden buried in Italian soil who could tell her another story. She withered, my child. She was life itself,—an incarnate ray of her own Southern sun. She died of De Grey's kisses. Don't ask me how it began, it's always been so. It goes back to the night of time. One of the race, they say, came home from the East, from the crusades, infected with the germs of the plague. He had pledged his love-faith to a young girl before his departure, and it had been arranged that the wedding should immediately succeed his return. Feeling unwell, he consulted an elder brother of the bride, a man versed in fantastic medical lore, and supposed to be gifted with magical skill. By him he was assured that he was plague-stricken, and that he was in duty bound to defer the marriage. The young knight refused to comply, and the physician, infuriated, pronounced a curse upon his race. The marriage took place; within a week the bride expired, in horrible agony; the young man, after a slight illness, recovered; the curse took effect."

Margaret took the quaint old missal into her hand, and turned to the grisly register of death. Her heart grew cold as she thought of her own sad sisterhood with all those miserable women of the past. Miserable women, but ah! tenfold more miserable men,—helpless victims of their own baleful hearts. She remained silent, with her eyes fixed on the book, abstractedly; mechanically, as it were, she turned to another page, and read a familiar orison to the blessed Virgin. Then raising her head, with her deep-blue eyes shining with the cold light of an immense resolve,—a prodigious act of volition,—"Father Herbert," she said, in low, solemn accents, "I revoke the curse. I undo it. *I curse it!*"

From this moment, nothing would induce her to bestow a moment's thought on salvation by flight. It was too late, she declared. If she was destined to die, she had already imbibed the fatal contagion. But they should see. She cast no discredit on the existence or the potency of the dreadful charm; she simply assumed, with deep self-confidence which filled the old priest with mingled wonder and anguish, that it would vainly expend its mystic force once and forever upon her own devoted, impassioned life. Father Herbert folded his trembling hands resignedly. He had done his duty; the rest was with God. At times, living as he had done for years in dread of the moment which had now arrived, with his whole life darkened by its shadow, it seemed to him among the strange possibilities of nature that this frail and pure young girl might indeed have sprung, at the command of outraged love, to the rescue of the unhappy line to which he had dedicated his manhood. And then at other moments it seemed as if she were joyously casting herself into the dark gulf. At all events, the sense of peril had filled Margaret herself with fresh energy and charm. Paul, if he had not been too enchanted with her feverish gayety and grace to trouble himself about their motive and origin, would have been at loss to explain their sudden morbid intensity. Forthwith, at her request, he announced his engagement to his mother, who put on a very gracious face, and honored Margaret with a sort of official kiss.

"Ah me!" muttered Father Herbert, "and now she thinks she has bound them fast." And later, the next day, when Mrs. De Grey, talking of the matter, avowed that it really did cost her a little to accept as a daughter a girl to whom she had paid a salary,—"A salary, madam!" cried the priest with a bitter laugh; "upon my word, I think it was the least you could do."

"Nous verrons," said Mrs. De Grey, composedly.

A week passed by, without ill omens. Paul was in a manly ecstasy of bliss. At moments he was almost bewildered by the fulness with which his love and faith had been requited. Margaret was transfigured, glorified, by the passion which burned in her heart. "Give a plain girl, a common girl, a lover," thought Paul, "and she grows pretty, charming. Give a charming girl a lover—" and if Margaret was present, his eloquent eyes uttered the conclusion; if she was absent, his restless steps wandered in search of her. Her beauty within the past ten days seemed to have acquired an unprecedented warmth and richness. Paul went so far as to fancy that her voice had grown more deep and mellow. She looked older; she seemed in an instant to have overleaped a year of her development, and to have arrived at the perfect maturity of her youth. One might have imagined that, instead of the further, she stood just on the hither verge of marriage. Meanwhile Paul grew conscious of he hardly knew what delicate change in his own emotions. The exquisite feeling of pity, the sense of her appealing weakness, her heavenly dependence, which had lent its tender strain to swell the concert of his affections, had died away, and given place to a vague, profound instinct of respect. Margaret was, after all, no such simple body; her nature, too, had its mysteries. In truth, thought Paul, tenderness, gentleness, is its own reward. He had bent to pluck this pallid flower of sunless household growth; he had dipped its slender stem in the living waters of his love, and lo! it had lifted its head, and spread its petals, and brightened into splendid purple and green. This glowing potency of loveliness filled him with a tremor which was almost a foreboding. He longed to possess her; he watched her with covetous eyes; he wished to call her utterly his own.

"Margaret," he said to her, "you fill me with a dreadful delight. You grow more beautiful every day. We must be married immediately, or, at this rate, by our wedding-day, I shall have grown mortally afraid of you. By the soul of my father, I didn't bargain for this! Look at yourself in that glass." And he turned her about to a long mirror; it was in his mother's dressing-room; Mrs. De Grey had gone into the adjoining chamber.

Margaret saw herself reflected from head to foot in the glassy depths, and perceived the change in her appearance. Her head rose with a sort of proud serenity from the full curve of her shoulders; her eyes were brilliant, her lips trembled, her bosom rose and fell with all the insolence of her deep devotion. "Blanche Ferrars, of Castle Ferrars," she silently repeated, "Isabel Stirling, Magdalen Scrope,—poor foolish women! You were not women, you were children. It's your fault, Paul," she cried, aloud, "if I look other than I should! Why is there such a love between us?" And then, seeing the young man's face beside her own, she fancied he looked pale. "My Paul," she said, taking his hands, "you're pale. What a face for a happy lover! You're impatient. Well-a-day, sir! it shall be when you please."

The marriage was fixed for the last of September; and the two women immediately began to occupy themselves with the purchase of the bridal garments. Margaret, out of her salary, had saved a sufficient sum to buy a handsome wedding gown; but, for the other articles of her wardrobe, she was obliged to be indebted to the liberality of Mrs. De Grey. She made no scruple, indeed, of expending large sums of money, and, when they were expended, of asking for more. She took an active, violent delight in procuring quantities of the richest stuffs. It seemed to her that, for the time, she had parted with all flimsy dignity and conventional reticence and coyness, as if she had flung away her conscience to be picked up by vulgar, happy, unimperilled women. She gathered her marriage finery together in a sort of fierce defiance of impending calamity. She felt excited to outstrip it, to confound it, to stare it out of countenance.

One day she was crossing the hall, with a piece of stuff just sent from the shop. It was a long morsel of vivid pink satin, and, as she held it, a portion of it fell over her arm to her feet. Father Herbert's door stood ajar; she stopped, and went in.

"Excuse me, reverend sir," said Margaret; "but I thought it a pity not to show you this beautiful bit of satin. Isn't it a lovely pink?—it's almost red,—it's carnation. It's the color of our love,—of my death. Father Herbert," she cried, with a shrill, resounding laugh, "*it's my shroud!* Don't you think it would be a pretty shroud?—pink satin, and blond-lace, and pearls?"

The old man looked at her with a haggard face. "My daughter," he said, "Paul will have an incomparable wife."

"Most assuredly, if you compare me with those ladies in your prayer-book. Ah! Paul shall have a wife, at least. That's very certain."

"Well," said the old man, "you're braver than I. You frighten me."

"Dear Father Herbert, didn't you once frighten me?"

The old man looked at Margaret with mingled tenderness and horror. "Tell me, child," he said, "in the midst of all this, do you ever pray?"

"God forbid!" cried the poor creature. "I have no heart for prayer."

She had long talks with Paul about their future pleasures, and the happy life they should lead. He declared that he would set their habits to quite another tune, and that the family should no longer be buried in silence and gloom. It was an absurd state of things, and he marvelled that it should ever have come about. They should begin to live like other people, and occupy their proper place in society. They should entertain company, and travel, and go to the play of an evening. Margaret had never seen a play; after their marriage, if she wished, she should see one every week for a year. "Have no fears, my dear," cried Paul, "I don't mean to bury you alive; I'm not digging your grave. If I expected you to be content to live as my poor mother lives, we might as well be married by the funeral service."

When Paul talked with this buoyant energy, looking with a firm, undoubting gaze on the long, blissful future, Margaret drew from his words fortitude and joy, and scorn of all danger. Father Herbert's secret seemed a vision, a fantasy, a dream, until, after a while, she found herself again face to face with the old man, and read in his haggard features that to him, at least, it was a deep reality. Nevertheless, among all her feverish transitions from hope to fear, from exaltation to despair, she never, for a moment, ceased to keep a cunning watch upon her physical sensations, and to lie in wait for morbid symptoms. She wondered that, with this ghastly burden on her consciousness, she had not long since been goaded to insanity, or crushed into utter idiocy. She fancied that, sad as it would have been to rest in ignorance of the mystery in which her life had been involved, it was yet more terrible to know it. During the week after her interview with Father Herbert, she had not slept half an hour of the daily twenty-four; and yet, far from missing her sleep, she felt, as I have attempted to show, intoxicated, electrified, by the unbroken vigilance and tension of her will. But she well knew that this could not last forever. One afternoon, a couple of days after Paul had uttered those brilliant promises, he mounted his horse for a ride. Margaret stood at the gate, watching him regretfully, and, as he galloped away, he kissed her his hand. An hour before tea she came out of her room, and entered the parlor, where Mrs. De Grey had established herself for the evening. A moment later, Father Herbert, who was in the act of lighting his study-lamp, heard a piercing shriek resound through the house.

His heart stood still. "The hour is come," he said. "It would be a pity to miss it." He hurried to the drawing-room, together with the servants, also startled by the cry. Margaret lay stretched on the sofa, pale, motionless, panting, with her eyes closed and her hand pressed to her side. Herbert exchanged a rapid glance with Mrs. De Grey, who was bending over the young girl, holding her other hand.

"Let us at least have no scandal," she said, with dignity, and straightway dismissed the servants. Margaret gradually revived, declared that it was nothing,—a mere sudden pain,—that she felt better, and begged her companions to make no commotion. Mrs. De Grey went to her room, in search of a phial of smelling-salts, leaving Herbert alone with Margaret. He was on his knees on the floor, holding her other hand. She raised herself to a sitting posture.

"I know what you are going to say," she cried, "but it's false. Where's Paul?"

"Do you mean to tell him?" asked Herbert.

"Tell him?" and Margaret started to her feet. "If I were to die, I should wring his heart; if I were to tell him, I should break it."

She started up, I say; she had heard and recognized her lover's rapid step in the passage. Paul opened the door and came in precipitately, out of breath and deadly pale. Margaret came towards him with her hand still pressed to her side, while Father Herbert mechanically rose from his kneeling posture. "What has happened?" cried the young man. "You've been ill!"

"Who told you that anything has happened?" said Margaret.

"What is Herbert doing on his knees?"

"I was praying, sir," said Herbert.

"Margaret," repeated Paul, "in Heaven's name, what *is* the matter?"

"What's the matter with you, Paul? It seems to me that I should ask the question."

De Grey fixed a dark, searching look on the young girl, and then closed his eyes, and grasped at the back of a chair, as if his head were turning. "Ten minutes ago," he said, speaking slowly, "I was riding along by the river-side; suddenly I heard in the air the sound of a distant cry, which I knew to be yours. I turned and galloped. I made three miles in eight minutes."

"A cry, dear Paul? what should I cry about? and to be heard three miles! A pretty compliment to my lungs."

"Well," said the young man, "I suppose, then, it was my fancy. But my horse heard it too; he lifted his ears, and plunged and started."

"It must have been his fancy too! It proves you an excellent riders,—you and your horse feeling as one man!"

"Ah, Margaret, don't trifle!"

"As one horse, then."

"Well, whatever it may have been, I'm not ashamed to confess that I'm thoroughly shaken. I don't know what has become of my nerves."

"For pity's sake, then, don't stand there shivering and staggering like a man in an ague-fit. Come, sit down on the sofa." She took hold of his arm, and led him to the couch. He, in turn, clasped her arm in his own hand, and drew her down beside him. Father Herbert silently made his exit, unheeded. Outside of the door he met Mrs. De Grey, with her smelling-salts.

"I don't think she needs them now," he said. "She has Paul." And the two adjourned together to the tea-table. When the meal was half finished, Margaret came in with Paul.

"How do you feel, dear?" said Mrs. De Grey.

"He feels much better," said Margaret, hastily.

Mrs. De Grey smiled complacently. "Assuredly," she thought, "my future daughter-in-law has a very pretty way of saying things."

The next day, going into Mrs. De Grey's room, Margaret found Paul and his mother together. The latter's eyes were red, as if she had been weeping; and Paul's face wore an excited look, as if he had been making some painful confession. When Margaret came in, he walked to the window and looked out, without speaking to her. She feigned to have come in search of a piece of needle-work, obtained it, and retired. Nevertheless, she felt deeply wounded. What had Paul been doing, saying? Why had he not spoken to her? Why had he turned his back upon her? It was only the evening before, when they were alone in the drawing-room, that he had been so unutterably tender. It was a cruel mystery; she would have no rest until she learned it,—although, in truth, she had little enough as it was. In the afternoon, Paul again ordered his horse, and dressed himself for a ride. She waylaid him as he came down stairs, booted and spurred; and, as his horse was not yet at the door, she made him go with her into the garden.

"Paul," she said, suddenly, "what were you telling your mother this morning? Yes," she continued, trying to smile, but without success, "I confess it,—I'm jealous."

"O my soul!" cried the young man, wearily, putting both his hands to his face.

"Dear Paul," said Margaret, taking his arm, "that's very beautiful, but it's not an answer."

Paul stopped in the path, took the young girl's hands and looked steadfastly into her face, with an expression that was in truth a look of weariness,—of worse than weariness, of despair. "Jealous, you say?"

"Ah, not now!" she cried, pressing his hands.

"It's the first foolish thing I have heard you say."

"Well, it was foolish to be jealous of your mother; but I'm still jealous of your solitude,—of these pleasures in which I have no share,—of your horse,—your long rides."

"You wish me to give up my ride?"

"Dear Paul, where are your wits? To wish it is—to wish it. To say I wish it is to make a fool of myself."

"My wits are with—with something that's forever gone!" And he closed his eyes and contracted his forehead as if in pain. "My youth, my hope,—what shall I call it?—my happiness."

"Ah!" said Margaret, reproachfully, "you have to shut your eyes to say that."

"Nay, what is happiness without youth?"

"Upon my word, one would think I was forty," cried Margaret.

"Well, so long as I'm sixty!"

The young girl perceived that behind these light words there was something very grave. "Paul," she said, "the trouble simply is that you're unwell."

He nodded assent, and with his assent it seemed to her that an unseen hand had smitten the life out of her heart.

"That is what you told your mother?"

He nodded again.

"And what you were unwilling to tell me?"

He blushed deeply. "Naturally," he said.

She dropped his hands and sat down, for very faintness, on a garden bench. Then rising suddenly, "Go, and take your ride," she rejoined. "But, before you go, kiss me once."

And Paul kissed her, and mounted his horse. As she went into the house, she met Father Herbert, who had been watching the young man ride away, from beneath the porch, and who was returning to his study.

"My dear child," said the priest, "Paul is very ill. God grant that, if you manage not to die, it may not be at his expense!"

For all answer, Margaret turned on him, in her passage, a face so cold, ghastly, and agonized, that it seemed a vivid response to his heart-shaking fears. When she reached her room, she sat down on her little bed, and strove to think clearly and deliberately. The old man's words had aroused a

deep-sounding echo in the vast spiritual solitudes of her being. She was to find, then, after her long passion, that the
curse was absolute, inevitable, eternal. It could be shifted, but
not eluded; in spite of the utmost strivings of human agony,
it insatiably claimed its victim. Her own strength was exhausted; what was she to do? All her borrowed splendor of
brilliancy and bravery suddenly deserted her, and she sat
alone, shivering in her weakness. Deluded fool that she was,
for a day, for an hour, to have concealed her sorrow from her
lover! The greater her burden, the greater should have been
her confidence. What neither might endure alone, they might
have surely endured together. But she blindly, senselessly, re-
morselessly drained the life from his being. As she bloomed
and prospered, he drooped and languished. While she was living for him, he was dying of her. Execrable, infernal comedy!
What would help her now? She thought of suicide, and she
thought of flight;—they were about equivalent. If it were certain that by the sudden extinction of her own life she might
liberate, exonerate Paul, it would cost her but an instant's delay to plunge a knife into her heart. But who should say that,
enfeebled, undermined as he was, the shock of her death
might not give him his own quietus? Worse than all was the
suspicion that he had begun to dislike her, and that a dim perception of her noxious influence had already taken possession
of his senses. He was cold and distant. Why else, when he had
begun really to feel ill, had he not spoken first to her? She was
distasteful, loathsome. Nevertheless, Margaret still grasped,
with all the avidity of despair, at the idea that it was still not
too late to take him into her counsels, and to reveal to him all
the horrors of her secret. Then at least, whatever came, death
or freedom, they should meet it together.

Now that the enchantment of her fancied triumph had
been taken from her, she felt utterly exhausted and overwhelmed. Her whole organism ached with the desire for sleep
and forgetfulness. She closed her eyes, and sank into the very
stupor of repose. When she came to her senses, her room was
dark. She rose, and went to her window, and saw the stars.
Lighting a candle, she found that her little clock indicated
nine. She had slept five hours. She hastily dressed herself, and
went down stairs.

In the drawing-room, by an open window, wrapped in a shawl, with a lighted candle, sat Mrs. De Grey.

"You're happy, my dear," she cried, "to be able to sleep so soundly, when we are all in such a state."

"What state, dear lady?"

"Paul has not come in."

Margaret made no reply; she was listening intently to the distant sound of a horse's steps. She hurried out of the room, to the front door, and across the court-yard to the gate. There, in the dark starlight, she saw a figure advancing, and the rapid ring of hoofs. The poor girl suffered but a moment's suspense. Paul's horse came dashing along the road—riderless. Margaret, with a cry, plunged forward, grasping at his bridle; but he swerved, with a loud neigh, and, scarcely slackening his pace, swept into the enclosure at a lower entrance, where Margaret heard him clattering over the stones on the road to the stable, greeted by shouts and ejaculations from the hostler.

Madly, precipitately, Margaret rushed out into the darkness, along the road, calling upon Paul's name. She had not gone a quarter of a mile, when she heard an answering voice. Repeating her cry, she recognized her lover's accents.

He was upright, leaning against a tree, and apparently uninjured, but with his face gleaming through the darkness like a mask of reproach, white with the phosphorescent dews of death. He had suddenly felt weak and dizzy, and in the effort to keep himself in the saddle had frightened his horse, who had fiercely plunged, and unseated him. He leaned on Margaret's shoulder for support, and spoke with a faltering voice.

"I have been riding," he said, "like a madman. I felt ill when I went out, but without the shadow of a cause. I was determined to work it off by motion and the open air." And he stopped, gasping.

"And you feel better, dearest?" murmured Margaret.

"No, I feel worse. I'm a dead man."

Margaret clasped her lover in her arms with a long, piercing moan, which resounded through the night.

"I'm yours no longer, dear unhappy soul,—I belong, by I don't know what fatal, inexorable ties, to darkness and death and nothingness. They stifle me. Do you hear my voice?"

"Ah, senseless clod that I am, I have killed you!"

"I believe it's true. But it's strange. What is it, Margaret?—you're enchanted, baleful, fatal!" He spoke barely above a whisper, as if his voice were leaving him; his breath was cold on her cheek, and his arm heavy on her neck.

"Nay," she cried, "in Heaven's name, go on! Say something that will kill me."

"Farewell, farewell!" said Paul, collapsing.

Margaret's cry had been, for the startled household she had left behind her, an index to her halting-place. Father Herbert drew near hastily, with servants and lights. They found Margaret sitting by the roadside, with her feet in a ditch, clasping her lover's inanimate head in her arms, and covering it with kisses, wildly moaning. The sense had left her mind as completely as his body, and it was likely to come back to one as little as to the other.

A great many months naturally elapsed before Mrs. De Grey found herself in the humor to allude directly to the immense calamity which had overwhelmed her house; and when she did so, Father Herbert was surprised to find that she still refused to accept the idea of a supernatural pressure upon her son's life, and that she quietly cherished the belief that he had died of the fall from his horse.

"And suppose Margaret had died? Would to Heaven she had!" said the priest.

"Ah, suppose!" said Mrs. De Grey. "Do you make that wish for the sake of your theory?"

"Suppose that Margaret had had a lover,—a passionate lover,—who had offered her his heart before Paul had ever seen her; and then that Paul had come, bearing love and death."

"Well, what then?"

"Which of the three, think you, would have had most cause for sadness?"

"It's always the survivors of a calamity who are to be pitied," said Mrs. De Grey.

"Yes, madam, it's the survivors,—even after fifty years."

Osborne's Revenge

PHILIP OSBORNE and Robert Graham were intimate friends. The latter had been spending the summer at certain medicinal springs in New York, the use of which had been recommended by his physician. Osborne, on the other hand—a lawyer by profession, and with a rapidly increasing practice—had been confined to the city, and had suffered June and July to pass, not unheeded, heaven knows, but utterly unhonored. Toward the middle of July he began to feel uneasy at not hearing from his friend, habitually the best of correspondents. Graham had a charming literary talent, and plenty of leisure, being without a family, and without business. Osborne wrote to him, asking the reason of his silence, and demanding an immediate reply. He received in the course of a few days the following letter:

> DEAR PHILIP: I am, as you conjectured, not well. These infernal waters have done me no good. On the contrary—they have poisoned me. They have poisoned my life, and I wish to God I had never come to them. Do you remember the *White Lady* in *The Monastery*, who used to appear to the hero at the spring? There is such a one here, at this spring—which you know tastes of sulphur. Judge of the quality of the young woman. She has charmed me, and I can't get away. But I mean to try again. Don't think I'm cracked, but expect me next week. Yours always, R.G.

The day after he received this letter, Osborne met, at the house of a female friend detained in town by the illness of one of her children, a lady who had just come from the region in which Graham had fixed himself. This lady, Mrs. Dodd by name, and a widow, had seen a great deal of the young man, and she drew a very long face and threw great expression into her eyes as she spoke of him. Seeing that she was inclined to be confidential, Osborne made it possible that she should converse with him privately. She assured him, behind her fan, that his friend was dying of a broken heart. Something should be done. The story was briefly this. Graham had made the acquaintance, in the early part of the summer, of a young lady,

a certain Miss Congreve, who was living in the neighborhood
with a married sister. She was not pretty, but she was clever,
graceful, and pleasing, and Graham had immediately fallen in
love with her. She had encouraged his addresses, to the
knowledge of all their friends, and at the end of a month
—heart-histories are very rapid at the smaller watering places
—their engagement, although not announced, was hourly expected. But at this moment a stranger had effected an entrance into the little society of which Miss Congreve was one
of the most brilliant ornaments—a Mr. Holland, out of the
West—a man of Graham's age, but better favored in person.
Heedless of the circumstance that her affections were notoriously preoccupied, he had immediately begun to be attentive
to the young girl. Equally reckless of the same circumstance,
Henrietta Congreve had been all smiles—all seduction. In the
course of a week, in fact, she had deliberately transferred her
favors from the old love to the new. Graham had been turned
out into the cold; she had ceased to look at him, to speak to
him, to think of him. He nevertheless remained at the
springs, as if he found a sort of fascination in the sense of his
injury, and in seeing Miss Congreve and Holland together.
Besides, he doubtless wished people to fancy that, for good
reasons, he had withdrawn his suit, and it was therefore not
for him to hide himself. He was proud, reserved, and silent,
but his friends had no difficulty in seeing that his pain was
intense, and that his wound was almost mortal. Mrs. Dodd
declared that unless he was diverted from his sorrow, and
removed from contact with the various scenes and objects
which reminded him of his unhappy passion—and above all,
deprived of the daily chance of meeting Miss Congreve—she
would not answer for his sanity.

Osborne made all possible allowance for exaggeration. A
woman, he reflected, likes so to round off her story—especially if it is a dismal one. Nevertheless he felt very anxious,
and he forthwith wrote his friend a long letter, asking him to
what extent Mrs. Dodd's little romance was true, and urging
him to come immediately to town, where, if it was substantially true, he might look for diversion. Graham answered by
arriving in person. At first, Osborne was decidedly relieved.
His friend looked better and stronger than he had looked for

months. But on coming to talk with him, he found him morally, at least, a sad invalid. He was listless, abstracted, and utterly inactive in mind. Osborne observed with regret that he made no response to his attempts at interrogation and to his proffered sympathy. Osborne had by nature no great respect for sentimental woes. He was not a man to lighten his tread because his neighbor below stairs was laid up with a broken heart. But he saw that it would never do to poke fun at poor Graham, and that he was quite proof against the contagion of gayety. Graham begged him not to think him morbid or indifferent to his kindness, and to allow him not to speak of his trouble until it was over. He had resolved to forget it. When he had forgotten it—as one forgets such things —when he had contrived to push the further end of it at least into the past—then he would tell him all about it. For the present he must occupy his thoughts with something else. It was hard to decide what to do. It was hard to travel without an aim. Yet the intolerable heat made it impossible that he should stay in New York. He might go to Newport.

"A moment," said Osborne. "Has Miss Congreve gone to Newport?"

"Not that I know of."

"Does she intend to go?"

Graham was silent. "Good heavens!" he cried, at last, "forbid it then! All I want is to have it forbidden. *I* can't forbid it. Did you ever see a human creature so degraded?" he added, with a ghastly smile. "Where *shall* I go?"

Philip went to his table and began to overhaul a mass of papers fastened with red tape. He selected several of these documents and placed them apart. Then turning to his friend, "You're to go out to Minnesota," he said, looking him in the eyes. The proposal was a grave one, and gravely as it was meant, Osborne would have been glad to have Graham offer some resistance. But he sat looking at him with a solemn stare which (in the light of subsequent events) cast a lugubrious shade over the whole transaction. "The deuce!" thought Osborne. "Has it made him stupid?—What you need," he said aloud, "is to have something else to think about. An idle man can't expect to get over such troubles. I have some business to be done at St. Paul, and I know that if you'll give your attention to it, you're as well able to do it as any man. It's a simple matter, but it needs a trustworthy person. So I shall depend upon you."

Graham came and took up the papers and looked over them mechanically.

"Never mind them now," said Osborne; "its past midnight; you must go to bed. To-morrow morning I'll put you *au fait*, and the day after, if you like, you can start."

The next morning Graham seemed to have recovered a considerable portion of his old cheerfulness. He talked about indifferent matters, laughed, and seemed for a couple of hours to have forgotten Miss Congreve. Osborne began to doubt that the journey was necessary, and he was glad to be able to think, afterwards, that he had expressed his doubts, and that his friend had strongly combatted them and insisted upon having the affair explained to him. He mastered it, to Osborne's satisfaction, and started across the continent.

During the ensuing week Philip was so pressed with business that he had very little time to think of the success of Graham's mission. Within the fortnight he received the following letter:

DEAR PHILIP: Here I am, safe, but anything but sound. I don't know what to think of it, but I have completely forgotten the terms of my embassy. I can't for my life remember what I'm to do or say, and neither the papers nor your notes assist me a whit. 12th.—I wrote so much yesterday and then went out to take a walk and collect my thoughts. I *have* collected them, once for all. Do you understand, dearest Philip? Don't call me insane, or impious, or anything that merely expresses your own impatience and intolerance, without throwing a ray of light on the state of my own mind. He only can understand it who has felt it, and he who has felt it can do but as I do. Life has lost, I don't say its charm—that I could willingly dispense with—but its meaning. I shall live in your memory and your love, which is a vast deal better than living in my own self-contempt. Farewell.   R.G.

Osborne learned the circumstances of his friend's death three days later, through his correspondent at St. Paul—the person to whom Graham had been addressed. The unhappy young man had shot himself through the head in his room at the hotel. He had left money, and written directions for the

disposal of his remains—directions which were, of course, observed. As Graham possessed no near relative, the effect of his
death was confined to a narrow circle; to the circle, I may say,
of Philip Osborne's capacious personality. The two young
men had been united by an almost passionate friendship.
Now that Graham had ceased to be, Osborne became sensible of the strength of this bond; he felt that he cared more for
it than for any human tie. They had known each other ten
years, and their intimacy had grown with their growth during
the most active period of their lives. It had been strengthened
within and without by the common enjoyment of so many
pleasures, the experience of so many hazards, the exchange of
so much advice, so much confidence, and so many pledges of
mutual interest, that each had grown to regard it as the single
absolute certainty in life, the one fixed fact in a shifting world.
As constantly happens with intimate friends, the two were
perfectly diverse in character, tastes and appearance. Graham
was three years the elder, slight, undersized, feeble in health,
sensitive, indolent, whimsical, generous, and in reality of a far
finer clay than his friend, as the latter, moreover, perfectly well
knew. Their intimacy was often a puzzle to observers. Disinterested parties were at loss to discover how Osborne had
come to set his heart upon an insignificant, lounging invalid,
who, in general company, talked in monosyllables, in a weak
voice, and gave himself the airs of one whom nature had endowed with the right to be fastidious, without ever having
done a stroke of work. Graham's partisans, on the other hand,
who were chiefly women (which, by the way, effectually re-
lieves him from the accusation occasionally brought against
him of being "effeminate") were quite unable to penetrate
the motives of his interest in a commonplace, hard-working
lawyer, who addressed a charming woman as if he were ex-
horting a jury of grocers and undertakers, and viewed the
universe as one vast "case." This account of Osborne's mind
and manners would have been too satirical to be wholly just,
and yet it would have been excusable as an attempt to depict
a figure in striking contrast with poor Graham. Osborne was
in all respects a large fellow. He was six feet two in height,
with a chest like a boxing-master, and a clear, brown complexion, which successfully resisted the deleterious action of a

sedentary life. He was, in fact, without a particle of vanity, a particularly handsome man. His character corresponded to his person, or, as one may say, continued and completed it, and his mind kept the promise of his character. He was all of one piece—all health and breadth, capacity and energy. Graham had once told his friend somewhat brutally—for in his little, weak voice Graham said things far more brutal than Osborne, just as he said things far more fine—he had told him that he worked like a horse and loved like a dog.

Theoretically, Osborne's remedy for mental trouble was work. He redoubled his attention to his professional affairs, and strove to reconcile himself, once for all, to his loss. But he found his grief far stronger than his will, and felt that it obstinately refused to be pacified without some act of sacrifice or devotion. Osborne had an essentially kind heart and plenty of pity and charity for deserving objects; but at the bottom of his soul there lay a well of bitterness and resentment which, when his nature was strongly shaken by a sense of wrong, was sure to ferment and raise its level, and at last to swamp his conscience. These bitter waters had been stirred, and he felt that they were rising fast. His thoughts travelled back with stubborn iteration from Graham's death to the young girl who figured in the prologue to the tragedy. He felt in his breast a savage need of hating her. Osborne's friends observed in these days that he looked by no means pleasant; and if he had not been such an excellent fellow he might easily have passed for an intolerable brute. He was not softened and mellowed by suffering; he was exasperated. It seemed to him that justice cried aloud that Henrietta Congreve should be confronted with the results of her folly, and made to carry forever in her thoughts, in all the hideousness of suicide, the image of her miserable victim. Osborne was, perhaps, in error, but he was assuredly sincere; and it is strong evidence of the energy of genuine affection that this lusty intellect should have been brought, in the interest of another, to favor a scheme which it would have deemed wholly, ludicrously impotent to assuage the injured dignity of its own possessor. Osborne must have been very fond of his friend not to have pronounced him a drivelling fool. It is true that he had always pitied him as much as he loved him, although Graham's incontestable gifts and virtues had kept this feeling in the background. Now that he was gone, pity came uppermost, and bade fair to drive him to a merciless disallowance of all claims to extenuation on the part of the accused. It was unlikely that, for a long time at least, he would listen to anything but that Graham had been foully wronged, and that the light of his life had been wantonly quenched. He found it impossible to sit down in resignation. The best that he could do, indeed, would not call Graham back to life; but he might at least discharge his gall, and have the comfort of feeling that Miss Congreve was the worse for it. He was quite unable to work. He roamed about for three days in a disconsolate, angry fashion. On the third, he called upon Mrs. Dodd, from whom he learned that Miss Congreve had gone to Newport, to stay with a second married sister. He went home and packed up a valise, and—without knowing why, feeling only that to do so was to do something, and to put himself in the way of doing more—drove down to the Newport boat.

II.

His first inquiry on his arrival, after he had looked up several of his friends and encountered a number of acquaintances, was about Miss Congreve's whereabouts and habits. He found that she was very little known. She lived with her sister, Mrs. Wilkes, and as yet had made but a single appearance in company. Mrs. Wilkes, moreover, he learned, was an invalid and led a very quiet life. He ascertained the situation of her house and gave himself the satisfaction of walking past it. It was a pretty place, on a secluded by-road, marked by various tokens of wealth and comfort. He heard, as he passed, through the closed shutters of the drawing-room window, the sound of a high, melodious voice, warbling and trilling to the accompaniment of a piano. Osborne had no soul for music, but he stopped and listened, and as he did so, he remembered Graham's passion for the charming art and fancied that these were the very accents that had lured him to his sorrow. Poor Graham! here too, as in all things, he had showed his taste. The singer discharged a magnificent volley of roulades and flourishes and became silent. Osborne, fancying he heard a

movement of the lattice of the shutters, slowly walked away.
A couple of days later he found himself strolling, alone and
disconsolate, upon the long avenue which runs parallel to the
Newport cliffs, which, as all the world knows, may be reached
by five minutes' walk from any part of it. He had been on the
field, now, for nearly a week, and he was no nearer his revenge. His unsatisfied desire haunted his steps and hovered in
a ghostly fashion about thoughts which perpetual contact
with old friends and new, and the entertaining spectacle of
a heterogeneous throng of pleasure seekers and pleasure
venders, might have made free and happy. Osborne was very
fond of the world, and while he still clung to his resentment,
he yet tacitly felt that it lurked as a skeleton at his banquet.
He was fond of nature, too, and betwixt these two predilec-
tions, he grew at moments ashamed of his rancor. At all
events, he felt a grateful sense of relief when as he pursued his
course along this sacred way of fashion, he caught a glimpse
of the deep blue expanse of the ocean, shining at the end of
a cross road. He forthwith took his way down to the cliffs. At
the point where the road ceased, he found an open barouche,
whose occupants appeared to have wandered out of sight.
Passing this carriage, he reached a spot where the surface of
the cliff communicates with the beach, by means of an abrupt
footpath. This path he descended and found himself on a
level with the broad expanse of sand and the rapidly rising
tide. The wind was blowing fresh from the sea and the little
breakers tumbling in with their multitudinous liquid clamor.
In a very few moments Osborne felt a sensible exhilaration of
spirits. He had not advanced many steps under the influence
of this joyous feeling, when, on turning a slight projection in
the cliff, he descried a sight which caused him to hasten forward. On a broad flat rock, at about a dozen yards from the
shore, stood a child of some five years—a handsome boy, fair-
haired and well dressed—stamping his feet and wringing his
hands in an apparent agony of terror. It was easy to understand the situation. The child had ventured out on the rock
while the water was still low, and had become so much absorbed in paddling with his little wooden spade among the
rich marine deposits on its surface, that he had failed to observe the advance of the waves, which had now completely

covered the intermediate fragments of rock and were foaming
and weltering betwixt him and the shore. The poor little
fellow stood screaming to the winds and waters, and quite
unable to answer Osborne's shouts of interrogation and comfort. Meanwhile, the latter prepared to fetch him ashore. He
saw with some disgust that the channel was too wide to warrant a leap, and yet, as the child's companions might at any
moment appear, in the shape of distracted importunate
women, he judged it imprudent to divest himself of any part
of his apparel. He accordingly plunged in without further
ado, waded forward, seized the child and finally restored him
to *terra firma*. He felt him trembling in his arms like a frightened bird. He set him on his feet, soothed him, and asked
him what had become of his guardians.

The boy pointed toward a rock, lying at a certain distance,
close under the cliff, and Osborne, following his gesture, distinguished what seemed to be the hat and feather of a lady sitting on the further side of it.

"That's Aunt Henrietta," said the child.

"Aunt Henrietta deserves a scolding," said Osborne.
"Come, we'll go and give it to her." And he took the boy's
hand and led him toward his culpable relative. They walked
along the beach until they came abreast of the rock, and approached the lady in front. At the sound of their feet on the
stones, she raised her head. She was a young woman, seated
on a boulder, with an album in her lap, apparently absorbed
in the act of sketching. Seeing at a glance that something was
amiss, she rose to her feet and thrust the album into her
pocket. Osborne's wet trousers and the bespattered garments
and discomposed physiognomy of the child revealed the nature of the calamity. She held out her arms to her little
nephew. He dropped Philip's hand, and ran and threw himself on his aunt's neck. She raised him up and kissed him, and
looked interrogatively at Osborne.

"I couldn't help seeing him safely in your hands," said the
latter, removing his hat. "He has had a terrific adventure."

"What is it, darling?" cried the young lady, again kissing the
little fellow's bloodless face.

"He came into the water after me," cried the boy. "Why
did you leave me there?"

"What has happened, sir?" asked the young girl, in a somewhat peremptory tone.

"You had apparently left him on that rock, madam, with a channel betwixt him and the shore deep enough to drown him. I took the liberty of displacing him. But he's more frightened than hurt."

The young girl had a pale face and dark eyes. There was no beauty in her features; but Osborne had already perceived that they were extremely expressive and intelligent. Her face flushed a little, and her eyes flashed; the former, it seemed to Philip, with mortification at her own neglect, and the latter with irritation at the reproach conveyed in his accents. But he may have been wrong. She sat down on the rock, with the child on her knees, kissing him repeatedly and holding him with a sort of convulsive pressure. When she looked up, the flashes in her eyes had melted into a couple of tears. Seeing that Philip was a gentleman, she offered a few words of self-justification. She had kept the boy constantly within sight, and only within a few minutes had allowed her attention to be drawn away. Her apology was interrupted by the arrival of a second young woman—apparently a nursery-maid—who emerged from the concealment of the neighboring rocks, leading a little girl by the hand. Instinctively, her eyes fell upon the child's wet clothes.

"Ah! Miss Congreve," she cried, in true nursery-maid style, "what'll Mrs. Wilkes say to that?"

"She will say that she is very thankful to this gentleman," said Miss Congreve, with decision.

Philip had been looking at the young girl as she spoke, forcibly struck by her face and manner. He detected in her appearance a peculiar union of modesty and frankness, of youthful freshness and elegant mannerism, which suggested vague possibilities of further acquaintance. He had already found it pleasant to observe her. He had been for ten days in search of a wicked girl, and it was a momentary relief to find himself suddenly face to face with a charming one. The nursery-maid's apostrophe was like an electric shock.

It is, nevertheless, to be supposed that he concealed his surprise, inasmuch as Miss Congreve gave no sign of having perceived that he was startled. She had come to a tardy sense of his personal discomfort. She besought him to make use of her carriage, which he would find on the cliff, and quickly return home. He thanked her and declined her offer, declaring that it was better policy to walk. He put out his hand to his little friend and bade him good-by. Miss Congreve liberated the child and he came and put his hand in Philip's.

"One of these days," said Osborne, "you'll have long legs, too, and then you'll not mind the water." He spoke to the boy, but he looked hard at Miss Congreve, who, perhaps, thought he was asking for some formal expression of gratitude.

"His mother," she said, "will give herself the pleasure of thanking you."

"The trouble," said Osborne, "the very unnecessary trouble. Your best plan," he added, with a smile (for, wonderful to tell, he actually smiled) "is to say nothing about it."

"If I consulted my own interests alone," said the young girl, with a gracious light in her dark eyes, "I should certainly hold my tongue. But I hope my little victim is not so ungrateful as to promise silence."

Osborne stiffened himself up; for this was more or less of a compliment. He made his bow in silence and started for home at a rapid pace. On the following day he received this note by post:

Mrs. Wilkes begs to thank Mr. Osborne most warmly for the prompt and generous relief afforded to her little boy. She regrets that Mr. Osborne's walk should have been interrupted, and hopes that his exertions have been attended with no bad effects.

Enclosed in the note was a pocket-handkerchief, bearing Philip's name, which he remembered to have made the child take, to wipe his tears. His answer was, of course, brief.

Mr. Osborne begs to assure Mrs. Wilkes that she exaggerates the importance of the service rendered to her son, and that he has no cause to regret his very trifling efforts. He takes the liberty of presenting his compliments to Master Wilkes, and of hoping that he has recovered from his painful sensations.

The correspondence naturally went no further, and for some days no additional light was thrown upon Miss Congreve. Now that Philip had met her, face to face, and found her a commonplace young girl—a clever girl, doubtless, for she looked it, and an agreeable one—but still a mere young lady, mindful of the proprieties, with a face innocent enough, and even a trifle sad, and a couple of pretty children who called her "aunt," and whom, indeed, in a moment of enthusiastic devotion to nature and art, she left to the mercy of the waves, but whom she finally kissed and comforted and handled with all due tenderness—now that he had met Miss Congreve under these circumstances, he felt his mission sitting more lightly on his conscience. Ideally she had been repulsive; actually, she was a person whom, if he had not been committed to detest her, he would find it very pleasant to like. She had been humanized, to his view, by the mere accidents of her flesh and blood. Philip was by no means prepared to to give up his resentment. Poor Graham's ghost sat grim and upright in his memory, and fed the flickering flame. But it was something of a problem to reconcile the heroine of his vengeful longings, with the heroine of the little scene on the beach, and to accommodate this inoffensive figure, in turn, to the color of his retribution. A dozen matters conspired to keep him from coming to the point, and to put him in a comparatively good humor. He was invited to the right and the left; he lounged and bathed, and talked, and smoked, and rode, and dined out, and saw an endless succession of new faces, and in short, reduced the vestments of his outward mood to a suit of very cheerful half-mourning. And all this, moreover, without any sense of being faithless to his friend. Oddly enough, Graham had never seemed so living as now that he was dead. In the flesh, he had possessed but a half-vitality. His spirit had been exquisitely willing, but his flesh had been fatally weak. He was at best a baffled, disappointed man. It was his spirit, his affections, his sympathies and perceptions, that were warm and active, and Osborne knew that he had fallen sole heir to these. He felt his bosom swell with a wholesome sense of the magnitude of the heritage, and he was conscious with each successive day, of less desire to invoke poor Graham in dark corners, and mourn him in lonely places. By a single solemn, irrevocable aspiration, he had placed his own tough organism and his energetic will at the service of his friend's virtues. So as he found his excursion turning into a holiday, he stretched his long limbs and with the least bit of a yawn whispered *Amen*.

Within a week after his encounter with Miss Congreve, he
went with a friend to witness some private theatricals, given in
the house of a lady of great social repute. The entertainment
consisted of two plays, the first of which was so flat and poor
that when the curtain fell Philip prepared to make his escape,
thinking he might easily bring the day to some less impotent
conclusion. As he passed along the narrow alley between the
seats and the wall of the drawing-room, he brushed a printed
programme out of a lady's hand. Stooping to pick it up, his
eye fell upon the name of Miss Congreve among the per-
formers in the second piece. He immediately retraced his
steps. The overture began, the curtain rose again, and several
persons appeared on the stage, arrayed in the powder and
patches of the last century. Finally, amid loud acclamations,
walked on Miss Congreve, as the heroine, powdered and
patched in perfection. She represented a young countess—a
widow in the most interesting predicament—and for all good
histrionic purposes, she was irresistibly beautiful. She was
dressed, painted, and equipped with great skill and in the very
best taste. She looked as if she had stepped out of the frame
of one of those charming full-length pastel portraits of fine
ladies in Louis XV.'s time, which they show you in French
palaces. But she was not alone all grace and elegance and *finesse*; she had dignity; she was serious at moments, and severe;
she frowned and commanded; and, at the proper time, she
wept the most natural tears. It was plain that Miss Congreve
was a true artist. Osborne had never seen better acting—
never, indeed, any so good; for here was an actress who was
at once a perfect young lady and a consummate mistress of
dramatic effect. The audience was roused to the highest pitch
of enthusiasm, and Miss Congreve's fellow-players were left
quite in the lurch. The beautiful Miss Latimer, celebrated in
polite society for her face and figure, who had undertaken the
second female part, was compelled for the nonce to have neither figure nor face. The play had been marked in the bills as
adapted from the French "especially for this occasion;" and
when the curtain fell for the last time, the audience, in great
good humor, clamored for the adapter. Some time elapsed
before any notice was taken of their call, which they took as a
provocation of their curiosity. Finally, a gentleman made his

way before the curtain, and proclaimed that the version of the piece which his associates had had the honor of performing was from the accomplished pen of the young lady who had won their applause in the character of the heroine. At this announcement, a dozen enthusiasts lifted their voices and demanded that Miss Congreve should be caused to re-appear; but the gentleman cut short their appeal by saying that she had already left the house. This was not true, as Osborne subsequently learned. Henrietta was sitting on a sofa behind the scenes, waiting for her carriage, fingering an immense bouquet, and listening with a tired smile to compliments—hard by Miss Latimer, who sat eating an ice beside her mother, the latter lady looking in a very grim fashion at that very plain, dreadfully thin Miss Congreve.

Osborne walked home thrilled and excited, but decidedly bewildered. He felt that he had reckoned without his host, and that Graham's fickle mistress was not a person to be snubbed and done for. He was utterly at a loss as to what to think of her. She broke men's hearts and turned their heads; whatever she put her hand to she marked with her genius. She was a coquette, a musician, an artist, an actress, an author—a prodigy. Of what stuff was she made? What had she done with her heart and her conscience? She painted her face, and frolicked among lamps and flowers to the clapping of a thousand hands, while poor Graham lay imprisoned in eternal silence. Osborne was put on his mettle. To draw a penitent tear from those deep and charming eyes was assuredly a task for a clever man.

The plays had been acted on a Wednesday. On the following Saturday Philip was invited to take part in a picnic, organized by Mrs. Carpenter, the lady who had conducted the plays, and who had a mania for making up parties. The persons whom she had now enlisted were to proceed by water to a certain pastoral spot consecrated by nature to picnics, and there to have lunch upon the grass, to dance and play nursery-games. They were carried over in two large sailing boats, and during the transit Philip talked awhile with Mrs. Carpenter, whom he found a very amiable, loquacious person. At the further end of the boat in which, with his hostess, he had taken his place, he observed a young girl in a white dress, with a thick, blue veil drawn over her face. Through the veil, directed toward his own person, he perceived the steady glance of two fine dark eyes. For a moment he was at a loss to recognize their possessor; but his uncertainty was rapidly dispelled.

"I see you have Miss Congreve," he said to Mrs. Carpenter—"the actress of the other evening."

"Yes," said Mrs. Carpenter, "I persuaded her to come. She's all the fashion since Wednesday."

"Was she unwilling to come?" asked Philip.

"Yes, at first. You see she's a good, quiet girl; she hates to have a noise made about her."

"She had enough noise the other night. She has wonderful talent."

"Wonderful, wonderful. And heaven knows where she gets it. Do you know her family? The most matter-of-fact, least dramatic, least imaginative people in the world—people who are shy of the theatre on moral grounds."

"I see. They won't go to the theatre; the theatre comes to them."

"Exactly. It serves them right. Mrs. Wilkes, Henrietta's sister, was in a dreadful state about her attempting to act. But now, since Henrietta's success, she's talking about it to all the world."

When the boat came to shore, a plank was stretched from the prow to an adjacent rock for the accommodation of the ladies. Philip stood at the head of the plank, offering his hand for their assistance. Mrs. Carpenter came last, with Miss Congreve, who declined Osborne's aid but gave him a little bow, through her veil. Half an hour later Philip again found himself at the side of his hostess, and again spoke of Miss Congreve. Mrs. Carpenter warned him that she was standing close at hand, in a group of young girls.

"Have you heard," he asked, lowering his voice, "of her being engaged to be married—or of her having been?"

"No," said Mrs. Carpenter, "I've heard nothing. To whom?—stay. I've heard vaguely of something this summer at Sharon. She had a sort of flirtation with some man, whose name I forget."

"Was it Holland?"

"I think not. He left her for that very silly little Mrs. Dodd —who hasn't been a widow six months. I think the name was Graham."

Osborne broke into a peal of laughter so loud and harsh that his companion turned upon him in surprise. "Excuse me," said he. "It's false."

"You ask questions, Mr. Osborne," said Mrs. Carpenter, "but you seem to know more about Miss Congreve than I do."

"Very likely. You see I knew Robert Graham." Philip's words were uttered with such emphasis and resonance that two or three of the young girls in the adjoining group turned about and looked at him.

"She heard you," said Mrs. Carpenter.

"She didn't turn round," said Philip.

"That proves what I say. I meant to introduce you, and now I can't."

"Thank you," said Philip. "I shall introduce myself." Osborne felt in his bosom all the heat of his old resentment. This perverse and heartless girl, then, his soul cried out, not content with driving poor Graham to impious self-destruction, had caused it to be believed that he had killed himself from remorse at his own misconduct. He resolved to strike while the iron was hot. But although he was an avenger, he was still a gentleman, and he approached the young girl with a very civil face.

"If I am not mistaken," he said, removing his hat, "you have already done me the honor of recognizing me."

Miss Congreve's bow, as she left the boat, had been so obviously a sign of recognition, that Philip was amazed at the vacant smile with which she received his greeting. Something had happened in the interval to make her change her mind. Philip could think of no other motive than her having overheard his mention of Graham's name.

"I have an impression," she said, "of having met you before; but I confess that I'm unable to place you."

Osborne looked at her a moment. "I can't deny myself," he said, "the pleasure of asking about little Mr. Wilkes."

"I remember you now," said Miss Congreve, simply. "You carried my nephew out of the water."

"I hope he has got over his fright."

"He denies, I believe, that he was frightened. Of course, for my credit, I don't contradict him."

Miss Congreve's words were followed by a long pause, by which she seemed in no degree embarrassed. Philip was confounded by her apparent self-possession—to call it by no worse name. Considering that she had Graham's death on her conscience, and that, hearing his name on Osborne's lips, she must have perceived the latter to be identical with that dear friend of whom Graham must often have spoken, she was certainly showing a very brave face. But had she indeed heard of Graham's death? For a moment Osborne gave her the benefit of the doubt. He felt that he would take a grim satisfaction in being bearer of the tidings. In order to confer due honor on the disclosure, he saw that it was needful to detach the young girl from her companions. As, therefore, the latter at this moment began to disperse in clusters and couples along the shore, he proposed that they should stroll further a-field. Miss Congreve looked about at the other young girls as if to call one of them to her side, but none of them seemed available. So she slowly moved forward under Philip's guidance, with a half-suppressed look of reluctance. Philip began by paying her a very substantial compliment upon her acting. It was a most inconsequential speech, in the actual state of his feelings, but he couldn't help it. She was perhaps as wicked a girl as you shall easily meet, but her acting was perfect. Having paid this little tribute to equity, he broke ground for Graham.

"I don't feel, Miss Congreve," he said, "as if you were a new acquaintance. I have heard you a great deal talked about." This was not literally true, the reader will remember. All Philip's information had been acquired in his half hour with Mrs. Dodd.

"By whom, pray?" asked Henrietta.

"By Robert Graham."

"Ah, yes. I was half prepared to hear you speak of him. I remember hearing him speak of a person of your name."

Philip was puzzled. Did she know, or not? "I believe you knew him quite well yourself," he said, somewhat peremptorily.

"As well as he would let me—I doubt if any one knew him well."

"So you've heard of his death," said Philip.

"Yes, from himself."

"How, from himself?"

"He wrote me a letter, in his last hours, leaving his ap-proaching end to be inferred, rather than positively announc-ing it. I wrote an answer, with the request that if my letter was not immediately called for, it should be returned by the post office. It was returned within a week.—And now, Mr. Osborne," the young girl added, "let me make a request."

Philip bowed.

"I shall feel particularly obliged if you will say no more about Mr. Graham."

This was a stroke for which Osborne was not prepared. It had at least the merit of directness. Osborne looked at his companion. There was a faint flush in her cheeks, and a seri-ous light in her eyes. There was plainly no want of energy in her wish. He felt that he must suspend operations and make his approach from another quarter. But it was some moments before he could bring himself to accede to her request. She looked at him, expecting an answer, and he felt her dark eyes on his face.

"Just as you please," he said, at last, mechanically.

They walked along for some moments in silence. Then, suddenly coming upon a young married woman, whom Mrs. Carpenter had pressed into her service as a lieutenant, Miss Congreve took leave of Philip, on a slight pretext, and en-tered into talk with this lady. Philip strolled away and walked about for an hour alone. He had met with a check, but he was resolved that, though he had fallen back, it would be only to leap the further. During the half-hour that Philip sauntered along by the water, the dark cloud suspended above poor Miss Congreve's head doubled its portentous volume. And, indeed, from Philip's point of view, could anything well be more shameless and more heartless than the young girl's re-quest?

At last Osborne remembered that he was neglecting the duties laid upon him by Mrs. Carpenter. He retraced his steps and made his way back to the spot devoted to the banquet. Mrs. Carpenter called him to her, said that she had been look-ing for him for an hour, and, when she learned how he had been spending his time, slapped him with her parasol, called him a horrid creature, and declared she would never again invite him to anything of hers. She then introduced him to her niece, a somewhat undeveloped young lady, with whom he went and sat down over the water. They found very little to talk about. Osborne was thinking of Miss Congreve, and Mrs. Carpenter's niece, who was very timid and fluttering, having but one foot yet, as one may say, in society, was abashed and unnerved at finding herself alone with so very tall and mature and handsome a gentleman as Philip. He gave her a little confidence in the course of time, however, by making little stones skip over the surface of the water for her amusement. But he still kept thinking of Henrietta Congreve, and he at last bethought himself of asking his companion whether she knew her. Yes, she knew her slightly; but she threw no light on the subject. She was evidently not of an analytical turn of mind, and she was too innocent to gossip. She contented herself with saying that she believed Henrietta was wonderfully clever, and that she read Latin and Greek.

"Clever, clever," said Philip, "I hear nothing else. I shall begin to think she's a demon."

"No, Henrietta Congreve is very good," said his companion. "She's very religious. She visits the poor and reads sermons. You know the other night she acted for the poor. She's anything but a demon. I think she's so nice."

Before long the party was summoned to lunch. Straggling couples came wandering into sight, gentlemen assisting young girls out of rocky retreats into which no one would have supposed them capable of penetrating, and to which—more wonderful still—no one had observed them to direct their steps.

The table was laid in the shade, on the grass, and the feasters sat about on rugs and shawls. As Osborne took his place along with Mrs. Carpenter's niece, he noticed that Miss Congreve had not yet re-appeared. He called his companion's attention to the circumstance, and she mentioned it to her aunt, who said that the young girl had last been seen in company with Mr. Stone—a person unknown to Osborne—and that she would, doubtless, soon turn up.

"I suppose she's quite safe," said Philip's neighbor—

innocently or wittily, he hardly knew which; "she's with a clergyman."

In a few moments the missing couple appeared on the crest of an adjacent hill. Osborne watched them as they came down. Mr. Stone was a comely-faced young man, in a clerical necktie and garments of an exaggerated sacerdotal cut—a divine, evidently of strong "ritualistic" tendencies. Miss Congreve drew near, pale, graceful, and grave, and Philip, with his eyes fixed on her in the interval, lost not a movement of her person, nor a glance of her eyes. She wore a white muslin dress, short, in the prevailing fashion, with trimmings of yellow ribbon inserted in the skirt; and round her shoulders a shawl of heavy black lace, crossed over her bosom and tied in a big knot behind. In her hand she carried a great bunch of wild flowers, with which, as Philip's neighbor whispered to him, she had "ruined" her gloves. Osborne wondered whether there was any meaning in her having taken up with a clergyman. Had she suddenly felt the tardy pangs of remorse, and been moved to seek spiritual advice? Neither on the countenance of her ecclesiastical gallant, nor on her own, were there any visible traces of pious discourse. On the contrary, poor Mr. Stone looked sadly demoralized; their conversation had been wholly of profane things. His white cravat had lost its conservative rigidity, and his hat its unimpassioned equipoise. Worse than all, a little blue forget-me-not had found its way into his button-hole. As for Henrietta, her face wore that look of half-severe serenity which was its wonted expression, but there was no sign of her having seen her lover's ghost.

Osborne went mechanically through the movements of being attentive to the insipid little person at his side. But his thoughts were occupied with Miss Congreve and his eyes constantly turning to her face. From time to time, they met her own. A fierce disgust muttered in his bosom. What Henrietta Congreve needed, he said to himself, was to be used as she used others, as she was evidently now using this poor little parson. He was already over his ears in love—vainly feeling for bottom in midstream, while she sat dry-shod on the brink. She needed a lesson; but who should give it? She knew more than all her teachers. Men approached her only to be dazzled and charmed. If she could only find her equal or her master! one with as clear a head, as lively a fancy, as relentless a will as her own; one who would turn the tables, anticipate her, fascinate her, and then suddenly look at his watch and bid her good morning. Then, perhaps, Graham might settle to sleep in his grave. Then she would feel what it was to play with hearts, for then her own would have been as glass against bronze. Osborne looked about the table, but none of Mrs. Carpenter's male guests bore the least resemblance to the hero of his vision—a man with a heart of bronze and a head of crystal. They were, indeed very proper swains for the young ladies at their sides, but Henrietta Congreve was not one of these. She was not a mere twaddling ball-room flirt. There was in her coquetry something serious and exalted. It was an intellectual joy. She drained honest men's hearts to the last drop, and bloomed white upon the monstrous diet. As Philip glanced around the circle, his eye fell upon a young girl who seemed for a moment to have forgotten her neighbors, her sandwiches and her champagne, and was very innocently contemplating his own person. As soon as she perceived that he had observed her, she of course dropped her eyes on her plate. But Philip had read the meaning of her glance. It seemed to say—this lingering virginal eyebeam—in language easily translated, Thou art the man! It said, in other words, in less transcendental fashion, My dear Mr. Osborne, you are a very good looking fellow. Philip felt his pulse quicken; he had received his baptism. Not that good looks were a sufficient outfit for breaking Miss Congreve's heart; but they were the outward sign of his mission.

The feasting at last came to an end. A fiddler, who had been brought along, began to tune his instrument, and Mrs. Carpenter proceeded to organize a dance. The *débris* of the collation was cleared away, and the level space thus uncovered converted into a dancing floor. Osborne, not being a dancing man, sat at a distance, with two or three other spectators, among whom was the Rev. Mr. Stone. Each of these gentlemen watched with close attention the movements of Henrietta Congreve. Osborne, however, occasionally glanced at his companion, who, on his side, was quite too absorbed in looking at Miss Congreve to think of anyone else.

"They look very charming, those young ladies," said Philip, addressing the young clergyman, to whom he had just been introduced. "Some of them dance particularly well."

"Oh, yes!" said Mr. Stone, with fervor. And then, as if he feared that he had committed himself to an invidious distinction unbecoming his cloth: "I think they all dance well."

But Philip, as a lawyer, naturally took a different view of the matter from Mr. Stone, as a clergyman. "Some of them very much better than others, it seems to me. I had no idea that there could be such a difference. Look at Miss Congreve, for instance."

Mr. Stone, whose eyes were fixed on Miss Congreve, obeyed this injunction by moving them away for a moment, and directing them to a very substantial and somewhat heavy-footed young lady, who was figuring beside her. "Oh, yes, she's very graceful," he said, with unction. "So light, so free, so quiet!"

Philip smiled. "You, too, most excellent simpleton," he said, to himself—"you, too, shall be avenged." And then—"Miss Congreve is a very remarkable person," he added, aloud.

"Oh, very!"

"She has extraordinary versatility."

"Most extraordinary."

"Have you seen her act?"

"Yes—yes; I infringed upon my usage in regard to entertainments of that nature, and went the other evening. It was a most brilliant performance."

"And you know she wrote the play."

"Ah, not exactly," said Mr. Stone, with a little protesting gesture; "she translated it."

"Yes; but she had to write it quite over. Do you know it in French?"—and Philip mentioned the original title.

Mr. Stone signified that he was unacquainted with the work.

"It would never have done, you know," said Philip, "to play it as it stands. I saw it in Paris. Miss Congreve eliminated the little difficulties with uncommon skill."

Mr. Stone was silent. The violin uttered a long-drawn note, and the ladies curtsied low to their gentlemen. Miss

Congreve's partner stood with his back to our two friends, and her own obeisance was, therefore, executed directly in front of them. As she bent toward the ground, she raised her eyes and looked at them. If Mr. Stone's enthusiasm had been damped by Philip's irreverent freedom, it was rekindled by this glance. "I suppose you've heard her sing," he said, after a pause.

"Yes, indeed," said Philip, without hesitation.

"She sings sacred music with the most beautiful fervor."

"Yes, so I'm told. And I'm told, moreover, that she's very learned—that she has a passion for books."

"I think it very likely. In fact, she's quite an accomplished theologian. We had this morning a very lively discussion."

"You differed, then?" said Philip.

"Oh," said Mr. Stone, with charming *naïveté*, "*I* didn't differ. It was she!"

"Isn't she a little—the least bit—" and Philip paused, to select his word.

"The least bit?" asked Mr. Stone, in a benevolent tone. And then, as Philip still hesitated—"The least bit heterodox?"

"The least bit of a coquette?"

"Oh, Mr. Osborne!" cried the young divine—"that's the last thing I should call Miss Congreve."

At this moment, Mrs. Carpenter drew nigh. "What is the last thing you should call Miss Congreve?" she asked, overhearing the clergyman's words.

"A coquette."

"It seems to me," said the lady, "that it's the first thing I should call her. You have to come to it, I fancy. You always do, you know. I should get it off my mind at once, and then I should sing her charms."

"Oh, Mrs. Carpenter!" said Mr. Stone.

"Yes, my dear young man. She's quiet but she's deep—I see Mr. Osborne knows," and Mrs. Carpenter passed on.

"She's deep—that's what I say," said Mr. Stone, with mild firmness.—"What do you know, Mr. Osborne?"

Philip fancied that the poor fellow had turned pale; he certainly looked grave.

"Oh, I know nothing," said Philip. "I affirmed nothing. I merely inquired."

"Well then, my dear sir"—and the young man's candid visage flushed a little with the intensity of his feelings—"I give you my word for it, that I believe Miss Congreve to be not only the most accomplished, but the most noble-minded, the most truthful, the most truly christian young lady—in this whole assembly."

"I'm sure, I'm much obliged to you for the assurance," said Philip. "I shall value it and remember it."

It would not have been hard for Philip to set down Mr. Stone as a mere soft-hearted, philandering parson—a type ready made to his hand. Mrs. Carpenter, on the other hand, was a shrewd sagacious woman. But somehow he was impressed by the minister's words, and quite untouched by those of the lady. At last those of the dancers who were tired of the sport, left the circle and wandered back to the shore. The afternoon was drawing to a close, the western sky was beginning to blush crimson and the shadows to grow long on the grass. Only half an hour remained before the moment fixed for the return to Newport. Philip resolved to turn it to account. He followed Miss Congreve to a certain rocky platform, overlooking the water, whither, with a couple of elderly ladies, she had gone to watch the sunset. He found no difficulty in persuading her to wander aside from her companions. There was no mistrust in her keen and delicate face. It was incredible that she should have meant defiance; but her very repose and placidity had a strangely irritating action upon Philip. They affected him as the climax of insolence. He drew from his breast-pocket a small portfolio, containing a dozen letters, among which was the last one he had received from Graham.

"I shall take the liberty, for once, Miss Congreve," he said, "of violating the injunction which you laid upon me this morning with regard to Robert Graham. I have here a letter which I should like you to see."

"From Mr. Graham himself?"

"From Graham himself—written just before his death." He held it out, but Henrietta made no movement to take it.

"I have no desire to see it," she said. "I had rather not. You know he wrote also to me at that moment."

"I'm sure," said Philip, "I should not refuse to see your letter."

"I can't offer to show it to you. I immediately destroyed it."

"Well, you see I've kept mine.—It's not long," Osborne pursued.

Miss Congreve, as if with a strong effort, put out her hand and took the document. She looked at the direction for some moments, in silence, and then raised her eyes toward Osborne. "Do you value it?" she asked. "Does it contain anything you wish to keep?"

"No; I give it to you, for that matter."

"Well then!" said Henrietta. And she tore the letter twice across, and threw the scraps into the sea.

"Ah!" cried Osborne, "what the devil have you done?"

"Don't be violent, Mr. Osborne," said the young girl. "I hadn't the slightest intention of reading it. You are properly punished for having disobeyed me."

Philip swallowed his rage at a gulp, and followed her as she turned away.

III.

In the middle of September Mrs. Dodd came to Newport, to stay with a friend—somewhat out of humor at having been invited at the fag end of the season, but on the whole very much the same Mrs. Dodd as before; or rather not quite the same, for, in her way, she had taken Graham's death very much to heart. A couple of days after her arrival, she met Philip in the street, and stopped him. "I'm glad to find *some one* still here," she said; for she was with her friend, and having introduced Philip to this lady, she begged him to come and see her. On the next day but one, accordingly, Philip presented himself, and saw Mrs. Dodd alone. She began to talk about Graham; she became very much affected, and with a little more encouragement from Osborne, she would certainly have shed tears. But, somehow, Philip was loth to countenance her grief; he made short responses. Mrs. Dodd struck him as weak and silly and morbidly sentimental. He wondered whether there could have been any truth in the rumor that Graham had cared for her. Not certainly if there was any truth in the story of his passion for Henrietta Congreve. It was impossible that he should have cared for both. Philip made this reflection, but he stopped short of adding that Mrs. Dodd failed signally to please him, because during the past three weeks he had constantly enjoyed Henrietta's society.

For Mrs. Dodd, of course, the transition was easy from Graham to Miss Congreve. "I'm told Miss Congreve is still here," she said. "Have you made her acquaintance?"

"Perfectly," said Philip.

"You seem to take it very easily. I hope you have brought her to a sense of her iniquities. There's a task, Mr. Osborne. You ought to convert her."

"I've not attempted to convert her. I've taken her as she is."

"Does she wear mourning for Mr. Graham? It's the least she can do."

"Wear mourning?" said Philip. "Why, she has been going to a party every other night."

"Of course I don't suppose she has put on a black dress. But does she mourn *here*?" And Mrs. Dodd laid her hand on her heart.

"You mean in her heart? Well, you know, it's problematical that she has one."

"I suppose she disapproves of suicide," said Mrs. Dodd, with a little acrid smile. "Bless my soul, so do I."

"So do I, Mrs. Dodd," said Philip. And he remained for a moment thoughtful. "I wish to heaven," he cried, "that Graham were here! It seems to me at moments that he and Miss Congreve might have come to an understanding again."

Mrs. Dodd threw out her hands in horror. "Why, has she given up her last lover?"

"Her last lover? Whom do you mean?"

"Why, the man I told you of—Mr. Holland."

Philip appeared quite to have forgotten this point in Mrs. Dodd's recital. He broke into a loud, nervous laugh. "I'll be hanged," he cried, "if I know! One thing is certain," he pursued, with emphasis, recovering himself; "Mr. Holland—

whoever he is—has for the past three weeks seen nothing of Miss Congreve."

Mrs. Dodd sat silent, with her eyes lowered. At last, looking up, "You, on the other hand, I infer," she said, "have seen a great deal of her."

"Yes, I've seen her constantly."

Mrs. Dodd raised her eyebrows and distended her lips in a smile which was emphatically not a smile. "Well, you'll think it an odd question, Mr. Osborne," she said, "but how do you reconcile your intimacy with Miss Congreve with your devotion to Mr. Graham?"

Philip frowned—quite too severely for good manners. Decidedly, Mrs. Dodd was extremely silly. "Oh," he rejoined, "I reconcile the two things perfectly. Moreover, my dear Mrs. Dodd, allow me to say that it's my own business. At all events," he added, more gently, "perhaps, one of these days, you'll read the enigma."

"Oh, if it's an enigma," cried the lady, "perhaps I can guess it."

Philip had risen to his feet to take his leave, and Mrs. Dodd threw herself back on the sofa, clasped her hands in her lap, and looked up at him with a penetrating smile. She shook her finger at him reproachfully. Philip saw that she had an idea; perhaps it was the right one. At all events, he blushed. Upon this Mrs. Dodd cried out.

"I've guessed it," she said. "Oh, Mr. Osborne!"

"What have you guessed?" asked Philip, not knowing why in the world he should blush.

"If I've guessed right," said Mrs. Dodd, "it's a charming idea. It does you credit. It's quite romantic. It would do in a novel."

"I doubt," said Philip, "whether I know what you are talking about."

"Oh, yes, you do. I wish you good luck. To another man I should say it was a dangerous game. But to you!"—and with an insinuating movement of her head, Mrs. Dodd measured with a glance the length and breadth of Philip's fine person.

Osborne was inexpressibly disgusted, and without further delay he took his leave.

The reader will be at a loss to understand why Philip should have been disgusted with the mere foreshadowing on the part of another, of a scheme which, three weeks before, he had thought a very happy invention. For we may as well say outright, that although Mrs. Dodd was silly, she was not so silly but that she had divined his original intentions with regard to Henrietta. The fact is that in three weeks Philip's humor had undergone a great change. The reader has gathered for himself that Henrietta Congreve was no ordinary girl, that she was, on the contrary, a person of distinguished gifts and remarkable character. Until within a very few months she had seen very little of the world, and her mind and talents had been gradually formed in seclusion, study, and it is not too much to say, meditation. Thanks to her circumscribed life and her long contemplative leisures, she had reached a pitch of rare intellectual perfection. She was educated, one may say, in a sense in which the term may be used of very few young girls, however richly endowed by nature. When at a later period than most girls, owing to domestic circumstances which it is needless to unfold, she made her entrance into society and learned what it was to be in the world and of the world, to talk and listen, to please and be pleased, to be admired, flattered and interested, her admirable faculties and beautiful intellect, ripened in studious solitude, burst into luxuriant bloom and bore the fairest fruit. Miss Congreve was accordingly a person for whom a man of taste and of feeling could not help entertaining a serious regard. Philip Osborne was emphatically such a man; the manner in which he was affected by his friend's death proves, I think, that he had feeling; and it is ample evidence of his taste that he had chosen such a friend. He had no sooner begun to act in obedience to the impulse mystically bestowed, as it were, at the close of Mrs. Carpenter's feast—he had no sooner obtained an introduction at Mrs. Wilkes's, and, with excellent tact and discretion, made good his footing there, than he began to feel in his inmost heart that in staking his life upon Miss Congreve's favor, poor Graham had indeed revealed the depths of his exquisite sensibility. For a week at least—a week during which, with unprecedented good fortune and a degree of assurance worthy of a better cause, Philip contrived in one way and another to

talk with his fair victim no less than a dozen times—he was
under the empire of a feverish excitement which kept him
from seeing the young girl in all her beautiful integrity. He
was pre-occupied with his own intentions and the effect of his
own manœuvres. But gradually he quite forgot himself while
he was in her presence, and only remembered that he had a
sacred part to play, after he had left the house. Then it was
that he conceived the intensity of Graham's despair, and then
it was that he began to be sadly, wofully puzzled by the idea
that a woman could unite so much loveliness with so much
treachery, so much light with so much darkness. He was as
certain of the bright surface of her nature as of its cold and
dark reverse, and he was utterly unable to discover a link of
connection between the two. At moments he wondered how
in the world he had become saddled with this metaphysical
burden: *que diable venait-il faire dans cette galère?* But nevertheless he was afloat; he must row his boat over the current
to where the restless spirit of his friend paced the opposite
shore.

Henrietta Congreve, after a first movement of apparent
aversion, was very well pleased to accept Osborne as a friend
and as an *habitué* of her sister's house. Osborne fancied that
he might believe without fatuity—for whatever the reader
may think, it is needless to say that Philip was very far from
supposing his whole course to be a piece of infatuated cox-
combry—that she preferred him to most of the young men of
her circle. Philip had a just estimate of his own endowments,
and he knew that for the finer social purposes, if not for
strictly sentimental ones, he contained the stuff of an important personage. He had no taste for trivialities, but trivialities
played but a small part in Mrs. Wilkes's drawing-room. Mrs.
Wilkes was a simple woman, but she was neither silly nor frivolous; and Miss Congreve was exempt from these foibles for
even better reasons. "Women really care only for men who
can tell them something," Osborne remembered once to have
heard Graham say, not without bitterness. "They are always
famished for news." Philip now reflected with satisfaction that
he could give Miss Congreve more news than most of her
constituted gossips. He had an admirable memory and a very
lively observation. In these respects Henrietta was herself

equally well endowed; but Philip's experience of the world had of course been tenfold more extensive, and he was able continually to complete her partial inductions and to rectify her false conjectures. Sometimes they seemed to him wonderfully shrewd, and sometimes delightfully innocent. He nevertheless frequently found himself in a position to make her acquainted with facts possessing the charm of absolute novelty. He had travelled and seen a great variety of men and women, and of course he had read a number of books which a woman is not expected to read. Philip was keenly sensible of these advantages; but it nevertheless seemed to him that if the exhibition of his mental treasures furnished Miss Congreve with a great deal of entertainment, her attention, on the other hand, had a most refreshing effect upon his mind.

At the end of three weeks Philip might, perhaps not unreasonably, have supposed himself in a position to strike his blow. It is true that, for a woman of sense, there is a long step between thinking a man an excellent friend and a charming talker, and surrendering her heart to him. Philip had every reason to believe that Henrietta thought these good things of himself; but if he had hereupon turned about to make his exit, with the conviction that when he had closed the parlor-door behind him he should, by lending an attentive ear, hear her fall in a swoon on the carpet, he might have been sadly snubbed and disappointed. He longed for an opportunity to test the quality of his empire. If he could only pretend for a week to be charmed by another woman, Miss Congreve might perhaps commit herself. Philip flattered himself that he could read very small signs. But what other woman could decently serve as the object of a passion thus extemporized? The only woman Philip could think of was Mrs. Dodd; and to think of Mrs. Dodd was to give it up. For a man who was intimate with Miss Congreve to pretend to care for any other woman (except a very old friend) was to act in flagrant contempt of all verisimilitude. Philip had, therefore, to content himself with playing off his own assumed want of heart against Henrietta's cordial regard. But at this rate the game moved very slowly. Work was accumulating at a prodigious rate at his office, and he couldn't dangle about Miss Congreve forever. He bethought himself of a harmless artifice for drawing her out. It seemed to him that his move was not altogether unsuccessful, and that, at a pinch, Henrietta might become jealous of a rival in his affections. Nevertheless, he was strongly tempted to take up his hand and leave the game. It was too confoundedly exciting.

The incident of which I speak happened within a few days after Osborne's visit to Mrs. Dodd. Finding it impossible to establish an imaginary passion for an actual, visible young lady, Philip resolved to invent not only the passion, but the young lady, too. One morning, as he was passing the show-case of one of the several photographers who came to Newport for the season, he was struck by the portrait of a very pretty young girl. She was fair in color, graceful, well dressed, well placed, her face was charming, she was plainly a lady. Philip went in and asked who she was. The photographer had destroyed the negative and had kept no register of her name. He remembered her, however, distinctly. The portrait had not been taken during the summer; it had been taken during the preceding winter, in Boston, the photographer's headquarters. "I kept it," he said, "because I thought it so very perfect a picture. And such a charming sitter! We haven't many like that." He added, however, that it was too good to please the masses, and that Philip was the first gentleman who had had the taste to observe it.

"So much the better," thought Philip, and forthwith proposed to the man to part with it. The latter, of course, had conscientious scruples; it was against his principles to dispose of the portraits of ladies who came to him in confidence. To do him justice, he adhered to his principles, and Philip was unable to persuade him to sell it. He consented, however, to give it to Mr. Osborne, *gratis*. Mr. Osborne deserved it, and he had another for himself. By this time Philip had grown absolutely fond of the picture; at this latter intelligence he looked grave, and suggested that if the artist would not sell one, perhaps he would sell two. The photographer declined, reiterated his offer, and Philip finally accepted. By way of compensation, however, he proceeded to sit for his own portrait. In the course of half an hour the photographer gave him a dozen reflections of his head and shoulders, distinguished by as many different attitudes and expressions.

"You sit first-rate, sir," said the artist. "You take beautifully. You're quite a match for my young lady."

Philip went off with his dozen prints, promising to examine them at his leisure, select and give a liberal order.

In the evening he went to Mrs. Wilkes's. He found this lady on her verandah, drinking tea in the open air with a guest, whom in the darkness he failed to recognize. As Mrs. Wilkes proceeded to introduce him, her companion graciously revealed herself as Mrs. Dodd. "How on earth," thought Philip, "did she get here?" To find Mrs. Dodd instead of Miss Congreve was, of course, a gross discomfiture. Philip sat down, however, with a good grace, to all appearance, hoping that Henrietta would turn up. Finally, moving his chair to a line with the drawing room window, he saw the young girl within, reading by the lamp. She was alone and intent upon her book. She wore a dress of white grenadine, covered with ornaments and arabesques of crimson silk, which gave her a somewhat fantastical air. For the rest, her expression was grave enough, and her brows contracted, as if she were completely absorbed in her book. Her right elbow rested on the table, and with her hand she mechanically twisted the long curl depending from her *chignon*. Watching his opportunity, Osborne escaped from the ladies on the verandah and made his way into the drawing-room. Miss Congreve received him as an old friend, without rising from her chair.

Philip began by pretending to scold her for shirking the society of Mrs. Dodd.

"Shirking!" said Henrietta. "You are very polite to Mrs. Dodd."

"It seems to me," rejoined Osborne, "that I'm quite as polite as you."

"Well, perhaps you are. To tell the truth, I'm not very polite. At all events, she don't care to see me. She must have come to see my sister."

"I didn't know she knew Mrs. Wilkes."

"It's an acquaintance of a couple of hours' standing. I met her, you know, at Sharon in July. She was once very impertinent to me, and I fancied she had quite given me up. But this afternoon, during our drive, as my sister and I got out of the carriage, on the rocks, who should I see but Mrs. Dodd, wandering about alone, with a bunch of sea-weed as big as her head. She rushed up to me; I introduced her to Anna, and finding that she had walked quite a distance, Anna made her get into the carriage. It appears that she's staying with a friend, who has no carriage, and she's very miserable. We drove her about for an hour. Mrs. Dodd was fascinating, she threw away her sea-weed, and Anna asked her to come home to tea. After tea, having endured her for two mortal hours, I took refuge here."

"If she was fascinating," said Philip, "why do you call it enduring her?"

"It's all the more reason, I assure you."

"I see, you have not forgiven her impertinence."

"No, I confess I have not. The woman was positively revolting."

"She appears nevertheless, to have forgiven you."

"She has nothing to forgive."

In a few moments, Philip took his photographs out of his pocket, handed them to Henrietta, and asked her advice as to which he should choose. Miss Congreve inspected them attentively, and selected but one. "This one is excellent," she said. "All the others are worthless in comparison."

"You advise me then to order that alone?"

"Why, you'll do as you please. I advise you to order that, at any rate. If you do, I shall ask you for one; but I shall care nothing for the rest."

Philip protested that he saw very little difference between this favored picture and the others, and Miss Congreve declared that there was all the difference in the world. As Philip replaced the specimens in his pocket-book, he dropped on the carpet the portrait of the young lady of Boston.

"Ah," said Henrietta, "a young lady. I suppose I may see it."

"On one condition," said Philip, picking it up. "You'll please not to look at the back of the card."

I am very much ashamed to have to tell such things of poor Philip; for in point of fact, the back of the card was a most innocent blank. If Miss Congreve had ventured to disobey him, he would have made a very foolish figure. But there was so little that was boisterous in Henrietta's demeanor, that Osborne felt that he ran no risk.

"Who is she?" asked Henrietta, looking at the portrait. "She's charming."

"She's a Miss Thompson, of Philadelphia."

"Dear me, not Dora Thompson, assuredly."

"No indeed," said Philip, a little nervously. "Her name's not Dora—nor anything like it."

"You needn't resent the insinuation, sir. Dora's a very pretty name."

"Yes, but her own is prettier."

"I'm very curious to hear it."

Philip suddenly found himself in deep waters. He struck out blindly and answered at random, "Angelica."

Miss Congreve smiled—somewhat ironically, it seemed to Philip. "Well," she said, "I like her face better than her name."

"Dear me, if you come to that, so do I!" cried Philip, with a laugh.

"Tell me about her, Mr. Osborne," pursued Henrietta. "She must be, with that face and figure, just the nicest girl in the world."

"Well, well, well," said Philip, leaning back in his chair, and looking at the ceiling—"perhaps she is—or at least, you'll excuse me if I say *I* think she is."

"I should think it inexcusable if you didn't say so," said Henrietta, giving him the card. "I'm sure I've seen her somewhere."

"Very likely. She comes to New York," said Philip. And he thought it prudent, on the whole, to divert the conversation to another topic. Miss Congreve remained silent and he fancied pensive. Was she jealous of Angelica Thompson? It seemed to Philip that, without fatuity, he might infer that she was, and that she was too proud to ask questions.

Mrs. Wilkes had enabled Mrs. Dodd to send tidings to her hostess of her whereabouts, and had promised to furnish her with an escort on her return. When Mrs. Dodd prepared to take her leave, Philip, finding himself also ready to depart, offered to walk home with her.

"Well, sir," said the lady, when they had left the house, "your little game seems to be getting on."

Philip said nothing.

"Ah, Mr. Osborne," said Mrs. Dodd, with ill-concealed impatience, "I'm afraid you're too good for it."

"Well, I'm afraid I am."

"If you hadn't been in such a hurry to agree with me," said Mrs. Dodd, "I should have said that I meant, in other words, that you're too stupid."

"Oh, I agree to that, too," said Philip.

The next day he received a letter from his partner in business, telling him of a great pressure of work, and urging him to return at his earliest convenience. "We are told," added this gentleman, "of a certain Miss——, I forget the name. If she's essential to your comfort, bring her along; but, at any rate, come yourself. In your absence the office is at a standstill—a fearful case of repletion without digestion."

This appeal came home to Philip's mind, to use a very old metaphor, like the sound of the brazen trumpet to an old cavalry charger. He felt himself overwhelmed with a sudden shame at the thought of the precious hours he had wasted and the long mornings he had consigned to perdition. He had been burning incense to a shadow, and the fumes had effaced it. In the afternoon he walked down toward the cliffs, feeling wofully perplexed, and exasperated in mind, and longing only to take a farewell look at the sea. He was not prepared to admit that he had played with fire and burned his fingers; but it was certain that he had gained nothing at the game. How the deuce had Henrietta Congreve come to thrust herself into his life—to steal away his time and his energies and to put him into a savage humor with himself? He would have given a great deal to be able to banish her from his thoughts; but she remained, and, while she remained, he hated her. After all, he had not been wholly cheated of his revenge. He had begun by hating her and he hated her still. On his way to the cliffs he met Mrs. Wilkes, driving alone. Henrietta's place, vacant beside her, seemed to admonish him that she was at home, and almost, indeed, that she expected him. At all events, instead of going to bid farewell to the sea, he went to bid farewell to Miss Congreve. He felt that his farewell might easily be cold and formal, and indeed bitter.

He was admitted, he passed through the drawing-room to the verandah, and found Henrietta sitting on the grass, in the garden, holding her little nephew on her knee and reading him a fairy tale. She made room for him on the garden bench beside her, but kept the child. Philip felt himself seriously discomposed by this spectacle. In a few moments he took the boy upon his own knees. He then told Miss Congreve briefly that he intended that evening to leave Newport. "And you," he said, "when are you coming?"

"My sister," said Henrietta, "means to stay till Christmas. I hope to be able to remain as long."

Poor Philip bowed his head and heard his illusions tumbling most unmusically about his ears. His blow had smitten but the senseless air. He waited to see her color fade, or to hear her voice tremble. But he waited in vain. When he looked up and his eyes met Henrietta's, she was startled by the expression of his face.

"Tom," she said to the child, "go and ask Jane for my fan."

The child walked off, and Philip rose to his feet. Henrietta, hesitating a moment, also rose. "Must you go?" she asked.

Philip made no answer, but stood looking at her with blood-shot eyes, and with an intensity which puzzled and frightened the young girl.

"Miss Congreve," he said, abruptly, "I'm a miserable man!"

"Oh, no!" said Henrietta, gently.

"I love a woman who doesn't care a straw for me!"

"Are you sure?" said Henrietta, innocently.

"Sure! I adore her!"

"Are you sure she doesn't care for you?"

"Ah, Miss Congreve!" cried Philip. "If I could imagine, if I could hope—" and he put out his hand, as if to take her own.

Henrietta drew back, pale and frowning, carrying her hand to her heart. "Hope for nothing!" she said.

At this moment, little Tom Wilkes re-appeared, issuing from the drawing-room window. "Aunt Henrietta," he cried, "here's a new gentleman!"

Miss Congreve and Philip turned about, and saw a young

man step out upon the verandah from the drawing-room. Henrietta, with a little cry, hastened to meet him. Philip stood in his place. Miss Congreve exchanged a cordial greeting with the stranger, and led him down to the lawn. As she came toward him, Philip saw that Henrietta's pallor had made way for a rosy flush. She was beautiful.

"Mr. Osborne," she said, "Mr. Holland."

Mr. Holland bowed graciously; but Philip bowed not at all. "Good-by, then," he said, to the young girl.

She bowed, without speaking.

"Who's your friend, Henrietta?" asked her companion, when they were alone.

"He's a Mr. Osborne, of New York," said Miss Congreve; "a friend of poor Mr. Graham."

"By the way, I suppose you've heard of poor Graham's death."

"Oh, yes; Mr. Osborne told me. And, indeed—what do you think? Mr. Graham wrote to me that he expected to die."

"Expected? Is that what he said?"

"I don't remember his words. I destroyed the letter."

"I must say, I think it would have been in better taste not to write."

"Taste! He had long since parted company with taste."

"I don't know. There was a method in his madness; and, as a rule, when a man kills himself, he shouldn't send out circulars."

"Kills himself? Good heavens, George! what do you mean?" Miss Congreve had turned pale, and stood looking at her companion with eyes dilated with horror.

"Why, my dear Henrietta," said the young man, "excuse my abruptness. Didn't you know it?"

"How strange—how fearful!" said Henrietta, slowly. "I wish I had kept his letter."

"I'm glad you didn't," said Holland. "It's a horrible business. Forget it."

"Horrible—horrible," murmured the young girl, in a tremulous tone. Her voice was shaken with irrepressible tears. Poor girl! in the space of five minutes, she had been three times surprised. She gave way to her emotion and burst into sobs. George Holland drew her against him, and pressed his arm about her, and kissed her, and whispered comfort in her ear.

In the evening, Philip started for New York. On the steamer, he found Mrs. Dodd, who had come to an end of her visit. She was accompanied by a certain Major Dodd, of the Army, a brother of her deceased husband, and in addition, as it happened, her cousin. He was an unmarried man, a good-natured man, and a very kind friend to his sister-in-law, who had no family of her own, and who was in a position to be grateful for the services of a gentleman. In spite of a general impression to the contrary, I may affirm that the Major had no desire to make his little services a matter of course. "I'm related to Maria twice over already," he had been known to say, in a moment of expansion. "If I ever marry, I shall prefer to do it not quite so much in the family." He had come to Newport to conduct his sister home, who forthwith introduced him to Philip.

It was a clear, mild night, and, when the steamer had got under way, Mrs. Dodd and the two gentlemen betook themselves to the upper deck, and sat down in the starlight. Philip, it may be readily imagined, was in no humor for conversation; but he felt that he could not wholly neglect Mrs. Dodd. Under the influence of the beautiful evening, the darkly-shining sea, the glittering constellations, this lady became rabidly sentimental. She talked of friendship, and love, and death, and immortality. Philip saw what was coming. Before many moments, she had the bad taste (considering the Major's presence, as it seemed to Philip) to take poor Graham as a text for a rhapsody. Osborne lost patience, and interrupted her by asking if she would mind his lighting a cigar. She was scandalized, and immediately announced that she would go below. Philip had no wish to be uncivil. He attempted to restore himself to her favor by offering to see her down to the cabin. She accepted his escort, and he went with her to the door of her state-room, where she gave him her hand for good-night.

"Well," she said—"and Miss Congreve?"

Philip positively scowled. "Miss Congreve," he said, "is engaged to be married."

"To Mr.——?"

"To Mr. Holland."

"Ah!" cried Mrs. Dodd, dropping his hand, "why didn't you break the engagement!"

"My dear Mrs. Dodd," said Philip, "you don't know what you're talking about."

Mrs. Dodd smiled a pitiful smile, shrugged her shoulders, and turned away. "Poor Graham!" she said.

Her words came to Philip like a blow in the face. "Graham!" he cried. "Graham was a fool!" He had struck back; he couldn't help it.

He made his way up stairs again, and came out on the deck, still trembling with the violence of his retort. He walked to the edge of the boat and leaned over the railing, looking down into the black gulfs of water which foamed and swirled in the wake of the vessel. He knocked off the end of his cigar, and watched the red particles fly downward and go out in the darkness. He was a disappointed, saddened man. There in the surging, furious darkness, yawned instant death. Did it tempt him, too? He drew back with a shudder, and returned to his place by Major Dodd.

The Major preserved for some moments a meditative silence. Then, at last, with a half apologetic laugh, "Mrs. Dodd," he said, "labors under a singular illusion."

"Ah?" said Philip.

"But you knew Mr. Graham yourself?" pursued the Major.

"Oh, yes; I knew him."

"It was a very melancholy case," said Major Dodd.

"A very melancholy case;" and Philip repeated his words.

"I don't know how it is that Mrs. Dodd was beguiled into such fanaticism on the subject. I believe she went so far as once to blow out at the young lady."

"The young lady?" said Philip.

"Miss Congreve, you know, the object of his persecutions."

"Oh, yes," said Philip, painfully mystified.

"The fact is," said the Major, leaning over, and lowering his voice confidentially, "Mrs. Dodd was in love with him—as far, that is, as a woman can be in love with a man in that state."

"Is it possible?" said Philip, disgusted and revolted at he knew not what; for his companion's allusions were an enigma.

"Oh, I was at Sharon for three weeks," the Major continued; "I went up for my sister-in-law; I saw it all. I wanted to bring poor Graham away, but he wouldn't listen to me—not that he wasn't very quiet. He made no talk, and opened himself only to Mrs. Dodd and me—we lived in the same house, you know. Of course, I very soon saw through it, and I felt very sorry for poor Miss Congreve. She bore it very well, but it must have been very annoying."

Philip started up from his chair. "For heaven's sake, Major Dodd," he cried, "what are you talking about?"

The Major stared a moment, and then burst into a peal of laughter. "You agree, then, with Mrs. Dodd?" he said, recovering himself.

"I understand Mrs. Dodd no better than I do you."

"Why, my dear sir," said the Major, rising to his feet and extending his hand, "I beg a hundred pardons. But you must excuse me if I adhere to my opinion."

"First, please, be so good as to inform me of your opinion."

"Why, sir, the whole story is simply bosh."

"Good heavens," cried Philip, "that's no opinion!"

"Well, then, sir, if you will have it: the man was as mad as a March hare."

"Oh!" cried Philip. His exclamation said a great many things, but the Major took it as a protest.

"He was a monomaniac."

Philip said nothing.

"The idea is not new to you?"

"Well," said Philip, "to tell the truth, it is."

"Well," said the Major, with a courteous flourish, "there you have it—for nothing."

Philip drew a long breath. "Ah, no!" he said, gravely, "not for nothing." He stood silent for some time, with his eyes fixed on the deck. Major Dodd puffed his cigar and eyed him askance. At last Philip looked up. "And Henrietta Congreve?"

"Henrietta Congreve," said the major, with military freedom and gallantry, "is the sweetest girl in the world. Don't talk to me! I know her."

"She never became engaged to Graham?"

"Engaged? She never looked at him."

"But he was in love with her."

"Ah, that was his own business. He worried her to death. She tried gentleness and kindness—it made him worse. Then, when she declined to see him, the poor fellow swore that she had jilted him. It was a fixed idea. He got Mrs. Dodd to believe it."

Philip's silent reflections—the hushed eloquence of his amazed unburdened heart—we have no space to interpret. But as the major lightened the load with one hand, he added to it with the other. Philip had never pitied his friend till now. "I knew him well," he said, aloud. "He was the best of men. She might very well have cared for him."

"Good heavens! my dear sir, how could the woman love a madman?"

"You use strong language. When I parted with him in June, he was as sane as you or I."

"Well, then, apparently, he lost his mind in the interval. He was in wretched health."

"But a man doesn't lose his mind without a cause."

"Let us admit, then," said the major, "that Miss Congreve was the cause. I insist that she was the innocent cause. How should she have trifled with him? She was engaged to another man. The ways of the Lord are inscrutable. Fortunately," continued the Major, "she doesn't know the worst."

"How, the worst?"

"Why, you know he shot himself."

"Bless your soul, Miss Congreve knows it."

"I think you're mistaken. She didn't know it this morning."

Philip was sickened and bewildered by the tissue of horrors in which he found himself entangled. "Oh," he said, bitterly, "she has forgotten it then. She knew it a month ago."

"No, no, no," rejoined the major, with decision. "I took the liberty, this morning, of calling upon her, and as we had had some conversation upon Mr. Graham at Sharon, I touched upon his death. I saw she had heard of it, and I said nothing more—"

"Well then?" said Philip.

"Well, then, my dear sir, she thinks he died in his bed. May she never think otherwise!"

In the course of that night—he sat out on deck till two o'clock, alone—Philip, revolving many things, fervently echoed this last wish of Major Dodd.

Aux grands maux les grands remèdes. Philip is now a married man; and curious to narrate, his wife bears a striking likeness to the young lady whose photograph he purchased for the price of six dozen of his own. And yet her name is not Angelica Thompson—nor even Dora.

A Light Man

And I—what I seem to my friend, you see—
What I soon shall seem to his love, you guess.
What I seem to myself, do you ask of me?
No hero, I confess.

A LIGHT WOMAN.
BROWNING'S MEN AND WOMEN.

A PRIL 4, 1857.—I have changed my sky without changing my mind. I resume these old notes in a new world. I hardly know of what use they are; but it's easier to preserve the habit than to break it. I have been at home now a week—at home, forsooth! And yet after all, it is home. I'm dejected, I'm bored, I'm blue. How can a man be more at home than that? Nevertheless, I'm the citizen of a great country, and for that matter, of a great city. I walked to-day some ten miles or so along Broadway, and on the whole I don't blush for my native land. We're a capable race and a good-looking withal; and I don't see why we shouldn't prosper as well as another. This, by the way, ought to be a very encouraging reflection. A capable fellow and a good looking withal; I don't see why he shouldn't die a millionaire. At all events he must set bravely to work. When a man has, at thirty-two, a net income of considerably less than nothing, he can scarcely hope to overtake a fortune before he himself is overtaken by age and philosophy—two deplorable obstructions. I'm afraid that one of them has already planted itself in my path. What am I? What do I wish? Whither do I tend? What do I believe? I am constantly beset by these impertinent whisperings. Formerly it was enough that I was Maximus Austin; that I was endowed with a cheerful mind and a good digestion; that one day or another, when I had come to the end, I should return to America and begin at the beginning; that, meanwhile, existence was sweet in—in the Rue Tranchet. But now! Has the sweetness really passed out of life? Have I eaten the plums and left nothing but the bread and milk and corn-starch, or whatever the horrible concoction is?—we had it to-day for dinner.

Pleasure, at least, I imagine—pleasure pure and simple, pleasure crude, brutal and vulgar—this poor flimsy delusion has lost all its prettiness. I shall never again care for certain things—and indeed for certain persons. Of such things, of such persons, I firmly maintain, however, that I was never an enthusiastic votary. It would be more to my credit, I suppose, if I had been. More would be forgiven me if I had loved a little more, if into all my folly and egotism I had put a little more *naïveté* and sincerity. Well, I did the best I could, I was at once too bad and too good for it all. At present, it's far enough off; I've put the sea between us. I'm stranded. I sit high and dry, scanning the horizon for a friendly sail, or waiting for a high tide to set me afloat. The wave of pleasure has planted me here in the sand. Shall I owe my rescue to the wave of pain? At moments my heart throbs with a sort of ecstatic longing to expiate my stupid peccadilloes. I see, as through a glass, darkly, the beauty of labor and love. Decidedly, I'm willing to work. It's written.

7th.—My sail is in sight; it's at hand; I've all but boarded the vessel. I received this morning a letter from the best man in the world. Here it is:

DEAR MAX: I see this very moment, in the old newspaper which had already passed through my hands without yielding up its most precious item, the announcement of your arrival in New York. To think of your having perhaps missed the grasp of my hand. Here it is, dear Max—to rap on the knuckles, if you like. When I say I have just read of your arrival, I mean that twenty minutes have elapsed by the clock. These have been spent in conversation with my excellent friend Mr. Frederick Sloane—your excellent self being the subject. I haven't time to say more about Mr. Sloane than that he is very anxious to make your acquaintance, and that, if your time is not otherwise predestined, he would esteem it a particular favor to have you pass a month under his roof—the ample roof which covers my own devoted head. It appears that he knew your mother very intimately, and he has a taste for visiting the amenities of the parents upon the children; the original ground of my own connection with him was that he had been a particular friend of my father. You may have heard your mother speak of him—a perfect eccentric, but a charming one. He will make you most welcome. But whether or no you come for his sake, come for mine. I have a hundred questions on the end of my pen, but I can't drop them, lest I should lose the mail.

You'll not refuse me without an excellent reason, and I shan't excuse
you, even then. So the sooner the better. Yours more than ever,
THEODORE LISLE.

Theodore's letter is of course very kind, but it's perfectly
obscure. My mother may have had the highest regards for Mr.
Sloane, but she never mentioned his name in my hearing.
Who is he, what is he, and what is the nature of his relations
with Theodore? I shall learn betimes. I have written to
Theodore that I gladly accept (I believe I suppressed the
"gladly" though) his friend's invitation, and that I shall immediately present myself. What better can I do? I shall, at the
narrowest calculation, obtain food and lodging while I invoke
the fates. I shall have a basis of operations. D., it appears, is a
long day's journey, but delicious when you reach it. I'm curious to see a delicious American town. And a month's stay!
Mr. Frederick Sloane, whoever you are, *vous faites bien les
choses*, and the little that I know of you is very much to your
credit. You enjoyed the friendship of my dear mother, you
possess the esteem of my incomparable Theodore, you commend yourself to my own affection. At this rate, I shan't
grudge it.

D——, 14th.—I have been here since Thursday evening—
three days. As we rattled up to the tavern in the village, I perceived from the top of the coach, in the twilight, Theodore
beneath the porch, scanning the vehicle, with all his affectionate soul in his eyes. I made hardly more than two downward strides into his arms—or, at all events, into his hands.
He has grown older, of course, in these five years, but less so
than I had expected. His is one of those smooth unwrinkled
souls that infuse a perennial fairness and freshness into the
body. As tall as ever, moreover, and as lean and clean. How
short and fat and dark and debauched he makes one feel! By
nothing he says or means, of course, but merely by his old
unconscious purity and simplicity—that slender aspiring rectitude which makes him remind you of the tower of an English
abbey. He greeted me with smiles, and stares, and formidable
blushes. He assures me that he never would have known me,
and that five years have quite transformed my physiognomy. I
asked him if it was for the better? He looked at me hard for a

moment, with his eyes of blue, and then, for all answer, he blushed again.

On my arrival we agreed to walk over from the village. He dismissed his wagon with my trunk, and we went arm-in-arm through the dusk. The town is seated at the foot of certain mountains, whose names I have yet to learn, and at the head of a vast sheet of water which, as yet, too, I know only as "The Lake." The road hitherward soon leaves the village and wanders in rural loveliness by the lake side. Sometimes the water is hidden by clumps of trees, behind which we heard it lapping and gurgling in the darkness; sometimes it stretches out from your feet in unspotted beauty, offering its broad white bosom to the embrace of the dark fraternal hills. The walk from the tavern takes some half an hour, in which space Theodore had explained his position to my comparative satisfaction. Mr. Sloane is old, widowed and rich; his age is seventy-two, and as his health is thoroughly broken, is practically even greater; and his fortune—Theodore, characteristically, doesn't know its numerical formula. It's probably a round million. He has lived much abroad, and in the thick of things; he has had adventures and passions and all that sort of thing; and now, in the evening of his days, like an old French diplomat, he takes it into his head to write his memoirs. To this end he has taken poor Theodore to his generous side, to serve as his guide, philosopher and friend. He has been a great scribbler, says Theodore, all his days, and he proposes to incorporate a large amount of promiscuous literary matter into this singular record of his existence. Theodore's principal function seems to be to get him to leave things out. In fact, the poor boy seems troubled in conscience. His patron's lucubrations have taken the turn of all memoirs, and become *tout bonnement* immoral. On the whole, he declares they are a very odd mixture—a jumble of pretentious trash and of excellent good sense. I can readily understand it. The old man bores me, puzzles me, and amuses me.

He was in waiting to receive me. We found him in his library—which, by the way, is simply the most delightful apartment that I ever smoked a cigar in—a room for a lifetime. At one end stands a great fireplace, with a florid, fantastic mantelpiece in carved white marble—an importation, of course, and as one may say, an interpolation; the groundwork of the house, the "fixtures," being throughout plain, solid and domestic. Over the mantel-shelf is a large landscape painting, a *soi-disant* Gainsborough, full of the mellow glory of an English summer. Beneath it stands a fantastic litter of French bronzes and outlandish *chinoiseries*. Facing the door, as you enter, is a vast window set in a recess, with cushioned seats and large clear panes, stationed as it were at the very apex of the lake (which forms an almost perfect oval) and commanding a view of its whole extent. At the other end, opposite the fire-place, the wall is studded, from floor to ceiling, with choice foreign paintings, placed in relief against the orthodox crimson screen. Elsewhere the walls are covered with books, arranged neither in formal regularity nor quite helter-skelter, but in a sort of genial mutual incongruity, which tells that sooner or later each volume feels sure of leaving the ranks and returning into different company. Mr. Sloane uses his books. His two passions, according to Theodore, are reading and talking; but to talk he must have a book in his hand. The charm of the room lies in the absence of the portentous soberness—the browns, and blacks, and greys—which distinguish most rooms of its class. It's a sort of female study. There are half a dozen light colors scattered about—pink in the carpet, tender blue in the curtains, yellow in the chairs. The result is a general look of brightness, and lightness, and unpedantic elegance. You perceive the place to be the home, not of a man of learning, but of a man of fancy.

He rose from his chair—the man of fancy, to greet me—the man of fact. As I looked upon him, in the lamp-light, it seemed to me, for the first five minutes, that I had seldom seen a worse-favored human creature. It took me then five minutes to get the point of view; then I began to admire. He is undersized, or at best of my own moderate stature, bent and contracted with years; thin, however, where I am stout, and light where I am heavy. In color we're about equally dark. Mr. Sloane, however, is curiously pale, with a dead opaque yellow pallor. Literally, it's a magnificent yellow. His skin is of just the hue and apparent texture of some old crumpled Oriental scroll. I know a dozen painters who would give more than they have to arrive at the exact "tone" of his thick-veined saffron-colored hands—his polished ivory knuckles. His eyes are circled with red, but within their unhealthy orbits they scintillate like black diamonds. His nose, owing to the falling away of other portions of his face, has assumed a grotesque, unnatural prominence; it describes an immense arch, gleaming like parchment stretched on ivory. He has kept his teeth, but replaced his hair by a dead black wig; of course he's clean shaven. In his dress he has a muffled, wadded look, and an apparent aversion to linen, inasmuch as none is visible on his person. He seems neat enough, but not fastidious. At first, as I say, I fancied him monstrously ugly; but on further acquaintance I perceived that what I had taken for ugliness is nothing but the incomplete remains of remarkable good looks. The lines of his features are delicate; his nose, *ceteris paribus*, would be extremely handsome; his eyes are the eyes of a mind, not of a body. There is intelligence on his brow and sweetness on his lips.

He offered his two hands, as Theodore introduced me; I gave him my own, and he stood smiling upon me like some quaint old image in ivory and ebony, scanning my face with the sombre sparkle of his gaze. "Good heaven!" he said, at last, "how much you look like your father." I sat down, and for half an hour we talked of many things; of my journey, of my impressions of home, of my reminiscences of Europe, and, by implication, of my prospects. His voice is aged and cracked, but he uses it with immense energy. Mr. Sloane is not yet in his dotage, by a long shot. He nevertheless makes himself out a wofully old man. In reply to an inquiry I made about his health, he favored me with a long list of his infirmities (some of which are very trying, certainly) and assured me that he had but a mere pinch of vitality left.

"I live," he said, "out of mere curiosity."

"I have heard of people dying," I answered, "from the same motive."

He looked at me a moment, as if to ascertain whether I was making light of his statement. And then, after a pause, "Perhaps you don't know," said he, with a certain vague pomposity, "that I disbelieve in a future life."

Poor Theodore! at these words he got up and walked to the fire.

"Well, we shan't quarrel about that," said I. Theodore turned round, staring.

"Do you mean that you agree with me?" the old man asked.

"I certainly haven't come here to talk theology. Dear me, Mr. Sloane," I said, "don't ask me to disbelieve, and I'll never ask you to believe."

"Come," cried Mr. Sloane, rubbing his hands, "you'll not persuade me you're a Christian—like your friend Theodore there."

"Like Theodore—assuredly not." And then, somehow, I don't know why, at the thought of Theodore's Christianism, I burst into a laugh. "Excuse me, my dear fellow," I said, "you know, for the last ten years I have lived in Catholic countries."

"Good, good, good!" cried Mr. Sloane, rubbing his hands and clapping them together, and laughing with high relish.

"Dear me," said Theodore, smiling, but vaguely apprehensive, too—and a little touched, perhaps, by my involuntary reflection upon the quality of his faith, "I hope you're not a Roman Catholic."

I saw the old man, with his hands locked, eyeing me shrewdly, and waiting for my answer. I pondered a moment in mock gravity. "I shall make my confession," I said. "I've been in the East, you know. I'm a Mohammedan!"

Hereupon Mr. Sloane broke out into a wheezy ecstasy of glee. Verily, I thought, if he lives for curiosity, he's easily satisfied.

We went into dinner, in the constitution of which I should have been at loss to suggest the shadow of an improvement. I observed, by the way, that for a victim of paralysis, neuralgia, dyspepsia, and a thousand other ills, Mr. Sloane plies a most inconsequential knife and fork. Sweets, and spices, and condiments seem to be the chief of his diet. After dinner he dismissed us, in consideration of my natural desire to see my friend in private. Theodore has capital quarters—a chamber and sitting-room as luxurious as a man (or as a woman, for that matter) could possibly wish. We talked till near midnight—of ourselves and of our lemon-colored host below. That is, I spoke of myself, and Theodore listened; and then

Theodore told of Mr. Sloane and I listened. His commerce with the old man has sharpened his wits. Sloane has taught him to observe and judge, and Theodore turns around, observes, judges—him! He has become quite the critic and analyst. There is something very pleasant in the sagacity of virtue, in discernment without bitterness, penetration without spite. Theodore has all these unalloyed graces, to say nothing of an angelic charity. At midnight we repaired to the library to take leave of our host till the morrow—an attention which, under all circumstances, he formally exacts. As I gave him my hand he held it again and looked at me as he had done on my arrival. "Good heaven," he said, at last, "how much you look like your mother!"

To night, at the end of my third day, I begin to feel decidedly at home. The fact is, I'm supremely comfortable. The house is pervaded by an indefinable, irresistible air of luxury and privacy. Mr. Frederick Sloane must be a horribly corrupt old mortal. Already in his hateful, delightful presence I have become heartily reconciled to doing nothing. But with Theodore on one side, I honestly believe I can defy Mr. Sloane on the other. The former asked me this morning, with real solicitude, in allusion to the bit of dialogue I have quoted above on matters of faith, if I had actually ceased to care for divine things. I assured him that I would rather utterly lose my sense of the picturesque, than do anything to detract from the splendor of religious worship. Some of the happiest hours of my life, I told him, have been spent in cathedrals. He looked at me awhile, in friendly sadness. "I hardly know," he said, "whether you are worse than Mr. Sloane, or better."

But Theodore is, after all, in duty bound to give a man a long rope in these matters. His own rope is one of the longest. He reads Voltaire with Mr. Sloane, and Emerson in his own room. He's the stronger man of the two; he has the bigger stomach. Mr. Sloane delights, of course, in Voltaire, but he can't read a line of Emerson. Theodore delights in Emerson, and has excellent taste in the matter of Voltaire. It appears that since we parted in Paris, five years ago, his conscience has dwelt in many lands. *C'est toute une histoire*— which he tells very nicely. He left college determined to enter the ministry, and came abroad to lay the basis of his theological greatness in some German repository of science. He appears to have studied, not wisely but too well. Instead of faith full-armed and serene, there sprang from the labor of his brain a myriad abortive doubts, piping for sustenance. He went for a winter to Italy, where, I take it, he was not quite so much afflicted as he ought to have been, at the sight of the beautiful spiritual repose which he had missed. It was after this that we spent those three months together in Brittany—the best-spent three months of my whole ten years abroad. Theodore inoculated me, I think, with a little of his sacred fermentation, and I infused into his conscience something of my vulgar indifference; and we agreed together that there were a few good things left—health, friendship, a summer sky, and the lovely by-ways of an old French province. He came home, returned to theology, accepted a "call," and made an attempt to respond to it. But the inner voice failed him. His outlook was cheerless enough. During his absence his married sister, the elder one, had taken the other to live with her, relieving Theodore of the charge of contribution to her support. But suddenly, behold the husband, the brother-in-law, dies, leaving a mere fragment of property; and the two ladies, with their two little girls, are afloat in the wide world. Theodore finds himself at twenty-six without an income, without a profession, and with a family of four females to support. Well, in his quiet way, he draws on his courage. The history of the two years which preceded his initiation here is a simple record of practical manly devotion. He rescued his sisters and nieces from the deep waters, placed them high and dry, established them somewhere in decent gentility—and then found at last that his strength had left him—had dropped dead like an over-ridden horse. In short, he had worked himself ill. It was now his sisters' turn. They nursed him with all the added tenderness of gratitude for the past and terror of the future, and brought him safely through a grievous malady. Meanwhile Mr. Sloane, having decided to treat himself to a private secretary and suffered dreadful mischance in three successive experiments, had heard of Theodore's situation and his merits; had furthermore recognized in him the son of an early and intimate friend, and had finally offered him the very comfortable position which he now occupies. There is a decided incongruity between Theodore as a man—as Theodore, in fine—and the dear fellow as the intellectual agent, confidant, complaisant, purveyor, pander—what you will—of a battered old cynic and worldly dilettante. There seems at first sight a perfect want of agreement between his character and his function. One is gold and the other brass, or something very like it. But on reflection I perfectly conceive that he should, under the circumstances, have accepted Mr. Sloane's offer and been content to do his duties. Just heaven! Theodore's contentment in such a case is a theme for the moralist—a better moralist than I. The best and purest mortals are an odd mixture, and in none of us does honesty exist *totus, teres, atque rotundus.* Ideally, Theodore hasn't the smallest business *dans cette galère.* It offends my sense of propriety to find him here. I feel like admonishing him as a friend that he has knocked at the wrong door, and that he had better retreat before he is brought to the blush. Really, as I say, I suppose he might as well be here, as reading Emerson "evenings," in the back parlor, to those two very plain sisters—judging from their photographs. Practically it hurts no one to compromise with his tendencies. Poor Theodore was weak, depressed, out of work. Mr. Sloane offers him a lodging and a salary in return for— after all, merely a little forbearance. All he has to do is to read to the old man, lay down the book awhile, with his finger in the place, and let him talk; take it up again, read another dozen pages and submit to another commentary. Then to write a dozen pages under his dictation—to suggest a word, polish off a period, or help him out with a reluctant idea or a half-remembered fact. This is all, I say; and yet this is much. Theodore's apparent success proves it to be much, as well as the old man's satisfaction. It's a part; he plays it. He uses tact; he has taken a reef in his pride; he has clipped the sting of his conscience, he listens, he talks, conciliates, accommodates, flatters—does it as well as many a worse man—does it far better than I. I might dominate Mr. Sloane, but I doubt that I could serve him. But after all, it's not a matter of better and worse. In every son of woman there are two men—the practical man and the dreamer. We live for our dreams—but, meanwhile, we live by our wits. When the dreamer is a poet, his brother is an artist. Theodore is essentially a man of taste. If he were not destined to become a high priest among moralists, he might be a prince among connoisseurs. He plays his part then, artistically, with taste, with relish—with all the *finesse* of his delicate fancy. How can Mr. Sloane fail to believe that he possesses a paragon? He is no such fool as to misconceive a *belle âme* when a *belle âme* comes in his way. He confidentially assured me this morning that Theodore has the most beautiful mind in the world, but that it's a pity he's so simple as not to suspect it. If he only doesn't ruin him with his flattery!

19th.—I'm certainly fortunate among men. This morning when, tentatively, I spoke of understaying my month, Mr. Sloane rose from his seat in horror, and declared that for the present I must regard his house as my home. "Come, come," he said, "when you leave this place where do you intend to go?" Where, indeed? I graciously allowed Mr. Sloane to have the best of the argument. Theodore assures me that he appreciates these and other affabilities, and that I have made what he calls a "conquest" of his venerable heart. Poor, battered, bamboozled old organ! he would have one believe that it has a most tragical record of capture and recapture. At all events, it appears that I'm master of the citadel. For the present I have no wish to evacuate. I feel, nevertheless, in some far-off corner of my soul, that I ought to shoulder my victorious banner and advance to more fruitful triumphs.

I blush for my slothful inaction. It isn't that I'm willing to stay here a month, but that I'm willing to stay here six. Such is the charming, disgusting truth. Have I actually outlived the age of energy? Have I survived my ambition, my integrity, my self-respect? Verily I ought to have survived the habit of asking myself silly questions. I made up my mind long ago that I care deeply for nothing save my own personal comfort, and I don't care for that sufficiently to secure it at the cost of acute temporary suffering. I have a passion for nothing—not even for life. I know very well the appearance I make in the world. I pass for intelligent, well-informed, accomplished, amiable, strong. I'm supposed to have a keen relish for letters, for music, for science, for art. There was a time when I fancied I cared for scientific research; but I know now that I care for it as little as I really do for Shakespeare, for Rubens, for Rossini. When I was younger, I used to find a certain entertainment in the contemplation of men and women. I liked to see them hurrying on each other's heels across the stage. But I'm sick and tired of them now; not that I'm a misanthrope, God forbid. They're not worth hating. I never knew but one creature who was, and her I went and loved. To be consistent, I ought to have hated my mother—and now I ought to hate Theodore. But I don't—truly, on the whole, I don't—any more than I love him. I firmly believe that a large portion of his happiness rests upon his devout conviction that I really care for him. He believes in that, as he believes in all the rest of it—in my knowledge, my music, my underlying "earnestness," my sense of beauty and love of truth. Oh, for a *man* among them all—a fellow with eyes in his head—eyes that would look me through and through, and flash out in scorn of my nothingness. Then, perhaps, I might answer him with rage; *then*, perhaps, I might feel a simple, healthy emotion.

In the name of bare nutrition—in the fear of starvation— what am I to do? (I was obliged this morning to borrow ten dollars from Theodore, who remembered gleefully that he has been owing me no less than twenty-five dollars for the past four years, and in fact has preserved a note to this effect). Within the last week I have hatched a desperate scheme. I have deliberately conceived the idea of marrying money. Why not accept and utilize the goods of the gods? It is not my fault, after all, if I pass for a superior fellow. Why not admit that practically, mechanically—as I may say—maritally, I *may* be a superior fellow? I warrant myself, at least, thoroughly gentle. I should never beat my wife; I doubt that I should ever snub her. Assume that her fortune has the proper number of zeros and that she herself is one of them, and I can actually imagine her adoring me. It's not impossible that I've hit the nail and solved my riddle. Curiously, as I look back upon my brief career, it all seems to tend in a certain way to this consummation. It has its graceful curves and crooks, indeed, and here and there a passionate tangent; but on the whole, if I were to unfold it here *à la* Hogarth, what better legend could I scrawl beneath the series of pictures than So-and-So's Progress to a Mercenary Marriage?

Coming events do what we all know with their shadows. My glorious destiny is, perhaps, not far off. I already feel throughout my person a magnificent languor—as from the possession of past opulence. Or is it simply my sense of perfect well-being in this perfectly appointed home? Is it simply the absolutely comfortable life I lead in this delicious old house? At all events, the house *is* delicious, and my only complaint of Mr. Sloane is, that instead of an old widower, he's not an old widow (or I a young maid), so that I might marry him, survive him, and dwell forever in this rich and mellow home. As I write here, at my bedroom table, I have only to stretch out an arm and raise the window curtain, to see the thick-planted garden budding and breathing, and growing in the moonshine. Far above, in the liquid darkness, sails the glory-freighted orb of the moon; beneath, in its light, lies the lake, in murmuring, troubled sleep; around stand the gentle mountains, wearing the cold reflection on their shoulders, or hiding it away in their glens. So much for midnight. To-morrow the sun will be lovely with the beauty of day. Under one aspect or another I have it always before me. At the end of the garden is moored a boat, in which Theodore and I have repeatedly explored the surface of the lake, and visited the mild wilderness of its shores. What lovely landward caves and bays—what alder-smothered creeks—what lily-sheeted pools—what sheer steep hill-sides, darkening the water with the downward image of their earthy greenness. I confess that in these excursions Theodore does the rowing and I the contemplation. Mr. Sloane avoids the water—on account of the dampness, he says; but because he's afraid of drowning, I suspect.

22d.—Theodore is right. The *bonhomme* has taken me into his favor. I protest I don't see how he was to escape it. I doubt that there has ever been a better flattered man. I don't blush for it. In one coin or another I must repay his hospitality—which is certainly very liberal. Theodore advises him, helps him, comforts him; I amuse him, surprise him, deprave him. This is speaking vastly well for my power. He pretends to be surprised at nothing, and to possess in perfection—poor, pitiable old fop—the art *nil admirari*; but repeatedly, I know, I have clear outskipped his fancy. As for his depravity, it's a very pretty piece of wickedness, but it strikes me as a purely intellectual matter. I imagine him never to have had any downright senses. He may have been unclean; morally, he's not over savory now; but he never can have been what the French call a *viveur*. He's too delicate, he's of a feminine turn; and what woman was ever a *viveur*? He likes to sit in his chair, and read scandal, talk scandal, make scandal, so far as he may without catching a cold or incurring a headache. I already feel as if I had known him a lifetime. I read him as clearly, I think, as if I had. I know the type to which he belongs; I have encountered, first and last, a round dozen of specimens. He's neither more nor less than a gossip—a gossip flanked by a coxcomb and an egotist. He's shallow, vain, cold, superstitious, timid, pretentious, capricious; a pretty jumble of virtues! And yet, for all this, he has his good points. His caprices are sometimes generous, I imagine; and his aversion to the harsh, cruel, and hideous, frequently takes the form of positive kindness and charity. His memory (for trifles) is remarkable, and (where his own performances are not involved) his taste is excellent. He has no will for evil more than for good. He is the victim, however, of more illusions with regard to himself than I ever knew a human heart to find lodging for. At the age of twenty, poor, ignorant and remarkably handsome, he married a woman of immense wealth, many years his senior. At the end of three years she very considerately went out of the world, and left him to the enjoyment of his freedom and riches. If he had remained poor, he might from time to time have rubbed at random against the truth, and would still be wearing a few of its sacred smutches on his sleeve. But he wraps himself in his money as in a wadded dressing gown, and goes trundling through life on his little gold wheels, as warm and close as an unweaned baby. The greater part of his career, from his marriage to within fifteen years ago, was spent in Europe, which, superficially, he knows very well. He has lived in fifty places, known hundreds of people, and spent thousands of dollars. At one time, I believe, he spent a few thousands too many, trembled for an instant on the verge of a pecuniary crash; but recovered himself, and found himself more frightened than hurt, but loudly admonished to lower his pitch. He passed five years in a species of

penitent seclusion on the lake of—I forget what (his genius
seems to be partial to lakes), and formed the rudiments of his
present magnificent taste for literature; I can't call it anything
but magnificent, so long as it must needs have Theodore Lisle
as a ministrant. At the close of this period, by economy, he
had become a rich man again. The control and discipline exercised during these years upon his desires and his natural
love of luxury, must have been the sole act of real resolution
in the history of Mr. Sloane's life. It was rendered possible by
his morbid, his actually pusillanimous dread of poverty; he
doesn't feel safe without half a million between him and starvation. Meanwhile he had turned from a young man into an
old man; his health was broken, his spirit was jaded, and I
imagine, to do him justice, that he began to feel certain natural, filial longings for this dear American mother of us all.
They say the most hopeless truants and triflers have come to
it. He came to it, at all events; he packed up his books and
pictures and gimcracks, and bade farewell to Europe. This
house which he now occupies belonged to his wife's estate.
She had, for sentimental reasons of her own, commended it
to his particular regard. On his return he came to see it, fancied it, turned a parcel of carpenters and upholsterers into it,
and by inhabiting it for twelve years, transformed it into the
perfect dwelling which I find it. Here he has spent all his
time, with the exception of a regular winter's visit to New
York—a practice recently discontinued, owing to the aggravation of his physical condition and the projection of these
famous memoirs. His life has finally come to be passed in
comparative solitude. He tells of various distant relatives, as
well as intimate friends of both sexes, who used formerly to
be largely entertained at his cost, but with each of them, in
the course of time, he seems to have clipped the thread of intercourse. Throughout life, evidently, he has shown great delicacy of tact in keeping himself clean of parasites. Rich, lonely
and vain, he must have been fair game for the race of social
sycophants and cormorants; and it's richly to the credit of his
shrewdness and good sense, that he has suffered so little
havoc in substance and happiness. Apparently they've been a
sad lot of bunglers. I maintain that he's to be—how shall I say
it?—possessed. But you must work in obedience to certain

definite laws. Doctor Jones, his physician, tells me that in point of fact he has had for the past ten years an unbroken series of favorites, *protégés*, and heirs presumptive; but that each, in turn, by some fatally false movement, has fairly unjointed his nose. The doctor declares, moreover, that they were, at best, a wofully common set of people. Gradually the old man seems to have developed a preference for two or three strictly exquisite intimates, over a throng of your vulgar charmers. His tardy literary schemes, too—fruit of his all but sapless senility—have absorbed more and more of his time and attention. The end of it all is, therefore, that Theodore and I have him quite to ourselves, and that it behooves us to keep our noses on our faces, and our heads on our shoulders.

Poor, pretentious old simpleton! It's not his fault, after all, that he fancies himself a great little man. How are you to judge of the stature of mankind when men have forever addressed you on their knees? Peace and joy to his innocent fatuity! He believes himself the most rational of men; in fact, he's the most vapidly sentimental. He fancies himself a philosopher, a thinker, a student. His philosophy and his erudition are quite of a piece; they would lie at ease in the palm of Theodore's hand. He prides himself on his good manners, his urbanity, his unvarying observance of the becoming. My private impression is, that his cramped old bosom contains unsuspected treasures of cunning impertinence. He takes his stand on his speculative audacity—his direct undaunted gaze at the universe; in truth, his mind is haunted by a hundred dingy old-world spectres and theological phantasms. He fancies himself one of the weightiest of men; he is essentially one of the lightest. He deems himself ardent, impulsive, passionate, magnanimous—capable of boundless enthusiasm for an idea or a sentiment. It is clear to me that, on no occasion of pure, disinterested action can he ever have taken a timely, positive second step. He fancies, finally, that he has drained the cup of life to the dregs; that he has known, in its bitterest intensity, every emotion of which the human spirit is capable; that he has loved, struggled, and suffered. Stuff and nonsense, all of it. He has never loved anyone but himself; he has never suffered from anything but an undigested supper or an exploded pretension; he has never touched with the end of his lips the vulgar bowl from which the mass of mankind quaffs its great floods of joy and sorrow. Well, the long and short of it all is, that I honestly pity him. He may have given sly knocks in his life, but he can't hurt *me*. I pity his ignorance, his weakness, his timidity. He has tasted the real sweetness of life no more than its bitterness; he has never dreamed, or wandered, or dared; he has never known any but mercenary affection; neither men nor women have risked aught for *him*—for his good spirits, his good looks, and his poverty. How I should like to give him, for once, a real sensation!

26th.—I took a row this morning with Theodore a couple of miles along the lake, to a point where we went ashore and lounged away an hour in the sunshine, which is still very comfortable. Poor Theodore seems troubled about many things. For one, he is troubled about me; he is actually more anxious about my future than I myself; he thinks better of me than I do of myself; he is so deucedly conscientious, so scrupulous, so averse to giving offence or to *brusquer* any situation before it has played itself out, that he shrinks from betraying his apprehensions or asking any direct questions. But I know that he is dying to extort from me some positive profession of practical interest and faith. I catch myself in the act of taking—heaven forgive me!—a half-malicious joy in confounding his expectations—leading his generous sympathies off the scent by various extravagant protestations of mock cynicism and malignity. But in Theodore I have so firm a friend that I shall have a long row to hoe if I ever find it needful to make him forswear his devotion—abjure his admiration. He admires me—that's absolute; he takes my moral infirmities for the eccentricities of genius, and they only impart an extra flavor—a *haut goût*—to the richness of my charms. Nevertheless, I can see that he is disappointed. I have even less to show, after this lapse of years, than he had hoped. Heaven help us! little enough it must strike him as being. What an essential absurdity there is in our being friends at all. I honestly believe we shall end with hating each other. They are all very well now—our diversity, our oppugnancy, our cross purposes; now that we are at play together they serve as a theme for jollity. But when we settle down to work—ah me! for the tug of war. I wonder, as it is, that Theodore keeps his patience with me. His education since we parted should tend logically to make him despise me. He has studied, thought, suffered, loved—loved those very plain sisters and nieces. Poor me! how should I be virtuous? I have no sisters, plain or pretty!— nothing to love, work for, live for. Friend Theodore, if you are going one of these days to despise me and drop me—in the sacred name of comfort, come to the point at once, and make an end of our common agony!

He is troubled, too, about Mr. Sloane. His attitude toward the *bonhomme* quite passes my comprehension. It's the queerest jumble of contraries. He penetrates him, contemns him— yet respects and admires him. It all comes of the poor boy's shrinking New England conscience. He's afraid to give his perceptions a fair chance, lest, forsooth, they should look over his neighbor's wall. He'll not understand that he may as well sacrifice the old man for a lamb as for a sheep. His view of the gentleman, therefore, is a perfect tissue of cobwebs—a jumble of half-way sorrows, and wide-drawn charities, and hair-breadth 'scapes from utter damnation, and sudden platitudes of generosity; fit, all of it, to make an angel curse!

"The man's a perfect egotist and fool," say I, "but I like him." Now Theodore likes him—or rather wants to like him; but he can't reconcile it to his self-respect—fastidious deity!— to like a fool. Why the deuce can't he leave it alone altogether? It's a purely practical matter. He ought to do the duties of his place all the better for having his head clear of officious sentiment. I don't believe in disinterested service; and Theodore is too desperately bent on preserving his disinterestedness. With me, it's different. I'm perfectly free to love the *bonhomme*—for a fool. I'm neither a scribe nor a Pharisee; I'm—ah me, *what* am I?

And then, Theodore is troubled about his sisters. He's afraid he's not doing his duty by them. He thinks he ought to be with them—to be getting a larger salary—to be teaching his nieces. I'm not versed in such questions. Perhaps he ought.

MAY 3d.—This morning Theodore sent me word that he was ill and unable to get up; upon which I immediately repaired to his bedside. He had caught cold, was sick and a little feverish. I urged him to make no attempt to leave his

room, and assured him that I would do what I could to reconcile Mr. Sloane to his non-attendance. This I found an easy
matter. I read to him for a couple of hours, wrote four letters—one in French—and then talked a good two hours
more. I have done more talking, by the way, in the last fortnight, than in any previous twelve months—much of it, too,
none of the wisest, nor, I may add, of the most fastidiously
veracious. In a little discussion, two or three days ago, with
Theodore, I came to the point and roundly proclaimed that
in gossiping with Mr. Sloane I made no scruple, for our common satisfaction, of discreetly using the embellishments of fiction. My confession gave him "that turn," as Mrs. Gamp
would say, that his present illness may be the result of it.
Nevertheless, poor, dear fellow, I trust he'll be on his legs to-
morrow. This afternoon, somehow, I found myself really in
the humor of talking. There was something propitious in the
circumstances; a hard, cold rain without, a wood-fire in the
library, the *bonhomme* puffing cigarettes in his arm-chair, beside him a portfolio of newly imported prints and photographs, and—Theodore tucked safely away in bed. Finally,
when I brought our *tête-à-tête* to a close (taking good care to
understay my welcome) Mr. Sloane seized me by both hands
and honored me with one of his venerable grins. "Max," he
said—"you must let me call you Max—you're the most delightful man I ever knew."

Verily, there's some virtue left in me yet. I believe I fairly
blushed.

"Why didn't I know you ten years ago?" the old man went
on. "Here are ten years lost."

"Ten years ago, my dear Mr. Sloane," quoth Max, "I was
hardly worth your knowing."

"But I did know you!" cried the *bonhomme*. "I knew you in
knowing your mother."

Ah! my mother again. When the old man begins that chapter I feel like telling him to blow out his candle and go to
bed.

"At all events," he continued, "we must make the most of
the years that remain. I'm a poor sick old fellow, but I've no
notion of dying. You'll not get tired of me and want to go
away?"

"I'm devoted to you, sir," I said. "But I must be looking up some work, you know."

"Work! Bah! I'll give you work. I'll give you wages."

"I'm afraid," I said, with a smile, "that you'll want to give me the wages without the work." And then I declared that I must go up and look at poor Theodore.

The *bonhomme* still kept my hands. "I wish very much," he said, "that I could get you to love me as well as you do poor Theodore."

"Ah, don't talk about love, Mr. Sloane. I'm no lover."

"Don't you love your friend?"

"Not as he deserves."

"Nor as he loves you, perhaps?"

"He loves me, I'm afraid, far more than I deserve."

"Well, Max," my host pursued, "we can be good friends, all the same. We don't need a hocus-pocus of false sentiment. We are *men*, aren't we?—men of sublime good sense." And just here, as the old man looked at me, the pressure of his hands deepened to a convulsive grasp, and the bloodless mask of his countenance was suddenly distorted with a nameless fear. "Ah, my dear young man!" he cried, "come and be a son to me—the son of my age and desolation! For God's sake don't leave me to pine and die alone!"

I was amazed—and I may say I was moved. Is it true, then, that this poor old heart contains such measureless depths of horror and longing? I take it that he's mortally afraid of death. I assured him on my honor that he may henceforth call upon me for any service.

8th.—Theodore's indisposition turned out more serious than I expected. He has been confined to his room till to-day. This evening he came down to the library in his dressing gown. Decidedly, Mr. Sloane is an eccentric, but hardly, as Theodore thinks, a "charming" one. There is something extremely curious in the exhibition of his caprices—the incongruous fits and starts, as it were, of his taste. For some reason, best known to himself, he took it into his head to deem it a want of delicacy, of respect, of *savoir-vivre*—of heaven knows what—that poor Theodore, who is still weak and languid, should enter the sacred precinct of his study in the vulgar drapery of a dressing-gown. The sovereign trouble with the *bonhomme* is an absolute lack of the instinct of justice. He's of the real feminine turn—I believe I have written it before—without a ray of woman's virtues. I honestly believe that I might come into his study in my night-shirt and he would smile upon it as a picturesque *déshabillé*. But for poor Theodore to-night there was nothing but scowls and frowns, and barely a civil inquiry about his health. But poor Theodore is not such a fool, either; he'll not die of a snubbing; I never said he was a weakling. Once he fairly saw from what quarter the wind blew, he bore the master's brutality with the utmost coolness and gallantry. Can it be that Mr. Sloane really wishes to drop him? The delicious old brute! He understands favor and friendship only as a selfish rapture—a reaction, an infatuation, an act of aggressive, exclusive patronage. It's not a bestowal with him, but a transfer, and half his pleasure in causing his sun to shine is that—being wofully near its setting—it will produce a number of delectable shadows. He wants to cast my shadow, I suppose, on Theodore; fortunately I'm not altogether an opaque body. Since Theodore was taken ill he has been into his room but once, and has sent him none but the scantiest messages. I, too, have been much less attentive than I should have wished to be; but my time has not been my own. It has been, every moment of it, at Mr. Sloane's disposal. He actually runs after me; he devours me; he makes a fool of himself, and is trying hard to make one of me. I find that he will stand—that, in fact, he actually enjoys—a certain kind of humorous snubbing. He likes anything that will tickle his fancy, impart a flavor to our relations, remind him of his old odds and ends of novels and memoirs. I have fairly stepped into Theodore's shoes, and done—with what I feel in my bones to be vastly inferior skill and taste—all the reading, writing, condensing, expounding, transcribing and advising that he has been accustomed to do. I have driven with the *bonhomme*; played chess and cribbage with him; and beaten him, bullied him, contradicted him; and forced him into going out on the water under my charge. Who shall say, after this, that I haven't done my best to discourage his advances, confound his benevolence? As yet, my efforts are vain; in fact they quite turn to my own confusion. Mr. Sloane is so vastly thankful at having escaped from the lake with his life that he seems actually to look upon me as a kind of romantic preserver and protector. Faugh! what tiresome nonsense it all is! But one thing is certain, it can't last forever. Admit that he *has* cast Theodore out and taken me in. He will speedily discover that he has made a pretty mess of it, and that he had much better have left well enough alone. He likes my reading and writing now, but in a month he'll begin to hate them. He'll miss Theodore's healthy, unerring, impersonal judgment. What an advantage that pure and luminous nature has over mine, after all. I'm for days, he's for years; he for the long run, I for the short. I, perhaps, am intended for success, but he alone for happiness. He holds in his heart a tiny sacred particle, which leavens his whole being and keeps it pure and sound—a faculty of admiration and respect. For him human nature is still a wonder and a mystery; it bears a divine stamp—Mr. Sloane's tawdry organism as well as the best.

13th.—I have refused, of course, to supplant Theodore further, in the exercise of his functions, and he has resumed his morning labors with Mr. Sloane. I, on my side, have spent these morning hours in scouring the country on that capital black mare, the use of which is one of the perquisites of Theodore's place. The days have been magnificent—the heat of the sun tempered by a murmuring, wandering wind, the whole north a mighty ecstasy of sound and verdure, the sky a far-away vault of bended blue. Not far from the mill at M., the other end of the lake, I met, for the third time, that very pretty young girl, who reminds me so forcibly of A. L. She makes so very frank and fearless a use of her eyes that I ventured to stop and bid her good-morning. She seems nothing loth to an acquaintance. She's an out-and-out barbarian in speech, but her eyes look as if they had drained the noon-day heavens of their lustre. These rides to me good; I had got into a sadly worrying, brooding habit of thought.

What has got into Theodore I know not; his illness seems to have left him strangely affected. He has fits of sombre reserve, alternating with spasms of extravagant gayety. He avoids me at times for hours together, and then he comes and looks at me with an inscrutable smile, as if he were on the verge of a burst of confidence—which again is swallowed up in the darkness of his silence. Is he hatching some astounding benefit to his species? Is he working to bring about my removal to a higher sphere of action? *Nous verrons bien.*

18th.—Theodore threatens departure. He received this morning a letter from one of his sisters—the young widow—announcing her engagement to a minister whose acquaintance she has recently made, and intimating her expectation of an immediate union with the gentleman—a ceremony which would require Theodore's attendance. Theodore, in high good humor, read the letter aloud at breakfast—and to tell the truth a charming letter it was. He then spoke of his having to go on to the wedding; a proposition to which Mr. Sloane graciously assented—but with truly startling amplitude. "I shall be sorry to lose you after so happy a connection," said the old man. Theodore turned pale, stared a moment, and then, recovering his color and his composure, declared that he should have no objection in life to coming back.

"Bless your soul!" cried the *bonhomme*, "you don't mean to say you'll leave your little sister all alone?"

To which Theodore replied that he would arrange for her to live with his brother-in-law. "It's the only proper thing," he declared, in a tone which was not to be gainsaid. It has come to this, then, that Mr. Sloane actually wants to turn him out of the house. Oh, the precious old fool! He keeps smiling an uncanny smile, which means, as I read it, that if the poor boy once departs he shall never return on the old footing—for all his impudence!

20th.—This morning, at breakfast, we had a terrific scene. A letter arrives for Theodore; he opens it, turns white and red, frowns, falters, and then informs us that the clever widow has broken off her engagement. No wedding, therefore, and no departure for Theodore. The *bonhomme* was furious. In his fury he took the liberty of calling poor Mrs. Parker (the sister) a very impolite name. Theodore rebuked him, with perfect good taste, and kept his temper.

"If my opinions don't suit you, Mr. Lisle," the old man broke out, "and my mode of expressing them displeases you, you know you can easily remove yourself from within my jurisdiction."

"My dear Mr. Sloane," said Theodore, "your opinions, as a general rule, interest me deeply, and have never ceased to act most beneficially upon the formation of my own. Your mode of expressing them is charming, and I wouldn't for the world, after all our pleasant intercourse, separate from you in bitterness. Only, I repeat, your qualification of my sister's conduct was perfectly uncalled for. If you knew her, you would be the first to admit it."

There was something in Theodore's aspect and manner, as he said these words, which puzzled me all the morning. After dinner, finding myself alone with him, I told him I was glad he was not obliged to go away. He looked at me with the mysterious smile I have mentioned—a smile which actually makes him handsome—thanked me and fell into meditation. As this bescribbled chronicle is the record of my follies, as well as of my *haut faits*, I needn't hesitate to say that, for a moment, I was keenly exasperated. What business has poor, transparent Theodore to put on the stony mask of the sphinx and play the inscrutable? What right has he to do so with me especially, in whom he has always professed an absolute confidence? Just as I was about to cry out, "Come, my dear boy, this affectation of mystery has lasted quite long enough—favor me at last with the result of your cogitation!"—as I was on the point of thus expressing my impatience of his continued solemnity of demeanor, the oracle at last addressed itself to utterance.

"You see, my dear Max," he said, "I can't, in justice to myself, go away in obedience to any such intimation as that vouchsafed to me this morning. What do you think of my actual footing here?"

Theodore's actual footing here seemed to me essentially uncomfortable; of course I said so.

"Nay, I assure you it's not," he answered. "I should feel, on the contrary, very uncomfortable to think that I'd come away, except by my own choice. You see a man can't afford to cheapen himself. What are you laughing at?"

"I'm laughing, in the first place, my dear fellow, to hear on your lips the language of cold calculation; and in the second place, at your odd notion of the process by which a man keeps himself up in the market."

"I assure you that it's the correct notion. I came here as a favor to Mr. Sloane; it was expressly understood so. The occupation was distasteful to me. I had from top to bottom to accommodate myself to my duties. I had to compromise with a dozen convictions, preferences, prejudices. I don't take such things easily; I take them hard; and when once the labor is achieved I can't consent to have it thrown away. If Mr. Sloane needed me then, he needs me still. I am ignorant of any change having taken place in his intentions, or in his means of satisfying them. I came not to amuse him, but to do a certain work; I hope to remain until the work is completed. To go away sooner is to make a confession of incapacity which, I protest, costs too great a sacrifice to my vanity."

Theodore spoke these words with a face which I have never seen him wear; a fixed, mechanical smile; a hard, dry glitter in his eyes; a harsh, strident tone in his voice—in his whole physiognomy a gleam, as it were, a note of defiance. Now I confess that for defiance I have never been conscious of an especial relish. When I'm defied, I'm ugly. "My dear man," I replied, "your sentiments do you prodigious credit. Your very ingenious theory of your present situation, as well as your extremely pronounced sense of your personal value, are calculated to insure you a degree of practical success which can very well dispense with the furtherance of my poor good wishes." Oh, the grimness of his listening smile—and I suppose I may add of my own physiognomy! But I have ceased to be puzzled. Theodore's conduct for the past ten days is suddenly illumined with a backward, lurid ray. Here are a few plain truths, which it behooves me to take to heart—commit to memory. Theodore is jealous of me. Theodore hates me. Theodore has been seeking for the past three months to see his name written, last but not least, in a certain testamentary document: "Finally, I bequeath to my dear young friend, Theodore Lisle, in return for invaluable services and unfailing devotion, the bulk of my property, real and personal, consisting of—" (hereupon follows an exhaustive enumeration of houses, lands, public securities, books, pictures, horses, and dogs). It is for this that he has toiled, and watched, and prayed; submitted to intellectual weariness and spiritual torture; made his terms with levity, blasphemy, and insult. For

this he sets his teeth and tightens his grasp; for this he'll fight.
Merciful powers! it's an immense weight off one's mind.
There are nothing, then, but vulgar, common laws; no sublime exceptions, no transcendent anomalies. Theodore's a
knave, a hypo—nay, nay; stay, irreverent hand!—Theodore's a
man! Well, that's all I want. *He* wants fight—he shall have it.
Have I got, at last, my simple, natural emotion?

21st.—I have lost no time. This evening, late, after I had
heard Theodore go to his room (I had left the library early,
on the pretext of having letters to write), I repaired to Mr.
Sloane, who had not yet gone to bed, and informed him that
it is necessary I shall at once leave him, and seek some occupation in New York. He felt the blow; it brought him straight
down on his marrow-bones. He went through the whole
gamut of his arts and graces; he blustered, whimpered, en-
treated, flattered. He tried to drag in Theodore's name; but
this I, of course, prevented. But, finally, why, *why*, WHY, after
all my promises of fidelity, must I thus cruelly desert him?
Then came my supreme avowal: I have spent my last penny;
while I stay, I'm a beggar. The remainder of this extraordinary
scene I have no power to describe: how the *bonhomme*,
touched, inflamed, inspired, by the thought of my destitu-
tion, and at the same time annoyed, perplexed, bewildered at
having to commit himself to any practical alleviation of it,
worked himself into a nervous frenzy which deprived him of
a clear sense of the value of his words and his actions; how I,
prompted by the irresistible spirit of my desire to leap astride
of his weakness, and ride it hard into the goal of my dreams,
cunningly contrived to keep his spirit at the fever point, so
that strength, and reason, and resistance should burn themselves out. I shall probably never again have such a sensation
as I enjoyed to-night—actually feel a heated human heart
throbbing, and turning, and struggling in my grasp; know its
pants, its spasms, its convulsions, and its final senseless quiescence. At half-past one o'clock, Mr. Sloane got out of his
chair, went to his secretary, opened a private drawer, and took
out a folded paper. "This is my will," he said, "made some
seven weeks ago. If you'll stay with me, I'll destroy it."

"Really, Mr. Sloane," I said, "if you think my purpose is to
exert any pressure upon your testamentary inclinations—"

"I'll tear it in pieces," he cried; "I'll burn it up. I shall be as sick as a dog to-morrow; but I'll do it. A-a-h!"

He clapped his hand to his side, as if in sudden, overwhelming pain, and sank back fainting into his chair. A single glance assured me that he was unconscious. I possessed myself of the paper, opened it, and perceived that the will is almost exclusively in Theodore's favor. For an instant, a savage, puerile feeling of hate sprang erect in my bosom, and I came within an ace of obeying my foremost impulse—that of casting the document into the fire. Fortunately, my reason overtook my passion, though for a moment 'twas an even race. I replaced the paper in the secretary, closed it, and rang the bell for Robert (the old man's servant). Before he came I stood watching the poor, pale remnant of mortality before me, and wondering whether those feeble life-gasps were numbered. He was as white as a sheet, grimacing with pain—horribly ugly. Suddenly, he opened his eyes; they met my own; I fell on my knees and took his hands. They closed on mine with a grasp strangely akin to the rigidity of death. Nevertheless, since then he has revived, and has relapsed again into a comparatively healthy sleep. Robert seems to know how to deal with him.

22d.—Mr. Sloane is seriously ill—out of his mind and unconscious of people's identity. The doctor has been here, off and on, all day, but this evening reports improvement. I have kept out of the old man's room, and confined myself to my own, reflecting largely upon the odd contingency of his immediate death. Does Theodore know of the will? Would it occur to him to divide the property? Would it occur to me, in his place? We met at dinner, and talked in a grave, desultory, friendly fashion. After all, he's an excellent fellow. I don't hate him. I don't even dislike him. He jars on me, *il m'agace*; but that's no reason why I should do him an evil turn. Nor shall I. The property is a fixed idea, that's all. I shall get it if I can. We're fairly matched. Before heaven, no, we're not fairly matched! Theodore has a conscience.

23d.—I'm restless and nervous—and for good reasons. Scribbling here keeps me quiet. This morning Mr. Sloane is better; feeble and uncertain in mind, but unmistakably on the mend. I may confess now that I feel relieved of a weighty

burden. Last night I hardly slept a wink. I lay awake listening
to the pendulum of my clock. It seemed to say "He lives—he
dies." I fully expected to have it stop suddenly at *dies.* But it
kept going all the morning, and to a decidedly more lively
tune. In the afternoon the old man sent for me. I found him
in his great muffled bed, with his face the color of damp
chalk, and his eyes glowing faintly, like torches half-stamped
out. I was forcibly struck with the utter loneliness of his lot.
For all human attendance, my villainous self grinning at his
bedside, and old Robert without, listening, doubtless, at the
keyhole. The *bonhomme* stared at me stupidly; then seemed to
know me, and greeted me with a sickly smile. It was some
moments before he was able to speak. At last he faintly bade
me to descend into the library, open the secret drawer of the
secretary (which he contrived to direct me how to do), possess myself of his will, and burn it up. He appears to have
forgotten his having removed it, night before last. I told
him that I had an insurmountable aversion to any personal
dealings with the document. He smiled, patted the back of
my hand, and requested me, in that case, to get it, at least,
and bring it to him. I couldn't deny him that favor? No, I
couldn't, indeed. I went down to the library, therefore, and
on entering the room found Theodore standing by the fire-
place with a bundle of papers. The secretary was open. I
stood still, looking from the ruptured cabinet to the documents in his hand. Among them I recognized, by its shape
and size, the paper of which I had intended to possess myself.
Without delay I walked straight up to him. He looked surprised, but not confused. "I'm afraid I shall have to trouble
you," I said, "to surrender one of those papers."

"Surrender, Max? To anything of your own you are perfectly welcome. I didn't know, however, that you made use of
Mr. Sloane's secretary. I was looking up some notes of my
own making, in which I conceive I have a property."

"This is what I want, Theodore," I said; and I drew the
will, unfolded, from between his hands. As I did so his eyes
fell upon the superscription, "Last Will and Testament.
March. F. S." He flushed a splendid furious crimson. Our
eyes met. Somehow—I don't how or why, or for that matter

why not—I burst into a violent peal of laughter. Theodore stood staring, with two hot, bitter tears in his eyes.

"Of course you think," he said, "that I came to ferret out that thing."

I shrugged my shoulders—those of my body only. I confess, morally, I was on my knees with contrition, but there was a fascination in it—a fatality. I remembered that in the hurry of my movements, the other evening, I had replaced the will simply in one of the outer drawers of the cabinet, among Theodore's own papers; doubtless where he had taken it up. "Mr. Sloane sent me for it," I said.

"Very good, I'm glad to hear he's well enough to think of such things."

"He means to destroy it."

"I hope, then, he has another made."

"Mentally, I suppose he has."

"Unfortunately, his weakness isn't mental—or exclusively so."

"Oh, he'll live to make a dozen more," I said. "Do you know the purport of this one?"

Theodore's color, by this time, had died away into a sombre paleness. He shook his head. The doggedness of the movement provoked me. I wished to arouse his curiosity. "I have his commission," I rejoined, "to destroy it."

Theodore smiled superbly. "It's not a task I envy you," he said.

"I should think not—especially if you knew the import of the will." He stood with folded arms, regarding me with the remote contempt of his rich blue eyes. I couldn't stand it. "Come, it's your property," I cried. "You're sole legatee. I give it up to you." And I thrust the paper into his hand.

He received it mechanically; but after a pause, bethinking himself, he unfolded it and cast his eyes over the contents. Then he slowly refolded it and held it a moment with a tremulous hand. "You say that Mr. Sloane directed you to destroy it?" he finally asked.

"I say so."

"And that you know the contents?"

"Exactly."

"And that you were about to comply?"

"On the contrary, I declined."

Theodore fixed his eyes, for a moment, on the superscription, and then raised them again to my face. "Thank you, Max," he said. "You've left me a real satisfaction." He tore the sheet across and threw the bits into the fire. We stood watching them burn. "Now he can make another," said Theodore.

"Twenty others," I replied.

"No," said Theodore, "you'll take care of that."

"Upon my soul," I cried, "you're bitter!"

"No, not now. I worked off all my bitterness in these few words."

"Well, in consideration of that, I excuse them."

"Just as you please."

"Ah," said I, "there's a little bitterness left!"

"No, nothing but indifference. Farewell." And he put out his hand.

"Are you going away?"

"Of course I am. Farewell."

"Farewell, then. But isn't your departure rather sudden?"

"I ought to have gone three weeks ago—three weeks ago." I had taken his hand, he pulled it away, covered his face, and suddenly burst into tears.

"Is *that* indifference?" I asked.

"It's something you'll never know," he cried. "It's shame! I'm not sorry you should see it. It will suggest to you, perhaps, that my heart has never been in this filthy contest. Let me assure you, at any rate, that it hasn't; that it has had nothing but scorn for the base perversion of my pride and my ambition. These tears are tears of joy at their return—the return of the prodigals! Tears of sorrow—sorrow—"

He was unable to go on. He sank into a chair, burying his face in his handkerchief.

"For God's sake, Theodore," I said, "stick to the joy."

He rose to his feet again. "Well," he said, "it was for your sake that I parted with my self-respect; with your assistance I recover it."

"How for my sake?"

"For whom but you would I have gone as far as I did? For

what other purpose than that of keeping our friendship whole
would I have borne you company into this narrow pass? A
man whom I loved less I would long since have parted with.
You were needed—you and your incomparable gifts—to
bring me to this. You ennobled, exalted, enchanted the struggle. I *did* value my prospects of coming into Mr. Sloane's
property. I valued them for my poor sisters' sake, as well as for
my own, so long as they were the natural reward of conscientious service, and not the prize of hypocrisy and cunning.
With another man than you I never would have contested
such a prize. But I loved you, even as my rival. You played
with me, deceived me, betrayed me. I held my ground, hoping and longing to purge you of your error by the touch of
your old pledges of affection. I carried them in my heart. For
Mr. Sloane, from the moment that, under your magical influence, he revealed his extraordinary foibles, I had nothing but
contempt."

"And for me now?"

"Don't ask me. I don't trust myself."

"Hate, I suppose."

"Is that the best you can imagine? Farewell."

"Is it a serious farewell—farewell forever?"

"How can there be any other?"

"I'm sorry that such should be your point of view. It's
characteristic. All the more reason then that I should say a
word in self-defence. You accuse me of having 'played with
you, deceived you, betrayed you.' It seems to me that you're
quite off the track. You say you loved me. If so, you ought to
love me still. It wasn't for my virtue; for I never had any, or
pretended to any. In anything I have done recently, therefore,
there has been no inconsistency. I never pretended to love
you. I don't understand the word, in the sense you attach to
it. I don't understand the feeling, between men. To me, love
means quite another thing. You give it a meaning of your
own; you enjoy the profit of your invention; it's no more than
just that you should pay the penalty. Only, it seems to me
rather hard that *I* should pay it." Theodore remained silent;
but his brow slowly contracted into an inexorable frown. "Is
it still a 'serious farewell?' " I went on. "It seems a pity. After
this clearing up, it actually seems to me that I shall be on

better terms with you. No man can have a deeper appreciation of your excellent faculties, a keener enjoyment of your
society, your talk. I should very much regret the loss of
them."

"Have we, then, all this while," said Theodore, "understood each other so little?"

"Don't say 'we' and 'each other.' I think I have understood
you."

"Very likely. It's not for want of my having confessed myself."

"Well, Theodore, I do you justice. To me you've always
been over generous. Try now, and be just."

Still he stood silent, with his cold, hard frown. It was plain
that, if he was to come back to me, it would be from a vast
distance. What he was going to answer I know not. The door
opened, and Robert appeared, pale, trembling, his eyes starting in his head.

"I verily believe, gentlemen," he cried, "that poor Mr.
Sloane is dead in his bed."

There was a moment's perfect silence. "Amen," said I.
"Yes, Theodore, try and be just." Mr. Sloane had quietly died
in my absence.

24th.—Theodore went up to town this morning, having
shaken hands with me in silence before he started. Doctor
Jones, and Brookes the attorney, have been very officious;
and, by their advice, I have telegraphed to a certain Miss
Meredith, a maiden lady, by their account the nearest of kin;
or, in other words, simply a discarded half-niece of the de-
funct. She telegraphs back that she will arrive in person for
the funeral. I shall remain till she comes. I have lost a fortune;
but have I irretrievably lost a friend? I'm sure I can't say.

Gabrielle de Bergerac

Y GOOD old friend, in his white flannel dressing-gown, with his wig "removed," as they say of the dinner-service, by a crimson nightcap, sat for some moments gazing into the fire. At last he looked up. I knew what was coming. "Apropos, that little debt of mine—"

Not that the debt was really very little. But M. de Bergerac was a man of honor, and I knew I should receive my dues. He told me frankly that he saw no way, either in the present or the future, to reimburse me in cash. His only treasures were his paintings; would I choose one of them? Now I had not spent an hour in M. de Bergerac's little parlor twice a week for three winters, without learning that the Baron's paintings were, with a single exception, of very indifferent merit. On the other hand, I had taken a great fancy to the picture thus excepted. Yet, as I knew it was a family portrait, I hesitated to claim it. I refused to make a choice. M. de Bergerac, however, insisted, and I finally laid my finger on the charming image of my friend's aunt. I of course insisted, on my side, that M. de Bergerac should retain it during the remainder of his life, and so it was only after his decease that I came into possession of it. It hangs above my table as I write, and I have only to glance up at the face of my heroine to feel how vain it is to attempt to describe it. The portrait represents, in dimensions several degrees below those of nature, the head and shoulders of a young girl of two-and-twenty. The execution of the work is not especially strong, but it is thoroughly respectable, and one may easily see that the painter deeply appreciated the character of the face. The countenance is interesting rather than beautiful,—the forehead broad and open, the eyes slightly prominent, all the features full and firm and yet replete with gentleness. The head is slightly thrown back, as if in movement, and the lips are parted in a half-smile. And yet, in spite of this tender smile, I always fancy that the eyes are sad. The hair, dressed without powder, is rolled back over a high cushion (as I suppose), and adorned just above the left ear with a single white rose; while, on the other side, a heavy tress from behind hangs upon the neck with a sort of pastoral freedom. The neck is long and full, and the shoulders rather broad. The whole face has a look of mingled softness and decision, and seems to reveal a nature inclined to revery, affection, and repose, but capable of action and even of heroism. Mlle. de Bergerac died under the axe of the Terrorists. Now that I had acquired a certain property in this sole memento of her life, I felt a natural curiosity as to her character and history. Had M. de Bergerac known his aunt? Did he remember her? Would it be a tax on his good-nature to suggest that he should favor me with a few reminiscences? The old man fixed his eyes on the fire, and laid his hand on mine, as if his memory were fain to draw from both sources—from the ruddy glow and from my fresh young blood—a certain vital, quickening warmth. A mild, rich smile ran to his lips, and he pressed my hand. Somehow,—I hardly know why,—I felt touched almost to tears. Mlle. de Bergerac had been a familiar figure in her nephew's boyhood, and an important event in her life had formed a sort of episode in his younger days. It was a simple enough story; but such as it was, then and there, settling back into his chair, with the fingers of the clock wandering on to the small hours of the night, he told it with a tender, lingering garrulity. Such as it is, I repeat it. I shall give, as far as possible, my friend's words, or the English of them; but the reader will have to do without his inimitable accents. For them there is no English.

My father's household at Bergerac (said the Baron) consisted, exclusive of the servants, of five persons,—himself, my mother, my aunt (Mlle. de Bergerac), M. Coquelin (my preceptor), and M. Coquelin's pupil, the heir of the house. Perhaps, indeed, I should have numbered M. Coquelin among the servants. It is certain that my mother did. Poor little woman! she was a great stickler for the rights of birth. Her own birth was all she had, for she was without health, beauty, or fortune. My father, on his side, had very little of the last; his property of Bergerac yielded only enough to keep us without discredit. We gave no entertainments, and passed the whole year in the country; and as my mother was resolved that her weak health should do her a kindness as well as an injury, it was put forward as an apology for everything. We led at best a simple, somnolent sort of life. There was a terrible amount of leisure for rural gentlefolks in those good old days. We slept a great deal; we slept, you will say, on a volcano. It was a very different world from this patent new world of yours, and I may say that I was born on a different planet. Yes, in 1789, there came a great convulsion; the earth cracked and opened and broke, and this poor old *pays de France* went whirling through space. When I look back at my childhood, I look over a gulf. Three years ago, I spent a week at a country house in the neighborhood of Bergerac, and my hostess drove me over to the site of the chateau. The house has disappeared, and there's a homœopathic—hydropathic—what do you call it?—establishment erected in its place. But the little town is there, and the bridge on the river, and the church where I was christened, and the double row of lime-trees on the market-place, and the fountain in the middle. There's only one strik-ing difference: the sky is changed. I was born under the old sky. It was black enough, of course, if we had only had eyes to see it; but to me, I confess, it looked divinely blue. And in fact it was very bright,—the little patch under which I cast my juvenile shadow. An odd enough little shadow, you would have thought it. I was promiscuously cuddled and fondled. I was M. le Chevalier, and prospective master of Bergerac; and when I walked to church on Sunday, I had a dozen yards of lace on my coat and a little sword at my side. My poor mother did her best to make me good for nothing. She had her maid to curl my hair with the tongs, and she used with her own fingers to stick little black patches on my face. And yet I was a good deal neglected too, and I would go for days with black patches of another sort. I'm afraid I should have got very little education if a kind Providence hadn't given me poor M. Coquelin. A kind Providence, that is, and my father; for with my mother my tutor was no favorite. She thought him—and, indeed, she called him—a bumpkin, a clown. There was a very pretty abbé among her friends, M. Tiblaud by name, whom she wished to install at the chateau as my in-tellectual, and her spiritual, adviser; but my father, who, with-out being anything of an *esprit fort*, had an incurable aversion to a priest out of church, very soon routed this pious scheme.

My poor father was an odd figure of a man. He belonged to a type as completely obsolete as the biggest of those big-boned, pre-historic monsters discovered by M. Cuvier. He was not overburdened with opinions or principles. The only truth that was absolute to his perception was that the house of Bergerac was *de bonne noblesse*. His tastes were not delicate. He was fond of the open air, of long rides, of the smell of the game-stocked woods in autumn, of playing at bowls, of a drinking-cup, of a dirty pack of cards, and a free-spoken tavern Hebe. I have nothing of him but his name. I strike you as an old fossil, a relic, a mummy. Good heavens! you should have seen him,—his good, his bad manners, his arrogance, his *bonhomie*, his stupidity and pluck.

My early years had promised ill for my health; I was listless and languid, and my father had been content to leave me to the women, who, on the whole, as I have said, left me a good deal to myself. But one morning he seemed suddenly to remember that he had a little son and heir running wild. It was I remember, in my ninth year, a morning early in June, after breakfast, at eleven o'clock. He took me by the hand and led me out on the terrace, and sat down and made me stand between his knees. I was engaged upon a great piece of bread and butter, which I had brought away from the table. He put his hand into my hair, and, for the first time that I could remember, looked me straight in the face. I had seen him take the forelock of a young colt in the same way, when he wished to look at its teeth. What did he want? Was he going to send me for sale? His eyes seemed prodigiously black and his eyebrows terribly thick. They were very much the eyebrows of that portrait. My father passed his other hand over the muscles of my arms and the sinews of my poor little legs.

"Chevalier," said he, "you're dreadfully puny. What's one to do with you?"

I dropped my eyes and said nothing. Heaven knows I felt puny.

"It's time you knew how to read and write. What are you blushing at?"

"I *do* know how to read," said I.

My father stared. "Pray, who taught you?"

"I learned in a book."

"What book?"

I looked up at my father before I answered. His eyes were bright, and there was a little flush in his face,—I hardly knew whether of pleasure or anger. I disengaged myself and went into the drawing-room, where I took from a cupboard in the wall an odd volume of Scarron's *Roman comique*. As I had to go through the house, I was absent some minutes. When I came back I found a stranger on the terrace. A young man in poor clothes, with a walking-stick, had come up from the avenue, and stood before my father, with his hat in his hand. At the farther end of the terrace was my aunt. She was sitting on the parapet, playing with a great black crow, which we kept in a cage in the dining-room window. I betook myself to my father's side with my book, and stood staring at our visitor. He was a dark-eyed, sun-burnt young man, of about twenty-eight, of middle height, broad in the shoulders and short in the neck, with a slight lameness in one of his legs. He looked travel-stained and weary and pale. I remember there was something prepossessing in his being pale. I didn't know that the paleness came simply from his being horribly hungry.

"In view of these facts," he said, as I came up, "I have ventured to presume upon the good-will of M. le Baron."

My father sat back in his chair, with his legs apart and a hand on each knee and his waistcoat unbuttoned, as was usual after a meal. "Upon my word," he said, "I don't know what I can do for you. There's no place for you in my own household."

The young man was silent a moment. "Has M. le Baron any children?" he asked, after a pause.

"I have my son whom you see here."

"May I inquire if M. le Chevalier is supplied with a preceptor?"

My father glanced down at me. "Indeed, he seems to be," he cried. "What have you got there?" And he took my book. "The little rascal has M. Scarron for a teacher. This is his preceptor!"

I blushed very hard, and the young man smiled. "Is that your only teacher?" he asked.

"My aunt taught me to read," I said, looking round at her.

"And did your aunt recommend this book?" asked my father.

"My aunt gave me M. Plutarque," I said.

My father burst out laughing, and the young man put his hat up to his mouth. But I could see that above it his eyes had a very good-natured look. My aunt, seeing that her name had been mentioned, walked slowly over to where we stood, still holding her crow on her hand. You have her there before you; judge how she looked. I remember that she frequently dressed in blue, my poor aunt, and I know that she must have dressed simply. Fancy her in a light stuff gown, covered with big blue flowers, with a blue ribbon in her dark hair, and the points of her high-heeled blue slippers peeping out under her stiff white petticoat. Imagine her strolling along the terrace of the chateau with a villanous black crow perched on her wrist. You'll admit it's a picture.

"Is all this true, sister?" said my father. "Is the Chevalier such a scholar?"

"He's a clever boy," said my aunt, putting her hand on my head.

"It seems to me that at a pinch he could do without a preceptor," said my father. "He has such a learned aunt."

"I've taught him all I know. He had begun to ask me questions that I was quite unable to answer."

"I should think he might," cried my father, with a broad laugh, "when once he had got into M. Scarron!"

"Questions out of Plutarch," said Mlle. de Bergerac, "which you must know Latin to answer."

"Would you like to know Latin, M. le Chevalier?" said the young man, looking at me with a smile.

"Do you know Latin,—you?" I asked.

"Perfectly," said the young man, with the same smile.

"Do you want to learn Latin, Chevalier?" said my aunt.

"Every gentleman learns Latin," said the young man.

I looked at the poor fellow, his dusty shoes and his rusty clothes. "But you're not a gentleman," said I.

He blushed up to his eyes. "Ah, I only teach it," he said.

In this way it was that Pierre Coquelin came to be my governor. My father, who had a mortal dislike to all kinds of cogitation and inquiry, engaged him on the simple testimony of his face and of his own account of his talents. His history, as he told it, was in three words as follows: He was of our province, and neither more nor less than the son of a village tailor. He is my hero: *tirez-vous de là*. Showing a lively taste for books, instead of being promoted to the paternal bench, he had been put to study with the Jesuits. After a residence of some three years with these gentlemen, he had incurred their displeasure by a foolish breach of discipline, and had been turned out into the world. Here he had endeavored to make capital out of his excellent education, and had gone up to Paris with the hope of earning his bread as a scribbler. But in Paris he scribbled himself hungry and nothing more, and was in fact in a fair way to die of starvation. At last he encountered an agent of the Marquis de Rochambeau, who was collecting young men for the little army which the latter was prepared to conduct to the aid of the American insurgents. He had engaged himself among Rochambeau's troops, taken part in several battles, and finally received a wound in his leg of which the effect was still perceptible. At the end of three years he had returned to France, and repaired on foot, with what speed he might, to his native town; but only to find that in his absence his father had died, after a tedious illness, in which he had vainly lavished his small earnings upon the physicians, and that his mother had married again, very little to his taste. Poor Coquelin was friendless, penniless, and homeless. But once back on his native soil, he found himself possessed again by his old passion for letters, and, like all starving members of his craft, he had turned his face to Paris. He longed to make up for his three years in the wilderness. He trudged along, lonely, hungry, and weary, till he came to the gates of Bergerac. Here, sitting down to rest on a stone, he saw us come out on the terrace to digest our breakfast in the sun. Poor Coquelin! he had the stomach of a gentleman. He was filled with an irresistible longing to rest awhile from his struggle with destiny, and it seemed to him that for a mess of smoking pottage he would gladly exchange his vague and dubious future. In obedience to this simple impulse,—an impulse touching in its humility, when you knew the man,—he made his way up the avenue. We looked affable enough,—an honest country gentleman, a young girl playing with a crow, and a little boy eating bread and butter; and it turned out, we were as kindly as we looked.

For me, I soon grew extremely fond of him, and I was glad to think in later days that he had found me a thoroughly docile child. In those days, you know, thanks to Jean Jacques Rousseau, there was a vast stir in men's notions of education, and a hundred theories afloat about the perfect teacher and the perfect pupil. Coquelin was a firm devotee of Jean Jacques, and very possibly applied some of his precepts to my own little person. But of his own nature Coquelin was incapable of anything that was not wise and gentle, and he had no need to learn humanity in books. He was, nevertheless, a great reader, and when he had not a volume in his hand he was sure to have two in his pockets. He had half a dozen little copies of the Greek and Latin poets, bound in yellow parchment, which, as he said, with a second shirt and a pair of white stockings, constituted his whole library. He had carried these books to America, and read them in the wilderness, and by the light of camp-fires, and in crowded, steaming barracks in winter-quarters. He had a passion for Virgil. M. Scarron was very soon dismissed to the cupboard, among the dice-boxes and the old packs of cards, and I was confined for the time to Virgil and Ovid and Plutarch, all of which, with the stimulus of Coquelin's own delight, I found very good reading. But better than any of the stories I read were those stories of his wanderings, and his odd companions and encounters, and charming tales of pure fantasy, which, with the best grace in the world, he would recite by the hour. We took long walks, and he told me the names of the flowers and the various styles of the stars, and I remember that I often had no small trouble to keep them distinct. He wrote a very bad hand, but he made very pretty drawings of the subjects then in vogue,—nymphs and heroes and shepherds and pastoral scenes. I used to fancy that his knowledge and skill were inexhaustible, and I pestered him so for entertainment that I certainly proved that there were no limits to his patience.

When he first came to us he looked haggard and thin and weary; but before the month was out, he had acquired a comfortable rotundity of person, and something of the sleek and polished look which befits the governor of a gentleman's son.

And yet he never lost a certain gravity and reserve of demeanor which was nearly akin to a mild melancholy. With me,
half the time, he was of course intolerably bored, and he must
have had hard work to keep from yawning in my face,—
which, as he knew I knew, would have been an unwarrantable
liberty. At table, with my parents, he seemed to be constantly
observing himself and inwardly regulating his words and gestures. The simple truth, I take it, was that he had never sat at
a gentleman's table, and although he must have known himself incapable of a real breach of civility,—essentially delicate
as he was in his feelings,—he was too proud to run the risk of
violating etiquette. My poor mother was a great stickler for
ceremony, and she would have had her majordomo to lift the
covers, even if she had had nothing to put into the dishes. I
remember a cruel rebuke she bestowed upon Coquelin,
shortly after his arrival. She could never be brought to forget
that he had been picked up, as she said, on the roads. At dinner one day, in the absence of Mlle. de Bergerac, who was indisposed, he inadvertently occupied her seat, taking me as a
vis-à-vis instead of a neighbor. Shortly afterwards, coming to
offer wine to my mother, he received for all response a stare
so blank, cold, and insolent, as to leave no doubt of her estimate of his presumption. In my mother's simple philosophy,
Mlle. de Bergerac's seat could be decently occupied only by
herself, and in default of her presence should remain conspic-
uously and sacredly vacant. Dinner at Bergerac was at best, indeed, a cold and dismal ceremony. I see it now,—the great
dining-room, with its high windows and their faded curtains,
and the tiles upon the floor, and the immense wainscots, and
the great white marble chimney-piece, reaching to the ceiling,—a triumph of delicate carving,—and the panels above
the doors, with their *galant* mythological paintings. All this
had been the work of my grandfather, during the Regency,
who had undertaken to renovate and beautify the chateau;
but his funds had suddenly given out, and we could boast but
a desultory elegance. Such talk as passed at table was between
my mother and the Baron, and consisted for the most part of
a series of insidious attempts on my mother's part to extort
information which the latter had no desire, or at least no faculty, to impart. My father was constitutionally taciturn and

apathetic, and he invariably made an end of my mother's interrogation by proclaiming that he hated gossip. He liked to take his pleasure and have done with it, or at best, to ruminate his substantial joys within the conservative recesses of his capacious breast. The Baronne's inquisitive tongue was like a lambent flame, flickering over the sides of a rock. She had a passion for the world, and seclusion had only sharpened the edge of her curiosity. She lived on old memories—shabby, tarnished bits of intellectual finery—and vagrant rumors, anecdotes, and scandals.

Once in a while, however, her curiosity held high revel; for once a week we had the Vicomte de Treuil to dine with us. This gentleman was, although several years my father's junior, his most intimate friend and the only constant visitor at Bergerac. He brought with him a sort of intoxicating perfume of the great world, which I myself was not too young to feel. He had a marvellous fluency of talk; he was polite and elegant; and he was constantly getting letters from Paris, books, newspapers, and prints, and copies of the new songs. When he dined at Bergerac, my mother used to rustle away from table, kissing her hand to him, and actually light-headed from her deep potations of gossip. His conversation was a constant popping of corks. My father and the Vicomte, as I have said, were firm friends,—the firmer for the great diversity of their characters. M. de Bergerac was dark, grave, and taciturn, with a deep, sonorous voice. He had in his nature a touch of melancholy, and, in default of piety, a broad vein of superstition. The foundations of his soul, moreover, I am satisfied, in spite of the somewhat ponderous superstructure, were laid in a soil of rich tenderness and pity. Gaston de Treuil was of a wholly different temper. He was short and slight, without any color, and with eyes as blue and lustrous as sapphires. He was so careless and gracious and mirthful, that to an unenlightened fancy he seemed the model of a joyous, reckless, gallant, impenitent *veneur*. But it sometimes struck me that, as he revolved an idea in his mind, it produced a certain flinty ring, which suggested that his nature was built, as it were, on rock, and that the bottom of his heart was hard. Young as he was, besides, he had a tired, jaded, exhausted look, which told of his having played high at the game of life, and, very possibly, lost. In fact, it was notorious that M. de Treuil had run through his property, and that his actual business in our neighborhood was to repair the breach in his fortunes by constant attendance on a wealthy kinsman, who occupied an adjacent chateau, and who was dying of age and his infirmities. But while I thus hint at the existence in his composition of these few base particles, I should be sorry to represent him as substantially less fair and clear and lustrous than he appeared to be. He possessed an irresistible charm, and that of itself is a virtue. I feel sure, moreover, that my father would never have reconciled himself to a real scantiness of masculine worth. The Vicomte enjoyed, I fancy, the generous energy of my father's good-fellowship, and the Baron's healthy senses were flattered by the exquisite perfume of the other's infallible *savoir-vivre*. I offer a hundred apologies, at any rate, to the Vicomte's luminous shade, that I should have ventured to cast a dingy slur upon his name. History has commemorated it. He perished on the scaffold, and showed that he knew how to die as well as to live. He was the last relic of the lily-handed youth of the *bon temps*; and as he looks at me out of the poignant sadness of the past, with a reproachful glitter in his cold blue eyes, and a scornful smile on his fine lips, I feel that, elegant and silent as he is, he has the last word in our dispute. I shall think of him henceforth as he appeared one night, or rather one morning, when he came home from a ball with my father, who had brought him to Bergerac to sleep. I had my bed in a closet out of my mother's room, where I lay in a most unwholesome fashion among her old gowns and hoops and cosmetics. My mother slept little; she passed the night in her dressing-gown, bolstered up in her bed, reading novels. The two gentlemen came in at four o'clock in the morning and made their way up to the Baronne's little sitting-room, next to her chamber. I suppose they were highly exhilarated, for they made a great noise of talking and laughing, and my father began to knock at the chamber door. He called out that he had M. de Treuil, and that they were cold and hungry. The Baronne said that she had a fire and they might come in. She was glad enough, poor lady, to get news of the ball, and to catch their impressions before they had been dulled by sleep. So they came in and sat by the fire, and M.

de Treuil looked for some wine and some little cakes where
my mother told him. I was wide awake and heard it all. I
heard my mother protesting and crying out, and the Vicomte
laughing, when he looked into the wrong place; and I am
afraid that in my mother's room there were a great many
wrong places. Before long, in my little stuffy, dark closet, I
began to feel hungry too; whereupon I got out of bed and
ventured forth into the room. I remember the whole picture,
as one remembers isolated scenes of childhood: my mother's
bed, with its great curtains half drawn back at the side, and
her little eager face and dark eyes peeping out of the recess;
then the two men at the fire,—my father with his hat on, sitting and looking drowsily into the flames, and the Vicomte
standing before the hearth, talking, laughing, and gesticulat-
ing, with the candlestick in one hand and a glass of wine in
the other,—dropping the wax on one side and the wine on
the other. He was dressed from head to foot in white velvet
and white silk, with embroideries of silver, and an immense
jabot. He was very pale, and he looked lighter and slighter
and wittier and more elegant than ever. He had a weak voice,
and when he laughed, after one feeble little spasm, it went off
into nothing, and you only knew he was laughing by his nodding his head and lifting his eyebrows and showing his handsome teeth. My father was in crimson velvet, with tarnished
gold facings. My mother bade me get back into bed, but my
father took me on his knees and held out my bare feet to the
fire. In a little while, from the influence of the heat, he fell
asleep in his chair, and I sat in my place and watched M. de
Treuil as he stood in the firelight drinking his wine and telling
stories to my mother, until at last I too relapsed into the innocence of slumber. They were very good friends, the
Vicomte and my mother. He admired the turn of her mind. I
remember his telling me several years later, at the time of her
death, when I was old enough to understand him, that she
was a very brave, keen little woman, and that in her musty
solitude of Bergerac she said a great many more good things
than the world ever heard of.

During the winter which preceded Coquelin's arrival, M.
de Treuil used to show himself at Bergerac in a friendly man-

ner; but about a month before this event, his visits became more frequent and assumed a special import and motive. In a word, my father and his friend between them had conceived it to be a fine thing that the latter should marry Mlle. de Bergerac. Neither from his own nor from his friend's point of view was Gaston de Treuil a marrying man or a desirable *parti*. He was too fond of pleasure to conciliate a rich wife, and too poor to support a penniless one. But I fancy that my father was of the opinion that if the Vicomte came into his kinsman's property, the best way to insure the preservation of it, and to attach him to his duties and responsibilities, would be to unite him to an amiable girl, who might remind him of the beauty of a domestic life and lend him courage to mend his ways. As far as the Vicomte was concerned, this was assuredly a benevolent scheme, but it seems to me that it made small account of the young girl's own happiness. M. de Treuil was supposed, in the matter of women, to have known everything that can be known, and to be as *blasé* with regard to their charms as he was proof against their influence. And, in fact, his manner of dealing with women, and of discussing them, indicated a profound disenchantment,—no bravado of contempt, no affectation of cynicism, but a cold, civil, absolute lassitude. A simply charming woman, therefore, would never have served the purpose of my father's theory. A very sound and liberal instinct led him to direct his thoughts to his sister. There were, of course, various auxiliary reasons for such disposal of Mlle. de Bergerac's hand. She was now a woman grown, and she had as yet received no decent proposals. She had no marriage portion of her own, and my father had no means to endow her. Her beauty, moreover, could hardly be called a dowry. It was without those vulgar allurements which, for many a poor girl, replace the glitter of cash. If within a very few years more she had not succeeded in establishing herself creditably in the world, nothing would be left for her but to withdraw from it, and to pledge her virgin faith to the chilly sanctity of a cloister. I was destined in the course of time to assume the lordship and the slender revenues of Bergerac, and it was not to be expected that I should be burdened on the very threshold of life with the maintenance of a dowerless maiden aunt. A marriage with M. de Treuil would be in all senses a creditable match, and, in the event of his be-coming his kinsman's legatee, a thoroughly comfortable one.

It was some time before the color of my father's intentions, and the milder hue of the Vicomte's acquiescence, began to show in our common daylight. It is not the custom, as you know, in our excellent France, to admit a lover on probation. He is expected to make up his mind on a view of the young lady's endowments, and to content himself before marriage with the bare cognition of her face. It is not thought decent (and there is certainly reason in it) that he should dally with his draught, and hold it to the light, and let the sun play through it, before carrying it to his lips. It was only on the ground of my father's warm good-will to Gaston de Treuil, and the latter's affectionate respect for the Baron, that the Vicomte was allowed to appear as a lover, before making his proposals in form. M. de Treuil, in fact, proceeded gradually, and made his approaches from a great distance. It was not for several weeks, therefore, that Mlle. de Bergerac became aware of them. And now, as this dear young girl steps into my story, where, I ask you, shall I find words to describe the broad loveliness of her person, to hint at the perfect beauty of her mind, to suggest the sweet mystery of her first suspicion of being sought, from afar, in marriage? Not in my fancy, surely; for there I should disinter the flimsy elements and tarnished properties of a superannuated comic opera. My taste, my son, was formed once for all fifty years ago. But if I wish to call up Mlle. de Bergerac, I must turn to my earliest memories, and delve in the sweet-smelling virgin soil of my heart. For Mlle. de Bergerac is no misty sylphid nor romantic moonlit nymph. She rises before me now, glowing with life, with the sound of her voice just dying in the air,—the more living for the mark of her crimson death-stain.

There was every good reason why her dawning conscious-ness of M. de Treuil's attentions—although these were little more than projected as yet—should have produced a serious tremor in her heart. It was not that she was aught of a co-quette; I honestly believe that there was no latent coquetry in her nature. At all events, whatever she might have become af-ter knowing M. de Treuil, she was no coquette to speak of in her ignorance. Her ignorance of men, in truth, was great. For the Vicomte himself, she had as yet known him only distantly, formally, as a gentleman of rank and fashion; and for others of his quality, she had seen but a small number, and not seen them intimately. These few words suffice to indicate that my aunt led a life of unbroken monotony. Once a year she spent six weeks with certain ladies of the Visitation, in whose convent she had received her education, and of whom she continued to be very fond. Half a dozen times in the twelve-month she went to a ball, under convoy of some haply ungrudging *châtelaine.* Two or three times a month, she received a visit at Bergerac. The rest of the time she paced, with the grace of an angel and the patience of a woman, the dreary corridors and unclipt garden walks of Bergerac. The discovery, then, that the brilliant Vicomte de Treuil was likely to make a proposal for her hand was an event of no small importance. With precisely what feelings she awaited its coming, I am unable to tell; but I have no hesitation in saying that even at this moment (that is, in less than a month after my tutor's arrival) her feelings were strongly modified by her acquaintance with Pierre Coquelin.

The word "acquaintance" perhaps exaggerates Mlle. de Bergerac's relation to this excellent young man. Twice a day she sat facing him at table, and half a dozen times a week she met him on the staircase, in the saloon, or in the park. Coquelin had been accommodated with an apartment in a small untenanted pavilion, within the enclosure of our domain, and except at meals, and when his presence was especially requested at the chateau, he confined himself to his own precinct. It was there, morning and evening, that I took my lesson. It was impossible, therefore, that an intimacy should have arisen between these two young persons, equally separated as they were by material and conventional barriers. Nevertheless, as the sequel proved, Coquelin must, by his mere presence, have begun very soon to exert a subtle action on Mlle. de Bergerac's thoughts. As for the young girl's influence on Coquelin, it is my belief that he fell in love with her the very first moment he beheld her,—that morning when he trudged wearily up our avenue. I need certainly make no apology for the poor fellow's audacity. You tell me that you fell in love at first sight with my aunt's portrait; you will readily excuse the poor youth for having been smitten with the original. It is less logical perhaps, but it is certainly no less natural, that Mlle. de Bergerac should have ventured to think of my governor as a decidedly interesting fellow. She saw so few men that one the more or the less made a very great difference. Coquelin's importance, moreover, was increased rather than diminished by the fact that, as I may say, he was a son of the soil. Marked as he was, in aspect and utterance, with the genuine plebeian stamp, he opened a way for the girl's fancy into a vague, unknown world. He stirred her imagination, I conceive, in very much the same way as such a man as Gaston de Treuil would have stirred—actually had stirred, of course—the grosser sensibilities of many a little *bourgeoise*. Mlle. de Bergerac was so thoroughly at peace with the consequences of her social position, so little inclined to derogate in act or in thought from the perfect dignity of her birth, that with the best conscience in the world, she entertained, as they came, the feelings provoked by Coquelin's manly virtues and graces. She had been educated in the faith that *noblesse oblige*, and she had seen none but gentlefolks and peasants. I think that she felt a vague, unavowed curiosity to see what sort of a figure you might make when you were under no obligations to nobleness. I think, finally, that unconsciously and in the interest simply of her unsubstantial dreams, (for in those long summer days at Bergerac, without finery, without visits, music, or books, or anything that a well-to-do grocer's daughter enjoys at the present day, she must, unless she was a far greater simpleton than I wish you to suppose, have spun a thousand airy, idle visions,) she contrasted Pierre Coquelin with the Vicomte de Treuil. I protest that I don't see how Coquelin bore the contrast. I frankly admit that, in her place, I would have given all my admiration to the Vicomte. At all events, the chief result of any such comparison must have been to show how, in spite of real trials and troubles, Coquelin had retained a certain masculine freshness and elasticity, and how, without any sorrows but those of his own wanton making, the Vicomte had utterly rubbed off this primal bloom of manhood. There was that about Gaston de Treuil that reminded you of an actor by daylight. His little row of foot-lights had burned itself out. But this is assuredly a more pedantic view of the case than any that Mlle. de Bergerac was capable of taking. The Vicomte had but to learn his part and declaim it, and the illusion was complete.

Mlle. de Bergerac may really have been a great simpleton, and my theory of her feelings—vague and imperfect as it is—may be put together quite after the fact. But I see you protest; you glance at the picture; you frown. *C'est bon*; give me your hand. She received the Vicomte's gallantries, then, with a modest, conscious dignity, and courtesied to exactly the proper depth when he made her one of his inimitable bows.

One evening—it was, I think, about ten days after Coquelin's arrival—she was sitting reading to my mother, who was ill in bed. The Vicomte had been dining with us, and after dinner we had gone into the drawing-room. At the drawing-room door Coquelin had made his bow to my father, and carried me off to his own apartment. Mlle. de Bergerac and the two gentlemen had gone into the drawing-room together. At dusk I had come back to the chateau, and, going up to my mother, had found her in company with her sister-in-law. In a few moments my father came in, looking stern and black.

"Sister," he cried, "why did you leave us alone in the drawing-room? Didn't you see I wanted you to stay?"

Mlle. de Bergerac laid down her book and looked at her brother before answering. "I had to come to my sister," she said: "I couldn't leave her alone."

My mother, I'm sorry to say, was not always just to my aunt. She used to lose patience with her sister's want of co-quetry, of ambition, of desire to make much of herself. She divined wherein my aunt had offended. "You're very devoted to your sister, suddenly," she said. "There are duties and duties, mademoiselle. I'm very much obliged to you for reading to me. You can put down the book."

"The Vicomte swore very hard when you went out," my father went on.

Mlle. de Bergerac laid aside her book. "Dear me!" she said, "if he was going to swear, it's very well I went."

"Are you afraid of the Vicomte?" said my mother. "You're twenty-two years old. You're not a little girl."

"Is she twenty-two?" cried my father. "I told him she was twenty-one."

"Frankly, brother," said Mlle. de Bergerac, "what does he want? Does he want to marry me?"

My father stared a moment. "*Pardieu!*" he cried.

"She looks as if she didn't believe it," said my mother. "Pray, did you ever ask him?"

"No, madam; did you? You are very kind." Mlle. de Bergerac was excited; her cheek flushed.

"In the course of time," said my father, gravely, "the Vicomte proposes to demand your hand."

"What is he waiting for?" asked Mlle. de Bergerac, simply.

"*Fi donc, mademoiselle!*" cried my mother.

"He is waiting for M. de Sorbières to die," said I, who had got this bit of news from my mother's waiting-woman.

My father stared at me, half angrily; and then,—"He expects to inherit," he said, boldly. "It's a very fine property."

"He would have done better, it seems to me," rejoined Mlle. de Bergerac, after a pause, "to wait till he had actually come into possession of it."

"M. de Sorbières," cried my father, "has given him his word a dozen times over. Besides, the Vicomte loves you."

Mlle. de Bergerac blushed, with a little smile, and as she did so her eyes fell on mine. I was standing gazing at her as a child gazes at a familiar friend who is presented to him in a new light. She put out her hand and drew me towards her. "The truth comes out of the mouths of children," she said. "Chevalier, does he love me?"

"Stuff!" cried the Baronne; "one doesn't speak to children of such things. A young girl should believe what she's told. I believed my mother when she told me that your brother loved me. He didn't, but I believed it, and as far as I know I'm none the worse for it."

For ten days after this I heard nothing more of Mlle. de Bergerac's marriage, and I suppose that, childlike, I ceased to think of what I had already heard. One evening, about midsummer, M. de Treuil came over to supper, and announced that he was about to set out in company with poor M. de Sorbières for some mineral springs in the South, by the use of which the latter hoped to prolong his life.

I remember that, while we sat at table, Coquelin was appealed to as an authority upon some topic broached by the Vicomte, on which he found himself at variance with my father. It was the first time, I fancy, that he had been so honored and that his opinions had been deemed worth hearing. The point under discussion must have related to the history of the American War, for Coquelin spoke with the firmness and fulness warranted by personal knowledge. I fancy that he was a little frightened by the sound of his own voice, but he acquitted himself with perfect good grace and success. We all sat attentive; my mother even staring a little, surprised to find in a beggarly pedagogue a perfect *beau diseur*. My father, as became so great a gentleman, knew by a certain rough instinct when a man had something amusing to say. He leaned back, with his hands in his pockets, listening and paying the poor fellow the tribute of a half-puzzled frown. The Vicomte, like a man of taste, was charmed. He told stories himself, he was a good judge.

After supper we went out on the terrace. It was a perfect summer night, neither too warm nor too cool. There was no moon, but the stars flung down their languid light, and the earth, with its great dark masses of vegetation and the gently swaying tree-tops, seemed to answer back in a thousand vague perfumes. Somewhere, close at hand, out of an enchanted tree, a nightingale raved and carolled in delirious music. We had the good taste to listen in silence. My mother sat down on a bench against the house, and put out her hand and made my father sit beside her. Mlle. de Bergerac strolled to the edge of the terrace, and leaned against the balustrade, whither M. de Treuil soon followed her. She stood motionless, with her head raised, intent upon the music. The Vicomte seated himself upon the parapet, with his face towards her and his arms folded. He may perhaps have been talking, under cover of the nightingale. Coquelin seated himself near the other end of the terrace, and drew me between his knees. At last the nightingale ceased. Coquelin got up, and bade good night to the company, and made his way across the park to his lodge. I went over to my aunt and the Vicomte.

"M. Coquelin is a clever man," said the Vicomte, as he

disappeared down the avenue. "He spoke very well this evening."

"He never spoke so much before," said I. "He's very shy."

"I think," said my aunt, "he's a little proud."

"I don't understand," said the Vicomte, "how a man with any pride can put up with the place of a tutor. I had rather dig in the fields."

"The Chevalier is much obliged to you," said my aunt, laughing. "In fact, M. Coquelin has to dig a little, hasn't he, Chevalier?"

"Not at all," said I. "But he keeps some plants in pots."

At this my aunt and the Vicomte began to laugh. "He keeps one precious plant," cried my aunt, tapping my face with her fan.

At this moment my mother called me away. "He makes them laugh," I heard her say to my father, as I went to her.

"She had better laugh about it than cry," said my father.

Before long, Mlle. de Bergerac and her companion came back toward the house.

"M. le Vicomte, brother," said my aunt, "invites me to go down and walk in the park. May I accept?"

"By all means," said my father. "You may go with the Vicomte as you would go with me."

"Ah!" said the Vicomte.

"Come then, Chevalier," said my aunt. "In my turn, I invite you."

"My son," said the Baronne, "I forbid you."

"But my brother says," rejoined Mlle. de Bergerac, "that I may go with M. de Treuil as I would go with himself. He would not object to my taking my nephew." And she put out her hand.

"One would think," said my mother, "that you were setting out for Siberia."

"For Siberia!" cried the Vicomte, laughing; "O no!"

I paused, undecided. But my father gave me a push. "After all," he said, "it's better."

When I overtook my aunt and her lover, the latter, losing no time, appeared to have come quite to the point.

"Your brother tells me, mademoiselle," he had begun, "that he has spoken to you."

The young girl was silent.

"You may be indifferent," pursued the Vicomte, "but I can't believe you're ignorant."

"My brother has spoken to me," said Mlle. de Bergerac at last, with an apparent effort,—"my brother has spoken to me of his project."

"I'm very glad he seemed to you to have espoused my cause so warmly that you call it his own. I did my best to convince him that I possess what a person of your merit is entitled to exact of the man who asks her hand. In doing so, I almost convinced myself. The point is now to convince you."

"I listen."

"You admit, then, that your mind is not made up in advance against me."

"*Mon Dieu!*" cried my aunt, with some emphasis, "a poor girl like me doesn't make up her mind. You frighten me, Vicomte. This is a serious question. I have the misfortune to have no mother. I can only pray God. But prayer helps me not to choose, but only to be resigned."

"Pray often, then, mademoiselle. I'm not an arrogant lover, and since I have known you a little better, I have lost all my vanity. I'm not a good man nor a wise one. I have no doubt you think me very light and foolish, but you can't begin to know how light and foolish I am. Marry me and you'll never know. If you don't marry me, I'm afraid you'll never marry."

"You're very frank, Vicomte. If you think I'm afraid of never marrying, you're mistaken. One can be very happy as an old maid. I spend six weeks every year with the ladies of the Visitation. Several of them are excellent women, charming women. They read, they educate young girls, they visit the poor—"

The Vicomte broke into a laugh. "They get up at five o'clock in the morning; they breakfast on boiled cabbage; they make flannel waistcoats, and very good sweetmeats! Why do you talk so, mademoiselle? Why do you say that you would like to lead such a life? One might almost believe it is coquetry. *Tenez*, I believe it's ignorance,—ignorance of your own feelings, your own nature, and your own needs." M. de Treuil paused a moment, and, although I had a very imperfect notion of the meaning of his words, I remember being struck with the vehement look of his pale face, which seemed fairly to glow in the darkness. Plainly, he was in love. "You are not made for solitude," he went on; "you are not made to be buried in a dingy old chateau, in the depths of a ridiculous province. You are made for the world, for the court, for pleasure, to be loved, admired, and envied. No, you don't know yourself, nor does Bergerac know you, nor his wife! I, at least, appreciate you. I know that you are supremely beautiful—"

"Vicomte," said Mlle. de Bergerac, "you forget—the child."

"Hang the child! Why did you bring him along? *You* are no child. You can understand me. You are a woman, full of intelligence and goodness and beauty. They don't know you here, they think you a little demoiselle in pinafores. Before Heaven, mademoiselle, there is that about you,—I see it, I feel it here at your side, in this rustling darkness,—there is that about you that a man would gladly die for."

Mlle. de Bergerac interrupted him with energy. "You talk extravagantly. I don't understand you; you frighten me."

"I talk as I feel. I frighten you? So much the better. I wish to stir your heart and get some answer to the passion of my own."

Mlle. de Bergerac was silent a moment, as if collecting her thoughts. "If I talk with you on this subject, I must do it with my wits about me," she said at last. "I must know exactly what we each mean."

"It's plain then that I can't hope to inspire you with any degree of affection."

"One doesn't promise to love, Vicomte; I can only answer for the present. My heart is so full of good wishes toward you that it costs me comparatively little to say I don't love you."

"And anything I may say of my own feelings will make no difference to you?"

"You have said you love me. Let it rest there."

"But you look as if you doubted my word."

"You can't see how I look; Vicomte, I believe you."

"Well then, there is one point gained. Let us pass to the others. I'm thirty years old. I have a very good name and a very bad reputation. I honestly believe that, though I've fallen below my birth, I've kept above my fame. I believe that I have no vices of temper; I'm neither brutal, nor jealous, nor

miserly. As for my fortune, I'm obliged to admit that it con-
sists chiefly in my expectations. My actual property is about
equal to your brother's, and you know how your sister-in-law
is obliged to live. My expectations are thought particularly
good. My great-uncle, M. de Sorbières, possesses, chiefly in
landed estates, a fortune of some three millions of livres. I
have no important competitors, either in blood or devotion.
He is eighty-seven years old and paralytic, and within the past
year I have been laying siege to his favor with such constancy
that his surrender, like his extinction, is only a question of
time. I received yesterday a summons to go with him to the
Pyrenees, to drink certain medicinal waters. The least he can
do, on my return, is to make me a handsome allowance,
which with my own revenues will make—*en attendant* better
things—a sufficient income for a reasonable couple."

There was a pause of some moments, during which we
slowly walked along in the obstructed starlight, the silence
broken only by the train of my aunt's dress brushing against
the twigs and pebbles.

"What a pity," she said, at last, "that you are not able to
speak of all this good fortune as in the present rather than in
the future."

"There it is! Until I came to know you, I had no thoughts
of marriage. What did I want of wealth? If five years ago I had
foreseen this moment, I should stand here with something
better than promises."

"Well, Vicomte," pursued the young girl, with singular
composure, "you do me the honor to think very well of me:
I hope you will not be vexed to find that prudence is one of
my virtues. If I marry, I wish to marry well. It's not only the
husband, but the marriage that counts. In accepting you as
you stand, I should make neither a sentimental match nor a
brilliant one."

"Excellent. I love you, prudence and all. Say, then, that I
present myself here three months hence with the titles and tokens of property amounting to a million and a half of livres,
will you consider that I am a *parti* sufficiently brilliant to
make you forget that you don't love me?"

"I should never forget that."

"Well, nor I either. It makes a sort of sorrowful harmony!

If three months hence, I repeat, I offer you a fortune instead of this poor empty hand, will you accept the one for the sake of the other?"

My aunt stopped short in the path. "I hope, Vicomte," she said, with much apparent simplicity, "that you are going to do nothing indelicate."

"God forbid, mademoiselle! It shall be a clean hand and a clean fortune."

"If you ask then a promise, a pledge—"

"You'll not give it. I ask then only for a little hope. Give it in what form you will."

We walked a few steps farther and came out from among the shadows, beneath the open sky. The voice of M. de Treuil, as he uttered these words, was low and deep and tender and full of entreaty. Mlle. de Bergerac cannot but have been deeply moved. I think she was somewhat awe-struck at having called up such a force of devotion in a nature deemed cold and inconstant. She put out her hand. "I wish success to any honorable efforts. In any case you will be happier for your wealth. In one case it will get you a wife, and in the other it will console you."

"Console me! I shall hate it, despise it, and throw it into the sea!"

Mlle. de Bergerac had no intention, of course, of leaving her companion under an illusion. "Ah, but understand, Vicomte," she said, "I make no promise. My brother claims the right to bestow my hand. If he wishes our marriage now, of course he will wish it three months hence. I have never gainsaid him."

"From now to three months a great deal may happen."

"To you perhaps, but not to me."

"Are you going to your friends of the Visitation?"

"No, indeed. I have no wish to spend the summer in a cloister. I prefer the green fields."

"Well, then, *va* for the green fields! They're the next best thing. I recommend you to the Chevalier's protection."

We had made half the circuit of the park, and turned into an alley which stretched away towards the house, and about midway in its course separated into two paths, one leading to the main avenue, and the other to the little pavilion inhabited

by Coquelin. At the point where the alley was divided stood
an enormous oak of great circumference, with a circular
bench surrounding its trunk. It occupied, I believe, the central point of the whole domain. As we reached the oak, I
looked down along the footpath towards the pavilion, and
saw Coquelin's light shining in one of the windows. I immediately proposed that we should pay him a visit. My aunt objected, on the ground that he was doubtless busy and would
not thank us for interrupting him. And then, when I insisted,
she said it was not proper.

"How not proper?"

"It's not proper for me. A lady doesn't visit young men in
their own apartments."

At this the Vicomte cried out. He was partly amused, I
think, at my aunt's attaching any compromising power to
poor little Coquelin, and partly annoyed at her not considering his own company, in view of his pretensions, a sufficient
guaranty.

"I should think," he said, "that with the Chevalier and me
you might venture—"

"As you please, then," said my aunt. And I accordingly led
the way to my governor's abode.

It was a small edifice of a single floor, standing prettily
enough among the trees, and still habitable, although very
much in disrepair. It had been built by that same ancestor to
whom Bergerac was indebted, in the absence of several of the
necessities of life, for many of its elegant superfluities, and had
been designed, I suppose, as a scene of pleasure,—such pleasure as he preferred to celebrate elsewhere than beneath the
roof of his domicile. Whether it had ever been used I know
not; but it certainly had very little of the look of a pleasure-
house. Such furniture as it had once possessed had long since
been transferred to the needy saloons of the chateau, and it
now looked dark and bare and cold. In front, the shrubbery
had been left to grow thick and wild and almost totally to ex-
clude the light from the windows; but behind, outside of the
two rooms which he occupied, and which had been provided
from the chateau with the articles necessary for comfort,
Coquelin had obtained my father's permission to effect a
great clearance in the foliage, and he now enjoyed plenty of

sunlight and a charming view of the neighboring country. It was in the larger of these two rooms, arranged as a sort of study, that we found him.

He seemed surprised and somewhat confused by our visit, but he very soon recovered himself sufficiently to do the honors of his little establishment.

"It was an idea of my nephew," said Mlle. de Bergerac. "We were walking in the park, and he saw your light. Now that we are here, Chevalier, what would you have us do?"

"M. Coquelin has some very pretty things to show you," said I.

Coquelin turned very red. "Pretty things, Chevalier? Pray, what do you mean? I have some of your nephew's copy-books," he said, turning to my aunt.

"Nay, you have some of your own," I cried. "He has books full of drawings, made by himself."

"Ah, you draw?" said the Vicomte.

"M. le Chevalier does me the honor to think so. My drawings are meant for no critics but children."

"In the way of criticism," said my aunt, gently, "we too are children." Her beautiful eyes, as she uttered these words, must have been quite as gentle as her voice. Coquelin looked at her, thinking very modestly of his little pictures, but loth to refuse the first request she had ever made him.

"Show them, at any rate," said the Vicomte, in a somewhat peremptory tone. In those days, you see, a man occupying Coquelin's place was expected to hold all his faculties and talents at the disposal of his patron, and it was thought an unwarrantable piece of assumption that he should cultivate any of the arts for his own peculiar delectation. In withholding his drawings, therefore, it may have seemed to the Vicomte that Coquelin was unfaithful to the service to which he was held,—that, namely, of instructing, diverting, and edifying the household of Bergerac. Coquelin went to a little cupboard in the wall, and took out three small albums and a couple of portfolios. Mlle. de Bergerac sat down at the table, and Coquelin drew up the lamp and placed his drawings before her. He turned them over, and gave such explanations as seemed necessary. I have only my childish impressions of the character of these sketches, which, in my eyes, of course, seemed prodigiously clever. What the judgment of my companions was worth I know not, but they appeared very well pleased. The Vicomte probably knew a good sketch from a poor one, and he very good-naturedly pronounced my tutor an extremely knowing fellow. Coquelin had drawn anything and everything,—peasants and dumb brutes, landscapes and Parisian types and figures, taken indifferently from high and low life. But the best pieces in the collection were a series of illustrations and reminiscences of his adventures with the American army, and of the figures and episodes he had observed in the Colonies. They were for the most part rudely enough executed, owing to his want of time and materials, but they were full of *finesse* and character. M. de Treuil was very much amused at the rude equipments of your ancestors. There were sketches of the enemy too, whom Coquelin had apparently not been afraid to look in the face. While he was turning over these designs for Mlle. de Bergerac, the Vicomte took up one of his portfolios, and, after a short inspection, drew from it, with a cry of surprise, a large portrait in pen and ink.

"*Tiens!*" said I; "it's my aunt!"

Coquelin turned pale. Mlle. de Bergerac looked at him, and turned the least bit red. As for the Vicomte, he never changed color. There was no eluding the fact that it was a likeness, and Coquelin had to pay the penalty of his skill.

"I didn't know," he said, at random, "that it was in that portfolio. Do you recognize it, mademoiselle?"

"Ah," said the Vicomte, dryly, "M. Coquelin meant to hide it."

"It's too pretty to hide," said my aunt; "and yet it's too pretty to show. It's flattered."

"Why should I have flattered you, mademoiselle?" asked Coquelin. "You were never to see it."

"That's what it is, mademoiselle," said the Vicomte, "to have such dazzling beauty. It penetrates the world. Who knows where you'll find it reflected next?"

However pretty a compliment this may have been to Mlle. de Bergerac, it was decidedly a back-handed blow to Coquelin. The young girl perceived that he felt it.

She rose to her feet. "My beauty," she said, with a slight

tremor in her voice, "would be a small thing without M. Coquelin's talent. We are much obliged to you. I hope that you'll bring your pictures to the chateau, so that we may look at the rest."

"Are you going to leave him this?" asked M. de Treuil, holding up the portrait.

"If M. Coquelin will give it to me, I shall be very glad to have it."

"One doesn't keep one's own portrait," said the Vicomte. "It ought to belong to me." In those days, before the invention of our sublime machinery for the reproduction of the human face, a young fellow was very glad to have his mistress's likeness in pen and ink.

But Coquelin had no idea of contributing to the Vicomte's gallery. "Excuse me," he said, gently, but looking the nobleman in the face. "The picture isn't good enough for Mlle. de Bergerac, but it's too good for any one else"; and he drew it out of the other's hands, tore it across, and applied it to the flame of the lamp.

We went back to the chateau in silence. The drawing-room was empty; but as we went in, the Vicomte took a lighted candle from a table and raised it to the young girl's face. "*Parbleu!*" he exclaimed, "the vagabond had looked at you to good purpose!"

Mlle. de Bergerac gave a half-confused laugh. "At any rate," she said, "he didn't hold a candle to me as if I were my old smoke-stained grandame, yonder!" and she blew out the light. "I'll call my brother," she said, preparing to retire.

"A moment," said her lover; "I shall not see you for some weeks. I shall start to-morrow with my uncle. I shall think of you by day, and dream of you by night. And meanwhile I shall very much doubt whether you think of me."

Mlle. de Bergerac smiled. "Doubt, doubt. It will help you to pass the time. With faith alone it would hang very heavy."

"It seems hard," pursued M. de Treuil, "that I should give you so many pledges, and that you should give me none."

"I give all I ask."

"Then, for Heaven's sake, ask for something!"

"Your kind words are all I want."

"Then give me some kind word yourself."

"What shall I say, Vicomte?"

"Say,—say that you'll wait for me."

They were standing in the centre of the great saloon, their figures reflected by the light of a couple of candles in the shining inlaid floor. Mlle. de Bergerac walked away a few steps with a look of agitation. Then turning about, "Vicomte," she asked, in a deep, full voice, "do you truly love me?"

"Ah, Gabrielle!" cried the young man.

I take it that no woman can hear her baptismal name uttered for the first time as that of Mlle. de Bergerac then came from her suitor's lips without being thrilled with joy and pride.

"Well, M. de Treuil," she said, "I will wait for you."

PART II.

I remember distinctly the incidents of that summer at Bergerac; or at least its general character, its tone. It was a hot, dry season; we lived with doors and windows open. M. Coquelin suffered very much from the heat, and sometimes, for days together, my lessons were suspended. We put our books away and rambled out for a long day in the fields. My tutor was perfectly faithful; he never allowed me to wander beyond call. I was very fond of fishing, and I used to sit for hours, like a little old man, with my legs dangling over the bank of our slender river, patiently awaiting the bite that so seldom came. Near at hand, in the shade, stretched at his length on the grass, Coquelin read and re-read one of his half dozen Greek and Latin poets. If we had walked far from home, we used to go and ask for some dinner at the hut of a neighboring peasant. For a very small coin we got enough bread and cheese and small fruit to keep us over till supper. The peasants, stupid and squalid as they were, always received us civilly enough, though on Coquelin's account quite as much as on my own. He addressed them with an easy familiarity, which made them feel, I suppose, that he was, if not quite one of themselves, at least by birth and sympathies much nearer to them than to the future Baron de Bergerac. He gave me in the course of these walks a great deal of good advice; and without perverting my signorial morals or

instilling any notions that were treason to my rank and position, he kindled in my childish breast a little democratic flame
which has never quite become extinct. He taught me the
beauty of humanity, justice, and tolerance; and whenever he
detected me in a precocious attempt to assert my baronial
rights over the wretched little *manants* who crossed my path,
he gave me morally a very hard drubbing. He had none of the
base complaisance and cynical nonchalance of the traditional
tutor of our old novels and comedies. Later in life I might
have found him too rigorous a moralist; but in those days I
liked him all the better for letting me sometimes feel the curb.
It gave me a highly agreeable sense of importance and maturity. It was a tribute to half-divined possibilities of naughtiness. In the afternoon, when I was tired of fishing, he would
lie with his thumb in his book and his eyes half closed and tell
me fairy-tales till the eyes of both of us closed together. Do
the instructors of youth nowadays condescend to the fairy-
tale pure and simple? Coquelin's stories belonged to the old,
old world: no political economy, no physics, no application to
anything in life. Do you remember in Doré's illustrations to
Perrault's tales, the picture of the enchanted castle of the
Sleeping Beauty? Back in the distance, in the bosom of an ancient park and surrounded by thick baronial woods which
blacken all the gloomy horizon, on the farther side of a great
abysmal hollow of tangled forest verdure, rise the long façade,
the moss-grown terraces, the towers, the purple roofs, of a
château of the time of Henry IV. Its massive foundations
plunge far down into the wild chasm of the woodland, and its
cold pinnacles of slate tower upwards, close to the rolling autumn clouds. The afternoon is closing in and a chill October
wind is beginning to set the forest a-howling. In the foreground, on an elevation beneath a mighty oak, stand a couple
of old woodcutters pointing across into the enchanted distance and answering the questions of the young prince. They
are the bent and blackened woodcutters of old France, of La
Fontaine's Fables and the *Médecin malgré lui*. What does the
castle contain? What secret is locked in its stately walls? What
revel is enacted in its long saloons? What strange figures stand
aloof from its vacant windows? You ask the question, and the
answer is a long revery. I never look at the picture without

thinking of those summer afternoons in the woods and of
Coquelin's long stories. His fairies were the fairies of the
Grand Siècle, and his princes and shepherds the godsons of
Perrault and Madame d'Aulnay. They lived in such palaces
and they hunted in such woods.

Mlle. de Bergerac, to all appearance, was not likely to break
her promise to M. de Treuil,—for lack of the opportunity,
quite as much as of the will. Those bright summer days must
have seemed very long to her, and I can't for my life imagine
what she did with her time. But she, too, as she had told the
Vicomte, was very fond of the green fields; and although she
never wandered very far from the house, she spent many an
hour in the open air. Neither here nor within doors was she
likely to encounter the happy man of whom the Vicomte
might be jealous. Mlle. de Bergerac had a friend, a single intimate friend, who came sometimes to pass the day with her,
and whose visits she occasionally returned. Marie de Chalais,
the granddaughter of the Marquis de Chalais, who lived some
ten miles away, was in all respects the exact counterpart and
foil of my aunt. She was extremely plain, but with that
sprightly, highly seasoned ugliness which is often so agreeable
to men. Short, spare, swarthy, light, with an immense mouth,
a most impertinent little nose, an imperceptible foot, a
charming hand, and a delightful voice, she was, in spite of her
great name and her fine clothes, the very ideal of the old stage
soubrette. Frequently, indeed, in her dress and manner, she
used to provoke a comparison with this incomparable type. A
cap, an apron, and a short petticoat were all sufficient; with
these and her bold, dark eyes she could impersonate the very
genius of impertinence and intrigue. She was a thoroughly
light creature, and later in life, after her marriage, she became
famous for her ugliness, her witticisms, and her adventures;
but that she had a good heart is shown by her real attachment
to my aunt. They were forever at cross-purposes, and yet they
were excellent friends. When my aunt wished to walk, Mlle.
de Chalais wished to sit still; when Mlle. de Chalais wished to
laugh, my aunt wished to meditate; when my aunt wished to
talk piety, Mlle. de Chalais wished to talk scandal. Mlle. de
Bergerac, however, usually carried the day and set the tune.
There was nothing on earth that Marie de Chalais so despised

as the green fields; and yet you might have seen her a dozen times that summer wandering over the domain of Bergerac, in a short muslin dress and a straw hat, with her arm entwined about the waist of her more stately friend. We used often to meet them, and as we drew near Mlle. de Chalais would always stop and offer to kiss the Chevalier. By this pretty trick Coquelin was subjected for a few moments to the influence of her innocent *agaceries*; for rather than have no man at all to prick with the little darts of her coquetry, the poor girl would have gone off and made eyes at the scarecrow in the wheatfield. Coquelin was not at all abashed by her harmless advances; for although, in addressing my aunt, he was apt to lose his voice or his countenance, he often showed a very pretty wit in answering Mlle. de Chalais.

On one occasion she spent several days at Bergerac, and during her stay she proffered an urgent entreaty that my aunt should go back with her to her grandfather's house, where, having no parents, she lived with her governess. Mlle. de Bergerac declined, on the ground of having no gowns fit to visit in; whereupon Mlle. de Chalais went to my mother, begged the gift of an old blue silk dress, and with her own cunning little hands made it over for my aunt's figure. That evening Mlle. de Bergerac appeared at supper in this renovated garment,—the first silk gown she had ever worn. Mlle. de Chalais had also dressed her hair, and decked her out with a number of trinkets and furbelows; and when the two came into the room together, they reminded me of the beautiful Duchess in Don Quixote, followed by a little dark-visaged Spanish waiting-maid. The next morning Coquelin and I rambled off as usual in search of adventures, and the day after that they were to leave the château. Whether we met with any adventures or not I forget; but we found ourselves at dinnertime at some distance from home, very hungry after a long tramp. We directed our steps to a little roadside hovel, where we had already purchased hospitality, and made our way in unannounced. We were somewhat surprised at the scene that met our eyes.

On a wretched bed at the farther end of the hut lay the master of the household, a young peasant whom we had seen a fortnight before in full health and vigor. At the head of the bed stood his wife, moaning, crying, and wringing her hands. Hanging about her, clinging to her skirts, and adding their piping cries to her own lamentations, were four little children, unwashed, unfed, and half clad. At the foot, facing the dying man, knelt his old mother—a horrible hag, so bent and brown and wrinkled with labor and age that there was nothing womanly left of her but her coarse, rude dress and cap, nothing of maternity but her sobs. Beside the pillow stood the priest, who had apparently just discharged the last offices of the Church. On the other side, on her knees, with the poor fellow's hand in her own, knelt Mlle. de Bergerac, like a consoling angel. On a stool near the door, looking on from a distance, sat Mlle. de Chalais, holding a little bleating kid in her arms. When she saw us, she started up. "Ah, M. Coquelin!" she cried, "do persuade Mlle. de Bergerac to leave this horrible place."

I saw Mlle. de Bergerac look at the curé and shake her head, as if to say that it was all over. She rose from her knees and went round to the wife, telling the same tale with her face. The poor, squalid *paysanne* gave a sort of savage, stupid cry, and threw herself and her rags on the young girl's neck. Mlle. de Bergerac caressed her, and whispered heaven knows what divinely simple words of comfort. Then, for the first time, she saw Coquelin and me, and beckoned us to approach.

"Chevalier," she said, still holding the woman on her breast, "have you got any money?"

At these words the woman raised her head. I signified that I was penniless.

My aunt frowned impatiently. "M. Coquelin, have you?"

Coquelin drew forth a single small piece, all that he possessed; for it was the end of his month. Mlle. de Bergerac took it, and pursued her inquiry.

"Curé, have you any money?"

"Not a sou," said the curé, smiling sweetly.

"Bah!" said Mlle. de Bergerac, with a sort of tragic petulance. "What can I do with twelve sous?"

"Give it all the same," said the woman, doggedly, putting out her hand.

"They want money," said Mlle. de Bergerac, lowering her

464 GABRIELLE DE BERGERAC

voice to Coquelin. "They have had this great sorrow, but a *louis d'or* would dull the wound. But we're all penniless. O for the sight of a little gold!"

"I have a *louis* at home," said I; and I felt Coquelin lay his hand on my head.

"What was the matter with the husband?" he asked.

"*Mon Dieu!*" said my aunt, glancing round at the bed. "I don't know."

Coquelin looked at her, half amazed, half worshipping.

"Who are they, these people? What are they?" she asked.

"Mademoiselle," said Coquelin, fervently, "you're an angel!"

"I wish I were," said Mlle. de Bergerac, simply; and she turned to the old mother.

We walked home together,—the curé with Mlle. de Chalais and me, and Mlle. de Bergerac in front with Coquelin. Asking how the two young girls had found their way to the death-bed we had just left, I learned from Mlle. de Chalais that they had set out for a stroll together, and, striking into a footpath across the fields, had gone farther than they supposed, and lost their way. While they were trying to recover it, they came upon the wretched hut where we had found them, and were struck by the sight of two children, standing crying at the door. Mlle. de Bergerac had stopped and questioned them to ascertain the cause of their sorrow, which with some difficulty she found to be that their father was dying of a fever. Whereupon, in spite of her companion's lively opposition, she had entered the miserable abode, and taken her place at the wretched couch, in the position in which we had discovered her. All this, doubtless, implied no extraordinary merit on Mlle. de Bergerac's part; but it placed her in a gracious, pleasing light.

The next morning the young girls went off in the great coach of M. de Chalais, which had been sent for them overnight, my father riding along as an escort. My aunt was absent a week, and I think I may say we keenly missed her. When I say we, I mean Coquelin and I, and when I say Coquelin and I, I mean Coquelin in particular; for it had come to this, that my tutor was roundly in love with my aunt. I didn't know it then, of course; but looking back, I see that he must already have been stirred to his soul's depths. Young as I was, moreover, I believe that I even then suspected his passion, and, loving him as I did, watched it with a vague, childish awe and sympathy. My aunt was to me, of course, a very old story, and I am sure she neither charmed nor dazzled my boyish fancy. I was quite too young to apprehend the meaning or the consequences of Coquelin's feelings; but I knew that he had a secret, and I wished him joy of it. He kept so jealous a guard on it that I would have defied my elders to discover the least reason for accusing him; but with a simple child of ten, thinking himself alone and uninterpreted, he showed himself plainly a lover. He was absent, restless, pre-occupied; now steeped in languid revery, now pacing up and down with the exaltation of something akin to hope. Hope it-self he could never have felt; for it must have seemed to him that his passion was so audacious as almost to be criminal. Mlle. de Bergerac's absence showed him, I imagine, that to know her had been the event of his life; to see her across the table, to hear her voice, her tread, to pass her, to meet her eye, a deep, consoling, healing joy. It revealed to him the force with which she had grasped his heart, and I think he was half frightened at the energy of his passion.

One evening, while Mlle. de Bergerac was still away, I sat in his window, committing my lesson for the morrow by the waning light. He was walking up and down among the shad-ows. "Chevalier," said he, suddenly, "what should you do if I were to leave you?"

My poor little heart stood still. "Leave me?" I cried, aghast; "why should you leave me?"

"Why, you know I didn't come to stay forever."

"But you came to stay till I'm a man grown. Don't you like your place?"

"Perfectly."

"Don't you like my father?"

"Your father is excellent."

"And my mother?"

"Your mother is perfect."

"And me, Coquelin?"

"You, Chevalier, are a little goose."

And then, from a sort of unreasoned instinct that Mlle. de

Bergerac was somehow connected with his idea of going away, "And my aunt?" I added.

"How, your aunt?"

"Don't you like her?"

Coquelin had stopped in his walk, and stood near me and above me. He looked at me some moments without answering, and then sat down beside me in the window-seat, and laid his hand on my head.

"Chevalier," he said, "I will tell you something."

"Well?" said I, after I had waited some time.

"One of these days you will be a man grown, and I shall have left you long before that. You'll learn a great many things that you don't know now. You'll learn what a strange, vast world it is, and what strange creatures men are—and women; how strong, how weak, how happy, how unhappy. You'll learn how many feelings and passions they have, and what a power of joy and of suffering. You'll be Baron de Bergerac and master of the château and of this little house. You'll sometimes be very proud of your title, and you'll sometimes feel very sad that it's so little more than a bare title. But neither your pride nor your grief will come to anything beside this, that one day, in the prime of your youth and strength and good looks, you'll see a woman whom you will love more than all these things,—more than your name, your lands, your youth, and strength, and beauty. It happens to all men, especially the good ones, and you'll be a good one. But the woman you love will be far out of your reach. She'll be a princess, perhaps she'll be the Queen. How can a poor little Baron de Bergerac expect her to look at him? You will give up your life for a touch of her hand; but what will she care for your life or your death? You'll curse your love, and yet you'll bless it, and perhaps—not having your living to get—you'll come up here and shut yourself up with your dreams and regrets. You'll come perhaps into this pavilion, and sit here alone in the twilight. And then, my child, you'll remember this evening; that I foretold it all and gave you my blessing in advance and—kissed you." He bent over, and I felt his burning lips on my forehead.

I understood hardly a word of what he said; but whether it was that I was terrified by his picture of the possible insignificance of a Baron de Bergerac, or that I was vaguely overawed by his deep, solemn tones, I know not; but my eyes very quietly began to emit a flood of tears. The effect of my grief was to induce him to assure me that he had no present intention of leaving me. It was not, of course, till later in life, that, thinking over the situation, I understood his impulse to arrest his hopeless passion for Mlle. de Bergerac by immediate departure. He was not brave in time.

At the end of a week she returned one evening as we were at supper. She came in with M. de Chalais, an amiable old man, who had been so kind as to accompany her. She greeted us severally, and nodded to Coquelin. She talked, I remember, with great volubility, relating what she had seen and done in her absence, and laughing with extraordinary freedom. As we left the table, she took my hand, and I put out the other and took Coquelin's.

"Has the Chevalier been a good boy?" she asked.

"Perfect," said Coquelin; "but he has wanted his aunt sadly."

"Not at all," said I, resenting the imputation as derogatory to my independence.

"You have had a pleasant week, mademoiselle?" said Coquelin.

"A charming week. And you?"

"M. Coquelin has been very unhappy," said I. "He thought of going away."

"Ah?" said my aunt.

Coquelin was silent.

"You think of going away?"

"I merely spoke of it, mademoiselle. I must go away some time, you know. The Chevalier looks upon me as something eternal."

"What's eternal?" asked the Chevalier.

"There is nothing eternal, my child," said Mlle. de Bergerac. "Nothing lasts more than a moment."

"O," said Coquelin, "I don't agree with you!"

"You don't believe that in this world everything is vain and fleeting and transitory?"

"By no means; I believe in the permanence of many things."

"Of what, for instance?"

"Well, of sentiments and passions."

"Very likely. But not of the hearts that hold them. 'Lovers die, but love survives.' I heard a gentleman say that at Chalais."

"It's better, at least, than if he had put it the other way. But lovers last too. They survive; they outlive the things that would fain destroy them,—indifference, denial, and despair."

"But meanwhile the loved object disappears. When it isn't one, it's the other."

"O, I admit that it's a shifting world. But I have a philosophy for that."

"I'm curious to know your philosophy."

"It's a very old one. It's simply to make the most of life while it lasts. I'm very fond of life," said Coquelin, laughing.

"I should say that as yet, from what I know of your history, you have had no great reason to be."

"Nay, it's like a cruel mistress," said Coquelin. "When once you love her, she's absolute. Her hard usage doesn't affect you. And certainly I have nothing to complain of now."

"You're happy here then?"

"Profoundly, mademoiselle, in spite of the Chevalier."

"I should suppose that with your tastes you would prefer something more active, more ardent."

"*Mon Dieu*, my tastes are very simple. And then—happiness, *cela ne se raisonne pas*. You don't find it when you go in quest of it. It's like fortune; it comes to you in your sleep."

"I imagine," said Mlle. de Bergerac, "that I was never happy."

"That's a sad story," said Coquelin.

The young girl began to laugh. "And never unhappy."

"Dear me, that's still worse. Never fear, it will come."

"What will come?"

"That which is both bliss and misery at once."

Mlle. de Bergerac hesitated a moment. "And what is this strange thing?" she asked.

On his side Coquelin was silent. "When it comes to you," he said, at last, "you'll tell me what you call it."

About a week after this, at breakfast, in pursuance of an urgent request of mine, Coquelin proposed to my father to allow him to take me to visit the ruins of an ancient feudal castle some four leagues distant, which he had observed and explored while he trudged across the country on his way to Bergerac, and which, indeed, although the taste for ruins was at that time by no means so general as since the Revolution (when one may say it was in a measure created), enjoyed a certain notoriety throughout the province. My father good-naturedly consented; and as the distance was too great to be achieved on foot, he placed his two old coach-horses at our service. You know that although I affected, in boyish sort, to have been indifferent to my aunt's absence, I was really very fond of her, and it occurred to me that our excursion would be more solemn and splendid for her taking part in it. So I appealed to my father and asked if Mlle. de Bergerac might be allowed to go with us. What the Baron would have decided had he been left to himself I know not; but happily for our cause my mother cried out that, to her mind, it was highly improper that her sister-in-law should travel twenty miles alone with two young men.

"One of your young men is a child," said my father, "and her nephew into the bargain; and the other,"—and he laughed, coarsely but not ill-humoredly,—"the other is—Coquelin!"

"Coquelin is not a child nor is mademoiselle either," said my mother.

"All the more reason for their going. Gabrielle, will you go?" My father I fear, was not remarkable in general for his tenderness or his *prévenance* for the poor girl whom fortune had given him to protect; but from time to time he would wake up to a downright sense of kinship and duty, kindled by the pardonable aggressions of my mother, between whom and her sister-in-law there existed a singular antagonism of temper.

Mlle. de Bergerac looked at my father intently and with a little blush. "Yes, brother, I'll go. The Chevalier can take me *en croupe.*"

So we started, Coquelin on one horse, and I on the other, with my aunt mounted behind me. Our sport for the first part of the journey consisted chiefly in my urging my beast into a somewhat ponderous gallop, so as to terrify my aunt, who was not very sure of her seat, and who, at moments, between pleading and laughing, had hard work to preserve her balance. At these times Coquelin would ride close alongside of us, at the same cumbersome pace, declaring himself ready to catch the young girl if she fell. In this way we jolted along, in a cloud of dust, with shouts and laughter.

"Madame the Baronne was wrong," said Coquelin, "in denying that we are children."

"O, this is nothing yet," cried my aunt.

The castle of Fossy lifted its dark and crumbling towers with a decided air of feudal arrogance from the summit of a gentle eminence in the recess of a shallow gorge among the hills. Exactly when it had flourished and when it had decayed I knew not, but in the year of grace of our pilgrimage it was a truly venerable, almost a formidable, ruin. Two great towers were standing,—one of them diminished by half its upper elevation, and the other sadly scathed and shattered, but still exposing its hoary head to the weather, and offering the sullen hospitality of its empty skull to a colony of swallows. I shall never forget that day at Fossy; it was one of those long raptures of childhood which seem to imprint upon the mind an ineffaceable stain of light. The novelty and mystery of the dilapidated fortress,—its antiquity, its intricacy, its sounding vaults and corridors, its inaccessible heights and impenetrable depths, the broad sunny glare of its grass-grown courts and yards, the twilight of its passages and midnight of its dungeons, and along with all this my freedom to rove and scramble, my perpetual curiosity, my lusty absorption of the sun-warmed air, and the contagion of my companions' careless and sensuous mirth,—all these things combined to make our excursion one of the memorable events of my youth. My two companions accepted the situation and drank in the beauty of the day and the richness of the spot with all my own reckless freedom. Coquelin was half mad with the joy of spending a whole unbroken summer's day with the woman whom he secretly loved. He was all motion and humor and resonant laughter; and yet intermingled with his random gayety there lurked a solemn sweetness and reticence, a feverish concentration of thought, which to a woman with a woman's senses must have fairly betrayed his passion. Mlle. de Bergerac, without quite putting aside her natural dignity and gravity of mien, lent herself with a charming girlish energy to the undisciplined spirit of the hour.

Our first thoughts, after Coquelin had turned the horses to pasture in one of the grassy courts of the castle, were naturally bestowed upon our little basket of provisions; and our first act was to sit down on a heap of fallen masonry and divide its contents. After that we wandered. We climbed the still practicable staircases, and wedged ourselves into the turrets and strolled through the chambers and halls; we started from their long repose every echo and bat and owl within the innumerable walls.

Finally, after we had rambled a couple of hours, Mlle. de Bergerac betrayed signs of fatigue. Coquelin went with her in search of a place of rest, and I was left to my own devices. For an hour I found plenty of diversion, at the end of which I returned to my friends. I had some difficulty in finding them. They had mounted by an imperfect and somewhat perilous ascent to one of the upper platforms of the castle. Mlle. de Bergerac was sitting in a listless posture on a block of stone, against the wall, in the shadow of the still surviving tower; opposite, in the light, half leaning, half sitting on the parapet of the terrace, was her companion.

"For the last half-hour, mademoiselle," said Coquelin, as I came up, "you've not spoken a word."

"All the morning," said Mlle. de Bergerac, "I've been scrambling and chattering and laughing. Now, by reaction, I'm *triste*."

"I protest, so am I," said Coquelin. "The truth is, this old feudal fortress is a decidedly melancholy spot. It's haunted with the ghost of the past. It smells of tragedies, sorrows, and cruelties." He uttered these words with singular emphasis. "It's a horrible place," he pursued, with a shudder.

Mlle. de Bergerac began to laugh. "It's odd that we should only just now have discovered it!"

"No, it's like the history of that abominable past of which it's a relic. At the first glance we see nothing but the great proportions, the show, and the splendor; but when we come to explore, we detect a vast underground world of iniquity and suffering. Only half this castle is above the soil; the rest is dungeons and vaults and *oubliettes*."

"Nevertheless," said the young girl, "I should have liked to live in those old days. Shouldn't you?"

"Verily, no, mademoiselle!" And then after a pause, with a certain irrepressible bitterness: "Life is hard enough now."

Mlle. de Bergerac stared but said nothing.

"In those good old days," Coquelin resumed, "I should have been a brutal, senseless peasant, yoked down like an ox, with my forehead in the soil. Or else I should have been a trembling, groaning, fasting monk, moaning my soul away in the ecstasies of faith."

Mlle. de Bergerac rose and came to the edge of the platform. "Was no other career open in those days?"

"To such a one as me,—no. As I say, mademoiselle, life is hard now, but it was a mere dead weight then. I know it was. I feel in my bones and pulses that awful burden of despair under which my wretched ancestors struggled. *Tenez*, I'm the great man of the race. My father came next; he was one of four brothers, who all thought it a prodigious rise in the world when he became a village tailor. If we had lived five hundred years ago, in the shadow of these great towers, we should never have risen at all. We should have stuck with our feet in the clay. As I'm not a fighting man, I suppose I should have gone into the Church. If I hadn't died from an overdose of inanition, very likely I might have lived to be a cardinal."

Mlle. de Bergerac leaned against the parapet, and with a meditative droop of the head looked down the little glen toward the plain and the highway. "For myself," she said, "I can imagine very charming things of life in this castle of Fossy."

"For yourself, very likely."

"Fancy the great moat below filled with water and sheeted with lilies, and the drawbridge lowered, and a company of knights riding into the gates. Within, in one of those vaulted, quaintly timbered rooms, the châtelaine stands ready to receive them, with her women, her chaplain, her physician, and her little page. They come clanking up the staircase, with ringing swords, sweeping the ground with their plumes. They are all brave and splendid and fierce, but one of them far more than the rest. They each bend a knee to the lady—"

"But he bends two," cried Coquelin. "They wander apart into one of those deep embrasures and spin the threads of perfect love. Ah, I could fancy a sweet life, in those days, mademoiselle, if I could only fancy myself a knight!"

"And you can't," said the young girl, gravely, looking at him.

"It's an idle game; it's not worth trying."

"Apparently then, you're a cynic; you have an equally small opinion of the past and the present."

"No; you do me injustice."

"But you say that life is hard."

"I speak not for myself, but for others; for my brothers and sisters and kinsmen in all degrees; for the great mass of *petits gens* of my own class."

"Dear me, M. Coquelin, while you're about it, you can speak for others still; for poor portionless girls, for instance."

"Are they very much to be pitied?"

Mlle. de Bergerac was silent. "After all," she resumed, "they oughtn't to complain."

"Not when they have a great name and beauty," said Coquelin.

"O heaven!" said the young girl, impatiently, and turned away. Coquelin stood watching her, his brow contracted, his lips parted. Presently, she came back. "Perhaps you think," she said, "that I care for my name,—my great name, as you call it."

"Assuredly, I do."

She stood looking at him, blushing a little and frowning. As he said these words, she gave an impatient toss of the head and turned away again. In her hand she carried an ornamented fan, an antiquated and sadly dilapidated instrument. She suddenly raised it above her head, swung it a moment, and threw it far across the parapet. "There goes the name of Bergerac!" she said; and sweeping round, made the young man a very low courtesy.

There was in the whole action a certain passionate freedom which set poor Coquelin's heart a-throbbing. "To have a good name, mademoiselle," he said, "and to be indifferent to it, is the sign of a noble mind." (In parenthesis, I may say that I think he was quite wrong.)

"It's quite as noble, monsieur," returned my aunt, "to have a small name and not to blush for it."

With these words I fancy they felt as if they had said enough; the conversation was growing rather too pointed.

"I think," said my aunt, "that we had better prepare to go." And she cast a farewell glance at the broad expanse of country which lay stretched out beneath us, striped with the long afternoon shadows.

Coquelin followed the direction of her eyes. "I wish very much," he said, "that before we go we might be able to make our way up into the summit of the great tower. It would be worth the attempt. The view from here, charming as it is, must be only a fragment of what you see from that topmost platform."

"It's not likely," said my aunt, "that the staircase is still in a state to be used."

"Possibly not; but we can see."

"Nay," insisted my aunt, "I'm afraid to trust the Chevalier. There are great breaches in the sides of the ascent, which are so many open doors to destruction."

I strongly opposed this view of the case; but Coquelin, after scanning the elevation of the tower and such of the fissures as were visible from our standpoint, declared that my aunt was right and that it was my duty to comply. "And you, too, mademoiselle," he said, "had better not try it, unless you pride yourself on your strong head."

"No, indeed, I have a particularly weak one. And you?"

"I confess I'm very curious to see the view. I always want to read to the end of a book, to walk to the turn of a road, and to climb to the top of a building."

"Good," said Mlle. de Bergerac. "We'll wait for you."

Although in a straight line from the spot which we occupied, the distance through the air to the rugged sides of the great cylinder of masonry which frowned above us was not more than thirty yards, Coquelin was obliged, in order to strike at the nearest accessible point the winding staircase which clung to its massive ribs, to retrace his steps through the interior of the castle and make a *détour* of some five minutes' duration. In ten minutes more he showed himself at an aperture in the wall, facing our terrace.

"How do you prosper?" cried my aunt, raising her voice.

"I've mounted eighty steps," he shouted; "I've a hundred

more." Presently he appeared again at another opening. "The steps have stopped," he cried.

"You've only to stop too," rejoined Mlle. de Bergerac. Again he was lost to sight and we supposed he was returning. A quarter of an hour elapsed, and we began to wonder at his not having overtaken us, when we heard a loud call high above our heads. There he stood, on the summit of the edifice, waving his hat. At this point he was so far above us that it was difficult to communicate by sounds, in spite of our curiosity to know how, in the absence of a staircase, he had effected the rest of the ascent. He began to represent, by gestures of pretended rapture, the immensity and beauty of the prospect. Finally Mlle. de Bergerac beckoned to him to descend, and pointed to the declining sun, informing him at the same time that we would go down and meet him in the lower part of the castle. We left the terrace accordingly, and, making the best of our way through the intricate passages of the edifice, at last, not without a feeling of relief, found ourselves on the level earth. We waited quite half an hour without seeing anything of our companion. My aunt, I could see, had become anxious, although she endeavored to appear at her ease. As the time elapsed, however, it became so evident that Coquelin had encountered some serious obstacle to his descent, that Mlle. de Bergerac proposed we should, in so far as was possible, betake ourselves to his assistance. The point was to approach him within speaking distance.

We entered the body of the castle again, climbed to one of the upper levels, and reached a spot where an extensive destruction of the external wall partially exposed the great tower. As we approached this crumbling breach, Mlle. de Bergerac drew back from its brink with a loud cry of horror. It was not long before I discerned the cause of her movement. The side of the tower visible from where we stood presented a vast yawning fissure, which explained the interruption of the staircase, the latter having fallen for want of support. The central column, to which the steps had been fastened, seemed, nevertheless, still to be erect, and to have formed, with the agglomeration of fallen fragments and various occasional projections of masonry, the means by which Coquelin, with extraordinary courage and skill, had reached the topmost platform. The ascent, then, had been possible; the descent, curiously enough, he seemed to have found another matter; and after striving in vain to retrace his footsteps, had been obliged to commit himself to the dangerous experiment of passing from the tower to the external surface of the main fortress. He had accomplished half his journey and now stood directly over against us in a posture which caused my young limbs to stiffen with dismay. The point to which he had directed himself was apparently the breach at which we stood; meanwhile he had paused, clinging in mid-air to heaven knows what narrow ledge or flimsy iron clump in the stone-work, and straining his nerves to an agonized tension in the effort not to fall, while his eyes vaguely wandered in quest of another footing. The wall of the castle was so immensely thick, that wherever he could embrace its entire section, progress was comparatively easy; the more especially as, above our heads, this same wall had been demolished in such a way as to maintain a rapid upward inclination to the point where it communicated with the tower.

I stood staring at Coquelin with my heart in my throat, forgetting (or rather too young to reflect) that the sudden shock of seeing me where I was might prove fatal to his equipoise. He perceived me, however, and tried to smile. "Don't be afraid," he cried, "I'll be with you in a moment." My aunt, who had fallen back, returned to the aperture, and gazed at him with pale cheeks and clasped hands. He made a long step forward, successfully, and, as he recovered himself, caught sight of her face and looked at her with fearful intentness. Then seeing, I suppose, that she was sickened by his insecurity, he disengaged one hand and motioned her back. She retreated, paced in a single moment the length of the enclosure in which we stood, returned and stopped just short of the point at which she would have seen him again. She buried her face in her hands, like one muttering a rapid prayer, and then advanced once more within range of her friend's vision. As she looked at him, clinging in mid-air and planting step after step on the jagged and treacherous edge of the immense perpendicular chasm, she repressed another loud cry only by thrusting her handkerchief into her mouth. He caught her eyes again, gazed into them with piercing keenness, as if to drink in coolness and confidence, and then, as she closed them again in horror, motioned me with his head to lead her away. She returned to the farther end of the apartment and leaned her head against the wall. I remained staring at poor Coquelin, fascinated by the spectacle of his mingled danger and courage. Inch by inch, yard by yard, I saw him lessen the interval which threatened his life. It was a horrible, beautiful sight. Some five minutes elapsed; they seemed like fifty. The last few yards he accomplished with a rush; he reached the window which was the goal of his efforts, swung himself in and let himself down by a prodigious leap to the level on which we stood. Here he stopped, pale, lacerated, and drenched with perspiration. He put out his hand to Mlle. de Bergerac, who, at the sound of his steps, had turned herself about. On seeing him she made a few steps forward and burst into tears. I took his extended hand. He bent over me and kissed me, and then giving me a push, "Go and kiss your poor aunt," he said. Mlle. de Bergerac clasped me to her breast with a most convulsive pressure. From that moment till we reached home, there was very little said. Both my companions had matter for silent reflection,—Mlle. de Bergerac in the deep significance of that offered hand, and Coquelin in the rich avowal of her tears.

PART III.

A week after this memorable visit to Fossy, in emulation of my good preceptor, I treated my friends, or myself at least, to a five minutes' fright. Wandering beside the river one day when Coquelin had been detained within doors to overlook some accounts for my father, I amused myself, where the bank projected slightly over the stream, with kicking the earth away in fragments, and watching it borne down the current. The result may be anticipated: I came very near going the way of those same fragments. I lost my foothold and fell into the stream, which, however, was so shallow as to offer no great obstacle to self-preservation. I scrambled ashore, wet to the bone, and, feeling rather ashamed of my misadventure, skulked about in the fields for a couple of hours, in my dripping clothes. Finally, there being no sun and my garments remaining inexorably damp, my teeth began to chatter and my limbs to ache. I went home and surrendered myself. Here again the result may be foreseen: the next day I was laid up with a high fever.

Mlle. de Bergerac, as I afterwards learned, immediately appointed herself my nurse, removed me from my little sleeping-closet to her own room, and watched me with the most tender care. My illness lasted some ten days, my convalescence a week. When I began to mend, my bed was transferred to an unoccupied room adjoining my aunt's. Here, late one afternoon, I lay languidly singing to myself and watching the western sunbeams shimmering on the opposite wall. If you were ever ill as a child, you will remember such moments. You look by the hour at your thin, white hands; you listen to the sounds in the house, the opening of doors and the tread of feet; you murmur strange odds and ends of talk; and you watch the fading of the day and the dark flowering of the night. Presently my aunt came in, introducing Coquelin, whom she left by my bedside. He sat with me a long time, talking in the old, kind way, and gradually lulled me to sleep with the gentle murmur of his voice. When I awoke again it was night. The sun was quenched on the opposite wall, but through a window on the same side came a broad ray of moonlight. In the window sat Coquelin, who had apparently not left the room. Near him was Mlle. de Bergerac.

Some time elapsed between my becoming conscious of their presence and my distinguishing the sense of the words that were passing between them. When I did so, if I had reached the age when one ponders and interprets what one hears, I should readily have perceived that since those last thrilling moments at Fossy their friendship had taken a very long step, and that the secret of each heart had changed place with its mate. But even now there was little that was careless and joyous in their young love; the first words of Mlle. de Bergerac that I distinguished betrayed the sombre tinge of their passion.

"I don't care what happens now," she said. "It will always be something to have lived through these days."

"You're stronger than I, then," said Coquelin. "I haven't

the courage to defy the future. I'm afraid to think of it. Ah, why can't we make a future of our own?"

"It would be a greater happiness than we have a right to. Who are you, Pierre Coquelin, that you should claim the right to marry the girl you love, when she's a demoiselle de Bergerac to begin with? And who am I, that I should expect to have deserved a greater blessing than that one look of your eyes, which I shall never, never forget? It is more than enough to watch you and pray for you and worship you in silence."

"What am I? what are you? We are two honest mortals, who have a perfect right to repudiate the blessings of God. If ever a passion deserved its reward, mademoiselle, it's the absolute love I bear you. It's not a spasm, a miracle, or a delusion; it's the most natural emotion of my nature."

"We don't live in a natural world, Coquelin. If we did, there would be no need of concealing this divine affection. Great heaven! who's natural? Is it my sister-in-law? Is it M. de Treuil? Is it my brother? My brother is sometimes so natural that he's brutal. Is it I myself? There are moments when I'm afraid of my nature."

It was too dark for me to distinguish my companions' faces in the course of this singular dialogue; but it's not hard to imagine how, as my aunt uttered these words, with a burst of sombre *naïveté*, her lover must have turned upon her face the puzzled brightness of his eyes.

"What do you mean?" he asked.

"*Mon Dieu!* think how I have lived! What a senseless, thoughtless, passionless life! What solitude, ignorance, and languor! What trivial duties and petty joys! I have fancied myself happy at times, for it was God's mercy that I didn't know what I lacked. But now that my soul begins to stir and throb and live, it shakes me with its mighty pulsations. I feel as if in the mere wantonness of strength and joy it might drive me to some extravagance. I seem to feel myself making a great rush, with my eyes closed and my heart in my throat. And then the earth sinks away from under my feet, and in my ears is the sound of a dreadful tumult."

"Evidently we have very different ways of feeling. For you our love is action, passion; for me it's rest. For you it's romance; for me it's reality. For me it's a necessity; for you (how shall I say it?) it's a luxury. In point of fact, mademoiselle, how should it be otherwise? When a demoiselle de Bergerac bestows her heart upon an obscure adventurer, a man born in poverty and servitude, it's a matter of charity, of noble generosity."

Mlle. de Bergerac received this speech in silence, and for some moments nothing was said. At last she resumed: "After all that has passed between us, Coquelin, it seems to me a matter neither of generosity nor of charity to allude again to that miserable fact of my birth."

"I was only trying to carry out your own idea, and to get at the truth with regard to our situation. If our love is worth a straw, we needn't be afraid of that. Isn't it true—blessedly true, perhaps, for all I know—that you shrink a little from taking me as I am? Except for my character, I'm so little! It's impossible to be less of a *personage*. You can't quite reconcile it to your dignity to love a nobody, so you fling over your weakness a veil of mystery and romance and exaltation. You regard your passion, perhaps, as more of an escapade, an adventure, than it needs to be."

"My 'nobody,'" said Mlle. de Bergerac, gently, "is a very wise man, and a great philosopher. I don't understand a word you say."

"Ah, so much the better!" said Coquelin with a little laugh.

"Will you promise me," pursued the young girl, "never again by word or deed to allude to the difference of our birth? If you refuse, I shall consider you an excellent pedagogue, but no lover."

"Will you in return promise me—"

"Promise you what?"

Coquelin was standing before her, looking at her, with folded arms. "Promise me likewise to forget it!"

Mlle. de Bergerac stared a moment, and also rose to her feet. "Forget it! Is this generous?" she cried. "Is it delicate? I had pretty well forgot it, I think, on that dreadful day at Fossy!" Her voice trembled and swelled; she burst into tears. Coquelin attempted to remonstrate, but she motioned him aside, and swept out of the room.

It must have been a very genuine passion between these

two, you'll observe, to allow this handling without gloves. Only a plant of hardy growth could have endured this chilling blast of discord and disputation. Ultimately, indeed, its effect seemed to have been to fortify and consecrate their love. This was apparent several days later; but I know not what manner of communication they had had in the interval. I was much better, but I was still weak and languid. Mlle. de Bergerac brought me my breakfast in bed, and then, having helped me to rise and dress, led me out into the garden, where she had caused a chair to be placed in the shade. While I sat watching the bees and butterflies, and pulling the flowers to pieces, she strolled up and down the alley close at hand, taking slow stitches in a piece of embroidery. We had been so occupied about ten minutes, when Coquelin came towards us from his lodge,—by appointment, evidently, for this was a roundabout way to the house. Mlle. de Bergerac met him at the end of the path, where I could not hear what they said, but only see their gestures. As they came along together, she raised both hands to her ears, and shook her head with vehemence, as if to refuse to listen to what he was urging. When they drew near my resting-place, she had interrupted him.

"No, no, no!" she cried, "I will never forget it to my dying day. How should I? How can I look at you without remembering it? It's in your face, your figure, your movements, the tones of your voice. It's you,—it's what I love in you! It was that which went through my heart that day at Fossy. It was the look, the tone, with which you called the place horrible; it was your bitter plebeian hate. When you spoke of the misery and baseness of your race, I could have cried out in an anguish of love! When I contradicted you, and pretended that I prized and honored all these tokens of your servitude,—just heaven! you know now what my words were worth!"

Coquelin walked beside her with his hands clasped behind him, and his eyes fixed on the ground with a look of repressed sensibility. He passed his poor little convalescent pupil without heeding him. When they came down the path again, the young girl was still talking with the same feverish volubility.

"But most of all, the first day, the first hour, when you came up the avenue to my brother! I had never seen any one like you. I had seen others, but you had something that went to my soul. I devoured you with my eyes,—your dusty clothes, your uncombed hair, your pale face, the way you held yourself not to seem tired. I went down on my knees, then; I haven't been up since."

The poor girl, you see, was completely possessed by her passion, and yet she was in a very strait place. For her life she wouldn't recede; and yet how was she to advance? There must have been an odd sort of simplicity in her way of bestowing her love; or perhaps you'll think it an odd sort of subtlety. It seems plain to me now, as I tell the story, that Coquelin, with his perfect good sense, was right, and that there was, at this moment, a large element of romance in the composition of her feelings. She seemed to feel no desire to realize her passion. Her hand was already bestowed; fate was inexorable. She wished simply to compress a world of bliss into her few remaining hours of freedom.

The day after this interview in the garden I came down to dinner; on the next I sat up to supper, and for some time afterwards, thanks to my aunt's preoccupation of mind. On rising from the table, my father left the château; my mother, who was ailing, returned to her room. Coquelin disappeared, under pretence of going to his own apartments; but, Mlle. de Bergerac having taken me into the drawing-room and detained me there some minutes, he shortly rejoined us.

"Great heaven, mademoiselle, this must end!" he cried, as he came into the room. "I can stand it no longer."

"Nor can I," said my aunt. "But I have given my word."

"Take back your word, then! Write him a letter—go to him—send me to him—anything! I can't stay here on the footing of a thief and an impostor. I'll do anything," he continued, as she was silent. "I'll go to him in person; I'll go to your brother; I'll go to your sister even. I'll proclaim it to the world. Or, if you don't like that, I'll keep it a mortal secret. I'll leave the château with you without an hour's delay. I'll defy pursuit and discovery. We'll go to America,—anywhere you wish, if it's only action. Only spare me the agony of seeing you drift along into that man's arms."

Mlle. de Bergerac made no reply for some moments. At last, "I will never marry M. de Treuil," she said.

To this declaration Coquelin made no response; but after a pause, "Well, well, well?" he cried.

"Ah, you're pitiless!" said the young girl.

"No, mademoiselle, from the bottom of my heart I pity you."

"Well, then, think of all you ask! Think of the inexpiable criminality of my love. Think of me standing here,—here before my mother's portrait,—murmuring out my shame, scorched by my sister's scorn, buffeted by my brother's curses! Gracious heaven, Coquelin, suppose after all I were a bad, hard girl!"

"I'll suppose nothing; this is no time for hair-splitting." And then, after a pause, as if with a violent effort, in a voice hoarse and yet soft: "Gabrielle, passion is blind. Reason alone is worth a straw. I'll not counsel you in passion, let us wait till reason comes to us." He put out his hand; she gave him her own; he pressed it to his lips and departed.

On the following day, as I still professed myself too weak to resume my books, Coquelin left the château alone, after breakfast, for a long walk. He was going, I suppose, into the woods and meadows in quest of Reason. She was hard to find, apparently, for he failed to return to dinner. He reappeared, however, at supper, but now my father was absent. My mother, as she left the table, expressed the wish that Mlle. de Bergerac should attend her to her own room. Coquelin, meanwhile, went with me into the great saloon, and for half an hour talked to me gravely and kindly about my studies, and questioned me on what we had learned before my illness. At the end of this time Mlle. de Bergerac returned.

"I got this letter to-day from M. de Treuil," she said, and offered him a missive which had apparently been handed to her since dinner.

"I don't care to read it," he said.

She tore it across and held the pieces to the flame of the candle. "He is to be here to-morrow," she added finally.

"Well?" asked Coquelin gravely.

"You know my answer."

"Your answer to him, perfectly. But what is your answer to me?"

She looked at him in silence. They stood for a minute, their eyes locked together. And then, in the same posture,—her arms loose at her sides, her head slightly thrown back,—"To you," she said, "my answer is—farewell."

The word was little more than whispered; but, though he heard it, he neither started nor spoke. He stood unmoved, all his soul trembling under his brows and filling the space between his mistress and himself with a sort of sacred stillness. Then, gradually, his head sank on his breast, and his eyes dropped on the ground.

"It's reason," the young girl began. "Reason has come to me. She tells me that if I marry in my brother's despite, and in opposition to all the traditions that have been kept sacred in my family, I shall neither find happiness nor give it. I must choose the simplest course. The other is a gulf; I can't leap it. It's harder than you think. Something in the air forbids it,— something in the very look of these old walls, within which I was born and I've lived. I shall never marry; I shall go into religion. I tried to fling away my name; it was sowing dragons' teeth. I don't ask you to forgive me. It's small enough comfort that you should have the right to think of me as a poor, weak heart. Keep repeating that: it will console you. I shall not have the compensation of doubting the perfection of what I love."

Coquelin turned away in silence. Mlle. de Bergerac sprang after him. "In Heaven's name," she cried, "say something! Rave, storm, swear, but don't let me think I've broken your heart."

"My heart's sound," said Coquelin, almost with a smile. "I regret nothing that has happened. O, how I love you!"

The young girl buried her face in her hands.

"This end," he went on, "is doubtless the only possible one. It's thinking very lightly of life to expect any other. After all, what call had I to interrupt your life,—to burden you with a trouble, a choice, a decision? As much as anything that I have ever known in you I admire your beautiful delicacy of conscience."

"Ah," said the young girl, with a moan, "don't kill me with fine names!"

And then came the farewell. "I feel," said poor Coquelin,

"that I can't see you again. We must not meet. I will leave Bergerac immediately,—to-night,—under pretext of having been summoned home by my mother's illness. In a few days I will write to your brother that circumstances forbid me to return."

My own part in this painful interview I shall not describe at length. When it began to dawn upon my mind that my friend was actually going to disappear, I was seized with a convulsion of rage and grief. "Ah," cried Mlle. de Bergerac bitterly, "that was all that was wanting!" What means were taken to restore me to composure, what promises were made me, what pious deception was practised, I forget; but, when at last I came to my senses, Coquelin had made his exit.

My aunt took me by the hand and prepared to lead me up to bed, fearing naturally that my ruffled aspect and swollen visage would arouse suspicion. At this moment I heard the clatter of hoofs in the court, mingled with the sound of voices. From the window, I saw M. de Treuil and my father alighting from horseback. Mlle. de Bergerac, apparently, made the same observation; she dropped my hand and sank down in a chair. She was not left long in suspense. Perceiving a light in the saloon, the two gentlemen immediately made their way to this apartment. They came in together, arm in arm, the Vicomte dressed in mourning. Just within the threshold they stopped; my father disengaged his arm, took his companion by the hand and led him to Mlle. de Bergerac. She rose to her feet as you may imagine a sitting statue to rise. The Vicomte bent his knee.

"At last, mademoiselle," said he,—"sooner than I had hoped,—my long probation is finished."

The young girl spoke, but no one would have recognized her voice. "I fear, M. le Vicomte," she said, "that it has only begun."

The Vicomte broke into a harsh, nervous laugh.

"Fol de rol, mademoiselle," cried my father, "your pleasantry is in very bad taste."

But the Vicomte had recovered himself. "Mademoiselle is quite right," he declared; "she means that I must now begin to deserve my happiness." This little speech showed a very brave fancy. It was in flagrant discord with the expression of the poor girl's figure, as she stood twisting her hands together and rolling her eyes,—an image of sombre desperation.

My father felt there was a storm in the air. "M. le Vicomte is in mourning for M. de Sorbières," he said. "M. le Vicomte is his sole legatee. He comes to exact the fulfilment of your promise."

"I made no promise," said Mlle. de Bergerac.

"Excuse me, mademoiselle; you gave your word that you'd wait for me."

"Gracious heaven!" cried the young girl; "haven't I waited for you!"

"*Ma toute belle*," said the Baron, trying to keep his angry voice within the compass of an undertone, and reducing it in the effort to a very ugly whisper, "if I had supposed you were going to make us a scene, *nom de Dieu!* I would have taken my precautions beforehand! You know what you're to expect. Vicomte, keep her to her word. I'll give you half an hour. Come, Chevalier." And he took me by the hand.

We had crossed the threshold and reached the hall, when I heard the Vicomte give a long moan, half plaintive, half indignant. My father turned, and answered with a fierce, inarticulate cry, which I can best describe as a roar. He straightway retraced his steps, I, of course, following. Exactly what, in the brief interval, had passed between our companions I am unable to say; but it was plain that Mlle. de Bergerac, by some cruelly unerring word or act, had discharged the bolt of her refusal. Her gallant lover had sunk into a chair, burying his face in his hands, and stamping his feet on the floor in a frenzy of disappointment. She stood regarding him in a sort of helpless, distant pity. My father had been going to break out into a storm of imprecations; but he suppressed them, and folded his arms.

"And now, mademoiselle," he said, "will you be so good as to inform me of your intentions."

Beneath my father's gaze the softness passed out of my aunt's face and gave place to an angry defiance, which he must have recognized as cousin-german, at least, to the passion in his own breast. "My intentions had been," she said, "to let M. le Vicomte know that I couldn't marry him, with as little offence as possible. But you seem determined, my brother, to thrust in a world of offence somewhere."

You must not blame Mlle. de Bergerac for the sting of her retort. She foresaw a hard fight; she had only sprung to her arms.

My father looked at the wretched Vicomte, as he sat sobbing and stamping like a child. His bosom was wrung with pity for his friend. "Look at that dear Gaston, that charming man, and blush for your audacity."

"I know a great deal more about my audacity than you, brother. I might tell you things that would surprise you."

"Gabrielle, you are mad!" the Baron broke out.

"Perhaps I am," said the young girl. And then, turning to M. de Treuil, in a tone of exquisite reproach, "M. le Vicomte, you suffer less well than I had hoped."

My father could endure no more. He seized his sister by her two wrists, so that beneath the pressure her eyes filled with tears. "Heartless fool!" he cried, "do you know what I can do to you?"

"I can imagine, from this specimen," said the poor creature.

The Baron was beside himself with passion. "Down, down on your knees," he went on, "and beg our pardon all round for your senseless, shameless perversity!" As he spoke, he increased the pressure of his grasp to that degree that, after a vain struggle to free herself, she uttered a scream of pain. The Vicomte sprang to his feet. "In heaven's name, Gabrielle," he cried,—and it was the only real *naïveté* that he had ever uttered,—"isn't it all a horrible jest?"

Mlle. de Bergerac shook her head. "It seems hard, Vicomte," she said, "that I should be answerable for your happiness."

"You hold it there in your hand. Think of what I suffer. To have lived for weeks in the hope of this hour, and to find it what you would fain make it! To have dreamed of rapturous bliss, and to wake to find it hideous misery! Think of it once again!"

"She shall have a chance to think of it," the Baron declared; "she shall think of it quite at her ease. Go to your room, mademoiselle, and remain there till further notice."

Gabrielle prepared to go, but, as she moved away, "I used to fear you, brother," she said with homely scorn, "but I don't fear you now. Judge whether it's because I love you more!"

"Gabrielle," the Vicomte cried out, "I haven't given you up."

"Your feelings are your own, M. le Vicomte. I would have given more than I can say rather than have caused you to suffer. Your asking my hand has been the great honor of my life; my withholding it has been the great trial." And she walked out of the room with the step of unacted tragedy. My father, with an oath, despatched me to bed in her train. Heavy-headed with the recent spectacle of so much half-appre-hended emotion, I speedily fell asleep.

I was aroused by the sound of voices, and the grasp of a heavy hand on my shoulder. My father stood before me, holding a candle, with M. de Treuil beside him. "Chevalier," he said, "open your eyes like a man, and come to your senses."

Thus exhorted, I sat up and stared. The Baron sat down on the edge of the bed. "This evening," he began, "before the Vicomte and I came in, were you alone with your aunt?"— My dear friend, you see the scene from here. I answered with the cruel directness of my years. Even if I had had the wit to dissemble, I should have lacked the courage. Of course I had no story to tell. I had drawn no inferences; I didn't say that my tutor was my aunt's lover. I simply said that he had been with us after supper, and that he wanted my aunt to go away with him. Such was my part in the play. I see the whole picture again,—my father brandishing the candlestick, and de-vouring my words with his great flaming eyes; and the Vicomte behind, portentously silent, with his black clothes and his pale face.

They had not been three minutes out of the room when the door leading to my aunt's chamber opened and Mlle. de Bergerac appeared. She had heard sounds in my apartment, and suspected the visit of the gentlemen and its motive. She immediately won from me the recital of what I had been forced to avow. "Poor Chevalier," she cried, for all commen-tary. And then, after a pause, "What made them suspect that M. Coquelin had been with us?"

"They saw him, or some one, leave the château as they came in."

"And where have they gone now?"

"To supper. My father said to M. de Treuil that first of all they must sup."

Mlle. de Bergerac stood a moment in meditation. Then suddenly, "Get up, Chevalier," she said, "I want you to go with me."

"Where are you going?"

"To M. Coquelin's."

I needed no second admonition. I hustled on my clothes; Mlle. de Bergerac left the room and immediately returned, clad in a light mantle. We made our way undiscovered to one of the private entrances of the château, hurried across the park and found a light in the window of Coquelin's lodge. It was about half past nine. Mlle. de Bergerac gave a loud knock at the door, and we entered her lover's apartment.

Coquelin was seated at his table writing. He sprang to his feet with a cry of amazement. Mlle. de Bergerac stood panting, with one hand pressed to her heart, while rapidly moving the other as if to enjoin calmness.

"They are come back," she began,—"M. de Treuil and my brother!"

"I thought he was to come to-morrow. Was it a deception?"

"Ah, no! not from him,—an accident. Pierre Coquelin, I've had such a scene! But it's not your fault."

"What made the scene?"

"My refusal, of course."

"You turned off the Vicomte?"

"Holy Virgin! You ask me?"

"Unhappy girl!" cried Coquelin.

"No, I was a happy girl to have had a chance to act as my heart bade me. I had faltered enough. But it was hard!"

"It's all hard."

"The hardest is to come," said my aunt. She put out her hand; he sprang to her and seized it, and she pressed his own with vehemence. "They have discovered our secret,— don't ask how. It was Heaven's will. From this moment, of course—"

"From this moment, of course," cried Coquelin, "I stay where I am!"

With an impetuous movement she raised his hand to her lips and kissed it. "You stay where you are. We have nothing to conceal, but we have nothing to avow. We have no confessions to make. Before God we have done our duty. You may expect them, I fancy, to-night; perhaps, too, they will honor me with a visit. They are supping between two battles. They will attack us with fury, I know; but let them dash themselves against our silence as against a wall of stone. I have taken my stand. My love, my errors, my longings, are my own affair. My reputation is a sealed book. Woe to him who would force it open!"

The poor girl had said once, you know, that she was afraid of her nature. Assuredly it had now sprung erect in its strength; it came hurrying into action on the wings of her indignation. "Remember, Coquelin," she went on, "you are still and always my friend. You are the guardian of my weakness, the support of my strength."

"Say it all, Gabrielle!" he cried. "I'm for ever and ever your lover!"

Suddenly, above the music of his voice, there came a great rattling knock at the door. Coquelin sprang forward; it opened in his face and disclosed my father and M. de Treuil. I have no words in my dictionary, no images in my rhetoric, to represent the sudden horror that leaped into my father's face as his eye fell upon his sister. He staggered back a step and then stood glaring, until his feelings found utterance in a single word: "*Coureuse!*" I have never been able to look upon the word as trivial since that moment.

The Vicomte came striding past him into the room, like a bolt of lightning from a rumbling cloud, quivering with baffled desire, and looking taller by the head for his passion. "And it was for this, mademoiselle," he cried, "and for *that!*" and he flung out a scornful hand toward Coquelin. "For a beggarly, boorish, ignorant pedagogue!"

Coquelin folded his arms. "Address me directly, M. le Vicomte," he said; "don't fling mud at me over mademoiselle's head."

"You? Who are you?" hissed the nobleman. "A man doesn't address you; he sends his lackeys to flog you!"

"Well, M. le Vicomte, you're complete," said Coquelin, eyeing him from head to foot.

"Complete?" and M. de Treuil broke into an almost hysterical laugh. "I only lack having married your mistress!"

"Ah!" cried Mlle. de Bergerac.

"O, you poor, insensate fool!" said Coquelin.

"Heaven help me," the young man went on, "I'm ready to marry her still."

While these words were rapidly exchanged, my father stood choking with the confusion of amazement and rage. He was stupefied at his sister's audacity,—at the dauntless spirit which ventured to flaunt its shameful passion in the very face of honor and authority. Yet that simple interjection which I have quoted from my aunt's lips stirred a secret tremor in his heart; it was like the striking of some magic silver bell, portending monstrous things. His passion faltered, and, as his eyes glanced upon my innocent head (which, it must be confessed, was sadly out of place in that pernicious scene), alighted on this smaller wrong. "The next time you go on your adventures, mademoiselle," he cried, "I'd thank you not to pollute my son by dragging him at your skirts."

"I'm not sorry to have my family present," said the young girl, who had had time to collect her thoughts. "I should be glad even if my sister were here. I wish simply to bid you farewell."

Coquelin, at these words, made a step towards her. She passed her hand through his arm. "Things have taken place— and chiefly within the last moment—which change the face of the future. You've done the business, brother," and she fixed her glittering eyes on the Baron; "you've driven me back on myself. I spared you, but you never spared me. I cared for my name; you loaded it with dishonor. I chose between happiness and duty,—duty as you would have laid it down: I preferred duty. But now that happiness has become one with simple safety from violence and insult, I go back to happiness. I give you back your name; though I have kept it more jealously than you. I have another ready for me. O Messieurs!" she cried, with a burst of rapturous exaltation, "for what you have done to me I thank you."

My father began to groan and tremble. He had grasped my

hand in his own, which was clammy with perspiration. "For the love of God, Gabrielle," he implored, "or the fear of the Devil, speak so that a sickened, maddened Christian can understand you! For what purpose did you come here tonight?"

"*Mon Dieu*, it's a long story. You made short work with it. I might in justice do as much. I came here, brother, to guard my reputation, and not to lose it."

All this while my father had neither looked at Coquelin nor spoken to him, either because he thought him not worth his words, or because he had kept some transcendent insult in reserve. Here my governor broke in. "It seems to me time, M. le Baron, that I should inquire the purpose of your own visit."

My father stared a moment. "I came, M. Coquelin, to take you by the shoulders and eject you through that door, with the further impulsion, if necessary, of a vigorous kick."

"Good! And M. le Vicomte?"

"M. le Vicomte came to see it done."

"Perfect! A little more and you had come too late. I was on the point of leaving Bergerac. I can put the story into three words. I have been so happy as to secure the affections of Mlle. de Bergerac. She asked herself, devoutly, what course of action was possible under the circumstances. She decided that the only course was that we should immediately separate. I had no hesitation in bringing my residence with M. le Chevalier to a sudden close. I was to have quitted the château early to-morrow morning, leaving mademoiselle at absolute liberty. With her refusal of M. de Treuil I have nothing to do. Her action in this matter seems to have been strangely precipitated, and my own departure anticipated in consequence. It was at her adjuration that I was preparing to depart. She came here this evening to command me to stay. In our relations there was nothing that the world had a right to lay a finger upon. From the moment that they were suspected it was of the first importance to the security and sanctity of Mlle. de Bergerac's position that there should be no appearance on my part of elusion or flight. The relations I speak of had ceased to exist; there was, therefore, every reason why for the present I should retain my place. Mlle. de Bergerac had been here some three minutes, and had just made known her wishes, when you arrived with the honorable intentions which you avow, and under that illusion the perfect stupidity of which is its least reproach. In my own turn, Messieurs, I thank you!"

"Gabrielle," said my father, as Coquelin ceased speaking, "the long and short of it appears to be that after all you needn't marry this man. Am I to understand that you intend to?"

"Brother, I mean to marry M. Coquelin."

My father stood looking from the young girl to her lover. The Vicomte walked to the window, as if he were in want of air. The night was cool and the window closed. He tried the sash, but for some reason it resisted. Whereupon he raised his sword-hilt and with a violent blow shivered a pane into fragments. The Baron went on: "On what do you propose to live?"

"It's for me to propose," said Coquelin. "My wife shall not suffer."

"Whither do you mean to go?"

"Since you're so good as to ask,—to Paris."

My father had got back his fire. "Well, then," he cried, "my bitterest unforgiveness go with you, and turn your unholy pride to abject woe! My sister may marry a base-born vagrant if she wants, but I shall not give her away. I hope you'll enjoy the mud in which you've planted yourself. I hope your marriage will be blessed in the good old fashion, and that you'll regard philosophically the sight of a half-dozen starving children. I hope you'll enjoy the company of chandlers and cobblers and scribblers!" The Baron could go no further. "Ah, my sister!" he half exclaimed. His voice broke; he gave a great convulsive sob, and fell into a chair.

"Coquelin," said my aunt, "take me back to the château."

As she walked to the door, her hand in the young man's arm, the Vicomte turned short about from the window, and stood with his drawn sword, grimacing horribly.

"Not if I can help it!" he cried through his teeth, and with a sweep of his weapon he made a savage thrust at the young girl's breast. Coquelin, with equal speed, sprang before her, threw out his arm, and took the blow just below the elbow.

"Thank you, M. le Vicomte," he said, "for the chance of calling you a coward! There was something I wanted."

Mlle. de Bergerac spent the night at the château, but by early dawn she had disappeared. Whither Coquelin betook himself with his gratitude and his wound, I know not. He lay, I suppose, at some neighboring farmer's. My father and the Vicomte kept for an hour a silent, sullen vigil in my preceptor's vacant apartment,—for an hour and perhaps longer, for at the end of this time I fell asleep, and when I came to my senses, the next morning, I was in my own bed.

M. de Bergerac had finished his tale.

"But the marriage," I asked, after a pause,—"was it happy?"

"Reasonably so, I fancy. There is no doubt that Coquelin was an excellent fellow. They had three children, and lost them all. They managed to live. He painted portraits and did literary work.

"And his wife?"

"Her history, I take it, is that of all good wives: she loved her husband. When the Revolution came, they went into politics; but here, in spite of his base birth, Coquelin acted with that superior temperance which I always associate with his memory. He was no *sans-culotte*. They both went to the scaffold among the Girondists."

Travelling Companions

THE MOST strictly impressive picture in Italy is incontestably the Last Supper of Leonardo at Milan. A part of its immense solemnity is doubtless due to its being one of the first of the great Italian masterworks that you encounter in coming down from the North. Another secondary source of interest resides in the very completeness of its decay. The mind finds a rare delight in filling each of its vacant spaces, effacing its rank defilement, and repairing, as far as possible, its sad disorder. Of the essential power and beauty of the work there can be no better evidence than this fact that, having lost so much, it has yet retained so much. An unquenchable elegance lingers in those vague outlines and incurable scars; enough remains to place you in sympathy with the unfathomable wisdom of the painter. The fresco covers a wall, the reader will remember, at the end of the former refectory of a monastery now suppressed, the precinct of which is occupied by a regiment of cavalry. Horses stamp, soldiers rattle their oaths, in the cloisters which once echoed to the sober tread of monastic sandals and the pious greetings of meek-voiced friars.

It was the middle of August, and summer sat brooding fiercely over the streets of Milan. The great brick-wrought dome of the church of St. Mary of the Graces rose black with the heat against the brazen sky. As my *fiacre* drew up in front of the church, I found another vehicle in possession of the little square of shade which carpeted the glaring pavement before the adjoining convent. I left the two drivers to share this advantage as they could, and made haste to enter the cooler presence of the Cenacolo. Here I found the occupants of the *fiacre* without, a young lady and an elderly man. Here also, besides the official who takes your tributary franc, sat a long-haired copyist, wooing back the silent secrets of the great fresco into the cheerfullest commonplaces of yellow and blue. The gentleman was earnestly watching this ingenious operation; the young lady sat with her eyes fixed on the picture, from which she failed to move them when I took my place on a line with her. I too, however, speedily became as unconscious of her presence as she of mine, and lost myself in the study of the work before us. A single glance had assured me that she was an American.

Since that day, I have seen all the great art treasures of Italy: I have seen Tintoretto at Venice, Michael Angelo at Florence and Rome, Correggio at Parma; but I have looked at no other picture with an emotion equal to that which rose within me as this great creation of Leonardo slowly began to dawn upon my intelligence from the tragical twilight of its ruin. A work so nobly conceived can never utterly die, so long as the half-dozen main lines of its design remain. Neglect and malice are less cunning than the genius of the great painter. It has stored away with masterly skill such a wealth of beauty as only perfect love and sympathy can fully detect. So, under my eyes, the restless ghost of the dead fresco returned to its mortal abode. From the beautiful central image of Christ I perceived its radiation right and left along the sadly broken line of the disciples. One by one, out of the depths of their grim dismemberment, the figures trembled into meaning and life, and the vast, serious beauty of the work stood revealed. What is the ruling force of this magnificent design? Is it art? is it science? is it sentiment? is it knowledge? I am sure I can't say; but in moments of doubt and depression I find it of excellent use to recall the great picture with all possible distinctness. Of all the works of man's hands it is the least superficial.

The young lady's companion finished his survey of the copyist's work and came and stood behind his chair. The reader will remember that a door has been rudely cut in the wall, a part of it entering the fresco.

"He hasn't got in that door," said the old gentleman, speaking apparently of the copyist.

The young lady was silent. "Well, my dear," he continued. "What do you think of it?"

The young girl gave a sigh. "I see it," she said.

"You see it, eh? Well, I suppose there is nothing more to be done."

The young lady rose slowly, drawing on her glove. As her eyes were still on the fresco, I was able to observe her. Beyond doubt she was American. Her age I fancied to be twenty-two. She was of middle stature, with a charming slender figure. Her hair was brown, her complexion fresh and clear. She wore a white piqué dress and a black lace shawl, and on her thick dark braids a hat with a purple feather. She was largely characterized by that physical delicacy and that personal elegance (each of them sometimes excessive) which seldom fail to betray my young countrywomen in Europe. The gentleman, who was obviously her father, bore the national stamp as plainly as she. A shrewd, firm, generous face, which told of many dealings with many men, of stocks and shares and current prices,—a face, moreover, in which there lingered the mellow afterglow of a sense of excellent claret. He was bald and grizzled, this perfect American, and he wore a short-bristled white moustache between the two hard wrinkles forming the sides of a triangle of which his mouth was the base and the ridge of his nose, where his eye-glass sat, the apex. In deference perhaps to this exotic growth, he was better dressed than is common with the typical American citizen, in a blue necktie, a white waistcoat, and a pair of gray trousers. As his daughter still lingered, he looked at me with an eye of sagacious conjecture.

"Ah, that beautiful, beautiful, beautiful Christ," said the young lady, in a tone which betrayed her words in spite of its softness. "O father, what a picture!"

"Hum!" said her father, "I don't see it."

"I must get a photograph," the young girl rejoined. She turned away and walked to the farther end of the hall, where the custodian presides at a table of photographs and prints. Meanwhile her father had perceived my Murray.

"English, sir?" he demanded.

"No, I'm an American, like yourself, I fancy."

"Glad to make your acquaintance, sir. From New York?"

"From New York. I have been absent from home, however, for a number of years."

"Residing in this part of the world?"

"No. I have been living in Germany. I have only just come into Italy."

"Ah, so have we. The young lady is my daughter. She is crazy about Italy. We were very nicely fixed at Interlaken, when suddenly she read in some confounded book or other that Italy should be seen in summer. So she dragged me over the mountains into this fiery furnace. I'm actually melting away. I have lost five pounds in three days."

I replied that the heat was indeed intense, but that I agreed with his daughter that Italy should be seen in summer. What could be pleasanter than the temperature of that vast cool hall?

"Ah, yes," said my friend; "I suppose we shall have plenty of this kind of thing. It makes no odds to me, so long as my poor girl has a good time."

"She seems," I remarked, "to be having a pretty good time with the photographs." In fact, she was comparing photographs with a great deal of apparent energy, while the salesman lauded his wares in the Italian manner. We strolled over to the table. The young girl was seemingly in treaty for a large photograph of the head of Christ, in which the blurred and fragmentary character of the original was largely intensified, though much of its exquisite pathetic beauty was also preserved. "They'll not think much of that at home," said the old gentleman.

"So much the worse for them," said his daughter, with an accent of delicate pity. With the photograph in her hand, she walked back to the fresco. Her father engaged in an English dialogue with the custodian. In the course of five minutes, wishing likewise to compare the copy and the original, I returned to the great picture. As I drew near it the young lady turned away. Her eyes then for the first time met my own. They were deep and dark and luminous,—I fancied streaming with tears. I watched her as she returned to the table. Her walk seemed to me peculiarly graceful; light, and rapid, and yet full of decision and dignity. A thrill of delight passed through my heart as I guessed at her moistened lids.

"Sweet fellow-countrywoman," I cried in silence, "you have the divine gift of feeling." And I returned to the fresco with a deepened sense of its virtue. When I turned around, my companions had left the room.

In spite of the great heat, I was prepared thoroughly to "do" Milan. In fact, I rather enjoyed the heat; it seemed to my Northern senses to deepen the Italian, the Southern, the local character of things. On that blazing afternoon, I have not forgotten, I went to the church of St. Ambrose, to the

Ambrosian Library, to a dozen minor churches. Every step distilled a richer drop into the wholesome cup of pleasure. From my earliest manhood, beneath a German sky, I had dreamed of this Italian pilgrimage, and, after much waiting and working and planning, I had at last undertaken it in a spirit of fervent devotion. There had been moments in Germany when I fancied myself a clever man; but it now seemed to me that for the first time I really *felt* my intellect. Imagination, panting and exhausted, withdrew from the game; and Observation stepped into her place, trembling and glowing with open-eyed desire.

I had already been twice to the Cathedral, and had wandered through the clustering inner darkness of the high arcades which support those light-defying pinnacles and spires. Towards the close of the afternoon I found myself strolling once more over the great column-planted, altar-studded pavement, with the view of ascending to the roof. On presenting myself at the little door in the right transept, through which you gain admission to the upper regions, I perceived my late fellow-visitors of the fresco preparing apparently for an upward movement, but not without some reluctance on the paternal side. The poor gentleman had been accommodated with a chair, on which he sat fanning himself with his hat and looking painfully apoplectic. The sacristan meanwhile held open the door with an air of invitation. But my corpulent friend, with his thumb in his Murray, balked at the ascent. Recognizing me, his face expressed a sudden sense of vague relief.

"Have you been up, sir?" he inquired, groaningly.

I answered that I was about to ascend; and recalling then the fact, which I possessed rather as information than experience, that young American ladies may not improperly detach themselves on occasion from the parental side, I ventured to declare that, if my friend was unwilling to encounter the fatigue of mounting to the roof in person, I should be most happy, as a fellow-countryman, qualified already perhaps to claim a traveller's acquaintance, to accompany and assist his daughter.

"You're very good, sir," said the poor man; "I confess that I'm about played out. I'd far rather sit here and watch these pretty Italian ladies saying their prayers. Charlotte, what do you say?"

"Of course if you're tired I should be sorry to have you make the effort," said Charlotte. "But I believe the great thing is to see the view from the roof. I'm much obliged to the gentleman."

It was arranged accordingly that we should ascend together. "Good luck to you," cried my friend, "and mind you take good care of her."

Those who have rambled among the marble immensities of the summit of Milan Cathedral will hardly expect me to describe them. It is only when they have been seen as a complete concentric whole that they can be properly appreciated. It was not as a whole that I saw them; a week in Italy had assured me that I have not the architectural *coup d'œil.* In looking back on the scene into which we emerged from the stifling spiral of the ascent, I have chiefly a confused sense of an immense skyward elevation and a fierce blinding efflorescence of fantastic forms of marble. There, reared for the action of the sun, you find a vast marble world. The solid whiteness lies in mighty slabs along the iridescent slopes of nave and transept, like the lonely snow-fields of the higher Alps. It leaps and climbs and shoots and attacks the unsheltered blue with a keen and joyous incision. It meets the pitiless sun with a more than equal glow; the day falters, declines, expires, but the marble shines forever, unmelted and unintermittent. You will know what I mean if you have looked upward from the Piazza at midnight. With confounding frequency too, on some uttermost point of a pinnacle, its plastic force explodes into satisfied rest in some perfect flower of a figure. A myriad carven statues, known only to the circling air, are poised and niched beyond reach of human vision, the loss of which to mortal eyes is, I suppose, the gain of the Church and the Lord. Among all the jewelled shrines and overwrought tabernacles of Italy, I have seen no such magnificent waste of labor, no such glorious synthesis of cunning secrets. As you wander, sweating and blinking, over the changing levels of the edifice, your eye catches at a hundred points the little profile of a little saint, looking out into the dizzy air, a pair of folded hands praying to the bright immediate heavens, a sandalled monkish foot planted on the edge of the white abyss. And then, besides this mighty world of the great Cathedral itself, you possess the view of all green Lombardy,—vast, lazy Lombardy, resting from its Alpine up-heavals.

My companion carried a little white umbrella, with a violet lining. Thus protected from the sun, she climbed and gazed with abundant courage and spirit. Her movements, her glance, her voice, were full of intelligent pleasure. Now that I could observe her closely, I saw that, though perhaps without regular beauty, she was yet, for youth, summer, and Italy, more than pretty enough. Owing to my residence in Germany, among Germans, in a small university town, Americans had come to have for me, in a large degree, the interest of novelty and remoteness. Of the charm of American women, in especial, I had formed a very high estimate, and I was more than ready to be led captive by the far-famed graces of their frankness and freedom. I already felt that in the young girl beside me there was a different quality of womanhood from any that I had recently known; a keenness, a maturity, a conscience, which deeply stirred my curiosity. It was positive, not negative maidenhood.

"You're an American," I said, as we stepped to look at the distance.

"Yes; and you?" In her voice alone the charm faltered. It was high, thin, and nervous.

"O, happily, I'm also one."

"I shouldn't have thought so. I should have taken you for a German."

"By education I am a German. I knew you were an American the moment I looked at you."

"I suppose so. It seems that American women are easily recognized. But don't talk about America." She paused and swept her dark eye over the whole immensity of prospect. "This is Italy," she cried, "Italy, Italy!"

"Italy indeed. What do you think of the Leonardo."

"I fancy there can be only one feeling about it. It must be the saddest and finest of all pictures. But I know nothing of art. I have seen nothing yet but that lovely Raphael in the Brera."

"You have a vast deal before you. You're going southward, I suppose."

"Yes, we are going directly to Venice. There I shall see Titian."

"Titian and Paul Veronese."

"Yes, I can hardly believe it. Have you ever been in a gondola?"

"No; this is my first visit to Italy."

"Ah, this is all new, then, to you as well."

"Divinely new," said I, with fervor.

She glanced at me, with a smile,—a ray of friendly pleasure in my pleasure. "And you are not disappointed!"

"Not a jot. I'm too good a German."

"I'm too good an American. I live at Araminta, New Jersey!"

We thoroughly "did" the high places of the church, concluding with an ascent into the little gallery of the central spire. The view from this spot is beyond all words, especially the view toward the long mountain line which shuts out the North. The sun was sinking: clear and serene upon their blue foundations, the snow-peaks sat clustered and scattered, and shrouded in silence and light. To the south the long shadows fused and multiplied, and the bosky Lombard flats melted away into perfect Italy. This prospect offers a great emotion to the Northern traveller. A vague, delicious impulse of conquest stirs in his heart. From his dizzy vantage-point, as he looks down at her, beautiful, historic, exposed, he embraces the whole land in the far-reaching range of his desire. "That is Monte Rosa," I said; "that is the Simplon pass; there is the triple glitter of those lovely lakes."

"Poor Monte Rosa," said my companion.

"I'm sure I never thought of Monte Rosa as an object of pity."

"You don't know what she represents. She represents the genius of the North. There she stands, frozen and fixed, resting her head upon that mountain wall, looking over at this lovely southern world and yearning towards it forever in vain."

"It is very well she can't come over. She would melt."

"Very true. She is beautiful, too, in her own way. I mean to fancy that I am her chosen envoy, and that I have come up here to receive her blessing."

I made an attempt to point out a few localities. "Yonder lies Venice, out of sight. In the interval are a dozen divine little towns. I hope to visit them all. I shall ramble all day in their streets and churches, their little museums, and their great palaces. In the evening I shall sit at the door of a café in the little piazza, scanning some lovely civic edifice in the moonlight, and saying, 'Ah! this is Italy!' "

"You gentlemen are certainly very happy. I'm afraid we must go straight to Venice."

"Your father insists upon it?"

"He wishes it. Poor father! in early life he formed the habit of being in a hurry, and he can't break it even now, when, being out of business, he has nothing on earth to do."

"But in America I thought daughters insisted as well as fathers."

The young girl looked at me, half serious, half smiling. "Have you a mother?" she asked; and then, blushing the least bit at her directness and without waiting for an answer, "This is not America," she said. "I should like to think I might become for a while a creature of Italy."

Somehow I felt a certain contagion in her momentary flash of frankness. "I strongly suspect," I said, "that you are American to the depths of your soul, and that you'll never be anything else; I hope not."

In this hope of mine there was perhaps a little impertinence; but my companion looked at me with a gentle smile, which seemed to hint that she forgave it. "You, on the other hand," she said, "are a perfect German, I fancy; and you'll never be anything else."

"I am sure I wish with all my heart," I answered, "to be a good American. I'm open to conversion. Try me."

"Thank you; I haven't the ardor; I'll make you over to my father. We mustn't forget, by the way, that he is waiting for us."

We did forget it, however, awhile longer. We came down from the tower and made our way to the balustrade which edges the front of the edifice, and looked down on the city and the piazza below. Milan had, to my sense, a peculiar

charm of temperate gayety,—the softness of the South without its laxity; and I felt as if I could gladly spend a month
there. The common life of the streets was beginning to stir
and murmur again, with the subsiding heat and the approaching night. There came up into our faces a delicious emanation
as from the sweetness of Transalpine life. At the little balconies
of the windows, beneath the sloping awnings, with their feet
among the crowded flower-pots and their plump bare arms on
the iron rails, lazy, dowdy Italian beauties would appear, still
drowsy with the broken *siesta*. Beautiful, slim young officers
had begun to dot the pavement, glorious with their clanking
swords, their brown moustaches, and their legs of azure. In
gentle harmony with these, various ladies of Milan were issuing forth to enjoy the cool; elegant, romantic, provoking, in
short black dresses and lace mantillas depending from their
chignons, with a little cloud of powder artfully enhancing the
darkness of their hair and eyes. How it all wasn't Germany!
how it couldn't have been Araminta, New Jersey! "It's the
South, the South," I kept repeating,—"the South in nature, in
man, in manners." It was a brighter world. "It's the South," I
said to my companion. "Don't you feel it in all your nerves?"

"O, it's very pleasant," she said.

"We must forget all our cares and duties and sorrows. We
must go in for the beautiful. Think of this great trap for the
sunbeams, in this city of yellows and russets and crimsons, of
liquid vowels and glancing smiles being, like one of our
Northern cathedrals, a temple to Morality and Conscience. It
doesn't belong to heaven, but to earth,—to love and light
and pleasure."

My friend was silent a moment. "I'm glad I'm not a
Catholic," she said at last. "Come, we must go down."

We found the interior of the Cathedral delightfully cool
and shadowy. The young lady's father was not at our place of
ingress, and we began to walk through the church in search
of him. We met a number of Milanese ladies, who charmed us
with their sombre elegance and the Spanish romance of their
veils. With these pale penitents and postulants my companion
had a lingering sisterly sympathy.

"Don't you wish you were a Catholic now?" I asked. "It
would be so pleasant to wear one of those lovely mantillas."

"The mantillas are certainly becoming," she said. "But who knows what horrible old-world sorrows and fears and remorses they cover? Look at this person." We were standing near the great altar. As she spoke, a woman rose from her knees, and as she drew the folds of her lace mantle across her bosom, fixed her large dark eyes on us with a peculiar significant intensity. She was of less than middle age, with a pale, haggard face, a certain tarnished elegance of dress, and a remarkable nobleness of gesture and carriage. She came towards us, with an odd mixture, in her whole expression, of decency and defiance. "Are you English?" she said in Italian. "You are very pretty. Is he a brother or a lover?"

"He is neither," said I, affecting a tone of rebuke.

"Neither? only a friend! You are very happy to have a friend, Signorina. Ah, you are pretty! You were watching me at my prayers just now; you thought me very curious, apparently. I don't care. You may see me here any day. But I devoutly hope you may never have to pray such bitter, bitter prayers as mine. A thousand excuses." And she went her way.

"What in the world does she mean?" said my companion.

"Monte Rosa," said I, "was the genius of the North. This poor woman is the genius of the Picturesque. She shows us the essential misery that lies behind it. It's not an unwholesome lesson to receive at the outset. Look at her sweeping down the aisle. What a poise of the head! The picturesque is handsome, all the same."

"I do wonder what is her trouble," murmured the young girl. "She has swept away an illusion in the folds of those black garments."

"Well," said I, "here is a solid fact to replace it." My eyes had just lighted upon the object of our search. He sat in a chair, half tilted back against a pillar. His chin rested on his shirt-bosom, and his hands were folded together over his waistcoat, where it most protruded. Shirt and waistcoat rose and fell with visible, audible regularity. I wandered apart and left his daughter to deal with him. When she had fairly aroused him, he thanked me heartily for my care of the young lady, and expressed the wish that we might meet again. "We start to-morrow for Venice," he said. "I want awfully to get a whiff of the sea-breeze and to see if there is anything to be got out of a gondola."

As I expected also to be in Venice before many days, I had little doubt of our meeting. In consideration of this circumstance, my friend proposed hat we should exchange cards; which we accordingly did, then and there, before the high altar, above the gorgeous chapel which enshrines the relics of St. Charles Borromeus. It was thus that I learned his name to be Mr. Mark Evans.

"Take a few notes for us!" said Miss Evans, as I shook her hand in farewell.

I spent the evening, after dinner, strolling among the crowded streets of the city, tasting of Milanese humanity. At the door of a café I perceived Mr. Evans seated at a little round table. He seemed to have discovered the merits of absinthe. I wondered where he had left his daughter. She was in her room, I fancied, writing her journal.

The fortnight which followed my departure from Milan was in all respects memorable and delightful. With an interest that hourly deepened as I read, I turned the early pages of the enchanting romance of Italy. I carried out in detail the programme which I had sketched for Miss Evans. Those few brief days, as I look back on them, seem to me the sweetest, fullest, calmest of my life. All personal passions, all restless egotism, all worldly hopes, regrets, and fears were stilled and absorbed in the steady perception of the material present. It exhaled the pure essence of romance. What words can reproduce the picture which these Northern Italian towns project upon a sympathetic retina? They are shabby, deserted, dreary, decayed, unclean. In those August days the southern sun poured into them with a fierceness which might have seemed fatal to any lurking shadow of picturesque mystery. But taking them as cruel time had made them and left them, I found in them an immeasurable instruction and charm. My perception seemed for the first time to live a sturdy creative life of its own. How it fed upon the mouldy crumbs of the festal past! I have always thought the observant faculty a windy impostor, so long as it refuses to pocket pride and doff its bravery and crawl on all-fours, if need be, into the unillumined corners and crannies of life. In these dead cities of Verona, Mantua, Padua, how life had revelled and postured in its strength! How sentiment and passion had blossomed and flowered! How much of history had been performed! What a wealth of mortality had ripened and decayed! I have never elsewhere got so deep an impression of the social secrets of mankind. In England, even, in those verdure-stifled haunts of domestic peace which muffle the sounding chords of British civilization, one has a fainter sense of the possible movement and fruition of individual character. Beyond a certain point you fancy it merged in the general medium of duty, business, and politics. In Italy, in spite of your knowledge of the strenuous public conscience which once inflamed these compact little states, the unapplied, spontaneous moral life of society seems to have been more active and more subtle. I walked about with a volume of Stendahl in my pocket; at every step I gathered some lingering testimony to the exquisite vanity of ambition.

But the great emotion, after all, was to feel myself among scenes in which art had ranged so freely. It had often enough been bad, but it had never ceased to be art. An invincible instinct of beauty had presided at life,—an instinct often ludicrously crude and primitive. Wherever I turned I found a vital principle of grace,—from the smile of a chambermaid to the curve of an arch. My memory reverts with an especial tenderness to certain hours in the dusky, faded saloons of those vacant, ruinous palaces which boast of "collections." The pictures are frequently poor, but the visitor's impression is generally rich. The brick-tiled floors are bare; the doors lack paint; the great windows, curtains; the chairs and tables have lost their gilding and their damask drapery; but the ghost of a graceful aristocracy treads at your side and does the melancholy honors of the abode with a dignity that brooks no sarcasm. You feel that art and piety here have been blind, generous instincts. You are reminded in persuasive accents of the old personal regimen in human affairs. Certain pictures are veiled and curtained *virginibus puerisque*. Through these tarnished halls lean and patient abbés led their youthful virginal pupils. Have you read Stendahl's *Chartreuse de Parme*? There was such a gallery in the palace of the Duchess of San Severino. After a long day of strolling, lounging, and staring, I found a singularly perfect pleasure in sitting at the door of a

café in the warm star-light, eating an ice and making an occasional experiment in the way of talk with my neighbors. I recall with peculiar fondness and delight three sweet sessions in
the delicious Piazza die Signori at Verona. The Piazza is small,
compact, private almost, accessible only to pedestrians, paved
with great slabs which have known none but a gentle human
tread. On one side of it rises in elaborate elegance and grace,
above its light arched *loggia*, the image-bordered mass of the
ancient palace of the Council; facing this stand two sterner,
heavier buildings, dedicated to municipal offices and to the
lodgement of soldiers. Step through the archway which leads
out of the Piazza and you will find a vast quadrangle with
a staircase climbing sunward, along the wall, a row of gen-
darmes sitting in the shade, a group of soldiers cleaning their
muskets, a dozen persons of either sex leaning downward
from the open windows. At one end of the little square rose
into the pale darkness the high slender shaft of a brick campanile; in the centre glittered steadily a colossal white statue
of Dante. Behind this statue was the Caffè Dante, where on
three successive days I sat till midnight, feeling the scene,
learning its sovereign "distinction." But of Verona I shall not
pretend to speak. As I drew near Venice I began to feel a soft
impatience, an expectant tremor of the heart. The day before
reaching it I spent at Vicenza. I wandered all day through the
streets, of course, looking at Palladio's palaces and enjoying
them in defiance of reason and Ruskin. They seemed to me
essentially rich and palatial. In the evening I resorted, as
usual, to the city's generous heart, the decayed ex-glorious
Piazza. This spot at Vicenza affords you a really soul-stirring
premonition of Venice. There is no Byzantine Basilica and no
Ducal Palace; but there is an immense impressive hall of
council, and a soaring campanile, and there are two dis-
crowned columns telling of defeated Venetian dominion.
Here I seated myself before a café door, in a group of gossiping votaries of the Southern night. The tables being mostly
occupied, I had some difficulty in finding one. In a short time
I perceived a young man walking through the crowd, seeking
where he might bestow himself. Passing near me, he stopped
and asked me with irresistible grace if he might share my
table. I cordially assented: he sat down and ordered a glass of

sugar and water. He was of about my own age, apparently, and full of the opulent beauty of the greater number of young Italians. His dress was simple even to shabbiness: he might have been a young prince in disguise, a Haroun-al-Raschid. With small delay we engaged in conversation. My companion was boyish, modest, and gracious; he nevertheless discoursed freely on the things of Vicenza. He was so good as to regret that we had not met earlier in the day; it would have given him such pleasure to accompany me on my tour of the city. He was passionately fond of art: he was in fact an artist. Was I fond of pictures? Was I inclined to purchase? I answered that I had no desire to purchase modern pictures, that in fact I had small means to purchase any. He informed me that he had a beautiful ancient work which, to his great regret, he found himself compelled to sell; a most divine little Correggio. Would I do him the favor to look at it? I had small belief in the value of this unrenowned masterpiece; but I felt a kindness for the young painter. I consented to have him call for me the next morning and take me to his house, where for two hundred years, he assured me, the work had been jealously preserved.

He came punctually, beautiful, smiling, shabby, as before. After a ten minutes' walk we stopped before a gaudy half-palazzo which rejoiced in a vague Palladian air. In the basement, looking on the court, lived my friend; with his mother, he informed me, and his sister. He ushered me in, through a dark antechamber, into which, through a gaping kitchen door, there gushed a sudden aroma of onions. I found myself in a high, half-darkened saloon. One of the windows was open into the court, from which the light entered verdantly through a row of flowering plants. In an arm-chair near the window sat a young girl in a dressing-gown, empty-handed, pale, with wonderful eyes, apparently an invalid. At her side stood a large elderly woman in a rusty black silk gown, with an agreeable face, flushed a little, apparently with the expectation of seeing me. The young man introduced them as his mother and his sister. On a table near the window, propped upright in such a way as to catch the light, was a small picture in a heavy frame. I proceeded to examine it. It represented in simple composition a Madonna and Child; the mother facing you, pressing the infant to her bosom, faintly smiling, and looking out of the picture with a solemn sweetness. It was pretty, it was good; but it was not Correggio. There was indeed a certain suggestion of his exquisite touch; but it was a likeness merely, and not the precious reality. One fact, however, struck swiftly home to my consciousness: the face of the Madonna bore a singular resemblance to that of Miss Evans. The lines, the character, the expression, were the same; the faint half-thoughtful smile was hers, the feminine frankness and gentle confidence of the brow, from which the dark hair waved back with the same even abundance. All this, in the Madonna's face, was meant for heaven; and on Miss Evans's in a fair degree, probably, for earth. But the mutual likeness was, nevertheless, perfect, and it quickened my interest in the picture to a point which the intrinsic merit of the work would doubtless have failed to justify; although I confess that I was now not slow to discover a great deal of agreeable painting in it.

"But I doubt of its being a Correggio," said I.

"A Correggio, I give you my word of honor, sir!" cried my young man.

"*Ecco!* my son's word of honor," cried his mother.

"I don't deny," I said, "that it is a very pretty work. It is perhaps Parmigianino."

"O no, sir," the elder insisted, "a true Correggio! We have had it two hundred years! Try another light; you will see. A true Correggio! Isn't it so, my daughter?"

The young man put his arm in mine, played his fingers airily over the picture, and whispered of a dozen beauties.

"O, I grant you," said I, "it's a very pretty picture." As I looked at it I felt the dark eyes of the young girl in the armchair fixed upon me with almost unpleasant intensity. I met her gaze for a moment: I found in it a strange union of defiant pride and sad despondent urgency.

"What do you ask for the picture?" I said.

There was a silence.

"Speak, *madre mia*," said the young man.

"*La senta!*" and the lady played with her broken fan. "We should like you to name a price."

"O, if I named a price, it would not be as for a Correggio.

I can't afford to buy Correggios. If this were a real Correggio, you would be rich. You should go to a duke, a prince, not to me."

"We would be rich! Do you hear, my children? We are very poor, sir. You have only to look at us. Look at my poor daughter. She was once beautiful, fresh, gay. A year ago she fell ill: a long story, sir, and a sad one. We have had doctors; they have ordered five thousand things. My daughter gets no better. There it is, sir. We are very poor."

The young girl's look confirmed her mother's story. That she had been beautiful I could easily believe; that she was ill was equally apparent. She was still remarkable indeed for a touching, hungry, unsatisfied grace. She remained silent and motionless, with her eyes fastened upon my face. I again examined the pretended Correggio. It was wonderfully like Miss Evans. The young American rose up in my mind with irresistible vividness and grace. How she seemed to glow with strength, freedom, and joy, beside this sombre, fading, Southern sister! It was a happy thought that, under the benediction of her image, I might cause a ray of healing sunshine to fall at this poor girl's feet.

"Have you ever tried to sell the picture before?"

"Never!" said the old lady, proudly. "My husband had it from his father. If we have made up our minds to part with it now,—most blessed little Madonna!—it is because we have had an intimation from heaven."

"From heaven?"

"From heaven, Signore. My daughter had a dream. She dreamed that a young stranger came to Vicenza, and that he wandered about the streets saying, 'Where, ah where, is my blessed Lady?' Some told him in one church, and some told him in another. He went into all the churches and lifted all the curtains, giving great fees to the sacristans! But he always came out shaking his head and repeating his question, 'Where is my blessed Lady? I have come from over the sea, I have come to Italy to find her!'" The woman delivered herself of this recital with a noble florid unction and a vast redundancy, to my Northern ear, of delightful liquid sounds. As she paused momentarily, her daughter spoke for the first time.

"And then I fancied," said the young girl, "that I heard his voice pausing under my window at night. 'His blessed Lady is here,' I said, 'we must not let him lose her.' So I called my brother and bade him go forth in search of you. I dreamed that he brought you back. We made an altar with candles and lace and flowers, and on it we placed the little picture. The stranger had light hair, light eyes, a flowing beard like you. He kneeled down before the little Madonna and worshipped her. We left him at his devotions and went away. When we came back the candles on the altar were out: the Madonna was gone, too; but in its place there burned a bright pure light. It was a purse of gold!"

"What a very pretty story!" said I. "How many pieces were there in the purse?"

The young man burst into a laugh. "Twenty thousand!" he said.

I made my offer for the picture. It was esteemed generous apparently; I was cordially thanked. As it was inconvenient, however, to take possession of the work at that moment, I agreed to pay down but half the sum, reserving the other half to the time of delivery. When I prepared to take my departure the young girl rose from her chair and enabled me to measure at once her weakness and her beauty. "Will you come back for the picture yourself?" she asked.

"Possibly. I should like to see you again. You must get better."

"O, I shall never get better."

"I can't believe that. I shall perhaps have a dream to tell you!"

"I shall soon be in heaven. I shall send you one."

"Listen to her!" cried the mother. "But she is already an angel."

With a farewell glance at my pictured Madonna I departed. My visit to this little Vicenza household had filled me with a painful, indefinable sadness. So beautiful they all were, so civil, so charming, and yet so mendacious and miserable! As I hurried along in the train toward the briny cincture of Venice, my heart was heavy with the image of that sombre, dying Italian maiden. Her face haunted me. What fatal wrong had she suffered? What hidden sorrow had blasted the freshness of her youth? As I began to smell the nearing Adriatic, my fancy

bounded forward to claim asylum in the calmer presence of
my bright American friend. I have no space to tell the story of
my arrival in Venice and my first impressions. Mr. Evans had
not mentioned his hotel. He was not at the Hotel de
l'Europe, whither I myself repaired. If he was still in Venice,
however, I foresaw that we should not fail to meet. The day
succeeding my arrival I spent in a restless fever of curiosity
and delight, now lost in the sensuous ease of my gondola,
now lingering in charmed devotion before a canvas of
Tintoretto or Paul Veronese. I exhausted three gondoliers
and saw all Venice in a passionate fury and haste. I wished to
probe its fulness and learn at once the best—or the worst.
Late in the afternoon I disembarked at the Piazzetta and took
my way haltingly and gazingly to the many-domed Basilica,
—that shell of silver with a lining of marble. It was that
enchanting Venetian hour when the ocean-touching sun sits
melting to death, and the whole still air seems to glow with
the soft effusion of his golden substance. Within the church,
the deep brown shadow-masses, the heavy thick-tinted air, the
gorgeous composite darkness, reigned in richer, quainter,
more fantastic gloom than my feeble pen can reproduce the
likeness of. From those rude concavities of dome and semi-
dome, where the multitudinous facets of pictorial mosaic
shimmer and twinkle in their own dull brightness; from the
vast antiquity of innumerable marbles, incrusting the walls in
roughly mated slabs, cracked and polished and triple-tinted
with eternal service; from the wavy carpet of compacted
stone, where a thousand once-bright fragments glimmer
through the long attrition of idle feet and devoted knees;
from sombre gold and mellow alabaster, from porphyry and
malachite, from long dead crystal and the sparkle of undying
lamps,—there proceeds a dense rich atmosphere of splendor
and sanctity which transports the half-stupefied traveller to
the age of a simpler and more awful faith. I wandered for half
an hour beneath those reverted cups of scintillating darkness,
stumbling on the great stony swells of the pavement as I
gazed upward at the long mosaic saints who curve gigantically
with the curves of dome and ceiling. I had left Europe; I was
in the East. An overwhelming sense of the sadness of man's
spiritual history took possession of my heart. The clustering

picturesque shadows about me seemed to represent the darkness of a past from which he had slowly and painfully struggled. The great mosaic images, hideous, grotesque, inhuman, glimmered like the cruel spectres of early superstitions and terrors. There came over me, too, a poignant conviction of the ludicrous folly of the idle spirit of travel. How with Murray and an opera-glass it strolls and stares where omniscient angels stand diffident and sad! How blunted and stupid are its senses! How trivial and superficial its imaginings! To this builded sepulchre of trembling hope and dread, this monument of mighty passions, I had wandered in search of pictorial effects. O vulgarity! Of course I remained, nevertheless, still curious of effects. Suddenly I perceived a very agreeable one. Kneeling on a low *prie-dieu*, with her hands clasped, a lady was gazing upward at the great mosaic Christ in the dome of the choir. She wore a black lace shawl and a purple hat. She was Miss Evans. Her attitude slightly puzzled me. Was she really at her devotions, or was she only playing at prayer? I walked to a distance, so that she might have time to move before I addressed her. Five minutes afterwards, however, she was in the same position. I walked slowly towards her, and as I approached her attracted her attention. She immediately recognized me and smiled and bowed, without moving from her place.

"I saw you five minutes ago," I said, "but I was afraid of interrupting your prayers."

"O, they were only half-prayers," she said.

"Half-prayers are pretty well for one who only the other day was thanking Heaven that she was not a Catholic."

"Half-prayers are no prayers. I'm not a Catholic yet."

Her father, she told me, had brought her to the church, but had returned on foot to the hotel for his pocket-book. They were to dine at one of the restaurants in the Piazza. Mr. Evans was vastly contented with Venice, and spent his days and nights in gondolas. Awaiting his return, we wandered over the church. Yes, incontestably, Miss Evans resembled my little Vicenza picture. She looked a little pale with the heat and the constant nervous tension of sight-seeing; but she pleased me now as effectually as she had pleased me before. There was an even deeper sweetness in the freedom and breadth of her utterance and carriage. I felt more even than before that she was an example of woman active, not of woman passive. We strolled through the great Basilica in serious, charmed silence. Miss Evans told me that she had been there much: she seemed to know it well. We went into the dark Baptistery and sat down on a bench against the wall, trying to discriminate in the vaulted dimness the harsh mediæval reliefs behind the altar and the mosaic Crucifixion above it.

"Well," said I, "what has Venice done for you?"

"Many things. Tired me a little, saddened me, charmed me."

"How have you spent your time?"

"As people spend it. After breakfast we get into our gondola and remain in it pretty well till bedtime. I believe I know every canal, every canaletto, in Venice. You must have learned already how sweet it is to lean back under the awning, to feel beneath you that steady, liquid lapse, to look out at all this bright, sad elegance of ruin. I have been reading two or three of George Sand's novels. Do you know *La Dernière Aldini*? I fancy a romance in every palace."

"The reality of Venice seems to me to exceed all romance. It's romance enough simply to be here."

"Yes; but how brief and transient a romance!"

"Well," said I, "we shall certainly cease to be here, but we shall never cease to have been here. You are not to leave directly, I hope."

"In the course of ten days or a fortnight we go to Florence."

"And then to Rome?"

"To Rome and Naples, and then by sea, probably, to Genoa, and thence to Nice and Paris. We must be at home by the new year. And you?"

"I hope to spend the winter in Italy."

"Are you never coming home again?"

"By no means. I shall probably return in the spring. But I wish you, too, were going to remain."

"You are very good. My father pronounces it impossible. I have only to make the most of it while I'm here."

"Are you going back to Araminta?"

Miss Evans was silent a moment. "O, don't ask!" she said.

"What kind of a place is Araminta?" I asked, maliciously.

Again she was silent. "That is John the Baptist on the cover of the basin," she said, at last, rising to her feet, with a light laugh.

On emerging from the Baptistery we found Mr. Evans who greeted me cordially and insisted on my coming to dine with them. I think most fondly of our little dinner. We went to the Caffè Quadri and occupied a table beside an open window, looking out into the Piazza, which was beginning to fill with evening loungers and listeners to the great band of music in the centre. Miss Evans took off her hat and sat facing me in friendly silence. Her father sustained the larger burden of conversation. He seemed to feel its weight, however, as the dinner proceeded and when he had attacked his second bottle of wine. Miss Evans then questioned me about my journey from Milan. I told her the whole story, and felt that I infused into it a great deal of color and heat. She sat charming me forward with her steady, listening smile. For the first time in my life I felt the magic of sympathy. After dinner we went down into the Piazza and established ourselves at one of Florian's tables. Night had become perfect; the music was magnificent. At a neighboring table was a group of young Venetian gentlemen, splendid in dress, after the manner of their kind, and glorious with the wondrous physical glory of the Italian race.

"They only need velvet and satin and plumes," I said, "to be subjects for Titian and Paul Veronese."

They sat rolling their dark eyes and kissing their white hands at passing friends, with smiles that were like the moon flashes on the Adriatic.

"They are beautiful exceedingly," said Miss Evans; "the most beautiful creatures in the world, except—"

"Except, you mean, this other gentleman."

She assented. The person of whom I had spoken was a young man who was just preparing to seat himself at a vacant table. A lady and gentleman, elderly persons, had passed near him and recognized him, and he had uncovered himself and now stood smiling and talking. They were all genuine Anglo Saxons. The young man was rather short of stature, but firm and compact. His hair was light and crisp, his eye a clear blue his face and neck violently tanned by exposure to the sun. He wore a pair of small blond whiskers.

"Do you call him beautiful?" demanded Mr. Evans. "He reminds me of myself when I was his age. Indeed, he looks like you, sir."

"He's not beautiful," said Miss Evans, "but he is handsome."

The young man's face was full of decision and spirit; his whole figure had been moulded by action, tempered by effort. He looked simple and keen, upright, downright.

"Is he English?" asked Miss Evans, "or American?"

"He is both," I said, "or either. He is made of that precious clay that is common to the whole English-speaking race."

"He's American."

"Very possibly," said I; and indeed we never learned. I repeat the incident because I think it has a certain value in my recital. Before we separated I expressed the hope that we might meet again on the morrow.

"It's very kind of you to propose it," said Miss Evans; "but you'll thank us for refusing. Take my advice, as for an old Venetian, and spend the coming three days alone. How can you enjoy Tintoretto and Bellini, when you are racking your brains for small talk for me?"

"With you, Miss Evans, I shouldn't talk small. But you shape my programme with a liberal hand. At the end of three days, pray, where will you be?"

They would still be in Venice, Mr. Evans declared. It was a capital hotel, and then those jolly gondolas! I was unable to impeach the wisdom of the young girl's proposition. To be so wise, it seemed to me, was to be extremely charming.

For three days, accordingly, I wandered about alone. I often thought of Miss Evans and I often fancied I should enjoy certain great pictures none the less for that deep associated contemplation and those fine emanations of assent and dissent which I should have known in her society. I wandered far; I penetrated deep, it seemed to me, into the heart of Venetian power. I shook myself free of the sad and sordid present, and embarked on that silent contemplative sea whose irresistible tides expire at the base of the mighty canvases in the Scuola di San Rocco. But on my return to the hither shore, I

always found my sweet young countrywoman waiting to re
ceive me. If Miss Evans had been an immense coquette, sh
could not have proceeded more cunningly than by this in
junction of a three days' absence. During this period, in m
imagination, she increased tenfold in value. I don't mean t
say that there were not hours together when I quite forgo
her, and when I had no heart but for Venice and the lesson
of Venice, for the sea and sky and the great painters an
builders. But when my mind had executed one of these grea
passages of appreciation, it turned with a sudden sense of soli
tude and lassitude to those gentle hopes, those fragrant hint
of intimacy, which clustered about the person of my friend
She remained modestly uneclipsed by the women of Titian
She was as deeply a woman as they, and yet so much more o
a person; as fit as the broadest and blondest to be loved fo
herself, yet full of serene superiority as an active friend. To th
old, old sentiment what an exquisite modern turn she migh
give! I so far overruled her advice as that, with her father, w
made a trio every evening, after the day's labors, at one o
Florian's tables. Mr. Evans drank absinthe and discourse
upon the glories of our common country, of which he de
clared it was high time I should make the acquaintance. H
was not the least of a bore: I relished him vastly. He was i
many ways an excellent representative American. Withou
taste, without culture or polish, he nevertheless produced a
impression of substance in character, keenness in perception
and intensity in will, which effectually redeemed him from
vulgarity. It often seemed to me, in fact, that his good
humored tolerance and easy morality, his rank self-confidence
his nervous decision and vivacity, his fearlessness of eithe
gods or men, combined in proportions of which the unio
might have been very fairly termed aristocratic. His voice,
admit, was of the nose, nasal; but possibly, in the matter of ut
terance, one eccentricity is as good as another. At all events
with his clear, cold gray eye, with that just faintly impudent
more than level poise of his ample chin, with those two har
lines which flanked the bristling wings of his gray moustache
with his general expression of unchallenged security and prac
tical aptitude and incurious scorn of tradition, he impresse
the sensitive beholder as a man of incontestable force. He wa

entertaining, too, partly by wit and partly by position. He was weak only in his love of absinthe. After his first glass he left his chair and strolled about the piazza, looking for possible friends and superbly unconscious of possible enemies. His daughter sat back in her chair, her arms folded, her ungloved hands sustaining them, her prettiness half defined, her voice enhanced and subdued by the gas-tempered starlight. We had infinite talk. Without question, she had an admirable feminine taste: she was worthy to know Venice. I remember telling her so in a sudden explosion of homage. "You are really worthy to know Venice, Miss Evans. We must learn to know it together. Who knows what hidden treasures we may help each other to find?"

II.

At the end of my three days' probation, I spent a week constantly with my friends. Our mornings were, of course, devoted to churches and galleries, and in the late afternoon we passed and repassed along the Grand Canal or betook ourselves to the Lido. By this time Miss Evans and I had become thoroughly intimate; we had learned to know Venice together, and the knowledge had helped us to know each other. In my own mind, Charlotte Evans and Venice had played the game most effectively into each other's hands. If my fancy had been called upon to paint her portrait, my fancy would have sketched her with a background of sunset-flushed palace wall, with a faint reflected light from the green lagoon playing up into her face. And if I had wished to sketch a Venetian scene, I should have painted it from an open window, with a woman leaning against the casement,—as I had often seen her lean from a window in her hotel. At the end of a week we went one afternoon to the Lido, timing our departure so as to allow us to return at sunset. We went over in silence, Mr. Evans sitting with reverted head, blowing his cigar-smoke against the dazzling sky, which told so fiercely of sea and summer; his daughter motionless and thickly veiled; I facing them, feeling the broken swerve of our gondola, and watching Venice grow level and rosy beyond the liquid interval. Near the landing-place on the hither side of the Lido is a

small *trattoria* for the refreshment of visitors. An arbor outside the door, a horizontal vine checkering still further a dirty
table-cloth, a pungent odor of *frittata*, an admiring circle of
gondoliers and beggars, are the chief attractions of this suburban house of entertainment,—attractions sufficient, however, to have arrested the inquisitive steps of an elderly
American gentleman, in whom Mr. Evans speedily recognized
a friend of early years, a comrade in affairs. A hearty greeting
ensued. This worthy man had ordered dinner: he besought
Mr. Evans at least to sit down and partake of a bottle of wine.
My friend vacillated between his duties as a father and the
prospect of a rich old-boyish revival of the delectable interests
of home; but his daughter graciously came to his assistance.
"Sit down with Mr. Munson, talk till you are tired, and then
walk over to the beach and find us. We shall not wander beyond call."

She and I accordingly started slowly for a stroll along the
barren strand which averts its shining side from Venice and
takes the tides of the Adriatic. The Lido has for me a peculiar
melancholy charm, and I have often wondered that I should
have felt the presence of beauty in a spot so destitute of any
exceptional elements of beauty. For beyond the fact that it
knows the changing moods and hues of the Adriatic, this narrow strip of sand-stifled verdure has no very rare distinction.
In my own country I know many a sandy beach, and many a
stunted copse, and many a tremulous ocean line of little less
purity and breadth of composition, with far less magical interest. The secret of the Lido is simply your sense of adjacent
Venice. It is the salt-sown garden of the city of the sea. Hither
came short-paced Venetians for a meagre taste of *terra firma*,
or for a wider glimpse of their parent ocean. Along a narrow
line in the middle of the island are market-gardens and
breeze-twisted orchards, and a hint of hedges and lanes and
inland greenery. At one end is a series of low fortifications
duly embanked and moated and sentinelled. Still beyond
these, half over-drifted with sand and over-clambered with
rank grasses and coarse thick shrubbery, are certain quaintly
lettered funereal slabs, tombs of former Jews of Venice.
Toward these we slowly wandered and sat down in the grass.
Between the sand-heaps, which shut out the beach, we saw in

a dozen places the blue agitation of the sea. Over all the scene there brooded the deep bright sadness of early autumn. I lay at my companion's feet and wondered whether I was in love. It seemed to me that I had never been so happy in my life. They say, I know, that to be in love is not pure happiness; that in the mood of the unconfessed, unaccepted lover there is an element of poignant doubt and pain. Should I at once confess myself and taste of the perfection of bliss? It seemed to me that I cared very little for the meaning of her reply. I only wanted to talk of love; I wanted in some manner to enjoy in that atmosphere of romance the woman who was so blessedly fair and wise. It seemed to me that all the agitation of fancy, the excited sense of beauty, the fervor and joy and sadness begotten by my Italian wanderings, had suddenly resolved themselves into a potent demand for expression. Miss Evans was sitting on one of the Hebrew tombs, her chin on her hand, her elbow on her knee, watching the broken horizon. I was stretched on the grass on my side, leaning on my elbow and on my hand, with my eyes on her face. She bent her own eyes and encountered mine; we neither of us spoke or moved, but exchanged a long steady regard; after which her eyes returned to the distance. What was her feeling toward me? Had she any sense of my emotion or of any answering trouble in her own wonderful heart? Suppose she should deny me: should I suffer, would I persist? At any rate, I should have struck a blow for love. Suppose she were to accept me; would my joy be any greater than in the mere translation of my heart-beats? Did I in truth long merely for a bliss which should be of that hour and that hour alone? I was conscious of an immense respect for the woman beside me. I was unconscious of the least desire even to touch the hem of her garment as it lay on the grass, touching my own. After all, it was but ten days that I had known her. How little I really knew of her! how little else than her beauty and her wit! How little she knew of me, of my vast out-lying, unsentimental, spiritual self! We knew hardly more of each other than had appeared in this narrow circle of our common impressions of Venice. And yet if into such a circle Love had forced his way, let him take his way! Let him widen the circle! Transcendent Venice! I rose to my feet with a violent movement, and walked ten steps away. I came back and flung myself again on the grass.

"The other day at Vicenza," I said, "I bought a picture."

"Ah? an 'original'?"

"No, a copy."

"From whom?"

"From you!"

She blushed. "What do you mean?"

"It was a little pretended Correggio; a Madonna and Child."

"Is it good?"

"No, it's rather poor."

"Why, then, did you buy it?"

"Because the Madonna looked singularly like you."

"I'm sorry, Mr. Brooke, you hadn't a better reason. I hope the picture was cheap."

"It was quite reason enough. I admire you more than any woman in the world."

She looked at me a moment, blushing again. "You don't know me."

"I have a suspicion of you. It's ground enough for admiration."

"O, don't talk about admiration. I'm tired of it all beforehand."

"Well, then," said I, "I'm in love."

"Not with me, I hope."

"With you, of course. With whom else?"

"Has it only just now occurred to you?"

"It has just occurred to me to say it."

Her blush had deepened a little; but a genuine smile came to its relief. "Poor Mr. Brooke!" she said.

"Poor Mr. Brooke indeed, if you take it in that way."

"You must forgive me if I doubt of your love."

"Why should you doubt?"

"Love, I fancy, doesn't come in just this way."

"It comes as it can. This is surely a very good way."

"I know it's a very pretty way, Mr. Brooke; Venice behind us, the Adriatic before us, these old Hebrew tombs! Its very prettiness makes me distrust it."

"Do you believe only in the love that is born in darkness

and pain? Poor love! it has trouble enough, first and last. Allow it a little ease."

"Listen," said Miss Evans, after a pause. "It's not with me you're in love, but with that painted picture. All this Italian beauty and delight has thrown you into a romantic state of mind. You wish to make it perfect. I happen to be at hand, so you say, 'Go to, I'll fall in love.' And you fancy me, for the purpose, a dozen fine things that I'm not."

"I fancy you beautiful and good. I'm sorry to find you so dogmatic."

"You mustn't abuse me, or we shall be getting serious."

"Well," said I, "you can't prevent me from adoring you."

"I should be very sorry to. So long as you 'adore' me, we're safe! I can tell you better things than that I'm in love with you."

I looked at her impatiently. "For instance?"

She held out her hand. "I like you immensely. As for love, I'm in love with Venice."

"Well, I like Venice immensely, but I'm in love with you."

"In that way I am willing to leave it. Pray don't speak of it again to-day. But my poor father is probably wandering up to his knees in the sand."

I had been happy before, but I think I was still happier for the words I had spoken. I had cast them abroad at all events; my heart was richer by a sense of their possible fruition. We walked far along the beach. Mr. Evans was still with his friend.

"What is beyond that horizon?" said my companion.

"Greece, among other things."

"Greece! only think of it! Shall you never go there?"

I stopped short. "If you will believe what I say, Miss Evans, we may both go there." But for all answer she repeated her request that I should forbear. Before long, retracing our steps, we met Mr. Evans, who had parted with his friend, the latter having returned to Venice. He had arranged to start the next morning for Milan. We went back over the lagoon in the glow of the sunset, in a golden silence which suffered us to hear the far-off ripple in the wake of other gondolas, a golden clearness so perfect that the rosy flush on the marble palaces seemed as light and pure as the life-blood on the forehead of a sleeping child. There is no Venice like the Venice of that magical hour. For that brief period her ancient glory returns. The sky arches over her like a vast imperial canopy crowded with its clustering mysteries of light. Her whole aspect is one of unspotted splendor. No other city takes the crimson evanescence of day with such magnificent effect. The lagoon is sheeted with a carpet of fire. All torpid, pallid hues of marble are transmuted to a golden glow. The dead Venetian tone brightens and quickens into life and lustre, and the spectator's enchanted vision seems to rest on an embodied dream of the great painter who wrought his immortal reveries into the ceilings of the Ducal Palace.

It was not till the second day after this that I again saw Miss Evans. I went to the little church of San Cassiano, to see a famous Tintoretto, to which I had already made several vain attempts to obtain access. At the door in the little bustling *campo* which adjoins the church I found her standing expectant. A little boy, she told me, had gone for the sacristan and his key. Her father, she proceeded to explain, had suddenly been summoned to Milan by a telegram from Mr. Munson, the friend whom he had met at the Lido, who had suddenly been taken ill.

"And so you're going about alone? Do you think that's altogether proper? Why didn't you send for me?" I stood lost in wonder and admiration at the exquisite dignity of her self-support. I had heard of American girls doing such things; but I had yet to see them done.

"Do you think it less proper for me to go about alone than to send for you? Venice has seen so many worse improprieties that she'll forgive me mine."

The little boy arrived with the sacristan and his key, and we were ushered into the presence of Tintoretto's Crucifixion. This great picture is one of the greatest of the Venetian school. Tintoretto, the travelled reader will remember, has painted two masterpieces on this tremendous theme. The larger and more complex work is at the Scuola di San Rocco: the one of which I speak is small, simple, and sublime. It occupies the left side of the narrow choir of the shabby little church which we had entered, and is remarkable as being, with two or three exceptions, the best preserved work of its incomparable author. Never, in the whole range of art, I

imagine, has so powerful an effect been produced by means
so simple and select; never has the intelligent choice of means
to an effect been pursued with such a refinement of perception. The picture offers to our sight the very central essence
of the great tragedy which it depicts. There is no swooning
Madonna, no consoling Magdalen, no mockery of contrast,
no cruelty of an assembled host. We behold the silent summit
of Calvary. To the right are the three crosses, that of the
Saviour foremost. A ladder pitched against it supports a tur-
baned executioner, who bends downward to receive the
sponge offered him by a comrade. Above the crest of the hill
the helmets and spears of a line of soldiery complete the grimness of the scene. The reality of the picture is beyond all
words: it is hard to say which is more impressive, the naked
horror of the fact represented, or the sensible power of the
artist. You breathe a silent prayer of thanks that you, for your
part, are without the terrible clairvoyance of genius. We sat
and looked at the picture in silence. The sacristan loitered
about; but finally, weary of waiting, he retired to the *campo*
without. I observed my companion: pale, motionless, oppressed, she evidently felt with poignant sympathy the commanding force of the work. At last I spoke to her; receiving
no answer, I repeated my question. She rose to her feet and
turned her face upon me, illumined with a vivid ecstasy of
pity. Then passing me rapidly, she descended into the aisle of
the church, dropped into a chair, and, burying her face in her
hands, burst into an agony of sobs. Having allowed time for
her feeling to expend itself, I went to her and recommended
her not to let the day close on this painful emotion. "Come
with me to the Ducal Palace," I said; "let us look at the Rape
of Europa." But before departing we went back to our
Tintoretto, and gave it another solemn half-hour. Miss Evans
repeated aloud a dozen verses from St. Mark's Gospel.

"What is it here," I asked, "that has moved you most, the
painter or the subject?"

"I suppose it's the subject. And you?"

"I'm afraid it's the painter."

We went to the Ducal Palace, and immediately made our
way to that transcendent shrine of light and grace, the room
which contains the masterpiece of Paul Veronese, and the

Bacchus and Ariadne of his solemn comrade. I steeped myself with unprotesting joy in the gorgeous glow and salubrity of that radiant scene, wherein, against her bosky screen of immortal verdure, the rosy-footed, pearl-circled, nymph-flattered victim of a divine delusion rustles her lustrous satin against the ambrosial hide of bovine Jove. "It makes one think more agreeably of life," I said to my friend, "that such visions have blessed the eyes of men of mortal mould. What has been may be again. We may yet dream as brightly, and some few of us translate our dreams as freely."

"This, I think, is the brighter dream of the two," she answered, indicating the Bacchus and Ariadne. Miss Evans, on the whole, was perhaps right. In Tintoretto's picture there is no shimmer of drapery, no splendor of flowers and gems; nothing but the broad, bright glory of deep-toned sea and sky, and the shining purity and symmetry of deified human flesh. "What do you think," asked my companion, "of the painter of that tragedy at San Cassiano being also the painter of this dazzling idyl; of the great painter of darkness being also the great painter of light?"

"He was a colorist! Let us thank the great man, and be colorists too. To understand this Bacchus and Ariadne we ought to spend a long day on the lagoon, beyond sight of Venice. Will you come to-morrow to Torcello?" The proposition seemed to me audacious; I was conscious of blushing a little as I made it. Miss Evans looked at me and pondered. She then replied with great calmness that she preferred to wait for her father, the excursion being one that he would probably enjoy. "Will you come, then,—somewhere?" I asked.

Again she pondered. Suddenly her face brightened. "I should very much like to go to Padua. It would bore my poor father to go. I fancy he would thank you for taking me. I should be almost willing," she said with a smile, "to go alone."

It was easily arranged that on the morrow we should go for the day to Padua. Miss Evans was certainly an American to perfection. Nothing remained for me, as the good American which I aspired to be, but implicitly to respect her confidence. To Padua, by an early train, we accordingly went. The day stands out in my memory delightfully curious and rich. Padua is a wonderful little city. Miss Evans was an excellent walker, and, thanks to the broad arcades which cover the foot-ways in the streets, we rambled for hours in perpetual shade. We spent an hour at the famous church of St. Anthony, which boasts one of the richest and holiest shrines in all church-burdened Italy. The whole edifice is nobly and darkly ornate and picturesque, but the chapel of its patron saint—a wondrous combination of chiselled gold and silver and alabaster and perpetual flame—splendidly outshines and outshadows the rest. In all Italy, I think, the idea of palpable, material sanctity is nowhere more potently enforced.

"O the Church, the Church!" murmured Miss Evans, as we stood contemplating.

"What a real pity," I said, "that we are not Catholics; that that dazzling monument is not something more to us than a mere splendid show! What a different thing this visiting of churches would be for us, if we occasionally felt the prompting to fall on our knees. I begin to grow ashamed of this perpetual attitude of bald curiosity. What a pleasant thing it must be, in such a church as this, for two good friends to say their prayers together!"

"*Ecco!*" said Miss Evans. Two persons had approached the glittering shrine,—a young woman of the middle class and a man of her own rank, some ten years older, dressed with a good deal of cheap elegance. The woman dropped on her knees; her companion fell back a few steps, and stood gazing idly at the chapel. "Poor girl!" said my friend, "she believes; he doubts."

"He doesn't look like a doubter. He's a vulgar fellow. They're a betrothed pair, I imagine. She is very pretty." She had turned round and flung at her companion a liquid glance of entreaty. He appeared not to observe it; but in a few moments he slowly approached her, and bent a single knee at her side. When presently they rose to their feet, she passed her arm into his with a beautiful, unsuppressed lovingness. As they passed us, looking at us from the clear darkness of their Italian brows, I keenly envied them. "They are better off than we," I said. "Be they husband and wife, or lovers, or simply friends, we, I think, are rather vulgar beside them."

"My dear Mr. Brooke," said Miss Evans, "go by all means and say your prayers." And she walked away to the other side of the church. Whether I obeyed her injunction or not, I feel under no obligation to report. I rejoined her at the beautiful frescoed chapel in the opposite transept. She was sitting listlessly turning over the leaves of her Murray. "I suppose," she said, after a few moments, "that nothing is more vulgar than to make a noise about having been called vulgar. But really, Mr. Brooke, don't call me so again. I have been of late so fondly fancying I am not vulgar."

"My dear Miss Evans, you are—"

"Come, nothing vulgar!"

"You're divine!"

"*A la bonne heure!* Divinities needn't pray. They are prayed to."

I have no space and little power to enumerate and describe the various curiosities of Padua. I think we saw them all. We left the best, however, for the last, and repaired in the late afternoon, after dining fraternally at a restaurant, to the Chapel of Giotto. This little empty church, standing unshaded and forlorn in the homely market-garden which was once a Roman arena, offers one of the deepest lessons of Italian travel. Its four walls are covered, almost from base to ceiling, with that wonderful series of dramatic paintings which usher in the golden prime of Italian art. I had been so ill-informed as to fancy that to talk about Giotto was to make more or less of a fool of one's self, and that he was the especial property of the mere sentimentalists of criticism. But you no sooner cross the threshold of that little ruinous temple—a mere empty shell, but coated as with the priceless substance of fine pearl, and vocal with a murmured eloquence as from the infinite of art—than you perceive with whom you have to deal: a complete painter of the very strongest sort. In one respect, as suredly, Giotto has never been surpassed,—in the art of presenting a story. The amount of dramatic expression compressed into those quaint little scenic squares would equip a thousand later masters. How, beside him, they seem to fumble and grope and trifle! And he, beside them, how direct he seems, how essential, how masculine! What a solid simplicity, what an immediate purity and grace! The exhibition suggested to my friend and me more wise reflections than we had the skill to utter. "Happy, happy art," we said, as we seemed to see it beneath Giotto's hand tremble and thrill and sparkle, almost, with a presentiment of its immense career, "for the next two hundred years what a glorious felicity will be yours!" The chapel door stood open into the sunny corn-field, and the lazy litter of verdure enclosed by the crumbling oval of Roman masonry. A loutish boy who had come with the key lounged on a bench, awaiting tribute, and gazing at us as we gazed. The ample light flooded the inner precinct, and lay hot upon the coarse, pale surface of the painted wall. There seemed an irresistible pathos in such a combination of shabbiness and beauty. I thought of this subsequently at the beautiful Museum at Bologna, where mediocrity is so richly enshrined. Nothing that we had yet seen together had filled us with so deep a sense of enjoyment. We stared, we laughed, we wept almost, we raved with a decent delight. We went over the little compartments one by one: we lingered and returned and compared; we studied; we melted together in unanimous homage. At last the light began to fade and the little saintly figures to grow quaint and terrible in the gathering dusk. The loutish boy had transferred himself significantly to the door-post: we lingered for a farewell glance.

"Mr. Brooke," said my companion, "we ought to learn from all this to be *real*; real even as Giotto is real; to discriminate between genuine and factitious sentiment; between the substantial and the trivial; between the essential and the superfluous; sentiment and sentimentality."

"You speak," said I, "with appalling wisdom and truth. You strike a chill to my heart of hearts."

She spoke unsmiling, with a slightly contracted brow and an apparent sense of effort. She blushed as I gazed at her.

"Well," she said, "I'm extremely glad to have been here. Good, wise Giotto! I should have liked to know you.—Nay, let me pay the boy." I saw the piece she put into his hand; he was stupefied by its magnitude.

"We shall not have done Padua," I said, as we left the garden, "unless we have been to the Caffè Pedrocchi. Come to the Caffè Pedrocchi. We have more than an hour before our train,—time to eat an ice." So we drove to the Caffè Pedrocchi, the most respectable *café* in the world; a *café* monumental, scholastic, classical.

We sat down at one of the tables on the cheerful external platform, which is washed by the gentle tide of Paduan life. When we had finished our ices, Miss Evans graciously allowed me a cigar. How it came about I hardly remember, but, prompted by some happy accident of talk, and gently encouraged perhaps by my smoke-wreathed quietude, she lapsed, with an exquisite feminine reserve, into a delicate autobiographical strain. For a moment she became egotistical; but with a modesty, a dignity, a lightness of touch which filled my eyes with admiring tears. She spoke of her home, her family, and the few events of her life. She had lost her mother in her early years; her two sisters had married young; she and her father were equally united by affection and habit. Upon one theme she touched, in regard to which I should be at loss to say whether her treatment told more, by its frankness, of our friendship, or, by its reticence, of her modesty. She spoke of having been engaged, and of having lost her betrothed in the Civil War. She made no story of it; but I felt from her words that she had tasted of sorrow. Having finished my cigar, I was proceeding to light another. She drew out her watch. Our train was to leave at eight o'clock. It was now a quarter past. There was no later evening train.

The reader will understand that I tell the simple truth when I say that our situation was most disagreeable and that we were deeply annoyed. "Of course," said I, "you are utterly disgusted."

She was silent. "I am extremely sorry," she said, at last, just vanquishing a slight tremor in her voice.

"Murray says the hotel is good," I suggested.

She made no answer. Then, rising to her feet, "Let us go immediately," she said. We drove to the principal inn and bespoke our rooms. Our want of luggage provoked, of course, a certain amount of visible surprise. This, however, I fancy, was speedily merged in a more flattering emotion, when my companion, having communed with the chambermaid, sent her forth with a list of purchases.

We separated early. "I hope," said I, as I bade her good night, "that you will be fairly comfortable."

She had recovered her equanimity. "I have no doubt of it."

"Good night."

"Good night." Thank God, I silently added, for the dignity of American women. Knowing to what suffering a similar accident would have subjected a young girl of the orthodox European training, I felt devoutly grateful that among my own people a woman and her reputation are more indissolubly one. And yet I was unable to detach myself from my Old-World associations effectually enough not to wonder whether, after all, Miss Evans's calmness might not be the simple calmness of despair. The miserable words rose to my lips, "Is she Compromised?" If she were, of course, as far as I was concerned, there was but one possible sequel to our situation.

We met the next morning at breakfast. She assured me that she had slept, but I doubted it. I myself had not closed my eyes,—not from the excitement of vanity. Owing partly, I suppose, to a natural reaction against our continuous talk on the foregoing day, our return to Venice was attended with a good deal of silence. I wondered whether it was a mere fancy that Miss Evans was pensive, appealing, sombre. As we entered the gondola to go from the railway station to the Hotel Danieli, she asked me to request the gondoliers to pass along the Canalezzo rather than through the short cuts of the smaller canals. "I feel as if I were coming home," she said, as we floated beneath the lovely façade of the Ca' Doro. Suddenly she laid her hand on my arm. "It seems to me," she said, "that I should like to stop for Mrs. L——,' and she mentioned the wife of the American Consul. "I have promised to show her some jewelry. This is a particularly good time. I shall ask her to come home with me." We stopped accordingly at the American Consulate. Here we found, on inquiry, to my great regret, that the Consul and his wife had gone for a week to the Lake of Como. For a moment my companion meditated. Then, "To the hotel," she said with decision. Our arrival attracted apparently little notice. I went with Miss Evans to the door of her father's sitting-room, where we met a servant, who informed us with inscrutable gravity that Monsieur had returned the evening before, but that he had gone out after breakfast and had not reappeared.

"Poor father," she said. "It was very stupid of me not to have left a note for him." I urged that our absence for the night was not to have been foreseen, and that Mr. Evans had in all likelihood very plausibly explained it. I withdrew with a hand-shake and permission to return in the evening.

I went to my hotel and slept, a long, sound, dreamless sleep. In the afternoon I called my gondola, and went over to the Lido. I crossed to the outer shore and sought the spot where a few days before I had lain at the feet of Charlotte Evans. I stretched myself on the grass and fancied her present. To say that I *thought* would be to say at once more and less than the literal truth. I was in a tremulous glow of feeling. I listened to the muffled rupture of the tide, vaguely conscious of my beating heart. Was I or was I not in love? I was able to settle nothing. I wandered musingly further and further from the point. Every now and then, with a deeper pulsation of the heart, I would return to it, but only to start afresh and follow some wire-drawn thread of fancy to a nebulous goal of doubt. That she was a most lovely woman seemed to me of all truths the truest, but it was a hard-featured fact of the senses rather than a radiant mystery of faith. I felt that I was not possessed by a passion; perhaps I was incapable of passion. At last, weary of self-bewilderment, I left the spot and wandered beside the sea. It seemed to speak more musingly than ever of the rapture of motion and freedom. Beyond the horizon was Greece, beyond and below was the wondrous Southern world which blooms about the margin of the Midland Sea. To marry, somehow, meant to abjure all this, and in the prime of youth and manhood to sink into obscurity and care. For a moment there stirred in my heart a feeling of anger and pain. Perhaps after all, I *was* in love!

I went straight across the lagoon to the Hotel Danieli, and as I approached it I became singularly calm and collected. From below I saw Miss Evans alone on her balcony, watching the sunset. She received me with perfect friendly composure. Her father had again gone out, but she had told him of my coming, and he was soon to return. He had not been painfully alarmed at her absence, having learned through a chambermaid, to whom she had happened to mention her intention, that she had gone for the day to Padua.

"And what have you been doing all day?" I asked.

"Writing letters,—long, tiresome, descriptive letters. I have also found a volume of Hawthorne, and have been reading 'Rappacini's Daughter.' You know the scene is laid in Padua." And what had I been doing?

Whether I was in a passion of love or not, I was enough in love to be very illogical. I was disappointed, Heaven knows why! that she should have been able to spend her time in this wholesome fashion. "I have been at the Lido, at the Hebrew tombs, where we sat the other day, thinking of what you told me there."

"What I told you?"

"That you liked me immensely."

She smiled; but now that she smiled, I fancied I saw in the movement of her face an undercurrent of pain. Had the peace of her heart been troubled? "You needn't have gone so far away to think of it."

"It's very possible," I said, "that I shall have to think of it, in days to come, farther away still."

"Other places, Mr. Brooke, will bring other thoughts."

"Possibly. This place has brought that one." At what prompting it was that I continued I hardly know; I *would* tell her that I loved her. "I value it beyond all other thoughts."

"I do like you, Mr. Brooke. Let it rest there."

"It may rest there for you. It can't for me. It begins there! Don't refuse to understand me."

She was silent. Then, bending her eyes on me, "Perhaps," she said, "I understand you too well."

"O, in Heaven's name, don't play at coldness and scepticism!"

She dropped her eyes gravely on a bracelet which she locked and unlocked on her wrist. "I think," she said, without raising them, "you had better leave Venice." I was about to reply, but the door opened and Mr. Evans came in. From his hard, grizzled brow he looked at us in turn; then, greeting me with an extended hand, he spoke to his daughter.

"I have forgotten my cigar-case. Be so good as to fetch it from my dressing-table."

For a moment Miss Evans hesitated and cast upon him a faint protesting glance. Then she lightly left the room. He stood holding my hand, with a very sensible firmness, with his eyes on mine. Then, laying his other hand heavily on my shoulder, "Mr. Brooke," he said, "I believe you are an honest man."

"I hope so," I answered.

He paused, and I felt his steady gray eyes. "How the devil," he said, "came you to be left at Padua?"

"The explanation is a very simple one. Your daughter must have told you."

"I have thought best to talk very little to my daughter about it."

"Do you regard it, Mr. Evans," I asked, "as a very serious calamity?"

"I regard it as an infernally disagreeable thing. It seems that the whole hotel is talking about it. There is a little beast of an Italian down stairs—"

"Your daughter, I think, was not seriously discomposed."

"My daughter is a d—d proud woman!"

"I can assure you that my esteem for her is quite equal to your own."

"What does that mean, Mr. Brooke?" I was about to answer, but Miss Evans reappeared. Her father, as he took his cigar-case from her, looked at her intently, as if he were on the point of speaking, but the words remained on his lips, and, declaring that he would be back in half an hour, he left the room.

His departure was followed by a long silence.

"Miss Evans," I said, at last, "will you be my wife?"

She looked at me with a certain firm resignation. "Do you *feel* that, Mr. Brooke? Do you know what you ask?"

"Most assuredly."

"Will you rest content with my answer?"

"It depends on what your answer is."

She was silent.

"I should like to know what my father said to you in my absence."

"You had better learn from himself."

"I think I know. Poor father!"

"But you give me no answer," I rejoined, after a pause.

She frowned a little. "Mr. Brooke," she said, "you disappoint me."

"Well, I'm sorry. Don't revenge yourself by disappointing me."

"I fancied that I had answered your proposal; that I had, at least, anticipated it, the other day at the Lido."

"O, that was very good for the other day; but do give me something different now."

"I doubt of your being more in earnest to-day than then."

"It seems to suit you wonderfully well to doubt!"

"I thank you for the honor of your proposal: but I can't be your wife, Mr. Brooke."

"That's the answer with which you ask me to remain satisfied!"

"Let me repeat what I said just now. You had better leave Venice, otherwise we must leave it."

"Ah, that's easy to say!"

"You mustn't think me unkind or cynical. You have done your duty."

"My duty,—what duty?"

"Come," she said, with a beautiful blush and the least attempt at a smile, "you imagine that I have suffered an injury by my being left with you at Padua. I don't believe in such injuries."

"No more do I."

"Then there is even less wisdom than before in your proposal. But I strongly suspect that if we had not missed the train at Padua, you would not have made it. There is an idea of reparation in it.—O Sir!" And she shook her head with a deepening smile.

"If I had flattered myself that it lay in my power to do you an injury," I replied, "I should now be rarely disenchanted. As little almost as to do you a benefit!"

"You have loaded me with benefits. I thank you from the bottom of my heart. I may be very unreasonable, but if I had doubted of my having to decline your offer three days ago, I should have quite ceased to doubt this evening."

"You are an excessively proud woman. I can tell you that."

"Possibly. But I'm not as proud as you think. I believe in my common sense."

"I wish that for five minutes you had a grain of imagination!"

"If only for the same five minutes you were without it. You have too much, Mr. Brooke. You imagine you love me."

"Poor fool that I am!"

"You imagine that I'm charming. I assure you I'm not in the least. Here in Venice I have not been myself at all. You should see me at home."

"Upon my word, Miss Evans, you remind me of a German philosopher. I have not the least objection to seeing you at home."

"Don't fancy that I think lightly of your offer. But we have been living, Mr. Brooke, in poetry. Marriage is stern prose. Do let me bid you farewell!"

I took up my hat. "I shall go from here to Rome and Naples," I said. "I must leave Florence for the last. I shall write you from Rome and of course see you there."

"I hope not. I had rather not meet you again in Italy. It perverts our dear good old American truth!"

"Do you really propose to bid me a final farewell?"

She hesitated a moment. "When do you return home?"

"Some time in the spring."

"Very well. If a year hence, in America, you are still of your present mind, I shall not decline to see you. I feel very safe. If you are not of your present mind, of course I shall be still more happy. Farewell." She put out her hand; I took it.

"Beautiful, wonderful woman!" I murmured.

"That's rank poetry! Farewell!"

I raised her hand to my lips and released it in silence. At this point Mr. Evans reappeared, considering apparently that his half-hour was up. "Are you going?" he asked.

"Yes. I start to-morrow for Rome."

"The deuce! Daughter, when are we to go?"

She moved her hand over her forehead, and a sort of nervous tremor seemed to pass through her limbs. "O, you must take me home!" she said. "I'm horribly homesick!" She flung her arms round his neck and buried her head on his shoulder. Mr. Evans with a movement of his head dismissed me.

At the top of the staircase, however, he overtook me. "You made your offer!" And he passed his arm into mine.

"Yes!"

"And she refused you?" I nodded. He looked at me squeezing my arm. "By Jove, sir, if she had accepted—"

"Well!" said I, stopping.

"Why, it wouldn't in the least have suited me! Not that I don't esteem you. The whole house shall see it." With his arm in mine we passed down stairs, through the hall, to the landing-place, where he called his own gondola and requested me to use it. He bade me farewell with a kindly hand-shake, and the assurance that I was too "nice a fellow not to keep as a friend."

I think, on the whole, that my uppermost feeling was a sense of freedom and relief. It seemed to me on my journey to Florence that I had started afresh, and was regarding things with less of nervous rapture than before, but more of sober insight. Of Miss Evans I forbade myself to think. In my deepest heart I admitted the truth, the partial truth at least, of her assertion of the unreality of my love. The reality I believed would come. The way to hasten its approach was, meanwhile, to study, to watch, to observe,—doubtless even to enjoy. I certainly enjoyed Florence and the three days I spent there. But I shall not attempt to deal with Florence in a parenthesis. I subsequently saw that divine little city under circumstances which peculiarly colored and shaped it. In Rome, to begin with, I spent a week and went down to Naples, dragging the heavy Roman chain which she rivets about your limbs forever. In Naples I discovered the real South—the Southern South,—in art, in nature, in man, and the least bit in woman. A German lady, an old kind friend, had given me a letter to a Neapolitan lady whom she assured me she held in high esteem. The Signora B—— was at Sorrento, where I presented my letter. It seemed to me that "esteem" was not exactly the word; but the Signora B—— was charming. She assured me on my first visit that she was a "true Neapolitan," and I think, on the whole, she was right. She told me that I was a true German, but in this she was altogether wrong. I spent four days in her house; on one of them we went to Capri, where the Signora had an infant—her only one—at nurse. We saw the Blue Grotto, the Tiberian ruins, the tarantella and the infant, and returned late in the evening by moonlight. The Signora sang on the water in a magnificent contralto. As I looked upward at Northern Italy, it seemed, in contrast, a cold, dark hyperborean clime, a land of order, conscience, and virtue. How my heart went out to that brave, rich, compact little Verona! How there Nature seemed to have mixed her colors with potent oil, instead of as here with crystalline water, drawn though it was from the Neapolitan Bay! But in Naples, too, I pursued my plan of vigilance and study. I spent long mornings at the Museum and learned to know Pompei; I wrote once to Miss Evans, about the statues in the Museum, without a word of wooing, but received no answer. It seemed to me that I returned to Rome a wiser man. It was the middle of October when I reached it. Unless Mr. Evans had altered his programme, he would at this moment be passing down to Naples.

A fortnight elapsed without my hearing of him, during which I was in the full fever of initiation into Roman wonders. I had been introduced to an old German archæologist, with whom I spent a series of memorable days in the exploration of ruins and the study of the classical topography. I thought, I lived, I ate and drank, in Latin, and German Latin at that. But I remember with especial delight certain long lonely rides on the Campagna. The weather was perfect Nature seemed only to slumber, ready to wake far on the hither side of wintry death. From time to time, after a passionate gallop, I would pull up my horse on the slope of some pregnant mound and embrace with the ecstasy of quickened senses the tragical beauty of the scene; strain my ear to the soft low silence, pity the dark dishonored plain, watch the heavens come rolling down in tides of light, and breaking in waves of fire against the massive stillness of temples and tombs. The aspect of all this sunny solitude and haunted vacancy used to fill me with a mingled sense of exaltation and dread. There were moments when my fancy swept that vast funereal desert with passionate curiosity and desire, moments when it felt only its potent sweetness and its high historic charm. But there were other times when the air seemed so heavy with the exhalation of unburied death, so bright with sheeted ghosts, that I turned short about and galloped back to the city. One afternoon after I had indulged in one of these super-sensitive flights on the Campagna, I betook myself to St. Peter's. It was shortly before the opening of the recent Council, and the city was filled with foreign ecclesiastics, the increase being of course especially noticeable in the churches

At St. Peter's they were present in vast numbers; great armies encamped in prayer on the marble plains of its pavement: an inexhaustible physiognomical study. Scattered among them were squads of little tonsured neophytes, clad in scarlet, marching and counter-marching, and ducking and flapping, like poor little raw recruits for the heavenly host. I had never before, I think, received an equal impression of the greatness of this church of churches, or, standing beneath the dome, beheld such a vision of erected altitude,—of the builded sublime. I lingered awhile near the brazen image of St. Peter, observing the steady procession of his devotees. Near me stood a lady in mourning, watching with a weary droop of the head the grotesque deposition of kisses. A peasant-woman advanced with the file of the faithful and lifted up her little girl to the well-worn toe. With a sudden movement of impatience the lady turned away, so that I saw her face to face. She was strikingly pale, but as her eyes met mine the blood rushed into her cheeks. This lonely mourner was Miss Evans. I advanced to her with an outstretched hand. Before she spoke I had guessed at the truth.

"You're in sorrow and trouble!"

She nodded, with a look of simple gravity.

"Why in the world haven't you written to me?"

"There was no use. I seem to have sufficed to myself."

"Indeed, you have not sufficed to yourself. You are pale and worn; you look wretchedly." She stood silent, looking about her with an air of vague unrest. "I have as yet heard nothing," I said. "Can you speak of it?"

"O Mr. Brooke!" she said with a simple sadness that went to my heart. I drew her hand through my arm and led her to the extremity of the left transept of the church. We sat down together, and she told me of her father's death. It had happened ten days before, in consequence of a severe apoplectic stroke. He had been ill but a single day, and had remained unconscious from first to last. The American physician had been extremely kind, and had relieved her of all care and responsibility. His wife had strongly urged her to come and stay in their house, until she should have determined what to do; but she had preferred to remain at her hotel. She had immediately furnished herself with an attendant in the person of a

French maid, who had come with her to the church and was now at confession. At first she had wished greatly to leave Rome, but now that the first shock of grief had passed away she found it suited her mood to linger on from day to day. "On the whole," she said, with a sober smile, "I have got through it all rather easily than otherwise. The common cares and necessities of life operate strongly to interrupt and dissipate one's grief. I shall feel my loss more when I get home again." Looking at her while she talked, I found a pitiful difference between her words and her aspect. Her pale face, her wilful smile, her spiritless gestures, spoke most forcibly of loneliness and weakness. Over this gentle weakness and dependence I secretly rejoiced; I felt in my heart an immense uprising of pity,—of the pity that goes hand in hand with love. At its bidding I hastily, vaguely sketched a magnificent scheme of devotion and protection.

"When I think of what you have been through," I said, "my heart stands still for very tenderness. Have you made any plans?" She shook her head with such a perfection of helplessness that I broke into a sort of rage of compassion: "One of the last things your father said to me was that you are a very proud woman."

She colored faintly. "I may have been! But there is not among the most abject peasants who stand kissing St. Peter's foot a creature more bowed in humility than I."

"How did you expect to make that weary journey home?"

She was silent a moment and her eyes filled with tears. "O don't cross-question me, Mr. Brooke!" she softly cried; "I expected nothing. I was waiting for my stronger self."

"Perhaps your stronger self has come." She rose to her feet as if she had not heard me, and went forward to meet her maid. This was a decent, capable-looking person, with a great deal of apparent deference of manner. As I rejoined them Miss Evans prepared to bid me farewell. "You haven't yet asked me to come and see you," I said.

"Come, but not too soon?"

"What do you call too soon? This evening?"

"Come to-morrow." She refused to allow me to go with her to her carriage. I followed her, however, at a short interval, and went as usual to my restaurant to dine. I remember that my dinner cost me ten francs,—it usually cost me five. Afterwards, as usual, I adjourned to the Caffè Greco, where I met my German archæologist. He discoursed with even more than his wonted sagacity and eloquence; but at the end of half an hour he rapped his fist on the table and asked me what the deuce was the matter; he would wager I hadn't heard a word of what he said.

I went forth the next morning into the Roman streets, doubting heavily of my being able to exist until evening without seeing Miss Evans. I felt, however, that it was due to her to make the effort. To help myself through the morning, I went into the Borghese Gallery. The great treasure of this collection is a certain masterpiece of Titian. I entered the room in which it hangs by the door facing the picture. The room was empty, save that before the great Titian, beside the easel of an absent copyist, stood a young woman in mourning. This time, in spite of her averted head, I immediately knew her and noiselessly approached her. The picture is one of the finest of its admirable author,—rich and simple and brilliant with the true Venetian fire. It unites the charm of an air of latent symbolism with a steadfast splendor and solid perfection of design. Beside a low sculptured well sit two young and beautiful women: one richly clad, and full of mild dignity and repose; the other with unbound hair, naked, ungirdled by a great reverted mantle of Venetian purple, and radiant with the frankest physical sweetness and grace. Between them a little winged cherub bends forward and thrusts his chubby arm into the well. The picture glows with the inscrutable chemistry of the prince of colorists.

"Does it remind you of Venice?" I said, breaking a long silence, during which she had not noticed me.

She turned and her face seemed bright with reflected color. We spoke awhile of common things; she had come alone. "What an emotion, for one who has loved Venice," she said, "to meet a Titian in other lands."

"They call it," I answered,—and as I spoke my heart was in my throat,—"a representation of Sacred and Profane Love. The name perhaps roughly expresses its meaning. The serious, stately woman is the likeness, one may say, of love as an experience,—the gracious, impudent goddess of love as a sentiment; this of the passion that fancies, the other of the passion that knows." And as I spoke I passed my arm, in its strength, around her waist. She let her head sink on my shoulders and looked up into my eyes.

"One may stand for the love I denied," she said; "and the other—"

"The other," I murmured, "for the love which, with this kiss, you accept." I drew her arm into mine, and before the envious eyes that watched us from gilded casements we passed through the gallery and left the palace. We went that afternoon to the Pamfili-Doria Villa. Saying just now that my stay in Florence was peculiarly colored by circumstances, I meant that I was there with my wife.

A Passionate Pilgrim

INTENDING to sail for America in the early part of June, I determined to spend the interval of six weeks in England, of which I had dreamed much but as yet knew nothing. I had formed in Italy and France a resolute preference for old inns, deeming that what they sometimes cost the ungratified body they repay the delighted mind. On my arrival in London, therefore, I lodged at a certain antique hostelry far to the east of Temple Bar, deep in what I used to denominate the Johnsonian city. Here, on the first evening of my stay, I descended to the little coffee-room and bespoke my dinner of the genius of decorum, in the person of the solitary waiter. No sooner had I crossed the threshold of this apartment than I felt I had mown the first swath in my golden-ripe crop of British "impressions." The coffee-room of the Red-Lion, like so many other places and things I was destined to see in England, seemed to have been waiting for long years, with just that sturdy sufferance of time written on its visage, for me to come and gaze, ravished but unamazed.

The latent preparedness of the American mind for even the most delectable features of English life is a fact which I never fairly probed to its depths. The roots of it are so deeply buried in the virgin soil of our primary culture, that, without some great upheaval of experience, it would be hard to say exactly when and where and how it begins. It makes an American's enjoyment of England an emotion more fatal and sacred than his enjoyment, say, of Italy or Spain. I had seen the coffee-room of the Red-Lion years ago, at home,—at Saragossa, Illinois,—in books, in visions, in dreams, in Dickens, in Smollett, and Boswell. It was small, and subdivided into six small compartments by a series of perpendicular screens of mahogany, something higher than a man's stature, furnished on either side with a narrow uncushioned ledge, denominated in ancient Britain a seat. In each of the little dining-boxes thus immutably constituted was a small table, which in crowded seasons was expected to accommodate the several agents of a fourfold British hungriness. But crowded seasons had passed away from the Red-Lion forever. It was crowded only with memories and ghosts and atmosphere. Round the room there marched, breast-high, a magnificent panelling of mahogany, so dark with time and so polished with unremitted friction, that by gazing awhile into its lucid blackness I fancied I could discern the lingering images of a party of gentlemen in periwigs and short-clothes, just arrived from York by the coach. On the dark yellow walls, coated by the fumes of English coal, of English mutton, of Scotch whiskey, were a dozen melancholy prints, sallow-toned with age,—the Derby favorite of the year 1807, the Bank of England, her Majesty the Queen. On the floor was a Turkey carpet,—as old as the mahogany, almost, as the Bank of England, as the Queen,—into which the waiter in his lonely revolutions had trodden so many massive soot-flakes and drops of overflowing beer, that the glowing looms of Smyrna would certainly not have recognized it. To say that I ordered my dinner of this superior being would be altogether to misrepresent the process, owing to which, having dreamed of lamb and spinach, and a charlotte-russe, I sat down in penitence to a mutton-chop and a rice pudding. Bracing my feet against the cross-beam of my little oaken table, I opposed to the mahogany partition behind me that vigorous dorsal resistance which expresses the old-English idea of repose. The sturdy screen refused even to creak; but my poor Yankee joints made up the deficiency. While I was waiting for my chop there came into the room a person whom I took to be my sole fellow-lodger. He seemed, like myself, to have submitted to proposals for dinner; the table on the other side of my partition had been prepared to receive him. He walked up to the fire, exposed his back to it, consulted his watch, and looked apparently out of the window, but really at me. He was a man of something less than middle age and more than middle stature, though indeed you would have called him neither young nor tall. He was chiefly remarkable for his exaggerated leanness. His hair, very thin on the summit of his head, was dark, short, and fine. His eye was of a pale, turbid gray, unsuited, perhaps, to his dark hair and brow, but not altogether out of harmony with his colorless, bilious complexion. His nose was aquiline and delicate; beneath it hung a thin, comely, dark mustache. His mouth and

chin were meagre and uncertain of outline; not vulgar, perhaps, but weak. A cold, fatal, gentlemanly weakness, indeed,
seemed expressed in his attenuated person. His eye was restless and deprecating; his whole physiognomy, his manner of
shifting his weight from foot to foot, the spiritless droop of
his head, told of exhausted purpose, of a will relaxed. His
dress was neat and careful, with an air of half-mourning. I
made up my mind on three points: he was unmarried, he was
ill, he was not an Englishman. The waiter approached him,
and they murmured momentarily in barely audible tones. I
heard the words "claret," "sherry," with a tentative inflection,
and finally "beer," with a gentle affirmative. Perhaps he was a
Russian in reduced circumstances; he reminded me of a certain type of Russian which I had met on the Continent. While
I was weighing this hypothesis,—for you see I was interested,—there appeared a short, brisk man with reddish-brown
hair, a vulgar nose, a sharp blue eye, and a red beard, confined
to his lower jaw and chin. My impecunious Russian was
still standing on the rug, with his mild gaze bent on vacancy;
the other marched up to him, and with his umbrella gave him
a playful poke in the concave frontage of his melancholy
waistcoat. "A penny-ha'penny for your thoughts!" said the
new-comer.

His companion uttered an exclamation, stared, then laid his
two hands on the other's shoulders. The latter looked round
at me keenly, compassing me in a momentary glance. I read
in its own high light that this was an American eyebeam; and
with such confidence that I hardly needed to see its owner, as
he prepared, with his friend, to seat himself at the table adjoining my own, take from his overcoat-pocket three New
York papers and lay them beside his plate. As my neighbors
proceeded to dine, I became conscious that, through no indiscretion of my own, a large portion of their conversation
made its way over the top of our dividing partition and mingled its savor with that of my simple repast. Occasionally their
tone was lowered, as with the intention of secrecy; but I
heard a phrase here and a phrase there distinctly enough to
grow very curious as to the burden of the whole, and, in fact,
to succeed at last in guessing it. The two voices were pitched
in an unforgotten key, and equally native to our Cisatlantic

air; they seemed to fall upon the muffled medium of surrounding parlance as the rattle of pease on the face of a drum. They were American, however, with a difference; and I had no hesitation in assigning the lighter and softer of the two to the pale, thin gentleman, whom I decidedly preferred to his comrade. The latter began to question him about his voyage.

"Horrible, horrible! I was deadly sick from the hour we left New York."

"Well, you do look considerably reduced," his friend affirmed.

"Reduced! I've been on the verge of the grave. I haven't slept six hours in three weeks." This was said with great gravity. "Well, I have made the voyage for the last time."

"The deuce you have! You mean to stay here forever?"

"Here, or somewhere! It's likely to be a short forever."

There was a pause; after which: "You're the same cheerful old boy, Searle. Going to die to-morrow, eh?"

"I almost wish I were."

"You're not in love with England, then? I've heard people say at home that you dressed and talked and acted like an Englishman. But I know Englishmen, and I know you. You're not one of them, Searle, not you. You'll go under here, sir, you'll go under as sure as my name is Simmons."

Following this, I heard a sudden clatter, as of the dropping of a knife and fork. "Well, you're a delicate sort of creature, Simmons! I have been wandering about all day in this accursed city, ready to cry with home-sickness and heart-sickness and every possible sort of sickness, and thinking, in the absence of anything better, of meeting you here this evening and of your uttering some syllable of cheer and comfort, and giving me some feeble ray of hope. Go under? Am I not under now? I can't sink lower, except to sink into my grave!"

Mr. Simmons seems to have staggered a moment under this outbreak of passion. But the next, "Don't cry, Searle," I heard him say. "Remember the waiter. I've grown Englishman enough for that. For heaven's sake, don't let us have any feelings. Feelings will do nothing for you here. It's best to come to the point. Tell me in three words what you expect of me."

I heard another movement, as if poor Searle had collapsed

in his chair. "Upon my word, Simmons, you are inconceivable. You got my letter?"

"Yes, I got your letter. I was never sorrier to get anything in my life."

At this declaration Mr. Searle rattled out an oath, which it was well perhaps that I but partially heard. "John Simmons," he cried, "what devil possesses you? Are you going to betray me here in a foreign land, to turn out a false friend, a heartless rogue?"

"Go on, sir," said sturdy Simmons. "Pour it all out. I'll wait till you have done.—Your beer is very bad," to the waiter. "I'll have some more."

"For God's sake, explain yourself!" cried Searle.

There was a pause, at the end of which I heard Mr. Simmons set down his empty tankard with emphasis. "You poor morbid man," he resumed, "I don't want to say anything to make you feel sore. I pity you. But you must allow me to say that you have acted like a blasted fool!"

Mr. Searle seemed to have made an effort to compose himself. "Be so good as to tell me what was the meaning of your letter."

"I was a fool, myself, to have written that letter. It came of my infernal meddlesome benevolence. I had much better have let you alone. To tell you the plain truth, I never was so horrified in my life as when I found that on the strength of that letter you had come out here to seek your fortune."

"What did you expect me to do?"

"I expected you to wait patiently till I had made further inquiries and had written to you again."

"You have made further inquiries now?"

"Inquiries! I have made assaults."

"And you find I have no claim?"

"No claim to call a claim. It looked at first as if you had a very pretty one. I confess the idea took hold of me—"

"Thanks to your preposterous benevolence!"

Mr. Simmons seemed for a moment to experience a difficulty in swallowing. "Your beer is undrinkable," he said to the waiter. "I'll have some brandy.—Come, Searle," he resumed, "don't challenge me to the arts of debate, or I'll settle right down on you. Benevolence, as I say, was part of it.

The reflection that if I put the thing through it would be a very pretty feather in my cap and a very pretty penny in my purse was part of it. And the satisfaction of seeing a poor nobody of a Yankee walk right into an old English estate was a good deal of it. Upon my word, Searle, when I think of it, I wish with all my heart that, erratic genius as you are, you had a claim, for the very beauty of it! I should hardly care what you did with the confounded property when you got it. I could leave you alone to turn it into Yankee notions,—into ducks and drakes, as they call it here. I should like to see you stamping over it and kicking up its sacred dust in their very faces!"

"You don't know me, Simmons!" said Searle, for all response to this untender benediction.

"I should be very glad to think I didn't, Searle. I have been to no small amount of trouble for you. I have consulted by main force three first-rate men. They smile at the idea. I should like you to see the smile negative of one of these London big-wigs. If your title were written in letters of fire, it wouldn't stand being sniffed at in that fashion. I sounded in person the solicitor of your distinguished kinsman. He seemed to have been in a manner forewarned and forearmed. It seems your brother George, some twenty years ago, put forth a feeler. So you are not to have the glory of even frightening them."

"I never frightened any one," said Searle. "I shouldn't begin at this time of day. I should approach the subject like a gentleman."

"Well, if you want very much to do something like a gentleman, you've got a capital chance. Take your disappointment like a gentleman."

I had finished my dinner, and I had become keenly interested in poor Mr. Searle's mysterious claim; so interested that it was vexatious to hear his emotions reflected in his voice without noting them in his face. I left my place, went over to the fire, took up the evening paper, and established a post of observation behind it.

Lawyer Simmons was in the act of choosing a soft chop from the dish,—an act accompanied by a great deal of prying and poking with his own personal fork. My disillusioned compatriot had pushed away his plate; he sat with his elbows on the table, gloomily nursing his head with his hands. His companion stared at him a moment, I fancied half tenderly; I am not sure whether it was pity or whether it was beer and brandy. "I say, Searle,"—and for my benefit, I think, taking me for an impressible native, he attuned his voice to something of a pompous pitch,—"in this country it is the inestimable privilege of a loyal citizen, under whatsoever stress of pleasure or of pain, to make a point of eating his dinner."

Searle disgustedly gave his plate another push. "Anything may happen, now!" he said. "I don't care a straw."

"You ought to care. Have another chop, and you *will* care. Have some brandy. Take my advice!"

Searle from between his two hands looked at him. "I have had enough of your advice!" he said.

"A little more," said Simmons, mildly; "I sha'n't trouble you again. What do you mean to do?"

"Nothing."

"O, come!"

"Nothing, nothing, nothing!"

"Nothing but starve. How about your money?"

"Why do you ask? You don't care."

"My dear fellow, if you want to make me offer you twenty pounds, you set most clumsily about it. You said just now I don't know you. Possibly! There is, perhaps, no such enormous difference between knowing you and not knowing you. At any rate, you don't know me. I expect you to go home."

"I won't go home! I have crossed the ocean for the last time."

"What is the matter? Are you afraid?"

"Yes, I'm afraid! 'I thank thee, Jew, for teaching me that word!'"

"You're more afraid to go than to stay?"

"I sha'n't stay. I shall die."

"O, are you sure of that?"

"One can always be sure of that."

Mr. Simmons started and stared: his mild cynic had turned grim stoic. "Upon my soul," he said, "one would think that Death had named the day!"

"We have named it, between us."

This was too much even for Mr. Simmons's easy morality. "I say, Searle," he cried, "I'm not more of a stickler than the next man, but if you are going to blaspheme, I shall wash my hands of you. If you'll consent to return home with me by the steamer of the 23d, I'll pay your passage down. More than that, I'll pay your wine bill."

Searle meditated. "I believe I never willed anything in my life," he said; "but I feel sure that I have willed this, that I stay here till I take my leave for a newer world than that poor old New World of ours. It's an odd feeling,—I rather like it! What should I do at home?"

"You said just now you were homesick."

"So I was—for a morning. But haven't I been all my life long sick for Europe? And now that I've got it, am I to cast it off again? I'm much obliged to you for your offer. I have enough for the present. I have about my person some forty pounds' worth of British gold and the same amount, say, of Yankee vitality. They'll last me out together! After they are gone, I shall lay my head in some English churchyard, beside some ivied tower, beneath an English yew."

I had thus far distinctly followed the dialogue; but at this point the landlord came in, and, begging my pardon, would suggest that No. 12, a most superior apartment, having now been vacated, it would give him pleasure, etc. The fate of No. 12 having been decreed, I transferred my attention back to my friends. They had risen to their feet; Simmons had put on his overcoat; he stood polishing his rusty black hat with his napkin. "Do you mean to go down to the place?" he asked.

"Possibly. I have dreamed of it so much I should like to see it."

"Shall you call on Mr. Searle?"

"Heaven forbid!"

"Something has just occurred to me," Simmons pursued, with an unhandsome grin, as if Mephistopheles were playing at malice. "There's a Miss Searle, the old man's sister."

"Well?" said the other, frowning.

"Well, sir! suppose, instead of dying, you should marry!"

Mr. Searle frowned in silence. Simmons gave him a tap on the stomach. "Line those ribs a bit first!" The poor gentleman blushed crimson and his eyes filled with tears. "You *are* a coarse brute," he said. The scene was pathetic. I was prevented from seeing the conclusion of it by the reappearance of the landlord, on behalf of No. 12. He insisted on my coming to inspect the premises. Half an hour afterwards I was rattling along in a Hansom toward Covent Garden, where I heard Madame Bosio in the Barber of Seville. On my return from the opera I went into the coffee-room, vaguely fancying I might catch another glimpse of Mr. Searle. I was not disappointed. I found him sitting before the fire, with his head fallen on his breast, sunk in the merciful stupor of tardy sleep. I looked at him for some moments. His face, pale and refined in the dim lamplight, impressed me with an air of helpless, ineffective delicacy. They say fortune comes while we sleep. Standing there I felt benignant enough to be poor Mr. Searle's fortune. As I walked away, I perceived amid the shadows of one of the little dining stalls which I have described the lonely ever-dressed waiter, dozing attendance on my friend, and shifting aside for a while the burden of waiterhood. I lingered a moment beside the old inn-yard, in which, upon a time, the coaches and postchaises found space to turn and disgorge. Above the upward vista of the enclosing galleries, from which lounging lodgers and crumpled chambermaids and all the picturesque domesticity of an antique tavern must have watched the great entrances and exits of the posting and coaching drama, I descried the distant lurid twinkle of the London constellations. At the foot of the stairs, enshrined in the glittering niche of her well-appointed bar, the landlady sat napping like some solemn idol amid votive brass and plate.

The next morning, not finding the innocent object of my benevolent curiosity in the coffee-room, I learned from the waiter that he had ordered breakfast in bed. Into this asylum I was not yet prepared to pursue him. I spent the morning running about London, chiefly on business, but snatching by the way many a vivid impression of its huge metropolitan interest. Beneath the sullen black and gray of that hoary civic world the hungry American mind detects the magic colors of association. As the afternoon approached, however, my impatient heart began to babble of green fields; it was of English meadows I had chiefly dreamed. Thinking over the suburban

lions, I fixed upon Hampton Court. The day was the more
propitious that it yielded just that dim, subaqueous light
which sleeps so fondly upon the English landscape.

At the end of an hour I found myself wandering through
the multitudinous rooms of the great palace. They follow
each other in infinite succession, with no great variety of interest or aspect, but with a sort of regal monotony, and a fine
specific flavor. They are most exactly of their various times.
You pass from great painted and panelled bedchambers and
closets, anterooms, drawing-rooms, council-rooms, through
king's suite, queen's suite, and prince's suite, until you feel as
if you were strolling through the appointed hours and stages
of some decorous monarchical day. On one side are the old
monumental upholsteries, the vast cold tarnished beds and
canopies, with the circumference of disapparelled royalty
attested by a gilded balustrade, and the great carved and
yawning chimney-places, where dukes-in-waiting may have
warmed their weary heels; on the other side, in deep recesses,
the immense windows, the framed and draped embrasures
where the sovereign whispered and favorites smiled, looking
out on the terraced gardens and the misty glades of Bushey
Park. The dark walls are gravely decorated by innumerable
dark portraits of persons attached to Court and State, more
especially with various members of the Dutch-looking *entourage* of William of Orange, the restorer of the palace; with
good store, too, of the lily-bosomed models of Lely and
Kneller. The whole tone of this long-drawn interior is immensely sombre, prosaic, and sad. The tints of all things have
sunk to a cold and melancholy brown, and the great palatial
void seems to hold no stouter tenantry than a sort of pungent
odorous chill. I seemed to be the only visitor. I held un-
grudged communion with the formal genius of the spot. Poor
mortalized kings! ineffective lure of royalty! This, or something like it, was the murmured burden of my musings. They
were interrupted suddenly by my coming upon a person
standing in devout contemplation before a simpering countess of Sir Peter Lely's creation. On hearing my footstep this
person turned his head, and I recognized my fellow-lodger at
the Red-Lion. I was apparently recognized as well; I detected
an air of overture in his glance. In a few moments, seeing I

had a catalogue, he asked the name of the portrait. On my ascertaining it, he inquired, timidly, how I liked the lady.

"Well," said I, not quite timidly enough, perhaps, "I confess she seems to me rather a light piece of work."

He remained silent, and a little abashed, I think. As we strolled away he stole a sidelong glance of farewell at his leering shepherdess. To speak with him face to face was to feel keenly that he was weak and interesting. We talked of our inn, of London, of the palace; he uttered his mind freely, but he seemed to struggle with a weight of depression. It was a simple mind enough, with no great culture, I fancied, but with a certain appealing native grace. I foresaw that I should find him a true American, full of that perplexing interfusion of refinement and crudity which marks the American mind. His perceptions, I divined, were delicate; his opinions, possibly, gross. On my telling him that I too was an American, he stopped short and seemed overcome with emotion: then silently passing his arm into my own, he suffered me to lead him through the rest of the palace and down into the gardens. A vast gravelled platform stretches itself before the basement of the palace, taking the afternoon sun. A portion of the edifice is reserved as a series of private apartments, occupied by state pensioners, reduced gentlewomen in receipt of the Queen's bounty, and other deserving persons. Many of these apartments have their little private gardens; and here and there, between their verdure-coated walls, you catch a glimpse of these dim horticultural closets. My companion and I took many a turn up and down this spacious level, looking down on the antique geometry of the lower garden and on the stoutly woven tapestry of vine and blossom which muffles the foundations of the huge red pile. I thought of the various images of old-world gentility, which, early and late, must have strolled upon that ancient terrace and felt the great protecting quietude of the solemn palace. We looked through an antique grating into one of the little private gardens, and saw an old lady with a black mantilla on her head, a decanter of water in one hand and a crutch in the other, come forth, followed by three little dogs and a cat, to sprinkle a plant. She had an opinion, I fancied, on the virtue of Queen Caroline. There are few sensations so exquisite in life as to stand with a companion in a foreign land and inhale to the depths of your consciousness the alien savor of the air and the tonic picturesqueness of things. This common relish of local color makes comrades of strangers. My companion seemed oppressed with vague amazement. He stared and lingered and scanned the scene with a gentle scowl. His enjoyment appeared to give him pain. I proposed, at last, that we should dine in the neighborhood and take a late train to town. We made our way out of the gardens into the adjoining village, where we found an excellent inn. Mr. Searle sat down to table with small apparent interest in the repast, but gradually warming to his work, he declared at the end of half an hour that for the first time in a month he felt an appetite.

"You're an invalid?" I said.

"Yes," he answered. "A hopeless one!"

The little village of Hampton Court stands clustered about the broad entrance of Bushey Park. After we had dined we lounged along into the hazy vista of the great avenue of horse-chestnuts. There is a rare emotion, familiar to every intelligent traveller, in which the mind, with a great passionate throb, achieves a magical synthesis of its impressions. You feel England; you feel Italy. The reflection for the moment has an extraordinary poignancy. I had known it from time to time in Italy, and had opened my soul to it as to the spirit of the Lord. Since my arrival in England I had been waiting for it to come. A bottle of excellent Burgundy at dinner had perhaps unlocked to it the gates of sense; it came now with a conquering tread. Just the scene around me was the England of my visions. Over against us, amid the deep-hued bloom of its ordered gardens, the dark red palace, with its formal copings and its vacant windows, seemed to tell of a proud and splendid past; the little village nestling between park and palace, around a patch of turfy common, with its tavern of gentility, its ivy-towered church, its parsonage, retained to my modernized fancy the lurking semblance of a feudal hamlet. It was in this dark composite light that I had read all English prose; it was this mild moist air that had blown from the verses of English poets; beneath these broad acres of rain-deepened greenness a thousand honored dead lay buried.

"Well," I said to my friend, "I think there is no mistake

about this being England. We may like it or not, it's positive! No more dense and stubborn fact ever settled down on an expectant tourist. It brings my heart into my throat."

Searle was silent. I looked at him; he was looking up at the sky, as if he were watching some visible descent of the elements. "On me too," he said, "it's settling down!" Then with a forced smile: "Heaven give me strength to bear it!"

"O mighty world," I cried, "to hold at once so rare an Italy and so brave an England!"

"To say nothing of America," added Searle.

"O," I answered, "America has a world to herself!"

"You have the advantage over me," my companion resumed, after a pause, "in coming to all this with an educated eye. You already know the old. I have never known it but by report. I have always fancied I should like it. In a small way at home, you know, I have tried to stick to the old. I must be a conservative by nature. People at home—a few people—used to call me a snob."

"I don't believe you were a snob," I cried. "You look too amiable."

He smiled sadly. "There it is," he said. "It's the old story! I'm amiable! I know what that means! I was too great a fool to be even a snob! If I had been I should probably have come abroad earlier in life—before—before—" He paused, and his head dropped sadly on his breast.

The bottle of Burgundy had loosened his tongue. I felt that my learning his story was merely a question of time. Something told me that I had gained his confidence and he would unfold himself. "Before you lost your health," I said.

"Before I lost my health," he answered. "And my property, —the little I had. And my ambition. And my self-esteem."

"Come!" I said. "You shall get them all back. This tonic English climate will wind you up in a month. And with the return of health, all the rest will return."

He sat musing, with his eyes fixed on the distant palace. "They are too far gone,—self-esteem especially! I should like to be an old genteel pensioner, lodged over there in the palace, and spending my days in maundering about these classic haunts. I should go every morning, at the hour when it gets the sun, into that long gallery where all those pretty women of Lely's are hung,—I know you despise them!—and stroll up and down and pay them compliments. Poor, precious, forsaken creatures! So flattered and courted in their day, so neglected now! Offering up their shoulders and ringlets and smiles to that inexorable solitude!"

I patted my friend on the shoulder. "You shall be yourself again yet," I said.

Just at this moment there came cantering down the shallow glade of the avenue a young girl on a fine black horse,—one of those lovely budding gentlewomen, perfectly mounted and equipped, who form to American eyes the sweetest incident of English scenery. She had distanced her servant, and, as she came abreast of us, turned slightly in her saddle and looked back at him. In the movement she dropped her whip. Drawing in her horse, she cast upon the ground a glance of maidenly alarm. "This is something better than a Lely," I said. Searle hastened forward, picked up the whip, and removing his hat with an air of great devotion, presented it to the young girl. Fluttered and blushing, she reached forward, took it with softly murmured gratitude, and the next moment was bounding over the elastic turf. Searle stood watching her; the servant, as he passed us, touched his hat. When Searle turned toward me again, I saw that his face was glowing with a violent blush. "I doubt of your having come abroad too late!" I said, laughing.

A short distance from where we had stopped was an old stone bench. We went and sat down on it and watched the light mist turning to sullen gold in the rays of the evening sun. "We ought to be thinking of the train back to London, I suppose," I said at last.

"O, hang the train!" said Searle.

"Willingly! There could be no better spot than this to feel the magic of an English twilight." So we lingered, and the twilight lingered around us,—a light and not a darkness. As we sat, there came trudging along the road an individual whom, from afar, I recognized as a member of the genus "tramp." I had read of the British tramp, but I had never yet encountered him, and I brought my historic consciousness to bear upon the present specimen. As he approached us he slackened pace and finally halted, touching his cap. He was a man of middle age, clad in a greasy bonnet, with greasy ear-locks depending from its sides. Round his neck was a grimy red scarf, tucked into his waistcoat; his coat and trousers had a remote affinity with those of a reduced hostler. In one hand he had a stick; on his arm he bore a tattered basket, with a handful of withered green stuff in the bottom. His face was pale, haggard, and degraded beyond description,—a singular mixture of brutality and finesse. He had a history. From what height had he fallen, from what depth had he risen? Never was a form of rascally beggarhood more complete. There was a merciless fixedness of outline about him which filled me with a kind of awe. I felt as if I were in the presence of a per-sonage,—an artist in vagrancy.

"For God's sake, gentlemen," he said, in that raucous tone of weather-beaten poverty suggestive of chronic sore-throat exacerbated by perpetual gin,—"for God's sake, gentlemen, have pity on a poor fern-collector!"—turning up his stale dan-delions. "Food hasn't passed my lips, gentlemen, in the last three days."

We gaped responsive, in the precious pity of guileless Yankeeism. "I wonder," thought I, "if half a crown would be enough?" And our fasting botanist went limping away through the park with a mystery of satirical gratitude super-added to his general mystery.

"I feel as if I had seen my *doppel-ganger*," said Searle. "He reminds me of myself. What am I but a tramp?"

Upon this hint I spoke. "What are you, my friend?" I asked. "Who are you?"

A sudden blush rose to his pale face, so that I feared I had offended him. He poked a moment at the sod with the point of his umbrella, before answering. "Who am I?" he said at last. "My name is Clement Searle. I was born in New York. I have lived in New York. What am I? That's easily told. Nothing! I assure you nothing."

"A very good fellow, apparently," I protested.

"A very good fellow! Ah, there it is! You've said more than you mean. It's by having been a very good fellow all my days that I've come to this. I have drifted through life. I'm a fail-ure, sir,—a failure as hopeless and helpless as any that ever swallowed up the slender investments of the widow and the orphan. I don't pay five cents on the dollar. Of what I was to begin with no memory remains. I have been ebbing away, from the start, in a steady current which, at forty, has left this arid sand-bank behind. To begin with, certainly, I was not a fountain of wisdom. All the more reason for a definite channel,—for will and purpose and direction. I walked by chance and sympathy and sentiment. Take a turn through New York and you'll find my tattered sympathies and sentiments dangling on every bush and fluttering in every breeze; the men to whom I lent money, the women to whom I made love, the friends I trusted, the dreams I cherished, the poisonous fumes of pleasure, amid which nothing was sweet or precious but the manhood they stifled! It was my fault that I believed in pleasure here below. I believe in it still, but as I believe in God and not in man! I believed in eating your cake and having it. I respected Pleasure, and she made a fool of me. Other men, treating her like the arrant strumpet she is, enjoyed her for the hour, but kept their good manners for plain-faced Business, with the larger dowry, to whom they are now lawfully married. My taste was to be delicate; well, perhaps I was so! I had a little money; it went the way of my little wit. Here in my pocket I have forty pounds of it left. The only thing I have to show for my money and my wit is a little volume of verses, printed at my own expense, in which fifteen years ago I made bold to sing the charms of love and idleness. Six months since I got hold of the volume; it reads like the poetry of fifty years ago. The form is incredible. I hadn't seen Hampton Court then. When I was thirty I married. It was a sad mistake, but a generous one. The young girl was poor and obscure, but beautiful and proud. I fancied she would make an incomparable woman. It was a sad mistake! She died at the end of three years, leaving no children. Since then I have idled long. I have had bad habits. To this impalpable thread of existence the current of my life has shrunk. To-morrow I shall be high and dry. Was I meant to come to this? Upon my soul I wasn't! If I say what I feel, you'll fancy my vanity quite equal to my folly, and set me down as one of those dreary theorizers after the fact, who draw any moral from their misfortunes but the damning moral that vice is vice and that's an end of it. Take it for what it's worth. I have always fancied

that I was meant for a gentler world. Before heaven, sir,—
whoever you are,—I'm in practice so absurdly tender-hearted
that I can afford to say it,—I came into the world an aristo-
crat. I was born with a soul for the picturesque. It condemns
me, I confess; but in a measure, too, it absolves me. I found
it nowhere. I found a world all hard lines and harsh lights,
without shade, without composition, as they say of pictures,
without the lovely mystery of color. To furnish color, I melted
down the very substance of my own soul. I went about with
my brush, touching up and toning down; a very pretty
chiaroscuro you'll find in my track! Sitting here, in this old
park, in this old land, I feel—I feel that I hover on the misty
verge of what might have been! I should have been born here
and not there; here my vulgar idleness would have been—
don't laugh now!—would have been elegant leisure. How it
was that I never came abroad is more than I can say. It might
have cut the knot; but the knot was too tight. I was always
unwell or in debt or entangled. Besides, I had a horror of the
sea,—with reason, heaven knows! A year ago I was reminded
of the existence of an old claim to a portion of an English estate, cherished off and on by various members of my family
for the past eighty years. It's undeniably slender and desperately hard to define. I am by no means sure that to this hour
I have mastered it. You look as if you had a clear head. Some
other time, if you'll consent, we'll puzzle it out, such as it is,
together. Poverty was staring me in the face; I sat down and
got my claim by heart, as I used to get nine times nine as a
boy. I dreamed about it for six months, half expecting to
wake up some fine morning to hear through a latticed casement the cawing of an English rookery. A couple of months
since there came out here on business of his own a sort of
half-friend of mine, a sharp New York lawyer, an extremely
common fellow, but a man with an eye for the weak point and
the strong point. It was with him yesterday that you saw me
dining. He undertook, as he expressed it, to 'nose round' and
see if anything could be made of this pretended right. The
matter had never seriously been taken up. A month later I got
a letter from Simmons, assuring me that things looked mighty
well, that he should be vastly amazed if I hadn't a case. I took
fire in a humid sort of way; I acted, for the first time in my

life; I sailed for England. I have been here three days: it seems three months. After keeping me waiting for thirty-six hours, last evening my precious Simmons makes his appearance and informs me, with his mouth full of mutton, that I was a blasted fool to have taken him at his word; that he had been precipitate; that I had been precipitate; that my claim was moonshine; and that I must do penance and take a ticket for another fortnight of seasickness in his agreeable society. My friend, my friend! Shall I say I was disappointed? I'm already resigned. I doubted the practicability of my claim. I felt in my deeper consciousness that it was the crowning illusion of a life of illusions. Well, it was a pretty one. Poor Simmons! I forgive him with all my heart. But for him I shouldn't be sitting in this place, in this air, with these thoughts. This is a world I could have loved. There's a great fitness in its having been kept for the last. After this nothing would have been tolerable. I shall now have a month of it, I hope, and I shall not have a chance to be disenchanted. There's one thing!"—and here, pausing, he laid his hand on mine; I rose and stood before him,—"I wish it were possible you should be with me to the end."

"I promise you," I said, "to leave you only at your own request. But it must be on condition of your omitting from your conversation this intolerable flavor of mortality. The end! Perhaps it's the beginning."

He shook his head. "You don't know me. It's a long story. I'm incurably ill."

"I know you a little. I have a strong suspicion that your illness is in great measure a matter of mind and spirits. All that you've told me is but another way of saying that you have lived hitherto in yourself. The tenement's haunted! Live abroad! Take an interest!"

He looked at me for a moment with his sad weak eyes. Then with a faint smile: "Don't cut down a man you find hanging. He has had a reason for it. I'm bankrupt."

"O, health is money!" I said. "Get well, and the rest will take care of itself. I'm interested in your claim."

"Don't ask me to expound it now! It's a sad muddle. Let it alone. I know nothing of business. If I myself were to take the matter in hand, I should break short off the poor little silken thread of my expectancy. In a better world than this I think I should be listened to. But in this hard world there's small bestowal of ideal justice. There is no doubt, I fancy, that, a hundred years ago, we suffered a palpable wrong. But we made no appeal at the time, and the dust of a century now lies heaped upon our silence. Let it rest!"

"What is the estimated value of your interest?"

"We were instructed from the first to accept a compromise. Compared with the whole property, our utmost right is extremely small. Simmons talked of eighty-five thousand dollars. Why eighty-five I'm sure I don't know. Don't beguile me into figures."

"Allow me one more question. Who is actually in possession?"

"A certain Mr. Richard Searle. I know nothing about him."

"He is in some way related to you?"

"Our great-grandfathers were half-brothers. What does that make?"

"Twentieth cousins, say. And where does your twentieth cousin live?"

"At Lockley Park, Herefordshire."

I pondered awhile. "I'm interested in you, Mr. Searle," I said. "In your story, in your title, such as it is, and in this Lockley Park, Herefordshire. Suppose we go down and see it."

He rose to his feet with a certain alertness. "I shall make a sound man of him, yet," I said to myself.

"I shouldn't have the heart," he said, "to accomplish the melancholy pilgrimage alone. But with you I'll go anywhere."

On our return to London we determined to spend three days there together, and then to go into the country. We felt to excellent purpose the sombre charm of London, the mighty mother-city of our mighty race, the great distributing heart of our traditional life. Certain London characteristics—monuments, relics, hints of history, local moods and memories—are more deeply suggestive to an American soul than anything else in Europe. With an equal attentive piety my friend and I glanced at these things. Their influence on Searle was deep and singular. His observation I soon perceived to be extremely acute. His almost passionate relish for the old, the artificial, and social, wellnigh extinct from its long inanition, began now to tremble and thrill with a tardy vitality. I watched in silent wonderment this strange metaphysical renascence.

Between the fair boundaries of the counties of Hereford and Worcester rise in a long undulation the sloping pastures of the Malvern Hills. Consulting a big red book on the castles and manors of England, we found Lockley Park to be seated near the base of this grassy range,—though in which county I forget. In the pages of this genial volume, Lockley Park and its appurtenances made a very handsome figure. We took up our abode at a certain little wayside inn, at which in the days of leisure the coach must have stopped for lunch, and burnished pewters of rustic ale been tenderly exalted to "outsides" athirst with breezy progression. Here we stopped, for sheer admiration of its steep thatched roof, its latticed windows, and its homely porch. We allowed a couple of days to elapse in vague, undirected strolls and sweet sentimental observance of the land, before we prepared to execute the especial purpose of our journey. This admirable region is a compendium of the general physiognomy of England. The noble friendliness of the scenery, its subtle old-friendliness, the magical familiarity of multitudinous details, appealed to us at every step and at every glance. Deep in our souls a natural affection answered. The whole land, in the full, warm rains of the last of April, had burst into sudden perfect spring. The dark walls of the hedge-rows had turned into blooming screens; the sodden verdure of lawn and meadow was streaked with a ranker freshness. We went forth without loss of time for a long walk on the hills. Reaching their summits, you find half England unrolled at your feet. A dozen broad counties, within the vast range of your vision, commingle their green exhalations. Closely beneath us lay the dark, rich flats of hedgy Worcestershire and the copse-checkered slopes of rolling Hereford, white with the blossom of apples. At widely opposite points of the large expanse two great cathedral towers rise sharply, taking the light, from the settled shadow of their circling towns,—the light, the ineffable English light! "Out of England," cried Searle, "it's but a garish world!"

The whole vast sweep of our surrounding prospect lay answering in a myriad fleeting shades the cloudy process of the tremendous sky. The English heaven is a fit antithesis to the complex English earth. We possess in America the infinite beauty of the blue; England possesses the splendor of combined and animated clouds. Over against us, from our station on the hills, we saw them piled and dissolved, compacted and shifted, blotting the azure with sullen rain spots, stretching, breeze-fretted, into dappled fields of gray, bursting into a storm of light or melting into a drizzle of silver. We made our way along the rounded summits of these well-grazed heights, —mild, breezy inland downs,—and descended through long-drawn slopes of fields, green to cottage doors, to where a rural village beckoned us from its seat among the meadows. Close beside it, I admit, the railway shoots fiercely from its tunnel in the hills; and yet there broods upon this charming hamlet an old-time quietude and privacy, which seems to make it a violation of confidence to tell its name so far away. We struck through a narrow lane, a green lane, dim with its height of hedges; it led us to a superb old farmhouse, now jostled by the multiplied lanes and roads which have curtailed its ancient appanage. It stands in stubborn picturesqueness, at the receipt of sad-eyed contemplation and the sufferance of "sketches." I doubt whether out of Nuremberg—or Pompeii! —you may find so forcible an image of the domiciliary genius of the past. It is cruelly complete; its bended beams and joists, beneath the burden of its gables, seem to ache and groan with memories and regrets. The short, low windows, where lead and glass combine in equal proportions to hint to the wondering stranger of the mediæval gloom within, still prefer their darksome office to the grace of modern day. Such an old house fills an American with an indefinable feeling of respect. So propped and patched and tinkered with clumsy tenderness, clustered so richly about its central English sturdiness, its oaken vertebrations, so humanized with ages of use and touches of beneficent affection, it seemed to offer to our grateful eyes a small, rude synthesis of the great English social order. Passing out upon the high-road, we came to the common browsing-patch, the "village green" of the tales of our youth. Nothing was wanting; the shaggy, mouse-colored donkey, nosing the turf with his mild and huge proboscis, the geese, the old woman,—*the* old woman, in person, with her red cloak and her black bonnet, frilled about the face and double-frilled beside her decent, placid cheeks,—the towering ploughman with his white smock-frock, puckered on chest and back, his short corduroys, his mighty calves, his big, red, rural face. We greeted these things as children greet the loved pictures in a story-book, lost and mourned and found again. It was marvellous how well we knew them. Beside the road we saw a ploughboy straddle, whistling, on a stile. Gainsborough might have painted him. Beyond the stile, across the level velvet of a meadow, a footpath lay, like a thread of darker woof. We followed it from field to field and from stile to stile. It was the way to church. At the church we finally arrived, lost in its rook-haunted churchyard, hidden from the work-day world by the broad stillness of pastures,—a gray, gray tower, a huge black yew, a cluster of village graves, with crooked headstones, in grassy, low relief. The whole scene was deeply ecclesiastical. My companion was overcome.

"You must bury me here," he cried. "It's the first church I have seen in my life. How it makes a Sunday where it stands!"

The next day we saw a church of statelier proportions. We walked over to Worcester, through such a mist of local color, that I felt like one of Smollett's pedestrian heroes, faring tavernward for a night of adventures. As we neared the provincial city we saw the steepled mass of the cathedral, long and high, rise far into the cloud-freckled blue. And as we came nearer still, we stopped on the bridge and viewed the solid minster reflected in the yellow Severn. And going farther yet we entered the town,—where surely Miss Austen's heroines, in chariots and curricles, must often have come a shopping for swan's-down boas and high lace mittens;—we lounged about the gentle close and gazed insatiably at that most soul-soothing sight, the waning, wasting afternoon light, the visible ether which feels the voices of the chimes, far aloft on the broad perpendicular field of the cathedral tower; saw it linger and nestle and abide, as it loves to do on all bold architectural spaces, converting them graciously into registers and witnesses of nature; tasted, too, as deeply of the peculiar stillness of this clerical precinct; saw a rosy English lad come forth and lock the door of the old foundation school, which marries its hoary basement to the soaring Gothic of the church, and carry his big responsible key into one of the quiet canonical houses; and then stood musing together on the effect on one's mind of having in one's boyhood haunted such cathedral shades as a King's scholar, and yet kept ruddy with much cricket in misty meadows by the Severn. On the third morning we betook ourselves to Lockley Park, having learned that the greater part of it was open to visitors, and that, indeed, on application, the house was occasionally shown.

Within its broad enclosure many a declining spur of the great hills melted into parklike slopes and dells. A long avenue wound and circled from the outermost gate through an untrimmed woodland, whence you glanced at further slopes and glades and copses and bosky recesses,—at everything except the limits of the place. It was as free and wild and untended as the villa of an Italian prince; and I have never seen the stern English fact of property put on such an air of innocence. The weather had just become perfect; it was one of the dozen exquisite days of the English year,—days stamped with a refinement of purity unknown in more liberal climes. It was as if the mellow brightness, as tender as that of the primroses which starred the dark waysides like petals wind-scattered over beds of moss, had been meted out to us by the cubic foot,—tempered, refined, recorded! From this external region we passed into the heart of the park, through a second lodge-gate, with weather-worn gilding on its twisted bars, to the smooth slopes where the great trees stood singly and the tame deer browsed along the bed of a woodland stream. Hence, before us, we perceived the dark Elizabethan manor among its blooming parterres and terraces.

"Here you can wander all day," I said to Searle, "like a proscribed and exiled prince, hovering about the dominion of the usurper."

"To think," he answered, "of people having enjoyed this all these years! I know what I am,—what might I have been? What does all this make of you?"

"That it makes you happy," I said, "I should hesitate to believe. But it's hard to suppose that such a place has not some beneficent action of its own."

"What a perfect scene and background it forms!" Searle

went on. "What legends, what histories it knows! My heart is breaking with unutterable visions. There's Tennyson's Talking Oak. What summer days one could spend here! How I could lounge my bit of life away on this shady stretch of turf! Haven't I some maiden-cousin in yon moated grange who would give me kind leave?" And then turning almost fiercely upon me: "Why did you bring me here? Why did you drag me into this torment of vain regrets?"

At this moment there passed near us a servant who had emerged from the gardens of the great house. I hailed him and inquired whether we should be likely to gain admittance. He answered that Mr. Searle was away from home, and that he thought it probable the housekeeper would consent to do the honors of the mansion. I passed my arm into Searle's. "Come," I said. "Drain the cup, bitter-sweet though it be. We shall go in." We passed another lodge-gate and entered the gardens. The house was an admirable specimen of complete Elizabethan, a multitudinous cluster of gables and porches, oriels and turrets, screens of ivy and pinnacles of slate. Two broad terraces commanded the great wooded horizon of the adjacent domain. Our summons was answered by the butler in person, solemn and *tout de noir habillé*. He repeated the statement that Mr. Searle was away from home, and that he would present our petition to the housekeeper. We would be so good, however, as to give him our cards. This request, following so directly on the assertion that Mr. Searle was absent, seemed to my companion not distinctly pertinent. "Surely not for the housekeeper," he said.

The butler gave a deferential cough. "Miss Searle is at home."

"Yours alone will suffice," said Searle. I took out a card and pencil, and wrote beneath my name, *New York*. Standing with the pencil in my hand I felt a sudden impulse. Without in the least weighing proprieties or results, I yielded to it. I added above my name, *Mr. Clement Searle*. What would come of it?

Before many minutes the housekeeper attended us,—a fresh rosy little old woman in a dowdy clean cap and a scanty calico gown; an exquisite specimen of refined and venerable servility. She had the accent of the country, but the manners of the house. Under her guidance we passed through a dozen apartments, duly stocked with old pictures, old tapestry, old carvings, old armor, with all the constituent properties of an English manor. The pictures were especially valuable. The two Vandykes, the trio of rosy Rubenses, the sole and sombre Rembrandt, glowed with conscious authenticity. A Claude, a Murillo, a Greuze, and a Gainsborough hung gracious in their chosen places. Searle strolled about silent, pale, and grave, with bloodshot eyes and lips compressed. He uttered no comment and asked no question. Missing him, at last, from my side, I retraced my steps and found him in a room we had just left, on a tarnished silken divan, with his face buried in his hands. Before him, ranged on an antique buffet, was a magnificent collection of old Italian majolica; huge platters radiant with their steady colors, jugs and vases nobly bellied and embossed. There came to me, as I looked, a sudden vision of the young English gentleman, who, eighty years ago, had travelled by slow stages to Italy and been waited on at his inn by persuasive toymen. "What is it, Searle?" I asked. "Are you unwell?"

He uncovered his haggard face and showed a burning blush. Then smiling in hot irony: "A memory of the past! I was thinking of a china vase that used to stand on the parlor mantel-shelf while I was a boy, with the portrait of General Jackson painted on one side and a bunch of flowers on the other. How long do you suppose that majolica has been in the family?"

"A long time probably. It was brought hither in the last century, into old, old England, out of old, old Italy, by some old young buck of this excellent house with a taste for *chinoiseries*. Here it has stood for a hundred years, keeping its clear, firm hues in this aristocratic twilight."

Searle sprang to his feet. "I say," he cried, "in heaven's name take me away! I can't stand this. Before I know it I shall do something I shall be ashamed of. I shall steal one of their d—d majolicas. I shall proclaim my identity and assert my rights! I shall go blubbering to Miss Searle and ask her in pity's name to keep me here for a month!"

If poor Searle could ever have been said to look "dangerous," he looked so now. I began to regret my officious presentation of his name, and prepared without delay to lead him out of the house. We overtook the housekeeper in the last room of the suite, a small, unused boudoir, over the chimney-piece of which hung a noble portrait of a young man in a powdered wig and a brocaded waistcoat. I was immediately struck with his resemblance to my companion.

"This is Mr. Clement Searle, Mr. Searle's great-uncle, by Sir Joshua Reynolds," quoth the housekeeper. "He died young, poor gentleman. He perished at sea, going to America."

"He's the young buck," I said, "who brought the majolica out of Italy."

"Indeed, sir, I believe he did," said the housekeeper, staring.

"He's the image of you, Searle," I murmured.

"He's wonderfully like the gentleman, saving his presence," said the housekeeper.

My friend stood gazing. "Clement Searle—at sea—going to America—" he muttered. Then harshly, to the housekeeper, "Why the deuce did he go to America?"

"Why, indeed, sir? You may well ask. I believe he had kins-folk there. It was for them to come to him."

Searle broke into a laugh. "It was for them to have come to him! Well, well," he said, fixing his eyes on the little old woman, "they have come to him at last!"

She blushed like a wrinkled rose-leaf. "Indeed, sir," she said, "I verily believe that you are one of *us*!"

"My name is the name of that lovely youth," Searle went on. "Kinsman, I salute you! Attend!" And he grasped me by the arm. "I have an idea! He perished at sea. His spirit came ashore and wandered forlorn till it got lodgment again in my poor body. In my poor body it has lived, homesick, these forty years, shaking its rickety cage, urging me, stupid, to carry it back to the scenes of its youth. And I never knew what was the matter with me! Let me exhale my spirit here!"

The housekeeper essayed a timorous smile. The scene was embarrassing. My confusion was not allayed when I suddenly perceived in the doorway the figure of a lady. "Miss Searle!" whispered the housekeeper. My first impression of Miss Searle was that she was neither young nor beautiful. She stood with a timid air on the threshold, pale, trying to smile, and twirling my card in her fingers. I immediately bowed. Searle, I think, gazed marvelling.

"If I am not mistaken," said the lady, "one of you gentlemen is Mr. Clement Searle."

"My friend is Mr. Clement Searle," I replied. "Allow me to add that I alone am responsible for your having received his name."

"I should have been sorry not to receive it," said Miss Searle, beginning to blush. "Your being from America has led me to—to interrupt you."

"The interruption, madam, has been on our part. And with just that excuse,—that we are from America."

Miss Searle, while I spoke, had fixed her eyes on my friend, as he stood silent beneath Sir Joshua's portrait. The housekeeper, amazed and mystified, took a liberty. "Heaven preserve us, Miss! It's your great-uncle's picture come to life."

"I'm not mistaken, then," said Miss Searle. "We are distantly related." She had the aspect of an extremely modest woman. She was evidently embarrassed at having to proceed unassisted in her overture. Searle eyed her with gentle wonder from head to foot. I fancied I read his thoughts. This, then, was Miss Searle, his maiden-cousin, prospective heiress of these manorial acres and treasures. She was a person of about thirty-three years of age, taller than most women, with health and strength in the rounded amplitude of her shape. She had a small blue eye, a massive chignon of yellow hair, and a mouth at once broad and comely. She was dressed in a lustreless black satin gown, with a short train. Around her neck she wore a blue silk handkerchief, and over this handkerchief, in many convolutions, a string of amber beads. Her appearance was singular; she was large, yet not imposing; girlish, yet mature. Her glance and accent, in addressing us, were simple, too simple. Searle, I think, had been fancying some proud cold beauty of five-and-twenty; he was relieved at finding the lady timid and plain. His person was suddenly illumined with an old disused gallantry.

"We are distant cousins, I believe. I am happy to claim a relationship which you are so good as to remember. I had not in the least counted on your doing so."

"Perhaps I have done wrong," and Miss Searle blushed anew and smiled. "But I have always known of there being people of our blood in America, and I have often wondered

and asked about them; without learning much, however. To-
day, when this card was brought me and I knew of a Clement
Searle wandering about the house like a stranger, I felt as if I
ought to do something. I hardly knew what! My brother is in
London. I have done what I think he would have done.
Welcome, as a cousin." And with a gesture at once frank and
shy, she put out her hand.

"I'm welcome indeed," said Searle, taking it, "if he would
have done it half as graciously."

"You've seen the show," Miss Searle went on. "Perhaps
now you'll have some lunch." We followed her into a small
breakfast-room, where a deep bay-window opened on the
mossy flags of the great terrace. Here, for some moments, she
remained silent and shy, in the manner of a person resting
from a great effort. Searle, too, was formal and reticent, so
that I had to busy myself with providing small-talk. It was of
course easy to descant on the beauties of park and mansion.
Meanwhile I observed our hostess. She had small beauty and
scanty grace; her dress was out of taste and out of season; yet
she pleased me well. There was about her a sturdy sweetness,
a homely flavor of the sequestered *châtelaine* of feudal days.
To be so simple amid this massive luxury, so mellow and yet
so fresh, so modest and yet so placid, told of just the spacious
leisure in which I had fancied human life to be steeped in
many a park-circled home. Miss Searle was to the Belle au
Bois Dormant what a fact is to a fairy-tale, an interpretation
to a myth. We, on our side, were to our hostess objects of no
light scrutiny. The best possible English breeding still marvels
visibly at the native American. Miss Searle's wonderment was
guileless enough to have been more overt and yet inoffensive;
there was no taint of offence indeed in her utterance of the
unvarying amenity that she had met an American family on
the Lake of Como whom she would have almost taken to be
English.

"If I lived here," I said, "I think I should hardly need to go
away, even to the Lake of Como."

"You might perhaps get tired of it. And then the Lake of
Como! If I could only go abroad again!"

"You have been but once?"

"Only once. Three years ago my brother took me to Switzerland. We thought it extremely beautiful. Except for this journey, I have always lived here. Here I was born. It's a dear old place, indeed, and I know it well. Sometimes I fancy I'm a little tired." And on my asking her how she spent her time and what society she saw, "It's extremely quiet," she went on, proceeding by short steps and simple statements, in the manner of a person summoned for the first time to define her situation and enumerate the elements of her life. "We see very few people. I don't think there are many nice people hereabouts. At least we don't know them. Our own family is very small. My brother cares for little else but riding and books. He had a great sorrow ten years ago. He lost his wife and his only son, a dear little boy, who would have succeeded him in the estates. Do you know that I'm likely to have them now? Poor me! Since his loss my brother has preferred to be quite alone. I'm sorry he's away. But you must wait till he comes back. I expect him in a day or two." She talked more and more, with a rambling, earnest vapidity, about her circumstances, her solitude, her bad eyes, so that she couldn't read, her flowers, her ferns, her dogs, and the curate, recently inducted by her brother and warranted sound orthodox, who had lately begun to light his altar candles; pausing every now and then to blush in self-surprise, and yet moving steadily from point to point in the deepening excitement of temptation and occasion. Of all the old things I had seen in England, this mind of Miss Searle's seemed to me the oldest, the quaintest, the most ripely verdant; so fenced and protected by convention and precedent and usage; so passive and mild and docile. I felt as if I were talking with a potential heroine of Miss Burney. As she talked, she rested her dull, kind eyes upon her kinsman with a sort of fascinated stare. At last, "Did you mean to go away," she demanded, "without asking for us?"

"I had thought it over, Miss Searle, and had determined not to trouble you. You have shown me how unfriendly I should have been."

"But you knew of the place being ours and of our relationship?"

"Just so. It was because of these things that I came down here,—because of them, almost, that I came to England. I have always liked to think of them."

"You merely wished to look, then? We don't pretend to be much to look at."

"You don't know what you are, Miss Searle," said my friend, gravely.

"You like the old place, then?"

Searle looked at her in silence. "If I could only tell you," he said at last.

"Do tell me! You must come and stay with us."

Searle began to laugh. "Take care, take care," he cried. "I should surprise you. At least I should bore you. I should never leave you."

"O, you'd get homesick for America!"

At this Searle laughed the more. "By the way," he cried to me, "tell Miss Searle about America!" And he stepped through the window out upon the terrace, followed by two beautiful dogs, a pointer and a young stag-hound, who from the moment we came in had established the fondest relation with him. Miss Searle looked at him as he went, with a certain tender wonder in her eye. I read in her glance, methought, that she was interested. I suddenly recalled the last words I had heard spoken by my friend's adviser in London: "Instead of dying you'd better marry." If Miss Searle could be gently manipulated. O for a certain divine tact! Something assured me that her heart was virgin soil; that sentiment had never bloomed there. If I could but sow the seed! There lurked within her the perfect image of one of the patient wives of old.

"He has lost his heart to England," I said. "He ought to have been born here."

"And yet," said Miss Searle, "he's not in the least an Englishman."

"How do you know that?"

"I hardly know how. I never talked with a foreigner before; but he looks and talks as I have fancied foreigners."

"Yes, he's foreign enough!"

"Is he married?"

"He's a widower,—without children."

"Has he property?"

"Very little."

"But enough to travel?"

I meditated. "He has not expected to travel far," I said at last. "You know he's in poor health."

"Poor gentleman! So I fancied."

"He's better, though, than he thinks. He came here because he wanted to see your place before he dies."

"Poor fellow!" And I fancied I perceived in her eye the lustre of a rising tear. "And he was going off without my seeing him?"

"He's a modest man, you see."

"He's very much of a gentleman."

"Assuredly!"

At this moment we heard on the terrace a loud, harsh cry. "It's the great peacock!" said Miss Searle, stepping to the window and passing out. I followed her. Below us on the terrace, leaning on the parapet, stood our friend, with his arm round the neck of the pointer. Before him, on the grand walk, strutted a splendid peacock, with ruffled neck and expanded tail. The other dog had apparently indulged in a momentary attempt to abash the gorgeous fowl; but at Searle's voice he had bounded back to the terrace and leaped upon the parapet, where he now stood licking his new friend's face. The scene had a beautiful old-time air; the peacock flaunting in the foreground, like the very genius of antique gardenry; the broad terrace, which flattered an innate taste of mine for all deserted promenades to which people may have adjourned from formal dinners, to drink coffee in old Sèvres, and where the stiff brocade of women's dresses may have rustled autumnal leaves; and far around us, with one leafy circle melting into another, the timbered acres of the park. "The very beasts have made him welcome," I said, as we rejoined our companion.

"The peacock has done for you, Mr. Searle," said his cousin, "what he does only for very great people. A year ago there came here a duchess to see my brother. I don't think that since then he has spread his tail as wide for any one else by a dozen feathers."

"It's not alone the peacock," said Searle. "Just now there

came slipping across my path a little green lizard, the first I ever saw, the lizard of literature! And if you have a ghost, broad daylight though it be, I expect to see him here. Do you know the annals of your house, Miss Searle?"

"O dear, no! You must ask my brother for all those things."

"You ought to have a book full of legends and traditions. You ought to have loves and murders and mysteries by the roomful. I count upon it."

"O Mr. Searle! We have always been a very well-behaved family. Nothing out of the way has ever happened, I think."

"Nothing out of the way? O horrors! We have done better than that in America. Why, I myself!"—and he gazed at her a moment with a gleam of malice, and then broke into a laugh. "Suppose I should turn out a better Searle than you? Better than you, nursed here in romance and picturesqueness. Come, don't disappoint me. You have some history among you all, you have some poetry. I have been famished all my days for these things. Do you understand? Ah, you can't understand! Tell me something! When I think of what must have happened here! when I think of the lovers who must have strolled on this terrace and wandered through those glades! of all the figures and passions and purposes that must have haunted these walls! of the births and deaths, the joys and sufferings, the young hopes and the old regrets, the intense experience—" And here he faltered a moment, with the increase of his vehemence. The gleam in his eye, which I have called a gleam of malice, had settled into a deep unnatural light. I began to fear he had become over-excited. But he went on with redoubled passion. "To see it all evoked before me," he cried, "if the Devil alone could do it, I'd make a bargain with the Devil! O Miss Searle, I'm a most unhappy man!"

"O dear, O dear!" said Miss Searle.

"Look at that window, that blessed oriel!" And he pointed to a small, protruding casement above us, relieved against the purple brick-work, framed in chiselled stone, and curtained with ivy.

"It's my room," said Miss Searle.

"Of course it's a woman's room. Think of the forgotten loveliness which has peeped from that window; think of the

old-time women's lives which have known chiefly that outlook on this bosky world. O gentle cousins! And you, Miss
Searle, you're one of them yet." And he marched towards her
and took her great white hand. She surrendered it, blushing
to her eyes, and pressing her other hand to her breast.
"You're a woman of the past. You're nobly simple. It has
been a romance to see you. It doesn't matter what I say to
you. You didn't know me yesterday, you'll not know me to-
morrow. Let me to-day do a mad, sweet thing. Let me fancy
you the soul of all the dead women who have trod these
terrace-flags, which lie here like sepulchral tablets in the pavement of a church. Let me say I worship you!" And he raised
her hand to his lips. She gently withdrew it, and for a moment averted her face. Meeting her eyes the next moment, I
saw that they were filled with tears. The Belle au Bois
Dormant was awake.

There followed an embarrassed pause. An issue was suddenly presented by the appearance of the butler bearing a
letter. "A telegram, Miss," he said.

"Dear me!" cried Miss Searle, "I can't open a telegram.
Cousin, help me."

Searle took the missive, opened it, and read aloud: *"I shall
be home to dinner. Keep the American."*

II.

"Keep the American!" Miss Searle, in compliance with the injunction conveyed in her brother's telegram (with something
certainly of telegraphic curtness), lost no time in expressing
the pleasure it would give her to have my companion remain.
"Really you must," she said; and forthwith repaired to the
housekeeper, to give orders for the preparation of a room.

"How in the world," asked Searle, "did he know of my
being here?"

"He learned, probably," I expounded, "from his solicitor of
the visit of your friend Simmons. Simmons and the solicitor
must have had another interview since your arrival in
England. Simmons, for reasons of his own, has communicated to the solicitor your journey to this neighborhood, and
Mr. Searle, learning this, has immediately taken for granted

that you have formally presented yourself to his sister. He's hospitably inclined, and he wishes her to do the proper thing by you. More, perhaps! I have my little theory that he is the very Phœnix of usurpers, that his nobler sense has been captivated by the exposition of the men of law, and that he means gracefully to surrender you your fractional interest in the estate."

"I give it up!" said my friend, musing. "Come what come will!"

"You of course," said Miss Searle, reappearing and turning to me, "are included in my brother's invitation. I have bespoken your lodging as well. Your luggage shall immediately be sent for."

It was arranged that I in person should be driven over to our little inn, and that I should return with our effects in time to meet Mr. Searle at dinner. On my arrival, several hours later, I was immediately conducted to my room. The servant pointed out to me that it communicated by a door and a private passage with that of my companion. I made my way along this passage,—a low, narrow corridor, with a long latticed casement, through which there streamed, upon a series of grotesquely sculptured oaken closets and cupboards, the lurid animating glow of the western sun,—knocked at his door, and, getting no answer, opened it. In an arm-chair by the open window sat my friend, sleeping, with arms and legs relaxed and head placidly reverted. It was a great relief to find him resting from his rhapsodies, and I watched him for some moments before waking him. There was a faint glow of color in his cheek and a light parting of his lips, as in a smile; something nearer to mental soundness than I had yet seen in him. It was almost happiness, it was almost health. I laid my hand on his arm and gently shook it. He opened his eyes, gazed at me a moment, vaguely recognized me, then closed them again. "Let me dream, let me dream!" he said.

"What are you dreaming about?"

A moment passed before his answer came. "About a tall woman in a quaint black dress, with yellow hair, and a sweet, sweet smile, and a soft, low, delicious voice! I'm in love with her."

"It's better to see her," I said, "than to dream about her.

Get up and dress, and we shall go down to dinner and meet her."

"Dinner—dinner—" And he gradually opened his eyes again. "Yes, upon my word, I shall dine!"

"You're a well man!" I said, as he rose to his feet. "You'll live to bury Mr. Simmons." He had spent the hours of my absence, he told me, with Miss Searle. They had strolled together over the park and through the gardens and greenhouses. "You must already be intimate!" I said, smiling.

"She is intimate with me," he answered. "Heaven knows what rigmarole I've treated her to!" They had parted an hour ago, since when, he believed, her brother had arrived.

The slow-fading twilight still abode in the great drawing-room as we entered it. The housekeeper had told us that this apartment was rarely used, there being a smaller and more convenient one for the same needs. It seemed now, however, to be occupied in my comrade's honor. At the farther end of it, rising to the roof, like a ducal tomb in a cathedral, was a great chimney-piece of chiselled white marble, yellowed by time, in which a light fire was crackling. Before the fire stood a small short man with his hands behind him; near him stood Miss Searle, so transformed by her dress that at first I scarcely knew her. There was in our entrance and reception something profoundly chilling and solemn. We moved in silence up the long room. Mr. Searle advanced slowly a dozen steps to meet us. His sister stood motionless. I was conscious of her masking her visage with a large white tinselled fan, and of her eyes, grave and expanded, watching us intently over the top of it. The master of Lockley Park grasped in silence the proffered hand of his kinsman, and eyed him from head to foot, suppressing, I think, a start of surprise at his resemblance to Sir Joshua's portrait. "This is a happy day!" he said. And then turning to me with a bow, "My cousin's friend is my friend." Miss Searle lowered her fan.

The first thing that struck me in Mr. Searle's appearance was his short and meagre stature, which was less by half a head than that of his sister. The second was the preternatural redness of his hair and beard. They intermingled over his ears and surrounded his head like a huge lurid nimbus. His face was pale and attenuated, like the face of a scholar, a dilettante,

a man who lives in a library, bending over books and prints
and medals. At a distance it had an oddly innocent and youthful look; but on a nearer view it revealed a number of finely
etched and scratched wrinkles, of a singularly aged and cunning effect. It was the complexion of a man of sixty. His nose
was arched and delicate, identical almost with the nose of my
friend. In harmony with the effect of his hair was that of his
eyes, which were large and deep-set, with a sort of vulpine
keenness and redness, but full of temper and spirit. Imagine
this physiognomy—grave and solemn in aspect, grotesquely
solemn, almost, in spite of the bushy brightness in which it
was encased—set in motion by a smile which seemed to whisper terribly, "I am *the* smile, the sole and official, the grin to
command," and you will have an imperfect notion of the remarkable presence of our host; something better worth seeing
and knowing, I fancied as I covertly scrutinized him, than
anything our excursion had yet introduced us to. Of how
thoroughly I had entered into sympathy with my companion
and how effectually I had associated my sensibilities with his,
I had small suspicion until, within the short five minutes
which preceded the announcement of dinner, I distinctly perceived him place himself, morally speaking, on the defensive.
To neither of us was Mr. Searle, as the Italians would say,
sympathetic. I might have fancied from her attitude that Miss
Searle apprehended our thoughts. A signal change had been
wrought in her since the morning; during the hour, indeed
(as I read in the light of the wondering glance he cast at her),
that had elapsed since her parting with her cousin. She had
not yet recovered from some great agitation. Her face was
pale and her eyes red with weeping. These tragic betrayals
gave an unexpected dignity to her aspect, which was further
enhanced by the rare picturesqueness of her dress.

Whether it was taste or whether it was accident, I know
not; but Miss Searle, as she stood there, half in the cool twilight, half in the arrested glow of the fire as it spent itself in
the vastness of its marble cave, was a figure for a cunning
painter. She was dressed in the faded splendor of a beautiful
tissue of combined and blended silk and crape of a tender sea-
green color, festooned and garnished and puffed into a massive *bouillonnement*; a piece of millinery which, though it

must have witnessed a number of stately dinners, preserved still an air of admirable elegance. Over her white shoulders she wore an ancient web of the most precious and venerable lace, and about her rounded throat a necklace of heavy pearls. I went with her in to dinner, and Mr. Searle, following with my friend, took his arm (as the latter afterwards told me) and pretended sportively to conduct him. As dinner proceeded, the feeling grew within me that a drama had begun to be played in which the three persons before me were actors, each of a most exacting part. The part of my friend, however, seemed the most heavily charged, and I was filled with a strong desire that he should acquit himself with honor. I seemed to see him summon his shadowy faculties to obey his shadowy will. The poor fellow sat playing solemnly at self-esteem. With Miss Searle, credulous, passive, and pitying, he had finally flung aside all vanity and propriety, and shown her the bottom of his fantastic heart. But with our host there might be no talking of nonsense nor taking of liberties; there and then, if ever, sat a double-distilled conservative, breathing the fumes of hereditary privilege and security. For an hour, then, I saw my poor friend turn faithfully about to speak graciously of barren things. He was to prove himself a sound American, so that his relish of this elder world might seem purely disinterested. What his kinsman had expected to find him, I know not; but, with all his finely adjusted urbanity, he was unable to repress a shade of annoyance at finding him likely to speak graciously at all. Mr. Searle was not the man to show his hand, but I think his best card had been a certain implicit confidence that this exotic parasite would hardly have good manners. Our host, with great decency, led the conversation to America, talking of it rather as if it were some fabled planet, alien to the British orbit, lately proclaimed indeed to have the proportion of atmospheric gases required to support animal life, but not, save under cover of a liberal afterthought, to be admitted into one's regular conception of things. I, for my part, felt nothing but regret that the spheric smoothness of his universe should be strained to cracking by the intrusion of our square shoulders.

"I knew in a general way," said Mr. Searle, "of my having relations in America; but you know one hardly realizes those things. I could hardly more have imagined people of our blood there, than I could have imagined being there myself. There was a man I knew at college, a very odd fellow, a nice fellow too; he and I were rather cronies; I think he afterwards went to America; to the Argentine Republic, I believe. Do you know the Argentine Republic? What an extraordinary name, by the way! And then, you know, there was that great-uncle of mine whom Sir Joshua painted. He went to America, but he never got there. He was lost at sea. You look enough like him to have one fancy he *did* get there, and that he has lived along till now. If you are he, you've not done a wise thing to show yourself here. He left a bad name behind him. There's a ghost who comes sobbing about the house every now and then, the ghost of one against whom he wrought a great evil!"

"O brother!" cried Miss Searle, in simple horror.

"Of course you know nothing of such things," said Mr. Searle. "You're too sound a sleeper to hear the sobbing of ghosts."

"I'm sure I should like immensely to hear the sobbing of a ghost!" said my friend, with the light of his previous eagerness playing up into his eyes. "Why does it sob? Unfold the wondrous tale."

Mr. Searle eyed his audience for a moment gaugingly; and then, as the French say, *se recueillit*, as if he were measuring his own imaginative force.

He wished to do justice to his theme. With the five finger-nails of his left hand nervously playing against the tinkling crystal of his wineglass, and his bright eye telling of a gleeful sense that, small and grotesque as he sat there, he was for the moment profoundly impressive, he distilled into our untutored minds the sombre legend of his house. "Mr. Clement Searle, from all I gather, was a young man of great talents but a weak disposition. His mother was left a widow early in life, with two sons, of whom he was the older and the more promising. She educated him with the utmost fondness and care. Of course, when he came to manhood she wished him to marry well. His means were quite sufficient to enable him to overlook the want of means in his wife; and Mrs. Searle selected a young lady who possessed, as she conceived, every good gift save a fortune,—a fine, proud, handsome girl, the daughter of an old friend,—an old lover, I fancy, of her own. Clement, however, as it appeared, had either chosen otherwise or was as yet unprepared to choose. The young lady discharged upon him in vain the battery of her attractions; in vain his mother urged her cause. Clement remained cold, insensible, inflexible. Mrs. Searle possessed a native force of which in its feminine branch the family seems to have lost the trick. A proud, passionate, imperious woman, she had had great cares and a number of law-suits; they had given her a great will. She suspected that her son's affections were lodged elsewhere, and lodged amiss. Irritated by his stubborn defiance of her wishes, she persisted in her urgency. The more she watched him the more she believed that he loved in secret. If he loved in secret, of course he loved beneath him. He went about sombre, sullen, and preoccupied. At last, with the fatal indiscretion of an angry woman, she threatened to bring the young lady of her choice—who, by the way, seems to have been no shrinking blossom—to stay in the house. A stormy scene was the result. He threatened that if she did so, he would leave the country and sail for America. She probably disbelieved him; she knew him to be weak, but she overrated his weakness. At all events, the fair rejected arrived and Clement departed. On a dark December day he took ship at Southampton. The two women, desperate with rage and sorrow, sat alone in this great house, mingling their tears and imprecations. A fortnight later, on Christmas eve, in the midst of a great snow-storm, long famous in the country, there came to them a mighty quickening of their bitterness. A young woman, soaked and chilled by the storm, gained entrance to the house and made her way into the presence of the mistress and her guest. She poured out her tale. She was a poor curate's daughter of Hereford. Clement Searle had loved her; loved her all too well. She had been turned out in wrath from her father's house; his mother, at least, might pity her; if not for herself, then for the child she was soon to bring forth. The poor girl had been a second time too trustful. The women, in scorn, in horror, with blows, possibly, turned her forth again into the storm. In the storm she wandered, and in the deep snow she died. Her lover, as you know, perished in that hard winter weather at sea; the news came to his mother late, but soon enough. We are haunted by the curate's daughter!"

There was a pause of some moments. "Ah, well we may be!" said Miss Searle, with a great pity.

Searle blazed up into enthusiasm. "Of course you know,"— and suddenly he began to blush violently,—"I should be sorry to claim any identity with my faithless namesake, poor fellow. But I shall be hugely tickled if this poor ghost should be deceived by my resemblance and mistake me for her cruel lover. She's welcome to the comfort of it. What one can do in the case I shall be glad to do. But can a ghost haunt a ghost? I *am* a ghost!"

Mr. Searle stared a moment, and then smiling superbly: "I could almost believe you are!" he said.

"O brother—cousin!" cried Miss Searle, with the gentlest, yet most appealing dignity, "how can you talk so horribly?"

This horrible talk, however, evidently possessed a potent magic for my friend; and his imagination, chilled for a while by the frigid contact of his kinsman, began to glow again with its earlier fire. From this moment he ceased to steer his cockle-shell, to care what he said or how he said it, so long as he expressed his passionate satisfaction in the scene about him. As he talked I ceased even mentally to protest. I have wondered since that I should not have resented the exhibition of so rank and florid an egotism. But a great frankness for the time makes its own law, and a great passion its own channel. There was, moreover, an immense sweetness in the manner of my friend's speech. Free alike from either adulation or envy, the very soul of it was a divine apprehension, an imaginative mastery, free as the flight of Ariel, of the poetry of his companions' situation and of the contrasted prosiness of their attitude.

"How does the look of age come?" he demanded, at dessert. "Does it come of itself, unobserved, unrecorded, unmeasured? Or do you woo it and set baits and traps for it, and watch it like the dawning brownness of a meerschaum pipe, and nail it down when it appears, just where it peeps out, and light a votive taper beneath it and give thanks to it daily? Or do you forbid it and fight it and resist it, and yet feel it settling and deepening about you, as irresistible as fate?"

"What the deuce is the man talking about?" said the smile of our host.

"I found a gray hair this morning," said Miss Searle.

"Good heavens! I hope you respected it," cried Searle.

"I looked at it for a long time in my little glass," said his cousin, simply.

"Miss Searle, for many years to come, can afford to be amused at gray hairs," I said.

"Ten years hence I shall be forty-three," she answered.

"That's my age," said Searle. "If I had only come here ten years ago! I should have had more time to enjoy the feast, but I should have had less of an appetite. I needed to get famished for it."

"Why did you wait for the starving point?" asked Mr. Searle. "To think of these ten years that we might have been enjoying you!" And at the thought of these wasted ten years Mr. Searle broke into a violent nervous laugh.

"I always had a notion,—a stupid, vulgar notion, if there ever was one,—that to come abroad properly one ought to have a pot of money. My pot was too nearly empty. At last I came with my empty pot!"

Mr. Searle coughed with an air of hesitation. "You're a— you're in limited circumstances?"

My friend apparently was vastly tickled to have his bleak situation called by so soft a name. "Limited circumstances!" he cried with a long, light laugh; "I'm in no circumstances at all!"

"Upon my word!" murmured Mr. Searle, with an air of being divided between his sense of the indecency and his sense of the rarity of a gentleman taking just that tone about his affairs. "Well—well—well!" he added, in a voice which might have meant everything or nothing; and proceeded, with a twinkle in his eye, to finish a glass of wine. His sparkling eye, as he drank, encountered mine over the top of his glass, and, for a moment, we exchanged a long deep glance,—a glance so keen as to leave a slight embarrassment on the face of each. "And you," said Mr. Searle, by way of carrying it off, "how about your circumstances?"

"O, his," said my friend, "his are unlimited! He could buy up Lockley Park!" He had drunk, I think, a rather greater number of glasses of port—I admit that the port was infinitely drinkable—than was to have been desired in the interest of perfect self-control. He was rapidly drifting beyond any tacit dissuasion of mine. A certain feverish harshness in his glance and voice warned me that to attempt to direct him would simply irritate him. As we rose from the table he caught my troubled look. Passing his arm for a moment into mine, "This is the great night!" he whispered. "The night of fatality, the night of destiny!"

Mr. Searle had caused the whole lower region of the house to be thrown open and a multitude of lights to be placed in convenient and effective positions. Such a marshalled wealth of ancient candlesticks and flambeaux I had never beheld. Niched against the dark panellings, casting great luminous circles upon the pendent stiffness of sombre tapestries, enhancing and completing with admirable effect the vastness and mystery of the ancient house, they seemed to people the great rooms, as our little group passed slowly from one to another, with a dim, expectant presence. We had a delightful hour of it. Mr. Searle at once assumed the part of cicerone, and—I had not hitherto done him justice—Mr. Searle became agreeable. While I lingered behind with Miss Searle, he walked in advance with his kinsman. It was as if he had said, "Well, if you want the old place, you shall have it—metaphysically!" To speak vulgarly, he rubbed it in. Carrying a great silver candlestick in his left hand, he raised it and lowered it and cast the light hither and thither, upon pictures and hangings and bits of carving and a hundred lurking architectural treasures. Mr. Searle knew his house. He hinted at innumerable traditions and memories, and evoked with a very pretty wit the figures of its earlier occupants. He told a dozen anecdotes with an almost reverential gravity and neatness. His companion attended, with a sort of brooding intelligence. Miss Searle and I, meanwhile, were not wholly silent.

"I suppose that by this time," I said, "you and your cousin are almost old friends."

She trifled a moment with her fan, and then raising her homely candid gaze: "Old friends, and at the same time strangely new! My cousin,—my cousin,"—and her voice lingered on the word,—"it seems so strange to call him my cousin, after thinking these many years that I had no cousin! He's a most singular man."

"It's not so much he as his circumstances that are singular," I ventured to say.

"I'm so sorry for his circumstances. I wish I could help him in some way. He interests me so much." And here Miss Searle gave a rich, mellow sigh. "I wish I had known him a long time ago. He told me that he is but the shadow of what he was."

I wondered whether Searle had been consciously playing upon the fancy of this gentle creature. If he had, I believed he had gained his point. But in fact, his position had become to my sense so charged with opposing forces, that I hardly ventured wholly to rejoice. "His better self just now," I said, "seems again to be taking shape. It will have been a good deed on your part, Miss Searle, if you help to restore him to soundness and serenity."

"Ah, what can I do?"

"Be a friend to him. Let him like you, let him love you! You see in him now, doubtless, much to pity and to wonder at. But let him simply enjoy awhile the grateful sense of your nearness and dearness. He will be a better and stronger man for it, and then you can love him, you can respect him without restriction."

Miss Searle listened with a puzzled tenderness of gaze. "It's a hard part for poor me to play!"

Her almost infantine gentleness left me no choice but to be absolutely frank. "Did you ever play any part at all?" I asked.

Her eyes met mine, wonderingly; she blushed, as with a sudden sense of my meaning. "Never! I think I have hardly lived."

"You've begun now, perhaps. You have begun to care for something outside the narrow circle of habit and duty. (Excuse me if I am rather too outspoken: you know I'm a foreigner.) It's a great moment: I wish you joy!"

"I could almost fancy you are laughing at me. I feel more trouble than joy."

"Why do you feel trouble?"

She paused, with her eyes fixed on our two companions. "My cousin's arrival," she said at last, "is a great disturbance."

"You mean that you did wrong in recognizing him? In that case the fault is mine. He had no intention of giving you the opportunity."

"I did wrong, after a fashion! But I can't find it in my heart to regret it. I never shall regret it! I did what I thought proper. Heaven forgive me!"

"Heaven bless you, Miss Searle! Is any harm to come of it? I did the evil; let me bear the brunt!"

She shook her head gravely. "You don't know my brother!"

"The sooner I do know him, then, the better!" And hereupon I felt a dull irritation which had been gathering force for more than hour explode into sudden wrath. "What on earth *is* your brother?" I demanded. She turned away. "Are you afraid of him?" I asked.

She gave me a tearful sidelong glance. "He's looking at me!" she murmured.

I looked at him. He was standing with his back to us, holding a large Venetian hand-mirror, framed in rococo silver, which he had taken from a shelf of antiquities, in just such a position that he caught the reflection of his sister's person. Shall I confess it? Something in this performance so tickled my sense of the picturesque, that it was with a sort of blunted anger that I muttered, "The sneak!" Yet I felt passion enough to urge me forward. It seemed to me that by implication I, too, was being covertly watched. I should not be watched for nothing! "Miss Searle," I said, insisting upon her attention, "promise me something."

She turned upon me with a start and the glance of one appealing from some great pain. "O, don't ask me!" she cried. It was as if she were standing on the verge of some sudden lapse of familiar ground and had been summoned to make a leap. I felt that retreat was impossible, and that it was the greater kindness to beckon her forward.

"Promise me," I repeated.

Still with her eyes she protested. "O, dreadful day!" she cried, at last.

"Promise me to let him speak to you, if he should ask you, any wish you may suspect on your brother's part notwithstanding."

She colored deeply. "You mean," she said,—"you mean that he—has something particular to say."

"Something most particular!"

"Poor cousin!"

I gave her a deeply questioning look. "Well, poor cousin! But promise me."

"I promise," she said, and moved away across the long room and out of the door.

"You're in time to hear the most delightful story!" said my friend, as I rejoined the two gentlemen. They were standing before an old sombre portrait of a lady in the dress of Queen Anne's time, with her ill-painted flesh-tints showing livid in the candlelight against her dark drapery and background. "This is Mistress Margaret Searle,—a sort of Beatrix Esmond, —who did as she pleased. She married a paltry Frenchman, a penniless fiddler, in the teeth of her whole family. Fair Margaret, my compliments! Upon my soul, she looks like Miss Searle! Pray go on. What came of it all?"

Mr. Searle looked at his kinsman for a moment with an air of distaste for his boisterous homage, and of pity for his crude imagination. Then resuming, with a very effective dryness of tone: "I found a year ago, in a box of very old papers, a letter from Mistress Margaret to Cynthia Searle, her elder sister. It was dated from Paris and dreadfully ill-spelled. It contained a most passionate appeal for—a—for pecuniary assistance. She had just been confined, she was starving, and neglected by her husband; she cursed the day she left England. It was a most dismal effusion. I never heard that she found means to return."

"So much for marrying a Frenchman!" I said, sententiously.

Mr. Searle was silent for some moments. "This was the first," he said, finally, "and the last of the family who has been so d—d un-English!"

"Does Miss Searle know her history?" asked my friend, staring at the rounded whiteness of the lady's heavy cheek.

"Miss Searle knows nothing!" said our host, with zeal.

This utterance seemed to kindle in my friend a generous opposing zeal. "She shall know at least the tale of Mistress

Margaret," he cried, and walked rapidly away in search of her.

Mr. Searle and I pursued our march through the lighted rooms. "You've found a cousin," I said, "with a vengeance."

"Ah, a vengeance?" said my host, stiffly.

"I mean that he takes as keen an interest in your annals and possessions as yourself."

"O, exactly so!" and Mr. Searle burst into resounding laughter. "He tells me," he resumed, in a moment, "that he is an invalid. I should never have fancied it."

"Within the past few hours," I said, "he's a changed man. Your place and your kindness have refreshed him immensely."

Mr. Searle uttered the little shapeless ejaculation with which many an Englishman is apt to announce the concussion of any especial courtesy of speech. He bent his eyes on the floor frowningly, and then, to my surprise, he suddenly stopped and looked at me with a penetrating eye. "I'm an honest man!" he said. I was quite prepared to assent; but he went on, with a sort of fury of frankness, as if it was the first time in his life that he had been prompted to expound himself, as if the process was mightily unpleasant to him and he was hurrying through it as a task. "An honest man, mind you! I know nothing about Mr. Clement Searle! I never expected to see him. He has been to me a—a—" And here Mr. Searle paused to select a word which should vividly enough express what, for good or for ill, his kinsman had been to him. "He has been to me an *amazement*! I have no doubt he is a most amiable man! You'll not deny, however, that he's a very odd style of person. I'm sorry he's ill! I'm sorry he's poor! He's my fiftieth cousin! Well and good! I'm an honest man. He shall not have it to say that he was not received at my house."

"He, too, thank heaven! is an honest man!" I said, smiling.

"Why the deuce, then," cried Mr. Searle, turning almost fiercely upon me, "has he established this underhand claim to my property?"

This startling utterance flashed backward a gleam of light upon the demeanor of our host and the suppressed agitation of his sister. In an instant the jealous soul of the unhappy gentleman revealed itself. For a moment I was so amazed and scandalized at the directness of his attack that I lacked words to respond. As soon as he had spoken, Mr. Searle appeared to feel that he had struck too hard a blow. "Excuse me, sir," he hurried on, "if I speak of this matter with heat. But I have seldom suffered so grievous a shock as on learning, as I learned this morning from my solicitor, the monstrous proceedings of Mr. Clement Searle. Great heaven, sir, for what does the man take me? He pretends to the Lord knows what fantastic passion for my place. Let him respect it, then. Let him, with his tawdry parade of imagination, imagine a tithe of what I feel. I love my estate; it's my passion, my life, myself! Am I to make a great hole in it for a beggarly foreigner, a man without means, without proof, a stranger, an adventurer, a Bohemian? I thought America boasted that she had land for all men! Upon my soul, sir, I have never been so shocked in my life."

I paused for some moments before speaking, to allow his passion fully to expend itself and to flicker up again if it chose; for on my own part it seemed well that I should answer him once for all. "Your really absurd apprehensions, Mr. Searle," I said at last,—"your terrors, I may call them,—have fairly overmastered your common-sense. You are attacking a man of straw, a creature of base illusion; though I'm sadly afraid you have wounded a man of spirit and of conscience. Either my friend has no valid claim on your estate, in which case your agitation is superfluous; or he *has* a valid claim—"

Mr. Searle seized my arm and glared at me, as I may say; his pale face paler still with the horror of my suggestion, his great keen eyes flashing, and his flamboyant hair erect and quivering.

"A valid claim!" he whispered. "Let him try it!"

We had emerged into the great hall of the mansion and stood facing the main doorway. The door stood open into the porch, through whose stone archway I saw the garden glittering in the blue light of a full moon. As Mr. Searle uttered the words I have just repeated, I beheld my companion come slowly up into the porch from without, bareheaded, bright in the outer moonlight, dark then in the shadow of the archway, and bright again in the lamplight on the threshold of the hall. As he crossed the threshold the butler made his appearance at the head of the staircase on our left, faltered visibly a moment on seeing Mr. Searle; but then, perceiving my friend, he gravely descended. He bore in his hand a small plated salver. On the salver, gleaming in the light of the suspended lamp, lay a folded note. Clement Searle came forward, staring a little and startled, I think, by some fine sense of a near explosion. The butler applied the match. He advanced toward my friend, extending salver and note. Mr. Searle made a movement as if to spring forward, but controlled himself. "Tottenham!" he shouted, in a strident voice.

"Yes, sir!" said Tottenham, halting.

"Stand where you are. For whom is that note?"

"For Mr. Clement Searle," said the butler, staring straight before him as if to discredit a suspicion of his having read the direction.

"Who gave it to you?"

"Mrs. Horridge, sir." (The housekeeper.)

"Who gave it Mrs. Horridge?"

There was on Tottenham's part just an infinitesimal pause before replying.

"My dear sir," broke in Searle, completely sobered by the sense of violated courtesy, "isn't that rather my business?"

"What happens in my house is my business; and mighty strange things seem to be happening." Mr. Searle had become exasperated to that point that, a rare thing for an Englishman, he compromised himself before a servant.

"Bring me the note!" he cried. The butler obeyed.

"Really, this is too much!" cried my companion, affronted and helpless.

I was disgusted. Before Mr. Searle had time to take the note, I possessed myself of it. "If you have no regard for your sister," I said, "let a stranger, at least, act for her." And I tore the disputed thing into a dozen pieces.

"In the name of decency," cried Searle, "what does this horrid business mean?"

Mr. Searle was about to break out upon him; but at this moment his sister appeared on the staircase, summoned evidently by our high-pitched and angry voices. She had exchanged her dinner-dress for a dark dressing-gown, removed her ornaments, and begun to disarrange her hair, a heavy tress of which escaped from the comb. She hurried downward, with a pale, questioning face. Feeling distinctly that, for ourselves, immediate departure was in the air, and divining Mr. Tottenham to be a butler of remarkable intuitions and extreme celerity, I seized the opportunity to request him, *sotto voce*, to send a carriage to the door without delay. "And put up our things," I added.

Our host rushed at his sister and seized the white wrist which escaped from the loose sleeve of her dress. "What was in that note?" he demanded.

Miss Searle looked first at its scattered fragments and then at her cousin. "Did you read it?" she asked.

"No, but I thank you for it!" said Searle.

Her eyes for an instant communed brightly with his own; then she transferred them to her brother's face, where the light went out of them and left a dull, sad patience. An inexorable patience he seemed to find it: he flushed crimson with rage and the sense of his unhandsomeness, and flung her away. "You're a child!" he cried. "Go to bed."

In poor Searle's face as well the gathered serenity was twisted into a sickened frown, and the reflected brightness of his happy day turned to blank confusion. "Have I been dealing these three hours with a madman?" he asked plaintively.

"A madman, yes, if you will! A man mad with the love of his home and the sense of its stability. I have held my tongue till now, but you have been too much for me. Who are you, what are you? From what paradise of fools do you come, that you fancy I shall cut off a piece of my land, my home, my heart, to toss to you? Forsooth, I shall share my land with you? Prove your infernal claim! There isn't *that* in it!" And he kicked one of the bits of paper on the floor.

Searle received this broadside gaping. Then turning away, he went and seated himself on a bench against the wall and rubbed his forehead amazedly. I looked at my watch, and listened for the wheels of our carriage.

Mr. Searle went on. "Wasn't it enough that you should have practised against my property? Need you have come into my very house to practise against my sister?"

Searle put his two hands to his face. "Oh, oh, oh!" he softly roared.

Miss Searle crossed rapidly and dropped on her knees at his side.

"Go to bed, you fool!" shrieked her brother.

"Dear cousin," said Miss Searle, "it's cruel that you are to have to think of us so!"

"O, I shall think of you!" he said. And he laid a hand on her head.

"I believe you have done nothing wrong!" she murmured.

"I've done what I could," her brother pursued. "But it's arrant folly to pretend to friendship when this abomination lies between us. You were welcome to my meat and my wine, but I wonder you could swallow them. The sight spoiled my appetite!" cried the furious little man, with a laugh. "Proceed with your case! My people in London are instructed and prepared."

"I have a fancy," I said to Searle, "that your case has vastly improved since you gave it up."

"Oho! you don't feign ignorance, then?" and he shook his flaming *chevelure* at me. "It is very kind of you to give it up!" And he laughed resoundingly. "Perhaps you will also give up my sister!"

Searle sat in his chair in a species of collapse, staring at his adversary. "O miserable man!" he moaned at last. "I fancied we had become such friends!"

"Boh! you imbecile!" cried our host.

Searle seemed not to hear him. "Am I seriously expected," he pursued, slowly and painfully,—"am I seriously expected—to—to sit here and defend myself—to prove I have done nothing wrong? Think what you please." And he rose, with an effort, to his feet. "I know what *you* think!" he added, to Miss Searle.

The carriage wheels resounded on the gravel, and at the same moment the footman descended with our two portmanteaus. Mr. Tottenham followed him with our hats and coats.

"Good God!" cried Mr. Searle; "you are not going away!" This ejaculation, under the circumstances, had a grand comicality which prompted me to violent laughter. "Bless my soul!" he added; "of course you are going."

"It's perhaps well," said Miss Searle, with a great effort, inexpressibly touching in one for whom great efforts were visibly new and strange, "that I should tell you what my poor little note contained."

"That matter of your note, madam," said her brother, "you and I will settle together!"

"Let me imagine its contents," said Searle.

"Ah! they have been too much imagined!" she answered simply. "It was only a word of warning. I knew something painful was coming."

Searle took his hat. "The pains and the pleasures of this day," he said to his kinsman, "I shall equally never forget. Knowing you," and he offered his hand to Miss Searle, "has been the pleasure of pleasures. I hoped something more was to come of it."

"A deal too much has come of it!" cried our host, irrepressibly.

Searle looked at him mildly, almost benignantly, from head to foot; and then closing his eyes with an air of sudden physical distress: "I'm afraid so! I can't stand more of this." I gave him my arm, and crossed the threshold. As we passed out I heard Miss Searle burst into a torrent of sobs.

"We shall hear from each other yet, I take it!" cried her brother, harassing our retreat.

Searle stopped and turned round on him sharply, almost fiercely. "O ridiculous man!" he cried.

"Do you mean to say you shall not prosecute?" screamed the other. "I shall force you to prosecute! I shall drag you into court, and you shall be beaten—beaten—beaten!" And this soft vocable continued to ring in our ears as we drove away.

We drove, of course, to the little wayside inn whence we had departed in the morning so unencumbered, in all broad England, with either enemies or friends. My companion, as the carriage rolled along, seemed utterly overwhelmed and exhausted. "What a dream!" he murmured stupidly. "What an awakening! What a long, long day! What a hideous scene! Poor me! Poor woman!" When we had resumed possession of our two little neighboring rooms, I asked him if Miss Searle's note had been the result of anything that had passed between them on his going to rejoin her. "I found her on the terrace," he said, "walking a restless walk in the moonlight. I was greatly excited; I hardly know what I said. I asked her, I think, if she knew the story of Margaret Searle. She seemed frightened and troubled, and she used just the words her brother had used, 'I know nothing.' For the moment, somehow, I felt as a man drunk. I stood before her and told her, with great emphasis, how sweet Margaret Searle had married a beggarly foreigner, in obedience to her heart and in defiance of her family. As I talked the sheeted moonlight seemed to close about us, and we stood in a dream, in a solitude, in a romance. She grew younger, fairer, more gracious. I trembled with a divine loquacity. Before I knew it I had gone far. I was taking her hand and calling her 'Margaret!' She had said that it was impossible; that she could do nothing; that she was a fool, a child, a slave. Then, with a sudden huge conviction, I spoke of my claim against the estate. 'It exists, then?' she said. 'It exists,' I answered, 'but I have foregone it. Be generous! Pay it from your heart!' For an instant her face was radiant. 'If I marry you,' she cried, 'it will repair the trouble.' 'In our marriage,' I affirmed, 'the trouble will melt away like a raindrop in the ocean.' 'Our marriage!' she repeated, wonderingly; and the deep, deep ring of her voice seemed to shatter the crystal walls of our illusion. 'I must think, I must think!' she said; and she hurried away with her face in her hands. I walked up and down the terrace for some moments, and then came in and met you. This is the only witchcraft I have used!"

The poor fellow was at once so excited and so exhausted by the day's events, that I fancied he would get little sleep. Conscious, on my own part, of a stubborn wakefulness, I but partly undressed, set my fire a blazing, and sat down to do some writing. I heard the great clock in the little parlor below strike twelve, one, half past one. Just as the vibration of this last stroke was dying on the air the door of communication into Searle's room was flung open, and my companion stood on the threshold, pale as a corpse, in his nightshirt, standing like a phantom against the darkness behind him. "Look at me!" he said, in a low voice, "touch me, embrace me, revere me! You see a man who has seen a ghost!"

"Great heaven, what do you mean?"

"Write it down!" he went on. "There, take your pen. Put it

into dreadful words. Make it of all ghost-stories the ghost-liest, the truest! How do I look? Am I human? Am I pale? Am I red? Am I speaking English? A ghost, sir! Do you understand?"

I confess, there came upon me, by contact, a great supernatural shock. I shall always feel that I, too, have seen a ghost. My first movement—I can't smile at it even now—was to spring to the door, close it with a great blow, and then turn the key upon the gaping blackness from which Searle had emerged. I seized his two hands; they were wet with perspiration. I pushed my chair to the fire and forced him to sit down in it. I kneeled down before him and held his hands as firmly as possible. They trembled and quivered; his eyes were fixed, save that the pupil dilated and contracted with extraordinary force. I asked no questions, but waited with my heart in my throat. At last he spoke. "I'm not frightened, but I'm—O, EXCITED! This is life! This is living! My nerves—my heart—my brain! They are throbbing with the wildness of a myriad lives! Do you feel it? Do you tingle? Are you hot? Are you cold? Hold me tight—tight—tight! I shall tremble away into waves—waves—waves, and know the universe and approach my Maker!" He paused a moment and then went on: "A woman—as clear as that candle.—No, far clearer! In a blue dress, with a black mantle on her head, and a little black muff. Young, dreadfully pretty, pale and ill, with the sadness of all the women who ever loved and suffered pleading and accusing in her dead dark eyes. God knows I never did any such thing! But she took me for my elder, for the other Clement. She came to me here as she would have come to me there. She wrung her hands and spoke to me. 'Marry me!' she moaned; 'marry me and right me!' I sat up in bed just as I sit here, looked at her, heard her,—heard her voice melt away, watched her figure fade away. Heaven and earth! Here I am!"

I made no attempt either to explain my friend's vision or to discredit it. It is enough that I felt for the hour the irresistible contagion of his own agitation. On the whole, I think my own vision was the more interesting of the two. He beheld but the transient, irresponsible spectre: I beheld the human subject, hot from the spectral presence. Nevertheless, I soon recovered my wits sufficiently to feel the necessity of guarding my friend's health against the evil results of excitement and exposure. It was tacitly established that, for the night, he was not to return to his room; and I soon made him fairly comfortable in his place by the fire. Wishing especially to obviate a chill, I removed my bedding and wrapped him about with multitudinous blankets and counterpanes. I had no nerves either for writing or sleep; so I put out my lights, renewed the fire, and sat down on the opposite side of the hearth. I found a kind of solemn entertainment in watching my friend. Silent, swathed and muffled to his chin, he sat rigid and erect with the dignity of his great adventure. For the most part his eyes were closed; though from time to time he would open them with a vast steady expansion and gaze unblinking into the firelight, as if he again beheld, without terror, the image of that blighted maid. With his cadaverous, emaciated face, his tragic wrinkles, intensified by the upward glow from the hearth, his drooping black mustache, his transcendent gravity, and a certain high fantastical air in the flickering alternations of his brow, he looked like the vision-haunted knight of La Mancha, nursed by the Duke and Duchess. The night passed wholly without speech. Towards its close I slept for half an hour. When I awoke the awakened birds had begun to twitter. Searle sat unperturbed, staring at me. We exchanged a long look; I felt with a pang that his glittering eyes had tasted their last of natural sleep. "How is it? are you comfortable?" I asked.

He gazed for some time without replying. Then he spoke with a strange, innocent grandiloquence, and with pauses between his words, as if an inner voice were slowly prompting him. "You asked me, when you first knew me, what I was. 'Nothing,' I said,—'nothing.' Nothing I have always deemed myself. But I have wronged myself. I'm a personage! I'm rare among men! I'm a haunted man!"

Sleep had passed out of his eyes: I felt with a deeper pang that perfect sanity had passed out of his voice. From this moment I prepared myself for the worst. There was in my friend, however, such an essential gentleness and conservative patience, that to persons surrounding him the worst was likely to come without hurry or violence. He had so confirmed a habit of good manners that, at the core of reason, the process of disorder might have been long at work without finding an issue. As morning began fully to dawn upon us, I brought our grotesque vigil to an end. Searle appeared so weak that I gave him my hands to help him to rise from his chair; he retained them for some moments after rising to his feet, from an apparent inability to keep his balance. "Well," he said, "I've seen one ghost, but I doubt of my living to see another. I shall soon be myself as brave a ghost as the best of them. I shall haunt Mr. Searle! It can only mean one thing,—my near, dear death."

On my proposing breakfast, "This shall be my breakfast!" he said; and he drew from his travelling-sack a phial of morphine. He took a strong dose and went to bed. At noon I found him on foot again, dressed, shaved, and apparently refreshed. "Poor fellow!" he said, "you have got more than you bargained for,—a ghost-encumbered comrade. But it won't be for long." It immediately became a question, of course, whither we should now direct our steps.

"As I have so little time," said Searle, "I should like to see the best, the best alone." I answered that, either for time or eternity, I had imagined Oxford to be the best thing in England; and for Oxford in the course of an hour we accordingly departed.

Of Oxford I feel small vocation to speak in detail. It must long remain for an American one of the supreme gratifications of travel. The impression it produces, the emotions it stirs, in an American mind, are too large and various to be compassed by words. It seems to embody with undreamed completeness a kind of dim and sacred ideal of the Western intellect,—a scholastic city, an appointed home of contemplation. No other spot in Europe, I imagine, extorts from our barbarous hearts so passionate an admiration. A finer pen than mine must enumerate the splendid devices by which it performs this great office; I can bear testimony only to the dominant tone of its effect. Passing through the various streets in which the obverse longitude of the hoary college walls seems to maintain an antique stillness, you feel this to be the most dignified of towns. Over all, through all, the great corporate fact of the University prevails and penetrates, like some steady bass in a symphony of lighter chords, like the mediæval and mystical presence of the Empire in the linked dispersion of lesser states. The plain Gothic of the long street-fronts of the colleges—blessed seraglios of culture and leisure—irritate the fancy like the blank harem-walls of Eastern towns. Within their arching portals, however, you perceive more sacred and sunless courts, and the dark verdure grateful and restful to bookish eyes. The gray-green quadrangles stand forever open with a noble and trustful hospitality. The seat of the humanities is stronger in the admonitory shadow of her great name than in a marshalled host of wardens and beadles. Directly after our arrival my friend and I strolled eagerly forth in the luminous early dusk. We reached the bridge which passes beneath the walls of Magdalen and saw the eight-spired tower, embossed with its slender shaftings, rise in temperate beauty,—the perfect prose of Gothic,—wooing the eyes to the sky, as it was slowly drained of day. We entered the little monkish doorway and stood in that dim, fantastic outer court, made narrow by the dominant presence of the great tower, in which the heart beats faster, and the swallows niche more lovingly in the tangled ivy, I fancied, than elsewhere in Oxford. We passed thence into the great cloister, and studied the little sculptured monsters along the entablature of the arcade. I was pleased to see that Searle became extremely interested; but I very soon began to fear that the influence of the place would prove too potent for his unbalanced imagination. I may say that from this time forward, with my unhappy friend, I found it hard to distinguish between the play of fancy and the labor of thought, and to fix the balance between perception and illusion. He had already taken a fancy to confound his identity with that of the earlier Clement Searle; he now began to speak almost wholly as from the imagined consciousness of his old-time kinsman.

"This was my college, you know," he said, "the noblest in all Oxford. How often I have paced this gentle cloister, side by side with a friend of the hour! My friends are all dead, but many a young fellow as we meet him, dark or fair, tall or short, reminds me of them. Even Oxford, they say, feels about its massive base the murmurs of the tide of time; there are things eliminated, things insinuated! Mine was ancient Oxford,—the fine old haunt of rank abuses, of precedent and privilege. What cared I, who was a perfect gentleman, with my pockets full of money? I had an allowance of two thousand a year."

It became evident to me, on the following day, that his strength had begun to ebb, and that he was unequal to the labor of regular sight-seeing. He read my apprehension in my eyes, and took pains to assure me that I was right. "I am going down hill. Thank heaven it's an easy slope, coated with English turf and with an English churchyard at the foot." The almost hysterical emotion produced by our adventure at Lockley Park had given place to a broad, calm satisfaction, in which the scene around us was reflected as in the depths of a lucid lake. We took an afternoon walk through Christ-Church Meadow, and at the river-bank procured a boat, which I pulled up the stream to Iffley and to the slanting woods of Nuneham,—the sweetest, flattest, reediest stream-side landscape that the heart need demand. Here, of course, we encountered in hundreds the mighty lads of England, clad in white flannel and blue, immense, fair-haired, magnificent in their youth, lounging down the current in their idle punts, in friendly couples or in solitude possibly portentous of scholastic honors; or pulling in straining crews and hoarsely exhorted from the near bank. When, in conjunction with all this magnificent sport, you think of the verdant quietude and the silvery sanctities of the college gardens, you cannot but consider that the youth of England have their porridge well salted. As my companion found himself less and less able to walk, we repaired on three successive days to these scholastic domains, and spent long hours sitting in their greenest places. They seemed to us the fairest things in England and the ripest and sweetest fruits of the English system. Locked in their antique verdure, guarded (as in the case of New College) by gentle battlements of silver-gray, outshouldering the matted leafage of centenary vines, filled with perfumes and privacy and memories, with students lounging bookishly on the turf (as if tenderly to spare it the pressure of their boot-heels), and with the great conservative presence of the college front appealing gravely from the restless outer world, they seem places to lie down on the grass in forever, in the happy faith that life is all a vast old English garden, and time an endless English afternoon. This charmed seclusion was especially grateful to my friend, and his sense of it reached its climax, I remember, on the last afternoon of our three, as we sat dreaming in the spacious garden of St. John's. The long college façade here, perhaps, broods over the lawn with a more effective air of property than elsewhere. Searle fell into unceasing talk and exhaled his swarming impressions with a tender felicity, compounded of the oddest mixture of wisdom and folly. Every student who passed us was the subject of an extemporized romance, and every feature of the place the theme of a lyric rhapsody.

"Isn't it all," he demanded, "a delightful lie? Mightn't one fancy this the very central point of the world's heart, where all the echoes of the world's life arrive only to falter and die? Listen! The air is thick with arrested voices. It is well there should be such places, shaped in the interest of factitious needs; framed to minister to the book-begotten longing for a medium in which one may dream unwaked, and believe unconfuted; to foster the sweet illusion that all is well in this weary world, all perfect and rounded, mellow and complete in this sphere of the pitiful unachieved and the dreadful uncommenced. The world's made! Work's over! Now for leisure! England's safe! Now for Theocritus and Horace, for lawn and sky! What a sense it all gives one of the composite life of England, and how essential a factor of the educated, British consciousness one omits in not thinking of Oxford! Thank heaven they had the wit to send me here in the other time. I'm not much with it, perhaps; but what should I have been without it? The misty spires and towers of Oxford seen far off on the level have been all these years one of the constant things of memory. Seriously, what does Oxford do for these people? Are they wiser, gentler, richer, deeper? At moments when its massive influence surges into my mind like a tidal wave, I take it as a sort of affront to my dignity. My soul reverts to the naked background of our own education, the dead white wall before which we played our parts. I assent to it all with a sort of desperate calmness; I bow to it with a dogged pride. We are nursed at the opposite pole. Naked come we into a naked world. There is a certain grandeur in the absence of a *mise en scène*, a certain heroic strain in those

young imaginations of the West, which find nothing made to
their hands, which have to concoct their own mysteries, and
raise high into our morning air, with a ringing hammer and
nails, the castles in which they dwell. *Noblesse oblige*: Oxford
obliges. What a horrible thing not to respond to such obligations. If you pay the pious debt to the last farthing of interest, you may go through life with her blessing; but if you let
it stand unhonored, you are a worse barbarian than we! But
for better or worse, in a myriad private hearts, think how she
must be loved! How the youthful sentiment of mankind
seems visibly to brood upon her! Think of the young lives
now taking color in her corridors and cloisters. Think of the
centuries' tale of dead lads,—dead alike with the close of the
young days to which these haunts were a present world and
the ending of the larger lives which a sterner mother-scene
has gathered into her massive history! What are those two
young fellows kicking their heels over on the grass there? One
of them has the Saturday Review; the other—upon my soul—
the other has Artemus Ward! Where do they live, how do
they live, to what end do they live? Miserable boys! How can
they read Artemus Ward under those windows of Elizabeth?
What do you think loveliest in all Oxford? The poetry of certain windows. Do you see that one yonder, the second of
those lesser bays, with the broken mullion and open casement? That used to be the window of my *fidus Achates*, a
hundred years ago. Remind me to tell you the story of that
broken mullion. Don't tell me it's not a common thing to
have one's *fidus Achates* at another college. Pray, was I
pledged to common things? He was a charming fellow. By the
way, he was a good deal like you. Of course his cocked hat,
his long hair in a black ribbon, his cinnamon velvet suit, and
his flowered waistcoat made a difference! We gentlemen used
to wear swords."

There was something surprising and impressive in my
friend's gushing magniloquence. The poor disheartened loafer
had turned rhapsodist and seer. I was particularly struck with
his having laid aside the diffidence and shy self-consciousness
which had marked him during the first days of our acquaintance. He was becoming more and more a disembodied observer and critic; the shell of sense, growing daily thinner and

more transparent, transmitted the tremor of his quickened spirit. He revealed an unexpected faculty for becoming acquainted with the lounging gownsmen whom we met in our vague peregrinations. If I left him for ten minutes, I was sure to find him, on my return, in earnest conversation with some affable wandering scholar. Several young men with whom he had thus established relations invited him to their rooms and entertained him, as I gathered, with boisterous hospitality. For myself, I chose not to be present on these occasions; I shrunk partly from being held in any degree responsible for his vagaries, and partly from witnessing that painful aggravation of them which I feared might be induced by champagne and youthful society. He reported these adventures with less eloquence than I had fancied he might use; but, on the whole, I suspect that a certain method in his madness, a certain firmness in his most melting *bonhomie*, had insured him perfect respect. Two things, however, became evident,—that he drank more champagne than was good for him, and that the boyish grossness of his entertainers tended rather, on reflection, to disturb in his mind the pure image of Oxford. At the same time it completed his knowledge of the place. Making the acquaintance of several tutors and fellows, he dined in Hall in half a dozen colleges, and alluded afterwards to these banquets with a sort of religious unction. One evening, at the close of one of these entertainments, he came back to the hotel in a cab, accompanied by a friendly student and a physician, looking deadly pale. He had swooned away on leaving table, and had remained so stubbornly unconscious as to excite great alarm among his companions. The following twenty-four hours, of course, he spent in bed; but on the third day he declared himself strong enough to go out. On reaching the street his strength again forsook him, and I insisted upon his returning to his room. He besought me with tears in his eyes not to shut him up. "It's my last chance," he said. "I want to go back for an hour to that garden of St. John's. Let me look and feel; to-morrow I die." It seemed to me possible that with a Bath-chair the expedition might be accomplished. The hotel, it appeared, possessed such a convenience: it was immediately produced. It became necessary hereupon that we should have a person to propel the chair. As there was no one available on the spot, I prepared to perform the office; but just as Searle had got seated and wrapped (he had come to suffer acutely from cold), an elderly man emerged from a lurking-place near the door, and, with a formal salute, offered to wait upon the gentleman. We assented, and he proceeded solemnly to trundle the chair before him. I recognized him as an individual whom I had seen lounging shyly about the hotel doors, at intervals during our stay, with a depressed air of wanting employment and a hopeless doubt of finding any. He had once, indeed, in a half-hearted way, proposed himself as an amateur cicerone for a tour through the colleges; and I now, as I looked at him, remembered with a pang that I had declined his services with untender curtness. Since then, his shyness, apparently, had grown less or his misery greater; for it was with a strange, grim avidity that he now attached himself to our service. He was a pitiful image of shabby gentility and the dinginess of "reduced circumstances." He imparted an original force to the term "seedy." He was, I suppose, some fifty years of age; but his pale, haggard, unwholesome visage, his plaintive, drooping carriage, and the irremediable decay of his apparel, seemed to add to the burden of his days and experience. His eyes were bloodshot and weak-looking, his handsome nose had turned to purple, and his sandy beard, largely streaked with gray, bristled with a month's desperate indifference to the razor. In all this rusty forlornness there lurked a visible assurance of our friend's having known better days. Obviously, he was the victim of some fatal depreciation in the market value of pure gentility. There had been something terribly pathetic in the way he fiercely merged the attempt to touch the greasy rim of his antiquated hat into a rounded and sweeping bow, as from jaunty equal to equal. Exchanging a few words with him as we went along, I was struck with the refinement of his tone.

"Take me by some long roundabout way," said Searle, "so that I may see as many college walls as possible."

"You can wander without losing your way?" I asked of our attendant.

"I ought to be able to, sir," he said, after a moment, with pregnant gravity. And as we were passing Wadham College, "That's my college, sir," he added.

At these words, Searle commanded him to stop and come and stand in front of him. "You say that is *your* college?" he demanded.

"Wadham might deny me, sir; but Heaven forbid I should deny Wadham. If you'll allow me to take you into the quad, I'll show you my windows, thirty years ago!"

Searle sat staring, with his huge, pale eyes, which now had come to usurp the greatest place in his wasted visage, filled with wonder and pity. "If you'll be so kind," he said, with immense politeness. But just as this degenerate son of Wadham was about to propel him across the threshold of the court, he turned about, disengaged his hands, with his own hand, from the back of the chair, drew him alongside of him and turned to me. "While we are here, my dear fellow," he said, "be so good as to perform this service. You understand?" I smiled sufferance at our companion, and we resumed our way. The latter showed us his window of thirty years ago, where now a rosy youth in a scarlet smoking-fez was puffing a cigarette in the open lattice. Thence we proceeded into the little garden, the smallest, I believe, and certainly the sweetest of all the bosky resorts in Oxford. I pushed the chair along to a bench on the lawn, wheeled it about toward the façade of the college, and sat down on the grass. Our attendant shifted himself mournfully from one foot to the other. Searle eyed him open-mouthed. At length he broke out: "God bless my soul, sir, you don't suppose that I expect you to stand! There's an empty bench."

"Thank you," said our friend, bending his joints to sit.

"You English," said Searle, "are really fabulous! I don't know whether I most admire you or despise you! Now tell me: who are you? what are you? what brought you to this?"

The poor fellow blushed up to his eyes, took off his hat, and wiped his forehead with a ragged handkerchief. "My name is Rawson, sir. Beyond that, it's a long story."

"I ask out of sympathy," said Searle. "I have a fellow-feeling! You're a poor devil; I'm a poor devil too."

"I'm the poorer devil of the two," said the stranger, with a little emphatic nod of the head.

"Possibly. I suppose an English poor devil is the poorest of all poor devils. And then, you have fallen from a height. From

Wadham College as a gentleman commoner (is that what they called you?) to Wadham College as a Bath-chair man! Good heavens, man, the fall's enough to kill you!"

"I didn't take it all at once, sir. I dropped a bit one time and a bit another."

"That's me, that's me!" cried Searle, clapping his hands.

"And now," said our friend, "I believe I can't drop further."

"My dear fellow," and Searle clasped his hand and shook it, "there's a perfect similarity in our lot."

Mr. Rawson lifted his eyebrows. "Save for the difference of sitting in a Bath-chair and walking behind it!"

"O, I'm at my last gasp, Mr. Rawson."

"I'm at my last penny, sir."

"Literally, Mr. Rawson?"

Mr. Rawson shook his head, with a world of vague bitterness. "I have almost come to the point," he said, "of drinking my beer and buttoning my coat figuratively; but I don't talk in figures."

Fearing that the conversation had taken a turn which might seem to cast a rather fantastic light upon Mr. Rawson's troubles, I took the liberty of asking him with great gravity how he made a living.

"I don't make a living," he answered, with tearful eyes, "I can't make a living. I have a wife and three children, starving, sir. You wouldn't believe what I have come to. I sent my wife to her mother's, who can ill afford to keep her, and came to Oxford a week ago, thinking I might pick up a few half-crowns by showing people about the colleges. But it's no use. I haven't the assurance. I don't look decent. They want a nice little old man with black gloves, and a clean shirt, and a silver-headed stick. What do I look as if I knew about Oxford, sir?"

"Dear me," cried Searle, "why didn't you speak to us before?"

"I wanted to; half a dozen times I have been on the point of it. I knew you were Americans."

"And Americans are rich!" cried Searle, laughing. "My dear Mr. Rawson, American as I am, I'm living on charity."

"And I'm not, sir! There it is. I'm dying for the want of charity. You say you're a pauper; it takes an American pauper to go bowling about in a Bath-chair. America's an easy country."

"Ah me!" groaned Searle. "Have I come to Wadham gardens to hear the praise of America?"

"Wadham gardens are very well!" said Mr. Rawson; "but one may sit here hungry and shabby, so long as one isn't too shabby, as well as elsewhere. You'll not persuade me that it's not an easier thing to keep afloat yonder than here. I wish I were there, that's all!" added Mr. Rawson, with a sort of feeble-minded energy. Then brooding for a moment on his wrongs: "Have you a brother? or you, sir? It matters little to you. But it has mattered to me with a vengeance! Shabby as I sit here, I have a brother with his five thousand a year. Being a couple of years my senior, he gorges while I starve. There's England for you! A very pretty place for *him*!"

"Poor England!" said Searle, softly.

"Has your brother never helped you?" I asked.

"A twenty-pound note now and then! I don't say that there have not been times when I have sorely tried his generosity. I have not been what I should. I married dreadfully amiss. But the devil of it is that he started fair and I started foul; with the tastes, the desires, the needs, the sensibilities of a gentleman,—and nothing else! I can't afford to live in England."

"This poor gentleman," said I, "fancied a couple of months ago that he couldn't afford to live in America."

"I'd change chances with him!" And Mr. Rawson gave a passionate slap to his knee.

Searle reclined in his chair with his eyes closed and his face twitching with violent emotion. Suddenly he opened his eyes with a look of awful gravity. "My friend," he said, "you're a failure! Be judged! Don't talk about chances. Don't talk about fair starts and foul starts. I'm at that point myself that I have a right to speak. It lies neither in one's chance nor one's start to make one a success; nor in anything one's brother can do or can undo. It lies in one's will! You and I, sir, have had none; that's very plain! We have been weak, sir; as weak as water. Here we are, sitting staring in each other's faces and reading our weakness in each other's eyes. We are of no account!"

Mr. Rawson received this address with a countenance in

which heartfelt conviction was oddly mingled with a vague suspicion that a proper self-respect required him to resent its unflattering candor. In the course of a minute a proper self-respect yielded to the warm, comfortable sense of his being understood, even to his light dishonor. "Go on, sir, go on," he said. "It's wholesome truth." And he wiped his eyes with his dingy handkerchief.

"Dear me!" cried Searle. "I've made you cry. Well! we speak as from man to man. I should be glad to think that you had felt for a moment the side-light of that great undarkening of the spirit which precedes—which precedes the grand illumination of death."

Mr. Rawson sat silent for a moment, with his eyes fixed on the ground and his well-cut nose more deeply tinged by the force of emotion. Then at last, looking up: "You're a very good-natured man, sir; and you'll not persuade me that you don't come of a good-natured race. Say what you please about a chance; when a man's fifty,—degraded, penniless, a husband and father,—a chance to get on his legs again is not to be despised. Something tells me that my chance is in your country,—that great home of chances. I can starve here, of course; but I don't want to starve. Hang it, sir, I want to live. I see thirty years of life before me yet. If only, by God's help, I could spend them there! It's a fixed idea of mine. I've had it for the last ten years. It's not that I'm a radical. I've no ideas! Old England's good enough for me, but I'm not good enough for old England. I'm a shabby man that wants to get out of a room full of staring gentlefolks. I'm forever put to the blush. It's a perfect agony of spirit. Everything reminds me of my younger and better self. O, for a cooling, cleansing plunge into the unknowing and the unknown! I lie awake thinking of it."

Searle closed his eyes and shivered with a long-drawn tremor which I hardly knew whether to take for an expression of physical or of mental pain. In a moment I perceived it was neither. "O my country, my country, my country!" he murmured in a broken voice; and then sat for some time abstracted and depressed. I intimated to our companion that it was time we should bring our *séance* to a close, and he, without hesitating, possessed himself of the little handrail of the

Bath-chair and pushed it before him. We had got half-way home before Searle spoke or moved. Suddenly in the High Street, as we were passing in front of a chop-house, from whose open doors there proceeded a potent suggestion of juicy joints and suet puddings, he motioned us to halt. "This is my last five pounds," he said, drawing a note from his pocket-book. "Do me the favor, Mr. Rawson, to accept it. Go in there and order a colossal dinner. Order a bottle of Burgundy and drink it to my immortal health!" Mr. Rawson stiffened himself up and received the gift with momentarily irresponsive fingers. But Mr. Rawson had the nerves of a gentleman. I saw the titillation of his pointed finger-tips as they closed upon the crisp paper; I noted the fine tremor in his empurpled nostril as it became more deeply conscious of the succulent flavor of the spot. He crushed the crackling note in his palm with a convulsive pressure.

"It shall be Chambertin!" he said, jerking a spasmodic bow. The next moment the door swung behind him.

Searle relapsed into his feeble stupor, and on reaching the hotel I helped him to get to bed. For the rest of the day he lay in a half-somnolent state, without motion or speech. The doctor, whom I had constantly in attendance, declared that his end was near. He expressed great surprise that he should have lasted so long; he must have been living for a month on a cruelly extorted strength. Toward evening, as I sat by his bedside in the deepening dusk, he aroused himself with a purpose which I had vaguely felt gathering beneath his quietude. "My cousin, my cousin," he said, confusedly. "Is she here?" It was the first time he had spoken of Miss Searle since our exit from her brother's house. "I was to have married her," he went on. "What a dream! That day was like a string of verses —rhymed hours. But the last verse is bad measure. What's the rhyme to 'love'? *Above!* Was she a simple person, a sweet person? Or have I dreamed it? She had the healing gift; her touch would have cured my madness. I want you to do something. Write three lines, three words: 'Good by; remember me; be happy.'" And then, after a long pause: "It's strange a man in my condition should have a wish. Need a man eat his breakfast before his hanging? What a creature is man! what a farce is life! Here I lie, worn down to a mere throbbing fever-point; I breathe and nothing more, and yet I *desire*! My desire lives. If I could see her! Help me out with it and let me die."

Half an hour later, at a venture, I despatched a note to Miss Searle: *"Your cousin is rapidly dying. He asks to see you."* I was conscious of a certain unkindness in doing so. It would bring a great trouble, and no power to face the trouble. But out of her distress I fondly hoped a sufficient energy might be born. On the following day my friend's exhaustion had become so total that I began to fear that his intelligence was altogether gone. But towards evening he rallied awhile, and talked in a maundering way about many things, confounding in a ghastly jumble the memories of the past weeks and those of bygone years. "By the way," he said suddenly, "I have made no will. I haven't much to bequeath. Yet I've something." He had been playing listlessly with a large signet-ring on his left hand, which he now tried to draw off. "I leave you this," working it round and round vainly, "if you can get it off. What mighty knuckles! There must be such knuckles in the mummies of the Pharaohs. Well, when I'm gone! Nay, I leave you something more precious than gold,—the sense of a great kindness. But I have a little gold left. Bring me those trinkets." I placed on the bed before him several articles of jewelry, relics of early elegance: his watch and chain, of great value, a locket and seal, some shirt-buttons and scarf-pins. He trifled with them feebly for some moments, murmuring various names and dates associated with them. At last, looking up with a sudden energy, "What's become of Mr. Rawson?"

"You want to see him?"

"How much are these things worth?" he asked, without heeding me. "How much would they bring?" And he held them up in his weak hands. "They have a great weight. Two hundred pounds? I am richer than I thought! Rawson— Rawson—you want to get out of this awful England."

I stepped to the door and requested the servant, whom I kept in constant attendance in the adjoining sitting-room, to send and ascertain if Mr. Rawson was on the premises. He returned in a few moments, introducing our shabby friend. Mr. Rawson was pale, even to his nose, and, with his suppressed agitation, had an air of great distinction. I led him up to the bed. In Searle's eyes, as they fell on him, there shone for a moment the light of a high fraternal greeting.

"Great God!" said Mr. Rawson, fervently.

"My friend," said Searle, "there is to be one American the less. Let there be one the more. At the worst, you'll be as good a one as I. Foolish me! Take these trinkets; let them help you on your way. They are gifts and memories, but this is a better use. Heaven speed you! May America be kind to you. Be kind, at the last, to your own country!"

"Really, this is too much; I can't," our friend protested in a tremulous voice. "Do get well, and I'll stop here!"

"Nay; I'm booked for my journey, you for yours. I hope you don't suffer at sea."

Mr. Rawson exhaled a groan of helpless gratitude, appealing piteously from so awful a good fortune. "It's like the angel of the Lord," he said, "who bids people in the Bible to rise and flee!"

Searle had sunk back upon his pillow, exhausted: I led Mr. Rawson back into the sitting-room, where in three words I proposed to him a rough valuation of our friend's trinkets. He assented with perfect good breeding; they passed into my possession and a second bank-note into his.

From the collapse into which this beneficent interview had plunged him, Searle gave few signs of being likely to emerge. He breathed, as he had said, and nothing more. The twilight deepened: I lit the night-lamp. The doctor sat silent and official at the foot of the bed; I resumed my constant place near the head. Suddenly Searle opened his eyes widely. "She'll not come," he murmured. "Amen! she's an English sister." Five minutes passed. He started forward. "She has come, she is here!" he whispered. His words conveyed to my mind so absolute an assurance, that I lightly rose and passed into the sitting-room. At the same moment, through the opposite door, the servant introduced a lady. A lady, I say; for an instant she was simply such; tall, pale, dressed in deep mourning. The next moment I had uttered her name—"Miss Searle!" She looked ten years older.

She met me, with both hands extended, and an immense question in her face. "He has just spoken your name," I said.

And then, with a fuller consciousness of the change in her dress and countenance: "What has happened?"

"O death, death!" said Miss Searle. "You and I are left."

There came to me with her words a sort of sickening shock, the sense of poetic justice having been grimly shuffled away. "Your brother?" I demanded.

She laid her hand on my arm, and I felt its pressure deepen as she spoke. "He was thrown from his horse in the park. He died on the spot. Six days have passed.—Six months!"

She took my arm. A moment later we had entered the room and approached the bedside. The doctor withdrew. Searle opened his eyes and looked at her from head to foot. Suddenly he seemed to perceive her mourning. "Already!" he cried, audibly; with a smile, as I believe, of pleasure.

She dropped on her knees and took his hand. "Not for you, cousin," she whispered. "For my poor brother."

He started in all his deathly longitude as with a galvanic shock. "Dead! *he* dead! Life itself!" And then, after a moment, with a slight rising inflection: "You are free?"

"Free, cousin. Sadly free. And now—*now*—with what use for freedom?"

He looked steadily a moment into her eyes, dark in the heavy shadow of her musty mourning veil. "For me," he said, "wear colors!"

In a moment more death had come, the doctor had silently attested it, and Miss Searle had burst into sobs.

We buried him in the little churchyard in which he had expressed the wish to lie; beneath one of the mightiest of English yews and the little tower than which none in all England has a softer and hoarier gray. A year has passed. Miss Searle, I believe, has begun to wear colors.

At Isella

MY STORY begins properly, I suppose, with my journey, and my journey began properly at Lucerne. It had been on the point of beginning a number of times before. About the middle of August I actually started. I had been putting it off from day to day in deference to the opinion of several discreet friends, who solemnly assured me that a man of my make would never outweather the rage of an Italian August. But ever since deciding to winter in Italy, instead of subsiding unimaginatively upon Paris, I had had a standing quarrel with Switzerland. What was Switzerland after all? Little else but brute Nature surely, of which at home we have enough and to spare. What we seek in Europe is Nature re-fined and transmuted to art. In Switzerland, what a pale historic coloring; what a penury of relics and monuments! I pined for a cathedral or a gallery. Instead of dutifully conning my Swiss Bädeker, I had fretfully deflavored my Murray's North Italy. Lucerne indeed is a charming little city, and I had learned to know it well. I had watched the tumbling Reuss, blue from the melting pinnacles which know the blue of heaven, come rushing and swirling beneath those quaintly-timbered bridges, vaulted with mystical paintings in the manner of Holbein, and through the severed mass of the white, compact town. I had frequented the great, bald, half-hand-some, half-hideous church of the Jesuits, and listened in the twilight to the seraphic choir which breathes through its mighty organ-tubes. I had taken the most reckless pleasure in the fact that this was Catholic Switzerland. I had strolled and restrolled across the narrow market-place at Altorf, and kept my countenance in the presence of that ludicrous plaster-cast of the *genius loci* and his cross-bow. I had peregrinated further to the little hamlet of Bürglen, and peeped into the fres-coed chapel which commemorates the hero's natal scene. I had also investigated that sordid lake-side sanctuary, with its threshold lapped by the waves and its walls defiled by cock-neys, which consecrates the spot at which the great moun-taineer, leaping from among his custodians in Gesler's boat, spurned the stout skiff with his invincible heel. I had contemplated from the deck of the steamer the images of the immortal trio, authors of the oath of liberation, which adorn the pier at Brunnen. I had sojourned at that compact little State of Gersau; sandwiched between the lake and the great wall of the Righi, and securely niched somewhere in history as the smallest and most perpetual of republics. The traveller's impatience hereabouts is quickened by his nearness to one of the greatest of the Alpine highways. Here he may catch a balmy side-wind, stirred from the ranks of southward-trooping pilgrims. The Saint Gothard route begins at Lucerne, where you take your place in the diligence and register your luggage. I used to fancy that a great wave of Southern life rolled down this mighty channel to expire visibly in the blue lake, and ripple to its green shores. I used to imagine great gusts of warm wind hovering about the coach office at Fluelen, scented with oleander and myrtle. I used to buy at Fluelen, to the great peril of my digestion, certain villanous peaches and plums, offered by little girls at the steamboat landing, and of which it was currently whispered that they had ripened on those further Italian slopes.

One fine morning I marked my luggage *Milan!* with a great imaginative flourish which may have had something to do with my subsequent difficulty in recovering it in the Lombard capital, banished it for a fortnight from sight and mind, and embarked on the steamboat at Lucerne with the interval's equipment in a knapsack. It is noteworthy how readily, on leaving Switzerland, I made my peace with it. What a pleasure-giving land it is, in truth! Besides the massive glory of its mountains, how it heaps up the measure of delight with the unbargained grace of town and tower, of remembered name and deed! As we passed away from Lucerne, my eyes lingered with a fresher fondness than before upon an admirable bit of the civic picturesque—a great line of mellow-stuccoed dwellings, with verdurous water-steps and grated basements, rising squarely from the rushing cobalt of the Reuss. It was a palpable foretaste of Venice. I am not ashamed to say how soon I began to look out for premonitions of Italy. It was better to begin too soon than too late; so, to miss nothing, I began to note "sensations" at Altorf, the historic heart of Helvetia. I remember here certain formal burgher mansions, standing back from the dusty highroad beyond spacious, well-swept courts, into which the wayfarer glances through immense gates of antique wrought iron. I had a notion that deserted Italian palazzos took the lingering sunbeams at somewhat such an angle, with just that coarse glare. I wondered of course who lived in them, and how they lived, and what was society in Altorf; longing plaintively, in the manner of roaming Americans, for a few stray crumbs from the native social board; with my fancy vainly beating its wings against the great blank wall, behind which, in travel-haunted Europe, all gentle private interests nestle away from intrusion. Here, as everywhere, I was struck with the mere surface-relation of the Western tourist to the soil he treads. He filters and trickles through the dense social body in every possible direction, and issues forth at last the same virginal water drop. "Go your way," these antique houses seemed to say, from their quiet courts and gardens; "the road is yours and welcome, but the land is ours. You may pass and stare and wonder, but you may never know us." The Western tourist consoles himself, of course, by the reflection that the gentry of Altorf and other ancient burghs gain more from the imagination possibly than they might bestow upon it.

I confess that so long as I remained in the land, as I did for the rest of the afternoon—a pure afternoon of late summer, charged with mellow shadows from the teeming verdure of the narrow lowland, beyond which to-morrow and Italy seemed merged in a vague bright identity—I felt that I was not fairly under way. The land terminates at Amstaeg, where I lay that night. Early the next morning I attacked the mighty slopes. Just beyond Amstaeg, if I am not mistaken, a narrow granite bridge spans the last mountain-plunge of the Reuss; and just here the great white road begins the long toil of its ascent. To my sense, these mighty Alpine highways have a grand poetry of their own. I lack, doubtless, that stout stomach for pure loneliness which leads your genuine mountaineer to pronounce them a desecration of the mountain stillness. As if the mountain stillness were not inviolable! Gleaming here and there against the dark sides of the gorges, unrolling their measured bands further and higher, doubling and stretching and spanning, but always climbing, they break it only to the anxious eye. The Saint Gothard road is immensely long drawn, and, if the truth be told, somewhat monotonous. As you follow it to its uppermost reaches, the landscape takes on a darker local color. Far below the wayside, the yellow Reuss tumbles and leaps and foams over a perfect torture-bed of broken rock. The higher slopes lie naked and raw, or coated with slabs of gray. The valley lifts and narrows and darkens into the scenic mountain pass of the fancy. I was haunted as I walked by an old steel plate in a French book that I used to look at as a child, lying on my stomach on the parlor floor. Under it was written "Saint Gothard." I remembered distinctly the cold, gray mood which this picture used to generate; the same tone of feeling is produced by the actual scene. Coming at last to the Devil's Bridge, I recognized the source of the steel plate of my infancy. You have no impulse here to linger fondly. You hurry away after a moment's halt, with an impression fierce and chaotic as the place itself. A great torrent of wind, sweeping from a sudden outlet and snatching uproar and spray from the mad torrent of water leaping in liquid thunderbolts beneath; a giddy, deafened, deluged stare, with my two hands my hat, and a rapid shuddering retreat—these are my chief impressions of the Devil's Bridge. If, on leaving Amstaeg in the morning, I had been asked whither I was bending my steps, "To Italy!" I would have answered, with a grand absence of detail. The radiance of this broad fact had quenched the possible side-lights of reflection. As I approached the summit of the pass, it became a profoundly solemn thought that I might, by pushing on with energy, lay my weary limbs on an Italian bed. There was something so delightful in the mere protracted, suspended sense of approach, that it seemed a pity to bring it to so abrupt a close. And then suppose, metaphysical soul of mine, that Italy should not, in vulgar parlance, altogether come up to time? Why not prolong awhile the possible bliss of ignorance—of illusion? Something short of the summit of the Saint Gothard pass, the great road of the Furca diverges to the right, passes the Rhône Glacier, enters the Rhône Valley, and conducts you to Brieg and the foot of the Simplon. Reaching in due course this divergence of the Furca road, I tarried awhile beneath the

mountain sky, debating whether or not delay would add to
pleasure. I opened my Bädeker and read that within a couple
of hours' walk from my halting-place was the *Albergo di San
Gothardo, vaste et sombre auberge Italienne*. To think of being
at that distance from a vast, sombre Italian inn! On the other
hand, there were some very pretty things said of the Simplon.
I tossed up a napoleon; the head fell uppermost. I trudged
away to the right. The road to the Furca lies across one of
those high desolate plateaux which represent the hard prose
of mountain scenery. Naked and stern it lay before me, rock
and grass, without a shrub, without a tree, without a grace—
like the dry bed of some gigantic river of prehistoric times.

The stunted hamlet of Realp, beside the road dwarfed by
the huge scale of things, seemed little more than a cluster of
naked, sun-blackened bowlders. It contained an inn, however,
and the inn contained the usual Alpine larder of cold veal and
cheese, and, as I remember, a very affable maid-servant, who
spoke excellent lowland French, and confessed in the course
of an after-dinner conversation that the winters in Realp were
un peu tristes. This conversation took place as I sat resting
outside the door in the late afternoon, watching the bright,
hard light of the scene grow gray and cold beneath a clear sky,
and wondering to find humanity lodged in such an exaltation
of desolation.

The road of the Furca, as I discovered the next morning, is
a road and little else. Its massive bareness, however, gives it an
incontestable grandeur. The broad, serpentine terrace uncoils
its slanting *cordons* with a multiplicity of curves and angles
and patient reaches of circumvention, which give it the air of
some wanton revelry of engineering genius. Finally, after a
brief level of repose, it plunges down to the Rhône Glacier. I
had the good fortune to see this great spectacle on the finest
day of the year. Its perfect beauty is best revealed beneath the
scorching glare of an untempered sun. The sky was without a
cloud—the air incredibly lucid. The glacier dropped its bil-
lowy sheet—a soundless tumult of whiteness, a torrent of
rolling marble—straight from the blue of heaven to the glassy
margin of the road. It seems to gather into its bosom the
whole diffused light of the world, so that round about it all
objects lose their color. The rocks and hills stand sullen and

neutral; the lustre of the sky is turned to blackness. At the lit-tle hotel near the glacier I waited for the coach to Brieg, and started thitherward in the early afternoon, sole occupant of the *coupé*.

Let me not, however, forget to commemorate the French priest whom we took in at one of the squalid villages of the dreary Haut-Valais, through which on that bright afternoon we rattled so superbly. It was a Sunday, and throughout this long dark chain of wayside hamlets the peasants were strad-dling stolidly about the little central *place* in the hideous fes-tal accoutrements of the rustic Swiss. He came forth from the tavern, gently cleaving the staring crowd, accompanied by two brother ecclesiastics. These were portly, elderly men; he was young and pale and priestly in the last degree. They had a little scene of adieux at the coach door. They whispered gently, gently holding each other's hands and looking lov-ingly into each other's eyes, and then the two elders saluted their comrade on each cheek, and, as we departed, blew after him just the least little sacramental kiss. It was all, dramatically speaking, delightfully low in tone. Before we reached Brieg the young priest had gained a friend to console him for those he had lost. He proved to be a most amiable person; full of homely frankness and appealing innocence of mundane things; and invested withal with a most pathetic air of sitting there as a mere passive object of transmission—a simple priestly particle in the great ecclesiastical body, transposed by the logic of an inscrutable *thither!* and *thus!* On learning that I was an American, he treated me so implicitly as a travelled man of the world, that he almost persuaded me for the time I was one. He was on pins and needles with his sense of the possible hazards of travel. He asked questions the most inno-cently *saugrenues.* He was convinced on general grounds that our driver was drunk, and that he would surely overturn us into the Rhône. He seemed possessed at the same time with a sort of school-boy relish for the profane humor of things. Whenever the coach made a lurch toward the river-bank or swung too broadly round a turn, he would grasp my arm and whisper that our hour had come; and then, before our pace was quite readjusted, he would fall to nursing his elbows and snickering gently to himself. It seemed altogether a larger

possibility than any he had been prepared for that on his complaining of the cold I should offer him the use of my overcoat. Of this and of other personal belongings he ventured to
inquire the price, and indeed seemed oppressed with the sudden expensiveness of the world. But now that he was fairly
launched he was moving in earnest. He was to reach Brieg, if
possible, in time for the night diligence over the Simplon,
which was to deposit him at the Hospice on the summit.

By a very early hour the next morning I had climbed apace
with the sun. Brieg was far below me in the valley. I had measured an endless number of the giant elbows of the road, and
from the bosky flank of the mountain I looked down at
nestling gulfs of greenness, cool with shade; at surging billows
of forest crested with the early brightness; at slopes in light
and cliffs in shadow; at all the heaving mountain zone which
belongs to the verdant nearness of earth; and then straight
across to the sacred pinnacles which take their tone from
heaven.

If weather could bless an enterprise, mine was blessed beyond words. It seemed to me that Nature had taken an interest in my little project and was determined to do the thing
handsomely. As I mounted higher, the light flung its dazzling
presence on all things. The air stood still to take it; the green
glittered within the green, the blue burned beyond it; the
dew on the forests gathered to dry into massive crystals, and
beyond the brilliant void of space the clear snow-fields stood
out like planes of marble inserted in a field of lapis-lazuli. The
Swiss side of the Simplon has the beauty of a boundless luxury of green; the view remains gentle even in its immensity.
The ascent is gradual and slow, and only when you reach the
summit do you get a sense of proper mountain grimness. On
this favoring day of mine the snowy horrors of the opposite
Aletsch Glacier seemed fairly to twinkle with serenity. It
seemed to me when I reached the Hospice that I had been
winding for hours along the inner hollow of some mighty cup
of verdure toward a rim of chiselled silver crowned with
topaz. At the Hospice I made bold to ask leave to rest. It
stands on the bare topmost plateau of the pass, bare itself as
the spot it consecrates, and stern as the courage of the pious
brothers who administer its charities. It broods upon the

scene with the true, bold, convent look, with rugged yellow
walls and grated windows, striving to close in human weakness from blast and avalanche, as in valleys and cities to close
it in from temptation and pollution. A few St. Bernard dogs
were dozing outside in the chilly sunshine. I climbed the
great stone steps which lift the threshold above the snowland,
and tinkled the bell of appeal. Here for a couple of hours I
was made welcome to the cold, hard fare of the convent.
There was to my mind a solemn and pleasant fitness in my
thus entering church-burdened Italy through the portal of
the church, for from the convent door to the plain of
Lombardy it was all to be downhill work. I seemed to feel on
my head the hands of especial benediction, and to hear in my
ears the premonition of countless future hours to be passed in
the light of altar-candles. The inner face of the Hospice is
well-nigh as cold and bare as the face it turns defiant to the
Alpine snows. Huge stone corridors and ungarnished rooms,
in which poor unacclimatized friars must sit aching and itching with chilblains in high midsummer; everywhere that peculiar perfume of churchiness—the *odeur de sacristie* and
essence of incense—which impart throughout the world an
especial pungency to Catholicism. Having the good fortune,
as it happened, to be invited to dine with the Prior, I found
myself in fine priestly company. A dozen of us sat about the
board in the greasy, brick-paved refectory, lined with sombre
cupboards of ponderous crockery, all in stole and cassock but
myself. Several of the brothers were *in transitu* from below.
Among them I had the pleasure of greeting my companion in
the *coupé* to Brieg, slightly sobered perhaps by his relapse into
the clerical ranks, but still timidly gracious and joyous. The
Prior himself, however, especially interested me, so every inch
was he a prior—a priest dominant and militant. He was still
young, and familiar, I should say, with the passions of youth;
tall and powerful in frame, stout-necked and small-headed,
with a brave beak of a nose and closely placed, fine, but sinister eyes. The simple, childish cut of his black cassock, with its
little linen band across his great pectoral expanse as he sat at
meat, seemed to denote a fantastical, ironical humility. Was it
a mere fancy of a romantic Yankee tourist that he was more
evil than gentle? Heaven grant, I mused as I glanced at him,

that his fierce and massive manhood be guided by the Lord's example. What was such a man as that doing up there on a lonely mountain top, watching the snow clouds from closed windows and doling out restorative cognac to frost-bitten wagoners? He ought to be down in the hard, dense world, fighting and sinning for his mother Church. But he was one who could bide his time. Unless I'm scribbling nonsense, it will come. In deference probably to the esoteric character of a portion of the company, our conversation at dinner was not rigidly clerical. In fact, when my attention wandered back to its theme, I found the good brothers were talking of Alexandre Dumas with a delightful air of protest and hearsay, and a spice of priestly malice. The great romancer, I believe, had among his many fictions somewhere promulgated an inordinate fiction touching the manners and customs of the Hospice. The game being started, each of them said his say and cast his pebble, weighted always with an "*on dit*," and I was amazed to find they were so well qualified to reprobate the author of "Monte Cristo." When we had dined my young Frenchman came and took me by the arm and led me in great triumph over the whole convent, delighted to have something to show me—me who had come from America and had lent him my overcoat. When at last I had under his auspices made my farewell obeisance to the Prior, and started on my downward course, he bore me company along the road. But before we lost sight of the Hospice he gave me his fraternal blessing. "*Allons!*" he was pleased to say, "the next time I shall know an American;" and he gathered up his gentle petticoat, and, as I looked behind, I saw his black stockings frolicking back over the stones by a short cut to the monastery.

I should like to be able to tell the veracious tale of that divine afternoon. I should like to be able to trace the soft stages by which those rugged heights melt over into a Southern difference. Now at last in good earnest I began to watch for the *symptoms* of Italy. Now that the long slope began to tend downward unbroken, it was not absurd to fancy a few adventurous tendrils of Southern growth might have crept and clambered upward. At a short distance beyond the Hospice stands the little village of Simplon, where I believe the coach stops for dinner; the uttermost outpost, I deemed it, of the

lower world, perched there like an empty shell, with its murmur not yet quenched, tossed upward and stranded by some
climbing Southern wave. The little inn at the Italian end of
the street, painted in a bright Italian medley of pink and blue,
must have been decorated by a hand which had learned its
cunning in the land of the fresco. The Italian slope of the
Simplon road commands a range of scenery wholly different
from the Swiss. The latter winds like a thread through the
blue immensity; the former bores its way beneath crag and
cliff, through gorge and mountain crevice. But though its
channel narrows and darkens, Italy nears and nears none the
less. You suspect it first in—what shall I say?—the growing
warmth of the air, a fancied elegance of leaf and twig; a little
while yet, and they will curl and wanton to your heart's content. The famous Gorge of Gando, at this stage of the road,
renews the sombre horrors of the Via Mala. The hills close together above your head, and the daylight filters down their
corrugated sides from three inches of blue. The mad torrent
of the Dauria, roaring through the straitened vale, fills it forever with a sounding din, as—to compare poetry to prose—a
railway train a tunnel. Emerging from the Gorge of Gando,
you fairly breathe Italian air. The gusts of a mild climate come
wandering along the road to meet you. Lo! suddenly, by the
still wayside, I came upon a sensation: a little house painted a
hot salmon color, with a withered pine-twig over the door in
token of entertainment, and above this inscribed in square
chirography—literally in Italics—*Osteria!* I stopped devotedly
to quaff a glass of sour wine to Italy gained. The place seemed
wrapped in a desolation of stillness, save that as I stood and
thumped the doorpost, the piping cry of a baby rose from the
left above and tickled the mountain echoes. Anon came clattering down the stairs a nursing mother of peasants; she gave
me her only wine, out of her own bottle, out of her only
glass. While she stood to wait on me, the terrible cry of her
infant became so painful that I bade her go and fetch him before he strangled; and in a moment she reappeared, holding
him in her arms, pacified and utterly naked. Standing there
with the little unswaddled child on her breast, and smiling
simply from her glowing brow, she made a picture which, in
coming weeks, I saw imitated more or less vividly over many

an altar and in many a palace. Onward still, through its long-drawn evolutions, the valley keeps darkly together, as if to hold its own to the last against the glittering breadth of level Lombardy. In truth, I had gained my desire. If Italy meant stifling heat, this was the essence of Italy. The afternoon was waning, and the early shadows of the valley deepening into a dead summer night. But the hotter the better, and the more Italian! At last, at a turn in the road, glimpsed the first houses of a shallow village, pressed against the mountain wall. It was Italy—the Dogana Isella! so I quickened my jaded steps. I met a young officer strolling along the road in sky-blue trousers, with a moustache *à la* Victor Emanuel, puffing a cigarette, and yawning with the sensuous *ennui* of Isella—the first of that swarming company of warriors whose cerulean presence, in many a rich street-scene, in later hours touched up so brightly the foreground of the picture. A few steps more brought me to the Dogana, and to my first glimpse of those massive and shadowy arcades so delightfully native to the South. Here it was my privilege to hear for the first time the music of an Italian throat vibrate upon Italian air. "Nothing to declare—*niente?*" asked the dark-eyed functionary, emerging from the arcade. "*Niente*" seemed to me delicious; I would have told a fib for the sake of repeating the word. Just beyond stood the inn, which seemed to me somehow not as the inns of Switzerland. Perched something aloft against the hillside, a vague light tendency to break out into balconies and terraces and trellises seemed to enhance its simple façade. Its open windows had an air of being familiar with Southern nights; with balmy dialogues, possibly, passing between languid ladies leaning on the iron rails, and lounging gentlemen, star-gazing from the road beneath at their mistresses' eyes. Heaven grant it should not be fastidiously neat, scrubbed and furbished and *frotté* like those prosy taverns on the Swiss lakes! Heaven was generous. I was ushered into a room whereof the ceiling was frescoed with flowers and gems and cherubs, but whose brick-tiled floor would have been vastly amended by the touch of a wet cloth and broom. After repairing my toilet within the limits of my resources, I proceeded to order supper. The host, I remember, I decreed to have been the *chef de cuisine* of some princely house of

Lombardy. He wore a grizzled moustache and a red velvet cap, with little gold ear-rings. I could see him, under proper inspiration, whip a towel round his waist, turn back his sleeves, and elaborate a masterly pasticcio. "I shall take the liberty," he said, "of causing monsieur to be served at the same time with a lady."

"With a lady—an English lady?" I asked.

"An Italian lady. She arrived an hour ago." And mine host paused a moment and honored me with a genial smile. "She is alone—she is young—she is pretty."

Stolid child of the North that I was, surely my smile of response was no match for his! But, nevertheless, in my heart I felt that fortune was kind. I went forth to stroll down the road while my repast was being served, and while daylight still lingered, to reach forward as far as possible into the beckoning land beyond. Opposite the inn the mountain stream, still untamed, murmured and tumbled between the stout parapet which edged the road and the wall of rock which enclosed the gorge. I felt indefinably curious, expectant, impatient. Here was Italy at last; but what next? Was I to eat my supper and go contentedly to bed? Was there nothing I could see, or do, or feel? I had been deeply moved, but I was primed for a deeper emotion still. Would it come? Along the road toward Domo d'Ossola the evening shadows deepened and settled, and filled the future with mystery. The future would take care of itself; but ah, for an intenser present! I stopped and gazed wistfully along the broad dim highway. At this moment I perceived beyond me, leaning against the parapet, the figure of a woman, alone and in meditation. Her two elbows rested on the stone coping, her two hands were laid against her ears to deaden the din of the stream, and her face, between them, was bent over upon the waters. She seemed young and comely. She was bare-headed; a black organdy shawl was gathered round her shoulders; her dress, of a light black material, was covered with a multitude of little puffs and flounces, trimmed and adorned with crimson silk. There was an air of intense meditation in her attitude; I passed near her without her perceiving me. I observed her black-brown tresses, braided by a cunning hand, but slightly disarranged by travel, and the crumpled disorder of her half-fantastic dress. She was a lady and an Italian; she was alone, young, and pretty; was she possibly my destined companion? A few yards beyond the spot at which she stood, I retraced my steps; she had now turned round. As I approached her she looked at me from a pair of dark expressive eyes. Just a hint of suspicion and defiance I fancied that at this moment they expressed. "Who are you, what are you, roaming so close to me?" they seemed to murmur. We were alone in this narrow pass, I a new comer, she a daughter of the land; moreover, her glance had almost audibly challenged me; instinctively, therefore, and with all the deference I was master of, I bowed. She continued to gaze for an instant; then suddenly she perceived, I think, that I was utterly a foreigner and presumably a gentleman, and hereupon, briefly but graciously, she returned my salute. I went my way and reached the hotel. As I passed in, I saw the fair stranger come slowly along the road as if also to enter the inn. In the little dining-room I found mine host of the velvet cap bestowing the finishing touches upon a small table set *en tête-à-tête* for two. I had heard, I had read, of the gracious loquacity of the Italian race and their sweet familiarities of discourse. Here was a chance to test the quality of the matter. The landlord, having poised two fantastically folded napkins directly *vis-à-vis*, glanced at me with a twinkle in his eye which seemed to bespeak recognition of this cunning arrangement.

"*A propos*," I said, "this lady with whom I am to dine? Does she wear a black dress with red flounces?"

"Precisely, Signore. You have already had a glimpse of her? A pretty woman, isn't it so?"

"Extremely pretty. Who is the lady?"

"Ah!" And the landlord turned back his head and thrust out his chin, with just the least play of his shoulders. "That's the question! A lady of that age, with that face and those red flounces, who travels alone—not even a maid—you may well ask who she is! She arrived here an hour ago in a carriage from Domo d'Ossola, where, her vetturino told me, she had arrived only just before by the common coach from Arona. But though she travels by the common vehicle, she is not a common person; one may see that with half an eye. She comes in great haste, but ignorant of the ways and means. She wishes

to go by the diligence to Brieg. She ought to have waited at
Domo, where she could have found a good seat. She didn't
even take the precaution of engaging one at the office there.
When the diligence stops here, she will have to fare as she can.
She is pretty enough indeed to fare very well—or very ill;
isn't it so, Signore?" demanded the worthy Bonifazio, as I believe he was named. "Ah, but behold her strolling along the
road, bare-headed, in those red flounces! What is one to say?
After dusk, with the dozen officers in garrison here watching
the frontier! Watching the ladies who come and go, *per Dio!*
Many of them, saving your presence, Signore, are your own
compatriots. You'll not deny that some of them are a little
free—a little bold, What will you have? Out of their own
country! What else were the use of travel? But this one; eh!
she's not out of her own country yet. Italians are Italians,
Signore, up to the frontier—eh! eh!" And the Signor
Bonifazio indulged in a laugh the most *goguenard*. "Nevertheless, I have not kept an inn these twenty years without
learning to know the sheep from the goats. This is an honorable lady, Signore; it is for that reason that I have offered to
you to sup with her. The other sort! one can always sup with
them!"

It seemed to me that my host's fluent commentary was no
meagre foretaste of Italian frankness. I approached the window. The fair object of our conversation stood at the foot of
the stone staircase which ascended to the inn door, with the
toe of her shoe resting upon the first step. She was looking
fixedly and pensively up the road toward Switzerland. Her
hand clasped the knob of the iron balustrade and her slight
fingers played an impatient measure. She had begun to interest me. Her dark eyes, intent upon the distant turn of the
road, seemed to expand with a vague expectancy. Whom was
she looking for? Of what romance of Italy was she the heroine? The *maître d'hôtel* appeared at the head of the steps, and
with a flourish of his napkin announced that the Signora was
served. She started a little and then lightly shrugged her
shoulders. At the same moment I caught her eye as I stood
gazing from the window. With a just visible deepening of her
color, she slowly ascended the steps. I was suddenly seized
with a sense of being dingy, travel-stained, unpresentable to a

woman so charming. I hastily retreated to my room, and, sur-
veying myself in my dressing-glass, objurgated fortune that I
lacked the wherewithal to amend my attire. But I could at
least change my cravat. I had no sooner replaced my black
neck-tie by a blue one than it occurred to me that the Signora
would observe the difference; but what then? It would hardly
offend her. With a timid hope that it might faintly gratify her
as my only feasible tribute to the honor of her presence, I returned to the dining-room. She was seated and had languidly
addressed herself to the contents of her soup-plate. The worthy Bonifazio had adorned our little table with four lighted
candles and a centre-piece of Alpine flowers. As I installed
myself opposite my companion, after having greeted her and
received a murmured response, it seemed to me that I was sitting down to one of those factitious repasts which are served
upon the French stage, when the table has been moved close
to the footlights, and the ravishing young widow and the romantic young artist begin to manipulate the very *nodus* of the
comedy. Was the Signora a widow? Our attendant, with his
crimson cap, his well-salted discourse, his right-handed gestures, and his smile from behind the scenes, might have
passed for a classic *valet de théâtre*. I had the appetite of a man
who had been walking since sunrise, but I found ample occasion, while I plied my knife and fork, to inspect the Signora.
She merely pretended to eat; and to appeal, perhaps, from the
over-flattering intentness of my vision, she opened an idle
conversation with Bonifazio. I listened admiringly, while the
glancing shuttle of Italian speech passed rapidly from lip to
lip. It was evident, frequently, that she remained quite heedless of what he said, losing herself forever in a kind of fretful
intensity of thought. The repast was long and multifarious,
and as he time and again removed her plate with its contents
untouched, mine host would catch my eye and roll up his
own with an air of mock commiseration, turning back his
thumb at the same moment toward the region of his heart.
"*Un coup de tête*," he took occasion to murmur as he reached
over me to put down a dish. But the more I looked at the fair
unknown, the more I came to suspect that the source of her
unrest lay deeper than in the petulance of wounded vanity.
Her face wore to my eye the dignity of a deep resolution—a

resolution taken in tears and ecstasy. She was some twenty-eight years of age, I imagined; though at moments a painful gravity resting upon her brow gave her the air of a woman who in youth has anticipated old age. How beautiful she was by natural gift I am unable to say; for at this especial hour of her destiny, her face was too serious to be fair and too interesting to be plain. She was pale, worn, and weary-looking; but in the midst of her weariness there flickered a fierce impatience of delay and forced repose. She was a gentle creature, turned brave and adventurous by the stress of fate. It burned bright in her soft, grave eyes, this longing for the larger freedom of the tarrying morrow. A dozen chance gestures indicated the torment of her spirit—the constant rapping of her knife against the table, her bread crumbed to pieces but uneaten, the frequent change from posture to posture of her full and flexible figure, shifting through that broad range of attitude—the very gamut of gracefulness—familiar to Italian women.

The repast advanced without my finding a voice to address her. Her secret puzzled me, whatever it was, but I confess that I was afraid of it. A *coup de tête!* Heaven only knew how direful a *coup!* My mind was flooded by the memory of the rich capacity of the historic womanhood of Italy. I thought of Lucrezia Borgia, of Bianca Capello, of the heroines of Stendahl. My fair friend seemed invested with an atmosphere of candid passion, which placed her quite apart from the ladies of my own land. The gallant soul of the Signor Bonifazio, however, had little sufferance for this pedantic view of things. Shocked by my apparent indifference to the privilege of my rare position, he thrust me by the shoulders into the conversation. The Signora eyed me for a moment not ungraciously, and then, "Do you understand Italian?" she asked.

I had come to Italy with an ear quite unattuned, of course, to the spoken tongue; but the mellow cadence of the Signora's voice rang in upon my senses like music. "I understand *you*," I said.

She looked at me gravely, with the air of a woman used to receive compliments without any great flutter of vanity. "Are you English?" she abruptly asked.

"English is my tongue."

"Have you come from Switzerland?"

"He has walked from Brieg!" proclaimed our host.

"Ah, you happy men, who can walk—who can run—who needn't wait for coaches and conductors!" The Signora uttered these words with a smile of acute though transient irony. They were followed by a silence. Bonifazio, seeing the ice was broken, retired with a flourish of his napkin and a contraction of his eyelids as much in the nature of a wink as his respect for me, for the Signora, and for himself allowed. What was the motive of the Signora's impatience? I had a presentiment that I should learn. The Italians are confidential; of this I had already received sufficient assurance; and my companion, with her lucid eye and her fine pliable lips, was a bright example of the eloquent genius of her race. She sat idly pressing with her fork the crimson substance out of a plateful of figs, without raising them to her lips.

"You are going over into Switzerland," I said, "and you are in haste."

She eyed me a minute suspiciously. "Yes, I'm in haste!"

"I, who have just begun to feel the charm of Italy," I rejoined, "can hardly understand being in haste to leave it."

"The charm of Italy!" cried the Signora, with a slightly cynical laugh. "Foreigners have a great deal to say about it."

"But you, a good Italian, certainly know what we mean."

She shrugged her shoulders—an operation she performed more gracefully than any woman I ever saw, unless it be Mlle. Madeleine Brohan of the Théâtre Français. "For me it has no charm! I have been unhappy here. Happiness for me is *there!*" And with a superb nod of her head she indicated the Transalpine world. Then, as if she had spoken a thought too freely, she rose suddenly from her chair and walked away to the window. She stepped out on the narrow balcony, looked intently for an instant up and down the road and at the band of sky above it, and then turned back into the room. I sat in my place, divided between my sense of the supreme sweetness of figs and my wonder at my companion's mystery. "It's a fine night!" she said. And with a little jerk of impatience she flung herself into an arm-chair near the table. She leaned back, with her skirt making a great wave around her and her arms folded. I went on eating figs. There was a long silence.

"You've eaten at least a dozen figs. You'll be ill!" said the Signora at last.

This was friendly in its frankness. "Ah, if you only knew how I enjoy them!" I cried, laughing. "They are the first I ever tasted. And this the first Asti wine. We don't have either in the North. If figs and Asti wine are for anything in your happiness, Signora," I added, "you had better not cross the Alps. See, the figs are all gone. Do you think it would hurt me to have any more?"

"Truly," cried the Signora, "I don't know what you English are made of!"

"You think us very coarse, and given up altogether to eating and drinking?" She gave another shrug tempered by a smile. "To begin with, I am not an Englishman. And in the second place, you'd not call me coarse if you knew—if you only knew what I feel this evening. Eh! such thick-coming fancies!"

"What are your fancies?" she demanded, with a certain curiosity gleaming in her dark eye.

"I *must* finish this Asti!" This I proceeded to do. I am very glad I did, moreover, as I borrowed from its mild and luscious force something of the courage with which I came to express myself. "I don't know how it is that I'm talking Italian at such a rate. Somehow the words come to me. I know it only from books. I have never talked it."

"You speak as well," the Signora graciously affirmed, "as if you had lived six months in the country."

"Half an hour in your society," said I, "is as profitable as six months elsewhere."

"Bravo!" she responded. "An Italian himself couldn't say it better."

Sitting before me in the vague candlelight, beautiful, pale, dark-browed, sad, the Signora seemed to me an incorporate image of her native land. I had come to pay it my devotions. Why not perform them at her feet? "I have come on a pilgrimage," I said. "To understand what I mean, you must have lived, as I have lived, in a land beyond the seas, barren of romance and grace. This Italy of yours, on whose threshold I stand, is the home of history, of beauty, of the arts—of all that makes life splendid and sweet. Italy, for us dull strangers, is a

magic word. We cross ourselves when we pronounce it. We
are brought up to think that when we have earned leisure and
rest—at some bright hour, when fortune smiles—we may go
forth and cross oceans and mountains and see on Italian soil
the primal substance—the Platonic 'idea'—of our consoling
dreams and our richest fancies. I have been brought up in
these thoughts. The happy hour has come to me—Heaven be
praised!—while I am still young and strong and sensitive.
Here I sit for the first time in the enchanted air in which love
and faith and art and knowledge are warranted to become
deeper passions than in my own chilly clime. I begin to behold the promise of my dreams. It's Italy. How can I tell you
what that means to one of us? Only see already how fluent
and tender of speech I've become. The air has a perfume;
everything that enters my soul, at every sense, is a suggestion,
a promise, a performance. But the best thing of all is that I
have met *you, bella donna!* If I were to tell you how you seem
to me, you would think me either insincere or impertinent.
Ecco!"

She listened to me without changing her attitude or without removing her fathomless eyes from my own. Their blue-
black depths, indeed, seemed to me the two wells of poetic
unity, from which I drew my somewhat transcendental alloca-
tion. She was puzzled, I think, and a little amused, but not
offended. Anything from an Inglese! But it was doubtless
grateful to feel these rolling waves of sentiment break softly at
her feet, chained as she was, like Andromeda, to the rock of a
lonely passion. With an admirable absence of *minauderie*,
"How is it that I seem to you, Signore?" she asked.

I left my place and came round and stood in front of her.
"Ever since I could use my wits," I said, "I have done little
else than fancy dramas and romances and love-tales, and
lodge them in Italy. You seem to me as the heroine of all my
stories."

There was perhaps a slight movement of coquetry in her reply: "Your stories must have been very dull, Signore," and she
gave a sad smile.

"Nay, in future," I said, "my heroines shall be more like
you than ever. Where do you come from?" I seated myself in
the chair she had quitted. "But it's none of my business," I

added. "From anywhere. In Milan or Venice, in Bologna or Florence, Rome or Naples, every grave old palazzo I pass, I shall fancy your home. I'm going the whole length of Italy. My soul, what things I shall see!"

"You please me, Signore. I say to you what I wouldn't say to another. I came from Florence. Shall you surely go there?"

"I have reasons," I said, "for going there more than elsewhere. In Florence"—and I hesitated, with a momentary horror at my perfect unreserve—"in Florence I am to meet my—my *promessa sposa*."

The Signora's face was instantly irradiated by a generous smile. "Ah!" she said, as if now for the first time she really understood me.

"As I say, she has been spending the summer at the Baths of Lucca. She comes to Florence with her mother in the middle of September."

"Do you love her?"

"Passionately."

"Is she pretty?"

"Extremely. But not like you. Very fair, with blue eyes."

"How long since you have seen her?"

"A year."

"And when are you to be married?"

"In November, probably, in Rome."

She covered me for a moment with a glance of the largest sympathy. "Ah, what happiness!" she cried abruptly.

"After our marriage," I said, "we shall go down to Naples. Do you know Naples?"

Instead of answering, she simply gazed at me, and her beautiful eyes seemed to grow larger and more liquid. Suddenly, while I sat in the benignant shadow of her vision, I saw the tears rise to her lids. Her face was convulsed and she burst into sobs. I remember that in my amazement and regret I suddenly lost my Italian. "Dearest lady," I cried in my mother tongue, "forgive me that I have troubled you. Share with me at least the sorrow that I have aroused." In an instant, however, she had brushed away her tears and her face had recovered its pale composure. She tried even to smile.

"What will you think of me?" she asked. "What do you think of me already?"

"I think you are an extremely interesting woman. You are in trouble. If there is anything I can do for you, pray say the word."

She gave me her hand. I was on the point of raising it to my lips. "No—*à l'Anglaise*," she said, and she lightly shook my own. "I like you—you're an honest man—you don't try to make love to me. I should like to write a note to your *promessa sposa* to tell her she may trust you. You can't help me. Besides, it's only a little longer. Eh, it's a long story, Signore! What is said in your country of a woman who travels alone at night without even a servant?"

"Nothing is said. It's very common."

"Ah! women must be very happy there, or very unhappy! Is it never supposed of a woman that she has a lover? That is worst of all."

"Fewer things are 'supposed' of women there than here. They live more in the broad daylight of life. They make their own law."

"They must be very good then—or very bad. So that a man of fancy like you, with a taste for romance, has to come to poor Italy, where he can suppose at leisure! But we are not all romance, I assure you. With me, I promise you, it's no light-minded *coup de tête*." And the Signora enforced her candid assurance with an almost imperious nod. "I know what I'm doing. Eh! I'm an old woman. I've waited and waited. But now my hour has come! Ah, the heavenly freedom of it! Ah, the peace—the joy! Just God, I thank thee!" And sitting back in her chair, she folded her hands on her bosom and closed her eyes in a kind of ecstasy. Opening them suddenly, she perceived, I suppose, my somewhat intent and dilated countenance. Breaking then into a loud, excited laugh, "How you stare at me!" she cried. "You think I've at least poisoned my husband. No, he's safe and sound and strong! On the contrary, I've forgiven him. I forgive him with all my heart, with all my soul; there! I call upon you to witness it. I bear him no rancor. I wish never to think of him again; only let me never see him—never hear of him! Let him never come near me: I shall never trouble him! Hark!" She had interrupted herself and pressed her hand with a startled air upon my arm. I listened, and in a moment my ear caught the sound of rolling wheels on the hard highroad. With a great effort at self-composure, apparently, she laid her finger on her lips. "If it should be he—if it should be he!" she murmured. "Heaven preserve me! Do go to the window and see."

I complied, and perceived a two-horse vehicle advancing rapidly from the Italian quarter. "It's a carriage of some sort from Italy," I said. "But what—whom do you fear?"

She rose to her feet. "That my husband should overtake me," and she gave a half-frantic glance round the room, like a hunted stag at bay. "If it should be he, protect me! Do something, say something—anything! Say I'm not fit to go back to him. He wants me because he thinks me good. Say I'm not good—to your knowledge. Oh, Signore—Holy Virgin!" Recovering herself, she sank into a chair, and sat stiff and superb, listening to the deepening sound of the wheels. The vehicle approached, reached the inn, passed it, and went on to the Dogana.

"You're safe," I said. "It's not a posting-chaise, but a common wagon with merchandise."

With a hushed sigh of relief she passed her hand over her brow, and then looking at me: "I have lived these three days in constant terror. I believe in my soul he has come in pursuit of me; my hope is in my having gained time through his being absent when I started. My nerves are broken. I have neither slept nor eaten, nor till now have I spoken. But I *must* speak! I'm frank; it's good to take a friend when you find one."

I confess that to have been thus freely admitted by the fair fugitive into the whirling circle of her destiny was one of the keenest emotions of my life. "I know neither the motive of your flight nor the goal of your journey," I answered; "but if I may help you and speed you, I will joyfully turn back from the threshold of Italy and give you whatever furtherance my company may yield. To go with you," I added, smiling, "will be to remain in Italy, I assure you."

She acknowledged my offer with a glance more potent than words. "I'm going to a friend," she said, after a silence. "To accept your offer would be to make friendship cheap. He is lying ill at Geneva; otherwise I shouldn't be *thus!* But my head is on fire. This room is close; it smells of supper. Do me the favor to accompany me into the air."

She gathered her shawl about her shoulders, I offered her
my arm, and we passed into the entry toward the door. In the
doorway stood mine host, with his napkin under his arm. He
drew himself up as we approached, and, as if to deprecate a
possible imputation of scandal, honored us with a bow of the
most ceremonious homage. We descended the steps and
strolled along the road toward the Swiss frontier. A vague
remnant of daylight seemed to linger imprisoned in the narrow gorge. We passed the Dogana and left the village behind
us. My thoughts reverted as we went, to the aching blank of
my fancy as I entered Isella an hour before. It seemed to pal-
pitate now with a month's experience. Beyond the village a
narrow bridge spans the stream and leads to a path which
climbs the opposite hillside. We diverged from the road and
lingered on the bridge while the sounding torrent gushed beneath us, flashing in the light of the few stars which sparkled
in our narrow strip of sky, like diamonds tacked upon a band
of velvet. I remained silent, thinking a passive silence the most
graceful tribute to the Signora's generous intentions. "I will
tell you all!" she said at last. "Do you think me pretty? But
you needn't answer. The less you think so, the more you'll say
it. I *was* pretty! I don't pretend to be so now. I have suffered
too much. I have a miserable fear that when *he* sees me, after
these three years, he'll notice the loss of my beauty. But,
poverino! he is perhaps too ill to notice anything. He is young
—a year younger than I—twenty-seven. He is a painter; he
has a most beautiful talent. He loved me four years ago, before my marriage. He was a friend of my poor brother, who
was fatally wounded at the battle of Mentana, where he
fought with Garibaldi. My brother, Giuseppino, was brought
home with his wound; he died in a week. Ernesto came to
make a drawing of his face before we lost it forever. It was not
the first time I had seen him, but it was the first time we understood each other. I was sitting by poor Giuseppino's bedside, crying—crying! He, too, cried while he drew and made
great blisters on the paper. I know where to look for them
still. They loved each other devotedly. I, too, had loved my
brother! for my mother was dead, and my father was not a
mother—not even a father! Judge for yourself! We placed together the love which each of us had borne for Giuseppino,

and it made a great love for each other. It was a misfortune; but how could we help it? He had nothing but his talent, which as yet was immature. I had nothing at all but the poor little glory of my father's being a Marchese, without a *soldo*, and my prettiness! But you see what has become of that! My father was furious to have given his only son to that scoundrel of a Garibaldi, for he is of that way of thinking. You should have heard the scene he made me when poor Ernesto in despair asked leave to marry me. My husband, whom I had never seen or at least never noticed, was at that time in treaty for my hand. By his origin he was little better than a peasant, but he had made a fortune in trade, and he was very well pleased to marry a *marchesina*. It's not every man who is willing to take a penniless girl; it was the first chance and perhaps the best. So I was given over blindfold, bound hand and foot, to that brute. Eh! what I hadn't brought in cash I had to pay down in patience. If I were to tell you what I've suffered these three years, it would bring tears to your eyes—Inglese as you are. But they are things which can't be told. He is a peasant, with the soul of a peasant—the taste, the manners, the vices of a peasant. It was my great crime that I was proud. I had much to be proud of. If I had only been a woman of his own sort! to pay him in his own coin! Ernesto, of course, had been altogether suppressed. He proposed to me to escape with him before my marriage, and I confess to you that I would have done it if I could. I tried in vain; I was too well watched. I implored him then to go away till better days; and he at last consented to go to Paris and pursue his studies. A week after my marriage he came to bid me farewell. My husband had taken me to Naples, to make me believe I was not wretched. Ernesto followed me, and I contrived to see him. It lasted three minutes by the clock: I have not seen him since. In three years I have had five letters from him; they are here in my dress. I am sure of his love; I don't need to have him write, to tell me. I have answered him twice. These letters—seven in all, in three years!—are all my husband has to reproach me with. He is furious at not having more. He knows of course that I love another; he knows that to bear such things a woman must borrow strength somewhere. I have had faith, but it has not been all faith! My husband has none;

nothing is sacred to him, not the Blessed Virgin herself. If you were to hear the things he says about the Holy Father! I have waited and waited. I confess it, I have hoped at times that my husband would die. But he has the health of a peasant. He used to strike me—to starve me—to lock me up without light or fire. I appealed to my father, but, I'm sorry to say it, my father is a coward! Heaven forgive me! I'm saying dreadful things here! But, ah, Signore, let me breathe at last! I've waited and waited, as I say, for this hour! Heaven knows I have been good. Though I stand here now, I have not trifled with my duties. It's not coquetry! I determined to endure as long as I could, and then to break—to break forever! A month ago strength and courage left me; or rather, they came to me! I wrote to Ernesto that I would come to him. He answered that he would come down to meet me—if possible at Milan. Just afterwards he wrote me in a little scrawl in pencil that he had been taken ill in Geneva, and that if I could I must come alone, before he got worse. Here I am then, alone, pursued, frantic with ignorance and dread. Heaven only keep him till I come. I shall do the rest! Exactly how I left home, I can't tell you. It has been like a dream! My husband—God be praised!—was obliged to make a short absence on business, of which I took advantage. My great trouble was getting a little money. I never have any. I sold a few trinkets for a few francs—hardly enough! The people saw I was too frightened to make a stand, so that they cheated me. But if I can only come to the end! I'm certain that my husband has pursued me. Once I get to Switzerland, we can hide. Meanwhile I'm in a fever. I've lost my head. I began very well, but all this delay has so vexed and confused me. I hadn't even the wit to secure a place in the coach at Domo d'Ossola. But I shall go, if I have to sit on the roof—to crouch upon the doorstep. If I had only a little more money, so that I needn't wait for coaches. To overtake me my husband, for once in his life, won't count his *lire*!"

I listened with a kind of awe to this torrent of passionate confidence. I had got more even than I had bargained for. The current of her utterance seemed to gather volume as it came, and she poured out her tragic story with a sort of rapturous freedom. She had unburdened at last her heavy heart.

As she spoke, the hot breath of her eloquence seemed to pass far beyond my single attentive sense, and mingle joyously with the free air of the night. Her tale, in a measure, might be untrue or imperfect; but her passion, her haste, her sincerity, were imperiously real. I felt, as I had never felt it, the truth of the poet's claim for his touch of nature. I became conscious of a hurrying share in my companion's dread. I seemed to hear in the trembling torrent the sound of rapid wheels. I expected every moment to see the glare of lights along the road, before the inn, then a strong arm locked about her waist, and, in the ray of a lantern from the carriage window, to catch the mute agony of her solemn eyes. My heart beat fast; I was part and parcel of a romance! Come! the *dénouement* shouldn't fail by any prosy fault of mine.

"How I've talked!" cried the Signora, after a brief pause. "And how you stare at me! Eh! don't be afraid. I've said all, and it has done me good. You'll laugh with your *promessa sposa* about that crazy creature who was flying from her husband. The idea of people not being happy in marriage, you'll say to her!"

"I thank you with all my heart," I said, "for having trusted me as you have. But I'm almost sorry you have taken the time. You oughtn't to be lingering here while your husband is making the dust fly."

"That's easy to say, Signore; but I can't walk to Brieg, like you. A carriage costs a hundred and fifty francs. I have only just enough to pay my place in the coach."

I drew out my portemonnaie and emptied it in my hand; it contained a hundred and seventy francs. "*Ecco!*" I said, holding them out to her.

She glanced at them an instant, and then, with a movement which effectually rounded and completed my impression of her simple and passionate sincerity, seized with both her hands my own hand as it held them. "Ah, the Blessed Virgin be praised!" she cried. "Ah, you're an angel from heaven! Quick, quick! A carriage, a carriage!"

She thrust the money into her pocket, and, without waiting for an answer, hurried back to the road, and moved swiftly toward the inn. I overtook her as she reached the doorstep, where our host was enjoying a pipe in the cool. "A carriage!"

she cried. "I must be off. Quick, without delay! I have the money; you shall be well paid. Don't tell me you haven't one. There must be one here. Find one, prepare it, lose not a moment. Do you think I can lie tossing here all night? I shall put together my things, and give you ten minutes! You, sir, see that they hurry!" And she rapidly entered the house.

Bonifazio stared, somewhat aghast at the suddenness and the energy of her requisition. Fearing that he might not be equal to the occasion, I determined to take him by his gallantry. "Come, my friend," I said, "don't stand scratching your head, but *act*. I know you admire the Signora. You don't want to see so charming a woman in trouble. You don't wish to have a scandal in your inn. It is of the first importance that she should leave in ten minutes. Stir up your hostler."

A wise grin illumined his face. "Ah," said he, "it's as bad as that. I had my notions. I'll do what I can." He exerted himself to such good purpose that in the incredibly short period of twenty minutes a small closed carriage was drawn by a couple of stout horses to the door. Going in to summon the fair fugitive, I found her in the dining-room, where, fretting with impatience, and hooded and shawled, she had suffered a rather bungling chambermaid to attempt the insertion of a couple of necessary pins. She swept past me on her exit as if she had equally forgotten my face and her obligations, and entered the carriage with passionate adjurations of haste. I followed her and watched her take her place; but she seemed not even to see me. My hour was over. I had added an impulse to her straining purpose; its hurrying current had left me alone on the brink. I could not resist the influence of a poignant regret at having dropped from her consciousness. Learning from a peasant who was lounging near at hand that an easy footpath wound along the side of the mountain and struck the highroad at the end of half an hour's walk, I immediately discovered and followed it. I saw beneath me in the dimness as I went the white highroad, with the carriage slowly beginning its ascent. Descending at last from the slope, I met the vehicle well on its way up the mountain, and motioned to the driver to stop. The poor Signora, haunted with the fear of interruption, thrust her pale face from the window. Seeing me, she stared an instant almost vacantly, and then passing her hand over her face broke into a glorious smile. Flinging open the carriage door from within, she held out her two hands in farewell.

"Give me your blessing," she cried, "and take mine! I had almost forgotten you. Love is selfish, Signore. But I should have remembered you later and cried with gratitude. My Ernesto will write to you. Give me your card—write me your address, there in the carriage lamp. No? As you please, then. Think of me kindly. And the young girl you marry—use her well—love her if only a little—it will be enough. We ask but a little, but we need that. Addio!" and she raised her two hands to her lips, seemed for an instant to exhale her whole soul upon her finger tips, and flung into the air a magnificent Italian kiss.

I returned along the winding footpath more slowly, a wiser, possibly a sadder man than a couple of hours before. I had entered Italy, I had tasted of sentiment, I had assisted at a drama. It was a good beginning. I found Bonifazio finishing his pipe before the inn. "Well, well, Signore," he cried, "what does it all mean?"

"Aren't you enough of an Italian to guess?" I asked.

"Eh, eh, it's better to be an Inglese and to be told," cried Bonifazio with a twinkle.

"You must sleep to-night with an ear open," I said. "A personage will arrive post-haste from Domo. Stop him if you can."

Bonifazio scratched his head. "If a late supper or an early breakfast will stop him!" he murmured. I looked deep into his little round eye, expecting to read there the recipe for the infusion of a sleeping potion into *café au lait*.

My room that night was close and hot, and my bed none of the best. I tossed about in a broken sleep. I dreamed that I was lying ill in a poor tavern at Naples, waiting, waiting with an aching heart, for the arrival from the Baths of Lucca of a certain young lady, who had been forced by her mother, Mrs. B. of Philadelphia, into a cruel marriage with a wealthy Tuscan *contadino*. At last I seemed to hear a great noise without and a step on the stairs; through the opened door rushed in my *promessa sposa*. Her blue eyes were bright with tears, and she wore a flounced black dress trimmed with crimson silk. The next moment she was kneeling at my bedside crying, "Ernesto, Ernesto!" At this point I awoke into the early morning. The noise of horses and wheels and voices came up from outside. I sprang from my bed and stepped to my open window. The huge, high-piled, yellow diligence from Domo d'Ossola had halted before the inn. The door of the *coupé* was open; from the aperture half emerged the Personage. "A peasant," she had called him, but he was well *dicrotti*, though he *had* counted his *lire* and taken the diligence. He struck me as of an odd type for an Italian: dark sandy hair, a little sandy moustache, waxed at the ends, and sandy whiskers *à l'Anglaise*. He had a broad face, a large nose, and a small keen eye, without any visible brows. He wore a yellow silk hand-kerchief tied as a nightcap about his head, and in spite of the heat he was very much muffled. On the steps stood Bonifazio, cap in hand, smiling and obsequious.

"Is there a lady here?" demanded the gentleman from the *coupé*. "A lady alone—good-looking—with little luggage?"

"No lady, Signore," said Bonifazio. "Alas! I have an empty house. If *eccellenza* would like to descend——"

"Have you had a lady—yesterday, last night? Don't lie."

"We had three, *eccellenza*, a week ago—three Scotch ladies going to Baveno. Nay, three days since we had a *prima donna* on her way to Milan."

"Damn your Scotch *prima donna*!" said the other. "Have you had my wife?"

"The wife of *eccellenza*? Save the ladies I mention, we have had neither wife nor maid. Would *eccellenza* like a cup of coffee?"

"*Sangue di Dio!*" was *eccellenza's* sole response. The *coupé* door closed with a slam, the conductor mounted, the six horses started, and the great mountain coach rolled away.

Master Eustace

HAVING handed me my cup of tea, she proceeded to make her own; an operation she performed with a delicate old-maidish precision I delighted to observe.

The story is not my own—she then began—but that of persons with whom for a time I was intimately connected. I have led a quiet life. This is my only romance—and it's the romance of others. When I was a young woman of twenty-two my poor mother died, after a long, weary illness, and I found myself obliged to seek a new home. Making a home requires time and money. I had neither to spare, so I advertised for a "situation," rating my accomplishments modestly, and asking rather for kind treatment than high wages. Mrs. Garnyer immediately answered my advertisement. She offered me a fair salary and a peaceful asylum. I was to teach her little boy the rudiments of my slender stock of sciences and to make myself generally useful. Something in her tone and manner assured me that in accepting this latter condition I was pledging myself to no very onerous servitude, and I never found reason to repent of my bargain. I had always valued my freedom before all things, and it seemed to me that in trading it away even partially I was surrendering a priceless treasure; but Mrs. Garnyer made service easy. I liked her from the first, and I doubt that she ever fairly measured my fidelity and affection. She knew that she could trust me, and she always spoke of me as "a good creature;" but she never estimated the trouble I saved her, or the little burdens I lifted from her pretty, feeble shoulders. Both in her position and her person there was something singularly appealing. She was in those days—indeed she always remained—a very pretty little woman. But she had grace even more than beauty. She was young, and looked even younger than her years; slight, light of tread and of gesture, though not at all rapid (for in all her movements there was a kind of pathetic morbid languor), and fairer, whiter, purer in complexion than any woman I have seen. She reminded me of a sketch from which the "shading" has been omitted. She had her shadows indeed, as well as her lights;

but they were all turned inward. She might have seemed compounded of the airy substance of lights and shadows. Nature
in making her had left out that wholesome leaden ballast of
will, of logic, of worldly zeal, with which we are all more or
less weighted. Experience, however, had given her a burden to
carry; she was evidently sorrow-laden. She shifted the cruel
weight from shoulder to shoulder, she ached and sighed under it, and in the depths of her sweet natural smile you saw it
pressing the tears from her soul. Mrs. Garnyer's trouble, I
confess, was in my eyes an added charm. I was desperately
fond of a bit of romance, and as I was plainly never to have
one of my own, I made the most of my neighbor's. This secret sadness of hers would have covered more sins than I ever
had to forgive her. At first, naturally, I connected her unavowed sorrow with the death of her husband; but as time
went on, I found reason to believe that there had been little
love between the pair. She had married against her will. Mr.
Garnyer was fifteen years her senior, and, as she frankly intimated, coarsely and cruelly dissipated. Their married life had
lasted but three years, and had come to an end to her great
and obvious relief. Had he done her while it lasted some irreparable wrong? I fancied so; she was like a garden rose with
half its petals plucked. He had left her with diminished means,
though her property (mostly her own) was still ample for her
needs. These, with those of her son, were extremely simple.
To certain little luxuries she was obstinately attached; but her
manner of life was so monotonous and frugal that she must
have spent but a fraction of her income. It was her single
son—the heir of her hopes, the apple of her eye—that she intrusted to my care. He was five years old, and she had taught
him his letters—a great feat, she seemed to think; she was as
proud of it as if she had invented the alphabet for the occasion. She had called him Eustace, for she meant that he should
have the best of everything—the prettiest clothes, the prettiest playthings, and the prettiest name. He was himself as
pretty as his name, though but little like his mother. He was
slight like her, but far more nervous and decided, and he had
neither her features nor her coloring. Least of all had he her
expression. Mrs. Garnyer's attitude was one of tender, pensive
sufferance modified by hopes—a certain half-mystical hope

which seemed akin to religion, but which was not all religion, for the heaven she dreamed of was lodged here below. The boy from his early childhood wore an air of defiance and authority. He was not one to wait for things, good or evil, but to snatch boldly at the one sort and snap his fingers at the other. He had a pale, dark skin, not altogether healthy in tone; a mass of fine brown hair, which seemed given him just to emphasize by its dancing sweep the petulant little nods and shakes of his head; and a deep, wilful, malicious eye. His eyes told me from the first that I should have no easy work with him; and in spite of a vast expense of tact and tenderness, no easy work it turned out to be. His wits were so quick, however, and his imagination so lively, that I gradually managed to fill out his mother's meagre little programme of study. This had been drawn up with a sparing hand; her only fear was of his being overworked. The poor lady had but a dim conception of what a man of the world is expected to know. She thought, I believe, that with his handsome face, his handsome property, and his doting mother, he would need to know little more than how to sign that pretty name of Eustace to replies to invitations to dinners. I wonder now that with her constant interference I contrived to set the child intellectually on his legs. Later, when he had a tutor, I received a compliment for my perseverance.

The truth is, I became fond of him; his very imperfections fascinated me. He would soon enough have to take his chance of the world's tolerance, and society would cease to consist for him of a couple of coaxing women. I told Mrs. Garnyer that there was never an easier child to spoil, and that those caressing hands of hers would sow a crop of formidable problems for future years. But Mrs. Garnyer was utterly incapable of taking a rational view of matters, or of sacrificing to-day to to-morrow; and her folly was the more incurable as it was founded on a strange, moonshiny little principle—a crude, passionate theory that love, love, pure love is the sum and substance of maternal duty; and that the love which reasons and exacts and denies is cruel and wicked and hideous. "I know you think I'm a silly goose," she said, "and not fit to have a child at all. But you're wrong—I promise you you're wrong. I'm very reasonable, I'm very patient; I have a great deal to bear—more than you know—and I bear it very well. But one can't be always on the stretch—always hard and wise and good. In some things one must break down and be one's poor, natural, lonely self. Eustace can't turn out wrong; it's impossible; it would be too cruel. You mustn't say it nor hint it. I shall do with him as my heart bids me; he's all I have; he consoles me."

My notions perhaps were a little old-fashioned; but surely it will never altogether go out of fashion to teach a child that he is not to have the moon by crying for it. Now Eustace had a particular fancy for the moon—for everything bright and inaccessible and absurd. His will was as sharp as a steel spring, and it was vain to attempt to bend it or break it. He had an indefeasible conviction that he was number one among men; and if he had been born in the purple, as they say, of some far-off Eastern court, or the last consummate fruit of a shadowy line of despots, he couldn't have been more closely curtained in this superb illusion. I pierced it here and there as roughly as I dared; but his mother's light fingers speedily repaired my punctures. The poor child had no sense of justice. He had the graceful virtues, but not the legal ones. He could condescend, he could forgive, he could permit this, that, and the other, with due leave asked; but he couldn't endure the hint of conflicting right. Poor puny little mortal, sitting there wrapped in his golden mist, listening to the petty trickle of his conscious favor and damming it—a swelling fountain of privileges! He could love, love passionately; but he was so jealous and exacting that his love cost you very much more than it was worth. I found it no sinecure to possess the confidence I had striven so cunningly to obtain. He fancied it a very great honor that he should care to harness me up as his horse, to throw me his ball by the hour, to have me joggle with him (sitting close to the middle) on the see-saw till my poor bones ached. Nevertheless, in this frank, childish arrogance there was an almost irresistible charm, and I was absurdly flattered by enjoying his favor. Poor me! at twenty-three I was his first "conquest"—the first in a long list, as I believe it came to be. If he demanded great license, he used it with a peculiar grace of his own, and he admitted the corresponding obligation of being clever and brilliant. As a child even, he seemed to be in a sort

of occult sympathy with the picturesque. His talents were excellent, and teaching him, whatever it may have been, was at
least not dull work. It was indeed less to things really needful
than to the luxuries of learning that he took most kindly. He
had an excellent ear for music, and though he never fairly
practised, he turned off an air as neatly as you could have
wished. In this he resembled his mother, who was a natural
musician. She, however, was always at the piano, and whenever I think of her in those early years, I see her sitting before
it musingly, half sadly, with her pretty head on one side, her
fair braids thrust behind her ears—ears from which a couple of
small but admirable diamonds were never absent—and her
white hands wandering over the notes, seeking vaguely for an
air which they seemed hardly to dare to remember. Eustace
had an insatiable appetite for stories, though he was one of
the coolest and most merciless of critics. I can fancy him now
at my knee with his big, superbly-expectant eyes fastened on
my lips, demanding more wonders and more, till my poor
little short-winded invention had to cry mercy for its impotence. Do my best, I could never startle him; my giants were
never big enough and my fairies never small enough, and my
enchanters, my prisoners, my castles never on the really grand
scale of his own imaginative needs. I felt pitifully prosaic. At
last he would always open his wilful little mouth and gape in
my face with a dreadfully dry want of conviction. I felt flattered when by chance I had pleased him, for, by a precocious
instinct, he knew tinsel from gold. "Look here," he would say,
"you're dreadfully ugly; what makes you so ugly? Your nose is
so big at the end." (You needn't protest; I *was* ugly. Like most
very plain women, I have improved with time.) Of course I
used to rebuke him for his rudeness, though I secretly
thanked it, for it taught me a number of things. Once he said
something, I forget what, which made me burst into tears. It
was the first time, and the last; for I found that, instead of stirring his pity, tears only moved his contempt, and apparently a
kind of cynical, physical disgust. The best way was to turn the
tables on him by pretending to be cool and indifferent and superior. In that case he himself would condescend to tears—
bitter, wrathful tears. Then you had perhaps gained nothing,
but you had lost nothing. In every other case you had.

Of course these close relations lasted but a couple of years. I had made him very much wiser than myself; he was growing tall and boyish and terribly inquisitive. My poor little stories ceased to have any illusion for him; and he would spend hours lying on his face on the carpet, kicking up his neat little legs and poring over the "Arabian Nights," the "Fairy Queen," the dozen prime enchanters of childhood. My advice would have been to pack him off to school; but I might as well have asked his mother to send him to the penitentiary. He was to be educated *en prince*; he was to have a teacher to himself. I thought sympathetically of the worthy pedagogue who was to enjoy Eustace without concurrence. But such a one was easily found—in fact, he was found three times over. Three private tutors came and went successively. They fell in love, categorically, with Mrs. Garnyer. Their love indeed she might have put up with; but unhappily, unlike Viola, they told their love—by letter—with an offer of their respective hands. Their letters were different, but to Mrs. Garnyer their hands were all alike, and alike distasteful. "The horrid creatures!" was her invariable commentary. "I wouldn't speak to them for the world. My dear, you must do it." And I, who had never declined an offer on my own account, went to work in this wholesale fashion for my friend! You will say that young as she was, pretty, independent, lovely, Mrs. Garnyer would have looked none the worse for a spice of coquetry. Nay, in her own eyes, she would have been hideous. Her greatest charm for me was a brave little passion of scorn for this sort of levity, and indeed a general contempt for cheap sentimental effects. It was as if, from having drunk at the crystal head-spring, she had lost her taste for standing water. She was absolutely indifferent to attention; in fact, she seemed to shrink from it. She hadn't a trace of personal vanity; she was even without visible desire to please. Unfortunately, as you see, she pleased in spite of herself. As regards love, she had an imposing array of principles; on this one point her floating imagination found anchorage. "It's either a passion," she said, "or it's nothing. You can know it by being willing to give up everything for it—name and fame, past and future, this world and the next. Do you keep back a feather's weight of tenderness or trust? Then you're not in love. You must risk everything, for you

get everything—if you're happy. I can't understand a woman
trifling with love. They talk about the unpardonable sin;
that's it, it seems to me. Do you know the word in the language I most detest? *Flirtation.* Poh! it makes me ill." When
Mrs. Garnyer uttered this hint of an esoteric doctrine, her
clear blue eyes would become clouded with the gathered
mists of memory. In this matter she understood herself and
meant what she said.

Defiant as she was of admiration, she saw little of the
world. She met her few friends but two or three times a year,
and was without a single intimate. As time went on, she came
to care more for me than for any one. When Eustace had out-
grown my teaching, she insisted on my remaining in any
capacity I chose—as housekeeper, companion, seamstress,
guest; I might make my own terms. I became a little of each
of these, and with the increasing freedom of our intercourse
grew to regard her as a younger and weaker sister. I gave her,
for what it was worth, my frankest judgment on all things.
Her own confidence always stopped short of a certain point.
A little curtain of reticence seemed always to hang between
us. Sometimes I fancied it growing thinner and thinner, becoming almost transparent and revealing the figures behind it.
Sometimes it seemed to move and flutter in the murmur of
our talk, so that in a moment it might drop or melt away into
air. But it was a magical web; it played a hundred tormenting
tricks, and year after year it hung in its place. Of course this
inviolate mystery stirred my curiosity, but I can't say more for
the disinterested tenderness I felt for Mrs. Garnyer than that
it never unduly irritated it. I lingered near the door of her
Blue-Beard's chamber, but I never peeped through the keyhole. She was a poor lady with a secret; I took her into my
heart, secret and all. She proclaimed that her isolation was her
own choice, and pretended to be vastly content that society
let her so well alone. She made her widowhood serve as a motive for her lonesome days, and declared that her boy's education amply filled them. She was a widow, however, who
never of her own accord mentioned her husband's name, and
she wore her weeds very lightly. She was very fond of white,
and for six months of the year was rarely seen in a dark dress.
Occasionally, on certain fixed days, she would flame forth in

some old-fashioned piece of finery from a store which she religiously preserved, and would flash about the house in rose-color or blue. One day, her boy's birthday, she kept with fantastic solemnity. It fell in the middle of September. On this occasion she would put on a faded ball-dress, overload herself with jewels and trinkets, and dress her hair with flowers. Eustace, too, she would trick out in a suit of crimson velvet, and in this singular guise the pair would walk with prodigious gravity about the garden and up and down the avenue. Every now and then she would stoop and give him a convulsive hug. The child himself seemed to feel the magnitude of this festival, and played his part with precocious discretion. He would appear at dark with the curl still in his hair, his velvet trousers unstained, his ruffles uncrumpled. In the evening the coachman let off rockets in the garden; we feasted on ice-cream, and a bottle of champagne was sent to the kitchen. No wonder Master Eustace took on the graces of an heir-apparent! Once, I remember, the mother and son were overtaken in their festal promenade by some people who had come to live in the neighborhood, and who drove up rather officiously to leave their cards. They stared in amazement from the carriage window, and were told Mrs. Garnyer was not at home. A few days later we heard that Mrs. Garnyer was out of her mind; she had been found masquerading in her grounds with her little boy, in the most indecent costume. From time to time she received an invitation, and occasionally she accepted one. When she went out she deepened her mourning, but she always came home in a fret. "It is the last house I will go to," she declared, as I helped her to undress. "People's neglect I can bear, and thank them for it; but Heaven deliver me from their kindness! I won't be patronized—I won't, I won't! Shall I, my boy? We'll wait till you grow up, shan't we, my darling? Then his poor little mother shan't be patronized, shall she, my brave little man?" The child was constantly dangling at his mother's skirts, and was seldom beyond the reach of some such passionate invocation.

A preceptor had at last been found of a less inflammable composition than the others—a worthy, elderly German of fair attainments, with a stout, sentimental wife—she gave music lessons in town—who monopolized his ardors. He was a

mild, patient man—a nose of wax, as the saying is. A pretty
nose it grew to be in Eustace's supple fingers! I'll answer for
it that in all those years he never carried a point. I believe
that, like me, he had begun with tears; but finding this an altogether losing game, he was content now to take off his
spectacles, drop his head on one side, look imploringly at his
pupil with his weak blue eyes, and then exhale his renunciation in a plaintive *Lieber Gott!* Under this discipline the boy
bloomed like a flower. But it was to my sense a kind of hot-
house growth. His tastes were sedentary, and he lived largely
within doors. He kept a horse and took long lonely rides; but
most of the time he spent lounging over a book, trifling at the
piano, or fretting over a water-color sketch, which he was sure
to throw aside in disgust. One amusement he pursued with
unwearying constancy; it was a sign of especial good humor,
and I never knew it to fail him. He would sit for hours lounging in a chair, with his head thrown back and his legs extended, staring at vacancy, or what seemed to us so, but a
vacancy filled with the silent revel of his fancy and the images
it evoked. What was the substance of these beatific visions?
The broad, happy life before him, the great world whose far-
off murmurs caressed his ear—the joys of consummate manhood—pleasure, success, prosperity—a kind of triumphant
and transfigured egotism. His reveries swarmed with ideal
shapes and transcendent delights; his handsome young face,
his idle, insolent smile were the cold reflections of their
brightness. His mother, after watching him for a while in
these moods, would steal up behind him and kiss him softly
on the forehead, as if to marry his sweet illusions to sweet reality. For my part, I wanted to divorce them. It was a sad pity,
I thought, that desire and occasion in the lad's life played so
deftly into each other's hands. I longed to spoil the game, to
shuffle the cards afresh and give him a taste of bad luck. I felt
as if between them—she by her measureless concessions, he
by his consuming arrogance—they were sowing a crop of
dragon's teeth. This sultry summer of youth couldn't last for
ever, and I knew that the poor lady would be the first to suffer by a change of weather. He would turn some day in his
passionate vanity and rend the gentle creature who had fed it
with the delusive wine of her love. And yet he had a better

angel as well as a worse. It was a marvel to see how this sturdy
seraph tussled with the fiends, and, in spite of bruises and ruffled pinions, returned again and again to the onset. There
were days when his generous, boyish gayety—the natural sunshine of youth and intelligence—warmed our women's hearts
to their depths and kindled our most trusting smiles. Me, as
he grew older, he treated as a licensed old-time friend. I was
the prince's jester. I used to tell him his truths, as the French
say. He believed them just enough to feel an agreeable irritation in listening; for the rest, doubtless, they seemed as vague
and remote as a croaking good-wife's gossip. There were moments, I think, when the eternal blue sky of his mother's temper wearied his capricious brain. At such times he would come
and sprawl on the sofa near my little work-table, clipping my
threads, mixing my spools, mislaying my various utensils, and
criticising my work without reserve—chattering, gossiping,
complaining, boasting. With all his faults Eustace had one
sovereign merit—that merit without which even the virtues
he lacked lose half their charms: he was superbly frank. He
was only too transparent. The light of truth played through
his rank pretensions, and against it they stood relieved in this
hard tenacity, like young trees against a sunset. He uttered his
passions, and uttered them only too loudly; you received ample notice of his vengeance. It came as a matter of course; he
never took it out in talk; but you were warned.

If these intense meditations of which I have spoken followed exclusively the vista of his personal fortunes, his conversation was hardly more disinterested. It was altogether
about himself—his ambitions, his ailments, his dreams, his
needs, his intentions. He talked a great deal of his property,
and, though he had a great aversion to figures, he knew the
amount of his expectations before he was out of jackets. He
had a shrewd relish for luxury—and indeed, as he respected
pretty things and used them with a degree of tenderness
which he by no means lavished upon animated objects, saving, sparing, and preserving them, this seemed to me one of
his most human traits, though, I admit, an expensive virtue—
and he promised to spend his fortune in books and pictures,
in art and travel. His mother was imperiously appealed to to
do the honors of his castles in the air. She would look at him

always with her doting smile, and with a little glow of melancholy in her eyes—a faint tribute to some shadowy chance
that even her Eustace might reckon without his host. She
would shake her head tenderly, or lean it on his shoulder and
murmur, "Who knows, who knows? It's perhaps as foolish,
my son, to try and forecast happiness as to attempt to take the
measure of misery. We know them each when they come.
Whatever comes to us, at all events, we shall meet it together." Resting in this delicious contact, with her arm round
his neck and her cheek on his hair, she would close her eyes
in a kind of tremor of ecstasy. As I have never had a son myself, I can speak of maternity but by hearsay; but I feel as if I
knew some of its secrets, as if I had gained from Mrs. Garnyer
a revelation of maternal passion. The perfect humility of her
devotion, indeed, seemed to me to point to some motive
deeper than vulgar motherhood. It looked like a kind of
penance, a kind of pledge. Had she done him some early
wrong? Did she meditate some wrong to come? Did she wish
to purchase pardon for the past or impunity for the future?
One might have fancied from the lad's calm relish of her incense—as if it were the fumes of some perfumed chibouque
palpitating lazily through his own lips—that he had a comfortable sense of something to forgive. In fact, he had something to forgive us all—our dulness, our vulgarity, our not
guessing his unuttered desires—the want of a supercelestial
harmony between our wills and his. I fancied, however, that
there were even moments when he turned dizzy on the cope
of this awful gulf of his mother's self-sacrifice. Fixing his eyes,
then, an instant to steady himself, he took comfort in the
thought that she had ceased to suffer—her personal ambitions
lay dead at the bottom. He could vaguely see them—distant,
dim, motionless. It was to be hoped that no adventurous
ghost of these shuffled passions would climb upward to the
light.

A frequent source of complaint with Eustace, when he had
no more immediate displeasure, was that he had not known
his father. He had formed a mental image of the late Mr.
Garnyer which I am afraid hardly tallied at all points with
the original. He knew that his father had been a man of pleasure, and he had painted his portrait in ideal hues. What a

charming father—a man of pleasure! the boy thought, fancying that gentlemen of this stamp take their pleasure in the
nursery. What pleasure they might have shared; what rides,
what talks, what games, what adventures—what far other
hours than those he passed in the deserted billiard-room (this
had been one of Mr. Garnyer's pleasures) clicking the idle
balls in the stillness. He learned to talk very early of shaping
his life on his father's. What he had done his son would do. A
dozen odds and ends which had belonged to Mr. Garnyer he
carried to his room, where he arranged them on his mantel-
shelf like relics on a high altar. When he had turned seventeen
he began to smoke an old silver-mounted pipe which had his
father's initials embossed on the bowl. "It would be a great
blessing," he said as he puffed this pipe—it made him dismally sick, for he hated tobacco—"to have some man in the
house. It's so fearfully womanish here. No one but you two
and Hauff, and what's he but an old woman? Mother, why
have you always lived in this way? What's the matter with
you? You've got no *savoir vivre*. What are you blushing
about? That comes of moping here all your days—that you
blush for nothing. I don't want my mother to blush for anything or any one, not even for me. But I give you notice, I
can stand it no longer. Now I'm seventeen, it's time I should
see the world. I'm going to travel. My father travelled; he
went all over Europe. There's a little French book up stairs,
the poems of Parny—it's awfully French, too—with 'Henry
Garnyer, Paris, 1802,' on the fly-leaf. I must go to Paris. I
shan't go to college. I've never been to school. I want to be
complete—privately educated altogether. Very few people
are, here; it's quite a distinction. Besides, I know all I want
to know. Hauff brought me out some college catalogues.
They're absurd; he laughs at them. We did all that three years
ago. I know more about books than most young fellows;
what I want is knowledge of the world. My father had it, and
you haven't, mother. But he had plenty of taste, too. Hauff
says that little edition of Parny is very rare. I shall bring home
lots of such things. You'll see!" Mrs. Garnyer listened to such
effusions of filial emulation in sad, distracted silence. I couldn't
but pity her. She knew that her husband was no proper
model for her child; yet she couldn't in decency turn his heart

against his father's memory. She took refuge in that attitude of tremulous contemplation which committed her neither to condemnation of her husband nor to approval with her son.

She had recourse at this period, as I had known her to do before, to a friend attached to a mercantile house in India—an old friend, she had told me; "in fact," she had added, "my only friend, a man to whom I am under immense obligations." Once in six months there came to her from this distant benefactor a large square letter, heavily sealed and covered with foreign post-marks. I used to fancy it a kind of bulletin of advice for the coming half year. Advice about what? Her cares were so few, her habits so simple, that they offered scanty matter for discussion. But now, of course, came a packet of counsel as to Eustace's absence. I knew that she dreaded it; but since her oracle had spoken, she wore a brave face. She was certainly a devout postulant. She concealed from Eustace the extent of her dependence on this far-away adviser, for the boy would have resented such interference, even though it favored his own schemes. She had always read her friend's letters in secret; this was the only practice of her life she failed to share with her son. Me she now for the first time admitted into her confidence. "Mr. Cope strongly recommends my letting him go," she said. "He says it will make a man of him. He needs to rub against other men. I suppose at least," she cried with her usual sweet fatuity, "it will do other men no harm! Perhaps I don't love him as I ought, and that I must lose him awhile to learn to prize him. If I only get him back again! It would be monstrous that I shouldn't! But why are we cursed with these frantic woes and fears? It's a weary life!" She would have said more if she had known that it was not his departure but his return that was to be cruel.

The excellent Mr. Hauff was deemed too mild and infirm to cope with the hazards of travel; but a companion was secured in the person of his nephew, an amiable young German who claimed to possess erudition and discretion in equal manner. For a week before he left us Eustace was so serene and joyous of humor as to double his mother's sense of loss. "I give her into your care," he said to me. "If anything happens to her, I shall hold you responsible. She is very woebegone just now, but she'll cheer up yet. But, mother, you're not to be too cheerful, mind. You're not to forget me an instant. If you do, I'll never forgive you. I insist on being missed. There's little enough merit in loving me when I'm here; I wish to be loved in my absence." For many weeks after he left, he might have been satisfied. His mother wandered about like a churchyard ghost keeping watch near a buried treasure. When his letters began to come, she read them over a dozen times, and sat for hours with her eyes closed holding them in her hand. They were wretchedly meagre and hurried; but their very brevity gratified her. He was prosperous and happy, and could snatch but odd moments from his pleasure-taking.

One morning, after he had been away some three months, there came two letters, one from Eustace, the other from India, the latter very much in advance of its time. Mrs. Garnyer opened the Indian letter first. I was pouring out tea; I observed her from behind the urn. As her eyes ran over the pages she turned deadly pale; then raising her glance she met mine. Immediately her paleness turned to crimson. She rose to her feet and hurried out of the room, leaving Eustace's letter untouched on the table. This little fact was eloquent, and my curiosity was aroused. Later in the day it was partially satisfied. She came to me with a singular conscious look—the look of a sort of oppression of happiness—and announced that Mr. Cope was coming home. He had obtained release from his engagements in India, and would arrive in a fortnight. She uttered herewith no words of rejoicing, but I fancied her joy was of the unutterable sort. As the days elapsed, however, her emotion betrayed itself in a restless, aimless flutter of movement, so intense as to seem to me almost painful. She roamed about the house singing to herself, gazing out of the windows, shifting the chairs and tables, smoothing the curtains, trying vaguely to brighten the faded look of things. Before every mirror she paused and inspected herself, with that frank audacity of pretty women which I have always envied, tucking up a curl of her blond hair or smoothing a crease in those muslins which she always kept so fresh. Of Eustace for the moment she rarely spoke; the boy's prediction had not been so very much amiss. Who was this wonderful Mr. Cope, this mighty magician?

I very soon learned. He arrived on the day he had fixed, and took up his lodging in the house. From the moment I looked at him, I felt that here was a man I should like. My poor unflattered soul, I suppose, was won by the kindness of his greeting. He had often heard of me, he said; he knew how good a friend I had been to Mrs. Garnyer; he begged to bespeak a proportionate friendship for himself. I felt as if I were amply thanked for my years of household zeal. But in spite of this pleasant assurance, I had a sense of being for the moment altogether *de trop*. He was united to his friend by a closer bond than I had suspected. I left them alone with their mutual secrets and effusions, and confined myself to my own room; though indeed I had noticed between them a sort of sentimental intelligence, so deep and perfect that many words were exchanged without audible speech. Mrs. Garnyer underwent a singular change; I seemed to know her now for the first time. It was as if she had flung aside a veil which muffled her tones and blurred her features. There was a new decision in her tread, a deeper meaning in her smile. So, at thirty-eight her girlhood had come back to her! She was as full of blushes and random prattle and foolish falterings for very pleasure as a young bride. Upon Mr. Cope the years had set a more ineffaceable seal. He was a man of forty-five, but you would have given him ten years more. He had that look which I have always liked of people who have lived in hot climates, a bronzed complexion, and a cool deliberate gait, as if he had learned to think twice before moving. He was tall and lean, yet extremely massive in shape, like a stout man emaciated by circumstances. His hair was thin and perfectly white, and he wore a grizzled moustache. He dressed in loose light-colored garments of those fine Eastern stuffs. I had a singular impression of having seen him before, but I could never say when or where. He was extremely deaf—so deaf that I had to force my voice; though I observed that Mrs. Garnyer easily made him hear by speaking slowly and looking at him. He had peculiarly that patient appealing air which you find in very deaf persons less frequently than in the blind, but which has with them an even deeper eloquence, enforced as it is by the normal pathos of the eye. It has an especially mild dignity where, as in Mr. Cope, it overlies a truly masculine mind. He had been obliged to make good company of himself, and the glimpses that one got of this blessed fellowship in stillness were of a kind to make one long to share it. But with others, too, he was a charming talker, though he was obliged to keep the talk in his own hands. He took your response for granted with a kind of conciliating *bonhomie*, guessed with a glance at your opinion, and phrased it usually more wittily than you would have done.

For ten years I had been pitying Mrs. Garnyer; it was odd to find myself envying her. Patient waiting is no loss; at last her day had come. I had always rather wondered at her patience; it was spiced with a logic all its own. But she had lived by precept and example, by chapter and verse; for *his* sake it was easy to be wise. I say for "his" sake, because as a matter of course I now connected her visitor with that undefined secret which had been one of my earliest impressions of Mrs. Garnyer. Mr. Cope's presence renewed my memory of it. I fitted the key to the lock, but on coming to open the casket I was disappointed to find that the best of the mystery had evaporated. Mr. Cope, I imagined, had been her first and only love. Her parents had frowned on him and forced her into a marriage with poor dissolute Mr. Garnyer—a course the more untender as he had already spent half his own property and was likely to make sad havoc with his wife's. He had a high social value, which the girl's own family, who were plain enough people to have had certain primitive scruples in larger measure, deemed a compensation for his vices. The discarded lover, thinking she had not resisted as firmly as she might, embarked for India, and there, half in spite, half in despair, married as sadly amiss as herself. She had trifled with his happiness; he lived to repent. His wife lived as well to perpetuate his misery; it was my belief that she had only recently died, and that this event was the occasion of his return. When he arrived he wore a weed on his hat; the next day it had disappeared. Reunion had come to them in the afternoon of life, when the tricks and graces of passion are no longer becoming; but when these have spent themselves something of passion still is left, and this they were free to enjoy. They had begun to enjoy it with the chastened zeal of which I caught the aroma. Such was my reading of the riddle. Right or not, at least it made sense.

I had promised Eustace to write to him, and one afternoon as I sat alone, well pleased to have a theme, I despatched him a long letter full of the praises of Mr. Cope, and by implication of the echo of his mother's happiness. I wished to anticipate his possible suspicions and reconcile him with the altered situation. But after I had posted my letter, it seemed to me that I had spoken too frankly. I doubted whether, even amid the wholesome novelty of travel, he had unlearned the old trick of jealousy. Jealousy surely would have been quite misplaced, for Mr. Cope's affection for his hostess embraced her boy in its ample scope. He regretted the lad's absence; he manifested the kindliest interest in everything that spoke of him; he turned over his books, he looked at his sketches, he examined and compared the half dozen portraits which the fond mother had caused to be executed at various stages of his growth. One hot day, when poor old Mr. Hauff travelled out from town for news of his pupil, he made a point of being introduced and of shaking his hand. The old man stayed to dinner, and on Mr. Cope's proposition we drank the boy's health in brimming glasses. The old German of course wept profusely; it was Eustace's mission to make people cry. I fancied too I saw a tear on Mr. Cope's lid. The cup of his contentment was full; at a touch it overflowed. On the whole, however, he took this bliss of reunion more quietly than his friend. He was a melancholy man. He had the air of one for whom the moral of this fable of life has greater charms than the plot, and who has made up his mind to ask no favors of destiny. When he met me, he used to smile gently, frankly, saying little; but I had a vast relish for his smile. It seemed to say much—to murmur, "Receive my compliments. You and I are a couple of tested souls; we understand each other. We are not agog with the privileges of existence, like charity children on a picnic. We have had, each of us, to live for years without the thing we once fancied gave life its only value. We have tasted of bondage, and patience, taken up as a means, has grown grateful as an end. It has cured us of eagerness." So easily it gossiped, the smile of our guest. No wonder I liked it.

One evening, a month after his advent, Mrs. Garnyer came to me with a strange, embarrassed smile. "I have something to tell you," she said; "something that will surprise you. Do you consider me a very old woman? I am old enough to be wiser, you'll say. But I've never been so wise as to-day. I'm engaged to Mr. Cope. There! make the best of it. I have no apologies to make to any one," she went on with a kind of defiant manner. "It's between ourselves. If we suit each other, it's no one's business. I know what I'm about. He means to remain in this country; we should be constantly together and extremely intimate. As he says, I'm young enough to be— what do they call it?—compromised. Of course, therefore, I'm young enough to marry. It will make no difference with you; you'll stay with me all the same. Who cares, after all, what I do? No one but Eustace, and he will thank me for giving him such a father. Ah, I shall do well by my boy!" she cried, clasping her hands with ecstasy. "I shall do better than he knows. My property, it appears, is dreadfully entangled. Mr. Garnyer did as he pleased with it; I was given to him with my hands tied. Mr. Cope has been looking into it, and he tells me that it will be a long labor to restore order. I have been living all these years at the mercy of unprincipled strangers. But now I have given up everything to Mr. Cope. *He*'ll drive the money-changers from the temple! It's a small reward to marry him. Eustace has no head for money matters; he only knows how to spend. For years now he needn't think of them. Mr. Cope is our providence. Don't be afraid; Eustace won't blaspheme! and at last he'll have a companion—the best, the wisest, the kindest. You know how he used to long for one—how tired he was of me and you. It will be a new life. Oh, I'm a happy mother—at last—at last! Don't look at me so hard; I'm a blushing bride, remember. Smile, laugh, kiss me. There! You're a good creature. I shall make my boy a present—the handsomest that ever was made! Poor Mr. Cope! I'm happier than he. I have had my boy all these years, and he has had none. He has the heart of a father. He has longed for a son. Do you know," she added with a strange deepening of her smile, "that I think he marries me as much for my son's sake as for my own? He marries me at all events, boy and all!" This speech was uttered with a forced and hurried animation which betrayed the effort to cheat herself into pure enthusiasm. The matter was not quite so simple as she tried to believe. Nevertheless, I was deeply pleased, and I kissed her in genuine sympathy. The more I thought of it the better I liked the marriage. It relieved me personally of a burdensome sense of ineffectual care, and it filled out solidly a kind of defenceless breach which had always existed on the worldly face of Mrs. Garnyer's position. Moreover, it promised to be full of wholesome profit for Eustace. It was a pity that Eustace had but a slender relish for wholesome profit. I ventured to hope, however, that his high esteem for his father's memory had been, at bottom, the expression of a need for counsel and support, and of a capacity to grant respect if there should be something of inspiration in it. Yet I took the liberty of suggesting to Mrs. Garnyer that she perhaps counted too implicitly on her son's concurrence; that he was always in opposition; that a margin should be left for his possible jealousy. Of course I was called a suspicious wretch for my pains.

"For what do you take him?" she cried. "He'll thank me on his knees. I shall place them face to face. Eustace has instinct! A word to the wise, says the proverb. I know what I'm about."

She knew it, I think, hardly as well as she declared. I had deemed it my duty to make a modest little speech of congratulation to the bridegroom elect. He blushed—somewhat to my surprise—but he answered me with a grave, grateful bow. He was preoccupied; Mrs. Garnyer was of a dozen different minds about her wedding-day. I had taken for granted that they would wait for Eustace's return; but I was somewhat startled on learning that Mr. Cope disapproved of further delay. They had waited twenty years! Mrs. Garnyer told me that she had not announced the news to Eustace. She wished it to be a "surprise." She seemed, however, not altogether to believe in her surprise. Poor lady! she had made herself a restless couch. One evening, coming into the library, I found Mr. Cope pleading his cause. For the first time I saw him excited. This hint of autumnal ardor was very becoming. He turned appealingly to me. "You have great authority with this lady," he said. "Plead my case. Are we people to care for Mrs.

Grundy? Has she been so very civil to us? We don't marry to
please her; I don't see why she should arrange the wedding.
Mrs. Garnyer has no *trousseau* to buy, no cards to send. Indeed, I think any more airs and graces are rather ridiculous.
They don't belong to our years. There's little Master Grundy,
I know," he went on, smiling—"a most honorable youth! But
I'll take charge of him. I should like vastly, of course, to have
him at the wedding; but one of these days I shall make up for
the breach of ceremony by punctually attending his own." It
was only an hour before this, as it happened, that I had received Eustace's answer to my letter. It was brief and hasty, but
he had found time to insert some such words as this: "I don't
at all thank you for your news of Mr. Cope. I knew that my
mother only wanted a chance to forget me and console herself,
as they say in France. Demonstrative mothers always do. I'm
like Hamlet—I don't approve of mothers consoling themselves. Mr. Cope may be an excellent fellow—I've no doubt he
is; but I do hope he will have made his visit by the time I get
back. The house isn't large enough for both of us. You'll find
me a bigger man than when I left home. I give you warning.
I've got a roaring black moustache, and I'm proportionately
fiercer." I said nothing about this letter. A week later they were
married. The time will always be memorable to me, apart from
this matter of my story, from the intense and overwhelming
heat which then prevailed. It had lasted several days when the
wedding took place; it bade fair to continue unbroken. The
ceremony was performed by the little old Episcopal clergyman
whose ministrations Mrs. Garnyer had regularly attended, and
who had always given her a vague parochial countenance. His
sister, a mature spinster who wore her hair cut short, and
called herself "strong-minded," and, thus qualified, had made
overtures to Mrs. Garnyer—this lady and myself were the only
witnesses. The marriage had nothing of a festive air; it seemed
a grave sacrifice to the unknown god. Mrs. Garnyer was very
much oppressed by the heat; in the vestibule, on leaving the
church, she fainted. They had arranged to go for a week to the
seaside, to a place they had known of old. When she had revived we placed her in the carriage, and they immediately
started. I, of course, remained in charge of the empty house,
vastly envying them their seaside breezes.

On the morning after the wedding, sitting alone in the darkened library, I heard a rapid tread in the hall. My first thought of course was of burglars—my second of Eustace. In a moment he came striding into the room. His step, his glance, his whole outline foretold trouble. He was amazingly changed, and all for the better. He seemed taller, older, manlier. He was bronzed by travel and dressed with great splendor. The moustache he had mentioned, though but a slender thing as yet, gave him, to my eye, a formidable foreign look. He gave me no greeting.

"Where's my mother?" he cried.

My heart rose to my throat; his tone seemed to put us horribly in the wrong. "She's away—for a day," I said. "But you"—and I took his hand—"pray where have you dropped from?"

"From New York, from shipboard, from Southampton. Is this the way my mother receives me?"

"Why, she never dreamed you were coming."

"She got no letter? I wrote from New York."

"Your letter never came. She left town yesterday, for a week."

He looked at me hard. "How comes it you're not with her?"

"I am not needed. She has—she has——" But I faltered.

"Say it—say it!" he cried; and he stamped his foot. "She has a companion."

"Mr. Cope went with her," I said, in a still small voice. I was ashamed of my tremor, I was outraged by his imperious manner, but the thought of worse to come unnerved me.

"Mr. Cope—ah!" he answered, with an indefinable accent. He looked about the room with a kind of hungry desire to detect some invidious difference as a trace of Mr. Cope's passage. Then flinging himself into a chair, "What infernal heat!" he went on. "What a hideous climate you've got here! Do bring me a glass of water."

I brought him his glass, and stood before him as he quickly drank it. "Don't think you're not welcome," I ventured to say, "if I ask what has brought you home so suddenly."

He gave me another hard look over the top of his glass. "A suspicion. It's none too soon. Tell me what is going on between my mother and Mr. Cope."

"Eustace," I said, "before I answer you, let me remind you of the respect which under all circumstances you owe your mother."

He sprang from his chair. "Respect! I'm right then. They mean to marry! Speak!" And as I hesitated, "You needn't speak," he cried. "I see it in your face. Thank God I'm here!"

His violence aroused me. "If you have a will to enforce in the matter," I said, "you are indeed none too soon. You're too late. Your mother is married." I spoke passionately, but in a moment I repented of my words.

"MARRIED!" the poor boy shouted. "*Married*, you say!" He turned deadly pale and stood staring at me with his mouth wide open. Then, trembling in all his limbs, he dropped into a chair. For some moments he was silent, gazing at me with fierce stupefaction, overwhelmed by the treachery of fate. "Married!" he went on. "When, where, how? Without me—without notice—without shame! And you stood and watched it, as you stand and tell me now! I called you friend!" he cried, with the bitterest reproach. "But if my mother betrays me, what can I expect of *you*? Married!" he repeated. "Is the devil in it? I'll unmarry her! When—when—when?" And he seized me by the arm.

"Yesterday, Eustace. I entreat you to be calm."

"Calm? Is it a case for calmness? *She* was calm enough—that she couldn't wait for her son!" He flung aside the hand I had laid upon his to soothe him, and began a furious march about the room. "What has come to her? Is she mad? Has she lost her head, her heart, her memory—all that made her mine? You're joking—come, it's a horrible dream?" And he stopped before me, glaring through fiery tears. "Did she hope to keep it a secret? Did she hope to hide away her husband in a cupboard? Her husband! And I—I—I—what has she done with me? Where am I in this devil's game? Standing here crying like a schoolboy for a cut finger—for the bitterest of disappointments! She has blighted my life—she has blasted my rights. She has insulted me—dishonored me. Am I a man to treat in that fashion? Am I a man to be made light of? Brought up as a flower and trampled as a weed! Bound in cotton and steeped in vitriol! You needn't speak"—I had tried, for pity, to remonstrate. "You can say nothing but bald folly. There's

nothing to be said but this—that I'm *insulted*. Do you understand?" He uttered the word with a concentrated agony of
vanity. "I guessed it from the first. I knew it was coming. Mr.
Cope—Mr. Cope—always Mr. Cope. It poisoned my journey—it poisoned my pleasure—it poisoned Italy. You don't
know what that means. But what matter, so long as it has poisoned my home? I held my tongue—I swallowed my rage; I
was patient, I was gentle, I forbore. And for this! I could have
damned him with a word! At the seaside, hey? Enjoying the
breezes—splashing in the surf—picking up shells. It's idyllic,
it's ideal—great heavens, it's fabulous, it's monstrous! It's well
she's not here. I don't answer for myself. Yes, madam, stare,
stare, wring your hands! You see an angry man, an outraged
man, but a man, mind you! He means to act as one."

This sweeping torrent of unreason I had vainly endeavored
to arrest. He pushed me aside, strode out of the room, and
went bounding up stairs to his own chamber, where I heard
him close the door with a terrible bang and turn the key. My
hope was that his passion would expend itself in this first explosion; I was glad to bear the brunt of it. But I deemed it my
duty to communicate with his mother. I wrote her a hurried
line: "Eustace is back—very ill. Come home." This I intrusted
to the coachman, with injunctions to carry it in person to the
place of her sojourn. I believed that if she started immediately
on the receipt of it, she might reach home late at night.
Those were days of private conveyances. Meanwhile I did my
best to pacify the poor young man. There was something terrible and portentous in his rage; he seemed absolutely rabid.
This was the sweet compliance, the fond assent, on which his
mother had counted; this was the "surprise"! I went repeatedly to his chamber door with soft speeches and urgent
prayers and offers of luncheon, of wine, of vague womanly
comfort. But there came no answer but shouts and imprecations, and finally a sullen silence. Late in the day I heard him
from the window order the gardener to saddle his horse; and
in a short time he came stamping down stairs, booted and
spurred, pale, dishevelled, with bloodshot eyes. "Where are
you going," I said, "in this awful heat?"

"To ride—ride—ride myself cool!" he cried. "There's nothing so hot as my rage!" And in a moment he was in the saddle

and bounding out of the gate. I went up to his room. Its wild disorder bore vivid evidence of the tumult of his temper. A dozen things were strewn broken on the floor; old letters were lying crumpled and torn; I was sickened by the sight of a pearl necklace, snatched from his gaping valise, and evidently purchased as a present to his mother, ground into fragments on the carpet as if by his boot-heels. His father's relics were standing in a row untouched on the mantel-shelf, save for a couple of pistols mounted with his initials in silver, which were tossed upon the table. I made a brave effort to thrust them into a drawer and turn the key, but to my eternal regret I was afraid to touch them. Evening descended and wore away; but neither Eustace nor his mother returned. I sat gloomily enough on the verandah, listening for wheels or hoofs. Toward midnight a carriage rattled over the gravel; my friend descended with her husband at the door. She fluttered into my arms with a kind of shrinking yet impetuous dread. "Where is he—how is he?" she cried.

I was spared the pain of answering, for at the same moment I heard Eustace's horse clatter into the stable-yard. He had rapidly dismounted and passed into the house by one of the side windows, which opened from the piazza into the drawing-room. There the lamps were lighted. I led in my companions. Eustace had crossed the threshold of the window; the lamp-light fell upon him, relieving him against the darkness. His mother with a shriek flung herself toward him, but in an instant with a deeper cry she stopped short, pressing her hand to her heart. He had raised his hand, and, with a gesture which had all the spiritual force of a blow, he had cast her off. "Ah, my son, my son!" she cried with a piteous moan, and looking round at us in wild bewilderment.

"I'm not your son!" said the boy in a voice half stifled with passion. "I give you up! You're not my mother! Don't touch me! You've cheated me—you've betrayed me—you've *insulted* me!" In this mad peal of imprecations, it was still the note of vanity which rang clearest.

I looked at Mr. Cope. He was deadly pale. He had seen the lad's gesture; he was unable to hear his words. He sat down in the nearest chair and eyed him wonderingly. I hurried to his poor wife's relief. She seemed smitten with a sudden tremor, a deadly chill. She clasped her hands, but she could barely find her voice. "Eustace—my boy—my darling—my own—do you know what you say? Listen, listen, Eustace. It's all for you—that you should love me more. I've done my best. I seem to have been hasty, but hasty to do for you—to do for you——" Her strength deserted her; she burst into tears. "He curses me—he denies me!" she cried. "He has killed me!"

"Cry, cry!" Eustace retorted; "cry as I've been crying! But don't be falser than you have been. That you couldn't even wait! And you prate of my happiness! Is my happiness in a broken home—in a disputed heart—in a bullying stepfather! You've chosen him big and strong! Cry your eyes out—you're no mother of mine."

"He's killing me—he's killing me," groaned his mother. "O Heaven! if I dared to speak, I should kill *him*!" She turned to her husband. "Go to him—go to him!" she cried. "He's ill, he's mad—he doesn't know what he says. Take his hand in yours—look at him, soothe him, heal him. It's the hot weather," she rambled on. "Let him feel your touch! Eustace, Eustace, be healed!"

Poor Mr. Cope had risen to his feet, passing his handkerchief over his forehead, on which the perspiration stood in great drops. He went slowly toward the young man, bending his eyes on him half in entreaty, half in command. Before him he stopped and frankly held out his hand. Eustace eyed him defiantly from head to foot—him and his proffered friendship, enforced as it was by a gaze of the most benignant authority. Then pushing his hand savagely down, "Hypocrite!" he roared close to his face—"can you hear that?" and marched bravely out of the room. Mr. Cope shook his head with a world of tragic meaning, and for an instant exchanged with his wife a long look brimming with anguish. She fell upon his neck shaken with resounding sobs. But soon recovering herself, "Go to him," she urged, "follow him; say everything, spare nothing. No matter for me; I've got *my* blow."

I helped her up to her room. Her strength had completely left her; she but half undressed and let me lay her on her bed. She was in a state of the intensest excitement. Every nerve in her body was thrilling and ringing. She kept murmuring to herself, with a kind of heart-breaking incoherency. "Nothing can hurt me now; I needn't be spared. Nothing can disgrace me—or grace me. I've got my blow. It's my fault—all, all, all! I heaped up folly on folly and weakness on weakness. My heart's broken; it will never serve again. You have been right, my dear—I perverted him, I taught him to strike. Oh, what a blow! He's hard—he's hard. He's cruel. He has no heart. He's blind with vanity and egotism. But it matters little now; I shan't live to suffer. I've suffered enough. I'm dying, my friend, I'm dying."

In this broken strain the poor lady poured out the bitterness of her grief. I used every art to soothe and console her, but I felt that the tenderest spot in her gentle heart had received an irreparable bruise. "I don't want to live," she murmured. "I'm disillusioned. It could never be patched up; we should never be the same. He has shown the bottom of his soul. It's bad."

In spite of my efforts to restore her to calmness, she became—not more excited, for her strength seemed to be ebbing and her voice was low—but more painfully and incoherently garrulous. Nevertheless, from her distressing murmur I gathered the glimmer of a meaning. She seemed to wish to make a kind of supreme confession. I sat on the cope of her bed, with her hand in mine. From time to time, above her loud whispers, I heard the sound of the two gentlemen's voices. Adjoining her chamber was a large dressing-room; beyond this was Eustace's apartment. The three rooms opened upon a long uncovered balcony.

Mr. Cope had followed the young man to his own chamber, and was addressing him in a low, steady voice. Eustace apparently was silent; but there was something sullen and portentous to my ear in this unnatural absence of response.

"What have you thought of me, my friend, all these years?" his mother asked. "Have I seemed to you like other women? I haven't been like others. I have tried to be so—and you see—you see! Let me tell you. It don't matter whether you despise me—I shan't know it. These are my last words; let them be frank."

They were not, however, so frank as she intended. She seemed to lose herself in a dim wilderness of memories; her

faculty wandered, faltered, stumbled. Not from her words—
they were ambiguous—but from her silence and from the re-
bound of my own impassioned sympathy, as it were, I guessed
the truth. It blossomed into being vivid and distinct; it exhaled a long illuminating glow upon the past—a lurid light
upon the present. Strange it seemed now that my suspicions
had been so late to bear fruit; but our imagination is always
too timid. Now all things were clear! Heaven knows that in
this unpitying light I felt no contempt for the poor woman
who lay before me, panting from her violated soul.

Poor victims of destiny! If I could only bring them to
terms! For the moment, however, the unhappy mother and
wife demanded all my attention. I left her and passed along
the balcony, intending to summon her husband. The light in
Eustace's room showed me the young man and his companion. They sat facing each other in momentary silence. Mr.
Cope's two hands were on his knees, his eyes were fixed on
the carpet, his teeth were set—as if, baffled, irate, desperate,
he were preparing to play his last card. Eustace was looking at
him hard, with a terribly untender gaze. It made me sick. I
was on the point of rushing in and adjuring Eustace by the
truth. But suddenly Mr. Cope raised his eyes and exchanged
with the boy a look with which he seemed to read his very
soul. He waved his hand in the air as if to dismiss fond
patience.

"If you were to see yourself as I see you," he said, "you
would be vastly amazed; you would know your absurd appearance. Young as you are, you are rotten with arrogance
and pride. What would you say if I were to tell you that, least
of men, you have reason to be proud? Your stable boy there
has more. There's a leak in your vanity; there's a blot on your
escutcheon! You force me to strong measures. Let me tell
you, in the teeth of your monstrous egotism, what you are.
You're a——"

I knew what was coming, but I hadn't the heart to hear it.
The word, ringing out, overtook my ear as I hurried back to
Mrs. Cope. It was followed by a loud, incoherent cry, the
sound, prolonged for some moments, of a scuffle, and then
the report of a pistol. This was lost in the noise of crashing
glass. Mrs. Cope rose erect in bed and shrieked aloud, "He

has killed him—and me." I caught her in my arms; she breathed her last. I laid her gently on the bed and made my trembling way, by the balcony, to Eustace's room. The first glance reassured me. Neither of the men was visibly injured; the pistol lay smoking on the floor. Eustace had sunk into a chair with his head buried in his hands. I saw his face crimson through his fingers.

"It's not murder," Mr. Cope said to me as I crossed the threshold, "but it has just missed being suicide. It has been fatal only to the looking-glass." The mirror was shivered.

"It *is* murder," I answered, seizing Eustace by the arm and forcing him to rise. "You have killed your mother. This is your father!"

My friend paused and looked at me with a triumphant air, as if she was very proud of her effect. Of course I had foreseen it half an hour ago. "What a dismal tale," I said. "But it's interesting. Of course Mrs. Cope recovered."

She was silent an instant. "You're like me," she answered. "Your imagination is timid."

"I confess," I rejoined, "I am rather at a loss how to dispose of our friend Eustace. I don't see how the two could very well shake hands—nor yet how they couldn't."

"They did once—and but once. They were for years, each in his way, lonely men. They were never reconciled. The trench had been dug too deep. Even the poor lady buried there didn't avail to fill it up. Yet the son was forgiven—the father never!"

Guest's Confession

"ARRIVE half past eight. Sick. Meet me."

The telegrammatic brevity of my step-brother's missive gave that melancholy turn to my thoughts which was the usual result of his communications. He was to have come on the Friday; what had made him start off on Wednesday? The terms on which we stood were a perpetual source of irritation. We were utterly unlike in temper and taste and opinions, and yet, having a number of common interests, we were obliged, after a fashion, to compromise with each other's idiosyncrasies. In fact, the concessions were all on my side. He was altogether too much my superior in all that makes the man who counts in the world for me not to feel it, and it cost me less to let him take his way than to make a stand for my dignity. What I did through indolence and in some degree, I confess, through pusillanimity, I had a fancy to make it appear (by dint of much whistling, as it were, and easy thrusting of my hands into my pockets) that I did through a sort of generous condescension. Edgar cared little enough upon what recipe I compounded a salve for my vanity, so long as he held his own course; and I am afraid I played the slumbering giant to altogether empty benches. There had been, indeed, a vague tacit understanding that he was to treat me, in form, as a man with a mind of his own, and there was occasionally something most incisively sarcastic in his observance of the treaty. What made matters the worse for me, and the better for him, was an absurd physical disparity; for Musgrave was like nothing so much as Falstaff's description of Shallow,—a man made after supper of a cheese-paring. He was a miserable invalid, and was perpetually concerned with his stomach, his lungs, and his liver, and as he was both doctor and patient in one, they kept him very busy. His head was grotesquely large for his diminutive figure, his eye fixed and salient, and his complexion liable to flush with an air of indignation and suspicion. He practised a most resolute little strut on a most attenuated pair of little legs. For myself, I was tall, happily; for I was broad enough, if I had been shorter, to have perhaps

incurred that invidious monosyllabic epithet which haunted
Lord Byron. As compared with Edgar, I was at least fairly
good-looking; a stoutish, blondish, indolent, amiable, rather
gorgeous young fellow might have served as my personal formula. My patrimony, being double that of my step-brother
(for we were related by my mother), was largely lavished on
the adornment of this fine person. I dressed in fact, as I recollect, with a sort of barbaric splendor, and I may very well
have passed for one of the social pillars of a small watering-
place.

L—— was in those days just struggling into fame, and but
that it savored overmuch of the fresh paint lately lavished
upon the various wooden barracks in which visitors were to
be accommodated, it yielded a pleasant mixture of rurality
and society. The vile taste and the sovereign virtue of the
spring were fairly established, and Edgar was not the man to
forego the chance of trying the waters and abusing them.
Having heard that the hotel was crowded, he wished to secure a room at least a week beforehand; the upshot of which
was, that I came down on the 19th of July with the mission to
retain and occupy his apartment till the 26th. I passed, with
people in general, and with Edgar in particular, for so very
idle a person that it seemed almost a duty to saddle me with
some wholesome errand. Edgar had, first and always, his
health to attend to, and then that neat little property and
those everlasting accounts, which he was never weary of contemplating, verifying, and overhauling. I had made up my
mind to make over his room to him, remain a day or two for
civility's sake and then leave him to his cups. Meanwhile, on
the 24th, it occurred to me that I ought really to see something of the place. The weather had been too hot for going
about, and, as yet, I had hardly left the piazza of the hotel.
Towards afternoon the clouds gathered, the sun was obscured, and it seemed possible even for a large, lazy man to
take a walk. I went along beside the river, under the trees, rejoicing much in the midsummer prettiness of all the land and
in the sultry afternoon stillness. I was discomposed and irritated, and all for no better reason than that Edgar was coming. What was Edgar that his comings and goings should

affect me? Was I, after all, so excessively his younger brother? I would turn over a new leaf! I almost wished things would come to a crisis between us, and that in the glow of exasperation I might say or do something unpardonable. But there was small chance of my quarrelling with Edgar for vanity's sake. Somehow, I didn't believe in my own egotism, but I had an indefeasible respect for his. I was fatally good-natured, and I should continue to do his desire until I began to do that of some one else. If I might only fall in love and exchange my master for a mistress, for some charming goddess of unreason who would declare that Mr. Musgrave was simply intolerable and that was an end of it!

So, meditating vaguely, I arrived at the little Episcopal chapel, which stands on the margin of the village where the latter begins to melt away into the large river-side landscape. The door was slightly ajar: there came through it into the hot outer stillness the low sound of an organ,—the rehearsal, evidently, of the organist or of some gentle amateur. I was warm with walking, and this glimpse of the cool musical dimness within prompted me to enter and rest and listen. The body of the church was empty; but a feeble glow of color was diffused through the little yellow and crimson windows upon the pews and the cushioned pulpit. The organ was erected in a small gallery facing the chancel, into which the ascent was by a short stairway directly from the church. The sound of my tread was apparently covered by the music, for the player continued without heeding me, hidden as she was behind a little blue silk curtain on the edge of the gallery. Yes, that gentle, tentative, unprofessional touch came from a feminine hand. Uncertain as it was, however, it wrought upon my musical sensibilities with a sort of provoking force. The air was familiar, and, before I knew it, I had begun to furnish the vocal accompaniment,—first gently, then boldly. Standing with my face to the organ, I awaited the effect of my venture. The only perceptible result was that, for a moment, the music faltered and the curtains were stirred. I saw nothing, but I had been seen, and, reassured apparently by my aspect, the organist resumed the chant. Slightly mystified, I felt urged to sing my best, the more so that, as I continued, the player seemed to borrow confidence and emulation from my voice. The notes rolled out bravely, and the little vault resounded. Suddenly there seemed to come to the musician, in the ardor of success, a full accession of vigor and skill. The last chords were struck with a kind of triumphant intensity, and their cadence was marked by a clear soprano voice. Just at the close, however, voice and music were swallowed up in the roll of a huge thunder-clap. At the same instant, the storm-drops began to strike the chapel-windows, and we were sheeted in a summer rain. The rain was a bore; but, at least, I should have a look at the organist, concerning whom my curiosity had suddenly grown great. The thunder-claps followed each other with such violence that it was vain to continue to play. I waited, in the confident belief that that charming voice—half a dozen notes had betrayed it—denoted a charming woman. After the lapse of some moments, which seemed to indicate a graceful and appealing hesitancy, a female figure appeared at the top of the little stairway and began to descend. I walked slowly down the aisle. The stormy darkness had rapidly increased, and at this moment, with a huge burst of thunder, following a blinding flash, a momentary midnight fell upon our refuge. When things had become visible again, I beheld the fair musician at the foot of the steps, gazing at me with all the frankness of agitation. The little chapel was rattling to its foundations.

"Do you think there is any danger?" asked my companion.

I made haste to assure her there was none. "The chapel has nothing in the nature of a spire, and even if it had, the fact of our being in a holy place ought to insure us against injury."

She looked at me wonderingly, as if to see whether I was in jest. To satisfy her, I smiled as graciously as I might. Whereupon, gathering confidence, "I think we have each of us," she said, "so little right to be here that we can hardly claim the benefit of sanctuary."

"Are you too an interloper?" I asked.

She hesitated a moment. "I'm not an Episcopalian," she replied; "I'm a good Unitarian."

"Well, I'm a poor Episcopalian. It's six of one and half a dozen of the other." There came another long, many-sheeted flash and an immediate wild reverberation. My companion, as she stood before me, was vividly illumined from head to foot.

It was as if some fierce natural power had designed to interpose her image on my soul forever, in this merciless electric glare. As I saw her then, I have never ceased to see her since. I have called her fair, but the word needs explanation. Singularly pleasing as she was, it was with a charm that was all her own. Not the charm of beauty, but of a certain intense expressiveness, which seems to have given beauty the go-by in the very interest of grace. Slender, meagre, without redundancy of outline or brilliancy of color, she was a person you might never have noticed, but would certainly never forget. What there was was so charming, what there might be so interesting! There was none of the idleness of conscious beauty in her clear gray eyes; they seemed charged with the impatience of a restless mind. Her glance and smile, her step and gesture, were as light and distinct as a whispered secret. She was nervous, curious, zealous, slightly imperious, and delicately elegant withal; without which, possibly, she might have seemed a trifle too positive. There is a certain sweet unreason in a picturesque toilet. She was dressed in a modish adjustment of muslins and lace, which denoted the woman who may have fancied that even less beauty might yet please. While I drew my conclusions,—they were eminently flattering,—my companion was buttoning her gloves and looking anxiously at the dripping windows. Wishing, as far as I might, to beguile her impatience, I proceeded to apologize for the liberty I had taken in singing to her music. "My best excuse," I said, "is your admirable playing, and my own most sensitive ear!"

"You might have frightened me away," she answered. "But you sang too well for that, better than I played. In fact, I was afraid to stop, I thought you might be one of the—the hierarchy."

"A bishop!"

"A bishop,—a dean,—a deacon,—or something of that sort."

"The sexton, perhaps."

"Before the sexton I should have succumbed. I take it his business would have been to eject me as a meddlesome heretic. I came in for no better reason than that the church door was ajar."

"As a church door ought always to be."

She looked at me a moment. "No; see what comes of it."

"No great harm, it seems to me."

"O, that's very well for us! But a church shouldn't be made a place of convenience."

I wished, in the interest of our growing intimacy, to make a point. "If it is not a place of convenience," I ventured to propound, deprecating offence with a smile, "what is it?"

It was an observation I afterwards made, that in cases when many women drop their eyes and look prettily silly or prudishly alarmed, this young lady's lucid glance would become more unaffectedly direct and searching. "Indeed," she answered, "you *are* but an indifferent Episcopalian! I came in because the door was open, because I was warm with my walk, and because, I confess, I have an especial fondness for going into churches on week-days. One does it in Europe, you know; and it reminds me of Europe."

I cast a glance over the naked tabernacle, with the counterfeit graining scarcely dry on its beams and planks, and a strong aroma of turpentine and putty representing the odor of sanctity. She followed my glance; our eyes met, and we laughed. From this moment we talked with a freedom tempered less by the sanctity of the spot than by a certain luxury of deference with which I felt prompted to anticipate possible mistrust. The rain continued to descend with such steady good-will that it seemed needful to accept our situation frankly and conjure away the spirit of awkwardness. We spoke of L——, of the people there, of the hot weather, of music. She had as yet seen little of the place, having been confined to her apartments by domestic reasons. I wondered what her domestic reasons were. She had come forth at last to call upon a friend at one of the boarding-houses which adorned this suburb of the village. Her friend being out, but likely soon to return, she had sought entertainment in a stroll along the road, and so had wandered into the chapel. Our interview lasted half an hour. As it drew to a close, I fancied there had grown up between us some delicate bond, begotten of our mutual urbanity. I might have been indiscreet; as it was, I took my pleasure in tracing the gradual evanescence of my companion's sense of peril. As the moments elapsed, she sat down on the bench with an air of perfect equanimity, and looked patiently at the trickling windows. The still small voice of some familiar spirit of the Lord, haunting the dedicated vault, seemed to have audibly blessed our meeting. At last the rain abated and suddenly stopped, and through a great rift in the clouds there leaped a giant sunbeam and smote the trickling windows. Through little gaudy lozenges the chapel was flooded with prismatic light. "The storm is over," said my companion. She spoke without rising, as if she had been cheated of the sense of haste. Was it calculated civility, or was it momentary self-oblivion? Whatever it was, it lasted but a moment. We were on our feet and moving toward the door. As we stood in the porch, honest gallantry demanded its rights.

"I never knew before," I said, "the possible blessings of a summer rain."

She proceeded a few steps before she answered. Then glancing at the shining sky, already blue and free, "In ten minutes," she said, "there will be no trace of it!"

"Does that mean," I frankly demanded, "that we are not to meet again as friends?"

"Are we to meet again at all?"

"I count upon it."

"Certainly, then, not as enemies!" As she walked away, I imprecated those restrictions of modern civilization which forbade me to stand and gaze at her.

Who was she? What was she?—questions the more intense as, in the absence of any further evidence than my rapid personal impression, they were so provokingly vain. They occupied me, however, during the couple of hours which were to elapse before my step-brother's arrival. When his train became due, I went through the form, as usual, of feeling desperately like treating myself to the luxury of neglecting his summons and leaving him to shift for himself; as if I had not the most distinct prevision of the inevitable event,—of my being at the station half an hour too early, of my calling his hack and making his bargain and taking charge of his precious little hand-bag, full of medicine-bottles, and his ridiculous bundle of umbrellas and canes. Somehow, this evening, I felt unwontedly loath and indocile; but I contented myself with this bold flight of the imagination.

It is hard to describe fairly my poor step-brother's peculiar turn of mind, to give an adequate impression of his want of social charm, to put it mildly, without accusing him of wilful malevolence. He was simply the most consistent and incorruptible of egotists. He was perpetually affirming and defining and insuring himself, insisting upon a personal right or righting a personal wrong. And above all, he was a man of conscience. He asked no odds, and he gave none. He made honesty something unlovely, but he was rigidly honest. He demanded simply his dues, and he collected them to the last farthing. These things gave him a portentous solemnity. He smiled perhaps once a month, and made a joke once in six. There are jokes of his making which, to this day, give me a shiver when I think of them. But I soon perceived, as he descended from the train, that there would be no joke that evening. Something had happened. His face was hard and sombre, and his eye bright and fierce. "A carriage," he said, giving me his hand stiffly. And when we were seated and driving away, "First of all," he demanded, "are there any mosquitoes? A single mosquito would finish me. And is my room habitable, on the shady side, away from the stairs, with a view, with a hair-mattress?" I assured him that mosquitoes were unknown, and that his room was the best, and his mattress the softest in the house. Was he tired? how had he been?

"Don't ask me. I'm in an extremely critical state. Tired? Tired is a word for well people! When I'm tired I shall go to bed and die. Thank God, so long as I have any work to do, I can hold up my head! I haven't slept in a week. It's singular, but I'm never so well disposed for my duties as when I haven't slept! But be so good, for the present, as to ask me no questions. I shall immediately take a bath and drink some arrow-root; I have brought a package in my bag, I suppose I can get them to make it. I'll speak about it at the office. No, I think, on the whole, I'll make it in my room; I have a little machine for boiling water. I think I shall drink half a glass of the spring to-night, just to make a beginning."

All this was said with as profound a gravity as if he were dictating his will. But I saw that he was at a sort of white-heat exasperation, and I knew that in time I should learn where the shoe pinched. Meanwhile, I attempted to say something cheerful and frivolous, and offered some information as to who was at the hotel and who was expected; "No one you know or care about, I think."

"Very likely not. I'm in no mood for gossip."

"You seem nervous," I ventured to say.

"Nervous? Call it frantic! I'm not blessed with your apathetic temperament, nor with your elegant indifference to money-matters. Do you know what's the matter with me? I've lost twenty thousand dollars."

I, of course, demanded particulars; but, for the present, I had to content myself with the naked fact. "It's a mighty serious matter," said Edgar. "I can't talk of it further till I have bathed and changed my linen. The thermometer has been at ninety-one in my rooms in town. I've had this pretty piece of news to keep me cool."

I left him to his bath, his toilet, and his arrow-root and strolled about pondering the mystery of his disaster. Truly, if Edgar had lost money, shrewdness was out of tune. Destiny must have got up early to outwit my step-brother. And yet his misfortune gave him a sort of unwonted grace, and I believe I wondered for five minutes whether there was a chance of his being relaxed and softened by it. I had, indeed, a momentary vision of lending him money, and taking a handsome revenge as a good-natured creditor. But Edgar would never borrow. He would either recover his money or grimly do without it. On going back to his room I found him dressed and refreshed, screwing a little portable kettle upon his gas-burner.

"You can never get them to bring you water that really boils," he said. "They don't know what it means. You're altogether wrong about the mosquitoes; I'm sure I heard one, and by the sound, he's a monster. But I have a net folded up in my trunk, and a hook and ring which I mean to drive into the ceiling."

"I'll put up your net. Meanwhile, tell me about your twenty thousand dollars."

He was silent awhile, but at last he spoke in a voice forcibly attuned to composure. "You're immensely tickled, I suppose, to find me losing money! That comes of worrying too much and handling my funds too often. Yes, I *have* worried too much." He paused, and then, suddenly, he broke out into a kind of fury. "I hate waste, I hate shiftlessness, I hate nasty mismanagement! I hate to see money bring in less than it may. My imagination loves a good investment. I respect my property, I respect other people's. But your own honesty is all you'll find in this world, and it will go no farther than you're there to carry it. You've always thought me hard and suspicious and grasping. No, you never said so; should I have cared if you had? With your means, it's all very well to be a fine gentleman, to skip the items and glance at the total. But, being poor and sick, I have to be close. I wasn't close enough. What do you think of my having been cheated?— cheated under my very nose? I hope I'm genteel enough now!"

"I should like to see the man!" I cried.

"You shall see him. All the world shall see him. I've been looking into the matter. It has been beautifully done. If I were to be a rascal, I should like to be just such a one."

"Who is your rascal?"

"His name is John Guest."

I had heard the name, but had never seen the man.

"No, you don't know him," Edgar went on. "No one knows him but I. But I know him well. He had things in his hands for a week, while I was debating a transfer of my New Jersey property. In a week this is how he mixed matters."

"Perhaps, if you had given him time," I suggested, "he meant to get them straight again."

"O, I shall give him time. I mean he shall get 'em straight, or I shall twist him so crooked his best friend won't know him."

"Did you never suspect his honesty?"

"Do you suspect mine?"

"But you have legal redress?"

"It's no thanks to him. He had fixed things to a charm, he had done his best to cut me off and cover his escape. But I've got him, and he shall disgorge!"

I hardly know why it was; but the implacable firmness of my brother's position produced in my mind a sort of fantastic reaction in favor of Mr. John Guest. I felt a sudden gush of the most inconsequent pity. "Poor man!" I exclaimed. But to repair my weakness, I plunged into a series of sympathetic questions and listened attentively to Edgar's statement of his wrongs. As he set forth the case, I found myself taking a whimsical interest in Mr. Guest's own side of it, wondering whether he suspected suspicion, whether he dreaded conviction, whether he had an easy conscience, and how he was getting through the hot weather. I asked Edgar how lately he had discovered his loss and whether he had since communicated with the criminal.

"Three days ago, three nights ago, rather; for I haven't slept a wink since. I have spoken of the matter to no one; for the present I need no one's help, I can help myself. I haven't seen the man more than three or four times; our dealings have generally been by letter. The last person you'd suspect. He's as great a dandy as you yourself, and in better taste, too. I was told ten days ago, at his office, that he had gone out of town. I suppose I'm paying for his champagne at Newport."

II.

On my proposing, half an hour later, to relieve him of my society and allow him to prepare for rest, Edgar declared that our talk had put an end to sleep and that he must take a turn in the open air. On descending to the piazza, we found it in the deserted condition into which it usually lapsed about ten o'clock; either from a wholesome desire on the part of our fellow-lodgers to keep classic country hours, or from the soporific influences of excessive leisure. Here and there the warm darkness was relieved by the red tip of a cigar in suggestive proximity to a light corsage. I observed, as we strolled along, a lady of striking appearance, seated in the zone of light projected from a window, in conversation with a gentleman. "Really, I'm afraid you'll take cold," I heard her say as we passed. "Let me tie my handkerchief round your neck." And she gave it a playful twist. She was a pretty woman, of middle age, with great freshness of toilet and complexion, and a picturesque abundance of blond hair, upon which was coquettishly poised a fantastic little hat, decorated with an immense pink rose. Her companion was a seemingly affable man, with a bald head, a white waistcoat, and a rather florid air of distinction. When we passed them a second time, they had risen and the lady was preparing to enter the house. Her companion went with her to the door; she left him with a great deal of coquettish by-play, and he turned back to the piazza. At this moment his glance fell upon my step-brother. He started, I thought, and then, replacing his hat with an odd, nervous decision, came towards him with a smile. "Mr. Musgrave!" he said.

Edgar stopped short, and for a moment seemed to lack words to reply. At last he uttered a deep, harsh note: "Mr. Guest!"

In an instant I felt that I was in the presence of a "situation." Edgar's words had the sound of the "click" upon the limb of the entrapped fox. A scene was imminent; the actors were only awaiting their cues. Mr. Guest made a half-offer of his hand, but, perceiving no response in Edgar's, he gracefully dipped it into his pocket. "You must have just come!" he murmured.

"A couple of hours ago."

Mr. Guest glanced at me, as if to include me in the operation of his urbanity, and his glance stirred in my soul an impulse of that kindness which we feel for a man about to be executed. It's no more than human to wish to shake hands with him. "Introduce me, Edgar," I said.

"My step-brother," said Edgar, curtly. "This is Mr. Guest, of whom we have been talking."

I put out my hand; he took it with cordiality. "Really," he declared, "this is a most unexpected—a—circumstance."

"Altogether so to me," said Edgar.

"You've come for the waters, I suppose," our friend went on. "I'm sorry your health continues—a—unsatisfactory."

Edgar, I perceived, was in a state of extreme nervous exacerbation, the result partly of mere surprise and partly of keen disappointment. His plans had been checked. He had determined to do thus and so, and he must now extemporize a policy. Well, as poor, pompous Mr. Guest wished it, so he should have it! "I shall never be strong," said Edgar.

"Well, well," responded Mr. Guest, "a man of your parts may make a little strength serve a great purpose."

My step-brother was silent a moment, relishing secretly, I think, the beautiful pertinence of this observation. "I suppose I can defend my rights," he rejoined.

"Exactly! What more does a man need?" and he appealed to me with an insinuating smile. His smile was singularly frank and agreeable, and his glance full of a sort of conciliating gallantry. I noted in his face, however, by the gaslight, a haggard, jaded look which lent force to what he went on to say. "I have been feeling lately as if I hadn't even strength for that. The hot weather, an overdose of this abominable water, one thing and another, the inevitable premonitions of—a—mortality, have quite pulled me down. Since my arrival here, ten days ago, I have really been quite—a—the invalid. I've actually been in bed. A most unprecedented occurrence!"

"I hope you're better," I ventured to say.

"Yes, I think I'm myself again,—thanks to capital nursing. I think I'm myself again!" He repeated his words mechanically, with a sort of exaggerated gayety, and began to wipe his forehead with his handkerchief. Edgar was watching him narrowly, with an eye whose keenness it was impossible to veil; and I think Edgar's eye partly caused his disquiet. "The last thing I did, by the way, before my indisposition, was to write you ten lines, Mr. Musgrave, on—a little matter of business."

"I got your letter," said Edgar, grimly.

Mr. Guest was silent a moment. "And I hope my arrangements have met your approval?"

"We shall talk of that," said Edgar.

At this point, I confess, my interest in the situation had become painful. I felt sick. I'm not a man of ready-made resolution, as my story will abundantly prove. I am discountenanced and bullied by disagreeable things. Poor Mr. Guest was so infallibly booked for exposure that I instinctively retreated. Taking advantage of his allusion to business, I turned away and walked to the other end of the piazza. This genial gentleman, then, was embodied fraud! this sayer of civil things was a doer of monstrously shabby ones! that irreproachable white waistcoat carried so sadly spotted a conscience! Whom had he involved in his dishonor? Had he a wife, children, friends? Who was that so prosperously pretty woman, with her flattering solicitude for his health? I stood for some time reflecting how guilt is not the vulgar bugaboo we fancy it,—that it has organs, senses, affections, passions, for all the world like those of innocence. Indeed, from my

cursory observation of my friend, I had rarely seen innocence
so handsomely featured. Where, then, was the line which severed rectitude from error? Was manhood a baser thing than I
had fancied, or was sin a thing less base? As I mused thus, my
disgust ebbed away, and the return of the wave brought an
immense curiosity to see what it had come to betwixt guilt
and justice. Had Edgar launched his thunder? I retraced my
steps and rejoined my companions. Edgar's thunder was apparently still in the clouds; but there had been a premonitory
flash of lightning. Guest stood before him, paler than before,
staring defiantly, and stammering out some fierce denial. "I
don't understand you," he said. "If you mean what you seem
to mean, you mean rank insult."

"I mean the truth," said Edgar. "It's a pity the truth should
be insulting."

Guest glared a moment, like a man intently taking thought
for self-defence. But he was piteously unmasked. His genial
smile had taken flight and left mere vulgar confusion. "This is
between ourselves, sir," he cried, angrily turning to me.

"A thousand pardons," I said, and passed along. I began to
be doubtful as to the issue of the quarrel. Edgar had right on
his side, but, under the circumstances, he might not have
force. Guest was altogether the stouter, bigger, weightier person. I turned and observed them from a distance. Edgar's
thunderbolt had fallen and his victim stood stunned. He was
leaning against the balustrade of the piazza, with his chin on
his breast and his eyes sullenly fixed on his adversary, demoralized and convicted. His hat had dropped upon the floor.
Edgar seemed to have made a proposal; with a passionate
gesture he repeated it. Guest slowly stooped and picked up
his hat, and Edgar led the way toward the house. A series of
small sitting-rooms opened by long windows upon the
piazza. These were for the most part lighted and empty.
Edgar selected one of them, and, stopping before the window, beckoned to me to come to him. Guest, as I advanced,
bestowed upon me a scowl of concentrated protest. I felt, for
my own part, as if I were horribly indelicate. Between Edgar
and him it was a question of morals, but between him and
myself it was, of course, but one of manners. "Be so good
as to walk in," said Edgar, turning to me with a smile of un-

precedented suavity. I might have resisted his dictation; I couldn't his petition.

"In God's name, what do you mean to do?" demanded Guest.

"My duty!" said Edgar. "Go in."

We passed into the room. The door of the corridor was open; Guest closed it with a passionate kick. Edgar shut the long window and dropped the curtain. In the same fury of mortification, Guest turned out one of the two burners of the chandelier. There was still light enough, however, for me to see him more distinctly than on the piazza. He was tallish and stoutish, and yet sleek and jaunty. His fine blue eye was a trifle weak, perhaps, and his handsome grizzled beard was something too foppishly trimmed; but, on the whole, he was a most comely man. He was dressed with the punctilious elegance of a man who loved luxury and appreciated his own good points. A little moss-rosebud figured in the lappet of his dark-blue coat. His whole person seemed redolent of what are called the "feelings of a gentleman." Confronted and contrasted with him under the lamp, my step-brother seemed wofully mean and grotesque; though for a conflict of forces that lay beneath the surface, he was visibly the better equipped of the two. He seemed to tremble and quiver with inexorable purpose. I felt that he would heed no admonitory word of mine, that I could not in the least hope to blunt the edge of his resentment, and that I must on the instant decide either to stand by him or leave him. But while I stood thus ungraciously gazing at poor Guest, the instant passed. Curiosity and a mingled sympathy with each—to say nothing of a touch of that relish for a fight inherent in the truly masculine bosom—sealed my lips and arrested my steps. And yet my heart paid this graceful culprit the compliment of beating very violently on his behalf.

"I wish you to repeat before my brother," said Edgar, "the three succinct denials to which you have just treated me."

Guest looked at the ceiling with a trembling lip. Then dropping upon the sofa, he began to inspect his handsome finger-nails mechanically, in the manner of one who hears in some horrible hush of all nature the nearing footsteps of doom. "Come, repeat them!" cried Edgar. "It's really deli-

cious. You never wrote to Stevens that you had my assent in
writing to the sale of the bonds. You never showed Stevens
my telegram from Boston, and assured him that my 'Do as
you think best' was a permission to raise money on them. If
it's not forgery sir, it's next door to it, and a very flimsy partition between."

Guest leaned back on the sofa, with his hands grasping his
knees. "You might have let things stand a week or so," he
said, with unnatural mildness. "You might have had common
patience. Good God, there's a gentlemanly way of doing
things! A man doesn't begin to roar for a pinch. I would have
got things square again."

"O, it would have been a pity to spoil them! It was such a
pretty piece of knavery! Give the devil his due!"

"I would have rearranged matters," Guest went on. "It was
just a temporary convenience. I supposed I was dealing with
a man of common courtesy. But what are you to say to a gentleman who says, 'Sir, I trust you,' and then looks through
the keyhole?"

"Upon my word, when I hear you scuttling through the
window," cried Edgar, "I think it's time I should break down
the door. For God's sake, don't nauseate me with any more
lies! You know as well as you sit there, that you had neither
chance nor means nor desire to redeem your fraud. You'd cut
the bridge behind you! You thought you'd been knowing
enough to eat your cake and have it, to lose your virtue and
keep your reputation, to sink half my property through a
trap-door and then stand whistling and looking t' other way
while I scratched my head and wondered what the devil was
in it! Sit down there and write me your note for twenty thousand dollars at twenty days."

Guest was silent a moment. "Propose something reasonable," he said, with the same tragic gentleness.

"I shall let the law reason about it."

Guest gave a little start and fixed his eyes on the ground.
"The law wouldn't help you," he answered, without looking
up.

"Indeed! do you think it would help *you*? Stoddard and
Hale will help me. I spoke to them this morning."

Guest sprang to his feet. "Good heavens! I hope you mentioned no names."

"Only one!" said Edgar.

Guest wiped his forehead and actually tried to smile. "That was your own, of course! Well, sir, I hope they advised you to—a—temper justice with mercy."

"They are not parsons, Mr. Guest; they are lawyers. They accept the case."

Guest dropped on the sofa, buried his face in his hands, and burst into tears. "O my soul!" he cried. His soul, poor man! was a rough term for name and fame and comfort and all that made his universe. It was a pitiful sight.

"Look here, Edgar," I said. "Don't press things too hard. I'm not a parson either—"

"No, you've not that excuse for your sentimentality!" Edgar broke out. "Here it is, of course! Here come folly and fear and ignorance maundering against the primary laws of life! Is rascality alone of all things in the world to be handled without gloves? Didn't he press me hard? He's danced his dance,—let him pay the piper! Am I a child, a woman, a fool, to stand and haggle with a swindler? Am I to go to the wall to make room for impudent fraud? Not while I have eyes to know black from white! I'm a decent man. I'm this or I'm nothing. For twenty years I've done my best for order and thrift and honesty. I've never yielded an inch to the detestable sharp practice that meets one nowadays at every turn. I've hated fraud as I hate all bad economy; I've no more patience with it than a bull with a red rag. Fraud is fraud; it's waste, it's wantonness, it's chaos; and I shall never give it the go-by. When I catch it, I shall hold it fast, and call all honest men to see how vile and drivelling a thing it is!"

Guest sat rigidly fixed, with his eyes on the carpet. "Do you expect to get your money?" he finally demanded.

"My money be hanged! I expect to let people know how they may be served if they intrust their affairs to you! A man's property, sir, is a man's person. It's as if you had given me a blow in the chest!"

Guest came towards him and took him by the button-hole. "Now see here," he said, with the same desperate calmness.

"You call yourself a practical man. Don't go on like one of those d—d long-haired reformers. You're off the track. Don't attempt too much. Don't make me confoundedly uncomfortable out of pure fantasticality. Come, sir, you're a man of the world." And he patted him gently on the shoulder. "Give me a chance. I confess to not having been quite square. There! My very dear sir, let me get on my legs again."

"O, you confess!" cried Edgar. "That's a vast comfort. You'll never do it again! Not if I know it. But other people, eh? Suppose I had been a decent widow with six children, and not a penny but that! You'd confess again, I suppose. Would your confession butter their bread! Let your confession be public!"

"My confession *is* public!" and Guest, with averted eyes, jerked his head towards me.

"O, my step-brother! Why, he's the most private creature in the world. Cheat him and he'll thank you! David, I retain you as a witness that Mr. Guest has confessed."

"Nothing will serve you then? You mean to prosecute?"

"I mean to prosecute."

The poor man's face flushed crimson, and the great sweat-drops trickled from his temples. "O you blundering brute!" he cried. "Do you know what you mean when you say that? Do we live in a civilized world?"

"Not altogether," said Edgar. "But I shall help it along."

"Have you lived among decent people? Have you known women whom it was an honor to please? Have you cared for name and fame and love? Have you had a dear daughter?"

"If I had a dear daughter," cried Edgar, flinching the least bit at this outbreak, "I trust my dear daughter would have kept me honest! Not the sin, then, but the detection unfits a man for ladies' society!—Did you kiss your daughter the day you juggled away my bonds?"

"If it will avail with you, I didn't. Consider her feelings. My fault has been that I have been too tender a father,—that I have loved the poor girl better than my own literal integrity. I became embarrassed because I hadn't the heart to tell her that she must spend less money. As if to the wisest, sweetest girl in the world a whisper wouldn't have sufficed! As if five minutes of her divine advice wouldn't have set me straight again! But the stress of my embarrassment was such—"

"Embarrassment!" Edgar broke in. "That may mean any-thing. In the case of an honest man it may be a motive for leniency; in that of a knave it's a ground for increased suspicion."

Guest, I felt, was a good-natured sinner. Just as he lacked rectitude of purpose, he lacked rigidity of temper, and he found in the mysteries of his own heart no clew to my step-brother's monstrous implacability. Looking at him from head to foot with a certain dignity,—a reminiscence of his former pomposity,—"I do you the honor, sir," he said, "to believe you are insane."

"Stuff and nonsense! you believe nothing of the sort," cried Edgar.

I saw that Guest's opposition was acting upon him as a lively irritant. "Isn't it possible," I asked, "to adopt some compromise? You're not as forgiving a man under the circumstances as I should be."

"In these things," retorted Edgar, without ceremony, "a forgiving man is a fool."

"Well, take a fool's suggestion. You can perhaps get satisfaction without taking your victim into court.—Let Mr. Guest write his confession."

Guest had not directly looked at me since we entered the room. At these words he slowly turned and gave me a sombre stare by which the brilliancy of my suggestion seemed somewhat obscured. But my interference was kindly meant, and his reception of it seemed rather ungrateful. At best, however, I could be but a thorn in his side. I had done nothing to earn my sport. Edgar hereupon flourished his hand as if to indicate the superfluity of my advice. "All in good time, if you please. If I'm insane, there's a method in my madness!" He paused, and his eyes glittered with an intensity which might indeed, for the moment, have seemed to be that of a disordered brain. I wondered what was coming. "Do me the favor to get down on your knees." Guest jerked himself up as if he had received a galvanic shock. "Yes, I know what I say,—on your knees. Did you never say your prayers? You can't get out of a tight place without being squeezed. I won't take less. I sha'n't feel like an honest man till I've seen you there at my feet."

There was in the contrast between the inflated self-complacency of Edgar's face as he made this speech, and the blank horror of the other's as he received it, something so poignantly grotesque that it acted upon my nerves like a mistimed joke, and I burst into irrepressible laughter. Guest walked away to the window with some muttered imprecation, pushed aside the curtain, and stood looking out. Then, with a sudden turn, he marched back and stood before my brother. He was drenched with perspiration. "A moment," said Edgar. "You're very hot. Take off your coat." Guest, to my amazement, took it off and flung it upon the floor. "Your shirt-sleeves will serve as a kind of sackcloth and ashes. Fold your hands, so. Now, beg my pardon."

It was a revolting sight,—this man of ripe maturity and massive comeliness on his two knees, his pale face bent upon his breast, his body trembling with the effort to keep his shameful balance; and above him Edgar, with his hands behind his back, solemn and ugly as a miniature idol, with his glittering eyes fixed in a sort of rapture on the opposite wall. I walked away to the window. There was a perfect stillness, broken only by Guest's hard breathing. I have no notion how long it lasted; when I turned back into the room he was still speechless and fixed, as if he were ashamed to rise. Edgar pointed to a blotting-book and inkstand which stood on a small table against the wall. "See if there is pen and paper!" I obeyed and made a clatter at the table, to cover our companion's retreat. When I had laid out a sheet of paper he was on his feet again. "Sit down and write," Edgar went on. Guest picked up his coat and busied himself mechanically with brushing off the particles of dust. Then he put it on and sat down at the table.

"I dictate," Edgar began. "I hereby, at the command of Edgar Musgrave, Esq., whom I have grossly wronged, declare myself a swindler." At these words, Guest laid down the pen and sank back in his chair, emitting long groans, like a man with a violent toothache. But he had taken that first step which costs, and after a moment's rest he started afresh. "I have on my bended knees, in the presence of Mr. Musgrave and his step-brother, expressed my contrition; in consideration of which Mr. Musgrave forfeits his incontestable right to publish his injury in a court of justice. Furthermore, I solemnly declare myself his debtor in the sum of twenty thousand dollars; which, on his remission of the interest, and under pain of exposure in a contrary event, I pledge myself to repay at the earliest possible moment. I thank Mr. Musgrave for his generosity."

Edgar spoke very slowly, and the scratching of Guest's pen kept pace with his words. "Now sign and date," he said; and the other, with a great heroic dash, consummated this amazing document. He then pushed it away, and rose and bestowed upon us a look which I long remembered. An outraged human soul was abroad in the world, with which henceforth I felt I should have somehow to reckon.

Edgar possessed himself of the paper and read it coolly to the end, without blushing. Happy Edgar! Guest watched him fold it and put it into his great morocco pocket-book. "I suppose," said Guest, "that this is the end of your generosity."

"I have nothing further to remark," said Edgar.

"Have *you*, by chance, anything to remark, Mr. Stepbrother?" Guest demanded, turning to me, with a fierceness which showed how my presence galled him.

I had been, to my own sense, so abjectly passive during the whole scene that, to reinstate myself as a responsible creature, I attempted to utter an original sentiment. "I pity you," I said.

But I had not been happy in my choice. "Faugh, you great hulking brute!" Guest roared, for an answer.

The scene at this point might have passed into another phase, had it not been interrupted by the opening of the door from the corridor. "A lady!" announced a servant, flinging it back.

The lady revealed herself as the friend with whom Guest had been in conversation on the piazza. She was apparently, of his nature, not a person to mind the trifle of her friend's being accompanied by two unknown gentlemen, and she advanced, shawled as if for departure, and smiling reproachfully. "Ah, you ungrateful creature," she cried, "you've lost my rosebud!"

Guest came up smiling, as they say. "Your own hands fastened it!—Where is my daughter?"

"She's coming. We've been looking for you, high and low. What on earth have you been doing here? Business? You've no business with business. You came here to rest. Excuse me, gentlemen! My carriage has been waiting this ten minutes. Give me your arm."

It seemed to me time we should disembarrass the poor man of our presence. I opened the window and stepped out upon the piazza. Just as Edgar had followed me, a young lady hastily entered the room.

"My dearest father!" she exclaimed.

Looking at her unseen from without, I recognized with amazement my charming friend of the Episcopal chapel, the woman to whom—I felt it now with a sort of convulsion—I had dedicated a sentiment.

III.

My discovery gave me that night much to think of, and I thought of it more than I slept. My foremost feeling was one of blank dismay as if Misfortune, whom I had been used to regard as a good-natured sort of goddess, who came on with an easy stride, letting off signals of warning to those who stood in her path, should have blinded her lantern and muffled her steps in order to steal a march on poor me,—of all men in the world! It seemed a hideous practical joke. "If I had known,—if I had only known!" I kept restlessly repeating. But towards morning, "Say I had known," I asked myself, "could I have acted otherwise? I might have protested by my absence; but would I not thus have surrendered poor Guest to the vengeance of a very Shylock? Had not that suggestion of mine divested the current of Edgar's wrath and saved his adversary from the last dishonor? Without it, Edgar would have held his course and demanded his pound of flesh!" Say what I would, however, I stood confronted with this acutely uncomfortable fact, that by lending a hand at that revolting interview, I had struck a roundabout blow at the woman to whom I owed a signally sweet impression. Well, my blow would never reach her, and I would devise some kindness that should! So I consoled myself, and in the midst of my regret I found a still further compensation in the thought that chance, rough-handed though it had been, had forged between us a stouter bond than any I had ventured to dream of as I walked sentimental a few hours before. Her father's being a rascal threw her image into more eloquent relief. If she suspected it, she had all the interest of sorrow; if not, she wore the tender grace of danger.

The result of my meditations was that I determined to defer indefinitely my departure from L——. Edgar informed me, in the course of the following day, that Guest had gone by the early train to New York, and that his daughter had left the hotel (where my not having met her before was apparently the result of her constant attendance on her father during his illness) and taken up her residence with the lady in whose company we had seen her. Mrs. Beck, Edgar had learned this lady's name to be; and I fancied it was upon her that Miss Guest had made her morning call. To begin with, therefore, I knew where to look for her. "That's the charming girl," I said to Edgar, "whom you might have plunged into disgrace."

"How do you know she's charming?" he asked.

"I judge by her face."

"Humph! Judge her father by his face and *he*'s charming."

I was on the point of assuring my step-brother that no such thing could be said of him; but in fact he had suddenly assumed a singularly fresh and jovial air. "I don't know what it is," he said, "but I feel like a trump; I haven't stood so firm on my legs in a twelvemonth. I wonder whether the waters have already begun to act. Really, I'm elated. Suppose, in the afternoon of my life, I were to turn out a sound man. It winds me up, sir. I shall take another glass before dinner."

To do Miss Guest a kindness, I reflected, I must see her again. How to compass an interview and irradiate my benevolence, it was not easy to determine. Sooner or later, of course, the chances of watering-place life would serve me. Meanwhile, I felt most agreeably that here was something more finely romantic than that feverish dream of my youth, treating Edgar some fine day to the snub direct. Assuredly, I was not in love; I had cherished a youthful passion, and I knew the signs and symptoms; but I was in a state of mind that really gave something of the same zest to consciousness.

For a couple of days I watched and waited for my friend in those few public resorts in which the little world of L—— used most to congregate,—the drive, the walk, the post-office, and the vicinage of the spring. At last, as she was nowhere visible, I betook myself to the little Episcopal chapel, and strolled along the road, past a scattered cluster of decent boarding-houses, in one of which I imagined her hidden. But most of them had a shady strip of garden stretching toward the river, and thitherward, of course, rather than upon the public road, their inmates were likely to turn their faces. A happy accident at last came to my aid. After three or four days at the hotel, Edgar began to complain that the music in the evening kept him awake and to wonder whether he might find tolerable private lodgings. He was more and more interested in the waters. I offered, with alacrity, to make inquiries for him, and as a first step, I returned to the little colony of riverside boarding-houses. I began with one I had made especial note of,—the smallest, neatest, and most secluded. The mistress of the establishment was at a neighbor's, and I was requested to await her return. I stepped out of the long parlor window, and began hopefully to explore the garden. My hopes were brightly rewarded. In a shady summer-house, on a sort of rustic embankment, overlooking the stream, I encountered Miss Guest and her coquettish duenna. She looked at me for a moment with a dubious air, as if to satisfy herself that she was distinctly expected to recognize me, and then, as I stood proclaiming my hopes in an appealing smile, she bade me a frank good-morning. We talked, I lingered, and at last, when the proper moment came for my going my way again, I sat down and paid a call in form.

"I see you know my name," Miss Guest said, with the peculiar—the almost boyish—directness which seemed to be her most striking feature; "I can't imagine how you learned it, but if you'll be so good as to tell me your own, I'll introduce you to Mrs. Beck. You must learn that she's my deputed chaperon, my she-dragon, and that I'm not to know you unless she knows you first and approves."

Mrs. Beck poised a gold eye-glass upon her pretty *retroussé* nose,—not sorry, I think, to hold it there a moment with a plump white hand and acquit herself of one of her most ef-

fective manœuvres,—and glanced at me with mock severity.
"He's a harmless-looking young man, my dear," she declared,
"and I don't think your father would object." And with this
odd sanction I became intimate with Miss Guest,—intimate
as, by the soft operation of summer and rural juxtaposition,
an American youth is free to become with an American maid.
I had told my friends, of course, the purpose of my visit, and
learned, with complete satisfaction, that there was no chance
for Mr. Musgrave, as they occupied the only three comfortable rooms in the house,—two as bedrooms, the third as a
common parlor. Heaven forbid that I should introduce Edgar
dans cette galère. I inquired elsewhere, but saw nothing I
could recommend, and, on making my report to him, found
him quite out of conceit of his project. A lady had just been
telling him horrors of the local dietary and making him feel
that he was vastly well off with the heavy bread and cold gravy
of the hotel. It was then too, I think, he first mentioned the
symptoms of that relapse which subsequently occurred. He
would run no risks.

I had prepared Miss Guest, I fancy, to regard another visit
as a matter of course. I paid several in rapid succession; for,
under the circumstances, it would have been a pity to be shy.
Her father, she told me, expected to be occupied for three or
four weeks in New York, so that for the present I was at ease
on that score. If I was to please, I must go bravely to work.
So I burned my ships behind me, and blundered into gallantry with an ardor over which, in my absence, the two ladies
must have mingled their smiles. I don't suppose I passed for
an especially knowing fellow; but I kept my friends from
wearying of each other (for such other chance acquaintances
as the place afforded they seemed to have little inclination),
and by my services as a retailer of the local gossip, a reader of
light literature, an explorer and suggester of drives and strolls,
and, more particularly, as an oarsman in certain happy row-
ing-parties on the placid river whose slow, safe current made
such a pretty affectation of Mrs. Beck's little shrieks and shud-
ders, I very fairly earned my welcome. That detestable scene
at the hotel used to seem a sort of horrid fable as I sat in the
sacred rural stillness, in that peaceful streamside nook, learning what a divinely honest girl she was, this daughter of the

man whose dishonesty I had so complacently attested. I wasted many an hour in wondering on what terms she stood with her father's rankling secret, with his poor pompous peccability in general, if not with Edgar's particular grievance. I used to fancy that certain momentary snatches of revery in the midst of our gayety, and even more, certain effusions of wilful and excessive gayety at our duller moments, portended some vague torment in her filial heart. She would quit her place and wander apart for a while, leaving me to gossip it out with Mrs. Beck, as if she were oppressed by the constant need of seeming interested in us. But she would come back with a face that told so few tales that I always ended by keeping my compassion in the case for myself, and being reminded afresh, by my lively indisposition to be thus grossly lumped, as it were, with the duenna, of how much I was interested in the damsel. In truth, the romance of the matter apart, Miss Guest was a lovely girl. I had read her dimly in the little chapel, but I had read her aright. Felicity in freedom, that was her great charm. I have never known a woman so simply and sincerely original, so finely framed to enlist the imagination and hold expectation in suspense, and yet leave the judgment in such blissful quietude. She had a genius for frankness; this was her only coquetry and her only cleverness, and a woman could not have acquitted herself more naturally of the trying and ungracious *rôle* of being expected to be startling. It was the pure personal accent of Miss Guest's walk and conversation that gave them this charm; everything she did and said was gilded by a ray of conviction; and to a respectful admirer who had not penetrated to the sources of spiritual motive in her being, this sweet, natural, various emphasis of conduct was ineffably provoking. Her creed, as I guessed it, might have been resumed in the simple notion that a man should do his best; and nature had treated her, I fancied, to some brighter vision of uttermost manhood than illumined most honest fellows' consciences. Frank as she was, I imagined she had a remote reserve of holiest contempt. She made me feel deplorably ignorant and idle and unambitious, a foolish, boyish spendthrift of time and strength and means; and I speedily came to believe that to win her perfect favor was a matter of something more than undoing a stupid wrong,—doing, namely, some very pretty piece of right. And she was poor Mr. Guest's daughter, withal! Truly, fate was a master of irony.

I ought in justice to say that I had Mrs. Beck more particularly to thank for my welcome, and for the easy terms on which I had become an *habitué* of the little summer-house by the river. How could I know how much or how little the younger lady meant by her smiles and hand-shakes, by laughing at my jokes and consenting to be rowed about in my boat? Mrs. Beck made no secret of her relish for the society of a decently agreeable man, or of her deeming some such pastime the indispensable spice of life; and in Mr. Guest's absence, I was graciously admitted to competition. The precise nature of their mutual sentiments—Mr. Guest's and hers—I was slightly puzzled to divine, and in so far as my conjectures seemed plausible, I confess they served as but a scanty offset to my knowledge of the gentleman's foibles. This lady was, to my sense, a very artificial charmer, and I think that a goodly portion of my admiration for Miss Guest rested upon a little private theory that for her father's sake she thus heroically accepted a companion whom she must have relished but little. Mrs. Beck's great point was her "preservation." It was rather too great a point for my taste, and partook too much of the nature of a physiological curiosity. Her age really mattered little, for with as many years as you pleased one way or the other, she was still a triumph of juvenility. Plump, rosy, dimpled, frizzled, with rings on her fingers and rosettes on her toes, she used to seem to me a sort of fantastic vagary or humorous experiment of time. Or, she might have been fancied a strayed shepherdess from some rococo Arcadia, which had melted into tradition during some profane excursion of her own, so that she found herself saddled in our prosy modern world with this absurdly perpetual prime. All this was true, at least of her pretty face and figure; but there was another Mrs. Beck, visible chiefly to the moral eye, who seemed to me excessively wrinkled and faded and world-wise, and whom I used to fancy I could hear shaking about in this enamelled envelope, like a dried nut in its shell. Mrs. Beck's morality was not Arcadian; or if it was, it was that of a shepherdess with a keen eye to the state of the wool and the mutton market, and a lively perception of the possible advantages of judicious partnership. She had no design, I suppose, of proposing to me a consolidation of our sentimental and pecuniary interests, but she performed her duties of duenna with such conscientious precision that she shared my society most impartially with Miss Guest. I never had the good fortune of finding myself alone with this young lady. She might have managed it, I fancied, if she had wished, and the little care she took about it was a sign of that indifference which stirs the susceptible heart to effort. "It's really detestable," I at last ventured to seize the chance to declare, "that you and I should never be alone."

Miss Guest looked at me with an air of surprise. "Your remark is startling," she said, "unless you have some excellent reason for demanding this interesting seclusion."

My reason was not ready just yet, but it speedily ripened. A happy incident combined at once to bring it to maturity and to operate a diversion for Mrs. Beck. One morning there appeared a certain Mr. Crawford out of the West, a worthy bachelor who introduced himself to Mrs. Beck and claimed cousinship. I was present at the moment, and I could not but admire the skill with which the lady gauged her aspiring kinsman before saying yea or nay to his claims. I think the large diamond in his shirt-front decided her; what he may have lacked in elegant culture was supplied by this massive ornament. Better and brighter than his diamond, however, was his frank Western *bonhomie*, his simple friendliness, and a certain half-boyish modesty which made him give a humorous twist to any expression of the finer sentiments. He was a tall, lean gentleman, on the right side of forty, yellow-haired, with a somewhat arid complexion, an irrepressible tendency to cock back his hat and chew his toothpick, and a spasmodic liability, spasmodically repressed when in a sedentary posture, to a centrifugal movement of the heels. He had a clear blue eye, in which simplicity and shrewdness contended and mingled in so lively a fashion that his glance was the oddest dramatic twinkle. He was a genial sceptic. If he disbelieved much that he saw, he believed everything he fancied, and for a man who had seen much of the rougher and baser side of life, he was able to fancy some very gracious things of men, to say nothing of women. He took his place as a very convenient fourth in our little party, and without obtruding his eccentricities, or being too often reminded of a story, like many cooler humorists, he treated us to a hundred anecdotes of his adventurous ascent of the ladder of fortune. The upshot of his history was that he was now owner of a silver mine in Arizona, and that he proposed in his own words to "lay off and choose." Of the nature of his choice he modestly waived specification; it of course had reference to the sex of which Mrs. Beck was an ornament. He lounged about meanwhile with his hands in his pockets, watching the flies buzz with that air of ecstatically suspended resolve proper to a man who has sunk a shaft deep into the very stuff that dreams are made of. But in spite of shyness he exhaled an atmosphere of regretful celibacy which might have relaxed the conjugal piety of a more tenderly mourning widow than Mrs. Beck. His bachelor days were evidently numbered, and unless I was vastly mistaken, it lay in this lady's discretion to determine the residuary figure. The two were just nearly enough akin to save a deal of time in courtship.

Crawford had never beheld so finished a piece of ladyhood, and it pleased and puzzled him and quickened his honest grin very much as a remarkably neat mechanical toy might have done. Plain people who have lived close to frank nature often think more of a fine crisp muslin rose than of a group of dewy petals of garden growth. Before ten days were past, he had begun to fumble tenderly with the stem of this unfading flower. Mr. Crawford's *petits soins* had something too much of the ring of the small change of the Arizona silver-mine, consisting largely as they did of rather rudimentary nosegays compounded by amateur florists from the local front-yards, of huge bundles of "New York candy" from the village store, and of an infinite variety of birch-bark and bead-work trinkets. He was no simpleton, and it occurred to me, indeed, that if these offerings were not the tokens and pledges of a sentiment, they were the offset and substitute of a sentiment; but if they were profuse for that, they were scanty for this. Mrs. Beck, for her part, seemed minded to spin the thread of decision excessively fine. A silver-mine was all very well, but a lover fresh from the diggings was to be put on probation. Crawford lodged at the hotel, and our comings and goings were often made together. He indulged in many a dry compliment to his cousin, and, indeed, declared that she was a magnificent little woman. It was with surprise, therefore, that I learned that his admiration was divided. "I've never seen one just like her," he said; "one so out and out a woman,— smiles and tears and everything else! But Clara comes out with her notions, and a man may know what to expect. I guess I can afford a wife with a notion or so! Short of the moon, I can give her what she wants." And I seemed to hear his hands producing in his pockets that Arizonian tinkle which served with him as the prelude to renewed utterance. He went on, "And tells me I mustn't make love to my grandmother. That's a very pretty way of confessing to thirty-five. She's a bit of coquette, is Clara!" I handled the honest fellow's illusions as tenderly as I could, and at last he eyed me askance with a knowing air. "You praise my cousin," he said, "because you think I want you to. On the contrary, I want you to say something against her. If there is anything, I want to know it." I declared I knew nothing in the world; whereupon Crawford, after a silence, heaved an impatient sigh.

"Really," said I, laughing, "one would think you were disappointed."

"I wanted to draw you out," he cried; "but you're too confoundedly polite. I suppose Mrs. Beck's to be my fate; it's borne in on me. I'm being roped in fast. But I only want a little backing to hang off awhile. Look here," he added suddenly, "let's be frank!" and he stopped and laid his hand on my arm. "That other young lady isn't so pretty as Mrs. Beck, but it seems to me I'd kind of trust her further. You didn't know I'd noticed her. Well, I've taken her in little by little, just as she gives herself out. Jerusalem! there's a woman. But you know it, sir, if I'm not mistaken; and that's where the shoe pinches. First come, first served. I want to act on the square. Before I settle down to Mrs. Beck, I want to know distinctly whether you put in a claim to Miss Guest."

The question was unexpected and found me but half prepared. "A claim?" I said. "Well, yes, call it a claim!"

"Any way," he rejoined, "I've no chance. She'd never look at me. But I want to have her put out of my own head, so that I can concentrate on Mrs. B. If you're not in love with her, my boy, let me tell you you ought to be! If you are, I've nothing to do but to wish you success. If you're not, upon my word, I don't know but what I would go in! She could but refuse me. Modesty is all very well; but after all, it's the handsomest thing you can do by a woman to offer yourself. As a compliment alone, it would serve. And really, a compliment with a round million isn't so bad as gallantry goes hereabouts. You're young and smart and good-looking, and Mrs. Beck tells me you're rich. If you succeed, you'll have more than your share of good things. But Fortune has her favorites, and they're not always such nice young men. If you're in love, well and good! If you're not,—by Jove, I am!"

This admonition was peremptory. My companion's face in the clear star-light betrayed his sagacious sincerity. I felt a sudden satisfaction in being summoned to take my stand. I performed a rapid operation in sentimental arithmetic, combined my factors, and established my total. It exceeded expectation. "Your frankness does you honor," I said, "and I'm sorry I can't make a kinder return. But—I'm madly in love!"

IV.

My situation, as I defined it to Crawford, was not purely delightful. Close upon my perception of the state of my heart followed an oppressive sense of the vanity of my pretensions. I had cut the ground from under my feet; to offer myself to Miss Guest would be to add insult to injury. I may truly say, therefore, that, for a couple of days, this manifest passion of mine rather saddened than exalted me. For a dismal forty-eight hours I left the two ladies unvisited. I even thought of paying a supreme tribute to delicacy and taking a summary departure. Some day, possibly, Miss Guest would learn with grief and scorn what her father had to thank me for; and then later, as resentment melted into milder conjecture, she would read the riddle of my present conduct and do me justice,— guess that I had loved her, and that, to punish myself, I had renounced her forever. This fantastic magnanimity was followed by a wholesome reaction. I was punished enough, surely, in my regret and shame; and I wished now not to suffer, but to act. Viewing the matter reasonably, she need never

learn my secret; if by some cruel accident she should, the favor I had earned would cover that I had forfeited. I stayed,
then, and tried to earn this precious favor; but I encountered
an obstacle more serious, I fancied, than even her passionate
contempt would have been,—her serene and benevolent indifference. Looking back at these momentous days, I get an
impression of a period of vague sentimental ferment and trouble, rather than of definite utterance and action; though I believe that by a singular law governing human conduct in
certain cases, the very modesty and humility of my passion expressed itself in a sort of florid and hyperbolical gallantry; so
that, in so far as my claims were inadmissible, they might pass,
partly as a kind of compensatory homage, and partly as a jest.
Miss Guest refused to pay me the compliment of even being
discomposed, and pretended to accept my addresses as an
elaborate device for her amusement. There was a perpetual assurance in her tone of her not regarding me as a serious,
much less as a dangerous, man. She could not have contrived
a more effective irritant to my resolution; and I confess there
were certain impatient moods when I took a brutal glee in the
thought that it was not so very long since, on a notable occasion, my presence had told. In so far as I *was* serious, Miss
Guest frankly offered to accept me as a friend, and laughingly
intimated, indeed, that with a little matronly tuition of her
dispensing, I might put myself into condition to please some
simple maiden in her flower. I was an excellent, honest fellow;
but I was excessively young and—as she really wished to be-
friend me, she would risk the admonition—I was decidedly
frivolous. I lacked "character." I was fairly clever, but I was
more clever than wise. I liked overmuch to listen to my own
tongue. I had done nothing; I was idle; I had, by my own
confession, never made an effort; I was too rich and too indolent; in my very good-nature there was nothing moral, no
hint of principle; in short, I was—boyish. I must forgive a
woman upon whom life had forced the fatal habit of discrim-
ination. I suffered this genial scepticism to expend itself freely,
for her candor was an enchantment. It was all true enough. I
had been indolent and unambitious; I had made no effort; I
had lived in vulgar ignorance and ease; I had in a certain frivolous fashion tried life at first hand, but my shallow gains had

been in proportion to my small hazards. But I was neither so young nor so idle as she chose to fancy, and I could at any rate prove I was constant. Like a legendary suitor of old, I might even slay my dragon. A monstrous accident stood between us, and to dissipate its evil influence would be a fairly heroic feat.

Mr. Guest's absence was prolonged from day to day, and Laura's tone of allusion to her father tended indeed to make a sort of invincible chimera of her possible discovery of the truth. This fond filial reference only brought out the more brightly her unlikeness to him. I could as little fancy her doing an act she would need to conceal as I could fancy her arresting exposure by a concession to dishonor. If I was a friend, I insisted on being a familiar one; and while Mrs. Beck and her cousin floated away on perilous waters, we dabbled in the placid shallows of disinterested sentiment. For myself, I sent many a longing glance toward the open sea, but Laura remained firm in her preference for the shore. I encouraged her to speak of her father, for I wished to hear all the good that could be told of him. It sometimes seemed to me that she talked of him with a kind of vehement tenderness designed to obscure, as it were, her inner vision. Better—had she said to herself?—that she should talk fond nonsense about him than that she should harbor untender suspicions. I could easily believe that the poor man was a most lovable fellow, and could imagine how, as Laura judged him in spite of herself, the sweet allowances of a mother had grown up within the daughter. One afternoon Mrs. Beck brought forth her photograph-book, to show to her cousin. Suddenly, as he was turning it over, she stayed his hand and snatched one of the pictures from its place. He tried to recover it and a little tussle followed, in the course of which she escaped, ran to Miss Guest, and thrust the photograph into her hand. "You keep it," she cried; "he's not to see it." There was a great crying out from Crawford about Mrs. Beck's inconstancy and his *right* to see the picture, which was cut short by Laura's saying with some gravity that it was too childish a romp for a man of forty and a woman of—thirty! Mrs. Beck allowed us no time to relish the irony of this attributive figure; she caused herself to be pursued to the other end of the garden, where the amorous frolic was resumed over the following pages of the album. "Who is it?" I asked. Miss Guest, after a pause, handed me the card.

"Your father!" I cried precipitately.

"Ah, you've seen him?" she asked.

"I know him by his likeness to you."

"You prevent my asking you, as I meant, if he doesn't look like a dear good man. I do wish he'd drop his stupid business and come back."

I took occasion hereupon to ascertain whether she suspected his embarrassments. She confessed to a painful impression that something was wrong. He had been out of spirits for many days before his return to town; nothing indeed but mental distress could have affected his health, for he had a perfect constitution. "If it comes to that," she went on, after a long silence, and looking at me with an almost intimate confidence, "I wish he would give up business altogether. All the business in the world, for a man of his open, joyous temper, doesn't pay for an hour's depression. I can't bear to sit by and see him imbittered and spoiled by this muddle of stocks and shares. Nature made him a happy man; I insist on keeping him so. We are quite rich enough, and we need nothing more. He tries to persuade me that I have expensive tastes, but I've never spent money but to please him. I have a lovely little dream which I mean to lay before him when he comes back; it's very cheap, like all dreams, and more practicable than most. He's to give up business and take me abroad. We're to settle down quietly somewhere in Germany, in Italy, I don't care where, and I'm to study music seriously. I'm never to marry; but as he grows to be an old man, he's to sit by a window, with his cigar, looking out on the Arno or the Rhine, while I play Beethoven and Rossini."

"It's a very pretty programme," I answered, "though I can't subscribe to certain details. But do you know," I added, touched by a forcible appeal to sympathy in her tone, "although you refuse to believe me anything better than an ingenuous fool, this liberal concession to my interest in your situation is almost a proof of respect."

She blushed a little, to my great satisfaction. "I surely respect you," she said, "if you come to that! Otherwise we

should hardly be sitting here so simply. And I think, too," she
went on, "that I speak to you of my father with peculiar freedom, because—because, somehow, you remind me of him."
She looked at me as she spoke with such penetrating candor
that it was my turn to blush. "You are genial, and gentle, and
essentially honest, like him; and like him," she added with a
half-smile, "you're addicted to saying a little more than it
would be fair to expect you to stand to. You ought to be very
good friends. You'll find he has your own *jeunesse de cœur*."

I murmured what I might about the happiness of making
his acquaintance; and then, to give the conversation a turn,
and really to test the force of this sympathetic movement of
hers, I boldly mentioned my fancy that he was an admirer of
Mrs. Beck. She gave me a silent glance, almost of gratitude, as
if she needed to unburden her heart. But she did so in few
words. "He does admire her," she said. "It's my duty, it's my
pleasure, to respect his illusions. But I confess to you that I
hope this one will fade." She rose from her seat and we joined
our companions; but I fancied, for a week afterwards, that she
treated me with a certain gracious implication of deference.
Had I ceased to seem boyish? I struck a truce with urgency
and almost relished the idea of being patient.

A day or two later, Mr. Guest's "illusions" were put before
me in a pathetic light. It was a Sunday; the ladies were at
church, and Crawford and I sat smoking on the piazza. "I
don't know how things are going with you," he said; "you're
either perfectly successful or desperately resigned. But unless
it's rather plainer sailing than in my case, I don't envy you. I
don't know where I am, anyway! She will and she won't. She
may take back her word once too often, I can tell her that!
You see, she has two strings to her bow. She likes my money,
but she doesn't like *me*. Now, it's all very well for a woman to
relish a fortune, but I'm not prepared to have my wife despise—my *person*!" said Crawford with feeling. "The alternative, you know, is Mr. Guest, that girl's father. I suppose he's
handsome, and a wit, and a dandy; though I must say an old
dandy, to my taste, is an old fool. She tells me a dozen times
an hour that he's a fascinating man. I suppose if I were to
leave her alone for a week, I might seem a fascinating man. I
wish to heaven she wasn't so confoundedly taking. I can't

give her up; she amuses me too much. There was once a little actress in Galveston, but Clara beats that girl! If I could only have gone in for some simple wholesome girl who doesn't need to count on her fingers to know the state of her heart!"

That evening as we were gathered in the garden, poor Crawford approached Laura Guest with an air of desperate gallantry, as if from a desire to rest from the petty torment of Mrs. Beck's sentimental mutations. Laura liked him, and her manner to him had always been admirable in its almost sisterly frankness and absence of provoking arts; yet I found myself almost wondering, as they now strolled about the garden together, whether there was any danger of this sturdy architect of his own fortunes putting out my pipe. Mrs. Beck, however, left me no chance for selfish meditation. Her artless and pointless prattle never lacked a purpose; before you knew it she was, in vulgar parlance, "pumping" you, trying to pick your pocket of your poor little receipt for prosperity. She took an intense delight in imaginatively bettering her condition, and one was forced to carry bricks for her castles in the air.

"You needn't be afraid of my cousin," she said, laughing, as I followed his red cigar-tip along the garden-paths. "He admires Laura altogether too much to make love to her. There's modesty! Don't you think it's rather touching in a man with a million of dollars? I don't mind telling you that he has made love to me, that being no case for modesty. I suppose you'll say that my speaking of it is. But what's the use of being an aged widow, if one can't tell the truth?"

"There's comfort in being an aged widow," I answered gallantly, "when one has two offers a month."

"I don't know what you know about my offers; but even two swallows don't make a summer! However, since you've mentioned the subject, tell me frankly what you think of poor Crawford. Is he at all presentable? You see I like him, I esteem him, and I'm afraid of being blinded by my feelings. Is he so dreadfully rough? You see I like downright simple manliness and all that; but a little polish does no harm, even on fine gold. I do wish you'd take hold of my poor cousin and teach him a few of the amenities of life. I'm very fond of the amenities of life; it's very frivolous and wicked, I suppose, but I can't help it. I have the misfortune to be sensitive to ugly things. Can one really accept a man who wears a green cravat? Of course you can make him take it off; but you'll be knowing all the while that he pines for it, that he would put it on if he could. Now that's a symbol of that dear, kind, simple fellow,—a heart of gold, but a green cravat! I've never heard a word of wisdom about that matter yet. People talk about the sympathy of souls being the foundation of happiness in marriage. It's pure nonsense. It's not the great things, but the little, that we dispute about, and the chances are terribly against the people who have a different taste in colors."

It seemed to me that, thus ardently invoked, I might hazard the observation, "Mr. Guest would never wear a green cravat."

"What do you know about Mr. Guest's cravats?"

"I've seen his photograph, you know."

"Well, you do him justice. You should see him in the life. He looks like a duke. I never saw a duke, but that's my notion of a duke. Distinction, you know; perfect manners and tact and wit. If I'm right about its being perfection in small things that assures one's happiness, I might—well, in two words, I might be very happy with Mr. Guest!"

"It's Crawford and soul, then," I proposed, smiling, "or Guest and manners!"

She looked at me a moment, and then with a toss of her head and a tap of her fan, "You wretch!" she cried, "you want to make me say something very ridiculous. I'll not pretend I'm not worldly. I'm excessively worldly. I always make a point of letting people know it. Of course I know very well my cousin's rich, and that so long as he's good he's none the worse for that. But in my quiet little way I'm a critic, and I look at things from a high ground. I compare a rich man who is simply a good fellow to a perfect gentleman who has simply a nice little fortune. Mr. Guest has a nice property, a very nice property. I shouldn't have to make over my old bonnets. You may ask me if I'm not afraid of Laura. But you'll marry Laura and carry her off!"

I found nothing to reply for some moments to this little essay in "criticism"; and suddenly Mrs. Beck, fancying perhaps that she was indiscreetly committing herself, put an end to our interview. "I'm really very kind," she cried, "to be talking so graciously about a lover who leaves me alone for a month and never even drops me a line. It's not such good manners after all. If you're not jealous of Mr. Crawford, I am of Miss Guest. We'll go down and separate them."

Miss Guest's repose and dignity were decidedly over-shadowed. I brought her the next afternoon a letter from the post-office, superscribed in a hand I knew, and wandered away while she sat in the garden and read it. When I came back she looked strangely sad. I sat down near her and drew figures in the ground with the end of her parasol, hoping that she would do me the honor to communicate her trouble. At last she rose in silence, as if to return to the house. I begged her to remain. "You're in distress," I said, speaking as calmly and coldly as I could, "and I hoped it might occur to you that there is infinite sympathy close at hand. Instead of going to your own room to cry, why not stay here and talk of it with me?"

She gave me a brilliant, searching gaze; I met it steadily and felt that I was turning pale with the effort not to obey the passionate impulse of self-denunciation. She began slowly to walk away from the house, and I felt that a point was gained. "It's your father, of course," I said. It was all I could say. She silently handed me his unfolded letter. It ran as follows:—

MY DEAREST DAUGHTER:—I have sold the house and everything in it, except your piano and books, of course at a painful sacrifice. But I needed ready money. Forgive your poor blundering, cruel father. My old luck has left me; but only *trust me*, and we shall be happy again."

Her eyes, fortunately, were wandering while I read; for I felt myself blushing to my ears.

"It's not the loss of the house," she said at last; "though of course we were fond of it. I grew up there,—my mother died there. It's the trouble it indicates. Poor dear father! Why does he talk of 'luck'? I detest the word! Why does he talk of forgiving him and trusting him? There's a wretched tone about it all. If he would only come back and let me look at him!"

"Nothing is more common in business," I answered, "than a temporary embarrassment demanding ready money. Of course it must be met at a sacrifice. One throws a little something overboard to lighten the ship, and the ship sails ahead. As for the loss of the house, nothing could be better for going to Italy, you know. You've no excuse left for staying here. If your father will forgive me the interest I take in his affairs, I strongly recommend his leaving business and its sordid cares. Let him go abroad and forget it all."

Laura walked along in silence, and I led the way out of the garden into the road. We followed it slowly till we reached the little chapel. The sexton was just leaving it, shouldering the broom with which he had been sweeping it for the morrow's services. I hailed him and gained his permission to go in and try the organ, assuring him that we were experts. Laura said that she felt in no mood for music; but she entered and sat down in one of the pews. I climbed into the gallery and attacked the little instrument. We had had no music since our first meeting, and I felt an irresistible need to recall the circumstances of that meeting. I played in a simple fashion, respectably enough, and fancied, at all events, that by my harmonious fingers I could best express myself. I played for an hour, in silence, choosing what I would, without comment or response from my companion. The summer twilight overtook us; when it was getting too dark to see the keys, I rejoined Miss Guest. She rose and came into the aisle. "You play very well," she said, simply; "better than I supposed."

Her praise was sweet; but sweeter still was a fancy of mine that I perceived in the light gloom just the glimmer of a tear. "In this place," I said, "your playing once moved me greatly. Try and remember the scene distinctly."

"It's easily remembered," she answered, with an air of surprise.

"Believe, then, that when we parted, I was already in love with you."

She turned away abruptly. "Ah, my poor music!"

The next day, on my arrival, I was met by Mrs. Beck, whose pretty forehead seemed clouded with annoyance. With her own fair hand she button-holed me. "You apparently," she said, "have the happiness to be in Miss Guest's confidence. What on earth is going on in New York? Laura received an hour ago a letter from her father. I found her sitting with it in her hand as cheerful as a Quakeress in meeting. 'Something's wrong, my dear,' I said; 'I don't know what. In any case, be assured of my sympathy.' She gave me the most extraordinary stare. 'You'll be interested to know,' she said, 'that my father has lost half his property.' Interested to know! I verily believe the child meant an impertinence. What is Mr. Guest's property to me? Has he been speculating? Stupid man!" she cried, with vehemence.

I made a brief answer. I discovered Miss Guest sitting by the river, in pale contemplation of household disaster. I asked no questions. She told me of her own accord that her father was to return immediately, "to make up a month's sleep," she added, glancing at his letter. We spoke of other matters, but before I left her, I returned to this one. "I wish you to tell your father this," I said. "That there is a certain gentleman here, who is idle, indolent, ignorant, frivolous, selfish. That he has certain funds for which he is without present use. That he places them at Mr. Guest's absolute disposal in the hope that they may partially relieve his embarrassment." I looked at Laura as I spoke and watched her startled blush deepen to crimson. She was about to reply; but before she could speak, "Don't forget to add," I went on, "that he hopes his personal faults will not prejudice Mr. Guest's acceptance of his offer, for it is prompted by the love he bears his daughter."

"You must excuse me," Laura said, after a pause. "I had rather not tell him this. He would not accept your offer.'

"Are you sure of that?"

"I shouldn't allow him."

"And why not, pray? Don't you, after all, like me well enough to suffer me to do you so small a service?"

She hesitated; then gave me her hand with magnificent frankness. "I like you too well to suffer you to do me just that service. We take that from *les indifferents*."

v.

Before the month was out, Edgar had quarrelled with the healing waters of L——. His improvement had been most illusory; his old symptoms had returned in force, and though he now railed bitterly at the perfidious spring and roundly denounced the place, he was too ill to be moved away. He was altogether confined to his room. I made a conscience of offering him my company and assistance, but he would accept no nursing of mine. He would be tended by no one whom he could not pay for his trouble and enjoy a legal right to grumble at. "I expect a nurse to *be* a nurse," he said, "and not a fine gentleman, waiting on me in gloves. It would be fine work for me, lying here, to have to think twice whether I might bid you not to breathe so hard." Nothing had passed between us about John Guest, though the motive for silence was different on each side. For Edgar, I fancied, our interview with him was a matter too solemn for frequent allusion; for me it was a detestable thought. But wishing now to assure myself that, as I supposed, he had paid his ugly debt, I asked Edgar, on the evening I had extorted from Miss Guest those last recorded words of happy omen, whether he had heard from our friend in New York. It was a very hot night; poor Edgar lay sweltering under a sheet, with open windows. He looked pitifully ill, and yet somehow more intensely himself than ever. He drew a letter from under his pillow. "This came to-day," he said. "Stevens writes me that Guest yesterday paid down the twenty thousand dollars in full. It's quick work. I hope he's not robbed Peter to pay Paul."

"Mr. Guest has a conscience," I said; and I thought bitterly of the reverse of the picture. "I'm afraid he has half ruined himself to do it."

"Well, ruin for ruin, I prefer his. I've no doubt his affairs have gone to the dogs. The affairs of such a man must, sooner or later! I believe, by the way, you've been cultivating the young lady. What does the papa say to that?"

"Of course," I said, without heeding his question, "you've already enclosed him the—the little paper."

Edgar turned in his bed. "Of course I've done no such thing!"

"You mean to keep it?" I cried.

"Of course I mean to keep it. Where else would be his punishment?"

There was something vastly grotesque in the sight of this sickly little mortal erecting himself among his pillows as a dispenser of justice, an appraiser of the wages of sin; but I confess that his attitude struck me as more cruel even than ludicrous. I was disappointed. I had certainly not expected Edgar to be generous, but I had expected him to be just, and in the heat of his present irritation he was neither. He was angry with Guest for his excessive promptitude, which had given a sinister twist to his own conduct. "Upon my word," I cried, "you're a veritable Shylock!"

"And you're a veritable fool! Is it set down in the bond that I'm to give it up to him? The thing's mine, to have and to hold forever. The scoundrel would be easily let off indeed! This bit of paper in my hands is to keep him in order and prevent his being too happy. The thought will be wholesome company,—a *memento mori* to his vanity."

"He's to go through life, then, with possible exposure staring him in the face?"

Edgar's great protuberant eyes expanded without blinking. "He has committed his fate to Providence."

I was revolted. "You may have the providential qualities, but you have not the gentlemanly ones, I formally protest. But, after a decent delay, he'll of course demand the document."

"Demand it? He shall have it then, with a vengeance!"

"Well, I wash my hands of further complicity! I shall inform Mr. Guest that I count for nothing in this base negation of his right."

Edgar paused a moment to stare at me in my unprecedented wrath. Then making me a little ironical gesture of congratulation, "Inform him of what you please. I hope you'll have a pleasant talk over it! You made rather a bad beginning, but who knows, if you put your heads together to abuse me, you may end as bosom friends! I've watched you, sir!" he suddenly added, propping himself forward among his pillows; "you're in love!" I may wrong the poor fellow, but it seemed to me that in these words he discharged the bitterness of a lifetime. He too would have hoped to please, and he had lived in acrid assent to the instinct which told him such hope was vain. In one way or another a man pays his tax to manhood. "Yes, sir, you're grossly in love! What do I know about love, you ask? I know a drivelling lover when I see him. You've made a clever choice. Do you expect John Guest to give the girl away? He's a good-natured man, I know; but really, considering your high standard of gentlemanly conduct, you ask a good deal."

Edgar had been guilty on this occasion of a kind of reckless moral self-exposure, which seemed to betray a sense that he should never need his reputation again. I felt as if I were standing by something very like a death-bed, and forbearingly, without rejoinder, I withdrew. He had simply expressed more brutally, however, my own oppressive belief that the father's aversion stood darkly massed in the rear of the daughter's indifference. I had, indeed, for the present, the consolation of believing that with Laura the day of pure indifference was over; and I tried hard to flatter myself that my position was tenable in spite of Mr. Guest. The next day as I was wandering on the hotel piazza, communing thus sadly with my hopes, I met Crawford, who, with his hands in his pockets and his hat on the bridge of his nose, seemed equally a sullen probationer of fate.

"I'm going down to join our friends," I said; "I expected to find you with them."

He gave a gloomy grin. "My nose is out of joint," he said; "Mr. Guest has come back." I turned pale, but he was too much engaged with his own trouble to observe it. "What do you suppose my cousin is up to? She had agreed to drive with me and I had determined to come home, once for all, engaged or rejected. As soon as she heard of Guest's arrival, she threw me overboard and tripped off to her room, to touch up her curls. Go down there now and you'll find her shaking them at Mr. Guest. By the Lord, sir, she can whistle for me now! If there was a decently good-looking woman in this house, I'd march straight up to her and offer myself. You're a happy man, my boy, not to have a d—d fool to interfere with you, and not to be in love with a d—d fool either."

I had no present leisure to smooth the turbid waters of poor Crawford's passion; but I remembered a clever remark in a French book, to the effect that even the best men—and Crawford was one of the best—are subject to a momentary need not to respect what they love. I repaired alone to the house by the river, and found Laura in the little parlor which she shared with Mrs. Beck. The room was flooded with the glow of a crimson sunset, and she was looking out of the long window at two persons in the garden. In my great desire to obtain some firm assurance from her before her father's interference should become a certainty, I lost no time. "I've been able to think of nothing," I said, "but your reply to that poor offer of mine. I've been flattering myself that it really means something,—means, possibly, that if I were to speak—here—now—all that I long to speak, you would listen to me more kindly. Laura," I cried, passionately, "I repent of all my follies and I love you!"

She looked at me from head to foot with a gaze almost strange in its intensity. It betrayed trouble, but, I fancied, a grateful trouble. Then, with a smile, "My father has come," she said. The words set my heart a beating, and I had a horrible fancy that they were maliciously uttered. But as she went on I was reassured. "I want him to see you, though he knows nothing of your offer."

Somehow, by her tone, my mind was suddenly illumined with a delicious apprehension of her motive. She had heard the early murmur of that sentiment whose tender essence resents compulsion. "Let me feel then," I said, "that I am not to stand or fall by *his* choice."

"He's sure to like you," she answered; "don't you remember my telling you so? He judges better of men than of women," she added sadly, turning away from the window.

Mr. Guest had been advancing toward the house, side by side with Mrs. Beck. Before they reached it the latter was met by two ladies who had been ushered into the garden from the front gate, and with whom, with an air of smothered petulance, perceptible even at a distance, she retraced her steps toward the summer-house. Her companion entered our little parlor alone from the piazza. He stepped jauntily and looked surprisingly little altered by his month's ordeal. Mrs. Beck might still have taken him for a duke, or, at least, for an earl. His daughter immediately introduced me. "Happy to make your acquaintance, sir," he exclaimed, in a voice which I was almost shocked to find how well I knew. He offered his hand. I met it with my own, and the next moment we were fairly face to face. I was prepared for anything. Recognition faltered for a mere instant in his eyes; then I felt it suddenly leap forth in the tremendous wrench of his hand, "Ah, you—*you*—YOU!"

"Why, you know him!" exclaimed Laura.

Guest continued to wring my hand, and I felt to my cost that he was shocked. He panted a moment for breath, and then burst into a monstrous laugh. I looked askance at Laura; her eyes were filled with wonder. I felt that for the moment anger had made her father reckless, and anything was better than that between us the edge of our secret should peep out. "We have been introduced," I said, trying to smile. Guest dropped my hand as if it burned him, and walked the length of the room.

"You should have told me!" Laura added, in a tone of almost familiar reproach.

"Miss Guest," I answered, hardly knowing what I said, "the world is so wide—"

"Upon my soul, I think it's damnably narrow!" cried Guest, who had turned very pale.

I determined then that he should know the worst. "I'm here with a purpose, Mr. Guest," I said; "I love your daughter."

He stopped short, fairly glaring at me. Laura stepped toward him and laid her two hands on his arm. "Something is wrong," she said, "very wrong! It's your horrible money-matters! Weren't you really then so generous?" and she turned to me.

Guest laid his other hand on hers as they rested on his arm and patted them gently. "My daughter," he said solemnly, "do your poor father a favor. Dismiss him forever. Turn him out of the house," he added, fiercely.

"You wrong your daughter," I cried, "by asking her to act so blindly and cruelly."

"My child," Guest went on, "I expect you to obey!"

There was a silence. At last Laura turned to me, excessively pale. "Will you do me the very great favor," she said, with a trembling voice, "to leave us?"

I reflected a moment. "I appreciate your generosity; but in the interest of your own happiness, I beg you not to listen to your father until I have had a word with him alone."

She hesitated and looked, as if for assent, at her father. "Great heavens, girl!" he cried, "you don't mean you love him!" She blushed to her hair and rapidly left the room.

Guest took up his hat and removed a speck of dust from

the ribbon by a fillip of his finger-nail. "Young man," he said, "you waste words!"

"Not, I hope, when, with my hand on my heart, I beg your pardon."

"Now that you have something to gain. If you respect me, you should have protested before. If you don't, you've nothing to do with me or mine."

"I allow for your natural resentment, but you might keep it within bounds. I religiously forget, ignore, efface the past. Meet me half-way! When we met a month ago, I already loved your daughter. If I had dreamed of your being ever so remotely connected with her, I would have arrested that detestable scene even by force, brother of mine though your adversary was!"

Guest put on his hat with a gesture of implacable contempt. "That's all very well! You don't know me, sir, or you'd not waste your breath on *ifs*! The thing's done. Such as I stand here, I've been *dishonored*!" And two hot tears sprang into his eyes. "Such as I stand here, I carry in my poor, sore heart the vision of your great, brutal, staring, cruel presence. And now you ask me to accept that presence as perpetual! Upon my soul, I'm a precious fool to talk about it."

I made an immense effort to remain calm and courteous. "Is there nothing I can do to secure your good-will? I'll make any sacrifice."

"Nothing but to leave me at once and forever. Fancy my living with you for an hour! Fancy, whenever I met your eyes, my seeing in them the reflection of—of that piece of business! And your walking about looking wise and chuckling! My precious young man," he went on with a scorching smile, "if you knew how I hated you, you'd give me a wide berth."

I was silent for some moments, teaching myself the great patience which I foresaw I should need. "This is after all but the question of our personal relations, which we might fairly leave to time. Not only am I willing to pledge myself to the most explicit respect—"

"Explicit respect!" he broke out. "I should relish that vastly! Heaven deliver me from your explicit respect!"

"I can quite believe," I quietly continued, "that I should

get to like you. Your daughter has done me the honor to say that she believed you would like me."

"Perfect! You've talked it all over with her?"

"At any rate," I declared roundly, "I love her, and I have reason to hope that I may render myself acceptable to her. I can only add, Mr. Guest, that much as I should value your approval of my suit, if you withhold it I shall try my fortune without it!"

"Gently, impetuous youth!" And Guest laid his hand on my arm and lowered his voice. "Do you dream that if my daughter ever so faintly suspected the truth, she would even look at you again?"

"The truth? Heaven forbid she should dream of it! I wonder that in your position you should allude to it so freely."

"I was prudent once; I shall treat myself to a little freedom now. Give it up, I advise you. She may have thought you a pretty young fellow; I took you for one myself at first; but she'll keep her affection for a man with the bowels of compassion. She'll never love a coward, sir. Upon my soul, I'd sooner she married your beautiful brother. *He*, at least, had a grievance. Don't talk to me about my own child. She and I have an older love than yours; and if she were to learn that I've been weak—Heaven help me!—she would only love me the more. She would feel only that I've been outraged."

I confess that privately I flinched, but I stood to it bravely. "Miss Guest, doubtless, is as perfect a daughter as she would be a wife. But allow me to say that a woman's heart is not so simple a mechanism. Your daughter is a person of a very fine sense of honor, and I can imagine nothing that would give her greater pain than to be reduced to an attitude of mere compassion for her father. She likes to believe that men are strong. The sense of respect is necessary to her happiness. We both wish to assure that happiness. Let us join hands to preserve her illusions."

I saw in his eye no concession except to angry perplexity. "I don't know what you mean," he cried, "and I don't want to know. If you wish to intimate that my daughter is so very superior a person that she'll despise me, you're mistaken! She's beyond any compliment you can pay her. You can't frighten

me now; I don't care for things." He walked away a moment
and then turned about with flushed face and trembling lip.
"I'm broken, I'm ruined! I don't want my daughter's respect,
nor any other woman's. It's a burden, a mockery, a snare!
What's a woman worth who can be kind only while she believes? Ah, ah!" and he began to rub his hands with a sudden
air of helpless senility, "I should never be so kissed and cod-
dled and nursed. I can tell her what I please; I sha'n't mind
what I say now. I've ceased to care,—all in a month! Reputation's a farce; a pair of tight boots, worn for vanity. I used
to have a good foot, but I shall end my days in my slippers. I
don't care for anything!"

This mood was piteous, but it was also formidable, for I
was scantily disposed to face the imputation of having reduced an amiable gentleman, in however strictly just a cause,
to this state of plaintive cynicism. I could only hope that time
would repair both his vanity and his charity, seriously dam-
aged as they were. "Well," I said, taking my hat, "a man in
love, you know, is obstinate. Confess, yourself, that you'd not
think the better of me for accepting dismissal philosophically.
A single word of caution, keep cool; don't lose your head;
don't speak recklessly to Laura. I protest that, for myself, I'd
rather my mistress shouldn't doubt of her father."

Guest had seated himself on the sofa with his hat on, and
remained staring absently at the carpet, as if he were deaf to
my words. As I turned away, Mrs. Beck crossed the piazza and
stood on the threshold of the long window. Her shadow fell
at Mr. Guest's feet; she sent a searching glance from his face
to mine. He started, stared, rose, stiffened himself up, and removed his hat. Suddenly he colored to the temples, and after
a second's delay there issued from behind this ruby curtain a
wondrous imitation of a smile. I turned away, reassured. "My
case is not hopeless," I said to myself. "You *do* care for something, yet." Even had I deemed it hopeless, I might have
made my farewell. Laura met me near the gate, and I remember thinking that trouble was vastly becoming to her.

"Is your quarrel too bad to speak of?" she asked.

"Allow me to make an urgent request. Your father forbids
me to think of you, and you, of course, to think of me. You
see," I said, mustering a smile, "we're in a delightfully ro-

mantic position, persecuted by a stern parent. He will say hard things of me; I say nothing about your believing them, I leave that to your own discretion. But don't contradict them. Let him call me cruel, pusillanimous, false, whatever he will. Ask no questions; they will bring you no comfort. Be patient, be a good daughter, and—wait!"

Her brow contracted painfully over her intensely lucid eyes, and she shook her head impatiently. "Let me understand. Have you really done wrong?"

I felt that it was but a slender sacrifice to generosity to say Yes, and to add that I had repented. I even felt gratefully that whatever it might be to have a crime to confess to, it was not "boyish."

For a moment, I think, Laura was on the point of asking me a supreme question about her father, but she suppressed it and abruptly left me.

My step-brother's feeble remnant of health was now so cruelly reduced that the end of his troubles seemed near. He was in constant pain, and was kept alive only by stupefying drugs. As his last hour might strike at any moment, I was careful to remain within call, and for several days saw nothing of father or daughter. I learned from Crawford that they had determined to prolong their stay into the autumn, for Mr. Guest's "health." "I don't know what's the matter with his health," Crawford grumbled. "For a sick man he seems uncommonly hearty, able to sit out of doors till midnight with Mrs. B., and always as spick and span as a bridegroom. I'm the invalid of the lot," he declared; "the climate don't agree with me." Mrs. Beck, it appeared, was too fickle for patience; he would be made a fool of no more. If she wanted him, she must come and fetch him; and if she valued her chance, she must do it without delay. He departed for New York to try the virtue of missing and being missed.

On the evening he left us, the doctor told me that Edgar could not outlast the night. At midnight, I relieved the watcher and took my place by his bed. Edgar's soundless and motionless sleep was horribly like death. Sitting watchful by his pillow, I passed an oppressively solemn night. It seemed to me that a part of myself was dying, and that I was sitting in cold survival of youthful innocence and of the lavish self-surrender of youth. There is a certain comfort in an ancient grievance, and as I thought of having heard for the last time the strenuous quaver of Edgar's voice, I could have wept as for the effacement of some revered horizon-line of life. I heard his voice again, however; he was not even to die without approving the matter. With the first flash of dawn and the earliest broken bird-note, he opened his eyes and began to murmur disconnectedly. At length he recognized me, and, with me, his situation. "Don't go on tiptoe, and hold your breath, and pull a long face," he said; "speak up like a man. I'm doing the biggest job I ever did yet, you'll not interrupt me; I'm dying. One—two, three—four; I can almost count the ebbing waves. And to think that all these years they've been breaking on the strand of the universe! It's only when the world's din is shut out, at the last, that we hear them. I'll not pretend to say I'm not sorry; I've been a man of this world. It's a great one; there's a vast deal to do in it, for a man of sense. I've not been a fool, either. Write that for my epitaph, *He was no fool!*—except when he went to L. I'm not satisfied yet. I might have got better, and richer. I wanted to try galvanism, and to transfer that Pennsylvania stock. Well, I'm to be transferred myself. If dying's the end of it all, it's as well to die worse as to die better. At any rate, while time was mine, I didn't waste it. I went over my will, pen in hand, for the last time, only a week ago, crossed the *t*'s and dotted the *i*'s. I've left you—nothing. You need nothing for comfort, and of course you expect nothing for sentiment. I've left twenty thousand dollars to found an infirmary for twenty indigent persons suffering from tumor in the stomach. *There*'s sentiment! There will be no trouble about it, for my affairs are in perfect shape. Twenty snug little beds in my own little house in Philadelphia. They can get five into the dining-room." He was silent awhile, as if with a kind of ecstatic vision of the five little beds in a row. "I don't know that there is anything else," he said, at last, "except a few old papers to be burned. I hate leaving rubbish behind me; it's enough to leave one's mouldering carcass!"

At his direction I brought a large tin box from a closet and placed it on a chair by his bedside, where I drew from it a dozen useless papers and burned them one by one in the candle. At last, when but three or four were left, I laid my hand on a small sealed document labelled *Guest's Confession*. My hand trembled as I held it up to him, and as he recognized it a faint flush overspread his cadaverous pallor. He frowned, as if painfully confused. "How did it come there? I sent it back, I sent it back," he said. Then suddenly with a strangely erroneous recollection of our recent dispute, "I told you so the other day, you remember; and you said I was too generous. And what did you tell me about the daughter? You're in love with her? Ah yes! What a muddle!"

I respected his confusion. "You say you've left me nothing," I answered. "Leave me this."

For all reply, he turned over with a groan, and relapsed into stupor. The nurse shortly afterwards came to relieve me; but though I lay down, I was unable to sleep. The personal possession of that little scrap of paper acted altogether too potently on my nerves and my imagination. In due contravention of the doctor, Edgar outlasted the night and lived into another day. But as high noon was clashing out from the village church, and I stood with the doctor by his bedside, the latter, who had lifted his wrist a little to test his pulse, released it, not with the tenderness we render to suffering, but with a more summary reverence. Suffering was over.

By the close of the day I had finished my preparations for attending my step-brother's remains to burial in Philadelphia, among those of his own people; but before my departure, I measured once more that well-trodden road to the house by the river, and requested a moment's conversation with Mr. Guest. In spite of my attention being otherwise engaged, I had felt strangely all day that I carried a sort of magic talisman, a mystic key to fortune. I was constantly fumbling in my waistcoat-pocket to see whether the talisman was really there. I wondered that, as yet, Guest should not have demanded a surrender of his note; but I attributed his silence to shame, scorn, and defiance, and promised myself a sort of golden advantage by anticipating his claim with the cogent frankness of justice. But as soon as he entered the room I foresaw that Justice must show her sword as well as her scales. His resentment had deepened into a kind of preposterous arrogance, of a temper quite insensible to logic. He had more than recovered his native buoyancy and splendor; there was an air of feverish impudence in his stare, his light swagger, in the very hue and fashion of his crimson necktie. He had an evil genius with blond curls and innumerable flounces.

"I feel it to be a sort of duty," I said, "to inform you that my brother died this morning."

"Your brother? What's your brother to me? He's been dead to me these three days. Is that all you have to say?"

I was irritated by the man's stupid implacability, and my purpose received a check. "No," I answered, "I've several things more to touch upon."

"In so far as they concern my daughter, you may leave them unsaid. She tells me of your offer to—to *buy off* my opposition. Am I to understand that it was seriously made? You're a coarser young man than I fancied!"

"She told you of my offer?" I cried.

"O, you needn't build upon that! She hasn't mentioned your name since."

I was silent, thinking my own thoughts. I won't answer for it, that, in spite of his caution, I did *not* lay an immaterial brick or two. "You're still irreconcilable?" I contented myself with asking.

He assumed an expression of absolutely jovial contempt. "My dear sir, I detest the sight of you!"

"Have you no question to ask, no demand to make?"

He looked at me a moment in silence, with just the least little twitch and tremor of mouth and eye. His vanity, I guessed on the instant, was determined stoutly to ignore that I held him at an advantage and to refuse me the satisfaction of extorting from him the least allusion to the evidence of his disgrace. He had known bitter compulsion once; he would not do it the honor to concede that it had not spent itself. "No demand but that you will excuse my further attendance."

My own vanity took a hand in the game. Justice herself was bound to go no more than half-way. If he was not afraid of his little paper, he might try a week or two more of bravery. I bowed to him in silence and let him depart. As I turned to go I found myself face to face with Mrs. Beck, whose pretty visage was flushed with curiosity. "You and Mr. Guest have quarrelled," she said roundly.

"As you see, madam."

"As I see, madam! But what is it all about?"

"About—his daughter."

"His daughter and his ducats! You're a very deep young man, in spite of those boyish looks of yours. Why did you never tell me you knew him? You've quarrelled about money matters."

"As you say," I answered, "I'm very deep. Don't tempt me to further subterfuge."

"He has lost money, I know. Is it much? Tell me that."

"It's an enormous sum!" I said, with mock solemnity.

"Provoking man!" And she gave a little stamp of disgust.

"He's in trouble," I said. "To a woman of your tender sympathies he ought to be more interesting than ever."

She mused a moment, fixing me with her keen blue eye. "It's a sad responsibility to have a heart!" she murmured.

"In that," I said, "we perfectly agree."

VI.

It was a singular fact that Edgar's affairs turned out to be in by no means the exemplary order in which he had flattered himself he placed them. They were very much at sixes and sevens. The discovery, to me, was almost a shock. I might have drawn from it a pertinent lesson on the fallacy of human pretensions. The gentleman whom Edgar had supremely honored (as he seemed to assume in his will) by appointing his executor, responded to my innocent surprise by tapping his forehead with a peculiar smile. It was partly from curiosity as to the value of this explanation, that I helped him to look into the dense confusion which prevailed in my step-brother's estate. It revealed certainly an odd compound of madness and method. I learned with real regret that the twenty eleemosynary beds at Philadelphia must remain a superb conception. I was horrified at every step by the broad license with which his will had to be interpreted. All profitless as I was in the case, when I thought of the comfortable credit in which he had died, I felt like some greedy kinsman of tragedy making impious havoc with a sacred bequest. These matters detained me for a week in New York, where I had joined my brother's executor. At my earliest moment of leisure, I called upon Crawford at the office of a friend to whom he had addressed me, and learned that after three or four dismally restless days in town, he had taken a summary departure for L. A couple of days later, I was struck with a certain dramatic connection between his return and the following note from Mr. Guest, which I give verbally, in its pregnant brevity:—

SIR:—I possess a claim on your late brother's estate which it is needless to specify. You will either satisfy it by return of mail or forfeit forever the common respect of gentlemen.

J. G.

Things had happened with the poor man rather as I hoped than as I expected. He had borrowed his recent exaggerated defiance from the transient smiles of Mrs. Beck. They had gone to his head like the fumes of wine, and he had dreamed for a day that he could afford to snap his fingers at the past. What he really desired and hoped of Mrs. Beck I was puzzled to say. In this woful disrepair of his fortunes he could hardly have meant to hold her to a pledge of matrimony extorted in brighter hours. He was infatuated, I believed, partly by a weak, spasmodic optimism which represented his troubles as momentary, and enjoined him to hold firm till something turned up, and partly by a reckless and frivolous susceptibility to the lady's unscrupulous blandishments. While they prevailed, he lost all notion of the wholesome truth of things, and would have been capable of any egregious folly. Mrs. Beck was in love with him, in so far as she was capable of being in love; his gallantry, of all gallantries, suited her to a charm; but she reproached herself angrily with this amiable weakness, and prudence every day won back an inch of ground. Poor Guest indeed had clumsily snuffed out his candle. He had slept in the arms of Delilah, and he had waked to find that Delilah had guessed, if not his secret, something uncomfortably like it. Crawford's return had found Mrs. Beck with but a scanty remnant of sentiment and a large accession of prudence, which was graciously placed at his service. Guest, hereupon, as I conjectured, utterly disillusioned by the cynical frankness of her defection, had seen his horizon grow ominously dark, and begun to fancy, as I remained silent, that there was thunder in the air. His pompous waiving, in his note, of allusion both to our last meeting and to my own present claim, seemed to me equally characteristic of his weakness and of his distress. The bitter after-taste of Mrs. Beck's coquetry had, at all events, brought him back to reality. For myself, the real fact in the matter was the image of Laura Guest, sitting pensive, like an exiled princess.

I sent him nothing by return of mail. On my arrival in New York, I had enclosed the precious document in an envelope, addressed it, and stamped it, and put it back in my pocket. I could not rid myself of a belief that by that sign I should conquer. Several times I drew it forth and laid it on the table before me, reflecting that I had but a word to say to have it dropped into the post. Cowardly, was it, to keep it? But what was it to give up one's mistress without a battle? Which was the uglier, my harshness or Guest's? In a holy cause,—and holy, you may be sure, I had dubbed mine,—were not all arms sanctified? Possession meant peril, and peril to a manly sense, of soul and conscience, as much as of person and fortune. Mine, at any rate, should share the danger. It was a sinister-looking talisman certainly; but when it had failed, it would be time enough to give it up.

In these thoughts I went back to L. I had taken the morning train; I arrived at noon, and with small delay proceeded to the quiet little house which harbored such world-vexed spirits. It was one of the first days of September, and the breath of autumn was in the air. Summer still met the casual glance; but the infinite light of summer had found its term; it was as if there were a leak in the crystal vault of the firmament through which the luminous ether of June was slowly stealing away.

Mr. Guest, I learned from the servant, had started on a walk,—to the mill, she thought, three miles away. I sent in my card to Laura, and went into the garden to await her appearance—or her answer. At the end of five minutes, I saw her descend from the piazza and advance down the long path. Her light black dress swept the little box-borders, and over her head she balanced a white parasol. I met her, and she stopped, silent and grave. "I've come to learn," I said, "that absence has not been fatal to me."

"You've hardly been absent. You left a—an influence behind,—a very painful one. In Heaven's name!" she cried, with vehemence, "what horrible wrong have you done?"

"I have done no horrible wrong. Do you believe me?" She scanned my face searchingly for a moment; then she gave a long, gentle, irrepressible sigh of relief. "Do you fancy that if I had, I could meet your eyes, feel the folds of your dress? I've done that which I have bitterly wished undone; I did it in ignorance, weakness, and folly; I've repented in passion and truth. Can a man do more?"

"I never was afraid of the truth," she answered slowly; "I don't see that I need fear it now. I'm not a child. Tell me the absolute truth!"

"The absolute truth," I said, "is that your father once saw me in a very undignified position. It made such an impression on him that he's unable to think of me in any other. You see I was rather cynically indifferent to his observation, for I didn't know him then as your father."

She gazed at me with the same adventurous candor, and blushed a little as I became silent, then turned away and strolled along the path. "It seems a miserable thing," she said, "that two gentle spirits like yours should have an irreparable difference. When good men hate each other, what are they to do to the bad men? You must excuse my want of romance, but I cannot listen to a suitor of whom my father complains. Make peace!"

"Shall peace with him be peace with you?"

"Let me see you frankly shake hands," she said, not directly answering. "Be very kind! You don't know what he has suffered here lately." She paused, as if to conceal a tremor in her voice.

Had she read between the lines of that brilliant improvisation of mine, or was she moved chiefly with pity for his recent sentimental tribulations,—pitying them the more that she respected them the less? "He has walked to the mill," I said; "I shall meet him, and we'll come back arm in arm." I turned away, so that I might not see her face pleading for a clemency which would make me too delicate. I went down beside the river and followed the old towing-path, now grassy with disuse. Reaching the shabby wooden bridge below the mill, I stopped mid-way across it and leaned against the railing. Below, the yellow water swirled past the crooked piers. I took my little sealed paper out of my pocketbook and held it over the stream, almost courting the temptation to drop it; but the temptation never came. I had just put it back in my pocket when I heard a footstep on the planks behind me. Turning round, I beheld Mr. Guest. He looked tired and dusty with his walk, and had the air of a man who had been trying by violent exercise to shake off a moral incubus. Judging by his haggard brow and heavy eyes, he had hardly succeeded. As he recognized me, he started just perceptibly, as if he were too weary to be irritated. He was about to pass on without speaking, but I intercepted him. My movement provoked a flash in his sullen pupil. "I came on purpose to meet you," I said. "I have just left your daughter, and I feel more than ever how passionately I love her. Once more, I demand that you withdraw your opposition."

"Is that your answer to my letter?" he asked, eying me from under his brows.

"Your letter puts me in a position to make my demand with force. I refuse to submit to this absurd verdict of accident. I have just seen your daughter, and I have authority to bring you to reason."

"My daughter has received you?" he cried, flushing.

"Most kindly."

"You scoundrel!"

"Gently, gently. Shake hands with me here where we stand, and let me keep my promise to Laura of our coming back to her arm in arm, at peace, reconciled, mutually forgiving and forgetting, or I walk straight back and put a certain little paper into her hands."

He turned deadly pale, and a fierce oath broke from his lips. He had been beguiled, I think, by my neglect of his letter, into the belief that Edgar had not died without destroying his signature,—a belief rendered possible by an indefeasible faith he must have had in my step-brother's probity. "You've kept that thing!" he cried. "The Lord be praised! I'm as honest a man as either of you!"

"Say but two words,—'Take her!'—and we shall be honest together again. The paper's yours." He turned away and leaned against the railing of the bridge, with his head in his hands, watching the river.

"Take your time," I continued; "I give you two hours. Go home, look at your daughter, and choose. An hour hence I'll join you. If I find you've removed your veto, I undertake to make you forget you ever offered it: if I find you've maintained it, I expose you."

"In either case you lose your mistress. Whatever Laura may think of me, there can be no doubt as to what she will think of you."

"I shall be forgiven. Leave that to me! That's my last word. In a couple of hours I shall take the liberty of coming to learn yours."

"O Laura, Laura!" cried the poor man in his bitter trouble. But I left him and walked away. I turned as I reached the farther end of the bridge, and saw him slowly resume his course. I marched along the road to the mill, so excited with having uttered this brave *ultimatum* that I hardly knew whither I went. But at last I bethought me of a certain shady streamside nook just hereabouts, which a little exploration soon discovered. A shallow cove, screened from the road by dense clumps of willows, stayed the current a moment in its grassy bend. I had noted it while boating, as a spot where a couple of lovers might aptly disembark and moor their idle skiff; and I was now tempted to try its influence in ardent solitude. I flung myself on the ground, and as I listened to the light gurgle of the tarrying stream and to the softer rustle of the cool gray leafage around me, I suddenly felt that I was exhausted and sickened. I lay motionless, watching the sky and resting from my anger. Little by little it melted away and left me horribly ashamed. How long I lay there I know not, nor what was the logic of my meditations, but an ineffable change stole over my spirit. There are fathomless depths in spiritual mood and motive. Opposite me, on the farther side of the stream, winding along a path through the bushes, three or four cows had come down to drink. I sat up and watched them. A young man followed them, in a red shirt, with his trousers in his boots. While they were comfortably nosing the water into ripples, he sat down on a stone and began to light his pipe. In a moment I fancied I saw the little blue thread of smoke curl up from the bowl. From beyond, just droning through the air, came the liquid rumble of the mill. There seemed to me something in this vision ineffably pastoral, peaceful, and innocent; it smote me to my heart of hearts. I felt a nameless wave of impulse start somewhere in the innermost vitals of conscience and fill me with passionate shame. I fell back on the grass and burst into tears.

The sun was low and the breeze had risen when I rose to my feet. I scrambled back to the road, crossed the bridge, and hurried home by the towing-path. My heart, however, beat faster than my footfalls. I passed into the garden and advanced to the house; as I stepped upon the piazza, I was met by Mrs. Beck. "Answer me a simple question," she cried, laying her hand on my arm.

"I should like to hear you ask one!" I retorted, impatiently.

"Has Mr. Guest lost his mind?"

"For an hour! I've brought it back to him."

"You've a pretty quarrel between you. He comes up an hour ago, as I was sitting in the garden with—with Mr. Crawford, requests a moment's interview, leads me apart and —offers himself. 'If you'll have me, take me now; you won't an hour hence,' he cried. 'Neither now nor an hour hence, thank you,' said I. 'My affections are fixed—elsewhere.' "

"You've not lost your head, at any rate," said I; and, releasing myself, I went into the parlor. I had a horrible fear of being too late. The candles stood lighted on the piano, and tea had been brought in, but the kettle was singing unheeded. On the divan facing the window sat Guest, lounging back on the cushions, his hat and stick flung down beside him; his hands grasping his knees, his head thrown back, and his eyes closed. That he should have remained so for an hour, unbrushed and unfurbished, spoke volumes as to his mental state. Near him sat Laura, looking at him askance in mute anxiety. What had passed between them? Laura's urgent glance as I entered was full of trouble, but I fancied without reproach. He had apparently chosen neither way; he had simply fallen there, weary, desperate, and dumb.

"I'm disappointed!" Laura said to me gravely.

Her father opened his eyes, stared at me a moment, and then closed them. I answered nothing; but after a moment's hesitation went and took my seat beside Guest. I laid my hand on his own with a grasp of which he felt, first the force, then, I think, the kindness; for, after a momentary spasm of repulsion, he remained coldly passive. He must have begun to wonder. "Be so good," I said to Laura, "as to bring me one of the candles." She looked surprised; but she complied and came toward me, holding the taper, like some pale priestess expecting a portent. I drew out the note and held it to the flame. "Your father and I have had a secret," I said, "which has been a burden to both of us. Here it goes." Laura's hand trembled as she held the candle, and mine as I held the paper; but between us the vile thing blazed and was consumed. I glanced askance at Guest; he was staring wide-eyed at the dropping cinders. When the last had dropped, I took the candle, rose, and carried it back to the piano. Laura dropped on her knees before her father, and, while my back was turned, something passed between them with which I was concerned only in its consequences.

When I looked round, Guest had risen and was passing his fingers through his hair. "Daughter," he said, "when I came in, what was it I said to you?"

She stood for an instant with her eyes on the floor. Then, "I've forgotten!" she said, simply.

Mrs. Beck had passed in by the window in time to hear these last words. "Do you know what you said to me when you came in?" she cried, mirthfully shaking a finger at Guest. He laughed nervously, picked up his hat, and stood looking, with an air of odd solemnity, at his boots. Suddenly it seemed to occur to him that he was dusty and dishevelled. He settled his shirt-collar and levelled a glance at the mirror, in which he caught my eye. He tried hard to look insensible; but it was the glance of a man who felt more comfortable than he had done in a month. He marched stiffly to the door.

"Are you going to dress?" said Mrs. Beck.

"From head to foot!" he cried, with violence.

"Be so good, then, if you see Mr. Crawford in the hall, as to ask him to come in and have a cup of tea."

Laura had passed out to the piazza, where I immediately joined her. "Your father accepts me," I said; "there is nothing left but for you—"

Five minutes later, I looked back through the window to see if we were being observed. But Mrs. Beck was busy adding another lump of sugar to Crawford's cup of tea. His eye met mine, however, and I fancied he looked sheepish.

The Madonna of the Future

WE HAD been talking about the masters who had achieved but a single masterpiece—the artists and poets who but once in their lives had known the divine afflatus and touched the high level of perfection. Our host had been showing us a charming little cabinet picture by a painter whose name we had never heard, and who, after this single spasmodic bid for fame, had apparently relapsed into obscurity and mediocrity. There was some discussion as to the frequency of this phenomenon; during which, I observed, H—— sat silent, finishing his cigar with a meditative air, and looking at the picture, which was being handed round the table. "I don't know how common a case it is," he said at last, "but I have seen it. I have known a poor fellow who painted his one masterpiece, and"—he added with a smile—"he didn't even paint that. He made his bid for fame and missed it." We all knew H—— for a clever man who had seen much of men and manners, and had a great stock of reminiscences. Some one immediately questioned him further, and while I was engrossed with the raptures of my neighbour over the little picture, he was induced to tell his tale. If I were to doubt whether it would bear repeating, I should only have to re-member how that charming woman, our hostess, who had left the table, ventured back in rustling rose-colour, to pro-nounce our lingering a want of gallantry, and, finding us a lis-tening circle, sank into her chair in spite of our cigars, and heard the story out so graciously that when the catastrophe was reached she glanced across at me and showed me a tear in each of her beautiful eyes.

It relates to my youth, and to Italy: two fine things! (H—— began.) I had arrived late in the evening at Florence, and while I finished my bottle of wine at supper, had fancied that, tired traveller though I was, I might pay the city a finer compliment than by going vulgarly to bed. A narrow passage wandered darkly away out of the little square before my hotel, and looked as if it bored into the heart of Florence. I followed it, and at the end of ten minutes emerged upon a great piazza, filled only with the mild autumn moonlight. Opposite rose the Palazzo Vecchio, like some huge civic fortress, with the great bell-tower springing from its embattled verge as a mountain-pine from the edge of a cliff. At its base, in its projected shadow, gleamed certain dim sculptures which I wonderingly approached. One of the images, on the left of the palace door, was a magnificent colossus, shining through the dusky air like a sentinel who has taken the alarm. In a moment I recognised him as Michael Angelo's *David*. I turned with a certain relief from his sinister strength to a slender figure in bronze, stationed beneath the high, light loggia which opposes the free and elegant span of its arches to the dead masonry of the palace; a figure supremely shapely and graceful; gentle, almost, in spite of his holding out with his light, nervous arm the snaky head of the slaughtered Gorgon. His name is Perseus, and you may read his story, not in the Greek mythology, but in the memoirs of Benvenuto Cellini. Glancing from one of these fine fellows to the other, I probably uttered some irrepressible commonplace of praise, for, as if provoked by my voice, a man rose from the steps of the loggia, where he had been sitting in the shadow, and addressed me in good English—a small, slim personage, clad in a sort of black velvet tunic (as it seemed), and with a mass of auburn hair, which gleamed in the moonlight, escaping from a little mediæval birretta. In a tone of the most insinuating deference, he asked me for my "impressions." He seemed picturesque, fantastic, slightly unreal. Hovering there in this consecrated neighbourhood, he might have passed for the genius of æsthetic hospitality—if the genius of æsthetic hospitality were not commonly some shabby little custode, flourishing a calico pocket-handkerchief and openly resentful of the divided franc. This analogy was made none the less complete by the brilliant tirade with which he greeted my embarrassed silence.

"I have known Florence long, sir, but I have never known her so lovely as to-night. It's as if the ghosts of her past were abroad in the empty streets. The present is sleeping; the past hovers about us like a dream made visible. Fancy the old Florentines strolling up in couples to pass judgment on the last performance of Michael, of Benvenuto! We should come in for a precious lesson if we might overhear what they say. The plainest burgher of them, in his cap and gown, had a taste in the matter! That was the prime of art, sir. The sun stood high in heaven, and his broad and equal blaze made the darkest places bright and the dullest eyes clear. We live in the evening of time! We grope in the gray dusk, carrying each our poor little taper of selfish and painful wisdom, holding it up to the great models and to the dim idea, and seeing nothing but overwhelming greatness and dimness. The days of illumination are gone! But do you know I fancy—I fancy"—and he grew suddenly almost familiar in this visionary fervour—"I fancy the light of that time rests upon us here for an hour! I have never seen the David so grand, the Perseus so fair! Even the inferior productions of John of Bologna and of Baccio Bandinelli seem to realise the artist's dream. I feel as if the moonlit air were charged with the secrets of the masters, and as if, standing here in religious attention, we might—we might witness a revelation!" Perceiving at this moment, I suppose, my halting comprehension reflected in my puzzled face, this interesting rhapsodist paused and blushed. Then with a melancholy smile, "You think me a moonstruck charlatan, I suppose. It's not my habit to hang about the piazza and pounce upon innocent tourists. But to-night, I confess, I am under the charm. And then, somehow, I fancied you too were an artist!"

"I am not an artist, I am sorry to say, as you must understand the term. But pray make no apologies. I am also under the charm; your eloquent remarks have only deepened it."

"If you are not an artist you are worthy to be one!" he rejoined, with an expressive smile. "A young man who arrives at Florence late in the evening, and, instead of going prosaically to bed, or hanging over the travellers' book at his hotel, walks forth without loss of time to pay his devoirs to the beautiful, is a young man after my own heart!"

The mystery was suddenly solved; my friend was an American! He must have been, to take the picturesque so prodigiously to heart. "None the less so, I trust," I answered, "if the young man is a sordid New-Yorker."

"New-Yorkers have been munificent patrons of art!" he answered, urbanely.

For a moment I was alarmed. Was this midnight reverie mere Yankee enterprise, and was he simply a desperate brother of the brush who had posted himself here to extort an "order" from a sauntering tourist? But I was not called to defend myself. A great brazen note broke suddenly from the far-off summit of the bell-tower above us, and sounded the first stroke of midnight. My companion started, apologised for detaining me, and prepared to retire. But he seemed to offer so lively a promise of further entertainment, that I was indisposed to part with him, and suggested that we should stroll homeward together. He cordially assented; so we turned out of the Piazza, passed down before the statued arcade of the Uffizi, and came out upon the Arno. What course we took I hardly remember, but we roamed slowly about for an hour, my companion delivering by snatches a sort of moon-touched æsthetic lecture. I listened in puzzled fascination, and wondered who the deuce he was. He confessed with a melancholy but all-respectful head-shake to his American origin.

"We are the disinherited of Art!" he cried. "We are condemned to be superficial! We are excluded from the magic circle. The soil of American perception is a poor little barren, artificial deposit. Yes! we are wedded to imperfection. An American, to excel, has just ten times as much to learn as a European. We lack the deeper sense. We have neither taste, nor tact, nor power. How should we have them? Our crude and garish climate, our silent past, our deafening present, the constant pressure about us of unlovely circumstance, are as void of all that nourishes and prompts and inspires the artist, as my sad heart is void of bitterness in saying so! We poor aspirants must live in perpetual exile."

"You seem fairly at home in exile," I answered, "and Florence seems to me a very pretty Siberia. But do you know my own thought? Nothing is so idle as to talk about our want of a nutritive soil, of opportunity, of inspiration, and all the rest of it. The worthy part is to do something fine! There is no law in our glorious Constitution against that. Invent, create, achieve! No matter if you have to study fifty times as much as one of these! What else are you an artist for? Be you our Moses," I added, laughing, and laying my hand on his shoulder, "and lead us out of the house of bondage!"

"Golden words—golden words, young man!" he cried, with a tender smile. " 'Invent, create, achieve!' Yes, that's our business; I know it well. Don't take me, in Heaven's name, for one of your barren complainers—impotent cynics who have neither talent nor faith! I am at work!"—and he glanced about him and lowered his voice as if this were a quite peculiar secret—"I'm at work night and day. I have undertaken a *creation*! I am no Moses; I am only a poor patient artist; but it would be a fine thing if I were to cause some slender stream of beauty to flow in our thirsty land! Don't think me a monster of conceit," he went on, as he saw me smile at the avidity with which he adopted my illustration; "I confess that I am in one of those moods when great things seem possible! This is one of my nervous nights—I dream waking! When the south-wind blows over Florence at midnight, it seems to coax the soul from all the fair things locked away in her churches and galleries; it comes into my own little studio with the moonlight, and sets my heart beating too deeply for rest. You see I am always adding a thought to my conception! This evening I felt that I couldn't sleep unless I had communed with the genius of Buonarotti!"

He seemed deeply versed in local history and tradition, and he expatiated *con amore* on the charms of Florence. I gathered that he was an old resident, and that he had taken the lovely city into his heart. "I owe her everything," he declared. "It's only since I came here that I have really lived, intellectually. One by one, all profane desires, all mere worldly aims, have dropped away from me, and left me nothing but my pencil, my little note-book" (and he tapped his breast-pocket), "and the worship of the pure masters—those who were pure because they were innocent, and those who were pure because they were strong!"

"And have you been very productive all this time?" I asked sympathetically.

He was silent a while before replying. "Not in the vulgar sense!" he said at last. "I have chosen never to manifest myself by imperfection. The good in every performance I have re-absorbed into the generative force of new creations; the bad—there is always plenty of that—I have religiously destroyed. I may say, with some satisfaction, that I have not added a mite to the rubbish of the world. As a proof of my conscientiousness"—and he stopped short, and eyed me with extraordinary candour, as if the proof were to be overwhelming—"I have never sold a picture! 'At least no merchant traffics in my heart!' Do you remember that divine line in Browning? My little studio has never been profaned by superficial, feverish, mercenary work. It's a temple of labour, but of leisure! Art is long. If we work for ourselves, of course we must hurry. If we work for her, we must often pause. She can wait!"

This had brought us to my hotel door, somewhat to my relief, I confess, for I had begun to feel unequal to the society of a genius of this heroic strain. I left him, however, not without expressing a friendly hope that we should meet again. The next morning my curiosity had not abated; I was anxious to see him by common daylight. I counted upon meeting him in one of the many pictorial haunts of Florence, and I was gratified without delay. I found him in the course of the morning in the Tribune of the Uffizi—that little treasure-chamber of world-famous things. He had turned his back on the Venus de' Medici, and with his arms resting on the railing which protects the pictures, and his head buried in his hands, he was lost in the contemplation of that superb triptych of Andrea Mantegna—a work which has neither the material splendour nor the commanding force of some of its neighbours, but which, glowing there with the loveliness of patient labour, suits possibly a more constant need of the soul. I looked at the picture for some time over his shoulder; at last, with a heavy sigh, he turned away and our eyes met. As he recognised me a deep blush rose to his face; he fancied, perhaps, that he had made a fool of himself overnight. But I offered him my hand with a friendliness which assured him I was not a scoffer. I knew him by his ardent *chevelure*; otherwise he was much altered. His midnight mood was over, and he looked as haggard as an actor by daylight. He was far older than I had supposed, and he had less bravery of costume and gesture. He seemed the quite poor, patient artist he had proclaimed himself, and the fact that he had never sold a picture was more obvious than glorious. His velvet coat was threadbare, and his short slouched hat, of an antique pattern, revealed a rustiness which marked it an "original," and not one of the picturesque reproductions which brethren of his craft affect. His eye was mild and heavy, and his expression singularly gentle and acquiescent; the more so for a certain pallid leanness of visage, which I hardly knew whether to refer to the consuming fire of genius or to a meagre diet. A very little talk, however, cleared his brow and brought back his eloquence.

"And this is your first visit to these enchanted halls?" he cried. "Happy, thrice happy youth!" And taking me by the arm, he prepared to lead me to each of the pre-eminent works in turn and show me the cream of the gallery. But before we left the Mantegna, he pressed my arm and gave it a loving look. "*He* was not in a hurry," he murmured. "He knew nothing of 'raw Haste, half-sister to Delay!' " How sound a critic my friend was I am unable to say, but he was an extremely amusing one; overflowing with opinions, theories, and sympathies, with disquisition and gossip and anecdote. He was a shade too sentimental for my own sympathies, and I fancied he was rather too fond of superfine discriminations and of discovering subtle intentions in shallow places. At moments, too, he plunged into the sea of metaphysics and floundered a while in waters too deep for intellectual security. But his abounding knowledge and happy judgment told a touching story of long, attentive hours in this worshipful company; there was a reproach to my wasteful saunterings in so devoted a culture of opportunity. "There are two moods," I remember his saying, "in which we may walk through galleries—the critical and the ideal. They seize us at their pleasure, and we can never tell which is to take its turn. The critical mood, oddly, is the genial one, the friendly, the condescending. It relishes the pretty trivialities of art, its vulgar cleverness, its conscious graces. It has a kindly greeting for anything which looks as if, according to his light, the painter had enjoyed doing it—for the little Dutch cabbages and kettles, for the taper fingers and breezy mantles of late-coming Madonnas, for the little blue-hilled, pastoral, sceptical Italian landscapes. Then there are the days of fierce, fastidious longing—solemn church-feasts of the intellect—when all vulgar effort and all petty success is a weariness, and everything but the best—the best of the best—disgusts. In these hours we are relentless aristocrats of taste. We will not take Michael Angelo for granted, we will not swallow Raphael whole!"

The gallery of the Uffizi is not only rich in its possessions, but peculiarly fortunate in that fine architectural accident, as one may call it, which unites it—with the breadth of river and city between them—to those princely chambers of the Pitti Palace. The Louvre and the Vatican hardly give you such a sense of sustained inclosure as those long passages projected over street and stream to establish a sort of inviolate transition between the two palaces of art. We passed along the gallery in which those precious drawings by eminent hands hang chaste and gray above the swirl and murmur of the yellow Arno, and reached the ducal saloons of the Pitti. Ducal as they are, it must be confessed that they are imperfect as show-rooms, and that, with their deep-set windows and their massive mouldings, it is rather a broken light that reaches the pictured walls. But here the masterpieces hang thick, and you seem to see them in a luminous atmosphere of their own. And the great saloons, with their superb dim ceilings, their outer wall in splendid shadow, and the sombre opposite glow of mellow canvas and dusky gilding, make, themselves, almost as fine a picture as the Titians and Raphaels they imperfectly reveal. We lingered briefly before many a Raphael and Titian; but I saw my friend was impatient, and I suffered him at last to lead me directly to the goal of our journey—the most tenderly fair of Raphael's virgins, the Madonna in the Chair. Of all the fine pictures of the world, it seemed to me this is the one with which criticism has least to do. None betrays less effort, less of the mechanism of success and of the irrepressible discord between conception and result which shows dimly in so many consummate works. Graceful, human, near to our sympathies as it is, it has nothing of manner, of method, nothing, almost, of style; it blooms there in rounded softness, as instinct with harmony as if it were an immediate exhalation of genius. The figure melts away the spectator's mind into a sort of passionate tenderness which he knows not whether he has given to heavenly purity or to earthly charm. He is intoxicated with the fragrance of the tenderest blossom of maternity that ever bloomed on earth.

"That's what I call a fine picture," said my companion, after we had gazed a while in silence. "I have a right to say so, for I have copied it so often and so carefully that I could repeat it now with my eyes shut. Other works are of Raphael: this *is* Raphael himself. Others you can praise, you can qualify, you can measure, explain, account for: this you can only love and admire. I don't know in what seeming he walked among men, while this divine mood was upon him; but after it, surely, he could do nothing but die; this world had nothing more to teach him. Think of it a while, my friend, and you will admit that I am not raving. Think of his seeing that spotless image, not for a moment, for a day, in a happy dream, or a restless fever-fit; not as a poet in a five minutes' frenzy—time to snatch his phrase and scribble his immortal stanza; but for days together, while the slow labour of the brush went on, while the foul vapours of life interposed, and the fancy ached with tension, fixed, radiant, distinct, as we see it now! What a master, certainly! But ah! what a seer!"

"Don't you imagine," I answered, "that he had a model, and that some pretty young woman—"

"As pretty a young woman as you please! It doesn't diminish the miracle! He took his hint, of course, and the young woman, possibly, sat smiling before his canvas. But, meanwhile, the painter's idea had taken wings. No lovely human outline could charm it to vulgar fact. He saw the fair form made perfect; he rose to the vision without tremor, without effort of wing; he communed with it face to face, and resolved into finer and lovelier truth the purity which completes it as the fragrance completes the rose. That's what they call idealism; the word's vastly abused, but the thing is good. It's my own creed, at any rate. Lovely Madonna, model at once and muse, I call you to witness that I too am an idealist!"

"An idealist, then," I said, half jocosely, wishing to provoke him to further utterance, "is a gentleman who says to Nature in the person of a beautiful girl, 'Go to, you are all wrong! Your fine is coarse, your bright is dim, your grace is *gaucherie*. This is the way you should have done it!' Is not the chance against him?"

He turned upon me almost angrily, but perceiving the genial savour of my sarcasm, he smiled gravely. "Look at that picture," he said, "and cease your irreverent mockery! Idealism is *that*! There's no explaining it; one must feel the flame! It says nothing to Nature, or to any beautiful girl, that they will not both forgive! It says to the fair woman, 'Accept me as your artist-friend, lend me your beautiful face, trust me, help me, and your eyes shall be half my masterpiece!' No one so loves and respects the rich realities of nature as the artist whose imagination caresses and flatters them. He knows what a fact may hold (whether Raphael knew, you may judge by his portrait, behind us there of Tommaso Inghirami); but his fancy hovers above it, as Ariel hovered above the sleeping prince. There is only one Raphael, but an artist may still be an artist. As I said last night, the days of illumination are gone; visions are rare; we have to look long to see them. But in meditation we may still cultivate the ideal; round it, smooth it, perfect it. The result—the result," (here his voice faltered suddenly, and he fixed his eyes for a moment on the picture; when they met my own again they were full of tears—"the result may be less than this; but still it may be good, it may be *great*!" he cried with vehemence. "It may hang somewhere, in after years, in goodly company, and keep the artist's memory warm. Think of being known to mankind after some such fashion as this! of hanging here through the slow centuries in the gaze of an altered world; living on and on in the cunning of an eye and hand that are part of the dust of ages, a delight and a law to remote generations; making beauty a force and purity an example!"

"Heaven forbid," I said, smiling, "that I should take the wind out of your sails! But doesn't it occur to you that besides being strong in his genius Raphael was happy in a certain good faith of which we have lost the trick? There are people, I know, who deny that his spotless Madonnas are anything more than pretty blondes of that period, enhanced by the Raphaelesque touch, which they declare is a profane touch. Be that as it may, people's religious and æsthetic needs went arm in arm, and there was, as I may say, a demand for the Blessed Virgin, visible and adorable, which must have given firmness to the artist's hand. I am afraid there is no demand now."

My companion seemed painfully puzzled; he shivered, as it

were, in this chilling blast of scepticism. Then shaking his head with sublime confidence—"There is always a demand!" he cried; "that ineffable type is one of the eternal needs of man's heart; but pious souls long for it in silence, almost in shame. Let it appear, and their faith grows brave. How *should* it appear in this corrupt generation? It cannot be made to order. It could, indeed, when the order came, trumpet-toned, from the lips of the Church herself, and was addressed to genius panting with inspiration. But it can spring now only from the soil of passionate labour and culture. Do you really fancy that while, from time to time, a man of complete artistic vision is born into the world, that image can perish? The man who paints it has painted everything. The subject admits of every perfection—form, colour, expression, composition. It can be as simple as you please, and yet as rich; as broad and pure, and yet as full of delicate detail. Think of the chance for flesh in the little naked, nestling child, irradiating divinity; of the chance for drapery in the chaste and ample garment of the mother! think of the great story you compress into that simple theme! Think, above all, of the mother's face and its ineffable suggestiveness, of the mingled burden of joy and trouble, the tenderness turned to worship, and the worship turned to far-seeing pity! Then look at it all in perfect line and lovely colour, breathing truth and beauty and mastery!"

"Anch' io son pittore!" I cried. "Unless I am mistaken, you have a masterpiece on the stocks. If you put all that in, you will do more than Raphael himself did. Let me know when your picture is finished, and wherever in the wide world I may be, I will post back to Florence and pay my respects to—the *Madonna of the future!*"

He blushed vividly and gave a heavy sigh, half of protest, half of resignation. "I don't often mention my picture by name. I detest this modern custom of premature publicity. A great work needs silence, privacy, mystery even. And then, do you know, people are so cruel, so frivolous, so unable to imagine a man's wishing to paint a Madonna at this time of day, that I have been laughed at—laughed at, sir!" and his blush deepened to crimson. "I don't know what has prompted me to be so frank and trustful with you. You look as if you wouldn't laugh at me. My dear young man"—and he laid his hand on my arm—"I am worthy of respect. Whatever my talents may be, I am honest. There is nothing grotesque in a pure ambition, or in a life devoted to it."

There was something so sternly sincere in his look and tone, that further questions seemed impertinent. I had repeated opportunity to ask them, however, for after this we spent much time together. Daily for a fortnight, we met by appointment, to see the sights. He knew the city so well, he had strolled and lounged so often through its streets and churches and galleries, he was so deeply versed in its greater and lesser memories, so imbued with the local genius, that he was an altogether ideal *valet de place*, and I was glad enough to leave my Murray at home, and gather facts and opinions alike from his gossiping commentary. He talked of Florence like a lover and admitted that it was a very old affair; he had lost his heart to her at first sight. "It's the fashion to talk of all cities as feminine," he said, "but, as a rule, it's a monstrous mistake. Is Florence of the same sex as New York, as Chicago? She is the sole perfect lady of them all; one feels towards her as a lad in his teens feels to some beautiful older woman with a 'history.' She fills you with a sort of aspiring gallantry." This disinterested passion seemed to stand my friend in stead of the common social ties; he led a lonely life, and cared for nothing but his work. I was duly flattered by his having taken my frivolous self into his favour, and by his generous sacrifice of precious hours to my society. We spent many of these hours among those early paintings in which Florence is so rich, returning ever and anon, with restless sympathies, to wonder whether these tender blossoms of art had not a vital fragrance and savour more precious than the full-fruited knowledge of the later works. We lingered often in the sepulchral chapel of San Lorenzo, and watched Michael Angelo's dim-visaged warrior sitting there like some awful Genius of Doubt and brooding behind his eternal mask upon the mysteries of life. We stood more than once in the little convent chambers where Fra Angelico wrought as if an angel indeed had held his hand, and gathered that sense of scattered dews and early bird-notes which makes an hour among his relics seem like a morning stroll in some monkish garden. We did all this and much more—wandered into dark chapels, damp courts, and dusty palace-rooms, in quest of lingering hints of fresco and lurking treasures of carving.

I was more and more impressed with my companion's remarkable singleness of purpose. Everything was a pretext for some wildly idealistic rhapsody or reverie. Nothing could be seen or said that did not lead him sooner or later to a glowing discourse on the true, the beautiful, and the good. If my friend was not a genius, he was certainly a monomaniac; and I found as great a fascination in watching the odd lights and shades of his character as if he had been a creature from another planet. He seemed, indeed, to know very little of this one, and lived and moved altogether in his own little province of art. A creature more unsullied by the world it is impossible to conceive, and I often thought it a flaw in his artistic character that he had not a harmless vice or two. It amused me greatly at times to think that he was of our shrewd Yankee race; but, after all, there could be no better token of his American origin than this high æsthetic fever. The very heat of his devotion was a sign of conversion; those born to European opportunity manage better to reconcile enthusiasm with comfort. He had, moreover, all our native mistrust for intellectual discretion and our native relish for sonorous superlatives. As a critic he was very much more generous than just, and his mildest terms of approbation were "stupendous," "transcendent," and "incomparable." The small change of admiration seemed to him no coin for a gentleman to handle; and yet, frank as he was intellectually, he was personally altogether a mystery. His professions, somehow, were all half-professions, and his allusions to his work and circumstances left something dimly ambiguous in the background. He was modest and proud, and never spoke of his domestic matters. He was evidently poor; yet he must have had some slender independence, since he could afford to make so merry over the fact that his culture of ideal beauty had never brought him a penny. His poverty, I supposed, was his motive for neither inviting me to his lodging nor mentioning its whereabouts. We met either in some public place or at my hotel, where I entertained him as freely as I might without appearing to be prompted by charity. He seemed always hungry, and this was his nearest approach to human grossness. I made a point of asking no impertinent questions, but, each time we met, I ventured to make some respectful allusion to the *magnum opus*, to inquire, as it were, as to its health and progress. "We are getting on, with the Lord's help," he would say, with a grave smile. "We are doing well. You see I have the grand advantage that I lose no time. These hours I spend with you are pure profit. They are *suggestive*! Just as the truly religious soul is always at worship, the genuine artist is always in labour. He takes his property wherever he finds it, and learns some precious secret from every object that stands up in the light. If you but knew the rapture of observation! I gather with every glance some hint for light, for colour or relief! When I get home, I pour out my treasures into the lap of my Madonna. Oh, I am not idle! *Nulla dies sine linea.*"

I was introduced in Florence to an American lady whose drawing-room had long formed an attractive place of reunion for the foreign residents. She lived on a fourth floor, and she was not rich; but she offered her visitors very good tea, little cakes at option, and conversation not quite to match. Her conversation had mainly an æsthetic flavour, for Mrs. Coventry was famously "artistic." Her apartment was a sort of Pitti Palace *au petit pied*. She possessed "early masters" by the dozen—a cluster of Peruginos in her dining-room, a Giotto in her boudoir, an Andrea del Sarto over her drawing-room chimney-piece. Surrounded by these treasures, and by innumerable bronzes, mosaics, majolica dishes, and little worm-eaten diptychs covered with angular saints on gilded backgrounds, our hostess enjoyed the dignity of a sort of high-priestess of the arts. She always wore on her bosom a huge miniature copy of the Madonna della Seggiola. Gaining her ear quietly one evening, I asked her whether she knew that remarkable man, Mr. Theobald.

"Know him!" she exclaimed; "know poor Theobald! All Florence knows him, his flame-coloured locks, his black velvet coat, his interminable harangues on the beautiful, and his wondrous Madonna that mortal eye has never seen, and that mortal patience has quite given up expecting."

"Really," I cried, "you don't believe in his Madonna?"

"My dear ingenuous youth," rejoined my shrewd friend, "has he made a convert of you? Well, we all believed in him once; he came down upon Florence and took the town by storm. Another Raphael, at the very least, had been born among men, and the poor dear United States were to have the credit of him. Hadn't he the very hair of Raphael flowing down on his shoulders? The hair, alas, but not the head! We swallowed him whole, however; we hung upon his lips and proclaimed his genius on the house-tops. The women were all dying to sit to him for their portraits and be made immortal, like Leonardo's Joconde. We decided that his manner was a good deal like Leonardo's—mysterious, and inscrutable, and fascinating. Mysterious it certainly was; mystery was the beginning and the end of it. The months passed by, and the miracle hung fire; our master never produced his masterpiece. He passed hours in the galleries and churches, posturing, musing, and gazing; he talked more than ever about the beautiful, but he never put brush to canvas. We had all subscribed, as it were, to the great performance; but as it never came off, people began to ask for their money again. I was one of the last of the faithful; I carried devotion so far as to sit to him for my head. If you could have seen the horrible creature he made of me, you would admit that even a woman with no more vanity than will tie her bonnet straight must have cooled off then. The man didn't know the very alphabet of drawing! His strong point, he intimated, was his sentiment; but is it a consolation, when one has been painted a fright, to know it has been done with peculiar gusto? One by one, I confess, we fell away from the faith, and Mr. Theobald didn't lift his little finger to preserve us. At the first hint that we were tired of waiting, and that we should like the show to begin, he was off in a huff. 'Great work requires time, contemplation, privacy, mystery! O ye of little faith!' We answered that we didn't insist on a great work; that the five-act tragedy might come at his convenience; that we merely asked for something to keep us from yawning, some inexpensive little *lever de rideau.* Hereupon the poor man took his stand as a genius misconceived and persecuted, an *âme méconnue*, and washed his hands of us from that hour! No, I believe he does me the honour to consider me the head and front of the conspiracy formed to nip his glory in the bud—a bud that has taken twenty years to blossom. Ask him if he knows me, and he will tell you I am a horribly ugly old woman who has vowed his destruction because he won't paint her portrait as a pendant to Titian's Flora. I fancy that since then he has had none but chance followers, innocent strangers like yourself, who have taken him at his word. The mountain is still in labour; I have not heard that the mouse has been born. I pass him once in a while in the galleries, and he fixes his great dark eyes on me with a sublimity of indifference, as if I were a bad copy of a Sassoferrato! It is a long time ago now that I heard that he was making studies for a Madonna who was to be a *résumé* of all the other Madonnas of the Italian school—like that antique Venus who borrowed a nose from one great image and an ankle from another. It's certainly a masterly idea. The parts may be fine, but when I think of my unhappy portrait I tremble for the whole. He has communicated this striking idea under the pledge of solemn secrecy to fifty chosen spirits, to every one he has ever been able to button-hole for five minutes. I suppose he wants to get an order for it, and he is not to blame; for Heaven knows how he lives. I see by your blush," my hostess frankly continued, "that you have been honoured with his confidence. You needn't be ashamed, my dear young man; a man of your age is none the worse for a certain generous credulity. Only allow me to give you a word of advice: keep your credulity out of your pockets! Don't pay for the picture till it's delivered. You have not been treated to a peep at it, I imagine? No more have your fifty predecessors in the faith. There are people who doubt whether there is any picture to be seen. I fancy, myself, that if one were to get into his studio, one would find something very like the picture in that tale of Balzac's—a mere mass of incoherent scratches and daubs, a jumble of dead paint!"

I listened to this pungent recital in silent wonder. It had a painfully plausible sound, and was not inconsistent with certain shy suspicions of my own. My hostess was not only a clever woman, but presumably a generous one. I determined to let my judgment wait upon events. Possibly she was right; but if she was wrong, she was cruelly wrong! Her version of my friend's eccentricities made me impatient to see him again and examine him in the light of public opinion. On our next meeting I immediately asked him if he knew Mrs. Coventry.

He laid his hand on my arm and gave me a sad smile. "Has she taxed *your* gallantry at last?" he asked. "She's a foolish woman. She's frivolous and heartless, and she pretends to be serious and kind. She prattles about Giotto's second manner and Vittoria Colonna's liaison with 'Michael'—one would think that Michael lived across the way and was expected in to take a hand at whist—but she knows as little about art, and about the conditions of production, as I know about Buddhism. She profanes sacred words," he added more vehemently, after a pause. "She cares for you only as some one to hand teacups in that horrible mendacious little parlour of hers, with its trumpery Peruginos! If you can't dash off a new picture every three days, and let her hand it round among her guests, she tells them in plain English that you are an impostor!"

This attempt of mine to test Mrs. Coventry's accuracy was made in the course of a late afternoon walk to the quiet old church of San Miniato, on one of the hill-tops which directly overlook the city, from whose gates you are guided to it by a stony and cypress-bordered walk, which seems a very fitting avenue to a shrine. No spot is more propitious to lingering repose* than the broad terrace in front of the church, where, lounging against the parapet, you may glance in slow alternation from the black and yellow marbles of the church-façade, seamed and cracked with time and wind-sown with a tender flora of its own, down to the full domes and slender towers of Florence and over to the blue sweep of the wide-mouthed cup of mountains into whose hollow the little treasure-city has been dropped. I had proposed, as a diversion from the painful memories evoked by Mrs. Coventry's name, that Theobald should go with me the next evening to the opera, where some rarely played work was to be given. He declined, as I half expected, for I had observed that he regularly kept his evenings in reserve, and never alluded to his manner of passing them. "You have reminded me before," I said, smiling, "of that charming speech of the Florentine painter in Alfred de Musset's 'Lorenzaccio': *'I do no harm to any one. I pass my days in my studio. On Sunday I go to the Annunziata or to Santa Maria; the monks think I have a voice; they dress me*

* 1869.

in a white gown and a red cap, and I take a share in the cho-ruses; sometimes I do a little solo: these are the only times I go into public. In the evening, I visit my sweetheart; when the night is fine, we pass it on her balcony.' I don't know whether you have a sweetheart, or whether she has a balcony. But if you are so happy, it's certainly better than trying to find a charm in a third-rate prima donna."

He made no immediate response, but at last he turned to me solemnly. "Can you look upon a beautiful woman with reverent eyes?"

"Really," I said, "I don't pretend to be sheepish, but I should be sorry to think I was impudent." And I asked him what in the world he meant. When at last I had assured him that I could undertake to temper admiration with respect, he informed me, with an air of religious mystery, that it was in his power to introduce me to the most beautiful woman in Italy—"A beauty with a soul!"

"Upon my word," I cried, "you are extremely fortunate, and that is a most attractive description."

"This woman's beauty," he went on, "is a lesson, a moral-ity, a poem! It's my daily study."

Of course, after this, I lost no time in reminding him of what, before we parted, had taken the shape of a promise. "I feel somehow," he had said, "as if it were a sort of violation of that privacy in which I have always contemplated her beauty. This is friendship, my friend. No hint of her existence has ever fallen from my lips. But with too great a familiarity we are apt to lose a sense of the real value of things, and you perhaps will throw some new light upon it and offer a fresher interpretation."

We went accordingly by appointment to a certain ancient house in the heart of Florence—the precinct of the Mercato Vecchio—and climbed a dark, steep staircase, to the very sum-mit of the edifice. Theobald's beauty seemed as loftily exalted above the line of common vision as his artistic ideal was lifted above the usual practice of men. He passed without knocking into the dark vestibule of a small apartment, and, flinging open an inner door, ushered me into a small saloon. The room seemed mean and sombre, though I caught a glimpse of white curtains swaying gently at an open window. At a table, near a lamp, sat a woman dressed in black, working at a piece of embroidery. As Theobald entered, she looked up calmly, with a smile; but seeing me, she made a movement of surprise, and rose with a kind of stately grace. Theobald stepped forward, took her hand and kissed it, with an indescribable air of immemorial usage. As he bent his head, she looked at me askance, and I thought she blushed.

"Behold the Serafina!" said Theobald, frankly, waving me forward. "This is a friend, and a lover of the arts," he added, introducing me. I received a smile, a curtsey, and a request to be seated.

The most beautiful woman in Italy was a person of a generous Italian type and of a great simplicity of demeanour. Seated again at her lamp, with her embroidery, she seemed to have nothing whatever to say. Theobald, bending towards her in a sort of Platonic ecstasy, asked her a dozen paternally tender questions as to her health, her state of mind, her occupations, and the progress of her embroidery, which he examined minutely and summoned me to admire. It was some portion of an ecclesiastical vestment—yellow satin wrought with an elaborate design of silver and gold. She made answer in a full, rich voice, but with a brevity which I hesitated whether to attribute to native reserve or to the profane constraint of my presence. She had been that morning to confession; she had also been to market, and had bought a chicken for dinner. She felt very happy; she had nothing to complain of, except that the people for whom she was making her vestment, and who furnished her materials, should be willing to put such rotten silver thread into the garment, as one might say, of the Lord. From time to time, as she took her slow stitches, she raised her eyes and covered me with a glance which seemed at first to denote a placid curiosity, but in which, as I saw it repeated, I thought I perceived the dim glimmer of an attempt to establish an understanding with me at the expense of our companion. Meanwhile, as mindful as possible of Theobald's injunction of reverence, I considered the lady's personal claims to the fine compliment he had paid her.

That she was indeed a beautiful woman I perceived, after recovering from the surprise of finding her without the freshness of youth. Her beauty was of a sort which, in losing youth, loses little of its essential charm, expressed for the most part as it was in form and structure, and, as Theobald would have said, in "composition." She was broad and ample, low-browed and large-eyed, dark and pale. Her thick brown hair hung low beside her cheek and ear, and seemed to drape her head with a covering as chaste and formal as the veil of a nun. The poise and carriage of her head were admirably free and noble, and they were the more effective that their freedom was at moments discreetly corrected by a little sanctimonious droop, which harmonised admirably with the level gaze of her dark and quiet eye. A strong, serene, physical nature, and the placid temper which comes of no nerves and no troubles, seemed this lady's comfortable portion. She was dressed in plain dull black, save for a sort of dark blue kerchief which was folded across her bosom and exposed a glimpse of her massive throat. Over this kerchief was suspended a little silver cross. I admired her greatly and yet with a large reserve. A certain mild intellectual apathy belonged properly to her type of beauty, and had always seemed to round and enrich it; but this *bourgeoise* Egeria, if I viewed her right betrayed a rather vulgar stagnation of mind. There might have been once a dim spiritual light in her face; but it had long since begun to wane. And furthermore, in plain prose, she was growing stout. My disappointment amounted very nearly to complete disenchantment when Theobald, as if to facilitate my covert inspection, declaring that the lamp was very dim and that she would ruin her eyes without more light, rose and fetched a couple of candles from the mantelpiece, which he placed lighted on the table. In this brighter illumination I perceived that our hostess was decidedly an elderly woman. She was nei-ther haggard nor worn nor grey; she was simply coarse. The "soul" which Theobald had promised seemed scarcely worth making such a point of; it was no deeper mystery than a sort of matronly mildness of lip and brow. I should have been ready even to declare that that sanctified bend of the head was nothing more than the trick of a person constantly working at embroidery. It occurred to me even that it was a trick of a less innocent sort; for, in spite of the mellow quietude of her wits, this stately needlewoman dropped a hint that she took the sit-uation rather less seriously than her friend. When he rose to light the candles, she looked across at me with a quick, intelligent smile, and tapped her forehead with her forefinger; then, as from a sudden feeling of compassionate loyalty to poor Theobald, I preserved a blank face, she gave a little shrug and resumed her work.

What was the relation of this singular couple? Was he the most ardent of friends or the most reverent of lovers? Did she regard him as an eccentric swain whose benevolent admiration of her beauty she was not ill-pleased to humour at this small cost of having him climb into her little parlour and gossip of summer nights? With her decent and sombre dress, her simple gravity, and that fine piece of priestly needlework, she looked like some pious lay-member of a sisterhood, living by special permission outside her convent walls. Or was she maintained here aloft by her friend in comfortable leisure, so that he might have before him the perfect, eternal type, uncorrupted and untarnished by the struggle for existence? Her shapely hands, I observed, were very fair and white; they lacked the traces of what is called honest toil.

"And the pictures, how do they come on?" she asked of Theobald, after a long pause.

"Finely, finely! I have here a friend whose sympathy and encouragement give me new faith and ardour."

Our hostess turned to me, gazed at me a moment rather inscrutably, and then tapping her forehead with the gesture she had used a minute before, "He has a magnificent genius!" she said, with perfect gravity.

"I am inclined to think so," I answered, with a smile.

"Eh, why do you smile?" she cried. "If you doubt it, you must see the *bambino*!" And she took the lamp and conducted me to the other side of the room, where on the wall, in a plain black frame, hung a large drawing in red chalk. Beneath it was fastened a little bowl for holy-water. The drawing represented a very young child, entirely naked, half nestling back against his mother's gown, but with his two little arms outstretched, as if in the act of benediction. It was executed with singular freedom and power, and yet seemed vivid with the sacred bloom of infancy. A sort of dimpled elegance and grace, mingled with its boldness, recalled the touch of Correggio. "That's what he can do!" said my hostess. "It's the blessed little boy whom I lost. It's his very image, and the Signor Teobaldo gave it me as a gift. He has given me many things besides!"

I looked at the picture for some time and admired it immensely. Turning back to Theobald, I assured him that if it were hung among the drawings in the Uffizi and labelled with a glorious name, it would hold its own. My praise seemed to give him extreme pleasure; he pressed my hands, and his eyes filled with tears. It moved him apparently with the desire to expatiate on the history of the drawing, for he rose and made his adieux to our companion, kissing her hand with the same mild ardour as before. It occurred to me that the offer of a similar piece of gallantry on my own part might help me to know what manner of woman she was. When she perceived my intention, she withdrew her hand, dropped her eyes solemnly, and made me a severe curtsey. Theobald took my arm and led me rapidly into the street.

"And what do you think of the divine Serafina?" he cried with fervour.

"It is certainly an excellent style of good looks!" I answered.

He eyed me an instant askance, and then seemed hurried along by the current of remembrance. "You should have seen the mother and the child together, seen them as I first saw them—the mother with her head draped in a shawl, a divine trouble in her face, and the bambino pressed to her bosom. You would have said, I think, that Raphael had found his match in common chance. I was coming in, one summer night, from a long walk in the country, when I met this apparition at the city gate. The woman held out her hand. I hardly knew whether to say, 'What do you want?' or to fall down and worship. She asked for a little money. I saw that she was beautiful and pale; she might have stepped out of the stable of Bethlehem! I gave her money and helped her on her way into the town. I had guessed her story. She, too, was a maiden mother, and she had been turned out into the world in her shame. I felt in all my pulses that here was my subject marvellously realised. I felt like one of the old monkish artists who had had a vision. I rescued the poor creatures, cherished them, watched them as I would have done some precious work of art, some lovely fragment of fresco discovered in a mouldering cloister. In a month—as if to deepen and sanctify the sadness and sweetness of it all—the poor little child died. When she felt that he was going, she held him up to me for ten minutes, and I made that sketch. You saw a feverish haste in it, I suppose; I wanted to spare the poor little mortal the pain of his position. After that, I doubly valued the mother. She is the simplest, sweetest, most natural creature that ever bloomed in this brave old land of Italy. She lives in the memory of her child, in her gratitude for the scanty kindness I have been able to show her, and in her simple religion! She is not even conscious of her beauty; my admiration has never made her vain. Heaven knows that I have made no secret of it. You must have observed the singular transparency of her expression, the lovely modesty of her glance. And was there ever such a truly virginal brow, such a natural classic elegance in the wave of the hair and the arch of the forehead? I have studied her; I may say I know her. I have absorbed her little by little; my mind is stamped and imbued, and I have determined now to clinch the impression; I shall at last invite her to sit for me!"

" 'At last—at last'?" I repeated, in much amazement. "Do you mean that she has never done so yet?"

"I have not really had—a—a sitting," said Theobald, speaking very slowly. "I have taken notes, you know; I have got my grand fundamental impression. That's the great thing! But I have not actually had her as a model, posed and draped and lighted, before my easel."

What had become for the moment of my perception and my tact I am at a loss to say; in their absence, I was unable to repress a headlong exclamation. I was destined to regret it. We had stopped at a turning, beneath a lamp. "My poor friend," I exclaimed, laying my hand on his shoulder, "you have *dawdled*! She's an old, old woman—for a Madonna!"

It was as if I had brutally struck him; I shall never forget the long, slow, almost ghastly look of pain with which he answered me.

"Dawdled?—old, old?" he stammered. "Are you joking?"

"Why, my dear fellow, I suppose you don't take her for a woman of twenty?"

He drew a long breath and leaned against a house, looking at me with questioning, protesting, reproachful eyes. At last, starting forward, and grasping my arm—"Answer me solemnly: does she seem to you truly old? Is she wrinkled, is she faded, am I blind?"

Then at last I understood the immensity of his illusion; how, one by one, the noiseless years had ebbed away and left him brooding in charmed inaction, for ever preparing for a work for ever deferred. It seemed to me almost a kindness now to tell him the plain truth. "I should be sorry to say you are blind," I answered, "but I think you are deceived. You have lost time in effortless contemplation. Your friend was once young and fresh and virginal; but, I protest, that was some years ago. Still, she has *de beaux restes*. By all means make her sit for you!" I broke down; his face was too horribly reproachful.

He took off his hat and stood passing his handkerchief mechanically over his forehead. "*De beaux restes?* I thank you for sparing me the plain English. I must make up my Madonna out of *de beaux restes*! What a masterpiece she will be! Old—old! Old—old!" he murmured.

"Never mind her age," I cried, revolted at what I had done, "never mind my impression of her! You have your memory, your notes, your genius. Finish your picture in a month. I pronounce it beforehand a masterpiece, and I hereby offer you for it any sum you may choose to ask."

He stared, but he seemed scarcely to understand me. "Old —old!" he kept stupidly repeating. "If she is old, what am I? If her beauty has faded, where—where is my strength? Has life been a dream? Have I worshipped too long—have I loved too well?" The charm, in truth, was broken. That the chord of illusion should have snapped at my light accidental touch showed how it had been weakened by excessive tension. The poor fellow's sense of wasted time, of vanished opportunity, seemed to roll in upon his soul in waves of darkness. He suddenly dropped his head and burst into tears.

I led him homeward with all possible tenderness, but I attempted neither to check his grief, to restore his equanimity, nor to unsay the hard truth. When we reached my hotel I tried to induce him to come in. "We will drink a glass of wine," I said, smiling, "to the completion of the Madonna."

With a violent effort he held up his head, mused for a moment with a formidably sombre frown, and then giving me his hand, "I will finish it," he cried, "in a month! No, in a fortnight! After all, I have it *here*!" And he tapped his forehead. "Of course she's old! She can afford to have it said of her—a woman who has made twenty years pass like a twelvemonth! Old—old! Why, sir, she shall be eternal!"

I wished to see him safely to his own door, but he waved me back and walked away with an air of resolution, whistling and swinging his cane. I waited a moment, and then followed him at a distance, and saw him proceed to cross the Santa Trinità Bridge. When he reached the middle, he suddenly paused, as if his strength had deserted him, and leaned upon the parapet gazing over into the river. I was careful to keep him in sight; I confess that I passed ten very nervous minutes. He recovered himself at last, and went his way, slowly and with hanging head.

That I had really startled poor Theobald into a bolder use of his long-garnered stores of knowledge and taste, into the vulgar effort and hazard of production, seemed at first reason enough for his continued silence, and absence; but as day followed day without his either calling or sending me a line, and without my meeting him in his customary haunts, in the galleries, in the chapel at San Lorenzo, or strolling between the Arno-side and the great hedge-screen of verdure which, along the drive of the Cascine, throws the fair occupants of barouche and phaeton into such becoming relief—as for more than a week I got neither tidings nor sight of him, I began to fear that I had fatally offended him, and that, instead of giving a wholesome impetus to his talent, I had brutally paralysed it. I had a wretched suspicion that I had made him ill. My stay at Florence was drawing to a close, and it was important that, before resuming my journey, I should assure myself of the truth. Theobald, to the last, had kept his lodging a mystery, and I was altogether at a loss where to look for him. The simplest course was to make inquiry of the beauty of the Mercato Vecchio, and I confess that unsatisfied curiosity as to the lady herself counselled it as well. Perhaps I had done her injustice, and she was as immortally fresh and fair as he conceived her. I was, at any rate, anxious to behold once more the ripe enchantress who had made twenty years pass as a twelvemonth. I repaired accordingly, one morning, to her abode, climbed the interminable staircase, and reached her door. It stood ajar, and as I hesitated whether to enter, a little serving-maid came clattering out with an empty kettle, as if she had just performed some savoury errand. The inner door, too, was open; so I crossed the little vestibule and entered the room in which I had formerly been received. It had not its evening aspect. The table, or one end of it, was spread for a late breakfast, and before it sat a gentleman—an individual, at least, of the male sex—doing execution upon a beefsteak and onions, and a bottle of wine. At his elbow, in friendly proximity, was placed the lady of the house. Her attitude, as I entered, was not that of an enchantress. With one hand she held in her lap a plate of smoking maccaroni; with the other she had lifted high in air one of the pendulous filaments of this succulent compound, and was in the act of slipping it gently down her throat. On the uncovered end of the table, facing her companion, were ranged half a dozen small statuettes, of some snuff-coloured substance resembling terracotta. He, brandishing his knife with ardour, was apparently descanting on their merits.

Evidently I darkened the door. My hostess dropped her maccaroni—into her mouth, and rose hastily with a harsh exclamation and a flushed face. I immediately perceived that the Signora Serafina's secret was even better worth knowing than I had supposed, and that the way to learn it was to take it for granted. I summoned my best Italian, I smiled and bowed and apologised for my intrusion; and in a moment, whether or no I had dispelled the lady's irritation, I had at least stimulated her prudence. I was welcome, she said; I must take a seat. This was another friend of hers—also an artist, she declared with a smile which was almost amiable. Her companion wiped his moustache and bowed with great civility. I saw at a glance that he was equal to the situation. He was presumably the author of the statuettes on the table, and he knew a money-spending *forestiére* when he saw one. He was a small, wiry man, with a clever, impudent, tossed-up nose, a sharp little black eye, and waxed ends to his moustache. On the side of his head he wore jauntily a little crimson velvet smoking-cap, and I observed that his feet were encased in brilliant slippers. On Serafina's remarking with dignity that I was the friend of Mr. Theobald, he broke out into that fantastic French of which certain Italians are so insistently lavish, and declared with fervour that Mr. Theobald was a magnificent genius.

"I am sure I don't know," I answered with a shrug. "If you are in a position to affirm it, you have the advantage of me. I have seen nothing from his hand but the bambino yonder, which certainly is fine."

He declared that the bambino was a masterpiece, a pure Correggio. It was only a pity, he added with a knowing laugh, that the sketch had not been made on some good bit of honey-combed old panel. The stately Serafina hereupon protested that Mr. Theobald was the soul of honour, and that he would never lend himself to a deceit. "I am not a judge of genius," she said, "and I know nothing of pictures. I am but a poor simple widow; but I know that the Signor Teobaldo has the heart of an angel and the virtue of a saint. He is my benefactor," she added sententiously. The after-glow of the somewhat sinister flush with which she had greeted me still lingered in her cheek, and perhaps did not favour her beauty; I could not but fancy it a wise custom of Theobald's to visit her only by candlelight. She was coarse, and her poor adorer was a poet.

"I have the greatest esteem for him," I said; "it is for this reason that I have been uneasy at not seeing him for ten days. Have you seen him? Is he perhaps ill?"

"Ill! Heaven forbid!" cried Serafina, with genuine vehemence.

Her companion uttered a rapid expletive, and reproached her with not having been to see him. She hesitated a moment; then she simpered the least bit and bridled. "He comes to see me—without reproach! But it would not be the same for me to go to him, though, indeed, you may almost call him a man of holy life."

"He has the greatest admiration for you," I said. "He would have been honoured by your visit."

She looked at me a moment sharply. "More admiration than you. Admit that!" Of course I protested with all the eloquence at my command, and my mysterious hostess then confessed that she had taken no fancy to me on my former visit, and that, Theobald not having returned, she believed I had poisoned his mind against her. "It would be no kindness to the poor gentleman, I can tell you that," she said. "He has come to see me every evening for years. It's a long friendship! No one knows him as well as I."

"I don't pretend to know him, or to understand him," I said. "He's a mystery! Nevertheless, he seems to me a little—" And I touched my forehead and waved my hand in the air.

Serafina glanced at her companion a moment, as if for inspiration. He contented himself with shrugging his shoulders, as he filled his glass again. The *padrona* hereupon gave me a more softly insinuating smile than would have seemed likely to bloom on so candid a brow. "It's for that that I love him!" she said. "The world has so little kindness for such persons. It laughs at them, and despises them, and cheats them. He is too good for this wicked life! It's his fancy that he finds a little Paradise up here in my poor apartment. If he thinks so, how can I help it? He has a strange belief—really, I ought to be ashamed to tell you—that I resemble the Blessed Virgin: Heaven forgive me! I let him think what he pleases, so long as it makes him happy. He was very kind to me once, and I am not one that forgets a favour. So I receive him every evening civilly, and ask after his health, and let him look at me on this side and that! For that matter, I may say it without vanity, I was worth looking at once! And he's not always amusing, poor man! He sits sometimes for an hour without speaking a word, or else he talks away, without stopping, on art and nature, and beauty and duty, and fifty fine things that are all so much Latin to me. I beg you to understand that he has never said a word to me that I mightn't decently listen to. He may be a little cracked, but he's one of the blessed saints."

"Eh!" cried the man, "the blessed saints were all a little cracked!"

Serafina, I fancied, left part of her story untold; but she told enough of it to make poor Theobald's own statement seem intensely pathetic in its exalted simplicity. "It's a strange fortune, certainly," she went on, "to have such a friend as this dear man—a friend who is less than a lover and more than a friend." I glanced at her companion, who preserved an impenetrable smile, twisted the end of his moustache, and disposed of a copious mouthful. Was *he* less than a lover? "But what will you have?" Serafina pursued. "In this hard world one must not ask too many questions; one must take what comes and keep what one gets. I have kept my good friend for twenty years, and I do hope that, at this time of day, signore, you have not come to turn him against me!"

I assured her that I had no such design, and that I should vastly regret disturbing Mr. Theobald's habits or convictions. On the contrary, I was alarmed about him, and I should immediately go in search of him. She gave me his address and a florid account of her sufferings at his non-appearance. She had not been to him, for various reasons; chiefly because she was afraid of displeasing him, as he had always made such a mystery of his home. "You might have sent this gentleman!" I ventured to suggest.

"Ah," cried the gentleman, "he admires the Signora Serafina, but he wouldn't admire me." And then, confidentially, with his finger on his nose, "He's a purist!"

I was about to withdraw, after having promised that I would inform the Signora Serafina of my friend's condition, when her companion, who had risen from table and girded his loins apparently for the onset, grasped me gently by the arm, and led me before the row of statuettes. "I perceive by your conversation, signore, that you are a patron of the arts. Allow me to request your honourable attention for these modest products of my own ingenuity. They are brand-new, fresh from my atelier, and have never been exhibited in public. I have brought them here to receive the verdict of this dear lady, who is a good critic, for all she may pretend to the contrary. I am the inventor of this peculiar style of statuette—of subject, manner, material, everything. Touch them, I pray you; handle them freely—you needn't fear. Delicate as they look, it is impossible they should break! My various creations have met with great success. They are especially admired by Americans. I have sent them all over Europe—to London, Paris, Vienna! You may have observed some little specimens in Paris, on the Boulevard, in a shop of which they constitute the specialty. There is always a crowd about the window. They form a very pleasing ornament for the mantelshelf of a gay young bachelor, for the boudoir of a pretty woman. You couldn't make a prettier present to a person with whom you wished to exchange a harmless joke. It is not classic art, signore, of course; but, between ourselves, isn't classic art sometimes rather a bore? Caricature, burlesque, *la charge*, as the French say, has hitherto been confined to paper, to the pen and pencil. Now, it has been my inspiration to introduce it into statuary. For this purpose I have invented a peculiar plastic compound which you will permit me not to divulge. That's my secret, signore! It's as light, you perceive, as cork, and yet as firm as alabaster! I frankly confess that I really pride myself as much on this little stroke of chemical ingenuity as upon the other element of novelty in my creations—my types. What do you say to my types, signore? The idea is bold; does it strike you as happy? Cats and monkeys—monkeys and cats—all human life is there! Human life, of course, I mean, viewed with the eye of the satirist! To combine sculpture and satire, signore, has been my unprecedented ambition. I flatter myself that I have not egregiously failed."

As this jaunty Juvenal of the chimney-piece delivered himself of his persuasive allocution, he took up his little groups successively from the table, held them aloft, turned them about, rapped them with his knuckles, and gazed at them lovingly, with his head on one side. They consisted each of a cat and a monkey, fantastically draped, in some preposterously sentimental conjunction. They exhibited a certain sameness of motive, and illustrated chiefly the different phases of what, in delicate terms, may be called gallantry and coquetry; but they were strikingly clever and expressive, and were at once very perfect cats and monkeys and very natural men and women. I confess, however, that they failed to amuse me. I was doubtless not in a mood to enjoy them, for they seemed to me peculiarly cynical and vulgar. Their imitative felicity was revolting. As I looked askance at the complacent little artist, brandishing them between finger and thumb and caressing them with an amorous eye, he seemed to me himself little more than an exceptionally intelligent ape. I mustered an

admiring grin, however, and he blew another blast. "My figures are studied from life! I have a little menagerie of monkeys whose frolics I contemplate by the hour. As for the cats,
one has only to look out of one's back window! Since I have
begun to examine these expressive little brutes, I have made
many profound observations. Speaking, signore, to a man of
imagination, I may say that my little designs are not without
a philosophy of their own. Truly, I don't know whether the
cats and monkeys imitate us, or whether it's we who imitate
them." I congratulated him on his philosophy, and he resumed: "You will do me the honour to admit that I have handled my subjects with delicacy. Eh, it was needed, signore! I
have been free, but not too free—eh? Just a hint, you know!
You may see as much or as little as you please. These little
groups, however, are no measure of my invention. If you will
favour me with a call at my studio, I think that you will admit
that my combinations are really infinite. I likewise execute figures to command. You have perhaps some little motive—the
fruit of your philosophy of life, signore—which you would
like to have interpreted. I can promise to work it up to your
satisfaction; it shall be as malicious as you please! Allow me to
present you with my card, and to remind you that my prices
are moderate. Only sixty francs for a little group like that. My
statuettes are as durable as bronze—*ære perennius*, signore—
and, between ourselves, I think they are more amusing!"

As I pocketed his card, I glanced at Madonna Serafina,
wondering whether she had an eye for contrasts. She had
picked up one of the little couples and was tenderly dusting it
with a feather broom.

What I had just seen and heard had so deepened my compassionate interest in my deluded friend that I took a summary leave, making my way directly to the house designated
by this remarkable woman. It was in an obscure corner of the
opposite side of the town, and presented a sombre and
squalid appearance. An old woman in the doorway, on my inquiring for Theobald, ushered me in with a mumbled blessing and an expression of relief at the poor gentleman having
a friend. His lodging seemed to consist of a single room at
the top of the house. On getting no answer to my knock, I
opened the door, supposing that he was absent; so that it gave

me a certain shock to find him sitting there helpless and dumb. He was seated near the single window, facing an easel which supported a large canvas. On my entering, he looked up at me blankly, without changing his position, which was that of absolute lassitude and dejection, his arms loosely folded, his legs stretched before him, his head hanging on his breast. Advancing into the room, I perceived that his face vividly corresponded with his attitude. He was pale, haggard, and unshaven, and his dull and sunken eye gazed at me without a spark of recognition. I had been afraid that he would greet me with fierce reproaches, as the cruelly officious patron who had turned his contentment to bitterness, and I was relieved to find that my appearance awakened no visible resentment. "Don't you know me?" I asked, as I put out my hand. "Have you already forgotten me?"

He made no response, kept his position stupidly, and left me staring about the room. It spoke most plaintively for itself. Shabby, sordid, naked, it contained, beyond the wretched bed, but the scantiest provision for personal comfort. It was bedroom at once and studio—a grim ghost of a studio. A few dusty casts and prints on the walls, three or four old canvases turned face inward, and a rusty-looking colour-box formed, with the easel at the window, the sum of its appurtenances. The place savoured horribly of poverty. Its only wealth was the picture on the easel, presumably the famous Madonna. Averted as this was from the door, I was unable to see its face; but at last, sickened by the vacant misery of the spot, I passed behind Theobald, eagerly and tenderly. I can hardly say that I was surprised at what I found—a canvas that was a mere dead blank, cracked and discoloured by time. This was his immortal work! Though not surprised, I confess I was powerfully moved, and I think that for five minutes I could not have trusted myself to speak. At last, my silent nearness affected him; he stirred and turned, and then rose and looked at me with a slowly kindling eye. I murmured some kind, ineffective nothings about his being ill and needing advice and care, but he seemed absorbed in the effort to recall distinctly what had last passed between us. "You were right," he said with a pitiful smile, "I am a dawdler! I am a failure! I shall do nothing more in this world. You opened my eyes; and, though the truth is bitter, I bear you no grudge. Amen! I have been sitting here for a week, face to face with the truth, with the past, with my weakness and poverty and nullity. I shall never touch a brush! I believe I have neither eaten nor slept. Look at that canvas!" he went on, as I relieved my emotion in an urgent request that he would come home with me and dine. "That was to have contained my masterpiece! Isn't it a promising foundation? The elements of it are all *here*." And he tapped his forehead with that mystic confidence which had marked the gesture before. "If I could only transpose them into some brain that has the hand, the will! Since I have been sitting here taking stock of my intellects, I have come to believe that I have the material for a hundred masterpieces. But my hand is paralysed now, and they will never be painted. I never began! I waited and waited to be worthier to begin, and wasted my life in preparation. While I fancied my creation was growing, it was dying. I have taken it all too hard! Michael Angelo didn't, when he went at the Lorenzo! He did his best at a venture, and his venture is immortal. *That's* mine!" And he pointed with a gesture I shall never forget at the empty canvas. "I suppose we are a genus by ourselves in the providential scheme—we talents that can't act, that can't do nor dare! We take it out in talk, in plans and promises, in study, in visions! But our visions, let me tell you," he cried, with a toss of his head, "have a way of being brilliant, and a man has not lived in vain who has seen the things I have seen! Of course you will not believe in them when that bit of worm-eaten cloth is all I have to show for them; but to convince you, to enchant and astound the world, I need only the hand of Raphael. His brain I already have. A pity, you will say, that I haven't his modesty! Ah, let me boast and babble now; it's all I have left! I am the half of a genius! Where in the wide world is my other half? Lodged perhaps in the vulgar soul, the cunning, ready fingers of some dull copyist or some trivial artisan who turns out by the dozen his easy prodigies of touch! But it's not for me to sneer at him; he at least does something. He's not a dawdler! Well for me if I had been vulgar and clever and reckless, if I could have shut my eyes and taken my leap."

What to say to the poor fellow, what to do for him, seemed

hard to determine; I chiefly felt that I must break the spell of his present inaction, and remove him from the haunted atmosphere of the little room it was such a cruel irony to call a studio. I cannot say I persuaded him to come out with me; he simply suffered himself to be led, and when we began to walk in the open air I was able to appreciate his pitifully weakened condition. Nevertheless, he seemed in a certain way to revive, and murmured at last that he should like to go to the Pitti Gallery. I shall never forget our melancholy stroll through those gorgeous halls, every picture on whose walls seemed, even to my own sympathetic vision, to glow with a sort of insolent renewal of strength and lustre. The eyes and lips of the great portraits appeared to smile in ineffable scorn of the dejected pretender who had dreamed of competing with their triumphant authors; the celestial candour, even, of the Madonna of the Chair, as we paused in perfect silence before her, was tinged with the sinister irony of the women of Leonardo. Perfect silence indeed marked our whole progress—the silence of a deep farewell; for I felt in all my pulses, as Theobald, leaning on my arm, dragged one heavy foot after the other, that he was looking his last. When we came out, he was so exhausted that instead of taking him to my hotel to dine, I called a carriage and drove him straight to his own poor lodging. He had sunk into an extraordinary lethargy; he lay back in the carriage, with his eyes closed, as pale as death, his faint breathing interrupted at intervals by a sudden gasp, like a smothered sob or a vain attempt to speak. With the help of the old woman who had admitted me before, and who emerged from a dark back court, I contrived to lead him up the long steep staircase and lay him on his wretched bed. To her I gave him in charge, while I prepared in all haste to seek a physician. But she followed me out of the room with a pitiful clasping of her hands.

"Poor, dear, blessed gentleman," she murmured; "is he dying?"

"Possibly. How long has he been thus?"

"Since a certain night he passed ten days ago. I came up in the morning to make his poor bed, and found him sitting up in his clothes before that great canvas he keeps there. Poor, dear, strange man, he says his prayers to it! He had not been to bed, nor since then, properly! What has happened to him? Has he found out about the Serafina?" she whispered with a glittering eye and a toothless grin.

"Prove at least that one old woman can be faithful," I said, "and watch him well till I come back." My return was delayed, through the absence of the English physician, who was away on a round of visits and whom I vainly pursued from house to house before I overtook him. I brought him to Theobald's bedside none too soon. A violent fever had seized our patient, and the case was evidently grave. A couple of hours later I knew that he had brain-fever. From this moment I was with him constantly; but I am far from wishing to describe his illness. Excessively painful to witness, it was happily brief. Life burned out in delirium. One night in particular that I passed at his pillow, listening to his wild snatches of regret, of aspiration, of rapture and awe at the phantasmal pictures with which his brain seemed to swarm, comes back to my memory now like some stray page from a lost masterpiece of tragedy. Before a week was over we had buried him in the little Protestant cemetery on the way to Fiesole. The Signora Serafina, whom I had caused to be informed of his illness, had come in person, I was told, to inquire about its progress; but she was absent from his funeral, which was attended by but a scanty concourse of mourners. Half a dozen old Florentine sojourners, in spite of the prolonged estrangement which had preceded his death, had felt the kindly impulse to honour his grave. Among them was my friend Mrs. Coventry, whom I found, on my departure, waiting in her carriage at the gate of the cemetery.

"Well," she said, relieving at last with a significant smile the solemnity of our immediate greeting, "and the great Madonna? Have you seen her, after all?"

"I have seen her," I said; "she is mine—by bequest. But I shall never show her to you."

"And why not, pray?"

"My dear Mrs. Coventry, you would not understand her!"

"Upon my word, you are polite."

"Excuse me; I am sad and vexed and bitter." And with reprehensible rudeness, I marched away. I was excessively impatient to leave Florence; my friend's dark spirit seemed diffused through all things. I had packed my trunk to start for Rome that night, and meanwhile, to beguile my unrest, I aimlessly paced the streets. Chance led me at last to the church of San Lorenzo. Remembering poor Theobald's phrase about Michael Angelo—"He did his best at a venture"—I went in and turned my steps to the chapel of the tombs. Viewing in sadness the sadness of its immortal treasures, I fancied, while I stood there, that they needed no ampler commentary than these simple words. As I passed through the church again to leave it, a woman, turning away from one of the side-altars, met me face to face. The black shawl depending from her head draped picturesquely the handsome visage of Madonna Serafina. She stopped as she recognised me, and I saw that she wished to speak. Her eye was bright, and her ample bosom heaved in a way that seemed to portend a certain sharpness of reproach. But the expression of my own face, apparently, drew the sting from her resentment, and she addressed me in a tone in which bitterness was tempered by a sort of dogged resignation. "I know it was you, now, that separated us," she said. "It was a pity he ever brought you to see me! Of course, you couldn't think of me as he did. Well, the Lord gave him, the Lord has taken him. I have just paid for a nine days' mass for his soul. And I can tell you this, signore—I never deceived him. Who put it into his head that I was made to live on holy thoughts and fine phrases? It was his own fancy, and it pleased him to think so.—Did he suffer much?" she added more softly, after a pause.

"His sufferings were great, but they were short."

"And did he speak of me?" She had hesitated and dropped her eyes; she raised them with her question, and revealed in their sombre stillness a gleam of feminine confidence which, for the moment, revived and illumined her beauty. Poor Theobald! Whatever name he had given his passion, it was still her fine eyes that had charmed him.

"Be contented, madam," I answered, gravely.

She dropped her eyes again and was silent. Then exhaling a full, rich sigh, as she gathered her shawl together—"He was a magnificent genius!"

I bowed, and we separated.

Passing through a narrow side-street on my way back to my hotel, I perceived above a doorway a sign which it seemed to me I had read before. I suddenly remembered that it was identical with the superscription of a card that I had carried for an hour in my waistcoat-pocket. On the threshold stood the ingenious artist whose claims to public favour were thus distinctly signalised, smoking a pipe in the evening air, and giving the finishing polish with a bit of rag to one of his inimitable "combinations." I caught the expressive curl of a couple of tails. He recognised me, removed his little red cap with a most obsequious bow, and motioned me to enter his studio. I returned his salute and passed on, vexed with the apparition. For a week afterwards, whenever I was seized among the ruins of triumphant Rome with some peculiarly poignant memory of Theobald's transcendent illusions and deplorable failure, I seemed to hear a fantastic, impertinent murmur, "Cats and monkeys, monkeys and cats; all human life is there!"

The Sweetheart of M. Briseux

THE LITTLE picture gallery at M—— is a typical *musée de province*—cold, musty, unvisited, and enriched chiefly with miniature works by painters whose maturity was not to be powerful. The floors are tiled in brick, and the windows draped in faded moreen; the very light seems pale and neutral, as if the dismal lack-lustre atmosphere of the pictures were contagious. The subjects represented are of course of the familiar academic sort—the Wisdom of Solomon and the Fureurs d'Oreste; together with a few elegant landscapes exhibiting the last century view of nature, and half a dozen neat portraits of French gentlefolks of that period, in the act, as one may say, of taking the view in question. To me, I confess, the place had a melancholy charm, and I found none of the absurd old paintings too absurd to enjoy. There is always an agreeable finish in the French touch, even when the hand is not a master's. The catalogue, too, was prodigiously queer; a bit of very ancient literature, with comments, in the manner of the celebrated M. La Harpe. I wondered, as I turned its pages, into what measure of reprobation pictures and catalogue together had been compressed by that sole son of M——, who has achieved more than local renown in the arts. Conjecture was pertinent, for it was in these crepuscular halls that this deeply original artist must have heard the first early bird-notes of awakening genius: first, half credulously, as we may suppose, on festal Sundays, with his hand in his father's, gazing rosy and wide-eyed at the classical wrath of Achilles and the sallow flesh-tints of Dido; and later, with his hands in his pockets, an incipient critical frown and the mental vision of an Achilles somehow more in earnest and a Dido more deeply desirable. It was indeed doubly pertinent, for the little Musée had at last, after much watching and waiting and bargaining, become possessor of one of Briseux's pictures. I was promptly informed of the fact by the *concierge*, a person much reduced by years and chronic catarrh, but still robust enough to display his æsthetic culture to a foreigner presumably of distinction. He led me solemnly into the presence of the great work, and placed a chair for me in the proper light. The famous painter had left his native town early in life, before making his mark, and an inappreciative family—his father was a small apothecary with a proper admiration of the arts, but a horror of artists—had been at no pains to preserve his boyish sketches. The more fools they! The merest scrawl with his signature now brought hundreds of francs, and there were those of his blood still in the town with whom the francs were scarce enough. To obtain a serious picture had of course been no small affair, and little M——, though with the yearning heart of a mother, happened to have no scanty maternal savings. Yet the thing had been managed by subscription, and the picture paid for. To make the triumph complete, a fortnight after it had been hung on its nail, M. Briseux succumbs to a fever in Rome and his pictures rise to the most fantastic prices! This was the very work which had made the painter famous. The portrait of a Lady in a Yellow Shawl in the Salon of 1836 had *fait époque*. Every one had heard of the Yellow Shawl; people talked of it as they did of the Chapeau de Paille of Rubens or the "Torn Glove" of Titian; or if they didn't, posterity would! Such was the discursive murmur of the concierge as I examined this precious specimen of Briseux's first manner; and there was a plaintive cadence in this last assurance, which seemed to denote a too vivid prevision of the harvest of tributary francs to be reaped by his successors in office. It would be graceless praise to say that a glimpse of the picture is worth your franc. It is a superb performance, and I spent half an hour before it in such serene enjoyment that I forgot the concierge was a bore.

It is a half-length portrait representing a young woman, not exactly beautiful, yet very far from plain, draped with a singularly simple elegance in a shawl of yellow silk embroidered with fantastic arabesque. She is dark and grave, her dress is dark, the background is of a sober tone, and this brilliant scarf glows splendidly by contrast. It seems indeed to irradiate luminous color, and makes the picture brilliant in spite of its sombre accessories; and yet it leaves their full value to the tenderly glowing flesh portions. The portrait lacks a certain harmonious finish, that masterly interfusion of parts which the painter afterwards practised; the touch is hasty, and here and there a little heavy; but its splendid vivacity and energy, and the almost boyish good faith of some of its more venturesome strokes, make it a capital example of that momentous point in the history of genius when still tender promise blooms—in a night, as it were—into perfect force. It was little wonder that the picture had made a noise: judges of the more penetrating sort must have felt that it contained that invaluable something which an artist gives but once—the prime outgush of his effort—the flower of his originality. As I continued to look, however, I began to wonder whether it did not contain something better still—the reflection of a countenance very nearly as deep and ardent as the artist's talent. In spite of the expressive repose of the figure the brow and mouth wore a look of smothered agitation, the dark gray eye almost glittered, and the flash in the cheek burned ominously. Evidently this was the picture of something more than a yellow shawl. To the analytic eye it was the picture of a mind, or at least of a mood. "Who was the lady?" I asked of my companion.

He shrugged his shoulders, and for an instant looked uncertain. But, as a Frenchman, he produced his hypothesis as follows: "Mon Dieu! a sweetheart of M. Briseux!—*Ces artistes!*"

I left my place and passed into the adjoining rooms, where, as I have said, I found half an hour's diversion. On my return, my chair was occupied by a lady, apparently my only fellow-visitor. I noticed her no further than to see that, though comely, she was no longer young, that she was dressed in black, and that she was looking intently at the picture. Her intentness indeed at last attracted me, and while I lingered to gather a final impression, I covertly glanced at her. She was so far from being young that her hair was white, but with that charming and often premature brilliancy which belongs to fine brunettes. The concierge hovered near, narrating and expounding, and I fancied that her brief responses (for she asked no questions) betrayed an English accent. But I had doubtless no business to fancy anything, for my companion, as if with a sudden embarrassing sense of being watched, gathered her shawl about her, rose, and prepared to turn away. I should have immediately retreated, but that with this movement of hers our eyes met, and in the light of her rapid, just slightly deprecating glance, I read something which helped curiosity to get the better of politeness. She walked away, and I stood staring; and as she averted her head it seemed to me that my rather too manifest surprise had made her blush. I watched her slowly cross the room and pass into the next one, looking very vaguely at the pictures; and then addressed a keenly questioning glance at the Lady with the Yellow Shawl. Her startling vivid eyes answered my question most distinctly. I was satisfied, and I left the Musée.

It would perhaps be more correct to say that I was wholly unsatisfied. I strolled at haphazard through the little town, and emerged, as a matter of course, on the local promenade. The promenade at M—— is a most agreeable spot. It stretches along the top of the old town wall, over whose sturdy parapet, polished by the peaceful showers of many generations, you enjoy a view of the pale-hued but charming Provencal landscape. The middle of the rampart is adorned with a row of close-clipped lime-trees, with benches in the spaces between them; and, as you sit in the shade, the prospect is framed to your vision by the level parapet and the even limit of the far-projecting branches. What you see is therefore a long horizontal strip of landscape—a radiant stretch of white rocks and vaporous olives, scintillating in the southern light. Except a *bonne* or two, with a couple of children grubbing in the gravel, an idle apprentice in a blouse dozing on a bench, and a couple of red-legged soldiers leaning on the wall, I was the only lounger on the rampart, and this was a place to relish solitude. By nature a very sentimental traveller, there is nothing I like better than to light a cigar and lose myself in a meditative perception of local color. I love to ruminate the picturesque, and the scene before me was redolent of it. On this occasion, however, the shady rampart and the shining distance were less interesting than a figure, disembodied but distinct, which soon obtruded itself on my attention. The mute assurance gathered before leaving the Musée had done as much to puzzle as to enlighten me. Was that modest and venerable person, then, the sweetheart of the illustrious Briseux? one of *ces artistes*, as rumor loudly proclaimed him, in the invidious as well as in the most honorable sense of the term. Plainly, she was the original of the portrait.

In the days when her complexion would bear it, she had worn the yellow shawl. Time had changed, but not transformed her, as she must have fancied it had, to come and contemplate thus frankly this monument of her early charms. Why had she come? Was it accident, or was it vanity? How did it seem to her to find herself so strangely lifted out of her own possession and made a helpless spectator of her survival to posterity? The more I consulted my impression of her, the more certain I felt that she was no Frenchwoman, but a modest spinster of my own transatlantic race, on whom posterity had as little claim as this musty Musée, which indeed possessed much of that sepulchral chill which clings to such knowledge of us as posterity enjoys. I found it hard to reconcile the lady with herself, and it was with the restlessness of conjecture that I left my place and strolled to the further end of the rampart. Here conjecture paused, amazed at its opportunities; for M. Briseux's sweetheart was seated on a bench under the lime-trees. She was gazing almost as thoughtfully on the distant view as she had done on her portrait; but as I passed, she gave me a glance from which embarrassment seemed to have vanished. I slowly walked the length of the rampart again, and as I went an impulse, born somehow of the delicious mild air, the light-bathed landscape of rock and olive, and of the sense of a sort of fellowship in isolation in the midst of these deeply foreign influences, as well as of a curiosity which was after all but the frank recognition of an obvious fact, was transmuted into a decision sufficiently remarkable in a bashful man. I proceeded gravely to carry it out. I approached my companion and bowed. She acknowledged my bow with a look which, though not exactly mistrustful, seemed to demand an explanation. To give it, I seated myself beside her. Something in her face made explanation easy. I was sure that she was an old maid, and gently but frankly eccentric. Her age left her at liberty to be as frank as she chose, and though I was somewhat her junior, I had gray hairs enough in my moustache to warrant her in smiling at my almost ardent impatience. Her smile, when she perceived that my direct appeal was deeply respectful, broke into a genial laugh which completed our introduction. To her inner sense, as well, evidently, the gray indifference of the historic rampart, the olive-sown landscape, the sweet foreign climate, left the law very much in our own hands; and then moreover, as something in her eyes proclaimed, the well of memory in her soul had been so strongly stirred that it naturally over-flowed. I fancy that she looked more like her portrait for that hour or two than she had done in twenty years. At any rate, it had come to seem, before many minutes, a delightful matter of course that I should sit there—a perfect stranger—listening to the story into which her broken responses to my first questions gradually shaped themselves. I should add that I had made a point of appearing a zealous student of the lamented Briseux. This was no more than the truth, and I proved categorically that I knew his works. We were thus pilgrims in the same faith, and licensed to discuss its mysteries. I repeat her story literally, and I surely don't transgress the proper limits of editorial zeal in supplying a single absent clause: she must in those days have been a wonderfully charming girl.

I have been spending the winter (she said) with my niece at Cannes, where I accidentally heard from an English gentleman interested in such matters, that Briseux's "Yellow Shawl" had been purchased by this little Musée. He had stopped to see it on his way from Paris, and, though a famous *connoisseur*, poor man, do you know he never discovered what it took you but a moment to perceive? I didn't enlighten him, in spite of his kindness in explaining, "Bradshaw" in hand, just how I might manage to diverge on my way to Paris and give a day to M——. I contented myself with telling him that I had known M. Briseux thirty years ago, and had chanced to have the first glimpse of his first masterpiece. Even this suggested nothing. But in fact, why should it have suggested anything? As I sat before the picture just now, I felt in all my pulses that I am *not* the person who stands masquerading there with that strangely cynical smile. That poor girl is dead and buried; I should tell no falsehood in saying I'm not she. Yet as I looked at her, time seemed to roll backward and experience to repeat itself. Before me stood a pale young man in a ragged coat, with glowing dark eyes, brushing away at a great canvas, with gestures more like those of inspiration than any I have ever seen. I seemed to see myself—to *be* myself—

muffled in that famous shawl, *posing* there for hours in a sort of fever that made me unconscious of fatigue. I've often wondered whether, during those memorable hours, I was more or less myself than usual, and whether the singular episode they brought forth was an act of folly or of transcendent reason. Perhaps you can tell me.

It was in Paris, in my twenty-first year. I had come abroad with Mrs. Staines, an old and valued friend of my mother's, who during the last days of her life, a year before, had consigned me appealingly to this lady's protection. But for Mrs. Staines, indeed, I should have been homeless. My brother had recently married, but not happily, and experiment had shown me that under his roof I was an indifferent peacemaker. Mrs. Staines was what is called a very superior person—a person with an aquiline nose, who wore gloves in the house, and gave you her ear to kiss. My mother, who considered her the wisest of women, had written her every week since their schooldays a crossed letter beginning "My dearest Lucretia"; but it was my poor mother's nature to like being patronized and bullied. Mrs. Staines would send her by return of mail a budget of advice adapted to her "station"—this being a considerate mode of allusion to the fact that she had married a very poor clergyman. Mrs. Staines received me, however, with such substantial kindness, that I should have had little grace to complain that the manner of it was frigid. When I knew her better I forgave her frigidity, for it was that of a disappointed woman. She was ambitious, and her ambitions had failed. She had married a very clever man, a rising young lawyer, of political tendencies, who promised to become famous. She would have enjoyed above all things being the wife of a legal luminary, and she would have insisted on his expanding to the first magnitude. She believed herself born, I think, to be the lawful Egeria of a cabinet minister. A cabinet minister poor Mr. Staines might have become if he had lived; but he broke down at thirty-five from overwork, and a year later his wife had to do double mourning. As time went on she transferred her hopes to her only boy; but here her disappointment lay the heavier on her heart that maternal pride had bidden it be forever dumb. He would never tread in his father's steps, nor redeem his father's pledges. His genius—if genius it was—was bent in quite another way, and he was to be, not a useful, but an ornamental member of society. Extremely ornamental he seemed likely to become, and his mother found partial comfort as he grew older. He did his duty apparently in growing up so very handsome that, whatever else he might do, he would be praised less for that than for his good looks. They were those of a decorous young Apollo. When I first saw him, as he was leaving college, he might well have passed for an incipient great man. He had in perfection the *air* of distinction, and he carried it out in gesture and manner. Never was a handsomer, graver, better-bred young man. He was tall, slender, and fair, with the finest blonde hair curling close about his shapely head; a blue eye, as clear and cold as a winter's morning; a set of teeth so handsome that his infrequent smile might have seemed almost a matter of modesty; and a general expression of discretion and maturity which seemed to protest against the imputation of foppishness. After a while, probably, you would have found him too imperturbably neat and polite, and have liked him better if his manner had been sometimes at fault and his cravat occasionally awry. Me, I confess, he vastly impressed from the first, and I secretly worshipped him. I had never seen so fine a gentleman, and I doubted if the world contained such another. My experience of the world was small, and I had lived among what Harold Staines would have considered very shabby people—several of whom wore ill-brushed hats. I was, therefore, not sorry to find that I appreciated merit of the most refined sort; and in fact, ignorant though I was, my judgment was not at fault. Harold was perfectly honorable and amiable, and his only fault was that he looked wiser than he could reasonably be expected to be. In the evening especially, in a white cravat, leaning in a doorway, and overtopping the crowd by his whole handsome head, he seemed some inscrutable young diplomatist whose skepticism hadn't undermined his courtesy.

He had, through his mother, expectation of property sufficient to support him in ample ease; but though he had elegant tastes, idleness was not one of them, and he agreed with his mother that he ought to choose a profession. Then it was that she fully measured her disappointment. There had been nothing in her family but judges and bishops, and anything else was of questionable respectability. There was a great deal of talk on the matter between them; for superficially at least they were a most united pair, and if Harold had not asked her opinion from conviction he would have done so from politeness. In reality, I believe, there was but one person in the world whose opinion he greatly cared for—and that person was not Mrs. Staines; nor had it yet come to pass that he pretended for a while it was I. It was so far from being Mrs. Staines that one day, after a long talk, I found her leaving him in tears; and tears with this superior woman were an event of portentous rarity. Harold on the same day was not at home at dinner, and I thought the next day held his handsome head even higher than usual. I asked no questions, but a little later my curiosity was satisfied. Mrs. Staines informed me, with an air of dignity which evidently cost her some effort and seemed intended to deprecate criticism, that Harold had determined to be an—artist. "It's not the career I should have preferred," she said, "but my son has talent—and respectability—which will make it honorable." That Harold would do anything more for the profession of the brush than Raphael and Rembrandt had done, I was perhaps not prepared to affirm; but I answered that I was very glad, and that I wished him all success. Indeed, I was not surprised, for Mrs. Staines had what in any one else would have been called a mania for pictures and bronzes, old snuff-boxes and candlesticks. He had not apparently used his pencil very freely; but he had recently procured—indeed, I think he had himself designed—a "sketching apparatus" of the most lavish ingenuity. He was now going to use it in earnest, and I remember reflecting with a good deal of satisfaction that the great white umbrella which formed its principal feature was large enough to protect his handsome complexion from the sun.

It was at this time I came to Mrs. Staines to stay indefinitely—with doubts and fears so few that I must have been either very ignorant or very confident. I had indeed an ample measure of the blessed simplicity of youth; but if I judged my situation imperfectly, I did so at any rate with a conscience. I was stoutly determined to receive no favors that I couldn't repay, and to be as quietly useful and gracefully agreeable as I could modestly devise occasion for. I was a homeless girl, but I was not a poor relation. My fortune was slender, but I was ready to go out into the world and seek a better, rather than fall into an attitude of irresponsive dependence. Mrs. Staines thought at first that I was dull and amiable, and that as a companion I would do no great credit to anything but her benevolence. Later, for a time, as I gave proofs of some sagacity and perhaps of some decision, I think she fancied me a schemer and—Heaven forgive her!—a hypocrite. But at last, evidently—although to the end, I believe, she continued to compliment my shrewdness at the expense of that feminine sweetness by which I should have preferred to commend myself—she decided that I was a person of the best intentions, and—here comes my story—that I would make a suitable wife for her son.

To this unexpectedly flattering conclusion, of course, she was slow in coming; it was the result of the winter we passed together after Harold had "turned his attention," as his mother always publicly phrased it, "to art." He had declared that we must immediately go abroad that he might study the works of the masters. His mother, I believe, suggested that he might begin with the rudiments nearer home. But apparently he had mastered the rudiments, for she was overruled and we went to Rome. I don't know how many of the secrets of the masters Harold learned; but we passed a delightful winter. He began his studies with the solemn promptitude which he used in all things, and devoted a great deal of time to copying from the antique in the Vatican and the Capitol. He worked slowly, but with extraordinary precision and neatness, and finished his drawings with exquisite care. He was openly very little of a dogmatist, but on coming to know him you found that he had various principles of which he was extremely tenacious. Several of these related to the proportions of the human body, as ascertained by himself. They constituted, he affirmed, an infallible method for learning to draw. If other artists didn't know it, so much the worse for them. He applied this rare method persistently all winter, and carried away from Rome a huge portfolio full of neatly shaded statues and statuesque *contadini*. At first he had gone into a painter's studio with several other pupils, but he took no fancy to either

his teacher or his companions, and came home one day in disgust, declaring that he had washed his hands of them. As he
never talked about disagreeable things, he said nothing as to
what had vexed him; but I guessed that he had received some
mortal offence, and I was not surprised that he shouldn't care
to fraternize with the common herd of art-students. They had
long, untidy hair, and smoked bad tobacco; they lay no one
knew where, and borrowed money and took liberties. Mr.
Staines certainly was not a man to refuse a needy friend a
napoleon, but he couldn't forgive a liberty. He took none
with himself! We became very good friends, and it was especially for this that I liked him. Nothing is truer than that in
the long run we like our opposites; they're a change and a rest
from ourselves. I confess that my good intentions sometimes
clashed with a fatal light-headedness, of which a fair share of
trouble had not cured me. In moments of irritation I had a
trick of giving the reins to my "sarcasm;" so at least my partners in quadrilles had often called it. At my leisure I was sure
to repent, and frank public amends followed fast on the heels
of offence. Then I believe I was called generous—not only by
my partners in quadrilles. But I had a secret admiration for
people who were just, from the first and always, and whose
demeanor seemed to shape itself with a sort of harmonious
unity, like the outline of a beautiful statue. Harold Staines was
a finished gentleman, as we used to say in those days, and I
admired him the more that I still had ringing in my ears that
eternal refrain of my school-room days—"My child, my child,
when will you ever learn to be a lady?" He seemed to me an
embodiment of the serene amenities of life, and I didn't know
how very great a personage I thought him until I once overheard a young man in a crowd at St. Peter's call him *that confounded prig.* Then I came to the conclusion that it was a very
coarse and vulgar world, and that Mr. Staines was too good
for it.

This impression was not removed by—I hardly know what
to call it—the gallant propriety of his conduct toward me. He
had treated me at first with polite condescension, as a very
young and rather humble person, whose presence in the
house rested on his mother's somewhat eccentric benevolence, rather than on any very obvious merits of her own. But

later, as my native merit, whatever it was, got the better of my shyness, he approached me, especially in company, with a sort of ceremonious consideration which seemed to give notice to the world that if his mother and he treated me as their equal—why, I *was* their equal. At last, one fine day in Rome, I learned that I had the honor to please him. It had seemed to me so little of a matter of course that I should captivate Mr. Staines, that for a moment I was actually disappointed, and felt disposed to tell him that I had expected more of his taste. But as I grew used to the idea, I found no fault with it, and I felt prodigiously honored. I didn't take him for a man of genius, but his admiration pleased me more than if it had come in chorus from a dozen of the men of genius whom I had had pointed out to me at archæological picnics. They somehow were covered with the world's rust and haunted with the world's errors, and certainly on any vital question could not be trusted to make their poor wives the same answers two days running. Besides, they were dreadfully ugly. Harold was consistency itself, and his superior manner and fine blond beauty seemed a natural result of his spiritual serenity. The way he declared himself was very characteristic, and to some girls might have seemed prosaic. To my mind it had a peculiar dignity. I had asked him, a week before, as we stood on the platform before the Lateran, some question about the Claudian aqueduct, which he had been unable to answer at the moment, although on coming to Rome he had laid in a huge provision of books of reference which he consulted with unfailing diligence. "I'll look it up," he said gravely; but I thought no more about it, and a few days afterwards, when he asked me to ride with him on the Campagna, I never supposed I was to be treated to an archæological lecture. It was worthy of a wiser listener. He led the way to a swelling mound, overlooking the long stretch of the aqueduct, and poured forth the result of his researches. This was surely not a trivial compliment; and it seemed to me a finer sort of homage than if he had offered me a fifty-franc bouquet or put his horse at a six-foot wall. He told me the number of the arches, and very possibly of the stones; his story bristled with learning. I listened respectfully and stared hard at the long ragged ruin, as if it had suddenly become intensely interesting. But it was Mr. Staines who was interesting: all honor to the man who kept his polite promises so handsomely! I said nothing when he paused, and after a few minutes was going to turn away my horse. Then he laid his hand on the bridle, and, in the same tone, as if he were still talking of the aqueduct, informed me of the state of his affections. I, in my unsuspectingness, had enslaved them, and it was proper that I should know he adored me. Proper! I have always remembered the word, though I was far from thinking then that it clashed with his eloquence. It often occurred to me afterwards as the key-note of his character. In a moment more, he formally offered himself.

Don't be surprised at these details: to be just I must be perfectly frank, and if I consented to tell you my story, it is because I fancied I should find profit in hearing it myself. As I speak my words come back to me. I left Rome engaged to Mr. Staines, subject to his mother's approval. He might dispense with it, I told him, but I could not, and as yet I had no reason to expect it. She would, of course, wish him to marry a woman of more consequence. Mine of late had risen in her eyes, but she could hardly regard me as yet as a possible daughter-in-law. With time I hoped to satisfy her and to receive her blessing. Then I would ask for no further delay. We journeyed slowly up from Rome along the Mediterranean, stopping often for several days to allow Harold to sketch. He depicted mountains and villages with the same diligence as the statues in the Vatican, and presumably with the same success. As his winter's practice had given him great facility, he would dash off a magnificent landscape in a single morning. I always thought it strange that, being very sober in his speech and manner, he should be extremely fond of color in art. Such at least was the fact, and these rapid water-colors were a wonderful medley. Crimson and azure, orange and emerald— nothing less would satisfy him. But, for that matter, nature in those regions has a dazzling brightness. So at least it had for a lively girl of twenty, just engaged. So it had for a certain time afterwards. I'll not deny, the lustrous sea and sky began vaguely to reflect my own occasionally sombre mood. How to explain to you the process of my feeling at this time is more than I can say; how especially to make you believe that I was

neither perverse nor capricious. I give it up; I can only assure
you that I observed my emotions, even before I understood
them, with painful surprise. I was not disillusioned, but an
end had suddenly come to my elation. It was as if my heart
had had wings, which had been suddenly clipped. I have
never been especially fond of my own possessions, and I have
learned that if I wish to admire a thing in peace, I must remain at a respectful distance. My happiness in Harold's affection reached its climax too suddenly, and before I knew it I
found myself wondering, questioning, and doubting. It was
no fault of his, certainly, and he had promised me nothing
that he was not ready to bestow. He was all attention and
decorous devotion. If there was a fault, it was mine, for having judged like the very young and uninformed person I was.
Since my engagement I felt five years older, and the first use
I made of my maturity—cruel as it may seem—was to turn
round and look keenly at my lover and revise my judgment.
His rigid urbanity was still extremely impressive, but at times
I could have fancied that I was listening to a musical symphony, of which only certain brief, unresonant notes were audible. Was this all, and were there no others? It occurred to
me more than once, with a kind of dull dismay, in the midst
of my placid expectancy, that Harold's grave notes were the
beginning and the end of his character. If the human heart
were a less incurable skeptic, I might have been divinely
happy. I sat by my lover's side while he worked, gazing at the
loveliest landscape in the world, and admiring the imperturbable audacity with which he attacked it. Sooner than I expected, these rather silent interviews, as romantic certainly as
scenery could make them, received Mrs. Staines's sanction.
She had guessed our secret, and disapproved of nothing but
its secrecy. She was satisfied with her son's choice, and declared with great emphasis that she was not ambitious. She
was kindness itself (though, as you see, she indulged in no
needless flattery), and I wondered that I could ever have
thought her stern. From this time forward she talked to me a
great deal about her son; too much, I might have thought, if
I had cared less for the theme. I have said I was not perverse.
Do I judge myself too tenderly? Before long I found something oppressive—something almost irritating—in the fre-

quency and complacency of Mrs. Staines's maternal disquisitions. One day, when she had been reminding me at greater length than usual of what a prize I had drawn, I abruptly changed the subject in the midst of a sentence, and left her staring at my petulance. She was on the point, I think, of administering a reprimand, but she suppressed it and contented herself with approaching the topic more cautiously in future. Here is another reminiscence. One morning (it was near Spezia, I think) Harold had been sketching under a tree, not far from the inn, and I sitting by and reading aloud from Shelley, whom one might feel a kindness for there if nowhere else. We had had a little difference of opinion about one of the poems—the beautiful "Stanzas written in Dejection near Naples," which you probably remember. Harold pronounced them childish. I thought the term ill-chosen, and remember saying, to reinforce my opinion, that though I was no judge of painting, I pretended to be of poetry. He told me (I have not forgotten his words) that "I lacked cultivation in each department," and I believe I replied that I would rather lack cultivation than imagination. For a pair of lovers it was a very pretty quarrel as it stood. Shortly afterwards he discovered that he had left one of his brushes at the inn, and went off in search of it. He had trouble in finding it, and was absent for some time. His verdict on poor Shelley rang in my ears as I sat looking out on the blue iridescence of the sea, and murmuring the lines in which the poet has so wonderfully suggested it. Then I went and sat down on Harold's stool to see how he had rendered this enchanting effect. The picture was nearly finished, but unfortunately I had too little cultivation to enjoy it. The blue sea, however, seemed in all conscience blue enough. While I was comparing it with the far-fading azure of the original, I heard a voice behind me, and turning, saw two gentlemen from the inn, one of whom had been my neighbor the evening before at dinner. He was a foreigner, but he spoke English. On recognizing me he advanced gallantly, ushering his companion, and immediately fell into ecstasies over my picture. I informed him without delay that the picture was not mine; it was the work of Mr. Staines. Nothing daunted, he declared that it was pretty enough to be mine, and that I must have given suggestions; but his companion, a less superficial character apparently, and extremely near-sighted, after examining it minutely with his nose close to the paper, exclaimed with an annoying smile, "Monsieur Staines? Surprising! I should have sworn it was the work of a *jeune fille.*"

The compliment was doubtful, and not calculated to re-store my equanimity. As a *jeune fille* I suppose I ought to have been gratified, but as a betrothed I should have preferred Harold to paint like a man. I don't know how long after this it was that I allowed myself to wonder, by way of harmless conjecture, how a woman might feel who should find herself married to an ineffective mediocrity. Then I remembered—as if the case were my own—that I had never heard any one talk about his pictures, and that when I had seen them handed about before company by his mother, the buzz of admiration usual on such occasions seemed rather heavy-winged. But I quickly reminded myself that it was not because he painted better or worse that I cared for him, but because personally and morally he was the pink of perfection. This being settled, I fell to wondering whether one mightn't grow weary of per-fection—whether (Heaven forgive me!) I was not already the least bit out of patience with Harold's. I could fancy him a trifle too absolute, too imperturbable, too prolific in cut-and-dried opinions. Had he settled everything, then, in his mind? Yes, he had certainly made the most of his time, and I could only admire his diligence. From the moment that I observed that he wasted no time in moods, or reveries, or intellectual pleasantry of any sort, I decided without appeal that he was not a man of genius; and yet, to listen to him at times, you would have vowed at least that he might be. He dealt out his opinions as if they were celestial manna, and nothing was more common than for him to say, "You remember, a month ago, I told you so-and-so;" meaning that he had laid down the law on some point and expected me to engrave it on my heart. It often happened that I had forgotten the lesson, and was obliged to ask him to repeat it; but it left me more un-satisfied than before. Harold would settle his shirt collar as if he considered that he had exhausted the subject, and I would take refuge in a silence which from day to day covered more treacherous conjectures. Nevertheless (strange as you may think it), I believe I should have decided that, Harold being a paragon, my doubts were immoral, if Mrs. Staines, after his cause might have been supposed to be gained, had not persisted in pleading it in season and out. I don't know whether she suspected my secret falterings, but she seemed to wish to secure me beyond relapse. I was so very modest a match for her son, that if I had been more worldly-wise, her enthusiasm might have alarmed me. Later I understood it; then I only understood that there was a general flavor of insinuation in her talk which made me vaguely uneasy. I did the poor lady injustice, and if I had been quicker-witted (and possibly harder-hearted) we might have become sworn allies. She judged her son less with a mother's tenderness than with a mother's zeal, and foresaw the world's verdict—which I won't anticipate! She perceived that he must depend upon a clever wife to float him into success; he would never prosper on his own merits. She did me the honor to believe me socially a sufficiently buoyant body for this arduous purpose, and must have felt it a thousand pities that she couldn't directly speak her mind. A thousand pities indeed! My answer would have been to the point, and would have saved us all a vast deal of pain. Meanwhile, trying half to convince and half to entangle me, she did everything to hasten our marriage.

If there had been anything less than the happiness of a lifetime at stake, I think I should have felt that I owed Harold a sort of reparation for thinking him too great a man, and should still have offered him an affection none the less genuine for being transposed into a minor key. But it was hard for a girl who had dreamed blissfully of a grandly sentimental union, to find herself suddenly face to face with a sternly rational one. When, therefore, Harold mentioned a certain day as the latest for which he thought it proper to wait, I found it impossible to assent, and asked for another month's delay. What I wished to wait for I could hardly have told. Possibly for the first glow of illusion to return; possibly for the last uneasy throb which told that illusion was ebbing away. Harold received this request very gravely, and inquired whether I doubted of his affection.

"No," I said, "I believe it's greater than I deserve."

"Why then," he asked, "should you wait?"

"Suppose I were to doubt of my own?"

He looked as if I had said something in very bad taste, and I was almost frightened at his sense of security. But he at last consented to the delay. Perhaps on reflection he was alarmed, for the grave politeness with which he discharged his attentions took a still more formal turn, as if to remind me at every hour of the day that his was not a sentiment to be trifled with. To trifle, Heaven knows, was far enough from my thoughts; for I was fast losing my spirits, and I woke up one morning with the conviction that I was decidedly not happy.

We were to be married in Paris, where Harold had determined to spend six months in order that he might try his fortune again in the studio of a painter whom he especially esteemed—a certain Monsieur Martinet, an old man, and belonging, I believe, to a rather antiquated school of art. During our first days in Paris I went with Harold a great deal to the Louvre, where he was a very profitable companion. He had the history of the schools at his fingers' ends, and, as the phrase is, he knew what he liked. We had a fatal habit of not liking the same things; but I pretended to no critical insight, and desired nothing better than to agree with him. I listened devoutly to everything that could be said for Guido and Caravaggio. One day we were standing before the inscrutable "Joconde" of Leonardo, a picture disagreeable to most women. I had been expressing my great aversion to the lady's countenance, which Harold on this occasion seemed to share. I was surprised therefore, when, after a pause, he said quietly, "I believe I'll copy her."

I hardly knew why I should have smiled, but I did, apparently to his annoyance. "She must be very difficult," I said. "Try something easier."

"I want something difficult," he answered sternly.

"Truly?" I said. "You mean what you say?"

"Why not?"

"Why then copy a portrait when you can copy an original?"

"What original?"

"Your betrothed! Paint my portrait. I promise to be difficult enough. Indeed, I'm surprised you should never have proposed it." In fact the idea had just occurred to me; but I embraced it with a sort of relief. It seemed to me that it

would somehow test my lover, and that if he succeeded, I
might believe in him irremissibly. He stared a moment as if he
had hardly understood me, and I completed my thought.
"Paint my portrait, and the day you finish it I'll fix our wedding day."

The proposal was after all not very terrible, and before long
he seemed to relish it. The next day he told me that he had
composed his figure mentally, and that we might begin immediately. Circumstances favored us, for he had for the time
undisturbed all of M. Martinet's studio. This gentleman had
gone into the country to paint a portrait, and Harold just
then was his only pupil. Our first sitting took place without
delay. At his request I brought with me a number of draperies, among which was the yellow shawl you have just been
admiring. We wore such things then, just as we played on the
harp and read "Corinne." I tried on my scarfs and veils, one
after the other, but Harold was satisfied with none. The yellow shawl, in especial, he pronounced a meretricious ornament, and decided that I should be represented in a plain
dark dress, with as few accessories as possible. He quoted with
a bow the verse about beauty when unadorned, and began his
work.

After the first day or two it progressed slowly, and I felt at
moments as if I had saddled him with a cruel burden. He expressed no irritation, but he often looked puzzled and wearied, and sometimes would lay aside his brushes, fold his
arms, and stand gazing at his work with a sort of vacant scowl
which tried my patience. "Frown at me," I said more than
once; "don't frown at that blameless sheet of canvas. Don't
spare me, though I confess it's not my fault if I'm hard to
paint." Thus admonished, he would turn toward me without
smiling, often shading his eyes with his hand, and would walk
slowly round the room, examining me at a distance. Then
coming back to his easel, he would make half a dozen strokes
and pause again, as if his impetus had already expired. For
some time I was miserable; it seemed to me that I had been
wonderfully wise to withhold my hand till the picture was finished. He begged I would not look at it, but I knew it was
standing still. At last, one morning, after gazing at his work
for some time in silence, he laid down his palette gravely, but

with no further sign of discomposure than that he gently wiped his forehead with his pocket-handkerchief. "You make me nervous," he suddenly declared.

I fancied there was a tremor in his voice, and I began to pity him. I left my place and laid my hand on his arm. "If it wearies you," I said, "give it up."

He turned away and for some time made no answer. I knew what he was thinking about, and I suppose he knew that I knew it, and was hesitating to ask me seriously whether in giving up his picture he gave up something more. He decided apparently to give up nothing, but grasped his palette, and, with the short incisive gesture habitual to him, motioned me back to my seat. "I'll bother no longer over the drawing," he said; "I'll begin to paint." With his colors he was more prosperous, for the next day he told me that we were progressing fast.

We generally went together to the studio, but it happened one day that he was to be occupied during the early morning at the other end of Paris, and he arranged to meet me there. I was punctual, but he had not arrived, and I found myself face to face with my reluctant image. Opportunity served too well, and I looked at it in spite of his prohibition, meaning of course to confess my fault. It brought me less pleasure than faults are reputed to bring. The picture, as yet very slight and crude, was unpromising and unflattering. I chiefly distinguished a long white face with staring black eyes, and a terribly angular pair of arms. Was it in this unlovely form that I had impressed myself on Harold's vision? Absorbed by the question, it was some moments before I perceived that I was not alone. I heard a sound, looked round, and discovered a stranger, a young man, gazing over my shoulder at Harold's canvas. His gaze was intense and not expressive of pleasure, and some moments passed before he perceived that I had noticed him. He reminded me strongly of certain dishevelled copyists whom I had seen at work in the Louvre, and as I supposed he had some lawful errand in the studio, I contented myself with thinking that he hadn't the best manners in the world, and walked to the other end of the room. At last, as he continued to betray no definite intentions, I ventured to look at him again. He was young—twenty-five at most—and ex-

cessively shabby. I remember, among other details, that he
had a black cravat wound two or three times round his neck,
without any visible linen. He was short, thin, pale, and hun-
gry-looking. As I turned toward him, he passed his hand
through his hair, as if to do what he could to make himself
presentable, and called my attention to his prodigious shock
of thick black curls—a real *coiffure de rapin*. His face would
have been meagre and vulgar, if from beneath their umbra-
geous locks there had not glanced an extraordinary pair of
eyes—eyes really of fire. They were not tender nor appealing,
but they glittered with a sort of feverish intelligence and penetration, and stamped their possessor not, as the French say,
the first comer. He almost glared at me and stopped my
words short.

"That's your portrait?" he asked, with a toss of his head.

I assented with dignity.

"It's bad, bad, bad!" he cried. "Excuse my frankness, but
it's really too bad. It's a waste of colors, of money, of time."

His frankness certainly was extreme; but his words had an
accent of ardent conviction which doesn't belong to commonplace impertinence. "I don't know who you are, that I
should value your opinion," I said.

"Who I am? I'm an artist, mademoiselle. If I had money
to buy visiting-cards, I would present you with one. But I
haven't even money to buy colors—hardly to buy bread. I've
talent—I've imagination—too much!—I've ideas—I've promise—I've a future; and yet the machine won't work—for want
of fuel! I have to roam about with my hands in my pockets—
to keep them warm—for want of the very tools of my trade.
I've been a fool—an ignoble fool; I've thrown precious hours
to the dogs and made enemies of precious friends. Six months
ago I quarrelled with the père Martinet, who believed in me
and would have been glad to keep me. *Il faut que jeunesse se
passe!* Mine has passed at a rattling pace, ill-mounted though
it was; we have parted company forever. Now I only ask to do
a man's work with a man's will. Meanwhile the père Martinet,
justly provoked, has used his tongue so well that not a color-
man in Paris will trust me. There's a situation! And yet what
could I do with ten francs' worth of paint? I want a room and
light and a model, and a dozen yards of satin tumbling about

her feet. Bah! I shall have to want! There are things I want more. Behold the force of circumstances. I've come back with my pride in my pocket to make it up with the venerable author of the 'Apotheosis of Molière,' and ask him to lend me a louis."

I arrested this vehement effusion by informing him that M. Martinet was out of town, and that for the present the studio was—private. But he seemed too much irritated to take my hint. "That's not his work?" he went on, turning to the portrait. "Martinet is bad, but is not as bad as that. *Quel genre!* You deserve, mademoiselle, to be better treated; you're an excellent model. Excuse me, once for all; I know I'm atrociously impudent. But I'm an artist, and I find it pitiful to see a fine great canvas besmeared in such a fashion as that! There ought to be a society for the protection of such things."

I was at loss what to reply to this extraordinary explosion of contempt. Strange to say—it's the literal truth—I was neither annoyed nor disgusted; I simply felt myself growing extremely curious. This impudent little Bohemian was forcing me somehow to respect his opinion; he spoke with penetrating authority. Don't say that I was willing to be convinced; if you had been there, you would have let him speak. It would have been, of course, the part of propriety to request him in a chilling voice to leave the room, or to ring for the concierge, or to flee in horror. I did none of these things: I went back to the picture, and tried hard to see something in it which would make me passionately contradict him. But it seemed to exhale a mortal chill, and all I could say was: "Bad—bad? How bad?"

"Ridiculously bad; impossibly bad! You're an angel of charity, mademoiselle, not to see it!"

"Is it weak—cold—ignorant?"

"Weak, cold, ignorant, stiff, empty, hopeless! And, on top of all, pretentious—oh, pretentious as the *façade* of the Madeleine!"

I endeavored to force a skeptical smile. "After all, monsieur, I'm not bound to believe you."

"Evidently!" And he rubbed his forehead and looked gloomily round the room. "But one thing I can tell you"—fixing me suddenly with his extraordinary eyes, which seemed to expand and glow with the vividness of prevision—"the day will come when people will fight for the honor of having believed me, and of having been the first. 'I discovered him—I always said so. But for me you'd have let the poor devil starve!' You'll hear the chorus! So now's your chance, mademoiselle! Here I stand, a man of genius if there ever was one, without a son, without a friend, without a ray of reputation. Believe in me now, and you'll be the first, by many a day. You'd find it easier, you'll say, if I had a little more modesty. I assure you I don't go about blowing my trumpet in this fashion every day. This morning I'm in a kind of fever, and I've reached a crisis. I must do something—even make an ass of myself! I can't go on devouring my own heart. You see for these three months I've been *à sec*. I haven't dined every day. Perhaps a sinking at the stomach is propitious to inspiration: certainly, week by week, my brain has grown clearer, my imagination more restless, my desires more boundless, my visions more splendid! Within the last fortnight my last doubt has vanished, and I feel as strong as the sun in heaven! I roam about the streets and lounge in the public gardens for want of a better refuge, and everything I look at—the very sunshine in the gutter, the chimney-pots against the sky—seems a picture, a subject, an opportunity! I hang over the balustrade that runs before the pictures at the Louvre, and Titian and Correggio seem to turn pale, like people when you've guessed their secret. I don't know who the author of this masterpiece may be, but I fancy he would have more talent if he weren't so sure of his dinner. Do you know how I learned to look at things and use my eyes? By staring at the *charcutier's* windows when my pockets were empty. It's a great lesson to learn even the shape of a sausage and the color of a ham. This gentleman, it's easy to see, hasn't noticed such matters. He goes by the sense of taste. *Voilà le monde!* I—I—I—"—and he slapped his forehead with a kind of dramatic fury—"here as you see me—ragged, helpless, hopeless, with my soul aching with ambition and my fingers itching for a brush—and *he*, standing up here after a good breakfast, in this perfect light, among pictures and tapestries and carvings, with you in your blooming beauty for a model, and painting that—sign-board."

His violence was startling; I didn't know what might come next, and I took up my bonnet and mantle. He immediately protested with ardor. "A moment's reflection, mademoiselle, will tell you that, with the appearance I present, I don't talk about your beauty *pour vous faire la cour*. I repeat with all respect, you're a model to make a painter's fortune. I doubt if you've many attitudes or much flexibility; but for once—the portrait of Mlle. X.—you're perfect."

"I'm obliged to you for your—information," I answered gravely. "You see my artist is chosen. I expect him here at any moment, and I won't answer for his listening to you as patiently as I have done."

"He's coming?" cried my visitor. "*Quelle chance!* I shall be charmed to meet him. I shall vastly enjoy seeing the human head from which that conception issued. I see him already: I construct the author from the work. He's tall and blond, with eyes very much the color of his own china-blue there. He wears straw-colored whiskers, and doubtless he paints in straw-colored gloves. In short, he's *un homme magnifique!*"

This was sarcasm run mad; but I listened to it and resented it as little as I enjoyed it. My companion seemed to possess a sort of demonic veracity of which the influence was irresistible. I questioned his sincerity so little that, if I offered him charity, it was with no intention of testing it. "I dare say you've immense talent," I said, "but you've horrible manners. Nevertheless, I believe you will perceive that there is no reason why our conversation should continue; and I should pay you a poor compliment in thinking that you need to be bribed to withdraw. But since M. Martinet isn't here to lend you a louis, let me act for him." And I laid the piece of gold on the table.

He looked at it hard for a moment and then at me, and I wondered whether he thought the gift too meagre. "I won't go so far as to say that I'm proud," he answered at last. "But from a lady, *ma foi!* it's beggarly—it's humiliating. Excuse me then if I refuse; I mean to ask for something else. To do me justice, remember that I speak to you not as a man, but as an artist. Bestow your charity on the artist, and if it costs you an effort, remember that that is the charity which is of most account with heaven. Keep your louis; go and stand as you've been standing for this picture, in the same light and the same attitude, and then let me look at you for three little minutes." As he spoke he drew from his pocket a ragged note-book and the stump of a pencil. "The few scrawls I shall make here will be your alms."

He spoke of effort, but it is a fact that I made little to comply. While I resumed my familiar attitude in front of Harold's canvas, he walked rapidly across the room and stooped over a chair upon which a mass of draperies had been carelessly tossed. In a moment I saw what had attracted him. He had caught a glimpse of the famous yellow scarf, glowing splendidly beneath a pile of darker stuffs. He pulled out the beautiful golden-hued tissue with furious alacrity, held it up before him and broke into an ecstasy of admiration. "What a tone—what a glow—what a texture! In Heaven's name, put it on!" And without further ceremony he tossed it over my shoulders. I need hardly tell you that I obeyed but a natural instinct in gathering it into picturesque folds. He rushed away, and stood gazing and clapping his hands. "The harmony is perfect—the effect sublime! You possess that thing and you bury it out of sight? Wear it, wear it, I entreat you—and your portrait—but ah!" and he glared angrily askance at the picture: "you'll never wear it there!"

"We thought of using it, but it was given up."

"Given up? *Quelle horreur!* He hadn't the pluck to attack it! Oh, if I could just take a brush at it and rub it in for him!" And, as if possessed by an uncontrollable impulse, he seized poor Harold's palette. But I made haste to stop his hand. He flung down the brushes, buried his face in his hands, and pressed back, I could fancy, the tears of baffled eagerness. "You'll think me crazy!" he cried.

He was not crazy, to my sense; but he was a raging, aimless force, which I suddenly comprehended that I might use. I seemed to measure the full proportions of Harold's inefficiency, and to foresee the pitiful result of his undertaking. He wouldn't succumb, but he would doggedly finish his task and present me, in evidence of his claim, with a dreadful monument of his pretentious incapacity. Twenty strokes from this master-hand would make a difference; ten minutes' work would carry the picture forward. I thrust the palette into the young man's grasp again and looked at him solemnly. "Paint away for your life," I said; "but promise me this: to succeed!"

He waved his hand in the air, despatched me with a glance to my place, and let himself loose on the canvas; there are no other words for his tremulous eagerness. A quarter of an hour passed in silence. As I watched his motions grow every moment broader and more sweeping, I could fancy myself listening to some ardent pianist, plunging deeper into a passionate symphony and devouring the key-board with outstretched arms. Flushed and dishevelled, consuming me almost with his ardent stare, daubing, murmuring, panting, he seemed indeed to be painting for life.

At last I heard a tread in the vestibule. I knew it was Harold's, and I hurried to look at the picture. How would he take it? I confess I was prepared for the worst. The picture spoke for itself. Harold's work had disappeared with magical rapidity, and even my unskilled eye perceived that a graceful and expressive figure had been powerfully sketched in. As Harold appeared, I turned to meet him. He seemed surprised at not finding me alone, and I laid my finger gravely on my lips and led him to the front of the canvas. The position of things was so singular that for some moments it baffled his comprehension. My companion finished what he was immediately concerned with; then with an obsequious bow laid down his brushes. "It was a loan, monsieur," he said. "I return it with interest."

Harold flushed to his eyes, and sat down in silence. I had expected him to be irritated; but this was more than irritation. At last: "Explain this extraordinary performance," he said in a low voice.

I felt pain, and yet somehow I felt no regret. The situation was tense, as the phrase is, and yet I almost relished it. "This gentleman is a great artist," I said boldly. "Look for yourself. Your picture was lost; he has redeemed it."

Harold looked at the intruder slowly from head to foot. "Who is this person?" he demanded, as if he had not heard me.

The young man understood no English, but he apparently guessed at the question. "My name is Pierre Briseux; let *that*" (pointing to his work) "denote my profession. If you're affronted, monsieur, don't visit your displeasure on made-moiselle; I alone am responsible. You had got into a tight place; I wished to help you out of it; *sympathie de confrère!* I've done you no injury. I've made you a present of half a masterpiece. If I could only trust you not to spoil it!"

Harold's face betrayed his invincible disgust, and I saw that my offence was mortal. He had been wounded in his tender-est part, and his self-control was rapidly ebbing. His lips trem-bled, but he was too angry even to speak. Suddenly he seized a heavy brush which stood in a pot of dusky varnish, and I thought for a moment he was going to fling it at Briseux. He balanced it an instant, and then tossed it full in the face of the picture. I raised my hands to my face as if I felt the blow. Briseux, at least, felt it sorely.

"*Malheureux!*" he cried. "Are you blind as well? Don't you know a good thing when you see it? That's what I call a waste of material. *Allons,* you're very angry; let me explain. In med-dling with your picture I certainly took a great liberty. My misery is my excuse. You have money, materials, models—everything but talent. No, no, you're no painter; it's impossi-ble! There isn't an intelligent line on your canvas. I, on the other hand, am a born painter. I've talent and nothing more. I came here to see M. Martinet; learning he was absent, I staid for very envy! I looked at your work, and found it a botch; at your empty stool and idle palette, and found them an immense temptation; at mademoiselle, and found her a perfect model. I persuaded, frightened, convinced her, and out of charity she gave me a five minutes' sitting. Once the brush in my hand, I felt the divine afflatus; I hoped for a mir-acle—that you'd never come back, that you'd be run over in the street, or have an attack of apoplexy. If you had only let me go on, I should have served you up a great work, mon-sieur—a work to which, in spite of your natural irritation, you wouldn't have dared to do a violence. You'd have been afraid of it. That's the sort of thing I meant to paint. If you could only believe me, you'd not regret it. Give me a start, and ten years hence I shall see you buying my pictures, and not think-ing them dear. Oh, I thought I had my foot in the stirrup; I dreamed I was in the saddle and riding hard. But I've turned a somersault!"

I doubt that Harold, in his resentment, either understood M. Briseux's words or appreciated his sketch. He simply felt that he had been the victim of a monstrous aggression, in which I, in some painfully inexplicable way, had been half dupe and half accomplice. I was watching his anger and weighing its ominous significance. His cold fury, and the expression it threw into his face and gestures, told me more about him than weeks of placid love-making had done, and, following close upon my vivid sense of his incapacity, seemed suddenly to cut the knot that bound us together, and over which my timid fingers had been fumbling. "Put on your bonnet," he said to me; "get a carriage and go home."

I can't describe his tone. It contained an assumption of my confusion and compliance, which made me feel that I ought to lose no time in undeceiving him. Nevertheless I felt cruelly perplexed, and almost afraid of his displeasure. Mechanically I took up my bonnet. As I held it in my hand, my eyes met those of our terrible companion, who was evidently trying to read the riddle of my relations with Harold. Planted there with his trembling lips, his glittering, searching eyes, an indefinable something in his whole person that told of joyous impulse arrested, but pausing only for a more triumphant effort, he seemed a strangely eloquent embodiment of youthful genius. I don't know whether he read in my glance a ray of sympathy, but his lips formed a soundless "*Restez, madame,*" which quickened the beating of my heart. The feeling that then invaded it I despair of making you understand; yet it must help in your eyes to excuse me, and it was so profound that often in memory it seems more real and poignant than the things of the present. Poor little Briseux, ugly, shabby, disreputable, seemed to me some appealing messenger from the mysterious immensity of life; and Harold, beside him, comely, elegant, imposing, justly indignant, seemed to me simply his narrow, personal, ineffectual self. This was a wider generalization than the feminine heart is used to. I flung my bonnet on the floor and burst into tears.

"This is not an exhibition for a stranger," said Harold grimly. "Be so good as to follow me."

"You must excuse me; I can't follow you; I can't explain. I

have something more to say to M. Briseux. He's less of a stranger than you think."

"I'm to leave you here?" stammered Harold.

"It's the simplest way."

"With that dirty little Frenchman?"

"What should I care for his being clean? It's his genius that interests me."

Harold stared in dark amazement. "Are you insane? Do you know what you're doing?"

"An act, I believe, of real charity."

"Charity begins at home. It's an act of desperate folly. Must I *command* you to leave?"

"You've done that already. I can't obey you. If I were to do so, I should pretend what isn't true; and, let me say it, it's to undeceive you that I refuse."

"I don't understand you," cried Harold, "nor to what spell this meddlesome little beggar has subjected you! But I'm not a man to be trifled with, you know, and this is my last request; my last, do you understand? If you prefer the society of this abandoned person, you're welcome, but you forfeit mine forever. It's a choice! You give up the man who has offered you an honorable affection, a name, a fortune, who has trusted and cherished you, who stands ready to make you a devoted husband. What you get the Lord knows!"

I had sunk into a chair. I listened in silence, and for some time answered nothing. His words were vividly true. He offered me much, and I gave up everything. He had played an honorable part, and I was playing a very strange one. I asked myself sternly whether I was ready to rise and take his arm and let him lead me blindfold through life. When I raised my eyes Briseux stood before me, and from the expression of his face I could have fancied he had guessed at the meaning of Harold's words. "I'll make you immortal," he murmured; "I'll delight mankind—and I'll begin my own career!"

An ineffable prevision of the truth which after the lapse of years had brought about our meeting here seemed to raise me as if on wings, and made decision easy. We women are so habitually condemned by fate to act simply in what is called the domestic sphere, that there is something intoxicating in the opportunity to exert a far-reaching influence outside of it. To feel the charms of such an opportunity, one must perhaps be of a reprehensibly fanciful turn. Such at any rate was my mood for that hour. I seemed to be the end of an electric chain, of which the rest was throbbing away through time. I seemed to hold in my hand an immeasurable gift. "We had better part on the spot," I said to Harold. "I've foreseen our parting for weeks, only it has come more abruptly. Forgive the abruptness. To myself the pretext seems better than to you; perhaps some day you'll appreciate it. A single question," I added. "Could you ever have finished my portrait?"

He looked at me askance for some moments, with a strange mistrust, as if I had suddenly developed some monstrous and sinister slyness; then catching his breath with a little groan—almost a shudder—he marched out of the room.

Briseux clasped his hands in ecstasy. "You're magnificent!" he cried. "If you could only look so for three hours!"

"To business," I said sternly. "If you don't paint a perfect picture, you're the most shameless of impostors."

He had but a single sitting, but it was a long one; though how many hours it lasted, I doubt that either of us could have told. He painted till dusk, and then we had lamps. Before I left him I looked at the picture for the last and only time before seeing it to-day. It seemed to me as perfect as it seemed this morning, and I felt that my choice was justified and that Briseux's fortune was made. It gave me all the strength I needed for the immediate future. He was evidently of the same opinion and profoundly absorbed in it. When I bade him farewell, in very few words, he answered me almost absently. I had served his purpose and had already passed into that dusky limbo of unhonored victims, the experience—intellectual and other—of genius. I left him the yellow shawl, that he might finish this part of his work at his leisure, and, as for the picture, I told him to keep it, for that I should have little pleasure in seeing it again. Then he stared a moment, but the next he was painting hard.

I had the next morning what under other circumstances I might call an explanation with Mr. Staines, an explanation in which I explained nothing to his satisfaction but that he had been hideously wronged, and that I was a demon of inconstancy. He wrapped himself in an icy silence, and, I think, expected some graceful effusion of humility. I may not have been humble, but I was considerate and I perceived, for my reward, that the sore point with him was not that he had lost me, but that I had ventured to judge him. Mrs. Staines's manner, on the other hand, puzzled me, so strange a mixture was it of half-disguised elation and undisguised sarcasm. At last I guessed her meaning. Harold, after all, had had an escape; instead of being the shrewd, practical girl she had thought me, I was a terribly romantic one! Perhaps she was right; I was romantic enough to make no further claim on her hospitality, and with as little delay as possible I returned home. A month later I received an enclosure of half a dozen cuttings from newspapers, scrawled boldly across with the signature of Pierre Briseux. The Paris *salon* had opened and the critics had spoken. They had not neglected the portrait of Mademoiselle X——. The picture was an immense success, and M. Briseux was famous. There were a few protesting voices, but it was evident that his career had begun. For Mademoiselle X—— herself, I believe, there were none but compliments, several of which took the form of gallant conjecture as to her real identity. Mademoiselle X—— was an assumed name, and according to more than one voice the lady was an imperious Russian princess with a distaste for vulgar publicity. You know the rest of M. Briseux's history. Since then he has painted real princesses by the dozen. He has delighted mankind rarely. As for his having made me immortal, I feel as if it were almost true. It must be an eternity since the thing happened—so very unreservedly I've described it!

The Last of the Valerii

I HAD had the occasion to declare more than once that if my god-daughter married a foreigner I should refuse to give her away. And yet when the young Conte Valerio was presented to me, in Rome, as her accepted and plighted lover, I found myself looking at the happy fellow, after a momentary stare of amazement, with a certain paternal benevolence; thinking, indeed, that from the picturesque point of view (she with her yellow locks and he with his dusky ones), they were a strikingly well-assorted pair. She brought him up to me half proudly, half timidly, pushing him before her, and begging me with one of her dovelike glances to be very polite. I don't know that I am particularly addicted to rudeness; but she was so deeply impressed with his grandeur that she thought it impossible to do him honor enough. The Conte Valerio's grandeur was doubtless nothing for a young American girl, who had the air and almost the habits of a princess, to sound her trumpet about; but she was desperately in love with him, and not only her heart, but her imagination, was touched. He was extremely handsome, and with a more significant sort of beauty than is common in the handsome Roman race. He had a sort of sunken depth of expression, and a grave, slow smile, suggesting no great quickness of wit, but an unimpassioned intensity of feeling which promised well for Martha's happiness. He had little of the light, inexpensive urbanity of his countrymen, and more of a sort of heavy sincerity in his gaze which seemed to suspend response until he was sure he understood you. He was perhaps a little stupid, and I fancied that to a political or æsthetic question the response would be particularly slow. "He is good, and strong, and brave," the young girl however assured me; and I easily believed her. Strong the Conte Valerio certainly was; he had a head and throat like some of the busts in the Vatican. To my eye, which has looked at things now so long with the painter's purpose, it was a real perplexity to see such a throat rising out of the white cravat of the period. It sustained a head as massively round as that of the familiar bust of the Emperor Caracalla, and covered with the same dense sculptural crop of curls. The young man's hair grew superbly; it was such hair as the old Romans must have had when they walked bareheaded and bronzed about the world. It made a perfect arch over his low, clear forehead, and prolonged itself on cheek and chin in a close, crisp beard, strong with its own strength and unstiffened by the razor. Neither his nose nor his mouth was delicate; but they were powerful, shapely, and manly. His complexion was of a deep glowing brown which no emotion would alter, and his large, lucid eyes seemed to stare at you like a pair of polished agates. He was of middle stature, and his chest was of so generous a girth that you half expected to hear his linen crack with its even respirations. And yet, with his simple human smile, he looked neither like a young bullock nor a gladiator. His powerful voice was the least bit harsh, and his large, ceremonious reply to my compliment had the massive sonority with which civil speeches must have been uttered in the age of Augustus. I had always considered my god-daughter a very American little person, in all delightful meanings of the word, and I doubted if this sturdy young Latin would understand the transatlantic element in her nature; but, evidently, he would make her a loyal and ardent lover. She seemed to me, in her blond prettiness, so tender, so appealing, so bewitching, that it was impossible to believe he had not more thoughts for all this than for the pretty fortune which it yet bothered me to believe that he must, like a good Italian, have taken the exact measure of. His own worldly goods consisted of the paternal estate, a villa within the walls of Rome, which his scanty funds had suffered to fall into sombre disrepair. "It's the Villa she's in love with, quite as much as the Count," said her mother. "She dreams of converting the Count; that's all very well. But she dreams of refurnishing the Villa!"

The upholsterers were turned into it, I believe, before the wedding, and there was a great scrubbing and sweeping of saloons and raking and weeding of alleys and avenues. Martha made frequent visits of inspection while these ceremonies were taking place; but one day, on her return, she came into my little studio with an air of amusing horror. She had found them *scraping* the sarcophagus in the great ilex-walk;

divesting it of its mossy coat, disincrusting it of the sacred green mould of the ages! This was their idea of making the Villa comfortable. She had made them transport it to the dampest place they could find; for, next after that slow-coming, slow-going smile of her lover, it was the rusty complexion of his patrimonial marbles that she most prized. The young Count's conversion proceeded less rapidly, and indeed I believe that his betrothed brought little zeal to the affair. She loved him so devoutly that she believed no change of faith could better him, and she would have been willing for his sake to say her prayers to the sacred Bambino at Epiphany. But he had the good taste to demand no such sacrifice, and I was struck with the happy promise of a scene of which I was an accidental observer. It was at St. Peter's, one Friday afternoon, during the vesper service which takes place in the chapel of the Choir. I met my god-daughter wandering happily on her lover's arm, her mother being established on her camp-stool near the chapel door. The crowd was collected thereabouts, and the body of the church was empty. Now and then the high voices of the singers escaped into the outer vastness and melted slowly away in the incense-thickened air. Something in the young girl's step and the clasp of her arm in her lover's told me that her contentment was perfect. As she threw back her head and gazed into the magnificent immensity of vault and dome, I felt that she was in that enviable mood in which all consciousness revolves on a single centre, and that her sense of the splendors around her was one with the ecstasy of her trust. They stopped before that sombre group of confessionals which proclaims so portentously the world's sinfulness, and Martha seemed to make some almost passionate protestation. A few minutes later I overtook them.

"Don't you agree with me, dear friend," said the Count, who always addressed me with the most affectionate deference, "that before I marry so pure and sweet a creature as this, I ought to go into one of those places and confess every sin I ever was guilty of,—every evil thought and impulse and desire of my grossly evil nature?"

Martha looked at him, half in deprecation, half in homage, with a look which seemed at once to insist that her lover could have no vices, and to plead that, if he had, there would be something magnificent in them. "Listen to him!" she said, smiling. "The list would be long, and if you waited to finish it, you would be late for the wedding! But if you confess your sins for me, it's only fair I should confess mine for you. Do you know what I have been saying to Camillo?" she added, turning to me with the half-filial confidence she had always shown me and with a rosy glow in her cheeks; "that I want to do something more for him than girls commonly do for their lovers,—to take some step, to run some risk, to break some law, even! I'm willing to change my religion, if he bids me. There are moments when I'm terribly tired of simply staring at Catholicism; it will be a relief to come into a church to kneel. That's, after all, what they are meant for! Therefore, Camillo mio, if it casts a shade across your heart to think that I'm a heretic, I'll go and kneel down to that good old priest who has just entered the confessional yonder and say to him, 'My father, I repent, I abjure, I believe. Baptize me in the only faith.'"

"If it's as a compliment to the Count," I said, "it seems to me he ought to anticipate it by turning Protestant."

She had spoken lightly and with a smile, and yet with an undertone of girlish ardor. The young man looked at her with a solemn, puzzled face and shook his head. "Keep your religion," he said. "Every one his own. If you should attempt to embrace mine, I'm afraid you would close your arms about a shadow. I'm a poor Catholic! I don't understand all these chants and ceremonies and splendors. When I was a child I never could learn my catechism. My poor old confessor long ago gave me up; he told me I was a good boy but a *pagan*! You must not be a better Catholic than your husband. I don't understand your religion any better, but I beg you not to change it for mine. If it has helped to make you what you are, it must be good." And taking the young girl's hand, he was about to raise it affectionately to his lips; but suddenly remembering that they were in a place unaccordant with profane passions, he lowered it with a comical smile. "Let us go!" he murmured, passing his hand over his forehead. "This heavy atmosphere of St. Peter's always stupefies me."

They were married in the month of May, and we separated for the summer, the Contessa's mamma going to illuminate the domestic circle in New York with her reflected dignity. When I returned to Rome in the autumn, I found the young couple established at the Villa Valerio, which was being gradually reclaimed from its antique decay. I begged that the hand of improvement might be lightly laid on it, for as an unscrupulous old *genre* painter, with an eye to "subjects," I preferred that ruin should accumulate. My god-daughter was quite of my way of thinking, and she had a capital sense of the picturesque. Advising with me often as to projected changes, she was sometimes more conservative than myself; and I more than once smiled at her archæological zeal, and declared that I believed she had married the Count because he was like a statue of the Decadence. I had a constant invitation to spend my days at the Villa, and my easel was always planted in one of the garden-walks. I grew to have a painter's passion for the place, and to be intimate with every tangled shrub and twisted tree, every moss-coated vase and mouldy sarcophagus and sad, disfeatured bust of those grim old Romans who could so ill afford to become more meagre-visaged. The place was of small extent; but though there were many other villas more pretentious and splendid, none seemed to me more deeply picturesque, more romantically idle and untrimmed, more encumbered with precious antique rubbish, and haunted with half-historic echoes. It contained an old ilex-walk in which I used religiously to spend half an hour every day,—half an hour being, I confess, just as long as I could stay without beginning to sneeze. The trees arched and intertwisted here along their dusky vista in the quaintest symmetry; and as it was exposed uninterruptedly to the west, the low evening sun used to transfuse it with a sort of golden mist and play through it—over leaves and knotty boughs and mossy marbles—with a thousand crimson fingers. It was filled with disinterred fragments of sculpture,—nameless statues and noseless heads and rough-hewn sarcophagi, which made it deliciously solemn. The statues used to stand there in the perpetual twilight like conscious things, brooding on their gathered memories. I used to linger about them, half expecting they would speak and tell me their stony secrets,—whisper heavily the whereabouts of their mouldering fellows, still unrecovered from the soil.

My god-daughter was idyllically happy and absolutely in love. I was obliged to confess that even rigid rules have their exceptions, and that now and then an Italian count is an honest fellow. Camillo was one to the core, and seemed quite content to be adored. Their life was a childlike interchange of caresses, as candid and unmeasured as those of a shepherd and shepherdess in a bucolic poem. To stroll in the ilex-walk and feel her husband's arm about her waist and his shoulder against her cheek; to roll cigarettes for him while he puffed them in the great marble-paved rotunda in the centre of the house; to fill his glass from an old rusty red amphora,—these graceful occupations satisfied the young Countess.

She rode with him sometimes in the grassy shadow of aqueducts and tombs, and sometimes suffered him to show his beautiful wife at Roman dinners and balls. She played dominos with him after dinner, and carried out in a desultory way a daily scheme of reading him the newspapers. This observance was subject to fluctuations caused by the Count's invincible tendency to go to sleep,—a failing his wife never attempted to disguise or palliate. She would sit and brush the flies from him while he lay picturesquely snoozing, and, if I ventured near him, would place her finger on her lips and whisper that she thought her husband was as handsome asleep as awake. I confess I often felt tempted to reply to her that he was at least as entertaining, for the young man's happiness had not multiplied the topics on which he readily conversed. He had plenty of good sense, and his opinions on practical matters were always worth having. He would often come and sit near me while I worked at my easel and offer a friendly criticism. His taste was a little crude, but his eye was excellent, and his measurement of the resemblance between some point of my copy and the original as trustworthy as that of a mathematical instrument. But he seemed to me to have either a strange reserve or a strange simplicity; to be fundamentally unfurnished with "ideas." He had no beliefs nor hopes nor fears,—nothing but senses, appetites, and serenely luxurious tastes. As I watched him strolling about looking at his finger-nails, I often wondered whether he had anything that could properly be termed a soul, and whether good health and good-nature were not the sum of his advantages.

"It's lucky he's good-natured," I used to say to myself; "for if he were not, there is nothing in his conscience to keep him in order. If he had irritable nerves instead of quiet ones, he would strangle us as the infant Hercules strangled the poor little snakes. He's the natural man! Happily, his nature is gentle; I can mix my colors at my ease." I wondered what he thought about and what passed through his mind in the sunny leisure which seemed to shut him in from that modern work-a-day world of which, in spite of my passion for be-daubing old panels with ineffective portraiture of mouldy statues against screens of box, I still flattered myself I was a member. I went so far as to believe that he sometimes with-drew from the world altogether. He had moods in which his consciousness seemed so remote and his mind so irresponsive and dumb, that nothing but a powerful caress or a sudden vi-olence was likely to arouse him. Even his lavish tenderness for his wife had a quality which I but half relished. Whether or no he had a soul himself, he seemed not to suspect that she had one. I took a godfatherly interest in what it had not always seemed to me crabbed and pedantic to talk of as her moral development. I fondly believed her to be a creature suscepti-ble of the finer spiritual emotions. But what was becoming of her spiritual life in this interminable heathenish honeymoon? Some fine day she would find herself tired of the Count's *beaux yeux* and make an appeal to his mind. She had, to my knowledge, plans of study, of charity, of worthily playing her part as a Contessa Valerio,—a position as to which the family records furnished the most inspiring examples. But if the Count found the newspapers soporific, I doubted if he would turn Dante's pages very fast for his wife, or smile with much zest at the anecdotes of Vasari. How could he advise her, in-struct her, sustain her? And if she became a mother, how could he share her responsibilities? He doubtless would assure his little son and heir a stout pair of arms and legs and a mag-nificent crop of curls, and sometimes remove his cigarette to kiss a dimpled spot; but I found it hard to picture him lend-ing his voice to teach the lusty urchin his alphabet or his prayers, or the rudiments of infant virtue. One accomplish-ment indeed the Count possessed which would make him an agreeable playfellow: he carried in his pocket a collection of precious fragments of antique pavement,—bits of porphyry and malachite and lapis and basalt,—disinterred on his own soil and brilliantly polished by use. With these you might see him occupied by the half-hour, playing the simple game of catch-and-toss, ranging them in a circle, tossing them in rotation, and catching them on the back of his hand. His skill was remarkable; he would send a stone five feet into the air, and pitch and catch and transpose the rest before he received it again. I watched with affectionate jealousy for the signs of a dawning sense, on Martha's part, that she was the least bit strangely mated. Once or twice, as the weeks went by, I fancied I read them, and that she looked at me with eyes which seemed to remember certain old talks of mine in which I had declared—with such verity as you please—that a Frenchman, an Italian, a Spaniard, might be a very good fellow, but that he never really respected the woman he pretended to love. For the most part, however, these dusky broodings of mine spent themselves easily in the charmed atmosphere of our romantic home. We were out of the modern world and had no business with modern scruples. The place was so bright, so still, so sacred to the silent, imperturbable past, that drowsy contentment seemed a natural law; and sometimes when, as I sat at my work, I saw my companions passing arm-in-arm across the end of one of the long-drawn vistas, and, turning back to my palette, found my colors dimmer for the radiant vision, I could easily believe that I was some loyal old chronicler of a perfectly poetical legend.

It was a help to ungrudging feelings that the Count, yielding to his wife's urgency, had undertaken a series of systematic excavations. To excavate is an expensive luxury, and neither Camillo nor his latter forefathers had possessed the means for a disinterested pursuit of archæology. But his young wife had persuaded herself that the much-trodden soil of the Villa was as full of buried treasures as a bride-cake of plums, and that it would be a pretty compliment to the ancient house which had accepted her as mistress, to devote a portion of her dowry to bringing its mouldy honors to the light. I think she was not without a fancy that this liberal process would help to disinfect her Yankee dollars of the impertinent odor of trade. She took learned advice on the subject, and was soon ready to swear to you, proceeding from irrefutable premises, that a colossal gilt-bronze Minerva mentioned by Strabo was placidly awaiting resurrection at a point twenty rods from the northwest angle of the house. She had a couple of grotesque old antiquaries to lunch, whom having plied with unwonted potations, she walked off their legs in the grounds; and though they agreed on nothing else in the world, they individually assured her that properly conducted researches would probably yield an unequalled harvest of discoveries. The Count had been not only indifferent, but even averse, to the scheme, and had more than once arrested his wife's complacent allusions to it by an unaccustomed acerbity of tone. "Let them lie, the poor disinherited gods, the Minerva, the Apollo, the Ceres you are so sure of finding," he said, "and don't break their rest. What do you want of them? We can't worship them. Would you put them on pedestals to stare and mock at them? If you can't believe in them, don't disturb them. Peace be with them!" I remember being a good deal impressed by a vigorous confession drawn from him by his wife's playfully declaring in answer to some remonstrances in this strain that he was absolutely superstitious. "Yes, by Bacchus, I am superstitious!" he cried. "Too much so, perhaps! But I'm an old Italian, and you must take me as you find me. There have been things seen and done here which leave strange influences behind! They don't touch you, doubtless, who come of another race. But they touch me, often, in the whisper of the leaves and the odor of the mouldy soil and the blank eyes of the old statues. I can't bear to look the statues in the face. I seem to see other strange eyes in the empty sockets, and I hardly know what they say to me. I call the poor old statues ghosts. In conscience, we've enough on the place already, lurking and peering in every shady nook. Don't dig up any more, or I won't answer for my wits!"

This account of Camillo's sensibilities was too fantastic not to seem to his wife almost a joke; and though I imagined there was more in it, he made a joke so seldom that I should have been sorry to cut short the poor girl's smile. With her smile she carried her point, and in a few days arrived a kind of archæological detective, with a dozen workmen armed with pickaxes and spades. For myself, I was secretly vexed at these energetic measures; for, though fond of disinterred statues, I disliked the disinterment, and deplored the profane sounds which were henceforth to jar upon the sleepy stillness of the gardens. I especially objected to the personage who conducted the operations; an ugly little dwarfish man who seemed altogether a subterranean genius, an earthy gnome of the underworld, and went prying about the grounds with a malicious smile which suggested more delight in the money the Signor Conte was going to bury than in the expected marbles and bronzes. When the first sod had been turned, the Count's mood seemed to alter, and his curiosity got the better of his scruples. He sniffed delightedly the odor of the humid earth, and stood watching the workmen, as they struck constantly deeper, with a kindling wonder in his eyes. Whenever a pickaxe rang against a stone he would utter a sharp cry, and be deterred from jumping into the trench only by the little explorer's assurance that it was a false alarm. The near prospect of discoveries seemed to act upon his nerves, and I met him more than once strolling restlessly among his cedarn alleys, as if at last he had fallen a thinking. He took me by the arm and made me walk with him, and discoursed ardently of the chance of a "find." I rather marvelled at his sudden zeal, and wondered whether he had an eye to the past or to the future,—to the beauty of possible Minervas and Apollos or to their market value. Whenever the Count would come and denounce his little army of spadesmen for a set of loitering vagabonds, the little explorer would glance at me with a sarcastic twinkle which seemed to hint that excavations were a snare. We were kept some time in suspense, for several false beginnings were made. The earth was probed in the wrong places. The Count began to be discouraged and to prolong his abbreviated siesta. But the little expert, who had his own ideas, shrewdly continued his labors; and as I sat at my easel I heard the spades ringing against the dislodged stones. Now and then I would pause, with an uncontrollable acceleration of my heart-beats. "It *may* be," I would say, "that some marble masterpiece is stirring there beneath its lightening weight of earth! There are as good fish in the sea . . . . ! I *may* be summoned to welcome another Antinous back to fame,—a Venus, a Faun, an Augustus!"

One morning it seemed to me that I had been hearing for half an hour a livelier movement of voices than usual; but as I was preoccupied with a puzzling bit of work, I made no inquiries. Suddenly a shadow fell across my canvas, and I turned round. The little explorer stood beside me, with a glittering eye, cap in hand, his forehead bathed in perspiration. Resting in the hollow of his arm was an earth-stained fragment of marble. In answer to my questioning glance he held it up to me, and I saw it was a woman's shapely hand. "Come!" he simply said, and led the way to the excavation. The workmen were so closely gathered round the open trench that I saw nothing till he made them divide. Then, full in the sun and flashing it back, almost, in spite of her dusky incrustations, I beheld, propped up with stones against a heap of earth, a majestic marble image. She seemed to me almost colossal, though I afterwards perceived that she was of perfect human proportions. My pulses began to throb, for I felt she was something great, and that it was great to be among the first to know her. Her marvellous beauty gave her an almost human look, and her absent eyes seemed to wonder back at us. She was amply draped, so that I saw that she was not a Venus. "She's a Juno," said the excavator, decisively; and she seemed indeed an embodiment of celestial supremacy and repose. Her beautiful head, bound with a single band, could have bent only to give the nod of command; her eyes looked straight before her; her mouth was implacably grave; one hand, outstretched, appeared to have held a kind of imperial wand, the arm from which the other had been broken hung at her side with the most classical majesty. The workmanship was of the rarest finish; and though perhaps there was a sort of vaguely modern attempt at character in her expression, she was wrought, as a whole, in the large and simple manner of the great Greek period. She was a masterpiece of skill and a marvel of preservation. "Does the Count know?" I soon asked, for I had a guilty sense that our eyes were taking something from her.

"The Signor Conte is at his siesta," said the explorer, with his sceptical grin. "We don't like to disturb him."

"Here he comes!" cried one of the workmen, and we made

way for him. His siesta had evidently been suddenly broken, for his face was flushed and his hair disordered.

"Ah, my dream—my dream was right, then!" he cried, and stood staring at the image.

"What was your dream?" I asked, as his face seemed to betray more dismay than delight.

"That they'd found a Juno; and that she rose and came and laid her marble hand on mine. Eh?" said the Count, excitedly.

A kind of awe-struck, guttural *a-ah!* burst from the listening workmen.

"This is the hand!" said the little explorer, holding up his perfect fragment. "I've had it this half-hour, so it can't have touched you."

"But you're apparently right as to her being a Juno," I said. "Admire her at your leisure." And I turned away; for if the Count was superstitious, I wished to leave him free to relieve himself. I repaired to the house to carry the news to my god-daughter, whom I found slumbering—dreamlessly, it appeared—over a great archæological octavo. "They've touched bottom," I said. "They've found a Juno of Praxiteles at the very least!" She dropped her octavo, and rang for a parasol. I described the statue, but not graphically, I presume, for Martha gave a little sarcastic grimace.

"A long, fluted *peplum*?" she said. "How very odd! I don't believe she's beautiful."

"She's beautiful enough, *figlioccia mia*," I answered, "to make you jealous."

We found the Count standing before the resurgent goddess in fixed contemplation, with folded arms. He seemed to have recovered from the irritation of his dream, but I thought his face betrayed a still deeper emotion. He was pale, and gave no response as his wife caressingly clasped his arm. I'm not sure, however, that his wife's attitude was not a livelier tribute to the perfection of the image. She had been laughing at my rhapsody as we walked from the house, and I had bethought myself of a statement I had somewhere seen, that women lacked the perception of the purest beauty. Martha, however, seemed slowly to measure our Juno's infinite stateliness. She gazed a long time silently, leaning against her husband, and then stepped half timidly down on the stones which formed a rough base for the figure. She laid her two rosy, ungloved hands upon the stony fingers of the goddess, and remained for some moments pressing them in her warm grasp, and fixing her living eyes upon the inexpressive brow. When she turned round her eyes were bright with an admiring tear,—a tear which her husband was too deeply absorbed to notice. He had apparently given orders that the workmen should be treated to a cask of wine, in honor of their discovery. It was now brought and opened on the spot, and the little explorer, having drawn the first glass, stepped forward, hat in hand, and obsequiously presented it to the Countess. She only moistened her lips with it and passed it to her husband. He raised it mechanically to his own; then suddenly he stopped, held it a moment aloft, and poured it out slowly and solemnly at the feet of the Juno.

"Why, it's a libation!" I cried. He made no answer, and walked slowly away.

There was no more work done that day. The laborers lay on the grass, gazing with the native Roman relish of a fine piece of sculpture, but wasting no wine in pagan ceremonies. In the evening the Count paid the Juno another visit, and gave orders that on the morrow she should be transferred to the Casino. The Casino was a deserted garden-house, built in not ungraceful imitation of an Ionic temple, in which Camillo's ancestors must often have assembled to drink cool syrups from Venetian glasses, and listen to learned madrigals. It contained several dusty fragments of antique sculpture, and it was spacious enough to enclose that richer collection of which I began fondly to regard the Juno as but the nucleus. Here, with short delay, this fine creature was placed, serenely upright, a reversed funereal *cippus* forming a sufficiently solid pedestal. The little explorer, who seemed an expert in all the offices of restoration, rubbed her and scraped her with mysterious art, removed her earthy stains, and doubled the lustre of her beauty. Her mellow substance seemed to glow with a kind of renascent purity and bloom, and, but for her broken hand, you might have fancied she had just received the last stroke of the chisel. Her fame remained no secret. Within two or three days half a dozen inquisitive *conoscenti* posted out to obtain sight of her. I happened to be present when the first of these gentlemen (a German in blue spectacles, with a portfolio under his arm) presented himself at the Villa. The Count, hearing his voice at the door, came forward and eyed him coldly from head to foot.

"Your new Juno, Signor Conte," began the German, "is, in my opinion, much more likely to be a certain Proserpine—"

"I've neither a Juno nor a Proserpine to discuss with you," said the Count, curtly. "You're misinformed."

"You've dug up no statue?" cried the German. "What a scandalous hoax!"

"None worthy of your learned attention. I'm sorry you should have the trouble of carrying your little note-book so far." The Count had suddenly become witty!

"But you've something, surely. The rumor is running through Rome."

"The rumor be damned!" cried the Count, savagely. "I've *nothing*,—do you understand? Be so good as to say so to your friends."

The answer was explicit, and the poor archæologist departed, tossing his flaxen mane. But I pitied him, and ventured to remonstrate with the Count. "She might as well be still in the earth, if no one is to see her," I said.

"*I'm* to see her: that's enough!" he answered with the same unnatural harshness. Then, in a moment, as he caught me eying him askance in troubled surprise, "I hated his great portfolio. He was going to make some hideous drawing of her."

"Ah, that touches me," I said. "I too have been planning to make a little sketch."

He was silent for some moments, after which he turned and grasped my arm, with less irritation, but with extraordinary gravity. "Go in there towards twilight," he said, "and sit for an hour and look at her. I think you'll give up your sketch. If you don't, my good old friend,—you're welcome!"

I followed his advice, and, as a friend, I gave up my sketch. But an artist is an artist, and I secretly longed to attempt one. Orders strictly in accordance with the Count's reply to our German friend were given to the servants, who, with an easy Italian conscience and a gracious Italian persuasiveness, assured all subsequent inquirers that they had been regrettably misinformed. I have no doubt, indeed, that, in default of larger opportunity, they made condolence remunerative. Further excavation was, for the present, suspended, as implying an affront to the incomparable Juno. The workmen departed, but the little explorer still haunted the premises and sounded the soil for his own entertainment. One day he came to me with his usual ambiguous grimace. "The beautiful hand of the Juno," he murmured; "what has become of it?"

"I've not seen it since you called me to look at her. I remember when I went away it was lying on the grass near the excavation."

"Where I placed it myself! After that it disappeared. Ecco!"

"Do you suspect one of your workmen? Such a fragment as that would bring more scudi than most of them ever looked at."

"Some, perhaps, are greater thieves than the others. But if I were to call up the worst of them and accuse him, the Count would interfere."

"He must value that beautiful hand, nevertheless."

The little expert in disinterment looked about him and winked. "He values it so much that he himself purloined it. That's my belief, and I think that the less we say about it the better."

"Purloined it, my dear sir? After all, it's his own property."

"Not so much as that comes to! So beautiful a creature is more or less the property of every one; we've all a right to look at her. But the Count treats her as if she were a sacrosanct image of the Madonna. He keeps her under lock and key, and pays her solitary visits. What does he do, after all? When a beautiful woman is in stone, all he can do is to look at her. And what does he do with that precious hand? He keeps it in a silver box; he has made a relic of it!" And this cynical personage began to chuckle grotesquely and walked away.

He left me musing uncomfortably, and wondering what the deuce he meant. The Count certainly chose to make a mystery of the Juno, but this seemed a natural incident of the first rapture of possession. I was willing to wait for a free access to her, and in the mean time I was glad to find that there was a limit to his constitutional apathy. But as the days elapsed I

began to be conscious that his enjoyment was not communicative, but strangely cold and shy and sombre. That he
should admire a marble goddess was no reason for his despising mankind; yet he really seemed to be making invidious
comparisons between us. From this untender proscription his
charming wife was not excepted. At moments when I tried to
persuade myself that he was neither worse nor better company than usual, her face condemned my optimism. She said
nothing, but she wore a constant look of pathetic perplexity.
She sat at times with her eyes fixed on him with a kind of imploring curiosity, as if pitying surprise held resentment yet
awhile in check. What passed between them in private, I had,
of course, no warrant to inquire. Nothing, I imagined,—and
that was the misery! It was part of the misery, too, that he
seemed impenetrable to these mute glances, and looked over
her head with an air of superb abstraction. Occasionally he
noticed me looking at him in urgent deprecation, and then
for a moment his heavy eye would sparkle, half, as it seemed,
in defiant irony and half with a strangely stifled impulse to justify himself. But from his wife he kept his face inexorably
averted; and when she approached him with some persuasive
caress, he received it with an ill-concealed shudder. I inwardly
protested and raged. I grew to hate the Count and everything
that belonged to him. "I was a thousand times right," I cried;
"an Italian count may be mighty fine, but he won't *wear*!
Give us some wholesome young fellow of our own blood,
who'll play us none of these dusky old-world tricks. Painter as
I am, I'll never recommend a picturesque husband!" I lost my
pleasure in the Villa, in the purple shadows and glowing
lights, the mossy marbles and the long-trailing profile of the
Alban Hills. My painting stood still; everything looked ugly. I
sat and fumbled with my palette, and seemed to be mixing
mud with my colors. My head was stuffed with dismal
thoughts; an intolerable weight seemed to lie upon my heart.
The Count became, to my imagination, a dark efflorescence
of the evil germs which history had implanted in his line. No
wonder he was foredoomed to be cruel. Was not cruelty a
tradition in his race, and crime an example? The unholy passions of his forefathers stirred blindly in his untaught nature
and clamored dumbly for an issue. What a heavy heritage it

seemed to me, as I reckoned it up in my melancholy musings, the Count's interminable ancestry! Back to the profligate re-vival of arts and vices,—back to the bloody medley of mediæ-val wars,—back through the long, fitfully glaring dusk of the early ages to its ponderous origin in the solid Roman state,—back through all the darkness of history it seemed to stretch, losing every feeblest claim on my sympathies as it went. Such a record was in itself a curse; and my poor girl had expected it to sit as lightly and gratefully on her consciousness as her feather on her hat! I have little idea how long this painful sit-uation lasted. It seemed the longer from my god-daughter's continued reserve, and my inability to offer her a word of consolation. A sensitive woman, disappointed in marriage, exhausts her own ingenuity before she takes counsel. The Count's preoccupations, whatever they were, made him in-creasingly restless; he came and went at random, with nervous abruptness; he took long rides alone, and, as I inferred, rarely went through the form of excusing himself to his wife; and still, as time went on, he came no nearer explaining his mys-tery. With the lapse of time, however, I confess that my ap-prehensions began to be tempered with pity. If I had expected to see him propitiate his urgent ancestry by a crime, now that his native rectitude seemed resolute to deny them this satis-faction, I felt a sort of grudging gratitude. A man couldn't be so gratuitously sombre without being unhappy. He had al-ways treated me with that antique deference to a grizzled beard for which elderly men reserve the flower of their gen-eral tenderness for waning fashions, and I thought it possible he might suffer me to lay a healing hand upon his trouble. One evening, when I had taken leave of my god-daughter and given her my useless blessing in a silent kiss, I came out and found the Count sitting in the garden in the mild starlight, and staring at a mouldy Hermes, nestling in a clump of ole-ander. I sat down by him and informed him roundly that his conduct needed an explanation. He half turned his head, and his dark pupil gleamed an instant.

"I understand," he said, "you think me crazy!" And he tapped his forehead.

"No, not crazy, but unhappy. And if unhappiness runs its course too freely, of course, our poor wits are sorely tried."

He was silent awhile, and then, "I'm not unhappy!" he cried abruptly. "I'm prodigiously happy. You wouldn't believe the satisfaction I take in sitting here and staring at that old weather-worn Hermes. Formerly I used to be afraid of him: his frown used to remind me of a little bushy-browed old priest who taught me Latin and looked at me terribly over the book when I stumbled in my Virgil. But now it seems to me the friendliest, jolliest thing in the world, and suggests the most delightful images. He stood pouting his great lips in some old Roman's garden two thousand years ago. He saw the sandalled feet treading the alleys and the rose-crowned heads bending over the wine; he knew the old feasts and the old worship, the old Romans and the old gods. As I sit here he speaks to me, in his own dumb way, and describes it all! No, no, my friend, I'm the happiest of men!"

I had denied that I thought he was crazy, but I suddenly began to suspect it, for I found nothing reassuring in this singular rhapsody. The Hermes, for a wonder, had kept his nose; and when I reflected that my dear Countess was being neglected for this senseless pagan block, I secretly promised myself to come the next day with a hammer and deal him such a lusty blow as would make him too ridiculous for a sentimental tête-à-tête. Meanwhile, however, the Count's infatuation was no laughing matter, and I expressed my sincerest conviction when I said, after a pause, that I should recommend him to see either a priest or a physician.

He burst into uproarious laughter. "A priest! What should I do with a priest, or he with me? I never loved them, and I feel less like beginning than ever. A priest, my dear friend," he repeated, laying his hand on my arm, "don't set a priest at me, if you value *his* sanity! My confession would frighten the poor man out of his wits. As for a doctor, I never was better in my life; and unless," he added abruptly, rising, and eying me askance; "you want to poison me, in Christian charity I advise you to leave me alone."

Decidedly, the Count *was* unsound, and I had no heart, for some days, to go back to the Villa. How should I treat him, what stand should I take, what course did Martha's happiness and dignity demand? I wandered about Rome, revolving these questions, and one afternoon found myself in the

Pantheon. A light spring shower had begun to fall, and I hurried for refuge into the great temple which its Christian altars have but half converted into a church. No Roman monument retains a deeper impress of ancient life, or verifies more forcibly those prodigious beliefs which we are apt to regard as dim fables. The huge dusky dome seems to the spiritual ear to hold a vague reverberation of pagan worship, as a gathered shell holds the rumor of the sea. Three or four persons were scattered before the various altars; another stood near the centre, beneath the aperture in the dome. As I drew near I perceived this was the Count. He was planted with his hands behind him, looking up first at the heavy rain-clouds, as they crossed the great bull's-eye, and then down at the besprinkled circle on the pavement. In those days the pavement was rugged and cracked and magnificently old, and this ample space, in free communion with the weather, had become as mouldy and mossy and verdant as a strip of garden soil. A tender herbage had sprung up in the crevices of the slabs, and the little microscopic shoots were twinkling in the rain. This great weather-current, through the uncapped vault, deadens most effectively the customary odors of incense and tallow, and transports one to a faith that was on friendly terms with nature. It seemed to have performed this office for the Count; his face wore an indefinable expression of ecstasy, and he was so rapt in contemplation that it was some time before he noticed me. The sun was struggling through the clouds without, and yet a thin rain continued to fall and came drifting down into our gloomy enclosure in a sort of illuminated drizzle. The Count watched it with the fascinated stare of a child watching a fountain, and then turned away, pressing his hand to his brow, and walked over to one of the ornamental altars. Here he again stood staring, but in a moment wheeled about and returned to his former place. Just then he recognized me, and perceived, I suppose, the puzzled gaze I must have fixed on him. He saluted me frankly with his hand, and at last came toward me. I fancied that he was in a kind of nervous tremor and was trying to appear calm.

"This is the best place in Rome," he murmured. "It's worth fifty St. Peters'. But do you know I never came here till the other day? I left it to the *forestieri*. They go about with

their red books, and read about this and that, and think they
know it. Ah! you must *feel* it,—feel the beauty and fitness of
that great open skylight. Now, only the wind and the rain, the
sun and the cold, come down; but of old—of old"—and he
touched my arm and gave me a strange smile—"the pagan
gods and goddesses used to come sailing through it and take
their places at their altars. What a procession, when the eyes
of faith could see it! Those are the things they have given us
instead!" And he gave a pitiful shrug. "I should like to pull
down their pictures, overturn their candlesticks, and poison
their holy-water!"

"My dear Count," I said gently, "you should tolerate people's honest beliefs. Would you renew the Inquisition, and in
the interest of Jupiter and Mercury?"

"People wouldn't tolerate my belief, if they guessed it!" he
cried. "There's been a great talk about the pagan persecutions; but the Christians persecuted as well, and the old gods
were worshipped in caves and woods as well as the new. And
none the worse for that! It was in caves and woods and
streams, in earth and air and water, they dwelt. And there—
and here, too, in spite of all your Christian lustrations—a son
of old Italy may find them still!"

He had said more than he meant, and his mask had fallen.
I looked at him hard, and felt a sudden outgush of the compassion we always feel for a creature irresponsibly excited. I
seemed to touch the source of his trouble, and my relief was
great, for my discovery made me feel like bursting into laughter. But I contented myself with smiling benignantly. He
looked back at me suspiciously, as if to judge how far he had
betrayed himself; and in his glance I read, somehow, that he
had a conscience we could take hold of. In my gratitude, I
was ready to thank any gods he pleased. "Take care, take
care," I said, "you're saying things which if the sacristan there
were to hear and report—!" And I passed my hand through
his arm and led him away.

I was startled and shocked, but I was also amused and comforted. The Count had suddenly become for me a delightfully
curious phenomenon, and I passed the rest of the day in meditating on the strange ineffaceability of race-characteristics. A
sturdy young Latin I had called Camillo; sturdier, indeed,

than I had dreamed him! Discretion was now misplaced, and on the morrow I spoke to my god-daughter. She had lately been hoping, I think, that I would help her to unburden her heart, for she immediately gave way to tears and confessed that she was miserable. "At first," she said, "I thought it was all fancy, and not his tenderness that was growing less, but my exactions that were growing greater. But suddenly it settled upon me like a mortal chill,—the conviction that he had ceased to care for me, that something had come between us. And the puzzling thing has been the want of possible cause in my own conduct, or of any sign that there is another woman in the case. I have racked my brain to discover what I had said or done or thought to displease him! And yet he goes about like a man too deeply injured to complain. He has never uttered a harsh word or given me a reproachful look. He has simply renounced me. I have dropped out of his life."

She spoke with such an appealing tremor in her voice that I was on the point of telling her that I had guessed the riddle, and that this was half the battle. But I was afraid of her incredulity. My solution was so fantastic, so apparently far-fetched, so absurd, that I resolved to wait for convincing evidence. To obtain it, I continued to watch the Count, covertly and cautiously, but with a vigilance which disinterested curiosity now made intensely keen. I returned to my painting, and neglected no pretext for hovering about the gardens and the neighborhood of the Casino. The Count, I think, suspected my designs, or at least my suspicions, and would have been glad to remember just what he had suffered himself to say to me in the Pantheon. But it deepened my interest in his extraordinary situation that, in so far as I could read his deeply brooding face, he seemed to have grudgingly pardoned me. He gave me a glance occasionally, as he passed me, in which a sort of dumb desire for help appeared to struggle with the instinct of mistrust. I was willing enough to help him, but the case was prodigiously delicate, and I wished to master the symptoms. Meanwhile I worked and waited and wondered. Ah! I wondered, you may be sure, with an interminable wonder; and, turn it over as I would, I couldn't get used to my idea. Sometimes it offered itself to me with a perverse fascination which deprived me of all wish to interfere.

The Count took the form of a precious psychological study, and refined feeling seemed to dictate a tender respect for his delusion. I envied him the force of his imagination, and I used sometimes to close my eyes with a vague desire that when I opened them I might find Apollo under the opposite tree, lazily kissing his flute, or see Diana hurrying with long steps down the ilex-walk. But for the most part my host seemed to me simply an unhappy young man, with an unwholesome mental twist which should be smoothed away as speedily as possible. If the remedy was to match the disease, however, it would have to be an ingenious compound!

One evening, having bidden my god-daughter good night, I had started on my usual walk to my lodgings in Rome. Five minutes after leaving the villa-gate I discovered that I had left my eye-glass—an object in constant use—behind me. I immediately remembered that, while painting, I had broken the string which fastened it round my neck, and had hooked it provisionally upon a twig of a flowering-almond tree within arm's reach. Shortly afterwards I had gathered up my things and retired, unmindful of the glass; and now, as I needed it to read the evening paper at the Caffé Greco, there was no alternative but to retrace my steps and detach it from its twig. I easily found it, and lingered awhile to note the curious night-aspect of the spot I had been studying by daylight. The night was magnificent, and full-charged with the breath of the early Roman spring. The moon was rising fast and flinging her silver checkers into the heavy masses of shadow. Watching her at play, I strolled farther and suddenly came in sight of the Casino.

Just then the moon, which for a moment had been concealed, touched with a white ray a small marble figure which adorned the pediment of this rather factitious little structure. Its sudden illumination suggested that a rarer spectacle was at hand, and that the same influence must be vastly becoming to the imprisoned Juno. The door of the Casino was, as usual, locked, but the moonlight was flooding the high-placed windows so generously that my curiosity became obstinate—and inventive. I dragged a garden-seat round from the portico, placed it on end, and succeeded in climbing to the top of it and bringing myself abreast of one of the windows. The casement yielded to my pressure, turned on its hinges, and showed me what I had been looking for,—Juno visited by Diana. The beautiful image stood bathed in the radiant flood and shining with a purity which made her most persuasively divine. If by day her mellow complexion suggested faded gold, her substance now might have passed for polished silver. The effect was almost terrible; beauty so eloquent could hardly be inanimate. This was my foremost observation. I leave you to fancy whether my next was less interesting. At some distance from the foot of the statue, just out of the light, I perceived a figure lying flat on the pavement, prostrate apparently with devotion. I can hardly tell you how it completed the impressiveness of the scene. It marked the shining image as a goddess indeed, and seemed to throw a sort of conscious pride into her stony mask. I of course immediately recognized this recumbent worshipper as the Count, and while I stood gazing, as if to help me to read the full meaning of his attitude, the moonlight travelled forward and covered his breast and face. Then I saw that his eyes were closed, and that he was either asleep or swooning. Watching him attentively, I detected his even respirations, and judged there was no reason for alarm. The moonlight blanched his face, which seemed already pale with weariness. He had come into the presence of the Juno in obedience to that fabulous passion of which the symptoms had so wofully perplexed us, and, exhausted either by compliance or resistance, he had sunk down at her feet in a stupid sleep. The bright moonshine soon aroused him, however; he muttered something and raised himself, vaguely staring. Then recognizing his situation, he rose and stood for some time gazing fixedly at the glowing image with an expression which I fancied was not that of wholly unprotesting devotion. He uttered a string of broken words of which I was unable to catch the meaning, and then, after another pause and a long, melancholy moan, he turned slowly to the door. As rapidly and noiselessly as possible I descended from my post of vigilance and passed behind the Casino, and in a moment I heard the sound of the closing lock and of his departing footsteps.

The next day, meeting the little antiquarian in the grounds, I shook my finger at him with what I meant he should consider portentous gravity. But he only grinned like the malicious earth-gnome to which I had always compared him, and twisted his mustache as if my menace was a capital joke. "If you dig any more holes here," I said, "you shall be thrust into the deepest of them, and have the earth packed down on top of you. We have made enough discoveries, and we want no more statues. Your Juno has almost ruined us."

He burst out laughing. "I expected as much," he cried; "I had my notions!"

"What did you expect?"

"That the Signor Conte would begin and say his prayers to her."

"Good heavens! Is the case so common? Why did you expect it?"

"On the contrary, the case is rare. But I've fumbled so long in the monstrous heritage of antiquity, that I have learned a multitude of secrets; learned that ancient relics may work modern miracles. There's a pagan element in all of us,—I don't speak for you, *illustrissimi forestieri*,—and the old gods have still their worshippers. The old spirit still throbs here and there, and the Signor Conte has his share of it. He's a good fellow, but, between ourselves, he's an impossible Christian!" And this singular personage resumed his impertinent hilarity.

"If your previsions were so distinct," I said, "you ought to have given me a hint of them. I should have sent your spadesmen walking."

"Ah, but the Juno is so beautiful!"

"Her beauty be blasted! Can you tell me what has become of the Contessa's? To rival the Juno, she's turning to marble herself."

He shrugged his shoulders. "Ah, but the Juno is worth fifty thousand scudi!"

"I'd give a hundred thousand," I said, "to have her annihilated. Perhaps, after all, I shall want you to dig another hole."

"At your service!" he answered, with a flourish; and we separated.

A couple of days later I dined, as I often did, with my host and hostess, and met the Count face to face for the first time since his prostration in the Casino. He bore the traces of it, and sat plunged in sombre distraction. I fancied that the path of the antique faith was not strewn with flowers, and that the Juno was becoming daily a harder mistress to serve. Dinner was scarcely over before he rose from table and took up his hat. As he did so, passing near his wife, he faltered a moment, stopped and gave her—for the first time, I imagine—that vaguely imploring look which I had often caught. She moved her lips in inarticulate sympathy and put out her hands. He drew her towards him, kissed her with a kind of angry ardor, and strode away. The occasion was propitious, and further delay unnecessary.

"What I have to tell you is very strange," I said to the Countess, "very fantastic, very incredible. But perhaps you'll not find it so bad as you feared. There *is* a woman in the case! Your enemy is the Juno. The Count—how shall I say it?—the Count takes her *au sérieux*." She was silent; but after a moment she touched my arm with her hand, and I knew she meant that I had spoken her own belief. "You admired his antique simplicity: you see how far it goes. He has reverted to the faith of his fathers. Dormant through the ages, that imperious statue has silently aroused it. He believes in the pedigrees you used to dog's-ear your School Mythology with trying to get by heart. In a word, dear child, Camillo is a pagan!"

"I suppose you'll be terribly shocked," she answered, "if I say that he's welcome to any faith, if he will only share it with me. I'll believe in Jupiter, if he'll bid me! My sorrow's not for that: let my husband be himself! My sorrow is for the gulf of silence and indifference that has burst open between us. His Juno's the reality; I'm the fiction!"

"I've lately become reconciled to this gulf of silence, and to your fading for a while into a fiction. After the fable, the moral! The poor fellow has but half succumbed: the other half protests. The modern man is shut out in the darkness with his incomparable wife. How can he have failed to feel—vaguely and grossly if it must have been, but in every throb of his heart—that you are a more perfect experiment of nature, a riper fruit of time, than those primitive persons for whom Juno was a terror and Venus an example? He pays you the compliment of believing you an inconvertible modern. He has crossed the Acheron, but he has left you behind, as a pledge to the present. We'll bring him back to redeem it. The old ancestral ghosts ought to be propitiated when a pretty creature like you has sacrificed the fragrance of her life. He has proved himself one of the Valerii; we shall see to it that he is the last, and yet that his decease shall leave the Conte Camillo in excellent health."

I spoke with confidence which I had partly felt, for it seemed to me that if the Count was to be touched, it must be by the sense that his strange spiritual excursion had not made his wife detest him. We talked long and to a hopeful end, for before I went away my god-daughter expressed the desire to go out and look at the Juno. "I was afraid of her almost from the first," she said, "and have hardly seen her since she was set up in the Casino. Perhaps I can learn a lesson from her,—perhaps I can guess how she charms him!"

For a moment I hesitated, with the fear that we might intrude upon the Count's devotions. Then, as something in the poor girl's face suggested that she had thought of this and felt a sudden impulse to pluck victory from the heart of danger, I bravely offered her my arm. The night was cloudy, and on this occasion, apparently, the triumphant goddess was to depend upon her own lustre. But as we approached the Casino I saw that the door was ajar, and that there was lamplight within. The lamp was suspended in front of the image, and it showed us that the place was empty. But the Count had lately been there. Before the statue stood a roughly extemporized altar, composed of a nameless fragment of antique marble, engraved with an illegible Greek inscription. We seemed really to stand in a pagan temple, and we gazed at the serene divinity with an impulse of spiritual reverence. It ought to have been deepened, I suppose, but it was rudely checked, by our observing a curious glitter on the face of the low altar. A second glance showed us it was blood!

My companion looked at me in pale horror, and turned away with a cry. A swarm of hideous conjectures pressed into my mind, and for a moment I was sickened. But at last I remembered that there is blood and blood, and the Latins were posterior to the cannibals.

"Be sure it's very innocent," I said; "a lamb, a kid, or a sucking calf!" But it was enough for her nerves and her conscience that it was a crimson trickle, and she returned to the house in sad agitation. The rest of the night was not passed in a way to restore her to calmness. The Count had not come in, and she sat up for him from hour to hour. I remained with her and smoked my cigar as composedly as I might; but internally I wondered what in horror's name had become of him. Gradually, as the hours wore away, I shaped a vague interpretation of these dusky portents,—an interpretation none the less valid and devoutly desired for its being tolerably cheerful. The blood-drops on the altar, I mused, were the last instalment of his debt and the end of his delusion. They had been a happy necessity, for he was, after all, too gentle a creature not to hate himself for having shed them, not to abhor so cruelly insistent an idol. He had wandered away to recover himself in solitude, and he would come back to us with a repentant heart and an inquiring mind! I should certainly have believed all this more easily, however, if I could have heard his footstep in the hall. Toward dawn, scepticism threatened to creep in with the gray light, and I restlessly betook myself to the portico. Here in a few moments I saw him cross the grass, heavy-footed, splashed with mud, and evidently excessively tired. He must have been walking all night, and his face denoted that his spirit had been as restless as his body. He paused near me, and before he entered the house he stopped, looked at me a moment, and then held out his hand. I grasped it warmly, and it seemed to me to throb with all that he could not utter.

"Will you see your wife?" I asked.

He passed his hand over his eyes and shook his head. "Not now—not yet—some time!" he answered.

I was disappointed, but I convinced her, I think, that he had cast out the devil. She felt, poor girl, a pardonable desire to celebrate the event. I returned to my lodging, spent the day in Rome, and came back to the Villa toward dusk. I was told that the Countess was in the grounds. I looked for her cautiously at first, for I thought it just possible I might interrupt the natural consequences of a reconciliation; but failing to meet her, I turned toward the Casino, and found myself face to face with the little explorer.

"Does your excellency happen to have twenty yards of stout rope about him?" he asked gravely.

"Do you want to hang yourself for the trouble you've stood sponsor to?" I answered.

"It's a hanging matter, I promise you. The Countess has given orders. You'll find her in the Casino. Sweet-voiced as she is, she knows how to make her orders understood."

At the door of the Casino stood half a dozen of the laborers on the place, looking vaguely solemn, like outstanding dependants at a superior funeral. The Countess was within, in a position which was an answer to the surveyor's riddle. She stood with her eyes fixed on the Juno, who had been removed from her pedestal and lay stretched in her magnificent length upon a rude litter.

"Do you understand?" she said. "She's beautiful, she's noble, she's precious, but she must go back!" And, with a passionate gesture, she seemed to indicate an open grave.

I was hugely delighted, but I thought it discreet to stroke my chin and look sober. "She's worth fifty thousand scudi."

She shook her head sadly. "If we were to sell her to the Pope and give the money to the poor, it wouldn't profit us. She must go back,—she must go back! We must smother her beauty in the dreadful earth. It makes me feel almost as if she were alive; but it came to me last night with overwhelming force, when my husband came in and refused to see me, that he'll not be himself as long as she is above ground. To cut the knot we must bury her! If I had only thought of it before!"

"Not before!" I said, shaking my head in turn. "Heaven reward our sacrifice now!"

The little surveyor, when he reappeared, seemed hardly like an agent of the celestial influences, but he was deft and active, which was more to the point. Every now and then he uttered some half-articulate lament, by way of protest against the Countess's cruelty; but I saw him privately scanning the recumbent image with an eye which seemed to foresee a malicious glee in standing on a certain unmarked spot on the turf and grinning till people stared. He had brought back an abundance of rope, and having summoned his assistants, who vigorously lifted the litter, he led the way to the original excavation, which had been left unclosed with the project of further researches. By the time we reached the edge of the grave the evening had fallen and the beauty of our marble victim was shrouded in a dusky veil. No one spoke,—if not exactly for shame, at least for regret. Whatever our plea, our performance looked, at least, monstrously profane. The ropes were adjusted and the Juno was slowly lowered into her earthy bed. The Countess took a handful of earth and dropped it solemnly on her breast. "May it lie lightly, but forever!" she said.

"Amen!" cried the little surveyor with a strange mocking inflection; and he gave us a bow, as he departed, which betrayed an agreeable consciousness of knowing where fifty thousand scudi were buried. His underlings had another cask of wine, the result of which, for them, was a suspension of all consciousness, and a subsequent irreparable confusion of memory as to where they had plied their spades.

The Countess had not yet seen her husband, who had again apparently betaken himself to communion with the great god Pan. I was of course unwilling to leave her to encounter alone the results of her momentous deed. She wandered into the drawing-room and pretended to occupy herself with a bit of embroidery, but in reality she was bravely composing herself for an "explanation." I took up a book, but it held my attention as feebly. As the evening wore away I heard a movement on the threshold and saw the Count lifting the tapestried curtain which masked the door, and looking silently at his wife. His eyes were brilliant, but not angry. He had missed the Juno—and drawn a long breath! The Countess kept her eyes fixed on her work, and drew her silken stitches like an image of wifely contentment. The image seemed to fascinate him: he came in slowly, almost on tiptoe, walked to the chimney-piece, and stood there in a sort of rapt contemplation. What had passed, what was passing, in his mind, I leave to your own apprehension. My god-daughter's hand trembled as it rose and fell, and the color came into her cheek. At last she raised her eyes and sustained the gaze in which all his returning faith seemed concentrated. He hesitated a moment, as if her very forgiveness kept the gulf open between them, and then he strode forward, fell on his two knees and buried his head in her lap. I departed as the Count had come in, on tiptoe.

He never became, if you will, a thoroughly modern man; but one day, years after, when a visitor to whom he was showing his cabinet became inquisitive as to a marble hand, suspended in one of its inner recesses, he looked grave and turned the lock on it. "It is the hand of a beautiful creature," he said, "whom I once greatly admired."

"Ah,—a Roman?" said the gentleman, with a smirk.

"A Greek," said the Count, with a frown.

Madame de Mauves

THE VIEW from the terrace at Saint-Germain-en-Laye is immense and famous. Paris lies spread before you in dusky vastness, domed and fortified, glittering here and there through her light vapours, and girdled with her silver Seine. Behind you is a park of stately symmetry, and behind that a forest, where you may lounge through turfy avenues and light-checkered glades, and quite forget that you are within half an hour of the boulevards. One afternoon, however, in mid-spring, some five years ago, a young man seated on the terrace had chosen not to forget this. His eyes were fixed in idle wistfulness on the mighty human hive before him. He was fond of rural things, and he had come to Saint-Germain a week before to meet the spring half-way; but though he could boast of a six months' acquaintance with the great city, he never looked at it from his present standpoint without a feeling of painfully unsatisfied curiosity. There were moments when it seemed to him that not to be there just then was to miss some thrilling chapter of experience. And yet his winter's experience had been rather fruitless, and he had closed the book almost with a yawn. Though not in the least a cynic, he was what one may call a disappointed observer; and he never chose the right-hand road without beginning to suspect after an hour's wayfaring that the left would have been the interesting one. He now had a dozen minds to go to Paris for the evening, to dine at the Café Brébant and to repair afterwards to the Gymnase and listen to the latest exposition of the duties of the injured husband. He would probably have risen to execute this project, if he had not observed a little girl who, wandering along the terrace, had suddenly stopped short and begun to gaze at him with round-eyed frankness. For a moment he was simply amused, for the child's face denoted helpless wonderment; the next he was agreeably surprised. "Why, this is my friend Maggie," he said; "I see you have not forgotten me."

Maggie, after a short parley, was induced to seal her remembrance with a kiss. Invited then to explain her appear-

ance at Saint-Germain, she embarked on a recital in which the
general, according to the infantine method, was so fatally sacrificed to the particular, that Longmore looked about him for
a superior source of information. He found it in Maggie's
mamma, who was seated with another lady at the opposite
end of the terrace; so, taking the child by the hand, he led her
back to her companions.

Maggie's mamma was a young American lady, as you would
immediately have perceived, with a pretty and friendly face
and an expensive spring toilet. She greeted Longmore with
surprised cordiality, mentioned his name to her friend, and
bade him bring a chair and sit with them. The other lady,
who, though equally young and perhaps even prettier, was
dressed more soberly, remained silent, stroking the hair of the
little girl, whom she had drawn against her knee. She had
never heard of Longmore, but she now perceived that her
companion had crossed the ocean with him, had met him afterwards in travelling, and (having left her husband in Wall
Street) was indebted to him for various small services.

Maggie's mamma turned from time to time and smiled at
her friend with an air of invitation; the latter smiled back, and
continued gracefully to say nothing.

For ten minutes Longmore felt a revival of interest in his
interlocutress; then (as riddles are more amusing than commonplaces) it gave way to curiosity about her friend. His eyes
wandered; her volubility was less suggestive than the latter's
silence.

The stranger was perhaps not obviously a beauty nor obviously an American; but she was essentially both, on a closer
scrutiny. She was slight and fair, and, though naturally pale,
she was delicately flushed, apparently with recent excitement.
What chiefly struck Longmore in her face was the union of a
pair of beautifully gentle, almost languid grey eyes, with a
mouth peculiarly expressive and firm. Her forehead was a trifle more expansive than belongs to classic types, and her thick
brown hair was dressed out of the fashion, which was just
then very ugly. Her throat and bust were slender, but all the
more in harmony with certain rapid, charming movements of
the head, which she had a way of throwing back every now
and then, with an air of attention and a sidelong glance from

her dove-like eyes. She seemed at once alert and indifferent, contemplative and restless; and Longmore very soon discovered that if she was not a brilliant beauty, she was at least an extremely interesting one. This very impression made him magnanimous. He perceived that he had interrupted a confidential conversation, and he judged it discreet to withdraw, having first learned from Maggie's mamma—Mrs. Draper— that she was to take the six-o'clock train back to Paris. He promised to meet her at the station.

He kept his appointment, and Mrs. Draper arrived betimes, accompanied by her friend. The latter, however, made her farewells at the door and drove away again, giving Longmore time only to raise his hat. "Who is she?" he asked with visible ardour, as he brought Mrs. Draper her tickets.

"Come and see me to-morrow at the Hôtel de l'Empire," she answered, "and I will tell you all about her." The force of this offer in making him punctual at the Hôtel de l'Empire Longmore doubtless never exactly measured; and it was perhaps well that he did not, for he found his friend, who was on the point of leaving Paris, so distracted by procrastinating milliners and perjured lingères that she had no wits left for disinterested narrative. "You must find Saint-Germain dreadfully dull," she said, as he was going. "Why won't you come with me to London?"

"Introduce me to Madame de Mauves," he answered, "and Saint-Germain will satisfy me." All he had learned was the lady's name and residence.

"Ah! she, poor woman, will not make Saint-Germain cheerful for you. She's very unhappy."

Longmore's further inquiries were arrested by the arrival of a young lady with a bandbox; but he went away with the promise of a note of introduction, to be immediately despatched to him at Saint-Germain.

He waited a week, but the note never came; and he declared that it was not for Mrs. Draper to complain of her milliner's treachery. He lounged on the terrace and walked in the forest, studied suburban street life, and made a languid attempt to investigate the records of the court of the exiled Stuarts; but he spent most of his time in wondering where Madame de Mauves lived, and whether she ever walked on the terrace. Sometimes, he finally discovered; for one after-noon towards dusk he perceived her leaning against the para-pet, alone. In his momentary hesitation to approach her, it seemed to him that there was almost a shade of trepidation; but his curiosity was not diminished by the consciousness of this result of a quarter of an hour's acquaintance. She imme-diately recognised him, on his drawing near, with the manner of a person unaccustomed to encounter an embarrassing vari-ety of faces. Her dress, her expression, were the same as be-fore; her charm was there, like that of sweet music on a second hearing. She soon made conversation easy by asking him for news of Mrs. Draper. Longmore told her that he was daily expecting news, and, after a pause, mentioned the promised note of introduction.

"It seems less necessary now," he said—"for me, at least. But for you—I should have liked you to know the flattering things Mrs. Draper would probably have said about me."

"If it arrives at last," she answered, "you must come and see me and bring it. If it doesn't, you must come without it."

Then, as she continued to linger in spite of the thickening twilight, she explained that she was waiting for her husband, who was to arrive in the train from Paris, and who often passed along the terrace on his way home. Longmore well re-membered that Mrs. Draper had pronounced her unhappy, and he found it convenient to suppose that this same husband made her so. Edified by his six months in Paris—"What else is possible," he asked himself, "for a sweet American girl who marries an unclean Frenchman?"

But this tender expectancy of her lord's return undermined his hypothesis, and it received a further check from the gen-tle eagerness with which she turned and greeted an approach-ing figure. Longmore beheld in the fading light a stoutish gentleman, on the fair side of forty, in a high light hat, whose countenance, indistinct against the sky, was adorned by a fan-tastically pointed moustache. M. de Mauves saluted his wife with punctilious gallantry, and having bowed to Longmore, asked her several questions in French. Before taking his prof-fered arm to walk to their carriage, which was in waiting at the gate of the terrace, she introduced our hero as a friend of Mrs. Draper, and a fellow-countryman, whom she hoped to see at home. M. de Mauves responded briefly, but civilly, in very fair English, and led his wife away.

Longmore watched him as he went, twisting his picturesque moustache, with a feeling of irritation which he certainly would have been at a loss to account for. The only conceivable cause was the light which M. de Mauves's good English cast upon his own bad French. For reasons involved apparently in the very structure of his being, Longmore found himself unable to speak the language tolerably. He admired and enjoyed it, but the very genius of awkwardness controlled his phraseology. But he reflected with satisfaction that Madame de Mauves and he had a common idiom, and his vexation was effectually dispelled by his finding on his table that evening a letter from Mrs. Draper. It enclosed a short, formal missive to Madame de Mauves, but the epistle itself was copious and confidential. She had deferred writing till she reached London, where for a week, of course, she had found other amusements.

"I think it is the sight of so many women here who don't look at all like her, that has reminded me by the law of contraries of my charming friend at Saint-Germain and my promise to introduce you to her," she wrote. "I believe I told you that she was unhappy, and I wondered afterwards whether I had not been guilty of a breach of confidence. But you would have found it out for yourself, and besides, she told me no secrets. She declared she was the happiest creature in the world, and then, poor thing, she burst into tears, and I prayed to be delivered from such happiness. It's the miserable story of an American girl, born to be neither a slave nor a toy, marrying a profligate Frenchman, who believes that a woman must be one or the other. The silliest American woman is too good for the best foreigner, and the poorest of us have moral needs that the cleverest Frenchman is quite unable to appreciate. She was romantic and perverse—she thought Americans were vulgar. Matrimonial felicity perhaps *is* vulgar; but I think nowadays she wishes she were a little less elegant. M. de Mauves cared, of course, for nothing but her money, which he is spending royally on his *menus plaisirs*. I hope you appreciate the compliment I pay you when I recommend you to go and console an unhappy wife. I have never given a man such a proof of esteem, and if you were to disappoint me I should renounce the world. Prove to Madame de Mauves that an American friend may mingle admiration and respect better than a French husband. She avoids society and lives quite alone, seeing no one but a horrible French sister-in-law. Do let me hear that you have drawn some of the sadness from that desperate smile of hers. Make her smile with a good conscience."

These zealous admonitions left Longmore slightly disturbed. He found himself on the edge of a domestic tragedy from which he instinctively recoiled. To call upon Madame de Mauves with his present knowledge seemed a sort of fishing in troubled waters. He was a modest man, and yet he asked himself whether the effect of his attentions might not be to add to her discomfort. A flattering sense of unwonted opportunity, however, made him, with the lapse of time, more confident—possibly more reckless. It seemed a very inspiring idea to draw the sadness from his fair countrywoman's smile, and at least he hoped to persuade her that there was such a thing as an agreeable American. He immediately called upon her.

II.

She had been placed for her education, fourteen years before, in a Parisian convent, by a widowed mamma who was fonder of Homburg and Nice than of letting out tucks in the frocks of a vigorously growing daughter. Here, besides various elegant accomplishments—the art of wearing a train, of composing a bouquet, of presenting a cup of tea—she acquired a certain turn of the imagination which might have passed for a sign of precocious worldliness. She dreamed of marrying a title—not for the pleasure of hearing herself called Madame la Vicomtesse (for which it seemed to her that she should never greatly care), but because she had a romantic belief that the best birth is the guarantee of an ideal delicacy of feeling. Romances are rarely constructed in such perfect good faith, and Euphemia's excuse was the primitive purity of her imagination. She was essentially incorruptible, and she cherished this pernicious conceit as if it had been a dogma revealed by a white-winged angel. Even after experience had given her a hundred rude hints, she found it easier to believe in fables, when they had a certain nobleness of meaning, than in well-attested but sordid facts. She believed that a gentleman with a long pedigree must be of necessity a very fine fellow, and that the consciousness of a picturesque family tradition imparts an exquisite tone to the character. *Noblesse oblige*, she thought, as regards yourself, and insures, as regards your wife. She had never spoken to a nobleman in her life, and these convictions were but a matter of transcendent theory. They were the fruit, in part, of the perusal of various Ultramontane works of fiction—the only ones admitted to the convent library—in which the hero was always a Legitimist vicomte who fought duels by the dozen, but went twice a month to confession; and in part of the perfumed gossip of her companions, many of them *filles de haut lieu*, who in the convent garden, after Sundays at home, depicted their brothers and cousins as Prince Charmings and young Paladins. Euphemia listened and said nothing; she shrouded her visions of matrimony under a coronet in religious mystery. She was not of that type of young lady who is easily induced to declare that her husband must be six feet high and a little near-sighted, part his hair in the middle, and have amber lights in his beard. To her companions she seemed to have a very pallid fancy; and even the fact that she was a sprig of the transatlantic democracy never sufficiently explained her apathy on social questions. She had a mental image of that son of the Crusaders who was to suffer her to adore him, but like many an artist who has produced a masterpiece of idealisation, she shrank from exposing it to public criticism. It was the portrait of a gentleman rather ugly than handsome, and rather poor than rich. But his ugliness was to be nobly expressive, and his poverty delicately proud.

Euphemia had a fortune of her own, which, at the proper time, after fixing on her in eloquent silence those fine eyes which were to soften the feudal severity of his visage, he was to accept with a world of stifled protestations. One condition alone she was to make—that his blood should be of the very finest strain. On this she would stake her happiness.

It so chanced that circumstances were to give convincing colour to this primitive logic.

Though little of a talker, Euphemia was an ardent listener, and there were moments when she fairly hung upon the lips of Mademoiselle Marie de Mauves. Her intimacy with this chosen schoolmate was, like most intimacies, based on their points of difference. Mademoiselle de Mauves was very positive, very shrewd, very ironical, very French—everything that Euphemia felt herself unpardonable in not being. During her Sundays *en ville* she had examined the world and judged it, and she imparted her impressions to our attentive heroine with an agreeable mixture of enthusiasm and scepticism. She was moreover a handsome and well-grown person, on whom Euphemia's ribbons and trinkets had a trick of looking better than on their slender proprietress. She had, finally, the supreme merit of being a rigorous example of the virtue of exalted birth, having, as she did, ancestors honourably mentioned by Joinville and Commines, and a stately grandmother with a hooked nose, who came up with her after the holidays from a veritable *castel* in Auvergne. It seemed to Euphemia that these attributes made her friend more at home in the world than if she had been the daughter of even the most prosperous grocer. A certain aristocratic impudence Mademoiselle de Mauves abundantly possessed, and her raids among her friend's finery were quite in the spirit of her baronial ancestors in the twelfth century—a spirit which Euphemia considered but a large way of understanding friendship—a freedom from small deference to the world's opinions which would sooner or later justify itself in acts of surprising magnanimity. Mademoiselle de Mauves herself perhaps was but partially conscious of that sweet security which Euphemia envied her. She proved herself later in life such an accomplished schemer that her sense of having further heights to scale must have awakened early. Our heroine's ribbons and trinkets had much to do with the other's sisterly patronage, and her appealing pliancy of character even more; but the concluding motive of Marie's writing to her grandmamma to invite Euphemia for a three weeks' holiday to the *castel* in Auvergne involved altogether superior considerations. Mademoiselle de Mauves was indeed at this time seventeen years of age, and presumably capable of general views; and Euphemia, who was hardly less, was a very well-grown subject for experiment,

besides being pretty enough almost to pre-assure success. It is
a proof of the sincerity of Euphemia's aspirations that the *castel* was not a shock to her faith. It was neither a cheerful nor
a luxurious abode, but the young girl found it as delightful as
a play. It had battered towers and an empty moat, a rusty
drawbridge and a court paved with crooked, grass-grown
slabs, over which the antique coach-wheels of the old lady
with the hooked nose seemed to awaken the echoes of the
seventeenth century. Euphemia was not frightened out of her
dream; she had the pleasure of seeing it assume the consistency of a flattering presentiment. She had a taste for old servants, old anecdotes, old furniture, faded household colours,
and sweetly stale odours—musty treasures in which the
Château de Mauves abounded. She made a dozen sketches in
water-colours, after her conventual pattern; but sentimentally,
as one may say, she was for ever sketching with a freer hand.

Old Madame de Mauves had nothing severe but her nose,
and she seemed to Euphemia, as indeed she was, a graciously
venerable relic of an historic order of things. She took a great
fancy to the young American, who was ready to sit all day at
her feet and listen to anecdotes of the *bon temps* and quotations from the family chronicles. Madame de Mauves was a
very honest old woman, and uttered her thoughts with antique plainness. One day, after pushing back Euphemia's shining locks and blinking at her with some tenderness from
under her spectacles, she declared with an energetic shake of
the head that she didn't know what to make of her. And in
answer to the young girl's startled blush—"I should like to
advise you," she said, "but you seem to me so all of a piece
that I am afraid that if I advise you, I shall spoil you. It's easy
to see that you are not one of us. I don't know whether you
are better, but you seem to me to listen to the murmur of
your own young spirit, rather than to the voice from behind
the confessional or to the whisper of opportunity. Young girls,
in my day, when they were stupid, were very docile, but when
they were clever, were very sly. You are clever enough, I imagine, and yet if I guessed all your secrets at this moment, is
there one I should have to frown at? I can tell you a wickeder
one than any you have discovered for yourself. If you expect
to live in France, and you wish to be happy, don't listen too

hard to that little voice I just spoke of—the voice that is neither the curé's nor the world's. You will fancy it saying things
that it won't help your case to hear. They will make you sad,
and when you are sad you will grow plain, and when you are
plain you will grow bitter, and when you are bitter you will be
very disagreeable. I was brought up to think that a woman's
first duty is to please, and the happiest women I have known
have been the ones who performed this duty faithfully. As you
are not a Catholic, I suppose you can't be a *dévote*; and if you
don't take life as a fifty years' mass, the only way to take it is
as a game of skill. Listen to this. Not to lose at the game of
life, you must—I don't say cheat, but not be too sure your
neighbour won't, and not be shocked out of your self-possession if he does. Don't lose, my dear; I beseech you, don't
lose. Be neither suspicious nor credulous, and if you find your
neighbour peeping, don't cry out, but very politely wait your
own chance. I have had my *revanche* more than once in my
day, but I really think that the sweetest I could take against
life as a whole would be to have your blessed innocence profit
by my experience."

This was rather bewildering advice, but Euphemia understood it too little to be either edified or frightened. She sat listening to it very much as she would have listened to the
speeches of an old lady in a comedy, whose diction should
picturesquely correspond to the pattern of her mantilla and
the fashion of her head-dress. Her indifference was doubly
dangerous, for Madame de Mauves spoke at the prompting of
coming events, and her words were the result of a somewhat
troubled conscience—a conscience which told her at once
that Euphemia was too tender a victim to be sacrificed to an
ambition, and that the prosperity of her house was too precious a heritage to be sacrificed to a scruple. The prosperity in
question had suffered repeated and grievous breaches, and
the house of De Mauves had been pervaded by the cold comfort of an establishment in which people were obliged to
balance dinner-table allusions to feudal ancestors against the
absence of side-dishes; a state of things the more regrettable
as the family was now mainly represented by a gentleman
whose appetite was large and who justly maintained that its
historic glories had not been established by underfed heroes.

Three days after Euphemia's arrival, Richard de Mauves came down from Paris to pay his respects to his grandmother, and treated our heroine to her first encounter with a gentil-homme in the flesh. On coming in he kissed his grand-mother's hand, with a smile which caused her to draw it away with dignity, and set Euphemia, who was standing by, won-dering what had happened between them. Her unanswered wonder was but the beginning of a life of bitter perplexity, but the reader is free to know that the smile of M. de Mauves was a reply to a certain postscript affixed by the old lady to a letter promptly addressed to him by her granddaughter, after Euphemia had been admitted to justify the latter's promises. Mademoiselle de Mauves brought her letter to her grand-mother for approval, but obtained no more than was ex-pressed in a frigid nod. The old lady watched her with a sombre glance as she proceeded to seal the letter, and sud-denly bade her open it again and bring her a pen.

"Your sister's flatteries are all nonsense," she wrote; "the young lady is far too good for you, *mauvais sujet*. If you have a particle of conscience you will not come and disturb the re-pose of an angel of innocence."

The young girl, who had read these lines, made up a little face as she re-directed the letter; but she laid down her pen with a confident nod which might have seemed to mean that, to the best of her belief, her brother had not a conscience.

"If you meant what you said," the young man whispered to his grandmother on the first opportunity, "it would have been simpler not to let her send the letter!"

It was perhaps because she was wounded by this cynical in-sinuation that Madame de Mauves remained in her own apartment during a greater part of Euphemia's stay, so that the latter's angelic innocence was left entirely to the Baron's mercy. It suffered no worse mischance, however, than to be prompted to intenser communion with itself. M. de Mauves was the hero of the young girl's romance made real, and so completely accordant with this creature of her imagina-tion, that she felt afraid of him, very much as she would have been of a supernatural apparition. He was now thirty-five—young enough to suggest possibilities of ardent activity, and old enough to have formed opinions which a simple woman might deem it an intellectual privilege to listen to. He was perhaps a trifle handsomer than Euphemia's rather grim, Quixotic ideal, but a very few days reconciled her to his good looks, as effectually they would have reconciled her to his ugliness. He was quiet, grave, eminently distinguished. He spoke little, but his speeches, without being sententious, had a certain nobleness of tone which caused them to re-echo in the young girl's ears at the end of the day. He paid her very little direct attention, but his chance words—if he only asked her if she objected to his cigarette—were accompanied by a smile of extraordinary kindness.

It happened that shortly after his arrival, riding an unruly horse which Euphemia with shy admiration had watched him mount in the castle yard, he was thrown with a violence which, without disparaging his skill, made him for a fortnight an interesting invalid, lounging in the library with a bandaged knee. To beguile his confinement, Euphemia was repeatedly induced to sing to him, which she did with a little natural tremor in her voice which might have passed for an exquisite refinement of art. He never overwhelmed her with compliments, but he listened with unwandering attention, remembered all her melodies, and sat humming them to himself. While his imprisonment lasted, indeed, he passed hours in her company, and made her feel not unlike some unfriended artist who has suddenly gained the opportunity to devote a fortnight to the study of a great model. Euphemia studied with noiseless diligence what she supposed to be the "character" of M. de Mauves, and the more she looked, the more fine lights and shades she seemed to behold in this masterpiece of nature. M. de Mauves's character, indeed, whether from a sense of being generously scrutinised, or for reasons which bid graceful defiance to analysis, had never been so amiable; it seemed really to reflect the purity of Euphemia's interpretation of it. There had been nothing especially to admire in the state of mind in which he left Paris—a hard determination to marry a young girl whose charms might or might not justify his sister's account of them, but who was mistress, at the worst, of a couple of hundred thousand francs a year. He had not counted out sentiment; if she pleased him, so much the better; but he had left a meagre margin for it, and he would

hardly have admitted that so excellent a match could be improved by it. He was a placid sceptic, and it was a singular fate
for a man who believed in nothing to be so tenderly believed
in. What his original faith had been he could hardly have told
you; for as he came back to his childhood's home to mend his
fortunes by pretending to fall in love, he was a thoroughly
perverted creature, and overlaid with more corruptions than a
summer day's questioning of his conscience would have put
to flight. Ten years' pursuit of pleasure, which a bureau full of
unpaid bills was all he had to show for, had pretty well stifled
the natural lad whose violent will and generous temper might
have been shaped by other circumstances to a result which a
romantic imagination might fairly accept as a late-blooming
flower of hereditary honour. The Baron's violence had been
subdued, and he had learned to be irreproachably polite; but
he had lost the fineness of his generosity, and his politeness,
which in the long run society paid for, was hardly more than
a form of luxurious egotism, like his fondness for cambric
handkerchiefs, lavender gloves, and other fopperies by which
shopkeepers remained out of pocket. In after years he was terribly polite to his wife. He had formed himself, as the phrase
was, and the form prescribed to him by the society into which
his birth and his tastes introduced him was marked by some
peculiar features. That which mainly concerns us is its classifi-
cation of the fairer half of humanity as objects not essentially
different—say from the light gloves one soils in an evening
and throws away. To do M. de Mauves justice, he had in the
course of time encountered such plentiful evidence of this pli-
ant, glove-like quality in the feminine character, that idealism
naturally seemed to him a losing game.

Euphemia, as he lay on his sofa, seemed by no means a
refutation; she simply reminded him that very young women
are generally innocent, and that this, on the whole, is the
most charming stage of their development. Her innocence inspired him with profound respect, and it seemed to him that
if he shortly became her husband it would be exposed to a
danger the less. Old Madame de Mauves, who flattered herself that in this whole matter she was very laudably rigid,
might have learned a lesson from his gallant consideration.
For a fortnight the Baron was almost a blushing boy again.

He watched from behind the *Figaro*, and admired, and held his tongue. He was not in the least disposed towards a flirtation; he had no desire to trouble the waters he proposed to transfuse into the golden cup of matrimony. Sometimes a word, a look, a movement of Euphemia's, gave him the oddest sense of being, or of seeming at least, almost bashful; for she had a way of not dropping her eyes, according to the mysterious virginal mechanism—of not fluttering out of the room when she found him there alone, of treating him rather as a benignant than as a pernicious influence—a radiant frankness of demeanour, in fine, in spite of an evident natural reserve, which it seemed equally graceless not to make the subject of a compliment and indelicate not to take for granted. In this way there was wrought in the Baron's mind a vague, unwonted resonance of soft impressions, as we may call it, which indicated the transmutation of "sentiment" from a contingency into a fact. His imagination enjoyed it; he was very fond of music, and this reminded him of some of the best he had ever heard. In spite of the bore of being laid up with a lame knee, he was in a better humour than he had known for months; he lay smoking cigarettes and listening to the nightingales, with the comfortable smile of one of his country neighbours whose big ox should have taken the prize at a fair. Every now and then, with an impatient suspicion of the resemblance, he declared that he was pitifully *bête*; but he was under a charm which braved even the supreme penalty of seeming ridiculous. One morning he had half an hour's *tête-à-tête* with his grandmother's confessor, a soft-voiced old Abbé, whom, for reasons of her own, Madame de Mauves had suddenly summoned, and had left waiting in the drawing-room while she rearranged her curls. His reverence, going up to the old lady, assured her that M. le Baron was in a most edifying state of mind, and a promising subject for the operation of grace. This was a theological interpretation of the Baron's momentary good-humour. He had always lazily wondered what priests were good for, and he now remembered, with a sense of especial obligation to the Abbé, that they were excellent for marrying people.

A day or two after this he left off his bandages, and tried to walk. He made his way into the garden and hobbled successfully along one of the alleys; but in the midst of his progress he was seized with a spasm of pain which forced him to stop and call for help. In an instant Euphemia came tripping along the path and offered him her arm with the frankest solicitude.

"Not to the house," he said, taking it; "further on, to the bosquet." This choice was prompted by her having immediately confessed that she had seen him leave the house, had feared an accident, and had followed him on tiptoe.

"Why didn't you join me?" he had asked, giving her a look in which admiration was no longer disguised, and yet felt itself half at the mercy of her replying that a *jeune fille* should not be seen following a gentleman. But it drew a breath which filled its lungs for a long time afterwards, when she replied simply that if she had overtaken him he might have accepted her arm out of politeness, whereas she wished to have the pleasure of seeing him walk alone.

The bosquet was covered with an odorous tangle of blossoming creepers, and a nightingale overhead was shaking out love-notes with a profuseness which made the Baron consider his own conduct the perfection of propriety.

"In America," he said, "I have always heard that when a man wishes to marry a young girl, he offers himself simply, face to face, without any ceremony—without parents, and uncles, and cousins sitting round in a circle."

"Why, I believe so," said Euphemia, staring, and too surprised to be alarmed.

"Very well, then," said the Baron, "suppose our bosquet here to be America. I offer you my hand, à l'Américaine. It will make me intensely happy to see you accept it."

Whether Euphemia's acceptance was in the American manner is more than I can say; I incline to think that for fluttering, grateful, trustful, softly-amazed young hearts, there is only one manner all over the world.

That evening, in the little turret chamber which it was her happiness to inhabit, she wrote a dutiful letter to her mamma, and had just sealed it when she was sent for by Madame de Mauves. She found this ancient lady seated in her boudoir, in a lavender satin gown, with all her candles lighted, as if to celebrate her grandson's betrothal. "Are you very happy?"

Madame de Mauves demanded, making Euphemia sit down before her.

"I am almost afraid to say so," said the young girl, "lest I should wake myself up."

"May you never wake up, *belle enfant*," said the old lady, solemnly. "This is the first marriage ever made in our family in this way—by a Baron de Mauves proposing to a young girl in an arbour, like Jeannot and Jeannette. It has not been our way of doing things, and people may say it wants frankness. My grandson tells me he considers it the perfection of frankness. Very good. I am a very old woman, and if your differences should ever be as marked as your agreement, I should not like to see them. But I should be sorry to die and think you were going to be unhappy. You can't be, beyond a certain point; because, though in this world the Lord sometimes makes light of our expectations, He never altogether ignores our deserts. But you are very young and innocent, and easy to deceive. There never was a man in the world—among the saints themselves—as good as you believe the Baron. But he's a *galant homme* and a gentleman, and I have been talking to him to-night. To you I want to say this—that you're to forget the worldly rubbish I talked the other day about frivolous women being happy. It's not the kind of happiness that would suit you. Whatever befalls you, promise me this: to be yourself. The Baronne de Mauves will be none the worse for it. Yourself, understand, in spite of everything—bad precepts and bad examples, bad usage, even. Be persistently and patiently yourself, and a De Mauves will do you justice!"

Euphemia remembered this speech in after years, and more than once, wearily closing her eyes, she seemed to see the old woman sitting upright in her faded finery and smiling grimly, like one of the Fates who sees the wheel of fortune turning up her favourite event. But at the moment it seemed to her simply to have the proper gravity of the occasion; this was the way, she supposed, in which lucky young girls were addressed on their engagement by wise old women of quality.

At her convent, to which she immediately returned, she found a letter from her mother, which shocked her far more than the remarks of Madame de Mauves. Who were these people, Mrs. Cleve demanded, who had presumed to talk to her daughter of marriage without asking her leave? Questionable gentlefolk, plainly; the best French people never did such things. Euphemia would return straightway to her convent, shut herself up, and await her own arrival.

It took Mrs. Cleve three weeks to travel from Nice to Paris, and during this time the young girl had no communication with her lover beyond accepting a bouquet of violets, marked with his initials and left by a female friend. "I have not brought you up with such devoted care," she declared to her daughter at their first interview, "to marry a penniless Frenchman. I will take you straight home, and you will please to forget M. de Mauves."

Mrs. Cleve received that evening at her hotel a visit from the Baron which mitigated her wrath, but failed to modify her decision. He had very good manners, but she was sure he had horrible morals; and Mrs. Cleve, who had been a very good-natured censor on her own account, felt a genuine spiritual need to sacrifice her daughter to propriety. She belonged to that large class of Americans who make light of their native land in familiar discourse, but are startled back into a sense of moral responsibility when they find Europeans taking them at their word. "I know the type, my dear," she said to her daughter with a sagacious nod. "He will not beat you; sometimes you will wish he would."

Euphemia remained solemnly silent; for the only answer she felt capable of making her mother was that her mind was too small a measure of things, and that the Baron's type was one which it took some mystical illumination to appreciate. A person who confounded him with the common throng of her watering-place acquaintance was not a person to argue with. It seemed to Euphemia that she had no cause to plead; her cause was in the Lord's hands and her lover's.

M. de Mauves had been irritated and mortified by Mrs. Cleve's opposition, and hardly knew how to handle an adversary who failed to perceive that a De Mauves of necessity gave more than he received. But he had obtained information on his return to Paris which exalted the uses of humility. Euphemia's fortune, wonderful to say, was greater than its fame, and in view of such a prize, even a De Mauves could afford to take a snubbing.

The young man's tact, his deference, his urbane insistence, won a concession from Mrs. Cleve. The engagement was to be put off and her daughter was to return home, be brought out and receive the homage she was entitled to, and which would but too surely take a form dangerous to the Baron's suit. They were to exchange neither letters, nor mementos, nor messages; but if at the end of two years Euphemia had refused offers enough to attest the permanence of her attachment, he should receive an invitation to address her again.

This decision was promulgated in the presence of the parties interested. The Baron bore himself gallantly, and looked at the young girl, expecting some tender protestation. But she only looked at him silently in return, neither weeping, nor smiling, nor putting out her hand. On this they separated; but as the Baron walked away, he declared to himself that, in spite of the confounded two years, he was a very happy fellow—to have a fiancée who, to several millions of francs, added such strangely beautiful eyes.

How many offers Euphemia refused but scantily concerns us —and how the Baron wore his two years away. He found that he needed pastimes, and, as pastimes were expensive, he added heavily to the list of debts to be cancelled by Euphemia's millions. Sometimes, in the thick of what he had once called pleasure with a keener conviction than now, he put to himself the case of their failing him after all; and then he remembered that last mute assurance of her eyes, and drew a long breath of such confidence as he felt in nothing else in the world save his own punctuality in an affair of honour.

At last, one morning, he took the express to Havre with a letter of Mrs. Cleve's in his pocket, and ten days later made his bow to mother and daughter in New York. His stay was brief, and he was apparently unable to bring himself to view what Euphemia's uncle, Mr. Butterworth, who gave her away at the altar, called our great experiment in democratic self-government, in a serious light. He smiled at everything, and seemed to regard the New World as a colossal *plaisanterie.* It is true that a perpetual smile was the most natural expression of countenance for a man about to marry Euphemia Cleve.

III.

Longmore's first visit seemed to open to him so large an opportunity for tranquil enjoyment that he very soon paid a second, and, at the end of a fortnight, had spent a great many hours in the little drawing-room which Madame de Mauves rarely quitted except to drive or walk in the forest. She lived in an old-fashioned pavilion, between a high-walled court and an excessively artificial garden, beyond whose enclosure you saw a long line of tree-tops. Longmore liked the garden, and in the mild afternoons used to move his chair through the open window to the little terrace which overlooked it, while his hostess sat just within. After a while she came out and wandered through the narrow alleys and beside the thin-spouting fountain, and at last introduced him to a little gate in the garden-wall, opening upon a lane which led to the forest. Hitherward, more than once, she wandered with him, bareheaded and meaning to go but twenty rods, but always strolling good-naturedly further, and often taking a generous walk. They discovered many things to talk about, and to the pleasure of finding the hours tread inaudibly away, Longmore was able to add the satisfaction of suspecting that he was a "resource" for Madame de Mauves. He had made her acquaintance with the sense, not altogether comfortable, that she was a woman with a painful secret, and that seeking her acquaintance would be like visiting at a house where there was an invalid who could bear no noise. But he very soon perceived that her sorrow, since sorrow it was, was not an aggressive one; that it was not fond of attitudes and ceremonies, and that her earnest wish was to forget it. He felt that even if Mrs. Draper had not told him she was unhappy, he would have guessed it; and yet he could hardly have pointed to his evidence. It was chiefly negative—she never alluded to her husband. Beyond this it seemed to him simply that her whole being was pitched on a lower key than harmonious Nature meant; she was like a powerful singer who had lost her high notes. She never drooped nor sighed nor looked unutterable things; she indulged in no dusky sarcasms against fate; she had, in short, none of the coquetry of unhappiness. But Longmore was sure that her gentle gaiety was the result of strenuous effort, and that she was trying to interest herself in his thoughts to escape from her own. If she had wished to irritate his curiosity and lead him to take her confidence by storm, nothing could have served her purpose better than this ingenuous reserve. He declared to himself that there was a rare magnanimity in such ardent self-effacement, and that but one woman in ten thousand was capable of merging an intensely personal grief in thankless outward contemplation. Madame de Mauves, he instinctively felt, was not sweeping the horizon for a compensation or a consoler; she had suffered a personal deception which had disgusted her with persons. She was not striving to balance her sorrow with some strongly seasoned joy; for the present, she was trying to live with it, peaceably, reputably, and without scandal—turning the key on it occasionally, as you would on a companion liable to attacks of insanity. Longmore was a man of fine senses and of an active imagination, whose leading-strings had never been slipped. He began to regard his hostess as a figure haunted by a shadow which was somehow her intenser, more authentic self. This hovering mystery came to have for him an extraordinary charm. Her delicate beauty acquired to his eye the serious cast of certain blank-browed Greek statues; and sometimes, when his imagination, more than his ear, detected a vague tremor in the tone in which she attempted to make a friendly question seemed to have behind it none of the hollow resonance of absent-mindedness, his marvelling eyes gave her an answer more eloquent, though much less to the point, than the one she demanded.

She gave him indeed much to wonder about, and, in his ignorance he formed a dozen experimental theories on the subject of her marriage. She had married for love and staked her whole soul on it; of that he was convinced. She had not married a Frenchman to be near Paris and her base of supplies of millinery; he was sure she had seen conjugal happiness in a light of which her present life, with its conveniences for shopping and its moral aridity, was the absolute negation. But by what extraordinary process of the heart—through what mysterious intermission of that moral instinct which may keep pace with the heart, even when this organ is making unprecedented time—had she fixed her affections on an arrogantly frivolous Frenchman? Longmore needed no telling; he knew M. de Mauves was frivolous; it was stamped on his eyes, his nose, his mouth, his carriage. For Frenchwomen Longmore had but a scanty kindness, or at least (what with him was very much the same thing) but a scanty gallantry; they all seemed to belong to the type of a certain fine lady to whom he had ventured to present a letter of introduction, and whom, directly after his first visit to her, he had set down in his notebook as "metallic." Why should Madame de Mauves have chosen a Frenchwoman's lot—she whose character had a perfume which is absent from even the brightest metals? He asked her one day frankly if it had cost her nothing to transplant herself—if she were not oppressed with a sense of irreconcilable difference from "all these people." She was silent a while, and he fancied that she was hesitating as to whether she should resent so unceremonious an allusion to her husband. He almost wished she would; it would seem a proof that her deep reserve of sorrow had a limit.

"I almost grew up here," she said at last, "and it was here for me that those dreams of the future took shape that we all have when we cease to be very young. As matters stand, one may be very American and yet arrange it with one's conscience to live in Europe. My imagination perhaps—I had a little when I was younger—helped me to think I should find happiness here. And after all, for a woman, what does it signify? This is not America, perhaps, about me, but it's quite as little France. France is out there, beyond the garden, in the town, in the forest; but here, close about me, in my room and"—she paused a moment—"in my mind, it's a nameless country of my own. It's not her country," she added, "that makes a woman happy or unhappy."

Madame Clairin, Euphemia's sister-in-law, might have been supposed to have undertaken the graceful task of making Longmore ashamed of his uncivil jottings about her sex and nation. Mademoiselle de Mauves, bringing example to the confirmation of precept, had made a remunerative match and sacrificed her name to the millions of a prosperous and aspiring wholesale druggist—a gentleman liberal enough to consider his fortune a moderate price for being towed into circles unpervaded by pharmaceutic odours. His system, possibly, was sound, but his own application of it was unfortunate. M. Clairin's head was turned by his good luck. Having secured an aristocratic wife, he adopted an aristocratic vice and began to gamble at the Bourse. In an evil hour he lost heavily, and then staked heavily to recover himself. But he overtook his loss only by a greater one. Then he let everything go—his wits, his courage, his probity—everything that had made him what his ridiculous marriage had so promptly unmade. He walked up the Rue Vivienne one day with his hands in his empty pockets, and stood for half an hour staring confusedly up and down the glittering Boulevard. People brushed against him, and half a dozen carriages almost ran over him, until at last a policeman, who had been watching him for some time, took him by the arm and led him gently away. He looked at the man's cocked hat and sword with tears in his eyes; he hoped he was going to interpret to him the wrath of Heaven—to execute the penalty of his dead-weight of self-abhorrence. But the *sergent de ville* only stationed him in the embrasure of a door, out of harm's way, and walked away to supervise a financial contest between an old lady and a cabman. Poor M. Clairin had only been married a year, but he had had time to measure the lofty spirit of a De Mauves. When night had fallen, he repaired to the house of a friend and asked for a night's lodging; and as his friend, who was simply his old head book-keeper, and lived in a small way, was put to some trouble to accommodate him—"You must excuse me," Clairin said, "but I can't go home. I am afraid of my wife!" Towards morning he blew his brains out. His widow turned the remnants of his property to better account than could have been expected, and wore the very handsomest mourning. It was for this latter reason, perhaps, that she was obliged to retrench at other points, and accept a temporary home under her brother's roof.

Fortune had played Madame Clairin a terrible trick, but had found an adversary and not a victim. Though quite without beauty, she had always had what is called the grand air, and her air from this time forward was grander than ever. As she trailed about in her sable furbelows, tossing back her well-dressed head, and holding up her vigilant eye-glass, she seemed to be sweeping the whole field of society and asking

herself where she should pluck her revenge. Suddenly she espied it, ready made to her hand, in poor Longmore's wealth
and amiability. American dollars and American complaisance
had made her brother's fortune; why should they not make
hers? She over-estimated Longmore's wealth and misinter-
preted his amiability; for she was sure that a man could not be
so contented without being rich, nor so unassuming without
being weak. He encountered her advances with a formal politeness which covered a great deal of unflattering discomposure. She made him feel acutely uncomfortable; and though
he was at a loss to conceive how he could be an object of interest to a shrewd Parisienne, he had an indefinable sense of
being enclosed in a magnetic circle, like the victim of an in-
cantation. If Madame Clairin could have fathomed his
Puritanic soul, she would have laid by her wand and her book
and admitted that he was an impossible subject. She gave him
a kind of moral chill, and he never mentally alluded to her
save as that dreadful woman—that terrible woman. He did
justice to her grand air, but for his pleasure he preferred the
small air of Madame de Mauves; and he never made her his
bow, after standing frigidly passive for five minutes to one of
her gracious overtures to intimacy, without feeling a peculiar
desire to ramble away into the forest, fling himself down on
the warm grass, and, staring up at the blue sky, forget that
there were any women in nature who didn't please like the
swaying tree-tops. One day, on his arrival, she met him in the
court and told him that her sister-in-law was shut up with a
headache, and that his visit must be for her. He followed her
into the drawing-room with the best grace at his command,
and sat twirling his hat for half an hour. Suddenly he understood her; the caressing cadence of her voice was a distinct invitation to solicit the incomparable honour of her hand. He
blushed to the roots of his hair and jumped up with uncontrollable alacrity; then, dropping a glance at Madame
Clairin, who sat watching him with hard eyes over the edge
of her smile, as it were, perceived on her brow a flash of un-
forgiving wrath. It was not becoming, but his eyes lingered a
moment, for it seemed to illuminate her character. What he
saw there frightened him and he felt himself murmuring,
"Poor Madame de Mauves!" His departure was abrupt, and

this time he really went into the forest and lay down on the grass.

After this he admired Madame de Mauves more than ever; she seemed a brighter figure, with a darker shadow appended to it. At the end of a month he received a letter from a friend with whom he had arranged a tour through the Low Countries, reminding him of his promise to meet him promptly at Brussels. It was only after his answer was posted that he fully measured the zeal with which he had declared that the journey must either be deferred or abandoned—that he could not possibly leave Saint-Germain. He took a walk in the forest, and asked himself if this were irrevocably true. If it were, surely his duty was to march straight home and pack his trunk. Poor Webster, who, he knew, had counted ardently on this excursion, was an excellent fellow; six weeks ago he would have gone through fire and water to join Webster. It had never been in his books to throw overboard a friend whom he had loved for ten years for a married woman whom for six weeks he had—admired. It was certainly beyond question that he was lingering at Saint-Germain because this admirable married woman was there; but in the midst of all this admiration, what had become of prudence? This was the conduct of a man drifting rapidly into passion. If she were as unhappy as he believed, the passion of such a man would help her very little more than his indifference; if she were less so, she needed no help, and could dispense with his friendly offices. He was sure, moreover, that if she knew he was staying on her account she would be extremely annoyed. But this very feeling had much to do with making it hard to go; her displeasure would only enhance the gentle stoicism which touched him to the heart. At moments, indeed, he assured himself that to linger was simply impertinent; it was indelicate to make a daily study of such a shrinking grief. But inclination answered that some day her self-support would fail, and he had a vision of this admirable creature calling vainly for help. He would be her friend, to any length; it was unworthy to both of them to think about consequences. But he was a friend who carried about with him a muttering resentment that he had not known her five years earlier, and a brooding hostility to those who had anticipated him. It seemed one of fortune's most mocking strokes, that she should be surrounded by persons whose only merit was that they threw the charm of her character into radiant relief.

Longmore's growing irritation made it more and more difficult for him to see any other merit than this in the Baron de Mauves. And yet, disinterestedly, it would have been hard to give a name to the portentous vices which such an estimate implied, and there were times when our hero was almost persuaded against his finer judgment that he was really the most considerate of husbands, and that his wife liked melancholy for melancholy's sake. His manners were perfect, his urbanity was unbounded, and he seemed never to address her but, sentimentally speaking, hat in hand. His tone to Longmore (as the latter was perfectly aware) was that of a man of the world to a man not quite of the world; but what it lacked in deference it made up in easy friendliness. "I can't thank you enough for having overcome my wife's shyness," he more than once declared. "If we left her to do as she pleased, she would bury herself alive. Come often, and bring some one else. She will have nothing to do with my friends, but perhaps she will look at yours."

The Baron made these speeches with a remorseless placidity very amazing to our hero, who had an innocent belief that a man's head may point out to him the shortcomings of his heart, and make him ashamed of them. He could not fancy him capable both of neglecting his wife and taking an almost humorous view of her suffering. Longmore had, at any rate, an exasperating sense that the Baron thought rather the less of his wife on account of that very same fine difference of nature which so deeply stirred his own sympathies. He was rarely present during Longmore's visits, and he made a daily journey to Paris, where he had "business," as he once mentioned—not in the least with a tone of apology. When he appeared, it was late in the evening, and with an imperturbable air of being on the best of terms with every one and every thing, which was peculiarly annoying if you happened to have a tacit quarrel with him. If he was a good fellow, he was surely a good fellow spoiled. Something he had, however, which Longmore vaguely envied—a kind of superb positiveness—a manner rounded and polished by the traditions of centuries—

an urbanity exercised for his own sake and not his neighbours'—which seemed the result of something better than a
good conscience—of a vigorous and unscrupulous temperament. The Baron was plainly not a moral man, and poor
Longmore, who was, would have been glad to learn the secret
of his luxurious serenity. What was it that enabled him, without being a monster with visibly cloven feet, exhaling brim-
stone, to misprize so cruelly a lovely wife, and to walk about
the world with a candid smile under his moustache? It was the
essential grossness of his imagination, which had nevertheless
helped him to turn so many neat compliments. He could be
very polite, and he could doubtless be supremely impertinent;
but he was as unable to draw a moral inference of the finer
strain as a school-boy who has been playing truant for a week
to solve a problem in algebra. It was ten to one he did not
know his wife was unhappy; he and his brilliant sister had
doubtless agreed to consider their companion a Puritanical
little person, of meagre aspirations and slender accomplishments, contented with looking at Paris from the terrace, and,
as an especial treat, having a countryman very much like herself to supply her with homely transatlantic gossip. M. de
Mauves was tired of his companion; he relished a higher
flavour in female society. She was too modest, too simple, too
delicate; she had too few arts, too little coquetry, too much
charity. M. de Mauves, some day, lighting a cigar, had probably decided she was stupid. It was the same sort of taste,
Longmore moralised, as the taste for Gérôme in painting, and
for M. Charles Baudelaire in literature. The Baron was a
pagan and his wife was a Christian, and between them, accordingly, was a gulf. He was by race and instinct a *grand
seigneur*. Longmore had often heard of this distinguished
social type, and was properly grateful for an opportunity to
examine it closely. It had certainly a picturesque boldness of
outline, but it was fed from spiritual sources so remote from
those of which he felt the living gush of his own soul, that he
found himself gazing at it, in irreconcilable antipathy, across a
dim historic mist. "I am a modern *bourgeois*," he said, "and
not perhaps so good a judge of how far a pretty woman's
tongue may go at supper without prejudice to her reputation.
But I have not met one of the sweetest of women without

recognising her, and discovering that a certain sort of character offers better entertainment than Thérésa's songs, sung by a dissipated duchess. Wit for wit, I think mine carries me further." It was easy indeed to perceive that, as became a *grand seigneur*, M. de Mauves had a stock of social principles. He would not especially have desired, perhaps, that his wife should compete in amateur operettas with the duchesses in question, chiefly of recent origin; but he held that a gentleman may take his amusement where he finds it, that he is quite at liberty not to find it at home, and that the wife of a De Mauves who should hang her head and have red eyes, and allow herself to make any other response to officious condolence than that her husband's amusements were his own affair, would have forfeited every claim to having her finger-tips bowed over and kissed. And yet in spite of this definite faith, Longmore fancied that the Baron was more irritated than gratified by his wife's irreproachable reserve. Did it dimly occur to him that it was self-control and not self-effacement? She was a model to all the inferior matrons of his line, past and to come, and an occasional "scene" from her at a convenient moment would have something reassuring—would attest her stupidity a trifle more forcibly than her inscrutable tranquillity.

Longmore would have given much to know the principle of her submissiveness, and he tried more than once, but with rather awkward timidity, to sound the mystery. She seemed to him to have been long resisting the force of cruel evidence, and, though she had succumbed to it at last, to have denied herself the right to complain, because if faith was gone, her heroic generosity remained. He believed even that she was capable of reproaching herself with having expected too much, and of trying to persuade herself out of her bitterness by saying that her hopes had been illusions and that this was simply—life. "I hate tragedy," she once said to him; "I have a really pusillanimous dread of moral suffering. I believe that—without base concessions—there is always some way of escaping from it. I would almost rather never smile all my life than have a single violent explosion of grief." She lived evidently in nervous apprehension of being fatally convinced—of seeing to the end of her deception. Longmore, when he thought of this, felt an immense longing to offer her something of which she could be as sure as of the sun in heaven.

IV.

His friend Webster lost no time in accusing him of the basest infidelity, and asking him what he found at Saint-Germain to prefer to Van Eyck and Memling, Rubens and Rembrandt. A day or two after the receipt of Webster's letter, he took a walk with Madame de Mauves in the forest. They sat down on a fallen log, and she began to arrange into a bouquet the anemones and violets she had gathered. "I have a letter," he said at last, "from a friend whom I some time ago promised to join at Brussels. The time has come—it has passed. It finds me terribly unwilling to leave Saint-Germain."

She looked up with the candid interest which she always displayed in his affairs, but with no disposition, apparently, to make a personal application of his words. "Saint-Germain is pleasant enough," she said; "but are you doing yourself justice? Shall you not regret in future days that instead of travelling and seeing cities and monuments and museums and improving your mind, you sat here—for instance—on a log, pulling my flowers to pieces?"

"What I shall regret in future days," he answered after some hesitation, "is that I should have sat here and not spoken the truth on the matter. I am fond of museums and monuments and of improving my mind, and I am particularly fond of my friend Webster. But I can't bring myself to leave Saint-Germain without asking you a question. You must forgive me if it's indiscreet, and be assured that curiosity was never more respectful. Are you really as unhappy as I imagine you to be?"

She had evidently not expected his question, and she greeted it with a startled blush. "If I strike you as unhappy," she said, "I have been a poorer friend to you than I wished to be."

"I, perhaps, have been a better friend of yours than you have supposed. I have admired your reserve, your courage, your studied gaiety. But I have felt the existence of something beneath them that was more *you*—more you as I wished to know you—than they were; something that I have believed to be a constant sorrow."

She listened with great gravity, but without an air of offence, and he felt that while he had been timorously calculating the last consequences of friendship, she had serenely accepted them. "You surprise me," she said slowly, and her blush still lingered. "But to refuse to answer you would confirm an impression on your part which is evidently already too strong. An unhappiness that one can sit comfortably talking about, is an unhappiness with distinct limitations. If I were examined before a board of commissioners for investigating the felicity of mankind, I am sure I should be pronounced a very fortunate woman." There was something delightfully gentle to him in her tone, and its softness seemed to deepen as she continued. "But let me add, with all gratitude for your sympathy, that it's my own affair altogether. It need not disturb you, Mr. Longmore, for I have often found myself in your company a very contented person."

"You are a wonderful woman," he said, "and I admire you as I never have admired any one. You are wiser than anything I, for one, can say to you; and what I ask of you is not to let me advise or console you, but simply thank you for letting me know you." He had intended no such outburst as this, but his voice rang loud, and he felt a kind of unfamiliar joy as he uttered it.

She shook her head with some impatience. "Let us be friends—as I supposed we were going to be—without protestations and fine words. To have you paying compliments to my wisdom—that would be real wretchedness. I can dispense with your admiration better than the Flemish painters can —better than Van Eyck and Rubens, in spite of all their worshippers. Go join your friend—see everything, enjoy everything, learn everything, and write me an excellent letter, brimming over with your impressions. I am extremely fond of the Dutch painters," she added, with a slight faltering of the voice, which Longmore had noticed once before, and which he had interpreted as the sudden weariness of a spirit self-condemned to play a part.

"I don't believe you care a button about the Dutch

painters," he said, with an unhesitating laugh. "But I shall certainly write you a letter."

She rose and turned homeward, thoughtfully rearranging her flowers as she walked. Little was said; Longmore was asking himself, with a tremor in the unspoken words, whether all this meant simply that he was in love. He looked at the rooks wheeling against the golden-hued sky, between the tree-tops, but not at his companion, whose personal presence seemed lost in the felicity she had created. Madame de Mauves was silent and grave, because she was painfully disappointed. A sentimental friendship she had not desired; her scheme had been to pass with Longmore as a placid creature with a good deal of leisure, which she was disposed to devote to profitable conversation of an impersonal sort. She liked him extremely, and felt that there was something in him to which, when she made up her girlish mind that a needy French baron was the ripest fruit of time, she had done very scanty justice. They went through the little gate in the garden wall and approached the house. On the terrace Madame Clairin was entertaining a friend—a little elderly gentleman with a white moustache, and an order in his button-hole. Madame de Mauves chose to pass round the house into the court; whereupon her sister-in-law, greeting Longmore with a commanding nod, lifted her eyeglass and stared at them as they went by. Longmore heard the little old gentleman uttering some old-fashioned epigram about "la vieille galanterie Française," and then, by a sudden impulse, he looked at Madame de Mauves and wondered what she was doing in such a world. She stopped before the house, without asking him to come in. "I hope you will act upon my advice," she said, "and waste no more time at Saint-Germain."

For an instant there rose to his lips some faded compliment about his time not being wasted, but it expired before the simple sincerity of her look. She stood there as gently serious as the angel of disinterestedness, and Longmore felt as if he should insult her by treating her words as a bait for flattery. "I shall start in a day or two," he answered, "but I will not promise you not to come back."

"I hope not," she said, simply. "I expect to be here a long time."

"I shall come and say good-bye," he rejoined; on which she nodded with a smile, and went in.

He turned away, and walked slowly homeward by the terrace. It seemed to him that to leave her thus, for a gain on which she herself insisted, was to know her better and admire her more. But he was in a vague ferment of feeling which her evasion of his question half an hour before had done more to deepen than to allay. Suddenly, on the terrace, he encountered M. de Mauves, who was leaning against the parapet, finishing a cigar. The Baron, who, he fancied, had an air of peculiar affability, offered him his white plump hand. Longmore stopped; he felt a sudden angry desire to cry out to him that he had the loveliest wife in the world; that he ought to be ashamed of himself not to know it; and that for all his shrewdness he had never looked into the depths of her eyes. The Baron, we know, considered that he had; but there was something in Euphemia's eyes now that was not there five years before. They talked for a while about various things, and M. de Mauves gave a humorous account of his visit to America. His tone was not soothing to Longmore's excited sensibilities. He seemed to consider the country a gigantic joke, and his urbanity only went so far as to admit that it was not a bad one. Longmore was not, by habit, an aggressive apologist for his native institutions; but the Baron's narrative confirmed his worst impressions of French superficiality. He had understood nothing, he had felt nothing, he had learned nothing; and our hero, glancing askance at his aristocratic profile, declared that if the chief merit of a long pedigree was to leave one so fatuously stupid, he thanked his stars that the Longmores had emerged from obscurity in the present century, in the person of an enterprising timber-merchant. M. de Mauves dwelt of course on that prime oddity of ours—the liberty allowed to young girls; and related the history of his researches into the "opportunities" it presented to French noblemen—researches in which, during a fortnight's stay, he seemed to have spent many agreeable hours. "I am bound to admit," he said, "that in every case I was disarmed by the extreme candour of the young lady, and that they took care of themselves to better purpose than I have seen some mammas in France take care of them." Longmore greeted this handsome concession with the grimmest of smiles, and damned his impertinent patronage.

Mentioning at last that he was about to leave Saint-Germain, he was surprised, without exactly being flattered, by the Baron's quickened attention. "I am so very sorry!" the latter cried. "I hoped we had you for the whole summer." Longmore murmured something civil, and wondered why M. de Mauves should care whether he stayed or went. "You were a distraction to Madame de Mauves," the Baron added; "I assure you I mentally blessed your visits."

"They were a great pleasure to me," Longmore said, gravely. "Some day I expect to come back."

"Pray do;" and the Baron laid his hand urgently on his arm. "You see I have confidence in you." Longmore was silent for a moment, and the Baron puffed his cigar reflectively and watched the smoke. "Madame de Mauves," he said at last, "is a rather singular person."

Longmore shifted his position, and wondered whether he were going to "explain" Madame de Mauves.

"Being, as you are, her fellow-countryman," the Baron went on, "I don't mind speaking frankly. She's just a little morbid—the most charming woman in the world, as you see, but a little fanciful—a little *entêtée*. Now you see she has taken this extraordinary fancy for solitude. I can't get her to go anywhere—to see any one. When my friends present themselves she is perfectly polite, but she is simply freezing. She doesn't do herself justice, and I expect every day to hear two or three of them say to me, 'Your wife is *jolie à croquer*: what a pity she hasn't a little *esprit*.' You must have found out that she has really a great deal. But to tell the whole truth, what she needs is to forget herself. She sits alone for hours poring over her English books and looking at life through that terrible brown fog which they always seem to me to fling over the world. I doubt if your English authors," the Baron continued, with a serenity which Longmore afterwards characterised as sublime, "are very sound reading for young married women. I don't pretend to know much about them; but I remember that, not long after our marriage, Madame de Mauves undertook to read me one day a certain Wordsworth—a poet highly esteemed, it appears, *chez vous*. It seemed to me that she took me by the nape of the neck and held my head for half an hour over a basin of *soupe aux choux*, and that one ought to ventilate the drawing-room before any one called. But I suppose you know him—*ce génie-là*. I think my wife never forgave me, and that it was a real shock to her to find she had married a man who had very much the same taste in literature as in cookery. But you are a man of general culture—a man of the world," said the Baron, turning to Longmore and fixing his eyes on the seal of his watchguard. "You can talk about everything, and I am sure you like Alfred de Musset as well as Monsieur Wordsworth. Talk to her about everything, Alfred de Musset included. Bah! I forgot that you are going. Come back then as soon as possible and talk about your travels. If Madame de Mauves too would make a little voyage, it would do her good. It would enlarge her horizon"—and M. de Mauves made a series of short nervous jerks with his stick in the air—"it would wake up her imagination. She's too rigid, you know—it would show her that one may bend a trifle without breaking." He paused a moment and gave two or three vigorous puffs. Then, turning to his companion again, with a little nod and a confidential smile—"I hope you admire my candour. I wouldn't say all this to one of *us*!"

Evening was coming on, and the lingering light seemed to float in the air in faintly golden motes. Longmore stood gazing at these luminous particles; he could almost have fancied them a swarm of humming insects, murmuring as a refrain, "She has a great deal of *esprit*—she has a great deal of *esprit*." "Yes, she has a great deal," he said, mechanically, turning to the Baron. M. de Mauves glanced at him sharply, as if to ask what the deuce he was talking about. "She has a great deal of intelligence," said Longmore, deliberately, "a great deal of beauty, a great many virtues."

M. de Mauves busied himself for a moment in lighting another cigar, and when he had finished, with a return of his confidential smile, "I suspect you of thinking that I don't do my wife justice," he said. "Take care—take care, young man; that's a dangerous assumption. In general a man always does his wife justice. More than justice," cried the Baron with a laugh—"that we keep for the wives of other men!"

Longmore afterwards remembered it in favour of the

Baron's fine manner that he had not measured at this moment the dusky abyss over which it hovered. But a sort of deepening subterranean echo lingered on his spiritual ear. For the present his keenest sensation was a desire to get away and cry aloud that M. de Mauves was an arrogant fool. He bade him an abrupt good-night, which was to serve also, he said, as good-bye.

"Decidedly, then, you go?" said M. de Mauves, almost peremptorily.

"Decidedly."

"Of course you will come and say good-bye to Madame de Mauves?" His tone implied that the omission would be very uncivil; but there seemed to Longmore something so ludicrous in his taking a lesson in consideration from M. de Mauves, that he burst into a laugh. The Baron frowned, like a man for whom it was a new and most unpleasant sensation to be perplexed. "You are a queer fellow," he murmured, as Longmore turned away, not foreseeing that he should think him a very queer fellow indeed before he had done with him.

Longmore sat down to dinner at his hotel with his usual good intentions; but as he was lifting his first glass of wine to his lips, he suddenly fell to musing and set down his wine untasted. His reverie lasted long, and when he emerged from it, his fish was cold; but this mattered little, for his appetite was gone. That evening he packed his trunk with a kind of indignant energy. This was so effective that the operation was accomplished before bedtime, and as he was not in the least sleepy, he devoted the interval to writing two letters; one was a short note to Madame de Mauves, which he intrusted to a servant, to be delivered the next morning. He had found it best, he said, to leave Saint-Germain immediately, but he expected to be back in Paris in the early autumn. The other letter was the result of his having remembered a day or two before that he had not yet complied with Mrs. Draper's injunction to give her an account of his impressions of her friend. The present occasion seemed propitious, and he wrote half a dozen pages. His tone, however, was grave, and Mrs. Draper, on receiving them, was slightly disappointed—she would have preferred a stronger flavour of rhapsody. But what chiefly concerns us is the concluding sentences.

"The only time she ever spoke to me of her marriage," he wrote, "she intimated that it had been a perfect love-match. With all abatements, I suppose most marriages are; but in her case, I think, this would mean more than in that of most women; for her love was an absolute idealisation. She believed her husband was a hero of rose-coloured romance, and he turns out to be not even a hero of very sad-coloured reality. For some time now she has been sounding her mistake, but I don't believe she has touched the bottom of it yet. She strikes me as a person who is begging off from full knowledge—who has struck a truce with painful truth, and is trying a while the experiment of living with closed eyes. In the dark she tries to see again the gilding on her idol. Illusion of course is illusion, and one must always pay for it; but there is something truly tragical in seeing an earthly penalty levied on such divine folly as this. As for M. de Mauves, he's a Frenchman to his fingers' ends; and I confess I should dislike him for this if he were a much better man. He can't forgive his wife for having married him too sentimentally and loved him too well; for in some uncorrupted corner of his being he feels, I suppose, that as she saw him, so he ought to have been. It is a perpetual vexation to him that a little American bourgeoise should have fancied him a finer fellow than he is, or than he at all wants to be. He has not a glimmering of real acquaintance with his wife; he can't understand the stream of passion flowing so clear and still. To tell the truth, I hardly can understand it myself; but when I see the spectacle I can admire it furiously. M. de Mauves, at any rate, would like to have the comfort of feeling that his wife is as corruptible as himself; and you will hardly believe me when I tell you that he goes about intimating to gentlemen whom he deems worthy of the knowledge, that it would be a convenience to him that they should make love to her."

V.

On reaching Paris, Longmore straightway purchased a Murray's *Belgium*, to help himself to believe that he would start on the morrow for Brussels; but when the morrow came, it occurred to him that, by way of preparation, he ought to acquaint himself more intimately with the Flemish painters in the Louvre. This took a whole morning, but it did little to hasten his departure. He had abruptly left Saint-Germain, because it seemed to him that respect for Madame de Mauves demanded that he should allow her husband no reason to suppose that he had understood him; but now that he had satisfied the behest of delicacy, he found himself thinking more and more ardently of Euphemia. It was a poor expression of ardour to be lingering irresolutely on the deserted Boulevards, but he detested the idea of leaving Saint-Germain five hundred miles behind him. He felt very foolish, nevertheless, and wandered about nervously, promising himself to take the next train; but a dozen trains started, and Longmore was still in Paris. This sentimental tumult was more than he had bargained for, and, as he looked at the shop windows, he wondered whether it was a "passion." He had never been fond of the word, and had grown up with a kind of horror of what it represented. He had hoped that when he should fall in love, he should do it with an excellent conscience, with no greater agitation than a mild suffusion of cheerfulness. But here was a sentiment concocted of pity and anger, as well as of admiration, and bristling with scruples and doubts. He had come abroad to enjoy the Flemish painters and all others; but what fair-tressed saint of Van Eyck or Memling was so interesting a figure as Madame de Mauves? His restless steps carried him at last out of the long villa-bordered avenue which leads to the Bois de Boulogne.

Summer had fairly begun, and the drive beside the lake was empty, but there were various loungers on the benches and chairs, and the great café had an air of animation. Longmore's walk had given him an appetite, and he went into the establishment and demanded a dinner, remarking for the hundredth time, as he observed the smart little tables disposed in the open air, how much better they ordered this matter in France.

"Will monsieur dine in the garden, or in the saloon?" asked the waiter. Longmore chose the garden; and observing that a great cluster of June roses was trained over the wall of the house, placed himself at a table near by, where the best of dinners was served him on the whitest of linen, in the most shining of porcelain. It so happened that his table was near a window, and that as he sat he could look into a corner of the saloon. So it was that his attention rested on a lady seated just within the window, which was open, face to face apparently with a companion who was concealed by the curtain. She was a very pretty woman, and Longmore looked at her as often as was consistent with good manners. After a while he even began to wonder who she was, and to suspect that she was one of those ladies whom it is no breach of good manners to look at as often as you like. Longmore, too, if he had been so disposed, would have been the more free to give her all his attention, that her own was fixed upon the person opposite to her. She was what the French call a *belle brune*, and though our hero, who had rather a conservative taste in such matters, had no great relish for her bold outlines and even bolder colouring, he could not help admiring her expression of basking contentment.

She was evidently very happy, and her happiness gave her an air of innocence. The talk of her friend, whoever he was, abundantly suited her humour, for she sat listening to him with a broad, lazy smile, and interrupted him occasionally, while she crunched her bon-bons, with a murmured response, presumably as broad, which seemed to deepen his eloquence. She drank a great deal of champagne and ate an immense number of strawberries, and was plainly altogether a person with an impartial relish for strawberries, champagne, and what she would have called *bêtises*.

They had half finished dinner when Longmore sat down, and he was still in his place when they rose. She had hung her bonnet on a nail above her chair, and her companion passed round the table to take it down for her. As he did so, she bent her head to look at a wine-stain on her dress, and in the movement exposed the greater part of the back of a very handsome neck. The gentleman observed it, and observed also, apparently, that the room beyond them was empty; that he stood within eyeshot of Longmore, he failed to observe. He stooped suddenly and imprinted a gallant kiss on the fair expanse. Longmore then recognised M. de Mauves. The recipient of this vigorous tribute put on her bonnet, using his flushed smile as a mirror, and in a moment they passed through the garden, on their way to their carriage.

Then, for the first time, M. de Mauves perceived Longmore. He measured with a rapid glance the young man's relation to the open window, and checked himself in the impulse to stop and speak to him. He contented himself with bowing with great gravity as he opened the gate for his companion.

That evening Longmore made a railway journey, but not to Brussels. He had effectually ceased to care about Brussels; the only thing he now cared about was Madame de Mauves. The atmosphere of his mind had had a sudden clearing up; pity and anger were still throbbing there, but they had space to rage at their pleasure, for doubts and scruples had abruptly departed. It was little, he felt, that he could interpose between her resignation and the indignity of her position; but that little, if it involved the sacrifice of everything that bound him to the tranquil past, he could offer her with a rapture which at last made reflection appear a wofully halting substitute for faith. Nothing in his tranquil past had given such a zest to consciousness as this happy sense of choosing to go straight back to Saint-Germain. How to justify his return, how to explain his ardour, troubled him little. He was not sure, even, that he wished to be understood; he wished only to feel that it was by no fault of his that Madame de Mauves was alone with the ugliness of fate. He was conscious of no distinct desire to "make love" to her; if he could have uttered the essence of his longing, he would have said that he wished her to remember that in a world coloured gray to her vision by disappointment, there was one vividly honest man. She might certainly have remembered it, however, without his coming back to remind her; and it is not to be denied that, as he waited for the morrow he wished immensely to hear the sound of her voice.

He waited the next day till his usual hour of calling—the late afternoon; but he learned at the door that Madame de Mauves was not at home. The servant offered the information that she was walking in the forest. Longmore went through the garden and out of the little door into the lane, and, after half an hour's vain exploration, saw her coming toward him at the end of a green by-path. As he appeared, she stopped for a moment, as if to turn aside; then recognising him, she slowly advanced, and he was soon shaking hands with her.

"Nothing has happened," she said, looking at him fixedly. "You are not ill?"

"Nothing, except that when I got to Paris I found how fond I had grown of Saint-Germain."

She neither smiled nor looked flattered; it seemed indeed to Longmore that she was annoyed. But he was uncertain, for he immediately perceived that in his absence the whole character of her face had altered. It told him that something momentous had happened. It was no longer self-contained melancholy that he read in her eyes, but grief and agitation which had lately struggled with that passionate love of peace of which she had spoken to him, and forced him to know that deep experience is never peaceful. She was pale, and she had evidently been shedding tears. He felt his heart beating hard; he seemed now to know her secrets. She continued to look at him with a contracted brow, as if his return had given her a sense of responsibility too great to be disguised by a commonplace welcome. For some moments, as he turned and walked beside her, neither spoke; then abruptly—"Tell me truly, Mr. Longmore," she said, "why you have come back."

He turned and looked at her with an air which startled her into a certainty of what she had feared. "Because I have learned the real answer to the question I asked you the other day. You are not happy—you are too good to be happy on the terms offered you. Madame de Mauves," he went on with a gesture which protested against a gesture of her own, "I can't be happy if you are not! I don't care for anything so long as I see such an unfathomable sadness in your eyes. I found during three dreary days in Paris that the thing in the world I most care for is this daily privilege of seeing you. I know it's very brutal to tell you I admire you; it's an insult to you to treat you as if you had complained to me or appealed to me. But such a friendship as I waked up to there"—and he tossed his head toward the distant city—"is a potent force, I assure you; and when forces are compressed they explode. But if you had told me every trouble in your heart, it would have mattered little; I couldn't say more than I must say now—that if that in life from which you have hoped most has given you least, this devoted respect of mine will refuse no service and betray no trust."

She had begun to make marks in the earth with the point of her parasol; but she stopped and listened to him in perfect immobility. Rather, her immobility was not perfect; for when he stopped speaking a faint flush had stolen into her cheek. It told Longmore that she was moved, and his first perceiving it was the happiest instant of his life. She raised her eyes at last, and looked at him with what at first seemed a pleading dread of excessive emotion.

"Thank you—thank you!" she said, calmly enough; but the next moment her own emotion overcame her calmness, and she burst into tears. Her tears vanished as quickly as they came, but they did Longmore a world of good. He had always felt indefinably afraid of her; her being had somehow seemed fed by a deeper faith and a stronger will than his own; but her half-dozen smothered sobs showed him the bottom of her heart, and assured him that she was weak enough to be grateful.

"Excuse me," she said; "I am too nervous to listen to you. I believe I could have encountered an enemy to-day, but I can't endure a friend."

"You are killing yourself with stoicism—that is what is the matter with you!" he cried. "Listen to a friend for his own sake, if not for yours. I have never ventured to offer you an atom of compassion, and you can't accuse yourself of an abuse of charity."

She looked about her with a kind of weary confusion which promised a reluctant attention. But suddenly perceiving by the wayside the fallen log on which they had rested a few evenings before, she went and sat down on it in impatient resignation, and looked at Longmore, as he stood silent, watching her, with a glance which seemed to urge that, if she was charitable now, he must be very wise.

"Something came to my knowledge yesterday," he said as he sat down beside her, "which gave me an intense impression of your loneliness. You are truth itself, and there is no truth about you. You believe in purity and duty and dignity,

and you live in a world in which they are daily belied. I sometimes ask myself with a kind of rage how you ever came into
such a world—and why the perversity of fate never let me
know you before."

"I like my 'world' no better than you do, and it was not for
its own sake I came into it. But what particular group of people is worth pinning one's faith upon? I confess it sometimes
seems to me that men and women are very poor creatures. I
suppose I am romantic. I have an unfortunate taste for poetic
fitness. Life is hard prose, and one must learn to read prose
contentedly. I believe I once thought that all the prose was in
America, which was very foolish. What I thought, what I believed, what I expected, when I was an ignorant girl, fatally
addicted to falling in love with my own theories, is more than
I can begin to tell you now. Sometimes, when I remember
certain impulses, certain illusions of those days, they take
away my breath, and I wonder that my false point of view has
not led me into troubles greater than any I have now to
lament. I had a conviction which you would probably smile at
if I were to attempt to express it to you. It was a singular
form for passionate faith to take, but it had all of the sweetness and the ardour of passionate faith. It led me to take a
great step, and it lies behind me now in the distance, like a
shadow melting slowly in the light of experience. It has faded,
but it has not vanished. Some feelings, I am sure, die only
with ourselves; some illusions are as much the condition of
our life as our heart-beats. They say that life itself is an illusion—that this world is a shadow of which the reality is yet to
come. Life is all of a piece, then, and there is no shame in being miserably human. As for my loneliness, it doesn't greatly
matter; it is the fault, in part, of my obstinacy. There have
been times when I have been frantically distressed, and, to tell
you the truth, wretchedly homesick, because my maid—a
jewel of a maid—lied to me with every second breath. There
have been moments when I have wished I was the daughter
of a poor New England minister, living in a little white house
under a couple of elms, and doing all the housework."

She had begun to speak slowly, with an air of effort; but she
went on quickly, as if talking were a relief. "My marriage introduced me to people and things which seemed to me at first

very strange and then very horrible, and then, to tell the truth, very contemptible. At first I expended a great deal of sorrow and dismay and pity on it all; but there soon came a time when I began to wonder whether it were worth one's tears. If I could tell you the eternal friendships I have seen broken, the inconsolable woes consoled, the jealousies and vanities scrambling for precedence, you would agree with me that tempers like yours and mine can understand neither such troubles nor such compensations. A year ago, while I was in the country, a friend of mine was in despair at the infidelity of her husband; she wrote me a most dolorous letter, and on my return to Paris I went immediately to see her. A week had elapsed, and, as I had seen stranger things, I thought she might have recovered her spirits. Not at all; she was still in despair—but at what? At the conduct, the abandoned, shameless conduct of Madame de T. You'll imagine, of course, that Madame de T. was the lady whom my friend's husband preferred to his wife. Far from it; he had never seen her. Who, then, was Madame de T.? Madame de T. was cruelly devoted to M. de V. And who was M. de V.? M. de V.—in two words, my friend was cultivating two jealousies at once. I hardly know what I said to her; something, at any rate, that she found unpardonable, for she quite gave me up. Shortly afterward my husband proposed we should cease to live in Paris, and I gladly assented, for I believe I was falling into a state of mind that made me a detestable companion. I should have preferred to go quite into the country, into Auvergne, where my husband has a house. But to him, Paris, in some degree, is necessary, and Saint-Germain has been a sort of compromise."

"A sort of compromise!" Longmore repeated. "That's your whole life."

"It's the life of many people, of most people of quiet tastes, and it is certainly better than acute distress. One is at a loss theoretically to defend a compromise; but if I found a poor creature who had managed to invent one, I should think it questionable friendship to expose its weak side." Madame de Mauves had no sooner uttered these words than she smiled faintly, as if to mitigate their personal application.

"Heaven forbid that one should do that unless one has something better to offer," said Longmore. "And yet I am haunted by a vision of a life in which you should have found no compromises, for they are a perversion of natures that tend only to goodness and rectitude. As I see it, you should have found happiness serene, profound, complete; a *femme de chambre* not a jewel perhaps, but warranted to tell but one fib a day; a society possibly rather provincial, but (in spite of your poor opinion of mankind) a good deal of solid virtue; jealousies and vanities very tame, and no particular iniquities and adulteries. A husband," he added after a moment—"a husband of your own faith and race and spiritual substance, who would have loved you well."

She rose to her feet, shaking her head. "You are very kind to go to the expense of visions for me. Visions are vain things; we must make the best of the reality."

"And yet," said Longmore, provoked by what seemed the very wantonness of her patience, "the reality, if I am not mistaken, has very recently taken a shape that keenly tests your philosophy."

She seemed on the point of replying that his sympathy was too zealous; but a couple of impatient tears in his eyes proved that it was founded on a devotion of which it was impossible to make light. "Philosophy?" she said. "I have none. Thank Heaven!" she cried, with vehemence, "I have none. I believe, Mr. Longmore," she added in a moment, "that I have nothing on earth but a conscience—it's a good time to tell you so—nothing but a dogged, obstinate, clinging conscience. Does that prove me to be indeed of your faith and race, and have you one for which you can say as much? I don't say it in vanity, for I believe that if my conscience will prevent me from doing anything very base, it will effectually prevent me from doing anything very fine."

"I am delighted to hear it," cried Longmore. "We are made for each other. It's very certain I too shall never do anything fine. And yet I have fancied that in my case this unaccommodating organ might be blinded and gagged a while, in a fine cause, if not turned out of doors. In yours," he went on with the same appealing irony, "is it absolutely inexpugnable?"

But she made no concession to his sarcasm. "Don't laugh at your conscience," she answered gravely; "that's the only blasphemy I know."

She had hardly spoken when she turned suddenly at an un-expected sound, and at the same moment Longmore heard a footstep in an adjacent by-path which crossed their own at a short distance from where they stood.

"It's M. de Mauves," said Euphemia directly, and moved slowly forward. Longmore, wondering how she knew it, had overtaken her by the time her husband advanced into sight. A solitary walk in the forest was a pastime to which M. de Mauves was not addicted, but he seemed on this occasion to have resorted to it with some equanimity. He was smoking a fragrant cigar, and his thumb was thrust into the armhole of his waistcoat, with an air of contemplative serenity. He stopped short with surprise on seeing his wife and her com-panion, and to Longmore his surprise seemed impertinent. He glanced rapidly from one to the other, fixed Longmore's eye sharply for a single instant, and then lifted his hat with formal politeness.

"I was not aware," he said, turning to Madame de Mauves, "that I might congratulate you on the return of monsieur."

"You should have known it," she answered gravely, "if I had expected Mr. Longmore's return."

She had become very pale, and Longmore felt that this was a first meeting after a stormy parting. "My return was unex-pected to myself," he said. "I came last evening."

M. de Mauves smiled with extreme urbanity. "It is needless for me to welcome you. Madame de Mauves knows the du-ties of hospitality." And with another bow he continued his walk.

Madame de Mauves and her companion returned slowly home, with few words, but, on Longmore's part at least, many thoughts. The Baron's appearance had given him an an-gry chill; it was a dusky cloud reabsorbing the light which had begun to shine between himself and his companion.

He watched Euphemia narrowly as they went, and won-dered what she had last had to suffer. Her husband's presence had checked her disposition to talk, but nothing indicated that she had acknowledged the insulting meaning of his words. Matters were evidently at a crisis between them, and Longmore wondered vainly what it was on Euphemia's part that prevented an absolute rupture. What did she suspect?—

how much did she know? To what was she resigned?—how much had she forgiven? How, above all, did she reconcile with knowledge, or with suspicion, that ineradicable tenderness of which she had just now all but assured him? "She has loved him once," Longmore said with a sinking of the heart, "and with her to love once is to commit one's self for ever. Her husband thinks her too stiff! What would a poet call it?"

He relapsed with a kind of aching impotence into the sense of her being somehow beyond him, unattainable, immeasurable by his own fretful logic. Suddenly he gave three passionate switches in the air with his cane, which made Madame de Mauves look round. She could hardly have guessed that they meant that where ambition was so vain, it was an innocent compensation to plunge into worship.

Madame de Mauves found in her drawing-room the little elderly Frenchman, M. de Chalumeau, whom Longmore had observed a few days before on the terrace. On this occasion, too, Madame Clairin was entertaining him, but as her sister-in-law came in she surrendered her post and addressed herself to our hero. Longmore, at thirty, was still an ingenuous youth, and there was something in this lady's large coquetry which had the power of making him blush. He was surprised at finding he had not absolutely forfeited her favour by his deportment at their last interview, and a suspicion of her being prepared to approach him on another line completed his uneasiness.

"So you have returned from Brussels by way of the forest?" she said.

"I have not been to Brussels. I returned yesterday from Paris by the only way—by the train."

Madame Clairin stared and laughed. "I have never known a young man to be so fond of Saint-Germain. They generally declare it's horribly dull."

"That's not very polite to you," said Longmore, who was vexed at his blushes, and determined not to be abashed.

"Ah, what am I?" demanded Madame Clairin, swinging open her fan. "I am the dullest thing here. They have not had your success with my sister-in-law."

"It would have been very easy to have it. Madame de Mauves is kindness itself."

"To her own countrymen!"

Longmore remained silent; he hated the tone of this conversation. Madame Clairin looked at him a moment, and then turned her head and surveyed Euphemia, to whom M. de Chalumeau was serving up another epigram, which she was receiving with a slight droop of the head and her eyes absently wandering through the window. "Don't pretend to tell me," she murmured suddenly, "that you are not in love with that pretty woman."

"*Allons donc!*" cried Longmore, in the best French he had ever uttered. He rose the next minute, and took a hasty farewell.

VI.

He allowed several days to pass without going back; it seemed delicate to appear not to regard Madame de Mauves' frankness during their last interview as a general invitation. This cost him a great effort, for hopeless passions are not the most deferential; and he had, moreover, a constant fear that if, as he believed, the hour of supreme explanations had come, the magic of her magnanimity might convert M. de Mauves. Vicious men, it was abundantly recorded, had been so converted as to be acceptable to God, and the something divine in Euphemia's temper would sanctify any means she should choose to employ. Her means, he kept repeating, were no business of his, and the essence of his admiration ought to be to allow her to do as she liked; but he felt as if he should turn away into a world out of which most of the joy had departed, if she should like, after all, to see nothing more in his interest in her than might be repaid by a murmured "Thank you."

When he called again he found to his vexation that he was to run the gauntlet of Madame Clairin's officious hospitality. It was one of the first mornings of perfect summer, and the drawing-room, through the open windows, was flooded with a sweet confusion of odours and bird-notes which filled him with the hope that Madame de Mauves would come out and spend half the day in the forest. But Madame Clairin, with her hair not yet dressed, emerged like a brassy discord in a maze of melody.

At the same moment the servant returned with Euphemia's regrets; she was "indisposed," and was unable to see Mr. Longmore. The young man knew that he looked disappointed and that Madame Clairin was observing him, and this consciousness impelled him to give her a glance of almost aggressive frigidity. This was apparently what she desired. She wished to throw him off his balance, and, if she was not mistaken, she had the means.

"Put down your hat, Mr. Longmore," she said, "and be polite for once. You were not at all polite the other day when I asked you that friendly question about the state of your heart."

"I have no heart—to talk about," said Longmore, uncompromisingly.

"As well say you have none at all. I advise you to cultivate a little eloquence; you may have use for it. That was not an idle question of mine; I don't ask idle questions. For a couple of months now that you have been coming and going among us, it seems to me that you have had very few to answer of any sort."

"I have certainly been very well treated," said Longmore.

Madame Clairin was silent a moment, and then—

"Have you never felt disposed to ask any?" she demanded.

Her look, her tone, were so charged with roundabout meanings that it seemed to Longmore as if even to understand her would savour of dishonest complicity. "What is it you have to tell me?" he asked, frowning and blushing.

Madame Clairin flushed. It is rather hard, when you come bearing yourself very much as the sibyl when she came to the Roman king, to be treated as something worse than a vulgar gossip. "I might tell you, Mr. Longmore," she said, "that you have as bad a *ton* as any young man I ever met. Where have you lived—what are your ideas? I wish to call your attention to a fact which it takes some delicacy to touch upon. You have noticed, I suppose, that my sister-in-law is not the happiest woman in the world."

Longmore assented with a gesture.

Madame Clairin looked slightly disappointed at his want of enthusiasm. Nevertheless—"You have formed, I suppose," she continued, "your conjectures on the causes of her—dis-satisfaction."

"Conjecture has been superfluous. I have seen the causes—or at least a specimen of them—with my own eyes."

"I know perfectly what you mean. My brother, in a single word, is in love with another woman. I don't judge him; I don't judge my sister-in-law. I permit myself to say that in her position I would have managed otherwise. I would either have kept my husband's affection, or I would have frankly done without it. But my sister is an odd compound; I don't profess to understand her. Therefore it is, in a measure, that I appeal to you, her fellow-countryman. Of course you will be surprised at my way of looking at the matter, and I admit that it's a way in use only among people whose family traditions compel them to take a superior view of things." Madame Clairin paused, and Longmore wondered where her family traditions were going to lead her.

"Listen," she went on. "There has never been a De Mauves who has not given his wife the right to be jealous. We know our history for ages back, and the fact is established. It's a shame if you like, but it's something to have a shame with such a pedigree. Our men have been real Frenchmen, and their wives—I may say it—have been worthy of them. You may see all their portraits at our house in Auvergne; every one of them an 'injured' beauty, but not one of them hanging her head. Not one of them had the bad taste to be jealous, and yet not one in a dozen was guilty of an escapade—not one of them was talked about. There's good sense for you! How they managed—go and look at the dusky, faded canvases and pastels, and ask. They were femmes d'esprit! When they had a headache, they put on a little rouge and came to supper as usual; and when they had a heart-ache, they put a little rouge on their hearts. These are great traditions, and it doesn't seem to me fair that a little American bourgeoise should come in and pretend to alter them, and should hang her photograph, with her obstinate little *air penché*, in the gallery of our shrewd fine ladies. A De Mauves must be of the old race. When she married my brother, I don't suppose she took him for a member of a *société de bonnes œuvres*. I don't say we are right; who is right? But we are as history has made us, and if any one is to change, it had better be my sister-in-law herself." Again Madame Clairin paused, and opened and closed her fan. "Let her conform!" she said, with amazing audacity.

Longmore's reply was ambiguous; he simply said, "Ah!"

Madame Clairin's historical retrospect had apparently imparted an honest zeal to her indignation. "For a long time," she continued, "my sister has been taking the attitude of an injured woman, affecting a disgust with the world, and shutting herself up to read free-thinking books. I have never permitted myself any observation on her conduct, but I have quite lost patience with it. When a woman with her prettiness lets her husband stray away, she deserves her fate. I don't wish you to agree with me—on the contrary; but I call such a woman a goose. She must have bored him to death. What has passed between them for many months needn't concern us; what provocation my sister has had—monstrous, if you wish—what ennui my brother has suffered. It's enough that a week ago, just after you had ostensibly gone to Brussels, something happened to produce an explosion. She found a letter in his pocket—a photograph—a trinket—*que sais-je?* At any rate, the scene was terrible. I didn't listen at the keyhole, and I don't know what was said; but I have reason to believe that my brother was called to account as I fancy none of his ancestors have ever been—even by injured mistresses!"

Longmore had leaned forward in silent attention with his elbows on his knees; and now instinctively he dropped his face into his hands. "Ah, poor woman!" he groaned.

"Voilà!" said Madame Clairin. "You pity her."

"Pity her?" cried Longmore, looking up with ardent eyes and forgetting the spirit of Madame Clairin's narrative in the miserable facts. "Don't you?"

"A little. But I am not acting sentimentally; I am acting politically. We have always been a political family. I wish to arrange things—to see my brother free to do as he chooses—to see Euphemia contented. Do you understand me?"

"Very well, I think. You are the most immoral person I have lately had the privilege of conversing with."

Madame Clairin shrugged her shoulders. "Possibly. When was there a great politician who was not immoral?"

"Ah no," said Longmore in the same tone. "You are too superficial to be a great politician. You don't begin to know anything about Madame de Mauves."

Madame Clairin inclined her head to one side, eyed Longmore sharply, mused a moment, and then smiled with an excellent imitation of intelligent compassion. "It's not in my interest to contradict you."

"It would be in your interest to learn, Madame Clairin," the young man went on with unceremonious candour, "what honest men most admire in a woman—and to recognise it when you see it."

Longmore certainly did injustice to her talents for diplomacy, for she covered her natural annoyance at this sally with a pretty piece of irony. "So you *are* in love!" she quietly exclaimed.

Longmore was silent a while. "I wonder if you would understand me," he said at last, "if I were to tell you that I have for Madame de Mauves the most devoted friendship?"

"You underrate my intelligence. But in that case you ought to exert your influence to put an end to these painful domestic scenes."

"Do you suppose that she talks to me about her domestic scenes?" cried Longmore.

Madame Clairin stared. "Then your friendship isn't returned?" And as Longmore turned away, shaking his head— "Now, at least," she added, "she will have something to tell you. I happen to know the upshot of my brother's last interview with his wife." Longmore rose to his feet as a sort of protest against the indelicacy of the position in which he found himself; but all that made him tender made him curious, and she caught in his averted eyes an expression which prompted her to strike her blow. "My brother is monstrously in love with a certain person in Paris; of course he ought not to be; but he wouldn't be my brother if he were not. It was this irregular passion that dictated his words. 'Listen to me, madam,' he cried at last; 'let us live like people who understand life! It is unpleasant to be forced to say such things outright, but you have a way of bringing one down to the rudiments. I am faithless, I am heartless, I am brutal, I am everything horrible—it's understood. Take your revenge,

console yourself; you are too pretty a woman to have anything to complain of. Here is a handsome young man sighing
himself into a consumption for you. Listen to the poor fellow,
and you will find that virtue is none the less becoming for
being good-natured. You will see that it's not after all such a
doleful world, and that there is even an advantage in having
the most impudent of husbands.'" Madame Clairin paused;
Longmore had turned very pale. "You may believe it," she
said; "the speech took place in my presence; things were done
in order. And now, Mr. Longmore"—this with a smile which
he was too troubled at the moment to appreciate, but which
he remembered later with a kind of awe—"we count upon
you!"

"He said this to her, face to face, as you say it to me now?"
Longmore asked slowly, after a silence.

"Word for word, and with the greatest politeness."

"And Madame de Mauves—what did she say?"

Madame Clairin smiled again. "To such a speech as that a
woman says—nothing. She had been sitting with a piece of
needlework, and I think she had not seen her husband since
their quarrel the day before. He came in with the gravity of
an ambassador, and I am sure that when he made his *demande en mariage* his manner was not more respectful. He
only wanted white gloves!" said Madame Clairin. "Euphemia
sat silent a few moments, drawing her stitches, and then without a word, without a glance, she walked out of the room. It
was just what she should have done!"

"Yes," Longmore repeated, "it was just what she should
have done."

"And I, left alone with my brother, do you know what I
said?"

Longmore shook his head. "*Mauvais sujet!*" he suggested.

"'You have done me the honour,' I said, 'to take this step
in my presence. I don't pretend to qualify it. You know what
you are about, and it's your own affair. But you may confide
in my discretion.' Do you think he has had reason to complain of it?" She received no answer; Longmore was slowly
turning away and passing his gloves mechanically round the
band of his hat. "I hope," she cried, "you are not going to
start for Brussels!"

Plainly, Longmore was deeply disturbed, and Madame Clairin might congratulate herself on the success of her plea for old-fashioned manners. And yet there was something that left her more puzzled than satisfied in the reflective tone with which he answered, "No, I shall remain here for the present." The processes of his mind seemed provokingly subterranean, and she could have fancied for a moment that he was linked with her sister in some monstrous conspiracy of asceticism.

"Come this evening," she boldly resumed. "The rest will take care of itself. Meanwhile I shall take the liberty of telling my sister-in-law that I have repeated—in short, that I have put you *au fait.*"

Longmore started and coloured, and she hardly knew whether he were going to assent or to demur. "Tell her what you please. Nothing you can tell her will affect her conduct."

"Voyons! Do you mean to tell me that a woman young, pretty, sentimental, neglected—insulted, if you will—? I see you don't believe it. Believe simply in your own opportunity! But for Heaven's sake, if it is to lead anywhere, don't come back with that *visage de croquemort*. You look as if you were going to bury your heart—not to offer it to a pretty woman. You are much better when you smile—you are very nice then. Come, do yourself justice."

"Yes," he said, "I must do myself justice." And abruptly, with a bow, he took his departure.

VII.

He felt, when he found himself unobserved, in the open air, that he must plunge into violent action, walk fast and far, and defer the opportunity for thought. He strode away into the forest, swinging his cane, throwing back his head, gazing away into the verdurous vistas, and following the road without a purpose. He felt immensely excited, but he could hardly have said whether his emotion was a pain or a joy. It was joyous as all increase of freedom is joyous; something seemed to have been cleared out of his path; his destiny appeared to have rounded a cape and brought him into sight of an open sea. But his freedom resolved itself somehow into the need of despising all mankind, with a single exception; and the fact of Madame de Mauves inhabiting a planet contaminated by the presence of this baser multitude kept his elation from seeming a pledge of ideal bliss.

But she was there, and circumstances now forced them to be intimate. She had ceased to have what men call a secret for him, and this fact itself brought with it a sort of rapture. He had no prevision that he should "profit," in the vulgar sense, by the extraordinary position into which they had been thrown; it might be but a cruel trick of destiny to make hope a harsher mockery and renunciation a keener suffering. But above all this rose the conviction that she could do nothing that would not deepen his admiration.

It was this feeling that circumstance—odious as it was in itself—was to force the beauty of her character into more perfect relief, that made him stride along as if he were celebrating a kind of spiritual festival. He rambled at random for a couple of hours, and found at last that he had left the forest behind him and had wandered into an unfamiliar region. It was a perfectly rural scene, and the still summer day gave it a charm for which its meagre elements but half accounted.

Longmore thought he had never seen anything so characteristically French; all the French novels seemed to have described it, all the French landscapists to have painted it. The fields and trees were of a cool metallic green; the grass looked as if it might stain your trousers, and the foliage your hands. The clear light had a sort of mild greyness; the sunbeams were of silver rather than gold. A great red-roofed, high-stacked farmhouse, with white-washed walls and a straggling yard, surveyed the high road, on one side, from behind a transparent curtain of poplars. A narrow stream, half choked with emerald rushes and edged with grey aspens, occupied the opposite quarter. The meadows rolled and sloped away gently to the low horizon, which was barely concealed by the continuous line of clipped and marshalled trees. The prospect was not rich, but it had a frank homeliness which touched the young man's fancy. It was full of light atmosphere and diffused sunshine, and if it was prosaic, it was soothing.

Longmore was disposed to walk further, and he advanced along the road beneath the poplars. In twenty minutes he came to a village which straggled away to the right, among orchards and *potagers*. On the left, at a stone's throw from the road, stood a little pink-faced inn, which reminded him that he had not breakfasted, having left home with a prevision of hospitality from Madame de Mauves. In the inn he found a brick-tiled parlour and a hostess in sabots and a white cap, whom, over the omelette she speedily served him—borrowing licence from the bottle of sound red wine which accompanied it—he assured that she was a true artist. To reward his compliment, she invited him to smoke his cigar in her little garden behind the house.

Here he found a *tonnelle* and a view of ripening crops, stretching down to the stream. The tonnelle was rather close, and he preferred to lounge on a bench against the pink wall, in the sun, which was not too hot. Here, as he rested and gazed and mused, he fell into a train of thought which, in an indefinable fashion, was a soft influence from the scene about him. His heart, which had been beating fast for the past three hours, gradually checked its pulses and left him looking at life with a rather more level gaze. The homely tavern sounds coming out through the open windows, the sunny stillness of the fields and crops, which covered so much vigorous natural life, suggested very little that was transcendental, had very little to say about renunciation—nothing at all about spiritual zeal. They seemed to utter a message from plain ripe nature, to express the unperverted reality of things, to say that the common lot is not brilliantly amusing, and that the part of wisdom is to grasp frankly at experience, lest you miss it altogether. What reason there was for his falling a-wondering after this whether a deeply wounded heart might be soothed and healed by such a scene, it would be difficult to explain; certain it is that, as he sat there, he had a waking dream of an unhappy woman strolling by the slow-flowing stream before him, and pulling down the fruit-laden boughs in the orchards. He mused and mused, and at last found himself feeling angry that he could not somehow think worse of Madame de Mauves— or at any rate think otherwise. He could fairly claim that in a sentimental way he asked very little of life—he made modest demands on passion; why then should his only passion be born to ill-fortune? why should his first—his last—glimpse of positive happiness be so indissolubly linked with renunciation?

It is perhaps because, like many spirits of the same stock, he had in his composition a lurking principle of asceticism to whose authority he had ever paid an unquestioning respect, that he now felt all the vehemence of rebellion. To renounce —to renounce again—to renounce for ever—was this all that youth and longing and resolve were meant for? Was experience to be muffled and mutilated, like an indecent picture? Was a man to sit and deliberately condemn his future to be the blank memory of a regret, rather than the long reverberation of a joy? Sacrifice? The word was a trap for minds muddled by fear, an ignoble refuge of weakness. To insist now seemed not to dare, but simply to be, to live on possible terms.

His hostess came out to hang a cloth to dry on the hedge, and, though her guest was sitting quietly enough, she seemed to see in his kindled eyes a flattering testimony to the quality of her wine.

As she turned back into the house, she was met by a young man whom Longmore observed in spite of his pre-occupation. He was evidently a member of that jovial fraternity of artists whose very shabbiness has an affinity with the element of picturesqueness and unexpectedness in life—that element which provokes so much unformulated envy among people foredoomed to be respectable.

Longmore was struck first with his looking like a very clever man, and then with his looking like a very happy one. The combination, as it was expressed in his face, might have arrested the attention of even a less cynical philosopher. He had a slouched hat and a blond beard, a light easel under one arm, and an unfinished sketch in oils under the other.

He stopped and stood talking for some moments to the landlady, with a peculiarly good-humoured smile. They were discussing the possibilities of dinner; the hostess enumerated some very savoury ones, and he nodded briskly, assenting to everything. It couldn't be, Longmore thought, that he found such soft contentment in the prospect of lamb-chops and spinach and a *croûte aux fruits*. When the dinner had been ordered, he turned up his sketch, and the good woman fell a-wondering and looking away at the spot by the stream-side where he had made it.

Was it his work, Longmore wondered, that made him so happy? Was a strong talent the best thing in the world? The landlady went back to her kitchen, and the young painter stood, as if he were waiting for something, beside the gate which opened upon the path across the fields. Longmore sat brooding and asking himself whether it was better to cultivate one of the arts than to cultivate one of the passions. Before he had answered the question the painter had grown tired of waiting. He picked up a pebble, tossed it lightly into an upper window, and called, "Claudine!"

Claudine appeared; Longmore heard her at the window, bidding the young man to have patience. "But I am losing my light," he said; "I must have my shadows in the same place as yesterday."

"Go without me, then," Claudine answered; "I will join you in ten minutes." Her voice was fresh and young; it seemed to say to Longmore that she was as happy as her companion.

"Don't forget the Chénier," cried the young man; and turning away, he passed out of the gate and followed the path across the fields until he disappeared among the trees by the side of the stream. Who was Claudine? Longmore vaguely wondered; and was she as pretty as her voice? Before long he had a chance to satisfy himself; she came out of the house with her hat and parasol, prepared to follow her companion. She had on a pink muslin dress and a little white hat, and she was as pretty as a Frenchwoman needs to be to be pleasing. She had a clear brown skin and a bright dark eye, and a step which seemed to keep time to some slow music, heard only by herself. Her hands were encumbered with various articles which she seemed to intend to carry with her. In one arm she held her parasol and a large roll of needlework, and in the other a shawl and a heavy white umbrella, such as painters use for sketching. Meanwhile she was trying to thrust into her pocket a paper-covered volume which Longmore saw to be the Poems of André Chénier; but in the effort she dropped the large umbrella, and uttered a half-smiling exclamation of disgust. Longmore stepped forward and picked up the umbrella, and as she, protesting her gratitude, put out her hand to take it, it seemed to him that she was unbecomingly overburdened.

"You have too much to carry," he said; "you must let me help you."

"You are very good, monsieur," she answered. "My husband always forgets something. He can do nothing without his umbrella. He is *d'une étourderie*—"

"You must allow me to carry the umbrella," Longmore said; "it's too heavy for a lady."

She assented, after many compliments to his politeness; and he walked by her side into the meadow. She went lightly and rapidly, picking her steps and glancing forward to catch a glimpse of her husband. She was graceful, she was charming, she had an air of decision and yet of sweetness, and it seemed to Longmore that a young artist would work none the worse for having her seated at his side reading Chénier's iambics. They were newly married, he supposed, and evidently their path of life had none of the mocking crookedness of some others. They asked little; but what need one ask more than such quiet summer days, with the creature one loves, by a shady stream, with art and books and a wide, unshadowed horizon? To spend such a morning, to stroll back to dinner in the red-tiled parlour of the inn, to ramble away again as the sun got low—all this was a vision of bliss which floated before him only to torture him with a sense of the impossible. All Frenchwomen are not coquettes, he remarked, as he kept pace with his companion. She uttered a word now and then, for politeness' sake, but she never looked at him, and seemed not in the least to care that he was a well-favoured young man. She cared for nothing but the young artist in the shabby coat and the slouched hat, and for discovering where he had set up his easel.

This was soon done. He was encamped under the trees, close to the stream, and, in the diffused green shade of the little wood, seemed to be in no immediate need of his umbrella. He received a vivacious rebuke, however, for forgetting it, and was informed of what he owed to Longmore's complaisance. He was duly grateful; he thanked our hero warmly, and offered him a seat on the grass. But Longmore felt like a marplot, and lingered only long enough to glance at the young man's sketch, and to see it was a very clever rendering of the silvery stream and the vivid green rushes. The young wife had spread her shawl on the grass at the base of a tree, and meant to seat herself when Longmore had gone, and murmur Chénier's verses to the music of the gurgling river. Longmore looked a while from one to the other, barely stifled a sigh, bade them good morning, and took his departure.

He knew neither where to go nor what to do; he seemed afloat on the sea of ineffectual longing. He strolled slowly back to the inn, and in the doorway met the landlady coming back from the butcher's with the lamb-chops for the dinner of her lodgers.

"Monsieur has made the acquaintance of the *dame* of our young painter," she said with a broad smile—a smile too broad for malicious meanings. "Monsieur has perhaps seen the young man's picture. It appears that he has a great deal of talent."

"His picture was very pretty," said Longmore, "but his *dame* was prettier still."

"She's a very nice little woman; but I pity her all the more."

"I don't see why she's to be pitied," said Longmore; "they seem a very happy couple."

The landlady gave a knowing nod.

"Don't trust to it, monsieur! Those artists—*ça n'a pas de principes!* From one day to another he can plant her there! I know them, *allez*. I have had them here very often; one year with one, another year with another."

Longmore was puzzled for a moment. Then, "You mean she is not his wife?" he asked.

She shrugged her shoulders. "What shall I tell you? They are not *des hommes sérieux*, those gentlemen! They don't engage themselves for an eternity. It's none of my business, and I have no wish to speak ill of madame. She's a very nice little woman, and she loves her *jeune homme* to distraction."

"Who is she?" asked Longmore. "What do you know about her?"

"Nothing for certain; but it's my belief that she's better than he. I have even gone so far as to believe that she's a lady—a true lady—and that she has given up a great many things for him. I do the best I can for them, but I don't believe she has been obliged all her life to content herself with a dinner of two courses." And she turned over her lamb-chops tenderly, as if to say that though a good cook could imagine better things, yet if you could have but one course, lamb-chops had much in their favour. "I shall cook them with bread-crumbs. *Voilà les femmes, monsieur!*"

Longmore turned away with the feeling that women were indeed a measureless mystery, and that it was hard to say whether there was greater beauty in their strength or in their weakness. He walked back to Saint-Germain, more slowly than he had come, with less philosophic resignation to any event, and more of the urgent egotism of the passion which philosophers call the supremely selfish one. Every now and then the episode of the happy young painter and the charming woman who had given up a great many things for him rose vividly in his mind, and seemed to mock his moral unrest like some obtrusive vision of unattainable bliss.

The landlady's gossip had cast no shadow on its brightness; her voice seemed that of the vulgar chorus of the uninitiated, which stands always ready with its gross prose rendering of the inspired passages of human action. Was it possible a man could take *that* from a woman—take all that lent lightness to that other woman's footstep and intensity to her glance—and not give her the absolute certainty of a devotion as unalterable as the process of the sun? Was it possible that such a rapturous union had the seeds of trouble—that the charm of such a perfect accord could be broken by anything but death? Longmore felt an immense desire to cry out a thousand times "No!" for it seemed to him at last that he was somehow spiritually the same as the young painter, and that the latter's companion had the soul of Euphemia.

The heat of the sun, as he walked along, became oppressive, and when he re-entered the forest he turned aside into the deepest shade he could find, and stretched himself on the mossy ground at the foot of a great beech. He lay for a while staring up into the verdurous dusk overhead, and trying to conceive Madame de Mauves hastening towards some quiet stream-side where he waited, as he had seen that trusting creature do an hour before. It would be hard to say how well he succeeded; but the effort soothed him rather than excited

him, and as he had had a good deal both of moral and physical fatigue, he sank at last into a quiet sleep.

While he slept he had a strange, vivid dream. He seemed to
be in a wood, very much like the one on which his eyes had
lately closed; but the wood was divided by the murmuring
stream he had left an hour before. He was walking up and
down, he thought, restlessly and in intense expectation of
some momentous event. Suddenly, at a distance, through the
trees, he saw the gleam of a woman's dress, and hurried forward to meet her. As he advanced he recognised her, but he
saw at the same time that she was on the opposite bank of the
river. She seemed at first not to notice him, but when they
were opposite each other she stopped and looked at him very
gravely and pityingly. She made him no motion that he
should cross the stream, but he wished greatly to stand by her
side. He knew the water was deep, and it seemed to him that
he knew that he should have to plunge, and that he feared
that when he rose to the surface she would have disappeared.
Nevertheless, he was going to plunge, when a boat turned
into the current from above and came swiftly towards them,
guided by an oarsman who was sitting so that they could
not see his face. He brought the boat to the bank where
Longmore stood; the latter stepped in, and with a few strokes
they touched the opposite shore. Longmore got out, and,
though he was sure he had crossed the stream, Madame de
Mauves was not there. He turned with a kind of agony and
saw that now she was on the other bank—the one he had left.
She gave him a grave, silent glance, and walked away up the
stream. The boat and the boatman resumed their course, but
after going a short distance they stopped, and the boatman
turned back and looked at the still divided couple. Then
Longmore recognised him—just as he had recognised him a
few days before at the restaurant in the Bois de Boulogne.

VIII.

He must have slept some time after he ceased dreaming, for
he had no immediate memory of his dream. It came back to
him later, after he had roused himself and had walked nearly

home. No great ingenuity was needed to make it seem a rather striking allegory, and it haunted and oppressed him for the rest of the day. He took refuge, however, in his quickened conviction that the only sound policy in life is to grasp unsparingly at happiness; and it seemed no more than one of the vigorous measures dictated by such a policy, to return that evening to Madame de Mauves. And yet when he had decided to do so, and had carefully dressed himself, he felt an irresistible nervous tremor which made it easier to linger at his open window, wondering, with a strange mixture of dread and desire, whether Madame Clairin had told her sister-in-law what she had told him. His presence now might be simply a gratuitous annoyance; and yet his absence might seem to imply that it was in the power of circumstances to make them ashamed to meet each other's eyes. He sat a long time with his head in his hands, lost in a painful confusion of hopes and questionings. He felt at moments as if he could throttle Madame Clairin, and yet he could not help asking himself whether it were not possible that she had done him a service. It was late when he left the hotel, and as he entered the gate of the other house his heart was beating so fast that he was sure his voice would show it.

The servant ushered him into the drawing-room, which was empty, with the lamp burning low. But the long windows were open, and their light curtains swaying in a soft, warm wind, so that Longmore immediately stepped out upon the terrace. There he found Madame de Mauves alone, slowly pacing up and down. She was dressed in white, very simply, and her hair was arranged, not as she usually wore it, but in a single loose coil, like that of a person unprepared for company.

She stopped when she saw Longmore, seemed slightly startled, uttered an exclamation, and stood waiting for him to speak. He looked at her, tried to say something, but found no words. He knew it was awkward, it was offensive, to stand gazing at her; but he could not say what was suitable, and he dared not say what he wished.

Her face was indistinct in the dim light, but he could see that her eyes were fixed on him, and he wondered what they expressed. Did they warn him, did they plead, or did they confess to a sense of provocation? For an instant his head swam; he felt as if it would make all things clear to stride forward and fold her in his arms. But a moment later he was still standing looking at her; he had not moved; he knew that she had spoken, but he had not understood her.

"You were here this morning," she continued; and now, slowly, the meaning of her words came to him. "I had a bad headache and had to shut myself up." She spoke in her usual voice.

Longmore mastered his agitation and answered her without betraying himself. "I hope you are better now."

"Yes, thank you, I am better—much better."

He was silent a moment, and she moved away to a chair and seated herself. After a pause he followed her and stood before her, leaning against the balustrade of the terrace. "I hoped you might have been able to come out for the morning into the forest. I went alone; it was a lovely day, and I took a long walk."

"It was a lovely day," she said, absently, and sat with her eyes lowered, slowly opening and closing her fan. Longmore, as he watched her, felt more and more sure that her sister-in-law had seen her since her interview with him; that her attitude towards him was changed. It was this same something that chilled the ardour with which he had come, or at least converted the dozen passionate speeches that kept rising to his lips into a kind of reverential silence. No, certainly, he could not clasp her to his arms now, any more than some antique worshipper could have clasped the marble statue in his temple. But Longmore's statue spoke at last, with a full human voice, and even with a shade of human hesitation. She looked up, and it seemed to him that her eyes shone through the dusk.

"I am very glad you came this evening," she said. "I have a particular reason for being glad. I half expected you, and yet I thought it possible you might not come."

"As I have been feeling all day," Longmore answered, "it was impossible I should not come. I have spent the day in thinking of you."

She made no immediate reply, but continued to open and close her fan thoughtfully. At last—"I have something to say to you," she said abruptly. "I want you to know to a certainty that I have a very high opinion of you." Longmore started and shifted his position. To what was she coming? But he said nothing, and she went on—

"I take a great interest in you; there is no reason why I should not say it—I have a great friendship for you."

He began to laugh; he hardly knew why, unless that this seemed the very mockery of coldness. But she continued without heeding him—

"You know, I suppose, that a great disappointment always implies a great confidence—a great hope?"

"I have hoped," he said, "hoped strongly; but doubtless never rationally enough to have a right to bemoan my disappointment."

"You do yourself injustice. I have such confidence in your reason that I should be greatly disappointed if I were to find it wanting."

"I really almost believe that you are amusing yourself at my expense," cried Longmore. "My reason? Reason is a mere word! The only reality in the world is the thing one *feels!*"

She rose to her feet and looked at him gravely. His eyes by this time were accustomed to the imperfect light, and he could see that her look was reproachful, and yet that it was beseechingly kind. She shook her head impatiently, and laid her fan upon his arm with a strong pressure.

"If that were so, it would be a weary world. I know what you feel, however, nearly enough. You needn't try to express it. It's enough that it gives me the right to ask a favour of you—to make an urgent, a solemn request."

"Make it; I listen."

"*Don't disappoint me.* If you don't understand me now, you will to-morrow, or very soon. When I said just now that I had a very high opinion of you, I meant it very seriously. It was not a vain compliment. I believe that there is no appeal one may make to your generosity which can remain long unanswered. If this were to happen,—if I were to find you selfish where I thought you generous, narrow where I thought you large"—and she spoke slowly, with her voice lingering with emphasis on each of these words—"vulgar where I thought you rare—I should think worse of human nature. I should suffer—I should suffer keenly. I should say to myself in the dull days of the future, 'There was one man who might have done so and so; and he, too, failed.' But this shall not be. You have made too good an impression on me not to make the very best. If you wish to please me for ever, there is a way."

She was standing close to him, with her dress touching him, her eyes fixed on his. As she went on her manner grew strangely intense, and she had the singular appearance of a woman preaching reason with a kind of passion. Longmore was confused, dazzled, almost bewildered. The intention of her words was all remonstrance, refusal, dismissal; but her presence there, so close, so urgent, so personal, seemed a distracting contradiction of it. She had never been so lovely. In her white dress, with her pale face and deeply lighted eyes, she seemed the very spirit of the summer night. When she had ceased speaking she drew a long breath; Longmore felt it on his cheek, and it stirred in his whole being a sudden rapturous conjecture. Were her words in their soft severity a mere delusive spell, meant to throw into relief her almost ghostly beauty, and was this the only truth, the only reality, the only law?

He closed his eyes and felt that she was watching him, not without pain and perplexity herself. He looked at her again, met her own eyes, and saw a tear in each of them. Then this last suggestion of his desire seemed to die away with a stifled murmur, and her beauty, more and more radiant in the darkness, rose before him as a symbol of something vague which was yet more beautiful than itself.

"I may understand you to-morrow," he said, "but I don't understand you now."

"And yet I took counsel with myself to-day and asked myself how I had best speak to you. On one side I might have refused to see you at all." Longmore made a violent movement, and she added—"In that case I should have written to you. I might see you, I thought, and simply say to you that there were excellent reasons why we should part, and that I begged this visit should be your last. This I inclined to do; what made me decide otherwise was—simply friendship! I said to myself that I should be glad to remember in future days, not that I had dismissed you, but that you had gone away out of the fulness of your own wisdom."

"The fulness—the fulness!" cried Longmore.

"I am prepared, if necessary," Madame de Mauves continued after a pause, "to fall back upon my strict right. But, as I said before, I shall be greatly disappointed if I am obliged to do that."

"When I hear you say that," Longmore answered, "I feel so angry, so horribly irritated, that I wonder I don't leave you without more words."

"If you should go away in anger, this idea of mine about our parting would be but half realised. No, I don't want to think of you as angry; I don't want even to think of you as making a serious sacrifice. I want to think of you as——"

"As a creature who never has existed—who never can exist! A creature who knew you without loving you—who left you without regretting you!"

She turned impatiently away and walked to the other end of the terrace. When she came back, he saw that her impatience had become a cold sternness. She stood before him again, looking at him from head to foot, in deep reproachfulness, almost in scorn. Beneath her glance he felt a kind of shame. He coloured; she observed it and withheld something she was about to say. She turned away again, walked to the other end of the terrace, and stood there looking away into the garden. It seemed to him that she had guessed he understood her, and slowly—slowly—half as the fruit of his vague self-reproach—he did understand her. She was giving him a chance to do gallantly what it seemed unworthy of both of them he should do meanly.

She liked him, she must have liked him greatly, to wish so to spare him, to go to the trouble of conceiving an ideal of conduct for him. With this sense of her friendship—her strong friendship she had just called it—Longmore's soul rose with a new flight, and suddenly felt itself breathing a clearer air. The words ceased to seem a mere bribe to his ardour; they were charged with ardour themselves; they were a present happiness. He moved rapidly towards her with a feeling that this was something he might immediately enjoy.

They were separated by two-thirds of the length of the terrace, and he had to pass the drawing-room window. As he did so he started with an exclamation. Madame Clairin stood posted there, watching him. Conscious, apparently, that she might be suspected of eavesdropping, she stepped forward with a smile and looked from Longmore to his hostess.

"Such a *tête-à-tête* as that," she said, "one owes no apology for interrupting. One ought to come in for good manners."

Madame de Mauves turned round, but she answered nothing. She looked straight at Longmore, and her eyes had extraordinary eloquence. He was not exactly sure, indeed, what she meant them to say; but they seemed to say plainly something of this kind: "Call it what you will, what you have to urge upon me is the thing which this woman can best conceive. What I ask of you is something she cannot!" They seemed, somehow, to beg him to suffer her to be herself, and to intimate that that self was as little as possible like Madame Clairin. He felt an immense answering desire not to do anything which would seem natural to this lady. He had laid his hat and stick on the parapet of the terrace. He took them up, offered his hand to Madame de Mauves with a simple goodnight, bowed silently to Madame Clairin, and departed.

IX.

He went home, and without lighting his candle flung himself on his bed. But he got no sleep till morning; he lay hour after hour tossing, thinking, wondering; his mind had never been so active. It seemed to him that Euphemia had given him in those last moments an inspiring commission, and that she had expressed herself almost as largely as if she had listened assentingly to an assurance of his love. It was neither easy nor delightful thoroughly to understand her; but little by little her perfect meaning sank into his mind and soothed it with a sense of opportunity which somehow stifled his sense of loss. For, to begin with, she meant that she could love him in no degree or contingency, in no imaginable future. This was absolute; he felt that he could alter it no more than he could pull down the constellations he lay gazing at through his open window. He wondered what it was, in the background of her life, that she had so attached herself to. A sense of duty unquenchable to the end? A love that no outrage could stifle? "Good heavens!" he thought, "is the world so rich in the purest pearls of passion, that such tenderness as that can be wasted for ever—poured away without a sigh into bottomless darkness?" Had she, in spite of the detestable present, some precious memory which contained the germ of a shrinking hope? Was she prepared to submit to everything and yet to believe? Was it strength, was it weakness, was it a vulgar fear, was it conviction, conscience, constancy?

Longmore sank back with a sigh and an oppressive feeling that it was vain to guess at such a woman's motives. He only felt that those of Madame de Mauves were buried deep in her soul, and that they must be of the noblest, and contain nothing base. He had a dim, overwhelming sense of a sort of invulnerable constancy being the supreme law of her character—a constancy which still found a foothold among crumbling ruins. "She has loved once," he said to himself as he rose and wandered to his window; "that is for ever. Yes, yes— if she loved again she would be *common*." He stood for a long time looking out into the starlit silence of the town and forest, and thinking of what life would have been if his constancy had met hers before this had happened. But life was this, now, and he must live. It was living keenly to stand there with such a request from such a woman still ringing in one's ears. He was not to disappoint her, he was to justify a conception which it had beguiled her weariness to shape. Longmore's imagination expanded; he threw back his head and seemed to be looking for Madame de Mauves' conception among the blinking, mocking stars. But it came to him rather on the mild night-wind, wandering in over the house-tops which covered the rest of so many heavy human hearts. What she asked, he felt that she was asking not for her own sake (she feared nothing, she needed nothing), but for that of his own happiness and his own character. He must assent to destiny. Why else was he young and strong, intelligent and resolute? He must not give it to her to reproach him with thinking that she had a moment's attention for his love—to plead, to argue, to break off in bitterness; he must see everything from above, her indifference and his own ardour; he must prove his strength, he must do the handsome thing; he must decide that the handsome thing was to submit to the inevitable, to be supremely delicate, to spare her all pain, to stifle his passion, to ask no compensation, to depart without delay and try to believe that wisdom is its own reward. All this, neither more nor less, it was a matter of friendship with Madame de Mauves to expect of him. And what should he gain by it? He should have pleased her! . . . . He flung himself on his bed again, fell asleep at last, and slept till morning.

Before noon the next day he had made up his mind that he would leave Saint-Germain at once. It seemed easier to leave without seeing her, and yet if he might ask a grain of "compensation," it would be five minutes face to face with her. He passed a restless day. Wherever he went he seemed to see her standing before him in the dusky halo of evening, and looking at him with an air of still negation more intoxicating than the most passionate self-surrender. He must certainly go, and yet it was hideously hard. He compromised and went to Paris to spend the rest of the day. He strolled along the Boulevards and looked at the shops, sat a while in the Tuileries gardens and looked at the shabby unfortunates for whom this only was nature and summer; but simply felt, as a result of it all, that it was a very dusty, dreary, lonely world into which Madame de Mauves was turning him away.

In a sombre mood he made his way back to the Boulevards and sat down at a table on the great plain of hot asphalt, before a café. Night came on, the lamps were lighted, the tables near him found occupants, and Paris began to wear that peculiar evening look of hers which seems to say, in the flare of windows and theatre-doors, and the muffled rumble of swift-rolling carriages, that this is no world for you unless you have your pockets lined and your scruples drugged. Longmore, however, had neither scruples nor desires; he looked at the swarming city for the first time with an easy sense of repaying its indifference. Before long a carriage drove up to the pavement directly in front of him, and remained standing for several minutes without its occupant descending. It was one of those neat, plain coupés, drawn by a single powerful horse, in which one is apt to imagine a pale, handsome woman, buried among silk cushions, and yawning as she sees the gas-lamps glittering in the gutters. At last the door opened and out stepped M. de Mauves. He stopped and leaned on the window for some time, talking in an excited manner to a person within. At last he gave a nod and the carriage rolled away. He stood swinging his cane and looking up and down the Boulevard, with the air of a man fumbling, as one may say, with the loose change of time. He turned towards the café and was apparently, for want of anything better worth his attention, about to seat himself at one of the tables, when he perceived Longmore. He wavered an instant, and then, without a change in his nonchalant gait, strolled towards him with a bow and a vague smile.

It was the first time they had met since their encounter in the forest after Longmore's false start for Brussels. Madame Clairin's revelations, as we may call them, had not made the Baron especially present to his mind; he had another office for his emotions than disgust. But as M. de Mauves came towards him he felt deep in his heart that he abhorred him. He noticed, however, for the first time, a shadow upon the Baron's cool placidity, and his delight at finding that somewhere at last the shoe pinched *him*, mingled with his impulse to be as exasperatingly impenetrable as possible, enabled him to return the other's greeting with all his own self-possession.

M. de Mauves sat down, and the two men looked at each other across the table, exchanging formal greetings which did little to make their mutual scrutiny seem gracious. Longmore had no reason to suppose that the Baron knew of his sister's intimations. He was sure that M. de Mauves cared very little about his opinions, and yet he had a sense that there was that in his eyes which would have made the Baron change colour if keener suspicion had helped him to read it. M. de Mauves did not change colour, but he looked at Longmore with a half-defiant intentness which betrayed at once an irritating memory of the episode in the Bois de Boulogne, and such vigilant curiosity as was natural to a gentleman who had intrusted his "honour" to another gentleman's magnanimity— or to his artlessness.

It would appear that Longmore seemed to the Baron to possess these virtues in rather scantier measure than a few days before; for the cloud deepened on his face, and he turned away and frowned as he lighted a cigar.

The person in the coupé, Longmore thought, whether or no the same person as the heroine of the episode of the Bois

de Boulogne, was not a source of unalloyed delight. Longmore had dark blue eyes, of admirable lucidity—truth-telling
eyes which had in his childhood always made his harshest
taskmasters smile at his primitive fibs. An observer watching
the two men, and knowing something of their relations,
would certainly have said that what he saw in those eyes must
not a little have puzzled and tormented M. de Mauves. They
judged him, they mocked him, they eluded him, they threatened him, they triumphed over him, they treated him as no
pair of eyes had ever treated him. The Baron's scheme had
been to make no one happy but himself, and here was
Longmore already, if looks were to be trusted, primed for an
enterprise more inspiring than the finest of his own achieve-
ments. Was this candid young barbarian but a *faux bonhomme*
after all? He had puzzled the Baron before, and this was once
too often.

M. de Mauves hated to seem preoccupied, and he took up
the evening paper to help himself to look indifferent. As he
glanced over it he uttered some cold common-place on the
political situation, which gave Longmore a fair opportunity of
replying by an ironical sally which made him seem for the moment aggressively at his ease. And yet our hero was far from
being master of the situation. The Baron's ill-humour did him
good, so far as it pointed to a want of harmony with the lady
in the coupé; but it disturbed him sorely as he began to suspect that it possibly meant jealousy of himself. It passed
through his mind that jealousy is a passion with a double face,
and that in some of its moods it bears a plausible likeness to
affection. It recurred to him painfully that the Baron might
grow ashamed of his political compact with his wife, and he
felt that it would be far more tolerable in the future to think
of his continued turpitude than of his repentance. The two
men sat for half an hour exchanging stinted small-talk, the
Baron feeling a nervous need of playing the spy, and
Longmore indulging a ferocious relish of his discomfort.
These thin amenities were interrupted however by the arrival
of a friend of M. de Mauves—a tall, pale consumptive-looking
dandy, who filled the air with the odour of heliotrope. He
looked up and down the Boulevard wearily, examined the
Baron's toilet from head to foot, then surveyed his own in

the same fashion, and at last announced languidly that the Duchess was in town! M. de Mauves must come with him to call; she had abused him dreadfully a couple of evenings before—a sure sign she wanted to see him.

"I depend upon you," said M. de Mauves' friend with an infantine drawl, "to put her *en train.*"

M. de Mauves resisted, and protested that he was *d'une humeur massacrante*; but at last he allowed himself to be drawn to his feet, and stood looking awkwardly—awkwardly for M. de Mauves—at Longmore. "You will excuse me," he said dryly; "you, too, probably have occupation for the evening?"

"None but to catch my train," Longmore answered, looking at his watch.

"Ah, you go back to Saint-Germain?"

"In half an hour."

M. de Mauves seemed on the point of disengaging himself from his companion's arm, which was locked in his own; but on the latter uttering some persuasive murmur, he lifted his hat stiffly and turned away.

Longmore the next day wandered off to the terrace, to try and beguile the restlessness with which he waited for evening; for he wished to see Madame de Mauves for the last time at the hour of long shadows and pale, pink, reflected lights, as he had almost always seen her. Destiny, however, took no account of this humble plea for poetic justice; it was his fortune to meet her on the terrace sitting under a tree, alone. It was an hour when the place was almost empty; the day was warm, but as he took his place beside her a light breeze stirred the leafy edges of the broad circle of shadow in which she sat. She looked at him with candid anxiety, and he immediately told her that he should leave Saint-Germain that evening—that he must bid her farewell. Her eye expanded and brightened for a moment as he spoke; but she said nothing and turned her glance away towards distant Paris, as it lay twinkling and flashing through its hot exhalations. "I have a request to make of you," he added; "that you think of me as a man who has felt much and claimed little."

She drew a long breath which almost suggested pain. "I can't think of you as unhappy. That is impossible. You have a life to lead, you have duties, talents, and interests. I shall hear of your career. And then," she continued after a pause and with the deepest seriousness, "one can't be unhappy through having a better opinion of a friend, instead of a worse."

For a moment he failed to understand her. "Do you mean that there can be varying degrees in my opinion of you?"

She rose and pushed away her chair. "I mean," she said quickly, "that it's better to have done nothing in bitterness—nothing in passion." And she began to walk.

Longmore followed her, without answering. But he took off his hat and with his pocket-handkerchief wiped his forehead. "Where shall you go? what shall you do?" he asked at last, abruptly.

"Do? I shall do as I have always done—except perhaps that I shall go for a while to Auvergne."

"I shall go to America. I have done with Europe for the present."

She glanced at him as he walked beside her after he had spoken these words, and then bent her eyes for a long time on the ground. At last, seeing that she was going far, she stopped and put out her hand. "Good-by," she said; "may you have all the happiness you deserve!"

He took her hand and looked at her, but something was passing in him that made it impossible to return her hand's light pressure. Something of infinite value was floating past him, and he had taken an oath not to raise a finger to stop it. It was borne by the strong current of the world's great life and not of his own small one. Madame de Mauves disengaged her hand, gathered her shawl, and smiled at him almost as you would do at a child you should wish to encourage. Several moments later he was still standing watching her receding figure. When it had disappeared, he shook himself, walked rapidly back to his hotel, and without waiting for the evening train paid his bill and departed.

Later in the day M. de Mauves came into his wife's drawing-room, where she sat waiting to be summoned to dinner. He was dressed with a scrupulous freshness which seemed to indicate an intention of dining out. He walked up and down for some moments in silence, then rang the bell for a servant, and went out into the hall to meet him. He ordered the carriage to take him to the station, paused a moment with his hand on the knob of the door, dismissed the servant angrily as the latter lingered observing him, re-entered the drawing-room, resumed his restless walk, and at last stopped abruptly before his wife, who had taken up a book. "May I ask the favour," he said with evident effort, in spite of a forced smile of easy courtesy, "of having a question answered?"

"It's a favour I never refused," Madame de Mauves replied.

"Very true. Do you expect this evening a visit from Mr. Longmore?"

"Mr. Longmore," said his wife, "has left Saint-Germain." M. de Mauves started and his smile expired. "Mr. Longmore," his wife continued, "has gone to America."

M. de Mauves stared a moment, flushed deeply, and turned away. Then recovering himself—"Had anything happened?" he asked. "Had he a sudden call?"

But his question received no answer. At the same moment the servant threw open the door and announced dinner; Madame Clairin rustled in, rubbing her white hands, Madame de Mauves passed silently into the dining-room, and he stood frowning and wondering. Before long he went out upon the terrace and continued his uneasy walk. At the end of a quarter of an hour the servant came to inform him that the carriage was at the door. "Send it away," he said curtly. "I shall not use it." When the ladies had half finished dinner he went in and joined them, with a formal apology to his wife for his tardiness.

The dishes were brought back, but he hardly tasted them; on the other hand, he drank a great deal of wine. There was little talk; what there was, was supplied by Madame Clairin. Twice she saw her brother's eyes fixed on her own, over his wineglass, with a piercing, questioning glance. She replied by an elevation of the eyebrows which did the office of a shrug of the shoulders. M. de Mauves was left alone to finish his wine; he sat over it for more than an hour, and let the darkness gather about him. At last the servant came in with a letter and lighted a candle. The letter was a telegram, which M. de Mauves, when he had read it, burnt at the candle. After five minutes' meditation, he wrote a message on the back of a visiting-card and gave it to the servant to carry to the office.

The man knew quite as much as his master suspected about the lady to whom the telegram was addressed; but its contents puzzled him; they consisted of the single word, "*Impossible.*" As the evening passed without her brother reappearing in the drawing-room, Madame Clairin came to him where he sat by his solitary candle. He took no notice of her presence for some time; but he was the one person to whom she allowed this licence. At last, speaking in a peremptory tone, "The American has gone home at an hour's notice," he said. "What does it mean?"

Madame Clairin now gave free play to the shrug she had been obliged to suppress at the table. "It means that I have a sister-in-law whom I have not the honour to understand."

He said nothing more, and silently allowed her to depart, as if it had been her duty to provide him with an explanation, and he was disgusted with her levity. When she had gone, he went into the garden and walked up and down, smoking. He saw his wife sitting alone on the terrace, but remained below strolling along the narrow paths. He remained a long time. It became late, and Madame de Mauves disappeared. Towards midnight he dropped upon a bench, tired, with a kind of angry sigh. It was sinking into his mind that he, too, did not understand Madame Clairin's sister-in-law.

Longmore was obliged to wait a week in London for a ship. It was very hot, and he went out one day to Richmond. In the garden of the hotel at which he dined he met his friend Mrs. Draper, who was staying there. She made eager inquiry about Madame de Mauves; but Longmore at first, as they sat looking out at the famous view of the Thames, parried her questions and confined himself to small-talk. At last she said she was afraid he had something to conceal; whereupon, after a pause, he asked her if she remembered recommending him, in the letter she sent to him at Saint-Germain, to draw the sadness from her friend's smile. "The last I saw of her was her smile," said he—"when I bade her good-by."

"I remember urging you to 'console' her," Mrs. Draper answered, "and I wondered afterwards whether—a model of discretion as you are—I had not given you rather foolish advice."

"She has her consolation in herself," he said; "she needs

none that any one else can offer her. That's for troubles for which—be it more, be it less—our own folly has to answer. Madame de Mauves has not a grain of folly left."

"Ah, don't say that!" murmured Mrs. Draper. "Just a little folly is very graceful."

Longmore rose to go, with a quick, nervous movement. "Don't talk of grace," he said, "till you have measured her reason!"

For two years after his return to America he heard nothing of Madame de Mauves. That he thought of her intently, constantly, I need hardly say; most people wondered why such a clever young man should not "devote" himself to something; but to himself he seemed absorbingly occupied. He never wrote to her; he believed that she preferred it. At last he heard that Mrs. Draper had come home, and he immediately called on her. "Of course," she said after the first greetings, "you are dying for news of Madame de Mauves. Prepare yourself for something strange. I heard from her two or three times during the year after your return. She left Saint-Germain and went to live in the country, on some old property of her husband's. She wrote me very kind little notes, but I felt somehow that—in spite of what you said about 'consolation'—they were the notes of a very sad woman. The only advice I could have given her was to leave her wretch of a husband and come back to her own land and her own people. But this I didn't feel free to do, and yet it made me so miserable not to be able to help her that I preferred to let our correspondence die a natural death. I had no news of her for a year. Last summer, however, I met at Vichy a clever young Frenchman whom I accidentally learned to be a friend of Euphemia's charming sister-in-law, Madame Clairin. I lost no time in asking him what he knew about Madame de Mauves—a countrywoman of mine and an old friend. 'I congratulate you on possessing her friendship,' he answered. 'That's the charming little woman who killed her husband.' You may imagine that I promptly asked for an explanation, and he proceeded to relate to me what he called the whole story. M. de Mauves had *fait quelques folies*, which his wife had taken absurdly to heart. He had repented and asked her forgiveness, which she had inexorably refused. She was very pretty, and severity, apparently, suited her style; for whether or no her husband had been in love with her before, he fell madly in love with her now. He was the proudest man in France, but he had begged her on his knees to be re-admitted to favour. All in vain! She was stone, she was ice, she was outraged virtue. People noticed a great change in him; he gave up society, ceased to care for anything, looked shockingly. One fine day they learned that he had blown out his brains. My friend had the story, of course, from Madame Clairin."

Longmore was strongly moved, and his first impulse after he had recovered his composure was to return immediately to Europe. But several years have passed, and he still lingers at home. The truth is, that in the midst of all the ardent tenderness of his memory of Madame de Mauves, he has become conscious of a singular feeling—a feeling for which awe would be hardly too strong a name.

Adina

W E HAD been talking of Sam Scrope round the fire—
mindful, such of us, of the rule *de mortuis*. Our host,
however, had said nothing; rather to my surprise, as I knew he
had been particularly intimate with our friend. But when our
group had dispersed, and I remained alone with him, he
brightened the fire, offered me another cigar, puffed his own
awhile with a retrospective air, and told me the following tale:

Eighteen years ago Scrope and I were together in Rome. It
was the beginning of my acquaintance with him, and I had
grown fond of him, as a mild, meditative youth often does of
an active, irreverent, caustic one. He had in those days the
germs of the eccentricities,—not to call them by a hard name,
—which made him afterwards the most intolerable of the
friends we did not absolutely break with; he was already, as
they say, a crooked stick. He was cynical, perverse, conceited,
obstinate, brilliantly clever. But he was young, and youth,
happily, makes many of our vices innocent. Scrope had his
merits, or our friendship would not have ripened. He was not
an amiable man, but he was an honest one—in spite of the
odd caprice I have to relate; and half my kindness for him was
based in a feeling that at bottom, in spite of his vanity, he enjoyed his own irritability as little as other people. It was his
fancy to pretend that he enjoyed nothing, and that what sentimental travelers call picturesqueness was a weariness to his
spirit; but the world was new to him and the charm of fine
things often took him by surprise and stole a march on his
premature cynicism. He was an observer in spite of himself,
and in his happy moods, thanks to his capital memory and
ample information, an excellent critic and most profitable
companion. He was a punctilious classical scholar. My boyish
journal, kept in those days, is stuffed with learned allusions;
they are all Scrope's. I brought to the service of my Roman
experience much more loose sentiment than rigid science. It
was indeed a jocular bargain between us that in our wanderings, picturesque and archæological, I should undertake the

sentimental business—the raptures, the reflections, the sketching, the quoting from Byron. He considered me absurdly Byronic, and when, in the manner of tourists at that period, I breathed poetic sighs over the subjection of Italy to the foreign foe, he used to swear that Italy had got no more than she deserved, that she was a land of vagabonds and declaimers, and that he had yet to see an Italian whom he would call a man. I quoted to him from Alfieri that the "human plant" grew stronger in Italy than anywhere else, and he retorted, that nothing grew strong there but lying and cheating, laziness, beggary and vermin. Of course we each said more than we believed. If we met a shepherd on the Campagna, leaning on his crook and gazing at us darkly from under the shadow of his matted locks, I would proclaim that he was the handsomest fellow in the world, and demand of Scrope to stop and let me sketch him. Scrope would confound him for a filthy scare-crow and me for a drivelling album-poet. When I stopped in the street to stare up at some mouldering *palazzo* with a patched petticoat hanging to dry from the drawing-room window, and assured him that its haunted disrepair was dearer to my soul than the neat barred front of my Aunt Esther's model mansion in Mount Vernon street, he would seize me by the arm and march me off, pinching me till I shook myself free, and whelming me, my soul and my *palazzo* in a ludicrous torrent of abuse. The truth was that the picturesque of Italy, both in man and in nature, fretted him, depressed him, strangely. He was consciously a harsh note in the midst of so many mellow harmonies; every thing seemed to say to him—"Don't you wish you were as easy, as loveable, as carelessly beautiful as we?" In the bottom of his heart he did wish it. To appreciate the bitterness of this dumb disrelish of the Italian atmosphere, you must remember how very ugly the poor fellow was. He was uglier at twenty than at forty, for as he grew older it became the fashion to say that his crooked features were "distinguished." But twenty years ago, in the infancy of modern æsthetics, he could not have passed for even a bizarre form of ornament. In a single word, poor Scrope looked *common*: that was where the shoe pinched. Now you know that in Italy almost everything, has, to the outer sense, what artists call style.

In spite of our clashing theories, our friendship *did* ripen, and we spent together many hours, deeply seasoned with the sense of youth and freedom. The best of these, perhaps, were those we passed on horseback, on the Campagna; you remember such hours; you remember those days of early winter, when the sun is as strong as that of a New England June, and the bare, purple-drawn slopes and hollows lie bathed in the yellow light of Italy. On such a day, Scrope and I mounted our horses in the grassy terrace before St. John Lateran, and rode away across the broad meadows over which the Claudian Aqueduct drags its slow length—stumbling and lapsing here and there, as it goes, beneath the burden of the centuries. We rode a long distance—well towards Albano, and at last stopped near a low fragment of ruin, which seemed to be all that was left of an ancient tower. Was it indeed ancient, or was it a relic of one of the numerous mediæval fortresses, with which the grassy desert of the Campagna is studded? This was one of the questions which Scrope, as a competent classicist, liked to ponder; though when I called his attention to the picturesque effect of the fringe of wild plants which crowned the ruin, and detached their clear filaments in the deep blue air, he shrugged his shoulders, and said they only helped the brick-work to crumble. We tethered our horses to a wild fig tree hard by, and strolled around the tower. Suddenly, on the sunny side of it, we came upon a figure asleep on the grass. A young man lay there, all unconscious, with his head upon a pile of weed-smothered stones. A rusty gun was on the ground beside him, and an empty game-bag, lying near it, told of his being an unlucky sportsman. His heavy sleep seemed to point to a long morning's fruitless tramp. And yet he must have been either very unskilled, or very little in earnest, for the Campagna is alive with small game every month in the year—or was, at least, twenty years ago. It was no more than I owed to my reputation for Byronism, to discover a careless, youthful grace in the young fellow's attitude. One of his legs was flung over the other; one of his arms was thrust back under his head, and the other resting loosely on the grass; his head drooped backward, and exposed a strong, young throat; his hat was pulled over his eyes, so that we could see nothing but his mouth and chin. "An American rustic asleep is an ugly fellow," said I; "but this young Roman clodhopper, as he lies snoring there, is really statuesque;" "clodhopper," was for argument, for our rustic Endymion, judging by his garments, was something better than a mere peasant. He turned uneasily, as we stood above him, and muttered something. "It's not fair to wake him," I said, and passed my arm into Scrope's, to lead him away; but he resisted, and I saw that something had struck him.

In his change of position, our picturesque friend had opened the hand which was resting on the grass. The palm, turned upward, contained a dull-colored oval object, of the size of a small snuff-box. "What has he got there?" I said to Scrope; but Scrope only answered by bending over and looking at it. "Really, we are taking great liberties with the poor fellow," I said. "Let him finish his nap in peace." And I was on the point of walking away. But my voice had aroused him; he lifted his hand, and, with the movement, the object I have compared to a snuff-box caught the light, and emitted a dull flash.

"It's a gem," said Scrope, "recently disinterred and encrusted with dirt."

The young man awoke in earnest, pushed back his hat, stared at us, and slowly sat up. He rubbed his eyes, to see if he were not still dreaming, then glanced at the gem, if gem it was, thrust his hand mechanically into his pocket, and gave us a broad smile. "Gentle, serene Italian nature!" I exclaimed. "A young New England farmer, whom we should have disturbed in this fashion, would wake up with an oath and a kick."

"I mean to test his gentleness," said Scrope. "I'm determined to see what he has got there." Scrope was very fond of small *bric-a-brac*, and had ransacked every curiosity shop in Rome. It was an oddity among his many oddities, but it agreed well enough with the rest of them. What he looked for and relished in old prints and old china was not, generally, beauty of form nor romantic association; it was elaborate and patient workmanship, fine engraving, skillful method.

"Good day," I said to our young man; "we didn't mean to interrupt you."

He shook himself, got up, and stood before us, looking out

from under his thick curls, and still frankly smiling. There was something very simple,—a trifle silly,—in his smile, and I wondered whether he was not under-witted. He was young, but he was not a mere lad. His eyes were dark and heavy, but they gleamed with a friendly light, and his parted lips showed the glitter of his strong, white teeth. His complexion was of a fine, deep brown, just removed from coarseness by that vague suffused pallor common among Italians. He had the frame of a young Hercules; he was altogether as handsome a vagabond as you could wish for the foreground of a pastoral landscape.

"You've not earned your rest," said Scrope, pointing to his empty game-bag; "you've got no birds."

He looked at the bag and at Scrope, and then scratched his head and laughed. "I don't want to kill them," he said. "I bring out my gun because it's stupid to walk about pulling a straw! And then my uncle is always grumbling at me for not doing something. When he sees me leave the house with my gun, he thinks I may, at least, get my dinner. He didn't know the lock's broke; even if I had powder and shot, the old blunderbuss wouldn't go off. When I'm hungry I go to sleep." And he glanced, with his handsome grin, at his recent couch. "The birds might come and perch on my nose, and not wake me up. My uncle never thinks of asking me what I have brought home for supper. He is a holy man, and lives on black bread and beans."

"Who is your uncle?" I inquired.

"The Padre Girolamo at Lariccia."

He looked at our hats and whips, asked us a dozen questions about our ride, our horses, and what we paid for them, our nationality, and our way of life in Rome, and at last walked away to caress our browsing animals and scratch their noses. "He has got something precious there," Scrope said, as we strolled after him. "He has evidently found it in the ground. The Campagna is full of treasures yet." As we overtook our new acquaintance he thrust his indistinguishable prize behind him, and gave a foolish laugh, which tried my companion's patience. "The fellow's an idiot!" he cried. "Does he think I want to snatch the thing?"

"What is it you've got there?" I asked kindly.

"Which hand will you have?" he said, still laughing.

"The right."

"The left," said Scrope, as he hesitated.

He fumbled behind him a moment more, and then produced his treasure with a flourish. Scrope took it, wiped it off carefully with his handkerchief, and bent his near-sighted eyes over it. I left him to examine it. I was more interested in watching the Padre Girolamo's nephew. The latter stood looking at my friend gravely, while Scrope rubbed and scratched the little black stone, breathed upon it and held it up to the light. He frowned and scratched his head; he was evidently trying to concentrate his wits on the fine account he expected Scrope to give of it. When I glanced towards Scrope, I found he had flushed excitedly, and I immediately bent my nose over it too. It was of about the size of a small hen's-egg, of a dull brown color, stained and encrusted by long burial, and deeply corrugated on one surface. Scrope paid no heed to my questions, but continued to scrape and polish. At last—

"How did you come by this thing?" he asked dryly.

"I found it in the earth, a couple of miles from here, this morning." And the young fellow put out his hand nervously, to take it back. Scrope resisted a moment, but thought better, and surrendered it. As an old mouser, he began instinctively to play at indifference. Our companion looked hard at the little stone, turned it over and over, then thrust it behind him again, with his simple-souled laugh.

"Here's a precious chance," murmured Scrope.

"But in Heaven's name, what is it," I demanded, impatiently.

"Don't ask me. I don't care to phrase the conjecture audibly—it's immense—if it's what I think it is; and here stands this giggling lout with a prior claim to it. What shall I do with him? I should like to knock him in the head with the butt end of his blunderbuss."

"I suppose he'll sell you the thing, if you offer him enough."

"Enough? What does he know about enough? He don't know a topaz from a turnip."

"Is it a topaz, then?"

"Hold your tongue, and don't mention names. He must sell it as a turnip. Make him tell you just where he found it."

He told us very frankly, still smiling from ear to ear. He had observed in a solitary ilex-tree, of great age, the traces of a recent lightning-stroke. (A week of unseasonably sultry weather had, in fact some days before, culminated in a terrific thunder-storm.) The tree had been shivered and killed, and the earth turned up at its foot. The bolt, burying itself, had dug a deep, straight hole, in which one might have planted a stake. "I don't know why," said our friend, "but as I stood looking at it, I thrust the muzzle of my old gun into the aperture. It descended for some distance and stopped with a strange noise, as if it were striking a metallic surface. I rammed it up and down, and heard the same noise. Then I said to myself—'Something is hidden there—*quattrini*, perhaps; let us see.' I made a spade of one of the shivered ilex-boughs, dug, and scraped and scratched; and, in twenty minutes, fished up a little, rotten, iron box. It was so rotten that the lid and sides were as thin as letter-paper. When I gave them a knock, they crumbled. It was filled with other bits of iron of the same sort, which seemed to have formed the compartments of a case; and with the damp earth, which had oozed in through the holes and crevices. In the middle lay this stone, embedded in earth and mold. There was nothing else. I broke the box to pieces and kept the stone. *Ecco!*"

Scrope, with a shrug, repossessed himself of the moldy treasure, and our friend, as he gave it up, declared it was a thousand years old. Julius Cæsar had worn it in his crown!

"Julius Cæsar wore no crown, my dear friend," said Scrope urbanely. "It may be a thousand years old, and it may be ten. It may be an—agate, and it may be a flint! I don't know. But if you will sell it on the chance?——" And he tossed it three times high into the air, and caught it as it fell.

"I have my idea it's precious," said the young man. "Precious things are found here every day—why shouldn't I stumble on something as well as another? Why should the lightning strike just that spot, and no other? It was sent there by my patron, the blessed Saint Angelo!"

He was not such a simpleton, after all; or rather he was a puzzling mixture of simplicity and sense. "If you really want the thing," I said to Scrope, "make him an offer, and have done with it."

" 'Have done with it,' is easily said. How little do you suppose he will take?"

"I haven't the smallest idea of its value."

"Its value has nothing to do with the matter. Estimate it at its value and we may as well put it back into its hole—of its probable value, he knows nothing; he need never know," and Scrope, musing an instant, counted, and flung them down on the grass, ten silver *scudi*—the same number of dollars. Angelo,—he virtually told us his name,—watched them fall, one by one, but made no movement to pick them up. But his eyes brightened; his simplicity and his shrewdness were debating the question. The little heap of silver was most agreeable; to make a poor bargain, on the other hand, was not. He looked at Scrope with a dumb appeal to his fairness which quite touched me. It touched Scrope, too, a trifle; for, after a moment's hesitation, he flung down another *scudi*. Angelo gave a puzzled sigh, and Scrope turned short about and began to mount. In another moment we were both in the saddle. Angelo stood looking at his money. "Are you satisfied?" said my companion, curtly.

The young fellow gave a strange smile. "Have *you* a good conscience?" he demanded.

"Hang your impudence!" cried Scrope, very red. "What's my conscience to you?" And he thrust in his spurs and galloped away. I waved my hand to our friend and followed more slowly. Before long I turned in the saddle and looked back. Angelo was standing as we had left him, staring after us, with his money evidently yet untouched. But, of course, he would pick it up!

I rode along with my friend in silence; I was wondering over his off-hand justice. I was youthful enough to shrink from being thought a Puritan or a casuist, but it seemed to me that I scented sophistry in Scrope's double valuation of Angelo's treasure. If it was a prize for him, it was a prize for Angelo, and ten *scudi*,—and one over,—was meager payment for a prize. It cost me some discomfort to find rigid Sam Scrope, of all men, capable of a piece of bargaining which needed to be ingeniously explained. Such as it was, he offered his explanation at last—half angrily, as if he knew his logic was rather grotesque. "Say it out; say it, for Heaven's sake!" he cried. "I know what you're thinking—I've played that pretty-faced simpleton a trick, eh?—and I'm no better than a swindler, evidently! Let me tell you, once for all, that I'm not ashamed of having got my prize cheap. It was ten *scudi* or nothing! If I had offered a farthing more I should have opened those sleepy eyes of his. It was a case to pocket one's scruples and *act*. That silly boy was not to be trusted with the keeping of such a prize for another half hour; the deuce knows what might have become of it. I rescued it in the interest of art, of science, of taste. The proper price of the thing I couldn't have dreamed of offering; where was I to raise ten thousand dollars to buy a bauble? Say I had offered a hundred—forthwith our picturesque friend, thick-witted though he is, would have pricked up his ears and held fast! He would have asked time to reflect and take advice, and he would have hurried back to his village and to his uncle, the shrewd old priest, Padre Girolamo. The wise-heads of the place would have held a conclave, and decided—I don't know what; that they must go up to Rome and see Signor Castillani, or the director of the Papal excavations. Some knowing person would have got wind of the affair, and whispered to the Padre Girolamo that his handsome nephew had been guided by a miracle to a fortune, and might marry a *contessina*. And when all was done, where should I be for my pains? As it is, I discriminate; I look at the matter all round, and I decide. I get my prize; the ingenious Angelo gets a month's carouse,—he'll enjoy it,—and goes to sleep again. Pleasant dreams to him! What does he want of money? Money would have corrupted him! I've saved the *contessina*, too; I'm sure he would have beaten her. So, if we're all satisfied, is it for you to look black? My mind's at ease; I'm neither richer nor poorer. I'm not poorer, because against my eleven *scudi* may stand the sense of having given a harmless treat to an innocent lad; I'm not richer, because,—I hope you understand,—I mean never to turn my stone into money. There it is that delicacy comes in. It's a stone and nothing more; and all the income I shall derive from it will be enjoying the way people open their eyes and hold their breath when I make it sparkle under the lamp, and tell them just what stone it is."

"What stone is it, then, in the name of all that's demoralizing?" I asked, with ardor.

Scrope broke into a gleeful chuckle, and patted me on the arm. "*Pazienza!* Wait till we get under the lamp, some evening, and then I'll make it sparkle and tell you. I must be sure first," he added, with sudden gravity.

But it was the feverish elation of his tone, and not its gravity, that struck me. I began to hate the stone; it seemed to have corrupted him. His ingenious account of his motives left something vaguely unexplained—almost inexplicable. There are dusky corners in the simplest natures; strange, moral involutions in the healthiest. Scrope was not simple, and, in virtue of his defiant self-consciousness, he might have been called morbid; so that I came to consider his injustice in this particular case as the fruit of a vicious seed which I find it hard to name. Everything in Italy seemed mutely to reproach him with his meager faculty of pleasing; the indefinable gracefulness of nature and man murmured forever in his ears that he was an angular cynic. This was the real motive of his intolerance of my sympathetic rhapsodies, and it prompted him now to regale himself, once for all, with the sense of an advantage wrested, if not by fair means, then by foul, from some sentient form of irritating Italian felicity. This is a rather metaphysical account of the matter; at the time I guessed the secret, without phrasing it.

Scrope carried his stone to no appraiser, and asked no archæological advice about it. He quietly informed himself, as if from general curiosity, as to the best methods of cleaning, polishing, and restoring antique gems, laid in a provision of delicate tools and acids, turned the key in his door, and took the measure of his prize. I asked him no questions, but I saw that he was intensely preoccupied, and was becoming daily better convinced that it was a rare one. He went about whistling and humming odd scraps of song, like a lover freshly accepted. Whenever I heard him I had a sudden vision of our friend Angelo staring blankly after us, as we rode away like a pair of ravishers in a German ballad. Scrope and I lodged in the same house, and one evening, at the end of a week, after I had gone to bed, he made his way into my

room, and shook me out of my slumbers as if the house were
on fire. I guessed his errand before he had told it, shuffled on
my dressing-gown, and hurried to his own apartment. "I
couldn't wait till morning," he said, "I've just given it the last
touch; there it lies in its imperial beauty!"

There it lay, indeed, under the lamp, flashing back the light
from its glowing heart—a splendid golden topaz on a cushion
of white velvet. He thrust a magnifying glass into my hand,
and pushed me into a chair by the table. I saw the surface of
the stone was worked in elaborate intaglio, but I was not prepared for the portentous character of image and legend. In
the center was a full-length naked figure, which I supposed at
first to be a pagan deity. Then I saw the orb of sovereignty in
one outstretched hand, the chiselled imperial scepter in the
other, and the laurel-crown on the low-browed head. All
round the face of the stone, near the edges, ran a chain of
carven figures—warriors, and horses, and chariots, and young
men and women interlaced in elaborate confusion. Over the
head of the image, within this concave frieze, stood the
inscription:

DIVUS TIBERIUS CÆSAR TOTIUS ORBIS IMPERATOR.

The workmanship was extraordinarily delicate; beneath the
powerful glass I held in my hand, the figures revealed the perfection and finish of the most renowned of antique marbles.
The color of the stone was superb, and, now that its purity
had been restored, its size seemed prodigious. It was in every
way a gem among gems, a priceless treasure.

"Don't you think it was worth while getting up to shake
hands with the Emperor Tiberius?" cried Scrope, after observing my surprise. "Shabby Nineteenth Century Yankees, as
we are, we are having our audience. Down on your knees,
barbarian, we're in a tremendous presence! Haven't I worked
all these days and nights, with my little rags and files, to some
purpose? I've annulled the centuries—I've resuscitated a *totius
orbis imperator*. Do you conceive, do you apprehend, does
your heart thump against your ribs? Not as it should, evidently. This is where Cæsar wore it, dull modern—here, on
his breast, near the shoulder, framed in chiselled gold, circled
about with pearls as big as plums, clasping together the two

sides of his gold-stiffened mantle. It was the agraffe of the imperial purple. Tremble, sir!" and he took up the splendid jewel, and held it against my breast. "No doubts—no objections—no reflections—or we're mortal enemies. How do I know it—where's my warrant? It simply must be! It's too precious to have been anything else. It's the finest intaglio in the world. It has told me its secret; it has lain whispering classic Latin to me by the hour all this week past."

"And has it told you how it came to be buried in its iron box?"

"It has told me everything—more than I can tell you now. Content yourself for the present with admiring it."

Admire it I did for a long time. Certainly, if Scrope's hypothesis was not sound, it ought to have been, and if the Emperor Tiberius had never worn the topaz in his mantle, he was by so much the less imperial. But the design, the legend, the shape of the stone, were all very cogent evidence that the gem had played a great part. "Yes, surely," I said, "it's the finest of known intaglios."

Scrope was silent a while. "Say of unknown," he answered at last. "No one shall ever know it. You I hereby hold pledged to secrecy. I shall show it to no one else—except to my mistress, if I ever have one. I paid for the chance of its turning out something great. I couldn't pay for the renown of possessing it. That only a princely fortune could have purchased. To be known as the owner of the finest intaglio in the world would make a great man of me, and that would hardly be fair to our friend Angelo. I shall sink the glory, and cherish my treasure for its simple artistic worth."

"And how would you express that simple artistic worth in Roman *scudi*?"

"It's impossible. Fix upon any sum you please."

I looked again at the golden topaz, gleaming in its velvet nest; and I felt that there could be no successful effort to conceal such a magnificent negation of obscurity. "I recommend you," I said at last, "to think twice before showing it to your mistress."

I had no idea, when I spoke, that my words were timely; for I had vaguely taken for granted that my friend was foredoomed to dispense with this graceful appendage, very much

as Peter Schlemihl, in the tale, was condemned to have no
shadow. Nevertheless, before a month had passed, he was in a
fair way to become engaged to a charming girl. "Juxtaposition is much," says Clough; especially juxtaposition, he implies, in foreign countries; and in Scrope's case it had been
particularly close. His cousin, Mrs. Waddington, arrived in
Rome, and with her a young girl who, though really no relative, offered him all the opportunities of cousinship, added to
the remoter charm of a young lady to whom he had to be introduced. Adina Waddington was her companion's step-
daughter, the elder lady having, some eight years before,
married a widower with a little girl. Mr. Waddington had recently died, and the two ladies were just emerging from their
deep mourning. These dusky emblems of a common grief
helped them to seem united, as indeed they really were, although Mrs. Waddington was but ten years older than her
stepdaughter. She was an excellent woman, without a fault
that I know of, but that of thinking all the world as good as
herself and keeping dinner waiting sometimes while she
sketched the sunset. She was stout and fresh-colored, she
laughed and talked rather loud, and generally, in galleries and
temples, caused a good many stiff British necks to turn round.

She had a mania for excursions, and at Frascati and Tivoli
she inflicted her good-humored ponderosity on diminutive
donkeys with a relish which seemed to prove that a passion
for scenery, like all our passions, is capable of making the best
of us pitiless. I had often heard Scrope say that he detested
boisterous women, but he forgave his cousin her fine spirits,
and stepped into his place as her natural escort and adviser. In
the vulgar sense he was not selfish; he had a very definite theory as to the sacrifices a gentleman should make to formal
courtesy; but I was nevertheless surprised at the easy terms on
which the two ladies secured his services. The key to the mystery was the one which fits so many locks; he was in love with
Miss Waddington. There was a sweet stillness about her which
balanced the widow's exuberance. Her pretty name of Adina
seemed to me to have somehow a mystic fitness to her personality. She was short and slight and blonde, and her black
dress gave a sort of infantine bloom to her fairness. She wore
her auburn hair twisted into a thousand fantastic braids, like a

coiffure in a Renaissance drawing, and she looked out at you from grave blue eyes, in which, behind a cold shyness, there seemed to lurk a tremulous promise to be franker when she knew you better. She never consented to know me well enough to be very frank; she talked very little, and we hardly exchanged a dozen words a day; but I confess that I found a perturbing charm in those eyes. As it was all in silence, though, there was no harm.

Scrope, however, ventured to tell his love—or, at least, to hint at it eloquently enough. I was not so deeply smitten as to be jealous, and I drew a breath of relief when I guessed his secret. It made me think better of him again. The stand he had taken about poor Angelo's gem, in spite of my efforts to account for it philosophically, had given an uncomfortable twist to our friendship. I asked myself if he really had no heart; I even wondered whether there was not a screw lose in his intellect. But here was a hearty, healthy, natural passion, such as only an honest man could feel—such as no man could feel without being the better for it. I began to hope that the sunshine of his fine sentiment would melt away his aversion to giving Angelo his dues. He was charmed, soul and sense, and for a couple of months he really forgot himself, and ceased to send forth his unsweetened wit to do battle for his ugly face. His happiness rarely made him "gush," as they say; but I could see that he was vastly contented with his prospects. More than once, when we were together, he broke into a kind of nervous, fantastic laugh, over his own thoughts; and on his refusal to part with them for the penny which one offers under those circumstances, I said to myself that this was humorous surprise at his good luck. How had *he* come to please that exquisite creature? Of course, I learned even less from the young girl about her own view of the case; but Mrs. Waddington and I, not being in love with each other, had nothing to do but to gossip about our companions whenever (which was very often) they consigned us to a *tête-à-tête*.

"She tells me nothing," the good-humored widow said; "and if I'm to know the answer to a riddle, I must have it in black and white. My cousin is not what is called 'attractive,' but I think Adina, nevertheless, is interested in him. How do you and I know how passion may transfigure and exalt him?

And who shall say beforehand what a fanciful young girl shall do with that terrible little piece of machinery she calls her heart? Adina is a strange child; she is fanciful without being capricious. For all I know, she may admire my cousin for his very ugliness and queerness. She has decided, very likely, that she wants an 'intellectual' husband, and if Mr. Scrope is not handsome, nor frivolous, nor over-polite, there's a greater chance of his being wise." Why Adina should have listened to my friend, however, was her own business. Listen to him she did, and with a sweet attentiveness which may well have flattered and charmed him.

We rarely spoke of the imperial topaz; it seemed not a subject for light allusions. It might properly make a man feel solemn to possess it; the mere memory of its luster lay like a weight on my own conscience. I had felt, as we lost sight of our friend Angelo that, in one way or another, we should hear of him again; but the weeks passed by without his re-appearing, and my conjectures as to the sequel, on his side, of his remarkable bargain remained quite unanswered. Christmas arrived, and with it the usual ceremonies. Scrope and I took the requisite vigorous measures,—it was a matter, you know, of fists and elbows and knees,—and obtained places for the two ladies at the Midnight Mass at the Sistine Chapel. Mrs. Waddington was my especial charge, and on coming out we found we had lost sight of our companions in the crowd. We waited awhile in the Colonnade, but they were not among the passers, and we supposed that they had gone home independently, and expected us to do likewise. But on reaching Mrs. Waddington's lodging we found they had not come in. As their prolonged absence demanded an explanation, it occurred to me that they had wandered into Saint Peter's, with many others of the attendants at the Mass, and were watching the tapers twinkle in its dusky immensity. It was not perfectly regular that a young lady should be wandering about at three o'clock in the morning with a very "unattractive" young man; but "after all," said Mrs. Waddington, "she's almost his cousin." By the time they returned she was much more. I went home, went to bed, and slept as late as the Christmas bells would allow me. On rising, I knocked at Scrope's door to wish him the compliments of the season, but on his coming to open it for me, perceived that such common-place greetings were quite below the mark. He was but half un-dressed, and had flung himself, on his return, on the outside of his bed. He had gone with Adina, as I supposed, into Saint Peter's, and they had found the twinkling tapers as pic-turesque as need be. He walked about the room for some time restlessly, and I saw that he had something to say. At last he brought it out. "I say, I'm accepted. I'm engaged. I'm what's called a happy man."

Of course I wished him joy on the news; and could assure him, with ardent conviction, that he had chosen well. Miss Waddington was the loveliest, the purest, the most interesting of young girls. I could see that he was grateful for my sympa-thy, but he disliked "expansion," and he contented himself, as he shook hands with me, with simply saying—"Oh yes; she's the right thing." He took two or three more turns about the room, and then suddenly stopped before his toilet-table, and pulled out a tray in his dressing-case. There lay the great in-taglio; larger even than I should have dared to boast. "That would be a pretty thing to offer one's *fiancée*," he said, after gazing at it for some time. "How could she wear it—how could one have it set?"

"There could be but one way," I said; "as a massive medal-lion, depending from a necklace. It certainly would light up the world more, on the bosom of a beautiful woman, than thrust away here, among your brushes and razors. But, to my sense, only a beauty of a certain type could properly wear it—a splendid, dusky beauty, with the brow of a Roman Empress, and the shoulders of an antique statue. A fair, slender girl, with blue eyes, and sweet smile, would seem, somehow, to be overweighted by it, and if I were to see it hung, for instance, round Miss Waddington's white neck, I should feel as if it were pulling her down to the ground, and giving her a mys-terious pain."

He was a trifle annoyed, I think, by this rather fine-spun objection; but he smiled as he closed the tray. "Adina may not have the shoulders of the Venus of Milo," he said, "but I hope it will take more than a bauble like this to make her stoop."

I don't always go to church on Christmas Day; but I have

a life-long habit of taking a solitary walk, in all weathers, and harboring Christian thoughts if they come. This was a Southern Christmas, without snow on the ground, or sleigh-bells in the air, or the smoke of crowded firesides rising into a cold, blue sky. The day was mild, and almost warm, the sky gray and sunless. If I was disposed toward Christmas thoughts, I confess, I sought them among Pagan memories. I strolled about the forums, and then walked along to the Coliseum. It was empty, save for a single figure, sitting on the steps at the foot of the cross in the center—a young man, apparently, leaning forward, motionless, with his elbows on his knees, and his head buried in his hands. As he neither stirred nor observed me when I passed near him, I said to myself that, brooding there so intensely in the shadow of the sign of redemption, he might pass for an image of youthful remorse. Then, as he never moved, I wondered whether it was not a deeper passion even than repentance. Suddenly he looked up, and I recognized our friend Angelo—not immediately, but in response to a gradual movement of recognition in his own face. But seven weeks had passed since our meeting, and yet he looked three years older. It seemed to me that he had lost flesh, and gained expression. His simple-souled smile was gone; there was no trace of it in the shy mistrust of his greeting. He looked graver, manlier, and very much less rustic. He was equipped in new garments of a pretentious pattern, though they were carelessly worn, and bespattered with mud. I remember he had a flaming orange necktie, which harmonized admirably with his picturesque coloring. Evidently he was greatly altered; as much altered as if he had made a voyage round the world. I offered him my hand, and asked if he remembered me.

"*Per Dio!*" he cried. "With good reason." Even his voice seemed changed; it was fuller and harsher. He bore us a grudge. I wondered how his eyes had been opened. He fixed them on me with a dumb reproachfulness, which was half appealing and half ominous. He had been brooding and brooding on his meager bargain till the sense of wrong had become a kind of smothered fear. I observed all this with poignant compassion, for it seemed to me that he had parted with something more precious even than his imperial intaglio. He had lost his boyish ignorance—that pastoral peace of mind which had suffered him to doze there so gracefully with his head among the flowers. But even in his resentment he was simple still. "Where is the other one—your friend?" he asked.

"He's at home—he's still in Rome."

"And the stone—what has he done with it?"

"Nothing. He has it still."

He shook his head dolefully. "Will he give it back to me for twenty-five *scudi*?"

"I'm afraid not. He values it."

"I believe so. Will he let me see it?"

"That you must ask him. He shows it to no one."

"He's afraid of being robbed, eh? That proves its value! He hasn't shown it to a jeweler—to a, what do they call them?—a lapidary?"

"To no one. You must believe me."

"But he has cleaned it, and polished it, and discovered what it is?"

"It's very old. It's hard to say."

"Very old! Of course it's old. There are more years in it than it brought me *scudi*. What does it look like? Is it red, blue, green, yellow?"

"Well, my friend," I said, after a moment's hesitation, "it's yellow."

He gave me a searching stare; then quickly—"It's what's called a topaz," he cried.

"Yes, it's what's called a topaz."

"And it's sculptured—that I could see! It's an intaglio. Oh, I know the names, and I've paid enough for my learning. What's the figure? A king's head—or a Pope's, perhaps, eh? Or the portrait of some beautiful woman that you read about?"

"It is the figure of an Emperor."

"What is his name?"

"Tiberius."

"*Corpo di Cristo!*" his face flushed, and his eyes filled with angry tears.

"Come," I said, "I see you're sorry to have parted with the stone. Some one has been talking to you, and making you discontented."

"Every one, *per Dio!* Like the finished fool I was, I couldn't
keep my folly to myself. I went home with my eleven *scudi*,
thinking I should never see the end of them. The first thing I
did was to buy a gilt hair-pin from a peddler, and give it to
the Ninetta—a young girl of my village, with whom I had a
friendship. She stuck it into her braids, and looked at herself
in the glass, and then asked how I had suddenly got so rich!
'Oh, I'm richer than you suppose,' said I, and showed her my
money, and told her the story of the stone. She is a very clever
girl, and it would take a knowing fellow to have the last word
with her. She laughed in my face, and told me I was an idiot,
that the stone was surely worth five hundred *scudi*; that my
forestiere was a pitiless rascal; that I ought to have brought it
away, and shown it to my elders and betters; in fine, that I
might take her word for it, I had held a fortune in my hand,
and thrown it to the dogs. And, to wind up this sweet speech,
she took out her hairpin, and tossed it into my face. She never
wished to see me again; she had as lief marry a blind beggar
at a cross-road. What was I to say? She had a sister who was
waiting-maid to a fine lady in Rome,—a *marchesa*,—who had
a priceless necklace made of fine old stones picked up on the
Campagna. I went away hanging my head, and cursing my
folly: I flung my money down in the dirt, and spat upon it! At
last, to ease my spirit, I went to drink a *foglietta* at the wine-
shop. There I found three or four young fellows I knew; I
treated them all round; I hated my money, and wanted to get
rid of it. Of course they too wanted to know how I came by
my full pockets. I told them the truth. I hoped they would
give me a better account of things than that vixen of a
Ninetta. But they knocked their glasses on the table, and
jeered at me in chorus. Any donkey, out a-grazing, if he had
turned up such a treasure with his nose, would have taken it
in his teeth and brought it home to his master. This was cold
comfort; I drowned my rage in wine. I emptied one flask after another; for the first time in my life I got drunk. But I
can't speak of that night! The next day I took what was left of
my money to my uncle, and told him to give it to the poor,
to buy new candlesticks for his church, or to say masses for
the redemption of my blaspheming soul. He looked at it very
hard, and hoped I had come by it honestly. I was in for it; I

told *him* too! He listened to me in silence, looking at me over his spectacles. When I had done, he turned over the money in his hands, and then sat for three minutes with his eyes closed. Suddenly he thrust it back into my own hands. 'Keep it— keep it, my son,' he said, 'your wits will never help you to a supper, make the most of what you've got!' Since then, do you see, I've been in a fever. I can think of nothing else but the fortune I've lost."

"Oh, a fortune!" I said, deprecatingly. "You exaggerate."

"It would have been a fortune to me. A voice keeps ringing in my ear night and day, and telling me I could have got a thousand *scudi* for it."

I'm afraid I blushed; I turned away a moment; when I looked at the young man again, his face had kindled. "Tiberius, eh? A Roman emperor sculptured on a big topaz— that's fortune enough for me! Your friend's a rascal—do you know that? I don't say it for you; I like your face, and I believe that, if you can, you'll help me. But your friend is an ugly little monster. I don't know why the devil I trusted him; I saw he wished me no good. Yet, if ever there was a harmless fellow, I was. *Ecco!* it's my fate. That's very well to say; I say it and say it, but it helps me no more than an empty glass helps your thirst. I'm not harmless now. If I meet your friend, and he refuses me justice, I won't answer for these two hands. You see—they're strong; I could easily strangle him! Oh, at first, I shall speak him fair, but if he turns me off, and answers me with English oaths, I shall think only of my *revenge*!" And with a passionate gesture he pulled off his hat, and flung it on the ground, and stood wiping the perspiration from his forehead.

I answered him briefly but kindly enough. I told him to leave his case in my hands, go back to Lariccia and try and find some occupation which would divert him from his grievance. I confess that even as I gave this respectable advice, I but half believed in it. It was none of poor Angelo's mission to arrive at virtue through tribulation. His indolent nature, active only in immediate feeling, would have found my prescription of wholesome labor more intolerable even than his wrong. He stared gloomily and made no answer, but he saw that I had his interests at heart, and he promised me, at least, to leave Rome, and believe that I would fairly plead his cause. If I had good news for him I was to address him at Lariccia. It was thus I learned his full name,—a name, certainly, that ought to have been to its wearer a sort of talisman against trouble,—Angelo Beati.

PART II.

Sam Scrope looked extremely annoyed when I began to tell him of my encounter with our friend, and I saw there was still a cantankerous something in the depths of his heart intensely hostile to fairness. It was characteristic of his peculiar temper that his happiness, as an accepted lover, had not disposed him to graceful concessions. He treated his bliss as his own private property, and was as little in the humor to diffuse its influence as he would have been to send out in charity a choice dish from an unfinished dinner. Nevertheless, I think he might have stiffly admitted that there was a grain of reason in Angelo's claim, if I had not been too indiscreetly accurate in my report of our interview. I had been impressed, indeed, with something picturesquely tragic in the poor boy's condition, and, to do perfect justice to the picture, I told him he had flung down his hat on the earth as a gauntlet of defiance and talked about his *revenge*. Scrope hereupon looked fiercely disgusted and pronounced him a theatrical jackanapes; but he authorized me to drop him a line saying that he would speak with him a couple of days later. I was surprised at Scrope's consenting to see him, but I perceived that he was making a conscientious effort to shirk none of the disagreeables of the matter. "I won't have him stamping and shouting in the house here," he said. "I'll also meet him at the Coliseum." He named his hour and I despatched to Lariccia three lines of incorrect but courteous Italian.

It was better,—far better,—that they should not have met. What passed between them Scrope requested me on his return to excuse him from repeating; suffice it that Angelo was an impudent puppy, and that he hoped never to hear of him again. Had Angelo, at last, I asked, received any compensation? "Not a farthing!" cried Scrope, and walked out of the room. Evidently the two young men had been a source of immitigable offense to each other. Angelo had promised to speak to him fair, and I inclined to believe had done so; but the very change in his appearance, by seeming to challenge my companion's sympathy in too peremptory a fashion, had had the irritating effect of a menace. Scrope had been contemptuous, and his awkward, ungracious Italian had doubtless made him seem more so. One can't handle Italians with contempt; those who know them have learned what may be done with a moderate amount of superficial concession. Angelo had replied in wrath, and, as I afterwards learned, had demanded, as a right, the restitution of the topaz in exchange for the sum received for it. Scrope had rejoined that if he took that tone he should get nothing at all, and the injured youth had retorted with reckless and insulting threats. What had prevented them from coming to blows, I know not, no sign of flinching, certainly, on my companion's part. Face to face, he had not seemed to Angelo so easy to strangle, and that saving grain of discretion which mingles with all Italian passion had whispered to the young man to postpone his revenge. Without taking a melodramatic view of things, it seemed to me that Scrope had an evil chance in waiting for him. I had, perhaps, no definite vision of a cloaked assassin lurking under a dark archway, but I thought it perfectly possible that Angelo might make himself intolerably disagreeable. His simply telling his story up and down Rome to whomsoever would listen to him, might be a grave annoyance; though indeed Scrope had the advantage that most people might refuse to believe in the existence of a gem of which its owner was so little inclined to boast. The whole situation, at all events, made me extremely nervous. I cursed my companion one day for a hungrier Jew than Shylock, and pitied him the next as the victim of a moral hallucination. If we gave him time, he *would* come to his senses; he would repay poor Angelo with interest. Meanwhile, however, I could do nothing, for I felt that it was worse than useless to suggest to Scrope that he was in danger. He would have scorned the idea of a ranting Italian making him swerve an inch from his chosen path.

I am unable to say whether Angelo's "imprudence" had seemed to relieve him, generally, from his vow to conceal the intaglio; a few words, at all events, from Miss Waddington, a couple of evenings later, reminded me of the original reservation he had made to the vow. Mrs. Waddington was at the piano, deciphering a new piece of music, and Scrope, who was fond of a puzzle, as a puzzle, was pretending, half jocosely, to superintend and correct her. "I've seen it," Adina said to me, with grave, expanded eyes; "I've seen the wonderful topaz. He says you are in the secret. He won't tell me how he came by it. Honestly, I hope."

I tried to laugh. "You mustn't investigate too closely the honesty of hunters for antiquities. It's hardly dishonest in their code to treat loose cameos and snuff-boxes as pickpockets treat purses."

She looked at me in shy surprise, as if I had made a really cruel joke. "He says that I must wear it one of these days as a medallion," she went on. "But I shall not. The stone is beautiful, but I should feel most uncomfortable in carrying the Emperor Tiberius so near my heart. Wasn't he one of the bad Emperors—one of the worst? It is almost a pollution to have a thing that *he* had looked at and touched coming to one in such direct descent. His image almost spoils for me the beauty of the stone and I'm very glad Mr. Scrope keeps it out of sight." This seemed a very becoming state of mind in a blonde angel of New England origin.

The days passed by and Angelo's "revenge" still hung fire. Scrope never met his fate at a short turning of one of the dusky Roman streets; he came in punctually every evening at eleven o'clock. I wondered whether our brooding friend had already spent the sinister force of a nature formed to be lazily contented. I hoped so, but I was wrong. We had gone to walk one afternoon,—the ladies, Scrope and I,—in the charming Villa Borghese, and, to escape from the rattle of the fashionable world and its distraction, we had wandered away to an unfrequented corner where the old moldering wall and the slim black cypresses and the untrodden grass made, beneath the splendid Roman sky, the most harmonious of pictures. Of course there was a mossy stone hemicycle not far off, and cracked benches with griffins' feet, where one might sit and gossip and watch the lizards scamper in the sun. We had done so for some half an hour when Adina espied the first violet of the year glimmering at the root of a cypress. She made haste to rise and gather it, and then wandered further, in the hope of giving it a few companions. Scrope sat and watched her as she moved slowly away, trailing her long shadow on the grass and drooping her head from side to side in her charming quest. It was not, I know, that he felt no impulse to join her; but that he was in love, for the moment, with looking at her from where he sat. Her search carried her some distance and at last she passed out of sight behind a bend in the villa wall. Mrs. Waddington proposed in a few moments that we should overtake her, and we moved forward. We had not advanced many paces before she re-appeared, glancing over her shoulder as she came towards us with an air of suppressed perturbation. In an instant I saw she was being followed; a man was close behind her—a man in whom my second glance recognized Angelo Beati. Adina was pale; something had evidently passed between them. By the time she had met us, we were also face to face with Angelo. He was pale, as well, and, between these two pallors, Scrope had flushed crimson. I was afraid of an explosion and stepped toward Angelo to avert it. But to my surprise, he was evidently following another line. He turned the cloudy brightness of his eyes upon each of us and poised his hand in the air as if to say, in answer to my unspoken charge—"Leave me alone, I know what I am about." I exchanged a glance with Scrope, urging him to pass on with the ladies and let me deal with the intruder. Miss Waddington stopped; she was gazing at Angelo with soft intentness. Her lover, to lead her away, grasped her arm almost rudely, and as she went with him I saw her faintly flushing. Mrs. Waddington, unsuspicious of evil, saw nothing but a very handsome young man. "What a beautiful creature for a sketch!" I heard her exclaim, as she followed her step-daughter.

"I'm not going to make a noise," said Angelo, with a somber smile; "don't be frightened! I know what good manners are. These three weeks now that I've been hanging about Rome, I've learned to play the gentleman. Who is that young lady?"

"My dear young man, it's none of your business. I hope you had not the hardihood to speak to her."

He was silent a moment, looking after her as she retreated

on her companion's arm. "Yes, I spoke to her—and she understood me. Keep quiet; I said nothing she mightn't hear. But such as it was she understood it. She's your friend's *amica*; I know that. I've been watching you for half an hour from behind those trees. She is wonderfully beautiful. Farewell; I wish you no harm, but tell your friend I've not forgotten *him*. I'm only awaiting my chance; I think it will come. I don't want to kill him; I want to give him some hurt that he'll survive and *feel*—forever!" He was turning away, but he paused and watched my companions till they disappeared. At last—"He has more than his share of good luck," he said, with a sort of forced coldness. "A topaz—and a pearl! both at once! Eh, farewell!" And he walked rapidly away, waving his hand. I let him go. I was unsatisfied, but his unexpected sobriety left me nothing to say.

When a startling event comes to pass, we are apt to waste a good deal of time in trying to recollect the correct signs and portents which preceded it, and when they seem fewer than they should be, we don't scruple to imagine them—we invent them after the fact. Therefore it is that I don't pretend to be sure that I was particularly struck, from this time forward, with something strange in our quiet Adina. She had always seemed to me vaguely, innocently strange; it was part of her charm that in the daily noiseless movement of her life a mystic undertone seemed to murmur—"You don't half know me!" Perhaps we three prosaic mortals were not quite worthy to know her: yet I believe that if a practised man of the world had whispered to me, one day, over his wine, after Miss Waddington had rustled away from the table, that *there* was a young lady who, sooner or later, would treat her friends to a first class surprise, I should have laid my finger on his sleeve and told him with a smile that he phrased my own thought. Was she more silent than usual, was she preoccupied, was she melancholy, was she restless? Picturesquely, she ought to have been all these things; but in fact, she was still to the unillumined eye simply a very pretty blonde maiden, who smiled more than she spoke, and accepted her lover's devotion with a charming demureness which savored much more of humility than of condescension. It seemed to me useless to repeat to Scrope the young Italian's declaration that he had spoken to her, and poor Sam never intimated to me either that he had questioned her in suspicion of the fact, or that she had offered him any account of it. I was sure, however, that something must have passed between the young girl and her lover in the way of question and answer, and I privately wondered what the deuce Angelo had meant by saying she had understood him. What had she understood? Surely not the story of Scrope's acquisition of the gem; for granting—what was unlikely—that Angelo had had time to impart it, it was unnatural that Adina should not have frankly demanded an explanation. At last I broke the ice and asked Scrope if he supposed Miss Waddington had reason to connect the great intaglio with the picturesque young man she had met in the Villa Borghese.

My question caused him visible discomfort. "Picturesque?" he growled. "Did she tell you she thought him picturesque?"

"By no means. But he is! You must at least allow him that."

"He hadn't brushed his hair for a week—if that's what you mean. But it's a charm which I doubt that Adina appreciates. But she has certainly taken," he added in a moment, "an unaccountable dislike to the topaz. She says the Emperor Tiberius spoils it for her. It's carrying historical antipathies rather far: I supposed nothing could spoil a fine gem for a pretty woman. It appears," he finally said, "that that rascal spoke to her."

"What did he say?"

"He asked her if she was engaged to me."

"And what did she answer?"

"Nothing."

"I suppose she was frightened."

"She might have been; but she says she was not. He begged her not to be; he told her he was a poor harmless fellow looking for justice. She left him, without speaking. I told her he was crazy—it's not a lie."

"Possibly!" I rejoined. Then, as a last attempt—"You know it wouldn't be quite a lie," I added, "to say that *you* are not absolutely sane. You're very erratic, about the topaz; obstinacy, pushed under certain circumstances beyond a certain point, bears a dangerous likeness to craziness."

I suppose that if one could reason with a mule it would

make him rather more mulish to know one called him stubborn. Scrope gave me a chilling grin. "I deny your circumstances. If I'm mad, I claim the madman's privilege of
believing myself peculiarly sane. If you wish to preach to me,
you must catch me in a lucid interval."

The breath of early spring in Rome, though magical, as you
know, in its visible influence on the dark old city, is often
rather trying to the foreign constitution. After a fortnight of
uninterrupted sirocco, Mrs. Waddington's fine spirits confessed to depression. She was afraid, of course, that she was
going to have "the fever," and made haste to consult a physician. He reassured her, told her she simply needed change of
air, and recommended a month at Albano. To Albano, accordingly, the two ladies repaired, under Scrope's escort. Mrs.
Waddington kindly urged my going with them; but I was detained in Rome by the arrival of some relations of my own, for
whom I was obliged to play *cicerone*. I could only promise to
make an occasional visit to Albano. My uncle and his three
daughters were magnificent sight-seers, and gave me plenty to
do; nevertheless, at the end of a week I was able to redeem
my promise. I found my friends lodging at the inn, and the
two ladies doing their best to merge the sense of dirty stone
floors and crumpled yellow table-cloth in ecstatic contemplation, from their windows, of the great misty sea-like level of
the Campagna. The view apart, they were passing delightful
days. You remember the loveliness of the place and its picturesque neighborhood of strange old mountain towns. The
country was blooming with early flowers and foliage, and my
friends lived in the open air. Mrs. Waddington sketched in water colors. Adina gathered wild nosegays, and Scrope hovered
contentedly between them—not without an occasional frank
stricture on the elder lady's use of her pigments and Adina's
combinations of narcissus and cyclamen. All seemed to me
very happy and, without ill-nature, I felt almost tempted to
wonder whether the most desirable gift of the gods is not a
thick-and-thin conviction of one's own impeccability. Yet even
a lover with a bad conscience might be cheated into a disbelief
in retribution by the unbargained sweetness of such a presence in his life as Adina Waddington's.

I spent the night at Albano, but as I had pledged myself to

go the next morning to a funzione with my fair cousins in Rome,—"fair" is for rhetoric; but they were excellent girls:— I was obliged to rise and start at dawn. Scrope had offered to go with me part of the way, and walk back to the inn before breakfast; but I declined to accept so onerous a favor, and departed alone, in the early twilight. A rickety diligence made the transit across the Campagna, and I had a five minutes' walk to the post-office, while it stood waiting for its freight. I made my way through the little garden of the inn, as this saved me some steps. At the sound of my tread on the gravel, a figure rose slowly from a bench at the foot of a crippled grim statue, and I found myself staring at Angelo Beati. I greeted him with an exclamation, which was virtually a challenge of his right to be there. He stood and looked at me fixedly, with a strangely defiant, unembarrassed smile, and at last, in answer to my repeated inquiry as to what the deuce he was about, he said he supposed he had a right to take a stroll in a neighbor's garden.

"A neighbor?" said I. "How ——?"

"Eh, *per Dio!* don't I live at Lariccia?" And he laughed in almost as simple a fashion as when we had awaked him from his dreamless sleep in the meadows.

I had had so many other demands on my attention during my friend's absence that it never occurred to me that Scrope had lodged himself in the very jaws of the enemy. But I began to believe that, after all, the enemy was very harmless. If Angelo confined his machinations to sitting about in damp gardens at malarial hours, Scrope would not be the first to suffer. I had fancied at first that his sense of injury had made a man of him; but there seemed still to hang about him a sort of a romantic ineffectiveness. His painful impulsion toward maturity had lasted but a day and he had become again an irresponsible lounger in Arcady. But he must have had an Arcadian constitution to brave the Roman dews at that rate. "And you came here for a purpose," I said. "It ought to be a very good one to warrant your spending your nights out of doors in this silly fashion. If you are not careful you'll get the fever and die, and that will be the end of everything."

He seemed grateful for my interest in his health. "No, no, *Signorino mio*, I'll not get the fever. I've a fever here"—and he struck a blow on his breast—"that's a safeguard against the other. I've had a purpose in coming here, but you'll never guess it. Leave me alone; I shan't harm you! But now, that day is beginning, I must go; I must not be seen."

I grasped him by the arm, looked at him hard and tried to penetrate his meaning. He met my eyes frankly and gave a little contented laugh. Whatever his secret was, he was not ashamed of it; I saw with some satisfaction that it was teaching him patience. Something in his face, in the impression it gave me of his nature, reassured me, at the same time, that it contradicted my hypothesis of a moment before. There was no evil in it and no malignity, but a deep, insistent, natural desire which seemed to be slumbering for the time in a mysterious prevision of success. He thought, apparently, that his face was telling too much. He gave another little laugh, and began to whistle softly. "You are meant for something better," I said, "than to skulk about here like a burglar. How would you like to go to America and do some honest work?" I had an absurd momentary vision of helping him on his way, and giving him a letter of introduction to my brother-in-law, who was in the hardware business.

He took off his hat and passed his hand through his hair. "You think, then, I am meant for something good?"

"If you will! If you'll give up your idle idea of 'revenge' and trust to time to right your wrong."

"Give it up?—Impossible!" he said, grimly. "Ask me rather to chop off my arm. This is the same thing. It's part of my life. I *have* trusted to time—I've waited four long months, and yet here I stand as poor and helpless as at the beginning. No, no, I'm not to be treated like a dog. If he had been just, I would have done anything for him. I'm not a bad fellow; I never had an unkind thought. Very likely I was too simple, too stupid, too contented with being poor and shabby. The Lord does with us as he pleases; he thought I needed a little shaking up. I've got it, surely! But did your friend take counsel of the Lord? No, no! He took counsel of his own selfishness, and he thought himself clever enough to steal the sweet and never taste the bitter. But the bitter will come; and it will be my sweet."

"That's fine talk! Tell me in three words what it means."

"*Aspetti!*—If you are going to Rome by the coach, as I suppose, you should be moving. You may lose your place. I have an idea we shall meet again." He walked away, and in a moment I heard the great iron gate of the garden creaking on its iron hinges

I was puzzled, and for a moment, I had a dozen minds to stop over with my friends. But on the one hand, I saw no definite way in which I could preserve them from annoyance; and on the other, I was confidently expected in Rome. Besides, might not the dusky cloud be the sooner dissipated by letting Angelo's project,—substance or shadow, whatever it was,—play itself out? To Rome accordingly I returned; but for several days I was haunted with a suspicion that something ugly, something sad, something strange, at any rate, was taking place at Albano. At last it became so oppressive that I hired a light carriage and drove back again. I reached the inn toward the close of the afternoon, and but half expected to find my friends at home. They had in fact gone out to walk, and the landlord had not noticed in what direction. I had nothing to do but to stroll about the dirty little town till their return. Do you remember the Capuchin convent at the edge of the Alban lake? I walked up to it and, seeing the door of the church still open, made my way in. The dusk had gathered in the corners, but the altar, for some pious reason, was glowing with an unusual number of candles. They twinkled picturesquely in the gloom; here and there a kneeling figure defined itself vaguely; it was a pretty piece of chiaroscuro, and I sat down to enjoy it. Presently I noticed the look of intense devotion of a young woman sitting near me. Her hands were clasped on her knees, her head thrown back and her eyes fixed in strange expansion on the shining altar. We make out pictures, you know, in the glow of the hearth at home; this young girl seemed to be reading an ecstatic vision in the light of the tapers. Her expression was so peculiar that for some moments it disguised her face and left me to perceive with a sudden shock that I was watching Adina Waddington. I looked round for her companions, but she was evidently alone. It seemed to me then that I had no right to watch her covertly, and yet I was indisposed either to disturb her or to retire and leave her. The evening was approaching; how came

it that she was unaccompanied? I concluded that she was
waiting for the others; Scrope, perhaps, had gone in to see the
sunset from the terrace of the convent garden—a privilege denied to ladies; and Mrs. Waddington was lingering outside the
church to take memoranda for a sketch. I turned away,
walked round the church and approached the young girl on
the other side. This time my nearness aroused her. She removed her eyes from the altar, looked at me, let them rest on
my face, and yet gave no sign of recognition. But at last she
slowly rose and I saw that she knew me. Was she turning
Catholic and preparing to give up her heretical friends? I
greeted her, but she continued to look at me with intense
gravity, as if her thoughts were urging her beyond frivolous
civilities. She seemed not in the least flurried—as I had feared
she would be—at having been observed; she was preoccupied,
excited, in a deeper fashion. In suspecting that something
strange was happening at Albano, apparently I was not far
wrong—"What are you doing, my dear young lady," I asked
brusquely, "in this lonely church?"

"I'm asking for light," she said.

"I hope you've found it!" I answered smiling.

"I think so!" and she moved toward the door. "I'm alone,"
she added, "will you take me home?" She accepted my arm
and we passed out; but in front of the church she paused.
"Tell me," she said suddenly, "are you a very intimate friend
of Mr. Scrope's?"

"You must ask him," I answered, "if he considers me so. I
at least aspire to the honor." The intensity of her manner embarrassed me, and I tried to take refuge in jocosity.

"Tell me then this: will he bear a disappointment—a keen
disappointment?"

She seemed to appeal to me to say yes! But I felt that she
had a project in hand, and I had no warrant to give her a
license. I looked at her a moment; her solemn eyes seemed to
grow and grow till they made her whole face a mute entreaty.
"No;" I said resolutely, "decidedly not!"

She gave a heavy sigh and we walked on. She seemed
buried in her thoughts; she gave no heed to my attempts at
conversation, and I had to wait till we reached the inn for an
explanation of her solitary visit to Capuccini. Her companions

had come in, and from them, after their welcome, I learned that the three had gone out together, but that Adina had presently complained of fatigue, and obtained leave to go home. "If I break down on the way," she had said, "I will go into a church to rest." They had been surprised at not finding her at the inn, and were grateful for my having met her. Evidently, they, too, had discovered that the young girl was in a singular mood. Mrs. Waddington had a forced smile, and Scrope had no smile at all. Adina quietly sat down to her needlework, and we confessed, even tacitly, to no suspicion of her being "nervous." Common nervousness it certainly was not; she bent her head calmly over her embroidery, and drew her stitches with a hand innocent of the slightest tremor. At last we had dinner; it passed somewhat oppressively, and I was thankful for Scrope's proposal, afterwards, to go and smoke a cigar in the garden. Poor Scrope was unhappy; I could see that, but I hardly ventured to hope that he would tell me off-hand what was the matter with Adina. It naturally occurred to me that she had shown a disposition to retract her engagement. I gave him a dozen chances to say so, but he evidently could not trust himself to utter his fears. To give an impetus to our conversation, I reminded him of his nearness to Lariccia, and asked whether he had had a glimpse of Angelo Beati.

"Several," he said. "He has passed me in the village, or on the roads, some half a dozen times. He gives me an impudent stare and goes his way. He takes it out in looking daggers from his dark eyes; you see how much there is to be feared from him!"

"He doesn't quite take it out," I presently said, "in looking daggers. He hangs about the inn at night; he roams about the garden while you're in bed, as if he thought that he might give you bad dreams by staring at your windows." And I described our recent interview at dawn.

Scrope stared in great surprise, then slowly flushed in rising anger. "Curse the meddling idiot!" he cried. "If he doesn't know where to stop, I'll show him."

"Buy him off!" I said sturdily.

"I'll buy him a horsewhip and give it to him over his broad back!"

I put my hands in my pockets, I believe, and strolled away, whistling. Come what might, I washed my hands of mediation! But it was not irritation, for I felt a strange, half-reasoned increase of pity for my friend's want of pliancy. He stood puffing his cigar gloomily, and by way of showing him that I didn't altogether give up, I asked him at last whether it had yet been settled when he should marry. He had told me shortly before that this was still an open question, and that Miss Waddington preferred to leave it so.

He made no immediate answer, but looked at me hard, "Why do you ask—just now?"

"Why, my dear fellow, friendly curiosity—" I began.

He tossed the end of his cigar nervously upon the ground. "No, no; it's not friendly curiosity!" he cried. "You've noticed something—you suspect something!"

Since he insisted, I confessed that I did. "That beautiful girl," I said, "seems to me agitated and preoccupied; I wondered whether you had been having a quarrel."

He seemed relieved at being pressed to speak.

"That beautiful girl is a puzzle. I don't know what's the matter with her; it's all very painful; she's a very strange creature. I never dreamed there was an obstacle to our happiness—to our union. She has never protested and promised; it's not her way, nor her nature; she is always humble, passive, gentle; but always extremely grateful for every sign of tenderness. Till within three or four days ago, she seemed to me more so than ever; her habitual gentleness took the form of a sort of shrinking, almost suffering, deprecation of my attentions, my *petits soins*, my lover's nonsense. It was as if they oppressed and mortified her—and she would have liked me to bear more lightly. I did not see directly that it was not the excess of my devotion, but my devotion itself—the very fact of my love and her engagement that pained her. When I did it was a blow in the face. I don't know what under heaven I've done! Women are fathomless creatures. And yet Adina is not capricious, in the common sense. Mrs. Waddington told me that it was a 'girl's mood,' that we must not seem to heed it—it would pass over. I've been waiting, but the situation don't mend; you've guessed at trouble without a hint. So these are *peines d'amour?*" he went on, after brooding a moment. "I didn't know how fiercely I was in love!"

I don't remember with what well-meaning foolishness I was going to attempt to console him; Mrs. Waddington suddenly appeared and drew him aside. After a moment's murmured talk with her, he went rapidly into the house. She remained with me and, as she seemed greatly perplexed, and we had, moreover, often discussed our companion's situation and prospects, I immediately told her that Scrope had just been relating his present troubles. "They are very unexpected," she cried. "It's thunder in a clear sky. Just now Adina laid down her work and told me solemnly that she would like to see Mr. Scrope alone; would I kindly call him? Would she kindly tell me, I inquired, what in common sense was the matter with her, and what she proposed to say to him. She looked at me a moment as if I were a child of five years old interrupting family prayers; then came up gently and kissed me, and said I would know everything in good time. Does she mean to stand there in that same ghostly fashion and tell him that, on the whole, she has decided not to marry him? What has the poor man done?"

"She has ceased to love him," I suggested.

"Why ceased, all of a sudden?"

"Perhaps it's not so sudden as you suppose. Such things have happened, in young women's hearts, as a gradual revision of a first impression."

"Yes, but not without a particular motive—another fancy. Adina is fanciful, that I know; with all respect be it said, it was fanciful to accept poor Sam to begin with. But her choice deliberately made, what has put her out of humor with it?—in a word the only possible explanation would be that our young lady has transferred her affections. But it's impossible!"

"Absolutely so?" I asked.

"Absolutely. Judge for yourself. To whom, pray? She hasn't seen another man in a month. Who could have so mysteriously charmed her? The little hunchback who brings us mandarin oranges every morning? Perhaps she has lost her heart to Prince Doria! I believe he has been staying at his villa yonder."

I found no smile for this mild sarcasm. I was wondering—
wondering. "Has she literally seen no one else?" I asked when
my wonderings left me breath.

"I can't answer for whom she may have *seen*; she's not
blind. But she has spoken to no one else, nor been spoken to;
that's very certain. Love at sight—at sight only—used to be
common in the novels I devoured when I was fifteen; but I
doubt whether it exists anywhere else."

I had a question on my tongue's end, but I hesitated some
time to risk it. I debated some time in silence and at last I uttered it, with a prefatory apology. "On which side of the
house is Adina's room?"

"Pray, what are you coming to?" said my companion. "On
this side."

"It looks into the garden?"

"There it is in the second story."

"Be so good——which one?"

"The third window—the one with the shutters tied back
with a handkerchief."

The shutters and the handkerchief suddenly acquired a
mysterious fascination for me. I looked at them for some
time, and when I glanced back at my companion our eyes
met. I don't know what she thought—what she thought I
thought. I thought it *might* be out of a novel—such a thing
as love at sight; such a thing as an unspoken dialogue, between a handsome young Italian with a "wrong," in a starlit
garden, and a fanciful western maid at a window. From her
own sudden impression Mrs. Waddington seemed slowly to
recoil. She gathered her shawl about her, shivered, and turned
towards the house. "The thing to do," I said, offering her my
arm, "is to leave Albano to-morrow."

On the inner staircase we paused; Mrs. Waddington was
loth to interrupt Adina's interview with Scrope. While she
was hesitating whither to turn, the door of her sitting-room
opened, and the young girl passed out. Scrope stood behind
her, very pale, his face distorted with an emotion he was determined to repress. She herself was pale, but her eyes were
lighted up like two wind-blown torches. Meeting the elder
lady, she stopped, stood for a moment, looking down and
hesitating, and then took Mrs. Waddington's two hands and

silently kissed her. She turned to me, put out her hand, and said "Good night!" I shook it, I imagine, with sensible ardor, for somehow, I was deeply impressed. There was a nameless force in the girl, before which one had to stand back. She lingered but an instant and rapidly disappeared towards her room, in the dusky corridor. Mrs. Waddington laid her hand kindly upon Scrope's arm and led him back into the parlor. He evidently was not going to be plaintive; his pride was rankling and burning, and it seasoned his self-control.

"Our engagement is at an end," he simply said.

Mrs. Waddington folded her hands. "And for what reason?"

"None."

It was cruel, certainly; but what could we say? Mrs. Waddington sank upon the sofa and gazed at the poor fellow in mute, motherly compassion. Her large, caressing pity irritated him; he took up a book and sat down with his back to her. I took up another, but I couldn't read; I sat noticing that he never turned his own page. Mrs. Waddington at last transferred her gaze uneasily, appealingly, to me; she moved about restlessly in her place; she was trying to shape my vague intimations in the garden into something palpable to common credulity. I could give her now no explanation that would not have been a gratuitous offense to Scrope. But I felt more and more nervous; my own vague previsions oppressed me. I flung down my book at last, and left the room. In the corridor Mrs. Waddington overtook me, and requested me to tell her what I meant by my extraordinary allusions to—"in plain English," she said, "to an intrigue."

"It would be needless, and it would be painful," I answered, "to tell you now and here. But promise me to return to Rome to-morrow. There we can take breath and talk."

"Oh, we shall bundle off, I promise!" she cried. And we separated. I mounted the stairs to go to my room; as I did so I heard her dress rustling in the corridor, undecidedly. Then came the sound of a knock; she had stopped at Adina's door. Involuntarily I paused and listened. There was a silence, and then another knock; another silence and a third knock; after this, despairing, apparently, of obtaining admission, she moved away, and I went to my room. It was useless going to bed; I knew I should not sleep. I stood a long time at my open window, wondering whether I had anything to say to Scrope. At the end of half an hour I wandered down into the garden again, and strolled through all the alleys. They were empty, and there was a light in Adina's window. No; it seemed to me that there was nothing I could bring myself to say to Scrope, but that he should leave Albano the next day, and Rome and Italy as soon after as possible, wait a year, and then try his fortune with Miss Waddington again. Towards morning, I *did* sleep.

Breakfast was served in Mrs. Waddington's parlor, and Scrope appeared punctually, as neatly shaved and brushed as if he were still under tribute to a pair of blue eyes. He really, of course, felt less serene than he looked. It can never be comfortable to meet at breakfast the young lady who has rejected you over night. Mrs. Waddington kept us waiting some time, but at last she entered with surprising energy. Her comely face was flushed from brow to chin, and in her hand she clasped a crumpled note. She flung herself upon the sofa and burst into tears; I had only time to turn the grinning *cameriêra* out of the room. "She's gone, gone, gone!" she cried, among her sobs. "Oh the crazy, wicked, ungrateful girl!"

Scrope, of course, knew no more than a tea-pot what she meant; but I understood her more promptly—and yet I believe I gave a long whistle. Scrope stood staring at her as she thrust out the crumpled note: that she meant that Adina—that Adina had left us in the night—was too large a horror for his unprepared sense. His dumb amazement was an almost touching sign of the absence of a thought which could have injured the girl. He saw by my face that I knew something, and he let me draw the note from Mrs. Waddington's hand and read it aloud:

"Good-bye to everything! Think me crazy if you will. I could never explain. Only forget me and believe that I am happy, happy, happy!

Adina Beati."

I laid my hand on his shoulder; even yet he seemed powerless to apprehend. "Angelo Beati," I said gravely, "has at last taken his revenge!"

"Angelo Beati!" he cried. "An Italian beggar! It's a lie!"

I shook my head and patted his shoulder. "He has insisted on payment. He's a clever fellow!"

He saw that I knew, and slowly, distractedly he answered with a burning blush!

It was a most extraordinary occurrence; we had ample time to say so, and to say so again, and yet never really to understand it. Neither of my companions ever saw the young girl again; Scrope never mentioned her but once. He went about for a week in absolute silence; when at last he spoke I saw that the fold was taken, that he was going to be a professional cynic for the rest of his days. Mrs. Waddington was a good-natured woman, as I have said, and, better still, she was a just woman. But I assure you, she never forgave her step-daughter. In after years, as I grew older, I took an increasing satisfaction in having assisted, as they say, at this episode. As mere *action*, it seemed to me really superb, and in judging of human nature I often weighed it mentally against the perpetual spectacle of strong impulses frittered in weakness and perverted by prudence. There has been no prudence here, certainly, but there has been ardent, full-blown, positive passion. We see the one every day, the other once in five years. More than once I ventured to ventilate this heresy before the kindly widow, but she always stopped me short, "The thing was odious," she said; "I thank heaven the girl's father did not live to see it."

We didn't finish that dismal day at Albano, but returned in the evening to Rome. Before our departure I had an interview with the Padre Girolamo of Lariccia, who failed to strike me as the holy man whom his nephew had described. He was a swarthy, snuffy little old priest, with a dishonest eye—quite capable, I believed, of teaching his handsome nephew to play his cards. But I had no reproaches to waste upon him; I simply wished to know whither Angelo had taken the young girl. I obtained the information with difficulty and only after a solemn promise that if Adina should reiterate, *vivâ voce*, to a person delegated by her friends, the statement that she was happy, they would take no steps to recover possession of her. She was in Rome, and in that holy city they should leave her. "Remember," said the Padre, very softly, "that she is of age, and her own mistress, and can do what she likes with her money;—she has a good deal of it, eh?" She had less than he thought, but evidently the Padre knew his ground. It was he, he admitted, who had united the young couple in marriage, the day before; the ceremony had taken place in the little old circular church on the hill, at Albano, at five o'clock in the morning. "You see, Signor," he said, slowly rubbing his yellow hands, "she had taken a great fancy!" I gave him no chance, by any remark of my own, to remind me that Angelo had a grudge to satisfy, but he professed the assurance that his nephew was the sweetest fellow in the world. I heard and departed in silence; my curiosity, at least, had not yet done with Angelo.

Mrs. Waddington, also, had more of this sentiment than she confessed to; her kindness wondered, under protest of her indignation, how on earth the young girl was living, and whether the smells on her staircase were very bad indeed. It was, therefore, at her tacit request that I repaired to the lodging of the young pair, in the neighborhood of the Piazza Barberini. The quarters were modest, but they looked into the quaint old gardens of the Capuchin Friars; and in the way of smells, I observed nothing worse than the heavy breath of a great bunch of pinks in a green jug on the window sill. Angelo stood there, pulling one of the pinks to pieces, and looking quite the proper hero of his romance. He eyed me shyly and a trifle coldly at first, as if he were prepared to stand firm against a possible blowing up; but when he saw that I chose to make no allusions whatever to the past, he suffered his dark brow to betray his serene contentment. I was no more disposed than I had been a week before, to call him a bad fellow; but he was a mystery,—his character was as great an enigma as the method of his courtship. That he was in love I don't pretend to say; but I think he had already forgotten how his happiness had come to him, and that he was basking in a sort of primitive natural, sensuous delight in being adored. It was like the warm sunshine, or like plenty of good wine. I don't believe his fortune in the least surprised him; at the bottom of every genuine Roman heart,—even if it beats beneath a beggar's rags,—you'll find an ineradicable belief that we are all barbarians, and made to pay them tribute. He was welcome to all his grotesque superstitions, but what sort of a future did they promise for Adina? I asked leave to speak with her; he shrugged his shoulders, said she was free to choose, and went into an adjoining room with my proposal. Her choice apparently was difficult; I waited sometime, wondering how she would look on the other side of the ugly chasm she had so audaciously leaped. She came in at last, and I immediately saw that she was vexed by my visit. She wished to utterly forget her past. She was pale and very grave; she seemed to wear a frigid mask of reserve. If she had seemed to me a singular creature before, it didn't help me to understand her to see her there, beside her extraordinary husband. My eyes went from one to the other and, I suppose, betrayed my reflections; she suddenly begged me to inform her of my errand.

"I have been asked," I said, "to enquire whether you are contented. Mrs. Waddington is unwilling to leave Rome while there is a chance of your——" I hesitated for a word, and she interrupted me.

"Of my repentance, is what you mean to say?" She fixed her eyes on the ground for a moment, then suddenly raised them. "Mrs. Waddington may leave Rome," she said softly. I turned in silence, but waited a moment for some slight message of farewell. "I only ask to be forgotten!" she added, seeing me stand.

Love is said to be *par excellence* the egotistical passion; if so Adina was far gone. "I can't promise to forget you," I said; "you and my friend here deserve to be remembered!"

She turned away; Angelo seemed relieved at the cessation of our English. He opened the door for me, and stood for a moment with a significant, conscious smile.

"She's happy, eh?" he asked.

"So she says!"

He laid his hand on my arm, "So am I!—She's better than the topaz!"

"You're a queer fellow!" I cried; and, pushing past him, I hurried away.

Mrs. Waddington gave her step-daughter another chance to repent, for she lingered in Rome a fortnight more. She was disappointed at my being able to bring her no information as to how Adina had eluded observation—how she had played her game and kept her secret. My own belief was that there had been a very small amount of courtship, and that until she stole out of the house the morning before her flight, to meet the Padre Girolamo and his nephew at the church, she had barely heard the sound of her lover's voice. There had been signs, and glances, and other unspoken vows, two or three notes, perhaps. Exactly who Angelo was, and what had originally secured for us the honor of his attentions, Mrs. Waddington never learned; it was enough for her that he was a friendless, picturesque Italian. Where everything was a painful puzzle, a shade or two, more or less, of obscurity hardly mattered. Scrope, of course, never attempted to account for his own blindness, though to his silent thoughts it must have seemed bitterly strange. He spoke of Adina, as I said, but once.

He knew by instinct, by divination,—for I had not told him,—that I had been to see her, and late on the evening following my visit, he proposed to me to take a stroll through the streets. It was a soft, damp, night, with vague, scattered cloud masses through which the moon was slowly drifting. A warm south wind had found its way into the dusky heart of the city. "Let us go to St. Peter's," he said, "and see the fountains play in the fitful moonshine." When we reached the bridge of St. Angelo, he paused and leaned some time on the parapet, looking over into the Tiber. At last, suddenly raising himself—"You've seen her?" he asked.

"Yes."

"What did she say?"

"She said she was happy."

He was silent, and we walked on. Halfway over the bridge he stopped again and gazed at the river. Then he drew a small velvet case from his pocket, opened it, and let something shine in the moonlight. It was the beautiful, the imperial, the baleful topaz. He looked at me and I knew what his look meant. It made my heart beat, but I did not say—no! It had been a curse, the golden gem, with its cruel emblems; let it return to the moldering under-world of the Roman past! I shook his hand firmly, he stretched out the other and, with a great flourish, tossed the glittering jewel into the dusky river.

There it lies! Some day, I suppose, they will dredge the Tiber for treasures, and, possibly, disinter our topaz, and recognize it. But who will guess at this passionate human interlude to its burial of centuries?

CHRONOLOGY

NOTE ON THE TEXTS

NOTES

.

Chronology

1843   Born April 15 at 21 Washington Place, New York City, the second child (after William, born January 11, 1842, N.Y.C.) of Henry James of Albany and Mary Robertson Walsh of New York. Father lives on inheritance of $10,000 a year, his share of litigated $3,000,000 fortune of his Albany father, William James, an Irish immigrant who came to the U.S. immediately after the Revolution.

1843–45   Accompanied by mother's sister, Catharine Walsh, and servants, the James parents take infant children to England and later to France. Reside at Windsor, where father has nervous collapse ("vastation") and experiences spiritual illumination. He becomes a Swedenborgian (May 1844), devoting his time to lecturing and religious-philosophical writings. James later claimed his earliest memory was a glimpse, during his second year, of the Place Vendôme in Paris with its Napoleonic column.

1845–47   Family returns to New York. Garth Wilkinson James (Wilky) born July 21, 1845. Family moves to Albany at 50 N. Pearl St., a few doors from grandmother Catharine Barber James. Robertson James (Bob or Rob) born August 29, 1846.

1847–55   Family moves to a large house at 58 W. 14th St., New York. Alice James born August 7, 1848. Relatives and father's friends and acquaintances—Horace Greeley, George Ripley, Charles Anderson Dana, William Cullen Bryant, Bronson Alcott, and Ralph Waldo Emerson ("I knew he was great, greater than any of our friends")—are frequent visitors. Thackeray calls during his lecture tour on the English humorists. Summers at New Brighton on Staten Island and Fort Hamilton on Long Island's south shore. On steamboat to Fort Hamilton August 1850, hears Washington Irving tell his father of Margaret Fuller's drowning in shipwreck off Fire Island. Frequently visits Barnum's American Museum on free days. Taken to art shows and theaters; writes and draws stage scenes. Described by father as "a devourer of libraries." Taught in assorted private schools and by tutors in lower Broadway and Greenwich Village. But father claims in 1848 that American schooling fails to provide "sensuous education" for his children and plans to take them to Europe.

1855–58   Family (with Aunt Kate) sails for Liverpool, June 27. James is intermittently sick with malarial fever as they travel to Paris, Lyon, and Geneva. After Swiss summer, leaves for London where Robert Thomson (later Robert Louis Stevenson's tutor) is engaged. Early summer 1856, family moves to Paris. Another tutor engaged and children attend experimental Fourierist school. Acquires fluency in French. Family goes to Boulogne-sur-mer in summer, where James contracts typhoid. Spends late October in Paris, but American crash of 1857 returns family to Boulogne where they can live more cheaply. Attends public school (fellow classmate is Coquelin, the future French actor).

1858–59   Family returns to America and settles in Newport, Rhode Island. Goes boating, fishing, and riding. Attends the Reverend W. C. Leverett's Berkeley Institute, and forms friendship with classmate Thomas Sergeant Perry. Takes long walks and sketches with the painter John La Farge.

1859–60   Father, still dissatisfied with American education, returns family to Geneva in October. James attends a pre-engineering school, Institution Rochette, because parents, with "a flattering misconception of my aptitudes," feel he might benefit from less reading and more mathematics. After a few months withdraws from all classes except French, German, and Latin, and joins William as a special student at the Academy (later the University of Geneva) where he attends lectures on literary subjects. Studies German in Bonn during summer 1860.

1860–62   Family returns to Newport in September where William studies with William Morris Hunt, and James sits in on his classes. La Farge introduces him to works of Balzac, Merimée, Musset, and Browning. Wilky and Bob attend Frank Sanborn's experimental school in Concord with children of Hawthorne and Emerson and John Brown's daughter. Early in 1861, orphaned Temple cousins come to live in Newport. Develops close friendship with cousin

Mary (Minnie) Temple. Goes on a week's walking tour in July in New Hampshire with Perry. William abandons art in autumn 1861 and enters Lawrence Scientific School at Harvard. James suffers back injury in a stable fire while serving as a volunteer fireman. Reads Hawthorne ("an American could be an artist, one of the finest").

1862–63 Enters Harvard Law School (Dane Hall). Wilky enlists in the Massachusetts 44th Regiment, and later in Colonel Robert Gould Shaw's 54th, one of the first black regiments. Summer 1863, Bob joins the Massachusetts 55th, another black regiment, under Colonel Hollowell. James withdraws from law studies to try writing. Sends unsigned stories to magazines. Wilky is badly wounded and brought home to Newport in August.

1864 Family moves from Newport to 13 Ashburton Place, Boston. First tale, "A Tragedy of Error" (unsigned), published in *Continental Monthly* (Feb. 1864). Stays in Northampton, Massachusetts, early August–November. Begins writing book reviews for *North American Review* and forms friendship with its editor, Charles Eliot Norton, and his family, including his sister Grace (with whom he maintains a long-lasting correspondence). Wilky returns to his regiment.

1865 First signed tale, "The Story of a Year," published in *Atlantic Monthly* (March 1865). Begins to write reviews for the newly founded *Nation* and publishes anonymously in it during next fifteen years. William sails on a scientific expedition with Louis Agassiz to the Amazon. During summer James vacations in the White Mountains with Minnie Temple and her family; joined by Oliver Wendell Holmes Jr. and John Chipman Gray, both recently demobilized. Father subsidizes plantation for Wilky and Bob in Florida with black hired workers. (The idealistic but impractical venture fails in 1870.)

1866–68 Continues to publish reviews and tales in Boston and New York journals. William returns from Brazil and resumes medical education. James has recurrence of back ailment and spends summer in Swampscott, Massachusetts. Begins friendship with William Dean Howells. Family moves to 20 Quincy St., Cambridge. William, suffering from nervous ailments, goes to Germany in spring 1867. "Poor Richard," James's longest story to date, published in *Atlantic Monthly* (June–Aug. 1867). William begins intermittent criticism of Henry's story-telling and style (which will continue throughout their careers). Momentary meeting with Charles Dickens at Norton's house. Vacations in Jefferson, New Hampshire, summer 1868. William returns from Europe.

1869–70   Sails in February for European tour. Visits English towns and cathedrals. Through Nortons meets Leslie Stephen, William Morris, Dante Gabriel Rossetti, Edward Burne-Jones, John Ruskin, Charles Darwin, and George Eliot (the "one marvel" of his stay in London). Goes to Paris in May, then travels in Switzerland in summer and hikes into Italy in autumn, where he stays in Milan, Venice (Sept.), Florence, and Rome (Oct. 30–Dec. 28). Returns to England to drink the waters at Malvern health spa in Worcestershire because of digestive troubles. Stays in Paris en route and has first experience of Comédie Française. Learns that his beloved cousin, Minnie Temple, has died of tuberculosis.

1870–72   Returns to Cambridge in May. Travels to Rhode Island, Vermont, and New York to write travel sketches for *The Nation*. Spends a few days with Emerson in Concord. Meets Bret Harte at Howells' home April 1871. *Watch and Ward*, his first novel, published in *Atlantic Monthly* (Aug.–Dec. 1871). Serves as occasional art reviewer for the *Atlantic* January–March 1872.

1872–74   Accompanies Aunt Kate and sister Alice on tour of England, France, Switzerland, Italy, Austria, and Germany from May through October. Writes travel sketches for *The Nation*. Spends autumn in Paris, becoming friends with James Russell Lowell. Escorts Emerson through the Louvre. (Later, on Emerson's return from Egypt, will show him the Vatican.) Goes to Florence in December and from there to Rome, where he becomes friends with actress Fanny Kemble, her daughter Sarah Butler Wister, and William Wetmore Story and his family. In Italy sees old family friend Francis Boott and his daughter Elizabeth (Lizzie), expatriates who have lived for many years in Florentine villa on Bellosguardo. Takes up horseback riding on the Campagna. Encounters Matthew Arnold in April 1873 at Story's. Moves from Rome hotel to rooms of his own. Continues writing and now earns enough to support himself. Leaves Rome in June, spends summer in Bad Homburg. In October goes to Florence, where William joins him. They also visit Rome, William returning to America in March. In Baden-Baden June–August and returns to America September 4, with *Roderick Hudson* all but finished.

1875   *Roderick Hudson* serialized in *Atlantic Monthly* from January (published by Osgood at the end of the year). First book, *A Passionate Pilgrim and Other Tales*, published January 31. Tries living and writing in New York, in rooms at 111 E. 25th Street. Earns $200 a month from novel installments and continued reviewing, but finds New York too expensive. *Transatlantic Sketches*, published in April, sells almost 1,000 copies in three months. In Cambridge in July decides to return to Europe; arranges with John Hay, assistant to the publisher, to write Paris letters for the *New York Tribune*.

1875–76   Arriving in Paris in November, he takes rooms at 29 Rue de Luxembourg (since renamed Cambon). Becomes friend of Ivan Turgenev and is introduced by him to Gustave Flaubert's Sunday parties. Meets Edmond de Goncourt, Émile Zola, G. Charpentier (the publisher), Catulle Mendès, Alphonse Daudet, Guy de Maupassant, Ernest Renan, Gustave Doré. Makes friends with Charles Sanders Peirce, who is in Paris. Reviews (unfavorably) the early Impressionists at the Durand-Ruel gallery. By midsummer has received $400 for *Tribune* pieces, but editor asks for more Parisian gossip and James resigns. Travels in France during July, visiting Normandy and the Midi, and in September crosses to San Sebastian, Spain, to see a bullfight ("I thought the bull, in any case, a finer fellow than any of his tormentors"). Moves to London in December, taking rooms at 3 Bolton Street, Piccadilly, where he will live for the next decade.

1877   *The American* published. Meets Robert Browning and George du Maurier. Leaves London in midsummer for visit to Paris and then goes to Italy. In Rome rides again in Campagna and hears of an episode that inspires "Daisy

Miller." Back in England, spends Christmas at Stratford
with Fanny Kemble.

1878   Publishes first book in England, *French Poets and Novelists*
(Macmillan). Appearance of "Daisy Miller" in *Cornhill
Magazine*, edited by Leslie Stephen, is international success, but by publishing it abroad loses American copyright
and story is pirated in U.S. *Cornhill* also prints "An International Episode." *The Europeans* is serialized in *Atlantic*.
Now a celebrity, he dines out often, visits country houses,
gains weight, takes long walks, fences, and does weight-
lifting to reduce. Elected to Reform Club. Meets Tennyson, George Meredith, and James McNeill Whistler.
William marries Alice Howe Gibbens.

1879   Immersed in London society (". . . dined out during the
past winter 107 times!"). Meets Edmund Gosse and
Robert Louis Stevenson, who will later become his close
friends. Sees much of Henry Adams and his wife, Marian
(Clover), in London and later in Paris. Takes rooms in
Paris, September–December. *Confidence* is serialized in
Scribner's and published by Chatto & Windus. *Hawthorne*
appears in Macmillan's "English Men of Letters" series.

1880–81   Stays in Florence March–May to work on *The Portrait of
a Lady*. Meets Constance Fenimore Woolson, American
novelist and grandniece of James Fenimore Cooper. Returns to Bolton Street in June, where William visits him.
Washington Square serialized in *Cornhill Magazine* and
published in U.S. by Harper & Brothers (Dec. 1880). *The
Portrait of a Lady* serialized in *Macmillan's Magazine* (Oct.
1880–Nov. 1881) and *Atlantic Monthly*; published by Macmillan and Houghton, Mifflin (Nov. 1881). Publication
both in United States and in England yields him the then-
large income of $500 a month, though book sales are dis-
appointing. Leaves London in February for Paris, the
south of France, the Italian Riviera, and Venice, and returns home in July. Sister Alice comes to London with
her friend Katharine Loring. James goes to Scotland in
September.

1881–83   In November revisits America after absence of six years.
Lionized in New York. Returns to Quincy Street for
Christmas and sees ailing brother Wilky for the first time

in ten years. In January visits Washington and the Henry Adamses and meets President Chester A. Arthur. Summoned to Cambridge by mother's death January 29 ("the sweetest, gentlest, most beneficent human being I have ever known"). All four brothers are together for the first time in fifteen years at her funeral. Alice and father move from Cambridge to Boston. Prepares a stage version of "Daisy Miller" and returns to England in May. William, now a Harvard professor, comes to Europe in September. Proposed by Leslie Stephen, James becomes member, without the usual red tape, of the Atheneum Club. Travels in France in October to write *A Little Tour in France* (published 1884) and has last visit with Turgenev, who is dying. Returns to England in December and learns of father's illness. Sails for America but Henry James Sr. dies December 18, 1882, before his arrival. Made executor of father's will. Visits brothers Wilky and Bob in Milwaukee in January. Quarrels with William over division of property—James wants to restore Wilky's share. Macmillan publishes a collected pocket edition of James's novels and tales in fourteen volumes. *Siege of London* and *Portraits of Places* published. Returns to Bolton Street in September. Wilky dies in November. Constance Fenimore Woolson comes to London for the winter.

1884–86 Goes to Paris in February and visits Daudet, Zola, and Goncourt. Again impressed with their intense concern with "art, form, manner" but calls them "mandarins." Misses Turgenev, who had died a few months before. Meets John Singer Sargent and persuades him to settle in London. Returns to Bolton Street. Sargent introduces him to young Paul Bourget. During country visits encounters many British political and social figures, including W. E. Gladstone, John Bright, and Charles Dilke. Alice, suffering from nervous ailment, arrives in England for visit in November but is too ill to travel and settles near her brother. *Tales of Three Cities* ("The Impressions of a Cousin," "Lady Barberina," "A New England Winter") and "The Art of Fiction" published 1884. Alice goes to Bournemouth in late January. James joins her in May and becomes an intimate of Robert Louis Stevenson, who resides nearby. Spends August at Dover and is visited by Paul Bourget. Stays in Paris for the next two months. Moves into a flat at 34 De Vere Gardens in Kensington early in March 1886. Alice takes rooms in London. *The Bostonians* serialized in *Century* (Feb. 1885–Feb. 1886; published 1886), *The Princess Casamassima* serialized in *Atlantic Monthly* (Sept. 1885–Oct. 1886; published 1886).

1886–87   Leaves for Italy in December for extended stay, mainly in Florence and Venice. Sees much of Constance Fenimore Woolson and stays in her villa. Writes "The Aspern Papers" and other tales. Returns to De Vere Gardens in July and begins work on *The Tragic Muse*. Pays several country visits. Dines out less often ("I know it all—all that one sees by 'going out'—today, as if I had made it. But if I had, I would have made it better!").

1888   *The Reverberator, The Aspern Papers, Louisa Pallant, The Modern Warning,* and *Partial Portraits* published. Elizabeth Boott Duveneck dies. Robert Louis Stevenson leaves for the South Seas. Engages fencing teacher to combat "symptoms of a portentous corpulence." Goes abroad in October to Geneva (where he visits Woolson), Genoa, Monte Carlo, and Paris.

1889–90   Catharine Walsh (Aunt Kate) dies March 1889. William comes to England to visit Alice in August. James goes to Dover in September and then to Paris for five weeks. Writes account of Robert Browning's funeral in Westminster Abbey. Dramatizes *The American* for the Compton Comedy Company. Meets and becomes close friends with American journalist William Morton Fullerton and young American publisher Wolcott Balestier. Goes to Italy for the summer, staying in Venice and Florence, and takes a brief walking tour in Tuscany with W. W. Baldwin, an American physician practicing in Florence. Miss Woolson moves to Cheltenham, England, to be near James. *Atlantic Monthly* rejects his story "The Pupil," but it appears in England. Writes series of drawing-room comedies for theater. Meets Rudyard Kipling. *The Tragic Muse* serialized in *Atlantic Monthly* (Jan. 1889–May 1890; published 1890). *A London Life* (including "The Patagonia," "The Liar," "Mrs. Temperly") published 1889.

1891   *The American* produced at Southport is a success during road tour. After residence in Leamington, Alice returns to London, cared for by Katharine Loring. Doctors discover she has breast cancer. James circulates comedies (*Mrs. Vibert*, later called *Tenants*, and *Mrs. Jasper*, later named *Disengaged*) among theater managers who are cool to his work. Unimpressed at first by Ibsen, writes an appreciative review after seeing a performance of *Hedda Gabler* with Elizabeth Robins, a young Kentucky actress; persuades her to take the part of Mme. de Cintré in the London production of *The American*. Recuperates from flu in Ireland. James Russell Lowell dies. *The American* opens in London, September 26, and runs for seventy nights. Wolcott Balestier dies, and James attends his funeral in Dresden in December.

1892 Alice James dies March 6. James travels to Siena to be near the Paul Bourgets, and Venice, June–July, to visit the Daniel Curtises, then to Lausanne to meet William and his family, who have come abroad for sabbatical. Attends funeral of Tennyson at Westminster Abbey. Augustin Daly agrees to produce *Mrs. Jasper. The American* continues to be performed on the road by the Compton Company. *The Lesson of the Master* (with a collection of stories including "The Marriages," "The Pupil," "Brooksmith," "The Solution," and "Sir Edmund Orme") published.

1893 Fanny Kemble dies in January. Continues to write unproduced plays. In March goes to Paris for two months. Sends Edward Compton first act and scenario for *Guy Domville*. Meets William and family in Lucerne and stays a month, returning to London in June. Spends July completing *Guy Domville* in Ramsgate. George Alexander, actor-manager, agrees to produce the play. Daly stages first reading of *Mrs. Jasper*, and James withdraws it, calling the rehearsal a mockery. *The Real Thing and Other Tales* (including "The Wheel of Time," "Lord Beaupré," "The Visit") published.

1894 Constance Fenimore Woolson dies in Venice, January. Shocked and upset, James prepares to attend funeral in Rome but changes his mind on learning she is a suicide. Goes to Venice in April to help her family settle her affairs. Receives one of four copies, privately printed by Miss Loring, of Alice's diary. Finds it impressive but is concerned that so much gossip he told Alice in private has been included (later burns his copy). Robert Louis Stevenson dies in the South Pacific. *Guy Domville* goes into rehearsal. *Theatricals: Two Comedies* and *Theatricals: Second Series* published.

1895   *Guy Domville* opens January 5 at St. James's Theatre. At play's end James is greeted by a fifteen-minute roar of boos, catcalls, and applause. Horrified and depressed, abandons the theater. Play earns him $1,300 after five-week run. Feels he can salvage something useful from playwriting for his fiction ("a key that, working in the same *general* way fits the complicated chambers of *both* the dramatic and the narrative lock"). Writes scenario for *The Spoils of Poynton*. Visits Lord Wolseley and Lord Houghton in Ireland. In the summer goes to Torquay in Devonshire and stays until November while electricity is being installed in De Vere Gardens flat. Friendship with W. E. Norris, who resides at Torquay. Writes a one-act play ("Mrs. Gracedew") at request of Ellen Terry. *Terminations* (containing "The Death of the Lion," "The Coxon Fund," "The Middle Years," "The Altar of the Dead") published.

1896–97   Finishes *The Spoils of Poynton* (serialized in *Atlantic Monthly* April–Oct. 1896 as *The Old Things*; published 1897). *Embarrassments* ("The Figure in the Carpet," "Glasses," "The Next Time," "The Way It Came") published. Takes a house on Point Hill, Playden, opposite the old town of Rye, Sussex, August–September. Ford Madox Hueffer (later Ford Madox Ford) visits him. Converts play *The Other House* into novel and works on *What Maisie Knew* (published Sept. 1897). George du Maurier dies early in October. Because of increasing pain in wrist, hires stenographer William MacAlpine in February and then purchases a typewriter; soon begins direct dictation to MacAlpine at the machine. Invites Joseph Conrad to lunch at De Vere Gardens and begins their friendship. Goes to Bournemouth in July. Serves on jury in London before going to Dunwich, Suffolk, to spend time with Temple-Emmet cousins. In late September 1897 signs a twenty-one-year lease for Lamb House in Rye for £70 a year ($350). Takes on extra work to pay for setting up his house—the life of William Wetmore Story ($1,250 advance) and will furnish an "American Letter" for new magazine *Literature* (precursor of *Times Literary Supplement*) for $200 a month. Howells visits.

1898   "The Turn of the Screw" (serialized in *Collier's* Jan.–April; published with "Covering End" under the title *The Two Magics*) proves his most popular work since "Daisy Miller." Sleeps in Lamb House for first time June 28. Soon after is visited by William's son, Henry James Jr. (Harry), followed by a stream of visitors: future Justice Oliver Wendell Holmes, Mrs. J. T. Fields, Sarah Orne Jewett, the Paul Bourgets, the Edward Warrens, the Daniel Curtises, the Edmund Gosses, and Howard Sturgis. His witty friend Jonathan Sturges, a young, crippled New Yorker, stays for two months during autumn. *In the Cage* published. Meets neighbors Stephen Crane and H. G. Wells.

1899   Finishes *The Awkward Age* and plans trip to the Continent. Fire in Lamb House delays departure. To Paris in March and then visits the Paul Bourgets at Hyères. Stays with the Curtises in their Venice palazzo, where he meets and becomes friends with Jessie Allen. In Rome meets young American-Norwegian sculptor Hendrik C. Andersen; buys one of his busts. Returns to England in July and Andersen comes for three days in August. William, his wife, Alice, and daughter, Peggy, arrive at Lamb House in October. First meeting of brothers in six years. William now has confirmed heart condition. James B. Pinker becomes literary agent and for first time James's professional relations are systematically organized; he reviews copyrights, finds new publishers, and obtains better prices for work ("the germ of a new career"). Purchases Lamb House for $10,000 with an easy mortgage.

1900   Unhappy at whiteness of beard which he has worn since the Civil War, he shaves it off. Alternates between Rye and London. Works on *The Sacred Fount*. Works on and then sets aside *The Sense of the Past* (never finished). Begins *The Ambassadors*. *The Soft Side*, a collection of twelve tales, published. Niece Peggy comes to Lamb House for Christmas.

1901   Obtains permanent room at the Reform Club for London visits and spends eight weeks in town. Sees funeral of Queen Victoria. Decides to employ a typist, Mary Weld, to replace the more expensive overqualified shorthand stenographer, MacAlpine. Completes *The Ambassadors* and begins *The Wings of the Dove*. *The Sacred Fount* published.

Has meeting with George Gissing. William James, much improved, returns home after two years in Europe. Young Cambridge admirer Percy Lubbock visits. Discharges his alcoholic servants of sixteen years (the Smiths). Mrs. Paddington is new housekeeper.

1902   In London for the winter but gout and stomach disorder force him home earlier. Finishes *The Wings of the Dove* (published in August). William James Jr. (Billy) visits in October and becomes a favorite nephew. Writes "The Beast in the Jungle" and "The Birthplace."

1903   *The Ambassadors, The Better Sort* (a collection of eleven tales), and *William Wetmore Story and His Friends* published. After another spell in town, returns to Lamb House in May and begins work on *The Golden Bowl*. Meets and establishes close friendship with Dudley Jocelyn Persse, a nephew of Lady Gregory. First meeting with Edith Wharton in December.

1904–05 Completes *The Golden Bowl* (published Nov. 1904). Rents Lamb House for six months, and sails in August for America after twenty-year absence. Sees new Manhattan skyline from New Jersey on arrival and stays with Colonel George Harvey, president of Harper's, in Jersey shore house with Mark Twain as fellow guest. Goes to William's country house at Chocorua in the White Mountains, New Hampshire. Re-explores Cambridge, Boston, Salem, Newport, and Concord, where he visits brother Bob. In October stays with Edith Wharton in the Berkshires and motors with her through Massachusetts and New York. Later visits New York, Philadelphia (where he delivers lecture "The Lesson of Balzac"), and then Washington, D.C., as a guest in Henry Adams' house. Meets (and is critical of) President Theodore Roosevelt. Returns to Philadelphia to lecture at Bryn Mawr. Travels to Richmond, Charleston, Jacksonville, Palm Beach, and St. Augustine. Then lectures in St. Louis, Chicago, South Bend, Indianapolis, Los Angeles (with a short vacation at Coronado Beach near San Diego), San Francisco, Portland, and Seattle. Returns to explore New York City ("the terrible town"), May–June. Lectures on "The Question of Our Speech" at Bryn Mawr commencement. Elected to newly founded American Academy of Arts and Letters

(William declines). Returns to England in July; lectures had more than covered expenses of his trip. Begins revision of novels for the New York Edition.

1906–08   Writes "The Jolly Corner" and *The American Scene* (published 1907). Writes eighteen prefaces for the New York Edition (twenty-four volumes published 1907–09). Visits Paris and Edith Wharton in spring 1907 and motors with her in Midi. Travels to Italy for the last time, visiting Hendrik Andersen in Rome, and goes on to Florence and Venice. Engages Theodora Bosanquet as his typist in autumn. Again visits Edith Wharton in Paris, spring 1908. William comes to England to give a series of lectures at Oxford and receives an honorary Doctor of Science degree. James goes to Edinburgh in March to see a tryout by the Forbes-Robertsons of his play *The High Bid*, a rewrite in three acts of the one-act play originally written for Ellen Terry (revised earlier as the story "Covering End"). Play gets only five special matinees in London. Shocked by slim royalties from sales of the New York Edition.

1909   Growing acquaintance with young writers and artists of Bloomsbury, including Virginia and Vanessa Stephen and others. Meets and befriends young Hugh Walpole in February. Goes to Cambridge in June as guest of admiring dons and undergraduates and meets John Maynard Keynes. Feels unwell and sees doctors about what he believes may be heart trouble. They reassure him. Late in year burns forty years of his letters and papers at Rye. Suffers severe attacks of gout. *Italian Hours* published.

1910   Very ill in January ("food-loathing") and spends much time in bed. Nephew Harry comes to be with him in February. In March is examined by Sir William Osler, who finds nothing physically wrong. James begins to realize that he has had "a sort of nervous breakdown." William, in spite of now severe heart trouble, and his wife, Alice, come to England to give him support. Brothers and Alice go to Bad Nauheim for cure, then travel to Zurich, Lucerne, and Geneva, where they learn Robertson (Bob) James has died in America of heart attack. James's health begins to improve but William is failing. Sails with William and Alice for America in August. William dies at Choco-

rua soon after arrival, and James remains with the family
for the winter. *The Finer Grain* and *The Outcry* published.

1911   Honorary degree from Harvard in spring. Visits with
        Howells and Grace Norton. Sails for England July 30. On
        return to Lamb House, decides he will be too lonely there
        and starts search for a London flat. Theodora Bosanquet
        obtains two work rooms adjoining her flat in Chelsea and
        he begins autobiography, *A Small Boy and Others.* Con-
        tinues to reside at the Reform Club.

1912   Delivers "The Novel in *The Ring and the Book*," on the
        100th anniversary of Browning's birth, to the Royal Soci-
        ety of Literature. Honorary Doctor of Letters from Ox-
        ford University June 26. Spends summer at Lamb House.
        Sees much of Edith Wharton ("the Firebird"), who
        spends summer in England. (She secretly arranges to have
        Scribner's put $8,000 into James's account.) Takes 21 Car-
        lyle Mansions, in Cheyne Walk, Chelsea, as London quar-
        ters. Writes a long admiring letter for William Dean
        Howells' seventy-fifth birthday. Meets André Gide. Con-
        tracts bad case of shingles and is ill four months, much of
        the time not able to leave bed.

1913   Moves into Cheyne Walk flat. Two hundred and seventy
        friends and admirers subscribe for seventieth birthday por-
        trait by Sargent and present also a silver-gilt Charles II
        porringer and dish ("golden bowl"). Sargent turns over
        his payment to young sculptor Derwent Wood, who does
        a bust of James. Autobiography *A Small Boy and Others*
        published. Goes with niece Peggy to Lamb House for the
        summer.

1914   *Notes of a Son and Brother* published. Works on "The Ivory
        Tower." Returns to Lamb House in July. Niece Peggy
        joins him. Horrified by the war ("this crash of our civili-
        sation," "a nightmare from which there is no waking"). In
        London in September participates in Belgian Relief, visits
        wounded in St. Bartholomew's and other hospitals; feels
        less "finished and useless and doddering" and recalls Walt
        Whitman and his Civil War hospital visits. Accepts chair-
        manship of American Volunteer Motor Ambulance Corps
        in France. *Notes on Novelists* (essays on Balzac, Flaubert,
        Zola) published.

1915–16   Continues work with the wounded and war relief. Has occasional lunches with Prime Minister Asquith and family, and meets Winston Churchill and other war leaders. Discovers that he is considered an alien and has to report to police before going to coastal Rye. Decides to become a British national and asks Asquith to be one of his sponsors. Receives Certificate of Naturalization on July 26. H. G. Wells satirizes him in *Boon* ("leviathan retrieving pebbles") and James, in the correspondence that follows, writes: "Art *makes* life, makes interest, makes importance." Burns more papers and photographs at Lamb House in autumn. Has a stroke December 2 in his flat, followed by another two days later. Develops pneumonia and during delirium gives his last confused dictation (dealing with the Napoleonic legend) to Theodora Bosanquet, who types it on the familiar typewriter. Mrs. William James arrives December 13 to care for him. On New Year's Day, George V confers the Order of Merit. Dies February 28. Funeral services held at the Chelsea Old Church. The body is cremated and the ashes are buried in Cambridge Cemetery family plot.

Note on the Texts

This volume, one of five collecting the complete stories of Henry James, presents in the approximate chronological order of their composition 24 stories that were first published in periodicals between 1864 and 1874. For 20 of the stories, the texts printed here are taken from the periodicals where they were first published. Thirteen of these stories were never collected in book form by James; the other seven appeared in later collections in substantially revised forms that reflect James at a different stage in his career. The remaining four stories, "A Passionate Pilgrim," "The Madonna of the Future," "The Last of the Valerii," and "Madame de Mauves," were published in book form during the period immediately following their composition. For these stories, the texts printed here are the book versions representing James's latest revisions during this period: the text of "A Passionate Pilgrim" is taken from *A Passionate Pilgrim and Other Tales* (Boston: James R. Osgood, 1875); the texts of "The Madonna of the Future," "The Last of the Valerii," and "Madame de Mauves" are taken from *The Madonna of the Future and Other Tales* (London: Macmillan, 1979).

The following list gives the first periodical and the first American and English book publications of the stories printed in this volume. (James later included three of the stories, "A Passionate Pilgrim," "The Madonna of the Future," and "Madame de Mauves," in the 1907–9 New York Edition of his collected works.)

"A Tragedy of Error." *Continental Monthly*, February 1864. Uncollected by James.

"The Story of a Year." *Atlantic Monthly*, March 1865. Uncollected by James.

"A Landscape Painter." *Atlantic Monthly*, February 1866. No American book edition during James's lifetime. Revised for inclusion in *Stories Revived* (London: Macmillan, 1885).

"A Day of Days." *Galaxy*, June 15, 1866. No American book edition during James's lifetime. Revised for inclusion in *Stories Revived* (London: Macmillan, 1885).

"My Friend Bingham." *Atlantic Monthly*, March 1867. Uncollected by James.

"Poor Richard." *Atlantic Monthly*, June 1867 and July–August 1867. No American book edition during James's lifetime. Revised for inclusion in *Stories Revived* (London: Macmillan, 1885).

"The Story of a Masterpiece." *Galaxy*, January–February 1868. Uncollected by James.

"The Romance of Certain Old Clothes." *Atlantic Monthly*, February 1868. Revised for collection in *A Passionate Pilgrim* (Boston: James R. Osgood, 1875), and further revised for inclusion in *Stories Revived* (London: Macmillan, 1885).

"A Most Extraordinary Case." *Atlantic Monthly*, April 1868. No American book edition during James's lifetime. Revised for inclusion in *Stories Revived* (London: Macmillan, 1885).

"A Problem." *Galaxy*, June 1868. Uncollected by James.

"De Grey: A Romance." *Atlantic Monthly*, July 1868. Uncollected by James.

"Osborne's Revenge." *Galaxy*, July 1868. Uncollected by James.

"A Light Man." *Galaxy*, July 1869. Revised for inclusion in the anthology *Stories by American Authors* (New York: Charles Scribner's Sons, 1884). Further revised for *Stories Revived* (London: Macmillan, 1885).

"Gabrielle de Bergerac." *Atlantic Monthly*, July–September 1869. Uncollected by James.

"Travelling Companions." *Atlantic Monthly*, November–December 1870. Uncollected by James.

"A Passionate Pilgrim." *Atlantic Monthly*, March–April 1871. Revised for collection in *A Passionate Pilgrim* (Boston: James R. Osgood, 1875), and further revised for inclusion in *Stories Revived* (London: Macmillan, 1885).

"At Isella." *Galaxy*, August 1871. Uncollected by James.

"Master Eustace." *Galaxy*, November 1871. Revised for inclusion in *Stories Revived* (London: Macmillan, 1885).

"Guest's Confession." *Atlantic Monthly*, October–November 1872. Uncollected by James.

"The Madonna of the Future." *Atlantic Monthly*, March 1873. Lightly revised for collection in *A Passionate Pilgrim* (Boston: James R. Osgood, 1875). Further revised for inclusion in *The Madonna of the Future* (London: Macmillan, 1879).

"The Sweetheart of M. Briseux." *Galaxy*, June 1873. Uncollected by James.

"The Last of the Valerii." *Atlantic Monthly*, January 1874. Revised for collection in *A Passionate Pilgrim* (Boston: James R. Osgood, 1875). Further revised for inclusion in *The Madonna of the Future* (London: Macmillan, 1879).

"Madame De Mauves." *Galaxy*, February–March 1874 (title: Mme. De Mauves"). Lightly revised for collection as "Madame de Mauves" in *A Passionate Pilgrim* (Boston: James R. Osgood, 1875).

Further revised for inclusion in *The Madonna of the Future* (London: Macmillan, 1879).

"Adina." *Scribner's Monthly*, May–June 1874. Uncollected by James.

This volume presents the texts of the printings chosen for inclusion here but does not attempt to reproduce features of their typographic design. Spelling, punctuation, and capitalization often are expressive features, and they are not altered, even when inconsistent or irregular. The following is a list of typographical errors corrected, cited by page and line number: 3.26, 'not guilty,'; 8.33, but; 13.32, is is; 29.22, dont; 29.28, Mrs; 41.29, Littlefild; 112.16, read. And; 114.8, future.; 115.10, tribute.; 115.22, to slow; 161.1, be-/between; 191.29, Gertrude,; 229.16, could'nt; 230.3, hav'nt; 239.37, havn't; 280.26, well, said; 307.2, see.; 307.3, you.; 310.20, it?; 310.23, to sneered; 310.35, was old; 311.21 fashion; 312.7, know,; 390.14, anwered; 396.3, woulnd't; 397.18, health.; 429.7, sister's; 456.21, children.; 457.21, it's; 516.8, Caffé; 580.25, *receuillit*; 622.33, *frotte*; 644.12, inacessible; 668.3, room,; 705.19, it's; 753.38–39, epuanimity; 838.26, If your; 872.18, as his; 899.10, look; 908.27, Lariceia; 913.4, *Pazrinza!*; 921.1, piece; 921.36, *Corps*; 923.6, got?; 923.32, Lariceia; 924.2, Lariceia; 930.6, as,; 937.14, me,". . ."what; 937.15, him."; 643.7, she came.

Notes

In the notes below, the reference numbers denote page and line of this volume (the line count includes titles and headings). No note is made for material included in standard desk-reference books such as Webster's *Collegiate, Biographical,* and *Geographical* dictionaries. Quotations from Shakespeare are keyed to *The Riverside Shakespeare,* ed. G. Blakemore Evans (Boston: Houghton Mifflin, 1974). For further background than is provided in the notes, see *Henry James Letters,* ed. Leon Edel (Cambridge: The Belknap Press of Harvard University Press, Vol. I—1843–1875 [1974]; Vol. II—1875–1883 [1975]; Vol III—1883–1895 [1980]; Vol. IV—1895–1916 [1984]) and *The Complete Notebooks of Henry James,* ed. Leon Edel and Lyall H. Powers (New York and Oxford: Oxford University Press, 1987).

9.21   *empressé*]   Eager; assiduous.

13.28–29   *commissionaires*]   Messengers; errand boys.

14.10   *sergent de ville*]   Police constable.

14.14   *fournisseur's*]   Tradesman.

17.35   *Il faut fixer la somme*]   We must establish the price.

18.24   *Pas si bête!*]   Not so stupid!

29.28   Mrs. Grundy]   Proverbial arbiter of proper social behavior, from an offstage character in Thomas Morton's play *Speed the Plough* (1798).

31.7   *épanchements*]   Outpourings.

35.28   "Scottish Chiefs"]   Novel (1810) by Jane Porter (1776–1850).

59.25–26   "Home . . . cry."]   Tennyson, *The Princess,* Canto VI, lines 1–2.

69.5   If . . . fail]   Cf. *Macbeth* I.vii.59.

72.19   *Vogue la galère!*]   Come what may!

73.16   "Barkis is willing."]   Laconic proposal conveyed by the carrier Barkis to the family servant Clara Peggotty in Charles Dickens' *David Copperfield* (1850).

75.32   Zanoni]   Novel (1842) by Edward Bulwer-Lytton.

85.39   *Je ne demande pas mieux*]   I ask nothing better.

92.33   *criarde*]   Discordant.

100.25   *à refaire*]   To be done over.

123.19–20   the repose of the Veres of Vere]   Cf. Alfred Tennyson, "Lady Clara Vere de Vere" (1833), lines 39–40: "Her manners had not that repose / Which stamps the caste of Vere-de-Vere."

132.1–4   "God . . . albatross.'"]   Samuel Taylor Coleridge, "The Rime of the Ancient Mariner" (1798), lines 79–82.

159.4–5   *in loco sororis*]   In place of a sister.

163.34–35   Maud Muller]   Farm girl secretly in love with the judge who greets her as he rides by, in the poem of the same name by John Greenleaf Whittier.

168.4–5   *Je le suis bien*]   I certainly am.

173.15   *éclaircissement*]   Clarification.

180.32–33   "Porphyro . . . on St. Agnes' eve]   Cf. John Keats, "The Eve of St. Agnes" (1818), lines 224–25.

211.17   *petits soins*]   Little efforts.

213.5–6   *"Dans un flôt de velours traînant ses petits pieds."*]   "On a billow of velvet trailing her little feet."

223.32   *la mort dans l'âme*]   Sick at heart.

227.34–35   *façon de parler*]   Manner of speaking.

228.27   *à la bonne heure*]   Well done.

230.30   *Exegi monumentum*]   "I have built a monument" (from Horace, *Odes*, III.xxx).

243.26   Viola]   The character's name was changed to Rosalind in later editions.

245.21   *empressement*]   Alacrity.

273.40   *au mieux*]   On the best terms.

276.2   *vie intime*]   Private life.

295.24–25   'The funeral . . . tables.']   *Hamlet*, I.ii.180–81.

300.15   *bouillonnement*]   Agitation.

309.17   Magawisca]   Daughter of a Pequod chief in Catherine Maria Sedgwick's novel *Hope Leslie* (1827).

347.7   *Nous verrons*]   We shall see.

357.19   *The Monastery*]   Novel (1820) by Sir Walter Scott.

385.16   *que diable venait-il faire dans cette galère?*]   "But what the devil was he doing in that galley?": comic catchphrase in Molière's play *Les Fourberies du Scapin* (1670).

398.4   *Aux grand maux les grandes remèdes*]   For great evils, desperate remedies.

401.16–17   *vous faites bien les choses*]   You do things well.

402.32   *tout bonnement*]   Quite simply.

403.4   *soi-disant*]   So-called.

404.14–15   *ceteris paribus*]   All else being equal.

406.38   *C'est toute une histoire*]   It's a long story.

408.13   *totus, teres, atque rotundus*]   Complete in itself, smooth, and rounded (from Horace, *Satires*, II.vii.86).

410.38–40   *à la* Hogarth . . . Mercenary Marriage?]   Cf. William Hogarth's series of engravings "The Rake's Progress" (1735).

417.12   Mrs. Gamp]   The midwife Sairy Gamp, in Charles Dickens' *Martin Chuzzlewit* (1844).

422.16   *haut faits*]   Great deeds.

433.39   *esprit fort*]   Free-thinker.

441.20   *bon temps*]   The good times; that is, before the Revolution.

453.14   *en attendant*]   While waiting for.

460.6   *manants*]   Peasants.

460.36   *Médecin malgré lui*]   *The Doctor In Spite of Himself* (1666), comedy by Molière.

461.3   *Grand Siècle*]   The Great Century (the 17th).

462.8   *agaceries*]   Coquetries.

468.26   *cela ne se raisonne pas*]   It's not a matter of reason.

469.27   *prévenance*]   Kind attentions.

469.35   *en croupe*]   Riding behind.

490.28   *Coureuse!*]   Loose woman.

495.29   Cenacolo]   The "Last Supper" (c. 1495–97) of Leonardo da Vinci.

500.15   *coup d'œil*]   Comprehensive glance.

507.35   *virginibus puerisque*]   For maidens and youths.

516.21   Florian's]   Celebrated café with a large area of outdoor seating, established on the south side of the Piazza San Marco in 1720.

543.9   Temple Bar]   Gateway adjoining the Temple Inns of Court between Fleet Street and the Strand, built by Christopher Wren in 1670, that marked the western boundary of the City of London. It was removed in 1878.

549.31–32   'I thank thee, Jew, for teaching me that word!']   *The Merchant of Venice*, IV.i.338.

566.22   *tout de noir habillé*]   Dressed all in black.

575.15–16   Belle au Bois Dormant]   Sleeping Beauty.

580.25   *se recueillit*]   Collected himself.

587.14   Beatrix Esmond]   Proud beauty in William M. Thackeray's *The History of Henry Esmond, Esquire* (1852).

601.25   *fidus Achates*]   "Faithful Achates": byword for loyal companion, from Virgil's *Aeneid*.

612.25   church of the Jesuits]   St. Francis Xavier Church (built 1666–77).

612.31   the *genius loci*]   William Tell.

612.37   Gesler]   Or Gessler; Austrian bailiff who according to legend ordered William Tell to shoot an apple off his own son's head as punishment for defying Gessler's authority.

613.2–4   the images . . . Brunnen]   The Swiss oath of liberation was sworn on November 7, 1307, by representatives of the cantons of Uri, Schwyz, and Unterwalden led by Werner Stauffacher, Erny an der Halden, and Walter Fürst.

617.32   *saugrenues*]   Ridiculous.

620.17   *on dit*]   It is said.

625.17   *goguenard*]   Mocking.

626.36   *Un coup de tête*]   An impulsive act.

630.28   *minauderie*]   Simpering.

631.10   *promessa sposa*]   Fiancée.

634.29   Mentana]   Scene of defeat of Garibaldi by French and papal troops in 1867.

652.26   Parny]   Evariste-Désiré de Parny (1753–1814), French poet best known for his *Poésies érotiques*.

669.28   Falstaff's description of Shallow]   Cf. *2 Henry IV*, III.ii.309.

692.38   *retroussé*]   Turned-up.

703.9   *jeunesse de cœur*] Youthful heart.

735.4–5   'At least no merchant traffics in my heart!'] Robert Browning, *Pictor Ignotus* (1845), line 62.

736.15   'raw Haste, half-sister to Delay!'] Alfred Tennyson, "Love thou thy land, with love far-brought," line 96.

739.10–12 his fancy . . . prince] Cf. *The Tempest*, I.ii.375–408.

743.14   *Nulla dies sine linea*] No day without a line.

743.22   *au petit pied*] In a pale imitation.

743.30   the Madonna della Seggiola] Raphael's "The Madonna of the Chair," in the Pitti Palace in Florence.

744.34   *lever de rideau*] Curtain-raiser.

744.36   *âme méconnue*] Misunderstood soul.

745.30   that tale of Balzac's] "Le Chef-d'oeuvre inconnu" ("The Unknown Masterpiece," 1831).

746.5   'Michael'] Michelangelo.

753.14   *de beaux restes*] Beautiful traces.

755.39   *forestiére*] Foreigner.

768.18   *fait époque*] Marked an era.

772.25   "Bradshaw" in hand] *Bradshaw's Monthly Railway Guide*, a series of timetables begun in 1839 by George Bradshaw, a printer and engraver.

776.39   *contadini*] Peasants.

778.24   the Lateran] San Giovanni in Laterano, seat of the Bishop of Rome, has the oldest Christian basilica (fourth century) in the city. Its famous façade by Allessandro Galilei was built in 1733–36.

782.4–5   *jeune fille*] Girl.

785.16   "Corinne."] *Corinne; or, Italy* (1807), novel by Mme. de Staël.

785.21   verse . . . unadorned] Cf. James Thomson, "Autumn" (1730), lines 208–10: "For loveliness / Needs not the foreign aid of ornament, / But is when unadorned adorned the most."

787.7   *coiffure de rapin*] Art student's hair style.

787.33–34 *Il faut que jeunesse se passe!*] Youth must pass!

789.14   *à sec*] Short of money.

790.5   *pour vous faire la cour*] To pay court to you.

832.38   *menus plaisirs*] Little pleasures.

834.15	*filles de haut lieu*]	Well-born girls.

838.19	*mauvais sujet*]	Sly character.

853.28	Charles Baudelaire]	Earlier versions read "Gustave Flaubert."

857.26	"la vieille galanterie Française,"]	The old French gallantry.

859.23	*entêtée*]	Wayward.

859.28	*jolie à croquer*]	Extremely pretty.

860.2	*soupe aux choux*]	Cabbage soup.

860.4	*ce génie-là*]	That genius.

864.27	*bêtises*]	Foolishness.

874.29–30	as the sibyl . . . king]	The sybil was said to have offered nine prophetic books for sale to a Roman king identified variously as Tarquinius Priscus or Tarquinius Superbus; when he refused to pay her price, she destroyed six of the nine, and he settled for the remaining three at the price originally asked.

875.39	*société de bonnes œuvres*]	Charitable organization.

879.20	*visage de croquemort*]	Undertaker's expression.

881.1	*potagers*]	Kitchen-gardens.

881.11	*tonnelle*]	Arbor.

884.5	*d'une étourderie*]	So thoughtless.

885.23–24	*ça n'a pas de principes!*]	They have no principles!

885.30	*des hommes sérieux*]	Serious men.

897.14	*faux bonhomme*]	A disingenuous person.

898.7–8	*d'une humeur massacrante*]	In a foul humor.

902.38	*fait quelques folies*]	Behaved foolishly.

910.13	*quattrini*]	Money; coins.

914.21	DIVUS TIBERIUS CÆSAR TOTIUS ORBIS IMPERATOR]	The divine emperor Tiberius, ruler of the whole world.

916.1	Peter Schlemihl, in the tale]	In *The Wonderful Story of Peter Schlemihl* (1813), by Adelbert von Chamisso (1781–1838), the protagonist sells his shadow to the devil.

933.1	*Aspetti!*]	Wait!

940.20	*camerièra*]	Chambermaid.

Library of Congress Cataloging-in-Publication Data

James, Henry, 1843–1916.
  [Short stories. Selections]
  Complete stories 1864–1874 / Henry James.
    p. cm. — (The Library of America ; 111)
  ISBN 1–883011–70–1 (alk. paper)
    1. United States—Social life and customs—19th century—
Fiction. 2. Europe—Social life and customs—19th century—
Fiction. 3. Americans—Travel—Europe—Fiction. I. Title.
II. Series.
PS2112. 1999c
813′.4—dc21   98–53919
                                                          CIP

THE LIBRARY OF AMERICA SERIES

The Library of America fosters appreciation and pride in America's literary heritage by publishing, and keeping permanently in print, authoritative editions of its best and most significant writing. An independent nonprofit organization, it was founded in 1979 with seed money from the National Endowment for the Humanities and the Ford Foundation.

This book is set in 10 point Linotron Galliard,
a face designed for photocomposition by Matthew Carter
and based on the sixteenth-century face Granjon. The paper is
acid-free Ecusta Nyalite and meets the requirements for permanence
of the American National Standards Institute. The binding
material is Brillianta, a woven rayon cloth made by
Van Heek-Scholco Textielfabrieken, Holland.
The composition is by The Clarinda
Company. Printing and binding by
R.R.Donnelley & Sons Company.
Designed by Bruce Campbell.

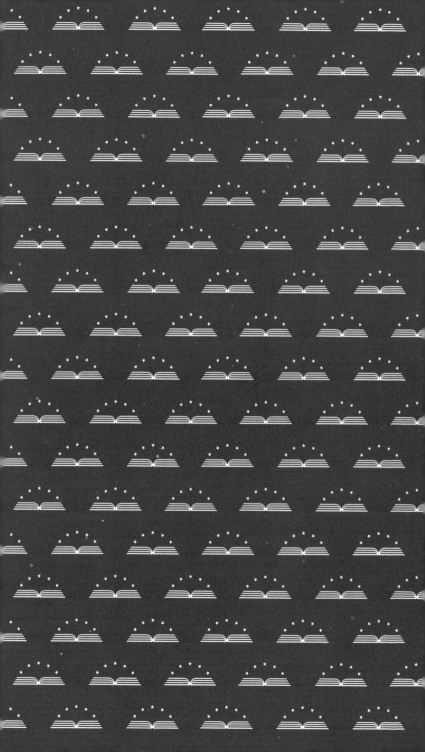